THE BIG BOOK OF

Classic Fantasy

ALSO EDITED BY ANN AND JEFF VANDERMEER

*The Thackery T. Lambshead Pocket Guide to Eccentric
& Discredited Diseases* (with Mark Roberts)

Best American Fantasy 1
(with Matthew Cheney)

Best American Fantasy 2
(with Matthew Cheney)

The New Weird

Steampunk

Steampunk II: Steampunk Reloaded

Fast Ships, Black Sails

*The Thackery T. Lambshead Cabinet
of Curiosities*

Last Drink Bird Head

ODD?

The Weird

The Time Traveler's Almanac

Sisters of the Revolution

The Kosher Guide to Imaginary Animals

The Big Book of Science Fiction

ALSO BY JEFF VANDERMEER

FICTION

The Southern Reach Trilogy

Annihilation

Authority

Acceptance

Dradin in Love

The Book of Lost Places (stories)

Veniss Underground

City of Saints and Madmen

Secret Life (stories)

Shriek: An Afterword

The Situation

Finch

The Third Bear (stories)

Borne

The Strange Bird

NONFICTION

Why Should I Cut Your Throat?

Booklife

Monstrous Creatures

The Steampunk Bible
(with S. J. Chambers)

The Steampunk User's Manual
(with Desirina Boskovich)

Wonderbook

ALSO BY ANN VANDERMEER

Steampunk III: Steampunk Revolution

The Bestiary

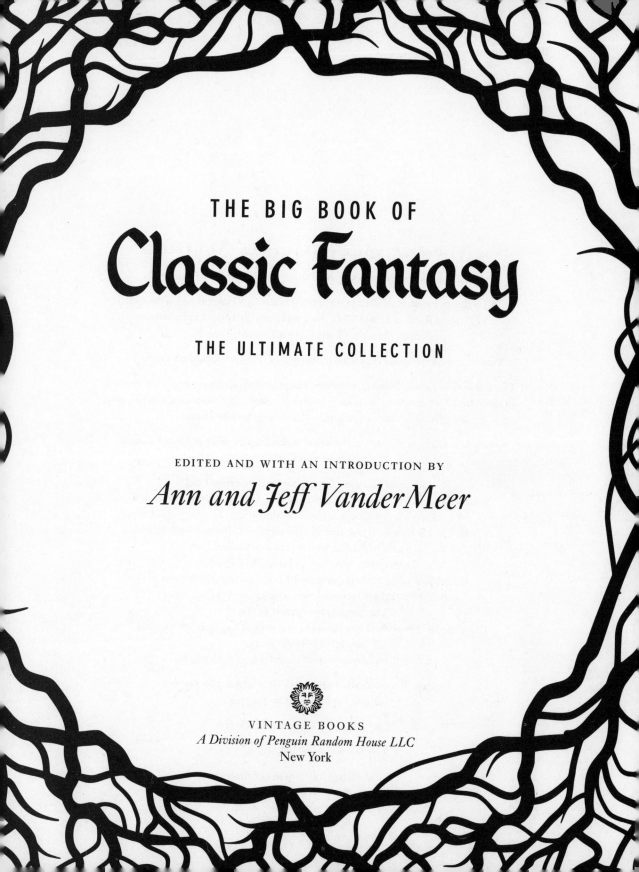

THE BIG BOOK OF
Classic Fantasy

THE ULTIMATE COLLECTION

EDITED AND WITH AN INTRODUCTION BY

Ann and Jeff VanderMeer

VINTAGE BOOKS
A Division of Penguin Random House LLC
New York

Library of Congress Cataloging-in-Publication Data
Names: VanderMeer, Ann, editor, writer of introduction. | VanderMeer, Jeff, editor, writer of introduction.
Title: The big book of classic fantasy : the ultimate collection / edited and with an introduction by Ann and Jeff VanderMeer.
Description: New York : Vintage Books, 2019.
Identifiers: LCCN 2018038439 (print) | LCCN 2018060576 (ebook) |
ISBN 9780525435570 (ebook) | ISBN 9780525435563 (paperback)
Subjects: LCSH: Fantasy fiction.
Classification: LCC PN6071.F25 (ebook) | LCC PN6071.F25 B535 2019 (print) |
DDC 808.83/8766—dc23
LC record available at https://lccn.loc.gov/2018038439

Vintage Books Trade Paperback ISBN: 978-0-525-43556-3
eBook ISBN: 978-0-525-43557-0

Book design by Christopher M. Zucker

www.vintagebooks.com

Printed in the United States of America
10 9 8 7 6 5 4 3 2 1

For Hans-My-Hedgehog

Contents

CONTENTS

CONTENTS

CONTENTS

Introduction

WILD DELIGHTS

IMAGINE BEING USHERED into a vast and palatial room on a sumptuous estate that rivals Versailles . . . and across from you on a golden table lies a smorgasbord of delights. A banquet fit for a king, a queen, or even an emperor. As you gaze upon this wonder, you're told you may partake of this magical repast for only one many-course dinner. After which, you will be ushered from the estate, from the enchanted gardens that surround it, with the little glints at dusk that might be fireflies or might be fairies. You will leave, never to return, left only with the memory of the most amazing meal you have ever eaten.

A banquet such as this could be said to be the dilemma of any anthologist, but especially ours when compiling *The Big Book of Classic Fantasy*. Defining "classic," as from the early 1800s to World War II—from the start of a nascent idea of "fantasy" as opposed to "folktale" to the moment before the rise of a commercial category of "fantasy"—one is still left with more than a century of fantastical stories. A feast almost beyond measure! But how to gorge oneself without getting sick? (Even with a larder as large as this book, there are limits.) How to sample as much

as one can without feeling slightly dissatisfied at not getting bigger bites of particular favorites? What to bring back, then, for readers, that isn't just the editors glutting themselves on their own particular tastes? How to be representative? Not everyone wants a steady diet of Turkish delight, even if it is accompanied by talking animals and a magical closet.

In short, the period in question was rich, deep, and wild for literature, and there is an inclination in even the most disciplined curator to succumb to that wildness and favor the word "treasury" over "anthology," to relinquish focus for a family-style buffet free-for-all. Yet the best meals are curated to some extent. They have a beginning, middle, and end. You remember them because of the selection of ingredients and the care with which they were put together. Thus, our decision has been to sample in such a way as to showcase certain themes and schools of thought while not forgetting that wonderful nostalgia for the fantasy treasuries of our collective childhood.

This predilection for a certain loosening of the reins of curation dovetails with the unpredictable nature of the period in question for fantasy. Fantasy, pre–World War II, often wasn't described as such, except, perhaps in the rise of pulp magazines like *Weird Tales* in the 1930s. Lawless, profound, visionary, phantasmagorical, these stories often eluded classification altogether on publication. Some were so personal, they were written before World War II but only discovered after (one, at least, published here for the first time). Fantasy grappled with or offered escape from some of the most horrific vistas of war and nascent industrialization and rubbed shoulders with formal new movements like surrealism, while at the same time navigating a difficult path out of the mythic by shedding or sublimating religious imagery and themes. (Which is to say, "fantasy" was like most other forms of literature during this time of vast upheaval and change.)

Whether it was fairy tales that contained warnings about real-life perils (at the time; most readers will not feel particularly threatened by giant hedgehogs these days) or the influence of the prior *contes philosophiques*, in which scientists presented their extrapolations in the form of dream journeys or quests, the beauty and dexterity of what would come to be termed "fantasy" became more fully formed during this era. The ideological war or debate over the value of non-realist fiction, including fantasy, would begin during the end of the period. The rise of pulp magazines gave writers in the United Kingdom and United States a home for work that couldn't be published elsewhere, even as pulp's own restrictions gave readers an incomplete (and often Anglo) idea of both the definition of and uses of fantasy.

None of this wildness or freedom means that writers of fantastical fiction were any less immune with regard to conveying racism or sexism. The world's first fantasy magazine, the *Orchid Garden* (established 1919 in Austria), published stories that have stood the test of time . . . but in a context of racist illustrations and at least one editor and contributor who later became a Nazi. Even some first-wave feminists (for example, the then-popular Mary Elizabeth Counselman) could be an example to white women while in her stories crafting depictions of African Americans that were based on the worst stereotypes. Today, many

of these stories are simply unreadable. Some of the omissions in this anthology occur for this reason.

However, as our selection shows, the creative minds writing short stories in the fantasy realm were more global and diverse than many past tables of contents may have suggested. As is alas ever true: editors can sometimes be more conservative than the period they cover. Inasmuch as we had a guiding principle, it was to push against conservative choices, within the range of material available. Thus, you will find many unusual and rare dishes among the banquet set out before you.

THE RATE OF THE "FEY" AS A BAROMETER FOR FANTASY

For purposes of this anthology, "fantasy" means any story in which an element of the unreal permeates the real world or any story that takes place within a secondary world that is identifiably not a version of ours, whether anything overtly "fantastical" occurs during the story. Beyond these basic parameters, fantasy is distinguished from horror or the weird in that fantasy isn't primarily concerned with the creation of terror or the exploration of an altered state of being frightened, alienated, or fascinated by an eruption of the uncanny.

"Classic fantasy," then, is that naive state of the unreal during which writers largely did not self-identify their work as "fantasy," during a transitional period that also loosely corresponds to the transition in history from religion to science and from agrarian, rural societies to industrialized, urban societies. This period also saw a marked devaluation of fantasy as for children, culminating in an association with the low cultural status of the pulp magazines.

Within this context, we searched for a useful word or phrase to further define "fantasy," much as science fiction has "sense of wonder," and "the uncanny" serves to support the weird. For us, that term is "the fey," a concept eight hundred years old and most commonly associated with fairies and a kind of twilit, magical meadow that blends "sense of wonder" and "uncanny" in a fantastical context.

Generalizations can be dangerous, but as editors we do have to make certain assertions, even if these just constitute scaffolding or an approximation. (Strict definers will, of course, be horrified by our unwillingness to euthanize the butterfly of taxonomy and pin it to a killing board.)

In this context, we can say that a fantasy story can be further defined by a wildness or an unease or ethereal alienness that emanates from the fey. The dictionary definition of "the fey" is "other-worldliness," which encapsulates how the most original fantasy seeks to elude locked-in, binary readings. "The rate of fey" (our construct) in fantasy provides some measure of whether a story is (1) escapist/non-escapist, (2) rational/irrational, or (3) employing familiar or unique symbolism. "Fey" also pertains to how much a fantasy story borrows from horror fiction or weird fiction. A high rate of fey, or strangeness, tends to fold in elements of horror or the weird because unfamiliarity creates unease and sometimes terror in the reader. In fact, many of the strangest fairy stories could also be classified as horror stories.

Inasmuch as fantasy seeks out or naturally accretes wonder and a particular kind of strangeness—like a pollinating bee becoming dusted with pollen—"fey" is a key indicator in fantasy fiction. The "kind of strangeness" emanates from the associations generated by elements like fairies, elves, talking animals, and the like, rather than ghosts or outright monsters.

In considering the "rate of fey," we must acknowledge that fantasy has baggage similar to certain modes of horror fiction. For example, just as vampires and werewolves tend to bring with them centuries of associations, so too fairies, mermaids, and talking animals bring along familiar symbolism—the comfort of a known baseline. Similarly, a modern discipline like psychology, especially Freudian dream interpretation, tends to want to "civilize" that which should remain wild, to confine and constrict symbolism into narrow dead-end channels—not unlike how

Christianity sought to colonize pagan rituals and symbols.

This comfort level can be subverted, weakened, strengthened, or presented as a familiar element in opposition to something else much stranger in the text, or, in a modern context, such stories can simply reinforce the status quo (for better or worse).

Another way of stating this is to say that "fey" has a concrete meaning or manifestation—"hey, presto, fairy!"—but that the fey (and thus fantasy) contains a streak of welcome irrationality that is quite logical because it reflects the dominant state of the human mind. It also harkens back to elements from our premodern past that trigger a visceral response in our reptile brain. ("Hey, presto, bear! Run!") For this reason, fantasy often produces a feeling akin to wonder or an ecstatic realignment of the spiritual, which can be felt deep in the body.

Fey can be elastic. Sometimes varying "rates of the fey" occur within the oeuvre of the same author. The work of the brothers Grimm and Hans Christian Andersen provide good examples because, in theory, they created versions of the same type of story over and over again: the classic modern fairy tale. Yet some of these tales prop up conservative values and outdated ideas about human and animal behavior—while others remain wild, unpredictable, hard to pin down as to their moral compass. They have retained a deep vein of the true fey.

As this thinking suggests, "the fey" in a story can have a half-life, undermined or reinforced by new science and new societal realizations. For this reason, what might have seemed revolutionary in even staid fairy tales—for example, portraying an animal sympathetically that was once thought of as predatory—can become stale, regardless of liveliness of plot. Repetition can also dilute the rate of fey. The glut of stories about mermaids doesn't mean a writer can't create a strikingly original mermaid story. But it does mean it becomes harder, because of all the past fictional, mythic, and pop-culture associations that readers bring with them when encountering the word "mermaid" in a text. (This is itself a kind of magical spell placed upon the reader—to create narrative from a single word.)

In general, we as editors wanted to foreground as much "fey" or as much "wildness" as possible, even as we recognize that in this effort we must include material that is, for lack of better words, pragmatic or logical or traditional. However, in doing so, we gently reject the trap of creating a more formal taxonomy for the inchoate, or to make claims for fantasy's origins that become so broad that they, for example, go all the way back to Gilgamesh, and become meaningless. Nor do we find it useful to engage in the thankless task of convincing readers or reviewers of the legitimacy of fantasy and thus of non-realist fiction. Too much time and energy has been expended by well-meaning editors of past anthologies invoking arguments such as the "Nathaniel Hawthorne Defense" to establish fantasy's bona fides. Such a position works to delegitimize the true power of fantasy via a "cultural cringe" that insists on claiming authors in the literary canon rather than suggesting that a narrow literary canon is itself already flawed and to some extent rigidly ideological. (Most variations on this defense are also too Anglocentric for an impulse that exists worldwide, across many cultures.)

Instead, we hope you simply enjoy the energy of a chaotic, miasmic period—one in which the fantastical is often playful and sui generis as it shakes off the expectations of the past. Far from being conservative, the best fantasy from before World War II was a bit like an overgrown garden rich and fertile with wildflowers, weeds, and odd nocturnal animals, under a full moon.

EXAMINING THE EVIDENCE

The best prior sources for an eclectic and inclusive selection of fantasy have been *The Book of Fantasy* (1940), edited by Silvina Ocampo, Jorge Luis Borges, and A. Bioy Casares; Alberto Manguel's two Black Water volumes, and Eric S. Rabin's *Fantastic Worlds: Myths, Tales, and Stories*. All three anthologies rely on excerpts overmuch and include a fair number of traditional ghost stories and horror stories, but they remain highly recommended benchmarks in the fantasy field.

Many other fantasy reprint anthologies have skewed Anglocentric in their selections, even when there was work with a higher rate of fey available. This excluded works in translation from other literary traditions and rendered invisible some works by African Americans and Native Americans—a problem compounded by very strict definitions of the term "fantasy." These kinds of editorial decisions were also often predicated on looking only at work published by genre imprints or magazines dedicated to fantasy stories, rather than casting a wider net.

For this reason, we have no qualms about letting the "fey" manifest where it will—to, in essence, look at the evidence rather than predetermine what that evidence might consist of. Beyond our usual remit of ignoring whether a story or author exists within the "genre" or "literary" world, we have also interrogated existing canon, dispensing with some oft-reprinted material, such as the heroic fantasy of William Morris, that seemed an echo of a bygone era as opposed to a precursor to the modern. Yet, we also tried to be objective about classic authors we have not included in anthologies before; for example, the inclusion herein of a superior example of Robert E. Howard's sword-and-sorcery stories.

Fiction from the more iconic authors in this anthology (including Carroll and Baum) benefits from being placed in conversation with the works of more obscure writers with similar themes or tendencies. From a historical perspective, this approach provides a more comprehensive context for stories that are more widely known—for example, compare Carroll's Alice to aspects of the Nesbit story in this collection or even "The Debutante" by Leonora Carrington. We hope readers will appreciate the resulting richness of certain time periods, while still enjoying that warm comfortable feeling of nostalgia of rediscovering classics last read in their childhood.

In the case of famous authors such as the brothers Grimm and Hans Christian Andersen, we purposefully selected more obscure stories. We did this because, quite frankly, it's boring to reprint "The Swan" or "Red Riding Hood" one more time. But we also wanted to showcase the extraordinary depth of these writers and to again emphasize the phantasmagorical wildness of pre–World War II fantasy. The brothers Grimm's "Hans-My-Hedgehog," for example, isn't just a complex and weird fairy tale—it is also a more interesting entry in the category "animal fables" than some of their better-known work. Andersen's "Will-o'-the-Wisps" cleverly provides several nested tales in one, but also comments on the idea of fairy tales in general, managing to be both earnest and meta at the same time.

GENERAL AREAS OF INTEREST

In creating this feast, we have tried to find a balance between the sprawling chaos of some medieval banquet and the refined curation of a tasting menu. A satisfying experience should feature both surprises and recurring motifs or themes.

For example, an animal tale can take any form and reflect any number of concerns, and this is not in any rigorous sense a "category." However, we do want to acknowledge the special attention we paid to the idea of animal (and human!) stereotypes in selecting material that features animals in a significant way. We did not want to perpetuate the worst of these clichés, which have led to gross misunderstandings of animal behavior and intelligence. Unique creations, like Franz Blei's remarkable bestiary of writers, displays another impulse with regard to use of animal characteristics: to emphasize a highly subjective view of biographical data in a satirical mode.

Other loose "categories" may exist at different levels of hierarchy but are still useful to mention to give an idea of the scaffolding of our curation. Many stories fall into multiple categories because, like most good fiction, they cannot be defined as just one thing.

Mysticism/Spiritualism—We have resisted the impulse to reclassify as "fantasy" those stories that are actually religious tales and thus sacrosanct among various cultures. We have also resisted reprinting, for the most part, overtly Christian texts in which the moral is too scriptural and thus didactic. However, a general spirituality or mysticism inhabits some of the best fantasy of the period. Some of this material comes from a utopian impulse, as in Paul Scheerbart's "The Dance of the Comets" (originally conceived of as a ballet) or otherworldly, as in E. M. Forster's "The Celestial Omnibus" or Maurice Renard's "Sound in the Mountain." Most exciting in this vein is the discovery of works in unexpected places. For example, H. P. Blavatskaya's excellent "The Ensouled Violin," originally written as a kind of advertisement for her spiritualist beliefs.

Satire/Humor—Fantasy lends itself readily to satire and absurdist humor because of the propulsive nature in such a tale to tumble head over heels through a "and then and then and then" approach. Oscar Wilde's "The Remarkable Rocket," a tale of braggadocio, is a good example of the kinetic energy in such works. Stella Benson's brilliant "Magic Comes to a Committee" showcases the humorous element in a more realist mode, while Marcel Aymé's "The Man Who Could Walk Through Walls" falls somewhere between with its understated approach.

Secondary World Fantasy—Any work of fiction set in a place not recognizable as a version of Earth can be considered "secondary world fantasy." Overlapping subsets of secondary world fantasy include "swords and sorcery" (focus on individual heroics of ragtag antiheroes, with or without quest), "heroic fantasy" (more likely to include broader societal context and upper classes, almost always with quest), and "science fantasy" (another way of saying the boundaries between science fiction and fantasy have been breached, with the uses of technology so advanced as to be indistinguishable from magic). The Oz novels and stories fit the broad definition of exploring a secondary world, while Howard's "The Shadow Kingdom" and Fritz Leiber's Lankhmar tales fit the criteria of swords and sorcery, and E. R. Eddison's "Ouroboros" represents a retro-modernist take on heroic fantasy. Alongside episodic novels by Edgar Rice Burroughs and David Lindsay, "Friend Island" by Francis Stevens, the *Night Land* excerpt from William Hope Hodgson, and "The Princess Steel" by W. E. B. Du Bois could be considered "science fantasy."

Science fantasy's blurring allows for hybrid effects in describing the fantastical (frequently employing the mythic alongside the empirical) and expresses itself most potently in the post–World War II fantasy of Jack Vance's Dying Earth and M. John Harrison's Viriconium cycle. A strict definition of fantasy might exclude this impulse, but in fact such tales tend to use fantasy tropes, not SF tropes, and are more recognizable to a fantasy reader as "fantasy" than to a science fiction reader as "science fiction." (Reluctantly but inevitably, see: *Star Wars*.)

Surrealism—Given our own love of surrealist fiction, we expected to include a number of examples. However, few full-on surrealists wrote fiction that seemed to fit even a wide definition of "fantasy." Some surrealist experiments, similar to formative Dadaist and Futurist writings, have not aged well; indeed, a definition of "painful" should include a reference to the fictions of Salvador Dalí. Therefore, the surrealists are directly represented by just two stories: Carrington's "The Debutante," and "The Influence of the Sun" by the obscure but often brilliant Belgian writer Fernand Dumont. A surrealist impulse may occur in aspects of other stories—for example Hagiwara Sakutarō's "The Town of Cats" (also classified as Japanese Modernism)—but not in the formal sense of being by self-identified surrealists. Even so, surrealism directly informed the works of such major post–World War II fantasists as Angela Carter.

Decadent Literature—The decadent movement manifested strongly in England, France, and Germany in the late 1800s, reaching its apogee in poetry and prose that celebrated artifice

and ritual while also grappling with the tactile nature of the body (in a pre-vaccine world). Although decadent fiction could be subversive and very much push back against middle-class sensibilities in a way similar to the Beat era in the United States, very few decadent-era stories fit our brief. Among those included are the aforementioned story by Oscar Wilde, two tales by Marcel Schwob (sometimes considered a symbolist); the completely over-the-top Meyrink story, "Blamol"; and "Sowbread" by the Sardinian writer Grazia Deledda. Yet, similar to our experience of exploring surrealism, decadent themes dealing with the decay of the body and ritualistic exploration of the darker sides of the human psyche do occur within these pages, even if not formally identified as decadence.

Within any or all of these categories, the form oft favored by writers is one that takes the apparatus of the folktale or fairy tale, even if updated to a modern context and delinked from place-specific culture. "Fairy tale," then, is not so much a category herein as a narrative strategy that allows effects like suspension of disbelief despite continual stacking of ever-more ridiculous situation atop absurdity; a devotion to the powerful engine of plot, relying on believable but two-dimensional characters; allusions to and symbolism that borrows from more religious or mystical times; and access to fantasy archetypes using a shorthand familiar to most readers.

SEEING THE WHOLE PICTURE

International fiction, in translation and originally written in English, is an indispensable part of any conversation about literature, and fantasy is no exception. While it is true that the issue of translation isn't as important for writers or readers in traditions that exist originally in non-English languages with large audiences, we English speakers are impoverished when we do not attempt to provide the widest possible survey. Dedicated to this principle, we aggressively pursued, through our many hardworking overseas contacts (including translators), information on fantasy fiction that may have been unknown to prior English-language anthologists, even little known in the countries of origin.

The result was astonishing: this volume contains more translations into English than any other anthology we have edited, and more, we believe, than any other general reprint fantasy anthology ever published. This did not occur by quota, but simply by looking at the whole landscape.

Statistics are perhaps not the most exciting things to discover in an anthology introduction, but it is worth noting that almost half of the stories in this anthology are translations, representing twenty-six countries. Seven come from writers never translated into English before, and two from writers with only one prior story in English. Fourteen are stories never before published in English. Six additional stories are new versions of previously translated stories, where we felt a new translation was long overdue.

The highlights are too many to mention here, but it is worth noting such significant stories as the underrated Aleksandr Grin's classic long story "The Ratcatcher" (translated by Ekaterina Sedia), the novella-length Korean tale "The Story of Jeon Unchi" (translated by Minsoo Kang), and the Yiddish philosopher Der Nister's "At the Border." This is Der Nister's second published story in English from his collection *Gedakht*, and to our knowledge his fiction is not widely known. It was unearthed by translator Joseph Tomaras while studying Der Nister's philosophical works.

Other notable stories include María Teresa León's "Rose-Cold, Moon Skater," which appears here in English for the first time. (Perhaps in part, León's late debut can be attributed to a terrible husband who had her committed so he could marry a younger woman, who then controlled León's estate.) The stories of the little-known Louis Fréchette capture a French Canadian impulse that is interesting to compare to the Paul Bunyan tales. Finally, we must again mention Franz Blei's remarkable "Bestiary," which has never appeared in English before, either. In some cases, his entry may provide the most information English-language readers will have on writers killed or murdered during World War II and long forgotten.

In no sense is this anthology a coherent, organized exploration of non-Anglo fantasy. However, it does, by our count, constitute the most extensive exploration of non-Anglo fantasy in a reprint anthology to date. We hope that this record will be broken by some other anthologist sooner rather than later.

Given that the "rate of fey" in this introduction is low and that the value of a good host is sometimes in being invisible, we will not keep you overlong. Instead, we now abandon you to the banquet: the sweet and the savory, in a vast and opulent dining room, from the corners of which the fairies blow raspberries and talking animals wait for you to finish that they may have their turn. We hope by the time you rise from your place you're sated and feel well served. Mind not that it is all enchantment, that the walls will fall away to reveal the dark forest beyond. Mind not the curious monsters staring from the shadows. Mind not the glint in the eyes of the fairies; they cannot hurt you this night.

But, still, don't tarry overlong, and keep to the road after. Thank you as ever for reading.

THE BIG BOOK OF
Classic Fantasy

Bettina von Arnim was the title of Elisabeth Katharina Ludovica Magdalena Brentano (1785–1859), a German writer, composer, and activist. She wrote in an exuberant style that matched her paradoxical personality. She was also a well-known artist and musician, fully encapsulating the spirit of a traditional German Romantic. Her most popular works are not her songs, poems, or short stories but edited versions of correspondence that she had with friends and family. An example would be *Clemens Brentano's Spring Garland* (1844), which was a series of letters Arnim wrote to her brother that blended journalist-like reportage with fiction. Although her fiction wasn't popular, she was close friends with the brothers Grimm as well as Johann Wolfgang von Goethe, the German dramatist known for his impact on the Gothic genre. Arnim wrote "The Queen's Son," her first fairy tale, as a gift for her fiancé, Achim von Arnim, in 1808. It is reminiscent of oral narration and notes the discord between those with power and those without.

The Queen's Son

Bettina von Arnim

Translated by Gio Clairval

THERE WAS ONCE A KING who ruled over a delightful land, and his burg stood on top of a high mountain, from which he could see far into the distance. Behind the burg there were beautiful gardens built for his pleasure, magnificent rivers, and thick woods full of wild animals. Lions and tigers lived there, wild cats perched in the trees, foxes and wolves roamed into the deepest parts of the forest, bears, white or with golden fur, often swam in pairs in the rivers and came into the King's garden. Atop the trees nested preying eagles, vultures and falcons. This forest, which girdled the King's realm, was seen by everyone as the animals' own realm.

Then the King took a wife, for her beauty and to have children. When the woman was blessed with child, the people rejoiced because their kingdom would have an heir to the throne, and they held the wife in high consideration. The day of the birth came and went and the King's wife did not deliver the child. The King was sad because he believed that his spouse was ill and would die soon. Still, she continued to eat and drink like any healthy woman. Seven years passed, and the Queen's belly remained swollen. The King, tired of her deformed body, grew angry. He believed that the woman must have sinned against God, since she was punished in such a harsh manner.

Finally, he left his wife's chambers, separated from her and sent her away from the castle, to live in a remote part of the burg.

Here, slowly and sadly, she carried her heavy burden through the deserted gardens, and watched the wild beasts wandering out of the forest on the opposite bank of the river, to drink and wade in the water. In the springtime, when lions or tigers came with their young and fed them, she often wished in deep despair to be a ravening beast, to snatch her food in the woods after fierce fighting, although she would only fight to feed the little child in her belly. "Why, must I . . ." she said, ". . . drag myself across the gardens in great misery? I can see you recover every year from bearing your fruit, and I observe how you bring up your young, following your wild, unruly nature; but I, the Princess's daughter, the Queen, shall not raise any of my noble progeny, I shall only be unhappy, and for that I hate my husband the King."

One day, as she sat in a solitary place under a palm, pain gripped her, and she gave birth to a son, who seemed to have the strength of a boy of seven years, for while he was being born, a she-bear had ventured across the river, and the little boy, barely freed from the womb, chased after the bear and clutched its fur. The animal swam back across the river, carrying him into the woods. Then the Queen cried in a powerful mother's voice: "My son, my only born, is in the forest and is going to be eaten by wild beasts!"

The King's guards came racing across the river into the woods, with maces, with bow, with arrow, to retrieve their master's son. But the animals, seeing the men invading their territory by force, galloped out of the forest onto the riverbank, ready to fight back. The bears sat upright and held out their paws, the lions bared their teeth and whipped their sides with their tails, the tigers with fiery glances ran up and down the shore, the wolves howled, the elephants ripped up the soil and hurled rocks into the water, the birds flew out of their nests, making the air heavy with wings, and gave terrible screeches, so that none of the bold knights dared to approach the river. So the armored men ran back to their abandoned Queen because they believed the King's son was lost, but when they arrived near her, they found that she was giving birth, and indeed she gave birth to six sons, each of whom seemed happier and stronger than the other. Therefore no one grieved much for the lost child. The woman was brought with her six infants as a glorious mother before the King, who received her with honor and joy.

Then the little ones grew up, and the Queen gave them nourishment and tended to them with great patience, but when evening fell, she laid them on their beds and went behind the castle to the spot where the she-bear had abducted her first child. There she walked by the water, hoping she might entice her son out of the bushes; for hours, she worried very little in her heart about the other children; she could only think of the lost one, and could not believe that he had perished, in which she resembled the shepherd who frets about the one lamb that is lost more than the whole flock, and believes this lamb was the best.

She no longer dreads the wild beasts when she hears them howling at night, and when wild animals roam into the garden, she runs after them and asks about her child; but the beasts refuse to listen. Then she becomes impatient and desperate, she threatens and begs and grabs the bears by their furs, saying: "You have stolen my son from me!" But they do not care about her pleas and go about their business; they know who the woman is and do not hurt her. When she returns to the castle, she wipes her tears and lowers her face to gaze at the children, who are restless, and thus she hides her tears and thinks, "My poor children are restless and cold, I must warm them, and must give nourishment to calm them again." All day long she conceals her sadness from the people around her and she avoids turning her face to the light, for she is ashamed to feel more love for the one lost child than for the other six. Still, she teaches her sons with great patience and wisdom during the day; but in the evening, when the children sleep, she searches the forest for her lost son. Then she addresses the great birds of prey that float high in the air, flying back and forth to bring food to their young, and she often addresses one of them: "Oh, you, winged animal, if only I could flutter in the air as you do, gazing down at the bushes, looking for my son! Oh, tell me, is he still alive, or have you seen him dead?"

When the birds in the air squeal incomprehensibly, she thinks she understands a few words and brushes her hair to the side to hear better. She often believes that the birds were telling her that her child is still alive and will come to her soon. She struggles to interpret the screeching, she even speaks to the little buzzing bees and beetles that hover above the water. The insects swarm around her, droning, humming, each in its own manner, and then flit away.—Oh, poor Queen, no wild, inscrutable animal will give you advice: they do not know what a human complaint is. Because the people, they persecute animals and have no fellowship with them, instead taking their lives for their pelts or to eat their flesh, but no human being has ever turned to a wild beast for comfort.

Many a noble animal complain about the freedom which human beings have deceitfully stolen from them: captive beasts are slaves, which is not in their nature, and they must eat dry fodder in payment of their services while in the forest they would nibble fresh foliage; moreover, masters put bridles around the beasts' mouths, and why on earth should a free animal let itself be governed with the whip? Therefore, wild beasts do not trust human creatures and avoid them; but, when cornered, animals often snatch and maul people in horrible ways, just to get their freedom or their offspring back.

Despite all this, the Queen's other children were raised quite well, in all wisdom. The boys showed very peaceful spirits and followed the noblest principles in every endeavor. The King could not decide to whom he should bequeath the crown, for one could not say who among his sons had been born earlier, or whether one or the other was less fit to rule. If he let them compete for the prize in any tournament, it often happened that everyone won the same prize, or that each of them excelled in his special way. Nor could the King love one more than the other, for everyone

was handsome, and their nature compared to the feathers of a splendid bird in the sunlight: under a certain angle, the red or green color shimmer most beautifully. Under a different angle, other dazzling colors appear, or, if the bird soars or dips, moving its wings, then the colors change as fast as lightning, each as ravishing as the other, and one cannot determine which is best; as with the rainbow, where all the colors are gracefully gathered and together span the wide sky, each blending and growing out of the other. But the King did not have the right to divide his land or hand down the crown to more than one ruler; he therefore had a crown made of pure gold, large enough to embrace the heads of his six children, and he said to them, "As long as your minds remain as pure as gold, and that you kiss one another with all your love, and you are so united that you think as one—the way your heads are encompassed in this ring—I will be able to declare: my country has only one lord, and although this lord has many bodies, he has one mind only."

Then he announced a magnificent feast, during which his subjects would admire the new kings. All the nobles gathered at the court; a tall dais was erected in the open, and a golden throne, upon which the six sons of the King sat together, and he placed the crown on their heads. The quiet, lonely mother was in full adornment and splendor, in veils and overcoats embroidered with threads of gold—a sheer jubilation. She is called the Glorious Mother, now, and all instruments play a splendid music to praise her; but she hides her face behind the veils and cries bitter tears for her lost child. Then the King's sons descend from their shared seat, fall on their knees and beg for their mother's blessing. She rises and with her right hand gives the blessing to her children, but the left hand she holds upon her heart. She recalls her lost son.

The wild animals, having heard the people exulting at the four corners of the country, had become restless; they swam across the river in droves. When the guards brought the gruesome news, the courtiers fled to their apartments, but the mother refused to leave because she was not afraid. The sons refused to leave their mother, as she did not allow her sons to lead her away for her protection. The hordes of beasts drew near, and in the midst of them a regal face could be seen looking straight up to the heavens, and it seemed a man's face, only more handsome and noble. The young man rides on the backs of a lion and a tiger, gracefully jumping from one to the other. The mother, seeing him, says: "This is my son." And with her courageous nature she walks up to him and lowers her head against his breast, sensing the heavy stone lodged in her heart unmoor and roll away. The animals know who the woman is, and do not harm her, but the youth had no human language, he could only express his will by signs. Therefore, he took the crown and turned it around his head seven times. With his strong hands he uprooted an olive tree from the ground and gave each of the six brothers one twig, keeping the trunk for himself—a manner for him to signify: "I am the one ruler! But you shall live in peace with me." And he became king over animals and humans in spirit, if not in language.

Jacob (1785–1863) and Wilhelm (1786–1859) Grimm, also known as the brothers Grimm, are who most people think of when someone says "fairy tale." Both brothers followed their father's footsteps and attended law school, but neither felt that law was their calling. The duo turned to literary research and began collecting folk stories to share with their friends at get-togethers. After realizing how much they relished discovering these tales, the German academics traveled Europe, collecting folk music and literature to share with the world. Their two-volume work *Kinder- und Hausmärchen* (1812–1815), better known as *Grimm's Fairy Tales*, led to a revolution in the study of folklore. "Hans-My-Hedgehog" (1815) made its way to the screen in 1987 when it was used as an episode in Jim Henson's television series *The Storyteller*. Much like the other Grimm fairy tales, "Hans" features an unusual protagonist who teaches us all a lesson—while remaining a deeply and wonderfully strange story.

Hans-My-Hedgehog

Jacob and Wilhelm Grimm

ONCE UPON A TIME there was a peasant who had money and land enough, but as rich as he was, there was still something missing from his happiness: He had no children with his wife. Often when he went to the city with the other peasants, they would mock him and ask him why he had no children. He finally became angry, and when he returned home, he said, "I will have a child, even if it is a hedgehog."

Then his wife had a baby, and the top half was a hedgehog and the bottom half a boy. When she saw the baby, she was horrified and said, "Now see what you have wished upon us!"

The man said, "It cannot be helped. The boy must be baptized, but we cannot ask anyone to be his godfather."

The woman said, "And the only name that we can give him is Hans-My-Hedgehog."

When he was baptized, the pastor said, "Because of his quills he cannot be given an ordinary bed." So they put a little straw behind the stove and laid him in it. And he could not drink from his mother, for he would have stuck her with his quills. He lay there behind the stove for eight years, and his father grew tired of him, and thought, "if only he would die." But he did not die, but just lay there.

Now it happened that there was a fair in the city, and the peasant wanted to go. He asked his wife what he should bring her.

"A little meat, some bread rolls, and things for the household," she said. Then he asked the servant girl, and she wanted a pair of slippers and some fancy stockings.

Finally, he also said, "Hans-My-Hedgehog, what would you like?"

"Father," he said, "bring me some bagpipes."

When the peasant returned home he gave his wife what he had brought for her, meat and bread rolls. Then he gave the servant girl the slippers and fancy stockings. And finally he went behind the stove and gave Hans-My-Hedgehog the bagpipes.

When Hans-My-Hedgehog had them, he said, "Father, go to the blacksmith's and have my cock-rooster shod, then I will ride away and never again come back." The father was happy to get rid of him, so he had his rooster shod, and when it was done, Hans-My-Hedgehog climbed on it and rode away. He took pigs and donkeys with him, to tend in the forest.

In the forest the rooster flew into a tall tree with him. There he sat and watched over the donkeys and the pigs. He sat there for years, until finally the herd had grown large. His father knew nothing about him. While sitting in the tree, he played his bagpipes and made beautiful music.

One day a king came by. He was lost and heard the music. He was amazed to hear it, and sent a servant to look around and see where it was coming from. He looked here and there but only saw a little animal sitting high in a tree. It looked like a rooster up there with a hedgehog sitting on it making the music.

The king said to the servant that he should ask him why he was sitting there, and if he knew the way back to his kingdom. Then Hans-My-Hedgehog climbed down from the tree and told him that he would show him the way if the king would promise in writing to give him the first thing that greeted him at the royal court upon his arrival home.

The king thought, "I can do that easily enough. Hans-My-Hedgehog cannot understand writing, and I can put down what I want to."

Then the king took pen and ink and wrote

something, and after he had done so, Hans-My-Hedgehog showed him the way, and he arrived safely at home. His daughter saw him coming from afar, and was so overjoyed that she ran to meet him and kissed him. He thought about Hans-My-Hedgehog and told her what had happened, that he was supposed to have promised the first thing that greeted him to a strange animal that rode a rooster and made beautiful music. But instead he had written that this would not happen, for Hans-My-Hedgehog could not read. The princess was happy about this, and said that it was a good thing, for she would not have gone with him in any event.

Hans-My-Hedgehog tended the donkeys and pigs, was of good cheer, and sat in the tree blowing on his bagpipes.

Now it happened that another king came this way with his servants and messengers. He too got lost and did not know the way back home because the forest was so large. He too heard the beautiful music from afar, and asked one of his messengers to go and see what it was and where it was coming from. The messenger ran to the tree where he saw Hans-My-Hedgehog astride the cock-rooster. The messenger asked him what he was doing up there.

"I am tending my donkeys and pigs. What is it that you want?" replied Hans-My-Hedgehog.

The messenger said that they were lost and could not find their way back to their kingdom, and asked him if he could not show them the way.

Then Hans-My-Hedgehog climbed down from the tree with his rooster and told the old king that he would show him the way if he would give him the thing that he first met at home before the royal castle.

The king said yes and signed a promise to Hans-My-Hedgehog.

When that was done, Hans-My-Hedgehog rode ahead on his rooster showing them the way, and the king safely reached his kingdom. When the king arrived at his court there was great joy. Now he had an only daughter who was very beautiful. She ran out to him, threw her arms around his neck and kissed him, and was ever so happy that her old father had returned.

She asked him where he had been during his long absence, and he told her how he had lost his way and almost not made it home again, but that as he was making his way through a great forest he had come upon a half hedgehog, half human astride a rooster sitting in a tall tree and making beautiful music who had shown him the way, but whom he had promised whatever first met him at the royal court, and it was she herself, and he was terribly sorry.

But she promised that she would go with him when he came, for the love of her old father.

Hans-My-Hedgehog tended his pigs, and the pigs had more pigs, until there were so many that the whole forest was full. Then Hans-My-Hedgehog let his father know that they should empty out all the stalls in the village, because he was coming with such a large herd of pigs that everyone who wanted to would be able to take part in the slaughter.

It saddened the father to hear this, for he thought that Hans-My-Hedgehog had long since died. But Hans-My-Hedgehog mounted his cock-rooster, drove the pigs ahead of himself into the village, and had them butchered. What a slaughter! What a commotion! They could hear the noise two hours away!

Afterward Hans-My-Hedgehog said, "Father, have my cock-rooster shod a second time at the blacksmith's. Then I will ride away and not come back again as long as I live." So the father had the cock-rooster shod, and was happy that Hans-My-Hedgehog was not coming back.

Hans-My-Hedgehog rode into the first kingdom. The king had ordered that if anyone should approach who was carrying bagpipes and riding on a rooster, that he should be shot at, struck down, and stabbed, to prevent him from entering the castle. Thus when Hans-My-Hedgehog rode up, they attacked him with bayonets, but he spurred his rooster on, flew over the gate and up to the king's window. Landing there, he shouted to him, to give him what he had prom-

ised, or it would cost him and his daughter their lives.

Then the king told the princess to go out to him, in order to save his life and her own as well. She put on a white dress, and her father gave her a carriage with six horses, magnificent servants, money, and property. She climbed aboard and Hans-My-Hedgehog took his place beside her with his rooster and bagpipes. They said farewell and drove off.

The king thought that he would never see them again. However, it did not go as he thought it would, for when they had traveled a short distance from the city, Hans-My-Hedgehog pulled off her beautiful clothes and stuck her with his quills until she was bloody all over. "This is the reward for your deceit. Go away. I do not want you." With that he sent her back home, and she was cursed as long as she lived.

Hans-My-Hedgehog, astride his cock-rooster and carrying his bagpipes, rode on to the second kingdom where he had also helped the king find his way. This one, in contrast, had ordered that if anyone looking like Hans-My-Hedgehog should arrive, he should be saluted and brought to the royal castle with honors and with a military escort.

When the princess saw him she was horrified, because he looked so strange, but she thought that nothing could be done about it, because she had promised her father to go with him. She welcomed Hans-My-Hedgehog, and they were married. Then he was taken to the royal table, and she sat next to him while they ate and drank.

That evening when it was time to go to bed, she was afraid of his quills, but he told her to have no fear, for he would not hurt her. He told the old king to have four men keep watch by their bedroom door. They should make a large fire. He said that he would take off his hedgehog skin after going into the bedroom, and before getting into bed. The men should immediately pick it up and throw it into the fire, and then stay there until it was completely consumed by the fire.

When the clock struck eleven, he went into the bedroom, took off the hedgehog skin, and laid it down by the bed. The men rushed in, grabbed it, and threw it into the fire, and as soon as the fire consumed it, he was redeemed, and he lay there in bed entirely in the shape of a human. But he was as black as coal, as though he had been charred. The king sent for his physician, who washed him with good salves and balms. Then he became a handsome young gentleman.

When the princess saw what had happened, she was overjoyed, and they got up and ate and drank. Now their wedding was celebrated for real, and Hans-My-Hedgehog inherited the old king's kingdom.

Some years later he traveled with his wife to his father, and said that he was his son. But the father said that he did not have a son. He had had one, but he had been born with quills like a hedgehog and had gone off into the world. Then he said that he was the one, and the old father rejoiced and returned with him to his kingdom.

Ernst Theodor Wilhelm Hoffmann (1776–1822), E. T. A. Hoffmann, was a German writer and composer who also had a love for painting. His stories showcase the more grotesque sides of human nature, and much of his oeuvre could be considered a precursor to the modern horror genre, including his classic "The Sandman." In honor of the composer Wolfgang Amadeus Mozart, Hoffmann changed his name to Ernst Theodor Amadeus Hoffmann when he was thirty-seven years old. Many of his short stories included characters that were possessed by their art, and Hoffmann portrayed them so realistically, one could imagine that he was writing from experience. The story within a story reprinted here, taken from his famous "The Nutcracker and the Mouse King," was later made into a ballet by Tchaikovsky.

The Story of the Hard Nut

E. T. A. Hoffmann

Translated by Major Alex. Ewing

PERLIPAT'S MOTHER was the wife of a king— that is, a queen; and, in consequence, Perlipat, the moment she was born, was a princess by birth. The king was beside himself for joy as he saw his beautiful little daughter lying in her cradle; he danced about, and hopped on one leg, and sang out, "Was anything ever so beautiful as my Perlipatkin?"

And all the ministers, presidents, generals, and staff-officers, hopped likewise on one leg, and cried out, "No, never!" However, the real fact is, that it is quite impossible, as long as the world lasts, that a princess should be born more beautiful than Perlipat. Her little face looked like a web of the most beautiful lilies and roses, her eyes were the brightest blue, and her hair was like curling threads of shining gold.

Besides all this, Perlipat came into the world with two rows of pearly teeth, with which, two hours after her birth, she bit the lord chancellor's thumb so hard that he cried out, "O gemini!"

Some say he cried out, "O dear!" but on this subject people's opinions are very much divided, even to the present day. In short, Perlipat bit the lord chancellor on the thumb, and all the kingdom immediately declared that she was the wittiest, sharpest, cleverest little girl, as well as the most beautiful.

Now, everybody was delighted except the queen—she was anxious and dispirited, and nobody knew the reason; everybody was puzzled to know why she caused Perlipat's cradle to be so strictly guarded. Besides having guards at the door, two nurses always sat close to the cradle, and six other nurses sat every night round the room; and what was most extraordinary, each of these six nurses was obliged to sit with a great tom-cat in her lap, and keep stroking him all night, to amuse him, and keep him awake.

Now, my dear little children, it is quite impossible that you should know why Perlipat's mother took all these precautions; but I know and will tell you all about it. It happened that, once on a time a great many excellent kings and agreeable princesses were assembled at the court of Perlipat's father, and their arrival was celebrated by all sorts of tournaments, and plays, and balls. The king, in order to show how rich he was, determined to treat them with a feast which should astonish them. So he privately sent for the upper court cook-master, and ordered him to order the upper court astronomer to fix the time for a general pig-killing, and a universal sausage-making; then he jumped into his carriage, and called, himself, on all the kings and queens; but he only asked them to eat a bit of mutton with him, in order to enjoy their surprise at the delightful entertainment he had prepared for them.

Then he went to the queen, and said, "You already know, my love, the partiality I entertain for sausages." Now the queen knew perfectly well what he was going to say, which was that she herself (as indeed she had often done before) should undertake to superintend the sausage-making. So the first lord of the treasury was obliged to hand out the golden sausage-pot and the silver saucepans; and a large fire was made of sandal-wood; the queen put on her damask kitchen-pinafore; and soon after the sausage soup was steaming and boiling in the kettle. The delicious smell penetrated as far as the privycouncil-chamber; the king was seized with such extreme delight, that he could not stand it any longer.

"With your leave," said he, "my lords and gentlemen"—jumped over the table, ran down into the kitchen, gave the queen a kiss, stirred about the sausagebrew with his golden scepter, and then returned back to the privycouncil-chamber in an easy and contented state of mind.

The queen had now come to the point in the sausage making, when the bacon was cut into little bits and roasted on little silver spits. The ladies of honor retired from the kitchen, for the queen, with a proper confidence in herself, and consideration for her royal husband, performed alone this important operation.

But just when the bacon began to roast, a little whispering voice was heard, "Sister, I am a queen as well as you, give me some roasted bacon, too"; then the queen knew it was Mrs. Mouserinks who was talking.

Mrs. Mouserinks had lived a long time in the palace; she declared she was a relation of the king's, and a queen into the bargain, and she had a great number of attendants and courtiers underground. The queen was a mild, good-natured woman; and although she neither acknowledged Mrs. Mouserinks for a queen nor for a relation, yet she could not, on such a holiday as this, grudge her a little bit of bacon. So she said, "Come out, Mrs. Mouserinks, and eat as much as you please of my bacon."

Out hops Mrs. Mouserinks, as merry as you please, jumped on the table, stretched out her pretty little paw, and ate one piece of bacon after the other, until, at last, the queen got quite tired of her. But then out came all Mrs. Mouserinks' relations, and her seven sons, ugly little fellows, and nibbled all over the bacon; while the poor queen was so frightened that she could not drive them away. Luckily, however, when there still remained a little bacon, the first lady of the bed-chamber happened to come in; she drove all the mice away, and sent for the court mathematician, who divided the little that was left as equally as possible among all the sausages.

Now sounded the drums and the trumpets; the princes and potentates who were invited rode forth in glittering garments, some under white canopies, others in magnificent coaches, to the sausage feast. The king received them with hearty friendship and elegant politeness; then, as master of the land, with scepter and crown, sat down at the head of the table. The first course was polonies. Even then it was remarked that the king grew paler and paler; his eyes were raised to heaven, his breast heaved with sighs; in fact, he seemed to be agitated by some deep and inward sorrow. But when, the blood-puddings came on, he fell back in his chair, groaning and moaning, sighing and crying. Everybody rose from table; the physicians in ordinary in vain endeavored to feel the king's pulse: a deep and unknown grief had taken possession of him.

At last—at last, after several attempts had been made, several violent remedies applied, such as burning feathers under his nose, and the like, the king came to himself, and almost inaudibly gasped out the words, "Too little bacon!" Then the queen threw herself in despair at his feet: "Oh, my poor unlucky royal husband," said she, "what sorrows have you had to endure! but see here the guilty one at your feet; strike strike and spare not. Mrs. Mouserinks and her seven sons, and all her relations, ate up the bacon, and—and—" Here the queen tumbled backwards in a fainting fit! But the king arose in a violent passion, and said he, "My lady of the bedchamber, explain this matter." The lady of the bedchamber explained as far as she knew, and the king swore vengeance on Mrs. Mouserinks and her family for having eaten up the bacon which was destined for the sausages.

The lord chancellor was called upon to institute a suit against Mrs. Mouserinks and to confiscate the whole of her property; but as the king thought that this would not prevent her from eating his bacon, the whole affair was entrusted to the court machine and watch maker. This man promised, by a peculiar and extraordinary operation, to expel Mrs. Mouserinks and her family from the palace forever. He invented curious machines, in which pieces of roasted bacon were hung on little threads, and which he set round about the dwelling of Mrs. Mouserinks. But Mrs. Mouserinks was far too cunning—not to see the artifices of the court watch and machine maker; still all her warnings, all her cautions, were vain; her seven sons, and a great number of her relations, deluded by the sweet smell of the bacon, entered the watchmaker's machines, where, as soon as they bit at the bacon, a trap fell on them, and then they were quickly sent to judgment and execution in the kitchen. Mrs. Mouserinks, with

the small remnants of her court, left the place of sorrow, doubt, and astonishment. The court was rejoiced; but the queen alone was sorrowful; for she knew well Mrs. Mouserinks' disposition and that she would never allow the murder of her sons and relations to go unrevenged. It happened as she expected.

One day, whilst she was cooking some tripe for the king, a dish to which he was particularly partial, appeared Mrs. Mouserinks and said, "You have murdered my sons, you have killed my cousins and relations, take good care that the mouse, queen, does not bite your little princess in two. Take care." After saying this, she disappeared; but the queen was so frightened, that she dropped the tripe into the fire, and thus for the second time Mrs. Mouserinks spoiled the dish the king liked best; and of course he was very angry.

And now you know why the queen took such extraordinary care of princess Perlipatkin: was not she right to fear that Mrs. Mouserinks would fulfill her threat, come back, and bite the princess to death? The machines of the machine-maker were not of the slightest use against the clever and cunning Mrs. Mouserinks; but the court astronomer, who was also upper-astrologer and star-gazer, discovered that only the tom-cat family could keep Mrs. Mouserinks from the princess's cradle; for this reason each of the nurses carried one of the sons of this family on her lap, and, by continually stroking him down the back, managed to render the otherwise unpleasant court service less intolerable.

It was once at midnight, as one of the two chief nurses, who sat close by the cradle, awoke as it were from a deep sleep; everything around lay in profound repose; no purring, but the stillness of death; but how astonished was the chief nurse when she saw close before her a great ugly mouse, who stood upon his hind legs, and already had laid his hideous head on the face of the princess. With a shriek of anguish, she sprung up; everybody awoke; but Mrs. Mouserinks (for she it was who had been in Perlipat's cradle), jumped down, and ran into the corner of the room. The tom-cats went after, but too late; she had escaped through a hole in the floor.

Perlipat awoke with the noise, and wept aloud. "Thank heaven," said the nurses, "she lives!" But what was their horror, when, on looking at the before beautiful child, they saw the change which had taken place in her! Instead of the lovely white and red cheeks which she had had before, and the shining golden hair, there was now a great deformed head on a little withered body; the blue eyes had changed into a pair of great green gogglers, and the mouth had stretched from ear to ear. The queen was almost mad with grief and vexation, and the walls of the king's study were obliged to be wadded, because he was always dashing his head against them for sorrow, and crying out, "O luckless monarch!"

He might have seen how that it would have been better to have eaten the sausage without bacon, and to have allowed Mrs. Mouserinks quietly to stay underground. Upon this subject, however, Perlipat's royal father did not think at all, but he laid all the blame on the court watch-maker, Christian Elias Drosselmeier, of Nurem-berg. He therefore issued this wise order, that Drosselmeier, should before four weeks restore the princess to her former state, or at least find out a certain and infallible means for so doing; or, in failure thereof, should suffer a shameful death under the ax of the executioner.

Drosselmeier was terribly frightened; but, trusting to his learning and good fortune, he immediately performed the first operation which seemed necessary to him. He carefully took Prin-cess Perlipat to pieces, took off her hands and feet, and thus was able to see the inward structure; but there, alas! he found that the princess would grow uglier as she grew older, and he had no remedy for it. He put the princess neatly together again, and sunk down in despair at her cradle; which he never was permitted to leave.

The fourth week had begun—yes, it was Wednesday! when the king, with eyes flash-ing with indignation, entered the room of the princess; and, waving his scepter, he cried out, "Christian Elias Drosselmeier, cure the prin-cess, or die!" Drosselmeier began to cry bitterly, but little Princess Perlipat went on cracking her nuts. Then first was the court watchmaker struck with the princess's extraordinary partiality for nuts, and the circumstance of her having come into the world with teeth. In fact, she had cried incessantly since her metamorphosis, until some-one by chance gave her a nut; she immediately cracked it, ate the kernel, and was quiet.

From that time the nurses found nothing so effectual as to bring her nuts. "O holy instinct of natural, eternal and unchangeable sympathy of all beings; thou showest me the door to the secret. I will knock, and thou wilt open it." He then asked permission to speak to the court astrono-mer, and was led out to him under a strong guard. These two gentlemen embraced with many tears, for they were great friends; they then entered into a secret cabinet, where they looked over a great number of books which treated of instincts, sym-pathies, and antipathies, and other deep subjects. The night came; the court astronomer looked to the stars, and made the horoscope of the princess, with the assistance of Drosselmeier, who was also very clever in this science. It was a troublesome business, for the lines were always wandering this way and that; at last, however, what was their joy to find that the princess Perlipat, in order to be freed from the enchantment which made her so ugly, and to become beautiful again, had only to eat the sweet kernel of the nut Krakatuk.

Now the nut Krakatuk had such a hard shell that an eight-and-forty-pound cannon could drive over without breaking it. But this nut was only to be cracked by a man who had never shaved, and never worn boots; he was to break it in the princess's presence, and then to present the kernel to her with his eyes shut; nor was he to open his eyes until he had walked seven steps backwards without stumbling. Drosselmeier and the astronomer worked without stopping three days and three nights; and, as the king was at din-ner on Saturday, Drosselmeier (who was to have had his head off Sunday morning early), rushed into the room, and declared he had found the means of restoring the princess Perlipat to her former beauty. The king embraced him with fervent affection, promised him a diamond sword, four orders, and two new coats for Sundays.

"We will go to work immediately after dinner," said the king in the most friendly manner, "and thou, dear watchmaker, must see that the young unshaven gentleman in shoes be ready with the nut Krakatuk. Take care, too, that he drink no wine before, that he may not stumble as he walks his seven steps backwards like a crab; afterwards he may get as tipsy as he pleases."

Drosselmeier was very much frightened at this speech of the king's; and it was not without fear and trembling that he stammered out that it was true that the means were known, but that both the nut Krakatuk, and the young man to crack it, were yet to be sought for; so that it was not impossible that nut and cracker would never be found at all. In tremendous fury the king swung his scepter over his crowned head, and cried, with a lion's voice, "Then you must be beheaded, as I said before."

It was a lucky thing for the anxious and unfortunate Drosselmeier that the king had found his dinner very good that day, and so was in a disposition to listen to any reasonable suggestions, which the magnanimous queen, who deplored Drosselmeier's fate, did not fail to bring forward. Drosselmeier took courage to plead that, as he had found out the remedy and the means whereby the princess might be cured, he was entitled to his life. The king said this was all stupid nonsense; but, after he had drunk a glass of cherry-brandy, concluded that both the watchmaker and the astronomer should immediately set off on their journey, and never return, except with the nut Krakatuk in their pocket. The man who was to crack the same was, at the queen's suggestion, to be advertised for in all the newspapers, in the country and out of it.

Drosselmeier and the court astronomer had been fifteen years on their journey without finding any traces of the nut Krakatuk. The countries in which they were, and the wonderful sights they saw, would take me a month at least to tell of. This, however, I shall not do: all I shall say is, that at last the miserable Drosselmeier felt an irresistible longing to see his native town Nuremberg. This longing came upon him most particularly as he and his friend were sitting together smoking a pipe in the middle of a wood; in Asia. "O Nuremberg, delightful city! Who's not seen thee, him I pity! All that beautiful is, in London, Petersburg, or Paris, are nothing when compared to thee! Nuremberg, my own city!"

As Drosselmeier deplored his fate in this melancholy manner, the astronomer, struck with pity for his friend, began to howl so loudly that it was heard all over Asia. But at last he stopped crying, wiped his eyes, and said, "Why do we sit here and howl, my worthy colleague? Why don't we set off at once for Nuremberg? Is it not perfectly the same where and how we seek this horrid nut Krakatuk?"

"You are right," said Drosselmeier; so they both got up, emptied their pipes, and walked from the wood in the middle of Asia to Nuremberg at a stretch.

As soon as they had arrived in Nuremberg, Drosselmeier hastened to the house of a cousin of his, called Christopher Zachariah Drosselmeier, who was a carver and gilder, and whom he had not seen for a long, long time. To him the watchmaker related the whole history of Princess Perlipat, of Mrs. Mouserinks, and the nut Krakatuk; so that Christopher Zachariah clapped his hands for wonder, and said, "O, cousin, cousin, what extraordinary stories are these!" Drosselmeier then told his cousin of the adventures which befell him on his travels: how he had visited the grand duke of Almonds, and the king of Walnuts; how he had inquired of the Horticultural Society of Acornshausen; in short, how he had sought everywhere, but in vain, to find some traces of the nut Krakatuk.

During this recital Christopher Zachariah had been snapping his fingers, and opening his eyes, calling out, hum! and ha! and oh! and ah! At last, he threw his cap and wig up to the ceiling, embraced his cousin, and said, "Cousin, I'm very much mistaken, very much mistaken, I say, if I don't myself possess this nut Krakatuk!" He then fetched a little box, out of which he took a gilded nut, of a middling size. "Now," said he, as he showed his cousin the nut, "the history of this nut is this: Several years ago, a man came here on Christmas Eve with a sackful of nuts, which he offered to sell cheap. He put the sack just before my booth, to guard it against the nut-sellers of the town, who could not bear that a foreigner should sell nuts in their native city. At that moment a heavy wagon passed over his sack, and cracked every nut in it except one, which the man, laughing in an extraordinary way, offered to sell me for a silver half-crown of the year 1720. This seemed odd to me. I found just such a half-crown in my pocket, bought the nut, and gilded it, not knowing myself why I bought it so dear and valued it so much." Every doubt with respect to its being the nut which they sought was removed by the astronomer, who, after removing the gilding, found written on the shell, in Chinese characters, the word "Krakatuk."

The joy of the travelers was excessive, and Drosselmeier's cousin, the gilder, the happiest man under the sun, on being promised a handsome pension and the gilding of all the gold in the treasury into the bargain. The two gentlemen, the watchmaker and the astronomer, had put on their night caps and were going to bed, when the latter (that is, the astronomer) said, "My worthy friend and colleague, you know one piece of luck follows another, and I believe that we have not only found the nut Krakatuk, but also the young man who shall crack it, and present the kernel of beauty to the princess; this person I conceive to be the son of your cousin!" "Yes," continued he, "I am determined not to sleep until I have cast the youth's horoscope." With these words he took his night cap from his head, and instantly commenced his observations.

In fact, the gilder's son was a handsome well-grown lad, who had never shaved, and never worn boots. At Christmas he used to wear an elegant red coat embroidered with gold; a sword, and a hat under his arm, besides having his hair beautifully powdered and curled. In this way he used to stand before his father's booth, and with a gallantry which was born with him, crack the nuts for the young ladies, who, from this peculiar quality of his, had already called him "Nutcrackerkin."

Next morning the astronomer fell delighted on the neck of the watchmaker, and cried, "We have him—he is found! but there are two things of which, my dear friend and colleague, we must take particular care: first, we must strengthen the under-jaw of your excellent nephew with a tough piece of wood, and then, on returning home, we must carefully conceal having brought with us the young man who is to bite the nut; for I read by the horoscope that the king, after several people have broken their teeth in vainly attempting to crack the nut, will promise to him who shall crack it, and restore the princess to her former beauty—will promise, I say, to this man the princess for a wife, and his kingdom after his death."

Of course the gilder was delighted with the idea of his son marrying the Princess Perlipat and becoming a prince and king; and delivered him over to the two deputies. The wooden jaw which Drosselmeier had fixed in his young and hopeful nephew answered to admiration, so that in cracking the hardest peachstones he came off with distinguished success.

As soon as Drosselmeier and his comrade had made known the discovery of the nut, the requisite advertisements were immediately issued; and as the travelers had returned with the means of restoring the princess's beauty, many hundred young men, among whom several princes might be found, trusting to the soundness of their teeth, attempted to remove the enchantment of the princess. The ambassadors were not a little frightened when they saw the princess again. The little body with the wee hands and feet could scarcely support the immense deformed head! The hideousness of the countenance was increased by a woolly beard, which spread over mouth and chin. Everything happened as the astronomer had foretold. One dandy in shoes after another broke teeth and jaws upon the nut Krakatuk, without in the slightest degree helping the princess, and as they were carried away half-dead to the dentist (who was always ready), groaned out—that was a hard nut!

When now the king in the anguish of his heart had promised his daughter and kingdom to the man who would break the enchantment, the gentle Drosselmeier made himself known, and begged to be allowed the trial. No one had pleased the princess so much as this young man; she laid her little hand on her heart, and sighed inwardly, Ah! if he were the person destined to crack Krakatuk, and be my husband! Young Drosselmeier, approaching the queen, the king, and the princess Perlipat in the most elegant manner, received from the hands of the chief master of ceremonies the nut Krakatuk, which he immediately put into his mouth,—and crack! crack!—broke the shell in a dozen pieces; he neatly removed the bits of shell which yet remained on the kernel, and then with a most profound bow presented it to the princess, shut his eyes, and proceeded to step backwards. The princess swallowed the kernel; and oh! wonderful wonder! her ugliness disappeared, and, instead, was seen a form of angel beauty, with a countenance like lilies and roses mixed, the eyes of glancing azure, and the full locks curling like threads of gold. Drums and trumpets mingled with the rejoicings of the people. The king and the whole court danced upon one leg, as before, at Perlipat's birth, and the queen was obliged to be sprinkled all over with eau de Cologne, since she had fainted with excessive joy.

This great tumult did not a little disturb young Drosselmeier, who had yet his seven steps to accomplish: however, he recollected himself, and had just put his right foot back for the seventh step, when Mrs. Mouserinks, squeaking in a most hideous manner, raised herself from the floor, so that Drosselmeier, as he put his foot backwards, trod on her, and stumbled,—nay, almost fell down. What a misfortune! The young man became at that moment just as ugly as ever was the princess Perlipat. The body was squeezed together, and could scarcely support the thick deformed head, with the great goggling eyes and wide gaping mouth. Instead of the wooden roof for his mouth, a little wooden mantel hung out from behind his back.

The watchmaker and astronomer were beside themselves with horror and astonishment; but they saw how Mrs. Mouserinks was creeping along the floor all bloody. Her wickedness, however, was not unavenged, for Drosselmeier had struck her so hard on the neck with the sharp heel of his shoe, that she was at the point of death; but just as she was in her last agonies, she squeaked out in the most piteous manner, "O Krakatuk, from thee I die! but Nutcracker dies as well as I; and thou, my son, with the seven crowns, revenge thy mother's horrid wounds! Kill the man who did attack her, that naughty, ugly wicked Nutcracker!" Quick with this cry died Mrs. Mouserinks, and was carried off by the royal housemaid.

Nobody had taken the least notice of young Drosselmeier. The princess, however, reminded the king of his promise, and he immediately ordered the young hero to be brought before him. But when that unhappy young man appeared in his deformed state, the princess put her hands before her and cried out, "Away with that nasty Nutcracker!" So the court marshal took him by his little shoulder and pushed him out of the door.

The king was in a terrible fury that anybody should ever think of making a nutcracker his son-in-law: he laid all the blame on the watchmaker and astronomer, and banished them both from his court and kingdom. This had not been seen by the astronomer in casting his horoscope; however, he found, on reading the stars a second time, that young Drosselmeier would so well behave himself in his new station, that, in spite of his ugliness, he would become prince and king. In the meantime, but with the fervent hope of soon seeing the end of these things, Drosselmeier remains as ugly as ever; so much so, that the nutcrackers in Nuremberg have always been made after the exact model of his countenance and figure.

Washington Irving (1783–1859) was an American historian and writer born the last of eleven children. In 1802, he published his first book—a collection of letters under the pseudonym Geoffrey Crayon. Continuing in the same vein, many of his earlier essays were centered on society, told with a satirical whimsy. After the death of his fiancée, Matilda Hoffman, in 1809, Irving stopped writing until he met Sir Walter Scott. Scott energized Irving, and with a renewed zeal, Irving completed *The Sketch Book of Geoffrey Crayon, Gent.* (1819), a collection of stories and essays. His famous short stories, "The Legend of Sleepy Hollow" and "Rip Van Winkle," both Americanized retellings of German folktales, were a part of this collection. Never again did he take a literary hiatus until, in the year 1859, Irving was laid to rest in the Sleepy Hollow Cemetery.

Rip Van Winkle

Washington Irving

A POSTHUMOUS WRITING OF DIEDRICH KNICKERBOCKER.

By Woden, God of Saxons,
From whence comes Wensday, that is Wodensday,
Truth is a thing that ever I will keep
Unto thylke day in which I creep into
My sepulchre—
CARTWRIGHT.

[THE FOLLOWING TALE was found among the papers of the late Diedrich Knickerbocker, an old gentleman of New York, who was very curious in the Dutch History of the province and the manners of the descendants from its primitive settlers. His historical researches, however, did not lie so much among books as among men; for the former are lamentably scanty on his favorite topics; whereas he found the old burghers, and still more, their wives, rich in that legendary lore, so invaluable to true history. Whenever, therefore, he happened upon a genuine Dutch family, snugly shut up in its low-roofed farm-house, under a spreading sycamore, he looked upon it as a little clasped volume of black-letter, and studied it with the zeal of a bookworm.

———

The result of all these researches was a history of the province, during the reign of the Dutch governors, which he published some years since. There have been various opinions as to the literary character of his work, and, to tell the truth, it is not a whit better than it should be. Its chief merit is its scrupulous accuracy, which indeed was a little questioned on its first appearance, but has since been completely established; and it is now admitted into all historical collections, as a book of unquestionable authority.

The old gentleman died shortly after the publication of his work; and now that he is dead and gone, it cannot do much harm to his memory to say that his time might have been much better employed in weightier labors. He, however, was apt to ride his hobby his own way; and though it did now and then kick up the dust a little in the eyes of his neighbors, and grieve the spirit of some friends, for whom he felt the truest deference and affection, yet his errors and follies are remembered "more in sorrow than in anger," and it begins to be suspected, that he never intended to injure or offend. But however his memory may be appreciated by critics, it is still held dear among many folks, whose good opinion is well worth having; particularly by certain biscuit-bakers, who have gone so far as to imprint his likeness on their new-year cakes, and have thus given him a chance for immortality, almost equal to the being stamped on a Waterloo medal, or a Queen Anne's farthing.]

Whoever has made a voyage up the Hudson must remember the Kaatskill mountains. They are a dismembered branch of the great Appalachian family, and are seen away to the west of the river, swelling up to a noble height, and lording it over the surrounding country. Every change of season, every change of weather, indeed, every hour of the day produces some change in the magical hues and shapes of these mountains; and they are regarded by all the good wives, far and near, as perfect barometers. When the weather is fair and settled, they are clothed in blue and purple, and print their bold outlines on the clear evening sky; but sometimes, when the rest of the landscape is cloudless, they will gather a hood of gray vapors about their summits, which, in the last rays of the setting sun, will glow and light up like a crown of glory.

At the foot of these fairy mountains, the voyager may have descried the light smoke curling up from a Village, whose shingle roofs gleam among the trees, just where the blue tints of the upland melt away into the fresh green of the nearer landscape. It is a little village of great antiquity, having been founded by some of the Dutch colonists, in the early times of the province, just about the beginning of the government of the good Peter Stuyvesant (may he rest in peace!), and there were some of the houses of the original settlers standing within a few years, built of small yellow bricks, brought from Holland, having latticed windows and gable fronts, surmounted with weathercocks.

In that same village, and in one of these very houses (which, to tell the precise truth, was sadly time-worn and weather-beaten), there lived, many years since, while the country was yet a province of Great Britain, a simple, good-natured fellow, of the name of Rip Van Winkle. He was a descendant of the Van Winkles who figured so gallantly in the chivalrous days of Peter Stuyvesant, and accompanied him to the siege of Fort Christina. He inherited, however, but little of the martial character of his ancestors. I have observed that he was a simple, good-natured man; he was, moreover, a kind neighbor, and an obedient henpecked husband. Indeed, to the latter circumstance might be owing that meekness of spirit which gained him such universal popularity; for those men are apt to be obsequious and conciliating abroad, who are under the discipline of shrews at home. Their tempers, doubtless, are rendered pliant and malleable in the fiery furnace of domestic tribulation, and a curtain-lecture is worth all the sermons in the world for teaching the virtues of patience and long-suffering. A termagant wife may, therefore, in some respects, be considered a tolerable blessing, and if so, Rip Van Winkle was thrice blessed.

Certain it is, that he was a great favorite

among all the good wives of the village, who, as usual with the amiable sex, took his part in all family squabbles, and never failed, whenever they talked those matters over in their evening gossipings, to lay all the blame on Dame Van Winkle. The children of the village, too, would shout with joy whenever he approached. He assisted at their sports, made their playthings, taught them to fly kites and shoot marbles, and told them long stories of ghosts, witches, and Indians. Whenever he went dodging about the village, he was surrounded by a troop of them hanging on his skirts, clambering on his back, and playing a thousand tricks on him with impunity; and not a dog would bark at him throughout the neighborhood.

The great error in Rip's composition was an insuperable aversion to all kinds of profitable labor. It could not be for want of assiduity or perseverance; for he would sit on a wet rock, with a rod as long and heavy as a Tartar's lance, and fish all day without a murmur, even though he should not be encouraged by a single nibble. He would carry a fowling-piece on his shoulder, for hours together, trudging through woods and swamps, and up hill and down dale, to shoot a few squirrels or wild pigeons. He would never refuse to assist a neighbor even in the roughest toil, and was a foremost man in all country frolics for husking Indian corn, or building stone fences; the women of the village, too, used to employ him to run their errands, and to do such little odd jobs as their less obliging husbands would not do for them. In a word, Rip was ready to attend to anybody's business but his own; but as to doing family duty, and keeping his farm in order, he found it impossible.

In fact, he declared it was of no use to work on his farm; it was the most pestilent little piece of ground in the whole country; everything about it went wrong, in spite of him. His fences were continually falling to pieces; his cow would either go astray, or get among the cabbages; weeds were sure to grow quicker in his fields than anywhere else; the rain always made a point of setting in just as he had some out-door work to do; so that though his patrimonial estate had dwindled

away under his management, acre by acre, until there was little more left than a mere patch of Indian corn and potatoes, yet it was the worst-conditioned farm in the neighborhood.

His children, too, were as ragged and wild as if they belonged to nobody. His son Rip, an urchin begotten in his own likeness, promised to inherit the habits, with the old clothes, of his father. He was generally seen trooping like a colt at his mother's heels, equipped in a pair of his father's cast-off galligaskins, which he had much ado to hold up with one hand, as a fine lady does her train in bad weather.

Rip Van Winkle, however, was one of those happy mortals, of foolish, well-oiled dispositions, who take the world easy, eat white bread or brown, whichever can be got with least thought or trouble, and would rather starve on a penny than work for a pound. If left to himself, he would have whistled life away, in perfect contentment; but his wife kept continually dinning in his ears about his idleness, his carelessness, and the ruin he was bringing on his family. Morning, noon, and night, her tongue was incessantly going, and every thing he said or did was sure to produce a torrent of household eloquence. Rip had but one way of replying to all lectures of the kind, and that, by frequent use, had grown into a habit. He shrugged his shoulders, shook his head, cast up his eyes, but said nothing. This, however, always provoked a fresh volley from his wife, so that he was fain to draw off his forces, and take to the outside of the house—the only side which, in truth, belongs to a henpecked husband.

Rip's sole domestic adherent was his dog Wolf, who was as much henpecked as his master; for Dame Van Winkle regarded them as companions in idleness, and even looked upon Wolf with an evil eye, as the cause of his master's going so often astray. True it is, in all points of spirit befitting in honorable dog, he was as courageous an animal as ever scoured the woods—but what courage can withstand the evil-doing and all-besetting terrors of a woman's tongue? The moment Wolf entered the house, his crest fell, his tail drooped to the ground, or curled between his legs, he sneaked about with a gallows air, casting many a sidelong glance at Dame Van Winkle, and at the least flourish of a broomstick or ladle, he would fly to the door with yelping precipitation.

Times grew worse and worse with Rip Van Winkle as years of matrimony rolled on; a tart temper never mellows with age, and a sharp tongue is the only edged tool that grows keener with constant use. For a long while he used to console himself, when driven from home, by frequenting a kind of perpetual club of the sages, philosophers, and other idle personages of the village, which held its sessions on a bench before a small inn, designated by a rubicund portrait of his Majesty George the Third. Here they used to sit in the shade through a long, lazy summer's day, talking listlessly over village gossip, or telling endless, sleepy stories about nothing. But it would have been worth any statesman's money to have heard the profound discussions which sometimes took place, when by chance an old newspaper fell into their hands from some passing traveller. How solemnly they would listen to the contents, as drawled out by Derrick Van Bummel, the school-master, a dapper learned little man, who was not to be daunted by the most gigantic word in the dictionary; and how sagely they would deliberate upon public events some months after they had taken place.

The opinions of this junto were completely controlled by Nicholas Vedder, a patriarch of the village, and landlord of the inn, at the door of which he took his seat from morning till night, just moving sufficiently to avoid the sun, and keep in the shade of a large tree; so that the neighbors could tell the hour by his movements as accurately as by a sun-dial. It is true, he was rarely heard to speak, but smoked his pipe incessantly. His adherents, however (for every great man has his adherents), perfectly understood him, and knew how to gather his opinions. When any thing that was read or related displeased him, he was observed to smoke his pipe vehemently, and to send forth, frequent, and angry puffs; but when pleased, he would inhale the smoke slowly and tranquilly, and emit it in light and placid clouds, and sometimes, taking the pipe from his mouth, and letting the fragrant vapor curl about his nose, would gravely nod his head in token of perfect approbation.

From even this stronghold the unlucky Rip was at length routed by his termagant wife, who would suddenly break in upon the tranquility of the assemblage, and call the members all to naught; nor was that august personage, Nicholas Vedder himself, sacred from the daring tongue of this terrible virago, who charged him outright with encouraging her husband in habits of idleness.

Poor Rip was at last reduced almost to despair; and his only alternative, to escape from the labor of the farm and the clamor of his wife, was to take gun in hand, and stroll away into the woods. Here he would sometimes seat himself at the foot of a tree, and share the contents of his wallet with Wolf, with whom he sympathized as a fellow-sufferer in persecution. "Poor Wolf," he would say, "thy mistress leads thee a dog's life of it; but never mind, my lad, whilst I live thou shalt never want a friend to stand by thee!" Wolf would wag his tail, look wistfully in his master's face, and if dogs can feel pity, I verily believe he reciprocated the sentiment with all his heart.

In a long ramble of the kind, on a fine autumnal day, Rip had unconsciously scrambled to one of the highest parts of the Kaatskill mountains. He was after his favorite sport of squirrel-shooting, and the still solitudes had echoed and re-echoed with the reports of his gun. Panting and fatigued, he threw himself, late in the afternoon, on a green knoll, covered with mountain herbage, that crowned the brow of a precipice. From an opening between the trees, he could overlook all the lower country for many a mile of rich woodland. He saw at a distance the lordly Hudson, far, far below him, moving on its silent but majestic course, with the reflection of a purple cloud, or the sail of a lagging bark, here and there sleeping on its glassy bosom and at last losing itself in the blue highlands.

On the other side he looked down into a deep mountain glen, wild, lonely, and shagged, the bottom filled with fragments from the impending cliffs, and scarcely lighted by the reflected rays of the setting sun. For some time Rip lay musing on this scene; evening was gradually advancing; the mountains began to throw their long blue shadows over the valleys; he saw that it would be dark long before he could reach the village; and he heaved a heavy sigh when he thought of encountering the terrors of Dame Van Winkle.

As he was about to descend, he heard a voice from a distance hallooing: "Rip Van Winkle! Rip Van Winkle!" He looked around, but could see nothing but a crow winging its solitary flight across the mountain. He thought his fancy must have deceived him, and turned again to descend, when he heard the same cry ring through the still evening air, "Rip Van Winkle! Rip Van Winkle!"—at the same time Wolf bristled up his back, and giving a low growl, skulked to his master's side, looking fearfully down into the glen. Rip now felt a vague apprehension stealing over him; he looked anxiously in the same direction, and perceived a strange figure slowly toiling up the rocks, and bending under the weight of something he carried on his back. He was surprised to see any human being in this lonely and unfrequented place, but supposing it to be some one of the neighborhood in need of his assistance, he hastened down to yield it.

On nearer approach, he was still more surprised at the singularity of the stranger's appearance. He was a short, square-built old fellow, with thick bushy hair, and a grizzled beard. His dress was of the antique Dutch fashion—a cloth jerkin strapped round the waist—several pairs of breeches, the outer one of ample volume, decorated with rows of buttons down the sides, and bunches at the knees. He bore on his shoulders a stout keg, that seemed full of liquor, and made signs for Rip to approach and assist him with the load. Though rather shy and distrustful of this new acquaintance, Rip complied with his usual alacrity; and mutually relieving each other, they clambered up a narrow gully, apparently the dry bed of a mountain torrent. As they ascended, Rip every now and then heard long rolling peals, like distant thunder, that seemed to issue out of a deep ravine, or rather cleft between lofty rocks, toward which their rugged path conducted. He paused for an instant, but supposing it to be the muttering of one of those transient thundershowers which often take place in the mountain heights, he proceeded. Passing through the ravine, they came to a hollow, like a small amphitheater, surrounded by perpendicular precipices, over the brinks of which impending trees shot their branches, so that you only caught glimpses of the azure sky, and the bright evening cloud. During the whole time Rip and his companion had labored on in silence; for though the former marveled greatly what could be the object of carrying a keg of liquor up this wild mountain, yet there was something strange and incomprehensible about the unknown, that inspired awe, and checked familiarity.

On entering the amphitheater, new objects of wonder presented themselves. On a level spot in the center was a company of odd-looking personages playing at ninepins. They were dressed in quaint outlandish fashion; some wore short doublets, others jerkins, with long knives in their belts, and most of them had enormous breeches, of similar style with that of the guide's. Their visages, too, were peculiar; one had a large head, broad face, and small piggish eyes; the face of another seemed to consist entirely of nose, and was surmounted by a white sugar-loaf hat, set off with a little red cock's tail. They all had beards, of various shapes and colors. There was one who seemed to be the commander. He was a stout old gentleman, with a weather-beaten countenance; he wore a laced doublet, broad belt and hanger, high-crowned hat and feather, red stockings, and high-heeled shoes, with roses in them. The whole group reminded Rip of the figures in an old Flemish painting, in the parlor of Dominie Van Schaick, the village parson, and which had been brought over from Holland at the time of the settlement.

What seemed particularly odd to Rip was, that though these folks were evidently amusing themselves, yet they maintained the gravest faces, the most mysterious silence, and were, withal, the most melancholy party of pleasure he had ever witnessed. Nothing interrupted the stillness of the scene but the noise of the balls, which, whenever they were rolled, echoed along the mountains like rumbling peals of thunder.

As Rip and his companion approached them, they suddenly desisted from their play, and stared at him with such a fixed statue-like gaze, and such strange uncouth, lack-luster countenances, that his heart turned within him, and his knees smote together. His companion now emptied the contents of the keg into large flagons, and made signs to him to wait upon the company. He obeyed with fear and trembling; they quaffed the liquor in profound silence, and then returned to their game.

By degrees, Rip's awe and apprehension subsided. He even ventured, when no eye was fixed upon him, to taste the beverage which he found had much of the flavor of excellent Hollands. He was naturally a thirsty soul, and was soon tempted to repeat the draught. One taste provoked another; and he reiterated his visits to the flagon so often, that at length his senses were overpowered, his eyes swam in his head, his head gradually declined, and he fell into a deep sleep.

On waking, he found himself on the green knoll whence he had first seen the old man of the glen. He rubbed his eyes—it was a bright sunny morning. The birds were hopping and twittering among the bushes, and the eagle was wheeling aloft, and breasting the pure mountain breeze. "Surely," thought Rip, "I have not slept here all night." He recalled the occurrences before he fell asleep. The strange man with the keg of liquor—the mountain ravine—the wild retreat among the rocks—the woe-begone party at ninepins—the flagon—"Oh! that flagon! that wicked flagon!" thought Rip—"what excuse shall I make to Dame Van Winkle?"

He looked round for his gun, but in place of the clean well-oiled fowling-piece, he found an old firelock lying by him, the barrel encrusted with rust, the lock falling off, and the stock worm-eaten. He now suspected that the grave roisterers

of the mountains had put a trick upon him, and, having dosed him with liquor, had robbed him of his gun. Wolf, too, had disappeared, but he might have strayed away after a squirrel or partridge. He whistled after him and shouted his name, but all in vain; the echoes repeated his whistle and shout, but no dog was to be seen.

He determined to revisit the scene of the last evening's gambol, and if he met with any of the party, to demand his dog and gun. As he rose to walk, he found himself stiff in the joints, and wanting in his usual activity. "These mountain beds do not agree with me," thought Rip, "and if this frolic, should lay me up with a fit of the rheumatism, I shall have a blessed time with Dame Van Winkle." With some difficulty he got down into the glen: he found the gully up which he and his companion had ascended the preceding evening; but to his astonishment a mountain stream was now foaming down it, leaping from rock to rock, and filling the glen with babbling murmurs. He, however, made shift to scramble up its sides, working his toilsome way through thickets of birch, sassafras, and witch-hazel; and sometimes tripped up or entangled by the wild grape vines that twisted their coils and tendrils from tree to tree, and spread a kind of network in his path.

At length he reached to where the ravine had opened through the cliffs to the amphitheater; but no traces of such opening remained. The rocks presented a high impenetrable wall, over which the torrent came tumbling in a sheet of feathery foam, and fell into a broad deep basin, black from the shadows of the surrounding forest. Here, then, poor Rip was brought to a stand. He again called and whistled after his dog; he was only answered by the cawing of a flock of idle crows, sporting high in the air about a dry tree that overhung a sunny precipice; and who, secure in their elevation, seemed to look down and scoff at the poor man's perplexities. What was to be done? The morning was passing away, and Rip felt famished for want of his breakfast. He grieved to give up his dog and gun; he dreaded to meet his wife; but it would not do to starve among the mountains. He shook his head, shouldered the rusty firelock, and, with a heart full of trouble and anxiety, turned his steps homeward.

As he approached the village, he met a number of people, but none whom he knew, which somewhat surprised him, for he had thought himself acquainted with every one in the country round. Their dress, too, was of a different fashion from that to which he was accustomed. They all stared at him with equal marks of surprise, and whenever they cast eyes upon him, invariably stroked their chins. The constant recurrence of this gesture, induced Rip, involuntarily, to do, the same, when, to his astonishment, he found his beard had grown a foot long!

He had now entered the skirts of the village. A troop of strange children ran at his heels, hooting after him, and pointing at his gray beard. The dogs, too, not one of which he recognized for an old acquaintance, barked at him as he passed. The very village was altered: it was larger and more populous. There were rows of houses which he had never seen before, and those which had been his familiar haunts had disappeared. Strange names were over the doors—strange faces at the windows—everything was strange. His mind now misgave him; he began to doubt whether both he and the world around him were not bewitched. Surely this was his native village, which he had left but a day before. There stood the Kaatskill mountains—there ran the silver Hudson at a distance—there was every hill and dale precisely as it had always been—Rip was sorely perplexed—"That flagon last night," thought he, "has addled my poor head sadly!"

It was with some difficulty that he found the way to his own house, which he approached with silent awe, expecting every moment to hear the shrill voice of Dame Van Winkle. He found the house gone to decay—the roof had fallen in, the windows shattered, and the doors off the hinges. A half-starved dog, that looked like Wolf, was skulking about it. Rip called him by name, but the cur snarled, showed his teeth, and passed on. This was an unkind cut indeed. "My very dog," sighed poor Rip, "has forgotten me!"

He entered the house, which, to tell the truth, Dame Van Winkle had always kept in neat order. It was empty, forlorn, and apparently abandoned. This desolateness overcame all his connubial fears—he called loudly for his wife and children—the lonely chambers rang for a moment with his voice, and then all again was silence.

He now hurried forth, and hastened to his old resort, the village inn—but it too was gone. A large rickety wooden building stood in its place, with great gaping windows, some of them broken, and mended with old hats and petticoats, and over the door was painted, "The Union Hotel, by Jonathan Doolittle." Instead of the great tree that used to shelter the quiet little Dutch inn of yore, there now was reared a tall naked pole, with something on the top that looked like a red nightcap, and from it was fluttering a flag, on which was a singular assemblage of stars and stripes—all this was strange and incomprehensible. He recognized on the sign, however, the ruby face of King George, under which he had smoked so many a peaceful pipe, but even this was singularly metamorphosed. The red coat was changed for one of blue and buff, a sword was held in the hand instead of a sceptre, the head was decorated with a cocked hat, and underneath was painted in large characters, "GENERAL WASHINGTON."

There was, as usual, a crowd of folk about the door, but none that Rip recollected. The very character of the people seemed changed. There was a busy, bustling, disputatious tone about it, instead of the accustomed phlegm and drowsy tranquility. He looked in vain for the sage Nicholas Vedder, with his broad face, double chin, and fair long pipe, uttering clouds of tobacco-smoke, instead of idle speeches; or Van Bummel, the schoolmaster, doling forth the contents of an ancient newspaper. In place of these, a lean, bilious-looking fellow, with his pockets full of handbills, was haranguing, vehemently about rights of citizens—elections—members of Congress—liberty—Bunker's hill—heroes of seventy-six—and other words, which were a perfect Babylonish jargon to the bewildered Van Winkle.

The appearance of Rip, with his long, grizzled beard, his rusty fowling-piece, his uncouth dress, and the army of women and children at his heels, soon attracted the attention of the tavern politicians. They crowded round him, eying him from head to foot, with great curiosity. The orator bustled up to him, and, drawing him partly aside, inquired, "on which side he voted?" Rip stared in vacant stupidity. Another short but busy little fellow pulled him by the arm, and, rising on tiptoe, inquired in his ear, "whether he was Federal or Democrat." Rip was equally at a loss to comprehend the question; when a knowing, self-important old gentleman, in a sharp cocked hat, made his way through the crowd, putting them to the right and left with his elbows as he passed, and planting himself before Van Winkle, with one arm akimbo, the other resting on his cane, his keen eyes and sharp hat penetrating, as it were, into his very soul, demanded in an austere tone, "What brought him to the election with a gun on his shoulder, and a mob at his heels; and whether he meant to breed a riot in the village?"

"Alas! gentlemen," cried Rip, somewhat dismayed, "I am a poor, quiet man, a native of the place, and a loyal subject of the King, God bless him!"

Here a general shout burst from the bystanders—"a tory! a tory! a spy! a refugee! hustle him! away with him!" It was with great difficulty that the self-important man in the cocked hat restored order; and having assumed a tenfold austerity of brow, demanded again of the unknown culprit, what he came there for, and whom he was seeking. The poor man humbly assured him that he meant no harm, but merely came there in search of some of his neighbors, who used to keep about the tavern.

"Well—who are they?—name them."

Rip bethought himself a moment, and inquired, Where's Nicholas Vedder?

There was a silence for a little while, when an old man replied, in a thin, piping voice, "Nicho-las Vedder? why, he is dead and gone these eighteen years! There was a wooden tombstone in the churchyard that used to tell all about him, but that's rotten and gone too."

"Where's Brom Dutcher?"

"Oh, he went off to the army in the beginning of the war; some say he was killed at the storming of Stony-Point—others say he was drowned in a squall at the foot of Antony's Nose. I don't know—he never came back again."

"Where's Van Bummel, the schoolmaster?"

"He went off to the wars, too; was a great militia general, and is now in Congress."

Rip's heart died away, at hearing of these sad changes in his home and friends, and finding himself thus alone in the world. Every answer puzzled him too, by treating of such enormous lapses of time, and of matters which he could not understand: war—Congress—Stony-Point;—he had no courage to ask after any more friends, but cried out in despair, "Does nobody here know Rip Van Winkle?"

"Oh, Rip Van Winkle!" exclaimed two or three. "Oh, to be sure! that's Rip Van Winkle yonder, leaning against the tree."

Rip looked, and beheld a precise counterpart of himself as he went up the mountain; apparently as lazy, and certainly as ragged. The poor fellow was now completely confounded. He doubted his own identity, and whether he was himself or another man. In the midst of his bewilderment, the man in the cocked hat demanded who he was, and what was his name?

"God knows!" exclaimed he at his wit's end; "I'm not myself—I'm somebody else—that's me yonder—no—that's somebody else, got into my shoes—I was myself last night, but I fell asleep on the mountain, and they've changed my gun, and everything's changed, and I'm changed, and I can't tell what's my name, or who I am!"

The by-standers began now to look at each other, nod, wink significantly, and tap their fingers against their foreheads. There was a whisper, also, about securing the gun, and keeping the old fellow from doing mischief; at the very suggestion of which, the self-important man with the cocked hat retired with some precipitation. At this critical moment a fresh, comely woman pressed through the throng to get a peep at the gray-bearded man. She had a chubby child in her arms, which, frightened at his looks, began to cry. "Hush, Rip," cried she, "hush, you little fool; the old man won't hurt you." The name of the child, the air of the mother, the tone of her voice, all awakened a train of recollections in his mind.

"What is your name, my good woman?" asked he.

"Judith Cardenier."

"And your father's name?"

"Ah, poor man, Rip Van Winkle was his name, but it's twenty years since he went away from home with his gun, and never has been heard of since,—his dog came home without him; but whether he shot himself, or was carried away by the Indians, nobody can tell. I was then but a little girl."

Rip had but one more question to ask; but he put it with a faltering voice:

"Where's your mother?"

"Oh, she too had died but a short time since; she broke a blood-vessel in a fit of passion at a New-England pedler."

There was a drop of comfort, at least, in this intelligence. The honest man could contain himself no longer. He caught his daughter and her child in his arms. "I am your father!" cried he—"Young Rip Van Winkle once—old Rip Van Winkle now—Does nobody know poor Rip Van Winkle!"

All stood amazed, until an old woman, tottering out from among the crowd, put her hand to her brow, and peering under it in his face for a moment exclaimed, "sure enough! it is Rip Van Winkle—it is himself. Welcome home again, old neighbor. Why, where have you been these twenty long years?"

Rip's story was soon told, for the whole twenty years had been to him but as one night. The neighbors stared when they heard it; some were seen to wink at each other, and put their tongues in their cheeks; and the self-important man in the cocked hat, who, when the alarm was over, had returned to the field, screwed down the corners of his mouth, and shook his head—upon which there was a general shaking of the head throughout the assemblage.

It was determined, however, to take the opinion of old Peter Vanderdonk, who was seen slowly advancing up the road. He was a descendant of the historian of that name, who wrote one of the earliest accounts of the province. Peter was the most ancient inhabitant of the village, and well versed in all the wonderful events and traditions of the neighborhood. He recollected Rip at once, and corroborated his story in the most satisfactory manner. He assured the company that it was a fact, handed down from his ancestor, the historian, that the Kaatskill mountains had always been haunted by strange beings. That it was affirmed that the great Hendrick Hudson, the first discoverer of the river and country, kept a kind of vigil there every twenty years, with his crew of the Half-moon; being permitted in this way to revisit the scenes of his enterprise, and keep a guardian eye upon the river and the great city called by his name. That his father had once seen them in their old Dutch dresses playing at ninepins in the hollow of the mountain; and that he himself had heard, one summer afternoon, the sound of their balls, like distant peals of thunder.

To make a long story short, the company broke up, and returned to the more important concerns of the election. Rip's daughter took him home to live with her; she had a snug, well-furnished house, and a stout cheery farmer for a husband, whom Rip recollected for one of the urchins that used to climb upon his back. As to Rip's son and heir, who was the ditto of himself, seen leaning against the tree, he was employed to work on the farm; but evinced an hereditary disposition to attend to any thing else but his business.

Rip now resumed his old walks and habits; he soon found many of his former cronies, though all rather the worse for the wear and tear of time; and preferred making friends among the rising generation, with whom he soon grew into great favor.

Having nothing to do at home, and being arrived at that happy age when a man can be idle with impunity, he took his place once more on the bench, at the inn door, and was reverenced as one of the patriarchs of the village, and a chronicle of the old times "before the war." It was some time before he could get into the regular track of gossip, or could be made to comprehend the strange events that had taken place during his torpor. How that there had been a revolutionary war—that the country had thrown off the yoke of old England—and that, instead of being a subject to his Majesty George the Third, he was now a free citizen of the United States. Rip, in fact, was no politician; the changes of states and empires made but little impression on him; but there was one species of despotism under which he had long groaned, and that was—petticoat government. Happily, that was at an end; he had got his neck out of the yoke of matrimony, and could go in and out whenever he pleased, without dreading the tyranny of Dame Van Winkle. Whenever her name was mentioned, however, he shook his head, shrugged his shoulders, and cast up his eyes; which might pass either for an expression of resignation to his fate, or joy at his deliverance.

He used to tell his story to every stranger that arrived at Mr. Doolittle's hotel. He was observed, at first, to vary on some points every time he told it, which was, doubtless, owing to his having so recently awaked. It at last settled down precisely to the tale I have related, and not a man, woman, or child in the neighborhood, but knew it by heart. Some always pretended to doubt the reality of it, and insisted that Rip had been out of his head, and that this was one point on which he always remained flighty. The old Dutch inhabitants, however, almost universally gave it full credit. Even to this day, they never hear a thunder-storm of a summer afternoon about the Kaatskill, but they say Hendrick Hudson and his crew are at their game of ninepins; and it is a common wish of all henpecked husbands in the neighborhood, when life hangs heavy on their hands, that they might have a quieting draught out of Rip Van Winkle's flagon.

NOTE.

The foregoing tale, one would suspect, had been suggested to Mr. Knickerbocker by a little German superstition about the Emperor Frederick der Rothbart and the Kypphauser mountain; the subjoined note, however, which had appended to the tale, shows that it is an absolute fact, narrated with his usual fidelity.

"The story of Rip Van Winkle may seem incredible to many, but nevertheless I give it my full belief, for I know the vicinity of our old Dutch settlements to have been very subject to marvellous events and appearances. Indeed, I have heard many stranger stories than this, in the villages along the Hudson; all of which were too well authenticated to admit of a doubt. I have even talked with Rip Van Winkle myself, who, when last I saw him, was a very venerable old man, and so perfectly rational and consistent on every other point, that I think no conscientious person could refuse to take this into the bargain; nay, I have seen a certificate on the subject taken before a country justice, and signed with cross, in the justice's own handwriting. The story, therefore, is beyond the possibility of doubt. D. K."

POSTSCRIPT.

The following are travelling notes from a memorandum-book of Mr. Knickerbocker:

The Kaatsberg or Catskill mountains have always been a region full of fable. The Indians considered them the abode of spirits, who influenced the weather, spreading sunshine or clouds over the landscape, and sending good or bad hunting seasons. They were ruled by an old squaw spirit, said to be their mother. She dwelt on the highest peak of the Catskills, and had charge of the doors of day and night to open and shut them at the proper hour. She hung up the new moons in the skies, and cut up the old ones into stars. In times of drought, if properly propitiated, she would spin light summer clouds out of cobwebs and morning dew, and send them off from the crest of the mountain, flake after flake, like flakes of carded cotton, to float in the air; until, dissolved by the heat of the sun, they would fall in gentle showers, causing the grass to spring, the fruits to ripen, and the corn to grow an inch an hour. If displeased, however, she would brew up clouds black as ink, sitting in the midst of them like a bottle-bellied spider in the midst of its web; and when these clouds broke, woe betide the valleys!

In old times, say the Indian traditions, there was a kind of Manitou or Spirit, who kept about the wildest recesses of the Catskill mountains, and took a mischievous pleasure in wreaking all kind of evils and vexations upon the red men. Sometimes he would assume the form of a bear, a panther, or a deer, lead the bewildered hunter a weary chase through tangled forests and among ragged rocks, and then spring off with a loud ho! ho! leaving him aghast on the brink of a beetling precipice or raging torrent.

The favorite abode of this Manitou is still shown. It is a rock or cliff on the loneliest port of the mountains, and, from the flowering vines which clamber about it, and the wild flowers which abound in its neighborhood, is known by the name of the Garden Rock. Near the foot of it is a small lake, the haunt of the solitary bittern, with water-snakes basking in the sun on the leaves of the pond-lilies which lie on the surface. This place was held in great awe by the Indians, insomuch that the boldest hunter would not pursue his game within its precincts. Once upon a time, however, a hunter who had lost his way penetrated to the Garden Rock, where he beheld a number of gourds placed in the crotches of trees. One of these he seized and made off with it, but in the hurry of his retreat he let it fall among the rocks, when a great stream gushed forth, which washed him away and swept him down precipices, where he was dished to pieces, and the stream made its way to the Hudson, and continues to flow to the present day, being the identical stream known by the name of the Kaaterskill.

Jean Charles Emmanuel Nodier (1780–1844), who wrote as Charles Nodier, was a French author and librarian. Although considered a great writer in his time, Nodier is best known now for the influence he had on French Romanticism, in part by bringing Victor Hugo, Alfred de Musset, and many others together. The only works by Nodier that remain somewhat known are his masterful fantasy short stories, not those he published in the Romantic style. Nodier used short fictions to explore dreams and madness, much like Goethe and Shakespeare, both of whom influenced his writing. "The Luck of the Bean-Rows" is a fairy tale by Nodier that has been reprinted as "The Luck of the Bean Rows: A Fairy Tale" and "The Luck of the Bean-Rows: A Fairy-Tale for Lucky Children." Although there are many versions of the tale, the exact date of its first publication is a mystery.

The Luck of the Bean-Rows

A FAIRY-TALE FOR LUCKY CHILDREN

Charles Nodier

ONCE UPON A TIME there was a man and his wife who were poor and very old. They had never had any children, and this was a great trouble to them, for they foresaw that in a few years more they would not be able to grow their beans and take them to market.

One day while they were weeding in their field (that with a little cabin was all they possessed—I wish *I* owned as much!)—one day, I say, while they were getting rid of the weeds the old woman spied in a corner, where they grew thickest, a small bundle very carefully tied up; and what should she find in it but a lovely boy, eight or ten months old to look at, but quite two years in intelligence! He had been weaned; at all events he needed no pressing to partake of boiled beans, which he raised to his mouth very prettily.

On hearing his wife's cries of surprise, the old man hurried from the end of the field; and when he too had gazed at the beautiful child God had given them these old people embraced each other with tears of joy, and then returned quickly to their cabin lest the falling dew should hurt their boy. When they were snug in the chimney corner it was a fresh delight to them to see the little fellow reach out his hands to them, laughing winsomely, and calling them *mamma* and *pappa*, as though he had known no other father or mother.

The old man took him on his knee and danced him gently up and down, in "the way the ladies ride in the Park," and said all sorts of droll things to amuse him; and the child responded in his own prattling fashion, for who would like to seem backward in such jolly talk?

Meanwhile the old woman lit up the house with a fire of dry bean pods, which gladdened the little body of the newcomer, and prepared an excellent bean-pap which a spoonful of honey made delicious eating. Then she laid him to sleep in his fine white night clothes in the best bed of bean-chaff in the house; for these poor folk knew nothing of feather-beds and eider-downs. When he was fast asleep, "There is one thing that bothers me," said the old man to his wife, "and that is what we are to call this bonny boy, for we know neither his parents nor where he comes from."

"We must call him," said the old woman, for though she was but a simple peasant she was quick-witted, "The Luck of the Bean-rows, for it was in our bean field he came to us, the best of luck, to comfort us in our old age."

"There could not be a better name," the old man agreed.

It would make the story too long to tell what happened in the days and in all the years that followed; it is enough to know that the old people kept getting older and older, while one could almost see Luck of the Bean-rows putting on strength and good looks. Not that he was mighty of his inches, for at twelve he was only two and a half feet, and when he was at work in the bean field, of which he was very fond, you could hardly have seen him from the road, but his small figure was so shapely, and he was so winning in his looks and ways, so gentle, and yet so sure of his words, and he appeared so gallant in his sky-blue smock, red belt and gay Sunday bonnet with bean blossoms for feathers, that people wondered at him and many believed that he was really an elf or a fairy.

Many things, I grant, encouraged this notion. First of all, the cabin and the bean field—the bean field in which a few years ago a cow would have found nothing to graze on—had become one of the fine estates of the country-side; and not a soul could tell how it had happened. Well, to see beanstalks sprouting, to see them flowering, to see the blossom fading and the beans swelling ripe in the pods—there is nothing out of the common in that, but to see a whole bean field expanding, spreading out, with never a strip of land added, whether bought or knavishly taken from a neighbor's holding—that gets beyond understanding.

And all the while the bean field went on growing and spreading. It spread to the south wind, it spread to the north wind, it spread towards the dawn, it spread towards the sunset. And the neighbors measured their land to no purpose; they always found it full measure with a rod or two to the good, so they naturally concluded that the whole country was getting bigger.

Then again the beans bore so heavily that the cabin could never have contained the crop, had it not also grown larger. And yet for more than five leagues round the bean-crop failed, so that beans had become priceless because of the quantities sought for the tables of lords and kings.

In the midst of this abundance the Luck of the Bean-rows saw to everything himself, turning the soil, sorting the seed, cleansing the plants, weeding, digging, hoeing, harvesting, shelling, and, over and above, trimming hedges and mending wattle-fences. What time was left he spent bargaining with the market people, for he could read, write and keep accounts, though he had had no schooling. He was indeed a very blessing of a boy.

One night, when the Luck was asleep, the old man said to his wife: "There is Luck of the Bean-rows now, who has done so much to make us comfortable that we can spend the few years that are left us in peace and without labor. In making him heir to all we own we have given him only what is already his; and we should be thankless indeed if we did not try to secure him a more becoming position in life than that of a bean-merchant. A pity he is too modest for a professor's chair in the universities, and he is just a trifle too short for a general."

"It's a pity," said the old woman, "he hasn't studied enough to pick up the Latin names for five or six diseases. Eh, but they would be glad to make him a doctor right off!"

"Then as to law-suits," the old man went on, "I am afraid he has too much brains and good sense to clear up one of them."

"I have always had a fancy," said the old woman, "that when he came of age he would marry Pea-Blossom."

"Pea-Blossom," rejoined the old man, shaking his head, "is far too great a princess to marry a poor foundling, worth no more than a cabin and a bean field. Pea-Blossom, old dear, is a match for a squire or a justice of the peace, or for the king himself, if he came to be a widower. We are talking of a serious matter, do speak sense."

"Luck of the Bean-rows has more sense than both of us together," said his wife after a moment's thought. "Besides, it is his business, and it would not be proper to press it further without asking his opinion."

Whereupon the old couple turned over and went to sleep.

Day was just breaking when the Luck leaped out of bed to begin work in the field as usual. Who but he was surprised to find his Sunday clothes laid out on the chest where he had left his others at bedtime? "It is a week-day, anyway," he said to himself, "if the almanack hasn't gone wrong. Mother must be keeping some holiday of her own to have set out my best things. Well, let it be as she wishes. I would not cross her in anything at her great age, and after all it is easy to make up for an hour or two by rising earlier or working later."

So after a prayer to God for the health of his parents and the progress of the beans, he dressed as handsomely as he could. He was about to go out of doors if only to cast an eye at the fences before the old couple awoke, when his mother appeared on the threshold with a bowl of good steaming porridge, which she placed with a wooden spoon on his little table.

"Eat it up, eat it up!" she said; "do not be sparing of this porridge sweetened with honey and a pinch of green aniseed, just as you liked it when you were a little fellow; for the road is before you, laddie, and it is a long road you will travel to-day."

"That is good to hear," said Luck of the Bean-rows, looking at her in surprise; "and where are you sending me?"

The old woman sat down on a stool, and with her two hands on her knees, replied with a laugh: "Into the world, into the wide world, little Luck. You have never seen anyone but ourselves, and a few poor market folk you sell your beans to, to keep the house going, good lad. Now one day, one day, you will be a big man if the price of beans keeps up, so it will be well for you, dearie, to know some people in good society. I must tell you there is a great city four or five miles away where at every step one meets lords in cloth of gold and ladies in silver dresses with trails of roses. Your bonnie little face, so pleasant and so lively, will be sure to win them; and I shall be much mistaken if the day goes by without your getting some distinguished appointment at court or in the public offices, where you may earn much and do little. So eat it up and do not spare the good porridge sweetened with honey and a pinch of green aniseed.

"Now as you know more about the price of beans than about the value of money," the old woman went on, "you are to sell in the market these six quart measures of choice beans. I have not put more lest you should be overburdened. Besides, with beans as dear as they are now, you would be hard set to bring home the price even if they paid you only in gold. So we propose, father and I, that you should keep half of what you get to enjoy yourself properly, as young people should, or in buying yourself some pretty trinket to wear of a Sunday, such as a silver watch with ruby and emerald seals, or an ivory cup and ball or a Nuremberg humming-top. The rest of the money you can put in the bank.

"So away with you, my little Luck, since you have finished your porridge; and be sure that you do not lose time chasing butterflies, for we should die broken-hearted if you were not home before nightfall. And keep to the roads for fear of the wolves."

"I will do as you bid me, mother," replied the Luck of the Bean-rows, hugging the old woman, "though for my part I would sooner spend the day in the field. As for wolves, they don't trouble me with my weeding-hook."

So saying he slung his pronged hoe in his belt, and set out at a steady pace.

"Come back early," the old woman kept calling after him; she was already feeling sorry that she had let him go.

Luck of the Bean-rows tramped on and on, taking huge strides like a five-foot giant, and staring left and right at the strange things he saw by the way. He had never dreamed that the world was so big and so full of wonders.

When he had walked for an hour or more, as he reckoned by the height of the sun, and was puzzled that he had not yet reached the great city at the rate he was going, he thought he heard someone calling after him: "Whoo, whoo, whoo, whoo, twee! Please do stop, Master Luck of the Bean-rows."

"Who is it calling me?" cried Luck of the Bean-rows, clapping his hand on his pronged hoe.

"Please do stop at once. Whoo, whoo, whoo, whoo, twee! It is I who am calling you."

"Can it be possible?" asked Luck, raising his eyes to the top of an old pine, hollow and half dead, on which a great owl was swaying in the wind. "What is it we two can settle together, my bonnie bird?"

"It would be indeed a wonder if you recognised me," answered the owl, "for you had no notion that I was ever helping you, as a modest and honest owl should, by devouring at my own risk the swarms of rats which nibbled away half your crops, good year and bad year. That is why your field now brings you in what will buy you a pretty kingdom, if you know when you have enough. As for me, who have paid dearly for my care of others, I have not one wretched lean rat on the hooks of the larder against daylight, for now at night, with my eyes grown so dim in your service, I can scarcely see where I am going. So I called to you, generous Luck of the Bean-rows, to beg of you one of those good quart measures of beans hanging from your staff. It will keep me alive till my oldest son comes of age, and on his loyalty to you may reckon."

"Why that, Master Owl," cried Luck of the Bean-rows, taking one of his own three quart measures from the end of his staff, "is a debt of gratitude, and I am glad to repay it."

The owl darted down on the measure, caught it in his claws and beak, and with one flap of the wing carried it off to the tree-top.

"My word, but you are in a hurry to be off!" said the Luck. "May I ask, Master Owl, if I am still far from the great town mother is sending me to?"

"You are just going into it," answered the owl, as he flitted off to another tree.

Luck of the Bean-rows went on his way with a lighter staff; he felt sure he must be near the end of his journey, but he had hardly gone a hundred steps when he heard someone else calling:

"Behh, behh, bekky! Please stop, Master Luck of the Bean-rows!"

"I think I know that voice," said the Luck, turning round. "Why, yes, of course! It is that bare-faced rogue of a mountain she-goat, which prowls around my field with her kids for a toothsome snack. So it is you, is it, my lady raider?"

"What is that about raiding, fair Master Luck? I guess your hedges are too thick, your ditches too deep, your fences too close for any raiding. All one could do was to nip a few leaves that pushed through the chinks of the wattles, and our pruning makes the stalks thrive. You know the old saying:

Sheeps' teeth, loss and trouble,
Goats' teeth pay back double

"Say no more," broke in Luck of the Bean-rows; "and may all the ill I wished you fall upon my own head. But why did you stop me, and what can I do to please you, Madame Doe?"

"Misery me!" she sobbed, dropping big tears, "Behh, behh, bekky! it was to tell you that the wicked wolf had killed my husband, the buck; and now my little orphan and I are in sore need, for he will forage for us no more; and I fear my poor little kid will die of hunger if you cannot help her. So I called to you, noble Master Luck of the Bean-rows, to beg of pity one of those good quart measures of beans hanging from your staff. It will keep us till we get help from our kinsfolk."

"What you ask, Lady Doe," said the Luck, taking one of his two measures from his staff, "is an act of compassion and good will, and I am glad to do it for you."

The goat caught up the measure in her lips, and one bound carried her into the leafy thicket.

"My word, but you are in a hurry to be off!" cried Luck of the Bean-rows. "May I ask you, dear lady, if I am still far from the great town mother is sending me to?"

"You are there already," answered the goat as she buried herself deep among the bushes.

Once more the Luck went on his way, his staff the lighter by two quart measures. He was looking out for the walls of the big town when he noticed by a rustling along the skirt of the woods that someone was following him closely. He turned quickly towards the sound, with his pronged hoe gripped hard in his hand. Well for him that the prongs were open, for the prowler that was tracking him was a grim old wolf whose appearance promised no good.

"So it is you, evil beast!" cried Luck. "You hoped to give me the place of honor at your evening spread! By good fortune my two iron teeth," and he glanced at his hoe, "are worth all yours together, though I would not belittle *them*; so you may take it as settled, old crony, that you are to sup this evening without me. Consider yourself in luck, too, if I do not avenge the husband of the she-goat and the father of the kid who have been brought into pitiful straits by your cruelty. Perhaps I ought to, and it would only be justice, but I have been brought up with such a horror of blood that I am loth to shed even a wolf's."

So far the wolf had listened in deep humility; now he suddenly broke into a long and lamentable howl and turned up his eyes to heaven as if calling on it to bear witness.

"Oh, power divine, who clothed me as a wolf," he sobbed, "you know if ever I felt wicked desires in my heart. However, my lord," he added, with a bow of resignation towards Luck of the Bean-rows, "it lies with you to dispose of my wretched life. I place it at your mercy without fear and without remorse. If you think it right to make my death atone for the crimes of my race I shall die at your hands without repining; for ever since I fondled you in your cradle with pure delight, when your lady mother was not there, I have ever loved you dearly and truly honored you. Then you grew so handsome, so stately, that, only to look at you, one might have guessed you would become a great and magnanimous prince, as you have. Only I beg you to believe, before you condemn me, I did not stain these claws in the blood of the doe's luckless mate.

"I was brought up on principles of restraint and moderation; my fell is sprinkled with grey, but through all the years I have never swerved from them. At the time you mention I was abroad among my scattered tribesfolk, proclaiming sound moral doctrines in the hope of leading them by word and example to a frugal standard of living, that high aim of wolfish character. I will go further, my lord; that mountain goat was my good friend. I encouraged promising qualities in him; often we travelled together, discoursing by the way, for he had a bright wit and eagerness to learn. In my absence a sad quarrel for precedence (you know how touchy these rock people are on this point) was the cause of his death, which I have never got over."

The wolf wept—from the very depth of his heart it seemed, as inconsolable as the doe herself.

"For all that and all that," said the Luck of the Bean-rows, who had kept the prongs of his weeding-hook open, "you were stalking me."

"Following you, following you, yes," replied the wolf in wheedling tones, "in the hope of interesting you in my benevolent purpose, but in some more suitable place than this for conversation. Ah, I said to myself, if my lord Luck of the

Bean-rows, whose reputation is spread far and wide, would but share in my scheme of reform, he would have to-day a splendid opportunity. I warrant that one quart measure of those dainty beans hanging from his staff would convert a tribe of wolves, wolflings and cubs to a vegetable diet, and preserve countless generations of bucks, does and kids."

"It is the last of my measures," thought the Luck to himself, "but what do I want with cups and balls, rubies and humming-tops? And who would put child's play before something really useful?"

"There are your beans," he said as he took the last measure his mother had given him for his amusement. All the same he did not shut the prongs of his hoe. "It is all that was left of my own," said he, "but I don't regret it; and I shall be grateful to you, friend wolf, if you put it to the good use you have promised."

The wolf snapped his fangs on it and bounded away to his den.

"My word," said Luck of the Bean-rows, "you are in a hurry to be off! May I ask, Master Wolf, if I am still far from the great town mother is sending me to?"

"You have been there for long enough," replied the wolf, laughing out of the corner of his eyes; "and stay there a thousand years you will see nothing new."

Yet once more Luck of the Bean-rows went on his way, and kept looking about for the town walls, but never a glimpse of them was to be seen. He was beginning to feel tired when he was startled by piercing cries which came from a leafy by-path. He ran towards the sound.

"What is it?" he shouted, and gripped his weeding-hook. "Who is it crying for help? Speak; I cannot see you."

"It is I, it is Pea-Blossom," replied a low, sweet voice. "Oh, do come and get me out of this fix, Master Luck of the Bean-rows. It is easy as wishing and will cost you nothing."

"Believe me, madam," said the Luck, "it is not my way to count the cost when I can help. What-

ever I have is yours to command, except these three quart measures of beans on my staff; they are not mine, they belong to father and mother. Mine I have just given away to a venerable owl, to a saintly wolf, who is preaching like a hermit, and to the most charming of mountain does. I have not a bean left that I can offer you."

"You are laughing at me," returned Pea-Blossom, somewhat displeased. "Who spoke of beans, sir? I have no need for your beans; they are not known in my household. The service you can do me is to turn the door handle of my carriage and throw back the hood—it is nearly smothering me."

"I shall be delighted, madam," said Luck of the Bean-rows, "if I could only discover your carriage. No trace of a carriage here! And no room to drive on such a narrow path. Still I shall soon find it, for I can hear that you are quite close to me."

"What!" she cried with a merry laugh, "You cannot see my carriage! Why you almost trampled on it, running up in your wild way. It is right in front of you, dear Luck of the Bean-rows. You can tell it by its elegant appearance, which is something like a dwarf pea."

"It is so like a chick pea," thought the Luck as he bent down, "that if I hadn't looked very close I should have taken it for nothing but a chick pea."

One glance, however, showed him that it was really a very large dwarf pea, round as an orange, yellow as a lemon, mounted on four little golden wheels, equipped with a dainty "boot," or hold-all, made of a tiny peapod as bright and green as morocco.

He touched the handle; the door flew open; and Pea-Blossom sprang out like a grain of touch-me-not, and lighted nimbly and gaily on her feet.

The Luck stood up in amazement, never had he conceived of anyone so lovely as Pea-Blossom. Her face, indeed, was the most perfect a painter could have imagined—sparkling almond eyes of a wonderful violet, and a small frolicsome mouth which showed glimpses of bright teeth as white as alabaster. Her short dress, slightly puffed out and brocaded with sweet peas, came just below the knee. She wore tight stockings of white silk; and her adorable little feet why, one envied the lucky shoemaker who shod them in satin.

"What can you be staring at?" she asked, which shows, by the way, that Luck of the Bean-rows was not making a very brilliant appearance.

The Luck blushed, but quickly recovered himself. "I was wondering," he said modestly, "how so beautiful a princess, just about my own size too, could possibly find room in a dwarf pea."

"What a mistake to speak so slightingly of my carriage, Luck of the Bean-rows. It is a most comfortable carriage when it is open. And it is quite by chance that I have not my equerry, my almoner, my tutor, my secretary, and two or three of my ladies-in-waiting with me. But I like driving alone, and this fancy of mine caused the accident that has happened to me to-day.

"I don't know whether you have met the king of the crickets in company; no one could mistake his glittering black mask, like Harlequin's, with two straight movable horns, and his shrill sing song whenever he speaks. The king of the crickets condescended to fall in love with me. He was quite well aware that I come of age to-day, and that it is the custom for the princesses of our house to choose a husband when they are ten years old. So he put himself in my way—that too is the custom—and beset me with a frightful racket of piercing declarations. I answered him—also according to custom—by stopping my ears."

"Oh, joy!" exclaimed the Luck in rapture. "You are not going to marry the king of the crickets?"

"I am not going to marry him," Pea-Blossom declared with dignity. "My choice is made. But no sooner had I given my decision than the odious Crik-Crik (that is his name) flung himself on my carriage like a wild monster, and slammed down the hood. 'Get married now, saucy minx,' he shrieked, 'get married if anyone ever comes a-wooing you in this plight. *I* don't care a chick pea either for your kingdom or yourself.'"

"But do tell me," cried Luck of the Bean-rows, indignantly, "in what hole this king of the crickets is skulking. I will quickly ho him out and fling him bound hand and foot to your mercy. And yet," he continued, as he rested his head on his hand, "I can understand his desperation. But is it not my duty, princess, to escort you to your realm and protect you from pursuit?"

"That would certainly be advisable if I were far from the frontier," answered Pea-Blossom, "but yonder is a field of sweet-peas which my enemy dare not approach, and where I can count upon my faithful subjects."

As she spoke she struck the ground with her foot, and fell, clinging to two swaying stalks, which bent under her and then sprang up again, scattering their fragrant blossom over her hair.

As Luck of the Bean-rows watched her with delight—and I assure you I would have been delighted too—she pierced him with her bright eyes, and he was so spell-bound in the maze of her smile that he would have been happy to die watching her. At the least he might have been still standing there had she not spoken.

"I have delayed you too long already," she said, "for I know what a stirring business the trade in beans must be just at present; but my carriage—or rather your carriage—will enable you to recover the time you have lost. Please do not hurt my feelings by refusing so slight a gift. I have a thousand carriages like it in the corn-lofts of the castle, and when I would like a new one I pick it out of a handful and throw the rest to the mice."

"The least of your highness's favors would be the pride and joy of my life," replied the Luck of the Bean-rows, "but you have forgotten that I have luggage. I can easily imagine that however closely my bean measures may be filled I could manage to find room for your carriage in one of them, but to get my measures into your carriage, that would be impossible."

"Try it," laughed the princess as she swung up and down on the sprays of the sweet peas; "try it, and do not stand amazed at everything, as if you were a little child who had seen nothing."

And indeed Luck of the Bean-rows had no

difficulty in getting his three quart-measures into the body of the carriage—it could have held thirty and more, and he felt rather mortified.

"I am ready to start, madam," he said, as he took his place on a plump cushion, which was large enough to let him sit comfortably in any position, or even to lie at full length if he had been so minded.

"I owe it to my kind parents," he continued, "not to leave them in suspense as to what has become of me this first time of my ever leaving them; so I am waiting only for your coachman, who fled, no doubt in terror at the outbreak of the king of the crickets, and took the horses and shafts with him. I shall then leave this spot with everlasting regret that I should have seen you without hope of ever seeing you again."

The princess did not appear to notice the marked feeling of the Luck's last words.

"Why," she said, "my carriage does not need either coachman, shafts, or horses; it goes by steam, and at any hour it can easily do fifty thousand miles. You see you will have no trouble in getting home whenever it suits you. You have just to remember the gesture and words with which I start it.

"In the boot you will find various things that may be useful on the journey; they are every one of them yours. You open the boot as you would shell a green pea. There you will see three caskets, the shape and size of a pea, each fastened by a thread which keeps them in their cases like peas in a pod, so that they cannot jolt against each other when you travel or when you remove them. It is a wonderful contrivance!

"They will open at the pressure of your finger like the hood of my carriage. Then all you have to do is to make a hole in the ground with your hoe, and sow some of their contents in it, to see whatever you may wish spring up, sprout and blossom. Is not that wonderful?

"Only remember this!—when the third casket is empty I have nothing else to offer you; for I have only three green peas, just as you had three measures of beans; and the prettiest girl in the world can give you no more than she has."

"Are you ready to set out now?"

The Luck of the Bean-rows bowed; he felt that he could not speak. Pea-Blossom snapped her thumb and middle finger: "Off, chick pea!" she cried; and the field of sweet peas was left nine hundred miles behind while Luck of the Bean-rows was still turning this way and that, looking in vain for Pea-Blossom.

"Alas!" he sighed.

It would be doing scant justice to the speed of the magic carriage to say that it shot through space at the rate of a rifle bullet. Woods, towns, mountains, seas swept by quicker than magic lantern pictures. Far away horizons had scarcely risen in outline from the deep-down distance before they had plunged under the flying carriage. The Luck would have striven in vain to see them; when he turned to look back—flick! they had gone. At last, when he had several times outraced the sun, swept round the globe, caught it up and again outstripped it, with rapid changes from day to night and from night to day, it suddenly struck the Luck of the Bean-rows that he had passed the great town he was going to and the market for his beans.

"The springs of this carriage are a trifle lively," he thought to himself (he was nimble-witted, remember); "it started off on its giddy race before Pea-Blossom could tell me whither I was bound. I don't see why this journey should not last for ages and ages, for that lovely princess, who is young enough to be something of a madcap, told me how to start the carriage, but had no time to say how I was to stop it."

The Luck of the Bean-rows tried all the cries he had heard from carters, wagoners, and muleteers to bring it to a standstill, but it was all to no purpose. Every shout seemed but to quicken its wild career.

It sped from the tropics to the poles and back from the poles to the tropics, across all the parallels and meridians, quite unconcerned by the unhealthy changes of temperature. It was enough to broil them or to turn them to ice before long, if the Luck had not been gifted, as we have frequently remarked, with admirable intelligence.

"Ay," he said to himself, "considering that Pea-Blossom sent her carriage flying through the world with 'Off, chick pea!' it is just possible we can stop it by saying the exact opposite."

It was a logical idea.

"Stop, chick pea!" he cried, snapping his finger and thumb as Pea-Blossom had done.

Could a whole learned society have come to a more sensible conclusion? The fairy carriage came to a standstill so suddenly, you could not have stopped it quicker if you had nailed it down. It did not even shake.

The Luck of the Bean-rows alighted, picked up the carriage, and let it slip into a leather wallet which he carried at his belt for bean samples, but not before he had taken out the hold-all.

The spot where the flying carriage was pulled up in this fashion has not been described by travelers. Bruce says it was at the sources of the Nile. M. Douville places it on the Congo, and M. Saillé at Timbuctoo. It was a boundless plain, so parched, so stony, so wild that there was never a bush to lie under, not a desert moss to lay one's head upon and sleep, not a leaf to appease hunger or thirst. But Luck of the Bean-rows was not in the least anxious. He prized open the hold-all with his fingernail, and untied one of the three little caskets which Pea-Blossom had described to him. He opened it as he had opened the magic carriage, and planted its contents in the sand at the points of his hoe.

"Come of this what must come!" he said, "but I do badly want a tent to shelter me to-night, were it only a cluster of peas in flower; a little supper to keep me going, were it but a bowl of pea-soup sweetened, and a bed to lie upon, if only one feather of a hummingbird—and all the more as I cannot get back home to-day I am so worn out with hunger and aching fatigue."

The words had scarcely left his lips when he saw rising out of the sand a splendid pavilion in the shape of a pergola of sweet-peas. It grew up, it spread; from point to point it was supported upon ten props of gold; it dropped down leafy curtains strewn with pea-blossom; it curved into numberless arches, and from the center of each hung a crystal luster set with perfumed wax lights. The background of this arcade was lined with Venetian mirrors, which reflected a blaze of light that would have dazzled a seven-year-old eagle a league away. From overhead a pea leaf dropped by chance at the Luck's feet. It spread out into a magnificent carpet variegated with all the colors of the rainbow and many more. Around its border stood little round tables loaded with pastry and sweetmeats; and iced fruits in gilded porcelain cups encircled a brimming bowl of sweet-pea soup, sprinkled over with currants black as jet, green pistachio nuts, coriander comfits and slices of pineapple. Amid all this gorgeous show the Luck quickly discovered his bed, and that was the hummingbird's feather which he had wished for. It sparkled in a corner like a jewel dropped from the crown of the Grand Mogul, although it was so tiny that a grain of millet might have concealed it.

At first he thought this pigmy bed was not quite in keeping with the rich furnishing of the pavilion, but the longer he looked at it, the larger it grew, till hummingbirds' feathers were soon lying knee-deep on the floor a dream-couch of topazes so soft, sapphires so yielding, opals so elastic, that a butterfly would have sunk deep if he had lighted on them.

"That will do, that will do," cried the Luck of the Bean-rows; "I shall sleep too soundly as it is."

I need not say that our traveler did justice to the feast that was spread for him, and lost no time in preparing for bed. Thoughts of love ran through his mind, but at twelve years of age, love does not keep one awake; and Pea-Blossom, of whom he had had only a glimpse, had left him with no more than the impression of a delightful dream, the enchantment of which could only return in sleep. Another good reason for going to sleep if you have remembrances like mine.

The Luck of the Bean-rows, however, was too cautious to yield to these idle fancies until he had made sure that all was safe outside the pavilion, the very splendor of which was likely to attract all the thieves and vagabonds for miles round. You will find them in every country.

So, with his weeding-hook in his hand as usual, he passed out of the magic circle, to make the round of his tent and see that all was quiet.

No sooner had he reached the limit of the grounds, a narrow ravine washed out by running water that a kid might have cleared at a bound, than he was brought to a standstill by such a shiver as a brave man feels, for the most valiant has his moments of fright which he can master only by his resolute will. And, faith, there was enough to make one hesitate in what he saw.

It was a battle-front where in the darkness of a starless night glistened two hundred fixed and burning eyes; and along the ranks, from right to left, from left to right, there ran incessantly two keen slanting eyes which bespoke an extremely alert commander.

Luck of the Bean-rows knew nothing of Lavater or Gall or Spurzheim, he had never heard of phrenology, but within him he felt the natural instinct which teaches every living creature to sense an enemy from afar. At a glance he recognized in the leader of this horde of wolves the wheedling coward who had tricked him, with his talk of enlightenment and self-control, out of his last measure of beans.

"Master Wolf has lost no time in setting his lambs on my track," said Luck of the Bean-rows; "but by what magic have they overtaken me, every one of them, if these ruffians too have not travelled by chick pea? It is possible," he added with a sigh, "that the secrets of science are not unknown to scoundrels, and I dare not be sworn, when I think of it, that it is not they who have invented them so as to persuade simple souls the more easily to take part in their hateful schemes."

Though the Luck was cautious in doing, he was quick in planning. He drew the hold-all hastily from his wallet, untied the second pea-casket, opened it as he had done the first, and planted the contents in the sand at point of his weeding-hook.

"Come of this what must come!" said he; "but to-night I do badly want a strong wall, were it no thicker than a cabin wall, and a close hedge if only

as strong as my wattle fence, to save me from my good friends the wolves."

In a twinkle walls arose, not cabin walls, but walls of a palace; hedges sprung up before the porches, not wattle fences, but a high lordly railing of blue steel with gilded shafts and spear-heads that never a wolf, badger or fox could have tried to clear without bruising himself or pricking his pointed muzzle. With the art of warfare at the stage it had then reached among the wolves there was nothing to be done. After testing several points the invaders retired in confusion. Thankful for this relief, the Luck returned to his pavilion. But now he passed on over marble pavements, along pillared walks lit up as if for a wedding, up staircases which seemed to ascend forever and through galleries that were endless. He was overjoyed to come upon his pavilion of pea-blossom in the midst of a vast garden, green and blooming, which he had never seen before, and to find his bed of hummingbirds' feathers, where, I take it, he slept happier than a king and I never exaggerate. Next day the first thing he did was to explore the gorgeous dwelling which had sprung out of a little pea. The beauty of the most trifling things in it filled him with astonishment; for the furnishing of it was admirably in keeping with its outward appearance.

He examined, one after another, his gallery of pictures, his cabinet of antiques, his collections of medals, insects, shells, his library, each of them a wonder and a delight quite new to him.

He was especially pleased at the admirable judgment with which the books had been chosen. The finest works in literature, the most useful in science had been gathered together for the entertainment and instruction of a long life—among them the Adventures of the ingenious Don Quixote; fairy tales of every kind, with beautiful engravings; a collection of curious and amusing travels and voyages (those of Gulliver and Robinson Crusoe so far the most authentic); capital almanacks, full of diverting anecdotes and infallible information as to the phases of the moon and the best times for sowing and planting; numberless treatises, very simply and clearly written, on agriculture, gardening, angling, netting game, and the art of taming nightingales—in short, all one can wish for when one has learned to value books and the spirit of their authors. For there have been no other scholars, no other philosophers, no other poets, and for this unquestionable reason that all learning, all philosophy, all poetry are to be found in their pages, and to be found only there. I can answer for that.

While he was thus taking account of his wealth, the Luck of the Bean-rows was struck by the reflection of himself in one of the mirrors with which all the apartments were adorned. If the glass was not fooling him, he must have grown—oh, wonder of wonders!—more than three feet since yesterday. And the brown moustache which darkened his upper lip plainly showed that he was passing from sturdy boyhood to youthful manliness.

He was puzzling over this extraordinary change, when, to his great regret, a costly timepiece, between two pier-glasses, enabled him to solve the riddle. One of the hands pointed to the date of the year, and the Luck saw, without a shadow of doubt, that he had grown six years older.

"Six years!" he exclaimed. "Unfortunate creature that I am! My poor parents have died of old age, and perhaps in want. Oh, pity me, perhaps they died of grief, fretting over the loss of me. What must they have thought in their last hours of my deserting them or of the misfortune that had befallen me!

"Now I understand, hateful carriage, how you came to travel so fast; days and days were swallowed up in your minutes. Off, then; off, chick pea!" he continued as he took the magic coach from the wallet and flung it out of the window; "out of my sight, and fly so far that no eye may ever look on you again!"

And to tell the truth, so far as I know, no one has ever since cast eyes on a chick pea in the shape of a post-chaise that went fifty leagues an hour.

Luck of the Bean-rows descended the marble steps more sorrowfully than ever he went down the ladder of his bean-loft. He turned his back on the palace without even seeing it; he traversed those desert plains with never a thought of the wolves that might have encamped there to besiege him. He tramped on in a dream, striking his forehead with his hand and at times weeping.

"What is there to wish for now that my parents are dead?" he asked himself as he listlessly turned the little hold-all in his fingers, "now that Pea-Blossom has been married six years?—for it was on the day I saw her that she came of age, and then the princesses of her house are married. Besides, she had already made her choice. What does the whole world matter—my world which was made up of no more than a cabin, a bean field which you, little green pea," and he untied the last of the caskets from its case, "will never bring back to me. The sweet days of boyhood return no more!

"Go, little green pea, go whither the will of God may carry you, and bring forth what you are destined to bring, to the glory of your mistress. All is over and done with—my old parents, the cabin, the bean field and Pea-Blossom. Go, little green pea, far and far away."

He flung it from him with such force that it might have overtaken the magic carriage had it been of that mind; then he sank down on the sand, hopeless and full of sorrow.

When Luck of the Bean-rows raised himself up again the entire appearance of the plain was changed. Right away to the horizon it was a sea of dusky or of sunny green, over which the wind rolled tossing waves of white keel-shaped flowers with butterfly wings. Here they were flecked with violet like bean-blossom, there with rose like pea-blossom, and when the wind shook them together they were lovelier than the flowers of the loveliest garden plots.

Luck of the Bean-rows sprang forward; he recognized it all—the enlarged field, the improved cabin, his father and mother alive, hastening now to meet him as eagerly as their old limbs would carry them, to tell him that not a day had passed since he went away without their receiving news of him in the evening, and with the news kindly gifts which had cheered them, and good hopes of his return, which had kept them alive.

The Luck embraced them fondly, and gave them each an arm to accompany him to his palace. Now they wondered more and more as they approached it! Luck of the Bean-rows was afraid of overshadowing their joy, yet he could not help saying: "Ah, if you had seen Pea-Blossom! But it is six years since she married."

"Since I married you," said a gentle voice, and Pea-Blossom threw wide the iron gates:

"My choice was made then, do you not remember? Do come in," she continued, kissing the old man and the old woman, who could not take their eyes off her, for she too had grown six years older and was now sixteen; "Do come in! This is your son's home, and it is in the land of the spirit and of day dreams where one no longer grows old and where no one dies."

It would have been difficult to welcome these poor people with better news.

The marriage festivities were held with all the splendor befitting such high personages; and their lives never ceased to be a perfect example of love, constancy and happiness. This is the usual lucky ending of all good fairy tales.

Mary Wollstonecraft Shelley (1797–1851), sometimes known as Mary Shelley, was an English novelist and poet best known for her novel *Frankenstein; or, The Modern Prometheus* (1818), which arose out of a competition with her literary friends. However, her dystopian novel about the destruction of mankind due to a malicious plague, *The Last Man* (1826), is often considered her finest work. Wollstonecraft Shelley's innovative style has placed her as an ancestor to modern science fiction and of certain offshoots of Gothic horror. What many do not know is that Wollstonecraft Shelley's life was very similar to a Cinderella tale; her mother died when she was young and her stepmother treated her very poorly. Yet, it would lead to her finding solace in her father's library and later writing stories. An early example of doppelgänger fiction, "Transformation" is believed to have first made an appearance in *The Keepsake for 1831*, a gift book that Wollstonecraft Shelley contributed to, with "the author of *Frankenstein*" appearing as the story's byline.

Transformation

Mary Wollstonecraft Shelley

> *Forthwith this frame of mine was wrench'd*
> *With a woful agony,*
> *Which forced me to begin my tale,*
> *And then it set me free.*
> *Since then, at an uncertain hour,*
> *That agony returns;*
> *And till my ghastly tale is told*
> *This heart within me burns.*
> —Coleridge's *Ancient Mariner.*

I HAVE HEARD IT SAID, that, when any strange, supernatural, and necromantic adventure has occurred to a human being, that being, however desirous he may be to conceal the same, feels at certain periods torn up as it were by an intellectual earthquake, and is forced to bare the inner depths of his spirit to another. I am a witness of the truth of this. I have dearly sworn to myself never to reveal to human ears the horrors to which I once, in excess of fiendly pride, delivered myself over. The holy man who heard my confession, and reconciled me to the church, is dead. None knows that once—

Why should it not be thus? Why tell a tale

of impious tempting of Providence, and soul-subduing humiliation? Why? answer me, ye who are wise in the secrets of human nature! I only know that so it is; and in spite of strong resolve—of a pride that too much masters me—of shame, and even of fear, so to render myself odious to my species—I must speak.

Genoa! my birth-place-proud city! looking upon the blue waves of the Mediterranean sea—dost thou remember me in my boyhood, when thy cliffs and promontories, thy bright sky and gay vineyards, were my world? Happy time! when to the young heart the narrow-bounded universe, which leaves, by its very limitation, free scope to the imagination, enchains our physical energies, and, sole period in our lives, innocence and enjoyment are united. Yet, who can look back to childhood, and not remember its sorrows and its harrowing fears? I was born with the most imperious, haughty, tameless spirit, with which ever mortal was gifted. I quailed before my father only; and he, generous and noble, but capricious and tyrannical, at once fostered and checked the wild impetuosity of my character, making obedience necessary, but inspiring no respect for the motives which guided his commands. To be a man, free, independent; or, in better words, insolent and domineering, was the hope and prayer of my rebel heart.

My father had one friend, a wealthy Genoese noble, who in a political tumult was suddenly sentenced to banishment, and his property confiscated. The Marchese Torella went into exile alone. Like my father, he was a widower: he had one child, the almost infant Juliet, who was left under my father's guardianship. I should certainly have been an unkind master to the lovely girl, but that I was forced by my position to become her protector. A variety of childish incidents all tended to one point,—to make Juliet see in me a rock of refuge; I in her, one, who must perish through the soft sensibility of her nature too rudely visited, but for my guardian care. We grew up together. The opening rose in May was not more sweet than this dear girl. An irradiation of beauty was spread over her face. Her form,

her step, her voice—my heart weeps even now, to think of all of relying, gentle, loving, and pure, that was enshrined in that celestial tenement. When I was eleven and Juliet eight years of age, a cousin of mine, much older than either—he seemed to us a man—took great notice of my playmate; he called her his bride, and asked her to marry him. She refused, and he insisted, drawing her unwillingly towards him. With the countenance and emotions of a maniac I threw myself on him—I strove to draw his sword—I clung to his neck with the ferocious resolve to strangle him: he was obliged to call for assistance to disengage himself from me. On that night I led Juliet to the chapel of our house: I made her touch the sacred relics—I harrowed her child's heart, and profaned her child's lips with an oath, that she would be mine, and mine only.

Well, those days passed away. Torella returned in a few years, and became wealthier and more prosperous than ever. When I was seventeen my father died; he had been magnificent to prodigality; Torella rejoiced that my minority would afford an opportunity for repairing my fortunes. Juliet and I had been affianced beside my father's deathbed—Torella was to be a second parent to me.

I desired to see the world, and I was indulged. I went to Florence, to Rome, to Naples; thence I passed to Toulon, and at length reached what had long been the bourne of my wishes, Paris. There was wild work in Paris then. The poor king, Charles the Sixth, now sane, now mad, now a monarch, now an abject slave, was the very mockery of humanity. The queen, the dauphin, the Duke of Burgundy, alternately friends and foes now meeting in prodigal feasts, now shedding blood in rivalry—were blind to the miserable state of their country, and the dangers that impended over it, and gave themselves wholly up to dissolute enjoyment or savage strife. My character still followed me. I was arrogant and selfwilled; I loved display, and above all, I threw all control far from me. Who could control me in Paris? My young friends were eager to foster passions which furnished them with pleasures. I was deemed handsome—I was master of every knightly accomplishment. I was disconnected with any political party. I grew a favourite with all: my presumption and arrogance were pardoned in one so young: I became a spoiled child. Who could control me? not the letters and advice of Torella—only strong necessity visiting me in the abhorred shape of an empty purse. But there were means to refill this void. Acre after acre, estate after estate, I sold. My dress, my jewels, my horses and their caparisons, were almost unrivalled in gorgeous Paris, while the lands of my inheritance passed into possession of others.

The Duke of Orleans was waylaid and murdered by the Duke of Burgundy. Fear and terror possessed all Paris. The dauphin and the queen shut themselves up; every pleasure was suspended. I grew weary of this state of things, and my heart yearned for my boyhood's haunts. I was nearly a beggar, yet still I would go there, claim my bride, and rebuild my fortunes. A few happy ventures as a merchant would make me rich again. Nevertheless, I would not return in humble guise. My last act was to dispose of my remaining estate near Albaro for half its worth, for ready money. Then I despatched all kinds of artificers, arras, furniture of regal splendour, to fit up the last relic of my inheritance, my palace in Genoa. I lingered a little longer yet, ashamed at the part of the prodigal returned, which I feared I should play. I sent my horses. One matchless Spanish jennet I despatched to my promised bride; its caparisons flamed with jewels and cloth of gold. In every part I caused to be entwined the initials of Juliet and her Guido. My present found favour in hers and in her father's eyes.

Still to return a proclaimed spendthrift, the mark of impertinent wonder, perhaps of scorn, and to encounter singly the reproaches or taunts of my fellow-citizens, was no alluring prospect. As a shield between me and censure, I invited some few of the most reckless of my comrades to accompany me: thus I went armed against the world, hiding a rankling feeling, half fear and half penitence, by bravado and an insolent display of satisfied vanity.

I arrived in Genoa. I trod the pavement of my ancestral palace. My proud step was no interpreter of my heart, for I deeply felt that, though surrounded by every luxury, I was a beggar. The first step I took in claiming Juliet must widely declare me such. I read contempt or pity in the looks of all. I fancied, so apt is conscience to imagine what it deserves, that rich and poor, young and old, all regarded me with derision. Torella came not near me. No wonder that my second father should expect a son's deference from me in waiting first on him. But, galled and stung by a sense of my follies and demerit, I strove to throw the blame on others. We kept nightly orgies in Palazzo Carega. To sleepless, riotous nights, followed listless, supine mornings. At the Ave Maria we showed our dainty persons in the streets, scoffing at the sober citizens, casting insolent glances on the shrinking women. Juliet was not among them—no, no; if she had been there, shame would have driven me away, if love had not brought me to her feet.

I grew tired of this. Suddenly I paid the Marchese a visit. He was at his villa, one among the many which deck the suburb of San Pietro d'Arena. It was the month of May—a month of May in that garden of the world the blossoms of the fruit trees were fading among thick, green foliage; the vines were shooting forth; the ground strewed with the fallen olive blooms; the fire-fly was in the myrtle hedge; heaven and earth wore a mantle of surpassing beauty. Torella welcomed me kindly, though seriously; and even his shade of displeasure soon wore away. Some resemblance to my father—some look and tone of youthful ingenuousness, lurking still in spite of my misdeeds, softened the good old man's heart. He sent for his daughter—he presented me to her as her betrothed. The chamber became hallowed by a holy light as she entered. Hers was that cherub look, those large, soft eyes, full dimpled cheeks, and mouth of infantine sweetness, that expresses the rare union of happiness and love. Admiration first possessed me; she is mine! was the second proud emotion, and my lips curled with haughty triumph. I had not been the *enfant gâté* of the beauties of France not to have learnt the art of pleasing the soft heart of woman. If towards men I was overbearing, the deference I paid to them was the more in contrast. I commenced my courtship by the display of a thousand gallantries to Juliet, who, vowed to me from infancy, had never admitted the devotion of others; and who, though accustomed to expressions of admiration, was uninitiated in the language of lovers.

For a few days all went well. Torella never alluded to my extravagance; he treated me as a favourite son. But the time came, as we discussed the preliminaries to my union with his daughter, when this fair face of things should be overcast. A contract had been drawn up in my father's lifetime. I had rendered this, in fact, void, by having squandered the whole of the wealth which was to have been shared by Juliet and myself. Torella, in consequence, chose to consider this bond as cancelled, and proposed another, in which, though the wealth he bestowed was immeasurably increased, there were so many restrictions as to the mode of spending it, that I, who saw independence only in free career being given to my own imperious will, taunted him as taking advantage of my situation, and refused utterly to subscribe to his conditions. The old man mildly strove to recall me to reason. Roused pride became the tyrant of my thought: I listened with indignation—I repelled him with disdain.

"Juliet, thou art mine! Did we not interchange vows in our innocent childhood? are we not one in the sight of God? and shall thy cold-hearted, cold-blooded father divide us? Be generous, my love, be just; take not away a gift, last treasure of thy Guido—retract not thy vows—let us defy the world, and setting at nought the calculations of age, find in our mutual affection a refuge from every ill."

Fiend I must have been, with such sophistry to endeavour to poison that sanctuary of holy thought and tender love. Juliet shrank from me affrighted. Her father was the best and kindest of men, and she strove to show me how, in obeying him, every good would follow. He would receive my tardy submission with warm affection; and

generous pardon would follow my repentance. Profitless words for a young and gentle daughter to use to a man accustomed to make his will, law; and to feel in his own heart a despot so terrible and stern, that he could yield obedience to nought save his own imperious desires! My resentment grew with resistance; my wild companions were ready to add fuel to the flame. We laid a plan to carry off Juliet. At first it appeared to be crowned with success. Midway, on our return, we were overtaken by the agonized father and his attendants. A conflict ensued. Before the city guard came to decide the victory in favour of our antagonists, two of Torella's servitors were dangerously wounded.

This portion of my history weighs most heavily with me. Changed man as I am, I abhor myself in the recollection. May none who hear this tale ever have felt as I. A horse driven to fury by a rider armed with barbed spurs, was not more a slave than I, to the violent tyranny of my temper. A fiend possessed my soul, irritating it to madness. I felt the voice of conscience within me; but if I yielded to it for a brief interval, it was only to be a moment after torn, as by a whirlwind, away—borne along on the stream of desperate rage—the plaything of the storms engendered by pride. I was imprisoned, and, at the instance of Torella, set free. Again I returned to carry off both him and his child to France; which hapless country, then preyed on by freebooters and gangs of lawless soldiery, offered a grateful refuge to a criminal like me. Our plots were discovered. I was sentenced to banishment; and, as my debts were already enormous, my remaining property was put in the hands of commissioners for their payment. Torella again offered his mediation, requiring only my promise not to renew my abortive attempts on himself and his daughter. I spurned his offers, and fancied that I triumphed when I was thrust out from Genoa, a solitary and penniless exile. My companions were gone: they had been dismissed the city some weeks before, and were already in France. I was alone—friendless; with nor sword at my side, nor ducat in my purse.

I wandered along the sea-shore, a whirlwind of

passion possessing and tearing my soul. It was as if a live coal had been set burning in my breast. At first I meditated on what I should do. I would join a band of freebooters. Revenge!—the word seemed balm to me:—I hugged it—caressed it—till, like a serpent, it stung me. Then again I would abjure and despise Genoa, that little corner of the world. I would return to Paris, where so many of my friends swarmed; where my services would be eagerly accepted; where I would carve out fortune with my sword, and might, through success, make my paltry birth-place, and the false Torella, rue the day when they drove me, a new Coriolanus, from her walls. I would return to Paris-thus, on foot—a beggar—and present myself in my poverty to those I had formerly entertained sumptuously? There was gall in the mere thought of it.

The reality of things began to dawn upon my mind, bringing despair in its train. For several months I had been a prisoner: the evils of my dungeon had whipped my soul to madness, but they had subdued my corporeal frame. I was weak and wan. Torella had used a thousand artifices to administer to my comfort; I had detected and scorned them all—and I reaped the harvest of my obduracy. What was to be done? Should I crouch before my foe, and sue for forgiveness?—Die rather ten thousand deaths!—Never should they obtain that victory! Hate—I swore eternal hate! Hate from whom?—to whom?—From a wandering outcast to a mighty noble. I and my feelings were nothing to them: already had they forgotten one so unworthy. And Juliet!—her angel-face and sylphlike form gleamed among the clouds of my despair with vain beauty; for I had lost her—the glory and flower of the world! Another will call her his!—that smile of paradise will bless another!

Even now my heart fails within me when I recur to this rout of grim-visaged ideas. Now subdued almost to tears, now raving in my agony, still I wandered along the rocky shore, which grew at each step wilder and more desolate. Hanging rocks and hoar precipices overlooked the tideless ocean; black caverns yawned; and for ever, among the seaworn recesses, murmured and dashed the unfruitful waters. Now my way was almost barred by an abrupt promontory, now rendered nearly impracticable by fragments fallen from the cliff. Evening was at hand, when, seaward, arose, as if on the waving of a wizard's wand, a murky web of clouds, blotting the late azure sky, and darkening and disturbing the till now placid deep. The clouds had strange fantastic shapes; and they changed, and mingled, and seemed to be driven about by a mighty spell. The waves raised their white crests; the thunder first muttered, then roared from across the waste of waters, which took a deep purple dye, flecked with foam. The spot where I stood, looked, on one side, to the wide-spread ocean; on the other, it was barred by a rugged promontory. Round this cape suddenly came, driven by the wind, a vessel. In vain the mariners tried to force a path for her to the open sea—the gale drove her on the rocks. It will perish!—all on board will perish!—Would I were among them! And to my young heart the idea of death came for the first time blended with that of joy. It was an awful sight to behold that vessel struggling with her fate. Hardly could I discern the sailors, but I heard them. It was soon all over!—A rock, just covered by the tossing waves, and so unperceived, lay in wait for its prey. A crash of thunder broke over my head at the moment that, with a frightful shock, the skiff dashed upon her unseen enemy. In a brief space of time she went to pieces. There I stood in safety; and there were my fellow-creatures, battling, how hopelessly, with annihilation. Methought I saw them struggling—too truly did I hear their shrieks, conquering the barking surges in their shrill agony. The dark breakers threw hither and thither the fragments of the wreck: soon it disappeared. I had been fascinated to gaze till the end: at last I sank on my knees—I covered my face with my hands: I again looked up; something was floating on the billows towards the shore. It neared and neared. Was that a human form?—It grew more distinct; and at last a mighty wave, lifting the whole freight, lodged it upon a rock. A human being bestriding a sea-chest!—A human being!—Yet was it one? Surely never such had existed before—a misshapen dwarf, with squinting eyes, distorted features, and body deformed, till it became a horror to behold. My blood, lately warming towards a fellow-being so snatched from a watery tomb, froze in my heart. The dwarf got off his chest; he tossed his straight, straggling hair from his odious visage:

"By St. Beelzebub!" he exclaimed, "I have been well bested." He looked round and saw me. "Oh, by the fiend! here is another ally of the mighty one. To what saint did you offer prayers, friend—if not to mine? Yet I remember you not on board."

I shrank from the monster and his blasphemy. Again he questioned me, and I muttered some inaudible reply. He continued:—

"Your voice is drowned by this dissonant roar. What a noise the big ocean makes! Schoolboys bursting from their prison are not louder than these waves set free to play. They disturb me. I will no more of their ill-timed brawling.— Silence, hoary One!—Winds, avaunt!—to your homes! Clouds, fly to the antipodes, and leave our heaven clear!"

As he spoke, he stretched out his two long lank arms, that looked like spider's claws, and seemed to embrace with them the expanse before him. Was it a miracle? The clouds became broken, and fled; the azure sky first peeped out, and then was spread a calm field of blue above us; the stormy gale was exchanged to the softly breathing west; the sea grew calm; the waves dwindled to riplets.

"I like obedience even in these stupid elements," said the dwarf. "How much more in the tameless mind of man! It was a well got up storm, you must allow—and all of my own making."

It was tempting Providence to interchange talk with this magician. But Power, in all its shapes, is venerable to man. Awe, curiosity, a clinging fascination, drew me towards him.

"Come, don't be frightened, friend," said the wretch: "I am good humoured when pleased; and something does please me in your well proportioned body and handsome face, though you look a little woebegone. You have suffered a land—I, a sea wreck. Perhaps I can allay the tempest of your fortunes as I did my own. Shall we be friends?" —And he held out his hand; I could not touch it. "Well, then, companions—that will do as well. And now, while I rest after the buffeting I underwent just now, tell me why, young and gallant as you seem, you wander thus alone and downcast on this wild sea-shore."

The voice of the wretch was screeching and horrid, and his contortions as he spoke were frightful to behold. Yet he did gain a kind of influence over me, which I could not master, and I told him my tale. When it was ended, he laughed long and loud: the rocks echoed back the sound: hell seemed yelling around me.

"Oh, thou cousin of Lucifer!" said he; "so thou too hast fallen through thy pride; and, though bright as the son of Morning, thou art ready to give up thy good looks, thy bride, and thy well-being, rather than submit thee to the tyranny of good. I honour thy choice, by my soul!—So thou hast fled, and yield the day; and mean to starve on these rocks, and to let the birds peck out thy dead eyes, while thy enemy and thy betrothed rejoice in thy ruin. Thy pride is strangely akin to humility, methinks."

As he spoke, a thousand fanged thoughts stung me to the heart.

"What would you that I should do?" I cried.

"I!—Oh, nothing, but lie down and say your prayers before you die. But, were I you, I know the deed that should be done."

I drew near him. His supernatural powers made him an oracle in my eyes; yet a strange unearthly thrill quivered through my frame as I said, "Speak!—teach me—what act do you advise?"

"Revenge thyself, man!—humble thy enemies!—set thy foot on the old man's neck, and possess thyself of his daughter!"

"To the east and west I turn," cried I, "and see no means! Had I gold, much could I achieve; but, poor and single, I am powerless."

The dwarf had been seated on his chest as he listened to my story. Now he got off; he touched a spring; it flew open!—What a mine of wealth—of blazing jewels, beaming gold, and pale silver—was displayed therein. A mad desire to possess this treasure was born within me.

"Doubtless," I said, "one so powerful as you could do all things."

"Nay," said the monster, humbly, "I am less omnipotent than I seem. Some things I possess which you may covet; but I would give them all for a small share, or even for a loan of what is yours."

"My possessions are at your service," I replied, bitterly—"my poverty, my exile, my disgrace—I make a free gift of them all."

"Good! I thank you. Add one other thing to your gift, and my treasure is yours."

"As nothing is my sole inheritance, what besides nothing would you have?"

"Your comely face and well-made limbs."

I shivered. Would this all-powerful monster murder me? I had no dagger. I forgot to pray—but I grew pale.

"I ask for a loan, not a gift," said the frightful thing: "lend me your body for three days—you shall have mine to cage your soul the while, and, in payment, my chest. What say you to the bargain?—Three short days."

We are told that it is dangerous to hold unlawful talk; and well do I prove the same. Tamely written down, it may seem incredible that I should lend any ear to this proposition; but, in spite of his unnatural ugliness, there was something fascinating in a being whose voice could govern earth, air, and sea. I felt a keen desire to comply; for with that chest I could command the world. My only hesitation resulted from a fear that he would not be true to his bargain. Then, I thought, I shall soon die here on these lonely sands, and the limbs he covets will be mine no more:—it is worth the chance. And, besides, I knew that, by all the rules of art-magic, there were formula and oaths which none of its practisers dared break. I hesitated to reply; and he went on, now displaying his wealth, now speaking of the petty price he demanded, till it seemed madness to refuse. Thus is it: place our bark in the current of the stream, and down, over fall and cataract it is hurried; give up our conduct to the wild torrent of passion, and we are away, we know not whither.

He swore many an oath, and I adjured him by many a sacred name; till I saw this wonder of power, this ruler of the elements, shiver like an autumn leaf before my words; and as if the spirit spake unwillingly and per force within him, at last, lie, with broken voice, revealed the spell whereby he might be obliged, did he wish to play me false, to render up the unlawful spoil. Our warm life-blood must mingle to make and to mar the charm.

Enough of this unholy theme. I was persuaded—the thing was done. The morrow dawned upon me as I lay upon the shingles, and I knew not my own shadow as it fell from me. I felt myself changed to a shape of horror, and cursed my easy faith and blind credulity. The chest was there—there the gold and precious stones for which I had sold the frame of flesh which nature had given me. The sight a little stilled my emotions: three days would soon be gone.

They did pass. The dwarf had supplied me with a plenteous store of food. At first I could hardly walk, so strange and out of joint were all my limbs; and my voice—it was that of the fiend. But I kept silent, and turned my face to the sun, that I might not see my shadow, and counted the hours, and ruminated on my future conduct. To bring Torella to my feet—to possess my Juliet in spite of him—all this my wealth could easily achieve. During dark night I slept, and dreamt of the accomplishment of my desires. Two suns had set—the third dawned. I was agitated, fearful. Oh expectation, what a frightful thing art thou, when kindled more by fear than hope! How dost thou twist thyself round the heart, torturing its pulsations! How dost thou dart unknown pangs all through our feeble mechanism, now seeming to shiver us like broken glass, to nothingness now giving us a fresh strength, which can do nothing, and so torments us by a sensation, such as the strong man must feel who cannot break his fetters, though they bend in his grasp. Slowly paced the bright, bright orb up the eastern sky; long it lingered in the zenith, and still more slowly wandered down the west: it touched the horizon's verge—it was lost! Its glories were on the summits of the cliff—they grew dun and gray. The evening star shone bright. He will soon be here.

He came not!—By the living heavens, he came not!—and night dragged out its weary length, and, in its decaying age, "day began to grizzle its dark hair"; and the sun rose again on the most miserable wretch that ever upbraided its light. Three days thus I passed. The jewels and the gold—oh, how I abhorred them!

Well, well—I will not blacken these pages with demoniac ravings. All too terrible were the thoughts, the raging tumult of ideas that filled my soul. At the end of that time I slept; I had not before since the third sunset; and I dreamt that I was at Juliet's feet, and she smiled, and then she shrieked—for she saw my transformation— and again she smiled, for still her beautiful lover knelt before her. But it was not I—it was he, the fiend, arrayed in my limbs, speaking with my voice, winning her with my looks of love. I strove to warn her, but my tongue refused its office; I strove to tear him from her, but I was rooted to the ground—I awoke with the agony. There were the solitary hoar precipices—there the plashing sea, the quiet strand, and the blue sky over all. What did it mean? was my dream but a mirror of the truth? was he wooing and winning my betrothed? I would on the instant back to Genoa—but I was banished. I laughed—the dwarf's yell burst from my lips—I banished! O, no! they had not exiled the foul limbs I wore; I might with these enter, without fear of incurring the threatened penalty of death, my own, my native city.

I began to walk towards Genoa. I was somewhat accustomed to my distorted limbs; none were ever so ill adapted for a straight-forward movement; it was with infinite difficulty that I proceeded. Then, too, I desired to avoid all the hamlets strewed here and there on the sea-beach, for I was unwilling to make a display of my hideousness. I was not quite sure that, if seen, the mere boys would not stone me to death as I passed, for a monster: some ungentle

salutations I did receive from the few peasants or fishermen I chanced to meet. But it was dark night before I approached Genoa. The weather was so balmy and sweet that it struck me that the Marchese and his daughter would very probably have quitted the city for their country retreat. It was from Villa Torella that I had attempted to carry off Juliet; I had spent many an hour reconnoitering the spot, and knew each inch of ground in its vicinity. It was beautifully situated, embosomed in trees, on the margin of a stream. As I drew near, it became evident that my conjecture was right; nay, moreover, that the hours were being then devoted to feasting and merriment. For the house was lighted up; strains of soft and gay music were wafted towards me by the breeze. My heart sank within me. Such was the generous kindness of Torella's heart that I felt sure that he would not have indulged in public manifestations of rejoicing just after my unfortunate banishment, but for a cause I dared not dwell upon.

The country people were all alive and flocking about; it became necessary that I should study to conceal myself; and yet I longed to address some one, or to hear others discourse, or in any way to gain intelligence of what was really going on. At length, entering the walks that were in immediate vicinity to the mansion, I found one dark enough to veil my excessive frightfulness; and yet others as well as I were loitering in its shade. I soon gathered all I wanted to know—all that first made my very heart die with horror, and then boil with indignation. To-morrow Juliet was to be given to the penitent, reformed, beloved Guido—to-morrow my bride was to pledge her vows to a fiend from hell! And I did this!—my accursed pride—my demoniac violence and wicked self-idolatry had caused this act. For if I had acted as the wretch who had stolen my form had acted—if, with a mien at once yielding and dignified, I had presented myself to Torella, saying, I have done wrong, forgive me; I am unworthy of your angel-child, but permit me to claim her hereafter, when my altered conduct shall manifest that I abjure my vices, and endeavour to become in some sort worthy of her. I go to serve against the infidels; and when my zeal for religion and my true penitence for the past shall appear to you to cancel my crimes, permit me again to call myself your son. Thus had he spoken; and the penitent was welcomed even as the prodigal son of scripture: the fatted calf was killed for him; and he, still pursuing the same path, displayed such open-hearted regret for his follies, so humble a concession of all his rights, and so ardent a resolve to reacquire them by a life of contrition and virtue, that he quickly conquered the kind, old man; and full pardon, and the gift of his lovely child, followed in swift succession.

O! had an angel from Paradise whispered to me to act thus! But now, what would be the innocent Juliet's fate? Would God permit the foul union—or, some prodigy destroying it, link the dishonoured name of Carega with the worst of crimes? To-morrow at dawn they were to be married: there was but one way to prevent this—to meet mine enemy, and to enforce the ratification of our agreement. I felt that this could only be done by a mortal struggle. I had no sword—if indeed my distorted arms could wield a soldier's weapon—but I had a dagger, and in that lay my every hope. There was no time for pondering or balancing nicely the question: I might die in the attempt; but besides the burning jealousy and despair of my own heart, honour, mere humanity, demanded that I should fall rather than not destroy the machinations of the fiend.

The guests departed—the lights began to disappear; it was evident that the inhabitants of the villa were seeking repose. I hid myself among the trees—the garden grew desert—the gates were closed—I wandered round and came under a window—ah! well did I know the same!—a soft twilight glimmered in the room—the curtains were half withdrawn. It was the temple of innocence and beauty. Its magnificence was tempered, as it were, by the slight disarrangements occasioned by its being dwelt in, and all the objects scattered around displayed the taste of her who hallowed it by her presence. I saw her enter with a quick light step—I saw her approach the window—she drew back the curtain yet further, and looked out into the night. Its breezy freshness played among her ringlets, and wafted them from the transparent marble of her brow. She clasped her hands, she raised her eyes to Heaven. I heard her voice. Guido! she softly murmured, Mine own Guido! and then, as if overcome by the fullness of her own heart, she sank on her knees:—her upraised eyes—her negligent but graceful attitude—the beaming thankfulness that lighted up her face—oh, these are tame words! Heart of mine, thou imagest ever, though thou canst not portray, the celestial beauty of that child of light and love.

I heard a step—a quick firm step along the shady avenue. Soon I saw a cavalier, richly dressed, young and, methought, graceful to look on, advance.—I hid myself yet closer.—The youth approached; he paused beneath the window. She arose, and again looking out she saw him, and said—I cannot, no, at this distant time I cannot record her terms of soft silver tenderness; to me they were spoken, but they were replied to by him.

"I will not go," he cried: "here where you have been, where your memory glides like some Heaven-visiting ghost, I will pass the long hours till we meet, never, my Juliet, again, day or night, to part. But do thou, my love, retire; the cold morn and fitful breeze will make thy cheek pale, and fill with languor thy love-lighted eyes. Ah, sweetest! could I press one kiss upon them, I could, methinks, repose."

And then he approached still nearer, and methought he was about to clamber into her chamber. I had hesitated, not to terrify her; now I was no longer master of myself. I rushed forward—I threw myself on him—I tore him away—I cried, "O loathsome and foul-shaped wretch!"

I need not repeat epithets, all tending, as it appeared, to rail at a person I at present feel some partiality for. A shriek rose from Juliet's lips. I neither heard nor saw—I felt only mine enemy, whose throat I grasped, and my dagger's hilt; he struggled, but could not escape: at length hoarsely he breathed these words: "Do!—strike home! destroy this body—you will still live: may your life be long and merry!"

The descending dagger was arrested at the word, and he, feeling my hold relax, extricated himself and drew his sword, while the uproar in the house, and flying of torches from one room to the other, showed that soon we should be separated—and I—oh! far better die: so that he did not survive, I cared not. In the midst of my frenzy there was much calculation:—fall I might, and so that he did not survive, I cared not for the death-blow I might deal against myself. While still, therefore, he thought I paused, and while I saw the villanous resolve to take advantage of my hesitation, in the sudden thrust he made at me, I threw myself on his sword, and at the same moment plunged my dagger, with a true desperate aim, in his side. We fell together, rolling over each other, and the tide of blood that flowed from the gaping wound of each mingled on the grass. More I know not—I fainted.

Again I returned to life: weak almost to death, I found myself stretched upon a bed—Juliet was kneeling beside it. Strange! my first broken request was for a mirror. I was so wan and ghastly, that my poor girl hesitated, as she told me afterwards; but, by the mass! I thought myself a right proper youth when I saw the dear reflection of my own well-known features. I confess it is a weakness, but I avow it, I do entertain a considerable affection for the countenance and limbs I behold, whenever I look at a glass; and have more mirrors in my house, and consult them oftener than any beauty in Venice. Before you too much condemn me, permit me to say that no one better knows than I the value of his own body; no one, probably, except myself, ever having had it stolen from him.

Incoherently I at first talked of the dwarf and his crimes, and reproached Juliet for her too easy admission of his love. She thought me raving, as well she might, and yet it was some time before I could prevail on myself to admit that the Guido whose penitence had won her back for me was myself; and while I cursed bitterly the monstrous dwarf, and blest the well-directed blow that had deprived him of life, I suddenly checked myself when I heard her say—Amen! knowing that him whom she reviled was my very self. A little reflection taught me silence—a little practice enabled me to speak of that frightful night without any very excessive blunder. The wound I had given myself was no mockery of one—it was long before I recovered—and as the benevolent and generous Torella sat beside me, talking such wisdom as might win friends to repentance, and mine own dear Juliet hovered near me, administering to my wants, and cheering me by her smiles, the work of my bodily cure and mental reform went on together. I have never, indeed, wholly recovered my strength, my cheek is paler since——my person a little bent. Juliet sometimes ventures to allude bitterly to the malice that caused this change, but I kiss her on the moment, and tell her all is for the best. I am a fonder and more faithful husband—and true is this—but for that wound, never had I called her mine.

I did not revisit the sea-shore, nor seek for the fiend's treasure; yet, while I ponder on the past, I often think, and my confessor was not backward in favoring the idea, that it might be a good rather than an evil spirit, sent by my guardian angel, to show me the folly and misery of pride. So well at least did I learn this lesson, roughly taught as I was, that I am known now by all my friends and fellow-citizens by the name of Guido il Cortese.

Théophile Gautier (1811–1872) was a prolific French dramatist and poet who helped change the sensibilities of French literature with his elegant and decadent tales. Gautier originally studied painting before deciding to try his hand at poetry; his first works appeared in the narrative *Albertus* (1830). Although he had long defended Romanticism, soon after *Albertus* was published he began advocating for aestheticism. During a trip to Greece, Gautier created "transposing art," a poetry technique that recorded his exact impressions while experiencing artwork. He believed in plasticity, the idea that words should be used as tools, in the same way that a sculptor uses clay or a painter uses a canvas and watercolors. His poetic vision is what helped make his short fiction so extraordinary. But he also loved cats, which didn't hurt. "The Nest of Nightingales" (1833) is classic Gautier, but also quite peculiar in the best of ways.

The Nest of Nightingales

Théophile Gautier

Translated by George Burnham Ives

ABOUT THE CHATEAU there was a beautiful park.

In the park there were birds of all kinds; nightingales, blackbirds, and linnets; all the birds of earth had made a rendezvous of the park.

In the spring there was such an uproar that one could not hear one's self talk; every leaf concealed a nest, every tree was an orchestra. All the little feathered musicians vied with one another in melodious contest. Some chirped, others cooed; some performed trills and pearly cadences, others executed bravura passages and elaborate flourishes; genuine musicians could not have done so well.

But in the chateau there were two fair cousins who sang better than all the birds in the park;

Fleurette was the name of one, and Isabeau that of the other. Both were lovely, alluring, and in good case; and on Sundays, when they wore their fine clothes, if their white shoulders had not proved that they were real maidens, one might have taken them for angels; they lacked only wings. When they sang, old Sire de Maulevrier, their uncle, sometimes held their hands, for fear that they might take it into their heads to fly away.

I leave you to imagine the gallant lance-thrusts that were exchanged at tournaments and carrousels in honour of Fleurette and Isabeau. Their reputation for beauty and talent had made the circuit of Europe, and yet they were none the prouder for it; they lived in retirement, seeing almost nobody save the little page Valentin, a pretty, fair-haired child, and Sire de Maulevrier, a hoary-headed old man, all tanned by the sun, and worn out by having borne his war-harness sixty years.

They passed their time in tossing seeds to the little birds, in saying their prayers, and above all, in studying the works of the masters and in rehearsing together some motet, madrigal, villanelle, or other music of the sort; they also had flowers which they themselves watered and tended. Their life passed in these pleasant and poetical maidenly occupations; they remained in the chateau, far from the eyes of the world, and yet the world busied itself about them. Neither the nightingale nor the rose can conceal itself; their melody and their perfume always betray them. Now, our two cousins were at once nightingales and roses.

There came dukes and princes to solicit their hands in marriage; the Emperor of Trebizond and the Sultan of Egypt sent ambassadors to propose an alliance to Sire de Maulevrier; the two cousins were not weary of being maidens and would not listen to any mention of the subject. Perhaps a secret instinct had informed them that their mission here on earth was to remain maidens and to sing, and that they would lower themselves by doing anything else.

They had come to that manor when they were very small. The window of their bedroom looked upon the park, and they had been lulled to sleep by the singing of the birds. When they could scarcely walk, old Blondiau, the old lord's minstrel, had placed their tiny hands on the ivory keys of the virginal; they had possessed no other toy and had learned to sing before they had learned to speak; they sang as others breathed; it was natural to them.

This sort of education had had a peculiar influence on their characters. Their melodious childhood had separated them from the ordinary boisterous and chattering one. They had never uttered a shriek or a discordant wail; they wept in rhythm and wailed in tune. The musical sense, developed in them at the expense of the other senses, made them quite insusceptible

to anything that was not music. They lived in melodious space, and had almost no perception of the real world otherwise than by musical notes. They understood wonderfully the rustling of the foliage, the murmur of streams, the striking of the clock, the sigh of the wind in the fireplace, the hum of the spinning-wheel, the dropping of the rain on the shivering grass, all varieties of harmony, without or within; but they did not feel, I am bound to say, great enthusiasm at the sight of a sunset, and they were as little capable of appreciating a painting as if their lovely blue and black eyes had been covered with a thick film. They had the music sickness; they dreamed of it, it deprived them of their appetite; they loved nothing else in the whole world. But, yes, they did love something else—Valentin and their flowers; Valentin because he resembled the roses, the roses because they resembled Valentin. But that love was altogether in the background. To be sure, Valentin was but thirteen years of age. Their greatest pleasure was to sing at their window in the evening the music which they had composed during the day.

The most celebrated masters came from long distances to hear them and to contend with them. The visitors had no sooner listened to one measure than they broke their instruments and tore up their scores, confessing themselves vanquished. In very truth, the music was so pleasant to the ear and so melodious, that the cherubim from heaven came to the window with the other musicians and learned it by heart to sing to the good Lord.

One evening in May the two cousins were singing a motet for two voices; never was a lovelier air more beautifully composed and executed. A nightingale in the park, perched upon a rosebush, listened attentively to them. When they had finished, he flew to the window, and said to them, in nightingale language:

"I would like to compete in song with you."

The two cousins replied that they would do it willingly, and that he might begin.

The nightingale began. He was a master among nightingales. His little throat swelled, his wings fluttered, his whole body trembled; he poured forth roulades, flourishes, arpeggios, and chromatic scales; he ascended and descended; he sang notes and trills with discouraging purity; one would have said that his voice, like his body, had wings. He paused, well assured that he had won the victory.

The two cousins performed in their turn; they surpassed themselves. The song of the nightingale, compared with theirs, seemed like the chirping of a sparrow.

The vanquished virtuoso made a last attempt; he sang a love romanza, then he executed a brilliant flourish, which he crowned by a shower of high, vibrating, and shrill notes, beyond the range of any human voice.

The two cousins, undeterred by that wonderful performance, turned the leaves of their book of music, and answered the nightingale in such wise that Saint Cecilia, who listened in heaven, turned pale with jealousy and let her viol fall to earth.

The nightingale tried again to sing, but the contest had utterly exhausted him; his breath failed him, his feathers drooped, his eyes closed, despite his efforts; he was at the point of death.

"You sang better than I," he said to the two cousins, "and my pride, by making me try to surpass you, has cost me my life. I ask one favor at your hands: I have a nest; in that nest there are three little ones; it is on the third eglantine in the broad avenue beside the pond; send someone to fetch them to you, bring them up and teach them to sing as you do, for I am dying."

Having spoken, the nightingale died. The two cousins wept bitterly for him, for he had sung well. They called Valentin, the fair-haired little page, and told him where the nest was. Valentin, who was a shrewd little rascal, readily found the place; he put the nest in his breast and carried it to the chateau without harm. Fleurette and Isabeau, leaning on the balcony rail, were awaiting him impatiently. Valentin soon arrived, holding the nest in his hands. The three little ones had their heads over the edge, with their beaks wide open. The girls were moved to pity by the

little orphans, and fed them each in turn. When they had grown a little they began their musical education, as they had promised the vanquished nightingale.

It was wonderful to see how tame they became, how well they sang. They went fluttering about the room, and perched now upon Isabeau's head, now upon Fleurette's shoulder. They lighted in front of the music-book, and in very truth one would have said that they were able to read the notes, with such an intelligent air did they scan the white ones and the black ones. They learned all Fleurette's and Isabeau's melodies and began to improvise some very pretty ones themselves.

The two cousins lived more and more in solitude, and at night strains of supernal melody were heard to issue from their chamber. The nightingales, perfectly taught, took their parts in the concert, and they sang almost as well as their mistresses, who themselves had made great progress.

Their voices assumed each day extraordinary brilliancy, and vibrated in metallic and crystalline tones far above the register of the natural voice. The young women grew perceptibly thin; their lovely colouring faded; they became as pale as agates and almost as transparent. Sire de Maulevrier tried to prevent their singing, but he could not prevail upon them.

As soon as they had sung a measure or two, a little red spot appeared upon their cheek-bones, and grew larger and larger until they had finished; then the spot disappeared, but a cold sweat issued from their skin, and their lips trembled as if they had a fever.

But their singing was more beautiful than ever; there was in it a something not of this world, and to one who heard those sonorous and powerful voices issuing from those two fragile maidens, it was not difficult to foresee what would happen— that the music would shatter the instrument.

They realized it themselves, and returned to their virginal, which they had abandoned for vocal music. But one night, the window was open, the birds were twittering in the park, the night wind sighed harmoniously; there was so much music in the air that they could not resist the temptation to sing a duet that they had composed the night before.

It was the "Swan's Song," a wondrous melody all drenched with tears, ascending to the most inaccessible heights of the scale, and redescending the ladder of notes to the lowest round; something dazzling and incredible; a deluge of trills, a fiery rain of chromatic flourishes, a display of musical fireworks impossible to describe; but meanwhile the little red spot grew rapidly larger and almost covered their cheeks. The three nightingales watched them and listened to them with painful anxiety; they flapped their wings, they went and came and could not remain in one place. At last the maidens reached the last bar of the duet; their voices assumed a sonority so extraordinary that it was easy to understand that they who sang were no longer living creatures. The nightingales had taken flight. The two cousins were dead; their souls had departed with the last note. The nightingales had ascended straight to heaven to carry that last song to the good Lord, who kept them all in His Paradise, to perform the music of the two cousins for Him.

Later, with these three nightingales, the good Lord made the souls of Palestrina, of Cimarosa, and of Gluck.

Vladimir Fedorovich Odoevsky (1803–1869) was a Russian writer, musicologist, and philosopher whose father was descended from royalty. Odoevsky published many mystical tales for children as well as phantasmagorical novels, which is why some claim him to be the Russian E. T. A. Hoffmann. His collection *Russian Nights* (1844) took more than two decades to complete. It includes essays, novellas, and some of his best-known fiction. Interestingly, his unpublished novel *The Year 4338* is said to have predicted blogging, although not the death of blogging. The story reprinted here, "The Fairytale About a Dead Body, Belonging to No One Knows Whom," also translated as "A Tale of a Dead Body Belonging to No One," is a fairy tale for old children. It examines the grotesquerie of bureaucracy and is often compared to the work of Gogol.

The Fairytale About a Dead Body, Belonging to No One Knows Whom

Vladimir Odoevsky

Translated by Ekaterina Sedia

> *In truth, the parish clerk as he left the tavern on all fours, saw that the new moon was dancing in the sky for no reason, and swore to it up and down the village; but the laity shook their heads and even made fun of him.*
> —Gogol, "Evenings on a Farm Near Dikanka"

THE COUNTY COURT has sent the following announcement to all trade villages of Rezhensky County:

"From the Rezhensky County Court it is announced that in its jurisdiction, on the pastures of Morkovkino-Natashino village, on the twenty-first of past November there was found an unidentified dead body of a male sex, dressed in an old grey flannel overcoat; embroidered cummerband; red and green flannel vest; in a red shirt and a speckled quilted leather-billed billed hat; the deceased appears to be about 43 years of age,

6 feet 1 inch tall, light brown hair, fair and smooth skinned, grey-eyed, beard shaven with some grey stubble, nose is large and slightly to the side; weak build. Theretofore, any relatives or owners of said body are asked to notify the authorities of Morkovino-Natashino where the investigation is situated; and if there are no such persons, also kindly notify to this end the same village Morkovino."

Three weeks passed in anticipation of the dead body's owners, but no one showed up, and finally the assessor and the county doctor set out to visit the Morkovino landowner; in the escheat cabin the clerk Sevastyanych was temporarily headquartered, as he too was sent there for the investigation. In the same cabin, in the larder, the dead body was kept, to be examined and buried the next day in the usual manner. The kind landowner, to cheer up Sevastyanych in his solitude, sent him from his own table a goose in gravy and a carafe of homemade digestive tincture.

It was already dark. Sevastyanych, a neat and responsible man, unlike most of his colleagues who would surely be already up in the bunkbed by the warm clay stove, decided it would be proper to work on the paperwork for tomorrow's meeting, seeing how the goose was nothing but bones but only a quarter of the carafe had been emptied. He adjusted the wick in the iron night lamp, maintained for just such an occasion by Morkovino's elder, and from his leather pouch he took out a worn, grimy notebook. Sevastyanych could not look at it without great delight: it contained excerpts and notes from various ukaze, and he inherited it from his father, blessed be his memory—a clerk dishonorably discharged in Rezhensk for libel, covetousness, and lewd behavior, with a special dispensation to never assign him to any position or accept any requests from him—the reason he was still greatly respected by the entire county.

Sevastyanych could not help but remember that this notebook was the only codex guiding the Rezhensky County Court; that only Sevastyanych alone could be the interpreter of the mysterious symbols of this Sybillian book; that

because of its magic power he held in his obedience the chief of police and the assessors, and required all citizens to come to him for advice and guidance; and this is why he guarded it like the apple of his eye, never showed it to anyone, and took it from its secret place only in the most dire necessity; he smiled as he leafed through the pages where in the hand of his deceased father and his own hand were scribbled and then crossed out various insignificant words, such as: not, or etc., and naturally his mind drifted to how stupid people were, and how smart were he and his father.

By the by he emptied the second quarter of the carafe, and started working; but as his habitual hand quickly curved letters on paper, his self-regard, inflamed by the sight of his notebook, worked as well: he reminisced of many times he transported dead bodies across county lines to save trouble to his chief of police; and just in general—put together a request, file a petition, interpret the law, to interact with the petitioners, report to the superiors that their demands cannot be met—Sevastyanych was everywhere and in everything; he smiled as he remembered a remedy of his own invention: to divert every general investigation to every possible direction; he remembered that only recently he had saved a good acquaintance of his using this very approach. The good acquaintance had done something, for which he could have easily undertaken a long and unpleasant journey to certain environs; he was questioned and investigated and during the investigation Sevastyanych advised his acquaintance to get a signed testimony from one well-educated and loyal fellow; they took the testimony from the educated fellow, which he signed after crossing himself, and Sevastyanych himself then started questioning local citizens— what about you, and you, and you?—and he was asking them so rapid-fire that while they were bowing and scratching their heads, and the well-educated fellow, since all others were illiterate, signed the testimony with their names, crossed himself, and thus recorded unanimous agreement with his testimony. And with no lesser delight Sevastyanych remembered when his chief of police was suspected in a significant embezzlement, he managed to drag fifteen more people into the case, divide the embezzled sum between all of them, and then work out a favorable plea for all. In short, Sevastyanych knew that that in all significant cases of Rezhensky Court, he was the only perpetrator, the only creator, and the only executor; that without him the assessor, the chief of police, the county judge and the marshal of nobility would all be goners; that he was the only man upholding the glory of Rezhenksy county— and the sweet awareness of his own importance filled his soul.

To tell the truth, from far away—as if from the clouds—he glimpsed the angry eyes of the governor and the accusatory face of the chairman of the criminal commission, but he looked at the windows covered with drifting snow, thought about three hundred miles separating him from this terrible apparition; to boost his cheer he drank the third quarter—and his thoughts became much more joyful: he thought of his cozy Rezhensk home, earned by his own wits; bottles of homemade schnapps on the windowsill between two flowerpots with basil; a china hutch with his favorite crystal peppermill on a porcelain saucer in the middle of it; and here is his stout, fair Lukerya Petrovna, a crusty loaf of homemade bread in her hands; here's a calf fattened for the Yule, looking at Sevastyanych; a large kettle is bowing to him and moving closer; and here is a warm cot and next to it a luxurious bed with feather mattress and jacquard duvet . . . and under the mattress, there is a folded quilt, and inside the quilt there is a white linen cloth, and in the linen cloth there is a leather billfold, and in the billfold there are grey papers . . . and then his imagination transported Sevastyanych to his youthful years, he imagined his destitute life in his father's house; how often he went hungry because of his mother's thrift; how they sent him away to study with a deacon—he laughed as he remembered climbing his teacher's apple trees and scaring him half to death when the deacon mistook him

for a real thief; how he was caned for his trespass and retaliated by breaking his master's Lent on the very Passion Friday; how finally he surpassed all his contemporaries and rose to read the Apostles in his parish church, starting in a thickest bass and finishing in the highest pitch possible, to everyone's amazement; how the local marshal, noticing his promise, assigned him to the county court; how he matured and married his Lukerya Petrovna; received the title of the Gubernatorial Registrar, which he held to this day, using it to increase his good fortune. His heart melted in gratitude, and he drained the last quarter of the charming beverage. It then occurred to Sevastyanych that not just in the court, but he was a true Jack of all trades: how they listened to him at nights, in the revelry hours, when he would spin tales of Bova the Prince and of the adventures of Vanka Cain, about the travels of trader Korobeynikov to Jerusalem—unstoppable gusli!—and then Sevastyanych started dreaming how nice it would be to have the strength of Bova the Prince, so if he grabbed someone's arm—the arm would come off, grabbed someone's head—the head would come off! Then he wondered the island named Cyprus described by Korobeynikov, rich with oil that came from a tree and Greek soap, where people ride donkeys and camels, and he started laughing at those natives who couldn't figure out to yoke them to the sleds, and as he kept reasoning he found that the books are filled with untruths, and the Greeks must be a very dumb people, because he asked the Greeks who came to Rezhensky Fair to sell soap and gingerbread, who you would think should know what was happening in their own land, why did they conquer Troy—as Korobeynikov noted—but gave up Constantinople to the Turks, and all in vain. There was no rhyme or reason with those people, what was that Troy? The Greek couldn't tell him, suggesting that the city must've been built and conquered during their absence— and as he conducted this important investigation, before his mind's eye marched the Arab thieves and the Rotten Sea; the funeral procession of a cat and the palace of the Pharaoh, all gilded on the inside, and the bird Ostricamel, as tall as a man, with a duck's face and stony hooves . . .

His daydreaming was interrupted by the following words someone spoke right next to him:

"Father Ivan Sevastyanych! I came to you with a most humble request."

These words reminded Sevastyanych of his role as a clerk, and he, out of habit, started writing much faster, bending his head as low as possible, and keeping his eyes on the paper answered in a monotone, "What can I do for you?"

"You sent the court request for the owners of the dead body found in Morkovino."

"It is so."

"So you see, that body is mine."

"Is it so."

"So would you be so kind and do me a kindness and let me collect it soonest?"

"Is it so."

"You can count on my gratitude."

"So the deceased was a serf of yours."

"No, Ivan Sevastyanych, what serf! This is my body, my very own . . ."

"Is it so."

"You can only imagine what it is like for me, without a body! So do me a kindness, help me as quickly as possible."

"Everything is possible but it is difficult to expedite such things—it's not a flapjack, can't just flip it over! I have to collect a lot of papers, send out requests . . . if only someone could butter things up."

"Of that you have no doubt! Just let me have my body and I will give you fifty rubles with no regrets!"

At those words, Sevastyanych lifted his head but seeing no one said, "Come on it, what's the point standing in the cold."

"I am here, Ivan Sevastyanych, standing right next to you."

Sevastyanych adjusted the light, rubbed his eyes and seeing nothing at all, mumbled, "Darn it to hell, have I gone blind? Can't see you, sir."

"That is not at all surprising! How would you see me? I am bodiless."

"Truly, I can make no sense of your words, let me see you."

"I'll oblige, show myself for just a moment . . . because it is a great effort for me."

And with those words a face without clear features appeared in the dark corner, appearing and fading away again—like a young man attending a ball for the first time, eager to approach the ladies but too shy, sticking his head out of the crowd and hiding from view again.

"Beg pardon," the voice was saying meanwhile, "do a kindness, I beg your pardon, you cannot imagine how difficult it is to show yourself without a body, do a kindness, give it to me soonest—I am telling you, fifty rubles . . ."

"I am glad to serve you, sir, but I cannot quite grasp what is it that you are asking of me, do you have a written query?"

"Have mercy, what query? How would I write anything without a body? Do me a kindness, labor to draft one yourself."

"Easy to say, sir, 'labor,' I keep telling you that I don't understand a damn thing here."

"Just write, and I will tell you what."

Sevastyanych took out a sheet of paper with the official crest. "Just tell me: do you have a title, name, patronymic, and surname?"

"Of course! My name is Sweerley John Louis."

"Title?"

"Foreigner."

Sevastyanych wrote in large letters on the crested sheet: "To Rezhensky County Court, from a foreign minor-aged nobleman Savely Zhaluev, an explanation."

"What's next?"

"Be so kind as to just keep writing, I will tell you what; write 'I possess . . .'"

"Land?"

"No; I possess an unfortunate weakness . . ."

"For strong beverages? Ah, that is not commendable."

"No; I possess an unfortunate weakness to exit my body . . ."

"What the devil!" Sevastyanych cried out,

throwing down the quill. "You are bamboozling me!"

"I assure you that I speak only truth, keep writing and know this: fifty rubles to you for the query alone, and fifty more if you successfully resolve it."

And Sevastyanych took up the quill again.

"On 20th October of this year, I was traveling in a wagon, on a personal business, along the Rezhensk Road, on a single rut, and since it was cold and the Rezhensk County roads are especially poor . . ."

"No, you will have to excuse me," Sevastyanych objected, "but I cannot write this down, it is a personal affront, and there is a ukaze forbidding personal attacks in official queries."

"As you wish; then just: it was so cold that I was afraid to freeze my soul, and I was in such a hurry to get to the place of my overnight stay that I lost patience and, as of my usual habit, jumped out of my body . . ."

"Have mercy!" Sevastyanych cried out.

"Easy, easy, no matter, just continue: what can you do if I have such a habit? There is nothing unlawful in it, is there?"

"It is so," Sevastyanych answered. "What's next?"

"Be so kind to write this down: jumped out of my body, laid it out nicely inside the wagon . . . tied its hands with reins so it wouldn't fall out and headed to the station, hoping that the horse will follow the familiar road to the inn."

"I must say," Sevastyanych observed, "that is this case you behaved quite imprudently."

"When I arrived at the station, I climbed the clay stove to warm up my soul and when, by my calculations, the horse should have returned to the inn, I went out to check on it, but that entire night neither the horse nor my body returned. The next morning I hurried to the place where I left my wagon . . . but even that was gone. I suspect that my non-breathing body fell out of the wagon while going over a bump and was found by local police, and the horse followed some traders . . . after three weeks of fruitless search-

ing, I, having found out today of the Rezhensky County Court announcement, calling for the owners of the found body, I request that said body is returned to me as I am its lawful owner, and to which I append a most humble request for the abovementioned court to kindly submerge my abovementioned body in cool water, to let it recover; and if in this frequently mentioned body there is some flaw due to the fall, or if it was damaged by the frost in places, I also request a county doctor to fix it up at my expense and to carry everything out in a lawful manner, to which I am signing."

"Well, then be so kind and sign," Sevastyanych said as he finished the document.

"Sign! Easy to say! I tell you, I don't have my hands with me—they stayed with my body! You sign for me, due to the absence of hands . . ."

"No! Beg your pardon," Sevastyanych objected, "there is no such protocol, and a query not signed according to proper protocol cannot be accepted by the court; if you so desire, illiteracy . . ."

"As you choose! It is all the same to me."

And Sevastyanych wrote, "To this explanation, for reasons of illiteracy, by the petitioner's own request, The Gubernatorial Registrar, Ivan Sevastyanovich Blagoserdov put down his signature."

"I am in your most sensitive debt, most respected Ivan Sevastyanovich! Well, now you please go ahead, solicit on my behalf, that this case is decided quickly; you cannot even imagine how awkward it is to exist without a body! . . . now I am going to run, to see my wife, but rest assured that I will not shortchange you!"

"Wait, wait, your honor!" Sevastyanych cried out. "There is a contradiction in your petition! How could you—without hands!—lie, or lay your body down in the wagon? Devil take it, I don't understand this at all!"

But there was no answer. Sevastyanych read the petition once more, started noodling over it, and thought, and thought . . .

When he woke up, the lamp had burned out

and the morning light was sifting in through the bladder-covered window. He looked with consternation at the empty carafe, standing before him, and this consternation forced the last night's incident from his mind; he gathered his papers without looking and sauntered to the landowner's mansion in hopes of finding a drink to treat his hangover.

As soon as he downed a shot of vodka, the assessor started looking over Sevastyanych's papers and found the petition from the foreign minor-age nobleman.

"Ah, brother Sevastyanych," he cried out after reading it, "yesterday I see you really indulged before sleep; look at this nonsense! Listen to this, Andrey Ignatyevich," he added, addressing the county doctor, "look at the petitioner Sevastyanych is bringing before us." And he read out loud the curious request to the county doctor, all the while near dying from laughter.

"Let's go, gentlemen," he said finally, "and cut that chatty body open, and if it doesn't respond, then we'll just bury it as is proper; it is time to go back to the city anyway."

These words brought Sevastyanych back to last night's incident, and although it did seem strange, he was also reminded of the fifty rubles, promised to him by the petitioner if he successfully solicited his body, and seriously demanded that the assessor and the doctor did not open the body because that could spoil it to such a degree that it would no longer be usable, and to record the petition in its proper order.

Of course they responded with advice for Sevastyanych to sober up, opened the body, and then buried it.

After this incident, the dead man's petition started making rounds; everywhere they copied it, and then embellished and elaborated, then read again, and Rezhenk old ladies crossed themselves in terror for a long while yet.

The story did not preserve the ending of this unusual incident: in one neighboring county they said that the moment the doctor touched the body with its cold instrument, the owner jumped into his body, the body stood up and ran off, and that Sevastyanych chased after it for a long while, screaming on top of his lungs, "Catch, catch the cadaver!"

But in the other county they aver that the owner to this day visits Sevastyanych every morning and every night, saying, "Father Ivan Sevastyanych, what about my body? When will they issue it to me?" and that Sevastyanych, never losing his cheerful demeanor, answers, "We are collecting references." It's been about twenty years.

Charles Dickens (1812–1870) was an iconic English writer and critic. He has become a household name because of such classics as *A Christmas Carol* (1843), *A Tale of Two Cities* (1859), *Great Expectations* (1861), and *David Copperfield* (1850), some of which are rightly or wrongly inflicted on high school students to this day. Dickens truly valued the affection of his audience, as it inspired his creativity and was a substitute for the lack of emotional support in his home. His later works showcase the depression he was battling. "The Story of the Goblins Who Stole a Sexton" (1836) is said to have been the inspiration for *A Christmas Carol*.

The Story of the Goblins Who Stole a Sexton

Charles Dickens

IN AN OLD ABBEY TOWN, down in this part of the country, a long, long while ago—so long, that the story must be a true one, because our great-grandfathers implicitly believed it—there officiated as sexton and grave-digger in the churchyard, one Gabriel Grub. It by no means follows that because a man is a sexton, and constantly surrounded by the emblems of mortality, therefore he should be a morose and melancholy man; your undertakers are the merriest fellows in the world; and I once had the honour of being on intimate terms with a mute, who in private life, and off duty, was as comical and jocose a little fellow as ever chirped out a devil-may-care song, without a hitch in his memory, or drained off a good stiff glass without stopping for breath. But notwithstanding these precedents to the contrary, Gabriel Grub was an ill-conditioned, cross-grained, surly fellow—a morose and lonely man, who consorted with nobody but himself, and an old wicker bottle which fitted into his large deep waistcoat pocket—and who eyed each merry face, as it passed him by, with such a deep scowl of malice and ill-humour, as it was difficult to meet without feeling something the worse for.

A little before twilight, one Christmas Eve, Gabriel shouldered his spade, lighted his lantern, and betook himself towards the old churchyard; for he had got a grave to finish by next morning, and, feeling very low, he thought it might raise his spirits, perhaps, if he went on with his work at once. As he went his way, up the ancient street, he saw the cheerful light of the blazing fires gleam through the old casements, and heard the loud laugh and the cheerful shouts of those who were assembled around them; he marked the bustling preparations for next day's cheer, and smelled the numerous savoury odours consequent thereupon, as they steamed up from the kitchen windows in clouds. All this was gall and wormwood to the heart of Gabriel Grub; and when groups of children bounded out of the houses, tripped across the road, and were met, before they could knock at the opposite door, by half a dozen curly-headed little rascals who crowded round them as they flocked upstairs to spend the evening in their Christmas games, Gabriel smiled grimly, and clutched the handle of his spade with a firmer grasp, as he thought of measles, scarlet fever, thrush, whooping-cough, and a good many other sources of consolation besides.

In this happy frame of mind, Gabriel strode along, returning a short, sullen growl to the good-humoured greetings of such of his neighbours as now and then passed him, until he turned into the dark lane which led to the churchyard. Now, Gabriel had been looking forward to reaching the dark lane, because it was, generally speaking, a nice, gloomy, mournful place, into which the townspeople did not much care to go, except in broad daylight, and when the sun was shining; consequently, he was not a little indignant to hear a young urchin roaring out some jolly song about a merry Christmas, in this very sanctuary which had been called Coffin Lane ever since the days of the old abbey, and the time of the shaven-headed monks. As Gabriel walked on, and the voice drew nearer, he found it proceeded from a small boy, who was hurrying along, to join one of the little parties in the old street, and who, partly to keep himself company, and partly to prepare himself for the occasion, was shouting out the song at the highest pitch of his lungs. So Gabriel waited until the boy came up, and then dodged him into a corner, and rapped him over the head with his lantern five or six times, just to teach him to modulate his voice. And as the boy hurried away with his hand to his head, singing quite a different sort of tune, Gabriel Grub chuckled very heartily to himself, and entered the churchyard, locking the gate behind him.

He took off his coat, set down his lantern, and getting into the unfinished grave, worked at it for an hour or so with right good-will. But the earth was hardened with the frost, and it was no very easy matter to break it up, and shovel it out; and although there was a moon, it was a very young one, and shed little light upon the grave, which was in the shadow of the church. At any other time, these obstacles would have made Gabriel Grub very moody and miserable, but he was so well pleased with having stopped the small boy's singing, that he took little heed of the scanty progress he had made, and looked down into the grave, when he had finished work for the night, with grim satisfaction, murmuring as he gathered up his things—

Brave lodgings for one, brave lodgings for one,
A few feet of cold earth, when life is done;
A stone at the head, a stone at the feet,
A rich, juicy meal for the worms to eat;
Rank grass overhead, and damp clay around,
Brave lodgings for one, these, in holy ground!

"Ho! ho!" laughed Gabriel Grub, as he sat himself down on a flat tombstone which was a favourite resting-place of his, and drew forth his wicker bottle. "A coffin at Christmas! A Christmas box! Ho! ho! ho!"

"Ho! ho! ho!" repeated a voice which sounded close behind him.

Gabriel paused, in some alarm, in the act of raising the wicker bottle to his lips, and looked round. The bottom of the oldest grave about him was not more still and quiet than the churchyard in the pale moonlight. The cold hoar frost glistened on the tombstones, and sparkled like rows of gems, among the stone carvings of the old church. The snow lay hard and crisp upon the ground; and spread over the thickly-strewn mounds of earth, so white and smooth a cover that it seemed as if corpses lay there, hidden only by their winding sheets. Not the faintest rustle broke the profound tranquillity of the solemn scene. Sound itself appeared to be frozen up, all was so cold and still.

"It was the echoes," said Gabriel Grub, raising the bottle to his lips again.

"It was NOT," said a deep voice.

Gabriel started up, and stood rooted to the spot with astonishment and terror; for his eyes rested on a form that made his blood run cold.

Seated on an upright tombstone, close to him, was a strange, unearthly figure, whom Gabriel felt at once, was no being of this world. His long, fantastic legs which might have reached the ground, were cocked up, and crossed after a quaint, fantastic fashion; his sinewy arms were bare; and his hands rested on his knees. On his short, round body, he wore a close covering, ornamented with small slashes; a short cloak dangled at his back; the collar was cut into curious peaks, which served the goblin in lieu of ruff or neckerchief; and his shoes curled up at his toes into long points. On his head, he wore a broad-brimmed sugar-loaf hat, garnished with a single feather. The hat was covered with the white frost; and the goblin looked as if he had sat on the same tombstone very comfortably, for two or three hundred years. He was sitting perfectly still; his tongue was put out, as if in derision; and he was grinning at Gabriel Grub with such a grin as only a goblin could call up.

"It was NOT the echoes," said the goblin.

Gabriel Grub was paralysed, and could make no reply.

"What do you do here on Christmas Eve?" said the goblin sternly.

"I came to dig a grave, Sir," stammered Gabriel Grub.

"What man wanders among graves and churchyards on such a night as this?" cried the goblin.

"Gabriel Grub! Gabriel Grub!" screamed a wild chorus of voices that seemed to fill the churchyard. Gabriel looked fearfully round—nothing was to be seen.

"What have you got in that bottle?" said the goblin.

"Hollands, sir," replied the sexton, trembling more than ever; for he had bought it of the smugglers, and he thought that perhaps his questioner might be in the excise department of the goblins.

"Who drinks Hollands alone, and in a churchyard, on such a night as this?" said the goblin.

"Gabriel Grub! Gabriel Grub!" exclaimed the wild voices again.

The goblin leered maliciously at the terrified sexton, and then raising his voice, exclaimed—

"And who, then, is our fair and lawful prize?"

To this inquiry the invisible chorus replied, in a strain that sounded like the voices of many choristers singing to the mighty swell of the old church organ—a strain that seemed borne to the sexton's ears upon a wild wind, and to die away as it passed onward; but the burden of the reply was still the same, "Gabriel Grub! Gabriel Grub!"

The goblin grinned a broader grin than before, as he said, "Well, Gabriel, what do you say to this?"

The sexton gasped for breath.

"What do you think of this, Gabriel?" said the goblin, kicking up his feet in the air on either side of the tombstone, and looking at the turned-up points with as much complacency as if he had been contemplating the most fashionable pair of Wellingtons in all Bond Street.

"It's—it's—very curious, Sir," replied the sexton, half dead with fright; "very curious, and very pretty, but I think I'll go back and finish my work, Sir, if you please."

"Work!" said the goblin, "what work?"

"The grave, Sir; making the grave," stammered the sexton.

"Oh, the grave, eh?" said the goblin; "who makes graves at a time when all other men are merry, and takes a pleasure in it?"

Again the mysterious voices replied, "Gabriel Grub! Gabriel Grub!"

"I am afraid my friends want you, Gabriel," said the goblin, thrusting his tongue farther into his cheek than ever—and a most astonishing tongue it was—"I'm afraid my friends want you, Gabriel," said the goblin.

"Under favour, Sir," replied the horror-stricken sexton, "I don't think they can, Sir; they don't know me, Sir; I don't think the gentlemen have ever seen me, Sir."

"Oh, yes, they have," replied the goblin; "we know the man with the sulky face and grim scowl, that came down the street to-night, throwing his evil looks at the children, and grasping his burying-spade the tighter. We know the man who struck the boy in the envious malice of his heart, because the boy could be merry, and he could not. We know him, we know him."

Here, the goblin gave a loud, shrill laugh, which the echoes returned twentyfold; and throwing his legs up in the air, stood upon his head, or rather upon the very point of his sugar-loaf hat, on the narrow edge of the tombstone, whence he threw a Somerset with extraordinary agility, right to the sexton's feet, at which he planted himself in the attitude in which tailors generally sit upon the shop-board.

"I—I—am afraid I must leave you, Sir," said the sexton, making an effort to move.

"Leave us!" said the goblin, "Gabriel Grub going to leave us. Ho! ho! ho!"

As the goblin laughed, the sexton observed, for one instant, a brilliant illumination within the windows of the church, as if the whole building were lighted up; it disappeared, the organ pealed forth a lively air, and whole troops of goblins, the very counterpart of the first one, poured into the churchyard, and began playing at leap-frog with the tombstones, never stopping for an instant to take breath, but "overing" the highest among them, one after the other, with the most marvellous dexterity. The first goblin was a most astonishing leaper, and none of the others could come near him; even in the extremity of his terror the sexton could not help observing, that while his friends were content to leap over the common-sized gravestones, the first one took the family vaults, iron railings and all, with as much ease as if they had been so many street-posts.

At last the game reached to a most exciting pitch; the organ played quicker and quicker, and the goblins leaped faster and faster, coiling themselves up, rolling head over heels upon the ground, and bounding over the tombstones like footballs. The sexton's brain whirled round with the rapidity of the motion he beheld, and his legs reeled beneath him, as the spirits flew before his eyes; when the goblin king, suddenly darting

towards him, laid his hand upon his collar, and sank with him through the earth.

When Gabriel Grub had had time to fetch his breath, which the rapidity of his descent had for the moment taken away, he found himself in what appeared to be a large cavern, surrounded on all sides by crowds of goblins, ugly and grim; in the centre of the room, on an elevated seat, was stationed his friend of the churchyard; and close behind him stood Gabriel Grub himself, without power of motion.

"Cold to-night," said the king of the goblins, "very cold. A glass of something warm here!"

At this command, half a dozen officious goblins, with a perpetual smile upon their faces, whom Gabriel Grub imagined to be courtiers, on that account, hastily disappeared, and presently returned with a goblet of liquid fire, which they presented to the king.

"Ah!" cried the goblin, whose cheeks and throat were transparent, as he tossed down the flame, "this warms one, indeed! Bring a bumper of the same, for Mr. Grub."

It was in vain for the unfortunate sexton to protest that he was not in the habit of taking anything warm at night; one of the goblins held him while another poured the blazing liquid down his throat; the whole assembly screeched with laughter, as he coughed and choked, and wiped away the tears which gushed plentifully from his eyes, after swallowing the burning draught.

"And now," said the king, fantastically poking the taper corner of his sugar-loaf hat into the sexton's eye, and thereby occasioning him the most exquisite pain; "and now, show the man of misery and gloom, a few of the pictures from our own great storehouse!"

As the goblin said this, a thick cloud which obscured the remoter end of the cavern rolled gradually away, and disclosed, apparently at a great distance, a small and scantily furnished, but neat and clean apartment. A crowd of little children were gathered round a bright fire, clinging to their mother's gown, and gambolling around her chair. The mother occasionally rose, and drew aside the window-curtain, as if to look for some expected object; a frugal meal was ready spread upon the table; and an elbow chair was placed near the fire. A knock was heard at the door; the mother opened it, and the children crowded round her, and clapped their hands for joy, as their father entered. He was wet and weary, and shook the snow from his garments, as the children crowded round him, and seizing his cloak, hat, stick, and gloves, with busy zeal, ran with them from the room. Then, as he sat down to his meal before the fire, the children climbed about his knee, and the mother sat by his side, and all seemed happiness and comfort.

But a change came upon the view, almost imperceptibly. The scene was altered to a small bedroom, where the fairest and youngest child lay dying; the roses had fled from his cheek, and the light from his eye; and even as the sexton looked upon him with an interest he had never felt or known before, he died. His young brothers and sisters crowded round his little bed, and seized his tiny hand, so cold and heavy; but they shrank back from its touch, and looked with awe on his infant face; for calm and tranquil as it was, and sleeping in rest and peace as the beautiful child seemed to be, they saw that he was dead, and they knew that he was an angel looking down upon, and blessing them, from a bright and happy Heaven.

Again the light cloud passed across the picture, and again the subject changed. The father and mother were old and helpless now, and the number of those about them was diminished more than half; but content and cheerfulness sat on every face, and beamed in every eye, as they crowded round the fireside, and told and listened to old stories of earlier and bygone days. Slowly and peacefully, the father sank into the grave, and, soon after, the sharer of all his cares and troubles followed him to a place of rest. The few who yet survived them, kneeled by their tomb, and watered the green turf which covered it with their tears; then rose, and turned away, sadly and mournfully, but not with bitter cries, or despairing lamentations, for they knew that they should

one day meet again; and once more they mixed with the busy world, and their content and cheerfulness were restored. The cloud settled upon the picture, and concealed it from the sexton's view.

"What do you think of THAT?" said the goblin, turning his large face towards Gabriel Grub.

Gabriel murmured out something about its being very pretty, and looked somewhat ashamed, as the goblin bent his fiery eyes upon him.

"You miserable man!" said the goblin, in a tone of excessive contempt. "You!" He appeared disposed to add more, but indignation choked his utterance, so he lifted up one of his very pliable legs, and, flourishing it above his head a little, to insure his aim, administered a good sound kick to Gabriel Grub; immediately after which, all the goblins in waiting crowded round the wretched sexton, and kicked him without mercy, according to the established and invariable custom of courtiers upon earth, who kick whom royalty kicks, and hug whom royalty hugs.

"Show him some more!" said the king of the goblins.

At these words, the cloud was dispelled, and a rich and beautiful landscape was disclosed to view—there is just such another, to this day, within half a mile of the old abbey town. The sun shone from out the clear blue sky, the water sparkled beneath his rays, and the trees looked greener, and the flowers more gay, beneath its cheering influence. The water rippled on with a pleasant sound, the trees rustled in the light wind that murmured among their leaves, the birds sang upon the boughs, and the lark carolled on high her welcome to the morning. Yes, it was morning; the bright, balmy morning of summer; the minutest leaf, the smallest blade of grass, was instinct with life. The ant crept forth to her daily toil, the butterfly fluttered and basked in the warm rays of the sun; myriads of insects spread their transparent wings, and revelled in their brief but happy existence. Man walked forth, elated with the scene; and all was brightness and splendour.

"YOU a miserable man!" said the king of the goblins, in a more contemptuous tone than before. And again the king of the goblins gave his leg a flourish; again it descended on the shoulders of the sexton; and again the attendant goblins imitated the example of their chief.

Many a time the cloud went and came, and many a lesson it taught to Gabriel Grub, who, although his shoulders smarted with pain from the frequent applications of the goblins' feet thereunto, looked on with an interest that nothing could diminish. He saw that men who worked hard, and earned their scanty bread with lives of labour, were cheerful and happy; and that to the most ignorant, the sweet face of Nature was a never-failing source of cheerfulness and joy. He saw those who had been delicately nurtured, and tenderly brought up, cheerful under privations, and superior to suffering, that would have crushed many of a rougher grain, because they bore within their own bosoms the materials of happiness, contentment, and peace. He saw that women, the tenderest and most fragile of all God's creatures, were the oftenest superior to sorrow, adversity, and distress; and he saw that it was because they bore, in their own hearts, an inexhaustible well-spring of affection and devotion. Above all, he saw that men like himself, who snarled at the mirth and cheerfulness of others, were the foulest weeds on the fair surface of the earth; and setting all the good of the world against the evil, he came to the conclusion that it was a very decent and respectable sort of world after all. No sooner had he formed it, than the cloud which had closed over the last picture, seemed to settle on his senses, and lull him to repose. One by one, the goblins faded from his sight; and, as the last one disappeared, he sank to sleep.

The day had broken when Gabriel Grub awoke, and found himself lying at full length on the flat gravestone in the churchyard, with the wicker bottle lying empty by his side, and his coat, spade, and lantern, all well whitened by the last night's frost, scattered on the ground. The stone on which he had first seen the goblin seated, stood bolt upright before him, and the grave at which he had worked, the night before, was not far off. At first, he began to doubt the reality of his adventures, but the acute pain in his shoulders when he attempted to rise, assured him that the kicking of the goblins was certainly not ideal. He was staggered again, by observing no traces of footsteps in the snow on which the goblins had played at leap-frog with the gravestones, but he speedily accounted for this circumstance when he remembered that, being spirits, they would leave no visible impression behind them. So, Gabriel Grub got on his feet as well as he could, for the pain in his back; and, brushing the frost off his coat, put it on, and turned his face towards the town.

But he was an altered man, and he could not bear the thought of returning to a place where his repentance would be scoffed at, and his reformation disbelieved. He hesitated for a few moments; and then turned away to wander where he might, and seek his bread elsewhere.

The lantern, the spade, and the wicker bottle were found, that day, in the churchyard. There were a great many speculations about the sexton's fate, at first, but it was speedily determined that he had been carried away by the goblins; and there were not wanting some very credible witnesses who had distinctly seen him whisked through the air on the back of a chestnut horse blind of one eye, with the hind-quarters of a lion, and the tail of a bear. At length all this was devoutly believed; and the new sexton used to exhibit to the curious, for a trifling emolument, a good-sized piece of the church weathercock which had been accidentally kicked off by the aforesaid horse in his aerial flight, and picked up by himself in the churchyard, a year or two afterwards.

Unfortunately, these stories were somewhat disturbed by the unlooked-for reappearance of Gabriel Grub himself, some ten years afterwards, a ragged, contented, rheumatic old man. He told his story to the clergyman, and also to the mayor; and in course of time it began to be received as a matter of history, in which form it has continued down to this very day. The believers in the weathercock tale, having misplaced their confidence once, were not easily prevailed upon to part with it again, so they looked as wise as they could, shrugged their shoulders, touched their foreheads, and murmured something about Gabriel Grub having drunk all the Hollands, and then fallen asleep on the flat tombstone; and they affected to explain what he supposed he had witnessed in the goblin's cavern, by saying that he had seen the world, and grown wiser. But this opinion, which was by no means a popular one at any time, gradually died off; and be the matter how it may, as Gabriel Grub was afflicted with rheumatism to the end of his days, this story has at least one moral, if it teach no better one—and that is, that if a man turn sulky and drink by himself at Christmas time, he may make up his mind to be not a bit the better for it: let the spirits be never so good, or let them be even as many degrees beyond proof, as those which Gabriel Grub saw in the goblin's cavern.

Nikolai (Vasilyevich) Gogol (1809–1852) was a Ukrainian-born Russian novelist, dramatist, and humorist whose body of work laid the foundation for Russian absurdist literature in the nineteenth and twentieth centuries. From an early age, Gogol was known for his biting tongue and only later, his nose, although there was always a whiff of genius about him. After some initial rejections, he found his place writing for periodicals. Combining Ukrainian folklore, romanticized memories of the past, and realistic incidents of the present, Gogol brought something fresh to Russian prose. As he matured he began documenting the vulgarity and evil of the world, exposing it with his words. Like most of his later work, his classic "The Nose" (1836) contains more than its share of the surreal and the grotesque.

The Nose

Nikolai Gogol

Translated by Claud Field

I

ON MARCH 25, 18—, a very strange occurrence took place in St. Petersburg. On the Ascension Avenue there lived a barber of the name of Ivan Jakovlevitch. He had lost his family name, and on his signboard, on which was depicted the head of a gentleman with one cheek soaped, the only inscription to be read was, "Bloodletting done here."

On this particular morning he awoke pretty early. Becoming aware of the smell of fresh-baked bread, he sat up a little in bed, and saw his wife, who had a special partiality for coffee, in the act of taking some fresh-baked bread out of the oven.

"Today, Prasskovna Ossipovna," he said, "I do not want any coffee; I should like a fresh loaf with onions."

"The blockhead may eat bread only as far as I am concerned," said his wife to herself; "then I shall have a chance of getting some coffee." And she threw a loaf on the table.

For the sake of propriety, Ivan Jakovlevitch drew a coat over his shirt, sat down at the table, shook out some salt for himself, prepared two onions, assumed a serious expression, and began to cut the bread. After he had cut the loaf in two halves, he looked, and to his great astonishment saw something whitish sticking in it. He carefully poked round it with his knife, and felt it with his finger.

"Quite firmly fixed!" he murmured in his beard. "What can it be?"

He put in his finger, and drew out—a nose!

Ivan Jakovlevitch at first let his hands fall from sheer astonishment; then he rubbed his eyes and began to feel it. A nose, an actual nose; and, moreover, it seemed to be the nose of an acquaintance! Alarm and terror were depicted in Ivan's face; but these feelings were slight in comparison with the disgust that took possession of his wife.

"Whose nose have you cut off, you monster?" she screamed, her face red with anger. "You scoundrel! You tippler! I myself will report you to the police! Such a rascal! Many customers have told me that while you were shaving them, you held them so tight by the nose that they could hardly sit still."

But Ivan Jakovlevitch was more dead than alive; he saw at once that this nose could belong to no other than to Kovaloff, a member of the Municipal Committee whom he shaved every Sunday and Wednesday.

"Stop, Prasskovna Ossipovna! I will wrap it in a piece of cloth and place it in the corner. There it may remain for the present; later on I will take it away."

"No, not there! Shall I endure an amputated nose in my room? You understand nothing except how to strop a razor. You know nothing of the duties and obligations of a respectable man. You vagabond! You good-for-nothing! Am I to undertake all responsibility for you at the police office? Ah, you soap smearer! You blockhead! Take it away where you like, but don't let it stay under my eyes!"

Ivan Jakovlevitch stood there flabbergasted. He thought and thought, and knew not what he thought.

"The devil knows how that happened!" he said at last, scratching his head behind his ear. "Whether I came home drunk last night or not, I really don't know; but in all probability this is a quite extraordinary occurrence, for a loaf is something baked and a nose is something different. I don't understand the matter at all." And Ivan Jakovlevitch was silent. The thought that the police might find him in unlawful possession of a nose and arrest him, robbed him of all presence of mind. Already he began to have visions of a red collar with silver braid and of a sword—and he trembled all over.

At last he finished dressing himself, and to the accompaniment of the emphatic exhortations of his spouse, he wrapped up the nose in a cloth and issued into the street.

He intended to lose it somewhere—either at somebody's door, or in a public square, or in a narrow alley; but just then, in order to complete his bad luck, he was met by an acquaintance, who showered inquiries upon him. "Hullo, Ivan Jakovlevitch! Whom are you going to shave so early in the morning?" etc., so that he could find no suitable opportunity to do what he wanted. Later on he did let the nose drop, but a sentry bore down upon him with his halberd, and said, "Look out! You have let something drop!" and Ivan Jakovlevitch was obliged to pick it up and put it in his pocket.

A feeling of despair began to take possession of him; all the more as the streets became more thronged and the merchants began to open their shops. At last he resolved to go to the Isaac Bridge, where perhaps he might succeed in throwing it into the Neva.

But my conscience is a little uneasy that I have not yet given any detailed information about Ivan Jakovlevitch, an estimable man in many ways.

Like every honest Russian tradesman, Ivan Jakovlevitch was a terrible drunkard, and although he shaved other people's faces every day, his own was always unshaved. His coat (he never wore an overcoat) was quite mottled, i.e. it had been black, but become brownish-yellow; the collar was quite shiny, and instead of the three buttons, only the threads by which they had been fastened were to be seen.

Ivan Jakovlevitch was a great cynic, and when Kovaloff, the member of the Municipal Committee, said to him, as was his custom while being shaved, "Your hands always smell, Ivan Jakovlevitch!" the latter answered, "What do they smell of?" "I don't know, my friend, but they smell very strong." Ivan Jakovlevitch after taking a pinch of snuff would then, by way of reprisals, set to work to soap him on the cheek, the upper lip, behind the ears, on the chin, and everywhere.

This worthy man now stood on the Isaac

Bridge. At first he looked round him, then he leaned on the railings of the bridge, as though he wished to look down and see how many fish were swimming past, and secretly threw the nose, wrapped in a little piece of cloth, into the water. He felt as though a weight had been lifted off him, and laughed cheerfully. Instead, however, of going to shave any officials, he turned toward a building, the signboard of which bore the legend "Teas served here," in order to have a glass of punch, when suddenly he saw at the other end of the bridge a police inspector of imposing exterior, with long whiskers, three-cornered hat, and sword hanging at his side. He nearly fainted; but the police inspector beckoned to him with his hand and said, "Come here, my dear sir."

Ivan Jakovlevitch, knowing how a gentleman should behave, took his hat off quickly, went toward the police inspector, and said, "I hope you are in the best of health."

"Never mind my health. Tell me, my friend, why you were standing on the bridge."

"By heaven, gracious sir, I was on the way to my customers, and only looked down to see if the river was flowing quickly."

"That is a lie! You won't get out of it like that. Confess the truth."

"I am willing to shave Your Grace two or even three times a week gratis," answered Ivan Jakovlevitch.

"No, my friend, don't put yourself out! Three barbers are busy with me already, and reckon it a high honor that I let them show me their skill. Now then, out with it! What were you doing there?"

Ivan Jakovlevitch grew pale. But here the strange episode vanishes in mist, and what further happened is not known.

II

Kovaloff, the member of the Municipal Committee, awoke fairly early that morning, and made a droning noise—"Brr! Brr!"—through his lips, as he always did, though he could not say why. He stretched himself, and told his valet to give him a little mirror which was on the table. He wished to look at the heat boil that had appeared on his nose the previous evening; but to his great astonishment, he saw that instead of his nose he had a perfectly smooth vacancy in his face. Thoroughly alarmed, he ordered some water to be brought, and rubbed his eyes with a towel. Sure enough, he had no longer a nose! Then he sprang out of bed, and shook himself violently! No, no nose anymore! He dressed himself and went at once to the police superintendent.

But before proceeding further, we must certainly give the reader some information about Kovaloff, so that he may know what sort of a man this member of the Municipal Committee really was. These committeemen, who obtain that title by means of certificates of learning, must not be compared with the committeemen appointed for the Caucasus district, who are of quite a different kind. The learned committeeman—but Russia is such a wonderful country that when one committeeman is spoken of all the others from Riga to Kamschatka refer it to themselves. The same is also true of all other titled officials. Kovaloff had been a Caucasian committeeman two years previously, and could not forget that he had occupied that position; but in order to enhance his own importance, he never called himself "committeeman" but "Major."

"Listen, my dear," he used to say when he met an old woman in the street who sold shirtfronts; "go to my house in Sadovaia Street and ask 'Does Major Kovaloff live here?' Any child can tell you where it is."

Accordingly we will call him, for the future, Major Kovaloff. It was his custom to take a daily walk on the Neffsky Avenue. The collar of his shirt was always remarkably clean and stiff. He wore the same style of whiskers as those that are worn by governors of districts, architects, and regimental doctors; in short, all those who have full red cheeks and play a good game of whist. These whiskers grow straight across the cheek toward the nose.

Major Kovaloff wore a number of seals, on

some of which were engraved armorial bearings, and others the names of the days of the week. He had come to St. Petersburg with the view of obtaining some position corresponding to his rank, if possible that of vice governor of a province; but he was prepared to be content with that of a bailiff in some department or other. He was, moreover, not disinclined to marry, but only such a lady who could bring with her a dowry of two hundred thousand roubles. Accordingly, the reader can judge for himself what his sensations were when he found in his face, instead of a fairly symmetrical nose, a broad, flat vacancy.

To increase his misfortune, not a single droshky was to be seen in the street, and so he was obliged to proceed on foot. He wrapped himself up in his cloak, and held his handkerchief to his face as though his nose bled. "But perhaps it is all only my imagination; it is impossible that a nose should drop off in such a silly way," he thought, and stepped into a confectioner's shop in order to look into the mirror.

Fortunately no customer was in the shop; only small shop boys were cleaning it out, and putting chairs and tables straight. Others with sleepy faces were carrying fresh cakes on trays, and yesterday's newspapers stained with coffee were still lying about. "Thank God no one is here!" he said to himself. "Now I can look at myself leisurely."

He stepped gingerly up to a mirror and looked.

"What an infernal face!" he exclaimed, and spat with disgust. "If there were only something there instead of the nose, but there is absolutely nothing."

He bit his lips with vexation, left the confectioner's, and resolved, quite contrary to his habit, neither to look nor smile at anyone on the street. Suddenly he halted as if rooted to the spot before a door, where something extraordinary happened. A carriage drew up at the entrance; the carriage door was opened, and a gentleman in uniform came out and hurried up the steps. How great was Kovaloff's terror and astonishment when he saw that it was his own nose!

At this extraordinary sight, everything seemed to turn around with him. He felt as though he could hardly keep upright on his legs; but, though trembling all over as though with fever, he resolved to wait till the nose should return to the carriage. After about two minutes the nose actually came out again. It wore a gold-embroidered uniform with a stiff, high collar, trousers of chamois leather, and a sword hanging at its side. The hat, adorned with a plume, showed that it held the rank of a state councillor. It was obvious that it was paying "duty calls." It looked around on both sides, called to the coachman "Drive on," and got into the carriage, which drove away.

Poor Kovaloff nearly lost his reason. He did not know what to think of this extraordinary procedure. And indeed how was it possible that the nose, which only yesterday he had on his face, and which could neither walk nor drive, should wear a uniform? He ran after the carriage, which fortunately had stopped a short way off before the Grand Bazar of Moscow. He hurried toward it and pressed through a crowd of beggar women with their faces bound up, leaving only two openings for the eyes, over whom he had formerly so often made merry.

There were only a few people in front of the Bazar. Kovaloff was so agitated that he could decide on nothing, and looked for the nose everywhere. At last he saw it standing before a shop. It seemed half buried in its stiff collar, and was attentively inspecting the wares displayed.

"How can I get at it?" thought Kovaloff. "Everything—the uniform, the hat, and so on—show that it is a state councillor. How the deuce has that happened?"

He began to cough discreetly near it, but the nose paid him not the least attention.

"Honorable sir," said Kovaloff at last, plucking up courage, "honorable sir."

"What do you want?" asked the nose, and turned around.

"It seems to me strange, most respected sir—you should know where you belong—and I find you all of a sudden—where? Judge yourself."

"Pardon me, I do not understand what you are talking about. Explain yourself more distinctly."

"How shall I make my meaning plainer to

him?" Then plucking up fresh courage, he continued, "Naturally—besides I am a Major. You must admit it is not befitting that I should go about without a nose. An old apple woman on the Ascension Bridge may carry on her business without one, but since I am on the lookout for a post; besides in many houses I am acquainted with ladies of high position—Madame Tchektyriev, wife of a state councillor, and many others. So you see—I do not know, honorable sir, what you—" (here the Major shrugged his shoulders). "Pardon me; if one regards the matter from the point of view of duty and honor—you will yourself understand—"

"I understand nothing," answered the nose. "I repeat, please explain yourself more distinctly."

"Honorable sir," said Kovaloff with dignity, "I do not know how I am to understand your words. It seems to me the matter is as clear as possible. Or do you wish—but you are after all my own nose!"

The nose looked at the Major and wrinkled its forehead. "There you are wrong, respected sir; I am myself. Besides, there can be no close relations between us. To judge by the buttons of your uniform, you must be in quite a different department to mine." So saying, the nose turned away.

Kovaloff was completely puzzled; he did not know what to do, and still less what to think. At this moment he heard the pleasant rustling of a lady's dress, and there approached an elderly lady wearing a quantity of lace, and by her side her graceful daughter in a white dress that set off her slender figure to advantage, and wearing a light straw hat. Behind the ladies marched a tall lackey with long whiskers.

Kovaloff advanced a few steps, adjusted his cambric collar, arranged his seals that hung by a little gold chain, and with smiling face fixed his eyes on the graceful lady, who bowed lightly like a spring flower, and raised to her brow her little white hand with transparent fingers. He smiled still more when he spied under the brim of her hat her little round chin, and part of her cheek faintly tinted with rose color. But suddenly he sprang back as though he had been scorched. He remembered that he had nothing but an absolute blank in place of a nose, and tears started to his eyes. He turned around in order to tell the gentleman in uniform that he was only a state councillor in appearance, but really a scoundrel and a rascal, and nothing else but his own nose; but the nose was no longer there. He had had time to go, doubtless in order to continue his visits.

His disappearance plunged Kovaloff into despair. He went back and stood for a moment under a colonnade, looking around him on all sides in hope of perceiving the nose somewhere. He remembered very well that it wore a hat with a plume in it and a gold-embroidered uniform; but he had not noticed the shape of the cloak, nor the color of the carriages and the horses, nor even whether a lackey stood behind it, and, if so, what sort of livery he wore. Moreover, so many carriages were passing that it would have been difficult to recognize one, and even if he had done so, there would have been no means of stopping it.

The day was fine and sunny. An immense crowd was passing to and fro in the Neffsky Avenue; a variegated stream of ladies flowed along the pavement. There was his acquaintance, the Privy Councillor, whom he was accustomed to style "General," especially when strangers were present. There was Iarygin, his intimate friend who always lost in the evenings at whist; and there another Major, who had obtained the rank of committeeman in the Caucasus, beckoned to him.

"Go to the deuce!" said Kovaloff sotto voce. "Hi! coachman, drive me straight to the superintendent of police." He got into a droshky and continued to shout to the coachman "Drive hard!"

"Is the police superintendent at home?" he asked on entering the front hall.

"No, sir," answered the porter, "he has just gone out."

"Ah, just as I thought!"

"Yes," continued the porter, "he has only just gone out; if you had been a moment earlier you would perhaps have caught him."

Kovaloff, still holding his handkerchief to

his face, reentered the droshky and cried in a despairing voice "Drive on!"

"Where?" asked the coachman.

"Straight on!"

"But how? There are crossroads here. Shall I go to the right or the left?"

This question made Kovaloff reflect. In his situation it was necessary to have recourse to the police; not because the affair had anything to do with them directly but because they acted more promptly than other authorities. As for demanding any explanation from the department to which the nose claimed to belong, it would, he felt, be useless, for the answers of that gentleman showed that he regarded nothing as sacred, and he might just as likely have lied in this matter as in saying that he had never seen Kovaloff.

But just as he was about to order the coachman to drive to the police station, the idea occurred to him that this rascally scoundrel who, at their first meeting, had behaved so disloyally toward him, might, profiting by the delay, quit the city secretly; and then all his searching would be in vain, or might last over a whole month. Finally, as though visited with a heavenly inspiration, he resolved to go directly to an advertisement office, and to advertise the loss of his nose, giving all its distinctive characteristics in detail, so that anyone who found it might bring it at once to him, or at any rate inform him where it lived. Having decided on this course, he ordered the coachman to drive to the advertisement office, and all the way he continued to punch him in the back— "Quick, scoundrel! quick!"

"Yes, sir!" answered the coachman, lashing his shaggy horse with the reins.

At last they arrived, and Kovaloff, out of breath, rushed into a little room where a gray-haired official, in an old coat and with spectacles on his nose, sat at a table holding his pen between his teeth, counting a heap of copper coins.

"Who takes in the advertisements here?" exclaimed Kovaloff.

"At your service, sir," answered the gray-haired functionary, looking up and then fastening his eyes again on the heap of coins before him.

"I wish to place an advertisement in your paper—"

"Have the kindness to wait a minute," answered the official, putting down figures on paper with one hand, and with the other moving two balls on his calculating frame.

A lackey, whose silver-laced coat showed that he served in one of the houses of the nobility, was standing by the table with a note in his hand, and speaking in a lively tone, by way of showing himself sociable. "Would you believe it, sir, this little dog is really not worth twenty-four kopecks, and for my own part I would not give a farthing for it; but the countess is quite gone upon it, and offers a hundred roubles' reward to anyone who finds it. To tell you the truth, the tastes of these people are very different from ours; they don't mind giving five hundred or a thousand roubles for a poodle or a pointer, provided it be a good one."

The official listened with a serious air while counting the number of letters contained in the note. At either side of the table stood a number of housekeepers, clerks, and porters, carrying notes. The writer of one wished to sell a barouche, which had been brought from Paris in 1814 and had been very little used; others wanted to dispose of a strong droshky that lacked one spring, a spirited horse seventeen years old, and so on. The room where these people were collected was very small, and the air was very close; but Kovaloff was not affected by it, for he had covered his face with a handkerchief, and because his nose itself was heaven knew where.

"Sir, allow me to ask you—I am in a great hurry," he said at last impatiently.

"In a moment! In a moment! Two roubles, twenty-four kopecks—one minute! One rouble, sixty-four kopecks!" said the gray-haired official, throwing their notes back to the housekeepers and porters. "What do you wish?" he said, turning to Kovaloff.

"I wish—" answered the latter, "I have just been swindled and cheated, and I cannot get hold of the perpetrator. I only want you to insert an advertisement to say that whoever brings this scoundrel to me will be well rewarded."

"What is your name, please?"

"Why do you want my name? I have many lady friends—Madame Tchektyriev, wife of a state councillor, Madame Podtotchina, wife of a Colonel. Heaven forbid that they should get to hear of it. You can simply write 'committeeman,' or, better, 'Major.'"

"And the man who has run away is your serf."

"Serf! If he was, it would not be such a great swindle! It is the nose which has absconded."

"H'm! What a strange name. And this Mr. Nose has stolen from you a considerable sum?"

"Mr. Nose! Ah, you don't understand me! It is my own nose which has gone, I don't know where. The devil has played a trick on me."

"How has it disappeared? I don't understand."

"I can't tell you how, but the important point is that now it walks about the city itself a state councillor. That is why I want you to advertise that whoever gets hold of it should bring it as soon as possible to me. Consider; how can I live without such a prominent part of my body? It is not as if it were merely a little toe; I would only have to put my foot in my boot and no one would notice its absence. Every Thursday I call on the wife of M. Tchektyriev, the state councillor; Madame Podtotchina, a Colonel's wife who has a very pretty daughter, is one of my acquaintances; and what am I to do now? I cannot appear before them like this."

The official compressed his lips and reflected. "No, I cannot insert an advertisement like that," he said after a long pause.

"What! Why not?"

"Because it might compromise the paper. Suppose everyone could advertise that his nose was lost. People already say that all sorts of nonsense and lies are inserted."

"But this is not nonsense! There is nothing of that sort in my case."

"You think so? Listen a minute. Last week there was a case very like it. An official came, just as you have done, bringing an advertisement for the insertion of which he paid two roubles, sixty-three kopecks; and this advertisement simply announced the loss of a black-haired poodle. There did not seem to be anything out of the way in it, but it was really a satire; by the poodle was meant the cashier of some establishment or other."

"But I am not talking of a poodle, but my own nose; i.e. almost myself."

"No, I cannot insert your advertisement."

"But my nose really has disappeared!"

"That is a matter for a doctor. There are said to be people who can provide you with any kind of nose you like. But I see that you are a witty man, and like to have your little joke."

"But I swear to you on my word of honor. Look at my face yourself."

"Why put yourself out?" continued the official, taking a pinch of snuff. "All the same, if you don't mind," he added with a touch of curiosity, "I should like to have a look at it."

The committeeman removed the handkerchief from before his face.

"It certainly does look odd," said the official. "It is perfectly flat like a freshly fried pancake. It is hardly credible."

"Very well. Are you going to hesitate anymore? You see it is impossible to refuse to advertise my loss. I shall be particularly obliged to you, and I shall be glad that this incident has procured me the pleasure of making your acquaintance." The Major, we see, did not even shrink from a slight humiliation.

"It certainly is not difficult to advertise it," replied the official; "but I don't see what good it would do you. However, if you lay so much stress on it, you should apply to someone who has a skillful pen, so that he may describe it as a curious, natural freak, and publish the article in the *Northern Bee*" (here he took another pinch) "for the benefit of youthful readers" (he wiped his nose), "or simply as a matter worthy of arousing public curiosity."

The committeeman felt completely discouraged. He let his eyes fall absentmindedly on a daily paper in which theatrical performances were advertised. Reading there the name of an actress whom he knew to be pretty, he involuntarily smiled, and his hand sought his pocket to see if he had a blue ticket—for in Kovaloff's opinion superior officers like himself should not take a lesser-priced seat; but the thought of his lost nose suddenly spoiled everything.

The official himself seemed touched at his difficult position. Desiring to console him, he tried to express his sympathy by a few polite words. "I much regret," he said, "your extraordinary mishap. Will you not try a pinch of snuff? It clears the head, banishes depression, and is a good preventive against hemorrhoids."

So saying, he reached his snuffbox out to Kovaloff, skillfully concealing at the same time the cover, which was adorned with the portrait of some lady or other.

This act, quite innocent in itself, exasperated Kovaloff. "I don't understand what you find to joke about in the matter," he exclaimed angrily. "Don't you see that I lack precisely the essential feature for taking snuff? The devil take your snuffbox. I don't want to look at snuff now, not even the best, certainly not your vile stuff!"

So saying, he left the advertisement office in a state of profound irritation, and went to the commissary of police. He arrived just as this dignitary was reclining on his couch, and saying to himself with a sigh of satisfaction, "Yes, I shall make a nice little sum out of that."

It might be expected, therefore, that the committeeman's visit would be quite inopportune.

This police commissary was a great patron of all the arts and industries; but what he liked above everything else was a check. "It is a thing," he used to say, "to which it is not easy to find an equivalent; it requires no food, it does not take up much room, it stays in one's pocket, and if it falls, it is not broken."

The commissary accorded Kovaloff a fairly frigid reception, saying that the afternoon was not the best time to come with a case, that nature required one to rest a little after eating (this showed the committeeman that the commissary was acquainted with the aphorisms of the ancient sages), and that respectable people did not have their noses stolen.

The last allusion was too direct. We must remember that Kovaloff was a very sensitive man. He did not mind anything said against him as an individual, but he could not endure any reflection on his rank or social position. He even believed that in comedies one might allow attacks on junior officers, but never on their seniors.

The commissary's reception of him hurt his feelings so much that he raised his head proudly, and said with dignity, "After such insulting expressions on your part, I have nothing more to say." And he left the place.

He reached his house quite wearied out. It was already growing dark. After all his fruitless search, his room seemed to him melancholy and even ugly. In the vestibule he saw his valet Ivan stretched on the leather couch and amusing himself by spitting at the ceiling, which he did very cleverly, hitting every time the same spot. His servant's equanimity enraged him; he struck him on the forehead with his hat, and said, "You good-for-nothing, you are always playing the fool!"

Ivan rose quickly and hastened to take off his master's cloak.

Once in his room, the Major, tired and depressed, threw himself in an armchair and, after sighing a while, began to soliloquize:

"In heaven's name, why should such a misfortune befall me? If I had lost an arm or a leg, it would be less insupportable; but a man without a nose! Devil take it!—what is he good for? He is only fit to be thrown out of the window. If it had been taken from me in war or in a duel, or if I had lost it by my own fault! But it has disappeared inexplicably. But no! it is impossible," he continued after reflecting a few moments, "it is incredible that a nose can disappear like that—quite incredible. I must be dreaming, or suffering from some hallucination; perhaps I swallowed, by mistake instead of water, the brandy with which I rub my chin after being shaved. That fool of an Ivan must have forgotten to take it away, and I must have swallowed it."

In order to find out whether he was really drunk, the Major pinched himself so hard that he involuntarily uttered a cry. The pain convinced him that he was quite wide awake. He walked slowly to the looking-glass and at first closed his eyes, hoping to see his nose suddenly in its proper place; but on opening them, he started back. "What a hideous sight!" he exclaimed.

It was really incomprehensible. One might easily lose a button, a silver spoon, a watch, or something similar; but a loss like this, and in one's own dwelling!

After considering all the circumstances, Major Kovaloff felt inclined to suppose that the cause of all his trouble should be laid at the door of Madame Podtotchina, the Colonel's wife, who wished him to marry her daughter. He himself paid her court readily, but always avoided coming to the point. And when the lady one day told him point-blank that she wished him to marry her daughter, he gently drew back, declaring that he was still too young, and that he had to serve five years more before he would be forty-two. This must be the reason why the lady, in revenge, had resolved to bring him into disgrace, and had hired two sorceresses for that object. One thing was certain—his nose had not been cut off; no one had entered his room, and as for Ivan Jakovlevitch—he had been shaved by him on Wednesday, and during that day and the whole of Thursday his nose had been there, as he knew and well remembered. Moreover, if his nose had been cut off he would naturally have felt pain, and doubtless the wound would not have healed so quickly, nor would the surface have been as flat as a pancake.

All kinds of plans passed through his head: should he bring a legal action against the wife of a superior officer, or should he go to her and charge her openly with her treachery?

His reflections were interrupted by a sudden light, which shone through all the chinks of the door, showing that Ivan had lit the wax candles in the vestibule. Soon Ivan himself came in with the lights. Kovaloff quickly seized a handkerchief and covered the place where his nose had been the evening before, so that his blockhead of a servant might not gape with his mouth wide open when he saw his master's extraordinary appearance.

Scarcely had Ivan returned to the vestibule than a stranger's voice was heard there.

"Does Major Kovaloff live here?" it asked.

"Come in!" said the Major, rising rapidly and opening the door.

He saw a police official of pleasant appearance, with gray whiskers and fairly full cheeks—the same who at the commencement of this story was standing at the end of the Isaac Bridge. "You have lost your nose?" he asked.

"Exactly so."

"It has just been found."

"What—do you say?" stammered Major Kovaloff.

Joy had suddenly paralyzed his tongue. He stared at the police commissary on whose cheeks and full lips fell the flickering light of the candle.

"How was it?" he asked at last.

"By a very singular chance. It has been arrested just as it was getting into a carriage for Riga. Its passport had been made out some time ago in the name of an official; and what is still more strange, I myself took it at first for a gentleman. Fortunately I had my glasses with me, and then I saw at once that it was a nose. I am shortsighted, you know, and as you stand before me I cannot distinguish your nose, your beard, or anything else. My mother-in-law can hardly see at all."

Kovaloff was beside himself with excitement. "Where is it? Where? I will hasten there at once."

"Don't put yourself out. Knowing that you need it, I have brought it with me. Another singular thing is that the principal culprit in the matter is a scoundrel of a barber living on the Ascension Avenue, who is now safely locked up. I had long suspected him of drunkenness and theft; only the day before yesterday he stole some buttons in a shop. Your nose is quite uninjured." So saying, the police commissary put his hand in his pocket and brought out the nose wrapped up in paper.

"Yes, yes, that is it!" exclaimed Kovaloff. "Will you not stay and drink a cup of tea with me?"

"I should like to very much, but I cannot. I must go at once to the House of Correction. The cost of living is very high nowadays. My mother-in-law lives with me, and there are several children; the eldest is very hopeful and intelligent, but I have no means for their education."

After the commissary's departure, Kovaloff remained for some time plunged in a kind of vague reverie, and did not recover full consciousness for several moments, so great was the effect of this unexpected good news. He placed the recovered nose carefully in the palm of his hand, and examined it again with the greatest attention.

"Yes, this is it!" he said to himself. "Here is the heat boil on the left side, which came out yesterday." And he nearly laughed aloud with delight.

But nothing is permanent in this world. Joy in the second moment of its arrival is already less keen than in the first, is still fainter in the third, and finishes by coalescing with our normal mental state, just as the circles which the fall of a pebble forms on the surface of water, gradually die away. Kovaloff began to meditate, and saw that his difficulties were not yet over; his nose had been recovered, but it had to be joined on again in its proper place.

And suppose it could not? As he put this question to himself, Kovaloff grew pale. With a feeling of indescribable dread, he rushed toward his dressing table, and stood before the mirror in order that he might not place his nose crookedly. His hands trembled.

Very carefully he placed it where it had been before. Horror! It did not remain there. He held it to his mouth and warmed it a little with his breath, and then placed it there again; but it would not hold.

"Hold on, you stupid!" he said.

But the nose seemed to be made of wood, and fell back on the table with a strange noise, as though it had been a cork. The Major's face began to twitch feverishly. "Is it possible that it won't stick?" he asked himself, full of alarm. But however often he tried, all his efforts were in vain.

He called Ivan, and sent him to fetch the doctor who occupied the finest flat in the mansion. This doctor was a man of imposing appearance, who had magnificent black whiskers and a healthy wife. He ate fresh apples every morning, and cleaned his teeth with extreme care, using five different toothbrushes for three-quarters of an hour daily.

The doctor came immediately. After having asked the Major when this misfortune had happened, he raised his chin and gave him a fillip with his finger just where the nose had been, in such a way that the Major suddenly threw back his head and struck the wall with it. The doctor said that did not matter; then, making him turn his face to the right, he felt the vacant place and said "H'm!" then he made him turn it to the left and did the same; finally he again gave him a fillip with his finger, so that the Major started like a horse whose teeth are being examined. After this experiment, the doctor shook his head and said, "No, it cannot be done. Rather remain as you are, lest something worse happen. Certainly one could replace it at once, but I assure you the remedy would be worse than the disease."

"All very fine, but how am I to go on without a nose?" answered Kovaloff. "There is nothing worse than that. How can I show myself with such a villainous appearance? I go into good society, and this evening I am invited to two parties. I know several ladies, Madame Tchektyriev, the wife of a state councillor, Madame Podtotchina—although after what she has done, I don't want to have anything to do with her except through the agency of the police. I beg you," continued Kovaloff in a supplicating tone, "find some way or other of replacing it; even if it is not quite firm, as long as it holds at all; I can keep it in place sometimes with my hand, whenever there is any risk. Besides, I do not even dance, so that it is not likely to be injured by any sudden movement. As to your fee, be in no anxiety about that; I can well afford it."

"Believe me," answered the doctor in a voice which was neither too high nor too low, but soft and almost magnetic, "I do not treat patients from love of gain. That would be contrary to my principles and to my art. It is true that I accept fees, but that is only not to hurt my patients' feelings by refusing them. I could certainly replace your nose, but I assure you on my word of honor, it would only make matters worse. Rather let Nature do her own work. Wash the place often with cold water, and I assure you that even without a nose, you will be just as well as if you had one. As to the nose itself, I advise you to have it preserved in a bottle of spirits, or, still better, of warm vinegar mixed with two spoonfuls of brandy, and then you can sell it at a good price. I would be willing to take it myself, provided you do not ask too much."

"No, no, I shall not sell it at any price. I would rather it were lost again."

"Excuse me," said the doctor, taking his leave. "I hoped to be useful to you, but I can do nothing more; you are at any rate convinced of my goodwill." So saying, the doctor left the room with a dignified air.

Kovaloff did not even notice his departure. Absorbed in a profound reverie, he only saw the edge of his snow-white cuffs emerging from the sleeves of his black coat.

The next day he resolved, before bringing a formal action, to write to the Colonel's wife and see whether she would not return to him, without further dispute, that of which she had deprived him.

The letter ran as follows:

To Madame Alexandra Podtotchina,

I hardly understand your method of action. Be sure that by adopting such a course you will gain nothing, and will certainly not succeed in making me marry your daughter. Believe me, the story of my nose has become well-known; it is you and no one else who have taken the principal part in it. Its unexpected separation from the place which it occupied, its flight and its appearances sometimes in the disguise of an official, sometimes in proper person, are nothing but the consequence of unholy spells employed by you or by persons who, like you, are addicted to such honorable pursuits. On my part, I wish to inform you, that if the above-mentioned nose is not restored today to its proper place, I shall be obliged to have recourse to legal procedure.

For the rest, with all respect, I have the honor to be your humble servant,
PLATON KOVALOFF.

The reply was not long in coming, and was as follows:

Major Platon Kovaloff,

Your letter has profoundly astonished me. I must confess that I had not expected such unjust reproaches on your part. I assure you that the official of whom you speak has not been at my house, either disguised or in his proper person. It is true that Philippe Ivanovitch Potantchikoff has paid visits at my house, and though he has actually asked for my daughter's hand, and was a man of good breeding, respectable and intelligent, I never gave him any hope.

Again, you say something about a nose. If you intend to imply by that that I wished to snub you, i.e. to meet you with a refusal, I am very astonished because, as you well know, I was quite of the opposite mind. If after this you wish to ask for my daughter's hand, I should be glad to gratify you, for such has also been the object of my most fervent desire, in the hope of the accomplishment of which, I remain, yours most sincerely,
ALEXANDRA PODTOTCHINA.

"No," said Kovaloff, after having reread the letter, "she is certainly not guilty. It is impossible. Such a letter could not be written by a criminal." The committeeman was experienced in such matters, for he had been often officially deputed to conduct criminal investigations while in the Caucasus. "But then how and by what trick of fate has the thing happened?" he said to himself with a gesture of discouragement. "The devil must be at the bottom of it."

Meanwhile the rumor of this extraordinary event had spread all over the city, and, as is generally the case, not without numerous additions. At that period there was a general disposition to believe in the miraculous; the public had recently been impressed by experiments in magnetism. The story of the floating chairs in Koniouchennaia Street was still quite recent, and there was nothing astonishing in hearing soon afterward that Major Kovaloff's nose was to be seen walking every day at three o'clock on the Neffsky Avenue. The crowd of curious spectators that gathered there daily was enormous. On one occasion someone spread a report that the nose was in Junker's stores and immediately the place was besieged by such a crowd that the police had to interfere and establish order. A certain speculator with a grave, whiskered face, who sold cakes at a theater door, had some strong wooden benches made, which he placed before the window of the stores, and obligingly invited the public to stand on them and look in, at the modest charge of twenty-four kopecks. A veteran colonel, leaving his house earlier than usual expressly for the purpose, had the greatest difficulty in elbowing his way through the crowd, but to his great indignation he saw nothing in the store window but an ordinary flannel waistcoat and a colored lithograph representing a young girl darning a stocking, while an elegant youth in a waistcoat with large lapels watched her from behind a tree. The picture had hung in the same place for more than ten years. The colonel went off, growling savagely to himself, "How can the fools let themselves be excited by such idiotic stories?"

Then another rumor got abroad, to the effect that the nose of Major Kovaloff was in the habit of walking not on the Neffsky Avenue but in the Tauris Gardens. Some students of the Academy of Surgery went there on purpose to see it. A highborn lady wrote to the keeper of the gardens asking him to show her children this rare phenomenon, and to give them some suitable instruction on the occasion.

All these incidents were eagerly collected by the town wits, who just then were very short of anecdotes adapted to amuse ladies. On the other hand, the minority of solid, sober people were very much displeased. One gentleman asserted with great indignation that he could not understand how in our enlightened age such absurdities could spread abroad, and he was astonished that the Government did not direct their attention to the matter. This gentleman evidently belonged to the category of those people who wish the Government to interfere in everything, even in their daily quarrels with their wives.

But here the course of events is again obscured by a veil.

III

Strange events happen in this world, events which are sometimes entirely improbable. The same nose which had masqueraded as a state councillor, and caused so much sensation in the town, was found one morning in its proper place, i.e. between the cheeks of Major Kovaloff, as if nothing had happened.

This occurred on April 7. On awaking, the Major looked by chance into a mirror and perceived a nose. He quickly put his hand to it; it was there beyond a doubt!

"Oh!" exclaimed Kovaloff. For sheer joy he was on the point of performing a dance barefooted across his room, but the entrance of Ivan prevented him. He told him to bring water, and after washing himself, he looked again in the glass. The nose was there! Then he dried his face with a towel and looked again. Yes, there was no mistake about it!

"Look here, Ivan, it seems to me that I have a heat boil on my nose," he said to his valet.

And he thought to himself at the same time, "That will be a nice business if Ivan says to me 'No, sir, not only is there no boil, but your nose itself is not there!' "

But Ivan answered, "There is nothing, sir; I can see no boil on your nose."

"Good! Good!" exclaimed the Major, and snapped his fingers with delight.

At this moment the barber, Ivan Jakovlevitch, put his head in at the door, but as timidly as a cat that has just been beaten for stealing lard.

"Tell me first, are your hands clean?" asked Kovaloff when he saw him.

"Yes, sir."

"You lie."

"I swear they are perfectly clean, sir."

"Very well; then come here."

Kovaloff seated himself. Jakovlevitch tied a napkin under his chin, and in the twinkling of an eye covered his beard and part of his cheeks with a copious creamy lather.

"There it is!" said the barber to himself, as he glanced at the nose. Then he bent his head a little and examined it from one side. "Yes, it actually is the nose—really, when one thinks—" he continued, pursuing his mental soliloquy and still looking at it. Then quite gently, with infinite precaution, he raised two fingers in the air in order to take hold of it by the extremity, as he was accustomed to do.

"Now then, take care!" Kovaloff exclaimed.

Ivan Jakovlevitch let his arm fall and felt more embarrassed than he had ever done in his life. At last he began to pass the razor very lightly over the Major's chin, and although it was very difficult to shave him without using the olfactory organ as a point of support, he succeeded, however, by placing his wrinkled thumb against the Major's lower jaw and cheek, thus overcoming all obstacles and bringing his task to a safe conclusion.

When the barber had finished, Kovaloff hastened to dress himself, took a droshky, and drove straight to the confectioner's. As he entered it, he ordered a cup of chocolate. He then stepped straight to the mirror; the nose was there!

He returned joyfully, and regarded with a satirical expression two officers who were in the shop, one of whom possessed a nose not much larger than a waistcoat button.

After that he went to the office of the department where he had applied for the post of vice governor of a province or Government bailiff. As he passed through the hall of reception, he cast a glance at the mirror; the nose was there! Then he went to pay a visit to another committeeman, a very sarcastic personage, to whom he was accustomed to say in answer to his raillery, "Yes, I know, you are the funniest fellow in St. Petersburg."

On the way he said to himself, "If the Major does not burst into laughter at the sight of me, that is a most certain sign that everything is in its accustomed place."

But the Major said nothing. "Very good!" thought Kovaloff.

As he returned, he met Madame Podtotchina with her daughter. He accosted them, and they responded very graciously. The conversation lasted a long time, during which he took more than one pinch of snuff, saying to himself, "No, you haven't caught me yet, coquettes that you are! And as to the daughter, I shan't marry her at all."

After that, the Major resumed his walks on the Neffsky Avenue and his visits to the theater as if nothing had happened. His nose also remained in its place as if it had never quitted it. From that time he was always to be seen smiling, in a good humor, and paying attentions to pretty girls.

IV

Such was the occurrence which took place in the northern capital of our vast empire. On considering the account carefully we see that there is a good deal which looks improbable about it. Not to speak of the strange disappearance of the nose, and its appearance in different places under the disguise of a councillor of state, how was it that Kovaloff did not understand that one cannot decently advertise for a lost nose? I do not mean to say that he would have had to pay too much for the advertisement—that is a mere trifle, and I am not one of those who attach too much importance to money; but to advertise in such a case is not proper nor befitting.

Another difficulty is—how was the nose found

in the baked loaf, and how did Ivan Jakovlevitch himself—no, I don't understand it at all!

But the most incomprehensible thing of all is, how authors can choose such subjects for their stories. That really surpasses my understanding. In the first place, no advantage results from it for the country; and in the second place, no harm results either.

All the same, when one reflects well, there really is something in the matter. Whatever may be said to the contrary, such cases do occur—rarely, it is true, but now and then actually.

Edgar Allan Poe (1809–1849) was born in Boston, Massachusetts, and is known for his iconic macabre short stories that created or helped create whole genres of fiction, like horror and mysteries. Poe was a theorist who believed in aestheticism, art for art's sake, who appreciated the French symbolists. Orphaned by the age of three, Poe was plagued by financial strain and the death of his closest relatives, dying at the age of forty—only to be resurrected as the artificial intelligence behind a hotel in Richard Morgan's novel and television series *Altered Carbon*. His poem "The Raven" (1845) is one of the most famous poems ever written and has been adapted numerous times, including into stage productions. "The Facts in the Case of M. Valdemar" (1845) is a suspenseful tale of mesmerism that has been adapted into the film *Tales of Terror* (1962) and the horror film *Two Evil Eyes* (1990).

The Facts in the Case of M. Valdemar

Edgar Allan Poe

OF COURSE I SHALL NOT pretend to consider it any matter for wonder, that the extraordinary case of M. Valdemar has excited discussion. It would have been a miracle had it not—especially under the circumstances. Through the desire of all parties concerned, to keep the affair from the public, at least for the present, or until we had farther opportunities for investigation—through our endeavors to effect this—a garbled or exaggerated account made its way into society, and became the source of many unpleasant misrepresentations, and, very naturally, of a great deal of disbelief.

It is now rendered necessary that I give the facts—as far as I comprehend them myself. They are, succinctly, these:

My attention, for the last three years, had been repeatedly drawn to the subject of Mesmerism; and, about nine months ago it occurred to me, quite suddenly, that in the series of experiments made hitherto, there had been a very remarkable and most unaccountable omission:—no person had as yet been mesmerized in articulo mortis. It remained to be seen, first, whether, in such condition, there existed in the patient any susceptibility to the magnetic influence; secondly, whether, if any existed, it was impaired or increased by the condition; thirdly, to what extent, or for how long a period, the encroachments of Death might be arrested by the process. There were other points to be ascertained, but these most excited my curiosity—the last in especial, from the immensely important character of its consequences.

In looking around me for some subject by whose means I might test these particulars, I was brought to think of my friend, M. Ernest Valdemar, the well-known compiler of the "Bibliotheca Forensica," and author (under the nom de plume of Issachar Marx) of the Polish versions of "Wallenstein" and "Gargantua." M. Valdemar, who has resided principally at Harlaem, N.Y., since the year 1839, is (or was) particularly noticeable for the extreme spareness of his person—his lower limbs much resembling those of John Randolph; and, also, for the whiteness of his whiskers, in violent contrast to the blackness of his hair—the latter, in consequence, being very generally mistaken for a wig. His temperament was markedly nervous, and rendered him a good subject for mesmeric experiment. On two or three occasions I had put him to sleep with little difficulty, but was disappointed in other results which his peculiar constitution had naturally led me to anticipate. His will was at no period positively, or thoroughly, under my control, and in regard to clairvoyance, I could accomplish with him nothing to be relied upon. I always attributed my failure at these points to the disordered state of his health. For some months previous to my becoming acquainted with him, his physicians had declared him in a confirmed phthisis. It was his custom, indeed, to speak calmly of his approaching dissolution, as of a matter neither to be avoided nor regretted.

When the ideas to which I have alluded first occurred to me, it was of course very natural that I should think of M. Valdemar. I knew the steady philosophy of the man too well to apprehend any scruples from him; and he had no relatives in America who would be likely to interfere. I spoke to him frankly upon the subject; and, to my surprise, his interest seemed vividly excited. I say to my surprise, for, although he had always yielded his person freely to my experiments, he had never before given me any tokens of sympathy with what I did. His disease was of that character which would admit of exact calculation in respect to the epoch of its termination in death; and it was finally arranged between us that he would send for me about twenty-four hours before the period announced by his physicians as that of his decease.

It is now rather more than seven months since I received, from M. Valdemar himself, the subjoined note:

My DEAR P——,

You may as well come now. D—— and F—— are agreed that I cannot hold out beyond to-morrow midnight; and I think they have hit the time very nearly.

VALDEMAR

I received this note within half an hour after it was written, and in fifteen minutes more I was in the dying man's chamber. I had not seen him for ten days, and was appalled by the fearful alteration which the brief interval had wrought in him. His face wore a leaden hue; the eyes were utterly lustreless; and the emaciation was so extreme that the skin had been broken through by the cheek-bones. His expectoration was excessive. The pulse was barely perceptible. He retained, nevertheless, in a very remarkable manner, both his mental power and a certain degree of physical strength. He spoke with distinctness—took some palliative medicines without aid—and, when I entered the room, was occupied in penciling memoranda in a pocket-book. He was propped up in the bed by pillows. Doctors D—— and F—— were in attendance.

After pressing Valdemar's hand, I took these gentlemen aside, and obtained from them a minute account of the patient's condition. The left lung had been for eighteen months in a semiosseous or cartilaginous state, and was, of course, entirely useless for all purposes of vitality. The right, in its upper portion, was also partially, if not thoroughly, ossified, while the lower region was merely a mass of purulent tubercles, running one into another. Several extensive perforations existed; and, at one point, permanent adhesion to the ribs had taken place. These appearances in the right lobe were of comparatively recent date. The ossification had proceeded with very unusual rapidity; no sign of it had been discovered a month before, and the adhesion had only been observed during the three previous days. Independently of the phthisis, the patient was suspected of aneurism of the aorta; but on this point the osseous symptoms rendered an exact diagnosis impossible. It was the opinion of both physicians that M. Valdemar would die about midnight on the morrow (Sunday). It was then seven o'clock on Saturday evening.

On quitting the invalid's bed-side to hold conversation with myself, Doctors D—— and F—— had bidden him a final farewell. It had not been their intention to return; but, at my request, they agreed to look in upon the patient about ten the next night.

When they had gone, I spoke freely with M. Valdemar on the subject of his approaching dissolution, as well as, more particularly, of the experiment proposed. He still professed himself quite willing and even anxious to have it made, and urged me to commence it at once. A male and a female nurse were in attendance; but I did not feel myself altogether at liberty to engage in a task of this character with no more reliable witnesses than these people, in case of sudden accident, might prove. I therefore postponed operations until about eight the next night, when the arrival of a medical student with whom I had some acquaintance, (Mr. Theodore L——l,) relieved me from farther embarrassment. It had been my design, originally, to wait for the physicians; but I was induced to proceed, first, by the urgent entreaties of M. Valdemar, and secondly, by my conviction that I had not a moment to lose, as he was evidently sinking fast.

Mr. L——l was so kind as to accede to my desire that he would take notes of all that occurred, and it is from his memoranda that what I now have to relate is, for the most part, either condensed or copied verbatim.

It wanted about five minutes of eight when, taking the patient's hand, I begged him to state, as distinctly as he could, to Mr. L——l, whether he (M. Valdemar) was entirely willing that I should make the experiment of mesmerizing him in his then condition.

He replied feebly, yet quite audibly, "Yes, I wish to be. I fear you have mesmerized"—adding immediately afterwards, "deferred it too long."

While he spoke thus, I commenced the passes which I had already found most effectual in subduing him. He was evidently influenced with the first lateral stroke of my hand across his forehead; but although I exerted all my powers, no further perceptible effect was induced until some minutes after ten o'clock, when Doctors D—— and F—— called, according to appointment. I explained to them, in a few words, what I designed, and as they opposed no objection, saying that the patient was already in the death agony, I proceeded without hesitation—exchanging, however, the lateral passes for downward ones, and directing my gaze entirely into the right eye of the sufferer.

By this time his pulse was imperceptible and his breathing was stertorous, and at intervals of half a minute.

This condition was nearly unaltered for a quarter of an hour. At the expiration of this period, however, a natural although a very deep sigh escaped the bosom of the dying man, and the stertorous breathing ceased—that is to say, its stertorousness was no longer apparent; the intervals were undiminished. The patient's extremities were of an icy coldness.

At five minutes before eleven I perceived unequivocal signs of the mesmeric influence. The glassy roll of the eye was changed for that expression of uneasy inward examination which is never seen except in cases of sleep-waking, and which it is quite impossible to mistake. With a few rapid lateral passes I made the lids quiver, as in incipient sleep, and with a few more I closed them altogether. I was not satisfied, however, with this, but continued the manipulations vigorously, and with the fullest exertion of the will, until I had completely stiffened the limbs of the slumberer, after placing them in a seemingly easy position. The legs were at full length; the arms were nearly so, and reposed on the bed at a moderate distance from the loin. The head was very slightly elevated.

When I had accomplished this, it was fully midnight, and I requested the gentlemen present to examine M. Valdemar's condition. After a few experiments, they admitted him to be an unusually perfect state of mesmeric trance. The curiosity of both the physicians was greatly excited. Dr. D—— resolved at once to remain with the patient all night, while Dr. F—— took leave with a promise to return at daybreak. Mr. L——l and the nurses remained.

We left M. Valdemar entirely undisturbed until about three o'clock in the morning, when I approached him and found him in precisely the same condition as when Dr. F—— went away—that is to say, he lay in the same position; the pulse was imperceptible; the breathing was gentle (scarcely noticeable, unless through the application of a mirror to the lips); the eyes were closed naturally; and the limbs were as rigid and as cold as marble. Still, the general appearance was certainly not that of death.

As I approached M. Valdemar I made a kind of half effort to influence his right arm into pursuit of my own, as I passed the latter gently to and fro above his person. In such experiments with this patient, I had never perfectly succeeded before, and assuredly I had little thought of succeeding now; but to my astonishment, his arm very readily, although feebly, followed every direction I assigned it with mine. I determined to hazard a few words of conversation.

"M. Valdemar," I said, "are you asleep?" He made no answer, but I perceived a tremor about the lips, and was thus induced to repeat the question, again and again. At its third repetition, his whole frame was agitated by a very slight shivering; the eyelids unclosed themselves so far as to display a white line of the ball; the lips moved sluggishly, and from between them, in a barely audible whisper, issued the words:

"Yes;—asleep now. Do not wake me!—let me die so!"

I here felt the limbs and found them as rigid as ever. The right arm, as before, obeyed the direction of my hand. I questioned the sleep-waker again:

"Do you still feel pain in the breast, M. Valdemar?"

The answer now was immediate, but even less audible than before: "No pain—I am dying."

I did not think it advisable to disturb him farther just then, and nothing more was said or done until the arrival of Dr. F——, who came a little before sunrise, and expressed unbounded astonishment at finding the patient still alive. After feeling the pulse and applying a mirror to the lips, he requested me to speak to the sleep-waker again. I did so, saying:

"M. Valdemar, do you still sleep?"

As before, some minutes elapsed ere a reply was made; and during the interval the dying man seemed to be collecting his energies to speak. At my fourth repetition of the question, he said very faintly, almost inaudibly:

"Yes; still asleep—dying."

It was now the opinion, or rather the wish, of the physicians, that M. Valdemar should be suffered to remain undisturbed in his present apparently tranquil condition, until death should supervene—and this, it was generally agreed, must now take place within a few minutes. I concluded, however, to speak to him once more, and merely repeated my previous question.

While I spoke, there came a marked change over the countenance of the sleep-waker. The eyes rolled themselves slowly open, the pupils disappearing upwardly; the skin generally assumed a cadaverous hue, resembling not so much parchment as white paper; and the circular hectic spots which, hitherto, had been strongly defined in the centre of each cheek, went out at once. I use this expression, because the suddenness of their departure put me in mind of nothing so much as the extinguishment of a candle by a puff of the breath. The upper lip, at the same time, writhed itself away from the teeth, which it had previously covered completely; while the lower jaw fell with an audible jerk, leaving the mouth widely extended, and disclosing in full view the swollen and blackened tongue. I presume that no member of the party then present had been unaccustomed to death-bed horrors; but so hideous beyond conception was the appearance of M. Valdemar at this moment, that there was a general shrinking back from the region of the bed.

I now feel that I have reached a point of this narrative at which every reader will be startled into positive disbelief. It is my business, however, simply to proceed.

There was no longer the faintest sign of vitality in M. Valdemar; and concluding him to be dead, we were consigning him to the charge of the nurses, when a strong vibratory motion was observable in the tongue. This continued for perhaps a minute. At the expiration of this period, there issued from the distended and motionless jaws a voice—such as it would be madness in me to attempt describing. There are, indeed, two or three epithets which might be considered as applicable to it in part; I might say, for example, that the sound was harsh, and broken and hollow; but the hideous whole is indescribable, for the simple reason that no similar sounds have ever jarred upon the ear of humanity. There were two particulars, nevertheless, which I thought then, and still think, might fairly be stated as characteristic of the intonation—as well adapted to convey some idea of its unearthly peculiarity. In the first place, the voice seemed to reach our ears—at least mine—from a vast distance, or from some deep cavern within the earth. In the second place, it impressed me (I fear, indeed, that it will be impossible to make myself comprehended) as gelatinous or glutinous matters impress the sense of touch.

I have spoken both of "sound" and of "voice." I mean to say that the sound was one of distinct—of even wonderfully, thrillingly distinct—syllabification. M. Valdemar spoke—obviously in reply to the question I had propounded to him a few minutes before. I had asked him, it will be remembered, if he still slept. He now said:

"Yes;—no;—I have been sleeping—and now—now—I am dead."

No person present even affected to deny, or attempted to repress, the unutterable, shudder-ing horror which these few words, thus uttered, were so well calculated to convey. Mr. L——l (the student) swooned. The nurses immediately left the chamber, and could not be induced to return. My own impressions I would not pretend to render intelligible to the reader. For nearly an hour, we busied ourselves, silently—without the utterance of a word—in endeavors to revive Mr. L——l. When he came to himself, we addressed ourselves again to an investigation of M. Valdemar's condition.

It remained in all respects as I have last described it, with the exception that the mirror no longer afforded evidence of respiration. An attempt to draw blood from the arm failed. I should mention, too, that this limb was no farther subject to my will. I endeavored in vain to make it follow the direction of my hand. The only real indication, indeed, of the mesmeric influence, was now found in the vibratory movement of the tongue, whenever I addressed M. Valdemar a question. He seemed to be making an effort to reply, but had no longer sufficient volition. To queries put to him by any other person than myself he seemed utterly insensible—although I endeavored to place each member of the company in mesmeric rapport with him. I believe that I have now related all that is necessary to an understanding of the sleep-waker's state at this epoch. Other nurses were procured; and at ten o'clock I left the house in company with the two physicians and Mr. L——l.

In the afternoon we all called again to see the patient. His condition remained precisely the same. We had now some discussion as to the propriety and feasibility of awakening him; but we had little difficulty in agreeing that no good purpose would be served by so doing. It was evident that, so far, death (or what is usually termed death) had been arrested by the mesmeric process. It seemed clear to us all that to awaken M. Valdemar would be merely to insure his instant, or at least his speedy dissolution.

From this period until the close of last week—an interval of nearly seven months—we continued to make daily calls at M. Valdemar's house, accompanied, now and then, by medical and other friends. All this time the sleep-waker remained exactly as I have last described him. The nurses' attentions were continual.

It was on Friday last that we finally resolved to make the experiment of awakening or attempting to awaken him; and it is the (perhaps) unfortunate result of this latter experiment which has given rise to so much discussion in private circles—to so much of what I cannot help thinking unwarranted popular feeling.

For the purpose of relieving M. Valdemar from the mesmeric trance, I made use of the customary passes. These, for a time, were unsuccessful. The first indication of revival was afforded by a partial descent of the iris. It was observed, as especially remarkable, that this lowering of the pupil was accompanied by the profuse out-flowing of a yellowish ichor (from beneath the lids) of a pungent and highly offensive odor.

It was now suggested that I should attempt to influence the patient's arm, as heretofore. I made the attempt and failed. Dr. F—— then intimated a desire to have me put a question. I did so, as follows:

"M. Valdemar, can you explain to us what are your feelings or wishes now?"

There was an instant return of the hectic circles on the cheeks; the tongue quivered, or rather rolled violently in the mouth (although the jaws and lips remained rigid as before) and at length the same hideous voice which I have already described, broke forth:

"For God's sake!—quick!—quick!—put me to sleep—or, quick!—waken me!—quick!—I say to you that I am dead!"

I was thoroughly unnerved, and for an instant remained undecided what to do. At first I made an endeavor to re-compose the patient; but, failing in this through total abeyance of the will, I retraced my steps and as earnestly struggled to awaken him. In this attempt I soon saw that I should be successful—or at least I soon fancied that my success would be complete—and I am sure that all in the room were prepared to see the patient awaken.

For what really occurred, however, it is quite impossible that any human being could have been prepared.

As I rapidly made the mesmeric passes, amid ejaculations of "dead! dead!" absolutely bursting from the tongue and not from the lips of the sufferer, his whole frame at once—within the space of a single minute, or even less, shrunk—crumbled—absolutely rotted away beneath my hands. Upon the bed, before that whole company, there lay a nearly liquid mass of loathsome—of detestable putridity.

"The Story of Jeon Unchi" is a classic of Korean fiction that incorporates the fantastic into the realistic. Unlike many of the moralistic works that came before it, "Jeon Unchi" is an adventure tale replete with action. Although no one knows who wrote the story, it has the characteristics of popular fiction written for commoners in the Korean vernacular script (hangul) that was produced in the late eighteenth and throughout the nineteenth centuries. Inspired by a historical figure with the slightly different name of Jeon Uchi (late fifteenth to early sixteenth century) who was reputed to be a master of the mystical arts, "The Story of Jeon Unchi" is the tale of a rebellious magician and has been adapted to the screen as both a Korean drama and a film. Originally published circa 1847, although even that fact isn't certain, this is the first time this work has been translated into English.

The Story of Jeon Unchi

Anonymous

Translated by Minsoo Kang

TOWARD THE END of the Goryeo dynasty,* in the southwestern part of the realm, there lived a gentleman scholar whose family name was Jeon, personal name was Suk, and literary name was Unhwa. Although he came from generations of illustrious statesmen, he had no desire to become a government official himself. So he moved into a mountain where he spent his days studying letters with reverence and occasionally gathering his friends to appreciate the mountains and the rivers, the winds and the moon. And so he came to be known by the people as the Mountain Scholar.

His wife, Lady Choe, was also from a family that produced many high-ranking officials. She was a person of decorous and modest character as well as of beauteous appearance and virtue. The husband and wife treated each other with respect and lived harmoniously together for about ten years, until they came to lament often that they had no child to care for. But then, one day,

---

* Goryeo dynasty: The kingdom that ruled over the Korean peninsula from 918 to 1392. It is unknown why the author of this story set it in the period, since there are a number of references to Korea during the subsequent Joseon dynasty (1392–1910), including the main character who is a fantasy version of a historical figure with the slightly different name Jeon Uchi, a scholar famed for his magical knowledge who lived in the late fifteenth and early sixteenth centuries. There is also the mention of Gyeongseong, which was the capital city of Joseon, rather than Goryeo, and a fantasy version of the historical figure Seo Gyeongdeok (1489–1546).

Lady Choe had a dream in which many clouds descended upon her to reveal in their midst a young boy in blue clothing holding a lotus flower.

The boy bowed twice before speaking to her. "I was a servant to the immortal spirits of the holy mountain of Yeongju, charged with gathering herbs for my masters. But due to an infraction I committed, I have been exiled to the realm of humans, so I bid you to treat me with affection."

Lady Choe, filled with joy, was about to ask the child a question when she suddenly woke from the dream. She happily informed Jeon Suk of her vision.

Her husband listened to her and replied. "I felt so sad thinking that we would remain childless due to some unfortunate fate. But this dream you had surely means that heaven will bless us with a precious child."

So they rejoiced. And sure enough, Lady Choe showed signs of pregnancy that month.

On a day before the passage of ten months, auspicious clouds surrounded their house and filled the place with a sweet fragrance. Jeon Suk cleaned the place thoroughly and waited for the birth. Lady Choe, disoriented from birth pangs, opened her eyes to see the boy from the dream enter into her. The joy she felt at the vision cleared her thoughts, and she soon gave birth to a wondrous boy. Jeon Suk, filled with happiness, took care of his wife and examined his son. The boy was of magnificent appearance as well as sturdy spirit.

Jeon Suk spoke out. "This child was seen in a cloud, so let us give him the name of Unchi, or 'cloud-sent,' the formal name of Mongjungseon, or 'a holy spirit in a dream,' and the household name of Gusipja."*

Jeon Suk thought Unchi very precious, and his love for him knew no bounds.

Once Unchi grew up and reached the age of nine, Jeon Suk began to teach him the letters.

The boy turned out to be so bright that learning one thing allowed him to understand ten things, which made his father love him even more.

Unfortunately, after Unchi turned ten, Jeon Suk suddenly fell ill and every medicine proved to be ineffectual. How sad it was! As it has always been the case, a happy event is often followed by a tragic one.

Jeon Suk summoned his wife and spoke to her. "It won't be long before I depart for the next world. My greatest regret is that I won't get to see my child grow up. I bid you to overcome your sorrow and raise Unchi well. I wish you much fortune, and I hope you will properly perform the rituals of reverence for our ancestors. May you live a long life without any illness."

His wife could not reply as she shed tears until she fell unconscious.

When Jeon Suk left this world a few days later, his wife hit herself on the chest and convulsed her entire body as she lamented. Unchi kept fainting as he thought of his father, whom he regarded as high as heaven, and the kindness he had shown him. His mother became concerned, so she consoled him even in midst of her own mourning. Although Unchi was still young, he took great care to perform all the funeral rituals properly as his father was buried at a gravesite on a mountain. He then displayed laudable filial piety in helping his mother and undergoing the three-year mourning period, earning the praise of the people of their village.

Jeon Suk's friend Yun Gong was a scholar who had mastered the world's learning so thoroughly that he could see far into the future. So Unchi picked up his books and went to Yun Gong to study under him.

One day, Unchi got up early and was walking to the school when he came across a woman

---

* Gusipja: Unchi's family name Jeon is signified by the Chinese character 田, meaning "field," which is a combination of the character for "opening" 口, which is pronounced "*gu*" in Korean, and the character for the number ten 十, which is pronounced "*sip*" in Korean. "*Ja*" is Korean for the character 子, meaning "son." So the name Gusipja is a rather elaborate way of signifying "son of the Jeon family."

dressed in mourning clothes, weeping by a forest of thick-leaved bamboo trees. He pretended not to see her and went on to learn the letters with Yun Gong, but on his way back home he saw that she was still crying at the same spot. He became curious, so he approached her. She was about fifteen or sixteen, and her jade-like beauty utterly captivated Unchi.

Unchi spoke to her in a gentle manner. "Where did you come from, and why are you crying so sadly from morning to the middle of the day?"

The girl stopped weeping and replied in embarrassment, "I live below this mountain, and I am crying because something terrible has happened to me."

She would not reveal the source of her sadness, so Unchi came even closer and earnestly asked her to tell him of her troubles until she finally relented.

"I am the daughter of Maeng the royal assistant. I lost my mother when I was five years old, and then a stepmother came into our household. She has been telling false tales of my wrongdoing to my father because she wants to see me die. I cry night and day, wondering if I should kill myself, but I cannot bring myself to do it. So there's nothing I can do but weep."

Unchi felt a great pity for her.

"Heaven alone should decide whether one lives or dies. Think of your body as a precious gift from your parents and find a way to live on."

When Unchi took her beauteous hand, she accepted his gesture without hesitation. And so they came together and joyfully shared their affection for each other. When it came time for them to part, they did so with sadness.

The next day, when Unchi came to the place on his way to Yun Gong, the girl appeared and called out to him. "I have been waiting for my young master for a long time."

Unchi took her hand with great joy, and they spent some time together.

"Wait for me here," he told her before going off to school.

When Yun Gong saw Unchi, he spoke to him.

"On your way here, you committed an unseemly act with a woman, who is actually a fox demon in disguise. She put a curse on you, so no matter how much you study, you will never fathom the ways of heaven and earth or the harmonious principles of the universe. If you want the curse lifted, go back now and see that woman again. You will find that she is keeping a marble in her mouth. Take that marble away from her and bring it to me."

Unchi followed Yun Gong's order and returned to the place where he had met the girl. When he saw her, he took her hand and led her into the bamboo forest, where they came together again. As they did so, he noticed that she indeed had a marble in her mouth. Unchi asked her to let him see it, but she refused. Unchi made a serious face.

"You are a maiden from a good family and I am a young bachelor. I thought we should tell our parents about us so that we can be together like a pair of faithful ducks that mate for life and live a hundred years or so in each other's company. But I suppose that you are not interested in that."

Hearing those words, the girl felt overcome with love for Unchi, so she rolled the marble out with her tongue and put it in his mouth. After a while, she asked for it back, but Unchi refused to return it. She pestered him, and then tried to forcibly open his mouth to retrieve it. At that point, Unchi swallowed the marble. She searched inside his mouth, but when she realized that it was gone, she got up without a word and left the forest while wailing in sorrow. Unchi felt ashamed, so he went to Yun Gong and told him the whole story.

Yun Gong spoke to him. "You have eaten the soul of a fox demon, so you will understand the ways of astrology and geomancy. You will also become the master of seventy-two spiritual powers. I also predict that in the fourth lunar month of this year, you will pass the preliminary civil examination and become a literary licentiate. After that, you must handle yourself carefully."

At the age of fifteen, Unchi's literary skills surpassed that of Yi Taebaek[*] and his calligraphy rivaled that of Wang Huiji.[†] After he had eaten the soul of the fox demon, he also became the master of thirty-six magical powers of transformation. The preliminary government civil examination was held at this time, so Unchi submitted his writings to the judges. He not only qualified but also attained first place among the candidates. After he made the rounds of visiting dignitaries and relatives for four days, he returned to his mother, who felt both joyful and sad.

"When your father was alive, he was averse to taking the civil examinations. But how could I not be happy to see you achieve such a distinction."

Time went on, and when it became spring, Unchi set off to tour the great mountains and rivers of the land. He came upon a Buddhist temple called Segeum, where he found the place of about a thousand rooms covered in cobwebs and empty of people, which he thought strange. He then went to another temple named Seongrim, where he met a few old monks.

When he asked them about Segeum Temple, one of them answered him. "Segeum Temple and Seongrim Temple here used to be the home of about a thousand monks, but four or five years ago something came over the two places, and they couldn't bear to live there anymore. They all scattered to unknown places, so Segeum Temple is now empty, and Seongrim Temple only has us old monks."

"This must be the work of some evil spirit."

Unchi returned home and related the story of Segeum Temple to his mother.

"You must be wary of places like that," Lady Choe told her son.

After the conversation, Unchi spent his time farming and taking care of his mother. But then, one day, Unchi told his mother that he would go to Segeum Temple to study for the final civil examination.

"You told me that the temple has evil spirits that harm people. Why would you go there?"

"What is evil can never overcome what is righteous, so how could such spirits harm me? Please do not worry."

He quickly prepared his travel gear and headed for Segeum Temple. On his way, he came to the top of a rough cliff, where he encountered an old man dressed in worn clothing and leaning on a staff.

When Unchi greeted him politely, the old man spoke to him. "And who might you be, taking the trouble to greet the likes of me in such a polite manner?"

"How could I carelessly pass by such a senior personage?"

"I have been waiting here for a long time so that I can give you something."

The old man took out of his sleeve some rope and a piece of paper with a talismanic symbol on it.

"A time will come when you will need to use these."

With those words, the old man disappeared. Unchi expressed his gratitude toward the air and proceeded to Segeum Temple. There, he ate dinner prepared for him by the monks of Seongrim Temple and then lit some candles to read. At around the third watch,[†] the door to his room suddenly opened, and a woman walked in to sit next to him. Unchi saw that she was only about fourteen years old but was so beautiful that she evoked the vision of a peony flower with morning dew on its leaves. And her bearing was so exquisite that it suggested willow leaves swaying in a spring breeze. It was enough to melt the heart of the toughest man.

Unchi felt disoriented with desire as he spoke

---

[*] Yi Taebaek: Korean for the great Chinese poet Li Tai Bai (701–62), one of the seminal figures of the literary golden age of the Tang dynasty (618–907).

[†] Wang Huiji: Korean for the great Chinese calligrapher Wang Xizhi (303–361).

[‡] Third watch: Traditionally, a day was divided into twelve units of roughly two modern hours each. The five units of nighttime were called *gyeong*, or "watch." The third watch fell into roughly eleven o'clock at night to one.

to her. "Where did you come from, and how did you end up here so late at night?"

"I am a respectable woman from a noble family who was accompanying her husband on his way to take up the position of magistrate in Jangyang District. But we were waylaid by bandits who killed everyone in our household and stole all our things. Only I survived and managed to run away. I hid in the mountains during the day and traveled homeward by night, but then I saw the light from this window and thought there must be people living here. From the outside, I could hear the sound of a man reading, but I am in such a pitiful state at the moment that I abandoned all sense of propriety and came in. If you would please save me, I promise to never forget what you did for me."

"Fortune and misfortune are things that are beyond our control. You were beset by bandits, but you managed to escape. Under the circumstances, it is fortunate that you came upon this place. Where is your home, and how old are you?"

"Our house is outside the South Gate of Gyeongseong,* and I am seventeen years old."

"We are of the same age. Gyeongseong is about three hundred *ri*† from here. It worries me that it's too far for a woman to travel by herself."

The woman replied in a plaintive voice. "Please take pity on me and allow me to stay the night here."

"Because I am from a poor family, I couldn't get myself a wife. I thought that if I am fortunate enough to pass the final civil examination next spring, I would be able to get married. But meeting you on this night, I think that this must be fate. How about we pledge to spend the rest of our lives in each other's company?"

When the woman heard those words, she bowed her head and did not say anything. In the candlelight, her modesty made her look even more beautiful.

Unchi pushed aside his reading table and

spoke to her. "I see that I have upset you with my words, which shames me. I bid you to think deeply and make a proper decision about your future."

The woman thought for a while before she replied. "I may be in a precarious situation now, but I am still a member of a noble family. I would rather die than allow myself to be dishonored. But your words have filled me with such gratitude that I cannot fully express it in words. If you promise to someday avenge the wrong I have suffered, how could I not follow your will?"

Unchi thought their minds were in agreement, so he lay with her.

"This is a wonderful day, so let us share liquor like a groom and bride and pledge our union to the gods of heaven and earth."

Unchi poured some liquor from a bamboo bottle into a cup and drank it, and then poured some for the woman. When Unchi tried to give her more, she firmly refused.

"Why don't you drink some more?" Unchi said.

As he insisted, she drank another. But when Unchi took some more and tried to give her another, she refused again. Unchi made an upset expression.

"A woman should obey a man, so why are you acting in such an improper manner?"

The woman saw how upset Unchi was, so she forced herself to drink until she became disoriented. When she finally lay down and began to snore, Unchi took her clothes off and wrote a magic spell on her chest with red ink. No trace of the writing appeared on her, so he became certain that she was a fox demon in disguise. He used the rope he was given to bind her hands and feet together, and then put a pick to the crown of her head and pounded it down with a hammer.

The woman woke up in fright and exclaimed, "Noble sir, what are you doing?"

"You evil fox demon! I know you committed heinous acts in this temple and murdered people.

---

* Gyeongseong: Capital of the kingdom, today's city of Seoul.
† *Ri*: A unit for measuring distance, a little under 450 meters (around 0.27 miles).

To prevent you from causing further mischief, I have been waiting here to kill you!"

Unchi hammered the pick into her head again until the demon could not stand the pain and revealed its true form.

When the golden-furred fox with nine tails begged Unchi for its life, he addressed her. "If you give me your fox soul, I will let you live."

"But my soul is in my belly. If you spare me, I will give you three books of Heavenly Wisdom, which is much better than a fox soul."

Since Unchi was a scholar first and foremost, he became glad at the mention of such books.

"Where are they?"

"They are in my cave, so if you release me, I'll go get them."

Unchi angrily hammered at the pick again.

"If you unbind my feet, I'll take you there and give you the books."

Unchi thought that would work, so he unbound the fox demon's feet and followed it to its cave. It was at the side of a great mountain, below a massive rock. Inside, he found a place full of blue-green pine and bamboo trees, as well as a calmly flowing stream illuminated by a fair light that also revealed countless shimmering dwellings.

As Unchi forced the fox demon to walk in front of him, maidens dressed in colorful clothing came out.

"Our young lady has returned from her hunt, so we are sure to eat well today."

Overcome with rage, Unchi beat those demons to death before hammering the nine-tailed fox with his pick yet again. The creature could not bear it, so it called out to others.

"Go quickly to my box of precious objects and bring three books that are in it."

A demon hurriedly brought the books.

When Unchi examined them, he could tell that they indeed contained Heavenly Wisdom, but he could not read their characters. He told the nine-tailed fox to teach him.

"I will teach you only if you unbind my hands."

When he raised his hammer, the nine-tailed fox relented.

Unchi spoke to her without unbinding her hands. "We will go back to the temple."

They returned to Segeum Temple, where Unchi drank some liquor and learned to read the book of Heavenly Wisdom, the first volume of which he mastered in a single night. Not even a supernatural spirit could fathom such an ability. It was only then that he unbound the fox demon's hands. He also attached to the first volume the paper with a talismanic symbol he was given.

"I was going to kill you to rid the world of your evil, but you have done me a favor, so I will let you live. Do not engage in unseemly acts ever again."

The nine-tailed fox bowed to him before leaving.

After some time had passed, a powerful wind suddenly blew open the door, and a voice came shouting from a blue cloud.

"Gusipja! Take the rope with you, but leave the talismanic paper behind."

Unchi hurried out as the blue cloud flew away. He expressed his gratitude toward the sky and returned to his room. Sometime later, a gentleman arrived outside the temple on a donkey and ascended the stone steps to the building. It was none other than Yun Gong.

After Unchi hurriedly informed him of all that had happened, Yun Gong addressed him. "This is not a book that a scholar should read, so how dare you even look at it?"

Unchi did not know how to reply to that. He then realized that Yun Gong had disappeared without a trace. He looked around in shock and found that one of the books was missing. As he wondered where it could be, he heard the sound of a wailing woman. When he went outside, he saw his former nanny coming with her hair undone.

She spoke to him while weeping. "Your mother was perfectly fine yesterday, but she passed away in the night. You must hurry home."

Unchi, in great shock, looked for his books

so that he could take them with him, but then he realized that both the nanny and another volume had disappeared.

Unchi spoke out in rage. "Those evil demons thought me so low as to trick me like this, so I will go to their cave, retrieve my books, and get rid of them all."

He went forth with his pick and hammer, but he found the mountains and valleys so rough and the road so long that he could not find the cave. He went back and thought to himself. "I don't know the full extent of those demons' magical powers, so I shouldn't stay here."

So he gathered his things and returned home. Because he had put the talismanic paper on the first volume of the book of Heavenly Wisdom, the demons could not steal it back as they did with the others.

Once Unchi studied the book of Heavenly Wisdom, he became the master of all forms of magic. He also lost interest in taking the final civil examination.

"It will take too long to provide my mother with a comfortable life by becoming a government official."

And he came up with an alternative plan.

With one shake of his body, he gave himself the appearance of a divine official of the Heavenly Realm. He then summoned many-colored clouds and rode them all the way to the royal residence of Daemyeong Palace, where he set himself down while spreading an air that filled the place with a sense of holiness. The palace servants ran about in panic, not knowing what to do, until some of them finally informed the king.

"An event of extreme rarity has occurred."

The king, in great surprise, questioned the servants about what they had seen.

Out of the thick clouds, Unchi sent forth a heavenly servant boy in a blue suit to announce his coming.

"King of Goryeo, receive the command of the Great Jade Emperor of the Heavenly Realm."

The king ordered that a carpet be laid out and a table with an incense burner placed on it. He then proceeded out to meet the heavenly official who was standing upright in the midst of many-colored clouds, dressed in a red robe, wearing a golden crown, and accompanied by servant boys at his sides.

After the king bowed down to him four times and then prostrated himself on the ground, Unchi spoke to him. "A palace in the Heavenly Realm has become old and worn. In order to make repairs, I came down to the world of humans and visited many countries to inform people of the upcoming work. I have received from them all the tributes that are needed for the construction, except for a girder of gold. The Great Jade Emperor knows that your kingdom is rich in gold, so he commands that you submit a golden girder by the seventh day of the seventh month, on the Hour of the Horse.* It has to be ten *cheok*†
and five *chon*‡ long, and three *cheok* and two *chon* thick. If you do not submit it by that time, a great calamity will fall upon you."

When he finished speaking, a serene tune was heard as the many-colored clouds flew away to the south. The king bowed down four times in the direction, then summoned all his officials to discuss the matter.

They spoke to him. "Official pronouncements should be sent out to all eight provinces of the land, ordering the gathering of gold to fulfill heaven's commandment. We think that is the right course."

The king agreed and immediately sent out orders to the provinces to collect gold. When all the necessary metal was brought to the capital, a master craftsman was tasked to fashion the girder

---

* Hour of the Horse: Roughly eleven o'clock in the morning to one in the afternoon.
† *Cheok*: A unit for measuring length, a little bit over 20 centimeters (0.218 yards).
‡ *Chon*: A unit for measuring length, a tenth of a *cheok*.

in the required dimensions. After it was completed, the king kept his mind and body pure for three days while waiting for the heavenly official to return.

At the end of the three days, in the Hour of the Dragon,* many-colored clouds came and filled the palace with a fragrant air before the heavenly official appeared. From either side of him boy servants in blue robes came riding on cranes, picked up the golden girder with metal hooks, and placed it inside the clouds. The clouds then dissipated to the east and the west.

The king went up to the incense table and bowed down four times before returning to his residence. There, his officials congratulated him for concluding the matter successfully.

Because Unchi tricked the king into giving him a golden girder, there was a shortage of gold in the kingdom. He knew that if he tried to sell the precious object, it would draw attention, so he came up with a plan. He cut off just the top part of the girder and took it to a city.

When a police officer saw it, he became suspicious. "Where did you get that gold, and how much is it?"

"It came from a legitimate source, and it is worth five hundred gold pieces."

"If you tell me where you live, I'll bring the money to you."

"I live in the southwestern side of Songak Mountain, and my name is Jeon Unchi."

After the police officer agreed to meet with Unchi, he went to the government office and reported everything to the governor.

"There has to be some story behind this. We should investigate this matter before arresting the wretch."

He then gave the police officer five hundred coins and told him to go and buy the gold. The officer immediately went to the southwest and met with Unchi, who sold the gold to him.

The officer returned to the governor, who examined it before exclaiming in surprise, "This is the top part of the golden girder for certain. We'll arrest the culprit and get the truth out of him before reporting the matter to the king."

The governor sent a team of policemen led by ten or so officers to the southwest to arrest Unchi. When they came, Unchi served them a sumptuous meal.

"I know you've exerted yourself coming all the way here, but I won't be going with you. Your governor is not powerful enough to bring me in. But if the king himself orders my arrest, then I'll surrender myself."

As Unchi sat stock-still, for some reason the officers could not bring themselves to lay their hands on him. So they ended up returning to the city and reporting everything to the governor, who became alarmed. He dispatched five hundred policemen to surround Unchi's house and sent a report to the king. The governor's story enraged the monarch, who gathered his officials to discuss the matter before ordering the Office of the State Tribunal to take charge of the case.

Unchi was serving his mother a plentiful meal that he was able to provide with the money he had made, when he heard of the order from the capital city to put him under arrest. He thought a great deal and came up with a stratagem.

When soldiers led by an officer of the State Tribunal arrived, Unchi picked up a water bottle and spoke to his mother. "Quickly, mother, get inside this bottle."

His mother somehow went in, followed by Unchi himself.

The officer thought it very strange, but he put a plug in the bottle's opening. As he then traveled to the capital night and day, he could hear a voice coming from inside the container.

"I went in here to avoid all the chaos outside. But someone plugged up the opening, so I'm suffocating. Remove the plug!"

The officer ignored the voice as he finally went before the king and reported everything that had occurred.

---

* Hour of the Dragon: Roughly seven o'clock in the morning to nine.

The king spoke out. "I've heard that Unchi knows magic, but how could he possibly get inside a bottle?"

Unchi's voice came from the bottle. "It's so stuffy in here. Please remove the plug."

When the king realized that Unchi was indeed inside, he asked his officials what he should do.

They answered him. "We don't know what kind of magic this wretch is capable of, so if we are not careful, he is liable to escape."

The king ordered oil to be boiled in an iron pot and had the water bottle placed in it.

Unchi spoke out from inside. "Because I was so poor, I have been shivering night and day from the cold. But now that I am in a hot place where I can warm my body, my gratitude knows no end."

The oil boiled from morning to night until it all dissipated. The king then ordered the bottle to be broken, but when it shattered on the ground, no one appeared. Instead, all the broken pieces hurriedly went before the king. "I am here, your lowly subject Jeon Unchi."

The alarmed king ordered that the pieces be gathered and boiled in oil once more. He also commanded that Jeon Unchi's house be destroyed and his land turned into a pond.

Upon his order to arrest Unchi again, his officials spoke up. "This wicked criminal seems hard to catch, so perhaps the best way to avoid further trouble is to put up a notice on all four gates of the city announcing that if Unchi surrenders on his own accord, his crime will be forgiven and he will be given an official position in the government. Once he appears, you could give him a very difficult task. And when he fails to carry it out, you could have him executed then. We believe that this is the right course."

After the king heard them out, he immediately ordered notices to be put up on the four gates, which read as follows.

"Jeon Unchi committed a great crime against the country, but given his special talents, he will be pardoned and given an official position. So come forth on your own accord."

Unchi took his mother into a mountain, where he spent his days riding on a cloud and wandering around as it pleased him. One day, he came to a place where a white-haired old man was weeping sadly. Unchi asked him why he was so sad.

"I am seventy years old and I have a son, but I am lamenting because he has been falsely accused of murder."

Unchi asked for details of the situation.

"In our village, there is a man named Wang whose wife is very beautiful. My son came to share his affection with her, so he went in and out of their house. But the wife, being a licentious woman, also shared affection with a man named Jo. One day, Wang caught his wife with Jo and the two of them ended up fighting. My son happened to come by and separated the two before sending Jo away, but Wang ended up dying of his wounds. Wang's cousin reported the death to the government office, turning it into a murder case. Jo is a houseguest of the magistrate Yang Mungi, so he was able to escape prosecution, so it was my son who ended up becoming written up as a murderous criminal. That's why I am so sad."

"If that is the truth, I will make sure that your son is safe."

After Unchi left the old man, he shook his body and turned himself into pure wind before flying to the house of Yang Mungi. There, he found Yang in the main chamber, looking at himself in a mirror. Unchi gave himself the appearance of Wang and stood next to Yang, who, surprised by the uncanny appearance, put down the mirror and looked around. But he saw no one else in the chamber.

"A ghost is playing a trick on me in broad daylight."

When he looked into the mirror again, he again saw the reflection of someone next to him who addressed him. "I am Wang who was killed by Jo. An official mistakenly arrested Yi for the murder while letting Jo go. If you do not avenge my death, I will not leave you alone."

And he disappeared.

Yang Mungi, taking great fright, quickly made

preparation for an interrogation and put Jo under arrest.

When he questioned him, Jo pleaded innocence, but then Wang appeared out of nowhere and yelled at him. "Jo, you evil bastard! Why did you have relations with my wife and then murder me? You are the unforgiveable culprit, yet you dare to put the guilt on Yi!"

And he disappeared. Jo became so frightened that he did not know what to do.

Yang Mungi put Jo under torture and interrogated him further until the prisoner could not bear the pain anymore and confessed to everything. And so Yi was released and Jo was punished.

After Unchi saved Yi, he flew around on a cloud again, until he came across two men fighting over a pig's head in the middle of a market street. Unchi came down and asked why they were struggling so.

One of them answered. "I bought this pig's head at a fair price, but this official is using his position to steal it from me. That's why we are fighting."

Unchi cast a spell, making the pig's head open its mouth and bite the official, who took fright and ran away.

And Unchi took to the sky once more and flew around until he heard the sounds of singing and musical instruments playing. He descended to the place and politely greeted the people he found there.

"I am a passing traveler who would like to join in your merriment."

A group of young scholars returned the greeting and exchanged names with him. They were in the company of ten or so courtesans, who played instruments and sang. As Unchi conversed with the scholars, he found two named So and Seol to be arrogant.

When food and liquor were served, Unchi addressed them. "I am so grateful to be tasting such precious food thanks to all of you."

Seol replied, "We may not be wealthy, but we can afford to keep the company of famous courtesans and eat fine food. Perhaps this is the first time you have experienced such things."

Unchi laughed. "That may be true, but there are things missing here."

"What might that be?"

"I see no refreshing watermelon, no tangy peach, and no sweet grapes, so why pretend that this is such a sumptuous feast?"

The scholars laughed. "How could you be so ignorant? This is late spring. Such fruits are not available now."

"I saw a place where all kinds of fruits were ripe."

Seol addressed him. "In that case, why don't you go and get some of them?"

Unchi took a servant and went up a hill where there were peaches hanging on trees. He had the servant pick some, and also grapes that were growing below them. They then went down to a field where there were plenty of watermelons growing on vines. They took about twenty of them and brought them to the scholars, who were astonished.

After Unchi got drunk, he decided to play a trick on So and Seol, so he cast a spell on them.

The two of them spoke. "My body feels so heavy, and my mind is in agony with dizziness. How strange this is."

Unchi addressed them. "You are arrogant and lack manners. And I don't think you are fit to be with these courtesans."

The two of them became angry. "We are not eunuchs, so why do you say that we are not fit to be with them?"

Unchi laughed. "Calm yourself and put your hands in your trousers."

Seol felt inside and addressed So. "My testicles have disappeared and everything is smooth down there. How could this be?"

So asked to see, so Seol showed him, and indeed there was nothing there. So reached into his own trousers and also found nothing there as well.

They exclaimed in shock, "Jeon ridiculed us and now this has happened. What do we do now?"

At this point, one of the courtesans discovered that the small opening below her belly had disappeared, while a new opening appeared above her belly. She knew not what to do.

Among the scholars, one named Eun was the brightest and the most learned, and he realized what was happening.

He begged Unchi. "In our blindness, we committed an offense against you. Please forgive us."

"Don't worry. Everything will return to normal."

The scholars and courtesan touched themselves again and were relieved to find that everything had returned to before.

They expressed their gratitude. "We did not realize that a heavenly personage had descended among us, and we nearly paid for our ignorance by turning into freaks."

Unchi flew on a cloud to the south until he came across a group of people who were talking anxiously among themselves.

"Jang the warehouse keeper is a good and filial man, so it would be a tragedy if he died unjustly."

When Unchi came down and asked for the story, one of them informed him, "There is a man named Jang Gyechang who works as a warehouse keeper at the Ministry of Taxation. He is a decent man who is good to his parents, and he also likes to help the unfortunate. But he made a mistake while writing an official report, so he ended up being blamed for the shortage of two thousand coins at the warehouse, which he did not take. We are sorry that he will be punished for it."

Unchi felt pity, so he rode his cloud and flew to the place where official punishments were administered. There, he saw a young man being brought forth in a wagon with his young wife following while weeping. When Unchi asked around, he was told that the man was indeed Jang Gyechang. A prison guard took the prisoner down from the wagon and announced that it was time for his punishment.

Unchi turned himself into wind and gathered Jang Gyechang and his wife to carry them into the sky. The official in charge of the punishment was astonished by the occurrence, so he reported

it to the king, who also took fright, as did all his officials who thought it all very strange.

Unchi brought the Jang couple home, where he fed them medicine, which awakened them from an unconscious state. As they had no idea what was going on, Unchi explained everything that had happened, also informing his mother.

Unchi took to the sky once more and flew about until he came across another person who was weeping.

When Unchi asked what was the matter, the man answered him, "My name is Han Jaegyeong. My father just passed away, and I have a seventy-year-old mother, but I have no money to pay for the funeral or to take care of my mother. That is why I am crying."

Unchi took pity on him, so he reached into his sleeve and took out a scroll.

"Take this scroll, hang it up at your house, and address it by the name of Gojik. If someone answers, ask for a hundred *nyang** and it will be given to you. Use the money to start a business, and then ask for just one *nyang* per day, and use that to take care of your mother. But if you ask for more than that, a calamity will fall upon you, so beware."

Jaegyeong felt both hopeful and skeptical of Unchi, so he asked for his name and where he lived before he went home. When he unrolled the scroll, he found no writing on it but a drawing of a big house with a locked gate and a young boy standing before it. Just to see what would happen, the man called out, "Gojik." The young boy answered and stepped out of the picture. When the astonished Jaegyeong asked for a hundred *nyang*, the boy took out the money and placed it in front of him. He subsequently started a business with it, and he called out "Gojik" every day to ask for one more *nyang*.

One day, Jaegyeong had the need for more money, so he thought to himself, "What harm would it be if I asked to borrow a hundred *nyang*?"

So he summoned Gojik and spoke to him. "I need a hundred *nyang*, so lend it to me."

* *Nyang*: Traditional currency.

When Gojik refused, Jaegyeong tried numerous times to persuade him. The boy went back into the picture without replying and unlocked the gate to the house before going inside. Jaegyeong became angry, so he went into the picture himself, kicked open the gate, and followed him in.

At this time, the minister of taxation was getting ready to begin his work for the day, when an official came to him.

"There's noise of someone inside the warehouse, which is very strange."

The minister thought it odd as well, so he summoned his lower officials and sent them to the warehouse. They opened the door and found a man holding coins, which surprised them.

"How did you get in here, you thief?"

The officials then put him under arrest and reported the incident to the minister, who had the prisoner brought before him. When Jaegyeong was forced to prostrate himself below a stone staircase, only then did he realize that he was no longer at his house but at a government building.

Jaegyeong spoke out in astonishment. "How did I come to this place? Is this a dream or reality?"

The minister addressed him. "For the crime of sneaking into the warehouse to steal money, you deserve to die. If you seek mercy, reveal the identities of your fellow outlaws."

Jaegyeong told the minister everything he knew, revealing his encounter with Jeon Unchi. The minister questioned him, "When do you see Jeon Unchi?"

"It's been four or five months, near where I live in the southwest."

After the minister put Jaegyeong in prison, he went to the warehouse, where he found the place empty of money but chock-full of frogs. Another warehouse was found to be full of yellow snakes but no coins. The enraged minister reported this to the king, who gathered his officials to discuss the matter.

At this time, officials in charge of other warehouses came and reported, "All the rice in the warehouse turned into insects."

Officials from military bases reported, "All the weapons have disappeared, replaced by stacks of tree branches."

Palace maidens reported, "All the hairpieces of palace maidens turned into golden crows and flew away, and a tiger appeared in the inner palace and killed a few servants."

The frightened king selected expert archers and dispatched them to the inner palace, where they found all the palace maidens there riding tigers. They couldn't bring themselves to kill them, so they returned to the king, who became enraged and ordered them to put them all down. The archers were about to shoot them when a black cloud suddenly appeared, enwrapped the tiger-riding maidens, and took them up to the sky.

The king spoke. "This is all the work of Jeon Unchi, so there will be no peace in the country until he is caught."

The minister of taxation addressed him, "The criminal who has been imprisoned is in league with Jeon Unchi, so I bid you to put him to death."

The king was about to order Jaegyeong's execution, when a great wind suddenly blew and the prisoner disappeared without a trace, which was also Unchi's doing.

Unchi was wandering around when he happened to see one of the notices put up on the four gates of the capital calling for his surrender. He scoffed at it at first, but he ended up going to the entrance to the royal palace.

"Your lowly subject Jeon Unchi has come to confess his guilt."

When the Office of the Royal Secretariat reported this to the king, he thought to himself, "This wretch possesses such powerful magic, he is liable to cause much mischief everywhere he goes. It would be a good idea to appease him by giving him an official position in the government. If he persists in making trouble after that, then I'll have him executed."

So he summoned Unchi to court.

Unchi prostrated himself before the monarch, who spoke to him, "Do you know your crime?"

At those words, Unchi flattened himself even more to the ground. "I have committed acts for which I deserve to be executed a hundred times, so I can make no excuse for myself."

"In consideration of your talents, I have decided to pardon you and grant you an official position. So you must fulfill your duties with utmost loyalty."

He made Unchi a royal messenger, putting him in charge of the office that took care of the horses and carriages used by the king's envoys. Unchi expressed much gratitude before leaving his presence.

After Unchi began working there, he noticed that the other royal messengers acted harshly toward their subordinates, often hitting them with clubs. One day, Unchi casually picked up a stone pillar and smashed it into their clubs, hitting their hands as well. That caused them such pain that they stopped abusing their subordinates.

A few months later, the other royal messengers sent their servants to Unchi with a demand that he show them respect by serving them a meal.

Unchi replied, "Tell them to come out to the nearby beach tomorrow at dawn."

The next day, all the royal messengers rode their horses and went to the beach, where they found tents of blue canopies with colorful sitting mats arranged decorously inside. Sonorous music was playing, and a plentiful feast was laid out. It was all a magnificent scene.

After everyone sat down to be served food and liquor, Unchi spoke. "All of you are here to enjoy yourself, but it would be no fun without women to keep us company. I know some women I used to be close to. Should I bring them here?"

Many who were already getting happily drunk spoke out. "Who would have known that such a junior official would demonstrate such enthusiasm? Do as you will."

So Unchi took a servant and headed for the south gate of the capital.

Many talked about him. "That junior official is so talented, I bet he could handle the most fearsome criminal." And so they praised him.

Unchi returned not long after, accompanied by many women whom he directed to stand outside the tents. He then had more food on large tables to be brought for the pleasure of the royal messengers.

Unchi spoke to them. "As per your wish, I brought all these women here. How about I have them sit by all of you so that you can enjoy yourself with them?"

When many assented happily, Unchi brought one woman and had her sit in front of the highest-ranking official. "Stay here and serve him well."

He then led the rest of the women and had them sit by the other officials, who only realized then that they were their wives. They were afraid to reveal what they had expected, so they kept quiet and kept their discontent to themselves. After they were done with the meal, they quickly left on their horses, which mystified their servants.

When the royal messengers returned home, all of them found their households in disarray, as they were beset by family members, some who came to deliver terrible news, some who were on their way to the pharmacy to obtain medicine, some who were bringing a doctor who practiced acupuncture, and some who were lamenting a death. When the officials questioned them, they found out that all their wives had died.

When a royal messenger named Kim came home, a servant girl informed him, "Your wife was fixing some clothes when she suddenly left this world."

Official Kim spoke out in rage, "That Jeon brought her to the party on the beach and reduced her to a courtesan. How could the wife of a nobleman bear such an insult? I am sure to lose my position now, and my family will be dishonored as well. How can I bear the sorrow of this calamity?"

A servant girl came in a hurry. "Your wife has woken up."

The official's rage died down as he ran to the woman's chamber, where his wife sat up and spoke to him. "A while ago, I fell asleep and saw a man in a red robe who took me away. Then a servant in yellow clothing covered me with a veil, put me on a horse, and led me to some place. There, I saw many women who were respectable wives like myself. Then that wretch Jeon the royal messenger grabbed me by the back of my head and pushed me in front of you and said 'serve him well.' He then had the other women sit next to officials. When all the royal messengers finished their meal, they all saw how angry you were as you got up and left on your horse. So they also left without looking back and scattered, all in rage. I and all the other women had no idea what was happening, so we were on the verge of panic. Then I woke up and realized that it was all a dream. Everyone in the household seemed to be lamenting because they thought I was dead. What is happening?"

When Official Kim heard this, he did not know what to say.

All the other royal messengers were filled with indignation. "That wicked criminal Jeon Unchi wormed his way into the royal palace, and now he dares to humiliate us all. We should allay our anger by killing that bastard!"

After Unchi tricked the royal messengers, he thought to himself, "The king did pardon me of my crime and gave me an official position, so I should be grateful for his great favor. I should turn over a new leaf and serve him with utmost loyalty."

And so he concentrated on fulfilling his duties well, taking good care of the horses under his charge until they gained weight and became healthy. The court became pleased with his work.

At Gadal Mountain, there was a man by the name of Yeom Jun who was extremely courageous and greatly skilled in martial arts. He gathered thousands of bandits and set up a lair in the mountain, from where they went forth to pillage villages and assault towns to steal weapons and provisions, murdering people in the process. As a result, every town in the area became frightened.

When the provincial governor sent a report of these events to the king, he became concerned enough that he summoned his officials to discuss the matter. "These bandits are so strong and flourishing, so who can destroy them?"

No one replied at first, but then one official stepped forward. "My gratitude for the favors Your Majesty has granted me knows no bounds. I may not be a person of much talent, but I would like to allay Your Majesty's concern by cutting off the head of Yeom Jun."

When the king looked up, he saw that it was none other than Jeon Unchi. He was greatly pleased.

He questioned the other officials. "What do you think?"

They all thought it was the right course, so the king spoke to Unchi, "How many soldiers do you need?"

"They say that the bandits are very powerful, so I think it would be best if I went by myself and spied on them first. Soldiers could be deployed later."

The king assented and granted him a sword with permission to proceed according to his will. Unchi expressed his gratitude and left the court.

The next day, Unchi rode a cloud and went southwest to visit his mother.

When he told her that he received the command of the king and was on his way to assess the strength of the bandits, she cautioned him, "It would be dangerous to go there not knowing the strengths and weaknesses of your enemy. Be very careful as you fulfill the king's mission."

Unchi returned to Gyeongseong, where he took ten or so police officers and set off at dawn. When they arrived at a provincial office, Unchi ordered the men to stay there for the time being. He then took up his sword and, with one shake of his body, turned himself into an eagle. He flew to Gadal Mountain, where he saw Yeom Jun riding a white horse beneath a large parasol. He was accompanied by many beautiful maidens in colorful dresses and about a hundred servants.

Yeom gave out an order. "Today is the day that chieftains from all eight provinces return. Tomorrow, slaughter ten large cows and prepare a feast."

Unchi considered Yeom Jun and saw that he was a man of grand appearance with a reddish complexion, eyes that were like large water drops, and a beard that looked like needles tied together.

Unchi came up with a stratagem and gathered leaves, which he transformed into so many spirit soldiers. He armed them with spears and swords and organized them in a well-defended camp with flying flags. He then put on a helmet with two phoenixes engraved on it and a red military coat, mounted a black-and-white horse, and proceeded to the enemies' position. He burst through the entrance to their lair, where he found a firmly locked gate. Unchi cast a spell, which forced the gate to open up by itself, and rode through to find a bustling place full of brightly colored houses. After he looked around a bit, he turned himself into an eagle again and flew to an enclosed garden, where he found Yeom Jun sitting on a golden chair with his chieftains all around him and a hundred or so beautiful maidens standing behind them, serving them liquor.

Unchi cast another spell, which brought countless eagles that covered the sky. They came down, picked up the tables in front of the chieftains, and bore them into the air. Then a great wind blew sand and pebbles all around, knocking down all the terrified people who could not even open their eyes. Canopies and floor mats flew into the sky as well. Yeom Jun became so disoriented that all he could do was climb up an incline and hold on to a tree stump while his soldiers tumbled through the air holding pieces of meat and cake, some of them vomiting in fright.

Everything was in chaos from the Hour of the Snake* to the Hour of the Horse, until Yeom Jun regained enough composure to look around and see that snow was falling in great profusion. Before he knew it, the snow had accumulated to a full *gil*.† As none could move or see, they were on the verge of panic, but then the wind suddenly ceased, and all the snow disappeared without a trace.

Yeom Jun went to the main hall of his headquarters and rang a large bell, summoning all his soldiers.

They all spoke of the strange occurrences and argued over their meaning, until a soldier came and reported, "A general leading an army has broken through the east gate and is coming inside."

Yeom Jun, in shock, ordered his men to go and ascertain the situation before he picked up a spear and went forth on a horse.

When Unchi saw him, he shouted at him, "What a lowly wretch you are, using your strength and ruthlessness to pillage villages and murder people. I mean to capture every single one of you ratlike bastards, so if you fear for your life, surrender at once and accept the will of heaven."

At that, Yeom Jun replied in rage, "I am following the will of heaven and the desire of the common people in seeking to topple the unrighteous king and save the multitudes who have fallen into misery. So how dare you get in my way!"

And he charged forward.

The two of them fought on horseback, exchanging blows of sword and spear in tens of rounds. Yeom Jun's mighty spear blocked the light of the sun, while Unchi's swift sword emitted light that produced a rainbow in the air. It was like a pair of tigers fighting over food in a mountain, or a pair of dragons over a pearl in the ocean. Both warriors became increasingly alert, so neither could overcome the other. Finally, it became so dark that gongs sounded from both camps, and the two of them fell back with their respective armies.

When Yeom Jun returned to his camp, his chieftains praised him. "Despite the surprise of the calamity that fell on us, you fought well against that tigerlike warrior. Heaven must be on your side. But the enemy also seems to be a man of great courage, so we bid you to take care."

Yeom Jun laughed. "He may be courageous,

---

* Hour of the Snake: Roughly nine o'clock in the morning to eleven.
† *Gil*: A unit for measuring length, a little over 2 meters (6.5 feet).

but I have no fear of him. I will surely capture him tomorrow and march on the capital."

The next day, he opened the camp's gate and went forth to shout out, "Come out quickly and face me and my blade. I swear that a victor will emerge on this day."

As he then dashed about, Unchi came riding out in fury, twirling his sword in a dance as he headed straight for Yeom Jun. Sword and spear clashed thirty or so times, Yeom Jun's skill with the spear proving flawless.

Unchi thought to himself, "I can't beat Yeom Jun through combat alone."

With a shake of his body, he raised himself into the air but left a phantom image of his body behind to keep fighting Yeom Jun.

He shouted at his foe, "I have never killed anyone, but I see no choice to put an end to one who dares to defy the will of heaven. So don't blame me for your demise."

Unchi was about to strike Yeom Jun with his sword, when he stopped to think. "I should not kill someone so casually. I should capture him alive."

From the air, he made his sword shine as he shouted, "Behold my power!"

Yeom Jun looked up in surprise and saw a massive cloud bursting with lightning, which was actually light coming out of Unchi's sword. Yeom Jun became pale with fright and tried to ride back to his camp but then found his way blocked by Unchi with his sword. Another Unchi chased him from behind, and two more Unchis appeared at his left and right to surround him. Yet another Unchi came flying down on a cloud, swinging his sword in a dance as he prepared to strike Yeom Jun in the head. When Yeom became so disoriented that he fell off his horse, Unchi came down from the cloud and ordered the other Unchis to bring up his soldiers to restrain Yeom Jun and take him to their camp. Unchi then rode into the enemy camp, where all the chieftains and soldiers, having witnessed Yeom Jun's capture, surrendered by binding their own hands together.

Unchi ordered them to prostrate themselves before him, but he spoke in a gentle manner. "Since you have engaged in acts of treason against the country, you deserve to be executed a hundred times. But I will grant you a special pardon, so go back to your hometowns, farm the land, and become good subjects."

The chieftains all bowed their heads twice and scattered. This was reminiscent of the time Jang Jabang, the meritorious official of the Han dynasty, scattered the enemy soldiers of the Kingdom of Cho at Gyemyeong Mountain.[*] On a moonlit night of autumn, he had the song of their homeland sung sadly, which made the Cho men from the Gangdong region homesick.[†]

Unchi went to Yeom Jun's dwelling place and released the hundred or so beautiful maidens, allowing them to return home. He then returned to the camp, where he sat down on the commander's chair and ordered that Yeom Jun be brought to him.

He reprimanded Yeom in a loud voice. "With all your talents and courage, you should have served the king with utmost loyalty, thereby earning royal favor for generations of your family. That is the righteous way. But you dared to act in a treasonous manner by causing disturbances across the country. There can be no pardon for that."

Unchi ordered a soldier to take him outside the camp's gate and behead him, at which point Yeom Jun begged plaintively for his life. "Mine is a crime that is deserving of the execution of three generations of my family, but if you would show benevolence and spare my life, I swear to mend my ways and follow you."

Unchi replied, "If you are truly repentant, that would be a good thing."

---

[*] "Jang Jabang" is Korean for the Chinese strategist "Zhang Zifang" (aka Zhang Liang, ?–189 BCE) who helped Liu Bang establish the Han dynasty in China. "Cho" is Korean for the "Kingdom of Chu," and "Gyemyeong Mountain" is Korean for "Jiming Mountain" in China.
[†] Gangdong: Korean for the Chinese region Jiangdong.

He ordered his soldier to unbind Yeom and consoled him before letting him return to his original home. He then gathered his spirit soldiers and sent a report to the king of his victory. When he returned to the royal palace and bowed down before the king, his sovereign questioned him on how he had defeated his enemy. After Unchi related everything to him, the king praised him profusely and gave him many awards.

Upon Unchi's return, all the government officials praised him for his achievement, except for those of the Office of the Royal Messengers, none of whom came to see him. This was because they still hated him for the humiliation he had inflicted on them at the party at the beach. So Unchi decided to trick them again.

One day, at the fourth watch,* the moon was shining brightly and there was not a single cloud in the sky. Unchi rode on a many-colored cloud and summoned a warrior spirit known as the Yellow Turban Strongman as well as all kinds of goblins.

He addressed the warrior spirit, "Go quickly and bring me all the royal messengers."

The spirit received the order and presently brought them one by one.

The frightened officials prostrated themselves on the ground and looked around at the most terrifying sight of ghosts and goblins all over the place.

Unchi reprimanded them in a loud voice. "I played a trick on you once by briefly humiliating your wives, but is that any reason to hate me so much as to treat me like dirt? I had planned a while ago to send all of you to the underworld, but I got busy fulfilling my duty as an official in the Heavenly Realm by night and an official of the earthly government by day, so I put it off. But now I feel obliged to send you down to suffer for your arrogance and contemptuous behavior."

Unchi then summoned the Yellow Turban Strongman. "Take these criminals and turn them over to the King of the Underworld. After they spend eighty thousand years there, they are to be reincarnated as animals."

When the royal messengers heard those words, they shook so badly in fright that it felt as if their souls were leaving their bodies.

They begged sorrowfully. "Out of our ignorance, we have done wrong. But please consider our bond as fellow officials and pardon us."

Unchi thought for a long time before he replied, "It is the right course for me to send you to the underworld to suffer, but considering that we were close once, I will pardon you for now. But I may change my mind depending on what I see in the future. Send them away!"

At that moment, all the royal messengers woke up from a dream. They had sweated so much that their blankets were all wet, and their minds were in a disoriented state. When they got together and spoke of their dreams, they realized that they were the same. After that, they all treated Unchi with utmost respect.

One day, the king summoned the minister of taxation and queried him. "You told me before that all the money at the ministry was transformed into other things. What is the situation now?"

The minister replied, "Nothing has changed."

As the king became concerned, Unchi stepped forward and spoke. "I bid you to allow me to thoroughly investigate the strange occurrence at the warehouses."

When the king assented, Unchi and the minister went to the warehouse and opened its door. There, they found all the money restored.

The minister exclaimed in surprise, "I inspected the warehouse yesterday, and it was full of frogs. But all the silver has returned overnight, so how strange this is."

They opened another warehouse and found

* Fourth watch: Roughly one o'clock in the morning to three.

all the weapons restored, which surprised everyone once again. When Unchi reported this to the king, he was pleased and guessed that it was all the work of Unchi's magic.

At this time, a royal censor came to the king and spoke to him. "An informant told me that four or five people were planning a revolt in Hoseo province. So I have come to report that I have put the informant under custody."

The king replied, "It is due to my lack of virtue that there are such criminals in the kingdom. How sad this is."

He ordered the State Tribunal and the Police Bureau to arrest and bring the traitors. When they were arrayed before the king, he interrogated them personally.

One of them spoke out. "We planned to make Jeon Unchi the king and so bring peace to the common people, but it has all come out. We deserve to be executed ten thousand times and more."

At this time, Unchi was working as the recorder of criminal investigations. He was standing at the king's side, writing down the words of the interrogation when his name unexpectedly came up in the testimony of the criminal. The king became enraged.

"I suspected that Jeon Unchi might plan treason one day, and now his name has appeared in this confession."

The king quickly ordered Unchi to be restrained and torture instruments to be brought. "I once pardoned you of your crimes and even granted you an official position. Yet, instead of serving me with loyalty, you committed an act that is deserving of the punishment of a traitor. I will hear no excuses but order you to die."

The king then commanded his servants, "Kill him with one blow."

One was about to hit him with all his strength, when his arm became beset with such pain that he could not proceed.

Unchi spoke out, "I deserve to be executed ten thousand times over for my past crimes, but I am innocent of the charge of treason that is being laid upon me now."

He thought to himself, "This is surely the work of someone trying to frame me."

"Since I am about to die, it saddens me that I won't be able to pass down a particular talent of mine. I beg Your Majesty to grant me the favor of displaying that talent."

The king thought to himself, "This wretch is quite skilled, so I should see this."

"What talent are you talking about?"

Unchi replied, "I am so good at painting that when I depict a tree, it actually grows, when I depict an animal, it walks about, and when I depict a mountain, trees and other plants appear on it. They call such a thing a radiant picture. If I do not leave behind such a painting before I die, I fear that I will turn into a discontented ghost."

The king thought to himself, "If this wretch returns as a ghost, that might cause some problems."

So he ordered his restraints to be removed, and a brush, ink, and paper to be brought.

Unchi drew mountains and rivers in layers upon layers of summits and valleys as well as a waterfall of ten thousand *gil* falling from a great height. Willow branches were arrayed on the bank of a stream where a donkey with a saddle was standing. Unchi threw away the brush and bowed four times to the king.

"Why are you bowing to me when you've been condemned to death?"

"I bid Your Majesty farewell as I mean to go into a mountain."

He then entered into the picture, got on the donkey, and headed for a mountain. He soon disappeared from sight.

The king spoke out in anger, "I have been tricked by this wretch again! What must be done!"

He ordered that the picture be burnt. He then interrogated the prisoners once more before they were beheaded.

Unable to allay his anger over being tricked by Unchi again, he sent out notices to all eight provinces, announcing that whoever captures Unchi will be awarded a hundred gold pieces along with other prizes and an official position in the government.

After Unchi used his magic to escape execution, he returned home and told his mother everything that had happened. She was shocked by what she heard.

"From now on, hide yourself and do not go to court ever again. Since you tricked the king, you won't obtain a pardon. How could you face your ancestors in the afterlife?"

She reprimanded him severely, so Unchi spent his days quietly in the mountain, concentrating on his studies.

One day, he was riding on a donkey and enjoying the scenery when he saw a young monk who was taking a pretty girl into the mountain. Unchi went on to drink some liquor at a country tavern, but on his way back, he saw the girl climb a tree and try to commit suicide by hanging herself. He quickly untied the noose and massaged her hands and feet to bring her back to consciousness. When she woke up, Unchi asked if she tried to kill herself.

"That monk you saw me with was a good friend of my husband when he was alive. Although I became a widow at a young age, I maintained my virtue. Today is the day of my husband's passing, so the monk came and said that we should perform a memorial ritual at the temple. I agreed to go with him without suspecting anything. But that bastard brought me to this place and raped me, violating my chastity. I saw no use in living on, so I tried to kill myself."

Unchi consoled her and sent her to his house. He then went up the mountain until he came to a large temple, where he saw the wretched monk. Unchi cast a spell and let out a strong breath, which transformed the monk so that he looked like Unchi.

An investigator from the Police Bureau, who happened to be staying at the temple to scout the area, saw the monk and thought he was Unchi and reported the sighting to the local magistrate.

The magistrate was pleased to hear this and sent soldiers to the temple, where they arrested the monk and transported him to Gyeongseong.

The king was preparing to interrogate him personally when officials of the Royal Secretariat reported to him, "Jeon Unchi has been arrested in every province and many towns, so there are three hundred sixty of them. This is surely the work of his magic."

The king became enraged but did not know how to handle the matter until Chief Royal Secretary Wang Yeonhui spoke. "It's hard to fathom Jeon Unchi's magic. Since this is liable to create much chaos, I think it would be best to behead them all rather than try to figure out which one is the real Jeon Unchi."

The king agreed and proceeded to a watchtower from where he ordered the beheading of all the Jeon Unchis. But then one of them spoke out. "I am not Jeon Unchi but the Chief Royal Secretary Wang Yeonhui."

The king looked at him closely and saw that it was indeed Wang.

When he asked his officials what was going on, they answered, "But he is Jeon Unchi."

The king lamented at that. "The fortunes of this country have fallen so low that it is rife with such demonic tricks. How am I to preserve this country? I can't allow so many innocent officials and commoners to die just so I can have one criminal executed."

And so he ended the interrogation.

At this time, Unchi changed his appearance to that of Wang Yeonhui inside a cloud, and then walked out of the palace gates. Servants hurried over with horses and escorted him to Wang's house. As Unchi went into the main chamber and conversed with Wang's wife, none in the household suspected anything.

The real Wang Yeonhui came out of the palace but could not find any of his servants. He thought it strange and borrowed a horse from a colleague and rode to his house. There he became very angry at his servants at the front door and demanded to know why they were home.

They answered him, "But we escorted Your Lordship here a while ago. How come Your Lordship is here again?"

And they looked at him strangely. As he proceeded to the main chamber, servant girls clapped their hands in astonishment.

"What is going on? How is His Lordship outside now? How is this happening?"

And so they talked in confusion.

Wang Yeonhui, unaware of anything, went into his sleeping chamber and found another Wang Yeonhui speaking with his wife.

He yelled in rage, "What kind of a wretch are you that you dare come into the house of a noble official and converse with his wife?"

He then commanded his servants, "Get that bastard now!"

Unchi spoke, "What kind of a wretch are you that you dare to wear my face, come into my chamber, and try to violate my wife? What calamity is this!"

He commanded the servants, "Get that bastard now!"

The servants looked back and forth but could not fathom the trick that was being performed before them.

As they did not know what to do, Unchi spoke out, "I've heard that demons cannot hold the appearance of a human for long."

Unchi threw water and red paint at Wang Yeonhui, which turned into a nine-tailed fox.

The servants came with swords and clubs to kill the animal, but Unchi stopped them. "This is such a strange event that it should be reported to the government and be handled officially. Until then, bind that creature tightly, put it in a chamber, and guard the place well."

The servants obeyed and restrained Wang Yeonhui before shutting him in.

When Wang Yeonhui tried to speak, fox noises came out of his mouth. He could only weep at the condition of having his human mind trapped inside an animal's body.

Unchi thought to himself, "He won't be able to live many days in such a state."

That night, at the fourth watch, he went to Wang Yeonhui.

"We had no cause to be enemies, but when I saw that you tried to earn merit by having me killed, I had no choice but to kill you first. But I would like to go through my life without taking any life, so I'm going to forgive you. So don't you dare try anything like that ever again."

Unchi then cast a spell that returned Wang Yeonhui to his true form.

When Wang realized only then that everything was the work of Unchi's magic, he spoke out in fear, "I did not know the extent of Master Jeon's power, so I committed a great wrong."

Wang Yeonhui then expressed his gratitude many times over, after which Unchi spoke to him again. "After I release you and leave this place, your household is going to fall into chaos, so do what you need to do."

He then left for the southwest.

Wang Yeonhui called out to his servants, "Come and look at the demon again."

The servants went into the room and found the creature gone.

When they exclaimed in astonishment, Wang Yeonhui spoke out in anger, "All this happened because you failed to guard the house properly."

He reprimanded them for a long time before dismissing them.

When Unchi went back to the mountain temple, he found that the monk had returned as well, but still with Unchi's appearance. He threw water on the monk and cast a spell that returned him to his true form.

Unchi reprimanded him severely, "As a monk, you should have abided by the ways of Buddhism. Instead, you lured away a virtuous woman and violated her. You deserve to be killed ten thousand times over, so I planned on having you executed as Jeon Unchi, but I just couldn't bring myself to take a life, so I saved you and turned you back into your true form. From now on, do not act like that again."

Unchi was returning home when he came across a group of young men who were fighting over a scroll and marveling at it. "The picture in this scroll is the greatest masterpiece."

Unchi looked at it and saw that it depicted a beautiful woman. It showed her holding a child while teasing it, her mouth and eyes drawn so well that she seemed to be alive and moving.

Unchi thought of a trick and spoke with a smile, "Why are you praising this picture like it's such a great work?"

A young man named O replied. "You may think that you have high taste, but you shouldn't speak of things you are ignorant of. See how the woman in the picture seems to be speaking and watching, so how could it not be a masterpiece?"

Unchi laughed at that and asked for the price of the painting.

O answered. "It is worth fifty *nyang*. That's actually cheap for such a quality work."

"I have scroll picture of my own, so come look at it."

He took a scroll out of his sleeve and unfurled it, revealing another picture of a beautiful woman. She was of great fairness, dressed in a blue jacket and red skirt. She also wore a golden coronet on her head. Her beauty was truly incomparable in the whole world.

All the youths looked and praised it. "She also looks alive, so this picture rivals ours."

Unchi laughed. "Your picture is fine, but mine has more liveliness. Witness its true quality."

Unchi hung up the scroll and quietly called to it. "Heavenly maiden Ju, where are you?"

The woman in the picture replied as she stepped out of the picture with a little boy.

Unchi spoke to her, "Pour all these gentlemen some liquor."

The heavenly maiden replied and poured drinks for everyone. Unchi drank his first and watched as all the young men received their liquor, all of them delighting in its taste. After everyone had their fill, the heavenly maiden cleared everything away before stepping back into the picture.

The men exclaimed in wonder, "I don't know if this picture is from the Heavenly Realm or something from a dream, but it is truly the most precious object of all time."

O spoke out, "Let me try it out. Allow me to ask Ju the heavenly maiden to bring us more liquor."

With Unchi's assent, O quietly called out to Ju, "We want more liquor, so please give us some."

Ju the heavenly maiden replied and stepped out of the picture bearing a liquor bottle, while the little boy brought a table. She bent down and poured liquor as before.

O drank his first and waited until everyone else had taken theirs before he got up and expressed his gratitude to Unchi. "I feel fortunate to have met you, to drink such fine liquor, and to witness such a marvel on this day."

"This picture may possess liveliness but it is a useless thing. So there is no need for you to be so grateful."

"If you think the picture is so useless, why don't you sell it to me?"

"If you really want it, I will."

When O asked for its price, Unchi replied, "Ju the heavenly maiden's bottle is a true marvel that never runs out of liquor. So I will take a thousand *nyang* for it."

"Let us not haggle over the price now. How about we go to my house and discuss it there?"

Unchi agreed and went to his house, where he gave O the scroll.

"I will return tomorrow, so have the money ready by then."

After Unchi left, O hung up the scroll at the outer chamber of his house and stared drunkenly at Ju the heavenly maiden holding a liquor bottle. He was so taken with her beauty that he took her fair hand and put it on his lap. Overcome with love, he then tried to drag her over to his mattress. Suddenly the chamber door burst open and O's wife, Lady Min, ran into the room. She was a woman given to jealousy and envy, and often got herself involved in other people's business. She became so enraged by the sight of her husband showing affection to Ju that she tried to beat her rival. But Ju went back into the painting, which made Min take the scroll down and rip it to pieces, leaving O in shock.

"I promised to pay a thousand *nyang* for that scroll. What have you done?"

"When the owner comes, I'm going to tell him off and curse him."

So the two of them argued.

When Unchi returned, O welcomed him and explained the situation. Unchi decided to play a trick on Lady Min and threw a net made of metal strings over her, which turned her into a giant snake. She found that when she tried to speak, no sound came out of her mouth, and when she tried to get up, she could not do so no matter how much she moved around.

Unchi spoke to O, "I left the scroll here as a favor to you, yet the marvel has been destroyed. So meeting you was a misfortune for me. A great calamity will fall upon your house, so take care of yourself."

"What calamity?"

"A demonic beast that has been waiting in this house for a thousand years will use your wife to create much chaos."

"How will the demon do that?"

"Because your wife ripped up my scroll, she turned into that demon. Go open the door and see."

O was skeptical of Unchi's words, but he opened the door and saw a snake the length of six arms on the ground with his wife nowhere in sight. O's face turned pale with terror.

"I see a giant snake. I must kill it."

Unchi stopped him. "This demon is a thousand-year-old spirit. If you kill it, a great harm will come to you. I will attach a talismanic paper to its back, which will make it disappear overnight."

He took out a talismanic paper and put it on the snake's back.

He warned O, "Close the door and do not open it until I return."

He then went home and waited until the new day dawned before he returned to O's house.

There, he went up to Lady Min and reprimanded her.

"You thought so low of your husband that you have acted in a violent and unrighteous manner. Out of jealousy, you ripped up my scroll and insulted me. So I was going to wrap you up in this metal net and put you in a hole in a rock to make you suffer. But if you promise to mend your ways, I will set you free."

Lady Min nodded her head, so Unchi cast a spell that released Lady Min from the net. She hurriedly got up and bowed down to him in gratitude.

On his way back home, Unchi stopped by the house of Yang Bongan, with whom he used to study. He found him lying down with an illness.

When Unchi queried him in concern, Yang answered him, "I have pains in my stomach and chest. And I can't partake in anything to eat or drink, so I don't think I'll be able to get up again."

Unchi checked his pulse and spoke, "Yours is not an illness that originated in the body but one that was caused by thoughts of another person. Who has made you so ill?"

"That's true. There is a woman named Lady Jeong who lives in Hoehyeon District, inside the south gate of the capital city. A person of incomparable beauty, she lost her husband early. She lives next to my uncle's house, so during a visit I happened to see her over the wall and fell so deeply in love that it has made me ill. And now I fear that I do not have long to live in this world."

"You should send a matchmaker who talks well to propose marriage."

"She has such a strict sense of virtue that she will not only reject the proposal but curse me for it."

"In that case, I will try to bring her to you."

"No matter how clever you are, she won't agree to come, so don't bother putting your effort into it."

"Don't worry."

Unchi then left and flew away on a cloud.

After Lady Jeong had lost her husband, she lived alone and spent day and night weeping over her loss, wishing she could die. She had an elderly mother but no siblings. The mother and daughter spent their days taking care of each other.

One day, Lady Jeong felt troubled for some reason and walked around in her chamber. Suddenly a cloud descended, and an official of the Heavenly Realm stepped forth, dressed in a red robe with a jade belt, wearing a gold crown, and bearing a jade tablet of officialdom.

He spoke to her in a clear and calm voice. "Lady Jeong, come out and hear the command of the Great Jade Emperor of the Heavenly Realm."

When Jeong told her mother of what she had heard, the elderly woman became astonished and quickly lit incense on a table. Lady Jeong came out to the garden and prostrated herself on the ground.

Unchi spoke, "Heavenly maiden Mun, how did you like living in the world of humans? It is time for you to return to the Heavenly Realm and attend the once-in-three-thousand-years party at the holy lake of Yoji."

Lady Jeong was astounded by the command of the Great Jade Emperor. "But I am only a human being with a base body who is guilty of many failings. So how could I possibly ascend to the Heavenly Realm?"

"Heavenly maiden Mun has partaken of so much impure water of the human world that she has lost all memory of the Heavenly Realm."

He then poured fragrant holy water into a gourd bottle and offered it to Jeong. When she drank it, she became so disoriented that she did not know what was happening. Unchi wrapped her inside his cloud and bore her into the air, leaving her mother to bow numerous times toward the sky.

At this time, a supernatural spirit called Heaven Sent Young Master was causing mischief by gathering beggars of all kinds to bother people in the marketplace for food and money. He suddenly became aware of a powerful fragrance and looked up to see a cloud traveling southeast. Heaven Sent Young Master lifted his hand and made a gesture, which created an open doorway on the cloud. A heavenly official and a beautiful woman fell out and dropped to the ground. It was Unchi and Lady Jeong.

Unchi looked around in astonishment but could find nothing amiss.

He was about to cast a spell when a beggar child suddenly appeared and reprimanded him loudly. "Mortal man Jeon Unchi, listen to me. You learned magic only to make use of the Heavenly Realm for your tricks and to deprive women of their virtue. Did you think that heaven would overlook that? I've been ordered to end the likes of you, so don't blame me for your demise."

Unchi unsheathed his sword in anger and tried to threaten the spirit with it, but the weapon turned into a white tiger and attacked Unchi. He tried to escape, but his feet became attached to the ground, making it impossible for him to move. He then attempted to transform himself, but his magic spells no longer worked. He looked up in shock and realized that while the beggar child had a shabby appearance, his magical power was superior.

Unchi got down on his knees and begged, "I may have eyes, but my vision is not clear, so I did not recognize you. I have committed crimes for which I deserve to be killed ten thousand times over. But I have an elderly mother whom I could not take care of properly because of my family's poverty, so I felt that I had no choice but to trick the king. Also, what I am doing now is not for the purpose of depriving this woman of her virtue but to save the life of a man who has fallen ill. I bid you, master, to pardon my crimes and to teach me the Ways of Heaven."

Heaven Sent Young Master replied, "I knew all that before you told me. Due to the unfortunate state of this country, the likes of you felt free to create disturbances with magic, so I was going to execute you. But given the situation with your elderly mother, I will let you live for now. Now, return Lady Jeong to her home, and think of some other clever way of saving the life of Yang Bongan. In fact, there is someone who can take the place of Lady Jeong, a woman who lost both her parents early and had to live in dire poverty with no one to depend on. Her name is also Jeong and she is twenty-four years old. If you dare to disobey me, you will come to great harm."

Unchi bowed down to him. "May I know your lofty name?"

"I am called Heaven Sent Young Master. I've been wandering around to have some fun in the world of humans."

And he returned Unchi's magical powers.

Unchi immediately took Lady Jeong and returned to her house, where he called out to her mother, "When I went up to the palace of the Great Jade Emperor, he proclaimed, 'The offenses committed by the heavenly maiden Mun have not been fully atoned for, so return her to the world of humans so that she may suffer some more.' I am bringing her back to you, so bid her to live virtuously."

He then put some fragrant medicine in Lady Jeong's mouth, which allowed her to eventually regain consciousness.

Unchi went back to Heaven Sent Young Master and asked where the woman he spoke of lived. The spirit gave him some magical medicine of transformation and directions to her house. Unchi bowed to him and went to the place, where he found a thatched hut on the verge of collapse. Inside, there was a woman sitting alone, drowning in depression.

Unchi approached her and spoke in a consoling tone, "I know that you are in a difficult situation. You are still unmarried at the age of twenty-four, and so you live a lonely life. I have taken pity on you and will act as your matchmaker."

She bowed down her head in embarrassment, but Unchi fed her the medicine, threw water on her, and cast a spell that changed her face to that of Lady Jeong. Unchi then told her the story of how Yang had fallen ill because of his love for Jeong and gave her instructions on what to do. He then wrapped her in cloth and transported her in a cloud to Yang's house. He put her in the outer chamber and went into the inner chamber to speak to Yang.

"Lady Jeong's sense of virtue is indeed so strong that I could not exchange a single word with her."

Yang lamented pitifully, "Even with all your skills, you could not persuade her, so how could I expect her to change her mind in the future?"

Unchi tried to console him. "I could not bring Lady Jeong, but I did bring a woman who is ten times more beautiful than her."

"I have seen a lot of beautiful women, but there is none like Lady Jeong. Don't joke about something you know nothing of."

"How could I joke around with an ill person? I put her in the outer chamber. Her beauty is truly incomparable. Go and you will see."

Yang was hopeful and skeptical in equal measure, but he was finally persuaded to go to the outer chamber, where he saw a woman in a white dress. The clarity of her face was that of a full moon on an autumn sky, and the brightness of her eyes was that of the morning star. Her beauty was indeed incomparable. As he continued to look at her, he saw that her appearance was that of Lady Jeong, who had been on his mind day and night. He felt so intoxicated with delight and affection that his illness faded away.

One day, Unchi left home to pay his respects to a senior personage, taking with him a bolt of silk to present as a gift.

At this time, the famed scholar Seo Hwadam* summoned a servant boy and spoke to him, "Today, at the Hour of the Horse, a man with the family name of Jeon will come. So clean up this cottage thoroughly."

Unchi came upon the entrance to a mountain path, which he walked through to climb up to a beauteous land, where he wandered leisurely to enjoy its scenery. The place was full of pine and

---

* Seo Hwadam: Hwadam was the literary name of the historical figure Seo Gyeongdeok (1489–1546), a revered Confucian philosopher who was famed for his brilliance, erudition, and commitment to scholarship.

bamboo trees, along with a calmly flowing river where deer looked for mushrooms and cranes danced about in joy. It was such a fair place that it appeared to be in a supernatural realm.

Unchi noticed a door made of twigs among bamboo trees and knocked on it.

A little boy came out. "Are you Master Jeon?"

"How do you know who I am?"

"My master told me this morning."

Unchi was greatly pleased, so he gave the boy the bolt of silk to present as a gift and asked to see his master. Hwadam invited him to his cottage, where they greeted each other politely before settling down to talk.

Unchi spoke. "You lofty name is so renowned that I decided to see you even if I had to travel a thousand *ri*. So I bid you to allow me to learn from you."

"So Master Jeon wants to follow my learning. But what profound knowledge do you think I possess that you should praise me so profusely? I have heard that your magical powers are so great that there is nothing that is unknown to you. So I hoped to meet you one day as well. Now that you are here, I feel most fortunate."

Unchi expressed his gratitude for his words, and they spent the entire day conversing leisurely. Hwadam summoned a maid and had her bring some liquor and food. He then grabbed a sword and stabbed it into a wall, which made holy liquor that supernatural spirits drank pour out, filling a bowl in an instant. On the north wall was a beautifully painted image of a magnificent tower. Hwadam reached into the picture and opened a silk-covered window through which they could see a maiden in a colorful dress approach with a table bearing liquor cups. She stepped out of the picture and sat by Unchi to present liquor to him. Unchi drank it and found it wonderfully fragrant.

"I have come to a place of supernatural beauty where I got to drink the liquor of holy spirits and partake in a sumptuous meal, so my gratitude toward you knows no bounds."

Hwadam laughed at that. "How excessively you praise such modest liquor and food."

They had been exchanging liquor for a while when suddenly a modestly dressed gentleman came in.

"Who is your guest?" he asked Hwadam.

"This is Master Jeon from the southwest." He then addressed Unchi. "This is my younger brother Yongdam. He has never seen you before, and he has forgotten how to act politely before a guest, so please forgive him."

Unchi looked at Yongdam and saw that he possessed clear eyes and outstanding eyebrows. He was of such grand appearance that his aura of dignity was liable to startle people.

Yongdam addressed Unchi in a polite manner. "For a long time I have heard of your great magical powers, so I have been wanting to meet you for a while. Could I possibly ask you to demonstrate your prowess?"

"How could a lowly person like myself pretend to know such things?"

But Yongdam made the request two or three more times until Unchi finally relented. He cast a spell, which turned Yongdam's hat into a bull's head with horns that stretched the length of six arms. It fell to the floor, twitched its eyes, and opened its mouth. Yongdam became upset and cast a spell of his own, which turned Unchi's hat into a pig's head. It fell to the ground as well, where it displayed its teeth and shook its ears.

Unchi thought to himself, "This man seems to possess some skills, so I'll take him on."

He cast a spell on the pig's head, transforming it into a long, three-pronged spear. Yongdam also cast a spell, turning the bull's head into a great sword.

The long spear and the great sword clashed in the air, their blades shimmering as they reflected the light of the sun. Yongdam then threw his fan into the mix and cast another spell, turning the sword and the fan into a red dragon and a blue dragon. Unchi threw in his own fan and cast a spell, turning the spear and the fan into a white dragon and a black dragon. As the four dragons fought, the place became filled with clouds and fog while thunder and lightning struck. Yet no clear winner emerged.

When Hwadam saw the blue dragon and the

red dragon losing strength, he thought to himself, "If the two of them keep competing like this, it will come to no good end."

He threw down a water plate, which turned everything back to their original shape.

Unchi put his hat back on, retrieved his fan, and spoke in a reconciliatory manner, which made Yongdam leave his hat and fan on the floor, all in good humor.

Unchi then bowed down to Hwadam. "I insulted you by daring to display my talent before your superior skills, which is a grievous thing. I will return later to apologize properly."

Hwadam saw Unchi off before he reprimanded Yongdam. "You used a blue dragon and a red dragon, while Unchi used a white dragon and a black dragon. Blue represents wood and red represents fire, while white represents gold and black represents water. Among the five basic elements, gold wins over wood and water wins over fire. So how did you expect to win against Unchi? And why did you get into such a silly contest with a guest in the first place?"

Yongdam pretended to apologize, but he bore a great resentment against Unchi, to the extent of wanting to do him harm.

Three days later, Unchi visited Hwadam again.

Hwadam spoke to him, "I have a favor to ask you, and I hope you will agree to it."

"What is it?"

"There is a great mountain in the south sea called Hwa. There is wise man there who is known as Master Unsu. I studied under him when I was young, and he has sent me many letters since then, but I have been unable to reply to him. Could you possibly go there for me?"

When Unchi readily agreed, Hwadam spoke to him, "Now that I think of it, Hwa Mountain is in the middle of the ocean, so it won't be easy for you to get there."

"I may be modest in my talents, but I can go and return in no time."

When Hwadam expressed skepticism at that, Unchi began to think that he underestimated his powers.

"If I do not return in good time, I will never leave this mountain again, even if I end up dying here."

"In that case, I wish you a good journey, but I still worry that you might make a mistake along the way."

When Hwadam gave him a letter to deliver, Unchi transformed himself into a hawk and flew toward the center of the ocean.

Suddenly a great net appeared out of nowhere and blocked his path. When Unchi tried to fly over it, it grew to block him further. No matter how high he flew, its size matched him to the extent of touching the sky. And its bottom knots were tied to ropes that were submerged in the water. When Unchi tried to fly around it, it spread wide as well, preventing him from reaching Hwa Mountain. After ten days of trying to break through, he had no choice but to return to Hwadam and relate the strange event in the middle of the ocean.

Hwadam spoke to him, "You boasted so much before but you failed in your mission, so why don't you try leaving the mountains now?"

Unchi, in great trepidation, tried to run, but Hwadam, predicting his action, transformed himself into a wildcat and attacked him. Unchi hurriedly turned himself into a hawk to escape, but then Hwadam became a blue lion and took Unchi in his mouth before knocking him to the ground.

Hwadam reprimanded him, "You used such measly magic to trick the king and cause mischief without thought. For your lack of manners, you deserve to die."

Unchi replied in a plaintive tone, "I was ignorant of how great your powers were, so I did act in defiance of your high dignity. I do deserve to die for that, but I have an elderly mother to take care of, so I ask that you spare my life."

"If I let you live just this once, you must promise never to act in an unrighteous manner again. Take care of your mother, but once she passes away, what do you say we go up to the holy mountain of Yeongju together and study the ways of heavenly spirits?"

"I will do as you say."

He bowed down to him before returning home. After that, he stopped using his magical powers and spent his time taking good care of his mother.

After time passed like the flowing of water, Unchi's mother passed away. He performed all the proper rituals as he buried her in a grave on a mountain. He then went through the three-year mourning period.

One day, Hwadam came to visit and Unchi hurried over to meet him. After they exchanged greetings, they went into his house and sat down.

Hwadam spoke to him, "We have made a promise before, so I came despite knowing that you are still in mourning. I have come to take you away, so prepare your travel gear."

Unchi, with great happiness, distributed his wealth to his servants. "This is my final farewell, so I bid you all to live well and perform proper rituals for my ancestors."

After Unchi bowed down before the graves of his ancestors, he and Hwadam got on a cloud and flew in the direction of Yeongju Mountain. No one knows what happened to them after that.

Nathaniel Hawthorne (1804–1864) was an American writer born in Salem, Massachusetts. The Salem witch trials were an influence on his life, even though they had taken place decades earlier, as one of his ancestors was an unrepentant judge in those cases. *The Scarlet Letter*, his most famous novel and in many ways an anti-puritan response to society, was one of the earliest books mass-produced in the United States and quickly reached bestseller status. This may be hard to believe today, given the number of high school students who have had to suffer through it. He flirted briefly with transcendentalism, even living on Brook Farm for a short time, although this was more for financial reasons than for any strong feelings in support of its utopian community. As a matter of fact, much of his later writing showed a negative side of this philosophical experiment. Hawthorne became close friends with Herman Melville while Melville was writing *Moby-Dick*. Melville later dedicated the book to Hawthorne. Not all of his contemporaries appreciated his work. Edgar Allan Poe was quite critical when writing reviews of Hawthorne's fiction. The story included here, "Feathertop," was very well received when it was first published in 1852 and later became the inspiration of an opera and theater, film, and television productions.

Feathertop: A Moralized Legend

Nathaniel Hawthorne

"DICKON," CRIED MOTHER RIGBY, "a coal for my pipe!"

The pipe was in the old dame's mouth when she said these words. She had thrust it there after filling it with tobacco, but without stooping to light it at the hearth, where indeed there was no appearance of a fire having been kindled that morning. Forthwith, however, as soon as the order was given, there was an intense red glow out of the bowl of the pipe, and a whiff of smoke came from Mother Rigby's lips. Whence the coal came, and how brought thither by an invisible hand, I have never been able to discover.

"Good!" quoth Mother Rigby, with a nod of her head. "Thank ye, Dickon! And now for making this scarecrow. Be within call, Dickon, in case I need you again."

The good woman had risen thus early (for as yet it was scarcely sunrise) in order to set about making a scarecrow, which she intended to put in the middle of her corn-patch. It was now the latter week of May, and the crows and blackbirds had already discovered the little, green, rolled-up leaf of the Indian corn just peeping out of the soil. She was determined, therefore, to contrive as lifelike a scarecrow as ever was seen, and to finish it immediately, from top to toe, so that it should begin its sentinel's duty that very morning. Now Mother Rigby (as everybody must have heard) was one of the most cunning and potent witches in New England, and might, with very little trouble, have made a scarecrow ugly enough to frighten the minister himself. But on this occasion, as she had awakened in an uncommonly pleasant humor, and was further dulcified by her pipe tobacco, she resolved to produce something fine, beautiful, and splendid, rather than hideous and horrible.

"I don't want to set up a hobgoblin in my own corn-patch, and almost at my own doorstep," said Mother Rigby to herself, puffing out a whiff of smoke; "I could do it if I pleased, but I'm tired of doing marvellous things, and so I'll keep within the bounds of every-day business just for variety's sake. Besides, there is no use in scaring the little children for a mile roundabout, though 't is true I'm a witch."

It was settled, therefore, in her own mind, that the scarecrow should represent a fine gentleman of the period, so far as the materials at hand would allow. Perhaps it may be as well to enumerate the chief of the articles that went to the composition of this figure.

The most important item of all, probably, although it made so little show, was a certain broomstick, on which Mother Rigby had taken many an airy gallop at midnight, and which now served the scarecrow by way of a spinal column, or, as the unlearned phrase it, a backbone. One of its arms was a disabled flail which used to be wielded by Goodman Rigby, before his spouse worried him out of this troublesome world; the other, if I mistake not, was composed of the pudding stick and a broken rung of a chair, tied loosely together at the elbow. As for its legs, the right was a hoe handle, and the left an undistinguished and miscellaneous stick from the woodpile. Its lungs, stomach, and other affairs of that kind were nothing better than a meal bag stuffed with straw. Thus we have made out the skeleton and entire corporosity of the scarecrow, with the exception of its head; and this was admirably supplied by a somewhat withered and shrivelled pumpkin, in which Mother Rigby cut two holes for the eyes and a slit for the mouth, leaving a bluish-colored knob in the middle to pass for a nose. It was really quite a respectable face.

"I've seen worse ones on human shoulders, at any rate," said Mother Rigby. "And many a fine gentleman has a pumpkin head, as well as my scarecrow."

But the clothes, in this case, were to be the making of the man. So the good old woman took down from a peg an ancient plum-colored coat of London make, and with relics of embroidery on its seams, cuffs, pocket-flaps, and button-holes, but lamentably worn and faded, patched at the elbows, tattered at the skirts, and threadbare all over. On the left breast was a round hole, whence either a star of nobility had been rent away, or else the hot heart of some former wearer had scorched it through and through. The neighbors said that this rich garment belonged to the Black Man's wardrobe, and that he kept it at Mother Rigby's cottage for the convenience of slipping it on whenever he wished to make a grand appearance at the governor's table. To match the coat there was a velvet waistcoat of very ample size, and formerly embroidered with foliage that had been as brightly golden as the maple leaves in October, but which had now quite vanished out of the substance of the velvet. Next came a pair of scarlet breeches, once worn by the French governor of Louisbourg, and the knees of which had touched the lower step of the throne of Louis le Grand. The Frenchman had given these small-clothes to an Indian powwow, who parted with them to the old witch for a gill of strong waters, at one of their dances in the forest. Furthermore, Mother Rigby produced a pair of silk stockings and put them on the figure's legs, where they showed as unsubstantial as a dream, with the wooden reality of the two sticks making itself miserably apparent through the holes. Lastly, she put her dead husband's wig on the bare scalp of the pumpkin, and surmounted the whole with a dusty three-cornered hat, in which was stuck the longest tail feather of a rooster.

Then the old dame stood the figure up in a corner of her cottage and chuckled to behold its yellow semblance of a visage, with its nobby little nose thrust into the air. It had a strangely self-satisfied aspect, and seemed to say, "Come look at me!"

"And you are well worth looking at, that's a fact!" quoth Mother Rigby, in admiration at her own handiwork. "I've made many a puppet since I've been a witch, but methinks this is the finest of them all. 'Tis almost too good for a scarecrow. And, by the by, I'll just fill a fresh pipe of tobacco and then take him out to the corn-patch."

While filling her pipe the old woman continued to gaze with almost motherly affection at the figure in the corner. To say the truth, whether it were chance, or skill, or downright witchcraft, there was something wonderfully human in this ridiculous shape, bedizened with its tattered finery; and as for the countenance, it appeared to shrivel its yellow surface into a grin—a funny kind of expression betwixt scorn and merriment, as if it understood itself to be a jest at mankind. The more Mother Rigby looked the better she was pleased.

"Dickon," cried she sharply, "another coal for my pipe!"

Hardly had she spoken, than, just as before, there was a red-glowing coal on the top of the tobacco. She drew in a long whiff and puffed it forth again into the bar of morning sunshine which struggled through the one dusty pane of her cottage window. Mother Rigby always liked to flavor her pipe with a coal of fire from the particular chimney corner whence this had been brought. But where that chimney corner might be, or who brought the coal from it,—further than that the invisible messenger seemed to respond to the name of Dickon,—I cannot tell.

"That puppet yonder," thought Mother Rigby, still with her eyes fixed on the scarecrow, "is too good a piece of work to stand all summer in a corn-patch, frightening away the crows and blackbirds. He's capable of better things. Why, I've danced with a worse one, when partners happened to be scarce, at our witch meetings in the

forest! What if I should let him take his chance among the other men of straw and empty fellows who go bustling about the world?"

The old witch took three or four more whiffs of her pipe and smiled.

"He'll meet plenty of his brethren at every street corner!" continued she. "Well; I didn't mean to dabble in witchcraft to-day, further than the lighting of my pipe, but a witch I am, and a witch I'm likely to be, and there's no use trying to shirk it. I'll make a man of my scarecrow, were it only for the joke's sake!"

While muttering these words, Mother Rigby took the pipe from her own mouth and thrust it into the crevice which represented the same feature in the pumpkin visage of the scarecrow.

"Puff, darling, puff!" said she. "Puff away, my fine fellow! your life depends on it!"

This was a strange exhortation, undoubtedly, to be addressed to a mere thing of sticks, straw, and old clothes, with nothing better than a shrivelled pumpkin for a head,—as we know to have been the scarecrow's case. Nevertheless, as we must carefully hold in remembrance, Mother Rigby was a witch of singular power and dexterity; and, keeping this fact duly before our minds, we shall see nothing beyond credibility in the remarkable incidents of our story. Indeed, the great difficulty will be at once got over, if we can only bring ourselves to believe that, as soon as the old dame bade him puff, there came a whiff of smoke from the scarecrow's mouth. It was the very feeblest of whiffs, to be sure; but it was followed by another and another, each more decided than the preceding one.

"Puff away, my pet! puff away, my pretty one!" Mother Rigby kept repeating, with her pleasantest smile. "It is the breath of life to ye; and that you may take my word for."

Beyond all question the pipe was bewitched. There must have been a spell either in the tobacco or in the fiercely-glowing coal that so mysteriously burned on top of it, or in the pungently-aromatic smoke which exhaled from the kindled weed. The figure, after a few doubtful attempts at length blew forth a volley of smoke extending all the way from the obscure corner into the bar of sunshine. There it eddied and melted away among the motes of dust. It seemed a convulsive effort; for the two or three next whiffs were fainter, although the coal still glowed and threw a gleam over the scarecrow's visage. The old witch clapped her skinny hands together, and smiled encouragingly upon her handiwork. She saw that the charm worked well. The shrivelled, yellow face, which heretofore had been no face at all, had already a thin, fantastic haze, as it were of human likeness, shifting to and fro across it; sometimes vanishing entirely, but growing more perceptible than ever with the next whiff from the pipe. The whole figure, in like manner, assumed a show of life, such as we impart to ill-defined shapes among the clouds, and half deceive ourselves with the pastime of our own fancy.

If we must needs pry closely into the matter, it may be doubted whether there was any real change, after all, in the sordid, wornout worthless, and ill-jointed substance of the scarecrow; but merely a spectral illusion, and a cunning effect of light and shade so colored and contrived as to delude the eyes of most men. The miracles of witchcraft seem always to have had a very shallow subtlety; and, at least, if the above explanation does not hit the truth of the process, I can suggest no better.

"Well puffed, my pretty lad!" still cried old Mother Rigby. "Come, another good stout whiff, and let it be with might and main. Puff for thy life, I tell thee! Puff out of the very bottom of thy heart, if any heart thou hast, or any bottom to it! Well done, again! Thou didst suck in that mouthful as if for the pure love of it."

And then the witch beckoned to the scarecrow, throwing so much magnetic potency into her gesture that it seemed as if it must inevitably be obeyed, like the mystic call of the loadstone when it summons the iron.

"Why lurkest thou in the corner, lazy one?" said she. "Step forth! Thou hast the world before thee!"

Upon my word, if the legend were not one which I heard on my grandmother's knee, and which had established its place among things credible before my childish judgment could analyze its probability, I question whether I should have the face to tell it now.

In obedience to Mother Rigby's word, and extending its arm as if to reach her outstretched hand, the figure made a step forward—a kind of hitch and jerk, however, rather than a step—then tottered and almost lost its balance. What could the witch expect? It was nothing, after all, but a scarecrow stuck upon two sticks. But the strong-willed old beldam scowled, and beckoned, and flung the energy of her purpose so forcibly at this poor combination of rotten wood, and musty straw, and ragged garments, that it was compelled to show itself a man, in spite of the reality of things. So it stepped into the bar of sunshine. There it stood, poor devil of a contrivance that it was!—with only the thinnest vesture of human similitude about it, through which was evident the stiff, rickety, incongruous, faded, tattered, good-for-nothing patchwork of its substance, ready to sink in a heap upon the floor, as conscious of its own unworthiness to be erect. Shall I confess the truth? At its present point of vivification, the scarecrow reminds me of some of the lukewarm and abortive characters, composed of heterogeneous materials, used for the thousandth time, and never worth using, with which romance writers (and myself, no doubt, among the rest) have so overpeopled the world of fiction.

But the fierce old hag began to get angry and show a glimpse of her diabolic nature (like a snake's head, peeping with a hiss out of her bosom), at this pusillanimous behavior of the thing which she had taken the trouble to put together.

"Puff away, wretch!" cried she, wrathfully. "Puff, puff, puff, thou thing of straw and emptiness! thou rag or two! thou meal bag! thou pumpkin head! thou nothing! Where shall I find a name vile enough to call thee by? Puff, I say, and suck in thy fantastic life with the smoke! else I snatch the pipe from thy mouth and hurl thee where that red coal came from."

Thus threatened, the unhappy scarecrow had

nothing for it but to puff away for dear life. As need was, therefore, it applied itself lustily to the pipe, and sent forth such abundant volleys of tobacco smoke that the small cottage kitchen became all vaporous. The one sunbeam struggled mistily through, and could but imperfectly define the image of the cracked and dusty window pane on the opposite wall. Mother Rigby, meanwhile, with one brown arm akimbo and the other stretched towards the figure, loomed grimly amid the obscurity with such port and expression as when she was wont to heave a ponderous nightmare on her victims and stand at the bedside to enjoy their agony. In fear and trembling did this poor scarecrow puff. But its efforts, it must be acknowledged, served an excellent purpose; for, with each successive whiff, the figure lost more and more of its dizzy and perplexing tenuity and seemed to take denser substance. Its very garments, moreover, partook of the magical change, and shone with the gloss of novelty and glistened with the skilfully embroidered gold that had long ago been rent away. And, half revealed among the smoke, a yellow visage bent its lustreless eyes on Mother Rigby.

At last the old witch clinched her fist and shook it at the figure. Not that she was positively angry, but merely acting on the principle—perhaps untrue, or not the only truth, though as high a one as Mother Rigby could be expected to attain—that feeble and torpid natures, being incapable of better inspiration, must be stirred up by fear. But here was the crisis. Should she fail in what she now sought to effect, it was her ruthless purpose to scatter the miserable simulacre into its original elements.

"Thou hast a man's aspect," said she, sternly. "Have also the echo and mockery of a voice! I bid thee speak!"

The scarecrow gasped, struggled, and at length emitted a murmur, which was so incorporated with its smoky breath that you could scarcely tell whether it were indeed a voice or only a whiff of tobacco. Some narrators of this legend hold the opinion that Mother Rigby's conjurations and the fierceness of her will had compelled a familiar spirit into the figure, and that the voice was his.

"Mother," mumbled the poor stifled voice, "be not so awful with me! I would fain speak; but being without wits, what can I say?"

"Thou canst speak, darling, canst thou?" cried Mother Rigby, relaxing her grim countenance into a smile. "And what shalt thou say, quotha! Say, indeed! Art thou of the brotherhood of the empty skull, and demandest of me what thou shalt say? Thou shalt say a thousand things, and saying them a thousand times over, thou shalt still have said nothing! Be not afraid, I tell thee! When thou comest into the world (whither I purpose sending thee forthwith) thou shalt not lack the wherewithal to talk. Talk! Why, thou shall babble like a mill-stream, if thou wilt. Thou hast brains enough for that, I trow!"

"At your service, mother," responded the figure.

"And that was well said, my pretty one," answered Mother Rigby. "Then thou speakest like thyself, and meant nothing. Thou shalt have a hundred such set phrases, and five hundred to the boot of them. And now, darling, I have taken so much pains with thee and thou art so beautiful, that, by my troth, I love thee better than any witch's puppet in the world; and I've made them of all sorts—clay, wax, straw, sticks, night fog, morning mist, sea foam, and chimney smoke. But thou art the very best. So give heed to what I say."

"Yes, kind mother," said the figure, "with all my heart!"

"With all thy heart!" cried the old witch, setting her hands to her sides and laughing loudly. "Thou hast such a pretty way of speaking. With all thy heart! And thou didst put thy hand to the left side of thy waistcoat as if thou really hadst one!"

So now, in high good humor with this fantastic contrivance of hers, Mother Rigby told the scarecrow that it must go and play its part in the great world, where not one man in a hundred, she affirmed, was gifted with more real substance than itself. And, that he might hold up his head with the best of them, she endowed him, on the spot, with an unreckonable amount of wealth. It consisted partly of a gold mine in Eldorado, and of ten thousand shares in a broken bubble, and of half a million acres of vineyard at the North Pole, and of a castle in the air, and a chateau in Spain, together with all the rents and income therefrom accruing. She further made over to him the cargo of a certain ship, laden with salt of Cadiz, which she herself, by her necromantic arts, had caused to founder, ten years before, in the deepest part of mid-ocean. If the salt were not dissolved, and could be brought to market, it would fetch a pretty penny among the fishermen. That he might not lack ready money, she gave him a copper farthing of Birmingham manufacture, being all the coin she had about her, and likewise a great deal of brass, which she applied to his forehead, thus making it yellower than ever.

"With that brass alone," quoth Mother Rigby, "thou canst pay thy way all over the earth. Kiss me, pretty darling! I have done my best for thee."

Furthermore, that the adventurer might lack no possible advantage towards a fair start in life, this excellent old dame gave him a token by which he was to introduce himself to a certain magistrate, member of the council, merchant, and elder of the church (the four capacities constituting but one man), who stood at the head of society in the neighboring metropolis. The token was neither more nor less than a single word, which Mother Rigby whispered to the scarecrow, and which the scarecrow was to whisper to the merchant.

"Gouty as the old fellow is, he'll run thy errands for thee, when once thou hast given him that word in his ear," said the old witch. "Mother Rigby knows the worshipful Justice Gookin, and the worshipful Justice knows Mother Rigby!"

Here the witch thrust her wrinkled face close to the puppet's, chuckling irrepressibly, and fidgeting all through her system, with delight at the idea which she meant to communicate.

"The worshipful Master Gookin," whispered she, "hath a comely maiden to his daughter. And hark ye, my pet! Thou hast a fair outside, and

a pretty wit enough of thine own. Yea, a pretty wit enough! Thou wilt think better of it when thou hast seen more of other people's wits. Now, with thy outside and thy inside, thou art the very man to win a young girl's heart. Never doubt it! I tell thee it shall be so. Put but a bold face on the matter, sigh, smile, flourish thy hat, thrust forth thy leg like a dancing-master, put thy right hand to the left side of thy waistcoat, and pretty Polly Gookin is thine own!"

All this while the new creature had been sucking in and exhaling the vapory fragrance of his pipe, and seemed now to continue this occupation as much for the enjoyment it afforded as because it was an essential condition of his existence. It was wonderful to see how exceedingly like a human being it behaved. Its eyes (for it appeared to possess a pair) were bent on Mother Rigby, and at suitable junctures it nodded or shook its head. Neither did it lack words proper for the occasion: "Really! Indeed! Pray tell me! Is it possible! Upon my word! By no means! Oh! Ah! Hem!" and other such weighty utterances as imply attention, inquiry, acquiescence, or dissent on the part of the auditor. Even had you stood by and seen the scarecrow made, you could scarcely have resisted the conviction that it perfectly understood the cunning counsels which the old witch poured into its counterfeit of an ear. The more earnestly it applied its lips to the pipe, the more distinctly was its human likeness stamped among visible realities, the more sagacious grew its expression, the more lifelike its gestures and movements, and the more intelligibly audible its voice. Its garments, too, glistened so much the brighter with an illusory magnificence. The very pipe, in which burned the spell of all this wonderwork, ceased to appear as a smoke-blackened earthen stump, and became a meerschaum, with painted bowl and amber mouthpiece.

It might be apprehended, however, that as the life of the illusion seemed identical with the vapor of the pipe, it would terminate simultaneously with the reduction of the tobacco to ashes. But the beldam foresaw the difficulty.

"Hold thou the pipe, my precious one," said she, "while I fill it for thee again."

It was sorrowful to behold how the fine gentleman began to fade back into a scarecrow while Mother Rigby shook the ashes out of the pipe and proceeded to replenish it from her tobacco-box.

"Dickon," cried she, in her high, sharp tone, "another coal for this pipe!"

No sooner said than the intensely red speck of fire was glowing within the pipe-bowl; and the scarecrow, without waiting for the witch's bidding, applied the tube to his lips and drew in a few short, convulsive whiffs, which soon, however, became regular and equable.

"Now, mine own heart's darling," quoth Mother Rigby, "whatever may happen to thee, thou must stick to thy pipe. Thy life is in it; and that, at least, thou knowest well, if thou knowest nought besides. Stick to thy pipe, I say! Smoke, puff, blow thy cloud; and tell the people, if any question be made, that it is for thy health, and that so the physician orders thee to do. And, sweet one, when thou shalt find thy pipe getting low, go apart into some corner, and (first filling thyself with smoke) cry sharply, 'Dickon, a fresh pipe of tobacco!' and, 'Dickon, another coal for my pipe!' and have it into thy pretty mouth as speedily as may be. Else, instead of a gallant gentleman in a gold-laced coat, thou wilt be but a jumble of sticks and tattered clothes, and a bag of straw, and a withered pumpkin! Now depart, my treasure, and good luck go with thee!"

"Never fear, mother!" said the figure, in a stout voice, and sending forth a courageous whiff of smoke, "I will thrive, if an honest man and a gentleman may!"

"Oh, thou wilt be the death of me!" cried the old witch, convulsed with laughter. "That was well said. If an honest man and a gentleman may! Thou playest thy part to perfection. Get along with thee for a smart fellow; and I will wager on thy head, as a man of pith and substance, with a brain and what they call a heart, and all else that a man should have, against any other thing on two legs. I hold myself a better witch than yesterday, for thy sake. Did not I make thee? And I defy any witch in New England to make such another! Here; take my staff along with thee!"

The staff, though it was but a plain oaken stick, immediately took the aspect of a gold-headed cane.

"That gold head has as much sense in it as thine own," said Mother Rigby, "and it will guide thee straight to worshipful Master Gookin's door. Get thee gone, my pretty pet, my darling, my precious one, my treasure; and if any ask thy name, it is Feathertop. For thou hast a feather in thy hat, and I have thrust a handful of feathers into the hollow of thy head, and thy wig, too, is of the fashion they call Feathertop,—so be Feathertop thy name!"

And, issuing from the cottage, Feathertop strode manfully towards town. Mother Rigby stood at the threshold, well pleased to see how the sunbeams glistened on him, as if all his magnificence were real, and how diligently and lovingly he smoked his pipe, and how handsomely he walked, in spite of a little stiffness of his legs. She watched him until out of sight, and threw a witch benediction after her darling, when a turn of the road snatched him from her view.

Betimes in the forenoon, when the principal street of the neighboring town was just at its acme of life and bustle, a stranger of very distinguished figure was seen on the sidewalk. His port as well as his garments betokened nothing short of nobility. He wore a richly-embroidered plum-colored coat, a waistcoat of costly velvet, magnificently adorned with golden foliage, a pair of splendid scarlet breeches, and the finest and glossiest of white silk stockings. His head was covered with a peruke, so daintily powdered and adjusted that it would have been sacrilege to disorder it with a hat; which, therefore (and it was a gold-laced hat, set off with a snowy feather), he carried beneath his arm. On the breast of his coat glistened a star. He managed his gold-headed cane with an airy grace, peculiar to the fine gentlemen of the period; and, to give the highest possible finish to his equipment, he had lace ruffles at his wrist, of a most ethereal delicacy, sufficiently avouching how idle and aristocratic must be the hands which they half concealed.

It was a remarkable point in the accoutrement of this brilliant personage that he held in his left hand a fantastic kind of a pipe, with an exquisitely painted bowl and an amber mouthpiece. This he applied to his lips as often as every five or six paces, and inhaled a deep whiff of smoke, which, after being retained a moment in his lungs, might be seen to eddy gracefully from his mouth and nostrils.

As may well be supposed, the street was all astir to find out the stranger's name.

"It is some great nobleman, beyond question," said one of the townspeople. "Do you see the star at his breast?"

"Nay; it is too bright to be seen," said another. "Yes; he must needs be a nobleman, as you say. But by what conveyance, think you, can his lordship have voyaged or travelled hither? There has been no vessel from the old country for a month past; and if he has arrived overland from the southward, pray where are his attendants and equipage?"

"He needs no equipage to set off his rank," remarked a third. "If he came among us in rags, nobility would shine through a hole in his elbow. I never saw such dignity of aspect. He has the old Norman blood in his veins, I warrant him."

"I rather take him to be a Dutchman, or one of your high Germans," said another citizen. "The men of those countries have always the pipe at their mouths."

"And so has a Turk," answered his companion. "But, in my judgment, this stranger hath been bred at the French court, and hath there learned politeness and grace of manner, which none understand so well as the nobility of France. That gait, now! A vulgar spectator might deem it stiff—he might call it a hitch and jerk—but, to my eye, it hath an unspeakable majesty, and must have been acquired by constant observation of the deportment of the Grand Monarque. The stranger's character and office are evident enough. He is a French ambassador, come to treat with our rulers about the cession of Canada."

"More probably a Spaniard," said another, "and hence his yellow complexion; or, most likely, he is from the Havana, or from some port on the Spanish main, and comes to make investigation about the piracies which our government is thought to connive at. Those settlers in Peru and Mexico have skins as yellow as the gold which they dig out of their mines."

"Yellow or not," cried a lady, "he is a beautiful man!—so tall, so slender! such a fine, noble face, with so well-shaped a nose, and all that delicacy of expression about the mouth! And, bless me, how bright his star is! It positively shoots out flames!"

"So do your eyes, fair lady," said the stranger, with a bow and a flourish of his pipe; for he was just passing at the instant. "Upon my honor, they have quite dazzled me."

"Was ever so original and exquisite a compliment?" murmured the lady, in an ecstasy of delight.

Amid the general admiration excited by the stranger's appearance, there were only two dissenting voices. One was that of an impertinent cur, which, after snuffing at the heels of the glistening figure, put its tail between its legs and skulked into its master's back yard, vociferating an execrable howl. The other dissentient was a young child, who squalled at the fullest stretch of his lungs, and babbled some unintelligible nonsense about a pumpkin.

Feathertop meanwhile pursued his way along the street. Except for the few complimentary words to the lady, and now and then a slight inclination of the head in requital of the profound reverences of the bystanders, he seemed wholly absorbed in his pipe. There needed no other proof of his rank and consequence than the perfect equanimity with which he comported himself, while the curiosity and admiration of the town swelled almost into clamor around him. With a crowd gathering behind his footsteps, he finally reached the mansion-house of the worshipful Justice Gookin, entered the gate, ascended the steps of the front door, and knocked. In the interim, before his summons was answered, the stranger was observed to shake the ashes out of his pipe.

"What did he say in that sharp voice?" inquired one of the spectators.

"Nay, I know not," answered his friend. "But the sun dazzles my eyes strangely. How dim and faded his lordship looks all of a sudden! Bless my wits, what is the matter with me?"

"The wonder is," said the other, "that his pipe, which was out only an instant ago, should be all alight again, and with the reddest coal I ever saw. There is something mysterious about this stranger. What a whiff of smoke was that! Dim and faded did you call him? Why, as he turns about the star on his breast is all ablaze."

"It is, indeed," said his companion; "and it will go near to dazzle pretty Polly Gookin, whom I see peeping at it out of the chamber window."

The door being now opened, Feathertop turned to the crowd, made a stately bend of his body like a great man acknowledging the reverence of the meaner sort, and vanished into the house. There was a mysterious kind of a smile, if it might not better be called a grin or grimace, upon his visage; but, of all the throng that beheld him, not an individual appears to have possessed insight enough to detect the illusive character of the stranger except a little child and a cur dog.

Our legend here loses somewhat of its continuity, and, passing over the preliminary explanation between Feathertop and the merchant, goes in quest of the pretty Polly Gookin. She was a damsel of a soft, round figure, with light hair and blue eyes, and a fair, rosy face, which seemed neither very shrewd nor very simple. This young lady had caught a glimpse of the glistening stranger while standing on the threshold, and had forthwith put on a laced cap, a string of beads, her finest kerchief, and her stiffest damask petticoat in preparation for the interview. Hurrying from her chamber to the parlor, she had ever since been viewing herself in the large

looking-glass and practising pretty airs—now a smile, now a ceremonious dignity of aspect, and now a softer smile than the former, kissing her hand likewise, tossing her head, and managing her fan; while within the mirror an unsubstantial little maid repeated every gesture and did all the foolish things that Polly did, but without making her ashamed of them. In short, it was the fault of pretty Polly's ability rather than her will if she failed to be as complete an artifice as the illustrious Feathertop himself; and, when she thus tampered with her own simplicity, the witch's phantom might well hope to win her.

No sooner did Polly hear her father's gouty footsteps approaching the parlor door, accompanied with the stiff clatter of Feathertop's high-heeled shoes, than she seated herself bolt upright and innocently began warbling a song.

"Polly! daughter Polly!" cried the old merchant. "Come hither, child."

Master Gookin's aspect, as he opened the door, was doubtful and troubled.

"This gentleman," continued he, presenting the stranger, "is the Chevalier Feathertop,—nay, I beg his pardon, my Lord Feathertop,—who hath brought me a token of remembrance from an ancient friend of mine. Pay your duty to his lordship, child, and honor him as his quality deserves."

After these few words of introduction, the worshipful magistrate immediately quitted the room. But, even in that brief moment, had the fair Polly glanced aside at her father instead of devoting herself wholly to the brilliant guest, she might have taken warning of some mischief nigh at hand. The old man was nervous, fidgety, and very pale. Purposing a smile of courtesy, he had deformed his face with a sort of galvanic grin, which, when Feathertop's back was turned, he exchanged for a scowl, at the same time shaking his fist and stamping his gouty foot—an incivility which brought its retribution along with it. The truth appears to have been that Mother Rigby's word of introduction, whatever it might be, had operated far more on the rich merchant's fears than on his good will. Moreover, being a man of wonderfully acute observation, he had noticed that these painted figures on the bowl of Feathertop's pipe were in motion. Looking more closely he became convinced that these figures were a party of little demons, each duly provided with horns and a tail, and dancing hand in hand, with gestures of diabolical merriment, round the circumference of the pipe bowl. As if to confirm his suspicions, while Master Gookin ushered his guest along a dusky passage from his private room to the parlor, the star on Feathertop's breast had scintillated actual flames, and threw a flickering gleam upon the wall, the ceiling, and the floor.

With such sinister prognostics manifesting themselves on all hands, it is not to be marvelled at that the merchant should have felt that he was committing his daughter to a very questionable acquaintance. He cursed, in his secret soul, the insinuating elegance of Feathertop's manners, as this brilliant personage bowed, smiled, put his hand on his heart, inhaled a long whiff from his pipe, and enriched the atmosphere with the smoky vapor of a fragrant and visible sigh. Gladly would poor Master Gookin have thrust his dangerous guest into the street; but there was a constraint and terror within him. This respectable old gentleman, we fear, at an earlier period of life, had given some pledge or other to the evil principle, and perhaps was now to redeem it by the sacrifice of his daughter.

It so happened that the parlor door was partly of glass, shaded by a silken curtain, the folds of which hung a little awry. So strong was the merchant's interest in witnessing what was to ensue between the fair Polly and the gallant Feathertop that, after quitting the room, he could by no means refrain from peeping through the crevice of the curtain.

But there was nothing very miraculous to be seen; nothing—except the trifles previously noticed—to confirm the idea of a supernatural peril environing the pretty Polly. The stranger it is true was evidently a thorough and practiced man of the world, systematic and self-possessed, and therefore the sort of a person to whom a parent ought not to confide a simple, young girl without due watchfulness for the result. The worthy magistrate who had been conversant with all degrees and qualities of mankind, could not but perceive every motion and gesture of the distinguished Feathertop came in its proper place; nothing had been left rude or native in him; a well-digested conventionalism had incorporated itself thoroughly with his substance and transformed him into a work of art. Perhaps it was this peculiarity that invested him with a species of ghastliness and awe. It is the effect of anything completely and consummately artificial, in human shape, that the person impresses us as an unreality and as having hardly pith enough to cast a shadow upon the floor. As regarded Feathertop, all this resulted in a wild, extravagant, and fantastical impression, as if his life and being were akin to the smoke that curled upward from his pipe.

But pretty Polly Gookin felt not thus. The pair were now promenading the room: Feathertop with his dainty stride and no less dainty grimace, the girl with a native maidenly grace, just touched, not spoiled, by a slightly affected manner, which seemed caught from the perfect artifice of her companion. The longer the interview continued, the more charmed was pretty Polly, until, within the first quarter of an hour (as the old magistrate noted by his watch), she was evidently beginning to be in love. Nor need it have been witchcraft that subdued her in such a hurry; the poor child's heart, it may be, was so very fervent that it melted her with its own warmth as reflected from the hollow semblance of a lover. No matter what Feathertop said, his words found depth and reverberation in her ear; no matter what he did, his action was heroic to her eye. And by this time it is to be supposed there was a blush on Polly's cheek, a tender smile about her mouth and a liquid softness in her glance; while the star kept coruscating on Feathertop's breast, and the little demons careered with more frantic merriment than ever about the circumference of his pipe bowl. O pretty Polly Gookin, why should these imps rejoice so madly that a silly maiden's heart was about to be given to a shadow! Is it so unusual a misfortune, so rare a triumph?

By and by Feathertop paused, and throwing himself into an imposing attitude, seemed to summon the fair girl to survey his figure and resist him longer if she could. His star, his embroidery, his buckles glowed at that instant with unutterable splendor; the picturesque hues of his attire took a richer depth of coloring; there was a gleam and polish over his whole presence betokening the perfect witchery of well-ordered manners. The maiden raised her eyes and suffered them to linger upon her companion with a bashful and admiring gaze. Then, as if desirous of judging what value her own simple comeliness might have side by side with so much brilliancy, she cast a glance towards the full-length looking-glass in front of which they happened to be standing. It was one of the truest plates in the world and incapable of flattery. No sooner did the images therein reflected meet Polly's eye than she shrieked, shrank from the stranger's side, gazed at him for a moment in the wildest dismay, and sank insensible upon the floor. Feathertop likewise had looked towards the mirror, and there beheld, not the glittering mockery of his outside show, but a picture of the sordid patchwork of his real composition stripped of all witchcraft.

The wretched simulacrum! We almost pity him. He threw up his arms with an expression of despair that went further than any of his previous manifestations towards vindicating his claims to be reckoned human, for perchance the only time since this so often empty and deceptive life of mortals began its course, an illusion had seen and fully recognized itself.

Mother Rigby was seated by her kitchen hearth in the twilight of this eventful day, and had just shaken the ashes out of a new pipe, when she heard a hurried tramp along the road. Yet it did not seem so much the tramp of human footsteps as the clatter of sticks or the rattling of dry bones.

"Ha!" thought the old witch, "what step is that? Whose skeleton is out of its grave now, I wonder?"

A figure burst headlong into the cottage door. It was Feathertop! His pipe was still alight; the star still flamed upon his breast; the embroidery still glowed upon his garments; nor had he lost, in any degree or manner that could be estimated, the aspect that assimilated him with our mortal brotherhood. But yet, in some indescribable way (as is the case with all that has deluded us when once found out), the poor reality was felt beneath the cunning artifice.

"What has gone wrong?" demanded the witch. "Did yonder sniffling hypocrite thrust my darling from his door? The villain! I'll set twenty fiends to torment him till he offer thee his daughter on his bended knees!"

"No, mother," said Feathertop despondingly; "it was not that."

"Did the girl scorn my precious one?" asked Mother Rigby, her fierce eyes glowing like two coals of Tophet. "I'll cover her face with pimples! Her nose shall be as red as the coal in thy pipe! Her front teeth shall drop out! In a week hence she shall not be worth thy having!"

"Let her alone, mother," answered poor Feathertop; "the girl was half won; and methinks a kiss from her sweet lips might have made me altogether human. But," he added, after a brief pause and then a howl of self-contempt, "I've seen myself, mother! I've seen myself for the wretched, ragged, empty thing I am! I'll exist no longer!"

Snatching the pipe from his mouth, he flung it with all his might against the chimney, and at the same instant sank upon the floor, a medley of straw and tattered garments, with some sticks protruding from the heap, and a shrivelled pumpkin in the midst. The eyeholes were now lustreless; but the rudely-carved gap, that just before had been a mouth still seemed to twist itself into a despairing grin, and was so far human.

"Poor fellow!" quoth Mother Rigby, with a rueful glance at the relics of her ill-fated contrivance. "My poor, dear, pretty Feathertop! There are thousands upon thousands of coxcombs and charlatans in the world, made up of just such a jumble of wornout, forgotten, and good-for-nothing trash as he was! Yet they live in fair repute, and never see themselves for what they are. And why should my poor puppet be the only one to know himself and perish for it?"

While thus muttering, the witch had filled a fresh pipe of tobacco, and held the stem between her fingers, as doubtful whether to thrust it into her own mouth or Feathertop's.

"Poor Feathertop!" she continued. "I could easily give him another chance and send him forth again tomorrow. But no; his feelings are too tender, his sensibilities too deep. He seems to have too much heart to bustle for his own advantage in such an empty and heartless world. Well! well! I'll make a scarecrow of him after all. 'Tis an innocent and useful vocation, and will suit my darling well; and, if each of his human brethren had as fit a one, 't would be the better for mankind; and as for this pipe of tobacco, I need it more than he."

So saying Mother Rigby put the stem between her lips. "Dickon!" cried she, in her high, sharp tone, "another coal for my pipe!"

Jules Gabriel Verne (1828–1905) was a French novelist, a playwright, and the master of the adventure tale. His fantastical worlds were considered plausible and detailed because Verne used scientific facts to support his narrative, even though H. G. Wells considered Verne a hopeless romantic. Verne's most popular works are *Journey to the Center of the Earth* (1863), *From the Earth to the Moon* (1865), and *Twenty Thousand Leagues Under the Sea* (1870), and were all published during his positivist period. After 1886, the tone in Verne's work began to change. Focusing more on the inherent dangers that came with hubris, his novels took a more pessimistic tone. Unlike the other tales Verne was publishing at the time, "Master Zacharius" (1854) is not an adventure tale. Originally published as "Master Zacharius, or the clockmaker who lost his soul," it is a tragedy about a proud old man, his daughter, and his creations.

Master Zacharius

Jules Verne

Translated by George Makepeace Towle

CHAPTER I

A WINTER NIGHT

THE CITY OF GENEVA lies at the west end of the lake of the same name. The Rhone, which passes through the town at the outlet of the lake, divides it into two sections, and is itself divided in the center of the city by an island placed in mid-stream. A topographical feature like this is often found in the great depôts of commerce and industry. No doubt the first inhabitants were influenced by the easy means of transport which the swift currents of the rivers offered them—those "roads which walk along of their own accord," as Pascal puts it. In the case of the Rhone, it would be the road that ran along.

Before new and regular buildings were con-structed on this island, which was enclosed like a Dutch galley in the middle of the river, the curious mass of houses, piled one on the other, presented a delightfully confused *coup-d'oeil*. The small area of the island had compelled some of the buildings to be perched, as it were, on the piles, which were entangled in the rough currents of the river. The huge beams, blackened by time, and worn by the water, seemed like the claws of an enormous crab, and presented a fantastic appearance. The little yellow streams, which were like cobwebs stretched amid this ancient foundation, quivered in the darkness, as if they had been the leaves of some old oak forest, while the river engulfed in this forest of piles, foamed and roared most mournfully.

One of the houses of the island was striking for

its curiously aged appearance. It was the dwelling of the old clockmaker, Master Zacharius, whose household consisted of his daughter Gerande, Aubert Thun, his apprentice, and his old servant Scholastique.

There was no man in Geneva to compare in interest with this Zacharius. His age was past finding out. Not the oldest inhabitant of the town could tell for how long his thin, pointed head had shaken above his shoulders, nor the day when, for the first time, he had walked through the streets, with his long white locks floating in the wind. The man did not live; he vibrated like the pendulum of his clocks. His spare and cadaverous figure was always clothed in dark colors. Like the pictures of Leonardo di Vinci, he was sketched in black.

Gerande had the pleasantest room in the whole house, whence, through a narrow window, she had the inspiriting view of the snowy peaks of Jura; but the bedroom and workshop of the old man were a kind of cavern close on to the water, the floor of which rested on the piles.

From time immemorial Master Zacharius had never come out except at meal times, and when he went to regulate the different clocks of the town. He passed the rest of his time at his bench, which was covered with numerous clockwork instruments, most of which he had invented himself. For he was a clever man; his works were valued in all France and Germany. The best workers in Geneva readily recognized his superiority, and showed that he was an honor to the town, by saying, "To him belongs the glory of having invented the escapement." In fact, the birth of true clockwork dates from the invention which the talents of Zacharius had discovered not many years before.

After he had worked hard for a long time, Zacharius would slowly put his tools away, cover up the delicate pieces that he had been adjusting with glasses, and stop the active wheel of his lathe; then he would raise a trapdoor constructed in the floor of his workshop, and, stooping down, used to inhale for hours together the thick vapors of the Rhone, as it dashed along under his eyes.

One winter's night the old servant Scholastique served the supper, which, according to old custom, she and the young mechanic shared with their master. Master Zacharius did not eat, though the food carefully prepared for him was offered him in a handsome blue-and-white dish. He scarcely answered the sweet words of Gerande, who evidently noticed her father's silence, and even the clatter of Scholastique herself no more struck his ear than the roar of the river, to which he paid no attention.

After the silent meal, the old clockmaker left the table without embracing his daughter, or saying his usual "Good night" to all. He left by the narrow door leading to his den, and the staircase groaned under his heavy footsteps as he went down.

Gerande, Aubert, and Scholastique sat for some minutes without speaking. On this evening the weather was dull; the clouds dragged heavily on the Alps, and threatened rain; the severe climate of Switzerland made one feel sad, while the south wind swept round the house, and whistled ominously.

"My dear young lady," said Scholastique, at last, "do you know that our master has been out of sorts for several days? Holy Virgin! I know he has had no appetite, because his words stick in his inside, and it would take a very clever devil to drag even one out of him."

"My father has some secret cause of trouble, that I cannot even guess," replied Gerande, as a sad anxiety spread over her face.

"Mademoiselle, don't let such sadness fill your heart. You know the strange habits of Master Zacharius. Who can read his secret thoughts in his face? No doubt some fatigue has overcome him, but tomorrow he will have forgotten it, and be very sorry to have given his daughter pain."

It was Aubert who spoke thus, looking into Gerande's lovely eyes. Aubert was the first apprentice whom Master Zacharius had ever admitted to the intimacy of his labors, for he appreciated his intelligence, discretion, and goodness of heart; and this young man had attached himself to Gerande with the earnest devotion natural to a noble nature.

Gerande was eighteen years of age. Her oval face recalled that of the artless Madonnas whom veneration still displays at the street corners of the antique towns of Brittany. Her eyes betrayed an infinite simplicity. One would love her as the sweetest realization of a poet's dream. Her apparel was of modest colors, and the white linen which was folded about her shoulders had the tint and perfume peculiar to the linen of the church. She led a mystical existence in Geneva, which had not as yet been delivered over to the dryness of Calvinism.

While, night and morning, she read her Latin prayers in her iron-clasped missal, Gerande had also discovered a hidden sentiment in Aubert Thun's heart, and comprehended what a profound devotion the young workman had for her. Indeed, the whole world in his eyes was condensed into this old clockmaker's house, and he passed all his time near the young girl, when he left her father's workshop, after his work was over.

Old Scholastique saw all this, but said nothing. Her loquacity exhausted itself in preference on the evils of the times, and the little worries of the household. Nobody tried to stop its course. It was with her as with the musical snuffboxes which they made at Geneva; once wound up, you must break them before you will prevent their playing all their airs through.

Finding Gerande absorbed in a melancholy silence, Scholastique left her old wooden chair, fixed a taper on the end of a candlestick, lit it, and placed it near a small waxen Virgin, sheltered in her niche of stone. It was the family custom to kneel before this protecting Madonna of the domestic hearth, and to beg her kindly watchfulness during the coming night; but on this evening Gerande remained silent in her seat.

"Well, well, dear demoiselle," said the astonished Scholastique, "supper is over, and it is time to go to bed. Why do you tire your eyes by sitting up late? Ah, Holy Virgin! It's much better to sleep, and to get a little comfort from happy dreams! In these detestable times in which we live, who can promise herself a fortunate day?"

"Ought we not to send for a doctor for my father?" asked Gerande.

"A doctor!" cried the old domestic. "Has Master Zacharius ever listened to their fancies and pompous sayings? He might accept medicines for the watches, but not for the body!"

"What shall we do?" murmured Gerande. "Has he gone to work, or to rest?"

"Gerande," answered Aubert softly, "some mental trouble annoys your father, that is all."

"Do you know what it is, Aubert?"

"Perhaps, Gerande."

"Tell us, then," cried Scholastique eagerly, economically extinguishing her taper.

"For several days, Gerande," said the young apprentice, "something absolutely incomprehensible has been going on. All the watches which your father has made and sold for some years have suddenly stopped. Very many of them have been brought back to him. He has carefully taken them to pieces; the springs were in good condition, and the wheels well set. He has put them together yet more carefully; but, despite his skill, they will not go."

"The devil's in it!" cried Scholastique.

"Why say you so?" asked Gerande. "It seems very natural to me. Nothing lasts forever in this world. The infinite cannot be fashioned by the hands of men."

"It is nonetheless true," returned Aubert, "that there is in this something very mysterious and extraordinary. I have myself been helping Master Zacharius to search for the cause of this derangement of his watches; but I have not been able to find it, and more than once I have let my tools fall from my hands in despair."

"But why undertake so vain a task?" resumed Scholastique. "Is it natural that a little copper instrument should go of itself, and mark the hours? We ought to have kept to the sundial!"

"You will not talk thus, Scholastique," said Aubert, "when you learn that the sundial was invented by Cain."

"Good heavens! What are you telling me?"

"Do you think," asked Gerande simply, "that we might pray to God to give life to my father's watches?"

"Without doubt," replied Aubert.

"Good! They will be useless prayers," muttered the old servant, "but Heaven will pardon them for their good intent."

The taper was relighted. Scholastique, Gerande, and Aubert knelt down together upon the tiles of the room. The young girl prayed for her mother's soul, for a blessing for the night, for travelers and prisoners, for the good and the wicked, and more earnestly than all for the unknown misfortunes of her father.

Then the three devout souls rose with some confidence in their hearts, because they had laid their sorrow on the bosom of God.

Aubert repaired to his own room; Gerande sat pensively by the window, while the last lights were disappearing from the city streets; and Scholastique, having poured a little water on the flickering embers, and shut the two enormous bolts on the door, threw herself upon her bed, where she was soon dreaming that she was dying of fright.

Meanwhile the terrors of this winter's night had increased. Sometimes, with the whirlpools of the river, the wind engulfed itself among the piles, and the whole house shivered and shook; but the young girl, absorbed in her sadness, thought only of her father. After hearing what Aubert told her, the malady of Master Zacharius took fantastic proportions in her mind; and it seemed to her as if his existence, so dear to her, having become purely mechanical, no longer moved on its worn-out pivots without effort.

Suddenly the penthouse shutter, shaken by the squall, struck against the window of the room. Gerande shuddered and started up without understanding the cause of the noise which thus disturbed her reverie. When she became a little calmer she opened the sash. The clouds had burst, and a torrent-like rain pattered on the surrounding roofs. The young girl leaned out of the window to draw to the shutter shaken by the wind, but she feared to do so. It seemed to her that

the rain and the river, confounding their tumultuous waters, were submerging the frail house, the planks of which creaked in every direction. She would have flown from her chamber, but she saw below the flickering of a light which appeared to come from Master Zacharius's retreat, and in one of those momentary calms during which the elements keep a sudden silence, her ear caught plaintive sounds. She tried to shut her window, but could not. The wind violently repelled her, like a thief who was breaking into a dwelling.

Gerande thought she would go mad with terror. What was her father doing? She opened the door, and it escaped from her hands, and slammed loudly with the force of the tempest. Gerande then found herself in the dark supper room, succeeded in gaining, on tiptoe, the staircase which led to her father's shop, and pale and fainting, glided down.

The old watchmaker was upright in the middle of the room, which resounded with the roaring of the river. His bristling hair gave him a sinister aspect. He was talking and gesticulating, without seeing or hearing anything. Gerande stood still on the threshold.

"It is death!" said Master Zacharius, in a hollow voice; "it is death! Why should I live longer, now that I have dispersed my existence over the earth? For I, Master Zacharius, am really the creator of all the watches that I have fashioned! It is a part of my very soul that I have shut up in each of these cases of iron, silver, or gold! Every time that one of these accursed watches stops, I feel my heart cease beating, for I have regulated them with its pulsations!"

As he spoke in this strange way, the old man cast his eyes on his bench. There lay all the pieces of a watch that he had carefully taken apart. He took up a sort of hollow cylinder, called a barrel, in which the spring is enclosed, and removed the steel spiral, but instead of relaxing itself, according to the laws of its elasticity, it remained coiled on itself like a sleeping viper. It seemed knotted, like impotent old men whose blood has long been congealed. Master Zacharius vainly essayed to uncoil it with his thin fingers, the outlines of which were exaggerated on the wall; but he tried in vain, and soon, with a terrible cry of anguish and rage, he threw it through the trapdoor into the boiling Rhone.

Gerande, her feet riveted to the floor, stood breathless and motionless. She wished to approach her father, but could not. Giddy hallucinations took possession of her. Suddenly she heard, in the shade, a voice murmur in her ears,—

"Gerande, dear Gerande! Grief still keeps you awake. Go in again, I beg of you; the night is cold."

"Aubert!" whispered the young girl. "You!"

"Ought I not to be troubled by what troubles you?"

These soft words sent the blood back into the young girl's heart. She leaned on Aubert's arm, and said to him,—

"My father is very ill, Aubert! You alone can cure him, for this disorder of the mind would not yield to his daughter's consolings. His mind is attacked by a very natural delusion, and in working with him, repairing the watches, you will bring him back to reason. Aubert," she continued, "it is not true, is it, that his life is mixed up with that of his watches?"

Aubert did not reply.

"But is my father's a trade condemned by God?" asked Gerande, trembling.

"I know not," returned the apprentice, warming the cold hands of the girl with his own. "But go back to your room, my poor Gerande, and with sleep recover hope!"

Gerande slowly returned to her chamber, and remained there till daylight, without sleep closing her eyelids. Meanwhile, Master Zacharius, always mute and motionless, gazed at the river as it rolled turbulently at his feet.

CHAPTER II

THE PRIDE OF SCIENCE

The severity of the Geneva merchant in business matters has become proverbial. He is rigidly honorable, and excessively just. What must, then, have been the shame of Master Zacharius, when he saw these watches, which he had so carefully constructed, returning to him from every direction?

It was certain that these watches had suddenly stopped, and without any apparent reason. The wheels were in a good condition and firmly fixed, but the springs had lost all elasticity. Vainly did the watchmaker try to replace them; the wheels remained motionless. These unaccountable derangements were greatly to the old man's discredit. His noble inventions had many times brought upon him suspicions of sorcery, which now seemed confirmed. These rumors reached Gerande, and she often trembled for her father, when she saw malicious glances directed toward him.

Yet on the morning after this night of anguish, Master Zacharius seemed to resume work with some confidence. The morning sun inspired him with some courage. Aubert hastened to join him in the shop, and received an affable "Good day."

"I am better," said the old man. "I don't know what strange pains in the head attacked me yesterday, but the sun has quite chased them away, with the clouds of the night."

"In faith, master," returned Aubert, "I don't like the night for either of us!"

"And thou art right, Aubert. If you ever become a great man, you will understand that day is as necessary to you as food. A great savant should be always ready to receive the homage of his fellow men."

"Master, it seems to me that the pride of science has possessed you."

"Pride, Aubert! Destroy my past, annihilate my present, dissipate my future, and then it will be permitted to me to live in obscurity! Poor boy, who comprehends not the sublime things to which my art is wholly devoted! Art thou not but a tool in my hands?"

"Yet. Master Zacharius," resumed Aubert, "I have more than once merited your praise for the manner in which I adjusted the most delicate parts of your watches and clocks."

"No doubt, Aubert; thou art a good workman, such as I love; but when thou workest, thou thinkest thou hast in thy hands but copper, silver, gold; thou dost not perceive these metals, which my genius animates, palpitating like living flesh! So that thou wilt not die, with the death of thy works!"

Master Zacharius remained silent after these words; but Aubert essayed to keep up the conversation.

"Indeed, master," said he, "I love to see you work so unceasingly! You will be ready for the festival of our corporation, for I see that the work on this crystal watch is going forward famously."

"No doubt, Aubert," cried the old watchmaker, "and it will be no slight honor for me to have been able to cut and shape the crystal to the durability of a diamond! Ah, Louis Berghem did well to perfect the art of diamond-cutting, which has enabled me to polish and pierce the hardest stones!"

Master Zacharius was holding several small watch pieces of cut crystal, and of exquisite workmanship. The wheels, pivots, and case of the watch were of the same material, and he had employed remarkable skill in this very difficult task.

"Would it not be fine," said he, his face flushing, "to see this watch palpitating beneath its transparent envelope, and to be able to count the beatings of its heart?"

"I will wager, sir," replied the young apprentice, "that it will not vary a second in a year."

"And you would wager on a certainty! Have I not imparted to it all that is purest of myself? And does my heart vary? My heart, I say?"

Aubert did not dare to lift his eyes to his master's face.

"Tell me frankly," said the old man sadly. "Have you never taken me for a madman? Do you not think me sometimes subject to dangerous folly? Yes; is it not so? In my daughter's eyes and yours, I have often read my condemnation. Oh!" he cried, as if in pain, "To be misunderstood by those whom one most loves in the world! But I will prove victoriously to thee, Aubert, that I am right! Do not shake thy head, for thou wilt be

astounded. The day on which thou understandest how to listen to and comprehend me, thou wilt see that I have discovered the secrets of existence, the secrets of the mysterious union of the soul with the body!"

As he spoke thus, Master Zacharius appeared superb in his vanity. His eyes glittered with a supernatural fire, and his pride illumined every feature. And truly, if ever vanity was excusable, it was that of Master Zacharius!

The watchmaking art, indeed, down to his time, had remained almost in its infancy. From the day when Plato, four centuries before the Christian era, invented the night watch, a sort of clepsydra which indicated the hours of the night by the sound and playing of a flute, the science had continued nearly stationary. The masters paid more attention to the arts than to mechanics, and it was the period of beautiful watches of iron, copper, wood, silver, which were richly engraved, like one of Cellini's ewers. They made a masterpiece of chasing, which measured time imperfectly, but was still a masterpiece. When the artist's imagination was not directed to the perfection of modelling, it set to work to create clocks with moving figures and melodious sounds, whose appearance took all attention. Besides, who troubled himself, in those days, with regulating the advance of time? The delays of the law were not as yet invented; the physical and astronomical sciences had not as yet established their calculations on scrupulously exact measurements; there were neither establishments which were shut at a given hour, nor trains which departed at a precise moment. In the evening the curfew bell sounded; and at night the hours were cried amid the universal silence. Certainly people did not live so long, if existence is measured by the amount of business done; but they lived better. The mind was enriched with the noble sentiments born of the contemplation of chefs d'oeuvre. They built a church in two centuries, a painter painted but few pictures in the course of his life, a poet only composed one great work; but these were so many masterpieces for after-ages to appreciate.

When the exact sciences began at last to make some progress, watch and clock making followed in their path, though it was always arrested by an insurmountable difficulty,—the regular and continuous measurement of time.

It was in the midst of this stagnation that Master Zacharius invented the escapement, which enabled him to obtain a mathematical regularity by submitting the movement of the pendulum to a sustained force. This invention had turned the old man's head. Pride, swelling in his heart, like mercury in the thermometer, had attained the height of transcendent folly. By analogy he had allowed himself to be drawn to materialistic conclusions, and as he constructed his watches, he fancied that he had discovered the secrets of the union of the soul with the body.

Thus, on this day, perceiving that Aubert listened to him attentively, he said to him in a tone of simple conviction,—

"Dost thou know what life is, my child? Hast thou comprehended the action of those springs which produce existence? Hast thou examined thyself? No. And yet, with the eyes of science, thou mightest have seen the intimate relation which exists between God's work and my own; for it is from his creature that I have copied the combinations of the wheels of my clocks."

"Master," replied Aubert eagerly, "can you compare a copper or steel machine with that breath of God which is called the soul, which animates our bodies as the breeze stirs the flowers? What mechanism could be so adjusted as to inspire us with thought?"

"That is not the question," responded Master Zacharius gently, but with all the obstinacy of a blind man walking toward an abyss. "In order to understand me, thou must recall the purpose of the escapement which I have invented. When I saw the irregular working of clocks, I understood that the movements shut up in them did not suffice, and that it was necessary to submit them to the regularity of some independent force. I then thought that the balance wheel might accomplish this, and I succeeded in regulating the movement! Now, was it not a sublime idea that came to me, to return to it its lost force by the action of the clock itself, which it was charged with regulating?"

Aubert made a sign of assent.

"Now, Aubert," continued the old man, growing animated, "cast thine eyes upon thyself! Dost thou not understand that there are two distinct forces in us, that of the soul and that of the body—that is, a movement and a regulator? The soul is the principle of life; that is, then, the movement. Whether it is produced by a weight, by a spring, or by an immaterial influence, it is nonetheless in the heart. But without the body this movement would be unequal, irregular, impossible! Thus the body regulates the soul, and, like the balance wheel, it is submitted to regular oscillations. And this is so true, that one falls ill when one's drink, food, sleep—in a word, the functions of the body—are not properly regulated; just as in my watches the soul renders to the body the force lost by its oscillations. Well, what produces this intimate union between soul and body, if not a marvelous escapement, by which the wheels of the one work into the wheels of the other? This is what I have discovered and applied; and there are no longer any secrets for me in this life, which is, after all, only an ingenious mechanism!"

Master Zacharius looked sublime in this hallucination, which carried him to the ultimate mysteries of the Infinite. But his daughter Gerande, standing on the threshold of the door, had heard all. She rushed into her father's arms, and he pressed her convulsively to his breast.

"What is the matter with thee, my daughter?" he asked.

"If I had only a spring here," said she, putting her hand on her heart, "I would not love you as I do, Father."

Master Zacharius looked intently at Gerande, and did not reply. Suddenly he uttered a cry, carried his hand eagerly to his heart, and fell fainting on his old leathern chair.

"Father, what is the matter?"

"Help!" cried Aubert. "Scholastique!"

But Scholastique did not come at once. Someone was knocking at the front door; she had gone to open it, and when she returned to the shop, before she could open her mouth, the old watch-maker, having recovered his senses, spoke:—

"I divine, my old Scholastique, that you bring me still another of those accursed watches which have stopped."

"Lord, it is true enough!" replied Scholastique, handing a watch to Aubert.

"My heart could not be mistaken!" said the old man, with a sigh.

Meanwhile Aubert carefully wound up the watch, but it would not go.

CHAPTER III

A STRANGE VISIT

Poor Gerande would have lost her life with that of her father, had it not been for the thought of Aubert, who still attached her to the world.

The old watchmaker was, little by little, passing away. His faculties evidently grew more feeble, as he concentrated them on a single thought. By a sad association of ideas, he referred everything to his monomania, and a human existence seemed to have departed from him, to give place to the extra-natural existence of the intermediate powers. Moreover, certain malicious rivals revived the sinister rumors which had spread concerning his labors.

The news of the strange derangements which his watches betrayed had a prodigious effect upon the master clockmakers of Geneva. What signified this sudden paralysis of their wheels, and why these strange relations which they seemed to have with the old man's life? These were the kind of mysteries which people never contemplate without a secret terror. In the various classes of the town, from the apprentice to the great lord who used the watches of the old horologist, there was no one who could not himself judge of the singularity of the fact. The citizens wished, but in vain, to get to see Master Zacharius. He fell very ill; and this enabled his daughter to withdraw him from those incessant visits which had degenerated into reproaches and recriminations.

Medicines and physicians were powerless in presence of this organic wasting away, the cause of which could not be discovered. It sometimes seemed as if the old man's heart had ceased to beat; then the pulsations were resumed with an alarming irregularity.

A custom existed in those days of publicly exhibiting the works of the masters. The heads of the various corporations sought to distinguish themselves by the novelty or the perfection of their productions; and it was among these that the condition of Master Zacharius excited the most lively, but most interested, commiseration. His rivals pitied him the more willingly because they feared him the less. They never forgot the old man's success, when he exhibited his magnificent clocks with moving figures, his repeaters, which provoked general admiration, and commanded such high prices in the cities of France, Switzerland, and Germany.

Meanwhile, thanks to the constant and tender care of Gerande and Aubert, his strength seemed to return a little; and in the tranquillity in which his convalescence left him, he succeeded in detaching himself from the thoughts which had absorbed him. As soon as he could walk, his daughter lured him away from the house, which was still besieged with dissatisfied customers. Aubert remained in the shop, vainly adjusting and readjusting the rebel watches; and the poor boy, completely mystified, sometimes covered his face with his hands, fearful that he, like his master, might go mad.

Gerande led her father toward the more pleasant promenades of the town. With his arm resting on hers, she conducted him sometimes through the quarter of Saint Antoine, the view from which extends toward the Cologny hill, and over the lake; on fine mornings they caught sight of the gigantic peaks of Mount Buet against the horizon. Gerande pointed out these spots to her father, who had well-nigh forgotten even their names. His memory wandered; and he took a childish interest in learning anew what had passed from his mind. Master Zacharius leaned upon his daughter; and the two heads, one white as snow and the other covered with rich golden tresses, met in the same ray of sunlight.

So it came about that the old watchmaker at last perceived that he was not alone in the world. As he looked upon his young and lovely daughter, and on himself old and broken, he reflected that after his death she would be left alone without support. Many of the young mechanics of Geneva had already sought to win Gerande's love; but none of them had succeeded in gaining access to the impenetrable retreat of the watchmaker's household. It was natural, then, that during this lucid interval, the old man's choice should fall on Aubert Thun. Once struck with this thought, he remarked to himself that this young couple had been brought up with the same ideas and the same beliefs; and the oscillations of their hearts seemed to him, as he said one day to Scholastique, "isochronous."

The old servant, literally delighted with the word, though she did not understand it, swore by her holy patron saint that the whole town should hear it within a quarter of an hour. Master Zacharius found it difficult to calm her; but made her promise to keep on this subject a silence which she never was known to observe.

So, though Gerande and Aubert were ignorant of it, all Geneva was soon talking of their speedy union. But it happened also that, while the worthy folk were gossiping, a strange chuckle was often heard, and a voice saying, "Gerande will not wed Aubert."

If the talkers turned round, they found themselves facing a little old man who was quite a stranger to them.

How old was this singular being? No one could have told. People conjectured that he must have existed for several centuries, and that was all. His big flat head rested upon shoulders the width of which was equal to the height of his body; this was not above three feet. This personage would have made a good figure to support a pendulum, for the dial would have naturally been placed on his face, and the balance wheel would have oscillated at its ease in his chest. His nose might readily have been taken for the style of a sundial, for it was narrow and sharp; his teeth, far apart, resembled the cogs of a wheel, and ground themselves between his lips; his voice had the metallic sound of a bell, and you could hear his heartbeat like the tick of a clock. This little man, whose arms moved like the hands on a dial, walked with jerks, without ever turning round. If any one followed him, it was found that he walked a league an hour, and that his course was nearly circular.

This strange being had not long been seen wandering, or rather circulating, around the town; but it had already been observed that, every day, at the moment when the sun passed the meridian, he stopped before the Cathedral of Saint Pierre, and resumed his course after the twelve strokes of noon had sounded. Excepting at this precise moment, he seemed to become a part of all the conversations in which the old watchmaker was talked of; and people asked each other, in terror, what relation could exist between him and Master Zacharius. It was remarked, too, that he never lost sight of the old man and his daughter while they were taking their promenades.

One day Gerande perceived this monster looking at her with a hideous smile. She clung to her father with a frightened motion.

"What is the matter, my Gerande?" asked Master Zacharius.

"I do not know," replied the young girl.

"But thou art changed, my child. Art thou going to fall ill in thy turn? Ah, well," he added, with a sad smile, "then I must take care of thee, and I will do it tenderly."

"O father, it will be nothing. I am cold, and I imagine that it is—"

"What, Gerande?"

"The presence of that man, who always follows us," she replied in a low tone.

Master Zacharius turned toward the little old man.

"Faith, he goes well," said he, with a satisfied air, "for it is just four o'clock. Fear nothing, my child; it is not a man, it is a clock!"

Gerande looked at her father in terror. How could Master Zacharius read the hour on this strange creature's visage?

"By-the-bye," continued the old watchmaker, paying no further attention to the matter, "I have not seen Aubert for several days."

"He has not left us, however, Father," said Gerande, whose thoughts turned into a gentler channel.

"What is he doing then?"

"He is working."

"Ah!" cried the old man. "He is at work repairing my watches, is he not? But he will never succeed; for it is not repair they need, but a resurrection!"

Gerande remained silent.

"I must know," added the old man, "if they have brought back any more of those accursed watches upon which the Devil has sent this epidemic!"

After these words Master Zacharius fell into complete silence, till he knocked at the door of his house, and for the first time since his convalescence descended to his shop, while Gerande sadly repaired to her chamber.

Just as Master Zacharius crossed the threshold of his shop, one of the many clocks suspended on the wall struck five o'clock. Usually the bells of these clocks—admirably regulated as they were—struck simultaneously, and this rejoiced the old man's heart; but on this day the bells struck one after another, so that for a quarter of an hour the ear was deafened by the successive noises. Master Zacharius suffered acutely; he could not remain still, but went from one clock to the other, and beat the time to them, like a conductor who no longer has control over his musicians.

When the last had ceased striking, the door of the shop opened, and Master Zacharius shuddered from head to foot to see before him the little old man, who looked fixedly at him and said,—

"Master, may I not speak with you a few moments?"

"Who are you?" asked the watchmaker abruptly.

"A colleague. It is my business to regulate the sun."

"Ah, you regulate the sun?" replied Master Zacharius eagerly, without wincing. "I can scarcely compliment you upon it. Your sun goes badly, and in order to make ourselves agree with it, we have to keep putting our clocks forward so much or back so much."

"And by the cloven foot," cried this weird personage, "you are right, my master! My sun does not always mark noon at the same moment as your clocks; but some day it will be known that this is because of the inequality of the earth's transfer, and a mean noon will be invented which will regulate this irregularity!"

"Shall I live till then?" asked the old man, with glistening eyes.

"Without doubt," replied the little old man, laughing. "Can you believe that you will ever die?"

"Alas! I am very ill now."

"Ah, let us talk of that. By Beelzebub! that will lead to just what I wish to speak to you about."

Saying this, the strange being leaped upon the old leather chair, and carried his legs one under the other, after the fashion of the bones which the painters of funeral hangings cross beneath death's heads. Then he resumed, in an ironical tone,—

"Let us see, Master Zacharius, what is going on in this good town of Geneva? They say that your health is failing, that your watches have need of a doctor!"

"Ah, do you believe that there is an intimate relation between their existence and mine?" cried Master Zacharius.

"Why, I imagine that these watches have faults, even vices. If these wantons do not preserve a regular conduct, it is right that they should bear the consequences of their irregularity. It seems to me that they have need of reforming a little!"

"What do you call faults?" asked Master Zacharius, reddening at the sarcastic tone in which these words were uttered. "Have they not a right to be proud of their origin?"

"Not too proud, not too proud," replied the

little old man. "They bear a celebrated name, and an illustrious signature is graven on their cases, it is true, and theirs is the exclusive privilege of being introduced among the noblest families; but for some time they have got out of order, and you can do nothing in the matter, Master Zacharius; and the stupidest apprentice in Geneva could prove it to you!"

"To me, to me,—Master Zacharius!" cried the old man, with a flush of outraged pride.

"To you, Master Zacharius,—you, who cannot restore life to your watches!"

"But it is because I have a fever, and so have they also!" replied the old man, as a cold sweat broke out upon him.

"Very well, they will die with you, since you cannot impart a little elasticity to their springs."

"Die! No, for you yourself have said it! I cannot die,—I, the first watchmaker in the world; I, who, by means of these pieces and diverse wheels, have been able to regulate the movement with absolute precision! Have I not subjected time to exact laws, and can I not dispose of it like a despot? Before a sublime genius had arranged these wandering hours regularly, in what vast uncertainty was human destiny plunged? At what certain moment could the acts of life be connected with each other? But you, man or devil, whatever you may be, have never considered the magnificence of my art, which calls every science to its aid! No, no! I, Master Zacharius, cannot die, for, as I have regulated time, time would end with me! It would return to the infinite, whence my genius has rescued it, and it would lose itself irreparably in the abyss of nothingness! No, I can no more die than the Creator of this universe, that submitted to His laws! I have become His equal, and I have partaken of His power! If God has created eternity, Master Zacharius has created time!"

The old watchmaker now resembled the fallen angel, defiant in the presence of the Creator. The little old man gazed at him, and even seemed to breathe into him this impious transport.

"Well said, master," he replied. "Beelzebub had less right than you to compare himself with

God! Your glory must not perish! So your servant here desires to give you the method of controlling these rebellious watches."

"What is it? what is it?" cried Master Zacharius.

"You shall know on the day after that on which you have given me your daughter's hand."

"My Gerande?"

"Herself!"

"My daughter's heart is not free," replied Master Zacharius, who seemed neither astonished nor shocked at the strange demand.

"Bah! She is not the least beautiful of watches; but she will end by stopping also—"

"My daughter,—my Gerande! No!"

"Well, return to your watches, Master Zacharius. Adjust and readjust them. Get ready the marriage of your daughter and your apprentice. Temper your springs with your best steel. Bless Aubert and the pretty Gerande. But remember, your watches will never go, and Gerande will not wed Aubert!"

Thereupon the little old man disappeared, but not so quickly that Master Zacharius could not hear six o'clock strike in his breast.

CHAPTER IV

THE CHURCH OF SAINT PIERRE

Meanwhile Master Zacharius became more feeble in mind and body every day. An unusual excitement, indeed, impelled him to continue his work more eagerly than ever, nor could his daughter entice him from it.

His pride was still more aroused after the crisis to which his strange visitor had hurried him so treacherously, and he resolved to overcome, by the force of genius, the malign influence which weighed upon his work and himself. He first repaired to the various clocks of the town which were confided to his care. He made sure, by a scrupulous examination, that the wheels were in good condition, the pivots firm, the weights exactly balanced. Every part, even to the bells, was examined with the minute attention of a physician studying the breast of a patient. Nothing indicated that these clocks were on the point of being affected by inactivity.

Gerande and Aubert often accompanied the old man on these visits. He would no doubt have been pleased to see them eager to go with him, and certainly he would not have been so much absorbed in his approaching end, had he thought that his existence was to be prolonged by that of these cherished ones, and had he understood that something of the life of a father always remains in his children.

The old watchmaker, on returning home, resumed his labors with feverish zeal. Though persuaded that he would not succeed, it yet seemed to him impossible that this could be so, and he unceasingly took to pieces the watches which were brought to his shop, and put them together again.

Aubert tortured his mind in vain to discover the causes of the evil.

"Master," said he, "this can only come from the wear of the pivots and gearing."

"Do you want, then, to kill me, little by little?" replied Master Zacharius passionately. "Are these watches child's work? Was it lest I should hurt my fingers that I worked the surface of these copper pieces in the lathe? Have I not forged these pieces of copper myself, so as to obtain a greater strength? Are not these springs tempered to a rare perfection? Could anybody have used finer oils than mine? You must yourself agree that it is impossible, and you avow, in short, that the devil is in it!"

From morning till night discontented purchasers besieged the house, and they got access to the old watchmaker himself, who knew not which of them to listen to.

"This watch loses, and I cannot succeed in regulating it," said one.

"This," said another, "is absolutely obstinate, and stands still, as did Joshua's sun."

"If it is true," said most of them, "that your health has an influence on that of your watches, Master Zacharius, get well as soon as possible."

The old man gazed at these people with hag-gard eyes, and only replied by shaking his head, or by a few sad words,—

"Wait till the first fine weather, my friends. The season is coming which revives existence in wearied bodies. We want the sun to warm us all!"

"A fine thing, if my watches are to be ill through the winter!" said one of the most angry. "Do you know, Master Zacharius, that your name is inscribed in full on their faces? By the Virgin, you do little honor to your signature!"

It happened at last that the old man, abashed by these reproaches, took some pieces of gold from his old trunk, and began to buy back the damaged watches. At news of this, the customers came in a crowd, and the poor watchmaker's money fast melted away; but his honesty remained intact. Gerande warmly praised his delicacy, which was leading him straight toward ruin; and Aubert soon offered his own savings to his master.

"What will become of my daughter?" said Master Zacharius, clinging now and then in the shipwreck to his paternal love.

Aubert dared not answer that he was full of hope for the future, and of deep devotion to Gerande. Master Zacharius would have that day called him his son-in-law, and thus refuted the sad prophecy, which still buzzed in his ears,—

"Gerande will not wed Aubert."

By this plan the watchmaker at last succeeded in entirely despoiling himself. His antique vases passed into the hands of strangers; he deprived himself of the richly carved panels which adorned the walls of his house; some primitive pictures of the early Flemish painters soon ceased to please his daughter's eyes, and everything, even the precious tools that his genius had invented, were sold to indemnify the clamorous customers.

Scholastique alone refused to listen to reason on the subject; but her efforts failed to prevent the unwelcome visitors from reaching her master, and from soon departing with some valuable object. Then her chattering was heard in all the streets of the neighborhood, where she had long been known. She eagerly denied the rumors of sorcery and magic on the part of Master Zacharius, which gained currency; but as at bottom she was persuaded of their truth, she said her prayers over and over again to redeem her pious falsehoods.

It had been noticed that for some time the old watchmaker had neglected his religious duties. Time was, when he had accompanied Gerande to church, and had seemed to find in prayer the intellectual charm which it imparts to thoughtful minds, since it is the most sublime exercise of the imagination. This voluntary neglect of holy practices, added to the secret habits of his life, had in some sort confirmed the accusations leveled against his labors. So, with the double purpose of drawing her father back to God, and to the world, Gerande resolved to call religion to her aid. She thought that it might give some vitality to his dying soul; but the dogmas of faith and humility had to combat, in the soul of Master Zacharius, an insurmountable pride, and came into collision with that vanity of science which connects everything with itself, without rising to the infinite source whence first principles flow.

It was under these circumstances that the young girl undertook her father's conversion; and her influence was so effective that the old watchmaker promised to attend high mass at the cathedral on the following Sunday. Gerande was in an ecstasy, as if heaven had opened to her view. Old Scholastique could not contain her joy, and at last found irrefutable arguments against the gossiping tongues which accused her master of impiety. She spoke of it to her neighbours, her friends, her enemies, to those whom she knew not as well as to those whom she knew.

"In faith, we scarcely believe what you tell us, dame Scholastique," they replied; "Master Zacharius has always acted in concert with the devil!"

"You haven't counted, then," replied the old servant, "the fine bells which strike for my master's clocks? How many times they have struck the hours of prayer and the mass!"

"No doubt," they would reply. "But has he not invented machines which go all by themselves, and which actually do the work of a real man?"

"Could a child of the devil," exclaimed dame Scholastique wrathfully, "have executed the fine iron clock of the château of Andernatt, which the town of Geneva was not rich enough to buy? A pious motto appeared at each hour, and a Christian who obeyed them, would have gone straight to Paradise! Is that the work of the devil?"

This masterpiece, made twenty years before, had carried Master Zacharius's fame to its acme; but even then there had been accusations of sorcery against him. But at least the old man's visit to the Cathedral ought to reduce malicious tongues to silence.

Master Zacharius, having doubtless forgotten the promise made to his daughter, had returned to his shop. After being convinced of his powerlessness to give life to his watches, he resolved to try if he could not make some new ones. He abandoned all those useless works, and devoted himself to the completion of the crystal watch, which he intended to be his masterpiece; but in vain did he use his most perfect tools, and employ rubies and diamonds for resisting friction. The watch fell from his hands the first time that he attempted to wind it up!

The old man concealed this circumstance from every one, even from his daughter; but from that time his health rapidly declined. There were only the last oscillations of a pendulum, which goes slower when nothing restores its original force. It seemed as if the laws of gravity, acting directly upon him, were dragging him irresistibly down to the grave.

The Sunday so ardently anticipated by Gerande at last arrived. The weather was fine, and the temperature inspiriting. The people of Geneva were passing quietly through the streets, gaily chatting about the return of spring. Gerande, tenderly taking the old man's arm, directed her steps toward the cathedral, while Scholastique followed behind with the prayer books. People looked curiously at them as they passed. The old watchmaker permitted himself to be led like a child, or rather like a blind man. The faithful of Saint Pierre were almost frightened when they saw him cross the threshold, and shrank back at his approach.

The chants of high mass were already resounding through the church. Gerande went to her accustomed bench, and kneeled with profound and simple reverence. Master Zacharius remained standing upright beside her.

The ceremonies continued with the majestic solemnity of that faithful age, but the old man had no faith. He did not implore the pity of Heaven with cries of anguish of the "Kyrie"; he did not, with the "Gloria in Excelsis," sing the splendors of the heavenly heights; the reading of the Testament did not draw him from his materialistic reverie, and he forgot to join in the homage of the "Credo." This proud old man remained motionless, as insensible and silent as a stone statue; and even at the solemn moment when the bell announced the miracle of transubstantiation, he did not bow his head, but gazed directly at the sacred host which the priest raised above the heads of the faithful. Gerande looked at her father, and a flood of tears moistened her missal. At this moment the clock of Saint Pierre struck half past eleven. Master Zacharius turned quickly toward this ancient clock which still spoke. It seemed to him as if its face was gazing steadily at him; the figures of the hours shone as if they had been engraved in lines of fire, and the hands shot forth electric sparks from their sharp points.

The mass ended. It was customary for the "Angelus" to be said at noon, and the priests, before leaving the altar, waited for the clock to strike the hour of twelve. In a few moments this prayer would ascend to the feet of the Virgin.

But suddenly a harsh noise was heard. Master Zacharius uttered a piercing cry.

The large hand of the clock, having reached twelve, had abruptly stopped, and the clock did not strike the hour.

Gerande hastened to her father's aid. He had fallen down motionless, and they carried him outside the church.

"It is the death blow!" murmured Gerande, sobbing.

When he had been borne home, Master Zacharius lay upon his bed utterly crushed. Life seemed only to still exist on the surface of his body, like the last whiffs of smoke about a lamp just extinguished. When he came to his senses, Aubert and Gerande were leaning over him. In these last moments the future took in his eyes the shape of the present. He saw his daughter alone, without a protector.

"My son," said he to Aubert, "I give my daughter to thee."

So saying, he stretched out his hands towards his two children, who were thus united at his deathbed.

But soon Master Zacharius lifted himself up in a paroxysm of rage. The words of the little old man recurred to his mind.

"I do not wish to die!" he cried; "I cannot die! I, Master Zacharius, ought not to die! My books—my accounts!—"

With these words he sprang from his bed toward a book in which the names of his customers and the articles which had been sold to them were inscribed. He seized it and rapidly turned over its leaves, and his emaciated finger fixed itself on one of the pages.

"There!" he cried, "there! this old iron clock, sold to Pittonaccio! It is the only one that has not been returned to me! It still exists—it goes—it lives! Ah, I wish for it—I must find it! I will take such care of it that death will no longer seek me!"

And he fainted away.

Aubert and Gerande knelt by the old man's bedside and prayed together.

CHAPTER V

THE HOUR OF DEATH

Several days passed, and Master Zacharius, though almost dead, rose from his bed and returned to active life under a supernatural excitement. He lived by pride. But Gerande did not deceive herself; her father's body and soul were forever lost.

The old man got together his last remaining resources, without thought of those who were dependent upon him. He betrayed an incredible energy, walking, ferreting about, and mumbling strange, incomprehensible words.

One morning Gerande went down to his shop. Master Zacharius was not there. She waited for him all day. Master Zacharius did not return.

Gerande wept bitterly, but her father did not reappear.

Aubert searched everywhere through the town, and soon came to the sad conviction that the old man had left it.

"Let us find my father!" cried Gerande, when the young apprentice told her this sad news.

"Where can he be?" Aubert asked himself.

An inspiration suddenly came to his mind. He remembered the last words which Master Zacharius had spoken. The old man only lived now in the old iron clock that had not been returned! Master Zacharius must have gone in search of it.

Aubert spoke of this to Gerande.

"Let us look at my father's book," she replied.

They descended to the shop. The book was open on the bench. All the watches or clocks made by the old man, and which had been returned to him because they were out of order, were stricken out excepting one:—

"Sold to M. Pittonaccio, an iron clock, with bell and moving figures; sent to his château at Andernatt."

It was this "moral" clock of which Scholastique had spoken with so much enthusiasm.

"My father is there!" cried Gerande.

"Let us hasten thither," replied Aubert. "We may still save him!"

"Not for this life," murmured Gerande, "but at least for the other."

"By the mercy of God, Gerande! The château of Andernatt stands in the gorge of the 'Dents-du-Midi' twenty hours from Geneva. Let us go!"

That very evening Aubert and Gerande, followed by the old servant, set out on foot by the road which skirts Lake Leman. They accomplished five leagues during the night, stopping neither at Bessinge nor at Ermance, where rises the famous château of the Mayors. They with difficulty forded the torrent of the Dranse, and everywhere they went they inquired for Master Zacharius, and were soon convinced that they were on his track.

The next morning, at daybreak, having passed Thonon, they reached Evian, whence the Swiss territory may be seen extended over twelve leagues. But the two betrothed did not even perceive the enchanting prospect. They went straight forward, urged on by a supernatural force. Aubert, leaning on a knotty stick, offered his arm alternately to Gerande and to Scholastique, and he made the greatest efforts to sustain his companions. All three talked of their sorrow, of their hopes, and thus passed along the beautiful road by the waterside, and across the narrow plateau which unites the borders of the lake with the heights of the Chalais. They soon reached Bouveret, where the Rhone enters the Lake of Geneva.

On leaving this town they diverged from the lake, and their weariness increased amid these mountain districts. Vionnaz, Chesset, Collombay, half lost villages, were soon left behind. Meanwhile their knees shook, their feet were lacerated by the sharp points which covered the ground like a brushwood of granite;—but no trace of Master Zacharius!

He must be found, however, and the two young people did not seek repose either in the isolated hamlets or at the château of Monthay, which, with its dependencies, formed the appanage of Margaret of Savoy. At last, late in the day, and half dead with fatigue, they reached the hermitage of Notre-Dame-du-Sex, which is situated at the base of the Dents-du-Midi, six hundred feet above the Rhone.

The hermit received the three wanderers as night was falling. They could not have gone another step, and here they must needs rest.

The hermit could give them no news of Master Zacharius. They could scarcely hope to find him still living amid these sad solitudes. The night was dark, the wind howled amid the mountains, and the avalanches roared down from the summits of the broken crags.

Aubert and Gerande, crouching before the hermit's hearth, told him their melancholy tale.

Their mantles, covered with snow, were drying in a corner; and without, the hermit's dog barked lugubriously, and mingled his voice with that of the tempest.

"Pride," said the hermit to his guests, "has destroyed an angel created for good. It is the stumbling block against which the destinies of man strike. You cannot reason with pride, the principal of all the vices, since, by its very nature, the proud man refuses to listen to it. It only remains, then, to pray for your father!"

All four knelt down, when the barking of the dog redoubled, and someone knocked at the door of the hermitage.

"Open, in the devil's name!"

The door yielded under the blows, and a disheveled, haggard, ill-clothed man appeared.

"My father!" cried Gerande.

It was Master Zacharius.

"Where am I?" said he. "In eternity! Time is ended—the hours no longer strike—the hands have stopped!"

"Father!" returned Gerande, with so piteous an emotion that the old man seemed to return to the world of the living.

"Thou here, Gerande?" he cried; "and thou, Aubert? Ah, my dear betrothed ones, you are going to be married in our old church!"

"Father," said Gerande, seizing him by the arm, "come home to Geneva,—come with us!"

The old man tore away from his daughter's embrace and hurried toward the door, on the threshold of which the snow was falling in large flakes.

"Do not abandon your children!" cried Aubert.

"Why return," replied the old man sadly, "to those places which my life has already quitted, and where a part of myself is forever buried?"

"Your soul is not dead," said the hermit solemnly.

"My soul? O no,—its wheels are good! I perceive it beating regularly—"

"Your soul is immaterial,—your soul is immortal!" replied the hermit sternly.

"Yes—like my glory! But it is shut up in the château of Andernatt, and I wish to see it again!"

The hermit crossed himself; Scholastique became almost inanimate. Aubert held Gerande in his arms.

"The château of Andernatt is inhabited by one who is lost," said the hermit, "one who does not salute the cross of my hermitage."

"My father, go not thither!"

"I want my soul! My soul is mine—"

"Hold him! Hold my father!" cried Gerande.

But the old man had leaped across the threshold, and plunged into the night, crying, "Mine, mine, my soul!"

Gerande, Aubert, and Scholastique hastened after him. They went by difficult paths, across which Master Zacharius sped like a tempest, urged by an irresistible force. The snow raged around them, and mingled its white flakes with the froth of the swollen torrents.

As they passed the chapel erected in memory of the massacre of the Theban legion, they hurriedly crossed themselves. Master Zacharius was not to be seen.

At last the village of Evionnaz appeared in the midst of this sterile region. The hardest heart would have been moved to see this hamlet, lost among these horrible solitudes. The old man sped on, and plunged into the deepest gorge of the Dents-du-Midi, which pierce the sky with their sharp peaks.

Soon a ruin, old and gloomy as the rocks at its base, rose before him.

"It is there—there!" he cried, hastening his pace still more frantically.

The château of Andernatt was a ruin even then. A thick, crumbling tower rose above it, and seemed to menace with its downfall the old gables which reared themselves below. The vast piles of jagged stones were gloomy to look on. Several dark halls appeared amid the debris, with caved-in ceilings, now become the abode of vipers.

A low and narrow postern, opening upon a ditch choked with rubbish, gave access to the château. Who had dwelt there none knew. No doubt some margrave, half lord, half brigand, had sojourned in it; to the margrave had succeeded bandits or counterfeit coiners, who had been hanged on the scene of their crime. The legend went that, on winter nights, Satan came to lead his diabolical dances on the slope of the deep gorges in which the shadow of these ruins was engulfed.

But Master Zacharius was not dismayed by their sinister aspect. He reached the postern. No one forbade him to pass. A spacious and gloomy court presented itself to his eyes; no one forbade him to cross it. He passed along the kind of inclined plane which conducted to one of the long corridors, whose arches seemed to banish daylight from beneath their heavy springings. His advance was unresisted. Gerande, Aubert, and Scholastique closely followed him.

Master Zacharius, as if guided by an irresistible hand, seemed sure of his way, and strode along with rapid step. He reached an old wormeaten door, which fell before his blows, whilst the bats described oblique circles around his head.

An immense hall, better preserved than the rest, was soon reached. High sculptured panels, on which serpents, ghouls, and other strange figures seemed to disport themselves confusedly, covered its walls. Several long and narrow windows, like loopholes, shivered beneath the bursts of the tempest.

Master Zacharius, on reaching the middle of this hall, uttered a cry of joy.

On an iron support, fastened to the wall, stood the clock in which now resided his entire life. This unequalled masterpiece represented an ancient Roman church, with buttresses of wrought iron, with its heavy bell tower, where there was a complete chime for the anthem of the day, the "Angelus," the mass, vespers, compline, and the benediction. Above the church door, which opened at the hour of the services, was placed a "rose," in the center of which two hands moved, and the archivault of which reproduced the twelve hours of the face sculptured in relief. Between the door and the rose, just as Scholas-tique had said, a maxim, relative to the employment of every moment of the day, appeared on a copper plate. Master Zacharius had once regulated this succession of devices with a really Christian solicitude; the hours of prayer, of work, of repast, of recreation, and of repose, followed each other according to the religious discipline, and were to infallibly ensure salvation to him who scrupulously observed their commands.

Master Zacharius, intoxicated with joy, went forward to take possession of the clock, when a frightful roar of laughter resounded behind him.

He turned, and by the light of a smoky lamp recognized the little old man of Geneva.

"You here?" cried he.

Gerande was afraid. She drew closer to Aubert.

"Good day, Master Zacharius," said the monster.

"Who are you?"

"Signor Pittonaccio, at your service! You have come to give me your daughter! You have remembered my words, 'Gerande will not wed Aubert.'"

The young apprentice rushed upon Pittonaccio, who escaped from him like a shadow.

"Stop, Aubert!" cried Master Zacharius.

"Good night," said Pittonaccio, and he disappeared.

"My father, let us fly from this hateful place!" cried Gerande. "My father!"

Master Zacharius was no longer there. He was pursuing the phantom of Pittonaccio across the rickety corridors. Scholastique, Gerande, and Aubert remained, speechless and fainting, in the large gloomy hall. The young girl had fallen upon a stone seat; the old servant knelt beside her, and prayed; Aubert remained erect, watching his betrothed. Pale lights wandered in the darkness, and the silence was only broken by the movements of the little animals which live in old wood, and the noise of which marks the hours of "death watch."

When daylight came, they ventured upon the endless staircase which wound beneath these ruined masses; for two hours they wandered thus without meeting a living soul, and hearing only a far-off echo responding to their cries. Sometimes they found themselves buried a hundred feet below the ground, and sometimes they reached places whence they could overlook the wild mountains.

Chance brought them at last back again to the vast hall, which had sheltered them during this night of anguish. It was no longer empty. Master Zacharius and Pittonaccio were talking there together, the one upright and rigid as a corpse, the other crouching over a marble table.

Master Zacharius, when he perceived Gerande, went forward and took her by the hand, and led her toward Pittonaccio, saying, "Behold your lord and master, my daughter. Gerande, behold your husband!"

Gerande shuddered from head to foot.

"Never!" cried Aubert, "for she is my betrothed."

"Never!" responded Gerande, like a plaintive echo.

Pittonaccio began to laugh.

"You wish me to die, then!" exclaimed the old man. "There, in that clock, the last which goes of all which have gone from my hands, my life is shut up; and this man tells me, 'When I have thy daughter, this clock shall belong to thee.' And this man will not rewind it. He can break it, and plunge me into chaos. Ah, my daughter, you no longer love me!"

"My father!" murmured Gerande, recovering consciousness.

"If you knew what I have suffered, far away from this principle of my existence!" resumed the old man. "Perhaps no one looked after this time-piece. Perhaps its springs were left to wear out, its wheels to get clogged. But now, in my own hands, I can nourish this health so dear, for I must not die,—I, the great watchmaker of Geneva. Look, my daughter, how these hands advance with certain step. See, five o'clock is about to strike. Listen well, and look at the maxim which is about to be revealed."

Five o'clock struck with a noise which re-sounded sadly in Gerande's soul, and these words appeared in red letters:

"YOU MUST EAT OF THE FRUITS OF THE TREE OF SCIENCE."

Aubert and Gerande looked at each other stupefied. These were no longer the pious sayings of the Catholic watchmaker. The breath of Satan must have passed over it. But Zacharius paid no attention to this, and resumed—

"Dost thou hear, my Gerande? I live, I still live! Listen to my breathing,—see the blood circulating in my veins! No, thou wouldst not kill thy father, and thou wilt accept this man for thy husband, so that I may become immortal, and at last attain the power of God!"

At these blasphemous words old Scholastique crossed herself, and Pittonaccio laughed aloud with joy.

"And then, Gerande, thou wilt be happy with him. See this man,—he is Time! Thy existence will be regulated with absolute precision. Gerande, since I gave thee life, give life to thy father!"

"Gerande," murmured Aubert, "I am thy betrothed."

"He is my father!" replied Gerande, fainting.

"She is thine!" said Master Zacharius. "Pittonaccio, thou wilt keep thy promise!"

"Here is the key of the clock," replied the horrible man.

Master Zacharius seized the long key, which resembled an uncoiled snake, and ran to the clock, which he hastened to wind up with fantastic rapidity. The creaking of the spring jarred upon the nerves. The old watchmaker wound and wound the key, without stopping a moment, and it seemed as if the movement were beyond his control. He wound more and more quickly, with strange contortions, until he fell from sheer weariness.

"There, it is wound up for a century!" he cried.

Aubert rushed from the hall as if he were mad.

After long wandering, he found the outlet of the hateful château, and hastened into the open air. He returned to the hermitage of Notre-Dame-du-Sex, and talked so despairingly to the holy recluse, that the latter consented to return with him to the château of Andernatt.

If, during these hours of anguish, Gerande had not wept, it was because her tears were exhausted.

Master Zacharius had not left the hall. He ran every moment to listen to the regular beating of the old clock.

Meanwhile the clock had struck, and to Scholastique's great terror, these words had appeared on the silver face:

> "MAN OUGHT TO BECOME
> THE EQUAL OF GOD."

The old man had not only not been shocked by these impious maxims, but read them deliriously, and flattered himself with thoughts of pride, while Pittonaccio kept close by him.

The marriage contract was to be signed at midnight. Gerande, almost unconscious, saw or heard nothing. The silence was only broken by the old man's words, and the chuckling of Pittonaccio.

Eleven o'clock struck. Master Zacharius shuddered, and read in a loud voice:—

> "MAN SHOULD BE THE SLAVE OF
> SCIENCE, AND SACRIFICE TO IT
> "RELATIVES AND FAMILY."

"Yes!" he cried, "there is nothing but science in this world!"

The hands slipped over the face of the clock with the hiss of a serpent, and the pendulum beat with accelerated strokes.

Master Zacharius no longer spoke. He had fallen to the floor, his throat rattled, and from his oppressed bosom came only these half-broken words: "Life—science!"

The scene had now two new witnesses, the hermit and Aubert. Master Zacharius lay upon the floor; Gerande was praying beside him, more dead than alive.

Of a sudden a dry, hard noise was heard, which preceded the strike.

Master Zacharius sprang up.

"Midnight!" he cried.

The hermit stretched out his hand toward the old clock,—and midnight did not sound.

Master Zacharius uttered a terrible cry, which must have been heard in hell, when these words appeared:—

> "WHO EVER SHALL ATTEMPT
> TO MAKE HIMSELF THE
> EQUAL OF GOD, SHALL BE
> FOREVER DAMNED!"

The old clock burst with a noise like thunder, and the spring, escaping, leaped across the hall with a thousand fantastic contortions; the old man rose, ran after it, trying in vain to seize it, and exclaiming, "My soul,—my soul!"

The spring bounded before him, first on one side, then on the other, and he could not reach it.

At last Pittonaccio seized it, and, uttering a horrible blasphemy, engulfed himself in the earth.

Master Zacharius fell backward. He was dead.

The old watchmaker was buried in the midst of the peaks of Andernatt.

Then Aubert and Gerande returned to Geneva, and during the long life which God accorded to them, they made it a duty to redeem by prayer the soul of the castaway of science.

Louisa May Alcott (1832–1888) was an American author and poet best known for her novel *Little Women*. A noted suffragist, Alcott's early works were inspired by her history teacher and her father's close friend, Henry David Thoreau and Ralph Waldo Emerson, respectively. "The Frost-King" is a story from the collection *Flower Fables* (1855), written when Alcott was only sixteen—after she decided to try her hand at fairy tales for Ellen Emerson, Ralph Waldo Emerson's young daughter. The tales had an oral tradition as well, in that Alcott served as a storyteller to a number of neighborhood children, not just Ellen Emerson. She also wrote fiction starring femme fatales and revenge under the pseudonym A. M. Barnard.

The Frost-King:
or,
The Power of Love

Louisa May Alcott

THREE LITTLE FAIRIES sat in the fields eating their breakfast; each among the leaves of her favorite flower, Daisy, Primrose, and Violet, were happy as Elves need be.

The morning wind gently rocked them to and fro, and the sun shone warmly down upon the dewy grass, where butterflies spread their gay wings, and bees with their deep voices sung among the flowers; while the little birds hopped merrily about to peep at them.

On a silvery mushroom was spread the breakfast; little cakes of flower-dust lay on a broad green leaf, beside a crimson strawberry, which, with sugar from the violet, and cream from the yellow milkweed, made a fairy meal, and their drink was the dew from the flowers' bright leaves.

"Ah me," sighed Primrose, throwing herself languidly back, "how warm the sun grows! give me another piece of strawberry, and then I must hasten away to the shadow of the ferns. But while I eat, tell me, dear Violet, why are you all so sad? I have scarce seen a happy face since my return from Rose Land; dear friend, what means it?"

"I will tell you," replied little Violet, the tears gathering in her soft eyes. "Our good Queen is ever striving to keep the dear flowers from the power of the cruel Frost-King; many ways she tried, but all have failed. She has sent messengers to his court with costly gifts; but all have returned sick for want of sunlight, weary and sad; we have watched over them, heedless of sun or shower, but still his dark spirits do their work, and we are left to weep over our blighted blossoms. Thus have we striven, and in vain; and this night our Queen holds council for the last time. Therefore are we sad, dear Primrose, for she has toiled and cared for us, and we can do nothing to help or advise her now."

"It is indeed a cruel thing," replied her friend; "but as we cannot help it, we must suffer patiently, and not let the sorrows of others disturb our happiness. But, dear sisters, see you not how high the sun is getting? I have my locks to curl, and my robe to prepare for the evening; therefore I must be gone, or I shall be brown as a withered leaf in this warm light." So, gathering a tiny mushroom for a parasol, she flew away; Daisy soon followed, and Violet was left alone.

Then she spread the table afresh, and to it came fearlessly the busy ant and bee, gay butterfly and bird; even the poor blind mole and humble worm were not forgotten; and with gentle words she gave to all, while each learned something of their kind little teacher; and the love that made her own heart bright shone alike on all.

The ant and bee learned generosity, the butterfly and bird contentment, the mole and worm confidence in the love of others; and each went to their home better for the little time they had been with Violet.

Evening came, and with it troops of Elves to counsel their good Queen, who, seated on her mossy throne, looked anxiously upon the throng below, whose glittering wings and rustling robes gleamed like many-colored flowers.

At length she rose, and amid the deep silence spoke thus:—

"Dear children, let us not tire of a good work, hard though it be and wearisome; think of the many little hearts that in their sorrow look to us for help. What would the green earth be without its lovely flowers, and what a lonely home for us! Their beauty fills our hearts with brightness, and

their love with tender thoughts. Ought we then to leave them to die uncared for and alone? They give to us their all; ought we not to toil unceasingly, that they may bloom in peace within their quiet homes? We have tried to gain the love of the stern Frost-King, but in vain; his heart is hard as his own icy land; no love can melt, no kindness bring it back to sunlight and to joy. How then may we keep our frail blossoms from his cruel spirits? Who will give us counsel? Who will be our messenger for the last time? Speak, my subjects."

Then a great murmuring arose, and many spoke, some for costlier gifts, some for war; and the fearful counselled patience and submission.

Long and eagerly they spoke, and their soft voices rose high.

Then sweet music sounded on the air, and the loud tones were hushed, as in wondering silence the Fairies waited what should come.

Through the crowd there came a little form, a wreath of pure white violets lay among the bright locks that fell so softly round the gentle face, where a deep blush glowed, as, kneeling at the throne, little Violet said:—

"Dear Queen, we have bent to the Frost-King's power, we have borne gifts unto his pride, but have we gone trustingly to him and spoken fearlessly of his evil deeds? Have we shed the soft light of unwearied love around his cold heart, and with patient tenderness shown him how bright and beautiful love can make even the darkest lot?

"Our messengers have gone fearfully, and with cold looks and courtly words offered him rich gifts, things he cared not for, and with equal pride has he sent them back.

"Then let me, the weakest of your band, go to him, trusting in the love I know lies hidden in the coldest heart.

"I will bear only a garland of our fairest flowers; these will I wind about him, and their bright faces, looking lovingly in his, will bring sweet thoughts to his dark mind, and their soft breath steal in like gentle words. Then, when he sees them fading on his breast, will he not sigh that there is no warmth there to keep them fresh and lovely? This will I do, dear Queen, and never leave his dreary home, till the sunlight falls on flowers fair as those that bloom in our own dear land."

Silently the Queen had listened, but now, rising and placing her hand on little Violet's head, she said, turning to the throng below:—"We in our pride and power have erred, while this, the weakest and lowliest of our subjects, has from the innocence of her own pure heart counselled us more wisely than the noblest of our train. All who will aid our brave little messenger, lift your wands, that we may know who will place their trust in the Power of Love."

Every fairy wand glistened in the air, as with silvery voices they cried, "Love and little Violet."

Then down from the throne, hand in hand, came the Queen and Violet, and till the moon sank did the Fairies toil, to weave a wreath of the fairest flowers. Tenderly they gathered them, with the night-dew fresh upon their leaves, and as they wove chanted sweet spells, and whispered fairy blessings on the bright messengers whom they sent forth to die in a dreary land, that their gentle kindred might bloom unharmed.

At length it was done; and the fair flowers lay glowing in the soft starlight, while beside them stood the Fairies, singing to the music of the wind-harps:—

> "We are sending you, dear flowers,
> Forth alone to die,
> Where your gentle sisters may not weep
> O'er the cold graves where you lie;
> But you go to bring them fadeless life
> In the bright homes where they dwell,
> And you softly smile that't is so,
> As we sadly sing farewell.
> O plead with gentle words for us,
> And whisper tenderly
> Of generous love to that cold heart,
> And it will answer ye;
> And though you fade in a dreary home,
> Yet loving hearts will tell
> Of the joy and peace that you have given:
> Flowers, dear flowers, farewell!"

The morning sun looked softly down upon the broad green earth, which like a mighty altar was sending up clouds of perfume from its breast, while flowers danced gayly in the summer wind, and birds sang their morning hymn among the cool green leaves. Then high above, on shining wings, soared a little form. The sunlight rested softly on the silken hair, and the winds fanned lovingly the bright face, and brought the sweetest odors to cheer her on.

Thus went Violet through the clear air, and the earth looked smiling up to her, as, with the bright wreath folded in her arms, she flew among the soft, white clouds.

On and on she went, over hill and valley, broad rivers and rustling woods, till the warm sunlight passed away, the winds grew cold, and the air thick with falling snow. Then far below she saw the Frost-King's home. Pillars of hard, gray ice supported the high, arched roof, hung with crystal icicles. Dreary gardens lay around, filled with withered flowers and bare, drooping trees; while heavy clouds hung low in the dark sky, and a cold wind murmured sadly through the wintry air.

With a beating heart Violet folded her fading wreath more closely to her breast, and with weary wings flew onward to the dreary palace.

Here, before the closed doors, stood many forms with dark faces and harsh, discordant voices, who sternly asked the shivering little Fairy why she came to them.

Gently she answered, telling them her errand, beseeching them to let her pass ere the cold wind blighted her frail blossoms. Then they flung wide the doors, and she passed in.

Walls of ice, carved with strange figures, were around her; glittering icicles hung from the high roof, and soft, white snow covered the hard floors. On a throne hung with clouds sat the Frost-King; a crown of crystals bound his white locks, and a dark mantle wrought with delicate frost-work was folded over his cold breast.

His stern face could not stay little Violet, and on through the long hall she went, heedless of the snow that gathered on her feet, and the bleak wind that blew around her; while the King with wondering eyes looked on the golden light that played upon the dark walls as she passed.

The flowers, as if they knew their part, unfolded their bright leaves, and poured forth their sweetest perfume, as, kneeling at the throne, the brave little Fairy said,—

"O King of blight and sorrow, send me not away till I have brought back the light and joy that will make your dark home bright and beautiful again. Let me call back to the desolate gardens the fair forms that are gone, and their soft voices blessing you will bring to your breast a never failing joy. Cast by your icy crown and sceptre, and let the sunlight of love fall softly on your heart.

"Then will the earth bloom again in all its beauty, and your dim eyes will rest only on fair forms, while music shall sound through these dreary halls, and the love of grateful hearts be yours. Have pity on the gentle flower-spirits, and do not doom them to an early death, when they might bloom in fadeless beauty, making us wiser by their gentle teachings, and the earth brighter by their lovely forms. These fair flowers, with the prayers of all Fairy Land, I lay before you; O send me not away till they are answered."

And with tears falling thick and fast upon their tender leaves, Violet laid the wreath at his feet, while the golden light grew ever brighter as it fell upon the little form so humbly kneeling there.

The King's stern face grew milder as he gazed on the gentle Fairy, and the flowers seemed to look beseechingly upon him; while their fragrant voices sounded softly in his ear, telling of their dying sisters, and of the joy it gives to bring happiness to the weak and sorrowing. But he drew the dark mantle closer over his breast and answered coldly,—

"I cannot grant your prayer, little Fairy; it is my will the flowers should die. Go back to your Queen, and tell her that I cannot yield my power to please these foolish flowers."

Then Violet hung the wreath above the throne, and with weary foot went forth again, out into the cold, dark gardens, and still the golden shadows followed her, and wherever they fell, flowers bloomed and green leaves rustled.

Then came the Frost-Spirits, and beneath their cold wings the flowers died, while the Spirits bore Violet to a low, dark cell, saying as they left her, that their King was angry that she had dared to stay when he had bid her go.

So all alone she sat, and sad thoughts of her happy home came back to her, and she wept bitterly. But soon came visions of the gentle flowers dying in their forest homes, and their voices ringing in her ear, imploring her to save them. Then she wept no longer, but patiently awaited what might come.

Soon the golden light gleamed faintly through the cell, and she heard little voices calling for help, and high up among the heavy cobwebs hung poor little flies struggling to free themselves, while their cruel enemies sat in their nets, watching their pain.

With her wand the Fairy broke the bands that held them, tenderly bound up their broken wings, and healed their wounds; while they lay in the warm light, and feebly hummed their thanks to their kind deliverer.

Then she went to the ugly brown spiders, and in gentle words told them, how in Fairy Land their kindred spun all the elfin cloth, and in return the Fairies gave them food, and then how happily they lived among the green leaves, spinning garments for their neighbors. "And you too," said she, "shall spin for me, and I will give you better food than helpless insects. You shall live in peace, and spin your delicate threads into a mantle for the stern King; and I will weave golden threads amid the gray, that when folded over his cold heart gentle thoughts may enter in and make it their home."

And while she gayly sung, the little weavers spun their silken threads, the flies on glittering wings flew lovingly above her head, and over all the golden light shone softly down.

When the Frost-Spirits told their King, he greatly wondered and often stole to look at the sunny little room where friends and enemies worked peacefully together. Still the light grew brighter, and floated out into the cold air, where it hung like bright clouds above the dreary gardens, whence all the Spirits' power could not drive it; and green leaves budded on the naked trees, and flowers bloomed; but the Spirits heaped snow upon them, and they bowed their heads and died.

At length the mantle was finished, and amid the gray threads shone golden ones, making it bright; and she sent it to the King, entreating him to wear it, for it would bring peace and love to dwell within his breast.

But he scornfully threw it aside, and bade his Spirits take her to a colder cell, deep in the earth; and there with harsh words they left her.

Still she sang gayly on, and the falling drops kept time so musically, that the King in his cold ice-halls wondered at the low, sweet sounds that came stealing up to him.

Thus Violet dwelt, and each day the golden light grew stronger; and from among the crevices of the rocky walls came troops of little velvet-coated moles, praying that they might listen to the sweet music, and lie in the warm light.

"We lead," said they, "a dreary life in the cold earth; the flower-roots are dead, and no soft dews descend for us to drink, no little seed or leaf can we find. Ah, good Fairy, let us be your servants: give us but a few crumbs of your daily bread, and we will do all in our power to serve you."

And Violet said, Yes; so day after day they labored to make a pathway through the frozen earth, that she might reach the roots of the withered flowers; and soon, wherever through the dark galleries she went, the soft light fell upon the roots of flowers, and they with new life spread forth in the warm ground, and forced fresh sap to the blossoms above. Brightly they bloomed and danced in the soft light, and the Frost-Spirits tried in vain to harm them, for when they came beneath the bright clouds their power to do evil left them.

From his dark castle the King looked out on the happy flowers, who nodded gayly to him, and in sweet colors strove to tell him of the good little Spirit, who toiled so faithfully below, that they might live. And when he turned from the bright-

ness without, to his stately palace, it seemed so cold and dreary, that he folded Violet's mantle round him, and sat beneath the faded wreath upon his ice-carved throne, wondering at the strange warmth that came from it; till at length he bade his Spirits bring the little Fairy from her dismal prison.

Soon they came hastening back, and prayed him to come and see how lovely the dark cell had grown. The rough floor was spread with deep green moss, and over wall and roof grew flowery vines, filling the air with their sweet breath; while above played the clear, soft light, casting rosy shadows on the glittering drops that lay among the fragrant leaves; and beneath the vines stood Violet, casting crumbs to the downy little moles who ran fearlessly about and listened as she sang to them.

When the old King saw how much fairer she had made the dreary cell than his palace rooms, gentle thoughts within whispered him to grant her prayer, and let the little Fairy go back to her friends and home; but the Frost-Spirits breathed upon the flowers and bid him see how frail they were, and useless to a King. Then the stern, cold thoughts came back again, and he harshly bid her follow him.

With a sad farewell to her little friends she followed him, and before the throne awaited his command. When the King saw how pale and sad the gentle face had grown, how thin her robe, and weak her wings, and yet how lovingly the golden shadows fell around her and brightened as they lay upon the wand, which, guided by patient love, had made his once desolate home so bright, he could not be cruel to the one who had done so much for him, and in kindly tone he said,—

"Little Fairy, I offer you two things, and you may choose between them. If I will vow never more to harm the flowers you may love, will you go back to your own people and leave me and my Spirits to work our will on all the other flowers that bloom? The earth is broad, and we can find them in any land, then why should you care what happens to their kindred if your own are safe? Will you do this?"

"Ah!" answered Violet sadly, "do you not know that beneath the flowers' bright leaves there beats a little heart that loves and sorrows like our own? And can I, heedless of their beauty, doom them to pain and grief, that I might save my own dear blossoms from the cruel foes to which I leave them? Ah no! sooner would I dwell for ever in your darkest cell, than lose the love of those warm, trusting hearts."

"Then listen," said the King, "to the task I give you. You shall raise up for me a palace fairer than this, and if you can work that miracle I will grant your prayer or lose my kingly crown. And now go forth, and begin your task; my Spirits shall not harm you, and I will wait till it is done before I blight another flower."

Then out into the gardens went Violet with a heavy heart; for she had toiled so long, her strength was nearly gone. But the flowers whispered their gratitude, and folded their leaves as if they blessed her; and when she saw the garden filled with loving friends, who strove to cheer and thank her for her care, courage and strength returned; and raising up thick clouds of mist, that hid her from the wondering flowers, alone and trustingly she began her work.

As time went by, the Frost–King feared the task had been too hard for the Fairy; sounds were heard behind the walls of mist, bright shadows seen to pass within, but the little voice was never heard. Meanwhile the golden light had faded from the garden, the flowers bowed their heads, and all was dark and cold as when the gentle Fairy came.

And to the stern King his home seemed more desolate and sad; for he missed the warm light, the happy flowers, and, more than all, the gay voice and bright face of little Violet. So he wandered through his dreary palace, wondering how he had been content to live before without sunlight and love.

And little Violet was mourned as dead in Fairy-Land, and many tears were shed, for the gentle Fairy was beloved by all, from the Queen down to the humblest flower. Sadly they watched over every bird and blossom which she had loved, and

strove to be like her in kindly words and deeds. They wore cypress wreaths, and spoke of her as one whom they should never see again.

Thus they dwelt in deepest sorrow, till one day there came to them an unknown messenger, wrapped in a dark mantle, who looked with wondering eyes on the bright palace, and flower-crowned elves, who kindly welcomed him, and brought fresh dew and rosy fruit to refresh the weary stranger. Then he told them that he came from the Frost-King, who begged the Queen and all her subjects to come and see the palace little Violet had built; for the veil of mist would soon be withdrawn, and as she could not make a fairer home than the ice-castle, the King wished her kindred near to comfort and to bear her home. And while the Elves wept, he told them how patiently she had toiled, how her fadeless love had made the dark cell bright and beautiful.

These and many other things he told them; for little Violet had won the love of many of the Frost-Spirits, and even when they killed the flowers she had toiled so hard to bring to life and beauty, she spoke gentle words to them, and sought to teach them how beautiful is love. Long stayed the messenger, and deeper grew his wonder that the Fairy could have left so fair a home, to toil in the dreary palace of his cruel master, and suffer cold and weariness, to give life and joy to the weak and sorrowing. When the Elves had promised they would come, he bade farewell to happy Fairy-Land, and flew sadly home.

At last the time arrived, and out in his barren garden, under a canopy of dark clouds, sat the Frost-King before the misty wall, behind which were heard low, sweet sounds, as of rustling trees and warbling birds.

Soon through the air came many-colored troops of Elves. First the Queen, known by the silver lilies on her snowy robe and the bright crown in her hair, beside whom flew a band of Elves in crimson and gold, making sweet music on their flower-trumpets, while all around, with smiling faces and bright eyes, fluttered her loving subjects.

On they came, like a flock of brilliant butterflies, their shining wings and many-colored garments sparkling in the dim air; and soon the leafless trees were gay with living flowers, and their sweet voices filled the gardens with music. Like his subjects, the King looked on the lovely Elves, and no longer wondered that little Violet wept and longed for her home. Darker and more desolate seemed his stately home, and when the Fairies asked for flowers, he felt ashamed that he had none to give them.

At length a warm wind swept through the gardens, and the mist-clouds passed away, while in silent wonder looked the Frost-King and the Elves upon the scene before them.

Far as eye could reach were tall green trees whose drooping boughs made graceful arches, through which the golden light shone softly, making bright shadows on the deep green moss below, where the fairest flowers waved in the cool wind, and sang, in their low, sweet voices, how beautiful is Love.

Flowering vines folded their soft leaves around the trees, making green pillars of their rough trunks. Fountains threw their bright waters to the roof, and flocks of silver-winged birds flew singing among the flowers, or brooded lovingly above their nests. Doves with gentle eyes cooed among the green leaves, snow-white clouds floated in the sunny sky, and the golden light, brighter than before, shone softly down.

Soon through the long aisles came Violet, flowers and green leaves rustling as she passed. On she went to the Frost-King's throne, bearing two crowns, one of sparkling icicles, the other of pure white lilies, and kneeling before him, said,—

"My task is done, and, thanks to the Spirits of earth and air, I have made as fair a home as Elfin hands can form. You must now decide. Will you be King of Flower-Land, and own my gentle kindred for your loving friends? Will you possess unfading peace and joy, and the grateful love of all the green earth's fragrant children? Then take this crown of flowers. But if you can find no pleasure here, go back to your own cold home, and dwell in solitude and darkness, where no ray of sunlight or of joy can enter.

"Send forth your Spirits to carry sorrow and desolation over the happy earth, and win for yourself the fear and hatred of those who would so gladly love and reverence you. Then take this glittering crown, hard and cold as your own heart will be, if you will shut out all that is bright and beautiful. Both are before you. Choose."

The old King looked at the little Fairy, and saw how lovingly the bright shadows gathered round her, as if to shield her from every harm; the timid birds nestled in her bosom, and the flowers grew fairer as she looked upon them; while her gentle friends, with tears in their bright eyes, folded their hands beseechingly, and smiled on her.

Kind thought came thronging to his mind, and he turned to look at the two palaces. Violet's, so fair and beautiful, with its rustling trees, calm, sunny skies, and happy birds and flowers, all created by her patient love and care. His own, so cold and dark and dreary, his empty gardens where no flowers could bloom, no green trees dwell, or gay birds sing, all desolate and dim;—and while he gazed, his own Spirits, casting off their dark mantles, knelt before him and besought him not to send them forth to blight the things the gentle Fairies loved so much. "We have served you long and faithfully," said they, "give us now our freedom, that we may learn to be beloved by the sweet flowers we have harmed so long. Grant the little Fairy's prayer; and let her go back to her own dear home. She has taught us that Love is mightier than Fear. Choose the Flower crown, and we will be the truest subjects you have ever had."

Then, amid a burst of wild, sweet music, the Frost-King placed the Flower crown on his head, and knelt to little Violet; while far and near, over the broad green earth, sounded the voices of flowers, singing their thanks to the gentle Fairy, and the summer wind was laden with perfumes, which they sent as tokens of their gratitude; and wherever she went, old trees bent down to fold their slender branches round her, flowers laid their soft faces against her own, and whispered blessings; even the humble moss bent over the little feet, and kissed them as they passed.

The old King, surrounded by the happy Fairies, sat in Violet's lovely home, and watched his icy castle melt away beneath the bright sunlight; while his Spirits, cold and gloomy no longer, danced with the Elves, and waited on their King with loving eagerness. Brighter grew the golden light, gayer sang the birds, and the harmonious voices of grateful flowers, sounding over the earth, carried new joy to all their gentle kindred.

Brighter shone the golden shadows;
On the cool wind softly came
The low, sweet tones of happy flowers,
Singing little Violet's name.
'Mong the green trees was it whispered,
And the bright waves bore it on
To the lonely forest flowers,
Where the glad news had not gone.
Thus the Frost-King lost his kingdom,

And his power to harm and blight.
Violet conquered, and his cold heart
Warmed with music, love, and light;
And his fair home, once so dreary,
Gay with lovely Elves and flowers,
Brought a joy that never faded
Through the long bright summer hours.
Thus, by Violet's magic power,
All dark shadows passed away,
And o'er the home of happy flowers
The golden light for ever lay.
Thus the Fairy mission ended,
And all Flower-Land was taught
The "Power of Love," by gentle deeds
That little Violet wrought.

As Sunny Lock ceased, another little Elf came forward; and this was the tale "Silver Wing" told.

Herman Melville (1819–1891) was an American novelist whose youth influenced many of the struggles seen within his work. Melville spent some time as a sailor and participated in a mutiny on a whaling expedition. This landed him in a Tahitian prison, and the experience would change him forever. Melville's second novel, *Omoo* (1847), although seemingly lighthearted, illustrates anger at the colonization and treatment of the Tahitian people. As he aged, Melville's work also began to take on a more serious tone, in part because Melville began to turn into a recluse. His best-known fictions are *Moby-Dick* (1851), "Bartleby the Scrivener" (1853), and *Typee* (1846). "The Tartarus of Maids" was originally published in *Harper's Magazine* in April 1855 and is often read in conjunction with Melville's "The Paradise of Bachelors" (1855), a closely related story.

The Tartarus of Maids

Herman Melville

IT LIES, NOT FAR from Woedolor Mountain in New England. Turning to the east, right out from among bright farms and sunny meadows, nodding in early June with odorous grasses, you enter ascendingly among bleak hills. These gradually close in upon a dusky pass, which, from the violent Gulf Stream of air unceasingly driving between its cloven walls of haggard rock, as well as from the tradition of a crazy spinster's hut having long ago stood somewhere hereabout, is called the Mad Maid's Bellows'-pipe.

Winding along at the bottom of the gorge is a dangerously narrow wheel-road, occupying the bed of a former torrent. Following this road to its highest point, you stand as within a Dantean gateway. From the steepness of the walls here, their strangely ebon hue, and the sudden contraction of the gorge, this particular point is called the Black Notch. The ravine now expandingly descends into a great, purple, hopper-shaped hollow, far sunk among many Plutonian, shaggy-wooded mountains. By the country people this hollow is called the Devil's Dungeon. Sounds of torrents fall on all sides upon the ear. These rapid waters unite at last in one turbid, brick-colored stream, boiling through a flume among enormous boulders. They call this strange-colored torrent Blood River. Gaining a dark precipice it wheels suddenly to the west, and makes one maniac spring of sixty feet into the arms of a stunted wood of gray-haired pines, between which it thence eddies on its further way down to the invisible lowlands.

Conspicuously crowning a rocky bluff high to one side, at the cataract's verge, is the ruin of an old saw-mill, built in those primitive times when vast pines and hemlocks superabounded throughout the neighboring region. The blackmossed bulk of those immense, rough-hewn, and spike-knotted logs, here and there tumbled all together, in long abandonment and decay, or left in solitary, perilous projection over the cataract's gloomy brink, impart to this rude wooden ruin not only much of the aspect of one of rough-quarried stone, but also a sort of feudal, Rhineland, and Thurmberg look, derived from the pinnacled wildness of the neighborhood scenery.

Not far from the bottom of the Dungeon stands a large whitewashed building, relieved, like some great white sepulchre, against the sullen background of mountain-side firs, and other hardy evergreens, inaccessibly rising in grim terraces for some two thousand feet.

The building is a paper-mill.

Having embarked on a large scale in the seedsman's business (so extensively and broadcast, indeed, that at length my seeds were distributed through all the Eastern and Northern States, and even fell into the far soil of Missouri and the Carolinas), the demand for paper at my place became so great, that the expenditure soon amounted to a most important item in the general account. It need hardly be hinted how paper comes into use with seedsmen, as envelopes. These are mostly made of yellowish paper, folded square; and when filled, are all but flat, and being stamped, and superscribed with the nature of the seeds contained, assume not a little the appearance of business letters ready for the mail. Of these small envelopes I used an incredible quantity—several hundred of thousands in a year. For a time I had purchased my paper from the wholesale dealers in a neighboring town. For economy's sake, and partly for the adventure of the trip, I now resolved to cross the mountains, some sixty miles, and order my future paper at the Devil's Dungeon paper-mill.

The sleighing being uncommonly fine toward the end of January, and promising to hold so for no small period, in spite of the bitter cold I started one gray Friday noon in my pung, well fitted with buffalo and wolf robes; and, spending one night on the road, next noon came in sight of Woedolor Mountain.

The far summit fairly smoked with frost; white vapors curled up from its white-wooded top, as from a chimney. The intense congelation made the whole country look like one petrification. The steel shoes of my pung craunched and gritted over the vitreous, chippy snow, as if it had been broken glass. The forests here and there skirting the route, feeling the same all-stiffening influence, their inmost fibres penetrated with the cold, strangely groaned—not in the swaying branches merely, but likewise in the vertical trunk—as the fitful gusts remorseless swept through them. Brittle with excessive frost, many colossal tough-grained maples, snapped in twain like pipe-stems, cumbered the unfeeling earth.

Flaked all over with frozen sweat, white as a milky ram, his nostrils at each breath sending forth two horn-shaped shoots of heated respiration, Black, my good horse, but six years old, started at a sudden turn, where, right across the track—not ten minutes fallen—an old distorted hemlock lay, darkly undulatory as an anaconda.

Gaining the Bellows'-pipe, the violent blast, dead from behind, all but shoved my high-backed pung up-hill. The gust shrieked through the shivered pass, as if laden with lost spirits bound to the unhappy world. Ere gaining the summit, Black, my horse, as if exasperated by the cutting wind, slung out with his strong hind legs, tore the light pung straight up-hill, and sweeping grazingly through the narrow notch, sped downward madly past the ruined saw-mill. Into the Devil's Dungeon horse and cataract rushed together.

With might and main, quitting my seat and robes, and standing backward, with one foot braced against the dashboard, I rasped and churned the bit, and stopped him just in time to avoid collision, at a turn, with the bleak nozzle of a rock, couchant like a lion in the way—a road-side rock.

At first I could not discover the paper-mill.

The whole hollow gleamed with the white, except, here and there, where a pinnacle of granite showed one wind-swept angle bare. The mountains stood pinned in shrouds—a pass of Alpine corpses. Where stands the mill? Suddenly a whirling, humming sound broke upon my ear. I looked, and there, like an arrested avalanche, lay the large whitewashed factory. It was subordinately surrounded by a cluster of other and smaller buildings, some of which, from their cheap, blank air, great length, gregarious windows, and comfortless expression, no doubt were boarding-houses of the operatives. A snow-white hamlet amidst the snows. Various rude, irregular squares and courts resulted from the somewhat picturesque clusterings of these buildings, owing to the broken, rocky nature of the ground, which forbade all method in their relative arrangement. Several narrow lanes and alleys, too, partly blocked with snow fallen from the roof, cut up the hamlet in all directions.

When, turning from the traveled highway, jingling with bells of numerous farmers—who, availing themselves of the fine sleighing, were dragging their wood to market—and frequently diversified with swift cutters dashing from inn to inn of the scattered villages—when, I say, turning from that bustling main-road, I by degrees wound into the Mad Maid's Bellows'-pipe, and saw the grim Black Notch beyond, then something latent, as well as something obvious in the time and scene, strangely brought back to my mind my first sight of dark and grimy Temple Bar. And when Black, my horse, went darting through the Notch, perilously grazing its rocky wall, I remembered being in a runaway London omnibus, which in much the same sort of style, though by no means at an equal rate, dashed through the ancient arch of Wren. Though the two objects did by no means correspond, yet this partial inadequacy but served to tinge the similitude not less with the vividness than the disorder of a dream. So that, when upon reining up at the protruding rock I at last caught sight of the quaint groupings of the factory-buildings, and with the traveled highway and the Notch behind, found myself all alone, silently and privily stealing through deep-cloven passages into this sequestered spot, and saw the long, high-gabled main factory edifice, with a rude tower—for hoisting heavy boxes—at one end, standing among its crowded outbuild-ings and boarding-houses, as the Temple Church amidst the surrounding offices and dormitories, and when the marvelous retirement of this mysterious mountain nook fastened its whole spell upon me, then, what memory lacked, all tributary imagination furnished, and I said to myself, "This is the very counterpart of the Paradise of Bachelors, but snowed upon, and frost-painted in a sepulchre."

Dismounting, and warily picking my way down the dangerous declivity—horse and man both sliding now and then upon the icy ledges—at length I drove, or the blast drove me, into the largest square, before one side of the main edifice. Piercingly and shrilly the shotted blast blew by the corner; and redly and demoniacally boiled Blood River at one side. A long woodpile, of many scores of cords, all glittering in mail of crusted ice, stood crosswise in the square. A row of horse-posts, their north sides plastered with adhesive snow, flanked the factory wall. The bleak frost packed and paved the square as with some ringing metal.

The inverted similitude recurred—"The sweet, tranquil Temple garden, with the Thames bordering its green beds," strangely meditated I.

But where are the gay bachelors?

Then, as I and my horse stood shivering in the wind-spray, a girl ran from a neighboring dormitory door, and throwing her thin apron over her bare head, made for the opposite building.

"One moment, my girl; is there no shed hereabouts which I may drive into?"

Pausing, she turned upon me a face pale with work, and blue with cold; an eye supernatural with unrelated misery.

"Nay," faltered I, "I mistook you. Go on; I want nothing."

Leading my horse close to the door from which she had come, I knocked. Another pale, blue girl appeared, shivering in the doorway as, to prevent the blast, she jealously held the door ajar.

"Nay, I mistake again. In God's name shut the door. But hold, is there no man about?"

That moment a dark-complexioned well-wrapped personage passed, making for the factory door, and spying him coming, the girl rapidly closed the other one.

"Is there no horse-shed here, Sir?"

"Yonder, the wood-shed," he replied, and disappeared inside the factory.

With much ado I managed to wedge in horse and pung between scattered piles of wood all sawn and split. Then, blanketing my horse, and piling my buffalo on the blanket's top, and tucking in its edges well around the breastband and breeching, so that the wind might not strip him bare, I tied him fast, and ran lamely for the factory door, still with frost, and cumbered with my driver's dread-naught.

Immediately I found myself standing in a spacious place, intolerably lighted by long rows of windows, focusing inward the snowy scene without.

At rows of blank-looking counters sat rows of blank-looking girls, white folders in their blank hands, all blankly folding blank paper.

In one corner stood some huge frame of ponderous iron, with a vertical thing like a piston periodically rising and falling upon a heavy wooden block. Before it—its tame minister—stood a tall girl, feeding the iron animal with half-quires of rose-hued note paper, which, at every downward dab of the piston-like machine, received in the corner the impress of a wreath of roses. I looked from the rosy paper to the pallid cheek, but said nothing.

Seated before a long apparatus, strung with long, slender strings like any harp, another girl was feeding it with foolscap sheets, which, so soon as they curiously traveled from her on the cords, were withdrawn at the opposite end of the machine by a second girl. They came to the first girl blank; they went to the second girl ruled.

I looked upon the first girl's brow, and saw it was young and fair; I looked upon the the second girl's brow, and saw it was ruled and wrinkled. Then, as I still looked, the two—for some small variety to the monotony—changed places; and where had stood the young, fair brow, now stood the ruled and wrinkled one.

Perched high upon a narrow platform, and still higher upon a high stool crowning it, sat another figure serving some other iron animal; while below the platform sat her mate in some sort of reciprocal attendance.

Not a syllable was breathed. Nothing was heard but the low, steady overruling hum of the iron animals. The human voice was banished from the spot. Machinery—that vaunted slave of humanity—here stood menially served by human beings, who served mutely and cringingly as the slave serves the Sultan. The girls did not so much seem accessory wheels to the general machinery as mere cogs to the wheels.

All this scene around me was instantaneously taken in at one sweeping glance—even before I had proceeded to unwind the heavy fur tippet from around my neck. But as soon as this fell from me the dark-complexioned man, standing close by, raised a sudden cry, and seizing my arm, dragged me out into the open air, and without pausing for a word instantly caught up some congealed snow and began rubbing both my cheeks.

"Two white spots like the whites of your eyes," he said; "man, your cheeks are frozen."

"That may well be," muttered I; "'tis some wonder the frost of the Devil's Dungeon strikes in no deeper. Rub away."

Soon a horrible, tearing pain caught at my reviving cheeks. Two gaunt blood-hounds, one on either side, seemed mumbling them. I seemed Actaeon.

Presently, when all was over, I re-entered the factory, made known my business, concluded it satisfactorily, and then begged to be conducted throughout the place to view it.

"Cupid is the boy for that," said the dark-complexioned man. "Cupid!" and by this odd fancy-name calling a dimpled, red-cheeked, spirited-looking, forward little fellow, who was rather impudently, I thought, gliding about among the passive-looking girls—like a gold fish through hueless waves—yet doing nothing in particular that I could see, the man bade him lead the stranger through the edifice.

"Come first and see the water-wheel," said

this lively lad, with the air of boyishly-brisk importance.

Quitting the folding-room, we crossed some damp, cold boards, and stood beneath a great wet shed, incessantly showered with foam, like the green barnacled bow of some East Indiaman in a gale. Round and round here went the enormous revolutions of the dark colossal water-wheel, grim with its one immutable purpose.

"This sets our whole machinery a-going, Sir; in every part of all these buildings; where the girls work and all."

I looked, and saw that the turbid waters of Blood River had not changed their hue by coming under the use of man.

"You make only blank paper; no printing of any sort, I suppose? All blank paper, don't you?"

"Certainly; what else should a paper-factory make?"

The lad here looked at me as if suspicious of my common-sense.

"Oh, to be sure!" said I, confused and stammering; "it only struck me as so strange that red waters should turn out pale chee—paper, I mean."

He took me up a wet and rickety stair to a great light room, furnished with no visible thing but rude, manger-like receptacles running all round its sides; and up to these mangers, like so many mares haltered to the rack stood rows of girls. Before each was vertically thrust up a long, glittering scythe, immovably fixed at bottom to the manger-edge. The curve of the scythe, and its having no snath to it, made it look exactly like a sword. To and fro, across the sharp edge, the girls forever dragged long strips of rags, washed white, picked from baskets at one side; thus ripping asunder every seam, and converting the tatters almost into lint. The air swam with the fine, poisonous particles, which from all sides darted, subtilely, as motes in sunbeams, into the lungs.

"This is the rag-room," coughed the boy.

"You find it rather stifling here," coughed I, in answer; "but the girls don't cough."

"Oh, they are used to it."

"Where do you get such hosts of rags?" picking up a handful from a basket.

"Some from the country round about; some from far over sea—Leghorn and London."

"'Tis not unlikely, then," murmured I, "that among these heaps of rags there may be some old shirts, gathered from the dormitories of the Paradise of Bachelors. But the buttons are all dropped off. Pray, my lad, do you ever find any bachelor's buttons hereabouts?"

"None grow in this part of the country. The Devil's Dungeon is no place for flowers."

"Oh! you mean the *flowers* so called—the Bachelor's Buttons?"

"And was not that what you asked about? Or did you mean the gold bosom-buttons of our boss, Old Bach, as our whispering girls all call him?"

"The man, then, I saw below is a bachelor, is he?"

"Oh, yes, he's a Bach."

"The edges of those swords, they are turned outward from the girls, if I see right; but their rags and fingers fly so, I can not distinctly see."

"Turned outward."

Yes, murmured I to myself; I see it now; turned outward; and each erected sword is so borne, edge-outward, before each girl. If my reading fails me not, just so, of old, condemned state-prisoners went from the hall of judgment to their doom; an officer before, bearing a sword, its edge turned outward, in significance of their fatal sentence. So, through consumptive pallors of this blank, raggy life, go these white girls to death.

"Those scythes look very sharp," again turning toward the boy.

"Yes; they have to keep them so. Look!"

That moment two of the girls, dropping their rags, plied each a whetstone up and down the sword-blade. My unaccustomed blood curdled at the sharp shriek of the tormented steel.

Their own executioners; themselves whetting the very swords that slay them; meditated I.

"What makes those girls so sheet-white, my lad?"

"Why"—with a roguish twinkle, pure igno-rant drollery, not knowing heartlessness—"I sup-pose the handling of such white bits of sheets all the time makes them so sheety."

"Let us leave the rag-room now, my lad."

More tragical and more inscrutably mysteri-ous than any mystic sight, human or machine, throughout the factory, was the strange innocence of cruel-heartedness in this usage-hardened boy.

"And now," said he, cheerily, "I suppose you want to see our great machine, which cost us twelve thousand dollars only last autumn. That's the machine that makes the paper, too. This way, Sir."

Following him I crossed a large, bespattered place, with two great round vats in it, full of a white, wet, woolly-looking stuff, not unlike the albuminous part of an egg, soft-boiled.

"There," said Cupid, tapping the vats care-lessly, "these are the first beginning of the paper; this white pulp you see. Look how it swims bub-bling round and round, moved by the paddle here. From hence it pours from both vats into the one common channel yonder; and so goes, mixed up and leisurely, to the great machine. And now for that."

He led me into a room, stifling with a strange, blood-like, abdominal heat, as if here, true enough, were being finally developed the germi-nous particles lately seen.

Before me, rolled out like some long Eastern manuscript, lay stretched one continuous length of iron framework—multitudinous and mystical, with all sorts of rollers, wheels, and cylinders, in slowly-measured and unceasing motion.

"Here first comes the pulp now," said Cupid, pointing to the nighest end of the machine.

"See; first it pours out and spreads itself upon this wide, sloping board; and then—look—slides, thin and quivering, beneath the first roller there. Follow on now, and see it as it slides from under that to the next cylinder. There; see how it has become just a very little less pulpy now. One step more, and it grows still more to some slight consistence. Still another cylinder, and it is so

knitted—though as yet mere dragon-fly wing—that it forms an air-bridge here, like a suspended cobweb, between two more separated rollers; and flowing over the last one, and under again, and doubling about there out of sight for a minute among all those mixed cylinders you indistinctly see, it reappears here, looking now at last a little less like pulp and more like paper, but still quite delicate and defective yet awhile. But—a little further onward, Sir, if you please—here now, at this further point, it puts on something of a real look, as if it might turn out to be something you might possibly handle in the end. But it's not yet done, Sir. Good way to travel yet, and plenty more of cylinders must roll it."

"Bless my soul!" said I, amazed at the elonga-tion, interminable convolutions, and deliberate slowness of the machine. "It must take a long time for the pulp to pass from end to end, and come out paper."

"Oh, not so long," smiled the precocious lad, with a superior and patronizing air; "only nine minutes. But look; you may try it for yourself. Have you a bit of paper? Ah! here's a bit on the floor. Now mark that with any word you please, and let me dab it on here, and we'll see how long before it comes out at the other end."

"Well, let me see," said I, taking out my pen-cil. "Come, I'll mark it with your name."

Bidding me take out my watch, Cupid adroitly dropped the inscribed slip on an exposed part of the incipient mass.

Instantly my eye marked the second-hand on my dial-plate.

Slowly I followed the slip, inch by inch: some-times pausing for full half a minute as it disap-peared beneath inscrutable groups of the lower cylinders, but only gradually to emerge again; and so, on, and on, and on—inch by inch; now in open sight, sliding along like a freckle on the quivering sheet; and then again wholly vanished; and so, on, and on, and on—inch by inch; all the time the main sheet growing more and more to final firmness—when, suddenly, I saw a sort of paper-fall, not wholly unlike a water-fall; a scissory sound smote my ear, as of some cord being snapped; and down dropped an unfolded sheet of perfect foolscap, with my "Cupid" half faded out of it, and still moist and warm.

My travels were at an end, for here was the end of the machine.

"Well, how long was it?" said Cupid.

"Nine minutes to a second," replied I, watch in hand.

"I told you so."

For a moment a curious emotion filled me, not wholly unlike that which one might experience at the fulfillment of some mysterious prophecy. But how absurd, thought I again; the thing is a mere machine, the essence of which is unvarying punctuality and precision.

Previously absorbed by the wheels and cylinders, my attention was now directed to a sad-looking woman standing by.

"That is rather an elderly person so silently tending the machine-end here. She would not seem wholly used to it either."

"Oh," knowingly whispered Cupid, through the din, "she only came last week. She was a nurse formerly. But the business is poor in these parts, and she's left it. But look at the paper she is piling there."

"Ay, foolscap," handling the piles of moist, warm sheets, which continually were being delivered into the woman's waiting hands. "Don't you turn out anything but foolscap at this machine?"

"Oh, sometimes, but not often, we turn out finer work—cream-laid and royal sheets, we call them. But foolscap being in chief demand we turn out foolscap most."

It was very curious. Looking at that blank paper continually dropping, dropping, dropping, my mind ran on in wonderings of those strange uses to which those thousand sheets eventually would be put. All sorts of writings would be writ on those now vacant things—sermons, lawyers' briefs, physicians' prescriptions, love-letters, marriage certificates, bills of divorce, registers of births, death-warrants, and so on, without end. Then, recurring back to them as they here lay all blank, I could not but bethink me of that celebrated comparison of John Locke, who, in demonstration of his theory that man had no innate ideas, compared the human mind at birth to a sheet of blank paper, something destined to be scribbled on, but what sort of characters no soul might tell.

Pacing slowly to and fro along the involved machine, still humming with its play, I was struck as well by the inevitability as the evolvement-power in all its motions.

"Does that thin cobweb there," said I, pointing to the sheet in its more imperfect stage, "does that never tear or break? It is marvelous fragile, and yet this machine it passes through is so mighty."

"It never is known to tear a hair's point."

"Does it never stop—get clogged?"

"No. It *must* go. The machinery makes it go just *so*; just that very way, and at that very pace you there plainly *see* it go. The pulp can't help going."

Something of awe now stole over me, as I gazed upon this inflexible iron animal. Always, more or less, machinery of this ponderous elaborate sort strikes, in some moods, strange dread into the human heart, as some living, panting Behemoth might. But what made the thing I saw so specially terrible to me was the metallic necessity, the unbudging fatality which governed it. Though, here and there, I could not follow the thin, gauzy veil of pulp in the course of its more mysterious or entirely invisible advance, yet it was indubitable that, at those points where it eluded me, it still marched on in unvarying docility to the autocratic cunning of the machine. A fascination fastened on me. I stood spellbound and wandering in my soul. Before my eyes—there, passing in slow procession along the wheeling cylinders, I seemed to see, glued to the pallid incipience of the pulp, the yet more pallid faces of all the pallid girls I had eyed that heavy day. Slowly, mournfully, beseechingly, yet unresistingly, they gleamed along, their agony dimly outlined on the imperfect paper, like the print of the tormented face on the handkerchief of Saint Veronica.

"Halloa! the heat of this room is too much for you," cried Cupid, staring at me.

"No—I am rather chill, if anything."

"Come out, Sir—out—out," and, with the protecting air of a careful father, the precocious lad hurried me outside.

In a few minutes, feeling revived a little, I went into the folding-room—the first room I had entered, and where the desk for transacting business stood, surrounded by the blank counters and blank girls engaged at them.

"Cupid here has led me a strange tour," said I to the dark-complexioned man before mentioned, whom I had ere this discovered not only to be an old bachelor, but also the principal proprietor. "Yours is a most wonderful factory. Your great machine is a miracle of inscrutable intricacy."

"Yes, all our visitors think it so. But we don't have many. We are in a very out-of-the-way corner here. Few inhabitants, too. Most of our girls come from far-off villages."

"The girls," echoed I, glancing round at their silent forms. "Why is it, Sir, that in most factories, female operatives, of whatever age, are indiscriminately called girls, never women?"

"Oh! as to that—why, I suppose, the fact of their being generally unmarried—that's the reason, I should think. But it never struck me before. For our factory here, we will not have married women; they are apt to be off-and-on too much. We want none but steady workers; twelve hours to the day, day after day, through the three hundred and sixty-five days, excepting Sundays, Thanksgiving, and Fast-days. That's our rule. And so, having no married women,

what females we have are rightly enough called girls."

"Then these are all maids," said I, while some pained homage to their pale virginity made me involuntarily bow.

"All maids."

Again the strange emotion filled me.

"Your cheeks look whitish yet, Sir," said the man, gazing at me narrowly. "You must be careful going home. Do they pain you at all now? It's a bad sign, if they do."

"No doubt, Sir," answered I, "when once I have got out of the Devil's Dungeon I shall feel them mending."

"Ah, yes; the winter air in valleys, or gorges, or any sunken place, is far colder and more bitter than elsewhere. You would hardly believe it now, but it is colder here than at the top of Woedolor Mountain."

"I dare say it is, Sir. But time presses me; I must depart."

With that, remuffling myself in dread-naught and tippet, thrusting my hands into my huge sealskin mittens, I sallied out into the nipping air, and found poor Black, my horse, all cringing and doubled up with the cold.

Soon, wrapped in furs and meditations, I ascended from the Devil's Dungeon.

At the Black Notch I paused, and once more bethought me of Temple-Bar. Then, shooting through the pass, all alone with inscrutable nature, I exclaimed—Oh! Paradise of Bachelors! and oh! Tartarus of Maids!

George MacDonald (1824–1905) was a Scottish writer and a Christian minister. The combination of his sermons, poems, novels, and children's stories has placed him as a forefather of the modern fantasy novel. Although ministering was his first profession, he was soon forced out of his pastoral position for not preaching more dogmatic sermons. He was even accused of heresy, which led him to abandon the doctrine of predestination. After his dismissal, he began to tutor and write full-time. MacDonald's first novel, *Phantastes: A Faerie Romance for Men and Women* (1858), was well received because readers of all ages could enjoy it. His work was admired by, among others, W. H. Auden, Lewis Carroll, C. S. Lewis, and J. R. R. Tolkien. *Phantastes* remains one of his most eminent works and stands beside his novels *The Princess and the Goblin* (1872), *At the Back of the North Wind* (1871), and *Lilith* (1895). "The Magic Mirror" is the thirteenth chapter of *Phantastes*.

The Magic Mirror

George MacDonald

COSMO VON WEHRSTAHL was a student at the University of Prague. Though of a noble family, he was poor, and prided himself upon the independence that poverty gives; for what will not a man pride himself upon, when he cannot get rid of it? A favourite with his fellow students, he yet had no companions; and none of them had ever crossed the threshold of his lodging in the top of one of the highest houses in the old town. Indeed, the secret of much of that complaisance which recommended him to his fellows, was the thought of his unknown retreat, whither in the evening he could betake himself and indulge undisturbed in his own studies and reveries. These studies, besides those subjects necessary to his course at the University, embraced some less commonly known and approved; for in a secret drawer lay the works of Albertus Magnus and Cornelius Agrippa, along with others less read and more abstruse. As yet, however, he had followed these researches only from curiosity, and had turned them to no practical purpose.

His lodging consisted of one large low-ceiled room, singularly bare of furniture; for besides a couple of wooden chairs, a couch which served for dreaming on both by day and night, and a great press of black oak, there was very little in the room that could be called furniture.

But curious instruments were heaped in the corners; and in one stood a skeleton, half-leaning against the wall, half-supported by a string about its neck. One of its hands, all of fingers, rested on the heavy pommel of a great sword that stood beside it.

Various weapons were scattered about over the floor. The walls were utterly bare of adornment;

for the few strange things, such as a large dried bat with wings dispread, the skin of a porcupine, and a stuffed sea-mouse, could hardly be reckoned as such. But although his fancy delighted in vagaries like these, he indulged his imagination with far different fare. His mind had never yet been filled with an absorbing passion; but it lay like a still twilight open to any wind, whether the low breath that wafts but odours, or the storm that bows the great trees till they strain and creak. He saw everything as through a rose-coloured glass. When he looked from his window on the street below, not a maiden passed but she moved as in a story, and drew his thoughts after her till she disappeared in the vista. When he walked in the streets, he always felt as if reading a tale, into which he sought to weave every face of interest that went by; and every sweet voice swept his soul as with the wing of a passing angel. He was in fact a poet without words; the more absorbed and endangered, that the springing-waters were dammed back into his soul, where, finding no utterance, they grew, and swelled, and undermined. He used to lie on his hard couch, and read a tale or a poem, till the book dropped from his hand; but he dreamed on, he knew not whether awake or asleep, until the opposite roof grew upon his sense, and turned golden in the sunrise. Then he arose too; and the impulses of vigorous youth kept him ever active, either in study or in sport, until again the close of the day left him free; and the world of night, which had lain drowned in the cataract of the day, rose up in his soul, with all its stars, and dim-seen phantom shapes. But this could hardly last long. Some one form must sooner or later step within the charmed circle, enter the house of life, and compel the bewildered magician to kneel and worship.

One afternoon, towards dusk, he was wandering dreamily in one of the principal streets, when a fellow student roused him by a slap on the shoulder, and asked him to accompany him into a little back alley to look at some old armour which he had taken a fancy to possess. Cosmo was considered an authority in every matter pertaining to arms, ancient or modern. In the use of weapons,

none of the students could come near him; and his practical acquaintance with some had principally contributed to establish his authority in reference to all. He accompanied him willingly.

They entered a narrow alley, and thence a dirty little court, where a low arched door admitted them into a heterogeneous assemblage of everything musty, and dusty, and old, that could well be imagined. His verdict on the armour was satisfactory, and his companion at once concluded the purchase. As they were leaving the place, Cosmo's eye was attracted by an old mirror of an elliptical shape, which leaned against the wall, covered with dust. Around it was some curious carving, which he could see but very indistinctly by the glimmering light which the owner of the shop carried in his hand. It was this carving that attracted his attention; at least so it appeared to him. He left the place, however, with his friend, taking no further notice of it. They walked together to the main street, where they parted and took opposite directions.

No sooner was Cosmo left alone, than the thought of the curious old mirror returned to him. A strong desire to see it more plainly arose within him, and he directed his steps once more towards the shop. The owner opened the door when he knocked, as if he had expected him. He was a little, old, withered man, with a hooked nose, and burning eyes constantly in a slow restless motion, and looking here and there as if after something that eluded them. Pretending to examine several other articles, Cosmo at last approached the mirror, and requested to have it taken down.

"Take it down yourself, master; I cannot reach it," said the old man.

Cosmo took it down carefully, when he saw that the carving was indeed delicate and costly, being both of admirable design and execution; containing withal many devices which seemed to embody some meaning to which he had no clue. This, naturally, in one of his tastes and temperament, increased the interest he felt in the old mirror; so much, indeed, that he now longed to possess it, in order to study its frame at his leisure. He pretended, however, to want it only for use; and saying he feared the plate could be of little service, as it was rather old, he brushed away a little of the dust from its face, expecting to see a dull reflection within. His surprise was great when he found the reflection brilliant, revealing a glass not only uninjured by age, but wondrously clear and perfect (should the whole correspond to this part) even for one newly from the hands of the maker. He asked carelessly what the owner wanted for the thing. The old man replied by mentioning a sum of money far beyond the reach of poor Cosmo, who proceeded to replace the mirror where it had stood before.

"You think the price too high?" said the old man.

"I do not know that it is too much for you to ask," replied Cosmo; "but it is far too much for me to give."

The old man held up his light towards Cosmo's face. "I like your look," said he.

Cosmo could not return the compliment. In fact, now he looked closely at him for the first time, he felt a kind of repugnance to him, mingled with a strange feeling of doubt whether a man or a woman stood before him.

"What is your name?" he continued.

"Cosmo von Wehrstahl."

"Ah, ah! I thought as much. I see your father in you. I knew your father very well, young sir. I dare say in some odd corners of my house, you might find some old things with his crest and cipher upon them still. Well, I like you: you shall have the mirror at the fourth part of what I asked for it; but upon one condition."

"What is that?" said Cosmo; for, although the price was still a great deal for him to give, he could just manage it; and the desire to possess the mirror had increased to an altogether unaccountable degree, since it had seemed beyond his reach.

"That if you should ever want to get rid of it again, you will let me have the first offer."

"Certainly," replied Cosmo, with a smile; adding, "a moderate condition indeed."

"On your honour?" insisted the seller.

"On my honour," said the buyer; and the bargain was concluded.

"I will carry it home for you," said the old man, as Cosmo took it in his hands.

"No, no; I will carry it myself," said he; for he had a peculiar dislike to revealing his residence to any one, and more especially to this person, to whom he felt every moment a greater antipathy. "Just as you please," said the old creature, and muttered to himself as he held his light at the door to show him out of the court: "Sold for the sixth time! I wonder what will be the upshot of it this time. I should think my lady had enough of it by now!"

Cosmo carried his prize carefully home. But all the way he had an uncomfortable feeling that he was watched and dogged. Repeatedly he looked about, but saw nothing to justify his suspicions. Indeed, the streets were too crowded and too ill lighted to expose very readily a careful spy, if such there should be at his heels. He reached his lodging in safety, and leaned his purchase against the wall, rather relieved, strong as he was, to be rid of its weight; then, lighting his pipe, threw himself on the couch, and was soon lapt in the folds of one of his haunting dreams.

He returned home earlier than usual the next day, and fixed the mirror to the wall, over the hearth, at one end of his long room.

He then carefully wiped away the dust from its face, and, clear as the water of a sunny spring, the mirror shone out from beneath the envious covering. But his interest was chiefly occupied with the curious carving of the frame. This he cleaned as well as he could with a brush; and then he proceeded to a minute examination of its various parts, in the hope of discovering some index to the intention of the carver. In this, however, he was unsuccessful; and, at length, pausing with some weariness and disappointment, he gazed vacantly for a few moments into the depth of the reflected room. But ere long he said, half aloud: "What a strange thing a mirror is! and what a wondrous affinity exists between it and a man's imagination! For this room of mine, as I behold it in the glass, is the same, and yet not the same. It is not the mere representation of the room I live in, but it looks just as if I were reading about it in a story I like. All its commonness has disappeared. The mirror has lifted it out of the region of fact into the realm of art; and the very representing of it to me has clothed with interest that which was otherwise hard and bare; just as one sees with delight upon the stage the representation of a character from which one would escape in life as from something unendurably wearisome. But is it not rather that art rescues nature from the weary and sated regards of our senses, and the degrading injustice of our anxious everyday life, and, appealing to the imagination, which dwells apart, reveals Nature in some degree as she really is, and as she represents herself to the eye of the child, whose every-day life, fearless and unambitious, meets the true import of the wonder-teeming world around him, and rejoices therein without questioning? That skeleton, now—I almost fear it, standing there so still, with eyes only for the unseen, like a watch-tower looking across all the waste of this busy world into the quiet regions of rest beyond. And yet I know every bone and every joint in it as well as my own fist. And that old battle-axe looks as if any moment it might be caught up by a mailed hand, and, borne forth by the mighty arm, go crashing through casque, and skull, and brain, invading the Unknown with yet another bewildered ghost. I should like to live in *that* room if I could only get into it."

Scarcely had the half-moulded words floated from him, as he stood gazing into the mirror, when, striking him as with a flash of amazement that fixed him in his posture, noiseless and unannounced, glided suddenly through the door into the reflected room, with stately motion, yet reluctant and faltering step, the graceful form of a woman, clothed all in white. Her back only was visible as she walked slowly up to the couch in the further end of the room, on which she laid herself wearily, turning towards him a face of unutterable loveliness, in which suffering, and dislike, and a sense of compulsion, strangely mingled with the beauty. He stood without the power of motion for some moments, with his eyes irrecoverably fixed

upon her; and even after he was conscious of the ability to move, he could not summon up courage to turn and look on her, face to face, in the veritable chamber in which he stood. At length, with a sudden effort, in which the exercise of the will was so pure, that it seemed involuntary, he turned his face to the couch. It was vacant. In bewilderment, mingled with terror, he turned again to the mirror: there, on the reflected couch, lay the exquisite lady-form. She lay with closed eyes, whence two large tears were just welling from beneath the veiling lids; still as death, save for the convulsive motion of her bosom.

Cosmo himself could not have described what he felt. His emotions were of a kind that destroyed consciousness, and could never be clearly recalled. He could not help standing yet by the mirror, and keeping his eyes fixed on the lady, though he was painfully aware of his rudeness, and feared every moment that she would open hers, and meet his fixed regard. But he was, ere long, a little relieved; for, after a while, her eyelids slowly rose, and her eyes remained uncovered, but unemployed for a time; and when, at length, they began to wander about the room, as if languidly seeking to make some acquaintance with her environment, they were never directed towards him: it seemed nothing but what was in the mirror could affect her vision; and, therefore, if she saw him at all, it could only be his back, which, of necessity, was turned towards her in the glass. The two figures in the mirror could not meet face to face, except he turned and looked at her, present in his room; and, as she was not there, he concluded that if he were to turn towards the part in his room corresponding to that in which she lay, his reflection would either be invisible to her altogether, or at least it must appear to her to gaze vacantly towards her, and no meeting of the eyes would produce the impression of spiritual proximity. By-and-by her eyes fell upon the skeleton, and he saw her shudder and close them. She did not open them again, but signs of repugnance continued evident on her countenance. Cosmo would have removed the obnoxious thing at once, but he feared to discompose her yet more by the assertion of his presence which the act would involve. So he stood and watched her. The eyelids yet shrouded the eyes, as a costly case the jewels within; the troubled expression gradually faded from the countenance, leaving only a faint sorrow behind; the features settled into an unchanging expression of rest; and by these signs, and the slow regular motion of her breathing, Cosmo knew that she slept. He could now gaze on her without embarrassment. He saw that her figure, dressed in the simplest robe of white, was worthy of her face; and so harmonious, that either the delicately moulded foot, or any finger of the equally delicate hand, was an index to the whole. As she lay, her whole form manifested the relaxation of perfect repose. He gazed till he was weary, and at last seated himself near the new-found shrine, and mechanically took up a book, like one who watches by a sick-bed. But his eyes gathered no thoughts from the page before him. His intellect had been stunned by the bold contradiction, to its face, of all its experience, and now lay passive, without assertion, or speculation, or even conscious astonishment; while his imagination sent one wild dream of blessedness after another coursing through his soul. How long he sat he knew not; but at length he roused himself, rose, and, trembling in every portion of his frame, looked again into the mirror. She was gone. The mirror reflected faithfully what his room presented, and nothing more. It stood there like a golden setting whence the central jewel has been stolen away—like a night-sky without the glory of its stars. She had carried with her all the strangeness of the reflected room. It had sunk to the level of the one without.

But when the first pangs of his disappointment had passed, Cosmo began to comfort himself with the hope that she might return, perhaps the next evening, at the same hour. Resolving that if she did, she should not at least be scared by the hateful skeleton, he removed that and several other articles of questionable appearance into a recess by the side of the hearth, whence they could not possibly cast any reflection into the mirror; and having made his poor room as tidy as he could, sought the solace of the open sky and of a night wind that had begun to blow, for he could not rest where he was. When he returned, somewhat composed, he could hardly prevail with himself to lie down on his bed; for he could not help feeling as if she had lain upon it; and for him to lie there now would be something like sacrilege. However, weariness prevailed; and laying himself on the couch, dressed as he was, he slept till day.

With a beating heart, beating till he could hardly breathe, he stood in dumb hope before the mirror, on the following evening. Again the reflected room shone as through a purple vapour in the gathering twilight. Everything seemed waiting like himself for a coming splendour to glorify its poor earthliness with the presence of a heavenly joy. And just as the room vibrated with the strokes of the neighbouring church bell, announcing the hour of six, in glided the pale beauty, and again laid herself on the couch. Poor Cosmo nearly lost his senses with delight. She was there once more! Her eyes sought the corner where the skeleton had stood, and a faint gleam of satisfaction crossed her face, apparently at seeing it empty. She looked suffering still, but there was less of discomfort expressed in her countenance than there had been the night before. She took more notice of the things about her, and seemed to gaze with some curiosity on the strange apparatus standing here and there in her room. At length, however, drowsiness seemed to overtake her, and again she fell asleep. Resolved not to lose sight of her this time, Cosmo watched the sleeping form. Her slumber was so deep and absorbing that a fascinating repose seemed to pass contagiously from her to him as he gazed upon her; and he started as if from a dream, when the lady moved, and, without opening her eyes, rose, and passed from the room with the gait of a somnambulist.

Cosmo was now in a state of extravagant delight. Most men have a secret treasure somewhere. The miser has his golden hoard; the virtuoso his pet ring; the student his rare book; the poet his favourite haunt; the lover his secret drawer; but Cosmo had a mirror with a lovely lady in it. And now that he knew by the skeleton, that she was affected by the things around her, he had a new object in life: he would turn the bare chamber in the mirror into a room such as no lady need disdain to call her own. This he could effect only by furnishing and adorning his. And Cosmo was poor. Yet he possessed accomplishments that could be turned to account; although, hitherto, he had preferred living on his slender allowance, to increasing his means by what his pride considered unworthy of his rank. He was the best swordsman in the University; and now he offered to give lessons in fencing and similar exercises, to such as chose to pay him well for the trouble. His proposal was heard with surprise by the students; but it was eagerly accepted by many; and soon his instructions were not confined to the richer students, but were anxiously sought by many of the young nobility of Prague and its neighbourhood. So that very soon he had a good deal of money at his command. The first thing he did was to remove his apparatus and oddities into a closet in the room. Then he placed his bed and a few other necessaries on each side of the hearth, and parted them from the rest of the room by two screens of Indian fabric. Then he put an elegant couch for the lady to lie upon, in the corner where his bed had formerly stood; and, by degrees, every day adding some article of luxury, converted it, at length, into a rich boudoir.

Every night, about the same time, the lady entered. The first time she saw the new couch, she started with a half-smile; then her face grew very sad, the tears came to her eyes, and she laid herself upon the couch, and pressed her face into the silken cushions, as if to hide from everything. She took notice of each addition and each change as the work proceeded; and a look of acknowledgment, as if she knew that some one was ministering to her, and was grateful for it, mingled with the constant look of suffering. At length, after

she had lain down as usual one evening, her eyes fell upon some paintings with which Cosmo had just finished adorning the walls. She rose, and to his great delight, walked across the room, and proceeded to examine them carefully, testifying much pleasure in her looks as she did so. But again the sorrowful, tearful expression returned, and again she buried her face in the pillows of her couch. Gradually, however, her countenance had grown more composed; much of the suffering manifest on her first appearance had vanished, and a kind of quiet, hopeful expression had taken its place; which, however, frequently gave way to an anxious, troubled look, mingled with something of sympathetic pity.

Meantime, how fared Cosmo? As might be expected in one of his temperament, his interest had blossomed into love, and his love—shall I call it *ripened*, or—*withered* into passion. But, alas! he loved a shadow. He could not come near her, could not speak to her, could not hear a sound from those sweet lips, to which his longing eyes would cling like bees to their honey-founts. Ever and anon he sang to himself:

"I shall die for love of the maiden"

and ever he looked again, and died not, though his heart seemed ready to break with intensity of life and longing. And the more he did for her, the more he loved her; and he hoped that, although she never appeared to see him, yet she was pleased to think that one unknown would give his life to her. He tried to comfort himself over his separation from her, by thinking that perhaps some day she would see him and make signs to him, and that would satisfy him; "for," thought he, "is not this all that a loving soul can do to enter into communion with another? Nay, how many who love never come nearer than to behold each other as in a mirror; seem to know and yet never know the inward life; never enter the other soul; and part at last, with but the vaguest notion of the universe on the borders of which they have been hovering for years? If I could but speak to her, and knew that she heard me, I should be satisfied." Once he contemplated painting a picture on the wall, which should, of necessity, convey to the lady a thought of himself; but, though he had some skill with the pencil, he found his hand tremble so much when he began the attempt, that he was forced to give it up. . . .

"Who lives, he dies; who dies, he is alive."

One evening, as he stood gazing on his treasure, he thought he saw a faint expression of self-consciousness on her countenance, as if she surmised that passionate eyes were fixed upon her. This grew; till at last the red blood rose over her neck, and cheek, and brow. Cosmo's longing to approach her became almost delirious. This night she was dressed in an evening costume, resplendent with diamonds. This could add nothing to her beauty, but it presented it in a new aspect; enabled her loveliness to make a new manifestation of itself in a new embodiment. For essential beauty is infinite; and, as the soul of Nature needs an endless succession of varied forms to embody her loveliness, countless faces of beauty springing forth, not any two the same, at any one of her heart-throbs; so the individual form needs an infinite change of its environments, to enable it to uncover all the phases of its loveliness. Diamonds glittered from amidst her hair, half hidden in its luxuriance, like stars through dark rain-clouds; and the bracelets on her white arms flashed all the colours of a rainbow of lightnings, as she lifted her snowy hands to cover her burning face. But her beauty shone down all its adornment. "If I might have but one of her feet to kiss," thought Cosmo, "I should be content." Alas! he deceived himself, for passion is never content. Nor did he know that there are *two* ways out of her enchanted house. But, suddenly, as if the pang had been driven into his heart from without, revealing itself first in pain, and afterwards in definite form, the thought darted into his mind, "She has a lover somewhere. Remembered words of his bring the colour on her face now. I am nowhere to her. She lives in another world all day, and all night, after she leaves me. Why does she come and make me love her, till I, a

strong man, am too faint to look upon her more?" He looked again, and her face was pale as a lily. A sorrowful compassion seemed to rebuke the glitter of the restless jewels, and the slow tears rose in her eyes. She left her room sooner this evening than was her wont. Cosmo remained alone, with a feeling as if his bosom had been suddenly left empty and hollow, and the weight of the whole world was crushing in its walls. The next evening, for the first time since she began to come, she came not.

And now Cosmo was in wretched plight. Since the thought of a rival had occurred to him, he could not rest for a moment. More than ever he longed to see the lady face to face. He persuaded himself that if he but knew the worst he would be satisfied; for then he could abandon Prague, and find that relief in constant motion, which is the hope of all active minds when invaded by distress. Meantime he waited with unspeakable anxiety for the next night, hoping she would return: but she did not appear. And now he fell really ill. Rallied by his fellow students on his wretched looks, he ceased to attend the lectures. His engagements were neglected. He cared for nothing. The sky, with the great sun in it, was to him a heartless, burning desert. The men and women in the streets were mere puppets, without motives in themselves, or interest to him. He saw them all as on the ever-changing field of a *camera obscura*. She—she alone and altogether—was his universe, his well of life, his incarnate good. For six evenings she came not. Let his absorbing passion, and the slow fever that was consuming his brain, be his excuse for the resolution which he had taken and begun to execute, before that time had expired.

Reasoning with himself, that it must be by some enchantment connected with the mirror, that the form of the lady was to be seen in it, he determined to attempt to turn to account what he had hitherto studied principally from curiosity. "For," said he to himself, "if a spell can force her presence in that glass (and she came unwillingly at first), may not a stronger spell, such as I know, especially with the aid of her half-presence in the mirror, if ever she appears again, compel her living form to come to me here? If I do her wrong, let love be my excuse. I want only to know my doom from her own lips." He never doubted, all the time, that she was a real earthly woman; or, rather, that there was a woman, who, somehow or other, threw this reflection of her form into the magic mirror.

He opened his secret drawer, took out his books of magic, lighted his lamp, and read and made notes from midnight till three in the morning, for three successive nights. Then he replaced his books; and the next night went out in quest of the materials necessary for the conjuration. These were not easy to find; for, in love-charms and all incantations of this nature, ingredients are employed scarcely fit to be mentioned, and for the thought even of which, in connexion with her, he could only excuse himself on the score of his bitter need. At length he succeeded in procuring all he required; and on the seventh evening from that on which she had last appeared, he found himself prepared for the exercise of unlawful and tyrannical power.

He cleared the centre of the room; stooped and drew a circle of red on the floor, around the spot where he stood; wrote in the four quarters mystical signs, and numbers which were all powers of seven or nine; examined the whole ring carefully, to see that no smallest break had occurred in the circumference; and then rose from his bending posture. As he rose, the church clock struck seven; and, just as she had appeared the first time, reluctant, slow, and stately, glided in the lady. Cosmo trembled; and when, turning, she revealed a countenance worn and wan, as with sickness or inward trouble, he grew faint, and felt as if he dared not proceed. But as he gazed on the face and form, which now possessed his whole soul, to the exclusion of all other joys and griefs, the longing to speak to her, to know that she heard him, to hear from her one word in return, became so unendurable, that he suddenly and hastily resumed his preparations. Stepping carefully from the circle, he put a small brazier into its centre. He then set fire to its contents of char-

coal, and while it burned up, opened his window and seated himself, waiting, beside it.

It was a sultry evening. The air was full of thunder. A sense of luxurious depression filled the brain. The sky seemed to have grown heavy, and to compress the air beneath it. A kind of purplish tinge pervaded the atmosphere, and through the open window came the scents of the distant fields, which all the vapours of the city could not quench. Soon the charcoal glowed. Cosmo sprinkled upon it the incense and other substances which he had compounded, and, stepping within the circle, turned his face from the brazier and towards the mirror. Then, fixing his eyes upon the face of the lady, he began with a trembling voice to repeat a powerful incantation. He had not gone far, before the lady grew pale; and then, like a returning wave, the blood washed all its banks with its crimson tide, and she hid her face in her hands. Then he passed to a conjuration stronger yet.

The lady rose and walked uneasily to and fro in her room. Another spell; and she seemed seeking with her eyes for some object on which they wished to rest. At length it seemed as if she suddenly espied him; for her eyes fixed themselves full and wide upon his, and she drew gradually, and somewhat unwillingly, close to her side of the mirror, just as if his eyes had fascinated her. Cosmo had never seen her so near before. Now at least, eyes met eyes; but he could not quite understand the expression of hers. They were full of tender entreaty, but there was something more that he could not interpret. Though his heart seemed to labour in his throat, he would allow no delight or agitation to turn him from his task. Looking still in her face, he passed on to the mightiest charm he knew. Suddenly the lady turned and walked out of the door of her reflected chamber. A moment after she entered his room with veritable presence; and, forgetting all his precautions, he sprang from the charmed circle, and knelt before her. There she stood, the living lady of his passionate visions, alone beside him, in a thundery twilight, and the glow of a magic fire.

"Why," said the lady, with a trembling voice, "didst thou bring a poor maiden through the rainy streets alone?"

"Because I am dying for love of thee; but I only brought thee from the mirror there."

"Ah, the mirror!" and she looked up at it, and shuddered. "Alas! I am but a slave, while that mirror exists. But do not think it was the power of thy spells that drew me; it was thy longing desire to see me, that beat at the door of my heart, till I was forced to yield."

"Canst thou love me then?" said Cosmo, in a voice calm as death, but almost inarticulate with emotion.

"I do not know," she replied sadly; "that I cannot tell, so long as I am bewildered with enchantments. It were indeed a joy too great, to lay my head on thy bosom and weep to death; for I think thou lovest me, though I do not know;—but—"

Cosmo rose from his knees.

"I love thee as—nay, I know not what—for since I have loved thee, there is nothing else."

He seized her hand: she withdrew it.

"No, better not; I am in thy power, and therefore I may not."

She burst into tears, and kneeling before him in her turn, said—

"Cosmo, if thou lovest me, set me free, even from thyself; break the mirror."

"And shall I see thyself instead?"

"That I cannot tell, I will not deceive thee; we may never meet again."

A fierce struggle arose in Cosmo's bosom. Now she was in his power. She did not dislike him at least; and he could see her when he would. To break the mirror would be to destroy his very life to banish out of his universe the only glory it possessed. The whole world would be but a prison, if he annihilated the one window that looked into the paradise of love. Not yet pure in love, he hesitated.

With a wail of sorrow the lady rose to her feet. "Ah! he loves me not; he loves me not even as I love him; and alas! I care more for his love than even for the freedom I ask."

"I will not wait to be willing," cried Cosmo; and sprang to the corner where the great sword stood.

Meantime it had grown very dark; only the embers cast a red glow through the room. He seized the sword by the steel scabbard, and stood before the mirror; but as he heaved a great blow at it with the heavy pommel, the blade slipped halfway out of the scabbard, and the pommel struck the wall above the mirror. At that moment, a terrible clap of thunder seemed to burst in the very room beside them; and ere Cosmo could repeat the blow, he fell senseless on the hearth. When he came to himself, he found that the lady and the mirror had both disappeared. He was seized with a brain fever, which kept him to his couch for weeks.

When he recovered his reason, he began to think what could have become of the mirror. For the lady, he hoped she had found her way back as she came; but as the mirror involved her fate with its own, he was more immediately anxious about that. He could not think she had carried it away. It was much too heavy, even if it had not been too firmly fixed in the wall, for her to remove it. Then again, he remembered the thunder; which made him believe that it was not the lightning, but some other blow that had struck him down. He concluded that, either by supernatural agency, he having exposed himself to the vengeance of the demons in leaving the circle of safety, or in some other mode, the mirror had probably found its way back to its former owner; and, horrible to think of, might have been by this time once more disposed of, delivering up the lady into the power of another man; who, if he used his power no worse than he himself had done, might yet give Cosmo abundant cause to curse the selfish indecision which prevented him from shattering the mirror at once. Indeed, to think that she whom he loved, and who had prayed to him for freedom, should be still at the mercy, in some degree, of the possessor of the mirror, and was at least exposed to his constant observation, was in itself enough to madden a chary lover.

Anxiety to be well retarded his recovery; but at length he was able to creep abroad. He first made his way to the old broker's, pretending to be in search of something else. A laughing sneer on the creature's face convinced him that he knew all about it; but he could not see it amongst his furniture, or get any information out of him as to what had become of it. He expressed the utmost surprise at hearing it had been stolen, a surprise which Cosmo saw at once to be counterfeited; while, at the same time, he fancied that the old wretch was not at all anxious to have it mistaken for genuine. Full of distress, which he concealed as well as he could, he made many searches, but with no avail. Of course he could ask no questions; but he kept his ears awake for any remotest hint that might set him in a direction of search. He never went out without a short heavy hammer of steel about him, that he might shatter the mirror the moment he was made happy by the sight of his lost treasure, if ever that blessed moment should arrive. Whether he should see the lady again, was now a thought altogether secondary, and postponed to the achievement of her freedom. He wandered here and there, like an anxious ghost, pale and haggard; gnawed ever at the heart, by the thought of what she might be suffering—all from his fault.

One night, he mingled with a crowd that filled the rooms of one of the most distinguished mansions in the city; for he accepted every invitation, that he might lose no chance, however poor, of obtaining some information that might expedite his discovery. Here he wandered about, listening to every stray word that he could catch, in the hope of a revelation. As he approached some ladies who were talking quietly in a corner, one said to another:

"Have you heard of the strange illness of the Princess von Hohenweiss?"

"Yes; she has been ill for more than a year now. It is very sad for so fine a creature to have such a terrible malady. She was better for some weeks lately, but within the last few days the same attacks have returned, apparently accompanied with more suffering than ever. It is altogether an inexplicable story."

"Is there a story connected with her illness?"

"I have only heard imperfect reports of it; but it is said that she gave offence some eighteen months ago to an old woman who had held an office of trust in the family, and who, after some incoherent threats, disappeared. This peculiar affection followed soon after. But the strangest part of the story is its association with the loss of an antique mirror, which stood in her dressing-room, and of which she constantly made use."

Here the speaker's voice sank to a whisper; and Cosmo, although his very soul sat listening in his ears, could hear no more. He trembled too much to dare to address the ladies, even if it had been advisable to expose himself to their curiosity. The name of the Princess was well known to him, but he had never seen her; except indeed it was she, which now he hardly doubted, who had knelt before him on that dreadful night. Fearful of attracting attention, for, from the weak state of his health, he could not recover an appearance of calmness, he made his way to the open air, and reached his lodgings; glad in this, that he at least knew where she lived, although he never dreamed of approaching her openly, even if he should be happy enough to free her from her hateful bondage. He hoped, too, that as he had unexpectedly learned so much, the other and far more important part might be revealed to him ere long.

"Have you seen Steinwald lately?"

"No, I have not seen him for some time. He is almost a match for me at the rapier, and I suppose he thinks he needs no more lessons."

"I wonder what has become of him. I want to see him very much. Let me see; the last time I saw him he was coming out of that old broker's den, to which, if you remember, you accompanied me once, to look at some armour. That is fully three weeks ago."

This hint was enough for Cosmo. Von Steinwald was a man of influence in the court, well known for his reckless habits and fierce passions. The very possibility that the mirror should be in his possession was hell itself to Cosmo. But violent or hasty measures of any sort were most unlikely to succeed. All that he wanted was an opportunity of breaking the fatal glass; and to obtain this he must bide his time. He revolved many plans in his mind, but without being able to fix upon any.

At length, one evening, as he was passing the house of Von Steinwald, he saw the windows more than usually brilliant. He watched for a while, and seeing that company began to arrive, hastened home, and dressed as richly as he could, in the hope of mingling with the guests unquestioned: in effecting which, there could be no difficulty for a man of his carriage.

In a lofty, silent chamber, in another part of the city, lay a form more like marble than a living woman. The loveliness of death seemed frozen upon her face, for her lips were rigid, and her eyelids closed. Her long white hands were crossed over her breast, and no breathing disturbed their repose. Beside the dead, men speak in whispers, as if the deepest rest of all could be broken by the sound of a living voice. Just so, though the soul was evidently beyond the reach of all intimations from the senses, the two ladies, who sat beside her, spoke in the gentlest tones of subdued sorrow. "She has lain so for an hour."

"This cannot last long, I fear."

"How much thinner she has grown within the last few weeks! If she would only speak, and explain what she suffers, it would be better for her. I think she has visions in her trances, but nothing can induce her to refer to them when she is awake."

"Does she ever speak in these trances?"

"I have never heard her; but they say she walks sometimes, and once put the whole household in a terrible fright by disappearing for a whole hour, and returning drenched with rain, and almost dead with exhaustion and fright. But

even then she would give no account of what had happened."

A scarce audible murmur from the yet motionless lips of the lady here startled her attendants. After several ineffectual attempts at articulation, the word "*Cosmo!*" burst from her. Then she lay still as before; but only for a moment. With a wild cry, she sprang from the couch erect on the floor, flung her arms above her head, with clasped and straining hands, and, her wide eyes flashing with light, called aloud, with a voice exultant as that of a spirit bursting from a sepulchre, "I am free! I am free! I thank thee!" Then she flung herself on the couch, and sobbed; then rose, and paced wildly up and down the room, with gestures of mingled delight and anxiety. Then turning to her motionless attendants—"Quick, Lisa, my cloak and hood!" Then lower—"I must go to him. Make haste, Lisa! You may come with me, if you will."

In another moment they were in the street, hurrying along towards one of the bridges over the Moldau. The moon was near the zenith, and the streets were almost empty. The Princess soon outstripped her attendant, and was half-way over the bridge, before the other reached it.

"Are you free, lady? The mirror is broken: are you free?"

The words were spoken close beside her, as she hurried on. She turned; and there, leaning on the parapet in a recess of the bridge, stood Cosmo, in a splendid dress, but with a white and quivering face.

"Cosmo!—I am free—and thy servant for ever. I was coming to you now."

"And I to you, for Death made me bold; but I could get no further. Have I atoned at all? Do I love you a little—truly?"

"Ah, I know now that you love me, my Cosmo; but what do you say about death?"

He did not reply. His hand was pressed against his side. She looked more closely: the blood was welling from between the fingers. She flung her arms around him with a faint bitter wail.

When Lisa came up, she found her mistress

kneeling above a wan dead face, which smiled on in the spectral moonbeams.

And now I will say no more about these wondrous volumes; though I could tell many a tale out of them, and could, perhaps, vaguely represent some entrancing thoughts of a deeper kind which I found within them. From many a sultry noon till twilight, did I sit in that grand hall, buried and risen again in these old books. And I trust I have carried away in my soul some of the exhalations of their undying leaves. In after hours of deserved or needful sorrow, portions of what I read there have often come to me again, with an unexpected comforting; which was not fruitless, even though the comfort might seem in itself groundless and vain.

Fitz-James O'Brien (1828–1862) was an Irish American writer of the uncanny and pseudoscience who died serving the Union as a soldier in the United States' Civil War. O'Brien began writing out of necessity after squandering his inheritance. Although he died very young, O'Brien made a huge contribution to fantasy and speculative fiction because his work existed on the cusp of the transition from the more traditional "tale" and the modern "short story." Brilliantly original, his stories include enigmatic characters, greedy narrators, disembodied eyes, and, perhaps we should quickly move past this, orgies. His best-known works are "The Diamond Lens" (1858), "What Was It?" (1859), and "The Wondersmith" (1859). "The Diamond Lens" is one of his most detailed short stories and subverts the idea of scientific genius. Since his death, O'Brien's stories have been collected in numerous editions, including *The Wondersmith and Others* (2008), which presents texts in their original magazine versions.

The Diamond Lens

Fitz-James O'Brien

I

FROM A VERY EARLY PERIOD of my life the entire bent of my inclinations had been toward microscopic investigations. When I was not more than ten years old, a distant relative of our family, hoping to astonish my inexperience, constructed a simple microscope for me by drilling in a disk of copper a small hole in which a drop of pure water was sustained by capillary attraction. This very primitive apparatus, magnifying some fifty diameters, presented, it is true, only indistinct and imperfect forms, but still sufficiently wonderful to work up my imagination to a preternatural state of excitement.

Seeing me so interested in this rude instrument, my cousin explained to me all that he knew about the principles of the microscope, related to me a few of the wonders which had been accomplished through its agency, and ended by promising to send me one regularly constructed, immediately on his return to the city. I counted the days, the hours, the minutes that intervened between that promise and his departure.

Meantime, I was not idle. Every transparent substance that bore the remotest resemblance to a lens I eagerly seized upon, and employed in vain attempts to realize that instrument the theory of whose construction I as yet only vaguely comprehended. All panes of glass containing those oblate spheroidal knots familiarly known as "bull's-eyes" were ruthlessly destroyed in the hope of obtaining lenses of marvelous power. I even went so far as to extract the crystalline humor from the eyes of fishes and animals, and endeavored to press it into the microscopic service. I plead guilty to having stolen the glasses from my Aunt Agatha's spectacles, with a dim idea of grinding them into lenses of wondrous magnifying properties—in which attempt it is scarcely necessary to say that I totally failed.

At last the promised instrument came. It was of that order known as Field's simple microscope, and had cost perhaps about fifteen dollars. As far as educational purposes went, a better apparatus could not have been selected. Accompanying it was a small treatise on the microscope—its history, uses, and discoveries. I comprehended then for the first time the "Arabian Nights' Entertainments." The dull veil of ordinary existence that hung across the world seemed suddenly to roll away, and to lay bare a land of enchantments. I felt toward my companions as the seer might feel toward the ordinary masses of men. I held conversations with nature in a tongue which they could not understand. I was in daily communication with living wonders such as they never imagined in their wildest visions, I penetrated beyond the external portal of things, and roamed through the sanctuaries. Where they beheld only a drop of rain slowly rolling down the window-glass, I saw a universe of beings animated with all the passions common to physical life, and convulsing their minute sphere with struggles as fierce and protracted as those of men. In the common spots of mould, which my mother, good housekeeper that she was, fiercely scooped away from her jam-pots, there abode for me, under the name of mildew, enchanted gardens, filled with dells and avenues of the densest foliage and most astonishing verdure, while from the fantastic boughs of these microscopic forests hung strange fruits glittering with green and silver and gold.

It was no scientific thirst that at this time filled my mind. It was the pure enjoyment of a poet to whom a world of wonders has been disclosed. I talked of my solitary pleasures to none. Alone with my microscope, I dimmed my sight, day after day and night after night, poring over the marvels which it unfolded to me. I was like one who, having discovered the ancient Eden still existing in all its primitive glory, should resolve to enjoy it in solitude, and never betray to mortal the secret of its locality. The rod of my life was bent at this moment. I destined myself to be a microscopist.

Of course, like every novice, I fancied myself a discoverer. I was ignorant at the time of the thousands of acute intellects engaged in the same pursuit as myself, and with the advantage of instruments a thousand times more powerful than mine. The names of Leeuwenhoek, Williamson, Spencer, Ehrenberg, Schultz, Dujardin, Schact, and Schleiden were then entirely unknown to me, or, if known, I was ignorant of their patient and wonderful researches. In every fresh specimen of cryptogamia which I placed beneath my instrument I believed that I discovered wonders of which the world was as yet ignorant. I remember well the thrill of delight and admiration that shot through me the first time that I discovered the common wheel animalcule (*Rotifera vulgaris*) expanding and contracting its flexible spokes and seemingly rotating through the water. Alas! as I grew older, and obtained some works treating of my favorite study, I found that I was only on the threshold of a science to the investigation of which some of the greatest men of the age were devoting their lives and intellects.

As I grew up, my parents, who saw but little likelihood of anything practical resulting from the examination of bits of moss and drops of water through a brass tube and a piece of glass, were anxious that I should choose a profession.

It was their desire that I should enter the counting-house of my uncle, Ethan Blake, a prosperous merchant, who carried on business in New York. This suggestion I decisively combated. I had no taste for trade; I should only make a failure; in short, I refused to become a merchant.

But it was necessary for me to select some pursuit. My parents were staid New England people, who insisted on the necessity of labor, and therefore, although, thanks to the bequest of my poor Aunt Agatha, I should, on coming of age, inherit a small fortune sufficient to place me above want, it was decided that, instead of waiting for this, I should act the nobler part, and employ the intervening years in rendering myself independent.

After much cogitation, I complied with the wishes of my family, and selected a profession. I determined to study medicine at the New York Academy. This disposition of my future suited me. A removal from my relatives would enable me to dispose of my time as I pleased without fear of detection. As long as I paid my Academy fees, I might shirk attending the lectures if I chose; and, as I never had the remotest intention of standing an examination, there was no danger of my being "plucked." Besides, a metropolis was the place for me. There I could obtain excellent instruments, the newest publications, intimacy with men of pursuits kindred with my own—in short, all things necessary to ensure a profitable devotion of my life to my beloved science. I had an abundance of money, few desires that were not bounded by my illuminating mirror on one side and my object-glass on the other; what, therefore, was to prevent my becoming an illustrious investigator of the veiled worlds? It was with the most buoyant hope that I left my New England home and established myself in New York.

II

My first step, of course, was to find suitable apartments. These I obtained, after a couple of days' search, in Fourth Avenue; a very pretty second floor, unfurnished, containing sitting-room, bedroom, and a smaller apartment which I intended to fit up as a laboratory. I furnished my lodgings simply, but rather elegantly, and then devoted all my energies to the adornment of the temple of my worship. I visited Pike, the celebrated optician, and passed in review his splendid collection of microscopes—Field's Compound, Hingham's, Spencer's, Nachet's Binocular (that founded on the principles of the stereoscope), and at length fixed upon that form known as Spencer's Trunnion Microscope, as combining

the greatest number of improvements with an almost perfect freedom from tremor. Along with this I purchased every possible accessory—draw-tubes, micrometers, a *camera lucida*, lever-stage, achromatic condensers, white cloud illuminators, prisms, parabolic condensers, polarizing apparatus, forceps, aquatic boxes, fishing-tubes, with a host of other articles, all of which would have been useful in the hands of an experienced microscopist, but, as I afterward discovered, were not of the slightest present value to me. It takes years of practice to know how to use a complicated microscope. The optician looked suspiciously at me as I made these valuable purchases. He evidently was uncertain whether to set me down as some scientific celebrity or a madman. I think he was inclined to the latter belief. I suppose I was mad. Every great genius is mad upon the subject in which he is greatest. The unsuccessful madman is disgraced and called a lunatic.

Mad or not, I set myself to work with a zeal which few scientific students have ever equaled. I had everything to learn relative to the delicate study upon which I had embarked—a study involving the most earnest patience, the most rigid analytic powers, the steadiest hand, the most untiring eye, the most refined and subtle manipulation.

For a long time half my apparatus lay inactively on the shelves of my laboratory, which was now most amply furnished with every possible contrivance for facilitating my investigations. The fact was that I did not know how to use some of my scientific implements—never having been taught microscopies—and those whose use I understood theoretically were of little avail until by practice I could attain the necessary delicacy of handling. Still, such was the fury of my ambition, such the untiring perseverance of my experiments, that, difficult of credit as it may be, in the course of one year I became theoretically and practically an accomplished microscopist.

During this period of my labors, in which I submitted specimens of every substance that came under my observation to the action of my lenses, I became a discoverer—in a small way, it is true, for I was very young, but still a discoverer. It was I who destroyed Ehrenberg's theory that the *Volvox globator* was an animal, and proved that his "monads" with stomachs and eyes were merely phases of the formation of a vegetable cell, and were, when they reached their mature state, incapable of the act of conjugation, or any true generative act, without which no organism rising to any stage of life higher than vegetable can be said to be complete. It was I who resolved the singular problem of rotation in the cells and hairs of plants into ciliary attraction, in spite of the assertions of Wenham and others that my explanation was the result of an optical illusion.

But notwithstanding these discoveries, laboriously and painfully made as they were, I felt horribly dissatisfied. At every step I found myself stopped by the imperfections of my instruments. Like all active microscopists, I gave my imagination full play. Indeed, it is a common complaint against many such that they supply the defects of their instruments with the creations of their brains. I imagined depths beyond depths in nature which the limited power of my lenses prohibited me from exploring. I lay awake at night constructing imaginary microscopes of immeasurable power, with which I seemed to pierce through all the envelopes of matter down to its original atom. How I cursed those imperfect mediums which necessity through ignorance compelled me to use! How I longed to discover the secret of some perfect lens, whose magnifying power should be limited only by the resolvability of the object, and which at the same time should be free from spherical and chromatic aberrations—in short, from all the obstacles over which the poor microscopist finds himself continually stumbling! I felt convinced that the simple microscope, composed of a single lens of such vast yet perfect power, was possible of construction. To attempt to bring the compound microscope up to such a pitch would have been commencing at the wrong end; this latter being simply a partially successful endeavor to remedy those very defects of the simplest instrument which, if conquered, would leave nothing to be desired.

It was in this mood of mind that I became a constructive microscopist. After another year passed in this new pursuit, experimenting on every imaginable substance—glass, gems, flints, crystals, artificial crystals formed of the alloy of various vitreous materials—in short, having constructed as many varieties of lenses as Argus had eyes—I found myself precisely where I started, with nothing gained save an extensive knowledge of glass-making. I was almost dead with despair. My parents were surprised at my apparent want of progress in my medical studies (I had not attended one lecture since my arrival in the city), and the expenses of my mad pursuit had been so great as to embarrass me very seriously.

I was in this frame of mind one day, experimenting in my laboratory on a small diamond—that stone, from its great refracting power, having always occupied my attention more than any other—when a young Frenchman who lived on the floor above me, and who was in the habit of occasionally visiting me, entered the room.

I think that Jules Simon was a Jew. He had many traits of the Hebrew character: a love of jewelry, of dress, and of good living. There was something mysterious about him. He always had something to sell, and yet went into excellent society. When I say sell, I should perhaps have said peddle; for his operations were generally confined to the disposal of single articles—a picture, for instance, or a rare carving in ivory, or a pair of duelling-pistols, or the dress of a Mexican *caballero*. When I was first furnishing my rooms, he paid me a visit, which ended in my purchasing an antique silver lamp, which he assured me was a Cellini—it was handsome enough even for that—and some other knick-knacks for my sitting-room. Why Simon should pursue this petty trade I never could imagine. He apparently had plenty of money, and had the *entrée* of the best houses in the city—taking care, however, I suppose, to drive no bargains within the enchanted circle of the Upper Ten. I came at length to the conclusion that this peddling was but a mask to cover some greater object, and even went so far as to believe my young acquaintance to be implicated in the slave-trade. That, however, was none of my affair.

On the present occasion, Simon entered my room in a state of considerable excitement.

"*Ah! mon ami!*" he cried, before I could even offer him the ordinary salutation, "it has occurred to me to be the witness of the most astonishing things in the world. I promenade myself to the house of Madame————. How does the little animal—*le renard*—name himself in the Latin?"

"Vulpes," I answered.

"Ah! yes—Vulpes. I promenade myself to the house of Madame Vulpes."

"The spirit medium?"

"Yes, the great medium. Great heavens! what a woman! I write on a slip of paper many of questions concerning affairs of the most secret—affairs that conceal themselves in the abysses of my heart the most profound; and behold, by example, what occurs? This devil of a woman makes me replies the most truthful to all of them. She talks to me of things that I do not love to talk of to myself. What am I to think? I am fixed to the earth!"

"Am I to understand you, M. Simon, that this Mrs. Vulpes replied to questions secretly written by you, which questions related to events known only to yourself?"

"Ah! more than that, more than that," he answered, with an air of some alarm. "She related to me things—But," he added after a pause, and suddenly changing his manner, "why occupy ourselves with these follies? It was all the biology, without doubt. It goes without saying that it has not my credence. But why are we here, *mon ami*? It has occurred to me to discover the most beautiful thing as you can imagine—a vase with green lizards on it, composed by the great Bernard Palissy. It is in my apartment; let us mount. I go to show it to you."

I followed Simon mechanically; but my thoughts were far from Palissy and his enameled ware, although I, like him, was seeking in the dark a great discovery. This casual mention of the spiritualist, Madame Vulpes, set me on a new track. What if, through communication with more subtle organisms than my own, I could reach at a single bound the goal which perhaps a life, of agonizing mental toil would never enable me to attain?

While purchasing the Palissy vase from my friend Simon, I was mentally arranging a visit to Madame Vulpes.

III

Two evenings after this, thanks to an arrangement by letter and the promise of an ample fee, I found Madame Vulpes awaiting me at her residence alone. She was a coarse-featured woman, with keen and rather cruel dark eyes, and an exceedingly sensual expression about her mouth and under jaw. She received me in perfect silence, in an apartment on the ground floor, very sparsely furnished. In the centre of the room, close to where Mrs. Vulpes sat, there was a common round mahogany table. If I had come for the purpose of sweeping her chimney, the woman could not have looked more indifferent to my appearance. There was no attempt to inspire the visitor with awe. Everything bore a simple and practical aspect. This intercourse with the spiritual world was evidently as familiar an occupation with Mrs. Vulpes as eating her dinner or riding in an omnibus.

"You come for a communication, Mr. Linley?" said the medium, in a dry, businesslike tone of voice.

"By appointment—yes."

"What sort of communication do you want—a written one?"

"Yes, I wish for a written one."

"From any particular spirit?"

"Yes."

"Have you ever known this spirit on this earth?"

"Never. He died long before I was born. I wish merely to obtain from him some information which he ought to be able to give better than any other."

"Will you seat yourself at the table, Mr. Linley," said the medium, "and place your hands upon it?"

I obeyed, Mrs. Vulpes being seated opposite to me, with her hands also on the table. We remained thus for about a minute and a half, when a violent succession of raps came on the table, on the back of my chair, on the floor immediately under my feet, and even on the window-panes. Mrs. Vulpes smiled composedly.

"They are very strong to-night," she remarked. "You are fortunate." She then continued, "Will the spirits communicate with this gentleman?"

Vigorous affirmative.

"Will the particular spirit he desires to speak with communicate?"

A very confused rapping followed this question.

"I know what they mean," said Mrs. Vulpes, addressing herself to me; "they wish you to write down the name of the particular spirit that you desire to converse with. Is that so?" she added, speaking to her invisible guests.

That it was so was evident from the numerous affirmatory responses. While this was going on, I tore a slip from my pocket-book and scribbled a name under the table.

"Will this spirit communicate in writing with this gentleman?" asked the medium once more.

After a moment's pause, her hand seemed to be seized with a violent tremor, shaking so forcibly that the table vibrated. She said that a spirit had seized her hand and would write. I handed her some sheets of paper that were on the table and a pencil. The latter she held loosely in her hand, which presently began to move over the paper with a singular and seemingly involuntary motion. After a few moments had elapsed, she handed me the paper, on which I found written, in a large, uncultivated hand, the words, "He is not here, but has been sent for." A pause of a minute or so ensued, during which Mrs. Vulpes remained perfectly silent, but the raps continued at regular intervals. When the short period I mention had elapsed, the hand of the medium was again seized with its convulsive tremor, and

she wrote, under this strange influence, a few words on the paper, which she handed to me. They were as follows:

"I am here. Question me.

"*Leeuwenhoek.*"

I was astounded. The name was identical with that I had written beneath the table, and carefully kept concealed. Neither was it at all probable that an uncultivated woman like Mrs. Vulpes should know even the name of the great father of microscopies. It may have been biology; but this theory was soon doomed to be destroyed. I wrote on my slip—still concealing it from Mrs. Vulpes—a series of questions which, to avoid tediousness, I shall place with the responses, in the order in which they occurred:

I.—Can the microscope be brought to perfection?

Spirit—Yes.

I.—Am I destined to accomplish this great task?

Spirit.—You are.

I.—I wish to know how to proceed to attain this end. For the love which you bear to science, help me!

Spirit—A diamond of one hundred and forty carats, submitted to electro-magnetic currents for a long period, will experience a rearrangement of its atoms *inter se* and from that stone you will form the universal lens.

I.—Will great discoveries result from the use of such a lens?

Spirit—So great that all that has gone before is as nothing.

I.—But the refractive power of the diamond is so immense that the image will be formed within the lens. How is that difficulty to be surmounted?

Spirit—Pierce the lens through its axis, and the difficulty is obviated. The image will be formed in the pierced space, which will itself serve as a tube to look through. Now I am called. Good-night.

I cannot at all describe the effect that these extraordinary communications had upon me. I felt completely bewildered. No biological theory could account for the *discovery* of the lens. The medium might, by means of biological *rapport* with my mind, have gone so far as to read my questions and reply to them coherently. But biology could not enable her to discover that magnetic currents would so alter the crystals of the diamond as to remedy its previous defects and admit of its being polished into a perfect lens. Some such theory may have passed through my head, it is true; but if so, I had forgotten it. In my excited condition of mind there was no course left but to become a convert, and it was in a state of the most painful nervous exaltation that I left the medium's house that evening. She accompanied me to the door, hoping that I was satisfied. The raps followed us as we went through the hall, sounding on the balusters, the flooring, and even the lintels of the door. I hastily expressed my satisfaction, and escaped hurriedly into the cool night air. I walked home with but one thought possessing me—how to obtain a diamond of the immense size required. My entire means multiplied a hundred times over would have been inadequate to its purchase. Besides, such stones are rare, and become historical. I could find such only in the regalia of Eastern or European monarchs.

IV

There was a light in Simon's room as I entered my house. A vague impulse urged me to visit him. As I opened the door of his sitting-room unannounced, he was bending, with his back toward me, over a Carcel lamp, apparently engaged in minutely examining some object which he held in his hands. As I entered, he started suddenly, thrust his hand into his breast pocket, and turned to me with a face crimson with confusion.

"What!" I cried, "poring over the miniature of some fair lady? Well, don't blush so much; I won't ask to see it."

Simon laughed awkwardly enough, but made none of the negative protestations usual on such occasions. He asked me to take a seat.

"Simon," said I, "I have just come from Madame Vulpes."

This time Simon turned as white as a sheet, and seemed stupefied, as if a sudden electric shock had smitten him. He babbled some incoherent words, and went hastily to a small closet where he usually kept his liquors. Although astonished at his emotion, I was too preoccupied with my own idea to pay much attention to anything else.

"You say truly when you call Madame Vulpes a devil of a woman," I continued. "Simon, she told me wonderful things to-night, or rather was the means of telling me wonderful things. Ah! if I could only get a diamond that weighed one hundred and forty carats!"

Scarcely had the sigh with which I uttered this desire died upon my lips when Simon, with the aspect of a wild beast, glared at me savagely, and, rushing to the mantelpiece, where some foreign weapons hung on the wall, caught up a Malay creese, and brandished it furiously before him.

"No!" he cried in French, into which he always broke when excited. "No! you shall not have it! You are perfidious! You have consulted with that demon, and desire my treasure! But I will die first! Me, I am brave! You cannot make me fear!"

All this, uttered in a loud voice, trembling with excitement, astounded me. I saw at a glance that I had accidentally trodden upon the edges of Simon's secret, whatever it was. It was necessary to reassure him.

"My dear Simon," I said, "I am entirely at a loss to know what you mean. I went to Madame Vulpes to consult with her on a scientific problem, to the solution of which I discovered that a diamond of the size I just mentioned was necessary. You were never alluded to during the evening, nor, so far as I was concerned, even thought of. What can be the meaning of this outburst? If you happen to have a set of valuable diamonds in your possession, you need fear nothing from me. The diamond which I require you could not possess; or, if you did possess it, you would not be living here."

Something in my tone must have completely reassured him, for his expression immediately changed to a sort of constrained merriment, combined however, with a certain suspicious attention to my movements. He laughed, and said that I must bear with him; that he was at certain moments subject to a species of vertigo, which betrayed itself in incoherent speeches, and that the attacks passed off as rapidly as they came.

He put his weapon aside while making this explanation, and endeavored, with some success, to assume a more cheerful air.

All this did not impose on me in the least. I was too much accustomed to analytical labors to be baffled by so flimsy a veil. I determined to probe the mystery to the bottom.

"Simon," I said gayly, "let us forget all this over a bottle of Burgundy. I have a case of Lausseure's *Clos Vougeot* downstairs, fragrant with the odors and ruddy with the sunlight of the Côte d'Or. Let us have up a couple of bottles. What say you?"

"With all my heart," answered Simon smilingly.

I produced the wine and we seated ourselves to drink. It was of a famous vintage, that of 1848, a year when war and wine throve together, and its pure but powerful juice seemed to impart renewed vitality to the system. By the time we had half finished the second bottle, Simon's head, which I knew was a weak one, had begun to yield, while I remained calm as ever, only that every draught seemed to send a flush of vigor through my limbs. Simon's utterance became more and more indistinct. He took to singing French *chansons* of a not very moral tendency. I rose suddenly from the table just at the conclusion of one of those incoherent verses, and, fixing my eyes on him with a quiet smile, said, "Simon, I have deceived you. I learned your secret this evening. You may as well be frank with me. Mrs. Vulpes—or rather, one of her spirits—told me all."

He started with horror. His intoxication seemed for the moment to fade away, and he made a movement toward the weapon that he had a short time before laid down. I stopped him with my hand.

"Monster!" he cried passionately, "I am ruined! What shall I do? You shall never have it! I swear by my mother!"

"I don't want it," I said; "rest secure, but be frank with me. Tell me all about it."

The drunkenness began to return. He protested with maudlin earnestness that I was entirely mistaken—that I was intoxicated; then asked me to swear eternal secrecy, and promised to disclose the mystery to me. I pledged myself, of course, to all. With an uneasy look in his eyes, and hands unsteady with drink and nervousness, he drew a small case from his breast and opened it. Heavens! How the mild lamplight was shivered into a thousand prismatic arrows as it fell upon a vast rose-diamond that glittered in the case! I was no judge of diamonds, but I saw at a glance that this was a gem of rare size and purity. I looked at Simon with wonder and—must I confess it?—with envy. How could he have obtained this treasure? In reply to my questions, I could just gather from his drunken statements (of which, I fancy, half the incoherence was affected) that he had been superintending a gang of slaves engaged in diamond-washing in Brazil; that he had seen one of them secrete a diamond, but, instead of informing his employers, had quietly watched the negro until he saw him bury his treasure; that he had dug it up and fled with it, but that as yet he was afraid to attempt to dispose of it publicly—so valuable a gem being almost certain to attract too much attention to its owner's antecedents—and he had not been able to discover any of those obscure channels by which such matters are conveyed away safely. He added that, in accordance with oriental practice, he had named his diamond with the fanciful title of "The Eye of Morning."

While Simon was relating this to me, I regarded the great diamond attentively. Never had I beheld anything so beautiful. All the glories of light ever imagined or described seemed to pulsate in its crystalline chambers. Its weight, as I learned from Simon, was exactly one hundred and forty carats. Here was an amazing coincidence. The hand of destiny seemed in it. On the very evening when the spirit of Leeuwenhoek communicates to me the great secret of the microscope, the priceless means which he directs me to employ start up within my easy reach! I determined, with the most perfect deliberation, to possess myself of Simon's diamond.

I sat opposite to him while he nodded over his glass, and calmly revolved the whole affair. I did not for an instant contemplate so foolish an act as a common theft, which would of course be discovered, or at least necessitate flight and concealment, all of which must interfere with my scientific plans. There was but one step to be taken—to kill Simon. After all, what was the life of a little peddling Jew in comparison with the interests of science? Human beings are taken every day from the condemned prisons to be experimented on by surgeons. This man, Simon, was by his own confession a criminal, a robber, and I believed on my soul a murderer. He deserved death quite as much as any felon condemned by the laws: why should I not, like government, contrive that his punishment should contribute to the progress of human knowledge?

The means for accomplishing everything I desired lay within my reach. There stood upon the mantelpiece a bottle half full of French laudanum. Simon was so occupied with his diamond, which I had just restored to him, that it was an affair of no difficulty to drug his glass. In a quarter of an hour he was in a profound sleep.

I now opened his waistcoat, took the diamond from the inner pocket in which he had placed it, and removed him to the bed, on which I laid him so that his feet hung down over the edge. I had possessed myself of the Malay creese, which I held in my right hand, while with the other I discovered as accurately as I could by pulsation the exact locality of the heart. It was essential that all the aspects of his death should lead to the surmise of self-murder. I calculated the exact angle at which it was probable that the weapon, if leveled by Simon's own hand, would enter his breast; then with one powerful blow I thrust it up to the hilt in the very spot which I desired to penetrate. A convulsive thrill ran through Simon's limbs. I heard a smothered sound issue from his throat, precisely like the bursting of a large air-bubble sent up by a diver when it reaches the surface of the water; he turned half round on his side, and, as if to assist my plans more effectually, his right hand, moved by some mere spasmodic impulse, clasped the handle of the creese, which it remained holding with extraordinary muscular tenacity. Beyond this there was no apparent struggle. The laudanum, I presume, paralyzed the usual nervous action. He must have died instantly.

There was yet something to be done. To make it certain that all suspicion of the act should be diverted from any inhabitant of the house to Simon himself, it was necessary that the door should be found in the morning *locked on the inside*. How to do this, and afterward escape myself? Not by the window; that was a physical impossibility. Besides, I was determined that the windows *also* should be found bolted. The solution was simple enough. I descended softly to my own room for a peculiar instrument which I had used for holding small slippery substances, such as minute spheres of glass, etc. This instrument was nothing more than a long, slender hand-vise, with a very powerful grip and a considerable leverage, which last was accidentally owing to the shape of the handle. Nothing was simpler than, when the key was in the lock, to seize the end of its stem in this vise, through the keyhole, from the outside, and so lock the door. Previously, however, to doing this, I burned a number of papers on Simon's hearth. Suicides almost always burn papers before they destroy themselves. I also emptied some more laudanum into Simon's glass—having first removed from it all traces of wine—cleaned the other wine-glass, and brought the bottles away with me. If traces of two persons drinking had been found in the room, the question naturally would have arisen, Who was the second? Besides, the wine-bottles might have been identified as belonging to me. The laudanum I poured out to account for its presence in his stomach, in case of a *post-mortem* examination. The theory naturally would be that he first intended to poison himself, but, after swallowing a little of the drug, was either disgusted with its taste, or changed his mind from other motives, and chose the dagger. These arrangements made, I walked out, leaving the gas burning, locked the door with my vise, and went to bed.

Simon's death was not discovered until nearly three in the afternoon. The servant, astonished at seeing the gas burning—the light streaming on the dark landing from under the door—peeped through the keyhole and saw Simon on the bed.

She gave the alarm. The door was burst open, and the neighborhood was in a fever of excitement.

Every one in the house was arrested, myself included. There was an inquest; but no clew to his death beyond that of suicide could be obtained. Curiously enough, he had made several speeches to his friends the preceding week that seemed to point to self-destruction. One gentleman swore that Simon had said in his presence that "he was tired of life." His landlord affirmed that Simon, when paying him his last month's rent, remarked that "he should not pay him rent much longer." All the other evidence corresponded—the door locked inside, the position of the corpse, the burned papers. As I anticipated, no one knew of the possession of the diamond by Simon, so that no motive was suggested for his murder. The jury, after a prolonged examination, brought in the usual verdict, and the neighborhood once more settled down to its accustomed quiet.

V

The three months succeeding Simon's catastrophe I devoted night and day to my diamond lens. I had constructed a vast galvanic battery, composed of nearly two thousand pairs of plates: a higher power I dared not use, lest the diamond should be calcined. By means of this enormous engine I was enabled to send a powerful current of electricity continually through my great diamond, which it seemed to me gained in lustre every day. At the expiration of a month I commenced the grinding and polishing of the lens, a work of intense toil and exquisite delicacy. The great density of the stone, and the care required to be taken with the curvatures of the surfaces of the lens, rendered the labor the severest and most harassing that I had yet undergone.

At last the eventful moment came; the lens was completed. I stood trembling on the threshold of new worlds. I had the realization of Alexander's famous wish before me. The lens lay on the table, ready to be placed upon its platform. My hand fairly shook as I enveloped a drop of water with a thin coating of oil of turpentine, preparatory to its examination, a process necessary in order to prevent the rapid evaporation of the water. I now placed the drop on a thin slip of glass under the lens, and throwing upon it, by the combined aid of a prism and a mirror, a powerful stream of light, I approached my eye to the minute hole drilled through the axis of the lens. For an instant I saw nothing save what seemed to be an illuminated chaos, a vast, luminous abyss. A pure white light, cloudless and serene, and seemingly limitless as space itself, was my first impression. Gently, and with the greatest care, I depressed the lens a few hairbreadths. The wondrous illumination still continued, but as the lens approached the object a scene of indescribable beauty was unfolded to my view.

I seemed to gaze upon a vast space, the limits of which extended far beyond my vision. An atmosphere of magical luminousness permeated the entire field of view. I was amazed to see no trace of animalculous life. Not a living thing, apparently, inhabited that dazzling expanse. I comprehended instantly that, by the wondrous power of my lens, I had penetrated beyond the grosser particles of aqueous matter, beyond the realms of infusoria and protozoa, down to the original gaseous globule, into whose luminous interior I was gazing as into an almost boundless dome filled with a supernatural radiance.

It was, however, no brilliant void into which I looked. On every side I beheld beautiful inorganic forms, of unknown texture, and colored with the most enchanting hues. These forms presented the appearance of what might be called, for want of a more specific definition, foliated clouds of the highest rarity—that is, they undulated and broke into vegetable formations, and were tinged with splendors compared with which the gilding of our autumn woodlands is as dross compared with gold. Far away into the illimitable distance stretched long avenues of these gaseous forests, dimly transparent, and painted with prismatic hues of unimaginable brilliancy. The pendent branches waved along the fluid glades until every vista seemed to break through half-lucent ranks of many-colored drooping silken pennons. What seemed to be either fruits or flowers, pied with a thousand hues, lustrous and ever-varying, bubbled from the crowns of this fairy foliage. No hills, no lakes, no rivers, no forms animate or inanimate, were to be seen, save those vast auroral copses that floated serenely in the luminous stillness, with leaves and fruits and flowers gleaming with unknown fires, unrealizable by mere imagination.

How strange, I thought, that this sphere should be thus condemned to solitude! I had hoped, at least, to discover some new form of animal life, perhaps of a lower class than any with which we are at present acquainted, but still some living organism. I found my newly discovered world, if I may so speak, a beautiful chromatic desert.

While I was speculating on the singular arrangements of the internal economy of Nature, with which she so frequently splinters into atoms our most compact theories, I thought I beheld a form moving slowly through the glades of one of the prismatic forests. I looked more attentively, and found that I was not mistaken. Words cannot depict the anxiety with which I awaited the nearer approach of this mysterious object. Was it merely some inanimate substance, held in suspense in the attenuated atmosphere of the globule, or was it an animal endowed with vitality and motion? It approached, flitting behind the gauzy, colored veils of cloud-foliage, for seconds dimly revealed, then vanishing. At last the violet pennons that trailed nearest to me vibrated; they were gently

pushed aside, and the form floated out into the broad light.

It was a female human shape. When I say human, I mean it possessed the outlines of humanity; but there the analogy ends. Its adorable beauty lifted it illimitable heights beyond the loveliest daughter of Adam.

I cannot, I dare not, attempt to inventory the charms of this divine revelation of perfect beauty. Those eyes of mystic violet, dewy and serene, evade my words. Her long, lustrous hair following her glorious head in a golden wake, like the track sown in heaven by a falling star, seems to quench my most burning phrases with its splendors. If all the bees of Hybla nestled upon my lips, they would still sing but hoarsely the wondrous harmonies of outline that inclosed her form.

She swept out from between the rainbow-curtains of the cloud-trees into the broad sea of light that lay beyond. Her motions were those of some graceful naiad, cleaving, by a mere effort of her will, the clear, unruffled waters that fill the chambers of the sea. She floated forth with the serene grace of a frail bubble ascending through the still atmosphere of a June day. The perfect roundness of her limbs formed suave and enchanting curves. It was like listening to the most spiritual symphony of Beethoven the divine, to watch the harmonious flow of lines. This, indeed was a pleasure cheaply purchased at any price. What cared I if I had waded to the portal of this wonder through another's blood. I would have given my own to enjoy one such moment of intoxication and delight.

Breathless with gazing on this lovely wonder, and forgetful for an instant of everything save her presence, I withdrew my eye from the microscope eagerly. Alas! as my gaze fell on the thin slide that lay beneath my instrument, the bright light from mirror and from prism sparkled on a colorless drop of water! There, in that tiny bead of dew, this beautiful being was forever imprisoned. The planet Neptune was not more distant from me than she. I hastened once more to apply my eye to the microscope.

Animula (let me now call her by that dear

name which I subsequently bestowed on her) had changed her position. She had again approached the wondrous forest, and was gazing earnestly upward. Presently one of the trees—as I must call them—unfolded a long ciliary process, with which it seized one of the gleaming fruits that glittered on its summit, and, sweeping slowly down, held it within reach of Animula. The sylph took it in her delicate hand and began to eat. My attention was so entirely absorbed by her that I could not apply myself to the task of determining whether this singular plant was or was not instinct with volition.

I watched her, as she made her repast, with the most profound attention. The suppleness of her motions sent a thrill of delight through my frame; my heart beat madly as she turned her beautiful eyes in the direction of the spot in which I stood. What would I not have given to have had the power to precipitate myself into that luminous ocean and float with her through those grooves of purple and gold! While I was thus breathlessly following her every movement, she suddenly started, seemed to listen for a moment, and then cleaving the brilliant ether in which she was floating, like a flash of light, pierced through the opaline forest and disappeared.

Instantly a series of the most singular sensations attacked me. It seemed as if I had suddenly gone blind. The luminous sphere was still before me, but my daylight had vanished. What caused this sudden disappearance? Had she a lover or a husband? Yes, that was the solution! Some signal from a happy fellow-being had vibrated through the avenues of the forest, and she had obeyed the summons.

The agony of my sensations, as I arrived at this conclusion, startled me. I tried to reject the conviction that my reason forced upon me. I battled against the fatal conclusion—but in vain. It was so. I had no escape from it. I loved an animalcule.

It is true that, thanks to the marvelous power of my microscope, she appeared of human proportions. Instead of presenting the revolting aspect of the coarser creatures, that live and struggle and die, in the more easily resolvable portions of the water-drop, she was fair and delicate and of surpassing beauty. But of what account was all that? Every time that my eye was withdrawn from the instrument it fell on a miserable drop of water, within which, I must be content to know, dwelt all that could make my life lovely.

Could she but see me once! Could I for one moment pierce the mystical walls that so inexorably rose to separate us, and whisper all that filled my soul, I might consent to be satisfied for the rest of my life with the knowledge of her remote sympathy.

It would be something to have established even the faintest personal link to bind us together—to know that at times, when roaming through these enchanted glades, she might think of the wonderful stranger who had broken the monotony of her life with his presence and left a gentle memory in her heart!

But it could not be. No invention of which human intellect was capable could break down the barriers that nature had erected. I might feast my soul upon her wondrous beauty, yet she must always remain ignorant of the adoring eyes that day and night gazed upon her, and, even when closed, beheld her in dreams. With a bitter cry of anguish I fled from the room, and flinging myself on my bed, sobbed myself to sleep like a child.

VI

I arose the next morning almost at daybreak, and rushed to my microscope, I trembled as I sought the luminous world in miniature that contained my all. Animula was there. I had left the gaslamp, surrounded by its moderators, burning when I went to bed the night before. I found the sylph bathing, as it were, with an expression of pleasure animating her features, in the brilliant light which surrounded her. She tossed her lustrous golden hair over her shoulders with innocent coquetry. She lay at full length in the transparent medium, in which she supported herself with ease, and gamboled with the enchanting grace that the nymph Salmacis might have exhibited when she sought to conquer the modest Hermaphroditus. I tried an experiment to satisfy myself if her powers of reflection were developed. I lessened the lamplight considerably. By the dim light that remained, I could see an expression of pain flit across her face. She looked upward suddenly, and her brows contracted. I flooded the stage of the microscope again with a full stream of light, and her whole expression changed. She sprang forward like some substance deprived of all weight. Her eyes sparkled and her lips moved. Ah! if science had only the means of conducting and reduplicating sounds, as it does rays of light, what carols of happiness would then have entranced my ears! what jubilant hymns to Adonais would have thrilled the illumined air!

I now comprehended how it was that the Count de Cabalis peopled his mystic world with sylphs—beautiful beings whose breath of life was lambent fire, and who sported forever in regions of purest ether and purest light. The Rosicrucian had anticipated the wonder that I had practically realized.

How long this worship of my strange divinity went on thus I scarcely know. I lost all note of time. All day from early dawn, and far into the night, I was to be found peering through that wonderful lens. I saw no one, went nowhere, and scarce allowed myself sufficient time for my meals. My whole life was absorbed in contemplation as rapt as that of any of the Romish saints. Every hour that I gazed upon the divine form strengthened my passion—a passion that was always overshadowed by the maddening conviction that, although I could gaze on her at will, she never, never could behold me!

At length I grew so pale and emaciated, from want of rest and continual brooding over my insane love and its cruel conditions, that I determined to make some effort to wean myself from it. "Come," I said, "this is at best but a fantasy. Your imagination has bestowed on Animula charms which in reality she does not possess. Seclusion from female society has produced this morbid condition of mind. Compare her with

the beautiful women of your own world, and this false enchantment will vanish."

I looked over the newspapers by chance. There I beheld the advertisement of a celebrated *danseuse* who appeared nightly at Niblo's. The Signorina Caradolce had the reputation of being the most beautiful as well as the most graceful woman in the world. I instantly dressed and went to the theatre.

The curtain drew up. The usual semicircle of fairies in white muslin were standing on the right toe around the enameled flower-bank of green canvas, on which the belated prince was sleeping. Suddenly a flute is heard. The fairies start. The trees open, the fairies all stand on the left toe, and the queen enters. It was the Signorina. She bounded forward amid thunders of applause, and, lighting on one foot, remained poised in the air. Heavens! was this the great enchantress that had drawn monarchs at her chariot-wheels? Those heavy, muscular limbs, those thick ankles, those cavernous eyes, that stereotyped smile, those crudely painted cheeks! Where were the vermeil blooms, the liquid, expressive eyes, the harmonious limbs of Animula?

The Signorina danced. What gross, discordant movements! The play of her limbs was all false and artificial. Her bounds were painful athletic efforts; her poses were angular and distressed the eye. I could bear it no longer; with an exclamation of disgust that drew every eye upon me, I rose from my seat in the very middle of the Signorina's *pas-de-fascination* and abruptly quitted the house.

I hastened home to feast my eyes once more on the lovely form of my sylph. I felt that henceforth to combat this passion would be impossible. I applied my eyes to the lens. Animula was there—but what could have happened? Some terrible change seemed to have taken place during my absence. Some secret grief seemed to cloud the lovely features of her I gazed upon. Her face had grown thin and haggard; her limbs trailed heavily; the wondrous lustre of her golden hair had faded. She was ill—ill, and I could not assist her! I believe at that moment I would have forfeited all claims to my human birthright if I could only have been dwarfed to the size of an animalcule, and permitted to console her from whom fate had forever divided me.

I racked my brain for the solution of this mystery. What was it that afflicted the sylph? She seemed to suffer intense pain. Her features contracted, and she even writhed, as if with some internal agony. The wondrous forests appeared also to have lost half their beauty. Their hues were dim and in some places faded away altogether. I watched Animula for hours with a breaking heart, and she seemed absolutely to wither away under my very eye. Suddenly I remembered that I had not looked at the water-drop for several days. In fact, I hated to see it; for it reminded me of the natural barrier between Animula and myself. I hurriedly looked down on the stage of the microscope. The slide was still there—but, great heavens, the water drop had vanished! The awful truth burst upon me; it had evaporated, until it had become so minute as to be invisible to the naked eye; I had been gazing on its last atom, the one that contained Animula—and she was dying!

I rushed again to the front of the lens and looked through. Alas! the last agony had seized her. The rainbow-hued forests had all melted away, and Animula lay struggling feebly in what seemed to be a spot of dim light. Ah! the sight was horrible: the limbs once so round and lovely shriveling up into nothings; the eyes—those eyes that shone like heaven—being quenched into black dust; the lustrous golden hair now lank and discolored. The last throe came. I beheld that final struggle of the blackening form—and I fainted.

When I awoke out of a trance of many hours, I found myself lying amid the wreck of my instrument, myself as shattered in mind and body as it. I crawled feebly to my bed, from which I did not rise for many months.

They say now that I am mad; but they are mistaken. I am poor, for I have neither the heart nor the will to work; all my money is spent, and I live on charity. Young men's associations that love a joke invite me to lecture on optics before them, for which they pay me, and laugh at me while I lecture. "Linley, the mad microscopist," is the name I go by. I suppose that I talk incoherently while I lecture. Who could talk sense when his brain is haunted by such ghastly memories, while ever and anon among the shapes of death I behold the radiant form of my lost Animula!

Christina Georgina Rossetti (1830–1894) was an English poet who also published under the name Ellen Alleyne. Most of her works were fantastical, but she also wrote both religious and children's poetry. Rossetti had the ability to write beautiful and elegant verse without making it feel forced or unnatural, turning even the most unlikely of scenes into something almost believable. The passion she conveys in some of her works is remarkable, and yet she was an advocate of self-denial, a theme that runs through all of her poetry. Some critics believed Rossetti would be the next Alfred Lord Tennyson, but cancer took her too soon. In 1896, her brother found some of her work and published it under the title *New Poems*. "Goblin Market" was originally to be published with a parental advisory warning, as Rossetti specifically told her publisher it was not appropriate for children. The only poem in this volume, "Goblin Market" definitely tells a tale.

Goblin Market

Christina Rossetti

Morning and evening
Maids heard the goblins cry:
"Come buy our orchard fruits,
Come buy, come buy:
Apples and quinces,
Lemons and oranges,
Plump unpecked cherries,
Melons and raspberries,
Bloom-down-cheeked peaches,
Swart-headed mulberries,
Wild free-born cranberries,
Crab-apples, dewberries,
Pine-apples, blackberries,
Apricots, strawberries;—
All ripe together
In summer weather,—
Morns that pass by,
Fair eves that fly;

Come buy, come buy:
Our grapes fresh from the vine,

Pomegranates full and fine,
Dates and sharp bullaces,
Rare pears and greengages,
Damsons and bilberries,
Taste them and try:
Currants and gooseberries,
Bright-fire-like barberries,
Figs to fill your mouth,
Citrons from the South,
Sweet to tongue and sound to eye;
Come buy, come buy."

Evening by evening
Among the brookside rushes,

Laura bowed her head to hear,
Lizzie veiled her blushes:
Crouching close together
In the cooling weather,
With clasping arms and cautioning lips,
With tingling cheeks and finger tips.
"Lie close," Laura said,
Pricking up her golden head:
"We must not look at goblin men,
We must not buy their fruits:
Who knows upon what soil they fed
Their hungry thirsty roots?"
"Come buy," call the goblins
Hobbling down the glen.
"Oh," cried Lizzie, "Laura, Laura,
You should not peep at goblin men."
Lizzie covered up her eyes,
Covered close lest they should look;
Laura reared her glossy head,
And whispered like the restless brook:
"Look, Lizzie, look, Lizzie,
Down the glen tramp little men.
One hauls a basket,
One bears a plate,
One lugs a golden dish
Of many pounds weight.
How fair the vine must grow
Whose grapes are so luscious;
How warm the wind must blow
Through those fruit bushes."
"No," said Lizzie, "No, no, no;
Their offers should not charm us,
Their evil gifts would harm us."
She thrust a dimpled finger
In each ear, shut eyes and ran:
Curious Laura chose to linger
Wondering at each merchant man.
One had a cat's face,
One whisked a tail,
One tramped at a rat's pace,
One crawled like a snail,
One like a wombat prowled obtuse and
    furry,
One like a ratel tumbled hurry skurry.
She heard a voice like voice of doves
Cooing all together:

They sounded kind and full of loves
In the pleasant weather.

Laura stretched her gleaming neck
Like a rush-imbedded swan,
Like a lily from the beck,
Like a moonlit poplar branch,
Like a vessel at the launch
When its last restraint is gone.
Backwards up the mossy glen
Turned and trooped the goblin men,
With their shrill repeated cry,
"Come buy, come buy."
When they reached where Laura was
They stood stock still upon the moss,
Leering at each other,
Brother with queer brother;
Signalling each other,
Brother with sly brother.
One set his basket down,
One reared his plate;
One began to weave a crown
Of tendrils, leaves, and rough nuts brown
(Men sell not such in any town);
One heaved the golden weight
Of dish and fruit to offer her:
"Come buy, come buy," was still their cry.
Laura stared but did not stir,
Longed but had no money:
The whisk-tailed merchant bade her taste
In tones as smooth as honey,
The cat-faced purr'd,
The rat-faced spoke a word
Of welcome, and the snail-paced even was
    heard;
One parrot-voiced and jolly
Cried "Pretty Goblin" still for "Pretty
    Polly;"—
One whistled like a bird.

But sweet-tooth Laura spoke in haste:
"Good folk, I have no coin;
To take were to purloin:
I have no copper in my purse,

I have no silver either,
And all my gold is on the furze
That shakes in windy weather
Above the rusty heather."
"You have much gold upon your head,"
They answered all together:
"Buy from us with a golden curl."
She clipped a precious golden lock,
She dropped a tear more rare than pearl,
Then sucked their fruit globes fair or red:
Sweeter than honey from the rock,
Stronger than man-rejoicing wine,
Clearer than water flowed that juice;
She never tasted such before,
How should it cloy with length of use?
She sucked and sucked and sucked the more
Fruits which that unknown orchard bore;
She sucked until her lips were sore;
Then flung the emptied rinds away
But gathered up one kernel stone,
And knew not was it night or day
As she turned home alone.

Lizzie met her at the gate
Full of wise upbraidings:
"Dear, you should not stay so late,
Twilight is not good for maidens;
Should not loiter in the glen
In the haunts of goblin men.
Do you not remember Jeanie,
How she met them in the moonlight,
Took their gifts both choice and many,
Ate their fruits and wore their flowers
Plucked from bowers
Where summer ripens at all hours?
But ever in the noonlight
She pined and pined away;
Sought them by night and day,
Found them no more, but dwindled and grew
    grey;
Then fell with the first snow,
While to this day no grass will grow
Where she lies low:
I planted daisies there a year ago

That never blow.
You should not loiter so."
"Nay, hush," said Laura:
"Nay, hush, my sister:
I ate and ate my fill,
Yet my mouth waters still;
To-morrow night I will
Buy more:" and kissed her:
"Have done with sorrow;
I'll bring you plums to-morrow
Fresh on their mother twigs,
Cherries worth getting;
You cannot think what figs
My teeth have met in,
What melons icy-cold
Piled on a dish of gold
Too huge for me to hold,
What peaches with a velvet nap,
Pellucid grapes without one seed:
Odorous indeed must be the mead
Whereon they grow, and pure the wave they
    drink
With lilies at the brink,
And sugar-sweet their sap."

Golden head by golden head,
Like two pigeons in one nest
Folded in each other's wings,
They lay down in their curtained bed:
Like two blossoms on one stem,
Like two flakes of new-fall'n snow,
Like two wands of ivory
Tipped with gold for awful kings.
Moon and stars gazed in at them,
Wind sang to them lullaby,
Lumbering owls forbore to fly,
Not a bat flapped to and fro
Round their rest:
Cheek to cheek and breast to breast
Locked together in one nest.

Early in the morning
When the first cock crowed his warning,

Neat like bees, as sweet and busy,
Laura rose with Lizzie:
Fetched in honey, milked the cows,
Aired and set to rights the house,
Kneaded cakes of whitest wheat,
Cakes for dainty mouths to eat,
Next churned butter, whipped up cream,
Fed their poultry, sat and sewed;
Talked as modest maidens should:
Lizzie with an open heart,
Laura in an absent dream,
One content, one sick in part;
One warbling for the mere bright day's
    delight,
One longing for the night.

At length slow evening came:
They went with pitchers to the reedy brook;
Lizzie most placid in her look,
Laura most like a leaping flame.
They drew the gurgling water from its deep;
Lizzie plucked purple and rich golden flags,
Then turning homeward said: "The sunset
    flushes
Those furthest loftiest crags;
Come, Laura, not another maiden lags,
No wilful squirrel wags,
The beasts and birds are fast asleep."
But Laura loitered still among the rushes
And said the bank was steep.

And said the hour was early still
The dew not fall'n, the wind not chill:
Listening ever, but not catching
The customary cry,
"Come buy, come buy,"
With its iterated jingle
Of sugar-baited words:
Not for all her watching
Once discerning even one goblin
Racing, whisking, tumbling, hobbling;
Let alone the herds
That used to tramp along the glen,

In groups or single,
Of brisk fruit-merchant men.

Till Lizzie urged, "O Laura, come;
I hear the fruit-call but I dare not look:
You should not loiter longer at this brook:
Come with me home.
The stars rise, the moon bends her arc,
Each glowworm winks her spark,
Let us get home before the night grows dark:
For clouds may gather
Though this is summer weather,
Put out the lights and drench us through;
Then if we lost our way what should we do?"

Laura turned cold as stone
To find her sister heard that cry alone,
That goblin cry,
"Come buy our fruits, come buy."
Must she then buy no more such dainty fruit?
Must she no more such succous pasture find,
Gone deaf and blind?
Her tree of life drooped from the root:
She said not one word in her heart's sore ache;
But peering thro' the dimness, nought
    discerning,
Trudged home, her pitcher dripping all the way;
So crept to bed, and lay
Silent till Lizzie slept;
Then sat up in a passionate yearning,
And gnashed her teeth for baulked desire, and
    wept
As if her heart would break.

Day after day, night after night,
Laura kept watch in vain
In sullen silence of exceeding pain.
She never caught again the goblin cry:
"Come buy, come buy;"—
She never spied the goblin men
Hawking their fruits along the glen:
But when the noon waxed bright

Her hair grew thin and grey;
She dwindled, as the fair full moon doth turn
To swift decay and burn
Her fire away.

One day remembering her kernel-stone
She set it by a wall that faced the south;
Dewed it with tears, hoped for a root,
Watched for a waxing shoot,
But there came none;
It never saw the sun,
It never felt the trickling moisture run:
While with sunk eyes and faded mouth
She dreamed of melons, as a traveller sees
False waves in desert drouth
With shade of leaf-crowned trees,
And burns the thirstier in the sandful breeze.

She no more swept the house,
Tended the fowls or cows,
Fetched honey, kneaded cakes of wheat,
Brought water from the brook:
But sat down listless in the chimney-nook
And would not eat.

Tender Lizzie could not bear
To watch her sister's cankerous care
Yet not to share.
She night and morning
Caught the goblins' cry:
"Come buy our orchard fruits,
Come buy, come buy:"—
Beside the brook, along the glen,
She heard the tramp of goblin men,
The voice and stir
Poor Laura could not hear;
Longed to buy fruit to comfort her,
But feared to pay too dear.

She thought of Jeanie in her grave,
Who should have been a bride;
But who for joys brides hope to have

Fell sick and died
In her gay prime,
In earliest Winter time
With the first glazing rime,
With the first snow-fall of crisp Winter time.

Till Laura dwindling
Seemed knocking at Death's door:
Then Lizzie weighed no more
Better and worse;
But put a silver penny in her purse,
Kissed Laura, crossed the heath with clumps
    of furze
At twilight, halted by the brook:
And for the first time in her life
Began to listen and look.

Laughed every goblin
When they spied her peeping:
Came towards her hobbling,
Flying, running, leaping,
Puffing and blowing,
Chuckling, clapping, crowing,
Clucking and gobbling,
Mopping and mowing,
Full of airs and graces,
Pulling wry faces,
Demure grimaces,
Cat-like and rat-like,
Ratel- and wombat-like,
Snail-paced in a hurry,
Parrot-voiced and whistler,
Helter skelter, hurry skurry,
Chattering like magpies,
Fluttering like pigeons,
Gliding like fishes,—
Hugged her and kissed her:
Squeezed and caressed her:
Stretched up their dishes,
Panniers, and plates:
"Look at our apples
Russet and dun,
Bob at our cherries,
Bite at our peaches,

Citrons and dates,
Grapes for the asking,
Pears red with basking
Out in the sun,
Plums on their twigs;
Pluck them and suck them,
Pomegranates, figs."—

"Good folk," said Lizzie,
Mindful of Jeanie:
"Give me much and many?"—
Held out her apron,
Tossed them her penny.
"Nay, take a seat with us,
Honour and eat with us,"
They answered grinning:
"Our feast is but beginning.
Night yet is early,
Warm and dew-pearly,
Wakeful and starry:
Such fruits as these
No man can carry;
Half their bloom would fly,
Half their dew would dry,
Half their flavour would pass by.
Sit down and feast with us,
Be welcome guest with us,
Cheer you and rest with us."—
"Thank you," said Lizzie: "But one waits
At home alone for me:
So without further parleying,
If you will not sell me any
Of your fruits though much and many,
Give me back my silver penny
I tossed you for a fee."—
They began to scratch their pates,
No longer wagging, purring,
But visibly demurring,
Grunting and snarling.
One called her proud,
Cross-grained, uncivil;
Their tones waxed loud,
Their looks were evil.
Lashing their tails
They trod and hustled her,

Elbowed and jostled her,
Clawed with their nails,
Barking, mewing, hissing, mocking,
Tore her gown and soiled her stocking,
Twitched her hair out by the roots,
Stamped upon her tender feet,
Held her hands and squeezed their fruits
Against her mouth to make her eat.

White and golden Lizzie stood,
Like a lily in a flood,—
Like a rock of blue-veined stone
Lashed by tides obstreperously,—
Like a beacon left alone
In a hoary roaring sea,
Sending up a golden fire,—
Like a fruit-crowned orange-tree
White with blossoms honey-sweet
Sore beset by wasp and bee,—
Like a royal virgin town
Topped with gilded dome and spire
Close beleaguered by a fleet
Mad to tug her standard down.

One may lead a horse to water,
Twenty cannot make him drink.
Though the goblins cuffed and caught her,
Coaxed and fought her,
Bullied and besought her,
Scratched her, pinched her black as ink,
Kicked and knocked her,
Mauled and mocked her,
Lizzie uttered not a word;
Would not open lip from lip
Lest they should cram a mouthful in:
But laughed in heart to feel the drip
Of juice that syrupped all her face,
And lodged in dimples of her chin,
And streaked her neck which quaked like curd.
At last the evil people,
Worn out by her resistance,
Flung back her penny, kicked their fruit
Along whichever road they took,
Not leaving root or stone or shoot;

Some writhed into the ground,
Some dived into the brook
With ring and ripple,
Some scudded on the gale without a sound,
Some vanished in the distance.

In a smart, ache, tingle,
Lizzie went her way;
Knew not was it night or day;
Sprang up the bank, tore thro' the furze,
Threaded copse and dingle,
And heard her penny jingle
Bouncing in her purse,—
Its bounce was music to her ear.
She ran and ran
As if she feared some goblin man
Dogged her with gibe or curse
Or something worse:
But not one goblin skurried after,
Nor was she pricked by fear;
The kind heart made her windy-paced
That urged her home quite out of breath with
    haste
And inward laughter.

She cried "Laura," up the garden,
"Did you miss me?
Come and kiss me.
Never mind my bruises,
Hug me, kiss me, suck my juices
Squeezed from goblin fruits for you,
Goblin pulp and goblin dew.
Eat me, drink me, love me;
Laura, make much of me:
For your sake I have braved the glen
And had to do with goblin merchant men."

Laura started from her chair,
Flung her arms up in the air,
Clutched her hair:
"Lizzie, Lizzie, have you tasted
For my sake the fruit forbidden?
Must your light like mine be hidden,

Your young life like mine be wasted,
Undone in mine undoing,
And ruined in my ruin,
Thirsty, cankered, goblin-ridden?"—
She clung about her sister,
Kissed and kissed and kissed her:
Tears once again
Refreshed her shrunken eyes,
Dropping like rain
After long sultry drouth;
Shaking with anguish, fear, and pain,
She kissed and kissed her with a hungry mouth.

Her lips began to scorch,
That juice was wormwood to her tongue,
She loathed the feast:
Writhing as one possessed she leaped and sung,
Rent all her robe, and wrung
Her hands in lamentable haste,
And beat her breast.
Her locks streamed like the torch
Borne by a racer at full speed,
Or like the mane of horses in their flight,
Or like an eagle when she stems the light
Straight toward the sun,
Or like a caged thing freed,
Or like a flying flag when armies run.

Swift fire spread through her veins, knocked at
    her heart,
Met the fire smouldering there
And overbore its lesser flame;
She gorged on bitterness without a name:
Ah! fool, to choose such part
Of soul-consuming care!
Sense failed in the mortal strife:
Like the watch-tower of a town
Which an earthquake shatters down,
Like a lightning-stricken mast,
Like a wind-uprooted tree
Spun about,
Like a foam-topped waterspout
Cast down headlong in the sea,
She fell at last;

Pleasure past and anguish past,
Is it death or is it life?

Life out of death.
That night long Lizzie watched by her,
Counted her pulse's flagging stir,
Felt for her breath,
Held water to her lips, and cooled her face
With tears and fanning leaves:
But when the first birds chirped about their
     eaves,
And early reapers plodded to the place
Of golden sheaves,
And dew-wet grass
Bowed in the morning winds so brisk to pass,
And new buds with new day
Opened of cup-like lilies on the stream,
Laura awoke as from a dream,
Laughed in the innocent old way,
Hugged Lizzie but not twice or thrice;
Her gleaming locks showed not one thread of
     grey,
Her breath was sweet as May
And light danced in her eyes.

Days, weeks, months, years
Afterwards, when both were wives
With children of their own;
Their mother-hearts beset with fears,
Their lives bound up in tender lives;
Laura would call the little ones
And tell them of her early prime,
Those pleasant days long gone
Of not-returning time:
Would talk about the haunted glen,
The wicked, quaint fruit-merchant men,
Their fruits like honey to the throat
But poison in the blood;
(Men sell not such in any town:)
Would tell them how her sister stood
In deadly peril to do her good,
And win the fiery antidote:
Then joining hands to little hands
Would bid them cling together,
"For there is no friend like a sister
In calm or stormy weather;
To cheer one on the tedious way,
To fetch one if one goes astray,
To lift one if one totters down,
To strengthen whilst one stands."

Hans Christian Andersen (1805–1875) was a Danish writer primarily known for his fairy tales, such as "The Princess and the Pea" (1835) and "The Emperor's New Suit" (1837), but he also wrote *The Mulatto* (1840), a play portraying the evils of slavery. In 1829, Andersen self-published a tale inspired by E. T. A. Hoffmann entitled "A Walk From Holmen's Canal to the East Point of the Island of Amager in the Years 1828 and 1829"; it became his first major success. Andersen used the vernacular, which was unheard of in his day, and combined his unique imagination with folklore to tell stories that both children and adults could enjoy—which may be why he remains one of the most translated writers of all time. "The Will-o'-the-Wisps Are in Town" (1865) is among the most unusual of his fantasy tales in that it is entertaining but also a commentary on such tales.

The Will-o'-the-Wisps Are in Town

Hans Christian Andersen

Translated by H. P. Paull

THERE WAS A MAN who once had known a great many new fairy tales, but he had forgotten them, he said. The fairy tale that used to come to visit him no longer came and knocked at his door; and why didn't it come any more? It's true that for a year and a day the man hadn't thought of it, hadn't really expected it to come and knock; and it certainly wouldn't have come anyway, for outside there was war and, inside, the misery and sorrow that war brings with it.

The stork and the swallow returned from their long journey, for they had no thought of danger. But when they arrived they found the nests burned, people's houses burned, the fences smashed, yes, and some even completely gone, and horses of the enemy were trampling down the old grave mounds. Those were hard, cruel times; but they always come to an end.

And now those times were past, people said; but still no fairy tale came to knock at the door or gave any sign of its presence.

"It may well be dead and gone, like so many other things," said the man. But then the fairy tale never dies!

More than a year passed, and he longed so for the fairy tale.

"I wonder if it will ever come back and knock again." And he remembered so vividly all the various forms in which it had come to him—sometimes as young and charming as spring itself, as a beautiful maiden with a thyme wreath in her hair and a birch branch in her hand, her eyes shining as clear as the deep woodland lakes in the bright sunshine. Sometimes the fairy tale had come to him in the likeness of a peddler and had opened its pack and let the silver ribbons inscribed with old verses flutter out. But it had been best of all when it had come as an old grandmother, with silvery hair and such large and kindly eyes. She knew so well the tales of the old, old times, of even long before the princesses spun with golden spindles, and the dragons, the serpents, lay outside, guarding them. She told her tales so vividly that black spots would dance before the eyes of her listeners and the floor become black with human blood; it was terrible to see and to hear, and yet very entertaining, since it had all happened so long ago.

"Will she ever knock at my door again?" said the man, and gazed at the door until black spots appeared before his eyes and on the floor, and he didn't know if it was blood or mourning crape from the dark and dismal days of yore.

As he sat there, the thought came to him that perhaps the fairy tale had hidden itself, like the princess in the very old tale, and if he should now go in search of it, and find it, it would shine in new splendor, lovelier than ever. "Who knows? Perhaps it is hidden in the discarded straw lying near the edge of the well. Careful, careful! Perhaps it's hidden in a faded flower, shut up in one of the big books on the shelf!"

So the man went to one of the newest books and opened it to find out, but there was no flower there. It was a book about Holger Danske, and the man read how the whole story had been invented and put together by a French monk, that it was only a romance, "translated and printed in the Danish language," and that since Holger Danske had never really lived he could never come again, as we have sung and wanted to believe. As with Holger Danske, so it was with William Tell; both were only popular legends, nothing we could depend on. Here it was all written down in a very learned manner.

"Yes, but I shall believe my own beliefs," said the man. "No road grows where no foot has trod!"

So he closed the book, put it back on the shelf, and walked over to the fresh flowers on the window sill; perhaps the fairy tale had hidden itself in the red tulips with the golden-yellow edges, or in the fresh roses, or in the brilliantly colored camellias. But only sunshine lay among the flowers—no fairy tale.

"The flowers which grew here in the days of misery were much more beautiful; but one after another was cut off, woven into wreaths, and laid in coffins, with the flag placed over them. Perhaps the fairy tale was buried with them; but then the flowers would have known of it, and the coffin would have heard of it, and every little blade of grass that shot up would have told of it. The fairy tale never dies!

"Maybe it was here and knocked, but who had ears for it or would have thought of it? Then people looked darkly, gloomily, almost angrily, at the spring sunshine, the singing birds, and all the cheerful greenery; yes, and their tongues wouldn't even repeat the merry old folk songs, and they were laid in the coffin with so much else that our heart cherished. The fairy tale may well have knocked but not been heard, and with no one to bid it welcome, it may have departed.

"I shall go out and search for it! In the country, in the woods, on the open beaches."

Out in the country stands an old manor house with red walls, pointed gables, and a flag waving from the tower. The nightingale sings under the fringed beech leaves while it gazes at the blooming apple trees in the garden and thinks they are rose trees. Here the bees labor busily in the summertime, hovering around their queen with humming song. Here the autumn storm tells much of the wild chase, of the falling leaves, and of the generations of men that pass away. At Christmastime the wild swans sing on the open water, while in the old manor house the guests beside the fire are happy to hear the ancient songs and legends.

Down into the old part of the garden, where the great avenue of old chestnut trees invites the wanderer to pause in their shade, went the man who was seeking the fairy tale. Here the wind had once told him of "Valdemar Daae and His Daughters"; here the dryad in the tree—the fairy-tale mother herself—had told him "The Old Oak Tree's Last Dream." In our grandmother's time clipped hedges stood here; now there grow only ferns and stinging nettles, hiding the broken fragments of old figures sculptured in stone; moss grows in their very eyes, but still they can see as well as ever, which the man seeking the fairy tale couldn't, for he didn't see it. Where could it be?

Hundreds of crows flew over him and the old trees, crying, "Caw! Caw!"

Then he left the garden and crossed the rampart surrounding the manor, into the alder grove. There a little six-sided house stands, with a poultry yard and a duck yard. In the midst of the living room in the house sat the old woman who managed everything and who knew exactly when every egg would be laid and when each chicken would creep out of its egg. But she wasn't the fairy tale the man was seeking; she could prove that with the certificates of Christian baptism and vaccination that she kept in her chest of drawers.

Outside, not far from the house, there is a hill covered with red thorn and broom; here lies an old gravestone, brought here many years ago from the churchyard of the near-by town in memory of one of the most honored councilmen of the neighborhood. Carved in stone, his wife and five daughters, all with folded hands and stiff ruffs, stand about him. If you looked at them for a long time it would affect your thoughts, which in turn would react on the stone, so that it would seem to tell of olden times. At least that was the way it had been with the man who was searching for the fairy tale.

As he approached, he noticed a living butterfly sitting right on the forehead of the sculptured councilman. The insect flapped its wings, flew a little bit away, then returned to sit close by the gravestone, as if to call attention to what was growing there. Four-leaved clovers grew there, seven in all, side by side. When good luck comes, it comes in bunches. The man plucked all the clovers and put them into his pocket. "Good luck is as good as ready cash," thought the man, "though a new, beautiful fairy tale would be better still." But he could find none here.

The sun went down, big and red, and vapor rose from the meadow; the Bog Witch was at her brewing.

That evening the man stood alone in his room, gazing out upon the sea, over the meadow, moor, and beach. The moon shone brightly; the mist over the meadow made it look like a great lake; indeed, legend tells us it once was a lake, and in the moonlight the eye can understand these myths.

Then the man thought of how he had been reading that Holger Danske and William Tell never really lived; yet they do live in the faith of the people, just like the lake out there, living evidence of the myth. Yes, Holger Danske will return again!

As he stood thinking, something struck heavily against the window. Was it a bird, an owl or a bat? We don't let those creatures in even when they knock. But the window burst open by itself, and an old woman looked in on the man.

"What is this?" he said. "What do you want? Who are you? Why, she's looking in at the second-floor window! Is she standing on a ladder?"

"You have a four-leaved clover in your pocket," she replied. "Or rather you have seven, but one of them has six leaves."

"Who are you?" asked the man.

"I am the Bog Witch," she said, "the Bog Witch who brews. I was busy at my brewing. The tap was in the cask, but one of those mischievous little marsh imps pulled it out and threw it over here, where it hit your window. Now the beer's running out of the barrel, and nobody can make money that way!"

"Please tell me—" said the man.

"Yes, but wait a little," said the Bog Witch. "I have something else to do right now." Then she was gone.

But as the man was about to close the window, she stood before him again.

"Now it's fixed," she said, "but I'll have to brew half the beer over again tomorrow, that is, if it's good weather. Well, what did you want to know? I came back, for I always keep my word, and besides, you have seven four-leaved clovers in your pocket, one of which has six leaves; that demands respect, for that type grows beside the roadside, and not many people find them. What did you want to ask me? Don't stand there looking foolish; I have to go back to my tap and my barrel very quickly."

Then the man asked her about the fairy tale, and if she had met it in her journeys. "For the love of my big brewing vat!" said the Bog Witch. "Haven't you told enough fairy tales? I certainly think most people have had enough of them. There are plenty of other things for you to do and take care of. Even the children have outgrown fairy tales! Give the small boys a cigar, and the little girls a new dress; they'll like that much better. But listen to fairy tales! No, indeed, there are certainly other things to attend to, more important things to do!"

"What do you mean?" the man asked. "And what do you know about the world? You never see anything but frogs and Will-o'-the-Wisps!"

"Beware of the Will-o'-the-Wisps!" said the Bog Witch. "They're out—they're on the loose! That's what we should talk about! Come to me at the marsh, for I must go there now; there I'll tell you about it. But you must hurry and come while your seven four-leaved clovers, one of them with six leaves, are still fresh and the moon is still high!"

And the Bog Witch was gone.

The town clock struck twelve, and before the last stroke had died away the man had left the house, crossed the garden, and stood in the meadow. The mist had cleared away; the Bog Witch had finished her brewing. "You took your time getting here!" said the woman. "Witches move much faster than men; I'm glad I'm a witch."

"What do you have to tell me now?" asked the man. "Anything about the fairy tale?"

"Is that all you can ever ask about?" said the woman.

"Is it something about the poetry of the future that you can tell me?"

"Don't become impatient," said the woman, "and I'll answer you. You now think only of poetry. You ask about the fairy tale as if she were the mistress of everything. She's the oldest, all right, but she always passes for the youngest; I know her very well. I was young once, and that's no children's disease! Once I was quite a pretty little elf maiden, and I danced with the others in the moonlight, listened to the nightingale, went into the forest, and met the fairy tale maiden there, where she was always running about. Sometimes she spent the night in a half-opened tulip or in some field flower; sometimes she would slip into the church and wrap herself in the mourning crape that hung down from the altar candles."

"You seem to know all about it," said the man.

"I should at least know as much as *you* do," said the Bog Witch. "Fairy tales and poetry— yes, they're like two pieces of the same material. They can go and lie where they wish. One can brew all their talk and goings-on and have it better and cheaper. I'll give it to you for nothing; I have a whole cabinet full of bottles of poetry, the essences, the best of it—both sweet and bitter herbs. I have all the poetry people might want, bottled up, and on holidays I put a little on my handkerchief to smell."

"Why, these are wonderful things you're telling me!" said the man. "You actually have poetry in bottles?"

"More than you can stand," said the woman. "I suppose you know the story of 'The Girl Who Trod on the Loaf,' so that she would not soil her shoes. That has been written down and printed, too."

"I told that story myself," said the man.

"Yes, then you know it, and you know, too, that the girl sank right into the earth, to the Bog Witch, just as the Devil's grandmother was there on a visit to inspect the brewery. She saw the girl come down and asked to have her as a souvenir of her visit, and she got her, too. I received a present from her which is of no good to me—a regular traveling drugstore, a whole cabinet full of bottled poetry. The grandmother told me where to put the cabinet, and it's still there. Now look here! You have your seven four-leaved clovers in your pocket, one of which has six leaves, so you should be able to see it!"

Sure enough, in the middle of the marsh was what looked like a great gnarled alder block, and that was the grandmother's cabinet. She explained that it was open to her and to everyone else in the world at any time, if they just knew where it was. It could be opened in front or at the back and at every side and corner; it was a real work of art and yet appeared to be only an alder stump. Poets of all countries, and especially of our own land, had been reproduced here; the essence of each had been extracted, refined, criticized, distilled, and then put into bottles. With great skill—as it's called, if one doesn't want to call it genius—the grandmother had taken a little of this poet and a little of that, added a touch of deviltry, and then corked up the bottles for the use of future ages.

"Please let me see," said the man.

"All right, but there are much more important things to listen to," said the Bog Witch.

"But we're right here at the cabinet," said the man, as he looked inside it. "Why, here are bottles of all sizes. What's in this one, and what's in that one over there?"

"This is what they call may-balm," said the woman. "I haven't tried it myself, but I know that if you spill only a little drop of it on the floor, you will see before you a lovely forest lake with water lilies, flowering rushes, and wild mint. You need pour only two drops on an old exercise book, even one from the lowest class in school, and the book becomes a complete, fragrant play that is good enough to be performed and to fall asleep over, so strong is its smell. It must be as a compliment to me that they labeled the bottle 'The Brew of the Bog Witch.'

"Here stands the bottle of scandal. It looks as if there is only dirty water in it, and, of course, it *is* dirty water, but with sparkling powder, three ounces of lies, and two grains of truth, stirred with a birch twig, not taken from a stalk pickled in salt and used on the bleeding backs of sinners, nor a piece of the schoolmaster's switch—no, but taken right from the broom that had been used to sweep the gutter.

"Here stands the bottle with the pious poetry set to psalm music. Every drop has a sound like the slamming of hell's gates and has been made from the blood and sweat of punishment. Some say it's only the gall of a dove; but doves are the gentlest of animals; they have no gall, say people who don't know their natural history.

"Here stood the bottle of all bottles; it took up half of the cabinet. It was the bottle with 'Stories of Everyday Life,' and it was covered with both hog skin and bladder so that it couldn't lose any of its strength. Every nation could get its own soup here; what would come forth would depend upon how you'd turn and tip the bottle. Here was an old German blood soup with robber dumplings, and there was also thin peasant soup, with genuine court officials, who lay like vegetables on the bottom, while fat, philosophical eyes floated on the top. There was English-governess soup, and French *potage à la coq*, made from chicken legs and sparrow eggs and, in Danish, called 'cancan soup.' But the best of all soups was Copenhagen soup; the whole family said so."

Here stood "Tragedy," in a champagne bottle; it could make a popping noise, and that was as it should be. "Comedy" looked like fine sand to throw into people's eyes—that is, the more refined comedy; the broader kind was also bottled, but consisted only of future playbills; there were some excellent comedy titles, such as, *Dare You Spit in the Machinery?*, *One on the Jaw*, *The Sweet Donkey!*

While the man was completely lost in his thoughts, the Bog Witch wanted to put an end to this.

"By now you must have seen enough of the hodgepodge chest," she said. "You know what it is now. But I haven't told you the important thing you must know. The Will-o'-the-Wisps are in town! That's much more important than poetry or fairy tales. I really should keep my mouth shut about it, but it seems that a compulsion—a force—something has come over me, and it sticks in my throat and wants to come out. The Will-o'-the-Wisps are in town! They are on the loose! Take care, you mortals!"

"I don't understand a word you're saying!" said the man.

"Please sit down on the cabinet," she said, "but be careful not to fall through and break the bottles—you know what's inside them. I'll tell you about the great event. It happened only yesterday; yet it has happened before. And now it has three hundred and sixty-four days to go. I suppose you know how many days there are in a year?"

And this was the story of the Bog Witch:

"There was a great commotion yesterday out here in the marsh! There was a christening feast! A little Will-o'-the-Wisp was born here; in fact, twelve of them were born all at once. And they have permission to go out among men, if they want to, and move around and command, just as if they were human beings! That was a great event in the marsh, and for that reason all Will-o'-the-Wisps, male and female, danced across the marsh and the meadow like little lights. Some of them are of the dog species, but they aren't worth talking about. I sat right there on my cabinet and held all the twelve little newborn Will-o'-the-Wisps on my lap. They glittered like glow-worms; already they had begun to hop, and they grew bigger every minute, and after a quarter of an hour each of them was as big as his father or uncle. Now it's an old-established law that when the moon stands just where it did yesterday, and the wind blows just the way it blew yesterday, it is granted to all Will-o'-the-Wisps born at that hour and at that minute that they may become human beings and each of them exercise their power for a whole year.

"The Will-o'-the-Wisp can go about in the country, or anywhere in the world, as long as it is not afraid of falling into the sea or being blown away by a great storm. It can go right into a person, and speak for him, and perform any action it wants. The Will-o'-the-Wisp can take any form it likes, man or woman, and act in his or her spirit, and so go to the extreme in doing what it wishes. But in the course of that year it must succeed in leading three hundred and sixty-five people into bad paths, and in grand style, too; it must lead them away from the right and truth, and then it will receive the highest honor a Will-o'-the-Wisp can, that of being a runner before the Devil's stagecoach; it can then wear a fiery yellow uniform and breathe flames from its mouth. That's enough to make a simple Will-o'-the-Wisp lick his lips in desire. But there's danger, too, and a lot of work for an ambitious Will-o'-the-Wisp who wants to reach that height. If the eyes of the person are opened and he realizes what is happening and can blow the Will-o'-the-Wisp away, it is done for and has to come back to the marsh. Or if, before the year is over, the Will-o'-the-Wisp is overcome with longing for its home and family, and so gives up and comes back, then it is also done for; it can't burn clearly any longer, and soon goes out, and can't be lighted again. And if, at the end of the year, it hasn't led three hundred and sixty-five people away from the truth and all that's fine and noble, it is condemned to lie in a rotten stump and shine without being able to move. That's the worst punishment of all for a lively Will-o'-the-Wisp.

"Now, I know all about this, and I told it all to the twelve little ones that I held on my lap, and they were quite wild with joy. I warned them that the safest and easiest way would be to give up the honor and just do nothing at all, but the little flames wouldn't listen to that; already they could imagine themselves dressed in fiery yellow uniforms, breathing flames from their mouths.

"'Stay here with us!' said some of the older ones.

"'Go and have your fun with the mortals!' others said.

"'Yes, they are draining our meadows and drying them up! What will become of our descendants?'

"'We want to flame with flames!' said the new-born Will-o'-the-Wisps, and that settled it.

"Then presently began the minute ball, which couldn't have been any shorter. The elf maidens whirled around three times with all the others, so as not to appear proud, but they always preferred dancing with each other. Then the godparents' gifts were given—'throwing pebbles,' it's called. The 'pebbles' were flung over the marsh water. Each of the elf maidens gave a little piece of her veil.

"'Take that,' they said, 'and you'll be able to do the highest dance, the most difficult turns and twists—that is, if you should ever need to. You'll have the best manners, so you can show your-selves in the highest of society.'

"The night raven taught the young Will-o'-the-Wisps to say, 'Goo-goo-good!' and to say it at the right times; and that's a great gift that brings its own reward.

"The owl and the stork dropped their gifts. But they said these weren't worth mentioning, and so we won't talk about it.

"The wild hunt of King Valdemar was just then rushing across the marsh, and when the nobles heard of the celebration they sent as a present a couple of handsome dogs which could hunt with the speed of the wind and carry a Will-o'-the-Wisp, or three, on their backs. A couple of old witches, who make a living riding broomsticks, were at the party, and they taught the young Will o'-the-Wisps how to slip through any keyhole as if the door stood open to them. These witches offered to carry the young ones to the town, which they knew quite well. They usually rode through the air on their own back hair fastened into a knot, for they prefer a hard seat. But now they sat on the hunting dogs and took on their laps the young Will-o'-the-Wisps, who were ready to go into town to start mislead-ing and bewildering human beings. Whiz! and they were gone!

"That's what happened last night. Today the Will-o'-the-Wisps are in town and have started to work—but how, and where? Can you tell me that?

Still, I have a lightning conductor in my big toe, and that always tells me something."

"That's a whole fairy tale!" said the man.

"Why, it's just the beginning of one," said the woman. "Can you tell me how the Will-o'-the-Wisps are behaving themselves and what they're doing, in what shapes they're appearing and lead-ing people astray?"

"I believe," said the man, "that one could tell quite a romance about the Will-o'-the-Wisps, in twelve parts; or better still, a complete comedy-drama could be written about them."

"You should write it," said the woman. "Or perhaps you'd better leave it undone."

"Yes, that's easier, and more pleasant," said the man. "Then we'll not be condemned by the newspapers, which is just as bad as it is for a Will-o'-the-Wisp to be shut in a rotten stump, shining, and afraid to say anything."

"It doesn't matter to me what you do," said the woman. "Let the others write, if they can, or even if they can't. I'll give you an old tap from my cask; that will open the cabinet where I keep the poetry in bottles, and you can take anything you want. But you, my good man, seem to have stained your fingers enough with ink, and at the age and stability you have reached, you don't have to be running around every year looking for fairy tales, especially as there are much more important things to be done. Have you under-stood what's happening?"

"The Will-o'-the-Wisps are in town," said the man. "I heard you, and I understand. But what do you think I ought to do about it? I'd be locked up if I were to go up to people and say, 'Look! There goes a Will-o'-the-Wisp in honest clothes!'"

"Sometimes they wear skirts!" said the woman. "The Will-o'-the-Wisp can take on any form and appear anywhere. It goes into the church, not for the sake of our Lord, but perhaps so that it can enter the minister. It speaks on election day, not for the good of state or coun-try, but only for itself. It is an artist with the paint pot, and in the theater, but when it gets complete power, then the pot's empty! Here I go, chattering on, but what's sticking in my throat must come out, even if it hurts my own family. But now I must be the woman to save a lot of people. But, truthfully, I'm not doing it with good intentions or for the sake of any medal. I do the most insane thing I possibly can; I tell a poet about it, and soon everybody in town gets to know about it."

"The town won't take it to heart," said the man. "It won't disturb a single person. They'll all think I'm only telling them a fairy tale if I say, 'The Will-o'-the-Wisps are in town, said the Bog Witch! Beware!'"

Aleksis Stenvall (1834–1872), more commonly known as Aleksis Kivi, was a Finnish novelist and poet who was often called the father of the Finnish novel, thanks to his *Seven Brothers* (1870). His imagination grew from a love of reading and can be seen in all his works, especially *Seven Brothers*. It was the first novel written in the Finnish language and is an adventure story full of romantic humor. Kivi's play *The Heath Cobblers* (1864) was also a noteworthy addition to the literary archive. In 1865, it was awarded the biggest literary prize in Finland and remains the most frequently produced play ever written in Finnish. Kivi had a magnificent sense of both tragedy and comedy. The novel *Seven Brothers* includes elements of both lyric and myth, and the excerpt published in this volume showcases that talent eloquently.

The Legend of the Pale Maiden

(EXCERPT FROM *SEVEN BROTHERS*)

Aleksis Kivi

Translated by David Hackston

Simeoni: Listen to the hoot of the eagle owl in the wilds—his hooting never foretells of good. Old folk say it bodes of fires, bloody battles and murders.

Tuomas: It is his job to hoot in the forest and it bodes nothing at all.

Eero: But this is the village; the turf-roofed house of Impivaara.

Simeoni: And now the seer has moved; look, there he hoots upon the mountain ridge. That is where, as legend tells us, the Pale Maiden prayed for the forgiveness of her sins; there she prayed every night in winter and in summer.

Juhani: This maiden gave Impivaara its name. I once heard this story as a child, but I fear it has mostly faded from my mind. Brother Aapo, tell us this tale to while away this sorry night.

Aapo: Timo is already snoring like a man; but let him lie in peace. I will gladly tell you this tale.

And thus Aapo recounted to his brothers the legend of the Pale Maiden:

In the caves beneath the mountain there once lived a terrible troll, bringing horror and death to many. Only two passions and pleasures did he have: to see and behold his treasures hidden deep within the mountain caves and to drink human blood, which he craved fervently. But only nine paces from the foot of the mountain did he have the strength to overpower his victims, and thus it was with stealth that he undertook his journeys into the woods. He could change his form at will; he could often be seen roaming these parts, sometimes as a handsome young man, sometimes as an enchanting maiden, depending on whether it was the blood of a man or a woman he craved. Many were ensnared by the demonic beauty of his eyes; many lost their lives in his abominable caves. In this manner did the monster lure his hapless victims into his lair.

It was a fine summer's night. Upon a green meadow there sat a youth holding in his arms a young woman, his beloved, who like a resplendent rose rested upon his breast. This was to be their final farewell, for the boy was to travel far away and leave his bosom friend for a time. "My love," spoke the young man, "I must leave you now, but barely shall a hundred suns rise and set before we meet again." And to this the maiden replied: "Not even the sun as it sets looks with such fondness upon its world as I upon my beloved as we part, nor as it rises does the blazing sky shine as gloriously as will my eyes as I run to meet you. And all that will fill my soul each bright day until then is the image of you, and through the mists of my dreams shall I walk beside you always."— Thus spoke the girl, but then the young man said: "You speak beautifully indeed, yet why does my soul sense evil? Fair maiden, let us swear eternal fidelity to one another, here beneath the face of heaven." And thus they swore a holy vow, sworn before God and the heavens, and the forest and the hillside listened, breathless, to their every word. Yet alas as day broke they embraced each other one last time and parted. The young man hastened away, but for a long time the maiden wandered through the forest twilight, thinking only of her handsome beloved.

And there as she wanders deep amongst the thick pine woods, what strange figure is this she sees approaching? She sees a young man, noble as a prince and as resplendent as the golden morning. The plume upon his hat shines and flickers like a flame. From his shoulders hangs a cloak, blue as the sky and like the sky lit with sparkling stars. His tunic is white as snow and around his waist is tied a purple belt. He looks towards the maiden and in his eyes a burning love smoulders, and most divine is the note in his voice as he says to the young lady: "Fear not, fair maiden; why, I am your friend and can bring you unending happiness, if but once I may take you into my arms. I am a powerful man, I have treasures and precious stones beyond number—I could buy the whole world, if I so wished. Follow me as my beloved and I shall take you to my wonderful castle and place you by my side upon a glorious throne." Thus spoke the man in a charming voice and the maiden stood in awe. She remembered the vow she had just sworn and turned away, but soon turned back towards the man once again, and a peculiar worry filled her mind. She turned towards the man, covering her face as if looking into the glaring sun; again she turned away, but glanced once more at the strange figure. His powerful charm beamed upon her, and all at once she fell into the arms of the handsome prince. Off sped the prince, his prey lying spellbound in his arms. Over steep hills, through deep dales they travelled, and the forest around them became ever darker. The maiden's heart throbbed restlessly and drops of pained sweat ran down her brow, for suddenly she saw something beastly, something terrifying amidst the captivating flames in the man's eyes. She looked around as thick spruce groves flew past as her bearer dashed on apace; she glanced at the man's face and she felt a terrible trembling throughout her body, yet still a strange attraction burned in her heart.

Onwards they travelled through the forest until finally they could see the great mountain and its dark caves. And now, as they were but a few paces from the foot of the mountain, something horrible took place. The man in his regal cloak turned suddenly into a terrible troll: horns burst forth upon his head, his neck began to bristle with thick hair, and the forlorn girl could feel the sting of his sharp claws in her breast; and thereupon the maiden began to shout, to struggle and kick in frantic agony, but all in vain. With a wicked cry of joy the troll dragged her deep into his cave and drank every last drop of her blood. But then a miracle occurred: her spirit did not leave the maiden's limbs, and she remained alive, bloodless and snow-white; a plaintive ghost from the realm of shadows. The troll saw this and, thus vexed, lashed out at his victim with his claws and teeth, with all his might, but still he could not bring death upon her. Finally he decided to keep her for himself, deep in the eternal night of his caves. But what service could she perform for him, what use could she have for the troll? He commanded the maiden to polish all his treasures and precious stones and to pile them endlessly in front of him, for never did he tire of admiring them.

And so for years this pale, bloodless maiden lives imprisoned in the mountain's womb. Yet by night she can be seen quietly praying high upon the ridge. Who could have given her such freedom? The power of the heavens?—But every night, come storm, rain or hard frost, she stands atop the mountain praying for the forgiveness of her sins. Bloodless, snow-white and like a picture, so motionless and silently she stands, her hands crossed upon her breast and her head bowed deeply. Not once does the poor maiden dare raise her head towards the heavens, for her gaze is fixed upon the church spire, far away at the edge of the forest. For always in her ear there whispers a voice of hope; though nothing more than a distant murmur across thousands of leagues, she catches a glimpse of this hope. And thus she spends her nights upon the mountain ridge, and never can a word of complaint be heard from her lips; nor does her praying breast rise or fall with sighs. And thus the dark nights pass, but come daybreak the ruthless troll drags her back into his caves.

Barely had a hundred suns shone upon the earth when the young man, the maiden's beloved, jubilantly returned home from his journey. But alas his fair maiden did not rush towards him to welcome him home. He enquired where his beauty may be, but not a soul knew of her whereabouts. He searched for her everywhere, every day and night, tirelessly, but in vain: like the morning dew the maiden had disappeared without a trace. At last he lost all hope, forgot all the joys of life and for many years he wandered these hills as a silent shadow. Finally, as another shining day broke, the endless night of death extinguished the light from his eyes.

Frightfully long were the years for the pale maiden: by day polishing incessantly the troll's treasures under the gaze of her cruel tormentor and piling them before his eyes; by night atop the mountain ridge. Bloodless, snow-white and like a picture, so motionless and silently she stands, her hands upon her breast and her head bowed deeply. Not once does she dare raise her head towards the heavens, for her gaze is fixed upon the church spire, far away at the edge of the forest. Never does she complain; never does her praying breast rise or fall with sighs.

It is a light summer's night. On the mountain ridge stands the maiden, remembering the agonising time she has spent in captivity; a hundred years have passed since the day she parted from her betrothed. Horrified, she swoons and cold pearls of sweat run from her brow down to the mossy soil at the foot of the mountain as she thinks of the terrible length of those bygone decades. At that moment she felt the courage, for the first time, to look up to the heavens, and a moment later she discerned a blinding light approaching her like a shooting star from the furthest outreaches of space. And the closer to her this light came, the more it began to change its form. This was no shooting star; it was the young man, transfigured, a flashing sword in his hand. And with that the maiden's heart began to beat feverishly, as the wonderful familiarity of that face dawned upon her; for now she recognised the face of her former groom. But why was he approaching with a sword in his hand? The maiden was vexed and said in a weak voice: "Will this sword finally end my pain? Here is my breast, young hero, strike your shining blade here and, if you can, bring me death, which for so long I have yearned after." Thus she spoke on the mountain ridge, but the young man did not bring her death, but the sweet breath of life, which like a fragrant, whispering morning breeze enveloped the pale maiden. The young man, his eyes filled with love, took her in his arms and kissed her, and at this the bloodless maiden felt the sweet ripple of blood running once again through her veins, her cheeks glowed like clouds at the glorious break of day and her fair brow brimmed with joy. And with that she threw her head of fine locks across her beloved's arm and looked up to the bright heavens, her breast sighing away the suffering of the bygone years; and the young man ran his fingers through her locks as they swayed gently in the breeze. How wonderful was the hour of her salvation and the morning of her deliverance! The birds chirped in the spruce trees along the sides of that steep mountain and from the north-east shone the first radiant sliver of the rising sun. This morning was indeed worthy of the morning the couple parted on the green meadow for so long a time.

But then the angry troll, his tail on end with rage, climbed up the mountain to drag the maiden back into his caverns. But no sooner had he bared his claws at the maiden than the young man's sword like lightning struck his breast, whereupon his black blood spurted across the mountain. The maiden turned her face away from this sight and pressed her brow into her beloved's breast, as shrieking wildly the troll breathed his last and plummeted down the mountainside. And so it was that the world was saved from this terrible monster. And upon the bright edge of a silver cloud the young man and the maiden rose up to the heavens. The bride rested upon the knee of her groom and with her brow against his breast she smiled with joy. Through the skies they flew, and into the infinite depths below them sank the forest, the mountains and undulating valleys and dales. And finally, as if into blue smoke, everything disappeared from their view.

And thus ends the legend of the Pale Maiden, which Aapo told his brothers that dreamless night in the turf-roofed cabin in the glades of Impivaara.

Lewis Carroll, born Charles Lutwidge Dodgson (1832–1898), was an English logician, photographer, and novelist whose novel *Alice's Adventures in Wonderland* (1865) became a classic of "nonsense literature." The sequel, *Through the Looking-Glass* (1871), was just as beloved. In fact, Alice's adventures in the second novel are a larger part of today's popular culture than the first. Unlike most books at the time, there was no political or religious meaning to Carroll's work. His stories are not allegorical, and they seem to be purely for entertainment, much like his pseudonym. "Looking-Glass House" is the first chapter of *Through the Looking-Glass* and is a good introduction to the surreal, absurdist world of the novel.

Looking-Glass House

(EXCERPT FROM *THROUGH THE LOOKING-GLASS*)

Lewis Carroll

ONE THING WAS CERTAIN, that the *white* kitten had had nothing to do with it:—it was the black kitten's fault entirely. For the white kitten had been having its face washed by the old cat for the last quarter of an hour (and bearing it pretty well, considering); so you see that it *couldn't* have had any hand in the mischief.

The way Dinah washed her children's faces was this: first she held the poor thing down by its ear with one paw, and then with the other paw she rubbed its face all over, the wrong way, beginning at the nose: and just now, as I said, she was hard at work on the white kitten, which was lying quite still and trying to purr—no doubt feeling that it was all meant for its good.

But the black kitten had been finished with earlier in the afternoon, and so, while Alice was sitting curled up in a corner of the great arm-chair, half talking to herself and half asleep, the kitten had been having a grand game of romps with the ball of worsted Alice had been trying to wind up, and had been rolling it up and down till it had all come undone again; and there it was, spread over the hearth-rug, all knots and tangles, with the kitten running after its own tail in the middle.

"Oh, you wicked little thing!" cried Alice, catching up the kitten, and giving it a little kiss to make it understand that it was in disgrace. "Really, Dinah ought to have taught you better manners! You *ought*, Dinah, you know you ought!" she added, looking reproachfully at the old cat, and speaking in as cross a voice as she could manage—and then she scrambled back into the arm-chair, taking the kitten and the worsted with her, and began winding up the ball again. But she didn't get on very fast, as she was talking all the time, sometimes to the kitten, and sometimes to herself. Kitty sat very demurely on her knee, pretending to watch the progress of the winding, and now and then putting out one paw and gently touching the ball, as if it would be glad to help, if it might.

"Do you know what to-morrow is, Kitty?" Alice began. "You'd have guessed if you'd been up in the window with me—only Dinah was making you tidy, so you couldn't. I was watching the boys getting in sticks for the bonfire—and it wants plenty of sticks, Kitty! Only it got so cold, and it snowed so, they had to leave off. Never mind, Kitty, we'll go and see the bonfire to-morrow." Here Alice wound two or three turns of the worsted round the kitten's neck, just to see how it would look: this led to a scramble, in which the ball rolled down upon the floor, and yards and yards of it got unwound again.

"Do you know, I was so angry, Kitty," Alice went on as soon as they were comfortably settled again, "when I saw all the mischief you had been doing, I was very nearly opening the window, and putting you out into the snow! And you'd have deserved it, you little mischievous darling! What have you got to say for yourself? Now don't interrupt me!" she went on, holding up one finger. "I'm going to tell you all your faults. Number one: you squeaked twice while Dinah was washing your face this morning. Now you can't deny it, Kitty: I heard you! What's that you say?" (pretending that the kitten was speaking). "Her paw went into your eye? Well, that's *your* fault, for keeping your eyes open—if you'd shut them tight up, it wouldn't have happened. Now don't make any more excuses, but listen! Number two: you pulled Snowdrop away by the tail just as I had put down the saucer of milk before her! What, you were thirsty, were you? How do you know she wasn't thirsty too? Now for number three: you unwound every bit of the worsted while I wasn't looking!

"That's three faults, Kitty, and you've not been punished for any of them yet. You know I'm saving up all your punishments for Wednesday week—Suppose they had saved up all *my* punishments!" she went on, talking more to herself than the kitten. "What *would* they do at the end of a year? I should be sent to prison, I suppose, when the day came. Or—let me see—suppose each punishment was to be going without a dinner: then, when the miserable day came, I should have to go without fifty dinners at once! Well, I shouldn't mind *that* much! I'd far rather go without them than eat them!

"Do you hear the snow against the window-panes, Kitty? How nice and soft it sounds! Just as if some one was kissing the window all over outside. I wonder if the snow *loves* the trees and fields, that it kisses them so gently? And then it covers them up snug, you know, with a white quilt; and perhaps it says, 'Go to sleep, darlings, till the summer comes again.' And when they wake up in the summer, Kitty, they dress themselves all in green, and dance about—whenever the wind blows—oh, that's very pretty!" cried Alice, dropping the ball of worsted to clap her hands. "And I do so *wish* it was true! I'm sure the woods look sleepy in the autumn, when the leaves are getting brown.

"Kitty, can you play chess? Now, don't smile, my dear, I'm asking it seriously. Because, when we were playing just now, you watched just as if you understood it: and when I said 'Check!' you purred! Well, it *was* a nice check, Kitty, and really I might have won, if it hadn't been for that nasty Knight, that came wiggling down among my pieces. Kitty, dear, let's pretend—" And here I wish I could tell you half the things Alice used to say, beginning with her favourite phrase "Let's pretend." She had had quite a long argument with her sister only the day before—all because Alice had begun with "Let's pretend we're kings and queens"; and her sister, who liked being very exact, had argued that they couldn't, because there were only two of them, and Alice had been reduced at last to say, "Well, *you* can be one of them then, and *I'll* be all the rest." And once she had really frightened her old nurse by shouting suddenly in her ear, "Nurse! Do let's pretend that I'm a hungry hyaena, and you're a bone."

But this is taking us away from Alice's speech

to the kitten. "Let's pretend that you're the Red Queen, Kitty! Do you know, I think if you sat up and folded your arms, you'd look exactly like her. Now do try, there's a dear!" And Alice got the Red Queen off the table, and set it up before the kitten as a model for it to imitate: however, the thing didn't succeed, principally, Alice said, because the kitten wouldn't fold its arms properly. So, to punish it, she held it up to the Looking-glass, that it might see how sulky it was—"and if you're not good directly," she added, "I'll put you through into Looking-glass House. How would you like *that*?

"Now, if you'll only attend, Kitty, and not talk so much, I'll tell you all my ideas about Looking-glass House. First, there's the room you can see through the glass—that's just the same as our drawing room, only the things go the other way. I can see all of it when I get upon a chair—all but the bit behind the fireplace. Oh! I do so wish I could see *that* bit! I want so much to know whether they've a fire in the winter: you never *can* tell, you know, unless our fire smokes, and then smoke comes up in that room too—but that may be only pretence, just to make it look as if they had a fire. Well then, the books are something like our books, only the words go the wrong way; I know that, because I've held up one of our books to the glass, and then they hold up one in the other room.

"How would you like to live in Looking-glass House, Kitty? I wonder if they'd give you milk in there? Perhaps Looking-glass milk isn't good to drink—But oh, Kitty! now we come to the passage. You can just see a little *peep* of the passage in Looking-glass House, if you leave the door of our drawing-room wide open: and it's very like our passage as far as you can see, only you know it may be quite different on beyond. Oh, Kitty! how nice it would be if we could only get through into Looking-glass House! I'm sure it's got, oh! such beautiful things in it! Let's pretend there's a way of getting through into it, somehow, Kitty. Let's pretend the glass has got all soft like gauze, so that we can get through. Why, it's turning into a sort of mist now, I declare! It'll be easy enough to get through—" She was up on the chimney-piece while she said this, though she hardly knew how she had got there. And certainly the glass *was* beginning to melt away, just like a bright silvery mist.

In another moment Alice was through the glass, and had jumped lightly down into the Looking-glass room. The very first thing she did was to look whether there was a fire in the fireplace, and she was quite pleased to find that there was a real one, blazing away as brightly as the one she had left behind. "So I shall be as warm here as I was in the old room," thought Alice: "warmer, in fact, because there'll be no one here to scold me away from the fire. Oh, what fun it'll be, when they see me through the glass in here, and can't get at me!"

Then she began looking about, and noticed that what could be seen from the old room was quite common and uninteresting, but that all the rest was as different as possible. For instance, the pictures on the wall next to the fire seemed to be all alive, and the very clock on the chimney-piece (you know you can only see the back of it in the Looking-glass) had got the face of a little old man, and grinned at her.

"They don't keep this room so tidy as the other," Alice thought to herself, as she noticed several of the chessmen down in the hearth among the cinders: but in another moment, with a little "Oh!" of surprise, she was down on her hands and knees watching them. The chessmen were walking about, two and two!

"Here are the Red King and the Red Queen," Alice said (in a whisper, for fear of frightening them), "and there are the White King and the White Queen sitting on the edge of the shovel—and here are two castles walking arm in arm—I don't think they can hear me," she went on, as she put her head closer down, "and I'm nearly sure they can't see me. I feel somehow as if I were invisible—"

Here something began squeaking on the table behind Alice, and made her turn her head just in time to see one of the White Pawns roll over and begin kicking: she watched it with great curiosity to see what would happen next.

"It is the voice of my child!" the White Queen cried out as she rushed past the King, so violently that she knocked him over among the cinders. "My precious Lily! My imperial kitten!" and she began scrambling wildly up the side of the fender.

"Imperial fiddlestick!" said the King, rubbing his nose, which had been hurt by the fall. He had a right to be a *little* annoyed with the Queen, for he was covered with ashes from head to foot.

Alice was very anxious to be of use, and, as the poor little Lily was nearly screaming herself into a fit, she hastily picked up the Queen and set her on the table by the side of her noisy little daughter.

The Queen gasped, and sat down: the rapid journey through the air had quite taken away her breath and for a minute or two she could do nothing but hug the little Lily in silence. As soon as she had recovered her breath a little, she called out to the White King, who was sitting sulkily among the ashes, "Mind the volcano!"

"What volcano?" said the King, looking up anxiously into the fire, as if he thought that was the most likely place to find one.

"Blew—me—up," panted the Queen, who was still a little out of breath. "Mind you come up—the regular way—don't get blown up!"

Alice watched the White King as he slowly struggled up from bar to bar, till at last she said, "Why, you'll be hours and hours getting to the table, at that rate. I'd far better help you, hadn't I?" But the King took no notice of the question: it was quite clear that he could neither hear her nor see her.

So Alice picked him up very gently, and lifted him across more slowly than she had lifted the Queen, that she mightn't take his breath away: but, before she put him on the table, she thought she might as well dust him a little, he was so covered with ashes.

She said afterwards that she had never seen in all her life such a face as the King made, when he found himself held in the air by an invisible hand, and being dusted: he was far too much astonished to cry out, but his eyes and his mouth went on getting larger and larger, and rounder and rounder, till her hand shook so with laughing that she nearly let him drop upon the floor.

"Oh! *please* don't make such faces, my dear!" she cried out, quite forgetting that the King couldn't hear her. "You make me laugh so that I can hardly hold you! And don't keep your mouth so wide open! All the ashes will get into it—there, now I think you're tidy enough!" she added, as she smoothed his hair, and set him upon the table near the Queen.

The King immediately fell flat on his back, and lay perfectly still: and Alice was a little alarmed at what she had done, and went round the room to see if she could find any water to throw over him. However, she could find nothing but a bottle of ink, and when she got back with it she found he had recovered, and he and the Queen were talking together in a frightened whisper—so low, that Alice could hardly hear what they said.

The King was saying, "I assure, you my dear, I turned cold to the very ends of my whiskers!"

To which the Queen replied, "You haven't got any whiskers."

"The horror of that moment," the King went on, "I shall never, *never* forget!"

"You will, though," the Queen said, "if you don't make a memorandum of it."

Alice looked on with great interest as the King took an enormous memorandum-book out of his pocket, and began writing. A sudden thought struck her, and she took hold of the end of the pencil, which came some way over his shoulder, and began writing for him.

The poor King looked puzzled and unhappy, and struggled with the pencil for some time without saying anything; but Alice was too strong for him, and at last he panted out, "My dear! I really *must* get a thinner pencil. I can't manage this one a bit; it writes all manner of things that I don't intend—"

"What manner of things?" said the Queen, looking over the book (in which Alice had put "*The White Knight is sliding down the poker. He balances very badly*"). "That's not a memorandum of *your* feelings!"

There was a book lying near Alice on the table, and while she sat watching the White King (for she was still a little anxious about him, and had the ink all ready to throw over him, in case he fainted again), she turned over the leaves, to find some part that she could read, "—for it's all in some language I don't know," she said to herself.

It was like this.

ЈАВВЕRWOCKY
'Twas brillig, and the slithy toves
Did gyre and gimble in the wabe;
All mimsy were the borogoves,
And the mome raths outgrabe.

She puzzled over this for some time, but at last a bright thought struck her. "Why, it's a Looking-glass book, of course! And if I hold it up to a glass, the words will all go the right way again."

This was the poem that Alice read.

JABBERWOCKY
'Twas brillig, and the slithy toves
Did gyre and gimble in the wabe;
All mimsy were the borogoves,
And the mome raths outgrabe.

"Beware the Jabberwock, my son!
The jaws that bite, the claws that catch!
Beware the Jubjub bird, and shun
The frumious Bandersnatch!"

He took his vorpal sword in hand:
Long time the manxome foe he sought—
So rested he by the Tumtum tree,
And stood awhile in thought.

And as in uffish thought he stood,
The Jabberwock, with eyes of flame,
Came whiffling through the tulgey wood,
And burbled as it came!

One, two! One, two! And through and through
The vorpal blade went snicker-snack!

He left it dead, and with its head
He went galumphing back.

"And hast thou slain the Jabberwock?
Come to my arms, my beamish boy!
O frabjous day! Callooh! Callay!"
He chortled in his joy.

'Twas brillig, and the slithy toves
Did gyre and gimble in the wabe;
All mimsy were the borogoves,
And the mome raths outgrabe.

"It seems very pretty," she said when she had finished it, "but it's *rather* hard to understand!" (You see she didn't like to confess, ever to herself, that she couldn't make it out at all.) "Somehow it seems to fill my head with ideas—only I don't exactly know what they are! However, *somebody* killed *something*: that's clear, at any rate—"

"But oh!" thought Alice, suddenly jumping up, "if I don't make haste I shall have to go back through the Looking-glass, before I've seen what the rest of the house is like! Let's have a look at the garden first!" She was out of the room in a moment, and ran down stairs—or, at least, it wasn't exactly running, but a new invention of hers for getting down stairs quickly and easily, as Alice said to herself. She just kept the tips of her fingers on the hand-rail, and floated gently down without even touching the stairs with her feet; then she floated on through the hall, and would have gone straight out at the door in the same way, if she hadn't caught hold of the door-post. She was getting a little giddy with so much floating in the air, and was rather glad to find herself walking again in the natural way.

Pauline Elisabeth Ottilie Luise zu Wied (1843–1916), known in the literary world as Carmen Sylva, was the queen consort of Romania. She began writing verse in her childhood and kept a secret diary full of her work. A compassionate woman, she founded schools, hospitals, and art galleries to help the cultural development of Romania. In 1881, Queen Elisabeth herself published Sylva's first book of poetry, entitled *Storms*. Soon after, her collection of Romanian myths, legends, and folklore, *From Carmen Sylva's Kingdom* (1883), came out. Sylva wrote poetry and short stories and even cowrote a few novels with her friend Madame Kremnitz under the pen names Idem and Ditto. It is through her stories that she first became known to the American public. "Furnica, or The Queen of the Ants," first appeared in 1893 and is a tale that juxtaposes love and responsibility. It has been collected in numerous anthologies.

Furnica, or The Queen of the Ants

Carmen Sylva

Translated by Gio Clairval

THERE WAS ONCE A BEAUTIFUL GIRL named Viorica; she had hair like gold, eyes like the sky, cheeks like carnations, lips like cherries, and her body was as lithe as reeds. All men were glad just to glimpse the attractive young woman, but not so much because of her beauty as because of her industriousness. When she went to the spring with a jar balancing on her head, she also carried a distaff in her girdle and busied herself spinning. She could weave, too, and sew like a fay. Her shirts were the finest of the entire village, black and red and with large traditional embroideries stitched on the shoulders. She had embellished her skirt with flowers, and even the stockings she wore on Sundays. Those little hands could never rest. In field or pasture, she worked as much as in the house, and whenever the young men glanced at the beautiful Viorica, they dreamed of the marvelous housewife she would become. She ignored them all, though, refused to think about marriage. She had no time because her mother needed to be taken care of. Her mother frowned, opined that an able son-in-law would be of great help. These words saddened the young woman, who asked whether she had become useless, given that Mother insisted on having a man in the house. "Men," she said, "just give us more work, as we must spin and weave and sew for them, too, and we can hardly find the time to work in the fields."

The mother sighed, thinking of her dead son, for whom she had made so many fine shirts,

213

which she washed so dazzlingly white that no young woman could pull her gaze away from him. She'd never minded the work, never found it tiring, but what wouldn't a mother do?

The day came when Viorica had to admit that Mother had been right in wanting a son-in-law in the house, as if she had known that she wouldn't be of this world for long. She took ill and all the love of her daughter could do nothing to keep her upon earth.

The beautiful young woman had to close her beloved mother's eyes and sat alone in the little house. For the first time her hands lay idle in her lap. For whom would she work now? She had nobody left.

One day, as she sat in her doorway and gazed dewy-eyed, she saw something on the ground, long and black, moving toward her. She saw ants advance in endless columns. Impossible to know where they came from: the processions stretched back in the distance. Then the ants stopped to form a formidable arc, encircling Viorica. A few of them stepped forth and spoke: "We know you well, Viorica, and on several occasions we have admired your industriousness, which resembles our own and is so rare among human beings. We also know that you are alone, and we entreat you to accept to live with us and be our queen. We shall build a palace for you, and it will be finer and larger than any house you have ever seen. In exchange you must promise us that you will never return to the world of humans, but you will forever remain with us."

"I shall gladly remain with you," said Viorica, "because nothing holds me here any longer, save for my mother's grave, and I must bring her flowers, cakes, and wine, and pray for her soul."

"You will visit your mother's grave, but you will speak to no one on the way. Should you be disloyal, the punishment will be terrible."

So did Viorica set forth with the ants until they found a place that seemed suitable for building a palace. Viorica saw that the ants were more skillful than she ever was. She could never have built such a building so quickly. There were galleries, one above the other, which opened onto vast spaces, deeper and deeper, to the innermost reaches dug out for the pupae, which would be transported to the surface to sunbathe and then quickly carried back to their quarters, sheltered from the rain. The chambers were decorated in the most graceful manner, petals held in place on the walls with fir needles. Viorica learned to spin spidersilk to fashion dais and blankets.

The building rose higher and higher. Viorica's bedroom was so enchanting she had never imagined anything like it, not even in a dream. Many galleries led to her quarters, so that she could be reached quickly by her subjects, at all times. The floors of the passageways were decked with poppy-petals, so that the queen's feet would tread on purple only. The doors were made of rose petals and the hinges were spider threads, to ensure that the doors would close and open noiselessly. The floor of her chamber was edelweiss, a thick, soft carpet in which Viorica's rosy toes sank—she needed no shoes there; they would have been too hard on the flower carpet. The walls were artistically woven of carnations, lilies of the valleys and forget-me-nots, and the flowers were continuously renewed, so that the decoration would retain freshness and scent. A canopy stretched out to form a ceiling of lily petals. The diligent ants had worked weeks to build the bed mattress with pollen of the softest kind and a spidersilk coverlet was spread over it. When she lay there asleep she was so beautiful the stars wished they could fall to earth and see her better. But the jealous ants guarded their queen well in the deepest recess of the castle-mound, hardly daring glance at her as she slept.

Life in the anthill could not have been more agreeable than it was. The ants, doing everything in their power to serve their industrious queen, vied for her approval. Each command was carried out at lightning speed, for she didn't give many orders, and none unreasonable; she would rather speak with a soft voice and her commands sounded like friendly advice or gentle hints; she thanked her subjects with a glance as warm as a kiss from the sun.

Often the ants would say that sunshine

dwelled in their house, and they praised their good luck. They had built a terrace especially for her to enjoy fresh air and daylight, whenever her chamber grew too narrow and confined. From her vantage point she could follow the progress of the construction, which was already as high as a mountain.

Every day she sat in her quarters, sewing butterflies' wings on a dress with silk threads spun by a caterpillar the ants had hauled in for her. Only her delicate fingers could accomplish such a fine work. But that day a loud scream resounded, a commotion of voices could be heard everywhere on the mountain. In a heartbeat, the small realm was roused and her subjects, breathless, came to circle around their queen. "They are destroying our house! Evil men are stomping all over us. Two, no, three galleries have caved in, and others will follow. What shall we do?"

"Is that all?" said Viorica in a calm voice. "I will bid them to go their way and in one or two days the galleries will be up again."

She dashed through the nearest exit into the maze of passageways and soon appeared onto her terrace. From there she spied a magnificent young man who had dismounted from his horse and endeavored with his retinue to upturn the anthill with swords and peaks. Upon her appearance they all stopped. The handsome youngster held a hand up to shield his eyes and observed the light-framed silhouette draped in shimmery garments. Viorica's golden locks flew around her, down to the tips of her feet, a gentle blush colored her cheeks, and her eyes gleamed like stars. She lowered her gaze before the young man's stare, but she soon looked up and through her pink lips she spoke with a strong, resounding voice.

"Who are you, whose hand is committing such outrage upon my queendom?"

"Forgiveness, my fair young lady!" cried the young man. "For if it is true that I am a knight and a king's son, I shall be your fervent defender! How could I guess that a goddess, or a fay, ruled over this realm?"

"I thank you," said Viorica, "but I need no servants other than my loyal subjects and I only demand that no human beings trample on my domain."

With these words, she disappeared as if the mountain had swallowed her, and those outside could not see the droves of ants kissing her feet and carrying her in triumph to her chambers, where she calmly resumed her work, as if nothing had happened. And outside, at the foot of the mountain, the king's son stood as if lost in a dream and for hours refused to mount on his horse, in the hope that the fair queen would reappear, even if proffering hard words and darting a reproachful stare, for he at least would see her again! He saw only ants, and more ants, in endless columns, efficiently striving to repair what he and his retinue, in their youthful mischief, had wrecked. In his anger and impatience, he could have crushed them under his boots, because the creatures didn't seem to understand his questions, or didn't even hear his words, instead scurrying boldly around, in their newfound sense of security. In the end, a sad prince mounted his steed, and began to plot and plan how to win the loveliest young woman he'd ever seen, riding on and on into the night, to his retinue's vast discontent, who wished both anthill and lady in Hell, as they thought of the supper table and pitchers of wine that had been long awaiting them.

Viorica had lain down to rest later than any of her subjects. She ordinarily visited the pupae every evening, to test the softness of their cots with her fingers; so she ambled down the passageways, lifting one flower-curtain after the other, a firefly perched on her fingertip, and looked after the young brood with tenderness. Now she went back to her quarters and dismissed all the glowing beetles that shed light over her long hours of needlework. Only one single glow-worm remained alongside her, while she undressed. She was used to falling at once into the deepest sleep, but that night she tossed and turned in her bed, twirled strands of hair around her finger, rose from bed and then lay down again, all along feeling so hot, so hot. She had never thought that her palace held so little fresh air but now she would have gladly hastened outside, only fearing that her wandering would be discovered, and that by her bad example she might corrupt others. Urged on by her councilors, she had passed many a harsh sentence, banishing a few because of their forbidden wanderings. She had also condemned others to death, and had to watch with a bleeding heart as the merciless stabbings were carried on.

The next morning she was up before everyone else and surprised her subjects by showing them a new gallery she had built all by herself.

Surely she was unaware of the many glances she had cast in the direction of the forest, and of the many times she had stood still, listening. No sooner had she regained her chambers than a few ants ran to her in terror. "The evil man has returned, and he is riding again around our mountain!"

"Let him be," replied Queen Viorica in utter calm. "He will do us no more harm."

But Viorica, our sweet young woman, heard her heart beating so loud she let out a deep sigh.

A peculiar unrest had come upon her. She wandered about much more than she used to, and she seemed to think that the pupae weren't getting enough sunshine; she often carried a few of them outside, only to bring them back again, and she gave contradictory orders. The ants didn't understand what was happening to her, and doubled their efforts to do everything perfectly, and they even tried to surprise her with a new splendid vaulted hall, at which she glanced in an absentminded way, scantily praising it. The sound of horse hooves roaming all over the mountain could be heard at any hour, but Viorica for many days didn't allow herself to be seen.

A longing for the companionship of other human beings, a sentiment she had never known before, had now seized hold of her heart. She recalled her village, the Hora dance, the hamlets, Mother and her grave, which she had never visited since her departure.

After a few days, she announced to her subjects that she was thinking of visiting her mother's grave, to which the ants, alarmed, asked whether her reminiscing meant that she could no longer find happiness with them. "Oh, no," said Viorica.

"I will be away only for a few hours, and I'll be back among you before nightfall."

She refused all escort, but a few ants followed her nonetheless, while endeavoring not to be seen.

Everything seemed different from what she remembered, and she realized that she must have spent a much longer time in the company of the ants than she had thought. Her subjects, she reckoned, had needed more than a few days to build the immense palace in which they lived. Maybe years had passed. Her mother's grave was impossible to find as weed and brambles had grown all over the place, and Viorica, weeping, wandered about the churchyard, which now seemed foreign to her. Evening approached, and she was still looking for the grave she could not find. Then the voice of the King's son reached her, close by. She wanted to flee, but the young man held her fast while he told her of his great love with so soft and so poignant words that she remained still, head bowed, and let herself listen. It was so sweet, to hear human speech again, and to hear words of love and friendship. Not until darkness had fallen did the thought strike her that she was a queen neglecting her duties, not an abandoned orphan, and that the ants had prohibited her from returning to the society of men. Viorica, running on swift feet, broke free from the king's son. He pursued her with caressing words not far from her mountain, where she implored him to leave her be. Finally he accepted to depart upon the promise that she would come to meet him again the following evening.

Viorica glided inside the anthill without making the faintest sound, feeling her way down the galleries, fearfully glancing over her shoulder. More than once she thought she had heard the scurrying of tiny feet, voices whispering around her. No doubt it was her heart beating too fast, for as soon as she halted silence enveloped her. At last she found her chamber and sank in exhaustion upon her bed, but no sleep came to soothe her. She couldn't help thinking that she had broken her promise, and that no one would respect her, now that her word was no longer sacred. She turned and tossed on her couch. Her pride balked at the idea of concealing her treason, and she knew the ants anyway, their implacable hatred and their cruel retribution. She often half rose, resting on her elbow to listen, and each time she had the impression that thousands of minuscule feet dashed in every direction, as if the entire mountain shuddered into life.

When morning felt near, she lifted one of the curtains of rose petals to hurry out in the open, but, to her amazement, she found the doorway filled with fir needles. She tried another, and then a third, until she had made the tour of all the passages. She called at the top of her lungs, and lo! through tiny, invisible openings did the ants enter, in droves. "Let me out!" she said with a strong voice. "In the open."

"No," said the ants. "We will not let you out. If we let you go out in the open, we would lose you."

"You won't obey my orders any longer?"

"Oh, yes, in all things, except this one. You can crush us under your feet, if you wish. We are ready to die for the greater good, to preserve our community, and to save the honor of our queen."

Viorica bowed her head, while tears streamed from her eyes. She supplicated the ants to give her freedom back, but the stern little creatures fell silent, and once more she found herself in complete solitude in those dark halls. Oh, how she wept and complained and tore her beautiful hair, and then she tried to dig a passage in the fir-needle wall with her delicate fingers, but, as soon as she clawed off a scoop of needles, more came to fill the hole, until, defeated, she slumped to the ground. The ants brought her the sweetest flowers and nectar, and dewdrops to quench her thirst, but her grievances went unheard. In fear that her laments could be heard outside, the ants built their mountain higher and higher, as high as the peak Vârful cu Dor, and named their mountain "Furnica" (Ant).

The king's son has long since ceased riding around the mountain, although in the quietest nights, one can still hear Viorica's cries.

Leo Tolstoy (1828–1910) was a Russian writer whose full name was Count Lev Nikolayevich Tolstoy. He is considered to be the greatest writer who had ever lived. Indeed, his novel *War and Peace* is the benchmark for all other novels, and *The Death of Ivan Ilyich* is said to be the perfect novella. Tolstoy was born into Russian nobility and grew up in a life of wealth and comfort. One of his earlier literary influences was Charles Dickens. He became very religious and spent much of his later years thinking and writing about religion and its contributions to the world. He became disillusioned with organized religion and was eventually excommunicated from the Russian Orthodox Church. His studies and essays on nonviolent resistance were a huge influence on such world changers as Martin Luther King, Jr., and Mahatma Gandhi. Although most of his fiction is realistic, he did enjoy writing tales of fantasy. The clever "The Story of Iván the Fool" (1886) may in part be based on Russian folktales, but Tolstoy's reinvention and expansion of the story is particular to him and reflected his anarchic-Christian tendencies (almost, in some senses, proto-Libertarian).

The Story of Iván the Fool

Leo Tolstoy

Translated by Louise and Aylmer Maude

I

ONCE UPON A TIME, in a certain province of a certain country, there lived a rich peasant, who had three sons: Simon the Soldier, Tarás the Stout, and Iván the Fool, besides an unmarried daughter, Martha, who was deaf and mute. Simon the Soldier went to the wars to serve the king; Tarás the Stout went to a merchant's in town to trade, and Iván the Fool stayed at home with the lass, to till the ground till his back bent.

Simon the Soldier obtained high rank and an estate, and married a nobleman's daughter. His pay was large and his estate was large, yet he could not make ends meet. What the husband earned his lady wife squandered, and they never had money enough.

So Simon the Soldier went to his estate to collect the income, but his steward said, "Where is any income to come from? We have neither cattle, nor tools, nor horse, nor plough, nor harrow. We must first get all these, and then the money will come."

Then Simon the Soldier went to his father

and said: "You, father, are rich, but have given me nothing. Divide what you have, and give me a third part, that I may improve my estate."

But the old man said: "You brought nothing into my house; why should I give you a third part? It would be unfair to Iván and to the girl."

But Simon answered, "He is a fool; and she is an old maid, and deaf and mute besides; what's the good of property to them?"

The old man said, "We will see what Iván says about it."

And Iván said, "Let him take what he wants."

So Simon the Soldier took his share of his father's goods and removed them to his estate, and went off again to serve the king.

Tarás the Stout also gathered much money, and married into a merchant's family, but still he wanted more. So he, also, came to his father and said, "Give me my portion."

But the old man did not wish to give Tarás a share either, and said, "You brought nothing here. Iván has earned all we have in the house, and why should we wrong him and the girl?"

But Tarás said, "What does he need? He is a fool! He cannot marry, no one would have him; and the mute lass does not need anything either. Look here, Iván!" said he, "Give me half the corn; I don't want the tools, and of the livestock I will take only the grey stallion, which is of no use to you for the plough."

Iván laughed and said, "Take what you want. I will work to earn some more."

So they gave a share to Tarás also; and he carted the corn away to town, and took the grey stallion. And Iván was left with one old mare, to lead his peasant life as before, and to support his father and mother.

II

Now the old Devil was vexed that the brothers had not quarrelled over the division, but had parted peacefully; and he summoned three imps.

"Look here," said he, "there are three brothers: Simon the Soldier, Tarás the Stout, and Iván the Fool. They should have quarrelled, but are living peaceably and meet on friendly terms. The fool Iván has spoilt the whole business for me. Now you three go and tackle those three brothers, and worry them till they scratch each other's eyes out! Do you think you can do it?"

"Yes, we'll do it," said they.

"How will you set about it?"

"Why," said they, "first we'll ruin them. And when they haven't a crust to eat we'll tie them up together, and then they'll fight each other, sure enough!"

"That's capital; I see you understand your business. Go, and don't come back till you've set them by the ears, or I'll skin you alive!"

The imps went off into a swamp, and began to consider how they should set to work. They argued and argued, each wanting the lightest job; but at last they decided to cast lots as to which of the brothers each imp should tackle. If one imp finished his task before the others, he was to come and help the other two. So the imps cast lots, and agreed on a time to meet again in the swamp to learn who had succeeded and who needed help.

The appointed time came round, and the imps met again in the swamp. And each began to tell how matters stood. The first, who had taken on the task of Simon the Soldier, began: "My business is going on well. Tomorrow Simon will return to his father's house."

His comrades asked, "How did you manage it?"

"First," says he, "I made Simon so bold that he offered to conquer the whole world for his king; and the king made him his general and sent him to fight the King of India. They met for battle, but the night before, I damped all the powder in Simon's camp, and made more straw soldiers for the Indian King than you could count. And when Simon's soldiers saw the straw soldiers surrounding them, they grew frightened. Simon ordered them to fire; but their cannons and guns would not go off. Then Simon's soldiers were quite frightened, and ran like sheep, and the Indian King slaughtered them. Simon was disgraced. He has been deprived of his estate, and tomorrow they intend to execute him. There is only one day's work left for me to do; I have to let him out of prison that he may escape home. Tomorrow I shall be ready to help whichever of you needs me."

Then the second imp, who had Tarás in hand, began to tell how he had fared. "I don't want any help," said he, "my job is going all right. Tarás can't hold out for more than a week. First, I caused him to grow greedy and fat. His covetousness became so great that whatever he saw he wanted to buy. He has spent all his money buying immense lots of goods, and still continues to buy. Already he has begun to use borrowed money. His debts hang like a weight round his neck, and he is so involved that he can never get clear. In a week his bills come due, and before then I will spoil all his stock. He will be unable to pay and will have to go home to his father."

Then they asked the third imp (Iván's), "And how are you getting on?"

"Well," said he, "my affair goes badly. First, I spat into his drink to make his stomach ache, and then I went into his field and hammered the ground hard as a stone that he should not be able to till it. I thought he wouldn't plough it, but like the fool that he is, he came with his plough and began to make a furrow. He groaned from the pain in his stomach, but went on ploughing. I broke his plough for him, but he went home, got out another, and again started ploughing. I crept under the earth and caught hold of the ploughshares, but there was no holding them; he leant heavily upon the plough, and the ploughshare was sharp and cut my hands. He has all but finished ploughing the field; only one little strip is left. Come, brothers, and help me; for if we don't get the better of him, all our labor is lost. If the fool holds out and keeps on working the land, his brothers will never know want, for he will feed them both."

Simon the Soldier's imp promised to come next day to help, and so they parted.

III

Iván had ploughed up the whole fallow, all but one little strip. He came to finish it. Though his stomach ached, the ploughing must be done. He freed the harness ropes, turned the plough, and began to work. He drove one furrow, but coming back the plough began to drag as if it had caught in a root. It was the imp, who had twisted his legs round the ploughshare and was holding it back.

"What a strange thing!" thought Iván. "There were no roots here at all, and yet here's a root."

Iván pushed his hand deep into the furrow, groped about, and, feeling something soft, seized hold of it and pulled it out. It was black like a root, but it wriggled. Why, it was a live imp!

"What a nasty thing!" said Iván, and he lifted his hand to dash it against the plough, but the imp squealed out:

"Don't hurt me, and I'll do anything you tell me to."

"What can you do?"

"Anything you tell me to."

Iván scratched his head.

"My stomach aches," said he; "can you cure that?"

"Certainly I can."

"Well then, do so."

The imp went down into the furrow, searched about, scratched with his claws, and pulled out a bunch of three little roots, which he handed to Iván.

"Here," says he, "whoever swallows one of these will be cured of any illness."

Iván took the roots, separated them, and swallowed one. The pain in his stomach was cured at once. The imp again begged to be let off. "I will jump right into the earth, and never come back," said he.

"All right," said Iván; "begone, and God be with you!"

And as soon as Iván mentioned God, the imp plunged into the earth like a stone thrown into the water. Only a hole was left.

Iván put the other two pieces of root into his cap and went on with his ploughing. He ploughed the strip to the end, turned his plough over, and went home. He unharnessed the horse, entered the hut, and there he saw his elder brother, Simon the Soldier, and his wife, sitting at supper.

Simon's estate had been confiscated, he himself had barely managed to escape from prison, and he had come back to live in his father's house.

Simon saw Iván, and said: "I have come to live with you. Feed me and my wife till I get another appointment."

"All right," said Iván, "you can stay with us."

But when Iván was about to sit down on the bench, the lady disliked the smell, and said to her husband: "I cannot sup with a dirty peasant."

Simon the Soldier said, "My lady says you don't smell nice. You'd better go and eat outside."

"All right," said Iván; "any way I must spend the night outside, for I have to pasture the mare."

So he took some bread, and his coat, and went with the mare into the fields.

IV

Having finished his work that night, Simon's imp came, as agreed, to find Iván's imp and help him to subdue the fool. He came to the field and searched and searched; but instead of his comrade he found only a hole.

"Clearly," thought he, "some evil has befallen my comrade. I must take his place. The field is ploughed up, so the fool must be tackled in the meadow."

The imp went to the meadows and flooded Iván's hayfield with water, which left the grass all covered with mud.

Iván returned from the pasture at dawn, sharpened his scythe, and went to mow the hayfield. He began to mow, but had only swung the scythe once or twice when the edge turned so that it would not cut at all, but needed resharpening. Iván struggled on for a while, and then said: "It's no good. I must go home and bring a tool to straighten the scythe, and I'll get a chunk of bread at the same time. If I have to spend a week here, I won't leave till the mowing's done."

The imp heard this and thought to himself, "This fool is a tough one; I can't get round him this way. I must try some other trick."

Iván returned, sharpened his scythe, and began to mow. The imp crept into the grass and began to catch the scythe by the heel, sending the point into the earth. Iván found the work very hard, but he mowed the whole meadow, except one little bit, which was in the swamp. The imp crept into the swamp and thought to himself, "Though I cut my paws I will not let him mow."

Iván reached the swamp. The grass didn't seem thick, but yet it resisted the scythe. Iván grew angry and began to swing the scythe with all his might. The imp had to give in; he could not keep up with the scythe, and, seeing it was a bad business, he scrambled into a bush. Iván swung the scythe, caught the bush, and cut off half the imp's tail. Then he finished mowing the grass, told his sister to rake it up, and went himself to mow the rye. He went with the scythe, but the dock-tailed imp was there first, and entangled the rye so that the scythe was of no use. But Iván went home and got his sickle, and began to reap with that and he reaped the whole of the rye.

"Now it's time," said he, "to start on the oats."

The dock-tailed imp heard this, and thought, "I couldn't get the better of him on the rye, but I shall on the oats. Only wait till the morning."

In the morning the imp hurried to the oat field, but the oats were already mowed down! Iván had mowed them that night, so less grain would shake out. The imp grew angry.

"He has cut me all over and tired me out—the fool. It is worse than war. The accursed fool never sleeps; one can't keep up with him. I will get into his stacks now and rot them."

So the imp entered the rye, and crept among the sheaves, and they began to rot. He heated them, grew warm himself, and fell asleep.

Iván harnessed the mare and went with the lass to cart the rye. He came to the heaps and began to pitch the rye into the cart. He tossed two sheaves and again thrust his fork—right into the imp's back.

He lifted the fork and saw on the prongs a live imp: dock-tailed, struggling, wriggling, and trying to jump.

"What, you nasty thing, are you here again?"

"I'm another," said the imp. "The first was my brother. I've been with your brother Simon."

"Well," said Iván, "whoever you are, you've met the same fate!"

He was about to dash him against the cart, but the imp cried out: "Let me off, and I will not only let you alone, but I'll do anything you tell me to do."

"What can you do?"

"I can make soldiers out of anything you like."

"But what use are they?"

"You can turn them to any use; they can do anything you please."

"Can they sing?"

"Yes, if you want them to."

"All right; you may make me some."

And the imp said, "Here, take a sheaf of rye, then bump it upright on the ground, and simply say:

'O sheaf! my slave
This order gave:
Where a straw has been
Let a soldier be seen!'"

Iván took the sheaf, struck it on the ground, and said what the imp had told him to. The sheaf fell asunder, and all the straws changed into soldiers, with a trumpeter and a drummer playing in front, so that there was a whole regiment.

Iván laughed.

"How clever!" said he. "This is fine! How pleased the girls will be!"

"Now let me go," said the imp.

"No," said Iván, "I must make my soldiers of thrashed straw, otherwise good grain will be wasted. Teach me how to change them back again into the sheaf. I want to thrash it."

And the imp said, "Repeat:

'Let each be a straw
Who was soldier before,
For my true slave
This order gave!'"

Iván said this, and the sheaf reappeared.

Again the imp began to beg, "Now let me go!"

"All right." And Iván pressed him against the side of the cart, held him down with his hand, and pulled him off the fork.

"God be with you," said he.

As soon as he mentioned God, the imp plunged into the earth like a stone into water. Only a hole was left.

Iván returned home, and there was his other brother, Tarás, with his wife, sitting at supper.

Tarás the Stout had failed to pay his debts, had run away from his creditors, and had come home to his father's house.

"Look here," said he, when he saw Iván, "until I can start in business again, I want you to keep me and my wife."

"All right," said Iván, "you can live here, if you like."

Iván took off his coat and sat down to table, but the merchant's wife said: "I cannot sit at table with this clown, he stinks of sweat."

Then Tarás the Stout said, "Iván, you smell too strong. Go and eat outside."

"All right," said Iván, taking some bread and going into the yard. "It is time, anyhow, for me to go and pasture the mare."

V

Tarás's imp, being also free that night, came, as agreed, to help his comrades subdue Iván the Fool. He arrived at the cornfield, looked and looked for his comrades—no one was there. He only found a hole. He went to the meadow, and there he found an imp's tail in the swamp, and another hole in the rye stubble.

"Evidently, some ill-luck has befallen my comrades," thought he. "I must take their place and tackle the fool."

So the imp went to look for Iván, who had already stacked the corn and was cutting trees in the wood. The two brothers had begun to feel crowded, living together, and had told Iván to cut down trees to build new houses for them.

The imp ran to the wood, climbed among the

branches, and began to hinder Iván from felling the trees. Iván undercut one tree so that it would fall clear, but in falling it turned askew and caught among some branches. Iván cut a pole with which to lever it aside, and with difficulty contrived to bring it to the ground. He set to work to fell another tree—again, the same thing occurred, so that despite all his efforts he could hardly get the tree clear. He began on a third tree, and again the same thing happened!

Iván had hoped to cut down half a hundred small trees, but had not felled even half a score, and now night had come and he was exhausted. The steam rising from him spread like a mist through the wood, but still he stuck to his work. He undercut another tree, but his back began to ache so that he could not stand. He drove his axe into the tree and sat down to rest.

The imp, noticing that Iván had stopped work, grew cheerful.

"At last," he thought, "Iván is tired out! He will give it up. Now I can take a rest myself."

He seated himself astride a branch and chuckled. But soon Iván got up, pulled the axe out, swung it, and smote the tree from the opposite side with such force that the tree gave way at once and came crashing down. The imp had not expected this, and had no time to get his feet clear, and the tree, in breaking, gripped his paw. Iván began to lop off the branches, when he noticed a live imp hanging in the tree! Iván was surprised.

"What, you nasty thing," says he, "so you are here again!'

"I am another one," says the imp. "I have been with your brother Tarás."

"Whoever you are, you have met your fate," said Iván, and, swinging his axe, he was about to strike the imp with the haft, but the imp begged for mercy: "Don't strike me," said he, "and I will do anything you tell me to."

"What can you do?"

"I can make money for you, as much as you want."

"All right, make some." So the imp showed him how to do it.

"Take some leaves from this oak and rub them in your hands, and gold will fall out on the ground."

Iván took some leaves and rubbed them, and gold ran down from his hands.

"This stuff will do fine," said he, "for the fellows to play with on their holidays."

"Now let me go," said the imp.

"All right," said Iván, and taking a lever he set the imp free. "Now begone! And God be with you," says he.

As soon as he mentioned God, the imp plunged into the earth, like a stone into water. Only a hole was left.

VI

So the brothers built houses, and began to live apart; and Iván finished the harvest work, brewed beer, and invited his brothers to spend the next holiday with him. His brothers would not come.

"We don't care about peasant feasts," they said.

So Iván entertained the peasants and their wives, and drank until he was rather tipsy. Then he went into the street to a circle of dancers; and going up to them he told the women to sing a song in his honor; "for," said he, "I will give you something you never saw in your lives before!"

The women laughed and sang his praises, and when they had finished they said, "Now let us have your gift!"

"I will bring it directly," said he.

He took a seed-basket and ran into the woods. The women laughed and said, "He is a fool!" and they began to talk of something else.

But soon Iván came running back, carrying the basket, now full of something heavy.

"Shall I give it you?"

"Yes! give it to us."

Iván took a handful of gold and threw it to the women. You should have seen them throw themselves upon it to pick it up! And the men around scrambled for it and snatched it from one another. One old woman was nearly crushed to death. Iván laughed.

"Oh, you fools!" says he. "Why did you nearly crush the old grandmother? Be quiet, and I will give you some more," and he threw them some more.

The people all crowded round, and Iván threw them all the gold he had. They asked for even more, but Iván said, "I have no more just now. Another time I'll give you some more. Now let us dance, and you can sing me your songs."

The women began to sing.

"Your songs are no good," says he.

"Where will you find better ones?" say they.

"I'll soon show you," says he.

He went to the barn, took a sheaf, thrashed it, stood it up, and bumped it on the ground.

"Now," said he:

"O sheaf! my slave
This order gave:
Where a straw has been
Let a soldier be seen!"

The sheaf fell asunder and became so many soldiers. The drums and trumpets began to play. Iván ordered the soldiers to play and sing. He led them out into the street, and the people were amazed. The soldiers played and sang, and then Iván (forbidding anyone to follow him) led them back to the thrashing ground, changed them into a sheaf again, and threw it in its place.

Then he went home and lay down in the stables to sleep.

VII

Simon the Soldier heard of all these things next morning and went to his brother.

"Tell me," says he, "where you got those soldiers from, and where you have taken them to."

"What does it matter to you?" said Iván.

"What does it matter? Why, with soldiers one can do anything. One can win a kingdom."

Iván pondered that.

"Really!" said he. "Why didn't you say so before? I'll make you as many as you like. It's well the lass and I have thrashed so much straw."

Iván took his brother to the barn and said: "Look here; if I make you some soldiers, you must take them away at once, for if we have to feed them, they will eat up the whole village in a day."

Simon the Soldier promised to lead the soldiers away, and Iván began to make them. He bumped a sheaf on the thrashing floor—a company appeared. He bumped another sheaf, and there was a second company. He made so many that they covered the field.

"Will that do?" he asked.

Simon was overjoyed and said: "That will do! Thank you, Iván!"

"All right," said Iván. "If you want more, come back, and I'll make them. There is plenty of straw this season."

Simon the Soldier at once took command of his army, organized it, and went off to make war.

Hardly had Simon the Soldier gone, when Tarás the Stout came along. He, too, had heard of yesterday's affair, and he said to his brother:

"Show me where you get gold money! If I only had some to start with, I could make it bring me in money from all over the world."

Iván was astonished.

"Really!" said he. "You should have told me sooner. I will make you as much as you like."

His brother was delighted.

"Give me three baskets-full to begin with."

"All right," said Iván. "Come into the forest; or better still, let us harness the mare, for you won't be able to carry it all."

They drove to the forest, and Iván began to rub the oak leaves. He made a great heap of gold.

"Will that do?"

Tarás was overjoyed.

"It will do for the present," he said. "Thank you, Iván!"

"All right," says Iván, "if you want more, come back for it. There are plenty of leaves left."

Tarás the Stout gathered up a whole cartload of money and went off to trade.

So the two brothers went away: Simon to fight, and Tarás to buy and sell. In time, Simon the Soldier conquered a kingdom for himself; and Tarás the Stout made much money in trade.

When the two brothers met, each told the other: Simon how he got the soldiers, and Tarás how he got the money.

Simon the Soldier said to his brother, I have conquered a kingdom and live in grand style, but I have not money enough to keep my soldiers."

Tarás the Stout said, "And I have made much money, but the trouble is, I have no one to guard it."

Then said Simon the Soldier, "Let us go to our brother. I will tell him to make more soldiers, and will give them to you to guard your money, and you can tell him to make money for me to feed my men."

And so they came again to Iván; and Simon said, "Dear brother, I have not enough soldiers; make me another couple of ricks or so."

Iván shook his head.

"No!" says he, "I will not make any more soldiers."

"But you promised you would."

"I know I promised, but I won't make any more."

"But why not, fool?"

"Because your soldiers killed a man. I was ploughing the other day near the road, and I saw a woman taking a coffin along in a cart and crying. I asked her who was dead. She said, "Simon's soldiers have killed my husband in the war." I thought the soldiers would only play tunes, but they have killed a man. I won't give you any more."

And he stuck to it, and would not make any more soldiers.

Tarás the Stout, too, began to beg Iván to make him more gold money. But Iván shook his head.

"No, I won't make any more," said he.

"Didn't you promise?"

"I did, but I'll make no more," said he.

"Why not, fool?"

"Because your gold coins took away the cow from Michael's daughter."

"How?"

"Simply took it away! Michael's daughter had a cow. Her children used to drink the milk. But

the other day her children came to me to ask for milk. I said, 'Where's your cow?' They answered, 'The steward of Tarás the Stout came and gave mother three bits of gold, and she gave him the cow, so we have nothing to drink.' I thought you were only going to play with the gold pieces, but you have taken the children's cow away. I will not give you any more."

Iván stuck to his decision and would not give him any more. So the brothers went away.

And as they went they discussed how they could meet their difficulties.

Simon said: "Look here, I tell you what to do. You give me money to feed my soldiers, and I will give you half my kingdom with soldiers enough to guard your money."

Tarás agreed. So the brothers divided what they possessed, and both became kings, and both were rich.

VIII

Iván lived at home, supporting his father and mother and working in the fields with his mute sister. Now it happened that Iván's yard-dog fell sick, grew mangy, and was near death. Iván, pitying it, got some bread from his sister, put it in his cap, carried it out, and threw it to the dog. But the cap was torn, and together with the bread one of the little roots fell to the ground. The old dog ate it up with the bread, and as soon as she had swallowed it she jumped up and began to play, bark, and wag her tail—in short, became quite well again.

The father and mother saw this and were amazed.

"How did you cure the dog?" they asked.

Iván answered: "I had two little roots to cure any pain, and she swallowed one."

Now, about that time, it happened that the King's daughter fell ill, and the King proclaimed in every town and village that he would reward anyone who could heal her, and if any unmarried man could heal the King's daughter he should have her for his wife. This news came to Iván's village as well as everywhere else.

His father and mother called to Iván, and said to him: "Have you heard what the King has proclaimed? You said you had a root that would cure any sickness. Go and heal the King's daughter, and you will be made happy for life."

"All right," he said.

Iván prepared to go, and they dressed him in his best. But as he went out of the door he met a beggar woman with a crippled hand.

"I have heard," said she, "that you can heal people. I pray you cure my arm, for I cannot even put on my boots myself."

"All right," said Iván, and giving the little root to the beggar woman he told her to swallow it.

She swallowed it and was cured. She was at once able to move her arm freely.

His father and mother came out to accompany Iván to the King, but when they heard that he had given away the root, and that he had nothing left to cure the King's daughter with, they began to scold him.

"You pity a beggar woman but aren't sorry for the King's daughter!"

But Iván felt sorry for the King's daughter also. So he harnessed the horse, put straw in the cart to sit on, and sat down to drive away.

"Where are you going, fool?"

"To cure the King's daughter."

"But you've nothing left to cure her with?"

"Never mind," he said, and went off.

He drove to the King's palace, and as soon as he stepped on the threshold the King's daughter got well.

The King was delighted, and had Iván brought to him, and had him dressed in fine robes.

"Be my son-in-law," said he.

"All right," Iván said.

So Iván married the Princess. Her father died soon after, and Iván became King. So all three brothers were now kings.

IX

The three brothers lived and reigned. The eldest brother, Simon the Soldier, prospered. With his straw soldiers he acquired real soldiers. He ordered throughout his whole kingdom a levy of one soldier from every ten houses, and each soldier had to be tall, and clean in body and in face. He gathered many such soldiers and trained them; and when any one opposed him, he sent these soldiers at once, and got his own way, so that everyone began to fear him, and his life was a comfortable one. Whatever he cast his eyes on and wished for, was his. All he had to do is send soldiers, and they brought him all he desired.

Tarás the Stout also lived comfortably. He did not waste the money he got from Iván but increased it greatly. He introduced law and order into his kingdom. He kept his money in coffers and taxed the people. He instituted a poll-tax, tolls for walking and driving, and a tax on shoes and stockings and dress trimmings. And whatever he wished for he got. For the sake of money, people brought him everything, and they offered to work for him—for everyone wanted money.

Iván the Fool did not live badly, either. As soon as he had buried his father-in-law, he took off all his royal robes and gave them to his wife to put away in a chest; and he again donned his hempen shirt, his breeches and peasant shoes, and started again to work.

"Life is dull for me," he said. "I'm getting fat and have lost my appetite and my sleep."

So he brought his father and mother and his mute sister to live with him, and worked as before.

People said, "But you are a king!"

"Yes," said he, "but even a king must eat."

One of his ministers came to him and said, "We have no money to pay salaries."

"All right," he said, "then don't pay them."

"Then no one will serve."

"All right; let them not serve. They will have more time to work; let them cart manure. There is plenty of scavenging to be done."

People came to Iván to be tried in court. One said, "He stole my money." And Iván said, "All right, that shows that he wanted it."

Soon everyone knew that Iván was a fool. Even his wife said to him, "People say that you are a fool."

"All right," Iván said.

His wife thought and thought about that, but she also was a fool.

"Shall I go against my husband? Where the needle goes the thread follows," she decided.

So she took off her royal dress, put it away in a chest, and went to the mute girl to learn to work. And she learned to work and began to help her husband.

All the wise men left Iván's kingdom; only the fools remained.

Nobody had money. They lived and worked. They fed themselves; and they fed others.

X

The old Devil waited and waited for news from the imps that they had finally ruined the three brothers. But no news came. So he went himself to inquire about it. He searched and searched, but instead of finding the three imps he found only the three holes!

"Evidently they have failed," he thought. "I shall have to tackle it myself."

So he went to look for the brothers, but they were no longer in their old places. He found them in three different kingdoms. All three were living and reigning. This annoyed the old Devil very much.

"Well," said he, "I must try my own hand at the job."

First, he went to King Simon. He did not go to him in his own shape, but disguised himself as a general, and arrived at Simon's palace.

"I hear, King Simon," he said, "that you are a great warrior, and as I know that business well, I desire to serve you."

King Simon questioned him, and thinking he was a wise man, took him into his service.

The new commander began to teach King Simon how to form a strong army.

"First," said he, "we must levy more soldiers, for there are in your kingdom many people unemployed. We must recruit all the young men without exception. Then you will have five times as many soldiers as before. Secondly, we must get new rifles and cannons. I will introduce rifles that will fire a hundred balls at once; they will fly out like peas. And I will get cannons that will consume with fire either man, or horse, or wall. They will burn up everything!"

Simon the King listened to the new commander, ordered all young men without exception to be enrolled as soldiers, and had new factories built in which he manufactured large quantities of improved rifles and cannons. Then he made haste to declare war against a neighboring king. As soon as he met the other army, King Simon ordered his soldiers to rain rifle balls against it and shoot fire from the cannons, and in one blow he burned and crippled half the enemy's army. The neighboring king was so thoroughly frightened that he gave up and surrendered.

King Simon was delighted.

"Now," he said, "I will conquer the King of India."

But the Indian King had heard about King Simon, and had adopted all his inventions, and added more of his own. The Indian King enlisted not only all the young men, but all the single women also, and gathered a greater army even than King Simon's. And he copied all King Simon's rifles and cannons, and invented a way of flying through the air to rain down bombs from above.

King Simon set out to fight the Indian King, expecting to beat him as he had beaten the other king; but the scythe that had cut so well had lost its edge. The King of India did not let Simon's army come within gunshot, but sent his women through the air to hurl down bombs onto Simon's army. The women began to rain down bombs onto the army like borax upon cockroaches. The army ran away, and Simon the King was left alone.

So the Indian King took Simon's kingdom, and Simon the Soldier fled as best he might.

Having finished with this brother, the old Devil went to King Tarás. Changing himself into a merchant, he settled in Tarás's kingdom, started a house of business, and began spending money. He paid high prices for everything, and everybody hurried to the new merchant to get money. And so much money spread among the people that they began to pay all their taxes promptly, and paid up all their arrears, and King Tarás rejoiced.

"Thanks to the new merchant," he thought, "I shall have more money than ever; and my life will be yet more comfortable."

Tarás the King began to form fresh plans and to build a new palace. He gave notice that people should bring him wood and stone, and he fixed high prices for everything. King Tarás thought people would come in crowds to work as before, but to his surprise all the wood and stone was taken to the merchant's, and all the workmen went there too. King Tarás increased his price, but the merchant bid yet more. King Tarás had money, but the merchant had still more, and outbid the King at every point.

The King's palace remained at a standstill as no building occurred.

King Tarás planned a garden, and when autumn came he called for the people to come and plant seedlings in the garden, but no one came. All the people were busy digging a pond for the merchant. Winter came, and King Tarás wanted to buy sable furs for a new overcoat. He sent servants to buy them, but they returned and said, "There are no sables left. The merchant has all the furs. He paid the best price and has made carpets of the skins."

Then King Tarás wanted to buy some stallions. He sent an emissary to buy them, but he returned saying, "The merchant has all the good stallions; they are carrying water to fill his pond."

All the King's affairs came to a standstill. No one would work for him, for everyone was busy working for the merchant; and they only brought King Tarás the merchant's money to pay their taxes.

The King collected so much money that he had nowhere to store it, and his life became wretched. He ceased to form plans, and would have been glad enough simply to live, but he was hardly able even to do that. He ran short of everything. One after another his cooks, coachmen, and servants left him for the merchant. Soon he lacked even food. When he sent to the market, there was nothing to be bought—the merchant had purchased everything, and people only brought the King money to pay their taxes.

Desperate and enraged, Tarás banished the merchant from the country. But the merchant settled just across the border and business went on as before. For the sake of the merchant's money, people took everything to him instead of to the King.

For days now the King had nothing to eat, and soon a rumor spread that the merchant was boasting that he would buy up the King himself! Frightened, King Tarás became frozen; he did not know what to do.

It was then that Simon the Soldier came to him, saying, "Help me, for the King of India has conquered my kingdom!"

But King Tarás himself was head over heels in difficulties.

"I myself," said he, "have had nothing to eat for two days. Thanks for asking."

XI

Having brought two brothers low, the old Devil went to Iván. He changed himself into a General and came before Iván to persuade him that he ought to have an army.

"It does not become a king," said the old Devil, "to be without an army. Only give me the order, and I will collect soldiers from among your people, and form one."

Iván listened to him. "All right," said Iván, "form an army, and teach them to sing songs well. I would like to hear them do that."

The old Devil went through Iván's kingdom to enlist men. He told them to enlist as soldiers, and each should have a quart of spirits and a fine red cap.

The people laughed.

"We have plenty of spirits," they said. "We

make it ourselves; and as for caps, the women make all kinds of them, even striped ones with tassels."

No one decided to enlist.

The old Devil went back to Iván and said: "Your fools won't enlist of their own free will. We shall have to make them."

"All right," said Iván, "you can try."

The old Devil gave notice that all the people must enlist, and that Iván would put to death anyone who refused.

The people came to the General and said, "You say that if we do not become soldiers the King will put us to death, but you don't say what will happen if we *do* enlist. We have heard it said that soldiers get killed!"

"Yes, that happens sometimes."

When the people heard this, they became obstinate.

"We won't go," they said. "Better to meet death at home. Either way we must die."

"Fools! You are fools!" the old Devil said. "A soldier may be killed or he may not, but if you don't go, King Iván will have you killed for certain."

The people were puzzled and went to Iván the Fool to consult him.

"A General has come," they said, "who says we must all become soldiers. 'If you become soldiers,' he says, 'you may be killed or you may not, but if you don't go, King Iván will certainly kill you.' Is this true?"

Iván laughed and said, "How can I, alone, put all of you to death? If I were not a fool I would explain it to you, but as it is, I don't understand it myself."

"Then," said they, "we will not serve."

"All right," said he, "don't."

The people went to the General and refused to enlist. And the old Devil saw that the jig was up, and he went off and ingratiated himself with the King of Tarakán.

"Let us make war," says he, "and conquer King Iván's country. It is true there is no money, but there is plenty of corn and cattle and everything else."

So the King of Tarakán prepared to make war. He mustered a great army, provided rifles and cannons, marched to the frontier, and entered Iván's kingdom.

The people came to Iván and said, "The King of Tarakán is coming to make war on us."

"All right," said Iván, "let him come."

Having crossed the frontier, the King of Tarakán sent scouts to look for Iván's army. They looked and looked, but there was no army! They waited and waited for one to appear, but there were no signs of an army, and nobody to fight with.

The King of Tarakán then made to seize the villages. The soldiers came to a village, and the people, both men and women, rushed out in astonishment to stare at the soldiers. The soldiers began to take their corn and cattle; the people let them have it and did not resist. The soldiers went on to another village; the same thing happened again. The soldiers went on for one day, and for two days, and everywhere the same thing happened. The people let them have everything, and no one resisted, but only invited the soldiers to live with them.

"Poor fellows," said they, "if you have a hard life in your own land, why don't you come and stay with us?"

The soldiers marched and marched: still no army, only people living and feeding themselves and others, and not resisting, but inviting the soldiers to stay and live with them. The soldiers found it dull work, and they came to the King of Tarakán and said, "We cannot fight here, lead us elsewhere. War is all right, but what is this? It is like cutting pea-soup! We cannot make war under these conditions."

The King of Tarakán grew angry, and ordered his soldiers to overrun the whole kingdom, to destroy the villages, to burn the grain and the houses, and to slaughter the cattle. "And if you do not obey my orders," he roared, "I will execute you all."

The soldiers were frightened, and began to act according to the King's orders. They began to burn houses and corn, and to kill cattle. But the fools still offered no resistance, and only wept. The old men wept, and the old women wept, and the young people wept.

"Why do you harm us?" they said. "Why do you waste good things? If you need them, why do you not take them for yourselves?"

At last the soldiers could stand it no longer. They refused to serve their king any longer, and the army disbanded and fled.

XII

The old Devil decided to give up. He could not get the better of Iván with soldiers. So he changed himself into a fine gentleman, and settled down in Iván's kingdom. He meant to overcome him by means of money, as he had overcome Tarás the Stout.

"I wish," he said, "to do you a good turn, to teach you sense and reason. I will build a house among you and organize a trade."

"All right," Iván said, "come and live among us if you like."

Next morning, the fine gentleman went out into the public square with a big sack of gold and a sheet of paper and said: "You all live like swine. I wish to teach you how to live properly. Build me a house according to this plan. You shall work, I will tell you how, and I will pay you with gold coins." And he showed them the gold.

The fools were astonished; there was no money in use among them; they bartered their goods and paid one another with labor. They looked at the gold coins with surprise.

"What nice little things they are!" said they.

And they began to exchange their goods and labor for the gentleman's gold pieces. And the old Devil began, as in Tarás's kingdom, to be free with his gold, and the people began to exchange everything for gold and to do all sorts of work for it.

The old Devil was delighted, and thought to himself, "Things are going right this time. Now I shall ruin the Fool as I did Tarás, and I shall buy him up body and soul."

But as soon as the fools had provided themselves with gold pieces they gave them to the women for necklaces. The lasses plaited them into their tresses, and at last the children in the street began to play with the gold.

Everyone had plenty of them, and they stopped taking them. But the fine gentleman's mansion was not yet half-built, and the grain and cattle for the year not yet provided. So he gave notice that he wished people to come and work for him, and that he wanted cattle and grain; for each thing, and for each service, he was ready to give many more pieces of gold.

But no one came to work and nothing was brought. Sometimes a boy or girl would run up to exchange an egg for a gold coin, but no one else, and he had nothing to eat. Being hungry, the fine gentleman went through the village to try and buy something for dinner. He stopped at one house, and offered a gold piece for a fowl, but the housewife wouldn't take it.

"I have a lot already," she said.

He tried at a widow's house to buy a herring and offered a gold piece.

"I don't want it, my good sir," said she. "I have no children to play with it, and I myself already have three coins as curiosities."

He tried at a peasant's house to get bread, but neither would the peasant take money.

"I don't need it," said he, "but if you are begging 'for Christ's sake,' wait a bit and I'll tell the housewife to cut you a piece of bread."

At that the Devil spat and ran away. To hear Christ's name mentioned—let alone the thought of receiving anything for Christ's sake—hurt him more than sticking a knife into him.

No bread was forthcoming. Everyone had gold, and no matter where the old Devil went, every one said, "Either bring something else, or come and work, or receive what you want in charity for Christ's sake."

But the old Devil had nothing but money; for work he had no liking, and as for taking anything "for Christ's sake" he could not do that. The old Devil grew very angry.

"What more do you want, when I give you money?" said he. "You can buy everything with gold and hire any kind of laborer." But the fools did not heed him.

"No, we do not want money," they said. "We have no payments to make, and no taxes, so what should we do with it?"

The old Devil lay down to sleep—supperless.

The affair was told to Iván the Fool. People came and asked him, "What are we to do? A fine gentleman has turned up, who likes to eat and drink and dress well, but he does not like to work, won't beg in 'Christ's name,' but only offers gold pieces to everyone. At first people gave him all he wanted, until they had plenty of gold pieces, but now no one gives him anything. What's to be done with him? He will die of hunger before long."

Iván listened.

"All right," he said, "we must feed him. Let him live by turn at each house as a shepherd does."

There was no help for it. The old Devil had to begin making the rounds, if he wanted any chance left of destroying the fool.

In due course, the turn came for him to go to Iván's house. The old Devil came in to dinner, and the mute girl was getting it ready.

She had often been deceived by lazy folk who came early to dinner, without having done their share of work, and then ate up all the porridge, so it had occurred to her to discover the sluggards by their hands. Those who had calloused hands she put at the table, but the others got only the leftover scraps.

The old Devil sat down at the table, but the mute girl seized him by the hands and looked at them—there were no hard places or whorls there: the hands were clean and smooth, with long nails. The mute girl gave a grunt and pulled the Devil away from the table.

Iván's wife said to him, "Don't be offended, fine gentleman. My sister-in-law does not allow anyone to come to table who hasn't calloused hands. But wait awhile—after the folk have eaten, you shall have what is left."

The old Devil was offended that in the King's house they wished him to feed like a pig. He said to Iván, "It is a foolish law you have in your kingdom that everyone must work with his hands. It's your stupidity that invented it. Do people work only with their hands? What do you think wise men work with?"

Iván said, "How are we fools to know? We do most of our work with our hands and our backs."

"That is because you are fools! But I will teach you how to work with the head. Then you will know that it is more profitable to work with the head than with the hands."

Iván was surprised.

"If that is so," said he, "then there is some sense in calling us fools!"

The old Devil went on: "Only it is not easy to work with one's head. You give me nothing to eat, because I have no hard places on my hands, but you do not know that it is a hundred times more difficult to work with the head. Sometimes one's head quite splits."

Iván became thoughtful.

"Why, then, friend, do you torture yourself so? Is it pleasant when the head splits? Would it not be better to do easier work with your hands and your back?"

The Devil said, "I do it all out of pity for you fools. If I didn't torture myself you would remain fools forever. But, having worked with my head, I can now teach you."

Iván was surprised.

"Do teach us!" he said, "so that when our hands get cramps and bruises we may use our heads for a change."

And the Devil promised to teach the people. So Iván gave notice throughout the kingdom that a fine gentleman had come who would teach everybody how to work with their heads; that with the head more could be done than with the hands; and that the people ought all to come and learn.

There was in Iván's kingdom a high tower, with many steps leading up to a lantern on the top. Iván took the gentleman up there that every one might see him.

The old Devil took his place on the top of the tower and began to speak, and the people came together to see him. They thought the gentleman would really show them how to work with the head without using the hands. But the old Devil only taught them in too many words how they might live without working. The people could make nothing of it. They stared and contemplated those words, and at last went off to attend to their affairs.

The old Devil stood on the tower a whole day and, after that, a second day, talking all the time. But standing there so long the old Devil grew hungry, and the fools never thought of taking food to him up in the tower. They thought that if he could work with his head better than with his hands, he could at any rate easily provide himself with bread.

The old Devil stood on the top of the tower yet another day, talking away. People came near, looked on for a while, and then went away.

Iván asked, "Well, has the gentleman begun to work with his head yet?"

"Not yet," the people said. "He's still spouting away."

The old Devil stood on the tower one day more, but he began to grow weak, so that he staggered and hit his head against one of the pillars of the lantern. One of the people noticed it and told Iván's wife, and she ran to her husband, who was in the field.

"Come and look," she said. "They say the gentleman is beginning to work with his head."

Iván was surprised.

"Really?" he said, and he turned his horse round, and went to the tower.

By the time he reached the tower the old Devil was quite exhausted with hunger and was staggering and knocking his head against the pillars. And just as Iván arrived at the tower, the Devil stumbled, fell, and came bump, bump, bump, straight down the stairs to the bottom, counting each step with a knock of his head!

"Well!" Iván said, "the fine gentleman told the truth when he said that 'sometimes one's head quite splits.' This is worse than blisters; after such work there will be swellings on the head."

The old Devil tumbled out at the foot of the stairs and struck his head against the ground.

Iván was about to go up to him to see how much work he had done—when suddenly the earth opened and the old Devil fell through. Only a hole was left.

Iván scratched his head.

"What a nasty thing," says he. "It's one of those devils again! What a whopper! He must be the father of them all."

Iván is still living and people crowd to his kingdom. His own brothers have come to live with him, and he feeds them, too.

To everyone who comes and says, "Give me food!" Iván says, "All right. You can stay with us; we have plenty of everything."

Only there is one special custom in his kingdom; whoever has calloused hands comes to table, but whoever has not . . . must eat what the others leave.

Charles Waddell Chestnutt (1858–1932) was an African American novelist and activist who used his novels and short stories to explore issues of race and social identity. He was a practicing attorney and used his free time to write stories. "The Goophered Grapevine" was the first work by an African American author published in the *Atlantic Monthly*. At the time, the *Atlantic* was the most prestigious literary magazine in the country. Like many of his other works, "Grapevine" uses subtle irony to discuss the authentic lives of blacks in America as well as to refute prejudice, not only racial but color prejudice among African American people. "Grapevine" (1887) was reprinted in Chestnutt's collection *The Conjure Woman* (1899) as well as in *Collected Stories of Charles W. Chestnutt* (1992), edited by William L. Andrews.

The Goophered Grapevine

Charles W. Chestnutt

SOME YEARS AGO my wife was in poor health, and our family doctor, in whose skill and honesty I had implicit confidence, advised a change of climate. I shared, from an unprofessional standpoint, his opinion that the raw winds, the chill rains, and the violent changes of temperature that characterized the winters in the region of the Great Lakes tended to aggravate my wife's difficulty, and would undoubtedly shorten her life if she remained exposed to them. The doctor's advice was that we seek, not a temporary place of sojourn, but a permanent residence, in a warmer and more equable climate. I was engaged at the time in grape-culture in northern Ohio, and, as I liked the business and had given it much study, I decided to look for some other locality suitable for carrying it on. I thought of sunny France, of sleepy Spain, of Southern California, but there were objections to them all. It occurred to me that I might find what I wanted in some one of

our own Southern States. It was a sufficient time after the war for conditions in the South to have become somewhat settled; and I was enough of a pioneer to start a new industry, if I could not find a place where grape-culture had been tried. I wrote to a cousin who had gone into the turpentine business in central North Carolina. He assured me, in response to my inquiries, that no better place could be found in the South than the State and neighborhood where he lived; the climate was perfect for health, and, in conjunction with the soil, ideal for grape-culture; labor was cheap, and land could be bought for a mere song. He gave us a cordial invitation to come and visit him while we looked into the matter. We accepted the invitation, and after several days of leisurely travel, the last hundred miles of which were up a river on a sidewheel steamer, we reached our destination, a quaint old town, which I shall call Patesville, because, for one reason, that is not its name. There was a red brick market-house in the public square, with a tall tower, which held a four-faced clock that struck the hours, and from which there pealed out a curfew at nine o'clock. There were two or three hotels, a court-house, a jail, stores, offices, and all the appurtenances of a county seat and a commercial emporium; for while Patesville numbered only four or five thousand inhabitants, of all shades of complexion, it was one of the principal towns in North Carolina, and had a considerable trade in cotton and naval stores. This business activity was not immediately apparent to my unaccustomed eyes. Indeed, when I first saw the town, there brooded over it a calm that seemed almost sabbatic in its restfulness, though I learned later on that underneath its somnolent exterior the deeper currents of life—love and hatred, joy and despair, ambition and avarice, faith and friendship—flowed not less steadily than in livelier latitudes.

We found the weather delightful at that season, the end of summer, and were hospitably entertained. Our host was a man of means and evidently regarded our visit as a pleasure, and we were therefore correspondingly at our ease, and in a position to act with the coolness of judgment desirable in making so radical a change in our lives. My cousin placed a horse and buggy at our disposal, and himself acted as our guide until I became somewhat familiar with the country.

I found that grape-culture, while it had never been carried on to any great extent, was not entirely unknown in the neighborhood. Several planters thereabouts had attempted it on a commercial scale, in former years, with greater or less success; but like most Southern industries, it had felt the blight of war and had fallen into desuetude.

I went several times to look at a place that I thought might suit me. It was a plantation of considerable extent, that had formerly belonged to a wealthy man by the name of McAdoo. The estate had been for years involved in litigation between disputing heirs, during which period shiftless cultivation had well-nigh exhausted the soil. There had been a vineyard of some extent on the place, but it had not been attended to since the war, and had lapsed into utter neglect. The vines—here partly supported by decayed and broken-down trellises, there twining themselves among the branches of the slender saplings which had sprung up among them—grew in wild and unpruned luxuriance, and the few scattered grapes they bore were the undisputed prey of the first comer. The site was admirably adapted to grape-raising; the soil, with a little attention, could not have been better; and with the native grape, the luscious scuppernong, as my main reliance in the beginning, I felt sure that I could introduce and cultivate successfully a number of other varieties.

One day I went over with my wife to show her the place. We drove out of the town over a long wooden bridge that spanned a spreading mill-pond, passed the long whitewashed fence surrounding the county fair-ground, and struck into a road so sandy that the horse's feet sank to the fetlocks. Our route lay partly up hill and partly down, for we were in the sand-hill county; we drove past cultivated farms, and then by abandoned fields grown up in scrub-oak and short-leaved pine, and once or twice through the solemn aisles of the virgin forest, where the tall pines, well-nigh meeting over the narrow road, shut out the sun, and wrapped us in cloistral solitude. Once, at a cross-roads, I was in doubt as to the turn to take, and we sat there waiting ten minutes—we had already caught some of the native infection of restfulness—for some human being to come along, who could direct us on our way. At length a little negro girl appeared, walking straight as an arrow, with a piggin full of water on her head. After a little patient investigation, necessary to overcome the child's shyness, we learned what we wished to know, and at the end of about five miles from the town reached our destination.

We drove between a pair of decayed gateposts— the gate itself had long since disappeared—and up a straight sandy lane, between two lines of rotting rail fence, partly concealed by jimson-weeds and briers, to the open space where a dwelling-house had once stood, evidently a spacious mansion, if we might judge from the ruined chimneys that were still standing, and the brick pillars on which the sills rested. The house itself, we had been informed, had fallen a victim to the fortunes of war.

We alighted from the buggy, walked about the yard for a while, and then wandered off into the adjoining vineyard. Upon Annie's complaining of weariness I led the way back to the yard, where a pine log, lying under a spreading elm, afforded a shady though somewhat hard seat. One end of the log was already occupied by a venerable-looking colored man. He held on his knees a hat full of grapes, over which he was smacking his lips with great gusto, and a pile of grapeskins near him indicated that the performance was no new thing. We approached him at an angle from the rear, and were close to him before he perceived us. He respectfully rose as we drew near, and was moving away, when I begged him to keep his seat.

"Don't let us disturb you," I said. "There is plenty of room for us all."

He resumed his seat with somewhat of embarrassment. While he had been standing, I had observed that he was a tall man, and, though slightly bowed by the weight of years, apparently quite vigorous. He was not entirely black, and this fact, together with the quality of his hair, which was about six inches long and very bushy, except on the top of his head, where he was quite bald, suggested a slight strain of other than negro blood. There was a shrewdness in his eyes, too, which was not altogether African, and which, as we afterwards learned from experience, was indicative of a corresponding shrewdness in his character. He went on eating the grapes, but did not seem to enjoy himself quite so well as he had apparently done before he became aware of our presence.

"Do you live around here?" I asked, anxious to put him at his ease.

"Yas, suh. I lives des ober yander, behine de nex' san'-hill, on de Lumberton plank-road."

"Do you know anything about the time when this vineyard was cultivated?"

"Lawd bless you, suh, I knows all about it. Dey ain' na'er a man in dis settlement w'at won' tell you ole Julius McAdoo 'uz bawn en raise' on dis yer same plantation. Is you de Norv'n gemman w'at's gwine ter buy de ole vimya'd?"

"I am looking at it," I replied; "but I don't know that I shall care to buy unless I can be reasonably sure of making something out of it."

"Well, suh, you is a stranger ter me, en I is a stranger ter you, en we is bofe strangers ter one anudder, but 'f I 'uz in yo' place, I wouldn' buy dis vimya'd."

"Why not?" I asked.

"Well, I dunno whe'r you b'lieves in cunj'in' er not,—some er de w'ite folks don't, er says dey don't,—but de truf er de matter is dat dis yer ole vimya'd is goophered."

"Is what?" I asked, not grasping the meaning of this unfamiliar word.

"Is goophered,—cunju'd, bewitch'."

He imparted this information with such solemn earnestness, and with such an air of confidential mystery, that I felt somewhat interested, while Annie was evidently much impressed, and drew closer to me.

"How do you know it is bewitched?" I asked.

"I wouldn' spec' fer you ter b'lieve me 'less you know all 'bout de fac's. But ef you en young miss dere doan' min' lis'nin' ter a ole nigger run on a minute er two w'ile you er restin', I kin 'splain to you how it all happen'."

We assured him that we would be glad to hear how it all happened, and he began to tell us. At first the current of his memory—or imagination—seemed somewhat sluggish; but as his embarrassment wore off, his language flowed more freely, and the story acquired perspective and coherence. As he became more and more absorbed in the narrative, his eyes assumed a dreamy expression, and he seemed to lose sight of his auditors, and to be living over again in monologue his life on the old plantation.

"Ole Mars Dugal' McAdoo," he began, "bought dis place long many years befo' de wah, en I 'member well w'en he sot out all dis yer part er de plantation in scuppernon's. De vimes growed monst'us fas', en Mars Dugal' made a thousan' gallon er scuppernon' wine eve'y year.

"Now, ef dey's an'thing a nigger lub, nex' ter 'possum, en chick'n, en watermillyums, it's scuppernon's. Dey ain' nuffin dat kin stan' up side'n de scuppernon' fer sweetness; sugar ain't a suckumstance ter scuppernon'. W'en de season is nigh 'bout ober, en de grapes begin ter swivel up des a little wid de wrinkles er ole age,—w'en de skin git sof' en brown,—den de scuppernon' make you smack yo' lip en roll yo' eye en wush fer mo'; so I reckon it ain' very 'stonishin' dat niggers lub scuppernon'.

"Dey wuz a sight er niggers in de naberhood er de vimya'd. Dere wuz ole Mars Henry Brayboy's niggers, en ole Mars Jeems McLean's niggers, en Mars Dugal's own niggers; den dey wuz a settlement er free niggers en po' buckrahs down by de Wim'l'ton Road, en Mars Dugal' had de only vimya'd in de naberhood. I reckon it ain' so much so nowadays, but befo' de wah, in slab'ry times, a nigger did n' mine goin' fi' er ten mile in a night, w'en dey wuz sump'n good ter eat at de yuther een'.

"So atter a w'ile Mars Dugal' begin ter miss his scuppernon's. Co'se he 'cuse' de niggers er it, but dey all 'nied it ter de las'. Mars Dugal' sot spring guns en steel traps, en he en de oberseah sot up nights once't er twice't, tel one night Mars Dugal'—he 'uz a monst'us keerless man—got his leg shot full er cow-peas. But somehow er nudder dey could n' nebber ketch none er de niggers. I dunner how it happen, but it happen des like I tell you, en de grapes kep' on a-goin' des de same.

"But bimeby ole Mars Dugal' fix' up a plan ter stop it. Dey wuz a cunjuh 'oman livin' down 'mongs' de free niggers on de Wim'l'ton Road, en all de darkies fum Rockfish ter Beaver Crick wuz feared er her. She could wuk de mos' powerfulles' kin' er goopher,—could make people hab fits, er rheumatiz, er make 'em des dwinel away en die; en dey say she went out ridin' de niggers at night, fer she wuz a witch 'sides bein' a cunjuh 'oman. Mars Dugal' hearn 'bout Aun' Peggy's doin's, en begun ter 'flect whe'r er no he could n' git her ter he'p him keep de niggers off'n de

grapevimes. One day in de spring er de year, ole miss pack' up a basket er chick'n en poun'-cake, en a bottle er scuppernon' wine, en Mars Dugal' tuk it in his buggy en driv ober ter Aun' Peggy's cabin. He tuk de basket in, en had a long talk wid Aun' Peggy.

"De nex' day Aun' Peggy come up ter de vimya'd. De niggers seed her slippin' 'roun', en dey soon foun' out what she 'uz doin' dere. Mars Dugal' had hi'ed her ter goopher de grapevimes. She sa'ntered 'roun' 'mongs' de vimes, en tuk a leaf fum dis one, en a grape-hull fum dat one, en a grape-seed fum anudder one; en den a little twig fum here, en a little pinch er dirt fum dere,—en put it all in a big black bottle, wid a snake's toof en a speckle' hen's gall en some ha'rs fum a black cat's tail, en den fill' de bottle wid scuppernon' wine. Wen she got de goopher all ready en fix', she tuk 'n went out in de woods en buried it under de root uv a red oak tree, en den come back en tole one er de niggers she done goopher de grapevimes, en a'er a nigger w'at eat dem grapes 'ud be sho ter die inside'n twel' mont's.

"Atter dat de niggers let de scuppernon's 'lone, en Mars Dugal' did n' hab no 'casion ter fine no mo' fault; en de season wuz mos' gone, w'en a strange gemman stop at de plantation one night ter see Mars Dugal' on some business; en his coachman, seein' de scuppernon's growin' so nice en sweet, slip 'roun' behine de smoke-house, en et all de scuppernon's he could hole. Nobody did n' notice it at de time, but dat night, on de way home, de gemman's hoss runned away en kill' de coachman. W'en we hearn de noos, Aun' Lucy, de cook, she up 'n say she seed de strange nigger eat'n' er de scuppernon's behine de smoke-house; en den we knowed de goopher had b'en er wukkin'. Den one er de nigger chilluns runned away fum de quarters one day, en got in de scuppernon's, en died de nex' week. W'ite folks say he die' er de fevuh, but de niggers knowed it wuz de goopher. So you k'n be sho de darkies did n' hab much ter do wid dem scuppernon' vimes.

"W'en de scuppernon' season 'uz ober fer dat year, Mars Dugal' foun' he had made fifteen hund'ed gallon er wine; en one er de niggers hearn him laffin' wid de oberseah fit ter kill, en sayin' dem fifteen hund'ed gallon er wine wuz monst'us good intrus' on de ten dollars he laid out on de vimya'd. So I 'low ez he paid Aun' Peggy ten dollars fer to goopher de grapevimes.

"De goopher did n' wuk no mo' tel de nex' summer, w'en 'long to'ds de middle er de season one er de fiel' han's died; en ez dat lef' Mars Dugal' sho't er han's, he went off ter town fer ter buy anudder. He fotch de noo nigger home wid 'im. He wuz er ole nigger, er de color er a gingy-cake, en ball ez a hoss-apple on de top er his head. He wuz a peart ole nigger, do', en could do a big day's wuk.

"Now it happen dat one er de niggers on de nex' plantation, one er ole Mars Henry Brayboy's niggers, had runned away de day befo', en tuk ter de swamp, en ole Mars Dugal' en some er de yuther nabor w'ite folks had gone out wid dere guns en dere dogs fer ter he'p 'em hunt fer de nigger; en de han's on our own plantation wuz all so flusterated dat we fuhgot ter tell de noo han' 'bout de goopher on de scuppernon' vimes. Co'se he smell de grapes en see de vimes, an atter dahk de fus' thing he done wuz ter slip off ter de grapevimes 'dout sayin' nuffin ter nobody. Nex' mawnin' he tole some er de niggers 'bout de fine bait er scuppernon' he et de night befo'.

"Wen dey tole 'im 'bout de goopher on de grapevimes, he 'uz dat tarrified dat he turn pale, en look des like he gwine ter die right in his tracks. De oberseah come up en axed w'at 'uz de matter; en w'en dey tole 'im Henry be'n eatin' er de scuppernon's, en got de goopher on 'im, he gin Henry a big drink er w'iskey, en 'low dat de nex' rainy day he take 'im ober ter Aun' Peggy's, en see ef she would n' take de goopher off'n him, seein' ez he did n' know nuffin erbout it tel he done et de grapes.

"Sho nuff, it rain de nex' day, en de oberseah went ober ter Aun' Peggy's wid Henry. En Aun' Peggy say dat bein' ez Henry did n' know 'bout de goopher, en et de grapes in ign'ance er de conseq'ences, she reckon she mought be able fer ter take de goopher off'n him. So she fotch out

er bottle wid some cunjuh medicine in it, en po'd some out in a go'd fer Henry ter drink. He manage ter git it down; he say it tas'e like whiskey wid sump'n bitter in it. She 'lowed dat 'ud keep de goopher off'n him tel de spring; but w'en de sap begin ter rise in de grapevimes he ha' ter come en see her ag'in, en she tell him w'at e's ter do.

"Nex' spring, w'en de sap commence' ter rise in de scuppernon' vime, Henry tuk a ham one night. Whar'd he git de ham? I doan know; dey wa'n't no hams on de plantation 'cep'n' w'at 'uz in de smoke-house, but I never see Henry 'bout de smoke-house. But ez I wuz a-sayin', he tuk de ham ober ter Aun' Peggy's; en Aun' Peggy tole 'im dat w'en Mars Dugal' begin ter prune de grapevimes, he mus' go en take 'n scrape off de sap whar it ooze out'n de cut een's er de vimes, en 'n'int his ball head wid it; en ef he do dat once't a year de goopher would n' wuk agin 'im long ez he done it. En bein' ez he fotch her de ham, she fix' it so he kin eat all de scuppernon' he want.

"So Henry 'n'int his head wid de sap out'n de big grapevime des ha'f way 'twix' de quarters en de big house, en de goopher nebber wuk agin him dat summer. But de beatenes' thing you eber see happen ter Henry. Up ter dat time he wuz ez ball ez a sweeten' 'tater, but des ez soon ez de young leaves begun ter come out on de grapevimes, de ha'r begun ter grow out on Henry's head, en by de middle er de summer he had de bigges' head er ha'r on de plantation. Befo' dat, Henry had tol'able good ha'r 'roun' de aidges, but soon ez de young grapes begun ter come, Henry's ha'r begun to quirl all up in little balls, des like dis yer reg'lar grapy ha'r, en by de time de grapes got ripe his head look des like a bunch er grapes. Combin' it did n' do no good; he wuk at it ha'f de night wid er Jim Crow, en think he git it straighten' out, but in de mawnin' de grapes 'ud be dere des de same. So he gin it up, en tried ter keep de grapes down by havin' his ha'r cut sho't.

"But dat wa'n't de quares' thing 'bout de goopher. When Henry come ter de plantation, he wuz gittin' a little ole an stiff in de j'ints. But dat summer he got des ez spry en libely ez any young nigger on de plantation; fac', he got so biggity dat

Mars Jackson, de oberseah, ha' ter th'eaten ter whip 'im, ef he did n' stop cuttin' up his didos en behave hisse'f. But de mos' cur'ouses' thing happen' in de fall, when de sap begin ter go down in de grapevimes. Fus', when de grapes 'uz gethered, de knots begun ter straighten out'n Henry's ha'r; en w'en de leaves begin ter fall, Henry's ha'r 'mence' ter drap out; en when de vimes 'uz bar', Henry's head wuz baller 'n it wuz in de spring, en he begin ter git ole en stiff in de j'ints ag'in, en paid no mo' 'tention ter de gals dyoin' er de whole winter. En nex' spring, w'en he rub de sap on ag'in, he got young ag'in, en so soopl en libely dat none er de young niggers on de plantation could n' jump, ner dance, ner hoe ez much cotton ez Henry. But in de fall er de year his grapes 'mence' ter straighten out, en his j'ints ter git stiff, en his ha'r drap off, en de rheumatiz begin ter wrastle wid 'im.

"Now, ef you'd 'a' knowed ole Mars Dugal' McAdoo, you'd 'a' knowed dat it ha' ter be a mighty rainy day when he could n' fine sump'n fer his niggers ter do, en it ha' ter be a mighty little hole he could n' crawl thoo, en ha' ter be a monst'us cloudy night when a dollar git by him in de dahkness; en w'en he see how Henry git young in de spring en ole in de fall, he 'lowed ter hisse'f ez how he could make mo' money out'n Henry dan by wukkin' him in de cotton-fiel'. 'Long de nex' spring, atter de sap 'mence' ter rise, en Henry 'n'int 'is head en sta'ted fer ter git young en soopl, Mars Dugal' up 'n tuk Henry ter town, en sole 'im fer fifteen hunder' dollars. Co'se de man w'at bought Henry did n' know nuffin 'bout de goopher, en Mars Dugal' did n' see no 'casion fer ter tell 'im. Long to'ds de fall, w'en de sap went down, Henry begin ter git ole ag'in same ez yuzhal, en his noo marster begin ter git skeered les'n he gwine ter lose his fifteen-hunder'-dollar nigger. He sent fer a mighty fine doctor, but de med'cine did n' 'pear ter do no good; de goopher had a good holt. Henry tole de doctor 'bout de goopher, but de doctor des laff at 'im.

"One day in de winter Mars Dugal' went ter town, en wuz santerin' 'long de Main Street, when who should he meet but Henry's noo marster. Dey said 'Hoddy,' en Mars Dugal' ax 'im ter hab a seegyar; en atter dey run on awhile 'bout de craps en de weather, Mars Dugal' ax 'im, sorter keerless, like ez ef he des thought of it,—

"'How you like de nigger I sole you las' spring?'

"Henry's marster shuck his head en knock de ashes off'n his seegyar.

"''Spec' I made a bad bahgin when I bought dat nigger. Henry done good wuk all de summer, but sence de fall set in he 'pears ter be sorter pinin' away. Dey ain' nuffin pertickler de matter wid 'im—leastways de doctor say so—'cep'n' a tech er de rheumatiz; but his ha'r is all fell out, en ef he don't pick up his strenk mighty soon, I spec' I'm gwine ter lose 'im.'

"Dey smoked on awhile, en bimeby ole mars say, 'Well, a bahgin 's a bahgin, but you en me is good fren's, en I doan wan' ter see you lose all de money you paid fer dat nigger; en ef w'at you say is so, en I ain't 'sputin' it, he ain't wuf much now. I 'spec's you wukked him too ha'd dis summer, er e'se de swamps down here don't agree wid de san'-hill nigger. So you des lemme know, en ef he gits any wusser I'll be willin' ter gib yer five hund'ed dollars fer 'im, en take my chances on his livin'.'

"Sho 'nuff, when Henry begun ter draw up wid de rheumatiz en it look like he gwine ter die fer sho, his noo marster sen' fer Mars Dugal', en Mars Dugal' gin him what he promus, en brung Henry home ag'in. He tuk good keer uv 'im dyoin' er de winter,—give 'im w'iskey ter rub his rheumatiz, en terbacker ter smoke, en all he want ter eat,—'caze a nigger w'at he could make a thousan' dollars a year off'n did n' grow on eve'y huckleberry bush.

"Nex' spring, w'en de sap ris en Henry's ha'r commence' ter sprout, Mars Dugal' sole 'im ag'in, down in Robeson County dis time; en he kep' dat sellin' business up fer five year er mo'. Henry nebber say nuffin 'bout de goopher ter his noo marsters, 'caze he know he gwine ter be tuk good keer uv de nex' winter, w'en Mars Dugal' buy him back. En Mars Dugal' made 'nuff money off'n Henry ter buy anudder plantation ober on Beaver Crick.

"But 'long 'bout de een' er dat five year dey come a stranger ter stop at de plantation. De fus' day he 'uz dere he went out wid Mars Dugal' en spent all de mawnin' lookin' ober de vimya'd, en atter dinner dey spent all de evenin' playin' kya'ds. De niggers soon 'skiver' dat he wuz a Yankee, en dat he come down ter Norf C'lina fer ter l'arn de w'ite folks how to raise grapes en make wine. He promus Mars Dugal' he c'd make de grapevimes b'ar twice't ez many grapes, en dat de noo wine-press he wuz a-sellin' would make mo' d'n twice't ez many gallons er wine. En ole Mars Dugal' des drunk it all in, des 'peared ter be bewitch' wid dat Yankee. Wen de darkies see dat Yankee run-nin' 'roun' de vimya'd en diggin' under de grape-vimes, dey shuk dere heads, en 'lowed dat dey feared Mars Dugal' losin' his min'. Mars Dugal' had all de dirt dug away fum under de roots er all de scuppernon' vimes, an' let 'em stan' dat away fer a week er mo'. Den dat Yankee made de nig-gers fix up a mixtry er lime en ashes en manyo, en po' it 'roun' de roots er de grapevimes. Den he 'vise Mars Dugal' fer ter trim de vimes close't, en Mars Dugal' tuck 'n done eve'ything de Yankee tole him ter do. Dyoin' all er dis time, mind yer, dis yer Yankee wuz libbin' off'n de fat er de lan', at de big house, en playin' kya'ds wid Mars Dugal' eve'y night; en dey say Mars Dugal' los' mo'n a thousan' dollars dyoin' er de week dat Yankee wuz a-ruinin' de grapevimes.

"Wen de sap ris nex' spring, ole Henry 'n'inted his head ez yuzhal, en his ha'r 'mence' ter grow des de same ez it done eve'y year. De scuppernon' vimes growed monst's fas', en de leaves wuz greener en thicker dan dey eber be'n dyoin' my rememb'ance; en Henry's ha'r growed out thicker dan eber, en he 'peared ter git younger 'n younger, en soopler 'n soopler; en seein' ez he wuz sho't er ban's dat spring, havin' tuk in consid'able noo groun', Mars Dugal' 'eluded he would n' sell Henry 'tel he git de crap in en de cotton chop'. So he kep' Henry on de plantation.

"But 'long 'bout time fer de grapes ter come on de scuppernon' vimes, dey 'peared ter come a change ober 'em; de leaves withered en swivel' up, en de young grapes turn' yaller, en bimeby eve'ybody on de plantation could see dat de whole vimya'd wuz dyin'. Mars Dugal' tuk'n water de vimes en done all he could, but 't wa'n' no use: dat Yankee had done bus' de watermil-lyum. One time de vimes picked up a bit, en Mars Dugal' 'lowed dey wuz gwine ter come out ag'in; but dat Yankee done dug too close under de roots, en prune de branches too close ter de vime, en all dat lime en ashes done burn' de life out'n de vimes, en dey des kep' a-with'in' en a-swivelin'.

"All dis time de goopher wuz a-wukkin'. When de vimes sta'ted ter wither, Henry 'mence' ter complain er his rheumatiz; en when de leaves begin ter dry up, his ha'r 'mence' ter drap out. When de vimes fresh' up a bit, Henry 'd git peart ag'in, en when de vimes wither' ag'in, Henry 'd git ole ag'in, en des kep' gittin' mo' en mo' fit-ten fer nuffin; he des pined away, en pined away, en fine'ly tuk ter his cabin; en when de big vime whar he got de sap ter 'n'int his head withered en turned yaller en died, Henry died too,—des went out sorter like a cannel. Dey didn't 'pear ter be nuffin de matter wid 'im, 'cep'n' de rheuma-tiz, but his strenk des dwinel' away 'tel he did n' hab ernuff lef ter draw his bref. De goopher had got de under holt, en th'owed Henry dat time fer good en all.

"Mars Dugal' tuk on might'ly 'bout losin' his vimes en his nigger in de same year; en he swo' dat ef he could git holt er dat Yankee he 'd wear 'im ter a frazzle, en den chaw up de frazzle; en he'd done it, too, for Mars Dugal' 'uz a monst'us brash man w'en he once git started. He sot de vimya'd out ober ag'in, but it wuz th'ee er fo' year befo' de vimes got ter b'arin' any scuppernon's.

"W'en de wah broke out, Mars Dugal' raise' a comp'ny, en went off ter fight de Yankees. He say he wuz mighty glad dat wah come, en he des want ter kill a Yankee fer eve'y dollar he los' 'long er dat grape-raisin' Yankee. En I 'spec' he would 'a' done it, too, ef de Yankees had n' s'picioned sump'n, en killed him fus'. Atter de s'render ole miss move' ter town, de niggers all scattered 'way fum de plantation, en de vimya'd ain' be'n culter-vated sence."

"Is that story true?" asked Annie doubtfully, but seriously, as the old man concluded his nar-rative.

"It's des ez true ez I'm a-settin' here, miss. Dey's a easy way ter prove it: I kin lead de way right ter Henry's grave ober yander in de planta-tion buryin'-groun'. En I tell yer w'at, marster, I would n' 'vise you to buy dis yer ole vimya'd, 'caze de goopher 's on it yit, en dey ain' no tellin' w'en it's gwine ter crap out."

"But I thought you said all the old vines died."

"Dey did 'pear ter die, but a few un 'em come out ag'in, en is mixed in 'mongs' de yuthers. I ain' skeered ter eat de grapes, 'caze I knows de old vimes fum de noo ones; but wid strangers dey ain' no tellin' w'at mought happen. I would n' 'vise yer ter buy dis vimya'd."

I bought the vineyard, nevertheless, and it has been for a long time in a thriving condition, and is often referred to by the local press as a striking illustration of the opportunities open to Northern capital in the development of South-ern industries. The luscious scuppernong holds first rank among our grapes, though we cultivate a great many other varieties, and our income from grapes packed and shipped to the Northern mar-kets is quite considerable. I have not noticed any developments of the goopher in the vineyard, although I have a mild suspicion that our col-ored assistants do not suffer from want of grapes during the season.

I found, when I bought the vineyard, that Uncle Julius had occupied a cabin on the place for many years, and derived a respectable rev-enue from the product of the neglected grape-vines. This, doubtless, accounted for his advice to me not to buy the vineyard, though whether it inspired the goopher story I am unable to state. I believe, however, that the wages I paid him for his services as coachman, for I gave him employment in that capacity, were more than an equivalent for anything he lost by the sale of the vineyard.

Frank Richard Stockton (1834–1902) was a Philadelphia-born American writer whose fairy tales were beloved toward the end of the nineteenth century. Before he began writing, Stockton was a wood engraver, although his father wanted him to go into medicine. In 1873, he became the assistant editor of the *St. Nicholas Magazine* and this also ignited his literary career. Although his earlier work was mostly for children, Stockton began publishing for adult readers in the latter half of the nineteenth century. Some of Stockton's most popular works include *Rudder Grange* (1879), "The Lady, or the Tiger?" (1884), and *Ting-a-Ling Tales* (1870). The funny and clever "The Bee-Man of Orn," reprinted here, was adapted into an episode of the BBC series *Jackanory* in 1971.

The Bee-Man of Orn

Frank R. Stockton

IN THE ANCIENT COUNTRY OF ORN, there lived an old man who was called the Bee-man, because his whole time was spent in the company of bees. He lived in a small hut, which was nothing more than an immense beehive, for these little creatures had built their honeycombs in every corner of the one room it contained, on the shelves, under the little table, all about the rough bench on which the old man sat, and even about the headboard and along the sides of his low bed. All day the air of the room was thick with buzzing insects, but this did not interfere in any way with the old Bee-man, who walked in among them, ate his meals, and went to sleep, without the slightest fear of being stung. He had lived with the bees so long, they had become so accustomed to him, and his skin was so tough and hard, that the bees no more thought of stinging him than they would of stinging a tree or a stone. A swarm of bees had made their hive in a pocket of his old leathern doublet; and when he put on this coat to take one of his long walks in the forest in search of wild bees' nests, he was very glad to have this hive with him, for, if he did not find any wild honey, he would put his hand in his pocket and take out a piece of a comb for a luncheon. The bees in his pocket worked very industriously, and he was always certain of having something to eat with him wherever he went. He lived principally upon honey; and when he needed bread or meat, he carried some fine combs to a village not far away and bartered them for other food. He was ugly, untidy, shriveled, and brown. He was poor, and the bees seemed to be his only friends. But, for all that, he was happy and contented; he had all the honey he wanted, and his bees, whom he considered the best company in the world, were as friendly and sociable as they could be, and seemed to increase in number every day.

One day, there stopped at the hut of the Bee-man a Junior Sorcerer. This young person, who was a student of magic, necromancy, and the kindred arts, was much interested in the Bee-man, whom he had frequently noticed in his wanderings, and he considered him an admirable subject for study. He had got a great deal of useful practice by endeavoring to find out, by the various rules and laws of sorcery, exactly why the old Bee-man did not happen to be something that he was not, and why he was what he happened to be. He had studied a long time at this matter, and had found out something.

"Do you know," he said, when the Bee-man came out of his hut, "that you have been transformed?"

"What do you mean by that?" said the other, much surprised.

"You have surely heard of animals and human beings who have been magically transformed into different kinds of creatures?"

"Yes, I have heard of these things," said the Bee-man; "but what have I been transformed from?"

"That is more than I know," said the Junior Sorcerer. "But one thing is certain—you ought to be changed back. If you will find out what you have been transformed from, I will see that you are made all right again. Nothing would please me better than to attend to such a case."

And, having a great many things to study and investigate, the Junior Sorcerer went his way.

This information greatly disturbed the mind of the Bee-man. If he had been changed from something else, he ought to be that other thing, whatever it was. He ran after the young man, and overtook him.

"If you know, kind sir," he said, "that I have been transformed, you surely are able to tell me what it is that I was."

"No," said the Junior Sorcerer, "my studies have not proceeded far enough for that. When I become a senior I can tell you all about it. But, in the meantime, it will be well for you to try to discover for yourself your original form, and when you have done that, I will get some of the learned masters of my art to restore you to it. It will be easy enough to do that, but you could not expect them to take the time and trouble to find out what it was."

And, with these words, he hurried away, and was soon lost to view.

Greatly disquieted, the Bee-man retraced his steps, and went to his hut. Never before had he heard any thing which had so troubled him.

"I wonder what I was transformed from?" he thought, seating himself on his rough bench.

"Could it have been a giant, or a powerful prince, or some gorgeous being whom the magicians or the fairies wished to punish? It may be that I was a dog or a horse, or perhaps a fiery dragon or a horrid snake. I hope it was not one of these. But, whatever it was, every one has certainly a right to his original form, and I am resolved to find out mine. I will start early tomorrow morning, and I am sorry now that I have not more pockets to my old doublet, so that I might carry more bees and more honey for my journey."

He spent the rest of the day in making a hive of twigs and straw, and, having transferred to this a number of honeycombs and a colony of bees which had just swarmed, he rose before sunrise the next day, and having put on his leathern doublet, and having bound his new hive to his back, he set forth on his quest; the bees who were to accompany him buzzing around him like a cloud.

As the Bee-man passed through the little village the people greatly wondered at his queer appearance, with the hive upon his back. "The Bee-man is going on a long expedition this time," they said; but no one imagined the strange business on which he was bent. About noon he sat down under a tree, near a beautiful meadow covered with blossoms, and ate a little honey. Then he untied his hive and stretched himself out on the grass to rest. As he gazed upon his bees hovering about him, some going out to the blossoms in the sunshine, and some returning laden with the sweet pollen, he said to himself, "They know just what they have to do, and they do it; but alas for me! I know not what I may have to do. And yet, whatever it may be, I am determined to do it. In some way or other I will find out what was my original form, and then I will have myself changed back to it."

And now the thought came to him that perhaps his original form might have been something very disagreeable, or even horrid.

"But it does not matter," he said sturdily. "Whatever I was that shall I be again. It is not right for any one to retain a form which does not properly belong to him. I have no doubt I shall discover my original form in the same way that I find the trees in which the wild bees hive. When I first catch sight of a bee-tree I am drawn toward it, I know not how. Something says to me: 'That is what you are looking for.' In the same way I believe that I shall find my original form. When I see it, I shall be drawn toward it. Something will say to me: 'That is it.'"

When the Bee-man was rested he started off again, and in about an hour he entered a fair domain. Around him were beautiful lawns, grand trees, and lovely gardens; while at a little distance stood the stately palace of the Lord of the Domain. Richly dressed people were walking about or sitting in the shade of the trees and arbors; splendidly caparisoned horses were waiting for their riders; and everywhere were seen signs of opulence and gaiety.

"I think," said the Bee-man to himself, "that I should like to stop here for a time. If it should happen that I was originally like any of these happy creatures it would please me much."

He untied his hive, and hid it behind some bushes, and taking off his old doublet, laid that beside it. It would not do to have his bees flying about him if he wished to go among the inhabitants of this fair domain.

For two days the Bee-man wandered about the palace and its grounds, avoiding notice as much as possible, but looking at everything. He saw handsome men and lovely ladies; the finest horses, dogs, and cattle that were ever known; beautiful birds in cages, and fishes in crystal globes, and it seemed to him that the best of all living things were here collected.

At the close of the second day, the Bee-man said to himself: "There is one being here toward whom I feel very much drawn, and that is the Lord of the Domain. I cannot feel certain that I was once like him, but it would be a very fine thing if it were so; and it seems impossible for me to be drawn toward any other being in the domain when I look upon him, so handsome, rich, and powerful. But I must observe him more closely, and feel more sure of the matter, before applying to the sorcerers to change me back into a lord of a fair domain."

The next morning, the Bee-man saw the Lord of the Domain walking in his gardens. He slipped along the shady paths, and followed him so as to observe him closely, and find out if he were really drawn toward this noble and handsome being. The Lord of the Domain walked on for some time, not noticing that the Bee-man was behind him. But suddenly turning, he saw the little old man.

"What are you doing here, you vile beggar?" he cried; and he gave him a kick that sent him into some bushes that grew by the side of the path.

The Bee-man scrambled to his feet, and ran as fast as he could to the place where he had hidden his hive and his old doublet.

"If I am certain of any thing," he thought, "it is that I was never a person who would kick a poor old man. I will leave this place. I was transformed from nothing that I see here."

He now traveled for a day or two longer, and then he came to a great black mountain, near the bottom of which was an opening like the mouth of a cave.

This mountain he had heard was filled with caverns and underground passages, which were the abodes of dragons, evil spirits, horrid creatures of all kinds.

"Ah me!" said the Bee-man with a sigh, "I suppose I ought to visit this place. If I am going to do this thing properly, I should look on all sides of the subject, and I may have been one of those horrid creatures myself."

Thereupon he went to the mountain, and as he approached the opening of the passage that led into its inmost recesses he saw, sitting upon the ground, and leaning his back against a tree, a Languid Youth.

"Good day," said this individual when he saw the Bee-man. "Are you going inside?"

"Yes," said the Bee-man, "that is what I intend to do."

"Then," said the Languid Youth, slowly rising to his feet, "I think I will go with you. I was told that if I went in there I should get my energies toned up, and they need it very much; but I did not feel equal to entering by myself, and I thought I would wait until someone came along. I am very glad to see you, and we will go in together."

So the two went into the cave, and they had proceeded but a short distance when they met a very little creature, whom it was easy to recognize as a Very Imp. He was about two feet high, and resembled in color a freshly polished pair of boots. He was extremely lively and active, and came bounding toward them.

"What did you two people come here for?" he asked.

"I came," said the Languid Youth, "to have my energies toned up."

"You have come to the right place," said the Very Imp. "We will tone you up. And what does that old Bee-man want?"

"He has been transformed from something, and wants to find out what it is. He thinks he may have been one of the things in here."

"I should not wonder if that were so," said the Very Imp, rolling his head on one side, and eyeing the Bee-man with a critical gaze.

"All right," said the Very Imp; "he can go around, and pick out his previous existence. We have here all sorts of vile creepers, crawlers, hissers, and snorters. I suppose he thinks any thing will be better than a Bee-man."

"It is not because I want to be better than I am," said the Bee-man, "that I started out on this search. I have simply an honest desire to become what I originally was."

"Oh! that is it, is it?" said the other. "There is an idiotic mooncalf here with a clam head that must be just like what you used to be."

"Nonsense," said the Bee-man. "You have not the least idea what an honest purpose is. I shall go about, and see for myself."

"Go ahead," said the Very Imp, "and I will attend to this fellow who wants to be toned up." So saying he joined the Languid Youth.

"Look here," said that individual, regarding him with interest, "do you black and shine yourself every morning?"

"No," said the other, "it is waterproof varnish. You want to be invigorated, don't you? Well, I will tell you a splendid way to begin. You see that Bee-man has put down his hive and his coat with the bees in it. Just wait till he gets out of sight, and then catch a lot of those bees, and squeeze them flat. If you spread them on a sticky rag, and make a plaster, and put it on the small of your back, it will invigorate you like every thing, especially if some of the bees are not quite dead."

"Yes," said the Languid Youth, looking at him with his mild eyes, "but if I had energy enough to catch a bee I would be satisfied. Suppose you catch a lot for me."

"The subject is changed," said the Very Imp. "We are now about to visit the spacious chamber of the King of the Snap-dragons."

"That is a flower," said the Languid Youth.

"You will find him a gay old blossom," said the other. "When he has chased you round his room, and has blown sparks at you, and has snorted and howled, and cracked his tail, and snapped his jaws like a pair of anvils, your energies will be toned up higher than ever before in your life."

"No doubt of it," said the Languid Youth; "but I think I will begin with something a little milder."

"Well then," said the other, "there is a flat-tailed Demon of the Gorge in here. He is generally asleep, and, if you say so, you can slip into the farthest corner of his cave, and I'll solder his tail to the opposite wall. Then he will rage and roar, but he can't get at you, for he doesn't reach all the way across his cave; I have measured him. It will tone you up wonderfully to sit there and watch him."

"Very likely," said the Languid Youth; "but I

would rather stay outside and let you go up in the corner. The performance in that way will be more interesting to me."

"You are dreadfully hard to please," said the Very Imp. "I have offered them to you loose, and I have offered them fastened to a wall, and now the best thing I can do is to give you a chance at one of them that can't move at all. It is the Ghastly Griffin and is enchanted. He can't stir so much as the tip of his whiskers for a thousand years. You can go to his cave and examine him just as if he were stuffed, and then you can sit on his back and think how it would be if you should live to be a thousand years old, and he should wake up while you are sitting there. It would be easy to imagine a lot of horrible things he would do to you when you look at his open mouth with its awful fangs, his dreadful claws, and his horrible wings all covered with spikes."

"I think that might suit me," said the Languid Youth. "I would much rather imagine the exercises of these monsters than to see them really going on."

"Come on, then," said the Very Imp, and he led the way to the cave of the Ghastly Griffin.

The Bee-man went by himself through a great part of the mountain, and looked into many of its gloomy caves and recesses, recoiling in horror from most of the dreadful monsters who met his eyes. While he was wandering about, an awful roar was heard resounding through the passages of the mountain, and soon there came flapping along an enormous dragon, with body black as night, and wings and tail of fiery red. In his great fore-claws he bore a little baby.

"Horrible!" exclaimed the Bee-man. "He is taking that little creature to his cave to devour it."

He saw the dragon enter a cave not far away, and following looked in. The dragon was crouched upon the ground with the little baby lying before him. It did not seem to be hurt, but was frightened and crying. The monster was looking upon it with delight, as if he intended to make a dainty meal of it as soon as his appetite should be a little stronger.

"It is too bad!" thought the Bee-man. "Some-body ought to do something." And turning around, he ran away as fast as he could.

He ran through various passages until he came to the spot where he had left his beehive. Picking it up, he hurried back, carrying the hive in his two hands before him. When he reached the cave of the dragon, he looked in and saw the monster still crouched over the weeping child. Without a moment's hesitation, the Bee-man rushed into the cave and threw his hive straight into the face of the dragon. The bees, enraged by the shock, rushed out in an angry crowd and immediately fell upon the head, mouth, eyes, and nose of the dragon. The great monster, astounded by this sudden attack, and driven almost wild by the numberless stings of the bees, sprang back to the farthest portion of his cave, still followed by his relentless enemies, at whom he flapped wildly with his great wings and struck with his paws. While the dragon was thus engaged with the bees, the Bee-man rushed forward, and, seizing the child, he hurried away. He did not stop to pick up his doublet, but kept on until he reached the entrance of the caves. There he saw the Very Imp hopping along on one leg, and rubbing his back and shoulders with his hands, and stopped to inquire what was the matter, and what had become of the Languid Youth.

"He is no kind of a fellow," said the Very Imp. "He disappointed me dreadfully. I took him up to the Ghastly Griffin, and told him the thing was enchanted, and that he might sit on its back and think about what it could do if it was awake; and when he came near it the wretched creature opened its eyes, and raised its head, and then you ought to have seen how mad that simpleton was. He made a dash at me and seized me by the ears; he kicked and beat me till I can scarcely move."

"His energies must have been toned up a good deal," said the Bee-man.

"Toned up! I should say so!" cried the other. "I raised a howl, and a Scissor-jawed Clipper came out of his hole, and got after him; but that lazy fool ran so fast that he could not be caught."

The Bee-man now ran on and soon overtook the Languid Youth.

"You need not be in a hurry now," said the latter, "for the rules of this institution don't allow the creatures inside to come out of this opening, or to hang around it. If they did, they would frighten away visitors. They go in and out of holes in the upper part of the mountain."

The two proceeded on their way.

"What are you going to do with that baby?" said the Languid Youth.

"I shall carry it along with me," said the Bee-man, "as I go on with my search, and perhaps I may find its mother. If I do not, I shall give it to somebody in that little village yonder. Anything would be better than leaving it to be devoured by that horrid dragon."

"Let me carry it. I feel quite strong enough now to carry a baby."

"Thank you," said the Bee-man, "but I can take it myself. I like to carry something, and I have now neither my hive nor my doublet."

"It is very well that you had to leave them behind," said the Youth, "for the bees would have stung the baby."

"My bees never sting babies," said the other.

"They probably never had a chance," remarked his companion.

They soon entered the village, and after walking a short distance the youth exclaimed: "Do you see that woman over there sitting at the door of her house? She has beautiful hair and she is tearing it all to pieces. She should not be allowed to do that."

"No," said the Bee-man. "Her friends should tie her hands."

"Perhaps she is the mother of this child," said the Youth, "and if you give it to her she will no longer think of tearing her hair."

"But," said the Bee-man, "you don't really think this is her child?"

"Suppose you go over and see," said the other.

The Bee-man hesitated a moment, and then he walked toward the woman. Hearing him coming, she raised her head, and when she saw the child she rushed toward it, snatched it into her arms, and screaming with joy she covered it with kisses. Then with happy tears she begged to know the story of the rescue of her child, whom she never expected to see again; and she loaded the Bee-man with thanks and blessings. The friends and neighbors gathered around and there was great rejoicing. The mother urged the Bee-man and the Youth to stay with her, and rest and refresh themselves, which they were glad to do as they were tired and hungry.

They remained at the cottage all night, and in the afternoon of the next day the Bee-man said to the Youth: "It may seem an odd thing to you, but never in all my life have I felt myself drawn toward any living being as I am drawn toward this baby. Therefore I believe that I have been transformed from a baby."

"Good!" cried the Youth. "It is my opinion that you have hit the truth. And now would you like to be changed back to your original form?"

"Indeed I would!" said the Bee-man, "I have the strongest yearning to be what I originally was."

The Youth, who had now lost every trace of languid feeling, took a great interest in the matter, and early the next morning started off to inform the Junior Sorcerer that the Bee-man had discovered what he had been transformed from, and desired to be changed back to it.

The Junior Sorcerer and his learned Masters were filled with enthusiasm when they heard this report, and they at once set out for the mother's cottage. And there by magic arts the Bee-man was changed back into a baby. The mother was so grateful for what the Bee-man had done for her that she agreed to take charge of this baby, and to bring it up as her own.

"It will be a grand thing for him," said the Junior Sorcerer, "and I am glad that I studied his case. He will now have a fresh start in life, and will have a chance to become something better than a miserable old man living in a wretched hut with no friends or companions but buzzing bees."

The Junior Sorcerer and his Masters then returned to their homes, happy in the success of their great performance; and the Youth went back to his home anxious to begin a life of activity and energy.

Years and years afterward, when the Junior Sorcerer had become a Senior and was very old indeed, he passed through the country of Orn, and noticed a small hut about which swarms of bees were flying. He approached it, and looking in at the door he saw an old man in a leathern doublet, sitting at a table, eating honey. By his magic art he knew this was the baby which had been transformed from the Bee-man.

"Upon my word!" exclaimed the Sorcerer, "He has grown into the same thing again!"

Oscar Fingal O'Flahertie Wills Wilde, better known as simply Oscar Wilde (1854–1900), was an Irish poet and dramatist best known for his only novel, *The Picture of Dorian Gray* (1891), and his play *The Importance of Being Earnest* (1895). Wilde was a spokesperson for the aestheticism movement and found himself, often for depressing reason, engaged in both civil and criminal suits. Both of Wilde's parents were published writers, and he soon proved himself as a literary genius when he won the Newdigate Prize in 1878 for his long poem "Ravenna" (1878). Although an excellent poet, Wilde did not publish much of his work until the latter half of his life, and his greatest successes were his comedies, which were imaginative and witty. "The Remarkable Rocket" (1888), originally published in the anthology *The Happy Prince and Other Tales*, is a comic fantastical children's story.

The Remarkable Rocket

Oscar Wilde

THE KING'S SON was going to be married, so there were general rejoicings. He had waited a whole year for his bride, and at last she had arrived. She was a Russian Princess, and had driven all the way from Finland in a sledge drawn by six reindeer. The sledge was shaped like a great golden swan, and between the swan's wings lay the little Princess herself. Her long ermine-cloak reached right down to her feet, on her head was a tiny cap of silver tissue, and she was as pale as the Snow Palace in which she had always lived. So pale was she that as she drove through the streets all the people wondered. "She is like a white rose!" they cried, and they threw down flowers on her from the balconies.

At the gate of the Castle the Prince was waiting to receive her. He had dreamy violet eyes, and his hair was like fine gold. When he saw her he sank upon one knee, and kissed her hand.

"Your picture was beautiful," he murmured, "but you are more beautiful than your picture"; and the little Princess blushed.

"She was like a white rose before," said a young Page to his neighbour, "but she is like a red rose now"; and the whole Court was delighted.

For the next three days everybody went about saying, "White rose, Red rose, Red rose, White rose"; and the King gave orders that the Page's salary was to be doubled. As he received no salary at all this was not of much use to him, but it was considered a great honour, and was duly published in the Court Gazette.

When the three days were over the marriage was celebrated. It was a magnificent ceremony, and the bride and bridegroom walked hand in hand under a canopy of purple velvet embroidered with little pearls. Then there was a State

Banquet, which lasted for five hours. The Prince and Princess sat at the top of the Great Hall and drank out of a cup of clear crystal. Only true lovers could drink out of this cup, for if false lips touched it, it grew grey and dull and cloudy.

"It's quite clear that they love each other," said the little Page, "as clear as crystal!" and the King doubled his salary a second time. "What an honour!" cried all the courtiers.

After the banquet there was to be a Ball. The bride and bridegroom were to dance the Rose-dance together, and the King had promised to play the flute. He played very badly, but no one had ever dared to tell him so, because he was the King. Indeed, he knew only two airs, and was never quite certain which one he was playing; but it made no matter, for, whatever he did, everybody cried out, "Charming! charming!"

The last item on the programme was a grand display of fireworks, to be let off exactly at midnight. The little Princess had never seen a firework in her life, so the King had given orders that the Royal Pyrotechnist should be in attendance on the day of her marriage.

"What are fireworks like?" she had asked the Prince, one morning, as she was walking on the terrace.

"They are like the Aurora Borealis," said the King, who always answered questions that were addressed to other people, "only much more natural. I prefer them to stars myself, as you always know when they are going to appear, and they are as delightful as my own flute-playing. You must certainly see them."

So at the end of the King's garden a great stand had been set up, and as soon as the Royal Pyrotechnist had put everything in its proper place, the fireworks began to talk to each other.

"The world is certainly very beautiful," cried a little Squib. "Just look at those yellow tulips. Why! if they were real crackers they could not be lovelier. I am very glad I have travelled. Travel improves the mind wonderfully, and does away with all one's prejudices."

"The King's garden is not the world, you foolish squib," said a big Roman Candle; "the world is an enormous place, and it would take you three days to see it thoroughly."

"Any place you love is the world to you," exclaimed a pensive Catherine Wheel, who had been attached to an old deal box in early life, and prided herself on her broken heart; "but love is not fashionable any more, the poets have killed it. They wrote so much about it that nobody believed them, and I am not surprised. True love suffers, and is silent. I remember myself once— But it is no matter now. Romance is a thing of the past."

"Nonsense!" said the Roman Candle, "Romance never dies. It is like the moon, and lives for ever. The bride and bridegroom, for instance, love each other very dearly. I heard all about them this morning from a brown-paper cartridge, who happened to be staying in the same drawer as myself, and knew the latest Court news."

But the Catherine Wheel shook her head. "Romance is dead, Romance is dead, Romance is dead," she murmured. She was one of those people who think that, if you say the same thing over and over a great many times, it becomes true in the end.

Suddenly, a sharp, dry cough was heard, and they all looked round.

It came from a tall, supercilious-looking Rocket, who was tied to the end of a long stick. He always coughed before he made any observation, so as to attract attention.

"Ahem! ahem!" he said, and everybody listened except the poor Catherine Wheel, who was still shaking her head, and murmuring, "Romance is dead."

"Order! order!" cried out a Cracker. He was something of a politician, and had always taken a prominent part in the local elections, so he knew the proper Parliamentary expressions to use.

"Quite dead," whispered the Catherine Wheel, and she went off to sleep.

As soon as there was perfect silence, the Rocket coughed a third time and began. He spoke with a very slow, distinct voice, as if he was dictating his memoirs, and always looked over the shoulder of the person to whom he was talking. In fact, he had a most distinguished manner.

"How fortunate it is for the King's son," he remarked, "that he is to be married on the very day on which I am to be let off. Really, if it had been arranged beforehand, it could not have turned out better for him; but, Princes are always lucky."

"Dear me!" said the little Squib, "I thought it was quite the other way, and that we were to be let off in the Prince's honour."

"It may be so with you," he answered; "indeed, I have no doubt that it is, but with me it is different. I am a very remarkable Rocket, and come of remarkable parents. My mother was the most celebrated Catherine Wheel of her day, and was renowned for her graceful dancing. When she made her great public appearance she spun round nineteen times before she went out, and each time that she did so she threw into the air seven pink stars. She was three feet and a half in diameter, and made of the very best gunpowder. My father was a Rocket like myself, and of French extraction. He flew so high that the people were afraid that he would never come down again. He did, though, for he was of a kindly disposition, and he made a most brilliant descent in a shower of golden rain. The newspapers wrote about his performance in very flattering terms. Indeed, the Court Gazette called him a triumph of Pylotechnic art."

"Pyrotechnic, Pyrotechnic, you mean," said a Bengal Light; "I know it is Pyrotechnic, for I saw it written on my own canister."

"Well, I said Pylotechnic," answered the Rocket, in a severe tone of voice, and the Bengal Light felt so crushed that he began at once to bully the little squibs, in order to show that he was still a person of some importance.

"I was saying," continued the Rocket, "I was saying—What was I saying?"

"You were talking about yourself," replied the Roman Candle.

"Of course; I knew I was discussing some interesting subject when I was so rudely inter-rupted. I hate rudeness and bad manners of every kind, for I am extremely sensitive. No one in the whole world is so sensitive as I am, I am quite sure of that."

"What is a sensitive person?" said the Cracker to the Roman Candle.

"A person who, because he has corns himself, always treads on other people's toes," answered the Roman Candle in a low whisper; and the Cracker nearly exploded with laughter.

"Pray, what are you laughing at?" inquired the Rocket; "I am not laughing."

"I am laughing because I am happy," replied the Cracker.

"That is a very selfish reason," said the Rocket angrily. "What right have you to be happy? You should be thinking about others. In fact, you should be thinking about me. I am always think-ing about myself, and I expect everybody else to do the same. That is what is called sympathy. It is a beautiful virtue, and I possess it in a high degree. Suppose, for instance, anything hap-pened to me to-night, what a misfortune that would be for every one! The Prince and Princess would never be happy again, their whole married life would be spoiled; and as for the King, I know he would not get over it. Really, when I begin to reflect on the importance of my position, I am almost moved to tears."

"If you want to give pleasure to others," cried the Roman Candle, "you had better keep yourself dry."

"Certainly," exclaimed the Bengal Light, who was now in better spirits; "that is only common sense."

"Common sense, indeed!" said the Rocket indignantly; "you forget that I am very uncom-mon, and very remarkable. Why, anybody can have common sense, provided that they have no imagination. But I have imagination, for I never think of things as they really are; I always think of them as being quite different. As for keeping myself dry, there is evidently no one here who can at all appreciate an emotional nature. Fortunately for myself, I don't care. The only thing that sustains one through life is the consciousness of the immense inferiority of everybody else, and this is a feeling that I have always cultivated. But none of you have any hearts. Here you are laughing and making merry just as if the Prince and Princess had not just been married."

"Well, really," exclaimed a small Fire-balloon, "why not? It is a most joyful occasion, and when I soar up into the air I intend to tell the stars all about it. You will see them twinkle when I talk to them about the pretty bride."

"Ah! what a trivial view of life!" said the Rocket; "but it is only what I expected. There is nothing in you; you are hollow and empty. Why, perhaps the Prince and Princess may go to live in a country where there is a deep river, and perhaps they may have one only son, a little fair-haired boy with violet eyes like the Prince himself; and perhaps some day he may go out to walk with his nurse; and perhaps the nurse may go to sleep under a great elder-tree; and perhaps the little boy may fall into the deep river and be drowned. What a terrible misfortune! Poor people, to lose their only son! It is really too dreadful! I shall never get over it."

"But they have not lost their only son," said the Roman Candle; "no misfortune has happened to them at all."

"I never said that they had," replied the Rocket; "I said that they might. If they had lost their only son there would be no use in saying anything more about the matter. I hate people who cry over spilt milk. But when I think that they might lose their only son, I certainly am very much affected."

"You certainly are!" cried the Bengal Light. "In fact, you are the most affected person I ever met."

"You are the rudest person I ever met," said the Rocket, "and you cannot understand my friendship for the Prince."

"Why, you don't even know him," growled the Roman Candle.

"I never said I knew him," answered the Rocket. "I dare say that if I knew him I should not be his friend at all. It is a very dangerous thing to know one's friends."

"You had really better keep yourself dry," said the Fire-balloon. "That is the important thing."

"Very important for you, I have no doubt," answered the Rocket, "but I shall weep if I choose"; and he actually burst into real tears, which flowed down his stick like rain-drops, and nearly drowned two little beetles, who were just thinking of setting up house together, and were looking for a nice dry spot to live in.

"He must have a truly romantic nature," said the Catherine Wheel, "for he weeps when there is nothing at all to weep about"; and she heaved a deep sigh, and thought about the deal box.

But the Roman Candle and the Bengal Light were quite indignant, and kept saying, "Humbug! humbug!" at the top of their voices. They were extremely practical, and whenever they objected to anything they called it humbug.

Then the moon rose like a wonderful silver shield; and the stars began to shine, and a sound of music came from the palace.

The Prince and Princess were leading the dance. They danced so beautifully that the tall white lilies peeped in at the window and watched them, and the great red poppies nodded their heads and beat time.

Then ten o'clock struck, and then eleven, and then twelve, and at the last stroke of midnight every one came out on the terrace, and the King sent for the Royal Pyrotechnist.

"Let the fireworks begin," said the King; and the Royal Pyrotechnist made a low bow, and marched down to the end of the garden. He had six attendants with him, each of whom carried a lighted torch at the end of a long pole.

It was certainly a magnificent display.

Whizz! Whizz! went the Catherine Wheel, as she spun round and round. Boom! Boom! went the Roman Candle. Then the Squibs danced all over the place, and the Bengal Lights made everything look scarlet. "Good-bye," cried the Fire-balloon, as he soared away, dropping tiny blue sparks. Bang! Bang! answered the Crackers, who were enjoying themselves immensely. Every one was a great success except the Remarkable Rocket. He was so damp with crying that he could not go off at all. The best thing in him was the gunpowder, and that was so wet with tears that it was of no use. All his poor relations, to whom he would never speak, except with a sneer, shot up into the sky like wonderful golden flowers with blossoms of fire. Huzza! Huzza! cried the Court; and the little Princess laughed with pleasure.

"I suppose they are reserving me for some grand occasion," said the Rocket; "no doubt that is what it means," and he looked more supercilious than ever.

The next day the workmen came to put everything tidy. "This is evidently a deputation," said the Rocket; "I will receive them with becoming dignity" so he put his nose in the air, and began to frown severely as if he were thinking about some very important subject. But they took no notice of him at all till they were just going away. Then one of them caught sight of him.

"Hallo!" he cried, "what a bad rocket!" and he threw him over the wall into the ditch.

"Bad Rocket? Bad Rocket?" he said, as he whirled through the air; "impossible! Grand Rocket, that is what the man said. Bad and Grand sound very much the same, indeed they often are the same"; and he fell into the mud.

"It is not comfortable here," he remarked, "but no doubt it is some fashionable watering-place, and they have sent me away to recruit my health. My nerves are certainly very much shattered, and I require rest."

Then a little Frog, with bright jewelled eyes, and a green mottled coat, swam up to him.

"A new arrival, I see!" said the Frog. "Well, after all there is nothing like mud. Give me rainy weather and a ditch, and I am quite happy. Do you think it will be a wet afternoon? I am sure I hope so, but the sky is quite blue and cloudless. What a pity!"

"Ahem! ahem!" said the Rocket, and he began to cough.

"What a delightful voice you have!" cried the Frog. "Really it is quite like a croak, and croaking is of course the most musical sound in the world. You will hear our glee-club this evening. We sit in the old duck pond close by the farmer's house, and as soon as the moon rises we begin. It is so entrancing that everybody lies awake to listen to us. In fact, it was only yesterday that I heard the farmer's wife say to her mother that she could not get a wink of sleep at night on account of us. It is most gratifying to find oneself so popular."

"Ahem! ahem!" said the Rocket angrily. He was very much annoyed that he could not get a word in.

"A delightful voice, certainly," continued the Frog; "I hope you will come over to the duck-pond. I am off to look for my daughters. I have six beautiful daughters, and I am so afraid the Pike may meet them. He is a perfect monster, and would have no hesitation in breakfasting off them. Well, good-bye: I have enjoyed our conversation very much, I assure you."

"Conversation, indeed!" said the Rocket. "You have talked the whole time yourself. That is not conversation."

"Somebody must listen," answered the Frog, "and I like to do all the talking myself. It saves time, and prevents arguments."

"But I like arguments," said the Rocket.

"I hope not," said the Frog complacently. "Arguments are extremely vulgar, for everybody in good society holds exactly the same opinions. Good-bye a second time; I see my daughters in the distance," and the little Frog swam away.

"You are a very irritating person," said the Rocket, "and very ill-bred. I hate people who talk about themselves, as you do, when one wants to talk about oneself, as I do. It is what I call selfishness, and selfishness is a most detestable thing, especially to any one of my temperament, for I am well known for my sympathetic nature. In fact, you should take example by me; you could not possibly have a better model. Now that you have the chance you had better avail yourself of it, for I am going back to Court almost immediately. I am a great favourite at Court; in fact, the Prince and Princess were married yesterday in my honour. Of course you know nothing of these matters, for you are a provincial."

"There is no good talking to him," said a Dragon-fly, who was sitting on the top of a large brown bulrush; "no good at all, for he has gone away."

"Well, that is his loss, not mine," answered the Rocket. "I am not going to stop talking to him merely because he pays no attention. I like hearing myself talk. It is one of my greatest pleasures. I often have long conversations all by myself, and I am so clever that sometimes I don't understand a single word of what I am saying."

"Then you should certainly lecture on Philosophy," said the Dragon-fly; and he spread a pair of lovely gauze wings and soared away into the sky.

"How very silly of him not to stay here!" said the Rocket. "I am sure that he has not often got such a chance of improving his mind. However, I don't care a bit. Genius like mine is sure to be appreciated some day"; and he sank down a little deeper into the mud.

After some time a large White Duck swam up to him. She had yellow legs, and webbed feet, and was considered a great beauty on account of her waddle.

"Quack, quack, quack," she said. "What a curious shape you are! May I ask were you born like that, or is it the result of an accident?"

"It is quite evident that you have always lived in the country," answered the Rocket, "otherwise you would know who I am. However, I excuse your ignorance. It would be unfair to expect other people to be as remarkable as oneself. You will no doubt be surprised to hear that I can fly up into the sky, and come down in a shower of golden rain."

"I don't think much of that," said the Duck, "as I cannot see what use it is to any one. Now, if you could plough the fields like the ox, or draw a cart like the horse, or look after the sheep like the collie-dog, that would be something."

"My good creature," cried the Rocket in a very haughty tone of voice, "I see that you belong to the lower orders. A person of my position is never useful. We have certain accomplishments, and that is more than sufficient. I have no sympathy myself with industry of any kind, least of all with such industries as you seem to recommend. Indeed, I have always been of the opinion that hard work is simply the refuge of people who have nothing whatever to do."

"Well, well," said the Duck, who was of a very peaceable disposition, and never quarrelled with any one, "everybody has different tastes. I hope, at any rate, that you are going to take up your residence here."

"Oh! dear no," cried the Rocket. "I am merely a visitor, a distinguished visitor. The fact is that I find this place rather tedious. There is neither society here, nor solitude. In fact, it is essentially suburban. I shall probably go back to Court, for I know that I am destined to make a sensation in the world."

"I had thoughts of entering public life once myself," remarked the Duck; "there are so many things that need reforming. Indeed, I took the chair at a meeting some time ago, and we passed resolutions condemning everything that we did not like. However, they did not seem to have much effect. Now I go in for domesticity, and look after my family."

"I am made for public life," said the Rocket, "and so are all my relations, even the humblest of them. Whenever we appear we excite great attention. I have not actually appeared myself, but when I do so it will be a magnificent sight. As for domesticity, it ages one rapidly, and distracts one's mind from higher things."

"Ah! the higher things of life, how fine they are!" said the Duck; "and that reminds me how hungry I feel": and she swam away down the stream, saying, "Quack, quack, quack."

"Come back! come back!" screamed the Rocket, "I have a great deal to say to you"; but the Duck paid no attention to him. "I am glad that she has gone," he said to himself, "she has a decidedly middle-class mind"; and he sank a little deeper still into the mud, and began to think about the loneliness of genius, when suddenly two little boys in white smocks came running down the bank, with a kettle and some faggots.

"This must be the deputation," said the Rocket, and he tried to look very dignified.

"Hallo!" cried one of the boys, "look at this old stick! I wonder how it came here"; and he picked the rocket out of the ditch.

"Old Stick!" said the Rocket, "impossible! Gold Stick, that is what he said. Gold Stick is very complimentary. In fact, he mistakes me for one of the Court dignitaries!"

"Let us put it into the fire!" said the other boy, "it will help to boil the kettle."

So they piled the faggots together, and put the Rocket on top, and lit the fire.

"This is magnificent," cried the Rocket, "they are going to let me off in broad day-light, so that every one can see me."

"We will go to sleep now," they said, "and when we wake up the kettle will be boiled"; and they lay down on the grass, and shut their eyes.

The Rocket was very damp, so he took a long time to burn. At last, however, the fire caught him.

"Now I am going off!" he cried, and he made himself very stiff and straight. "I know I shall go much higher than the stars, much higher than the moon, much higher than the sun. In fact, I shall go so high that—"

Fizz! Fizz! Fizz! and he went straight up into the air.

"Delightful!" he cried, "I shall go on like this for ever. What a success I am!"

But nobody saw him.

Then he began to feel a curious tingling sensation all over him.

"Now I am going to explode," he cried. "I shall set the whole world on fire, and make such a noise that nobody will talk about anything else for a whole year." And he certainly did explode. Bang! Bang! Bang! went the gunpowder. There was no doubt about it.

But nobody heard him, not even the two little boys, for they were sound asleep.

Then all that was left of him was the stick, and this fell down on the back of a Goose who was taking a walk by the side of the ditch.

"Good heavens!" cried the Goose. "It is going to rain sticks"; and she rushed into the water.

"I knew I should create a great sensation," gasped the Rocket, and he went out.

Helena Blavatskaya (1831–1891) is an esoteric Russian writer who founded the Theosophical Society in 1875. Her first major work, *Isis Unveiled* (1877), asserted the importance of mystical experience in attaining spiritual insight. Blavatskaya believed she had mystical powers, even though she was declared a fraud by many—including the London Society for Psychical Research in 1885. Although a well-known occultist, Blavatskaya wrote fiction as well. "The Ensouled Violin" (1892) is considered a masterpiece, inspired by one of Blavatskaya's nightmares. The rhythm of the tale perfectly fuses with its musical theme. Black magic occurs in many of her tales, and it is the author's passion for the subject that makes this tale so hauntingly relatable.

The Ensouled Violin

H. P. Blavatskaya

I

IN THE YEAR 1828, an old German, a music teacher, came to Paris with his pupil and settled unostentatiously in one of the quiet faubourgs of the metropolis. The first rejoiced in the name of Samuel Klaus; the second answered to the more poetical appellation of Franz Stenio. The younger man was a violinist, gifted, as rumor went, with extraordinary, almost miraculous talent. Yet as he was poor and had not hitherto made a name for himself in Europe, he remained for several years in the capital of France—the heart and pulse of capricious continental fashion—unknown and unappreciated. Franz was a Styrian by birth, and, at the time of the event to be presently described, he was a young man considerably under thirty. A philosopher and a dreamer by nature, imbued with all the mystic oddities of true genius, he reminded one of some of the heroes in Hoffmann's *Contes Fantastiques*. His earlier existence had been a very unusual, in fact, quite an eccentric one, and its history must be briefly told—for the better understanding of the present story.

Born of very pious country people, in a quiet burg among the Styrian Alps; nursed "by the native gnomes who watched over his cradle"; growing up in the weird atmosphere of the ghouls and vampires who play such a prominent part in the household of every Styrian and Slavonian in Southern Austria; educated later, as a student in the shadow of the old Rhenish castles of Germany; Franz from his childhood had passed through every emotional stage on the plane of the so-called "supernatural." He had also studied at one time the "occult arts" with an enthusiastic disciple of Paracelsus and Kunrath; alchemy had few theoretical secrets for him; and he had dabbled in "ceremonial magic" and "sorcery" with some Hungarian Tziganes. Yet he loved above all else music, and above music—his violin.

At the age of twenty-two he suddenly gave

up his practical studies in the occult, and from that day, though as devoted as ever in thought to the beautiful Grecian Gods, he surrendered himself entirely to his art. Of his classic studies he had retained only that which related to the muses—Euterpe especially, at whose altar he worshipped—and Orpheus whose magic lyre he tried to emulate with his violin. Except his dreamy belief in the nymphs and the sirens, on account probably of the double relationship of the latter to the muses, through Calliope and Orpheus, he was interested but little in the matters of this sublunary world. All his aspirations mounted, like incense, with the wave of the heavenly harmony that he drew from his instrument, to a higher and a nobler sphere. He dreamed awake, and lived a real though an enchanted life only during those hours when his magic bow carried him along the wave of sound to the Pagan Olympus, to the feet of Euterpe. A strange child he had ever been in his own home, where tales of magic and witchcraft grow out of every inch of the soil; a still stranger boy he had become, until finally he had blossomed into manhood, without one single characteristic of youth. Never had a fair face attracted his attention; not for one moment had his thoughts turned from his solitary studies to a life beyond that of a mystic Bohemian. Content with his own company, he had thus passed the best years of his youth and manhood with his violin for his chief idol, and with the Gods and Goddesses of old Greece for his audience, in perfect ignorance of practical life. His whole existence had been one long day of dreams, of melody and sunlight, and he had never felt any other aspirations.

How useless, but oh, how glorious those dreams! how vivid! and why should he desire any better fate? Was he not all that he wanted to be, transformed in a second of thought into one or another hero; from Orpheus, who held all nature breathless, to the urchin who piped away under the plane tree to the naiads of Calirrhoe's crystal fountain? Did not the swift-footed nymphs frolic at his beck and call to the sound of the magic flute of the Arcadian shepherd—who was him-

self? Behold, the Goddess of Love and Beauty herself descending from on high, attracted by the sweet-voiced notes of his violin! . . . Yet there came a time when he preferred Syrinx to Aphrodite—not as the fair nymph pursued by Pan, but after her transformation by the merciful Gods into the reed out of which the frustrated God of the Shepherds had made his magic pipe. For also, with time, ambition grows and is rarely satisfied. When he tried to emulate on his violin the enchanting sounds that resounded in his mind, the whole of Parnassus kept silent under the spell, or joined in heavenly chorus; but the audience he finally craved was composed of more than the Gods sung by Hesiod, verily of the most appreciative *melomanes* of European capitals. He felt jealous of the magic pipe, and would fain have had it at his command.

"Oh! that I could allure a nymph into my beloved violin!"—he often cried, after awakening from one of his daydreams. "Oh, that I could only span in spirit flight the abyss of Time! Oh, that I could find myself for one short day a partaker of the secret arts of the Gods, a God myself, in the sight and hearing of enraptured humanity; and, having learned the mystery of the lyre of Orpheus, or secured within my violin a siren, thereby benefit mortals to my own glory!"

Thus, having for long years dreamed in the company of the Gods of his fancy, he now took to dreaming of the transitory glories of fame upon this earth. But at this time he was suddenly called home by his widowed mother from one of the German universities where he had lived for the last year or two. This was an event which brought his plans to an end, at least so far as the immediate future was concerned, for he had hitherto drawn upon her alone for his meager pittance, and his means were not sufficient for an independent life outside his native place.

His return had a very unexpected result. His mother, whose only love he was on earth, died soon after she had welcomed her Benjamin back; and the good wives of the burg exercised their swift tongues for many a month after as to the real causes of that death.

Frau Stenio, before Franz's return, was a healthy, buxom, middle-aged body, strong and hearty. She was a pious and a God-fearing soul too, who had never failed in saying her prayers, nor had missed an early mass for years during his absence. On the first Sunday after her son had settled at home—a day that she had been longing for and had anticipated for months in joyous visions, in which she saw him kneeling by her side in the little church on the hill—she called him from the foot of the stairs. The hour had come when her pious dream was to be realized, and she was waiting for him, carefully wiping the dust from the prayer book he had used in his boyhood. But instead of Franz, it was his violin that responded to her call, mixing its sonorous voice with the rather cracked tones of the peal of the merry Sunday bells. The fond mother was somewhat shocked at hearing the prayer-inspiring sounds drowned by the weird, fantastic notes of the "Dance of the Witches"; they seemed to her so unearthly and mocking. But she almost fainted upon hearing the definite refusal of her well-beloved son to go to church. He never went to church, he coolly remarked. It was loss of time; besides which, the loud peals of the old church organ jarred on his nerves. Nothing should induce him to submit to the torture of listening to that cracked organ. He was firm, and nothing could move him. To her supplications and remonstrances he put an end by offering to play for her a "Hymn to the Sun" he had just composed.

From that memorable Sunday morning, Frau Stenio lost her usual serenity of mind. She hastened to lay her sorrows and seek for consolation at the foot of the confessional; but that which she heard in response from the stern priest filled her gentle and unsophisticated soul with dismay and almost with despair. A feeling of fear, a sense of profound terror, which soon became a chronic state with her, pursued her from that moment; her nights became disturbed and sleepless, her days passed in prayer and lamentations. In her maternal anxiety for the salvation of her beloved son's soul, and for his *post mortem* welfare, she made a series of rash vows. Finding that neither the Latin petition to the Mother of God written for her by her spiritual adviser, nor yet the humble supplications in German, addressed by herself to every saint she had reason to believe was residing in Paradise, worked the desired effect, she took to pilgrimages to distant shrines. During one of these journeys to a holy chapel situated high up in the mountains, she caught cold, amid the glaciers of the Tyrol, and redescended only to take to a sick bed, from which she arose no more. Frau Stenio's vow had led her, in one sense, to the desired result. The poor woman was now given an opportunity of seeking out in *propria persona* the saints she had believed in so well, and of pleading face to face for the recreant son, who refused adherence to them and to the Church, scoffed at monk and confessional, and held the organ in such horror.

Franz sincerely lamented his mother's death. Unaware of being the indirect cause of it, he felt no remorse; but selling the modest household goods and chattels, light in purse and heart, he resolved to travel on foot for a year or two, before settling down to any definite profession.

A hazy desire to see the great cities of Europe, and to try his luck in France, lurked at the bottom of this traveling project, but his Bohemian habits of life were too strong to be abruptly abandoned. He placed his small capital with a banker for a rainy day, and started on his pedestrian journey *via* Germany and Austria. His violin paid for his board and lodging in the inns and farms on his way, and he passed his days in the green fields and in the solemn silent woods, face to face with Nature, dreaming all the time as usual with his eyes open. During the three months of his pleasant travels to and fro, he never descended for one moment from Parnassus; but, as an alchemist transmutes lead into gold, so he transformed everything on his way into a song of Hesiod or Anacreon. Every evening, while fiddling for his supper and bed, whether on a green lawn or in the hall of a rustic inn, his fancy changed the whole scene for him. Village swains and maidens became transfigured into Arcadian shepherds and nymphs. The sand-covered floor was now a green sward; the uncouth couples spinning round in a measured waltz with the wild grace of tamed bears became priests and priestesses of Terpsichore; the bulky, cherry-cheeked and blue-eyed daughters of rural Germany were the Hesperides circling round the trees laden with the golden apples. Nor did the melodious strains of the Arcadian demigods piping on their syrinxes, and audible but to his own enchanted ear, vanish with the dawn. For no sooner was the curtain of sleep raised from his eyes than he would sally forth into a new magic realm of daydreams. On his way to some dark and solemn pine forest, he played incessantly, to himself and to everything else. He fiddled to the green hill, and forthwith the mountain and the moss-covered rocks moved forward to hear him the better, as they had done at the sound of the Orphean lyre. He fiddled to the merry-voiced brook, to the hurrying river, and both slakened their speed and stopped their waves, and, becoming silent seemed to listen to him in an entranced rapture. Even the long-legged stork who stood meditatively on one leg on the thatched top of the rustic mill, gravely resolving unto himself the problem of his too-long existence, sent out after him a long and strident cry, screeching, "Art thou Orpheus himself, O Stenio?"

It was a period of full bliss, of a daily and almost hourly exaltation. The last words of his dying mother, whispering to him of the horrors of eternal condemnation, had left him unaffected, and the only vision her warning evoked in him was that of Pluto. By a ready association of ideas, he saw the lord of the dark nether kingdom greeting him as he had greeted the husband of Eurydice before him. Charmed with the magic sounds of his violin, the wheel of Ixion was at a standstill once more, thus affording relief to the wretched seducer of Juno, and giving the lie to those who claim eternity for the duration of the punishment of condemned sinners. He perceived Tantalus forgetting his never-ceasing thirst, and smacking his lips as he drank in the heaven-born melody; the stone of Sisyphus becoming motion-less, the Furies themselves smiling on him, and the sovereign of the gloomy regions delighted, and awarding preference to his violin over the lyre of Orpheus. Taken *au serieux*, mythology thus seems a decided antidote to fear, in the face of theological threats, especially when strengthened with an insane and passionate love of music, with Franz, Euterpe proved always victorious in every contest, aye, even with Hell itself!

But there is an end to everything, and very soon Franz had to give up uninterrupted dreaming. He had reached the university town where dwelt his old violin teacher, Samuel Klaus. When this antiquated musician found that his beloved and favorite pupil, Franz, had been left poor in purse and still poorer in earthly affections, he felt his strong attachment to the boy awaken with tenfold force. He took Franz to his heart, and forthwith adopted him as his son.

The old teacher reminded people of one of those grotesque figures which look as if they had just stepped out of some mediaeval panel. And yet Klaus, with his fantastic *allures* of a night goblin, had the most loving heart, as tender as that of a woman, and the self-sacrificing nature of an old Christian martyr. When Franz had briefly narrated to him the history of his last few years, the professor took him by the hand, and leading him into his study simply said:

"Stop with me, and put an end to your Bohemian life. Make yourself famous. I am old and childless and will be your father. Let us live together and forget all save fame."

And forthwith he offered to proceed with Franz to Paris, *via* several large German cities, where they would stop to give concerts.

In a few days Klaus succeeded in making Franz forget his vagrant life and its artistic independence, and reawakened in his pupil his now dormant ambition and desire for worldly fame. Hitherto, since his mother's death, he had been content to receive applause only from the Gods and Goddesses who inhabited his vivid fancy; now he began to crave once more for the admiration of mortals. Under the clever and careful training of old Klaus his remarkable talent gained in strength and powerful charm with every day, and his reputation grew and expanded with every city and town wherein he made himself heard. His ambition was being rapidly realized; the presiding genii of various musical centers to whose patronage his talent was submitted soon proclaimed him *the one* violinist of the day, and the public declared loudly that he stood unrivaled by anyone whom they had ever heard. These laudations very soon made both master and pupil completely lose their heads.

But Paris was less ready with such appreciation. Paris makes reputations for itself, and will take none on faith. They had been living in it for almost three years, and were still climbing with difficulty the artist's Calvary, when an event occurred which put an end even to their most modest expectations. The first arrival of Niccolo Paganini was suddenly heralded, and threw Lutetia into a convulsion of expectation. The unparallel artist arrived, and—all Paris fell at once at his feet.

II

Now it is a well-known fact that a superstition born in the dark days of medieval superstition, and surviving almost to the middle of the present century, attributed all such abnormal, out-of-the-way talent as that of Paganini to "supernatural" agency. Every great and marvelous artist had been accused in his day of dealings with the devil. A few instances will suffice to refresh the reader's memory.

Tartini, the great composer and violinist of the XVIIth century, was denounced as one who got his best inspirations from the Evil One, with whom he was, it was said, in regular league. This accusation was of course due to the almost magical impression he produced upon his audiences. His inspired performance on the violin secured for him in his native country the title of "Master of Nations." The *Sonate du Diable*, also called "Tartini's Dream"—as everyone who has heard it will be ready to testify—is the most

weird melody ever heard or invented: hence, the marvelous composition has become the source of endless legends. Nor were they entirely baseless, since it was he, himself, who was shown to have originated them. Tartini confessed to having written it on awakening from a dream, in which he had heard his sonata performed by Satan, for his benefit, and in consequence of a bargain made with his infernal majesty.

Several famous singers, even, whose exceptional voices struck the hearers with superstitious admiration, have not escaped a like accusation. Pasta's splendid voice was attributed in her day to the fact that, three months before her birth, the diva's mother was carried during a trance to heaven, and there treated to a vocal concert of seraphs. Malibran was indebted for her voice to St. Cecilia while others said she owed it to a demon who watched over her cradle and sung the baby to sleep. Finally Paganini—the unrivaled performer, the mean Italian, who like Dryden's Jubal striking on the "chorded shell" forced the throngs that followed him to worship the divine sounds produced, and made people say that "less than a God could not dwell within the hollow of his violin"—Paganini left a legend too.

The almost supernatural art of the greatest violin player that the world has ever known was often speculated upon, never understood. The effect produced by him on his audience was literally marvelous, overpowering. The great Rossini is said to have wept like a sentimental German maiden on hearing him play for the first time. The Princess Elisa of Lucca, a sister of the great Napoleon, in whose service Paganini was, as director of her private orchestra, for a long time was unable to hear him play without fainting. In women he produced nervous fits and hysterics at his will; stouthearted men he drove to frenzy. He changed cowards into heroes and made the bravest soldiers feel like so many nervous schoolgirls. Is it to be wondered at, then, that hundreds of weird tales circulated for long years about and around the mysterious Genoese, that modern Orpheus of Europe. One of these was especially ghastly. It was rumored, and was believed by more people than would probably like to confess it, that the strings of his violin were made of *human intestines, according to all the rules and requirements of the Black Art.*

Exaggerated as this idea may seem to some, it has nothing impossible in it; and it is more than probable that it was this legend that led to the extraordinary events which we are about to narrate. Human organs are often used by the Eastern Black Magicians, so-called, and it is an averred fact that some Bengali Tantrikas (reciters of *tantras*, or "invocations to the demon," as a reverend writer has described them) use human corpses, and certain internal and external organs pertaining to them, as powerful magical agents for bad purposes.

However this may be, now that the magnetic and mesmeric potencies of hypnotism are recognized as facts by most physicians, it may be suggested with less danger than heretofore that the extraordinary effects of Paganini's violin playing were not, perhaps, entirely due to his talent and genius. The wonder and awe he so easily excited were as much caused by his external appearance, "which had something weird and demoniacal in it," according to certain of his biographers, as by the inexpressible charm of his execution and his remarkable mechanical skill. The latter is demonstrated by his perfect imitation of the flageolet, and his performance of long and magnificent melodies on the G string alone. In this performance, which many an artist has tried to copy without success, he remains unrivaled to this day.

It is owing to this remarkable appearance of his—termed by his friends eccentric, and by his too nervous victims, diabolical—that he experienced great difficulties in refuting certain ugly rumors. These were credited far more easily in his day than they would be now. It was whispered throughout Italy, and even in his own native town, that Paganini had murdered his wife, and, later on, a mistress, both of whom he had loved passionately, and both of whom he had not hesitated to sacrifice to his fiendish ambition. He had made himself proficient in magic arts, it was asserted,

and had succeeded thereby in imprisoning the souls of his two victims in his violin—his famous Cremona.

It is maintained by the immediate friends of Ernst T. W. Hoffmann, the celebrated author of *Die Elixire des Teufels, Meister Martin*, and other charming and mysterious tales, that Councilor Crespel, in the *Violin of Cremona*, was taken from the legend about Paganini. It is as all who have read it know, the history of a celebrated violin, into which the voice and the soul of a famous diva, a woman whom Crespel had loved and killed, had passed, and to which was added the voice of his beloved daughter, Antonia.

Nor was this superstition utterly ungrounded, nor was Hoffmann to be blamed for adopting it, after he had heard Paganini's playing. The extraordinary facility with which the artist drew out of his instrument, not only the most unearthly sounds, but positively human voices, justified the suspicion. Such effects might well have startled an audience and thrown terror into many a nervous heart. Add to this the impenetrable mystery connected with a certain period of Paganini's youth, and the most wild tales about him must be found in a measure justifiable, and even excusable; especially among a nation whose ancestors knew the Borgias and the Medicis of Black Art fame.

III

In those pre-telegraphic days, newspapers were limited, and the wings of fame had a heavier flight than they have now.

Franz had hardly heard of Paganini; and when he did, he swore he would rival, if not eclipse, the Geonese magician. Yes, he would either become the most famous of all living violinists, or he would break his instrument and put an end to his life at the same time.

Old Klaus rejoiced at such a determination. He rubbed his hands in glee, and jumping about on his lame leg like a crippled satyr, he flattered and incensed his pupil, believing himself all the while to be performing a sacred duty to the holy and majestic cause of art.

Upon first setting foot in Paris, three years before, Franz had all but failed. Musical critics pronounced him a rising star, but had all agreed that he required a few more years' practice, before he could hope to carry his audiences by storm. Therefore, after a desperate study of over two years and uninterrupted preparations, the Styrian artist had finally made himself ready for his first serious appearance in the great Opera House where a public concert before the most exacting critics of the old world was to be held; at this critical moment Paganini's arrival in the European metropolis placed an obstacle in the way of the realization of his hopes, and the old German professor wisely postponed his pupil's *debut*. At first he had simply smiled at the wild enthusiasm, the laudatory hymns sung about the Genoese violinist, and the almost superstitious awe with which his name was pronounced. But very soon Paganini's name became a burning iron in the hearts of both the artists, and a threatening phantom in the mind of Klaus. A few days more, and they shuddered at the very mention of their great rival, whose success became with every night more unprecedented.

The first series of concerts was over, but neither Klaus nor Franz had as yet had an opportunity of hearing him and of judging for themselves. So great and so beyond their means was the charge for admission, and so small the hope of getting a free pass from a brother artist justly regarded as the meanest of men in monetary transactions, that they had to wait for a chance, as did so many others. But the day came when neither master nor pupil could control their impatience any longer; so they pawned their watches, and with the proceeds bought two modest seats.

Who can describe the enthusiasm, the triumphs, of this famous, and at the same time fatal night! The audience was frantic; men wept and women screamed and fainted; while both Klaus and Stenio, sat looking paler than two ghosts.

At the first touch of Paganini's magic bow, both Franz and Samuel felt as if the icy hand of death had touched them. Carried away by an irresistible enthusiasm, which turned into a violent, unearthly mental torture, they dared neither look into each other's faces, nor exchange one word during the whole performance.

At midnight, while the chosen delegates of the Musical Societies and the Conservatory of Paris unhitched the horses, and dragged the carriage of the grand artist home in triumph, the two Germans returned to their modest lodging, and it was a pitiful sight to see them. Mournful and desperate, they placed themselves in their usual seats at the fire-corner, and neither for a while opened his mouth.

"Samuel!" at last exclaimed Franz, pale as death itself. "Samuel—it remains for us now but to die! . . . Do you hear me? . . . We are worthless! We were two madmen to have ever hoped that any one in this world would ever rival . . . him!"

The name of Paganini stuck in his throat, as in utter despair he fell into his armchair.

The old professor's wrinkles suddenly became purple. His little greenish eyes gleamed phosphorescently as, bending toward his pupil, he whispered to him in hoarse and broken tones:

"Nein, nein! Thou art wrong, my Franz! I have taught thee, and thou hast learned all of the great art that a simple mortal, and a Christian by baptism, can learn from another simple mortal. Am I to blame because these accursed Italians, in order to reign unequaled in the domain of art, have recourse to Satan and the diabolical effects of Black Magic?"

Franz turned his eyes upon his old master. There was a sinister light burning in those glittering orbs; a light telling plainly, that, to secure such a power, he, too, would not scruple to sell himself, body and soul, to the Evil One.

But he said not a word, and, turning his eyes from his old master's face, gazed dreamily at the dying embers.

The same long-forgotten incoherent dreams, which, after seeming such realities to him in his younger days, had been given up entirely, and had gradually faded from his mind, now crowded back into it with the same force and vividness as of old. The grimacing shades of Ixion, Sisyphus, and Tantalus resurrected and stood before him, saying:

"What matters hell—in which thou believest not. And even if hell there be, it is the hell described by the old Greeks, not that of the modern bigots—a locality full of conscious shadows, to whom thou canst be a second Orpheus."

Franz felt that he was going mad, and, turning instinctively, he looked his old master once more right in the face. Then his bloodshot eye evaded the gaze of Klaus.

Whether Samuel understood the terrible state of mind of his pupil, or whether he wanted to draw him out, to make him speak, and thus to divert his thoughts, must remain as hypothetical to the reader as it is to the writer. Whatever may have been in his mind, the German enthusiast went on, speaking with a feigned calmness:

"Franz, my dear boy, I tell you that the art of the accursed Italian is not natural; that it is due neither to study nor to genius. It never was acquired in the usual, natural way. You need not stare at me in that wild manner, for what I say is in the mouth of millions of people. Listen to what I now tell you, and try to understand. You have heard the strange tale whispered about the famous Tartini? He died one fine Sabbath night, strangled by his familiar demon, who had taught him how to endow his violin with a human voice, by shutting up in it, by means of incantations, the soul of a young virgin. Paganini—did more. In order to endow his instrument with the faculty of emitting human sounds, such as sobs, despairing cries, supplications, moans of love and fury—in short, the most heartrending notes of the human voice—Paganini became, the murderer not only of his wife and his mistress, but also of a friend, who was more tenderly attached to him than any other being on this earth. He then made the four chords of his magic violin out of the intestines of his last victim. This is the secret of his enchant-

ing talent, of that overpowering melody, that combination of sounds, which you will never be able to master unless . . ."

The old man could not finish the sentence. He staggered back before the fiendish look of his pupil, and covered his face with his hands.

Franz was breathing heavily, and his eyes had an expression that reminded Klaus of those of a hyena. His pallor was cadaverous. For some time he could not speak, but only gasped for breath. At last he slowly muttered, "Are you in earnest?"

"I am, as I hope to help you."

"And . . . and do you really believe that had I only the means of obtaining human intestines for strings, I could rival Paganini?" asked Franz, after a moment's pause, and casting down his eyes.

The old German unveiled his face, and, with a strange look of determination upon it, softly answered:

"Human intestines alone are not sufficient for our purpose; they must have belonged to someone who had loved us well, with an unselfish, holy love. Tartini endowed his violin with the life of a virgin; but that virgin had died of unrequited love for him. The fiendish artist had prepared beforehand a tube, in which he managed to catch her last breath as she expired, pronouncing his beloved name, and he then transferred this breath to his violin. As to Paganini, I have just told you his tale. It was with the consent of his victim, though, that he murdered him to get possession of his intestines.

"Oh, for the power of the human voice!" Samuel went on, after a brief pause. "What can equal the eloquence, the magic spell of the human voice? Do you think, my poor boy, I would not have taught you this great, this final secret, were it not that it throws one right into the clutches of him . . . who must remain unnamed at night?" he added, with a sudden return to the superstitions of his youth.

Franz did not answer; but with a calmness awful to behold, he left his place, took down his violin from the wall where it was hanging, and, with one powerful grasp of the chords, he tore them out and flung them into the fire.

Samuel suppressed a cry of horror. The chords were hissing upon the coals, where, among the blazing logs, they wriggled and curled like so many living snakes.

"By the witches of Thessaly and the dark arts of Circe!" he exclaimed, with foaming mouth and his eyes burning like coals; "by the Furies of Hell and Pluto himself, I now swear, in thy presence, O Samuel, my master, never to touch a violin again until I can string it with four human chords. May I be accursed for ever and ever if I do!" He fell senseless on the floor, with a deep sob, that ended like a funeral wail; old Samuel lifted him up as he would have lifted a child, and carried him to his bed. Then he sallied forth in search of a physician.

IV

For several days after this painful scene Franz was very ill, ill almost beyond recovery. The physician declared him to be suffering from brain fever and said that the worst was to be feared. For nine long days the patient remained delirious; and Klaus, who was nursing him night and day with the solicitude of the tenderest mother, was horrified at the work of his own hands. For the first time since their acquaintance began, the old teacher, owing to the wild ravings of his pupil, was able to penetrate into the darkest corners of that weird, superstitious, cold, and, at the same time, passionate nature; and—he trembled at what he discovered. For he saw that which he had failed to perceive before—Franz as he was in reality, and not as he seemed to superficial observers. Music was the life of the young man, and adulation was the air he breathed, without which that life became a burden; from the chords of his violin alone, Stenio drew his life and being, but the applause of men and even of Gods was necessary to its support. He saw unveiled before his eyes

a genuine, artistic, *earthly* soul, with its divine counterpart totally absent, a son of the Muses, all fancy and brain poetry, but without a heart. While listening to the ravings of that delirious and unhinged fancy Klaus felt as if he were for the first time in his long life exploring a marvelous and untraveled region, a human nature not of this world but of some incomplete planet. He saw all this, and shuddered. More than once he asked himself whether it would not be doing a kindness to his "boy" to let him die before he returned to consciousness.

But he loved his pupil too well to dwell for long on such an idea. Franz had bewitched his truly artistic nature, and now old Klaus felt as though their two lives were inseparably linked together. That he could thus feel was a revelation to the old man; so he decided to save Franz, even at the expense of his own old and, as he thought, useless life.

The seventh day of the illness brought on a most terrible crisis. For twenty-four hours the patient never closed his eyes, nor remained for a moment silent; he raved continuously during the whole time. His visions were peculiar, and he minutely described each. Fantastic, ghastly figures kept slowly swimming out of the penumbra of his small, dark room, in regular and uninterrupted procession, and he greeted each by name as he might greet old acquaintances. He referred to himself as Prometheus, bound to the rock by four bands made of human intestines. At the foot of the Caucasian Mount the black waters of the river Styx were running. . . . They had deserted Arcadia, and were now endeavoring to encircle within a seven-fold embrace the rock upon which he was suffering. . . .

"Wouldst thou know the name of the Promethean rock, old man?" he roared into his adopted father's ear. . . . "Listen then, . . . its name is . . . called Samuel Klaus . . .

"Yes, yes! . . ." the German murmured disconsolately. "It is I who killed him, while seeking to console. The news of Paganini's magic arts struck his fancy too vividly. . . . Oh, my poor, poor boy!"

"Ha, ha, ha, ha!" The patient broke into a loud and discordant laugh. "Aye, poor old man, sayest thou? . . . So, so, thou art of poor stuff, anyhow, and wouldst look well only when stretched upon a fine Cremona violin! . . ."

Klaus shuddered, but said nothing. He only bent over the poor maniac, and with a kiss upon his brow, a caress as tender and as gentle as that of a doting mother, he left the sickroom for a few instants to seek relief in his own garret. When he returned, the ravings were following another channel. Franz was singing, trying to imitate the sounds of a violin.

Toward the evening of that day, the delirium of the sick man became perfectly ghastly. He saw spirits of fire clutching at his violin. Their skeleton hands, from each finger of which grew a flaming claw, beckoned to old Samuel. . . . They approached and surrounded the old master, and were preparing to rip him open . . . him, "the only man on this earth who loves me with an unselfish, holy love, and . . . whose intestines can be of any good at all!" he went on whispering, with glaring eyes and demon laugh. . . .

By the next morning, however, the fever had disappeared, and by the end of the ninth day Stenio had left his bed, having no recollection of his illness, and no suspicion that he had allowed Klaus to read his inner thought. Nay; had he himself any knowledge that such a horrible idea as the sacrifice of his old master to his ambition had ever entered his mind? Hardly. The only immediate result of his fatal illness was, that as, by reason of his vow, his artistic passion could find no issue, another passion awoke, which might avail to feed his ambition and his insatiable fancy. He plunged headlong into the study of the Occult Arts, of Alchemy and of Magic. In the practice of Magic the young dreamer sought to stifle the voice of his passionate longing for his, as he thought, forever lost violin. . . .

Weeks and months passed away, and the conversation about Paganini was never resumed between the master and the pupil. But a profound melancholy had taken possession of Franz, the two hardly exchanged a word, the violin hung mute, chordless, full of dust, in its habitual place. It was as the presence of a soulless corpse between them.

The young man had become gloomy and sarcastic, even avoiding the mention of music. Once, as his old professor, after long hesitation, took out his own violin from its dust-covered case and prepared to play, Franz gave a convulsive shudder, but said nothing. At the first notes of the bow, however, he glared like a madman, and rushing out of the house, remained for hours, wandering in the streets. Then old Samuel in his turn threw his instrument down, and locked himself up in his room till the following morning.

One night as Franz sat, looking particularly pale and gloomy, old Samuel suddenly jumped from his seat, and after hopping about the room in a magpie fashion, approached his pupil, imprinted a fond kiss upon the young man's brow, and squeaked at the top of his shrill voice:

"Is it not time to put an end to all this?" . . .

Whereupon, starting from his usual lethargy, Franz echoed, as in a dream:

"Yes, it is time to put an end to this."

Upon which the two separated, and went to bed.

On the following morning, when Franz awoke, he was astonished not to see his old teacher in his usual place to greet him. But he had greatly altered during the last few months, and he at first paid no attention to his absence, unusual as it was. He dressed and went into the adjoining room, a little parlor where they had their meals, and which separated their two bedrooms. The fire had not been lighted since the embers had died out on the previous night, and no sign was anywhere visible of the professor's busy hand in his usual housekeeping duties. Greatly puzzled, but in no way dismayed, Franz took his usual place at the corner of the now cold fireplace, and fell into an aimless reverie. As he stretched himself in his old armchair, raising both his hands to clasp them behind his head in a favorite posture of his, his hand came into contact with something on a shelf at his back; he knocked against a case, and brought it violently on the ground.

It was old Klaus's violin case that came down to the floor with such a sudden crash that the case opened and the violin fell out of it, rolling to the feet of Franz. And then the chords striking against the brass fender emitted a sound, prolonged, sad and mournful as the sigh of an unrestful soul; it seemed to fill the whole room, and reverberated in the head and the very heart of the young man. The effect of that broken violin string was magical.

"Samuel!" cried Stenio, with his eyes starting from their sockets, and an unknown terror suddenly taking possession of his whole being. "Samuel! what has happened? . . . My good, my dear old master!" he called out, hastening to the professor's little room, and throwing the door violently open. No one answered, all was silent within.

He staggered back, frightened at the sound of his own voice, so changed and hoarse it seemed to him at this moment. No reply came in response to his call. Naught followed but a dead silence . . . that stillness which in the domain of sounds, usually denotes death. In the presence of a corpse, as in the lugubrious stillness of a tomb, such silence acquires a mysterious power, which strikes the sensitive soul with a nameless terror. . . . The little room was dark, and Franz hastened to open the shutters.

Samuel was lying on his bed, cold, stiff, and lifeless. . . . At the sight of the corpse of him who had loved him so well, and had been to him more than a father, Franz experienced a dreadful revulsion of feeling a terrible shock. But the ambition of the fanatical artist got the better of the despair of the man, and smothered the feelings of the latter in a few seconds.

A note bearing his own name was conspicuously placed upon a table near the corpse. With trembling hand, the violinist tore open the envelope, and read the following:

MY BELOVED SON, FRANZ,

When you read this, I shall have made the greatest sacrifice, that your best and only friend and teacher could have accomplished for your fame. He, who loved you most, is now but an inanimate lump of clay. Of your old teacher there now remains but a clod of cold organic matter. I need not prompt you as to what you have to do with it. Fear not stupid prejudices. It is for your future fame that I have made an offering of my body, and you would be guilty of the blackest ingratitude were you now to render useless this sacrifice. When you shall have replaced the chords upon your violin, and these chords a portion of my own self, under your touch it will acquire the power of that accursed sorcerer, all the magic voices of Paganini's instrument. You will find therein my voice, my sighs and groans, my song of welcome, the prayerful sobs of my infinite and sorrowful sympathy, my love for you. And now, my Franz, fear nobody! Take your instrument with you, and dog the steps of him who filled our lives with bitterness and despair! . . . Appear in every arena, where, hitherto, he has reigned without a rival, and bravely throw the gauntlet of defiance in his face. O Franz! then only wilt thou hear with what a magic power the full notes of unselfish love will issue forth from thy violin. Perchance, with a last caressing touch of its chords, thou wilt remember that they once formed a portion of thine old teacher, who now embraces and blesses thee for the last time.

SAMUEL.

Two burning tears sparkled in the eyes of Franz, but they dried up instantly. Under the fiery rush of passionate hope and pride, the two orbs of the future magician-artist, riveted to the ghastly face of the dead man, shone like the eyes of a demon.

Our pen refuses to describe that which took place on that day, after the legal inquiry was over. As another note, written with a view of satisfying the authorities, had been prudently provided by the loving care of the old teacher, the verdict was, "Suicide from causes unknown"; after this the coroner and the police retired, leaving the bereaved heir alone in the death room, with the remains of that which had once been a living man.

Scarcely a fortnight had elapsed from that day, ere the violin had been dusted, and four new, stout strings had been stretched upon it. Franz dared not look at them. He tried to play, but the bow trembled in his hand like a dagger in the grasp of a novice brigand. He then determined not to try again, until the portentous night should arrive, when he should have a chance of rivaling, nay, of surpassing, Paganini.

The famous violinist had meanwhile left Paris, and was giving a series of triumphant concerts at an old Flemish town in Belgium.

V

One night, as Paganini, surrounded by a crowd of admirers, was sitting in the dining room of the hotel at which he was staying, a visiting card, with a few words written on it in pencil, was handed to him by a young man with wild and staring eyes.

Fixing upon the intruder a look, which few persons could bear, but receiving back a glance as calm and determined as his own, Paganini slightly bowed, and then dryly said:

"Sir, it shall be as you desire. Name the night. I am at your service."

On the following morning the whole town was startled by the appearance of bills posted at the corner of every street, and bearing the strange notice:

On the night of . . . , at the Grand Theatre of . . . and for the first time, will appear before the public, Franz Stenio, a German violinist, arrived purposely to throw down the gauntlet to the world-famous Paganini and to challenge him to a duel—upon their violins. He purposes to compete with the great "virtuoso" in the execution of the most difficult of his compositions. The famous Paganini has accepted the challenge. Franz Stenio will play, in competition with the unrivaled violinist, the celebrated "Fantaisie Caprice" of the latter, known as "The Witches."

The effect of the notice was magical. Paganini, who, amid his greatest triumphs, never lost sight of a profitable speculation, doubled the usual price of admission, but still the theater could not hold the crowds that flocked to secure tickets for that memorable performance.

At last the morning of the concert day dawned, and the "duel" was in everyone's mouth. Franz Stenio, who, instead of sleeping, had passed the whole long hours of the preceding midnight in walking up and down his room like an encaged panther, had, toward morning, fallen on his bed from mere physical exhaustion. Gradually he passed into a deathlike and dreamless slumber. At the gloomy winter dawn he awoke, but finding it too early to rise he fell asleep again. And then he had a vivid dream—so vivid indeed, so lifelike, that from its terrible realism he felt sure that it was a vision rather than a dream.

He had left his violin on a table by his bedside, locked in its case, the key of which never left him. Since he had strung it with those terrible chords he never let it out of his sight for a moment. In accordance with his resolution he had not touched it since his first trial, and his bow had never but once touched the human strings, for he had since always practiced on another instrument. But now in his sleep he saw himself looking at the locked case. Something in it was attracting his attention, and he found himself incapable of detaching his eyes from it. Suddenly he saw the upper part of the case slowly rising, and, within the chink thus produced, he perceived two small, phosphorescent green eyes—eyes but too familiar to him—fixing themselves on his, lovingly, almost beseechingly. Then a thin, shrill voice, as if issuing from these ghastly orbs—the voice and orbs of Samuel Klaus himself—resounded in Stenio's horrified ear, and he heard it say:

"Franz, my beloved boy. . . . Franz, I cannot, no *I cannot* separate myself from . . . *them*!"

And "they" twanged piteously inside the case.

Franz stood speechless, horror-bound. He felt his blood actually freezing, and his hair moving and standing erect on his head.

"It's but a dream, an empty dream!" he attempted to formulate in his mind.

"I have tried my best, Franzchen. . . . I have tried my best to sever myself from these accursed strings, without pulling them to pieces. . . ." pleaded the same shrill, familiar voice. "Wilt thou help me to do so?"

Another twang, still more prolonged and dismal, resounded within the case, now dragged about the table in every direction, by some interior power, like some living, wriggling thing, the twangs becoming sharper and more jerky with every new pull.

It was not for the first time that Stenio heard those sounds. He had often remarked them before—indeed, ever since he had used his master's viscera as a footstool for his own ambition. But on every occasion a feeling of creeping horror had prevented him from investigating their cause, and he had tried to assure himself that the sounds were only a hallucination.

But now he stood face-to-face with the terrible fact, whether in dream or in reality he knew not, nor did he care, since the hallucination—if hallucination it were—was far more real and vivid than any reality. He tried to speak, to take a step forward; but as often happens in nightmares, he could neither utter a word nor move a finger. . . . He felt hopelessly paralyzed.

The pulls and jerks were becoming more desperate with each moment, and at last something inside the case snapped violently. The vision of his Stradivarius, devoid of its magical strings, flashed before his eyes, throwing him into a cold sweat of mute and unspeakable terror.

He made a superhuman effort to rid himself of the incubus that held him spellbound. But as the last supplicating whisper of the invisible Presence repeated:

"Do, oh, do . . . help me to cut myself off—"

Franz sprang to the case with one bound, like an enraged tiger defending its prey, and with one frantic effort breaking the spell.

"Leave the violin alone, you old fiend from hell!" he cried, in hoarse and trembling tones.

He violently shut down the self-raising lid, and while firmly pressing his left hand on it, he seized with the right a piece of rosin from the table and drew on the leather-covered top the sign of the six-pointed star—the seal used by King Solomon to bottle up the rebellious djins inside their prisons.

A wail, like the howl of a she-wolf moaning over her dead little ones, came out of the violin case:

"Thou art ungrateful . . . very ungrateful, my Franz!" sobbed the blubbering "spirit voice." "But I forgive . . . for I still love thee well. Yet thou canst not shut me in . . . boy. Behold!"

And instantly a grayish mist spread over and covered case and table, and rising upward formed itself into an indistinct shape. Then it began growing, and as it grew, Franz felt himself gradually enfolded in cold and damp coils, slimy as those of a huge snake. He gave a terrible cry and awoke; but, strangely enough, not on his bed, but near the table, just as he had dreamed, pressing the violin case desperately with both his hands.

"It was but a dream, . . . after all," he muttered, still terrified, but relieved of the load on his heaving breast.

With a tremendous effort he composed himself, and unlocked the case to inspect the violin. He found it covered with dust, but otherwise sound and in order, and he suddenly felt himself as cool and determined as ever. Having dusted the instrument he carefully rosined the bow, tightened the strings and tuned them. He even went so far as to try upon it the first notes of the "Witches"; first cautiously and timidly, then using his bow boldly and with full force.

The sound of that loud, solitary note—defiant as the war trumpet of a conquerer, sweet and majestic as the touch of a seraph on his golden harp in the fancy of the faithful—thrilled through the very soul of Franz it revealed to him a hitherto unsuspected potency in his bow, which ran on in strains that filled the room with the richest swell of melody, unheard by the artist until that night. Commencing in uninterrupted *legato* tones, his bow sang to him of sun-bright hope and beauty, of moonlit nights, when the soft and balmy still-ness endowed every blade of grass and all things animate and inanimate with a voice and a song of love. For a few brief moments it was a torrent of melody, the harmony of which, "tuned to soft woe," was calculated to make mountains weep, had there been any in the room, and to soothe.

. . . even th'inexorable powers of hell,

the presence of which was undeniably felt in this modest hotel room. Suddenly, the solemn *legato* chant, contrary to all laws of harmony, quivered, became *arpeggios*, and ended in shrill *staccatos*, like the notes of a hyena laugh. The same creeping sensation of terror, as he had before felt, came over him, and Franz threw the bow away. He had recognized the familiar laugh, and would have no more of it. Dressing, he locked the bedeviled violin securely in its case, and tak-ing it with him to the dining room, determined to await quietly the hour of trial.

VI

The terrible hour of the struggle had come, and Stenio was at his post—calm, resolute, almost smiling.

The theater was crowded to suffocation, and there was not even standing room to be got for any amount of hard cash or favoritism. The sin-gular challenge had reached every quarter to which the post could carry it, and gold flowed freely into Paganini's unfathomable pockets, to an extent almost satisfying even to his insatiate and venal soul.

It was arranged that Paganini should begin. When he appeared upon the stage, the thick walls of the theater shook to their foundations with the applause that greeted him. He began and ended his famous composition "The Witches" amid a storm of cheers. The shouts of public enthusi-asm lasted so long that Franz began to think his turn would never come. When, at last, Paganini, amid the roaring applause of a frantic public, was allowed to retire behind the scenes, his eye fell upon Stenio, who was tuning his violin, and he felt amazed at the serene calmness, the air of assurance, of the unknown German artist.

When Franz approached the footlights, he was received with icy coldness. But for all that, he did not feel in the least disconcerted. He looked very pale, but his thin white lips wore a scornful smile as response to this dumb unwelcome. He was sure of his triumph.

At the first notes of the prelude of "The Witches" a thrill of astonishment passed over the audience. It was Paganini's touch, and it was something more. Some—and they were the majority—thought that never in his best moments of inspiration, had the Italian artist himself, in executing that diabolical composition of his, exhibited such an extraordinary diabolical power. Under the pressure of the long muscular fingers of Franz, the chords shivered like the palpitating intestines of a disemboweled victim under the vivisector's knife. They moaned melodiously, like a dying child. The large blue eye of the artist, fixed with a satanic expression upon the sounding board, seemed to summon forth Orpheus himself from the infernal regions, rather than the musi-cal notes supposed to be generated in the depths of the violin. Sounds seemed to transform them-selves into objective shapes, thickly and precipi-tately gathering as at the evocation of a mighty magician, and to be whirling around him, like a host of fantastic, infernal figures, dancing the witches' "goat dance." In the empty depths of the shadowy background of the stage, behind the artist, a nameless phantasmagoria, produced by the concussion of unearthly vibrations, seemed to form pictures of shameless orgies, of the volup-tuous hymens of a real witches' Sabbat . . . A collective hallucination took hold of the public. Panting for breath, ghastly, and trickling with the icy perspiration of an inexpressible horror, they sat spellbound, and unable to break the spell of the music by the slightest motion. They experienced all the illicit enervating delights of the paradise of Mahommed, that come into the disordered fancy of an opium-eating Mussulman, and felt at the same time the abject terror, the agony of one who struggles against an attack of *delirium tremens*. . . . Many ladies shrieked aloud, others fainted, and strong men gnashed their teeth, in a state of utter helplessness. . . .

Then came the *finale*. Thundering uninterrupted applause delayed its beginning, expanding the momentary pause to a duration of almost a quarter of an hour. The bravos were furious, almost hysterical. At last, when after a profound and last bow, Stenio, whose smile was as sardonic as it was triumphant, lifted his bow to attack the famous finale, his eye fell upon Paganini, who, calmly seated in the manager's box, had been behind none in zealous applause. The small and piercing black eyes of the Genoese artist were riveted to the Stradivarius in the hands of Franz, but otherwise he seemed quite cool and unconcerned. His rival's face troubled him for one short instant, but he regained his self-possession and, lifting once more his bow, drew the first note.

Then the public enthusiasm reached its acme, and soon knew no bounds. The listeners heard and saw indeed. The witches' voices resounded in the air, and beyond all the other voices one voice was heard—

> *Discordant, and unlike to human sounds*
> *It seem'd of dogs the bark, of wolves the howl;*
> *The doleful screechings of the midnight owl;*
> *The hiss of snakes, the hungry lion's roar;*
> *The sounds of billows beating on the shore;*
> *The groan of winds among the leafy wood,*
> *And burst of thunder from the rending*
> *   cloud;—*
> *'Twas these, all these in one . . .*

The magic bow was drawing forth its last quivering sounds—famous among prodigious musical feats—imitating the precipitate flight of the witches before bright dawn; of the unholy women saturated with the fumes of their nocturnal Saturnalia, when—a strange thing came to pass on the stage. Without the slightest transition, the notes suddenly changed. In their aerial flight of ascension and descent, their melody was unexpectedly altered in character. The sounds became confused, scattered, disconnected . . . and then—it seemed from the sounding board of the violin—came out swearing, jarring tones, like those of a street Punch, screaming at the top of a senile voice:

"Art thou satisfied, Franz, my boy? . . . Have not I gloriously kept my promise, eh?"

The spell was broken. Though still unable to realize the whole situation, those who heard the voice and the *Punchinello*-like tones, were freed, as by enchantment, from the terrible charm under which they had been held. Loud roars of laughter, mocking exclamations of half-anger and half-irritation were now heard from every corner of the vast theatre. The musicians in the orchestra, with faces still blanched from weird emotion, were now seen shaking with laughter, and the whole audience rose, like one man, from their seats, unable yet to solve the enigma; they felt, nevertheless, too disgusted, too disposed to laugh to remain one moment longer in the building.

But suddenly the sea of moving heads in the stalls and the pit became once more motionless, and stood petrified, as though struck by lightning. What all saw was terrible enough—the handsome though wild face of the young artist suddenly aged, and his graceful, erect figure bent down, as though under the weight of years; but this was nothing to that which some of the most sensitive clearly perceived. Franz Stenio's person was now entirely enveloped in a semitransparent mist, cloud-like, creeping with serpentine motion, and gradually tightening round the living form, as though ready to engulf him. And there were those also who discerned in this tall and ominous pillar of smoke a clearly defined figure, a form showing the unmistakable outlines of a grotesque and grinning, but terribly awful-looking old man, whose viscera were protruding and the ends of the intestines stretched on the violin.

Within this hazy, quivering veil, the violinist was then seen, driving his bow furiously across the human chords, with the contortions of a demoniac, as we see them represented on medieval cathedral paintings!

An indescribable panic swept over the audience, and breaking now, for the last time, through the spell which had again bound them motionless, every living creature in the theater made one mad rush toward the door. It was like the sudden outburst of a dam, a human torrent, roaring amid a shower of discordant notes, idiotic squeakings, prolonged and whining moans, cacophonous cries of frenzy, above which, like the detonations of pistol shots, was heard the consecutive bursting of the four strings stretched upon the soundboard of that bewitched violin.

When the theater was emptied of the last man of the audience, the terrified manager rushed on the stage in search of the unfortunate performer. He was found dead and already stiff, behind the footlights, twisted up into the most unnatural of postures, with the "catguts" wound curiously round his neck and his violin shattered into a thousand fragments. . . .

When it became publicly known that the unfortunate would-be rival of Niccolo Paganini had not left a cent to pay for his funeral or his hotel bill, the Genoese, his proverbial meanness notwithstanding, settled the hotel bill and had poor Stenio buried at his own expense.

He claimed, however, in exchange, the fragments of the Stradivarius—as a memento of the strange event.

Mayer André Marcel Schwob (1867–1905), better known as Marcel Schwob, was a French symbolist whose stories were a precursor to surrealist fiction; he also often sought to uncover the bizarre quirks of the human psychology. Schwob's collection *The King in the Golden Mask* (1892) and his *The Book of Monelle* (1894), which many critics agree to be the story of his love for a woman named Louise, became an integral part of the French symbolist movement. His novels and short stories often allude to legends, forgotten myths, and characters who feel abandoned by history. Schwob's love for history may have come from his time living and working with his uncle, León Cahun, at the Mazarine Library. Whatever his inspiration, Schwob went on to write amazing tales such as *Imaginary Lives* (1896), *The Children's Crusade* (1896), and *The Lamp of Psyche* (1903). Although praised during his lifetime, Schwob has all but been forgotten except by the most faithful lovers of the strange and fantastical.

The Death of Odjigh

Marcel Schwob

Translated by Kit Schluter

TO J.-H. ROSNY

AT THAT TIME, the human race seemed close to perishing. The orb of the sun was as cold as the moon. An endless winter caused the soil to crack. The mountains which had erupted, spewing the earth's flaming entrails into the sky, were now gray with frozen lava. The lands were riveted by parallel or starry trenches; tremendous crevasses, suddenly yawning, engulfed the things above as they collapsed, and one could see, moving toward them in heavy sideslips, long lines of glacial erratics. The dark air was sequined with transparent needles; a sinister whiteness hung over the land; the universal silver glow seemed to sterilize the world.

No vegetation remained, save the seldom trace of pale lichen upon the boulders. The bones of the globe had been stripped of their flesh, which is made of soil, and the plains spread out like skeletons. And with this wintry death having first attacked life here below, the fish and beasts of the sea had perished, imprisoned in the ice, then the insects who swarmed over the crawling plants, and the animals who bore their young in their belly pouches, and the half-flying creatures who had haunted the great forests; for as far as the eye could see, there was neither tree nor greenery, and no living thing was to be found, save what chose to dwell in the caverns, grottoes, or dens.

And so, among the children of men, two races had already gone extinct; those who had inhabited the liana nests in the canopies of the great trees, and those who had withdrawn to the center of lakes in floating houses: the forests, woods, thickets, and bushes littered the sparkling land, and the water's surface was hard and resplendent like polished stone.

The Animal Hunters, who understood fire, the Troglodytes, who knew how to dig under the earth to its internal warmth, and the Fish Eaters, who had hoarded sea oil in their ice holes, still resisted the winter. But the beasts were growing scarce, taken by the frost as soon as their snouts broke aboveground, and the wood for making fires was soon to be exhausted, and the oil was as solid as a yellow rock with a white crest.

Nevertheless a wolf slayer, named Odjigh, who dwelled in a deep den and wielded an enormous, weighty, and formidable ax of green jade, took pity on living things. Standing on the shore of the great interior sea whose tip extends to the east of Minnesota, he cast his gaze over the Septentrional regions where the cold seemed to amass. Deep in his frozen grotto he took his sacred calumet carved of white stone, packed it with the aromatic herbs whence smoke puffs in rings, and blew this divine incense into the air. The rings mounted to the sky and the gray whorl drifted northward.

It was to the North that Odjigh, the slayer of wolves, set out walking. He covered his face with the furry, perforated pelt of a baby rat, whose plumed tail swayed above his head, tied a pouch of dried minced meat and lard around his waist with a lash of leather, and, swinging his ax of green jade, he started for the thick clouds piled on the horizon.

He went on, and all around him life was fading away. The rivers had long been killed. The opaque air bore naught but muffled sounds. The blue, white, and green heaps of ice, radiant with frost, seemed pillars along a monumental road.

Odjigh, deep in his heart, regretted the jigging of the nacreous fish in the meshing of the nets, the serpentine swimming of the conger eels, the heavy gait of the tortoises, the sidelong trot of the gigantic walleyed crabs, and the lively yawns of the earthly beasts, hairy beasts decked in scales, beasts spotted in an irregular fashion that pleased the eyes, beasts who loved their young and bounded adroitly, or twirled curiously, or took to perilous flight. But above all the other animals, he regretted the ferocious wolves, their coats of gray fur and their familiar howls, having been accustomed to hunting them with club and stone ax, through misty nights, by the red glow of the moon.

And now to his left appeared a den-dwelling beast who lives deep underground and digs its holes backward, a thin badger with ragged coat. Odjigh saw him and rejoiced, without a thought of killing him. The badger, keeping its distance, walked abreast.

Then to Odjigh's right suddenly appeared from an icy gulley a poor lynx with fathomless eyes. He looked awry at Odjigh, fearfully, and crept along with disquiet. But the slayer of wolves rejoiced again, walking between Badger and Lynx.

As he went on, with his pouch of meat beating against his side, he heard a feeble yip of hunger from behind. And turning around then to the sound of a familiar voice, he saw a bony wolf, trailing sadly. Odjigh felt pity for those whose skulls he had split. Wolf stuck out his steaming tongue, and his eyes were red.

So the slayer continued on his way with his animal companions, subterranean Badger to his left, and Lynx, who sees all on earth, to his right, and Wolf, with hunger in his gut, behind.

They came to the middle of the interior sea, indistinguishable from the continent save for the vast green of its ice. And there Odjigh, the slayer of wolves, sat upon a block of ice and placed before him the stone calumet. And before each of his living companions, he placed a block of ice, which he carved with the angle of his ax into the shape of the holy censer where one breathes smoke. Into the four calumets he packed the aromatic herbs; then he struck one firestone against another, and the herbs caught fire, and four thin columns of smoke rose toward the sky.

Yet the gray spire that rose before Badger drifted to the West; and the one that rose before Lynx curved to the East, and the one that rose before Wolf arced to the South. But the gray whorl from Odjigh's own calumet rose to the North.

The wolf slayer resumed his path. And, looking to his left, he grew sad: for Badger, who sees beneath the earth, drifted off to the West, and looking to his right, he lamented Lynx, who sees all on earth, and who fled to the East. He thought then of how these two animal companions were judicious and wise, each in the domain assigned him.

Nevertheless he walked on boldly, having behind him the red-eyed, hungry wolf, for whom he felt pity.

The mass of frigid clouds situated to the North seemed to touch the heavens. The winter grew crueler still. Odjigh's feet began to bleed, cut by the ice, and his blood froze into black scabs. But he went on for hours, days, weeks, no doubt, perhaps even months, sucking on a bit of dried meat, throwing scraps to his companion Wolf who followed him.

Odjigh walked with an indistinct hope. He pitied the world of men, animals, and plants that were dying off, and felt all the stronger for fighting the cause of the cold.

And finally, his path was blocked by an immense barrier of ice that enclosed the sky's somber dome, like a mountain range with invisible peaks. The great icicles that plunged into the ocean's solid sheet were of a limpid green; but they grew muddled in their accumulation; and as they mounted, they appeared an opaque blue, much like the color of the sky on the fairer days of time past: for they were composed of fresh water and snow.

Odjigh seized his ax of green jade, and carved steps into the escarpment. And so he climbed slowly to a prodigal height, where it seemed to him his head was enveloped in clouds and the ground had disappeared. And on the ledge just below him, Wolf sat and waited assuredly.

When he believed he was at the crest, he saw that it was constituted by a sparkling, vertical blue wall, and that one could not pass beyond it. But he looked behind him, and he saw the famished, living beast. His pity for the animate world gave him strength.

He sank his jade ax into the blue wall, and dug into the ice. Sparks of many colors flew around him. He dug for hours. His limbs were jaundiced and wrinkled by the cold. His pouch of meat had long since withered. He had chewed the aromatic herb of the calumet to trick his hunger, and, suddenly mistrustful of the Higher Powers, threw his calumet into the depths along with the two firestones.

He dug. He heard a dry grinding noise, and cried out: for he knew this sound originated from the blade of his jade ax, which the excessive cold was going to break. So he lifted it up and, with no other means of warming it, sank it powerfully into his right thigh. The green ax was stained with hot blood. And, once again, Odjigh dug into the blue wall. Wolf, sitting behind him, howled as he lapped at the red drops raining down.

And suddenly, the smooth wall burst. There was a tremendous gust of heat, as if the hot seasons had been building up on the other side at the barrier of the sky. The breach widened, and the mighty wind enveloped Odjigh. He heard the rustling of little spring shoots and felt summer's blaze. In the great current that carried him away, it seemed to him that the seasons were returning to the world, to save general life from its icy death. The current swept in the white rays of the sun, and warm rains, and caressing breezes, and clouds heavy with fecundity. And in this hot gust of life, the black clouds piled up and begat fire.

There was a great streak of fire and a crack of thunder, and the dazzling line struck Odjigh in the heart like a red gladius. He fell against the smooth wall, his back turned to the world, toward which the seasons were rushing back in the river of the storm, and the hungry wolf, timidly climbing upon him, setting his paws upon his shoulders, began to gnaw at the nape of his neck.

The Terrestrial Fire

Marcel Schwob

Translated by Kit Schluter

TO PAUL CLAUDEL

THE FINAL THRUST of faith that had swept the world was unable to save it. New prophets had arisen in vain. The mysteries of the will were expounded to no end; it was no longer a question of controlling it, but rather its quantity seemed simply to diminish. The energy of all living things dissipated. It had been gathered in one supreme effort toward a future religion, and the effort had failed. All withdrew into a very gentle selfishness. Every passion was tolerated. The world was as if in a hot lull. Vices bred there with the frenzy of great, poisonous plants. Immorality, become the very law of things, with the god Chance of Life; science obscured by mystical superstition; the Tartuffery of the heart, which the senses serve as tentacles; the seasons, once distinct, now mixed together in a series of rainy days that incubated the storm; nothing precise, nor traditional, but a disarray of old-fashioned things, and the reign of the vague.

It was at that point when, through an electric night, the omen of devastation appeared to fall from the sky. A heretofore unseen tempest blew on high, engendered by the Earth's corruption. The colds and warmths, the brightnesses of the sun and snows, the rains and the confused beams of light, had birthed forces of destruction that broke out without warning.

For an extraordinary cascade of aeroliths became visible and the night was scored by dazzling lines; the stars blazed like torches, and the clouds were heralds of fire, and the moon a red brazier hurling varicolored projectiles. All things were infused with a pale light that limned the last hovels, and the glare of which, however softened, caused tremendous pain. Then the night that had opened, again withdrew. From every volcano columns of ash blew into the sky like volutes of black basalt, the pillars of a supraterrestrial world. A rain of dark dust fell backward and a cloud emanated from the Earth, which covered the Earth.

And so passed the night, and the dawn was invisible. A gigantic wash of deep red coursed through the sky's embers from east to west. The atmosphere became fiery, and the air was pocked with black dots that clung to everything.

The crowds lay prostrate on the ground, not knowing where to flee. The bells of the churches, convents, and monasteries chimed uncertainly, as if struck by supernatural clappers. There were, from time to time, detonations in the forts, where siege cannons fired rounds of powder in an attempt to clear the air. Then, as the red globe touched the west and a day had slipped past, the general silence set in. No one had any strength left to pray, nor to beg.

And as the incandescent mass sank below the black horizon, the entire western sky burst into flames, and a sheet of fire retreated along the bygone route of the sun.

There was an exodus before the celestial and terrestrial fires. Two poor little bodies slid along a low window and ran wildly. Despite the maculations from the rancid air, her hair was very blond, her eyes limpid; he, golden-skinned, with a bright curtain of locks, where peculiar glints bore violet light. They knew nothing, neither one nor the other; they were hardly beyond the confines of childhood and, as neighbors, felt the affection of a brother and sister.

And so, holding each other's hand, they walked down the black streets, where the roofs and chimneys appeared rubbed with a sinister light, through the men laid out and the splayed, twitching horses, then on to the outer walls, the dispeopled suburbs, moving to the east, away from the flames.

They were stopped by a river that suddenly blocked their way, whose water coursed rapidly.

But there was a bark on the riverbank: they pushed it off and threw themselves in, letting it go with the flood.

The keel of the bark was seized by the current, its sides by the hurricane, and it shot off like a stone from the sling.

It was a very old fishing bark, browned and polished from use, with paddle-worn oarlocks and gunwales shiny from the passage of nets, like a primitive and honest tool of this perishing civilization.

They lay themselves down deep inside, still holding each other's hand and trembling before the unknown.

And the quick rowboat led them out to a mysterious sea, as they fled below the hot, swirling tempest.

They awoke upon a desolate ocean. Their boat was surrounded by mounds of pale algae, where the sea foam had deposited its dry slime, where iridescent creatures and pink starfish putrefied. The small waves buoyed up the white bellies of dead fish.

Half the sky was veiled by the growth of the fire, which crept sensibly forth and ate away at the other half's ashen fringe.

The sea appeared dead to them, like everything else. For its breath was pestilent and its clarity was streaked with veins of blue and deep green. Nevertheless the boat glided over its surface with unrelenting speed.

The western horizon held bluish flickers.

She dipped her hand in the water, and immediately withdrew it: the waves were already hot. A dreadful seething was perhaps going to cause the ocean to quake.

To the south, they saw the white clouds with pink aigrettes, and were uncertain if this was ignited gas.

The general silence and the growing fire transfixed them in a stupor: they preferred the great scream that had accompanied them, like the echo of a wheeze totalized in the wind.

The far reaches of the sea, where the dome of ash, still half dark, had come to plunge, were opened by a gash of light. A livid blue portion of circle there seemed to promise entrance to a new world.

"Ah! Look!" she said.

The wispy steam floating behind them on the ocean had just lit up with the selfsame glow as the pale and trembling sky: it was the sea aflame.

Why this universal destruction? Their heads, pounding from the overhot air, were filled with this multiplying question. They did not know. They were unaware of faults. Life embraced them; suddenly, they were living more quickly; adolescence seized them amid the burning of the world.

And in this ancient bark, in this first instrument of life here below, they were such a young Adam and such a little Eve: the lone survivors of this terrestrial Hell.

The sky was a dome of fire. Nothing remained on the horizon but a single distant blue point, over which the eyelid of fire was poised to close. They were already in the grip of a roaring sea.

She stood and undressed. Naked, their pale and willowy limbs were illuminated by the universal glow. They took each other's hands and kissed.

"Let's fall in love," she said.

Rabindranath Tagore (1861–1941) was a Bengali poet, composer, and writer known for transforming Bengali literature. Separating himself from the traditional Sanskrit, Tagore also helped introduce Indian culture to the Western world and vice versa. And thanks to the profound appreciation of his book *Gitanjali*, translated as *Song Offerings* (1910), in 1913 Tagore became the first non-European to receive the Nobel Prize for Literature. He wrote several volumes of short stories, including *Gora* (1910), *The Home and the World* (1916), and *Crosscurrents* (1929). His most magnificent stories examine the lives of the meek and unassuming as well as the sometimes difficult realities of their lives. Tagore also wrote more than two thousand songs and hundreds of poems, many of which cannot be translated. "The Kingdom of Cards" is a story about bureaucracy and absurdity. In 1933, Tagore wrote a play based on this story that has been produced numerous times since his death.

The Kingdom of Cards

Rabindranath Tagore

I

ONCE UPON A TIME there was a lonely island in a distant sea where lived the Kings and Queens, the Aces and the Knaves, in the Kingdom of Cards. The Tens and Nines, with the Twos and Threes, and all the other members, had long ago settled there also. But these were not twice-born people, like the famous Court Cards.

The Ace, the King, and the Knave were the three highest castes. The fourth caste was made up of a mixture of the lower Cards. The Twos and Threes were lowest of all. These inferior Cards were never allowed to sit in the same row with the great Court Cards.

Wonderful indeed were the regulations and rules of that island kingdom. The particular rank of each individual had been settled from time immemorial. Everyone had his own appointed work, and never did anything else. An unseen hand appeared to be directing them wherever they went,—according to the Rules.

No one in the Kingdom of Cards had any occasion to think: no one had any need to come to any decision: no one was ever required to debate any new subject. The citizens all moved along in a listless groove without speech. When they fell, they made no noise. They lay down on their backs, and gazed upward at the sky with each prim feature firmly fixed for ever.

There was a remarkable stillness in the Kingdom of Cards. Satisfaction and contentment were complete in all their rounded wholeness. There was never any uproar or violence. There was never any excitement or enthusiasm.

The great ocean, crooning its lullaby with one

unceasing melody, lapped the island to sleep with a thousand soft touches of its wave's white hands. The vast sky, like the outspread azure wings of the brooding mother-bird, nestled the island round with its downy plume. For on the distant horizon a deep blue line betokened another shore. But no sound of quarrel or strife could reach the Island of Cards, to break its calm repose.

II

In that far-off foreign land across the sea, there lived a young Prince whose mother was a sorrowing queen. This queen had fallen from favor, and was living with her only son on the seashore. The Prince passed his childhood alone and forlorn, sitting by his forlorn mother, weaving the net of his big desires. He longed to go in search of the Flying Horse, the Jewel in the Cobra's hood, the Rose of Heaven, the Magic Roads, or to find where the Princess Beauty was sleeping in the Ogre's castle over the thirteen rivers and across the seven seas.

From the Son of the Merchant at school the young Prince learned the stories of foreign kingdoms. From the Son of the Kotwal he learned the adventures of the Two Genii of the Lamp. And when the rain came beating down, and the clouds covered the sky, he would sit on the threshold facing the sea, and say to his sorrowing mother: "Tell me, mother, a story of some very far-off land."

And his mother would tell him an endless tale she had heard in her childhood of a wonderful country beyond the sea where dwelled the Princess Beauty. And the heart of the young Prince would become sick with longing, as he sat on the threshold, looking out on the ocean, listening to his mother's wonderful story, while the rain outside came beating down and the gray clouds covered the sky.

One day the Son of the Merchant came to the Prince, and said boldly: "Comrade, my studies are over. I am now setting out on my travels to seek my fortunes on the sea. I have come to bid you good-bye."

The Prince said: "I will go with you."

And the Son of Kotwal said also: "Comrades, trusty and true, you will not leave me behind. I also will be your companion."

Then the young Prince said to his sorrowing mother: "Mother, I am now setting out on my travels to seek my fortune. When I come back once more, I shall surely have found some way to remove all your sorrow."

So the Three Companions set out on their travels together. In the harbor were anchored the twelve ships of the merchant, and the Three Companions got on board. The south wind was blowing, and the twelve ships sailed away, as fast as the desires that rose in the Prince's breast.

At the Conch Shell Island they filled one ship with conchs. At the Sandal Wood Island they filled a second ship with sandalwood, and at the Coral Island they filled a third ship with coral.

Four years passed away, and they filled four more ships, one with ivory, one with musk, one with cloves, and one with nutmegs.

But when these ships were all loaded a terrible tempest arose. The ships were all of them sunk, with their cloves and nutmeg, and musk and ivory, and coral and sandalwood and conchs. But the ship with the Three Companions struck on an island reef, buried them safe ashore, and itself broke in pieces.

This was the famous Island of Cards, where lived the Ace and King and Queen and Knave, with the Nines and Tens and all the other Members—according to the Rules.

III

Up till now there had been nothing to disturb that island stillness. No new thing had ever happened. No discussion had ever been held.

And then, of a sudden, the Three Companions appeared, thrown up by the sea,—and the Great Debate began. There were three main points of dispute.

First, to what caste should these unclassed strangers belong? Should they rank with the Court Cards? Or were they merely lower-caste people, to be ranked with the Nines and Tens? No precedent could be quoted to decide this weighty question.

Secondly, what was their clan? Had they the fairer hue and bright complexion of the Hearts, or was theirs the darker complexion of the Clubs? Over this question there were interminable disputes. The whole marriage system of the island, with its intricate regulations, would depend on its nice adjustment.

Thirdly, what food should they take? With whom should they live and sleep? And should their heads be placed southwest, northwest, or only northeast? In all the Kingdom of Cards a series of problems so vital and critical had never been debated before.

But the Three Companions grew desperately hungry. They had to get food in some way or other. So while this debate went on, with its interminable silence and pauses, and while the Aces called their own meeting, and formed themselves into a Committee, to find some obsolete dealing with the question, the Three Companions themselves were eating all they could find, and drinking out of every vessel, and breaking all regulations.

Even the Twos and Threes were shocked at this outrageous behavior. The Threes said: "Brother Twos, these people are openly shameless!" And the Twos said: "Brother Threes, they are evidently of lower caste than ourselves!" After their meal was over, the Three Companions went for a stroll in the city.

When they saw the ponderous people moving in their dismal processions with prim and solemn faces, then the Prince turned to the Son of the Merchant and the Son of the Kotwal, and threw back his head, and gave one stupendous laugh.

Down Royal Street and across Ace Square and along the Knave Embankment ran the quiver of this strange, unheard-of laughter, the laughter that, amazed at itself, expired in the vast vacuum of silence.

The Son of the Kotwal and the Son of the Merchant were chilled through to the bone by the ghostlike stillness around them. They turned to the Prince, and said: "Comrade, let us away. Let us not stop for a moment in this awful land of ghosts."

But the Prince said: "Comrades, these people resemble men, so I am going to find out, by shaking them upside down and outside in, whether they have a single drop of warm living blood left in their veins."

IV

The days passed one by one, and the placid existence of the Island went on almost without a ripple. The Three Companions obeyed no rules nor regulations. They never did anything correctly either in sitting or standing or turning themselves round or lying on their back. On the contrary, wherever they saw these things going on precisely and exactly according to the Rules, they gave way to inordinate laughter. They remained unimpressed altogether by the eternal gravity of those eternal regulations.

One day the great Court Cards came to the Son of the Kotwal and the Son of the Merchant and the Prince.

"Why," they asked slowly, "are you not moving according to the Rules?"

The Three Companions answered: "Because that is our Ichcha (wish)."

The great Court Cards with hollow, cavernous voices, as if slowly awakening from an agelong dream, said together: "Ich-cha! And pray who is Ich-cha?"

They could not understand who Ichcha was then, but the whole island was to understand it by-and-by. The first glimmer of light passed the threshold of their minds when they found out, through watching the actions of the Prince, that they might move in a straight line in an opposite direction from the one in which they had always gone before. Then they made another startling discovery, that there was another side to the Cards that they had never yet noticed with attention. This was the beginning of the change.

Now that the change had begun, the Three Companions were able to initiate them more and more deeply into the mysteries of Ichcha. The Cards gradually became aware that life was not bound by regulations. They began to feel a secret satisfaction in the kingly power of choosing for themselves.

But with this first impact of Ichcha the whole pack of cards began to totter slowly, and then tumble down to the ground. The scene was like that of some huge python awaking from a long sleep, as it slowly unfolds its numberless coils with a quiver that runs through its whole frame.

V

Hitherto the Queens of Spades and Clubs and Diamonds and Hearts had remained behind curtains with eyes that gazed vacantly into space, or else remained fixed upon the ground.

And now, all of a sudden, on an afternoon in spring the Queen of Hearts from the balcony raised her dark eyebrows for a moment, and cast a single glance upon the Prince from the corner of her eye.

"Great God," cried the Prince, "I thought they were all painted images. But I am wrong. They are women after all."

Then the young Prince called to his side his two Companions, and said in a meditative voice: "My comrades! There is a charm about these ladies that I never noticed before. When I saw that glance of the Queen's dark, luminous eyes, brightening with new emotion, it seemed to me like the first faint streak of dawn in a newly created world."

The two Companions smiled a knowing smile, and said: "Is that really so, Prince?"

And the poor Queen of Hearts from that day went from bad to worse. She began to forget all rules in a truly scandalous manner. If, for instance, her place in the row was beside the Knave, she suddenly found herself quite acci-

dentally standing beside the Prince instead. At this, the Knave, with motionless face and solemn voice, would say: "Queen, you have made a mistake."

And the poor Queen of Hearts' red cheeks would get redder than ever. But the Prince would come gallantly to her rescue and say: "No! There is no mistake. From today I am going to be Knave!"

Now it came to pass that, while everyone was trying to correct the improprieties of the guilty Queen of Hearts, they began to make mistakes themselves. The Aces found themselves elbowed out by the Kings. The Kings got muddled up with the Knaves. The Nines and Tens assumed airs as though they belonged to the Great Court Cards. The Twos and Threes were found secretly taking the places specially resented for the Fours and Fives. Confusion had never been so confounded before.

Many spring seasons had come and gone in that Island of Cards. The Kokil, the bird of Spring, had sung its song year after year. But it had never stirred the blood as it stirred it now. In days gone by the sea had sung its tireless melody. But, then, it had proclaimed only the inflexible monotony of the Rule. And suddenly its waves were telling, through all their flashing light and luminous shade and myriad voices, the deepest yearnings of the heart of love!

VI

Where are vanished now their prim, round, regular, complacent features? Here is a face full of lovesick longing. Here is a heart heating wild with regrets. Here is a mind racked sore with doubts. Music and sighing, and smiles and tears, are filling the air. Life is throbbing; hearts are breaking; passions are kindling.

Every one is now thinking of his own appearance, and comparing himself with others. The Ace of Clubs is musing to himself, that the King of Spades may be just passably good-looking. "But," says he, "when I walk down the street you have only to see how people's eyes turn toward me." The King of Spades is saying: "Why on earth is that Ace of Clubs always straining his neck and strutting about like a peacock? He imagines all the Queens are dying of love for him, while the real fact is—" Here he pauses, and examines his face in the glass.

But the Queens were the worst of all. They began to spend all their time in dressing themselves up to the Nines. And the Nines would become their hopeless and abject slaves. But their cutting remarks about one another were more shocking still.

So the young men would sit listless on the leaves under the trees, lolling with outstretched limbs in the forest shade. And the young maidens, dressed in pale-blue robes, would come walking accidentally to the same shade of the same forest by the same trees, and turn their eyes as though they saw no one there, and look as though they came out to see nothing at all. And then one young man more forward than the rest in a fit of madness would dare to go near to a maiden in blue. But, as he drew near, speech would forsake him. He would stand there tongue-tied and foolish, and the favorable moment would pass.

The Kokil birds were singing in the boughs overhead. The mischievous South wind was blowing; it disarrayed the hair, it whispered in the ear, and stirred the music in the blood. The leaves of the trees were murmuring with rustling delight. And the ceaseless sound of the ocean made all the mute longings of the heart of man and maid surge backward and forward on the full springtide of love.

The Three Companions had brought into the dried-up channels of the Kingdom of Cards the full flood tide of a new life.

VII

And, though the tide was full, there was a pause as though the rising waters would not break into foam but remain suspended forever. There were no outspoken words, only a cautious going forward one step and receding two. All seemed busy heaping up their unfulfilled desires like castles in the air, or fortresses of sand. They were pale and speechless, their eyes were burning, their lips trembling with unspoken secrets.

The Prince saw what was wrong. He summoned everyone on the Island and said: "Bring hither the flutes and the cymbals, the pipes and drums. Let all be played together, and raise loud shouts of rejoicing. For the Queen of Hearts this very night is going to choose her Mate!"

So the Tens and Nines began to blow on their flutes and pipes; the Eights and Sevens played on their sackbuts and viols; and even the Twos and Threes began to beat madly on their drums.

When this tumultous gust of music came, it swept away at one blast all those sighings and mopings. And then what a torrent of laughter and words poured forth! There were daring proposals and locking refusals, and gossip and chatter, and jests and merriment. It was like the swaying and shaking, and rustling and soughing, in a summer gale, of a million leaves and branches in the depth of the primeval forest.

But the Queen of Hearts, in a rose-red robe, sat silent in the shadow of her secret bower, and listened to the great uproarious sound of music and mirth that came floating toward her. She shut her eyes, and dreamed her dream of lore. And when she opened them she found the Prince seated on the ground before her gazing up at her face. And she covered her eyes with both hands, and shrank back quivering with an inward tumult of joy.

And the Prince passed the whole day alone, walking by the side of the surging sea. He carried in his mind that startled look, that shrinking gesture of the Queen, and his heart beat high with hope.

That night the serried, gaily dressed ranks of young men and maidens waited with smiling faces at the Palace Gates. The Palace Hall was lighted with fairy lamps and festooned with the flowers of spring. Slowly the Queen of Hearts entered, and the whole assembly rose to greet her. With a jasmine garland in her hand, she stood before the Prince with downcast eyes. In her lowly bashfulness she could hardly raise the garland to the neck of the Mate she had chosen. But the Prince bowed his head, and the garland slipped to its place. The assembly of youths and maidens had waited her choice with eager, expectant hush. And when the choice was made, the whole vast concourse rocked and swayed with a tumult of wild delight. And the sound of their shouts was heard in every part of the island, and by ships far out at sea. Never had such a shout been raised in the Kingdom of Cards before.

And they carried the Prince and his Bride, and seated them on the throne, and crowned them then and there in the Ancient Island of Cards.

And the sorrowing Mother Queen, on the far-off island shore on the other side of the sea, came sailing to her son's new kingdom in a ship adorned with gold.

And the citizens are no longer regulated according to the Rules, but are good or bad, or both, according to their Ichcha.

Count Eric Stanislaus Stenbock (1860–1895) was a Baltic Swedish poet and writer known for his macabre fantasy and, as the Count of Bogesund, the heir to an Estonian estate. Stenbock has been acclaimed as the paragon of the decadent movement by some. His works often feature strange, supernatural, suicidal, and satanic themes. By the year 1885, Count Stenbock had developed very peculiar tastes as well as addiction to both alcohol and opium. He had a menagerie of exotic animals and lit his house with lamps made in the image of Buddha and Mary Shelley. Stenbock died after publishing only three volumes of poetry and one short story collection. "The Other Side: A Breton Legend" is a good example of his work, filled as it is with magical creatures and sinister danger.

The Other Side: A Breton Legend

Count Eric Stanlislaus Stenbock

NOT THAT I LIKE IT, but one does feel so much better after it—"oh, thank you, Mère Yvonne, yes just a little drop more." So the old crones fell to drinking their hot brandy and water (although of course they only took it medicinally, as a remedy for their rheumatics), all seated round the big fire and Mère Pinquèle continued her story.

"Oh, yes, then when they get to the top of the hill, there is an altar with six candles quite black and a sort of something in between, that nobody sees quite clearly, and the old black ram with the man's face and long horns begins to say Mass in a sort of gibberish nobody understands, and two black strange things like monkeys glide about with the book and the cruets—and there's music too, such music. There are things the top half like black cats, and the bottom part like men only their legs are all covered with close black hair, and they play on the bagpipes, and when they come to the elevation, then—" Amid the old crones there

was lying on the hearth rug, before the fire, a boy whose large lovely eyes dilated and whose limbs quivered in the very ecstacy of terror.

"Is that all true, Mère Pinquèle?" he said.

"Oh, quite true, and not only that, the best part is yet to come; for they take a child and—" Here Mère Pinquèle showed her fang-like teeth.

"Oh! Mère Pinquèle, are you a witch too?"

"Silence, Gabriel," said Mère Yvonne, "how can you say anything so wicked? Why, bless me, the boy ought to have been in bed ages ago."

Just then all shuddered, and all made the sign of the cross except Mère Pinquèle, for they heard that most dreadful of dreadful sounds—the howl of a wolf, which begins with three sharp barks and then lifts itself up in a long protracted wail of commingled cruelty and despair, and at last subsides into a whispered growl fraught with eternal malice.

There was a forest and a village and a brook,

the village was on one side of the brook, none had dared to cross to the other side. Where the village was, all was green and glad and fertile and fruitful; on the other side the trees never put forth green leaves, and a dark shadow hung over it even at noonday, and in the nighttime one could hear the wolves howling—the werewolves and the wolf-men and the men-wolves, and those very wicked men who for nine days in every year are turned into wolves; but on the green side no wolf was ever seen, and only one little running brook like a silver streak flowed between.

It was spring now and the old crones sat no longer by the fire but before their cottages sunning themselves, and everyone felt so happy that they ceased to tell stories of the "other side." But Gabriel wandered by the brook as he was wont to wander, drawn thither by some strange attraction mingled with intense horror.

His schoolfellows did not like Gabriel; all laughed and jeered at him, because he was less cruel and more gentle of nature than the rest, and even as a rare and beautiful bird escaped from a cage is hacked to death by the common sparrows, so was Gabriel among his fellows. Everyone wondered how Mère Yvonne, that buxom and worthy matron, could have produced a son like this, with strange dreamy eyes, who was as they said "*pas comme les autres gamins.*" His only friends were the Abbé Félicien, whose Mass he served each morning, and one little girl called Carmeille, who loved him, no one could make out why.

The sun had already set, Gabriel still wandered by the brook, filled with vague terror and irresistible fascination. The sun set and the moon rose, the full moon, very large and very clear, and the moonlight flooded the forest both this side and "the other side," and just on the "other side" of the brook, hanging over, Gabriel saw a large deep blue flower, whose strange intoxicating perfume reached him and fascinated him even where he stood.

"If I could only make one step across," he thought, "nothing could harm me if I only plucked that one flower, and nobody would know I had been over at all," for the villagers looked with hatred and suspicion on anyone who was said to have crossed to the "other side," so summing up courage, he leaped lightly to the other side of the brook. Then the moon breaking from a cloud shone with unusual brilliance, and he saw, stretching before him, long reaches of the same strange blue flowers each one lovelier than the last, till, not being able to make up his mind which one flower to take or whether to take several, he went on and on, and the moon shone very brightly and a strange unseen bird, somewhat like a nightingale, but louder and lovelier, sang, and his heart was filled with longing for he knew not what, and the moon shone and the nightingale sang. But on a sudden a black cloud covered the moon entirely, and all was black, utter darkness, and through the darkness he heard wolves howling and shrieking in the hideous ardor of the chase, and there passed before him a horrible procession of wolves (black wolves with red fiery eyes), and with them men that had the heads of wolves and wolves that had the heads of men, and above them flew owls (black owls with red fiery eyes), and bats and long serpentine black things, and last of all seated on an enormous black ram with hideous human face the wolf-keeper on whose face was eternal shadow; but they continued their horrid chase and passed him by, and when they had passed, the moon shone out more beautiful than ever, and the strange nightingale sang again, and the strange intense blue flowers were in long reaches in front to the right and to the left. But one thing was there that had not been before, among the deep blue flowers walked one with long gleaming golden hair, and she turned once round and her eyes were of the same color as the strange blue flowers, and she walked on and Gabriel could not choose but follow. But when a cloud passed over the moon he saw no beautiful woman but a wolf, so in utter terror he turned and fled, plucking one of the strange blue flowers on the way, and leaped again over the brook and ran home.

When he got home Gabriel could not resist showing his treasure to his mother, though he knew she would not appreciate it; but when she saw the strange blue flower, Mère Yvonne turned pale and said, "Why, child, where hast thou been? sure it is the witch flower"; and so saying she snatched it from him and cast it into the corner, and immediately all its beauty and strange fragrance faded from it and it looked charred as though it had been burned. So Gabriel sat down silently and rather sulkily, and having eaten no supper went up to bed, but he did not sleep but waited and waited till all was quiet within the house. Then he crept downstairs in his long white nightshirt and bare feet on the square cold stones and picked hurriedly up the charred and faded flower and put it in his warm bosom next his heart, and immediately the flower bloomed again lovelier than ever, and he fell into a deep sleep, but through his sleep he seemed to hear a soft low voice singing underneath his window in a strange language (in which the subtle sounds melted into one another), but he could distinguish no word except his own name.

When he went forth in the morning to serve Mass, he still kept the flower with him next his heart. Now when the priest began Mass and said "*Intriobo ad altare Dei*," then said Gabriel "*Qui nequiquam laetificavit juventutem meam.*" And the Abbé Félicien turned round on hearing this strange response, and he saw the boy's face deadly pale, his eyes fixed and his limbs rigid, and as the priest looked on him Gabriel fell fainting to the floor, so the sacristan had to carry him home and seek another acolyte for the Abbé Félicien.

Now when the Abbé Félicien came to see after him, Gabriel felt strangely reluctant to say anything about the blue flower and for the first time he deceived the priest.

In the afternoon as sunset drew nigh he felt better and Carmeille came to see him and begged him to go out with her into the fresh air. So they went out hand in hand, the dark-haired, gazelle-eyed boy, and the fair wavy-haired girl, and something, he knew not what, led his steps (half knowingly and yet not so, for he could not but walk thither) to the brook, and they sat down together on the bank.

Gabriel thought at least he might tell his secret to Carmeille, so he took out the flower from his bosom and said, "Look here, Carmeille, hast thou seen ever so lovely a flower as this?" but Carmeille turned pale and faint and said, "Oh, Gabriel what is this flower? I but touched it and I felt something strange come over me. No, no, I don't like its perfume, no there's something not quite right about it, oh, dear Gabriel, do let me throw it away," and before he had time to answer, she cast it from her, and again all its beauty and fragrance went from it and it looked charred as though it had been burned. But suddenly where the flower had been thrown on this side of the brook, there appeared a wolf, which stood and looked at the children.

Carmeille said, "What shall we do," and clung to Gabriel, but the wolf looked at them very steadfastly and Gabriel recognized in the eyes of the wolf the strange deep intense blue eyes of the wolf-woman he had seen on the "other side," so he said, "Stay here, dear Carmeille, see she is looking gently at us and will not hurt us."

"But it is a wolf," said Carmeille, and quivered all over with fear, but again Gabriel said languidly, "She will not hurt us." Then Carmeille seized Gabriel's hand in an agony of terror and dragged him along with her till they reached the village, where she gave the alarm and all the lads of the village gathered together. They had never seen a wolf on this side of the brook, so they excited themselves greatly and arranged a grand wolf hunt for the morrow, but Gabriel sat silently apart and said no word.

That night Gabriel could not sleep at all nor could he bring himself to say his prayers; but he sat in his little room by the window with his shirt open at the throat and the strange blue flower at his heart and again this night he heard a voice singing beneath his window in the same soft, subtle, liquid language as before—

Ma zála liral va jé Cwamûlo zhajéla je Cárma urádi el javé Járma, symai,—carmé—Zhála javály thra je al vú al vlaûle va azré Safralje vairálje va já? Cárma serâja Lâja lâja Luzhà!

And as he looked he could see the silvern shadows slide on the limmering light of golden hair, and the strange eyes gleaming dark blue through the night and it seemed to him that he could not but follow; so he walked half-clad and barefoot as he was with eyes fixed as in a dream silently down the stairs and out into the night.

And ever and again she turned to look on him with her strange blue eyes full of tenderness and passion and sadness beyond the sadness of things human—and as he foreknew his steps led him to the brink of the brook. Then she, taking his hand, familiarly said, "Won't you help me over Gabriel?"

Then it seemed to him as though he had known her all his life—so he went with her to the "other side" but he saw no one by him; and looking again beside him there were two wolves. In a frenzy of terror, he (who had never thought to kill any living thing before) seized a log of wood lying by and smote one of the wolves on the head.

Immediately he saw the wolf-woman again at his side with blood streaming from her forehead, staining her wonderful golden hair, and with eyes looking at him with infinite reproach, she said— "Who did this?"

Then she whispered a few words to the other wolf, which leaped over the brook and made its way toward the village, and turning again toward him she said, "Oh Gabriel, how could you strike me, who would have loved you so long and so well." Then it seemed to him again as though he had known her all his life but he felt dazed and said nothing—but she gathered a dark green strangely shaped leaf and holding it to her forehead, she said—"Gabriel, kiss the place, all will be well again." So he kissed as she had bidden him and he felt the salt taste of blood in his mouth and then he knew no more.

Again he saw the wolf-keeper with his horrible troupe around him, but this time not engaged in the chase but sitting in strange conclave in a circle and the black owls sat in the trees and the black bats hung downward from the branches. Gabriel stood alone in the middle with a hundred wicked eyes fixed on him. They seemed to deliberate about what should be done with him, speaking in that same strange tongue that he had heard in the songs beneath his window. Suddenly he felt a hand pressing in his and saw the mysterious wolf-woman by his side. Then began what seemed a kind of incantation where human or half human creatures seemed to howl, and beasts to speak with human speech but in the unknown tongue. Then the wolf-keeper whose face was ever veiled in shadow spake some words in a voice that seemed to come from afar off, but all he could distinguish was his own name, Gabriel, and her name, Lilith. Then he felt arms enlacing him.

Gabriel awoke—in his own room—so it was a dream after all—but what a dreadful dream. Yes, but was it his own room? Of course there was his coat hanging over the chair—yes but— the Crucifix—where was the Crucifix and the benetier and the consecrated palm branch and the antique image of Our Lady *perpetuae salutis*, with the little ever-burning lamp before it, before which he placed every day the flowers he had gathered, yet had not dared to place the blue flower.

Every morning he lifted his still dream-laden eyes to it and said Ave Maria and made the sign of the cross, which bringeth peace to the soul—but how horrible, how maddening, it was not there, not at all. No surely he could not be awake, at least not quite awake, he would make the benedictive sign and he would be freed from this fearful illusion—yes but the sign, he would make the sign—oh, but what was the sign? Had he forgotten? or was his arm paralyzed? No he could not move. Then he had forgotten—and the prayer—he must remember that. *A—vae— nunc—mortis—fructus.* No surely it did not run thus—but something like it surely—yes, he was awake he could move at any rate—he would reassure himself—he would get up—he would see the gray old church with the exquisitely pointed gables bathed in the light of dawn, and presently the deep solemn bell would toll and he would run down and don his red cassock and lace-worked cotta and light the tall candles on the altar and wait reverently to vest the good and gracious Abbé Félicien, kissing each vestment as he lifted it with reverent hands.

But surely this was not the light of dawn; it was like sunset! He leaped from his small white bed, and a vague terror came over him, he trembled and had to hold on to the chair before he reached the window. No, the solemn spires of the gray church were not to be seen—he was in the depths of the forest; but in a part he had never seen before—but surely he had explored every part, it must be the "other side." To terror succeeded a languor and lassitude not without charm—passivity, acquiescence, indulgence—he felt, as it were, the strong caress of another will flowing over him like water and clothing him with invisible hands in an impalpable garment; so he dressed himself almost mechanically and walked downstairs, the same stairs it seemed to him down which it was his wont to run and spring. The broad square stones seemed singularly beautiful and irridescent with many strange colors—how was it he had never noticed this before—but he was gradually losing the power of wondering—he entered the room below—the wonted coffee and bread rolls were on the table.

"Why, Gabriel, how late you are today." The voice was very sweet but the intonation strange—and there sat Lilith, the mysterious wolf-woman, her glittering gold hair tied in a loose knot and an embroidery whereon she was tracing strange serpentine patterns, lay over the lap of her maize-colored garment—and she looked at Gabriel steadfastly with her wonderful dark blue eyes and said, "Why, Gabriel, you are late today," and Gabriel answered, "I was tired yesterday, give me some coffee."

A dream within a dream—yes, he had known her all his life, and they dwelled together; had they not always done so? And she would take him through the glades of the forest and gather for him flowers, such as he had never seen before, and tell him stories in her strange, low deep voice, which seemed ever to be accompanied by the faint vibration of strings, looking at him fixedly the while with her marvelous blue eyes.

Little by little the flame of vitality which burned within him seemed to grow fainter and fainter, and his lithe lissom limbs waxed languor-

ous and luxurious—yet was he ever filled with a languid content and a will not his own perpetually overshadowed him.

One day in their wanderings he saw a strange dark blue flower like unto the eyes of Lilith, and a sudden half remembrance flashed through his mind.

"What is this blue flower?" he said, and Lilith shuddered and said nothing; but as they went a little farther there was a brook—the brook he thought, and felt his fetters falling off him, and he prepared to spring over the brook; but Lilith seized him by the arm and held him back with all her strength, and trembling all over she said, "Promise me, Gabriel, that you will not cross over." But he said, "Tell me what is this blue flower, and why you will not tell me?" And she said, "Look, Gabriel, at the brook." And he looked and saw that though it was just like the brook of separation it was not the same, the waters did not flow.

As Gabriel looked steadfastly into the still waters it seemed to him as though he saw voices—some impression of the Vespers for the Dead. "*Hei mihi quia incolatus sum,*" and again "*De profundis clamavi ad te*"—oh, that veil, that overshadowing veil! Why could he not hear properly and see, and why did he only remember as one looking through a threefold semitransparent curtain. Yes they were praying for him—but who were they? He heard again the voice of Lilith in whispered anguish, "Come away!"

Then he said, this time in monotone, "What is this blue flower, and what is its use?"

And the low thrilling voice answered, "It is called '*lûli uzhûri,*' two drops pressed upon the face of the sleeper and he will sleep."

He was as a child in her hand and suffered himself to be led from thence, nevertheless he plucked listlessly one of the blue flowers, holding it downward in his hand. What did she mean? Would the sleeper wake? Would the blue flower leave any stain? Could that stain be wiped off?

But as he lay asleep at early dawn he heard voices from afar off praying for him—the Abbé Félicien, Carmeille, his mother too, then some familiar words struck his ear: "*Libera mea porta inferi*." Mass was being said for the repose of his soul, he knew this. No, he could not stay, he would leap over the brook, he knew the way—he had forgotten that the brook did not flow. Ah, but Lilith would know—what should he do? The blue flower—there it lay close by his bedside—he understood now; so he crept very silently to where Lilith lay asleep, her long hair glistening gold, shining like a glory round about her. He pressed two drops on her forehead, she sighed once, and a shade of præternatural anguish passed over her beautiful face. He fled—terror, remorse, and hope tearing his soul and making fleet his feet. He came to the brook—he did not see that the water did not flow—of course it was the brook for separation; one bound, he should be with things human again. He leaped over and—

A change had come over him—what was it? He could not tell—did he walk on all fours? Yes surely. He looked into the brook, whose still waters were fixed as a mirror, and there, horror, he beheld himself; or was it himself? His head and face, yes; but his body transformed to that of a wolf. Even as he looked he heard a sound of hideous mocking laughter behind him. He turned round—there, in a gleam of red lurid light, he saw one whose body was human, but whose head was that of a wolf, with eyes of infinite malice; and, while this hideous being laughed with a loud human laugh, he, essaying to speak, could only utter the prolonged howl of a wolf.

But we will transfer our thoughts from the alien things on the "other side" to the simple human village where Gabriel used to dwell. Mère Yvonne was not much surprised when Gabriel did not turn up to breakfast—he often did not, so absent-minded was he; this time she said, "I suppose he has gone with the others to the wolf hunt." Not that Gabriel was given to hunting, but, as she sagely said, "there was no knowing what he might do next." The boys said, "Of course that muff Gabriel is skulking and hiding himself, he's afraid to join the wolf hunt; why, he wouldn't even kill a cat," for their one notion of excellence was slaughter—so the greater the

game the greater the glory. They were chiefly now confined to cats and sparrows, but they all hoped in after time to become generals of armies.

Yet these children had been taught all their life through with the gentle words of Christ—but alas, nearly all the seed falls by the wayside, where it could not bear flower or fruit; how little these know the suffering and bitter anguish or realize the full meaning of the words to those, of whom it is written "Some fell among thorns."

The wolf hunt was so far a success that they did actually see a wolf, but not a success, as they did not kill it before it leapt over the brook to the "other side," where, of course, they were afraid to pursue it. No emotion is more inrooted and intense in the minds of common people than hatred and fear of anything "strange."

Days passed by but Gabriel was nowhere seen—and Mère Yvonne began to see clearly at last how deeply she loved her only son, who was so unlike her that she had thought herself an object of pity to other mothers—the goose and the swan's egg. People searched and pretended to search, they even went to the length of dragging the ponds, which the boys thought very amusing, as it enabled them to kill a great number of water rats, and Carmeille sat in a corner and cried all day long. Mère Pinquèle also sat in a corner and chuckled and said that she had always said Gabriel would come to no good. The Abbé Félicien looked pale and anxious, but said very little, save to God and those that dwelt with God.

At last, as Gabriel was not there, they supposed he must be nowhere—that is dead. (Their knowledge of other localities being so limited, that it did not even occur to them to suppose he might be living elsewhere than in the village.) So it was agreed that an empty catafalque should be put up in the church with tall candles round it, and Mère Yvonne said all the prayers that were in her prayer book, beginning at the beginning and ending at the end, regardless of their appropriateness—not even omitting the instructions of the rubrics. And Carmeille sat in the corner of the little side chapel and cried, and cried. And the Abbé Félicien caused the boys to sing the Vespers for the Dead (this did not amuse them so much as dragging the pond), and on the following morning, in the silence of early dawn, said the Dirge and the Requiem—and this Gabriel heard.

Then the Abbé Félicien received a message to bring the Holy Viaticum to one sick. So they set forth in solemn procession with great torches, and their way lay along the brook of separation.

Essaying to speak he could only utter the prolonged howl of a wolf—the most fearful of all bestial sounds. He howled and howled again—perhaps Lilith would hear him! Perhaps she could rescue him? Then he remembered the blue flower—the beginning and end of all his woe. His cries aroused all the denizens of the forest—the wolves, the wolf-men, and the men-wolves. He fled before them in an agony of terror—behind him, seated on the black ram with human face, was the wolf-keeper, whose face was veiled in eternal shadow. Only once he turned to look behind—for among the shrieks and howls of bestial chase he heard one thrilling voice moan with pain. And there among them he beheld Lilith, her body too was that of a wolf, almost hidden in the masses of her glittering golden hair, on her forehead was a stain of blue, like in color to her mysterious eyes, now veiled with tears she could not shed.

The way of the Most Holy Viaticum lay along the brook of separation. They heard the fearful howlings afar off, the torch bearers turned pale and trembled—but the Abbé Félicien, holding aloft the Ciborium, said "They cannot harm us."

Suddenly the whole horrid chase came in sight. Gabriel sprang over the brook, the Abbé Félicien held the most Blessed Sacrament before him, and his shape was restored to him and he fell down prostrate in adoration. But the Abbé Félicien still held aloft the Sacred Ciborium, and the people fell on their knees in the agony of fear, but the face of the priest seemed to shine with divine effulgence. Then the wolf-keeper held up in his hands the shape of something horrible and inconceivable—a monstrance to the Sacrament of Hell, and three times he raised it, in mockery of the blessed rite of Benediction. And on the third time streams of fire went forth from his fingers, and all the "other side" of the forest took fire, and great darkness was over all.

All who were there and saw and heard it have kept the impress thereof for the rest of their lives—nor till in their death hour was the remembrance thereof absent from their minds. Shrieks, horrible beyond conception, were heard till nightfall—then the rain rained.

The "other side" is harmless now—charred ashes only; but none dares to cross but Gabriel alone—for once a year for nine days a strange madness comes over him.

Edith Wharton (1862–1937) was an American novelist and writer who wrote mainly about the lives of the upper class that she belonged to. Her first publication was a book of poetry when she was sixteen, but she did not begin a fervent writing career until after her marriage. The book that most are familiar with is *The House of Mirth* (1905), a bestselling novel of manners that can also be called a tragedy. Wharton also won a Pulitzer Prize for her novel *The Age of Innocence* (1920) and published four novelettes, a writing manual, and many more novels and travel books before her death in 1937. She wrote many short stories, and quite a few can be considered ghost stories, but "The Fulness of Life" is dissimilar from many of Wharton's other works in that it is neither a typical ghost story nor a tale of manners.

The Fulness of Life

Edith Wharton

I

FOR HOURS SHE HAD LAIN in a kind of gentle torpor, not unlike that sweet lassitude which masters one in the hush of a midsummer noon, when the heat seems to have silenced the very birds and insects, and, lying sunk in the tasselled meadow-grasses, one looks up through a level roofing of maple-leaves at the vast shadowless, and unsuggestive blue. Now and then, at ever-lengthening intervals, a flash of pain darted through her, like the ripple of sheet-lightning across such a midsummer sky; but it was too transitory to shake her stupor, that calm, delicious, bottomless stupor into which she felt herself sinking more and more deeply, without a disturbing impulse of resistance, an effort of reattachment to the vanishing edges of consciousness.

The resistance, the effort, had known their hour of violence; but now they were at an end.

Through her mind, long harried by grotesque visions, fragmentary images of the life that she was leaving, tormenting lines of verse, obstinate presentments of pictures once beheld, indistinct impressions of rivers, towers, and cupolas, gathered in the length of journeys half forgotten—through her mind there now only moved a few primal sensations of colorless well-being; a vague satisfaction in the thought that she had swallowed her noxious last draught of medicine . . . and that she should never again hear the creaking of her husband's boots—those horrible boots—and that no one would come to bother her about the next day's dinner . . . or the butcher's book. . . .

At last even these dim sensations spent themselves in the thickening obscurity which enveloped her; a dusk now filled with pale geometric roses, circling softly, interminably before her, now darkened to a uniform blue-blackness, the hue of a summer night without stars. And into this darkness she felt herself sinking, sinking, with the gentle sense of security of one upheld from beneath. Like a tepid tide it rose around her, gliding ever higher and higher, folding in its velvety embrace her relaxed and tired body, now submerging her breast and shoulders, now creeping gradually, with soft inexorableness, over her throat to her chin, to her ears, to her mouth. . . . Ah, now it was rising too high; the impulse to struggle was renewed; . . . her mouth was full; . . . she was choking. . . . Help!

"It is all over," said the nurse, drawing down the eyelids with official composure.

The clock struck three. They remembered it afterward. Someone opened the window and let in a blast of that strange, neutral air which walks the earth between darkness and dawn; someone else led the husband into another room. He walked vaguely, like a blind man, on his creaking boots.

II

She stood, as it seemed, on a threshold, yet no tangible gateway was in front of her. Only a wide vista of light, mild yet penetrating as the gathered glimmer of innumerable stars, expanded gradually before her eyes, in blissful contrast to the cavernous darkness from which she had of late emerged.

She stepped forward, not frightened, but hesitating, and as her eyes began to grow more familiar with the melting depths of light about her, she distinguished the outlines of a landscape, at first swimming in the opaline uncertainty of Shelley's vaporous creations, then gradually resolved into distincter shape—the vast unrolling of a sunlit plain, aerial forms of mountains, and presently the silver crescent of a river in the valley, and a blue stencilling of trees along its curve—something suggestive in its ineffable hue of an azure background of Leonardo's, strange, enchanting, mysterious, leading on the eye and the imagination into regions of fabulous delight.

As she gazed, her heart beat with a soft and rapturous surprise; so exquisite a promise she read in the summons of that hyaline distance.

"And so death is not the end after all," in sheer gladness she heard herself exclaiming aloud. "I always knew that it couldn't be. I believed in Darwin, of course. I do still; but then Darwin himself said that he wasn't sure about the soul—at least, I think he did—and Wallace was a spiritualist; and then there was St. George Mivart—"

Her gaze lost itself in the ethereal remoteness of the mountains.

"How beautiful! How satisfying!" she murmured. "Perhaps now I shall really know what it is to live."

As she spoke she felt a sudden thickening of her heart-beats, and looking up she was aware that before her stood the Spirit of Life.

"Have you never really known what it is to live?" the Spirit of Life asked her.

"I have never known," she replied, "that fulness of life which we all feel ourselves capable of knowing; though my life has not been without scattered hints of it, like the scent of earth which comes to one sometimes far out at sea."

"And what do you call the fulness of life?" the Spirit asked again.

"Oh, I can't tell you, if you don't know," she said, almost reproachfully. "Many words are supposed to define it—love and sympathy are those in commonest use, but I am not even sure that they are the right ones, and so few people really know what they mean."

"You were married," said the Spirit, "yet you did not find the fulness of life in your marriage?"

"Oh, dear, no," she replied, with an indulgent scorn, "my marriage was a very incomplete affair."

"And yet you were fond of your husband?"

"You have hit upon the exact word; I was fond of him, yes, just as I was fond of my grandmother, and the house that I was born in, and my old nurse. Oh, I was fond of him, and we were counted a very happy couple. But I have sometimes thought that a woman's nature is like a great house full of rooms: there is the hall, through which everyone passes in going in and out; the drawingroom, where one receives formal visits; the sitting-room, where the members of the family come and go as they list; but beyond that, far beyond, are other rooms, the handles of whose doors perhaps are never turned; no one knows the way to them, no one knows whither they lead; and in the innermost room, the holy of holies, the soul sits alone and waits for a footstep that never comes."

"And your husband," asked the Spirit, after a pause, "never got beyond the family sitting-room?"

"Never," she returned, impatiently; "and the worst of it was that he was quite content to remain there. He thought it perfectly beautiful, and sometimes, when he was admiring its commonplace furniture, insignificant as the chairs and tables of a hotel parlor, I felt like crying out to him: 'Fool, will you never guess that close at hand are rooms full of treasures and wonders, such as the eye of man hath not seen, rooms that no step has crossed, but that might be yours to live in, could you but find the handle of the door?'"

"Then," the Spirit continued, "those moments of which you lately spoke, which seemed to come to you like scattered hints of the fulness of life, were not shared with your husband?"

"Oh, no—never. He was different. His boots creaked, and he always slammed the door when he went out, and he never read anything but railway novels and the sporting advertisements in the papers—and—and, in short, we never understood each other in the least."

"To what influence, then, did you owe those exquisite sensations?"

"I can hardly tell. Sometimes to the perfume of a flower; sometimes to a verse of Dante or of Shakespeare; sometimes to a picture or a sunset, or to one of those calm days at sea, when one seems to be lying in the hollow of a blue pearl; sometimes, but rarely, to a word spoken by someone who chanced to give utterance, at the right moment, to what I felt but could not express."

"Someone whom you loved?" asked the Spirit.

"I never loved anyone, in that way," she said, rather sadly, "nor was I thinking of any one person when I spoke, but of two or three who, by touching for an instant upon a certain chord of my being, had called forth a single note of that strange melody which seemed sleeping in my soul. It has seldom happened, however, that I have owed such feelings to people; and no one ever gave me a moment of such happiness as it was my lot to feel one evening in the Church of Orsanmichele, in Florence."

"Tell me about it," said the Spirit.

"It was near sunset on a rainy spring afternoon in Easter week. The clouds had vanished, dispersed by a sudden wind, and as we entered the church the fiery panes of the high windows shone out like lamps through the dusk. A priest was at the high altar, his white cope a livid spot in the incense-laden obscurity, the light of the candles flickering up and down like fireflies about his head; a few people knelt near by. We stole behind them and sat down on a bench close to the tabernacle of Orcagna.

"Strange to say, though Florence was not new to me, I had never been in the church before; and in that magical light I saw for the first time the inlaid steps, the fluted columns, the sculptured bas-reliefs and canopy of the marvellous shrine. The marble, worn and mellowed by the subtle hand of time, took on an unspeakable rosy hue, suggestive in some remote way of the honey-colored columns of the Parthenon, but more mystic, more complex, a color not born of the sun's inveterate kiss, but made up of cryptal twilight, and the flame of candles upon martyrs' tombs, and gleams of sunset through symbolic panes of chrysoprase and ruby; such a light as illumines the missals in the library of Siena, or burns like a hidden fire through the Madonna of Gian Bellini in the Church of the Redeemer, at Venice; the light of the Middle Ages, richer, more solemn, more significant than the limpid sunshine of Greece.

"The church was silent, but for the wail of

the priest and the occasional scraping of a chair against the floor, and as I sat there, bathed in that light, absorbed in rapt contemplation of the marble miracle which rose before me, cunningly wrought as a casket of ivory and enriched with jewel-like incrustations and tarnished gleams of gold, I felt myself borne onward along a mighty current, whose source seemed to be in the very beginning of things, and whose tremendous waters gathered as they went all the mingled streams of human passion and endeavor. Life in all its varied manifestations of beauty and strangeness seemed weaving a rhythmical dance around me as I moved, and wherever the spirit of man had passed I knew that my foot had once been familiar.

"As I gazed the mediaeval bosses of the tabernacle of Orcagna seemed to melt and flow into their primal forms so that the folded lotus of the Nile and the Greek acanthus were braided with the runic knots and fish-tailed monsters of the North, and all the plastic terror and beauty born of man's hand from the Ganges to the Baltic quivered and mingled in Orcagna's apotheosis of Mary. And so the river bore me on, past the alien face of antique civilizations and the familiar wonders of Greece, till I swam upon the fiercely rushing tide of the Middle Ages, with its swirling eddies of passion, its heaven-reflecting pools of poetry and art; I heard the rhythmic blow of the craftsmen's hammers in the goldsmiths' workshops and on the walls of churches, the party-cries of armed factions in the narrow streets, the organroll of Dante's verse, the crackle of the fagots around Arnold of Brescia, the twitter of the swallows to which St. Francis preached, the laughter of the ladies listening on the hillside to the quips of the Decameron, while plague-struck Florence howled beneath them—all this and much more I heard, joined in strange unison with voices earlier and more remote, fierce, passionate, or tender, yet subdued to such awful harmony that I thought of the song that the morning stars sang together and felt as though it were sounding in my ears. My heart beat to suffocation, the tears burned my lids, the

joy, the mystery of it seemed too intolerable to be borne. I could not understand even then the words of the song; but I knew that if there had been someone at my side who could have heard it with me, we might have found the key to it together.

"I turned to my husband, who was sitting beside me in an attitude of patient dejection, gazing into the bottom of his hat; but at that moment he rose, and stretching his stiffened legs, said, mildly: 'Hadn't we better be going? There doesn't seem to be much to see here, and you know the table d'hote dinner is at half-past six o'clock.'"

Her recital ended, there was an interval of silence; then the Spirit of Life said: "There is a compensation in store for such needs as you have expressed."

"Oh, then you *do* understand?" she exclaimed. "Tell me what compensation, I entreat you!"

"It is ordained," the Spirit answered, "that every soul which seeks in vain on earth for a kindred soul to whom it can lay bare its inmost being shall find that soul here and be united to it for eternity."

A glad cry broke from her lips. "Ah, shall I find him at last?" she cried, exultant.

"He is here," said the Spirit of Life.

She looked up and saw that a man stood near whose soul (for in that unwonted light she seemed to see his soul more clearly than his face) drew her toward him with an invincible force.

"Are you really he?" she murmured.

"I am he," he answered.

She laid her hand in his and drew him toward the parapet which overhung the valley.

"Shall we go down together," she asked him, "into that marvellous country; shall we see it together, as if with the self-same eyes, and tell each other in the same words all that we think and feel?"

"So," he replied, "have I hoped and dreamed."

"What?" she asked, with rising joy. "Then you, too, have looked for me?"

"All my life."

"How wonderful! And did you never, never find anyone in the other world who understood you?"

"Not wholly—not as you and I understand each other."

"Then you feel it, too? Oh, I am happy," she sighed.

They stood, hand in hand, looking down over the parapet upon the shimmering landscape which stretched forth beneath them into sapphirine space, and the Spirit of Life, who kept watch near the threshold, heard now and then a floating fragment of their talk blown backward like the stray swallows which the wind sometimes separates from their migratory tribe.

"Did you never feel at sunset—"

"Ah, yes; but I never heard anyone else say so. Did you?"

"Do you remember that line in the third canto of the 'Inferno'?"

"Ah, that line—my favorite always. Is it possible—"

"You know the stooping Victory in the frieze of the Nike Apteros?"

"You mean the one who is tying her sandal? Then you have noticed, too, that all Botticelli and Mantegna are dormant in those flying folds of her drapery?"

"After a storm in autumn have you never seen—"

"Yes, it is curious how certain flowers suggest certain painters—the perfume of the incarnation, Leonardo; that of the rose, Titian; the tuberose, Crivelli—"

"I never supposed that anyone else had noticed it."

"Have you never thought—"

"Oh, yes, often and often; but I never dreamed that anyone else had."

"But surely you must have felt—"

"Oh, yes, yes; and you, too—"

"How beautiful! How strange—"

Their voices rose and fell, like the murmur of two fountains answering each other across a garden full of flowers. At length, with a certain tender impatience, he turned to her and said: "Love, why should we linger here? All eternity lies before us. Let us go down into that beautiful country together and make a home for ourselves on some blue hill above the shining river."

As he spoke, the hand she had forgotten in his was suddenly withdrawn, and he felt that a cloud was passing over the radiance of her soul.

"A home," she repeated, slowly, "a home for you and me to live in for all eternity?"

"Why not, love? Am I not the soul that yours has sought?"

"Y-yes—yes, I know—but, don't you see, home would not be like home to me, unless—"

"Unless?" he wonderingly repeated.

She did not answer, but she thought to herself, with an impulse of whimsical inconsistency, "Unless you slammed the door and wore creaking boots."

But he had recovered his hold upon her hand, and by imperceptible degrees was leading her toward the shining steps which descended to the valley.

"Come, O my soul's soul," he passionately implored; "why delay a moment? Surely you feel, as I do, that eternity itself is too short to hold such bliss as ours. It seems to me that I can see our home already. Have I not always seen it in my dreams? It is white, love, is it not, with polished columns, and a sculptured cornice against the blue? Groves of laurel and oleander and thickets of roses surround it; but from the terrace where we walk at sunset, the eye looks out over woodlands and cool meadows where, deep-bowered under ancient boughs, a stream goes delicately toward the river. Indoors our favorite pictures hang upon the walls and the rooms are lined with books. Think, dear, at last we shall have time to read them all. With which shall we begin? Come, help me to choose. Shall it be 'Faust' or the 'Vita Nuova,' the 'Tempest' or 'Les Caprices de Marianne,' or the thirty-first canto of the 'Paradise,' or 'Epipsychidion' or "Lycidas'? Tell me, dear, which one?"

As he spoke he saw the answer trembling joyously upon her lips; but it died in the ensuing silence, and she stood motionless, resisting the persuasion of his hand.

"What is it?" he entreated.

"Wait a moment," she said, with a strange hesitation in her voice. "Tell me first, are you quite sure of yourself? Is there no one on earth whom you sometimes remember?"

"Not since I have seen you," he replied; for, being a man, he had indeed forgotten.

Still she stood motionless, and he saw that the shadow deepened on her soul.

"Surely, love," he rebuked her, "it was not that which troubled you? For my part I have walked through Lethe. The past has melted like a cloud before the moon. I never lived until I saw you."

She made no answer to his pleadings, but at length, rousing herself with a visible effort, she turned away from him and moved toward the Spirit of Life, who still stood near the threshold.

"I want to ask you a question," she said, in a troubled voice.

"Ask," said the Spirit.

"A little while ago," she began, slowly, "you told me that every soul which has not found a kindred soul on earth is destined to find one here."

"And have you not found one?" asked the Spirit.

"Yes; but will it be so with my husband's soul also?"

"No," answered the Spirit of Life, "for your husband imagined that he had found his soul's mate on earth in you; and for such delusions eternity itself contains no cure."

She gave a little cry. Was it of disappointment or triumph?

"Then—then what will happen to him when he comes here?"

"That I cannot tell you. Some field of activity and happiness he will doubtless find, in due measure to his capacity for being active and happy."

She interrupted, almost angrily: "He will never be happy without me."

"Do not be too sure of that," said the Spirit.

She took no notice of this, and the Spirit continued: "He will not understand you here any better than he did on earth."

"No matter," she said; "I shall be the only sufferer, for he always thought that he understood me."

"His boots will creak just as much as ever—"

"No matter."

"And he will slam the door—"

"Very likely."

"And continue to read railway novels—"

She interposed, impatiently: "Many men do worse than that."

"But you said just now," said the Spirit, "that you did not love him."

"True," she answered, simply; "but don't you understand that I shouldn't feel at home without him? It is all very well for a week or two—but for eternity! After all, I never minded the creaking of his boots, except when my head ached, and I don't suppose it will ache *here*; and he was always so sorry when he had slammed the door, only he never *could* remember not to. Besides, no one else would know how to look after him, he is so helpless. His inkstand would never be filled, and he would always be out of stamps and visiting-cards. He would never remember to have his umbrella re-covered, or to ask the price of anything before he bought it. Why, he wouldn't even know what novels to read. I always had to choose the kind he liked, with a murder or a forgery and a successful detective."

She turned abruptly to her kindred soul, who stood listening with a mien of wonder and dismay.

"Don't you see," she said, "that I can't possibly go with you?"

"But what do you intend to do?" asked the Spirit of Life.

"What do I intend to do?" she returned, indignantly. "Why, I mean to wait for my husband, of course. If he had come here first *he* would have waited for me for years and years; and it would break his heart not to find me here when he comes." She pointed with a contemptuous gesture to the magic vision of hill and vale sloping away to the translucent mountains. "He wouldn't give a fig for all that," she said, "if he didn't find me here."

"But consider," warned the Spirit, "that you are now choosing for eternity. It is a solemn moment."

"Choosing!" she said, with a half-sad smile. "Do you still keep up here that old fiction about choosing? I should have thought that *you* knew better than that. How can I help myself? He will expect to find me here when he comes, and he would never believe you if you told him that I had gone away with someone else—never, never."

"So be it," said the Spirit. "Here, as on earth, each one must decide for himself."

She turned to her kindred soul and looked at him gently, almost wistfully. "I am sorry," she said. "I should have liked to talk with you again; but you will understand, I know, and I dare say you will find someone else a great deal cleverer—"

And without pausing to hear his answer she waved him a swift farewell and turned back toward the threshold.

"Will my husband come soon?" she asked the Spirit of Life.

"That you are not destined to know," the Spirit replied.

"No matter," she said, cheerfully; "I have all eternity to wait in."

And still seated alone on the threshold, she listens for the creaking of his boots.

Violet Paget (1856–1935) was a prolific British essayist and novelist who used the pseudonym of Vernon Lee in order to be taken more seriously. She began using the name personally as well as professionally and was known as Vernon Lee by writers such as Henry James. Lee often wrote strange fictions that included haunting scenery and supernatural activities such as possession. Although known for her speculative fiction, she also wrote essays, plays, and poetry. Her essays, collected in *Belcaro* (1881) and *Euphorion* (1884), display imaginative wit and scholarship and often call for social change and activism. Many of her stories, including "Prince Alberic and the Snake Lady" (1895) appeared in the literary magazine the *Yellow Book*. "Prince Alberic and the Snake Lady" can be described as a macabre fairy tale that explores desire, youth, and beauty. It also allows for delightful ambiguity as to the darkly fantastical.

Prince Alberic and the Snake Lady

Vernon Lee

TO H. H. THE RANEE BROOKE OF SARAWAK

IN THE YEAR 1701, the Duchy of Luna became united to the Italian dominions of the Holy Roman Empire, owing to the extinction of its famous ducal house in the persons of Duke Balthasar Maria and of his grandson Alberic, who should have been third of the name. Under this dry historical fact lies hidden the strange story of Prince Alberic and the Snake Lady.

I

The first act of hostility of old Duke Balthasar towards the Snake Lady, in whose existence he did not, of course, believe, was connected with the arrival at Luna of certain tapestries after the designs of the famous Monsieur Le Brun, a present from his most Christian Majesty King Lewis the XIV. These Gobelins, which represented the marriage of Alexander and Roxana, were placed in the throne room, and in the most gallant suit of chambers overlooking the great rockery garden, all of which had been completed by Duke Balthasar Maria in 1680; and, as a consequence, the already existing tapestries, silk hangings and mirrors painted by Marius of the Flowers, were transferred into other apartments, thus occasioning a general re-hanging of the Red Palace at Luna. These magnificent operations, in which, as the court poets sang, Apollo and the Graces lent their services to their beloved patron, aroused in Duke Balthasar's mind a sudden curiosity to see what might be made of the rooms occupied by his grandson and heir, and which he had not entered since Prince Alberic's christening. He found the apartments in a shocking state of neglect, and the youthful prince unspeakably shy and rustic; and he determined to give him at once an establishment befitting his age, to look out presently for a princess worthy to be his wife, and, somewhat earlier, for a less illustrious but more agreeable lady to fashion his manners. Meanwhile, Duke Balthasar Maria gave orders to change the tapestry in Prince Alberic's chamber. This tapestry was of old and Gothic taste, extremely worn, and represented Alberic the Blond and the Snake Lady Oriana, alluded to in the poems of Boiardo and the chronicles of the Crusaders. Duke Balthasar Maria was a prince of enlightened mind and delicate taste; the literature as well as the art of the dark ages found no grace in his sight; he reproved the folly of feeding the thoughts of youth on improbable events; besides, he disliked snakes and was afraid of the devil. So he ordered the tapestry to be removed and another, representing Susanna and the Elders, to be put in its stead. But when Prince Alberic discovered the change, he cut Susanna and the Elders into strips with a knife he had stolen out of the ducal kitchens (no dangerous instruments being allowed to young princes before they were of an age to learn to fence) and refused to touch his food for three days. The tapestry over which little Prince Alberic mourned so greatly had indeed been both tattered and Gothic. But for the boy it possessed an inexhaustible charm. It was quite full of things, and they were all delightful. The sorely frayed borders consisted of wonderful garlands of leaves, and fruits, and flowers, tied at intervals with ribbons, although they seemed all to grow, like tall, narrow bushes, each from a big vase in the bottom corner; and made of all manner of different plants. There were bunches of spiky bays, and of acorned oakleaves, sheaves of lilies and heads of poppies, gourds, and apples and pears, and hazelnuts and mulberries, wheat ears, and beans, and pine tufts. And in each of these plants, of which those above named are only a very few, there were curious live creatures of some sort, various birds, big and little, butter-flies on the lilies, snails, squirrels, and mice, and rabbits, and even a hare, with such pointed ears, darting among the spruce fir. Alberic learned the names of most of these plants and creatures from his nurse, who had been a peasant, and spent much ingenuity seeking for them in the palace gardens and terraces; but there were no live creatures there, except snails and toads, which the gardeners killed, and carp swimming about in the big tank, whom Alberic did not like, and who were not in the tapestry; and he had to supplement his nurse's information by that of the grooms and scullions, when he could visit them secretly. He was even promised a sight, one day, of a dead rabbit. The rabbit was the most fascinating of the inhabitants of the tapestry border but he came to the kitchen too late, and saw it with its pretty fur pulled off, and looking so sad and naked that it made him cry. But Alberic had grown so accustomed to never quitting the Red Palace and its gardens, that he was usually satisfied with seeing the plants and animals in the tapestry, and looked forward to seeing the real things when he should be grown up. "When I am a man," he would say to himself for his nurse scolded him for saying it to her, "I will have a live rabbit of my own."

The border of the tapestry interested Prince Alberic most when he was very little indeed, his remembrance of it was older than that of the Red Palace, its terraces and gardens but gradually he began to care more and more for the pictures in the middle.

There were mountains, and the sea with ships; and these first made him care to go on to the topmost palace terrace and look at the real mountains and the sea beyond the roofs and gardens; and there were woods of all manner of tall trees, with clover and wild strawberries growing beneath them, and roads, and paths, and rivers, in and out these were rather confused with the places where the tapestry was worn out, and with the patches and mendings thereof, but Alberic, in the course of time, contrived to make them all out, and knew exactly whence the river came which turned the big mill wheel, and how many bends it made before coming to the fishing nets; and how the horsemen must cross over the bridge, then wind behind the cliff with the chapel, and pass through the wood of firs in order to get from the castle in the left hand corner nearest the bottom to the town, over which the sun was shining with all its beams, and a wind blowing with inflated cheeks on the right hand close to the top.

The centre of the tapestry was the most worn and discoloured; and it was for this reason perhaps that little Alberic scarcely noticed it for some years, his eye and mind led away by the bright red and yellow of the border of fruit and flowers, and the still vivid green and orange of the background landscape. Red, yellow and orange, even green, had faded in the centre into pale blue and lilac; even the green had grown an odd dusky tint; and the figures seemed like ghosts, sometimes emerging and then receding again into vagueness. Indeed, it was only as he grew bigger that Alberic began to see any figures at all; and then, for a long time he would lose sight of them. But little by little, when the light was strong, he could see them always; and even in the dark make them out with a little attention. Among the spruce firs and pines, and against a hedge of roses, on which there still lingered a remnant of redness, a knight had reined in his big white horse, and was putting one arm round the shoulder of a lady, who was leaning against the horse's flank. The knight was all dressed in armour—not at all like that of the equestrian statue of Duke Balthasar Maria in the square, but all made of plates, with plates also on the legs, instead of having them bare like Duke Balthasar's statue; and on his head he had no wig, but a helmet with big plumes. It seemed a more reasonable dress than the other, but probably Duke Balthasar was right to go to battle with bare legs and a kilt and a wig, since he did so. The lady who was looking up into his face was dressed with a high collar and long sleeves, and on her head she wore a thick circular garland, from under which the hair fell about her shoulders. She was very lovely, Alberic got to think, particularly when, having climbed upon a chest of drawers, he saw that her hair was still full of threads of gold, some of them quite loose because the tapestry was so rubbed. The knight and his horse were of course very beautiful, and he liked the way in which the knight reined in the horse with one hand, and embraced the lady with the other arm. But Alberic got to love the lady most, although she was so very pale and faded, and almost the colour of the moonbeams through the palace windows in summer. Her dress also was so beautiful and unlike those of the ladies who got out of the coaches in the Court of Honour, and who had on hoops and no clothes at all on their upper part. This lady, on the contrary, had that collar like a lily, and a beautiful gold chain, and patterns in gold (Alberic made them out little by little) all over her bodice. He got to want so much to see her skirt; it was probably very beautiful too, but it so happened that the inlaid chest of drawers before mentioned stood against the wall in that place, and on it a large ebony and ivory crucifix, which covered the lower part of the lady's body. Alberic often tried to lift off the crucifix, but it was a great deal too heavy, and there was not room on the chest of drawers to push it aside; so the lady's skirt and feet remained invisible. But one day, when Alberic was eleven, his nurse suddenly took a fancy to having all the furniture shifted. It was time that the child should cease to sleep in her room, and plague her with his loud talking in his dreams. And she might as well have the handsome inlaid chest of drawers, and that nice pious crucifix for herself next door, in place of Alberic's little bed. So one morning there was a great shifting and dusting, and when Alberic came in from his walk on the terrace, there hung the tapestry entirely uncovered. He stood for a few minutes before it, riveted to the ground. Then he ran to his nurse, exclaiming, "Oh, nurse, dear nurse, look—the lady—!"

For where the big crucifix had stood, the lower part of the beautiful pale lady with the gold thread hair was now exposed. But instead of a skirt, she ended off in a big snake's tail, with scales of still most vivid (the tapestry not having faded there) green and gold.

The nurse turned round.

"Holy Virgin," she cried, "why she's a serpent!" Then noticing the boy's violent excitement, she added, "You little ninny, it's only Duke Alberic the Blond, who was your ancestor, and the Snake Lady."

Little Prince Alberic asked no questions, feeling that he must not. Very strange it was, but he loved the beautiful lady with the thread of gold hair only the more because she ended off in the long twisting body of a snake. And that, no doubt, was why the knight was so very good to her.

II

For want of that tapestry, poor Alberic, having cut its successor to pieces, began to pine away. It had been his whole world; and now it was gone he discovered that he had no other. No one had ever cared for him except his nurse, who was very cross. Nothing had ever been taught him except the Latin catechism; he had had nothing to make a pet of except the fat carp, supposed to be four hundred years old, in the tank; he had nothing to play with except a gala coral with bells by Benvenuto Cellini, which Duke Balthasar Maria had sent him on his eighth birthday. He had never had anything except a grandfather, and had never been outside the Red Palace.

Now, after the loss of the tapestry, the disappearance of the plants and flowers and birds and beasts on its borders, and the departure of the kind knight on the horse and the dear golden-haired Snake Lady, Alberic became aware that he had always hated both his grandfather and the Red Palace.

The whole world, indeed, were agreed that Duke Balthasar was the most magnanimous and fascinating of monarchs; and that the Red Palace of Luna was the most magnificent and delectable of residences. But the knowledge of this universal opinion, and the consequent sense of his own extreme unworthiness, merely exasperated Alberic's detestation, which, as it grew, came to identify the Duke and the Palace as the personification and visible manifestation of each other. He knew now oh how well every time that he walked on the terrace or in the garden (at the hours when no one else ever entered them) that he had always abominated the brilliant tomato-coloured plaster which gave the palace its name: such a pleasant, gay colour, people would remark, particularly against the blue of the sky. Then there were the Twelve Caesars—they were the Twelve Caesars, but multiplied over and over again—busts with flying draperies and spiky garlands, one over every first floor window, hundreds of them, all fluttering and grimacing round the place. Alberic had always thought them uncanny; but now he positively avoided looking out of the window, lest his eye should catch the stucco eyeball of one of those Caesars in the opposite wing of the building. But there was one thing more especially in the Red Palace, of which a bare glimpse had always filled the youthful Prince with terror, and which now kept recurring to his mind like a nightmare. This was no other than the famous grotto of the Court of Honour. Its roof was ingeniously inlaid with oyster shells, forming elegant patterns, among which you could plainly distinguish some colossal satyrs; the sides were built of rockery, and in its depths, disposed in a most natural and tasteful manner, was a herd of lifesize animals all carved out of various precious marbles. On holidays the water was turned on, and spurted about in a gallant fashion. On such occasions persons of taste would flock to Luna from all parts of the world to enjoy the spectacle. But ever since his earliest infancy Prince Alberic had held this grotto in abhorrence. The oyster shell satyrs on the roof frightened him into fits, particularly when the fountains were playing; and his terror of the marble animals was such that a bare allusion to the Porphyry Rhinoceros, the Giraffe of Cipollino, and the Verde Antique Monkeys, set him screaming for an hour. The grotto, moreover, had become associated in his mind with the other great glory of the Red Palace, to wit, the domed chapel in which Duke Balthasar Maria intended erecting monuments to his immediate ancestors, and in which he had already prepared a monument for himself. And the whole magnificent palace, grotto, chapel and all, had become mysteriously connected with Alberic's grandfather, owing to a particularly terrible dream. When the boy was eight years old, he was taken one day to see his grandfather. It was the feast of St. Balthasar, one of the Three Wise Kings from the East, as is well known. There had been firing of mortars and ringing of bells ever since daybreak. Alberic had his hair curled, was put into new clothes (his usual raiment was somewhat tattered), a large nosegay was put in his hand, and he and his nurse were conveyed by complicated relays of lackeys and of pages up to the Ducal apartments. Here, in a crowded outer room, he was separated from his nurse and received by a gaunt person in a long black robe like a sheath, and a long shovel hat, whom Alberic identified many years later as his grandfather's Jesuit confessor. He smiled a long smile, discovering a prodigious number of teeth, in a manner which froze the child's blood; and lifting an embroidered curtain, pushed Alberic into his grandfather's presence. Duke Balthasar Maria, known as the Ever Young Prince in all Italy, was at his toilet. He was wrapped in a green Chinese wrapper, embroidered with gold pagodas, and round his head was tied an orange scarf of delicate fabric. He was listening to the performance of some fiddlers, and of a lady dressed as a nymph, who was singing the birthday ode with many shrill trills and quavers; and meanwhile his face, in the hands of a valet, was being plastered with a variety of brilliant colours. In his green and gold wrapper and orange headdress, with the strange patches of vermilion and white on his cheeks, Duke Balthasar looked to the diseased fancy of his grandson as if he had been made of various precious metals, like the celebrated effigy he had erected of himself in the great burial chapel. But, just as Alberic was mustering up courage and approaching his magnificent grandparent, his eye fell upon a sight so mysterious and terrible that he fled wildly out of the Ducal presence. For through an open door he could see in an adjacent closet a man dressed in white, combing the long flowing locks of what he recognised as his grandfather's head, stuck on a short pole in the light of a window.

That night Alberic had seen in his dreams the ever young Duke Balthasar Maria descend from his niche in the burial-chapel; and, with his Roman lappets and corslet visible beneath the green bronze cloak embroidered with gold pagodas, march down the great staircase into the Court of Honour, and ascend to the empty place at the end of the rockery grotto (where, as a matter of fact, a statue of Neptune, by a pupil of Bernini, was placed some months later), and there, raising his sceptre, receive the obeisance of all the marble animals, the giraffe, the rhinoceros, the stag, the peacock, and the monkeys. And behold! suddenly his well-known features waxed dim, and beneath the great curly peruke there was a round blank thing—a barber's block! Alberic, who was an intelligent child, had gradually learned to disentangle this dream from reality; but its grotesque terror never vanished from his mind, and became the core of all his feelings towards Duke Balthasar Maria and the Red Palace.

III

The news—which was kept back as long as possible—of the destruction of Susanna and the Elders threw Duke Balthasar Maria into a most violent rage with his grandson. The boy should be punished by exile, and exile to a terrible place; above all, to a place where there was no furniture to destroy. Taking due counsel with his Jesuit, his Jester, and his Dwarf, Duke Balthasar decided that in the whole Duchy of Luna there was no place more fitted for the purpose than the Castle of Sparkling Waters.

For the Castle of Sparkling Waters was little better than a ruin, and its sole inhabitants were a family of peasants. The original cradle of the House of Luna, and its principal bulwark against invasion, the castle had been ignominiously discarded and forsaken a couple of centuries before, when the dukes had built the rectangular town in the plain; after which it had been used as a quarry for ready cut stone, and the greater part carted off to rebuild the city of Luna, and even the central portion of the Red Palace. The castle was therefore reduced to its outer circuit of walls, enclosing vineyards and orange-gardens, instead of moats and yards and towers, and to the large gate tower, which had been kept, with one or two smaller buildings, for the housing of the farmer, his cattle, and his stores.

Thither the misguided young prince was conveyed in a carefully shuttered coach and at a late hour of the evening, as was proper in the case of an offender at once so illustrious and so criminal. Nature, moreover, had clearly shared Duke Balthasar Maria's legitimate anger, and had done her best to increase the horror of this just though terrible sentence. For that particular night the long summer broke up in a storm of fearful violence; and Alberic entered the ruined castle amid the howling of wind, the rumble of thunder, and the rush of torrents of rain.

But the young prince showed no fear or reluctance; he saluted with dignity and sweetness the farmer and his wife and family, and took possession of his attic, where the curtains of an antique and crazy four-poster shook in the draught of the unglazed windows, as if he were taking possession of the gala chambers of a great palace. "And so," he merely remarked, looking round him with reserved satisfaction, "I am now in the castle which was built by my ancestor and namesake, Alberic the Blond."

He looked not unworthy of such illustrious lineage, as he stood there in the flickering light of the pine torch: tall for his age, slender and strong, with abundant golden hair falling about his very white face.

That first night at the Castle of Sparkling Waters, Alberic dreamed without end about his dear, lost tapestry. And when, in the radiant autumn morning, he descended to explore the place of his banishment and captivity, it seemed as if those dreams were still going on. Or had the tapestry been removed to this spot, and become a reality in which he himself was running about?

The gate tower in which he had slept was still intact and chivalrous. It had battlements, a drawbridge, a great escutcheon with the arms of Luna, just like the castle in the tapestry. Some vines, quite loaded with grapes, rose on the strong cords of their fibrous wood from the ground to the very roof of the tower, exactly like those borders of leaves and fruit which Alberic had loved so much. And, between the vines, all along the masonry, were strung long narrow ropes of maize, like garlands of gold. A plantation of orange trees filled what had once been the moat; lemons were espaliered against the delicate pink brickwork. There were no lilies, but big carnations hung down from the tower windows, and a tall oleander, which Alberic mistook for a special sort of rose-tree, shed its blossoms on to the drawbridge. After the storm of the night, birds were singing all round; not indeed as they sang in spring, which Alberic, of course, did not know, but in a manner quite different from the canaries in the ducal aviaries at Luna. Moreover other birds, wonderful white and gold creatures, some of them with brilliant tails and scarlet crests, were pecking and strutting and making curious noises in the yard. And—could it be true?—a little way further up the hill, for the castle walls climbed steeply from the seaboard, in the grass beneath the olive trees, white creatures were running in and out—white creatures with pinkish lining to their ears, undoubtedly—as Alberic's nurse had taught him on the tapestry—undoubtedly *rabbits*.

Thus Alberic rambled on, from discovery to discovery, with the growing sense that he was in the tapestry, but that the tapestry had become the whole world. He climbed from terrace to terrace of the steep olive yard, among the sage and the fennel tufts, the long red walls of the castle winding ever higher on the hill. And, on the very top of the hill was a high terrace surrounded by towers, and a white shining house with columns and windows, which seemed to drag him upwards.

It was, indeed, the citadel of the place, the very centre of the castle.

Alberic's heart beat strangely as he passed beneath the wide arch of delicate ivy-grown brick, and clambered up the rough paved path to the topmost terrace. And there he actually forgot the tapestry. The terrace was laid out as a vineyard, the vines trellised on the top of stone columns; at one end stood a clump of trees, pines, and a big ilex and a walnut, whose shrivelled leaves already strewed the grass. To the back stood a tiny little house all built of shining marble, with two large rounded windows divided by delicate pillars, of the sort (as Alberic later learned) which people built in the barbarous days of the Goths. Among the vines, which formed a vast arbour, were growing, in open spaces, large orange and lemon trees, and flowering bushes of rosemary, and pale pink roses. And in front of the house, under a great umbrella pine, was a well, with an arch over it and a bucket hanging to a chain.

Alberic wandered about in the vineyard, and then slowly mounted the marble staircase which flanked the white house. There was no one in it. The two or three small upper chambers stood open, and on their blackened floor were heaped sacks, and faggots, and fodder, and all manner of coloured seeds. The un-glazed windows stood open, framing in between their white pillars a piece of deep blue sea. For there, below, but seen over the tops of the olive trees and the green leaves of the oranges and lemons, stretched the sea, deep blue, speckled with white sails, bounded by pale blue capes and arched over by a dazzling pale blue sky. From the lower story there rose faint sounds of cattle, and a fresh, sweet smell as of cut grass and herbs and coolness, which Alberic had never known before. How long did Alberic stand at that window? He was startled by what he took to be steps close behind him, and a rustle as of silk. But the rooms were empty, and he could see nothing moving among the stacked up fodder and seeds. Still, the sounds seemed to recur, but now outside, and he thought he heard someone in a very low voice call his name. He descended into the vineyard; he walked round every tree and every shrub, and climbed upon the broken masses of rose-coloured masonry, crushing the scented rag-wort and peppermint with which they were overgrown. But all was still

and empty. Only, from far, far below, there rose a stave of peasant's song.

The great gold balls of oranges, and the delicate yellow lemons, stood out among their glossy green against the deep blue of the sea; the long bunches of grapes, hung, filled with sunshine, like clusters of rubies and jacinths and topazes, from the trellis which patterned the pale blue sky. But Alberic felt not hunger, but sudden thirst, and mounted the three broken marble steps of the well. By its side was a long narrow trough of marble, such as stood in the court at Luna, and which, Alberic had been told, people had used as coffins in pagan times. This one was evidently intended to receive water from the well, for it had a mask in the middle, with a spout; but it was quite dry and full of wild herbs and even of pale, prickly roses. There were garlands carved upon it, and people twisting snakes about them; and the carving was picked out with golden brown minute mosses. Alberic looked at it, for it pleased him greatly; and then he lowered the bucket into the deep well, and drank. The well was very, very deep. Its inner sides were covered, as far as you could see, with long delicate weeds like pale green hair, but this faded away in the darkness. At the bottom was a bright space, reflecting the sky, but looking like some subterranean country. Alberic, as he bent over, was startled by suddenly seeing what seemed a face filling up part of that shining circle; but he remembered it must be his own reflection, and felt ashamed. So, to give himself courage, he bent over again, and sang his own name to the image. But instead of his own boyish voice he was answered by wonderful tones, high and deep alternately, running through the notes of a long, long cadence, as he had heard them on holidays at the Ducal Chapel at Luna.

When he had slaked his thirst, Alberic was about to unchain the bucket, when there was a rustle hard by, and a sort of little hiss, and there rose from the carved trough, from among the weeds and roses, and glided on to the brick of the well, a long, green, glittering thing. Alberic recognised it to be a snake; only, he had no idea it had such a flat, strange little head and such a long forked tongue, for the lady on the tapestry was a woman from the waist upwards. It sat on the opposite side of the well, moving its long neck in his direction, and fixing him with its small golden eyes. Then, slowly, it began to glide round the well circle towards him. Perhaps it wants to drink, thought Alberic, and tipped the bronze pitcher in its direction. But the creature glided past, and came around and rubbed itself against Alberic's hand. The boy was not afraid, for he knew nothing about snakes; but he started, for, on this hot day, the creature was icy cold. But then he felt sorry. "It must be dreadful to be always so cold," he said, "come, try and get warm in my pocket."

But the snake merely rubbed itself against his coat, and then disappeared back into the carved sarcophagus.

IV

Duke Balthasar Maria, as we have seen, was famous for his unfading youth, and much of his happiness and pride was due to this delightful peculiarity. Any comparison, therefore, which might diminish it was distasteful to the ever young sovereign of Luna; and when his son had died with mysterious suddenness, Duke Balthasar Maria's grief had been tempered by the consolatory fact that he was now the youngest man at his own court. This very natural feeling explains why the Duke of Luna had put behind him for several years the fact of having a grandson, painful because implying that he was of an age to be a grandfather. He had done his best, and succeeded not badly, to forget Alberic while the latter abode under his own roof; and now that the boy had been sent away to a distance, he forgot him entirely for the space of several years.

But Balthasar Maria's three chief counsellors had no such reason for forgetfulness; and so in turn, each unknown to the other, the Jesuit, the Dwarf, and the Jester, sent spies to the Castle of Sparkling Waters, and even secretly visited that place in person. For by the coincidence of genius, the mind of each of these profound politi-cians, had been illuminated by the same remarkable thought, to wit: that Duke Balthasar Maria, unnatural as it seemed, would some day have to die, and Prince Alberic, if still alive, become duke in his stead. Those were the times of subtle statecraft; and the Jesuit, the Dwarf, and the Jester were notable statesmen even in their day. So each of them had provided himself with a scheme, which, in order to be thoroughly artistic, was twofold, and so to speak, double-barrelled. Alberic might live or he might die, and therefore Alberic must be turned to profit in either case. If, to invert the chances, Alberic should die before coming to the throne, the Jesuit, the Dwarf, and the Jester had each privately determined to represent this death as purposely brought about by himself for the benefit of one of three Powers which would claim the Duchy in case of extinction of the male line. The Jesuit had chosen to attribute the murder to devotion to the Holy See, the Dwarf had preferred to appear active in favour of the King of Spain, and the Jester had decided that he would lay claim to the gratitude of the Emperor; the very means which each would pretend to have used had been thought out: poison in each case; only while the Dwarf had selected arsenic, taken through a pair of perfumed gloves, and the Jester pounded diamonds mixed in champagne, the Jesuit had modestly adhered to the humble cup of chocolate, which whether real or fictitious, had always stood his order in such good stead. Thus had each of these wily courtiers disposed of Alberic in case that he should die.

There remained the alternative of Alberic continuing to live; and for this the three rival statesmen were also prepared. If Alberic lived, it was obvious that he must be made to select one of the three as his sole minister; and banish, imprison, or put to death the other two. For this purpose it was necessary to secure his affection by gifts, until he should be old enough to understand that he had actually owed his life to the passionate loyalty of the Jesuit, or the Dwarf, or the Jester, each of whom had saved him from the atrocious enterprises of the other two counsellors of Balthasar Maria—nay, who knows? perhaps from the malignity of Balthasar Maria himself.

In accordance with these subtle machinations, each of the three statesmen determined to outwit his rivals by sending young Alberic such things as would appeal most strongly to a poor young prince living in banishment among peasants, and wholly unsupplied with pocket-money. The Jesuit expended a considerable sum on books, magnificently bound with the arms of Luna; the Dwarf prepared several suits of tasteful clothes; and the Jester selected, with infinite care, a horse of equal and perfect gentleness and mettle. And, unknown to one another, but much about the same period, each of the statesmen sent his present most secretly to Alberic. Imagine the astonishment and wrath of the Jesuit, the Dwarf, and the Jester, when each saw his messenger come back from Sparkling Waters, with his gift returned, and the news that Prince Alberic was already supplied with a complete library, a handsome wardrobe and not one, but two horses of the finest breed and training; nay, more unexpected still, that while returning the gifts to their respective donors, he had rewarded the messengers with splendid liberality.

The result of this amazing discovery was much the same in the mind of the Jesuit, the Dwarf, and the Jester. Each instantly suspected one or both of his rivals; then, on second thoughts, determined to change the present to one of the other items (horse, clothes, or books, as the case might be) little suspecting that each of them had been supplied already; and, on further reflection, began to doubt the reality of the whole business, to suspect connivance of the messengers, intended insult on the part of the prince, and decided to trust only to the evidence of his own eyes in the matter.

Accordingly, within the same few months, the Jesuit, the Dwarf, and the Jester, feigned grievous illness to their Ducal Master, and while everybody thought them safe in bed in the Red Palace at Luna, hurried, on horseback, or in a litter, or in a coach, to the Castle of Sparkling Waters.

The scene with the peasant and his family, young Alberic's host, was identical on the three occasions; and, as the farmer saw that these personages were equally willing to pay liberally for absolute secrecy, he very consistently swore to supply that desideratum to each of the three great functionaries. And similarly, in all three cases, it was deemed preferable to see the young prince first from a hiding place, before asking leave to pay their respects.

The Dwarf, who was the first in the field, was able to hide very conveniently in one of the cut velvet plumes which surmounted Alberic's four-post bedstead, and to observe the young prince as he changed his apparel. But he scarcely recognised the Duke's grandson. Alberic was sixteen, but far taller and stronger than his age would warrant. His figure was at once manly and delicate, and full of grace and vigour of movement. His long hair, the colour of floss silk, fell in wavy curls, which seemed to imply almost a woman's care and coquetry. His hands also, though powerful, were, as the Dwarf took note, of princely form and whiteness. As to his garments, the open doors of his wardrobe displayed every variety that a young prince could need; and, while the Dwarf was watching, he was exchanging a russet and purple hunting dress, cut after the Hungarian fashion with cape and hood, and accompanied by a cap crowned with peacock's feathers, for a habit of white and silver, trimmed with Venetian lace, in which he intended to honour the wedding of one of the farmer's daughters. Never, in his most genuine youth, had Balthasar Maria, the ever young and handsome, been one quarter as beautiful in person or as delicate in apparel as his grandson in exile among poor country folk.

The Jesuit, in his turn, came to verify his messenger's extraordinary statements. Through the gap between two rafters he was enabled to look down on to Prince Alberic in his study. Magnificently bound books lined the walls of the closet, and in this gap hung valuable maps and prints. On the table were heaped several open volumes, among globes both terrestrial and celestial, and Alberic himself was leaning on the arm of a great chair, reciting the verses of Virgil in a most graceful chant. Never had the Jesuit seen a better-appointed study nor a more precocious young scholar.

As regards the Jester, he came at the very moment that Alberic was returning from a ride; and, having begun life as an acrobat, he was able to climb into a large ilex which commanded an excellent view of the Castle yard.

Alberic was mounted on a splendid jet-black barb, magnificently caparisoned in crimson and gold Spanish trappings. His groom—for he even had a groom—was riding a horse only a shade less perfect: it was white and he was black. When Alberic came in sight of the farmer's wife, who stood shelling peas on the door step, he waved his hat with infinite grace, caused his horse to caracole and rear three times in salutation, picked an apple up while cantering round the Castle yard, threw it in the air with his sword and cut it in two as it descended, and did a number of similar feats such as are taught only to the most brilliant cavaliers. Now, as he was going to dismount, a branch of the ilex cracked, the black barb reared, and Alberic, looking up, perceived the Jester moving in the tree.

"A wonderful parti-coloured bird!" he exclaimed, and seized the fowling-piece that hung by his saddle. But before he had time to fire the Jester had thrown himself down and alighted, making three somersaults, on the ground.

"My Lord," said the Jester, "you see before you a faithful subject who, braving the threats and traps of your enemies, and, I am bound to add, risking also your Highness's sovereign displeasure, has been determined to see his Prince once more, to have the supreme happiness of seeing him at last clad and equipped and mounted—"

"Enough!" interrupted Alberic sternly. "You need say no more. You would have me believe that it is to you I owe my horses and books and clothes, even as the Dwarf and the Jesuit tried to make me believe about themselves last month. Know, then, that Alberic of Luna requires gifts from none of you. And now, most miserable councillor of my unhappy grandfather, begone!"

The Jester checked his rage, and tried, all the way back to Luna, to get at some solution of this intolerable riddle. The Jesuit and the Dwarf—the scoundrels—had been trying their hand then! Perhaps, indeed, it was their blundering which had ruined his own perfectly concocted scheme. But for their having come and claimed gratitude for gifts they had not made, Alberic would perhaps have believed that the Jester had not merely offered the horse which was refused, but had actually given the two which had been accepted, and the books and clothes (since there had been books and clothes given) into the bargain. But then, had not Alberic spoken as if he were perfectly sure from what quarter all his possessions had come? This reminded the Jester of the allusion to the Duke Balthasar Maria; Alberic had spoken of him as unhappy. Was it, could it be, possible that the treacherous old wretch had been keeping up relations with his grandson in secret, afraid—for he was a miserable coward at bottom—both of the wrath of his three counsellors, and of the hatred of his grandson? Was it possible, thought the Jester, that not only the Jesuit and the Dwarf, but the Duke of Luna also, had been intriguing against him round young Prince Alberic? Balthasar Maria was quite capable of it; he might be enjoying the trick he was playing to his three masters—for they were his masters; he might be preparing to turn suddenly upon them with his long neglected grandson like a sword to smite them. On the other hand, might this not be a mere mistake and supposition on the part of Prince Alberic, who, in his silly dignity, preferred to believe in the liberality of his ducal grandfather than in that of his grandfather's servants? Might the horses, and all the rest, not really be the gift of either the Dwarf or the Jesuit, although neither had got the credit for it? "No, no," exclaimed the Jester, for he hated his fellow servants worse than his master, "anything better than that! Rather a thousand times that it were the Duke himself who had outwitted them."

Then, in his bitterness, having gone over the old arguments again and again, some additional circumstances returned to his memory. The black groom was deaf and dumb, and the peasants it appeared, had been quite unable to extract any information from him. But he had arrived with those particular horses only a few months ago; a gift, the peasants had thought, from the old Duke of Luna. But Alberic, they had said, had possessed other horses before, which they had also thus taken for granted, must have come from the Red Palace. And the clothes and books had been accumulating, it appeared, ever since the Prince's arrival in his place of banishment. Since this was the case, the plot, whether on the part of the Jesuit or the Dwarf, or on that of the Duke himself, had been going on for years before the Jester had bestirred himself! Moreover, the Prince not only possessed horses, but he had learned to ride; he not only had books, but he had learned to read, and even to read various tongues; and finally, the Prince was not only clad in princely garments, but he was every inch of him a Prince. He had then been consorting with other people than the peasants at Sparkling Waters. He must have been away—or—someone must have come. He had not been living in solitude.

But when—how—and above all, who?

And again the baffled Jester revolved the probabilities concerning the Dwarf, the Jesuit, and the Duke. It must be—it could be no other—it evidently could only be—

"Ah!" exclaimed the unhappy diplomatist; "if only one could believe in magic!"

And it suddenly struck him, with terror and mingled relief, "Was it magic?"

But the Jester, like the Dwarf and the Jesuit, and the Duke of Luna himself, was altogether superior to such foolish beliefs.

V

The young Prince of Luna had never attempted to learn the story of Alberic the Blond and the Snake Lady. Children sometimes conceive an inexplicable shyness, almost a dread, of knowing more on subjects which are uppermost in their thoughts; and such had been the case of Duke Balthasar Maria's grandson. Ever since the memorable morning when the ebony crucifix had been removed from in front of the faded tapestry, and the whole figure of the Snake Lady had been for the first time revealed, scarcely a day had passed without there coming to the boy's mind his nurse's words about his ancestor Alberic and the Snake Lady Oriana. But, even as he had asked no questions then, so he had asked no questions since; shrinking more and more from all further knowledge of the matter. He had never questioned his nurse, he had never questioned the peasants of Sparkling Waters, although the story, he felt quite sure, must be well known among the ruins of Alberic the Blond's own castle. Nay, stranger still, he had never mentioned the subject to his dear Godmother, to whom he had learned to open his heart about all things, and who had taught him all that he knew.

For the Duke's Jester had guessed rightly that, during these years at Sparkling Waters, the young Prince had not consorted solely with peasants. The very evening after his arrival, as he was sitting by the marble well in the vineyard, looking towards the sea, he had felt a hand placed lightly on his shoulder, and looked up into the face of a beautiful lady dressed in green.

"Do not be afraid," she had said, smiling at his terror. "I am not a ghost, but alive like you; and I am, though you do not know it, your Godmother. My dwelling is close to this castle, and I shall come every evening to play and talk with you, here by the little white palace with the pillars, where the fodder is stacked. Only, you must remember that I do so against the wishes of your grandfather and all his friends, and that if ever you mention me to anyone, or allude in any way to our meetings, I shall be obliged to leave the neighbourhood, and you will never see me again. Some day when you are big you will learn why; till then you must take me on trust. And now what shall we play at?"

And thus his Godmother had come every evening at sunset; just for an hour and no more, and had taught the poor solitary little prince to play (for he had never played) and to read, and to manage a horse, and, above all, to love: for, except the old tapestry in the Red Palace, he had never loved anything in the world.

Alberic told his dear Godmother everything, beginning with the story of the two pieces of tapestry, the one they had taken away and the one he had cut to pieces; and he asked her about all the things he ever wanted to know, and she was always able to answer. Only, about two things they were silent: she never told him her name nor where she lived, nor whether Duke Balthasar Maria knew her (the boy guessed that she had been a friend of his father's); and Alberic never revealed the fact that the tapestry had represented his ancestor and the beautiful Oriana; for, even to his dear Godmother, and most perhaps to her, he found it impossible even to mention Alberic the Blond and the Snake Lady.

But the story, or rather the name of the story he did not know, never loosened its hold on Alberic's mind. Little by little, as he grew up, it came to add to his life two friends, of whom he never told his Godmother. They were, to be sure, of such sort, however different, that a boy might find it difficult to speak about without feeling foolish. The first of the two friends was his own ancestor, Alberic the Blond: and the second that large tame grass snake whose acquaintance he had made the day after his arrival at the castle. About Alberic the Blond he knew indeed but little, save that he had reigned in Luna many hundreds of years ago, and that he had been a very brave and glorious prince indeed, who had helped to conquer the Holy Sepulchre with Godfrey and Tancred and the other heroes of Tasso. But, perhaps in proportion to this vagueness, Alberic the Blond served to personify all the notions of chivalry which the boy had learned from his Godmother, and those which bubbled up in his own breast. Nay, little by little the young Prince began to take his unknown ancestor as a model, and in a confused way, to identify himself with him. For was he not fair-haired too, and Prince of Luna, *Alberic*, third of the name, as the other had been first? Perhaps for this reason he could never speak of this ancestor with his Godmother. She might think it presumptuous and foolish; besides, she might perhaps tell him things about Alberic the Blond which might hurt him; the poor young

Prince, who had compared the splendid reputation of his own grandfather with the miserable reality, had grown up precociously sceptical. As to the Snake, with whom he played every day in the grass, and who was his only companion during the many hours of his Godmother's absence, he would willingly have spoken of her, and had once been on the point of doing so, but he had noticed that the mere name of such creatures seemed to be odious to his Godmother. Whenever, in their readings, they came across any mention of serpents, his Godmother would exclaim, "Let us skip that," with a look of intense pain in her usually cheerful countenance. It was a pity, Alberic thought, that so lovely and dear a lady should feel such hatred towards any living creature, particularly towards a kind, which like his own tame grass snake, was perfectly harmless. But he loved her too much to dream of thwarting her; and he was very grateful to his tame snake for having the tact never to show herself at the hour of his Godmother's visits.

But to return to the story represented on the dear, faded tapestry in the Red Palace.

When Prince Alberic, unconscious to himself, was beginning to turn into a full-grown and gallant-looking youth, a change began to take place in him, and it was about the story of his ancestor and the Lady Oriana. He thought of it more than ever, and it began to haunt his dreams; only it was now a vaguely painful thought, and, while dreading still to know more, he began to experience a restless, miserable, craving to know all. His curiosity was like a thorn in his flesh, working its way in and in; and it seemed something almost more than curiosity. And yet, he was still shy and frightened of the subject; nay, the greater his craving to know, the greater grew a strange certainty that the knowing would be accompanied by evil. So, although many people could have answered—the very peasants, the fishermen of the coast, and first, and foremost, his Godmother—he let months pass before he asked the question.

It, and the answer, came of a sudden.

There occasionally came to Sparkling Waters

an old man, who united in his tattered person the trades of mending crockery and reciting fairy tales. He would seat himself, in summer, under the spreading fig tree in the castle yard, and in winter, by the peasants' deep, black chimney, alternately boring holes in pipkins, or gluing plate edges, and singing, in a cracked, nasal voice, but not without dignity and charm of manner, the stories of the King of Portugal's Cowherd, of the Feathers of the Griffin, or some of the many stanzas of *Orlando* or *Jerusalem Delivered*, which he knew by heart. Our young Prince had always avoided him, partly from a vague fear of a mention of his ancestor and the Snake Lady, and partly because of something vaguely sinister in the old man's eye. But now he awaited with impatience the vagrant's periodical return, and on one occasion, summoned him to his own chamber.

"Sing me," he commanded, "the story of Alberic the Blond and the Snake Lady."

The old man hesitated, and answered with a strange look—

"My lord, I do not know it."

A sudden feeling, such as the youth had never experienced before, seized hold of Alberic. He did not recognise himself. He saw and heard himself, as if it were someone else, nod first at some pieces of gold, of those his Godmother had given him, and then at his fowling piece hung on the wall; and as he did so, he had a strange thought: "I must be mad." But he merely said, sternly—

"Old man, that is not true. Sing that story at once, if you value my money and your safety."

The vagrant took his white-bearded chin in his hand, mused, and then, fumbling among the files and drills and pieces of wire in his tool basket, which made a faint metallic accompaniment, he slowly began to chant the following stanzas—

VI

Now listen, courteous Prince, to what befell your ancestor, the valorous Alberic, returning from the Holy Land.

Already a year had passed since the strong-holds of Jerusalem had fallen beneath the blows of the faithful, and since the sepulchre of Christ had been delivered from the worshippers of Macomet. The great Godfrey was enthroned as its guardian, and the mighty barons, his companions, were wending their way homewards— Tancred, and Bohemund, and Reynold, and the rest.

The valorous Alberic, the honour of Luna, after many perilous adventures, brought by the anger of the Wizard Macomet, was ship-wrecked on his homeward way, and cast, alone of all his great following, upon the rocky shore of an unknown island. He wandered long about, among woods and pleasant pastures, but without ever seeing any signs of habitation; nourishing himself solely on the berries and clear water, and taking his rest in the green grass beneath the trees. At length, after some days of wandering, he came to a dense forest, the like of which he had never seen before, so deep was its shade and so tangled were its boughs. He broke the branches with his iron-gloved hand, and the air became filled with the croaking and screeching of dreadful night-birds. He pushed his way with shoulder and knee, trampling the broken leafage under foot, and the air was filled with the roaring of monstrous lions and tigers. He grasped his sharp double-edged sword and hewed through the interlaced branches, and the air was filled with the shrieks and sobs of a vanquished city. But the Knight of Luna went on, undaunted, cutting his way through the enchanted wood. And behold! as he issued thence, there rose before him a lordly castle, as of some great prince, situate in a pleasant meadow among running streams. And as Alberic approached the portcullis was raised, and the drawbridge lowered; and there arose sounds of fifes and bugles, but nowhere could he descry any living creature around. And Alberic entered the castle, and found therein guardrooms full of shining arms, and chambers spread with rich stuffs, and a banquetting hall, with a great table laid and a chair of state at the end. And as he entered a concert of invisible voices and instruments greeted him sweetly, and called him by name, and bid him be welcome; but not a living soul did he see. So he sat him down at the table, and as he did so, invisible hands filled his cup and his plate, and ministered to him with delicacies of all sorts. Now, when the good knight had eaten and drunken his fill, he drank to the health of his unknown host, declaring himself the servant thereof with his sword and heart. After which, weary with wandering, he prepared to take rest on the carpets which strewed the ground; but invisible hands unbuckled his armour, and clad him in silken robes, and led him to a couch all covered with rose-leaves. And when he had laid himself down, the concert of invisible singers and players put him to sleep with their melodies. It was the hour of sunset when the valorous Baron awoke, and buckled on his armour, and hung on his thigh his great sword Brillamorte; and the invisible hands helped him once more.

And the Knight of Luna went all over the enchanted castle, and found all manner of rarities, treasures of precious stones, such as great kings possess, and store of gold and silver vessels, and rich stuffs, and stables full of fiery coursers ready caparisoned; but never a human creature anywhere. And, wondering more and more, he went forth into the orchard, which lay within the walls of the castle. And such another orchard, sure, was never seen, since that in which the hero Hercules found the three golden apples and slew the great dragon. For you might see in this place fruit trees of all kinds, apples and pears, and peaches and plums, and the goodly orange, which bore at the same time fruit and delicate and scented blossom. And all around were set hedges of roses, whose scent was even like heaven; and there were other flowers of all kinds, those into which the vain Narcissus turned through love of himself, and those which grew, they tell us, from the blood-drops of fair Venus's minion; and lilies of which that Messenger carried a sheaf who saluted the Meek Damsel, glorious above all womankind. And in the trees sang innumerable birds; and others, of unknown breed, joined melody in hanging cages and aviaries. And in the orchard's midst was set a fountain, the most wonderful ever made, its waters running in green channels among the flowered grass. For that fountain was made in the likeness of twin naked maidens, dancing together, and pouring water out of pitchers as they did so; and the maidens were of fine silver, and the pitchers of wrought gold, and the whole so cunningly contrived by magic art that the maidens really moved and danced with the waters they were pouring out: a wonderful work, most truly. And when the Knight of Luna had feasted his eyes upon this marvel, he saw among the grass, beneath a flowering almond tree, a sepulchre of marble, cunningly carved and gilded, on which was written, "Here is imprisoned the Fairy Oriana, most miserable of all fairies, condemned for no fault, but by envious powers, to a dreadful fate,"—and as he read, the inscription changed, and the sepulchre showed these words: "O Knight of Luna, valorous Alberic, if thou wouldst show thy gratitude to the hapless mistress of this castle, summon up thy redoubtable courage, and, whatsoever creature issue from my marble heart, swear thou to kiss it three times on the mouth, that Oriana may be released."

And Alberic drew his great sword, and on its hilt, shaped like a cross, he swore.

Then wouldst thou have heard a terrible sound of thunder, and seen the castle walls rock. But Alberic, nothing daunted, repeats in a loud voice, "I swear," and instantly that sepulchre's lid up heaves, and there issues thence and rises up a great green snake, wearing a golden crown, and raises itself and fawns towards the valorous Knight of Luna. And Alberic starts and recoils in terror. For rather, a thousand times, confront alone the armed hosts of all the heathen, than put his lips to that cold, creeping beast! And the serpent looks at Alberic with great gold eyes, and big tears issue thence, and it drops prostrate on the grass, and Alberic summons courage and approaches; but when the serpent glides along his arm, a horror takes him, and he falls back unable. And the tears stream from the snake's golden eyes, and moans come from its mouth.

And Alberic runs forward, and seizes the serpent in both hands, and lifts it up, and three times presses his hot lips against its cold and slippery skin, shutting his eyes in horror, and when the Knight of Luna opens them again, behold! O wonder! in his arms no longer a dreadful snake, but a damsel, richly dressed and beautiful beyond comparison.

VII

Young Alberic sickened that very night, and lay for many days with raging fever. The peasant's wife and a good neighbouring priest nursed him unhelped, for when the messenger they sent arrived at Luna, Duke Balthasar was busy rehearsing a grand ballet in which he himself danced the part of Phoebus Apollo; and the ducal physician was therefore despatched to Sparkling Waters only when the young prince was already recovering.

Prince Alberic undoubtedly passed through a very bad illness, and went fairly out of his mind for fever and ague.

He raved so dreadfully in his delirium about enchanted tapestries and terrible grottoes, Twelve Caesars with rolling eye balls, barbers blocks with perukes on them, monkeys of verde antique, and porphyry rhinoceroses, and all manner of hellish creatures, that the good priest began to suspect a case of demoniac possession, and caused candles to be kept lighted all day and all night, and holy water to be sprinkled, and a printed form of exorcism, absolutely sovereign in such trouble, to be nailed against the bed-post. On the fourth day the young prince fell into a profound sleep, from which he awaked in apparent possession of his faculties.

"Then you are not the Porphyry Rhinoceros?" he said, very slowly as his eye fell upon the priest; "and this is my own dear little room at Sparkling Waters, though I do not understand all those candles. I thought it was the great hall in the Red Palace, and that all those animals of precious marbles, and my grandfather, the duke, in his bronze and gold robes, were beating me and

my tame snake to death with Harlequin's laths. It was terrible. But now I see it was all fancy and delirium."

The poor youth gave a sigh of relief, and feebly caressed the rugged old hand of the priest, which lay on his counterpane. The prince lay for a long while motionless, but gradually a strange light came into his eyes, and a smile on to his lips. Presently he made a sign that the peasants should leave the room, and taking once more the good priest's hand, he looked solemnly in his eyes, and spoke in an earnest voice. "My father," he said, "I have seen and heard strange things in my sickness, and I cannot tell for certain now what belongs to the reality of my previous life, and what is merely the remembrance of delirium. On this I would fain be enlightened. Promise me, my father, to answer my questions truly, for this is a matter of the welfare of my soul, and therefore of your own."

The priest nearly jumped on his chair. So he had been right. The demons had been trying to tamper with the poor young prince, and now he was going to have a fine account of it all.

"My son," he murmured, "as I hope for the spiritual welfare of both of us, I promise to answer all your interrogations to the best of my powers. Speak them without hesitation."

Alberic hesitated for a moment, and his eyes glanced from one long lit taper to the other.

"In that case," he said, slowly, "let me conjure you, my father, to tell me whether or not there exists a certain tradition in my family, of the loves of my ancestor, Alberic the Blond, with a certain Snake Lady, and how he was unfaithful to her, and failed to disenchant her, and how a second Alberic, also my ancestor, loved this same Snake Lady, but failed before the ten years of fidelity were over, and became a monk. . . . Does such a story exist, or have I imagined it all during my sickness?"

"My son," replied the good priest, testily, for he was most horribly disappointed by this speech, "it is scarce fitting that a young prince but just escaped from the jaws of death—and, perhaps, even from the insidious onslaught of the Evil One—should give his mind to idle tales like these."

"Call them what you choose," answered the prince, gravely, "but remember your promise, father. Answer me truly, and presume not to question my reasons."

The priest started. What a hasty ass he had been! Why these were probably the demons talking out of Alberic's mouth, causing him to ask silly irrelevant questions in order to prevent a good confession. Such were notoriously among their stock tricks! But he would outwit them. If only it were possible to summon up St. Paschal Baylon, that new fashionable saint who had been doing such wonders with devils lately! But St. Paschal Baylon required not only that you should say several rosaries, but that you should light four candles on a table and lay a supper for two; after that there was nothing he would not do. So the priest hastily seized two candlesticks from the foot of the bed, and called to the peasant's wife to bring a clean napkin and plates and glasses; and meanwhile endeavoured to detain the demons by answering the poor prince's foolish chatter, "Your ancestors, the two Alberics—a tradition in your Serene family—yes, my Lord—there is such—let me see, how does the story go?—ah yes—this demon, I mean this Snake Lady was a—what they call a fairy—or witch, malefica or stryx is, I believe, the proper Latin expression—who had been turned into a snake for her sins—good woman, woman, is it possible you cannot be a little quicker in bringing those plates for his Highness's supper? The Snake Lady—let me see—was to cease altogether being a snake if a cavalier remained faithful to her for ten years; and at any rate turned into a woman every time a cavalier was found who had the courage to give her a kiss as if she were not a snake—a disagreeable thing, besides being mortal sin. As I said just now, this enabled her to resume temporarily her human shape, which is said to have been fair enough; but how can one tell? I believe she was allowed to change into a woman for an hour at

sunset, in any case and without anybody kissing her, but only for an hour. A very unlikely story, my Lord, and not a very moral one to my thinking!"

And the good priest spread the table-cloth over the table, wondering secretly when the plates and glasses for St. Paschal Baylon would make their appearance. If only the demon could be prevented from beating a retreat before all was ready! "To return to the story about which your Highness is pleased to inquire," he continued, trying to gain time by pretending to humour the demon who was asking questions through the poor Prince's mouth, "I can remember hearing a poem before I took orders—a foolish poem too, in a very poor style, if my memory is correct—that related the manner in which Alberic the Blond met this Snake Lady, and disenchanted her by performing the ceremony I have alluded to. The poem was frequently sung at fairs and similar resorts of the uneducated, and, as remarked, was a very inferior composition indeed. Alberic the Blond afterwards came to his senses, it appears, and after abandoning the Snake Lady fulfilled his duty as a prince, and married the princess. . . . I cannot exactly remember what princess, but it was a very suitable marriage, no doubt, from which your Highness is of course descended.

"As regards the Marquis Alberic, second of the name, of whom it is accounted that he died in the odour of sanctity (and indeed it is said that the facts concerning his beatification are being studied in the proper quarters), there is a mention in a life of Saint Fredevaldus, bishop and patron of Luna, printed at the beginning of the present century at Venice, with approbation and license of the authorities and inquisition, a mention of the fact that this Marquis Alberic the second had contracted, having abandoned his lawful wife, a left-handed marriage with this same Snake Lady (such evil creatures not being subject to natural death), she having induced him thereunto in hope of his proving faithful ten years, and by this means restoring her altogether to human shape. But a certain holy hermit, having got wind of this scandal, prayed to St. Fredevaldus as patron of Luna, whereupon St. Fredevaldus took pity on the Marquis Alberic's sins, and appeared to him in a vision at the end of the ninth year of his irregular connection with the Snake Lady, and touched his heart so thoroughly that he instantly forswore her company, and handing the Marquisate over to his mother, abandoned the world and entered the order of St. Romuald, in which he died, as remarked, in odour of sanctity, in consequence of which the present Duke, your Highness's magnificent grandfather, is at this moment, as befits so pious a prince, employing his influence with the Holy Father for the beatification of so glorious an ancestor. And now, my son," added the good priest, suddenly changing his tone, for he had got the table ready, and lighted the candles, and only required to go through the preliminary invocation of St. Paschal Baylon—"and now, my son, let your curiosity trouble you no more, but endeavour to obtain some rest, and if possible—"

But the prince interrupted him.

"One word more, good father," he begged, fixing him with earnest eyes, "is it known what has been the fate of the Snake Lady?"

The impudence of the demons made the priest quite angry, but he must not scare them before the arrival of St. Paschal, so he controlled himself, and answered slowly by gulps, between the lines of the invocation he was mumbling under his breath:

"My Lord—it results from the same life of St. Fredevaldus, that . . . (in case of property lost, fire, flood, earthquake, plague) . . . that the Snake Lady (thee we invoke, most holy Paschal Baylon!)—the Snake Lady being of the nature of fairies, cannot die unless her head be severed from her trunk, and is still haunting the world, together with other evil spirits, in hopes that another member of the house of Luna (thee we invoke, most holy Paschal Baylon!)—may succumb to her arts and be faithful to her for the ten years needful to her disenchantments—(most holy Paschal Baylon!—and most of all on thee we call for aid against the . . .)"

But before the priest could finish his invoca-tion, a terrible shout came from the bed where the sick prince was lying—

"O Oriana, Oriana!" cried Prince Alberic, sitting up in his bed with a look which terrified the priest as much as his voice. "O Oriana, Oriana!" he repeated, and then fell back exhausted and broken.

"Bless my soul!" cried the priest, almost upsetting the table; "why the demon has already issued out of him! Who would have guessed that St. Paschal Baylon performed his miracles as quick as that!"

VIII

Prince Alberic was awakened by the loud trill of a nightingale. The room was bathed in moonlight, in which the tapers, left burning round the bed to ward off evil spirits, flickered yellow and ineffectual. Through the open casement came, with the scent of freshly cut grass, a faint concert of nocturnal sounds: the silvery vibration of the cricket, the reedlike quavering notes of the leaf frogs, and, every now and then, the soft note of an owlet, seeming to stroke the silence as the downy wings growing out of the temples of the Sleep god might stroke the air. The nightingale had paused; and Alberic listened breathless for its next burst of song. At last, and when he expected it least, it came, liquid, loud and triumphant; so near that it filled the room and thrilled through his marrow like an unison of Cremona viols. He was singing in the pomegranate close outside, whose first buds must be opening into flame-coloured petals. For it was May. Alberic listened; and collected his thoughts, and understood. He arose and dressed, and his limbs seemed suddenly strong, and his mind strangely clear, as if his sickness had been but a dream. Again the nightingale trilled out, and again stopped. Alberic crept noiselessly out of his chamber, down the stairs and into the open. Opposite, the moon had just risen, immense and golden, and the pines and the cypresses of the hill, the furthest battlements of the castle walls, were printed upon her like delicate lace. It was so light that the roses were pink, and the pomegranate flower scarlet, and the lemons pale yellow, and the grass bright green, only differently coloured from how they looked by day, and as if washed over with silver. The orchard spread up hill, its twigs and separate leaves all glittering as if made of diamonds, and its tree trunks and spalliers weaving strange black patterns of shadow. A little breeze shuddered up from the sea, bringing the scent of the irises grown for their root among the cornfields below. The nightingale was silent. But Prince Alberic did not stand waiting for its song. A spiral dance of fire-flies, rising and falling like a thin gold fountain, beckoned him upwards through the dewy grass. The circuit of castle walls, jagged and battlemented, and with tufts of trees profiled here and there against the resplendent blue pallor of the moon light, seemed turned and knotted like huge snakes around the world.

Suddenly, again, the nightingale sang; a throbbing, silver song. It was the same bird, Alberic felt sure; but it was in front of him now, and was calling him onwards. The fire-flies wove their golden dance a few steps in front, always a few steps in front, and drew him up-hill through the orchard.

As the ground became steeper, the long trellises, black and crooked, seemed to twist and glide through the blue moonlight grass like black gliding snakes, and, at the top, its marble pillarets, clear in the moonlight, slumbered the little Gothic palace of white marble. From the solitary sentinel pine broke the song of the nightingale. This was the place. A breeze had risen, and from the shining moonlit sea, broken into causeways and flotillas of smooth and of fretted silver, came a faint briny smell, mingling with that of the irises and blossoming lemons, with the scent of vague ripeness and freshness. The moon hung like a silver lantern over the orchard; the wood of the trellises patterned the blue luminous heaven, the vine leaves seemed to swim, transparent, in the shining air. Over the circular well, in the high grass, the fire-flies rose and fell like a thin fountain of gold. And, from the sentinel pine, the nightingale sang.

Prince Alberic leant against the brink of the well, by the trough carved with antique designs of serpent-bearing maenads. He was wonderfully calm, and his heart sang within him. It was, he knew, the hour and place of his fate.

The nightingale ceased: and the shrill songs of the crickets was suspended. The silvery luminous world was silent.

A quiver came through the grass by the well; a rustle through the roses. And, on the well's brink, encircling its central blackness, glided the Snake.

"Oriana!" whispered Alberic. "Oriana!" She paused, and stood almost erect. The Prince put out his hand, and she twisted round his arm, extending slowly her chilly coil to his wrist and fingers.

"Oriana!" whispered Prince Alberic again. And raising his hand to his face, he leaned down and pressed his lips on the little flat head of the serpent. And the nightingale sang. But a coldness seized his heart, the moon seemed suddenly extinguished, and he slipped away in unconsciousness.

When he awoke the moon was still high. The nightingale was singing its loudest. He lay in the grass by the well, and his head rested on the knees of the most beautiful of ladies. She was dressed in cloth of silver which seemed woven of moon mists, and shimmering moonlit green grass. It was his own dear Godmother.

IX

When Duke Balthasar Maria had got through the rehearsals of the ballet called Daphne Transformed, and finally danced his part of Phoebus Apollo to the infinite delight and glory of his subjects, he was greatly concerned, being benignly humoured, on learning that he had very nearly lost his grandson and heir. The Dwarf, the Jesuit, and the Jester, whom he delighted in pitting against one another, had severely accused each other of disrespectful remarks about the dancing of that ballet; so Duke Balthasar determined to disgrace all three together and inflict upon them the hated presence of Prince Alberic. It was, after all, very pleasant to possess a young grandson, whom one could take to one's bosom and employ in being insolent to one's own favourites. It was time, said Duke Balthasar, that Alberic should learn the habits of a court and take unto himself a suitable princess.

The young prince accordingly was sent for from Sparkling Waters, and installed at Luna in a wing of the Red Palace, overlooking the Court of Honour, and commanding an excellent view of the great rockery, with the verde antique apes and the Porphyry Rhinoceros. He found awaiting him on the great staircase a magnificent staff of servants, a master of the horse, a grand cook, a barber, a hairdresser and assistant, a fencing master, and four fiddlers. Several lovely ladies of the Court, the principal ministers of the Crown and the Jesuit, the Dwarf and the Jester, were also ready to pay their respects. Prince Alberic threw himself out of the glass coach before they had time to open the door, and bowing coldly, ascended the staircase, carrying under his cloak what appeared to be a small wicker cage. The Jesuit, who was the soul of politeness, sprang forward and signed to an officer of the household to relieve his highness of this burden. But Alberic waved the man off; and the rumour went abroad that a hissing noise had issued from under the prince's cloak, and, like lightning, the head and forked tongue of a serpent.

Half-an-hour later the official spies had informed Duke Balthasar that his grandson and heir had brought from Sparkling Waters no apparent luggage save two swords, a fowling piece, a volume of Virgil, a branch of pomegranate blossom, and a tame grass snake.

Duke Balthasar did not like the idea of the grass snake; but wishing to annoy the Jester, the Dwarf, and the Jesuit, he merely smiled when they told him of it, and said: "The dear boy! What a child he is! He probably, also, has a pet lamb, white as snow, and gentle as spring, mourning for him in his old home! How touching is the innocence of childhood! Heigho! I was just like that myself not so very long ago." Whereupon the three favourites and the whole Court of Luna

smiled and bowed and sighed: "How lovely is the innocence of youth!" while the Duke fell to humming the well-known air, "Thrysis was a shepherd boy," of which the ducal fiddlers instantly struck up the ritornello.

"But," added Balthasar Maria, with that subtle blending of majesty and archness in which he excelled all living princes, "but it is now time that the prince, my grandson, should learn"—here he put his hand on his sword and threw back slightly one curl of his jet black peruke—"the stern exercises of Mars; and, also, let us hope, the freaks and frolics of Venus."

Saying which, the old sinner pinched the cheek of a lady of the very highest quality, whose husband and father were instantly congratulated by all the court on this honour.

Prince Alberic was displayed next day to the people of Luna, standing on the balcony among a tremendous banging of mortars; while Duke Balthasar explained that he felt towards this youth all the fondness and responsibility of an elder brother. There was a grand ball, a gala opera, a review, a very high mass in the cathedral; the Dwarf, the Jesuit, and the Jester each separately offered his services to Alberic in case he wanted a loan of money, a love letter carried, or in case even (expressed in more delicate terms) he might wish to poison his grandfather. Duke Balthasar Maria, on his side, summoned his ministers, and sent couriers, booted and liveried, to three great dukes of Italy, carrying each of these in a morocco wallet emblazoned with the arms of Luna, an account of Prince Alberic's lineage and person, and a request for particulars of any marriageable princesses and dowries to be disposed of.

X

Prince Alberic did not give his grandfather that warm satisfaction which the old duke had expected. Balthasar Maria, entirely bent upon annoying the three favourites, had said, and had finally believed, that he intended to introduce his grandson to the delight and duties of life, and in the company of this beloved stripling to dream that he, too, was a youth once more: a statement which the court took with due deprecatory reverence, as the duke was well known never to have ceased to be young.

But Alberic did not lend himself to so touching an idyll. He behaved, indeed, with the greatest decorum, and manifested the utmost respect for his grandfather. He was marvellously assiduous in the council chamber, and still more so in following the military exercises and learning the trade of a soldier. He surprised everyone by his interest and intelligence in all affairs of state; he more than surprised the Court by his readiness to seek knowledge about the administration of the country and the condition of the people. He was a youth of excellent morals, courage and diligence; but, there was no denying it, he had positively no conception of sacrificing to the Graces. He sat out, as if he had been watching a review, the delicious operas and superb ballets which absorbed half the revenue of the duchy. He listened, without a smile of comprehension, to the witty innuendoes of the ducal table. But worst of all, he had absolutely no eyes, let alone a heart, for the fair sex. Now Balthasar Maria had assembled at Luna a perfect bevy of lovely nymphs, both ladies of the greatest birth, whose husbands received most honourable posts military and civil, and young females of humbler extraction, though not less expressive habits, ranging from singers and dancers to slave-girls of various colours, all dressed in their appropriate costume: a galaxy of beauty which was duly represented by the skill of celebrated painters on all the walls of the Red Palace, where you may still see their fading charms, habited as Diana, or Pallas, or in the spangles of Columbine, or the turban of Sibyls. These ladies were the object of Duke Balthasar's most munificently divided attentions; and in the delight of his newborn family affection, he had promised himself much tender interest in guiding the taste of his heir among such of these nymphs as had already received his own exquisite appreciation. Great, therefore, was the disappointment of the affectionate grandfather when his dream of companionship was dispelled, and it became hopeless to interest young Alberic in anything at Luna, save despatches and cannons.

The Court, indeed, found the means of consoling Duke Balthasar for this bitterness, by extracting therefrom a brilliant comparison between the unfading grace, the vivacious, though majestic, character of the grandfather, and the gloomy and pedantic personality of the grandson. But, although Balthasar Maria would only smile at every new proof of Alberic's bearish obtuseness, and ejaculate in French, "Poor child! he was born old, and I shall die young!" the reigning Prince of Luna grew vaguely to resent the peculiarities of his heir.

In this fashion things proceeded in the Red Palace at Luna, until Prince Alberic had attained his twenty-first year.

He was sent, in the interval, to visit the principal Courts of Italy, and to inspect its chief curiosities, natural and historical, as befitted the heir to an illustrious state. He received the golden rose from the Pope in Rome; he witnessed the festivities of Ascension Day from the Doge's barge at Venice; he accompanied the Marquis of Montferrat to the camp under Turin; he witnessed the launching of a galley against the Barbary corsairs by the Knights of St. Stephen in the port of Leghorn, and a grand bullfight and burning of heretics given by the Spanish Viceroy at Palermo; and he was allowed to be present when the celebrated Dr. Borri turned two brass buckles into pure gold before the Archduke at Milan. On all of which occasions the heir-apparent of Luna bore himself with a dignity and discretion most singular in one so young. In the course of these journeys he was presented to several of the most promising heiresses in Italy, some of whom were of so tender age as to be displayed in jewelled swaddling-clothes on brocade cushions; and a great many possible marriages were discussed behind his back. But Prince Alberic declared for his part that he had decided to lead a single life until the age of twenty-eight or thirty, and that he would then require the assistance of no ambassadors or chancellors, but find for himself the future Duchess of Luna.

All this did not please Balthasar Maria, as indeed nothing else about his grandson did please him much. But, as the old duke did not really relish the idea of a daughter-in-law at Luna, and as young Alberic's whimsicalities entailed no expense, and left him entirely free in his business and pleasure, he turned a deaf ear to the criticisms of his councillors, and letting his grandson inspect fortifications, drill soldiers, pore over parchments, and mope in his wing of the palace, with no amusement save his repulsive tame snake, Balthasar Maria composed and practised various ballets, and began to turn his attention very seriously to the completion of the rockery grotto and of the sepulchral chapel, which, besides the Red Palace itself, were the chief monuments of his glorious reign.

It was this growing desire to witness the fulfilment of these magnanimous projects which led the Duke of Luna into an expected conflict with his grandson. The wonderful enterprises above mentioned involved immense expenses, and had periodically been suspended for lack of funds. The collection of animals in the rockery was very far from complete. A camelopard of spotted alabaster, an elephant of Sardinian jasper, and the entire families of a cow and sheep, all of correspondingly rich marbles, were urgently required to fill up the corners. Moreover, the supply of water was at present so small that the fountains were dry save for a couple of hours on the very greatest holidays; and it was necessary for the perfect naturalness of this ingenious work that an aqueduct twenty miles long should pour perennial streams from a high mountain lake into the grotto of the Red Palace.

The question of the sepulchral chapel was, if possible, even worse; for, after every new ballet, Duke Balthasar went through a fit of contrition, during which he fixed his thoughts on death; and the possibilities of untimely release, and of burial in an unfinished mausoleum, filled him with terrors. It is true that Duke Balthasar had, immediately after building the vast domed cha-

pel, secured an effigy of his own person before taking thought for the monuments of his already buried ancestors; and the statue, twelve feet high, representing himself in coronation robes of green bronze brocaded with gold, holding a sceptre and bearing on his head, of purest silver, a spiky coronet set with diamonds, was one of the curiosities which travellers admired most in Italy. But this statue was unsymmetrical, and moreover had a dismal suggestiveness, so long as surrounded by empty niches; and the fact that only one half of the pavement was inlaid with discs of sardonyx, jasper, and cornelian, and that the larger part of the walls were rough brick without a vestige of the mosaic pattern of lapis-lazuli, malachite, pearl, and coral, which had been begun round the one finished tomb, rendered the chapel as poverty-stricken in one aspect as it was magnificent in another. The finishing of the chapel was therefore urgent, and two more bronze statues were actually cast, those to wit of the duke's father and grandfather, and mosaic workmen called from the Medicean works in Florence. But, all of a sudden the ducal treasury was discovered to be empty, and the ducal credit to be exploded.

State lotteries, taxes on salt, even a sham crusade against the Dey of Algiers, all failed to produce any money. The alliance, the right to pass troops through the duchy, the letting out of the ducal army to the highest bidder, had long since ceased to be a source of revenue either from the Emperor, the King of Spain, or the Most Christian One. The Serene Republics of Venice and Genoa publicly warned their subjects against lending a single sequin to the Duke of Luna; the Dukes of Parma and Modena began to worry about bad debts; the Pope himself had the atrocious bad taste to make complaints about suppression of church dues and interception of Peter's pence. There remained to the bankrupt Duke Balthasar Maria only one hope in the world, the marriage of his grandson.

There happened to exist at that moment a sovereign of incalculable wealth, with an only daughter of marriageable age. But this potentate, although the nephew of a recent Pope, by whose confiscations his fortunes were founded, had originally been a dealer in such goods as are comprehensively known as drysalting; and, rapacious as were the princes of the Empire, each was too much ashamed of his neighbours to venture upon alliance with a family of so obtrusive an origin. Here was Balthasar Maria's opportunity; the drysalter prince's ducats should complete the rockery, the aqueduct, and the chapel; the drysalter's daughter should be wedded to Alberic of Luna, that was to be third of the name.

XI

Prince Alberic sternly declined. He expressed his dutiful wish that the grotto and the chapel, like all other enterprises undertaken by his grandparent, might be brought to an end worthy of him. He declared that the aversion to drysalters was a prejudice unshared by himself. He even went so far as to suggest that the eligible princess should marry not the heir-apparent, but the reigning Duke of Luna. But, as regarded himself, he intended, as stated, to remain for many years single. Duke Balthasar had never in his life before seen a man who was determined to oppose him. He felt terrified and became speechless in the presence of young Alberic.

Direct influence having proved useless, the duke and his councillors, among whom the Jesuit, the Dwarf and the Jester had been duly re-instated, looked round for means of indirect persuasion or coercion. A celebrated Venetian beauty was sent for to Luna, a lady frequently employed in diplomatic missions, which she carried through by her unparalleled grace in dancing. But Prince Alberic, having watched her for half an hour, merely remarked to his equerry that his own tame grass snake made the same movements as the lady, infinitely better and more modestly. Whereupon this means was abandoned. The Dwarf then suggested a new method of acting on the young Prince's feelings. This, which he remembered to have been employed very successfully in the case of a certain Duchess of

Malfi, who had given her family much trouble some generations back, consisted in dressing up a certain number of lacqueys as ghosts and devils, hiring some genuine lunatics from a neighbouring establishment, and introducing them at dead of night into Prince Alberic's chamber. But the Prince, who was busy at his orisons, merely threw a heavy stool and two candlesticks at the apparitions; and, as he did so, the tame snake suddenly rose up from the floor, growing colossal in the act, and hissed so terrifically that the whole party fled down the corridor. The most likely advice was given by the Jesuit. This truly subtle diplomatist averred that it was useless trying to act upon the Prince by means which did not already affect him; instead of clumsily constructing a lever for which there was no fulcrum in the youth's soul, it was necessary to find out whatever leverage there might already exist.

Now, on careful inquiry, there was discovered a fact which the official spies, who always acted by precedent and pursued their inquiries according to the rules of the human heart as taught by the Secret Inquisition of the Republic of Venice, had naturally failed to perceive. This fact consisted in a rumour, very vague but very persistent, that Prince Alberic did not inhabit his wing of the palace in absolute solitude. Some of the pages attending on his person affirmed to have heard whispered conversations in the Prince's study, on entering which they had invariably found him alone; others maintained that, during the absence of the Prince from the palace, they had heard the sound of his private harpsichord, the one with the story of Orpheus and the view of Soracte on the cover, although he always kept its key on his person. A footman declared that he had found in the Prince's study, and among his books and maps, a piece of embroidery certainly not belonging to the Prince's furniture and apparel, moreover, half finished, and with a needle sticking in the canvas; which piece of embroidery the Prince had thrust into his pocket. But, as none of the attendants had ever seen any visitor entering or issuing from the Prince's apartments, and the professional spies had ransacked all possible hiding-places and modes of exit in vain, these curious indications had been neglected, and the opinion had been formed that Alberic, being, as everyone could judge, somewhat insane, had a gift of ventriloquism, a taste for musical-boxes, and a proficiency in unmanly handicrafts which he carefully dissimulated.

These rumours had at one time caused great delight to Duke Balthasar; but he had got tired of sitting in a dark cupboard in his grandson's chamber, and had caught a bad chill looking through his keyhole; so he had stopped all further inquiries as officious fooling on the part of impudent lacqueys.

But the Jesuit foolishly adhered to the rumour. "Discover *her*," he said, "and work through her on Prince Alberic." But Duke Balthasar, after listening twenty times to this remark with the most delighted interest, turned round on the twenty-first time and gave the Jesuit a look of Jove-like thunder; "My father," he said, "I am surprised, I may say more than surprised, at a person of your cloth descending so low as to make aspersions upon the virtue of a young Prince reared in my palace and born of my blood. Never let me hear another word about ladies of light manners being secreted within these walls." Whereupon the Jesuit retired, and was in disgrace for a fortnight, till Duke Balthasar woke up one morning with a strong apprehension of dying.

But no more was said of the mysterious female friend of Prince Alberic, still less was any attempt made to gain her intervention in the matter of the drysalter Princess's marriage.

XII

More desperate measures were soon resorted to. It was given out that Prince Alberic was engrossed in study, and he was forbidden to leave his wing of the Red Palace, with no other view than the famous grotto with the verde antique apes and the Porphyry Rhinoceros. It was published that

Prince Alberic was sick, and he was confined very rigorously to a less agreeable apartment in the rear of the palace, where he could catch sight of the plaster laurels and draperies, and the rolling plaster eyeball of one of the Twelve Caesars under the cornice. It was judiciously hinted that the Prince had entered into religious retreat, and he was locked and bolted into the State prison, alongside of the unfinished sepulchral chapel, whence a lugubrious hammering came as the only sound of life. In each of these places the recalcitrant youth was duly argued with by some of his grandfather's familiars, and even received a visit from the old duke in person. But threats and blandishments were all in vain, and Alberic persisted in his refusal to marry.

It was six months now since he had seen the outer world, and six weeks since he had inhabited the State prison, every stage in his confinement, almost every day thereof, having systematically deprived him of some luxury, some comfort, or some mode of passing his time. His harpsichord and foils had remained in the gala wing overlooking the grotto. His maps and books had not followed him beyond the higher story with the view of the Twelfth Caesar. And now they had taken away from him his Virgil, his inkstand and paper, and left him only a book of Hours.

Balthasar Maria and his councillors felt intolerably baffled. There remained nothing further to do; for if Prince Alberic were publicly beheaded, or privately poisoned, or merely left to die of want and sadness, it was obvious that Prince Alberic could no longer conclude the marriage with the drysalter Princess, and that no money to finish the grotto and the chapel, or to carry on Court expenses, would be forthcoming.

It was a burning day of August, a Friday, thirteenth of that month, and after a long prevalence of enervating sirocco, when the old duke determined to make one last appeal to the obedience of his grandson. The sun, setting among ominous clouds, sent a lurid orange beam into Prince Alberic's prison chamber, at the moment that his ducal grandfather, accompanied by the Jester, the

Dwarf and the Jesuit, appeared on its threshold after prodigious clanking of keys and clattering of bolts. The unhappy youth rose as they entered, and making a profound bow, motioned his grandparent to the only chair in the place. Balthasar Maria had never visited him before in this, his worst place of confinement; and the bareness of the room, the dust and cobwebs, the excessive hardness of the chair, affected his sensitive heart, and, joined with irritation at his grandson's obstinacy and utter depression about the marriage, the grotto, and the chapel, actually caused this magnanimous sovereign to burst into tears and bitter lamentations.

"It would indeed melt the heart of a stone," remarked the Jester sternly, while his two companions attempted to soothe the weeping duke "to see one of the greatest, wisest, and most valorous princes in Europe reduced to tears by the undutifulness of his child."

"Princes, nay, kings and emperors' sons," exclaimed the Dwarf, who was administering Melissa water to the duke, "have perished miserably for much less."

"Some of the most remarkable personages of sacred history are stated to have incurred eternal perdition for far slighter offences," added the Jesuit.

Alberic had sat down on the bed. The tawny sunshine fell upon his figure. He had grown very thin, and his garments were inexpressibly threadbare. But he was spotlessly neat, his lace band was perfectly folded, his beautiful blond hair flowed in exquisite curls about his pale face, and his whole aspect was serene and even cheerful. He might be twenty-two years old, and was of consummate beauty and stature.

"My lord," he answered slowly, "I entreat your Serene Highness to believe that no one could regret more deeply than I do such a spectacle as is offered by the tears of a Duke of Luna. At the same time, I can only reiterate that I accept no responsibility . . ."

A distant growling of thunder caused the old duke to start, and interrupted Alberic's speech.

"Your obstinacy, my lord," exclaimed the Dwarf, who was an excessively choleric person, "betrays the existence of a hidden conspiracy most dangerous to the state."

"It is an indication," added the Jester, "of a highly deranged mind."

"It seems to me," whispered the Jesuit, "o savour most undoubtedly of devilry."

Alberic shrugged his shoulders. He had risen from the bed to close the grated window, into which a shower of hail was suddenly blowing with unparalleled violence, when the old duke jumped on his seat, and, with eyeballs starting with terror, exclaimed, as he tottered convulsively, "The serpent! the serpent!"

For there, in a corner, the tame grass snake was placidly coiled up, sleeping.

"The snake! the devil! Prince Alberic's pet companion!" exclaimed the three favourites, and rushed towards that corner.

Alberic threw himself forward. But he was too late. The Jester, with a blow of his harlequin's lath, had crushed the head of the startled creature; and, even while he was struggling with him and the Jesuit, the Dwarf had given it two cuts with his Turkish scimitar.

"The snake! the snake!" shrieked Duke Balthasar, heedless of the desperate struggle.

The warders and equerries, waiting outside, thought that Prince Alberic must be murdering his grandfather, and burst into prison and separated the combatants.

"Chain the rebel! the wizard! the madman!" cried the three favourites.

Alberic had thrown himself on the dead snake, which lay crushed and bleeding on the floor, and he moaned piteously.

But the Prince was unarmed and overpowered in a moment. Three times he broke loose, but three times he was recaptured, and finally bound and gagged, and dragged away. The old duke recovered from his fright, and was helped up from the bed on to which he had sunk. As he prepared to leave, he approached the dead snake, and looked at it for some time. He kicked its mangled head with his ribboned shoe, and turned away laughing.

"Who knows," he said, "whether you were not the Snake Lady? That foolish boy made a great fuss, I remember, when he was scarcely out of long clothes, about a tattered old tapestry representing that repulsive story."

And he departed to supper.

XIII

Prince Alberic of Luna, who should have been third of his name, died a fortnight later, it was stated, insane. But those who approached him maintained that he had been in perfect possession of his faculties; and that if he refused all nourishment during his second imprisonment, it was from set purpose. He was removed at night from his apartments facing the grotto with the verde antique monkeys and the Porphyry Rhinoceros, and hastily buried under a slab, which remained without any name or date, in the famous mosaic sepulchral chapel.

Duke Balthasar Maria survived him only a few months. The old duke had plunged into excesses of debauchery with a view, apparently, to dismissing certain terrible thoughts and images which seemed to haunt him day and night, and against which no religious practices or medical prescription were of any avail. The origin of these painful delusions was probably connected with a very strange rumour, which grew to a tradition at Luna, to the effect that when the prison room, occupied by Prince Alberic, was cleaned, after that terrible storm of the 13th August of the year 1700, the persons employed found in a corner, not the dead grass-snake, which they had been ordered to cast into the palace drains, but the body of a woman, naked, and miserably disfigured with blows and sabre cuts.

Be this as it may, history records as certain, that the house of Luna became extinct in 1701, the duchy lapsing to the Empire. Moreover, that the mosaic chapel remained forever unfinished, with no statue save the green bronze and gold one of Balthasar Maria above the nameless slab covering Prince Alberic; and that the rockery also was never completed; only a few marble animals adorning it besides the Porphyry Rhinoceros and the verde antique apes, and the water supply being sufficient only for the greatest holidays. These things the traveller can confirm; also, that certain chairs and curtains in the porter's lodge of the now long deserted Red Palace are made of the various pieces of an extremely damaged arras, having represented the story of Alberic the Blond and the Snake Lady.

Madeline Yale Wynne (1847–1918) was an American metal worker and artisan and enthusiastically supported the arts and crafts movement. She founded both the Society of Deerfield Industries and Chicago Arts and Crafts Society. She often extolled the virtues of creative expression in articles and essays such as "Clay Paint and Other Wall Finishings" (1902), which was published in the magazine *House Beautiful*. In addition to writing, she had talent in metalworking, basket weaving, woodworking, and painting. "The Little Room," which first appeared in *Harper's Magazine*, was not her only creative publication, but it was Wynne's only story of any acclaim.

The Little Room

Madeline Yale Wynne

"HOW WOULD IT DO for a smoking-room?"

"Just the very place! only, you know, Roger, you must not think of smoking in the house. I am almost afraid that having just a plain, common man around, let alone a smoking man, will upset Aunt Hannah. She is New England—Vermont New England—boiled down."

"You leave Aunt Hannah to me; I'll find her tender side. I'm going to ask her about the old sea-captain and the yellow calico."

"Not yellow calico—blue chintz."

"Well, yellow *shell* then."

"No, no! don't mix it up so; you won't know yourself what to expect, and that's half the fun."

"Now you tell me again exactly what to expect; to tell the truth, I didn't half hear about it the other day; I was woolgathering. It was something queer that happened when you were a child, wasn't it?"

"Something that began to happen long before that, and kept happening, and may happen again; but I hope not."

"What was it?"

"I wonder if the other people in the car can hear us?"

"I fancy not; we don't hear them—not consecutively, at least."

"Well, mother was born in Vermont, you know; she was the only child by a second marriage. Aunt Hannah and Aunt Maria are only half-aunts to me, you know."

"I hope they are half as nice as you are."

"Roger, be still; they certainly will hear us."

"Well, don't you want them to know we are married?"

"Yes, but not just married. There's all the difference in the world."

"You are afraid we look too happy!"

"No; only I want my happiness all to myself."

"Well, the little room?"

"My aunts brought mother up; they were nearly twenty years older than she. I might say Hiram and they brought her up. You see, Hiram was bound out to my grandfather when he was a

321

boy, and when grandfather died Hiram said he 's'posed he went with the farm, long o' the critters,' and he has been there ever since. He was my mother's only refuge from the decorum of my aunts. They are simply workers. They make me think of the Maine woman who wanted her epitaph to be: 'She was a *hard* working woman.'"

"They must be almost beyond their working-days. How old are they?"

"Seventy, or thereabouts; but they will die standing; or, at least, on a Saturday night, after all the house-work is done up. They were rather strict with mother, and I think she had a lonely childhood. The house is almost a mile away from any neighbors, and off on top of what they call Stony Hill. It is bleak enough up there, even in summer.

"When mamma was about ten years old they sent her to cousins in Brooklyn, who had children of their own, and knew more about bringing them up. She staid there till she was married; she didn't go to Vermont in all that time, and of course hadn't seen her sisters, for they never would leave home for a day. They couldn't even be induced to go to Brooklyn to her wedding, so she and father took their wedding trip up there."

"And that's why we are going up there on our own?"

"Don't, Roger; you have no idea how loud you speak."

"You never say so except when I am going to say that one little word."

"Well, don't say it, then, or say it very, very quietly."

"Well, what was the queer thing?"

"When they got to the house, mother wanted to take father right off into the little room; she had been telling him about it, just as I am going to tell you, and she had said that of all the rooms, that one was the only one that seemed pleasant to her. She described the furniture and the books and paper and everything, and said it was on the north side, between the front and back room. Well, when they went to look for it, there was no little room there; there was only a shallow china-closet. She asked her sisters when the house had been altered and a closet made of the room that used to be there. They both said the house was exactly as it had been built—that they had never made any changes, except to tear down the old wood-shed and build a smaller one.

"Father and mother laughed a good deal over it, and when anything was lost they would always say it must be in the little room, and any exaggerated statement was called 'little-roomy.'

"When I was a child I thought that was a regular English phrase, I heard it so often.

"Well, they talked it over, and finally they concluded that my mother had been a very imaginative sort of a child, and had read in some book about such a little room, or perhaps even dreamed it, and then had 'made believe,' as children do, till she herself had really thought the room was there."

"Why, of course, that might easily happen."

"Yes, but you haven't heard the queer part yet; you wait and see if you can explain the rest as easily.

"They staid at the farm two weeks, and then went to New York to live. When I was eight years old my father was killed in the war, and mother was broken-hearted. She never was quite strong afterwards, and that summer we decided to go up to the farm for three months.

"I was a restless sort of a child, and the journey seemed very long to me; and finally, to pass the time, mamma told me the story of the little room, and how it was all in her own imagination, and how there really was only a china-closet there.

"She told it with all the particulars; and even to me, who knew beforehand that the room wasn't there, it seemed just as real as could be. She said it was on the north side, between the front and back rooms; that it was very small, and they sometimes called it an entry. There was a door also that opened out-of-doors, and that one was painted green, and was cut in the middle like the old Dutch doors, so that it could be used for a window by opening the top part only. Directly opposite the door was a lounge or couch; it was covered with blue chintz—India chintz—some that had been brought over by an old Salem sea-captain as a 'venture.' He had given it to Hannah when she was a young girl. She was sent to Salem for two years to school. Grandfather originally came from Salem."

"I thought there wasn't any room or chintz."

"*That is just it.* They had decided that mother had imagined it all, and yet you see how exactly everything was painted in her mind, for she had even remembered that Hiram had told her that Hannah could have married the sea-captain if she had wanted to!

"The India cotton was the regular blue stamped chintz, with the peacock figure on it. The head and body of the bird were in profile, while the tail was full front view behind it. It had seemed to take mamma's fancy, and she drew it for me on a piece of paper as she talked. Doesn't it seem strange to you that she could have made all that up, or even dreamed it?

"At the foot of the lounge were some hanging shelves with some old books on them. All the books were leather-colored except one; that was bright red, and was called the *Ladies' Album.* It made a bright break between the other thicker books.

"On the lower shelf was a beautiful pink sea-shell, lying on a mat made of balls of red shaded worsted. This shell was greatly coveted by mother, but she was only allowed to play with it when she had been particularly good. Hiram had shown her how to hold it close to her ear and hear the roar of the sea in it.

"I know you will like Hiram, Roger; he is quite a character in his way.

"Mamma said she remembered, or *thought* she remembered, having been sick once, and she had to lie quietly for some days on the lounge; then was the time she had become so familiar with everything in the room, and she had been allowed to have the shell to play with all the time. She had had her toast brought to her in there, with make-believe tea. It was one of her pleas-

ant memories of her childhood; it was the first time she had been of any importance to anybody, even herself.

"Right at the head of the lounge was a light-stand, as they called it, and on it was a very brightly polished brass candlestick and a brass tray, with snuffers. That is all I remember of her describing, except that there was a braided rag rug on the floor, and on the wall was a beautiful flowered paper—roses and morning-glories in a wreath on a light blue ground. The same paper was in the front room."

"And all this never existed except in her imagination?"

"She said that when she and father went up there, there wasn't any little room at all like it anywhere in the house; there was a china-closet where she had believed the room to be."

"And your aunts said there had never been any such room."

"That is what they said."

"Wasn't there any blue chintz in the house with a peacock figure?

"Not a scrap, and Aunt Hannah said there had never been any that she could remember; and Aunt Maria just echoed her—she always does that. You see, Aunt Hannah is an up-and-down New England woman. She looks just like herself; I mean, just like her character. Her joints move up and down or backward and forward in a plain square fashion. I don't believe she ever leaned on anything in her life, or sat in an easy-chair. But Maria is different; she is rounder and softer; she hasn't any ideas of her own; she never had any. I don't believe she would think it right or becoming to have one that differed from Aunt Hannah's, so what would be the use of having any? She is an echo, that's all.

"When mamma and I got there, of course I was all excitement to see the china-closet, and I had a sort of feeling that it would be the little room after all. So I ran ahead and threw open the door, crying, 'Come and see the little room.'

"And Roger," said Mrs. Grant, laying her hand in his, "there really was a little room there, exactly as mother had remembered it. There was the lounge, the peacock chintz, the green door, the shell, the morning-glory, and rose paper, *everything exactly as she had described it to me.*"

"What in the world did the sisters say about it?"

"Wait a minute and I will tell you. My mother was in the front hall still talking with Aunt Hannah. She didn't hear me at first, but I ran out there and dragged her through the front room, saying, 'The room *is* here—it is all right.'

"It seemed for a minute as if my mother would faint. She clung to me in terror. I can remember now how strained her eyes looked and how pale she was.

"I called out to Aunt Hannah and asked her when they had had the closet taken away and the little room built; for in my excitement I thought that that was what had been done.

"'That little room has always been there,' said Aunt Hannah, 'ever since the house was built.'

"'But mamma said there wasn't any little room here, only a china-closet, when she was here with papa,' said I.

"'No, there has never been any china-closet there; it has always been just as it is now,' said Aunt Hannah.

"Then mother spoke; her voice sounded weak and far off. She said, slowly, and with an effort, 'Maria, don't you remember that you told me that there had *never been any little room here*? and Hannah said so too, and then I said I must have dreamed it?'

"'No, I don't remember anything of the kind,' said Maria, without the slightest emotion. 'I don't remember you ever said anything about any china-closet. The house has never been altered; you used to play in this room when you were a child, don't you remember?'

"'I know it,' said mother, in that queer slow voice that made me feel frightened. 'Hannah, don't you remember my finding the china-closet here, with the gilt-edged china on the shelves, and then *you* said that the *china-closet* had always been here?'

"'No,' said Hannah, pleasantly but unemotionally—'no, I don't think you ever asked me about any china-closet, and we haven't any gilt-edged china that I know of.'

"And that was the strangest thing about it. We never could make them remember that there had ever been any question about it. You would think they could remember how surprised mother had been before, unless she had imagined the whole thing. Oh, it was so queer! They were always pleasant about it, but they didn't seem to feel any interest or curiosity. It was always this answer: 'The house is just as it was built; there have never been any changes, so far as we know.'

"And my mother was in an agony of perplexity. How cold their gray eyes looked to me! There was no reading anything in them. It just seemed to break my mother down, this queer thing. Many times that summer, in the middle of the night, I have seen her get up and take a candle and creep softly downstairs. I could hear the steps creak under her weight. Then she would go through the front room and peer into the darkness, holding her thin hand between the candle and her eyes. She seemed to think the little room might vanish. Then she would come back to bed and toss about all night, or lie still and shiver; it used to frighten me.

"She grew pale and thin, and she had a little cough; then she did not like to be left alone. Sometimes she would make errands in order to send me to the little room for something—a book, or her fan, or her handkerchief; but she would never sit there or let me stay in there long, and sometimes she wouldn't let me go in there for days together. Oh, it was pitiful!"

"Well, don't talk any more about it, Margaret, if it makes you feel so," said Mr. Grant.

"Oh yes, I want you to know all about it, and there isn't much more—no more about the room.

"Mother never got well, and she died that autumn. She used often to sigh, and say, with a wan little laugh, 'There is one thing I am glad of, Margaret: your father knows now all about the little room.' I think she was afraid I distrusted her. Of course, in a child's way, I thought there was something queer about it, but I did not brood over it. I was too young then, and took it as a part of her illness. But, Roger, do you know, it really did affect me. I almost hate to go there after talking about it; I somehow feel as if it might, you know, be a china-closet again."

"That's an absurd idea."

"I know it; of course it can't be. I saw the room, and there isn't any china-closet there, and no gilt-edged china in the house, either."

And then she whispered: "But, Roger, you may hold my hand as you do now, if you will, when we go to look for the little room."

"And you won't mind Aunt Hannah's gray eyes?"

"I won't mind *anything*."

It was dusk when Mr. and Mrs. Grant went into the gate under the two old Lombardy poplars and walked up the narrow path to the door, where they were met by the two aunts.

Hannah gave Mrs. Grant a frigid but not unfriendly kiss; and Maria seemed for a moment to tremble on the verge of an emotion, but she glanced at Hannah, and then gave her greeting in exactly the same repressed and noncommittal way.

Supper was waiting for them. On the table was the *gilt-edged china*. Mrs. Grant didn't notice it immediately, till she saw her husband smiling at her over his teacup; then she felt fidgety, and couldn't eat. She was nervous, and kept wondering what was behind her, whether it would be a little room or a closet.

After supper she offered to help about the dishes, but, mercy! she might as well have offered to help bring the seasons round; Maria and Hannah couldn't be helped.

So she and her husband went to find the little room, or closet, or whatever was to be there.

Aunt Maria followed them, carrying the lamp, which she set down, and then went back to the dish-washing.

Margaret looked at her husband. He kissed her, for she seemed troubled; and then, hand in hand, they opened the door. It opened into a *china-closet*. The shelves were neatly draped with scalloped paper; on them was the gilt-edged china, with the dishes missing that had been used at the supper, and which at that moment were being carefully washed and wiped by the two aunts.

Margaret's husband dropped her hand and looked at her. She was trembling a little, and turned to him for help, for some explanation, but in an instant she knew that something was wrong. A cloud had come between them; he was hurt; he was antagonized.

He paused for an appreciable instant, and then said, kindly enough, but in a voice that cut her deeply: "I am glad this ridiculous thing is ended; don't let us speak of it again."

"Ended!" said she. "How ended?" And somehow her voice sounded to her as her mother's voice had when she stood there and questioned her sisters about the little room. She seemed to have to drag her words out. She spoke slowly: "It seems to me to have only just begun in my case. It was just so with mother when she—"

"I really wish, Margaret, you would let it drop. I don't like to hear you speak of your mother in connection with it. It—" He hesitated, for was not this their wedding-day? "It doesn't seem quite the thing, quite delicate, you know, to use her name in the matter."

She saw it all now: *he didn't believe her.* She felt a chill sense of withering under his glance.

"Come," he added, "let us go out, or into the dining-room, somewhere, anywhere, only drop this nonsense."

He went out; he did not take her hand now—he was vexed, baffled, hurt. Had he not given her his sympathy, his attention, his belief—and his hand?—and she was fooling him. What did it mean?—she so truthful, so free from morbidness—a thing he hated. He walked up and down under the poplars, trying to get into the mood to go and join her in the house.

Margaret heard him go out; then she turned and shook the shelves; she reached her hand behind them and tried to push the boards away; she ran out of the house on to the north side and tried to find in the darkness, with her hands, a door, or some steps leading to one. She tore her dress on the old rose-trees, she fell and rose and stumbled, then she sat down on the ground and tried to think. What could she think—was she dreaming?

She went into the house and out into the kitchen, and begged Aunt Maria to tell her about the little room—what had become of it, when had they built the closet, when had they bought the gilt-edged china?

They went on washing dishes and drying them on the spotless towels with methodical exactness; and as they worked they said that there had never been any little room, so far as they knew; the china-closet had always been there, and the gilt-edged china had belonged to their mother, it had always been in the house.

"No, I don't remember that your mother ever asked about any little room," said Hannah. "She didn't seem very well that summer, but she never asked about any changes in the house; there hadn't ever been any changes."

There it was again: not a sign of interest, curiosity, or annoyance, not a spark of memory.

She went out to Hiram. He was telling Mr. Grant about the farm. She had meant to ask him about the room, but her lips were sealed before her husband.

Months afterwards, when time had lessened the sharpness of their feelings, they learned to speculate reasonably about the phenomenon, which Mr. Grant had accepted as something not to be scoffed away, not to be treated as a poor joke, but to be put aside as something inexplicable on any ordinary theory.

Margaret alone in her heart knew that her mother's words carried a deeper significance than she had dreamed of at the time. "One thing I am glad of, your father knows now," and she wondered if Roger or she would ever know.

Five years later they were going to Europe. The packing was done; the children were lying asleep, with their travelling things ready to be slipped on for an early start.

Roger had a foreign appointment. They were not to be back in America for some years. She had meant to go up to say good-by to her aunts; but a mother of three children intends to do a great many things that never get done. One thing she had done that very day, and as she paused for a moment between the writing of two notes that must be posted before she went to bed, she said:

"Roger, you remember Rita Lash? Well, she and Cousin Nan go up to the Adirondacks every autumn. They are clever girls, and I have intrusted to them something I want done very much."

"They are the girls to do it, then, every inch of them."

"I know it, and they are going to."

"Well?"

"Why, you see, Roger, that little room—"

"Oh—"

"Yes, I was a coward not to go myself, but I didn't find time, because I hadn't the courage."

"Oh! *that* was it, was it?"

"Yes, just that. They are going, and they will write us about it."

"Want to bet?"

"No; I only want to know."

Rita Lash and Cousin Nan planned to go to Vermont on their way to the Adirondacks. They found they would have three hours between trains, which would give them time to drive up to the Keys farm, and they could still get to the camp that night. But, at the last minute, Rita was prevented from going. Nan had to go to meet the Adirondack party, and she promised to telegraph her when she arrived at the camp. Imagine Rita's amusement when she received this message: "Safely arrived; went to the Keys farm; it is a little room."

Rita was amused, because she did not in the least think Nan had been there. She thought it was a hoax; but it put it into her mind to carry the joke further by really stopping herself when she went up, as she meant to do the next week.

She did stop over. She introduced herself to the two maiden ladies, who seemed familiar, as they had been described by Mrs. Grant.

They were, if not cordial, at least not disconcerted at her visit, and willingly showed her over the house. As they did not speak of any other stranger's having been to see them lately, she became confirmed in her belief that Nan had not been there.

In the north room she saw the roses and morning-glory paper on the wall, and also the door that should open into—what?

She asked if she might open it.

"Certainly," said Hannah; and Maria echoed, "Certainly."

She opened it, and found the china-closet. She experienced a certain relief; she at least was not under any spell. Mrs. Grant left it a china-closet; she found it the same. Good.

But she tried to induce the old sisters to remember that there had at various times been certain questions relating to a confusion as to whether the closet had always been a closet. It was no use; their stony eyes gave no sign.

Then she thought of the story of the sea-captain, and said, "Miss Keys, did you ever have a lounge covered with India chintz, with a figure of a peacock on it, given to you in Salem by a sea-captain, who brought it from India?"

"I dun'no' as I ever did," said Hannah. That was all. She thought Maria's cheeks were a little flushed, but her eyes were like a stone wall.

She went on that night to the Adirondacks. When Nan and she were alone in their room she said, "By-the-way, Nan, what did you see at the farmhouse? and how did you like Maria and Hannah?"

Nan didn't mistrust that Rita had been there, and she began excitedly to tell her all about her visit. Rita could almost have believed Nan had been there if she hadn't known it was not so. She let her go on for some time, enjoying her enthusiasm, and the impressive way in which she described her opening the door and finding the "little room." Then Rita said: "Now, Nan, that is

enough fibbing. I went to the farm myself on my way up yesterday, and there is *no* little room, and there *never* has been any; it is a china-closet, just as Mrs. Grant saw it last."

She was pretending to be busy unpacking her trunk, and did not look up for a moment; but as Nan did not say anything, she glanced at her over her shoulder. Nan was actually pale, and it was hard to say whether she was most angry or frightened. There was something of both in her look. And then Rita began to explain how her telegram had put her in the spirit of going up there alone. She hadn't meant to cut Nan out. She only thought—Then Nan broke in: "It isn't that; I am sure you can't think it is that. But I went myself, and you did not go; you can't have been there, for *it is a little room.*"

Oh, what a night they had! They couldn't sleep. They talked and argued, and then kept still for a while, only to break out again, it was so absurd. They both maintained that they had been there, but both felt sure the other one was either crazy or obstinate beyond reason. They were wretched; it was perfectly ridiculous, two friends at odds over such a thing; but there it was—"little room," "china-closet,"—"china-closet," "little room."

The next morning Nan was tacking up some tarlatan at a window to keep the midges out. Rita offered to help her, as she had done for the past ten years. Nan's "No, thanks," cut her to the heart.

"Nan," said she, "come right down from that stepladder and pack your satchel. The stage leaves in just twenty minutes. We can catch the afternoon express train, and we will go together to the farm. I am either going there or going home. You better go with me."

Nan didn't say a word. She gathered up the hammer and tacks, and was ready to start when the stage came round.

It meant for them thirty miles of staging and six hours of train, besides crossing the lake; but what of that, compared with having a lie lying round loose between them! Europe would have seemed easy to accomplish, if it would settle the question.

At the little junction in Vermont they found a farmer with a wagon full of meal-bags. They asked him if he could not take them up to the old Keys farm and bring them back in time for the return train, due in two hours.

They had planned to call it a sketching trip, so they said, "We have been there before, we are artists, and we might find some views worth taking; and we want also to make a short call upon the Misses Keys."

"Did ye calculate to paint the old *house* in the picture?"

They said it was possible they might do so. They wanted to see it, anyway.

"Waal, I guess you are too late. The *house* burnt down last night, and everything in it."

Herbert George Wells (1866–1946) was an English novelist and sociologist who became one of the most preeminent writers of his time. His first science fiction novel was *The Time Machine* (1895), which demonstrated his originality and is still somewhat edgy to this day. Wells was so prolific and convincing during his career that some believed that his inventions were actually predictions of the future, but his novel *The War of the Worlds* (1898) also laid the foundation for the Martian space invader trope. Of course, he wrote fantasy as well, and "The Plattner Story" was first published in a collection simply titled *The Plattner Story and Others* in 1897.

The Plattner Story

H. G. Wells

WHETHER THE STORY of Gottfried Plattner is to be credited or not, is a pretty question in the value of evidence. On the one hand, we have seven witnesses—to be perfectly exact, we have six and a half pairs of eyes, and one undeniable fact; and on the other we have—what is it?—prejudice, common sense, the inertia of opinion. Never were there seven more honest-seeming witnesses; never was there a more undeniable fact than the inversion of Gottfried Plattner's anatomical structure, and—never was there a more preposterous story than the one they have to tell! The most preposterous part of the story is the worthy Gottfried's contribution (for I count him as one of the seven). Heaven forbid that I should be led into giving countenance to superstition by a passion for impartiality, and so come to share the fate of Eusapia's patrons! Frankly, I believe there is something crooked about this business of Gottfried Plattner; but what that crooked factor is, I will admit as frankly, I do not know. I have been surprised at the credit accorded to the story in the most unexpected and authoritative quarters. The fairest way to the reader, however, will be for me to tell it without further comment.

Gottfried Plattner is, in spite of his name, a free-born Englishman. His father was an Alsatian who came to England in the Sixties, married a respectable English girl of unexceptionable antecedents, and died, after a wholesome and uneventful life (devoted, I understand, chiefly to the laying of parquet flooring), in 1887. Gottfried's age is seven-and-twenty. He is, by virtue of his heritage of three languages, Modern Languages Master in a small private school in the South of England. To the casual observer he is singularly like any other Modern Languages Master in any other small private school. His costume is neither very costly nor very fashionable, but, on the other hand, it is not markedly cheap or shabby; his complexion, like his height and his bearing, is inconspicuous. You would notice, perhaps, that, like the majority of people, his face was not absolutely symmetrical, his right eye a little larger than the left, and his jaw a trifle heavier on the right side. If you, as an ordinary careless person, were to bare his chest and feel his heart beating, you would probably find it quite like the heart of anyone else. But here you and the trained observer would part company. If you found his heart quite ordinary, the trained observer would find it quite otherwise. And once the thing was pointed out to you, you too would perceive the peculiarity easily enough. It is that Gottfried's heart beats on the right side of his body.

Now, that is not the only singularity of Gottfried's structure, although it is the only one that would appeal to the untrained mind. Careful sounding of Gottfried's internal arrangements, by a well-known surgeon, seems to point to the fact that all the other unsymmetrical parts of his body are similarly misplaced. The right lobe of his liver is on the left side, the left on his right; while his lungs, too, are similarly contraposed. What is still more singular, unless Gottfried is a consummate actor, we must believe that his right hand has recently become his left. Since the occurrences we are about to consider (as impartially as possible), he has found the utmost difficulty in writing, except from right to left across the paper with his left hand. He cannot throw with his right hand, he is perplexed at meal times between knife and fork, and his ideas of the rule of the road—he is a cyclist—are still a dangerous confusion. And there is not a scrap of evidence to show that before these occurrences Gottfried was at all left-handed.

There is yet another wonderful fact in this preposterous business. Gottfried produces three photographs of himself. You have him at the age of five or six, thrusting fat legs at you from under a plaid frock, and scowling. In that photograph his left eye is a little larger than his right, and his jaw is a trifle heavier on the left side. This is the reverse of his present living conditions. The photograph of Gottfried at fourteen seems to contradict these facts, but that is because it is one of those cheap "Gem" photographs that were then in vogue, taken direct upon metal, and therefore reversing things just as a looking-glass would. The third photograph represents him at one-and-twenty, and confirms the record of the others. There seems here evidence of the strongest confirmatory character that Gottfried has exchanged his left side for his right. Yet how a human being can be so changed, short of a fantastic and pointless miracle, it is exceedingly hard to suggest.

In one way, of course, these facts might be explicable on the supposition that Plattner has undertaken an elaborate mystification, on the strength of his heart's displacement. Photographs may be fudged, and left-handedness imitated. But the character of the man does not lend itself to any such theory. He is quiet, practical, unobtrusive, and thoroughly sane, from the Nordau standpoint. He likes beer, and smokes moderately, takes walking exercise daily, and has a healthily high estimate of the value of his teaching. He has a good but untrained tenor voice, and takes a pleasure in singing airs of a popular and cheerful character. He is fond, but not morbidly fond, of reading,—chiefly fiction pervaded with a vaguely pious optimism,—sleeps well, and rarely dreams. He is, in fact, the very last person to evolve a fantastic fable. Indeed, so far from forcing this story upon the world, he has been singularly reticent on the matter. He meets inquirers with a certain engaging—bashfulness is almost the word, that disarms the most suspicious. He seems genuinely ashamed that anything so unusual has occurred to him.

It is to be regretted that Plattner's aversion to the idea of post-mortem dissection may postpone, perhaps for ever, the positive proof that his entire body has had its left and right sides transposed. Upon that fact mainly the credibility of his story hangs. There is no way of taking a man and moving him about *in space*, as ordinary people understand space, that will result in our changing his sides. Whatever you do, his right is still his right, his left his left. You can do that with a perfectly thin and flat thing, of course. If you were to cut a figure out of paper, any figure with a right and left side, you could change its sides simply by lifting it up and turning it over. But with a solid it is different. Mathematical theorists tell us that the only way in which the right and left sides of a solid body can be changed is by taking that body clean out of space as we know it,—taking it out of ordinary existence, that is, and turning it somewhere outside space. This is a little abstruse, no doubt, but anyone with any knowledge of mathematical theory will assure the reader of its truth. To put the thing in technical language, the curious inversion of Plattner's right and left sides is proof that he has moved out of our space into what is called the Fourth Dimension, and that he has returned again to our world. Unless we choose to consider ourselves the victims of an elaborate and motiveless fabrication, we are almost bound to believe that this has occurred.

So much for the tangible facts. We come now to the account of the phenomena that attended his temporary disappearance from the world. It appears that in the Sussexville Proprietary School, Plattner not only discharged the duties of Modern Languages Master, but also taught chemistry, commercial geography, book-keeping, shorthand, drawing, and any other additional subject to which the changing fancies of the boys' parents might direct attention. He knew little or nothing of these various subjects, but in secondary as distinguished from Board or elementary schools, knowledge in the teacher is, very properly, by no means so necessary as high moral character and gentlemanly tone. In chemistry he was particularly deficient, knowing, he says, nothing beyond the Three Gases (whatever the three gases may be). As, however, his pupils began by knowing nothing, and derived all their information from him, this caused him (or anyone) but little inconvenience for several terms. Then a little boy named Whibble joined the school, who had been educated (it seems) by some mischievous relative into an inquiring habit of mind. This little boy followed Plattner's lessons with marked and sustained interest, and in order to exhibit his zeal on the subject, brought, at various times, substances for Plattner to analyse. Plattner, flattered by this evidence of his power of awakening interest, and trusting to the boy's ignorance, analysed these, and even made general statements as to their composition. Indeed, he was so far stimulated by his pupil as to obtain a work upon analytical chemistry, and study it during his supervision of the evening's preparation. He was surprised to find chemistry quite an interesting subject.

So far the story is absolutely commonplace. But now the greenish powder comes upon the scene. The source of that greenish powder seems, unfortunately, lost. Master Whibble tells a tortuous story of finding it done up in a packet in a disused limekiln near the Downs. It would have been an excellent thing for Plattner, and possibly for Master Whibble's family, if a match could have been applied to that powder there and then. The young gentleman certainly did not bring it to school in a packet, but in a common eight-ounce graduated medicine bottle, plugged with masticated newspaper. He gave it to Plattner at the end of the afternoon school. Four boys had been detained after school prayers in order to complete some neglected tasks, and Plattner was supervising these in the small classroom in which the chemical teaching was conducted. The appliances for the practical teaching of chemistry in the Sussexville Proprietary School, as in most small schools in this country, are characterised by a severe simplicity. They are kept in a small cupboard standing in a recess, and having about the same capacity as a common travelling trunk. Plattner, being bored with his passive superintendence, seems to have welcomed the intervention of Whibble with his green powder as an agreeable diversion, and, unlocking this cupboard, proceeded at once with his analytical experiments. Whibble sat, luckily for himself, at a safe distance, regarding him. The four malefactors, feigning a profound absorption in their work, watched him furtively with the keenest interest. For even within the limits of the Three Gases, Plattner's practical chemistry was, I understand, temerarious.

They are practically unanimous in their account of Plattner's proceedings. He poured a little of the green powder into a test-tube, and tried the substance with water, hydrochloric acid, nitric acid, and sulphuric acid in succession. Getting no result, he emptied out a little heap—nearly half the bottleful, in fact—upon a slate and tried a match. He held the medicine bottle in his left hand. The stuff began to smoke and melt, and then—exploded with deafening violence and a blinding flash.

The five boys, seeing the flash and being prepared for catastrophes, ducked below their desks, and were none of them seriously hurt. The window was blown out into the playground, and the blackboard on its easel was upset. The slate was smashed to atoms. Some plaster fell from the ceiling. No other damage was done to the school edifice or appliances, and the boys at first, seeing nothing of Plattner, fancied he was knocked down and lying out of their sight below the desks. They jumped out of their places to go to his assistance, and were amazed to find the space empty. Being still confused by the sudden violence of the report, they hurried to the open door, under the impression that he must have been hurt, and have rushed out of the room. But Carson, the foremost, nearly collided in the doorway with the principal, Mr. Lidgett.

Mr. Lidgett is a corpulent, excitable man with one eye. The boys describe him as stumbling into the room mouthing some of those tempered expletives irritable schoolmasters accustom themselves to use—lest worse befall. "Wretched mumchancer!" he said. "Where's Mr. Plattner?" The boys are agreed on the very words. ("Wobbler," "snivelling puppy," and "mumchancer" are, it seems, among the ordinary small change of Mr. Lidgett's scholastic commerce.)

Where's Mr. Plattner? That was a question that was to be repeated many times in the next few days. It really seemed as though that frantic hyperbole, "blown to atoms," had for once realised itself. There was not a visible particle of Plattner to be seen; not a drop of blood nor a stitch of clothing to be found. Apparently he had been blown clean out of existence and left not a wrack behind. Not so much as would cover a sixpenny piece, to quote a proverbial expression! The evidence of his absolute disappearance, as a consequence of that explosion, is indubitable.

It is not necessary to enlarge here upon the commotion excited in the Sussexville Proprietary School, and in Sussexville and elsewhere, by this event. It is quite possible, indeed, that some of the readers of these pages may recall the hearing of some remote and dying version of that excitement during the last summer holidays. Lidgett, it would seem, did everything in his power to suppress and minimise the story. He instituted a penalty of twenty-five lines for any mention of Plattner's name among the boys, and stated in the schoolroom that he was clearly aware of his assistant's whereabouts. He was afraid, he explains, that the possibility of an explosion happening, in spite of the elaborate precautions taken to minimise the practical teaching of chemistry, might injure the reputation of the school; and so might any mysterious quality in Plattner's departure. Indeed, he did everything in his power to make the occurrence seem as ordinary as possible. In particular, he cross-examined the five eye-witnesses of the occurrence so searchingly that they began to doubt the plain evidence of their senses. But, in spite of these efforts, the tale, in a magnified and distorted state, made a nine days' wonder in the district, and several parents withdrew their sons on colourable pretexts. Not the least remarkable point in the matter is the fact that a large number of people in the neighbourhood dreamed singularly vivid dreams of Plattner during the period of excitement before his return, and that these dreams had a curious uniformity. In almost all of them Plattner was seen, sometimes singly, sometimes in company, wandering about through a coruscating iridescence. In all cases his face was pale and distressed, and in some he gesticulated towards the dreamer. One or two of the boys, evidently under the influence of nightmare, fancied that Plattner approached them with remarkable swiftness, and seemed to look closely into their very eyes. Others fled with Plattner from the pursuit of vague and extraordinary creatures of a globular shape. But all these fancies were forgotten in inquiries and specula-tions when, on the Wednesday next but one after the Monday of the explosion, Plattner returned.

The circumstances of his return were as sin-gular as those of his departure. So far as Mr. Lidgett's somewhat choleric outline can be filled in from Plattner's hesitating statements, it would appear that on Wednesday evening, towards the hour of sunset, the former gentleman, having dismissed evening preparation, was engaged in his garden, picking and eating strawberries, a fruit of which he is inordinately fond. It is a large old-fashioned garden, secured from obser-vation, fortunately, by a high and ivy-covered red-brick wall. Just as he was stooping over a particularly prolific plant, there was a flash in the air and a heavy thud, and before he could look round, some heavy body struck him violently from behind. He was pitched forward, crushing the strawberries he held in his hand, and that so roughly, that his silk hat—Mr. Lidgett adheres to the older ideas of scholastic costume—was driven violently down upon his forehead, and almost over one eye. This heavy missile, which slid over him sideways and collapsed into a sit-ting posture among the strawberry plants, proved to be our long-lost Mr. Gottfried Plattner, in an extremely dishevelled condition. He was collar-less and hatless, his linen was dirty, and there was blood upon his hands. Mr. Lidgett was so indig-nant and surprised that he remained on all-fours, and with his hat jammed down on his eye, while he expostulated vehemently with Plattner for his disrespectful and unaccountable conduct.

This scarcely idyllic scene completes what I may call the exterior version of the Plattner story—its exoteric aspect. It is quite unneces-sary to enter here into all the details of his dis-missal by Mr. Lidgett. Such details, with the full names and dates and references, will be found in the larger report of these occurrences that was laid before the Society for the Investigation of Abnormal Phenomena. The singular transposi-tion of Plattner's right and left sides was scarcely observed for the first day or so, and then first in connection with his disposition to write from right to left across the blackboard. He concealed rather than ostended this curious confirmatory circumstance, as he considered it would unfa-vourably affect his prospects in a new situation. The displacement of his heart was discovered some months after, when he was having a tooth extracted under anæsthetics. He then, very unwillingly, allowed a cursory surgical examina-tion to be made of himself, with a view to a brief account in the *Journal of Anatomy*. That exhausts the statement of the material facts; and we may now go on to consider Plattner's account of the matter.

But first let us clearly differentiate between the preceding portion of this story and what is to follow. All I have told thus far is established by such evidence as even a criminal lawyer would approve. Every one of the witnesses is still alive; the reader, if he have the leisure, may hunt the lads out tomorrow, or even brave the terrors of the redoubtable Lidgett, and cross-examine and trap and test to his heart's content; Gottfried Plattner, himself, and his twisted heart and his three photographs are producible. It may be taken as proved that he did disappear for nine days as the consequence of an explosion; that he returned almost as violently, under circumstances in their nature annoying to Mr. Lidgett, what-ever the details of those circumstances may be; and that he returned inverted, just as a reflection returns from a mirror. From the last fact, as I have already stated, it follows almost inevitably that Plattner, during those nine days, must have been in some state of existence altogether out of space. The evidence to these statements is, indeed, far stronger than that upon which most murderers are hanged. But for his own particular account of where he had been, with its confused expla-nations and well-nigh self-contradictory details, we have only Mr. Gottfried Plattner's word. I do not wish to discredit that, but I must point out—what so many writers upon obscure psychic phe-nomena fail to do—that we are passing here from the practically undeniable to that kind of matter which any reasonable man is entitled to believe or reject as he thinks proper. The previous statements render it plausible; its discordance with common experience tilts it towards the incredible. I would prefer not to sway the beam of the reader's judgment either way, but simply to tell the story as Plattner told it me.

He gave me his narrative, I may state, at my house at Chislehurst, and so soon as he had left me that evening, I went into my study and wrote down everything as I remembered it. Subsequently he was good enough to read over a typewritten copy, so that its substantial correctness is undeniable.

He states that at the moment of the explosion he distinctly thought he was killed. He felt lifted off his feet and driven forcibly backward. It is a curious fact for psychologists that he thought clearly during his backward flight, and wondered whether he should hit the chemistry cupboard or the blackboard easel. His heels struck ground, and he staggered and fell heavily into a sitting position on something soft and firm. For a moment the concussion stunned him. He became aware at once of a vivid scent of singed hair, and he seemed to hear the voice of Lidgett asking for him. You will understand that for a time his mind was greatly confused.

At first he was distinctly under the impression that he was still in the classroom. He perceived quite distinctly the surprise of the boys and the entry of Mr. Lidgett. He is quite positive upon that score. He did not hear their remarks; but that he ascribed to the deafening effect of the experiment. Things about him seemed curiously dark and faint, but his mind explained that on the obvious but mistaken idea that the explosion had engendered a huge volume of dark smoke. Through the dimness the figures of Lidgett and the boys moved, as faint and silent as ghosts. Plattner's face still tingled with the stinging heat of the flash. He was, he says, "all muddled." His first definite thoughts seem to have been of his personal safety. He thought he was perhaps blinded and deafened. He felt his limbs and face in a gingerly manner. Then his perceptions grew clearer, and he was astonished to miss the old familiar desks and other schoolroom fur-

niture about him. Only dim, uncertain, grey shapes stood in the place of these. Then came a thing that made him shout aloud, and awoke his stunned faculties to instant activity. *Two of the boys, gesticulating, walked one after the other clean through him!* Neither manifested the slightest consciousness of his presence. It is difficult to imagine the sensation he felt. They came against him, he says, with no more force than a wisp of mist.

Plattner's first thought after that was that he was dead. Having been brought up with thoroughly sound views in these matters, however, he was a little surprised to find his body still about him. His second conclusion was that he was not dead, but that the others were: that the explosion had destroyed the Sussexville Proprietary School and every soul in it except himself. But that, too, was scarcely satisfactory. He was thrown back upon astonished observation.

Everything about him was extraordinarily dark: at first it seemed to have an altogether ebony blackness. Overhead was a black firmament. The only touch of light in the scene was a faint greenish glow at the edge of the sky in one direction, which threw into prominence a horizon of undulating black hills. This, I say, was his impression at first. As his eye grew accustomed to the darkness, he began to distinguish a faint quality of differentiating greenish colour in the circumambient night. Against this background the furniture and occupants of the classroom, it seems, stood out like phosphorescent spectres, faint and impalpable. He extended his hand, and thrust it without an effort through the wall of the room by the fireplace.

He describes himself as making a strenuous effort to attract attention. He shouted to Lidgett, and tried to seize the boys as they went to and fro. He only desisted from these attempts when Mrs. Lidgett, whom he (as an Assistant Master) naturally disliked, entered the room. He says the sensation of being in the world, and yet not a part of it, was an extraordinarily disagreeable one. He compared his feelings, not inaptly, to those of a cat watching a mouse through a window. Whenever he made a motion to communicate with the dim, familiar world about him, he found an invisible, incomprehensible barrier preventing intercourse.

He then turned his attention to his solid environment. He found the medicine bottle still unbroken in his hand, with the remainder of the green powder therein. He put this in his pocket, and began to feel about him. Apparently, he was sitting on a boulder of rock covered with a velvety moss. The dark country about him he was unable to see, the faint, misty picture of the schoolroom blotting it out, but he had a feeling (due perhaps to a cold wind) that he was near the crest of a hill, and that a steep valley fell away beneath his feet. The green glow along the edge of the sky seemed to be growing in extent and intensity. He stood up, rubbing his eyes.

It would seem that he made a few steps, going steeply down hill, and then stumbled, nearly fell, and sat down again upon a jagged mass of rock to watch the dawn. He became aware that the world about him was absolutely silent. It was as still as it was dark, and though there was a cold wind blowing up the hill-face, the rustle of grass, the soughing of the boughs that should have accompanied it, were absent. He could hear, therefore, if he could not see, that the hillside upon which he stood was rocky and desolate. The green grew brighter every moment, and as it did so a faint, transparent blood-red mingled with, but did not mitigate, the blackness of the sky overhead and the rocky desolations about him. Having regard to what follows, I am inclined to think that that redness may have been an optical effect due to contrast. Something black fluttered momentarily against the livid yellow-green of the lower sky, and then the thin and penetrating voice of a bell rose out of the black gulf below him. An oppressive expectation grew with the growing light.

It is probable that an hour or more elapsed while he sat there, the strange green light growing brighter every moment, and spreading slowly, in flamboyant fingers, upward towards the zenith. As it grew, the spectral vision of *our* world became relatively or absolutely fainter. Probably both, for the time must have been about that of our earthly sunset. So far as his vision of our world went, Plattner, by his few steps downhill, had passed through the floor of the classroom, and was now, it seemed, sitting in mid-air in the larger schoolroom downstairs. He saw the boarders distinctly, but much more faintly than he had seen Lidgett. They were preparing their evening tasks, and he noticed with interest that several were cheating with their Euclid riders by means of a crib, a compilation whose existence he had hitherto never suspected. As the time passed, they faded steadily, as steadily as the light of the green dawn increased.

Looking down into the valley, he saw that the light had crept far down its rocky sides, and that the profound blackness of the abyss was now broken by a minute green glow, like the light of a glow-worm. And almost immediately the limb of a huge heavenly body of blazing green rose over the basaltic undulations of the distant hills, and the monstrous hill-masses about him came out gaunt and desolate, in green light and deep, ruddy black shadows. He became aware of a vast number of ball-shaped objects drifting as thistledown drifts over the high ground. There were none of these nearer to him than the opposite side of the gorge. The bell below twanged quicker and quicker, with something like impatient insistence, and several lights moved hither and thither. The boys at work at their desks were now almost imperceptibly faint.

This extinction of our world, when the green sun of this other universe rose, is a curious point upon which Plattner insists. During the Other-World night it is difficult to move about, on account of the vividness with which the things of this world are visible. It becomes a riddle to explain why, if this is the case, we in this world catch no glimpse of the Other-World. It is due, perhaps, to the comparatively vivid illumination of this world of ours. Plattner describes the midday of the Other-World, at its brightest, as not being nearly so bright as this world at full moon, while its night is profoundly black. Consequently, the amount of light, even in an ordinary dark room, is sufficient to render the things of the Other-World invisible, on the same principle that faint phosphorescence is only visible in the profoundest darkness. I have tried, since he told me his story, to see something of the Other-World by sitting for a long space in a photographer's dark room at night. I have certainly seen indistinctly the form of greenish slopes and rocks, but only, I must admit, very indistinctly indeed. The reader may possibly be more successful. Plattner tells me that since his return he has dreamt and seen and recognised places in the Other-World, but this is probably due to his memory of these scenes. It seems quite possible that people with unusually keen eyesight may occasionally catch a glimpse of this strange Other-World about us.

However, this is a digression. As the green sun rose, a long street of black buildings became perceptible, though only darkly and indistinctly, in the gorge, and, after some hesitation, Plattner began to clamber down the precipitous descent towards them. The descent was long and exceedingly tedious, being so not only by the extraordinary steepness, but also by reason of the looseness of the boulders with which the whole face of the hill was strewn. The noise of his descent—now and then his heels struck fire from the rocks— seemed now the only sound in the universe, for the beating of the bell had ceased. As he drew nearer, he perceived that the various edifices had a singular resemblance to tombs and mausoleums and monuments, saving only that they were all uniformly black instead of being white, as most sepulchres are. And then he saw, crowding out of the largest building, very much as people disperse from church, a number of pallid, rounded, pale-green figures. These dispersed in several directions about the broad street of the place, some going through side alleys and reappearing upon the steepness of the hill, others entering some of the small black buildings which lined the way.

At the sight of these things drifting up towards him, Plattner stopped, staring. They were not walking, they were indeed limbless, and they had the appearance of human heads, beneath which a tadpole-like body swung. He was too astonished at their strangeness, too full, indeed, of strangeness, to be seriously alarmed by them. They drove towards him, in front of the chill wind that was blowing uphill, much as soap-bubbles drive before a draught. And as he looked at the nearest of those approaching, he saw it was indeed a human head, albeit with singularly large eyes, and wearing such an expression of distress and anguish as he had never seen before upon mortal countenance. He was surprised to find that it did not turn to regard him, but seemed to be watching and following some unseen moving thing. For a moment he was puzzled, and then it occurred to him that this creature was watching with its enormous eyes something that was happening in the world he had just left. Nearer it came, and nearer, and he was too astonished to cry out. It made a very faint fretting sound as it came close to him. Then it struck his face with a gentle pat— its touch was very cold—and drove past him, and upward towards the crest of the hill.

An extraordinary conviction flashed across Plattner's mind that this head had a strong likeness to Lidgett. Then he turned his attention to the other heads that were now swarming thickly up the hillside. None made the slightest sign of recognition. One or two, indeed, came close to his head and almost followed the example of the first, but he dodged convulsively out of the way. Upon most of them he saw the same expression of unavailing regret he had seen upon the first, and heard the same faint sounds of wretchedness from them. One or two wept, and one rolling swiftly uphill wore an expression of diabolical rage. But others were cold, and several had a look of gratified interest in their eyes. One, at least, was almost in an ecstasy of happiness. Plattner does not remember that he recognised any more likenesses in those he saw at this time.

For several hours, perhaps, Plattner watched these strange things dispersing themselves over the hills, and not till long after they had ceased to issue from the clustering black buildings in the gorge, did he resume his downward climb. The darkness about him increased so much that he had a difficulty in stepping true. Overhead the sky was now a bright, pale green. He felt neither hunger nor thirst. Later, when he did, he found a chilly stream running down the centre of the gorge, and the rare moss upon the boulders, when he tried it at last in desperation, was good to eat.

He groped about among the tombs that ran down the gorge, seeking vaguely for some clue to these inexplicable things. After a long time he came to the entrance of the big mausoleum-like building from which the heads had issued. In this he found a group of green lights burning upon a kind of basaltic altar, and a bell-rope from a belfry overhead hanging down into the centre of the place. Round the wall ran a lettering of fire in a character unknown to him. While he was still wondering at the purport of these things, he heard the receding tramp of heavy feet echoing far down the street. He ran out into the darkness again, but he could see nothing. He had a mind to pull the bell-rope, and finally decided to follow the footsteps. But, although he ran far, he never overtook them; and his shouting was of no avail. The gorge seemed to extend an interminable distance. It was as dark as earthly starlight throughout its length, while the ghastly green day lay along the upper edge of its precipices. There were none of the heads, now, below. They were all, it seemed, busily occupied along the upper slopes. Looking up, he saw them drifting hither and thither, some hovering stationary, some flying swiftly through the air. It reminded him, he said, of "big snowflakes"; only these were black and pale green.

In pursuing the firm, undeviating footsteps that he never overtook, in groping into new regions of this endless devil's dyke, in clambering up and down the pitiless heights, in wandering about the summits, and in watching the drifting faces, Plattner states that he spent the better part of seven or eight days. He did not keep count, he says. Though once or twice he found eyes watching him, he had word with no living soul. He slept among the rocks on the hillside. In the gorge things earthly were invisible, because, from the earthly standpoint, it was far underground. On the altitudes, so soon as the

earthly day began, the world became visible to him. He found himself sometimes stumbling over the dark green rocks, or arresting himself on a precipitous brink, while all about him the green branches of the Sussexville lanes were swaying; or, again, he seemed to be walking through the Sussexville streets, or watching unseen the private business of some household. And then it was he discovered, that to almost every human being in our world there pertained some of these drifting heads: that everyone in the world is watched intermittently by these helpless disembodiments.

What are they—these Watchers of the Living? Plattner never learned. But two, that presently found and followed him, were like his childhood's memory of his father and mother. Now and then other faces turned their eyes upon him: eyes like those of dead people who had swayed him, or injured him, or helped him in his youth and manhood. Whenever they looked at him, Plattner was overcome with a strange sense of responsibility. To his mother he ventured to speak; but she made no answer. She looked sadly, steadfastly, and tenderly—a little reproachfully, too, it seemed—into his eyes.

He simply tells this story: he does not endeavour to explain. We are left to surmise who these Watchers of the Living may be, or if they are indeed the Dead, why they should so closely and passionately watch a world they have left for ever. It may be—indeed to my mind it seems just—that, when our life has closed, when evil or good is no longer a choice for us, we may still have to witness the working out of the train of consequences we have laid. If human souls continue after death, then surely human interests continue after death. But that is merely my own guess at the meaning of the things seen. Plattner offers no interpretation, for none was given him. It is well the reader should understand this clearly. Day after day, with his head reeling, he wandered about this strange-lit world outside the world, weary and, towards the end, weak and hungry. By day—by our earthly day, that is—the ghostly vision of the old familiar scenery of Sussexville, all about him, irked and worried him. He could not see where to put his feet, and ever and again with a chilly touch one of these Watching Souls would come against his face. And after dark the multitude of these Watchers about him, and their intent distress, confused his mind beyond describing. A great longing to return to the earthly life that was so near and yet so remote consumed him. The unearthliness of things about him produced a positively painful mental distress. He was worried beyond describing by his own particular followers. He would shout at them to desist from staring at him, scold at them, hurry away from them. They were always mute and intent. Run as he might over the uneven ground, they followed his destinies.

On the ninth day, towards evening, Plattner heard the invisible footsteps approaching, far away down the gorge. He was then wandering over the broad crest of the same hill upon which he had fallen in his entry into this strange Other-World of his. He turned to hurry down into the gorge, feeling his way hastily, and was arrested by the sight of the thing that was happening in a room in a back street near the school. Both of the people in the room he knew by sight. The windows were open, the blinds up, and the setting sun shone clearly into it, so that it came out quite brightly at first, a vivid oblong of room, lying like a magic-lantern picture upon the black landscape and the livid green dawn. In addition to the sunlight, a candle had just been lit in the room.

On the bed lay a lank man, his ghastly white face terrible upon the tumbled pillow. His clenched hands were raised above his head. A little table beside the bed carried a few medicine bottles, some toast and water, and an empty glass. Every now and then the lank man's lips fell apart, to indicate a word he could not articulate. But the woman did not notice that he wanted anything, because she was busy turning out papers from an old-fashioned bureau in the opposite corner of the room. At first the picture was very vivid indeed, but as the green dawn behind it grew brighter and brighter, so it became fainter and more and more transparent.

As the echoing footsteps paced nearer and nearer, those footsteps that sound so loud in that Other-World and come so silently in this, Plattner perceived about him a great multitude of dim faces gathering together out of the darkness and watching the two people in the room. Never before had he seen so many of the Watchers of the Living. A multitude had eyes only for the sufferer in the room, another multitude, in infinite anguish, watched the woman as she hunted with greedy eyes for something she could not find. They crowded about Plattner, they came across his sight and buffeted his face, the noise of their unavailing regrets was all about him. He saw clearly only now and then. At other times the picture quivered dimly, through the veil of green reflections upon their movements. In the room it must have been very still, and Plattner says the candle flame streamed up into a perfectly vertical line of smoke, but in his ears each footfall and its echoes beat like a clap of thunder. And the faces! Two, more particularly near the woman's: one a woman's also, white and clear-featured, a face which might have once been cold and hard, but which was now softened by the touch of a wisdom strange to earth. The other might have been the woman's father. Both were evidently absorbed in the contemplation of some act of hateful meanness, so it seemed, which they could no longer guard against and prevent. Behind were others, teachers, it may be, who had taught ill, friends whose influence had failed. And over the man, too—a multitude, but none that seemed to be parents or teachers! Faces that might once have been coarse, now purged to strength by sorrow! And in the forefront one face, a girlish one, neither angry nor remorseful, but merely patient and weary, and, as it seemed to Plattner, waiting for relief. His powers of description fail him at the memory of this multitude of ghastly countenances. They gathered on the stroke of the bell. He saw them all in the space of a second. It would seem that he was so worked on by his excitement that, quite involuntarily, his restless fingers took the bottle of green powder out of his pocket and held it before him. But he does not remember that.

Abruptly the footsteps ceased. He waited for

the next, and there was silence, and then suddenly, cutting through the unexpected stillness like a keen, thin blade, came the first stroke of the bell. At that the multitudinous faces swayed to and fro, and a louder crying began all about him. The woman did not hear; she was burning something now in the candle flame. At the second stroke everything grew dim, and a breath of wind, icy cold, blew through the host of watchers. They swirled about him like an eddy of dead leaves in the spring, and at the third stroke something was extended through them to the bed. You have heard of a beam of light. This was like a beam of darkness, and looking again at it, Plattner saw that it was a shadowy arm and hand.

The green sun was now topping the black desolations of the horizon, and the vision of the room was very faint. Plattner could see that the white of the bed struggled, and was convulsed; and that the woman looked round over her shoulder at it, startled.

The cloud of watchers lifted high like a puff of green dust before the wind, and swept swiftly downward towards the temple in the gorge. Then suddenly Plattner understood the meaning of the shadowy black arm that stretched across his shoulder and clutched its prey. He did not dare turn his head to see the Shadow behind the arm. With a violent effort, and covering his eyes, he set himself to run, made, perhaps, twenty strides, then slipped on a boulder, and fell. He fell forward on his hands; and the bottle smashed and exploded as he touched the ground.

In another moment he found himself, stunned and bleeding, sitting face to face with Lidgett in the old walled garden behind the school.

There the story of Plattner's experiences ends. I have resisted, I believe successfully, the natural disposition of a writer of fiction to dress up incidents of this sort. I have told the thing as far as possible in the order in which Plattner told it to me. I have carefully avoided any attempt at style, effect, or construction. It would have been easy, for instance, to have worked the scene of the death-bed into a kind of plot in which Plattner might have been involved. But, quite apart from the objectionableness of falsifying a most extraordinary true story, any such trite devices would spoil, to my mind, the peculiar effect of this dark world, with its livid green illumination and its drifting Watchers of the Living, which, unseen and unapproachable to us, is yet lying all about us.

It remains to add, that a death did actually occur in Vincent Terrace, just beyond the school garden, and, so far as can be proved, at the moment of Plattner's return. Deceased was a rate-collector and insurance agent. His widow, who was much younger than himself, married last month a Mr. Whymper, a veterinary surgeon of Allbeeding. As the portion of this story given here has in various forms circulated orally in Sussexville, she has consented to my use of her name, on condition that I make it distinctly known that she emphatically contradicts every detail of Plattner's account of her husband's last moments. She burnt no will, she says, although Plattner never accused her of doing so: her husband made but one will, and that just after their marriage. Certainly, from a man who had never seen it, Plattner's account of the furniture of the room was curiously accurate.

One other thing, even at the risk of an irksome repetition, I must insist upon, lest I seem to favour the credulous superstitious view. Plattner's absence from the world for nine days is, I think, proved. But that does not prove his story. It is quite conceivable that even outside space hallucinations may be possible. That, at least, the reader must bear distinctly in mind.

Willa (Sibert) Cather (1873–1947) was a well-known American novelist recognized for her portrayals of the frontier and of settlers; the Great Plains was the inspiration for much of her fiction. Cather won the Pulitzer Prize in 1922 for her novel *One of Ours*. She clearly expresses her love of nature in her novels and short stories through the use of masterful description. Some of her more popular works include *Sapphira and the Slave Girl* (1940), which was her last novel, her short story collection *The Troll Garden* (1905), and *A Lost Lady* (1923), a tale about the loss of spirit in a small town. Cather first published "Princess Baladina—Her Adventure" in 1896 under the pseudonym Charles Douglass.

The Princess Baladina– Her Adventure

Willa Cather

THE PRINCESS BALADINA sat sullenly gazing out of her nursery window. There was no use in crying any more for there was no one there to see and pity her tears, and who ever cries unless there is some one to pity them? She had kicked at the golden door until it became evident that she was much more discomforted than the door, and then she gave it up and sat sullenly down and did nothing but watch the big bumble-bees buzzing about the honey-suckles outside the window. The Princess Baladina had been shut up in her nursery for being naughty. Indeed, she had been unusually naughty that day. In the first place she had scratched and bitten the nurse who had combed her golden hair in the morning. Later, while she was playing about the palace grounds, she had lost in the moat one of the three beau-

tiful golden balls which her father had bought for her of an old Jewish magician from Bagdad who was staying at the court, and who bought up the queen's old dresses and loaned the courtiers money on their diamonds. Then she had been so rude to her fairy godmother who came to luncheon with them that her mother had reprimanded her twice. Finally, when she poured custard in her fairy godmother's ear-trumpet, she was sent up to her nursery. Now she sat locked up there and thinking how cruelly her family had used her. She wondered what she could do to make them repent of their harsh behavior and wish they had been kinder to their little Princess Baladina. Perhaps if she should die they would realize how brutal they had been. O yes, if she were to die, then they would grieve and mourn and put flowers on her grave every day, and cry for their little Baladina who would never gather flowers any more. Baladina wept a little herself at the pathetic picture she had conjured up. But she decided not to die, that was such a very decisive thing to do; beside, then she could not see the remorse of her family, and what good is it to have your family repent if you cannot have the satisfaction of seeing them reduced to sackcloth and ashes? So the Princess cast about for another plan. She might cut off her beautiful golden hair, but then she had no scissors; besides, if a young Prince should happen to come that way it would be awkward not to have any golden hair. Princesses are taught to think of these things early. She began thinking over all the stories she had read about Princesses and their adventures, until suddenly she thought of the story of the Princess Alice, who had been enchanted by a wizard. Yes, that was it, that would be the best revenge of all, she would be enchanted by a wizard, and her family would be in despair; her father would offer his kingdom to the knight who should free her, and some young Prince would come and break the spell and bear her triumphantly off to his own realm, on his saddle bow. Then her unfeeling parents would never see her any more, and her sisters and brothers would have no dear sweet little Princess to wait on.

But the next question was where to find a wizard. The Princess went over all the gentlemen of her acquaintance, but could not think of one who belonged to that somewhat complicated profession. Never mind, she would find one, she had heard of Princesses wandering away from their palaces on strange missions before. She waited through all the hot afternoon, and when the nurse brought her tea she took two of the buns and a piece of raisin cake and did them up carefully in a handkerchief, and said her prayers and let them put her to bed. She lay awake for a time, half hoping that her mother would come up to see her and relieve her from the obvious necessity of running away. But there was a court ball that night and no one came, so listening to

the tempting strains of music and feeling more aggrieved and forgotten than ever, the little Princess fell asleep.

As soon as she had breakfasted in the morning, she took the buns tied up in the handkerchief and went down into the yard.

She waited awhile until there was no one looking and then slipped out through one of the rear gates. Once fairly outside, she drew a long breath and looked about her; yes, there was the green meadow and the blue sky, just as they always were in the Princess' books. She started off across the meadow, keeping a little under the shadow of the wild crab hedge to better screen herself from the palace windows. She saw some little peasant children down by the pool watching some white things that must be sheep. O yes, they were sheep and the boys were shepherds' sons, thought Baladina. She approached them and greeted them politely.

"Kind shepherds, why keep ye your sheep so near the town?"

"These are not sheep, but geese, Silly," replied the biggest boy surlily.

"That is not the way to speak to a Princess," said Baladina angrily.

"Princess, so that's what you call yourself, Miss Stuck Up?" cried the big boy, and with that he set the geese on her.

The Princess fled in the wildest alarm, with the squawking geese after her, while the little peasant children rolled over and over on the grass, screaming with merriment. The chase did not continue long, for the Princess' long silk gown tripped her and she fell, covering her eyes with her hands and screaming with fright, expecting to feel the sharp beaks of the geese in her face at any moment. But just then a chubby curly-headed boy rode up on a donkey. He chased the geese away with his staff, and sliding down from his beast picked up the little Princess and brushed the dust from her hair.

"Who are you, little girl?" he asked.

"I am the Princess Baladina, and those naughty boys set their geese on me because I corrected them for being rude. They don't believe I'm a Princess; you believe it, don't you?"

"If you say so, of course I do," returned the boy, looking wonderingly at her with his big blue eyes and then doubtfully at his bare feet and rough clothes. "But what are you doing out here?"

"I want to find a wizard, do you know of one?"

"O yes, there's Lean Jack, he lives back of the mill. If you'll get on my donkey I'll walk and lead him and we'll get there in no time."

The Princess accepted this homage as her due and was soon on the donkey, while the boy trotted along beside her.

"What do you want of a wizard anyway, a spell to cure something?" he asked curiously.

"No," said Baladina. "I wish to become enchanted because my family have been unkind to me. And then I want some Prince to come and free me. You are not a Prince in disguise, I suppose?" she added hopefully.

The boy shook his head regretfully. "No, I am only the miller's son."

When they came to Lean Jack's house, they found the old man out in his garden hoeing melon vines. They approached slowly and stood still for some time, Baladina expecting him to at once perceive her and cast his spell. But the old man worked on until the braying of the donkey attracted his attention.

"Well, youngsters, what is it?" he asked, leaning on his spade and wiping his brow.

"I believe you are a wizard, sir?" inquired Baladina politely.

He nodded. "So they say, what can I do for you?"

"I have come," said Baladina, "to allow you to cast a spell upon me, as my family are very unkind to me and if I am enchanted some Prince will come and free me from your power and carry me off to his own country."

The wizard smiled grimly and returned to his hoeing. "Sorry I can't accommodate you, but I can't leave my melons. There is a fat wizard who lives in a little red house over the hill yonder, he may be able to give you what you want."

"Dear me," sighed Baladina as they turned away, "how very rude everyone is. Most wizards would be glad enough to get a chance to enchant a Princess."

"I wish you wouldn't be enchanted at all. It must be very uncomfortable, and I shouldn't like to see you changed into an owl or a fox or anything," said the miller's boy as he trotted beside her.

"It must be," said Baladina firmly, "all Princesses should be enchanted at least once."

When they reached the red house behind the hill they had considerable trouble in finding the wizard, and the miller's boy pounded on the door until his knuckles were quite blue. At last a big, jolly looking man with a red cap on his head came to the window. The Princess rode her donkey up quite close to the window and told him what she wanted. The fat wizard leaned up against the window sill and laughed until the tears came to his eyes, and the Princess again felt that her dignity was hurt.

"So you want to be enchanted, do you, so a Prince can come and release you? Who sent you here? It was that lean rascal of a Jack, I'll warrant, he's always putting up jokes on me. This is a little the best yet. Has it occurred to you that when your Prince comes he will certainly kill me? That's the way they always do, you know, they slay the cruel enchanter and then bear off the maiden."

The Princess looked puzzled. "Well," she said thoughtfully, "in this case, if you leave me the power of speech, I will request him not to. It's unusual, but I should hate to have him kill you."

"Thank you, my dear, now I call that considerate. But there is another point. Suppose your Prince should not hear of you, and should never come?"

"But they always do come," objected Baladina.

"Not always, I've known them to tarry a good many years. No, I positively cannot enchant you until you find your Prince."

Baladina turned her donkey and went slowly down to the road leaving the fat wizard still laughing in the window.

"How disobliging these wizards seem to be, but this one seems to mean well. I believe they are afraid to undertake it with a Princess. Do you know where we can find a Prince?"

The miller's boy shook his head. "No, I don't know of any at all."

"Then I suppose we must just hunt for one," said Baladina.

They asked several carters whom they met if they knew where a Prince was to be found, but they all laughed so that Baladina grew quite discouraged. She stopped one boy on horseback and asked if he were a Prince in disguise, but he indignantly denied the charge.

So they went up the road and down a country lane that ran under the willow trees, and when they were both very tired and hungry Baladina opened her handkerchief and gave the miller's boy a bun. He refused the raisin cake, although he looked longingly at it, for he saw there was scarcely enough for two. Baladina sat down and ate it in the shade while he pulled some grass for the donkey. After their lunch they went on again. Just at the top of a hill they met a young man riding a black horse with a pack of hounds running beside him. "I know he is a Prince out hunting. You must stop him," whispered Baladina. So the miller's boy ran on ahead and shouted to the horseman.

"Are you a Prince, sir?" asked Baladina as she approached.

"Yes, miss, I am," he replied curtly.

Nothing daunted Baladina as she told her story. The young man laughed and said impatiently, "You foolish child, have you stopped me all this time to tell me a fairy tale? Go home to your parents and let me follow my dogs, I have no time to be playing with silly little girls," and rode away.

"How unkind of him to talk so," said the Princess, "besides, he is very little older than I."

"If he were here, I'd thrash him!" declared the miller's boy stoutly, clenching his fist.

They went on for a little while in a spiritless sort of way, but the boy hurt his toe on a stone until it bled and the Princess was hot and dusty and ached in every bone of her body. Suddenly she stopped the donkey and began to cry.

"There, there," said the miller's boy kindly, "don't do that. I'll find a Prince for you. You go home and rest and I'll hunt until I find one, if it takes for ever."

Baladina dried her tears and spoke with sudden determination.

"You shall be my Prince yourself. I know you are one, really. You must be a changeling left at the mill by some wicked fairy who stole you from your palace."

The boy shook his head stubbornly. "No, I wish I were, but I am only a miller's boy."

"Well, you are the only nice person I have met all day; you have walked till your feet are sore and have let me ride your donkey, and your face is all scratched by the briars and you have had no dinner, and if you are not a Prince, you ought to be one. You are Prince enough for me, anyway. But I am so tired and hungry now, we will go home to the palace to-night and I will be enchanted in the morning. Come, get on the donkey and take me in front of you."

In vain he protested that the donkey could not carry them both, the Princess said that a Prince could not walk.

"I wish you had on shoes and stockings, though," she said. "I think a Prince should always have those."

"I have some for Sunday," said the miller's boy, "if I had only known I would have brought them."

As they turned slowly out of the lane they met a party of horsemen who were hunting for the Princess, and the king himself was among them.

"Ha there, you precious run-away, so here you are, and who is this you have with you?"

"He is my Prince," said the Princess, "and he is to have half the kingdom."

"Oh-h, he is, is he? Who are you, my man?"

"Please, sir, I am only the miller's son, but the Princess was hunting for a Prince and couldn't find one, so she asked me to be one."

"Hear, gentlemen, the Princess is out Prince-hunting early. Come here you little baggage." He lifted her on the saddle in front of him.

"He must come too, for he is my Prince!" cried the wilful Princess.

But the king only laughed and gave the boy a gold piece, and rode away followed by his gentlemen, who were all laughing too. The miller's boy stood by his donkey, looking wistfully after them, and the Princess Baladina wept bitterly at the dearth of Princes.

Kenneth Grahame (1859–1932) was a Scottish author best known for his children's book *The Wind in the Willows* (1908), which was dramatized in 1930 by A. A. Milne as *Toad of Toad Hall*. What many do not know is that the book came out of stories he wrote to his son in letters and that when Grahame tried to publish the book, he was rejected by numerous publications. Before *Wind in the Willows*, Grahame wrote stories about an orphaned family and published his first collection *The Golden Age* (1895), which consisted of eighteen stories. Three years later, Grahame published his second collection, *Dream Days* (1898), the first chapter of which is the wonderful "The Reluctant Dragon." Although largely unknown today, these collections were popular in their day.

The Reluctant Dragon

Kenneth Grahame

FOOTPRINTS IN THE SNOW have been unfailing provokers of sentiment ever since snow was first a white wonder in this drab-coloured world of ours. In a poetry-book presented to one of us by an aunt, there was a poem by one Wordsworth in which they stood out strongly with a picture all to themselves, too—but we didn't think very highly either of the poem or the sentiment. Footprints in the sand, now, were quite another matter, and we grasped Crusoe's attitude of mind much more easily than Wordsworth's. Excitement and mystery, curiosity and suspense—these were the only sentiments that tracks, whether in sand or in snow, were able to arouse in us.

We had awakened early that winter morning, puzzled at first by the added light that filled the room. Then, when the truth at last fully dawned on us and we knew that snow-balling was no longer a wistful dream, but a solid certainty waiting for us outside, it was a mere brute fight for the necessary clothes, and the lacing of boots seemed a clumsy invention, and the buttoning of coats an unduly tedious form of fastening, with all that snow going to waste at our very door.

When dinner-time came we had to be dragged in by the scruff of our necks. The short armistice over, the combat was resumed; but presently Charlotte and I, a little weary of contests and of missiles that ran shudderingly down inside one's clothes, forsook the trampled battle-field of the lawn and went exploring the blank virgin spaces of the white world that lay beyond. It stretched away unbroken on every side of us, this mysterious soft garment under which our familiar world had so suddenly hidden itself. Faint imprints showed where a casual bird had alighted, but of other traffic there was next to no sign; which made these strange tracks all the more puzzling.

We came across them first at the corner of the shrubbery, and pored over them long, our hands on our knees. Experienced trappers that we knew ourselves to be, it was annoying to be brought up suddenly by a beast we could not at once identify.

"Don't you know?" said Charlotte, rather scornfully. "Thought you knew all the beasts that ever was."

This put me on my mettle, and I hastily rattled off a string of animal names embracing both the arctic and the tropic zones, but without much real confidence.

"No," said Charlotte, on consideration; "they won't any of 'em quite do. Seems like something lizardy. Did you say a iguanodon? Might be that, p'raps. But that's not British, and we want a real British beast. I think it's a dragon!"

"'T isn't half big enough," I objected.

"Well, all dragons must be small to begin with," said Charlotte: "like everything else. P'raps this is a little dragon who's got lost. A little dragon would be rather nice to have. He might scratch and spit, but he couldn't do anything really. Let's track him down!"

So we set off into the wide snow-clad world, hand in hand, our hearts big with expectation,—complacently confident that by a few smudgy traces in the snow we were in a fair way to capture a half-grown specimen of a fabulous beast.

We ran the monster across the paddock and along the hedge of the next field, and then he took to the road like any tame civilized tax-payer. Here his tracks became blended with and lost among more ordinary footprints, but imagination and a fixed idea will do a great deal, and we were sure we knew the direction a dragon would naturally take. The traces, too, kept reappearing at intervals—at least Charlotte maintained they did, and as it was her dragon I left the following of the slot to her and trotted along peacefully, feeling that it was an expedition anyhow and something was sure to come out of it.

Charlotte took me across another field or two, and through a copse, and into a fresh road; and I began to feel sure it was only her confounded pride that made her go on pretending to see dragon-tracks instead of owning she was entirely at fault, like a reasonable person. At last she

dragged me excitedly through a gap in a hedge of an obviously private character; the waste, open world of field and hedge row disappeared, and we found ourselves in a garden, well-kept, secluded, most undragon-haunted in appearance. Once inside, I knew where we were. This was the garden of my friend the circus-man, though I had never approached it before by a lawless gap, from this unfamiliar side. And here was the circus-man himself, placidly smoking a pipe as he strolled up and down the walks. I stepped up to him and asked him politely if he had lately seen a Beast.

"May I inquire," he said, with all civility, "what particular sort of a Beast you may happen to be looking for?"

"It's a lizardy sort of Beast," I explained. "Charlotte says it's a dragon, but she doesn't really know much about beasts."

The circus-man looked round about him slowly. "I don't think," he said, "that I've seen a dragon in these parts recently. But if I come across one I'll know it belongs to you, and I'll have him taken round to you at once."

"Thank you very much," said Charlotte, "but don't trouble about it, please, 'cos p'raps it isn't a dragon after all. Only I thought I saw his little footprints in the snow, and we followed 'em up, and they seemed to lead right in here, but maybe it's all a mistake, and thank you all the same."

"Oh, no trouble at all," said the circus-man, cheerfully. "I should be only too pleased. But of course, as you say, it may be a mistake. And it's getting dark, and he seems to have got away for the present, whatever he is. You'd better come in and have some tea. I'm quite alone, and we'll make a roaring fire, and I've got the biggest Book of Beasts you ever saw. It's got every beast in the world, and all of 'em coloured; and we'll try and find your beast in it!"

We were always ready for tea at any time, and especially when combined with beasts. There was marmalade, too, and apricot-jam, brought in expressly for us; and afterwards the beast-book was spread out, and, as the man had truly said, it contained every sort of beast that had ever been in the world.

The striking of six o'clock set the more prudent Charlotte nudging me, and we recalled ourselves with an effort from Beastland, and reluctantly stood up to go.

"Here, I'm coming along with you," said the circus-man. "I want another pipe, and a walk'll do me good. You needn't talk to me unless you like."

Our spirits rose to their wonted level again. The way had seemed so long, the outside world so dark and eerie, after the bright warm room and the highly-coloured beast-book. But a walk with a real Man—why, that was a treat in itself! We set off briskly, the Man in the middle. I looked up at him and wondered whether I should ever live to smoke a big pipe with that careless sort of majesty! But Charlotte, whose young mind was not set on tobacco as a possible goal, made herself heard from the other side.

"Now, then," she said, "tell us a story, please, won't you?"

The Man sighed heavily and looked about him. "I knew it," he groaned. "I knew I should have to tell a story. Oh, why did I leave my pleasant fireside? Well, I will tell you a story. Only let me think a minute."

So he thought a minute, and then he told us this story.

Long ago—might have been hundreds of years ago—in a cottage half-way between this village and yonder shoulder of the Downs up there, a shepherd lived with his wife and their little son. Now the shepherd spent his days—and at certain times of the year his nights too—up on the wide ocean-bosom of the Downs, with only the sun and the stars and the sheep for company, and the friendly chattering world of men and women far out of sight and hearing. But his little son, when he wasn't helping his father, and often when he was as well, spent much of his time buried in big volumes that he borrowed from the affable gentry and interested parsons of the country round about. And his parents were very fond of him, and rather proud of him too, though they didn't let on in his hearing, so he was left to go his own way and read as much as he liked; and instead of frequently getting a cuff on the side of the head, as might very well have happened to him, he was treated more or less as an equal by his parents, who sensibly thought it a very fair division of labour that they should supply the practical knowledge, and he the book-learning. They knew that book-learning often came in useful at a pinch, in spite of what their neighbours said. What the Boy chiefly dabbled in was natural history and fairy-tales, and he just took them as they came, in a sandwichy sort of way, without making any distinctions; and really his course of reading strikes one as rather sensible.

One evening the shepherd, who for some nights past had been disturbed and preoccupied, and off his usual mental balance, came home all of a tremble, and, sitting down at the table where his wife and son were peacefully employed, she with her seam, he in following out the adventures of the Giant with no Heart in his Body, exclaimed with much agitation:

"It's all up with me, Maria! Never no more can I go up on them there Downs, was it ever so!"

"Now don't you take on like that," said his wife, who was a very sensible woman: "but tell us all about it first, whatever it is as has given you this shake-up, and then me and you and the son here, between us, we ought to be able to get to the bottom of it!"

"It began some nights ago," said the shepherd. "You know that cave up there—I never liked it, somehow, and the sheep never liked it neither, and when sheep don't like a thing there's generally some reason for it. Well, for some time past there's been faint noises coming from that cave—noises like heavy sighings, with grunts mixed up in them; and sometimes a snoring, far away down—real snoring, yet somehow not honest snoring, like you and me o'nights, you know!"

"I know," remarked the Boy, quietly.

"Of course I was terrible frightened," the shepherd went on; "yet somehow I couldn't keep away. So this very evening, before I come down, I took a cast round by the cave, quietly. And there—O Lord! there I saw him at last, as plain as I see you!"

"Saw who?" said his wife, beginning to share in her husband's nervous terror.

"Why him, I'm a telling you!" said the shepherd. "He was sticking half-way out of the cave, and seemed to be enjoying of the cool of the evening in a poetical sort of way. He was as big as four cart-horses, and all covered with shiny scales—deep-blue scales at the top of him, shading off to a tender sort o' green below. As he breathed, there was that sort of flicker over his nostrils that you see over our chalk roads on a baking windless day in summer. He had his chin on his paws, and I should say he was meditating about things. Oh, yes, a peaceable sort o' beast enough, and not ramping or carrying on or doing anything but what was quite right and proper. I admit all that. And yet, what am I to do? Scales, you know, and claws, and a tail for certain, though I didn't see that end of him—I ain't used to 'em, and I don't hold with 'em, and that's a fact!"

The Boy, who had apparently been absorbed in his book during his father's recital, now closed the volume, yawned, clasped his hands behind his head, and said sleepily:

"It's all right, father. Don't you worry. It's only a dragon."

"Only a dragon?" cried his father. "What do you mean, sitting there, you and your dragons? Only a dragon indeed! And what do you know about it?"

"'Cos it is, and 'cos I do know," replied the Boy, quietly. "Look here, father, you know we've each of us got our line. You know about sheep, and weather, and things; I know about dragons. I always said, you know, that that cave up there was a dragon-cave. I always said it must have belonged to a dragon some time, and ought to belong to a dragon now, if rules count for anything. Well, now you tell me it has got a dragon, and so that's all right. I'm not half as much surprised as when you told me it hadn't got a dragon. Rules always come right if you wait quietly. Now, please, just leave this all to me. And I'll stroll up to-morrow morning—no, in the morning I can't, I've got a whole heap of things to do—well, perhaps in the evening, if I'm quite free, I'll go up

and have a talk to him, and you'll find it'll be all right. Only, please, don't you go worrying round there without me. You don't understand 'em a bit, and they're very sensitive, you know!"

"He's quite right, father," said the sensible mother. "As he says, dragons is his line and not ours. He's wonderful knowing about book-beasts, as every one allows. And to tell the truth, I'm not half happy in my own mind, thinking of that poor animal lying alone up there, without a bit o' hot supper or anyone to change the news with; and maybe we'll be able to do something for him; and if he ain't quite respectable our Boy'll find it out quick enough. He's got a pleasant sort o' way with him that makes everybody tell him everything."

Next day, after he'd had his tea, the Boy strolled up the chalky track that led to the summit of the Downs; and there, sure enough, he found the dragon, stretched lazily on the sward in front of his cave. The view from that point was a magnificent one. To the right and left, the bare and billowy leagues of Downs; in front, the vale, with its clustered homesteads, its threads of white roads running through orchards and well-tilled acreage, and, far away, a hint of grey old cities on the horizon. A cool breeze played over the surface of the grass and the silver shoulder of a large moon was showing above distant junipers. No wonder the dragon seemed in a peaceful and contented mood; indeed, as the Boy approached he could hear the beast purring with a happy regularity. "Well, we live and learn!" he said to himself. "None of my books ever told me that dragons purred!

"Hullo, dragon!" said the Boy, quietly, when he had got up to him.

The dragon, on hearing the approaching footsteps, made the beginning of a courteous effort to rise. But when he saw it was a Boy, he set his eyebrows severely.

"Now don't you hit me," he said; "or bung stones, or squirt water, or anything. I won't have it, I tell you!"

"Not goin' to hit you," said the Boy wearily, dropping on the grass beside the beast: "and don't, for goodness' sake, keep on saying 'Don't';

I hear so much of it, and it's monotonous, and makes me tired. I've simply looked in to ask you how you were and all that sort of thing; but if I'm in the way I can easily clear out. I've lots of friends, and no one can say I'm in the habit of shoving myself in where I'm not wanted!"

"No, no, don't go off in a huff," said the dragon, hastily; "fact is,—I'm as happy up here as the day's long; never without an occupation, dear fellow, never without an occupation! And yet, between ourselves, it is a trifle dull at times."

The Boy bit off a stalk of grass and chewed it. "Going to make a long stay here?" he asked, politely.

"Can't hardly say at present," replied the dragon. "It seems a nice place enough—but I've only been here a short time, and one must look about and reflect and consider before settling down. It's rather a serious thing, settling down. Besides—now I'm going to tell you something! You'd never guess it if you tried ever so!—fact is, I'm such a confoundedly lazy beggar!"

"You surprise me," said the Boy, civilly.

"It's the sad truth," the dragon went on, settling down between his paws and evidently delighted to have found a listener at last: "and I fancy that's really how I came to be here. You see all the other fellows were so active and earnest and all that sort of thing—always rampaging, and skirmishing, and scouring the desert sands, and pacing the margin of the sea, and chasing knights all over the place, and devouring damsels, and going on generally—whereas I liked to get my meals regular and then to prop my back against a bit of rock and snooze a bit, and wake up and think of things going on and how they kept going on just the same, you know! So when it happened I got fairly caught."

"When what happened, please?" asked the Boy.

"That's just what I don't precisely know," said the dragon. "I suppose the earth sneezed, or shook itself, or the bottom dropped out of something. Anyhow there was a shake and a roar and a general stramash, and I found myself miles away underground and wedged in as tight as tight. Well, thank goodness, my wants are few, and at

any rate I had peace and quietness and wasn't always being asked to come along and do something. And I've got such an active mind—always occupied, I assure you! But time went on, and there was a certain sameness about the life, and at last I began to think it would be fun to work my way upstairs and see what you other fellows were doing. So I scratched and burrowed, and worked this way and that way and at last I came out through this cave here. And I like the country, and the view, and the people—what I've seen of 'em—and on the whole I feel inclined to settle down here."

"What's your mind always occupied about?" asked the Boy. "That's what I want to know."

The dragon coloured slightly and looked away. Presently he said bashfully:

"Did you ever—just for fun—try to make up poetry—verses, you know?"

"'Course I have," said the Boy. "Heaps of it. And some of it's quite good, I feel sure, only there's no one here cares about it. Mother's very kind and all that, when I read it to her, and so's father for that matter. But somehow they don't seem to—"

"Exactly," cried the dragon; "my own case exactly. They don't seem to, and you can't argue with 'em about it. Now you've got culture, you have, I could tell it on you at once, and I should just like your candid opinion about some little things I threw off lightly, when I was down there. I'm awfully pleased to have met you, and I'm hoping the other neighbours will be equally agreeable. There was a very nice old gentleman up here only last night, but he didn't seem to want to intrude."

"That was my father," said the Boy, "and he is a nice old gentleman, and I'll introduce you some day if you like."

"Can't you two come up here and dine or something to-morrow?" asked the dragon eagerly. "Only, of course, if you've got nothing better to do," he added politely.

"Thanks awfully," said the Boy, "but we don't go out anywhere without my mother, and, to tell you the truth, I'm afraid she mightn't quite approve of you. You see there's no getting over the hard fact that you're a dragon, is there? And when you talk of settling down, and the neighbours, and so on, I can't help feeling that you don't quite realize your position. You're an enemy of the human race, you see!"

"Haven't got an enemy in the world," said the dragon, cheerfully. "Too lazy to make 'em, to begin with. And if I do read other fellows my poetry, I'm always ready to listen to theirs!"

"Oh, dear!" cried the Boy, "I wish you'd try and grasp the situation properly. When the other people find you out, they'll come after you with spears and swords and all sorts of things. You'll have to be exterminated, according to their way of looking at it! You're a scourge, and a pest, and a baneful monster!"

"Not a word of truth in it," said the dragon, wagging his head solemnly. "Character'll bear the strictest investigation. And now, there's a little sonnet-thing I was working on when you appeared on the scene—"

"Oh, if you won't be sensible," cried the Boy, getting up, "I'm going off home. No, I can't stop for sonnets; my mother's sitting up. I'll look you up to-morrow, sometime or other, and do for goodness' sake try and realize that you're a pestilential scourge, or you'll find yourself in a most awful fix. Good-night!"

The Boy found it an easy matter to set the mind of his parents' at ease about his new friend. They had always left that branch to him, and they took his word without a murmur. The shepherd was formally introduced and many compliments and kind inquiries were exchanged. His wife, however, though expressing her willingness to do anything she could—to mend things, or set the cave to rights, or cook a little something when the dragon had been poring over sonnets and forgotten his meals, as male things will do, could not be brought to recognize him formally. The fact that he was a dragon and "they didn't know who he was" seemed to count for everything with her. She made no objection, however, to her little son spending his evenings with the dragon quietly, so long as he was home by nine o'clock: and many

a pleasant night they had, sitting on the swan, while the dragon told stories of old, old times, when dragons were quite plentiful and the world was a livelier place than it is now, and life was full of thrills and jumps and surprises.

What the Boy had feared, however, soon came to pass. The most modest and retiring dragon in the world, if he's as big as four cart-horses and covered with blue scales, cannot keep altogether out of the public view. And so in the village tavern of nights the fact that a real live dragon sat brooding in the cave on the Downs was naturally a subject for talk. Though the villagers were extremely frightened, they were rather proud as well. It was a distinction to have a dragon of your own, and it was felt to be a feather in the cap of the village. Still, all were agreed that this sort of thing couldn't be allowed to go on. The dreadful beast must be exterminated, the country-side must be freed from this pest, this terror, this destroying scourge. The fact that not even a hen-roost was the worse for the dragon's arrival wasn't allowed to have anything to do with it. He was a dragon, and he couldn't deny it, and if he didn't choose to behave as such that was his own lookout. But in spite of much valiant talk no hero was found willing to take sword and spear and free the suffering village and win deathless fame; and each night's heated discussion always ended in nothing. Meanwhile the dragon, a happy Bohemian, lolled on the turf, enjoyed the sunsets, told antediluvian anecdotes to the Boy, and polished his old verses while meditating on fresh ones.

One day the Boy, on walking in to the village, found everything wearing a festal appearance which was not to be accounted for in the calendar. Carpets and gay-coloured stuffs were hung out of the windows, the church-bells clamoured noisily, the little street was flower-strewn, and the whole population jostled each other along either side of it, chattering, shoving, and ordering each other to stand back. The Boy saw a friend of his own age in the crowd and hailed.

"What's up?" he cried. "Is it the players, or bears, or a circus, or what?" "It's all right," his friend hailed back. "He's a-coming."

"Who's a-coming?" demanded the Boy, thrusting into the throng.

"Why, St. George, of course," replied his friend. "He's heard tell of our dragon, and he's comm' on purpose to slay the deadly beast, and free us from his horrid yoke. O my! won't there be a jolly fight!"

Here was news indeed! The Boy felt that he ought to make quite sure for himself, and he wriggled himself in between the legs of his good-natured elders, abusing them all the time for their unmannerly habit of shoving. Once in the front rank, he breathlessly awaited the arrival.

Presently from the far-away end of the line came the sound of cheering. Next, the measured tramp of a great war-horse made his heart beat quicker, and then he found himself cheering with the rest, as, amidst welcoming shouts, shrill cries of women, uplifting of babies and waving of handkerchiefs, St. George paced slowly up the street. The Boy's heart stood still and he breathed with sobs, the beauty and the grace of the hero were so far beyond anything he had yet seen. His fluted armour was inlaid with gold, his plumed helmet hung at his saddle-bow, and his thick fair hair framed a face gracious and gentle beyond expression till you caught the sternness in his eyes. He drew rein in front of the little inn, and the villagers crowded round with greetings and thanks and voluble statements of their wrongs and grievances and oppressions. The Boy heard the grave gentle voice of the Saint, assuring them that all would be well now, and that he would stand by them and see them righted and free them from their foe; then he dismounted and passed through the doorway and the crowd poured in after him. But the Boy made off up the hill as fast as he could lay his legs to the ground.

"It's all up, dragon!" he shouted as soon as he was within sight of the beast. "He's coming! He's here now! You'll have to pull yourself together and do something at last!"

The dragon was licking his scales and rubbing them with a bit of house-flannel the Boy's mother had lent him, till he shone like a great turquoise.

"Don't be violent, Boy," he said without look-ing round. "Sit down and get your breath, and try and remember that the noun governs the verb, and then perhaps you'll be good enough to tell me who's coming?"

"That's right, take it coolly," said the Boy. "Hope you'll be half as cool when I've got through with my news. It's only St. George who's coming, that's all; he rode into the village half-an-hour ago. Of course you can lick him—a great big fel-low like you! But I thought I'd warn you, 'cos he's sure to be round early, and he's got the longest, wickedest-looking spear you ever did see!" And the Boy got up and began to jump round in sheer delight at the prospect of the battle.

"O deary, deary me," moaned the dragon; "this is too awful. I won't see him, and that's flat. I don't want to know the fellow at all. I'm sure he's not nice. You must tell him to go away at once, please. Say he can write if he likes, but I can't give him an interview. I'm not seeing any-body at present."

"Now dragon, dragon," said the Boy implor-ingly, "don't be perverse and wrongheaded. You've got to fight him some time or other, you know, 'cos he's St. George and you're the dragon. Better get it over, and then we can go on with the sonnets. And you ought to consider other people a little, too. If it's been dull up here for you, think how dull it's been for me!"

"My dear little man," said the dragon sol-emnly, "just understand, once for all, that I can't fight and I won't fight. I've never fought in my life, and I'm not going to begin now, just to give you a Roman holiday. In old days I always let the other fellows—the earnest fellows—do all the fighting, and no doubt that's why I have the pleasure of being here now."

"But if you don't fight he'll cut your head off!" gasped the Boy, miserable at the prospect of los-ing both his fight and his friend.

"Oh, I think not," said the dragon in his lazy way. "You'll be able to arrange something. I've every confidence in you, you're such a manager. Just run down, there's a dear chap, and make it all right. I leave it entirely to you."

The Boy made his way back to the village in

a state of great despondency. First of all, there wasn't going to be any fight; next, his dear and honoured friend the dragon hadn't shown up in quite such a heroic light as he would have liked; and lastly, whether the dragon was a hero at heart or not, it made no difference, for St. George would most undoubtedly cut his head off. "Arrange things indeed!" he said bitterly to himself. "The dragon treats the whole affair as if it was an invitation to tea and croquet."

The villagers were straggling homewards as he passed up the street, all of them in the highest spirits, and gleefully discussing the splendid fight that was in store. The Boy pursued his way to the inn, and passed into the principal chamber, where St. George now sat alone, musing over the chances of the fight, and the sad stories of rapine and of wrong that had so lately been poured into his sympathetic ear.

"May I come in, St. George?" said the Boy politely, as he paused at the door. "I want to talk to you about this little matter of the dragon, if you're not tired of it by this time."

"Yes, come in, Boy," said the Saint kindly. "Another tale of misery and wrong, I fear me. Is it a kind parent, then, of whom the tyrant has bereft you? Or some tender sister or brother? Well, it shall soon be avenged."

"Nothing of the sort," said the Boy. "There's a misunderstanding somewhere, and I want to put it right. The fact is, this is a good dragon."

"Exactly," said St. George, smiling pleasantly, "I quite understand. A good dragon. Believe me, I do not in the least regret that he is an adversary worthy of my steel, and no feeble specimen of his noxious tribe."

"But he's not a noxious tribe," cried the Boy distressedly. "Oh dear, oh dear, how stupid men are when they get an idea into their heads! I tell you he's a good dragon, and a friend of mine, and tells me the most beautiful stories you ever heard, all about old times and when he was little. And he's been so kind to mother, and mother'd do anything for him. And father likes him too, though father doesn't hold with art and poetry

much, and always falls asleep when the dragon starts talking about style. But the fact is, nobody can help liking him when once they know him. He's so engaging and so trustful, and as simple as a child!"

"Sit down, and draw your chair up," said St. George. "I like a fellow who sticks up for his friends, and I'm sure the dragon has his good points, if he's got a friend like you. But that's not the question. All this evening I've been listening, with grief and anguish unspeakable, to tales of murder, theft, and wrong; rather too highly coloured, perhaps, not always quite convincing, but forming in the main a most serious roll of crime. History teaches us that the greatest rascals often possess all the domestic virtues; and I fear that your cultivated friend, in spite of the qualities which have won (and rightly) your regard, has got to be speedily exterminated."

"Oh, you've been taking in all the yarns those fellows have been telling you," said the Boy impatiently. "Why, our villagers are the biggest storytellers in all the country round. It's a known fact. You're a stranger in these parts, or else you'd have heard it already. All they want is a fight. They're the most awful beggars for getting up fights—it's meat and drink to them. Dogs, bulls, dragons— anything so long as it's a fight. Why, they've got a poor innocent badger in the stable behind here, at this moment. They were going to have some fun with him to-day, but they're saving him up now till your little affair's over. And I've no doubt they've been telling you what a hero you were, and how you were bound to win, in the cause of right and justice, and so on; but let me tell you, I came down the street just now, and they were betting six to four on the dragon freely!"

"Six to four on the dragon!" murmured St. George sadly, resting his cheek on his hand. "This is an evil world, and sometimes I begin to think that all the wickedness in it is not entirely bottled up inside the dragons. And yet—may not this wily beast have misled you as to his real character, in order that your good report of him may serve as a cloak for his evil deeds? Nay, may there not be, at this very moment, some hapless Princess immured within yonder gloomy cavern?"

The moment he had spoken, St. George was sorry for what he had said, the Boy looked so genuinely distressed.

"I assure you, St. George," he said earnestly, "there's nothing of the sort in the cave at all. The dragon's a real gentleman, every inch of him, and I may say that no one would be more shocked and grieved than he would, at hearing you talk in that—that loose way about matters on which he has very strong views!"

"Well, perhaps I've been over-credulous," said St. George. "Perhaps I've misjudged the animal. But what are we to do? Here are the dragon and I, almost face to face, each supposed to be thirsting for each other's blood. I don't see any way out of it, exactly. What do you suggest? Can't you arrange things, somehow?"

"That's just what the dragon said," replied the Boy, rather nettled. "Really, the way you two seem to leave everything to me—I suppose you couldn't be persuaded to go away quietly, could you?"

"Impossible, I fear," said the Saint. "Quite against the rules. You know that as well as I do."

"Well, then, look here," said the Boy, "it's early yet—would you mind strolling up with me and seeing the dragon and talking it over? It's not far, and any friend of mine will be most welcome."

"Well, it's irregular," said St. George, rising, "but really it seems about the most sensible thing to do. You're taking a lot of trouble on your friend's account," he added, good-naturedly, as they passed out through the door together. "But cheer up! Perhaps there won't have to be any fight after all."

"Oh, but I hope there will, though!" replied the little fellow, wistfully.

"I've brought a friend to see you, dragon," said the Boy, rather loud.

The dragon woke up with a start. "I was just—er—thinking about things," he said in his simple way. "Very pleased to make your acquaintance, sir. Charming weather we're having!"

"This is St. George," said the Boy, shortly. "St. George, let me introduce you to the dragon. We've come up to talk things over quietly, dragon, and now for goodness' sake do let us have a little straight common-sense, and come to some practical business-like arrangement, for I'm sick of views and theories of life and personal tendencies, and all that sort of thing. I may perhaps add that my mother's sitting up."

"So glad to meet you, St. George," began the dragon rather nervously, "because you've been a great traveller, I hear, and I've always been rather a stay-at-home. But I can show you many antiquities, many interesting features of our countryside, if you're stopping here any time—"

"I think," said St. George, in his frank, pleasant way, "that we'd really better take the advice of our young friend here, and try to come to some understanding, on a business footing, about this little affair of ours. Now don't you think that after all the simplest plan would be just to fight it out, according to the rules, and let the best man win? They're betting on you, I may tell you, down in the village, but I don't mind that!"

"Oh, yes, do, dragon," said the Boy, delightedly; "it'll save such a lot of bother!"

"My young friend, you shut up," said the dragon severely. "Believe me, St. George," he went on, "there's nobody in the world I'd sooner oblige than you and this young gentleman here. But the whole thing's nonsense, and conventionality, and popular thick-headedness. There's absolutely nothing to fight about, from beginning to end. And anyhow I'm not going to, so that settles it!"

"But supposing I make you?" said St. George, rather nettled.

"You can't," said the dragon, triumphantly. "I should only go into my cave and retire for a time down the hole I came up. You'd soon get heartily sick of sitting outside and waiting for me to come out and fight you. And as soon as you'd really gone away, why, I'd come up again gaily, for I tell you frankly, I like this place, and I'm going to stay here!"

St. George gazed for a while on the fair landscape around them. "But this would be a beautiful place for a fight," he began again persuasively. "These great bare rolling Downs for the arena,—and me in my golden armour showing up against your big blue scaly coils! Think what a picture it would make!"

"Now you're trying to get at me through my artistic sensibilities," said the dragon. "But it won't work. Not but what it would make a very pretty picture, as you say," he added, wavering a little.

"We seem to be getting rather nearer to business," put in the Boy. "You must see, dragon, that there's got to be a fight of some sort, 'cos you can't want to have to go down that dirty old hole again and stop there till goodness knows when."

"It might be arranged," said St. George, thoughtfully. "I must spear you somewhere, of course, but I'm not bound to hurt you very much. There's such a lot of you that there must be a few spare places somewhere. Here, for instance, just behind your foreleg. It couldn't hurt you much, just here!"

"Now you're tickling, George," said the dragon, coyly. "No, that place won't do at all. Even if it didn't hurt,—and I'm sure it would, awfully,—it would make me laugh, and that would spoil everything."

"Let's try somewhere else, then," said St. George, patiently. "Under your neck, for instance,—all these folds of thick skin,—if I speared you here you'd never even know I'd done it!"

"Yes, but are you sure you can hit off the right place?" asked the dragon, anxiously.

"Of course I am," said St. George, with confidence. "You leave that to me!"

"It's just because I've got to leave it to you that I'm asking," replied the dragon, rather testily. "No doubt you would deeply regret any error you might make in the hurry of the moment; but you wouldn't regret it half as much as I should! However, I suppose we've got to trust somebody, as we go through life, and your plan seems, on the whole, as good a one as any."

"Look here, dragon," interrupted the Boy, a little jealous on behalf of his friend, who seemed to be getting all the worst of the bargain: "I don't quite see where you come in! There's to be a fight, apparently, and you're to be licked; and what I want to know is, what are you going to get out of it?"

"St. George," said the dragon, "Just tell him, please,—what will happen after I'm vanquished in the deadly combat?"

"Well, according to the rules I suppose I shall lead you in triumph down to the market-place or whatever answers to it," said St. George.

"Precisely," said the dragon. "And then—"

"And then there'll be shoutings and speeches and things," continued St. George. "And I shall explain that you're converted, and see the error of your ways, and so on."

"Quite so," said the dragon. "And then—?"

"Oh, and then—" said St. George, "why, and then there will be the usual banquet, I suppose."

"Exactly," said the dragon; "and that's where I come in. Look here," he continued, addressing the Boy, "I'm bored to death up here, and no one really appreciates me. I'm going into Society, I am, through the kindly aid of our friend here, who's taking such a lot of trouble on my account; and you'll find I've got all the qualities to endear me to people who entertain! So now that's all settled, and if you don't mind—I'm an old-fashioned fellow—don't want to turn you out, but—"

"Remember, you'll have to do your proper share of the fighting, dragon!" said St. George, as he took the hint and rose to go; "I mean ramping, and breathing fire, and so on!"

"I can ramp all right," replied the dragon, confidently; "as to breathing fire, it's surprising how easily one gets out of practice, but I'll do the best I can. Good-night!"

They had descended the hill and were almost back in the village again, when St. George stopped short. "Knew I had forgotten something," he said. "There ought to be a Princess. Terror-stricken and chained to a rock, and all that sort of thing. Boy, can't you arrange a Princess?"

The Boy was in the middle of a tremendous yawn. "I'm tired to death," he wailed, "and I can't arrange a Princess, or anything more, at this time of night. And my mother's sitting up, and do stop asking me to arrange more things till to-morrow!"

Next morning the people began streaming up to the Downs at quite an early hour, in their Sunday clothes and carrying baskets with bottle-necks sticking out of them, every one intent on securing good places for the combat. This was not exactly a simple matter, for of course it was quite possible that the dragon might win, and in that case even those who had put their money on him felt they could hardly expect him to deal with his backers on a different footing to the rest. Places were chosen, therefore, with circumspection and with a view to a speedy retreat in case of emergency; and the front rank was mostly composed of boys who had escaped from parental control and now sprawled and rolled about on the grass, regardless of the shrill threats and warnings discharged at them by their anxious mothers behind.

The Boy had secured a good front place, well up towards the cave, and was feeling as anxious as a stage-manager on a first night. Could the dragon be depended upon? He might change his mind and vote the whole performance rot; or else, seeing that the affair had been so hastily planned, without even a rehearsal, he might be too nervous to show up. The Boy looked narrowly at the cave, but it showed no sign of life or occupation. Could the dragon have made a moon-light flitting?

The higher portions of the ground were now black with sightseers, and presently a sound of cheering and a waving of handkerchiefs told that something was visible to them which the Boy, far up towards the dragon-end of the line as he was, could not yet see. A minute more and St. George's red plumes topped the hill, as the Saint rode slowly forth on the great level space which stretched up to the grim mouth of the cave. Very gallant and beautiful he looked, on his tall war-horse, his golden armour glancing in the sun, his great spear held erect, the little white pennon, crimson-crossed, fluttering at its point. He drew rein and remained motionless. The lines of spectators began to give back a little, nervously; and even the boys in front stopped pulling hair and cuffing each other, and leaned forward expectant.

"Now then, dragon!" muttered the Boy impatiently, fidgeting where he sat. He need not have distressed himself, had he only known. The dramatic possibilities of the thing had tickled the dragon immensely, and he had been up from an early hour, preparing for his first public appearance with as much heartiness as if the years had run backwards, and he had been again a little dragonlet, playing with his sisters on the floor of their mother's cave, at the game of saints-and-dragons, in which the dragon was bound to win.

A low muttering, mingled with snorts, now made itself heard; rising to a bellowing roar that seemed to fill the plain. Then a cloud of smoke obscured the mouth of the cave, and out of the midst of it the dragon himself, shining, sea-blue, magnificent, pranced splendidly forth; and everybody said, "Oo-oo-oo!" as if he had been a mighty rocket! His scales were glittering, his long spiky tail lashed his sides, his claws tore up the turf and sent it flying high over his back, and smoke and fire incessantly jetted from his angry nostrils. "Oh, well done, dragon!" cried the Boy, excitedly. "Didn't think he had it in him!" he added to himself.

St. George lowered his spear, bent his head, dug his heels into his horse's sides, and came thundering over the turf. The dragon charged with a roar and a squeal,—a great blue whirling combination of coils and snorts and clashing jaws and spikes and fire.

"Missed!" yelled the crowd. There was a moment's entanglement of golden armour and blue-green coils, and spiky tail, and then the great horse, tearing at his bit, carried the Saint, his spear swung high in the air, almost up to the mouth of the cave.

The dragon sat down and barked viciously, while St. George with difficulty pulled his horse round into position.

"End of Round One!" thought the Boy. "How well they managed it! But I hope the Saint won't get excited. I can trust the dragon all right. What a regular play-actor the fellow is!"

St. George had at last prevailed on his horse to stand steady, and was looking round him as he wiped his brow. Catching sight of the Boy, he smiled and nodded, and held up three fingers for an instant.

"It seems to be all planned out," said the Boy to himself. "Round Three is to be the finishing one, evidently. Wish it could have lasted a bit longer. Whatever's that old fool of a dragon up to now?"

The dragon was employing the interval in giving a ramping-performance for the benefit of the crowd. Ramping, it should be explained, consists in running round and round in a wide circle, and sending waves and ripples of movement along the whole length of your spine, from your pointed ears right down to the spike at the end of your long tail. When you are covered with blue scales, the effect is particularly pleasing; and the Boy recollected the dragon's recently expressed wish to become a social success.

St. George now gathered up his reins and began to move forward, dropping the point of his spear and settling himself firmly in the saddle.

"Time!" yelled everybody excitedly; and the dragon, leaving off his ramping sat up on end, and began to leap from one side to the other with huge ungainly bounds, whooping like a Red Indian. This naturally disconcerted the horse, who swerved violently, the Saint only just saving himself by the mane; and as they shot past the dragon delivered a vicious snap at the horse's tail which sent the poor beast careering madly far over the Downs, so that the language of the Saint, who had lost a stirrup, was fortunately inaudible to the general assemblage.

Round Two evoked audible evidence of friendly feeling towards the dragon. The spectators were not slow to appreciate a combatant who could hold his own so well and clearly wanted to show good sport; and many encouraging remarks reached the ears of our friend as he strutted to and fro, his chest thrust out and his tail in the air, hugely enjoying his new popularity.

St. George had dismounted and was tightening his girths, and telling his horse, with quite an Oriental flow of imagery, exactly what he thought of him, and his relations, and his conduct on the present occasion; so the Boy made his way down to the Saint's end of the line, and held his spear for him.

"It's been a jolly fight, St. George!" he said with a sigh. "Can't you let it last a bit longer?"

"Well, I think I'd better not," replied the Saint. "The fact is, your simple-minded old friend's getting conceited, now they've begun cheering him, and he'll forget all about the arrangement and take to playing the fool, and there's no telling where he would stop. I'll just finish him off this round."

He swung himself into the saddle and took his spear from the Boy. "Now don't you be afraid," he added kindly. "I've marked my spot exactly, and he's sure to give me all the assistance in his power, because he knows it's his only chance of being asked to the banquet!"

St. George now shortened his spear, bringing the butt well up under his arm; and, instead of galloping as before, trotted smartly towards the dragon, who crouched at his approach, flicking his tail till it cracked in the air like a great cart-whip. The Saint wheeled as he neared his opponent and circled warily round him, keeping his eye on the spare place; while the dragon, adopting similar tactics, paced with caution round the same circle, occasionally feinting with his head. So the two sparred for an opening, while the spectators maintained a breathless silence.

Though the round lasted for some minutes, the end was so swift that all the Boy saw was a lightning movement of the Saint's arm, and then a whirl and a confusion of spines, claws, tail, and flying bits of turf. The dust cleared away, the spectators whooped and ran in cheering, and the Boy made out that the dragon was down, pinned to the earth by the spear, while St. George had dismounted, and stood astride of him.

It all seemed so genuine that the Boy ran in breathlessly, hoping the dear old dragon wasn't really hurt. As he approached, the dragon lifted one large eyelid, winked solemnly, and collapsed again. He was held fast to earth by the neck, but the Saint had hit him in the spare place agreed upon, and it didn't even seem to tickle.

"Bain't you goin' to cut 'is 'ed orf, master?" asked one of the applauding crowd. He had backed the dragon, and naturally felt a trifle sore.

"Well, not to-day, I think," replied St. George, pleasantly. "You see, that can be done at any time. There's no hurry at all. I think we'll all go down to the village first, and have some refreshment, and then I'll give him a good talking-to, and you'll find he'll be a very different dragon!"

At that magic word refreshment the whole crowd formed up in procession and silently awaited the signal to start. The time for talking and cheering and betting was past, the hour for action had arrived. St. George, hauling on his spear with both hands, released the dragon, who rose and shook himself and ran his eye over his spikes and scales and things, to see that they were all in order. Then the Saint mounted and led off the procession, the dragon following meekly in the company of the Boy, while the thirsty spectators kept at a respectful interval behind.

There were great doings when they got down to the village again, and had formed up in front of the inn. After refreshment St. George made a speech, in which he informed his audience that he had removed their direful scourge, at a great deal of trouble and inconvenience to himself, and now they weren't to go about grumbling and fancying they'd got grievances, because they hadn't. And they shouldn't be so fond of fights, because next time they might have to do the fighting themselves, which would not be the same thing at all. And there was a certain badger in the inn stables which had got to be released at once, and he'd come and see it done himself. Then he told them that the dragon had been thinking over things, and saw that there were two sides to every question, and he wasn't going to do it any more, and if they were good perhaps he'd stay and settle down there. So they must make friends, and not be prejudiced; and go about fancying they knew everything there was to be known, because they

didn't, not by a long way. And he warned them against the sin of romancing, and making up stories and fancying other people would believe them just because they were plausible and highly-coloured. Then he sat down, amidst much repentant cheering, and the dragon nudged the Boy in the ribs and whispered that he couldn't have done it better himself. Then every one went off to get ready for the banquet.

Banquets are always pleasant things, consisting mostly, as they do, of eating and drinking; but the specially nice thing about a banquet is, that it comes when something's over, and there's nothing more to worry about, and to-morrow seems a long way off. St. George was happy because there had been a fight and he hadn't had to kill anybody; for he didn't really like killing, though he generally had to do it. The dragon was happy because there had been a fight, and so far from being hurt in it he had won popularity and a sure footing in society. The Boy was happy because there had been a fight, and in spite of it all his two friends were on the best of terms. And all the others were happy because there had been a fight, and—well, they didn't require any other reasons for their happiness. The dragon exerted himself to say the right thing to everybody, and proved the life and soul of the evening; while the Saint and the Boy, as they looked on, felt that they were only assisting at a feast of which the honour and the glory were entirely the dragon's. But they didn't mind that, being good fellows, and the dragon was not in the least proud or forgetful. On the contrary, every ten minutes or so he leant over towards the Boy and said impressively: "Look here! you will see me home afterwards, won't you?" And the Boy always nodded, though he had promised his mother not to be out late.

At last the banquet was over, the guests had dropped away with many good-nights and congratulations and invitations, and the dragon, who had seen the last of them off the premises, emerged into the street followed by the Boy, wiped his brow, sighed, sat down in the road and gazed at the stars. "Jolly night it's been!" he murmured. "Jolly stars! Jolly little place this! Think

I shall just stop here. Don't feel like climbing up any beastly hill. Boy's promised to see me home. Boy had better do it then! No responsibility on my part. Responsibility all Boy's!" And his chin sank on his broad chest and he slumbered peacefully.

"Oh, get up, dragon," cried the Boy, piteously. "You know my mother's sitting up, and I'm so tired, and you made me promise to see you home, and I never knew what it meant or I wouldn't have done it!" And the Boy sat down in the road by the side of the sleeping dragon, and cried.

The door behind them opened, a stream of light illumined the road, and St. George, who had come out for a stroll in the cool night-air, caught sight of the two figures sitting there—the great motionless dragon and the tearful little Boy.

"What's the matter, Boy?" he inquired kindly, stepping to his side.

"Oh, it's this great lumbering pig of a dragon!" sobbed the Boy. "First he makes me promise to see him home, and then he says I'd better do it, and goes to sleep! Might as well try to see a haystack home! And I'm so tired, and mother's—" here he broke down again.

"Now don't take on," said St. George. "I'll stand by you, and we'll both see him home. Wake up, dragon!" he said sharply, shaking the beast by the elbow.

The dragon looked up sleepily. "What a night, George!" he murmured; "what a—"

"Now look here, dragon," said the Saint, firmly. "Here's this little fellow waiting to see you home, and you know he ought to have been in bed these two hours, and what his mother'll say I don't know, and anybody but a selfish pig would have made him go to bed long ago—"

"And he shall go to bed!" cried the dragon, starting up. "Poor little chap, only fancy his being up at this hour! It's a shame, that's what it is, and I don't think, St. George, you've been very considerate—but come along at once, and don't let us have any more arguing or shilly-shallying. You give me hold of your hand, Boy—thank you, George, an arm up the hill is just what I wanted!"

So they set off up the hill arm-in-arm, the Saint, the Dragon, and the Boy. The lights in the little village began to go out; but there were stars, and a late moon, as they climbed to the Downs together. And, as they turned the last corner and disappeared from view, snatches of an old song were borne back on the night-breeze. I can't be certain which of them was singing, but I think it was the Dragon!

"Here we are at your gate," said the man, abruptly, laying his hand on it. "Good-night. Cut along in sharp, or you'll catch it!"

Could it really be our own gate? Yes, there it was, sure enough, with the familiar marks on its bottom bar made by our feet when we swung on it.

"Oh, but wait a minute!" cried Charlotte. "I want to know a heap of things. Did the dragon really settle down? And did—"

"There isn't any more of that story," said the man, kindly but firmly. "At least, not to-night. Now be off! Good-bye!"

"Wonder if it's all true?" said Charlotte, as we hurried up the path. "Sounded dreadfully like nonsense, in parts!"

"P'raps it's true for all that," I replied encouragingly.

Charlotte bolted in like a rabbit, out of the cold and the dark; but I lingered a moment in the still, frosty air, for a backward glance at the silent white world without, ere I changed it for the land of firelight and cushions and laughter. It was the day for choir-practice, and carol-time was at hand, and a belated member was passing homewards down the road, singing as he went:—

"Then St. George: ee made rev'rence: in the stable so dim, Oo vanquished the dragon: so fearful and grim. So-o grim: and so-o fierce: that now may we say All peaceful is our wakin': on Chri-istmas Day!"

The singer receded, the carol died away. But I wondered, with my hand on the door-latch, whether that was the song, or something like it, that the dragon sang as he toddled contentedly up the hill.

Zitkala-Ša (which translates as Red Bird) was born Gertrude Simmons (1876–1938) in South Dakota and adopted her Lakota name as a teenager. She began publishing stories and biographical essays while she was teaching at Carlisle Indian Industrial School, a place that had eradicated the presence of Native Americans from the historical archive. Her first publications were in the *Atlantic Monthly* and *Harper's Monthly* and focused on her struggle to retain her identity while being pressured to assimilate to the dominant American culture. Zitkala-Ša began working with the composer William F. Hanson and in 1913, produced the first opera by a Native American, *The Sun Dance*. She collected Native American folklore, supported Native American civil rights, and worked to ensure better education for native populations. In 1901, she published *Old Indian Legends*, an anthology of Dakota folktales, from which comes "Iktomi Tales."

Iktomi Tales

Zitkala-Ša

IKTOMI AND THE DUCKS

IKTOMI IS A SPIDER FAIRY. He wears brown deerskin leggins with long soft fringes on either side, and tiny beaded moccasins on his feet. His long black hair is parted in the middle and wrapped with red, red bands. Each round braid hangs over a small brown ear and falls forward over his shoulders.

He even paints his funny face with red and yellow, and draws big black rings around his eyes. He wears a deerskin jacket, with bright colored beads sewed tightly on it. Iktomi dresses like a real Dakota brave. In truth, his paint and deerskins are the best part of him—if ever dress is part of man or fairy.

Iktomi is a wily fellow. His hands are always kept in mischief. He prefers to spread a snare rather than to earn the smallest thing with honest hunting. Why! he laughs outright with wide open mouth when some simple folk are caught in a trap, sure and fast.

He never dreams another lives so bright as he. Often his own conceit leads him hard against the common sense of simpler people.

Poor Iktomi cannot help being a little imp. And so long as he is a naughty fairy, he cannot find a single friend. No one helps him when he is in trouble. No one really loves him. Those who come to admire his handsome beaded jacket and long fringed leggins soon go away sick and tired of his vain, vain words and heartless laughter.

Thus Iktomi lives alone in a cone-shaped wigwam upon the plain. One day he sat hungry within his teepee. Suddenly he rushed out, dragging after him his blanket. Quickly spreading it on the ground, he tore up dry tall grass with both his hands and tossed it fast into the blanket.

Tying all the four corners together in a knot, he threw the light bundle of grass over his shoulder.

Snatching up a slender willow stick with his free left hand, he started off with a hop and a leap. From side to side bounced the bundle on his back, as he ran light-footed over the uneven ground. Soon he came to the edge of the great level land. On the hilltop he paused for breath. With wicked smacks of his dry parched lips, as if tasting some tender meat, he looked straight into space toward the marshy river bottom. With a thin palm shading his eyes from the western sun, he peered far away into the lowlands, munching his own cheeks all the while. "Ah-ha!" grunted he, satisfied with what he saw.

A group of wild ducks were dancing and feasting in the marshes. With wings outspread, tip to tip, they moved up and down in a large circle. Within the ring, around a small drum, sat the chosen singers, nodding their heads and blinking their eyes.

They sang in unison a merry dance-song, and beat a lively tattoo on the drum.

Following a winding footpath near by, came a bent figure of a Dakota brave. He bore on his back a very large bundle. With a willow cane he propped himself up as he staggered along beneath his burden.

"Ho! who is there?" called out a curious old duck, still bobbing up and down in the circular dance.

Hereupon the drummers stretched their necks till they strangled their song for a look at the stranger passing by.

"Ho, Iktomi! Old fellow, pray tell us what you carry in your blanket. Do not hurry off! Stop! halt!" urged one of the singers.

"Stop! stay! Show us what is in your blanket!" cried out other voices.

"My friends, I must not spoil your dance. Oh, you would not care to see if you only knew what is in my blanket. Sing on! dance on! I must not show you what I carry on my back," answered Iktomi, nudging his own sides with his elbows. This reply broke up the ring entirely. Now all the ducks crowded about Iktomi.

"We must see what you carry! We must know what is in your blanket!" they shouted in both his ears. Some even brushed their wings against the mysterious bundle. Nudging himself again, wily Iktomi said, "My friends, 't is only a pack of songs I carry in my blanket."

"Oh, then let us hear your songs!" cried the curious ducks.

At length Iktomi consented to sing his songs. With delight all the ducks flapped their wings and cried together, "Hoye! hoye!"

Iktomi, with great care, laid down his bundle on the ground.

"I will build first a round straw house, for I never sing my songs in the open air," said he.

Quickly he bent green willow sticks, planting both ends of each pole into the earth. These he covered thick with reeds and grasses. Soon the straw hut was ready. One by one the fat ducks waddled in through a small opening, which was the only entrance way. Beside the door Iktomi stood smiling, as the ducks, eyeing his bundle of songs, strutted into the hut.

In a strange low voice Iktomi began his queer old tunes. All the ducks sat round-eyed in a circle about the mysterious singer. It was dim in that straw hut, for Iktomi had not forgot to cover up the small entrance way. All of a sudden his song burst into full voice. As the startled ducks sat uneasily on the ground, Iktomi changed his tune into a minor strain. These were the words he sang:

"Istokmus wacipo, tuwayatunwanpi kinhan ista nisasapi kta," which is, "With eyes closed you must dance. He who dares to open his eyes, forever red eyes shall have."

Up rose the circle of seated ducks and holding their wings close against their sides began to dance to the rhythm of Iktomi's song and drum.

With eyes closed they did dance! Iktomi ceased to beat his drum. He began to sing louder and faster. He seemed to be moving about in the center of the ring. No duck dared blink a wink.

Each one shut his eyes very tight and danced even harder. Up and down! Shifting to the right of them they hopped round and round in that blind dance. It was a difficult dance for the curious folk.

At length one of the dancers could close his eyes no longer! It was a Skiska who peeped the least tiny blink at Iktomi within the center of the circle. "Oh! oh!" squawked he in awful terror! "Run! fly! Iktomi is twisting your heads and breaking your necks! Run out and fly! fly!" he cried. Hereupon the ducks opened their eyes. There beside Iktomi's bundle of songs lay half of their crowd—flat on their backs.

Out they flew through the opening Skiska had made as he rushed forth with his alarm.

But as they soared high into the blue sky they cried to one another: "Oh! your eyes are red-red!" "And yours are red-red!" For the warning words of the magic minor strain had proven true. "Ah-ha!" laughed Iktomi, untying the four corners of his blanket, "I shall sit no more hungry within my dwelling." Homeward he trudged along with nice fat ducks in his blanket. He left the little straw hut for the rains and winds to pull down.

Having reached his own teepee on the high level lands, Iktomi kindled a large fire out of doors. He planted sharp-pointed sticks around the leaping flames. On each stake he fastened a duck to roast. A few he buried under the ashes to bake. Disappearing within his teepee, he came out again with some huge seashells. These were his dishes. Placing one under each roasting duck, he muttered, "The sweet fat oozing out will taste well with the hard-cooked breasts."

Heaping more willows upon the fire, Iktomi sat down on the ground with crossed shins. A long chin between his knees pointed toward the red flames, while his eyes were on the browning ducks.

Just above his ankles he clasped and unclasped his long bony fingers. Now and then he sniffed impatiently the savory odor.

The brisk wind which stirred the fire also played with a squeaky old tree beside Iktomi's wigwam.

From side to side the tree was swaying and crying in an old man's voice, "Help! I'll break! I'll fall!" Iktomi shrugged his great shoulders, but did not once take his eyes from the ducks. The dripping of amber oil into pearly dishes, drop by drop, pleased his hungry eyes. Still the old tree man called for help. "He! What sound is it that makes my ear ache!" exclaimed Iktomi, holding a hand on his ear.

He rose and looked around. The squeaking came from the tree. Then he began climbing the tree to find the disagreeable sound. He placed his foot right on a cracked limb without seeing it. Just then a whiff of wind came rushing by and pressed together the broken edges. There in a strong wooden hand Iktomi's foot was caught.

"Oh! my foot is crushed!" he howled like a coward. In vain he pulled and puffed to free himself.

While sitting a prisoner on the tree he spied, through his tears, a pack of gray wolves roaming over the level lands. Waving his hands toward them, he called in his loudest voice, "He! Gray wolves! Don't you come here! I'm caught fast in the tree so that my duck feast is getting cold. Don't you come to eat up my meal."

The leader of the pack upon hearing Iktomi's words turned to his comrades and said:

"Ah! hear the foolish fellow! He says he has a duck feast to be eaten! Let us hurry there for our share!" Away bounded the wolves toward Iktomi's lodge.

From the tree Iktomi watched the hungry wolves eat up his nicely browned fat ducks. His foot pained him more and more. He heard them crack the small round bones with their strong long teeth and eat out the oily marrow. Now severe pains shot up from his foot through his whole body. "Hin-hin-hin!" sobbed Iktomi. Real tears washed brown streaks across his red-painted cheeks. Smacking their lips, the wolves began to leave the place, when Iktomi cried out like a pouting child, "At least you have left my baking under the ashes!"

"Ho! Po!" shouted the mischievous wolves; "he says more ducks are to be found under the ashes! Come! Let us have our fill this once!"

Running back to the dead fire, they pawed out the ducks with such rude haste that a cloud of ashes rose like gray smoke over them.

"Hin-hin-hin!" moaned Iktomi, when the wolves had scampered off. All too late, the sturdy breeze returned, and, passing by, pulled apart the broken edges of the tree. Iktomi was released. But alas! he had no duck feast.

IKTOMI'S BLANKET

Alone within his teepee sat Iktomi. The sun was but a handsbreadth from the western edge of land.

"Those, bad, bad gray wolves! They ate up all my nice fat ducks!" muttered he, rocking his body to and fro.

He was cuddling the evil memory he bore those hungry wolves. At last he ceased to sway his body backward and forward, but sat still and stiff as a stone image.

"Oh! I'll go to Inyan, the great-grandfather, and pray for food!" he exclaimed.

At once he hurried forth from his teepee and, with his blanket over one shoulder, drew nigh to a huge rock on a hillside.

With half-crouching, half-running strides, he fell upon Inyan with outspread hands.

"Grandfather! pity me. I am hungry. I am starving. Give me food. Great-grandfather, give me meat to eat!" he cried. All the while he stroked and caressed the face of the great stone god.

The all-powerful Great Spirit, who makes the trees and grass, can hear the voice of those who pray in many varied ways. The hearing of Inyan, the large hard stone, was the one most sought after. He was the great-grandfather, for he had sat upon the hillside many, many seasons. He had seen the prairie put on a snow-white blanket and then change it for a bright green robe more than a thousand times.

Still unaffected by the myriad moons he rested on the everlasting hill, listening to the prayers of Indian warriors. Before the finding of the magic arrow he had sat there.

Now, as Iktomi prayed and wept before the great-grandfather, the sky in the west was red like a glowing face. The sunset poured a soft mellow light upon the huge gray stone and the solitary figure beside it. It was the smile of the Great Spirit upon the grandfather and the wayward child.

The prayer was heard. Iktomi knew it. "Now, grandfather, accept my offering; 'tis all I have," said Iktomi as he spread his half-worn blanket upon Inyan's cold shoulders. Then Iktomi, happy with the smile of the sunset sky, followed a foot-path leading toward a thicketed ravine. He had not gone many paces into the shrubbery when before him lay a freshly wounded deer!

"This is the answer from the red western sky!" cried Iktomi with hands uplifted.

Slipping a long thin blade from out his belt, he cut large chunks of choice meat. Sharpening some willow sticks, he planted them around a wood-pile he had ready to kindle. On these stakes he meant to roast the venison.

While he was rubbing briskly two long sticks to start a fire, the sun in the west fell out of the sky below the edge of land. Twilight was over all. Iktomi felt the cold night air upon his bare neck and shoulders. "Ough!" he shivered as he wiped his knife on the grass. Tucking it in a beaded case hanging from his belt, Iktomi stood erect, looking about. He shivered again. "Ough! Ah! I am cold. I wish I had my blanket!" whispered he, hovering over the pile of dry sticks and the sharp stakes round about it. Suddenly he paused and dropped his hands at his sides.

"The old great-grandfather does not feel the cold as I do. He does not need my old blanket as I do. I wish I had not given it to him. Oh! I think I'll run up there and take it back!" said he, pointing his long chin toward the large gray stone.

Iktomi, in the warm sunshine, had no need of his blanket, and it had been very easy to part with a thing which he could not miss. But the chilly night wind quite froze his ardent thank-offering.

Thus running up the hillside, his teeth chattering all the way, he drew near to Inyan, the sacred symbol. Seizing one corner of the half-worn blanket, Iktomi pulled it off with a jerk.

"Give my blanket back, old grandfather! You do not need it. I do!" This was very wrong, yet Iktomi did it, for his wit was not wisdom. Drawing the blanket tight over his shoulders, he descended the hill with hurrying feet.

He was soon upon the edge of the ravine. A young moon, like a bright bent bow, climbed up from the southwest horizon a little way into the sky.

In this pale light Iktomi stood motionless as a ghost amid the thicket. His woodpile was not yet kindled. His pointed stakes were still bare as he had left them. But where was the deer—the venison he had felt warm in his hands a moment ago? It was gone. Only the dry rib bones lay on the ground like giant fingers from an open grave. Iktomi was troubled. At length, stooping over the white dried bones, he took hold of one and shook it. The bones, loose in their sockets, rattled together at his touch. Iktomi let go his hold. He sprang back amazed. And though he wore a blanket his teeth chattered more than ever. Then his blunted sense will surprise you, little reader; for instead of being grieved that he had taken back his blanket, he cried aloud, "Hin-hin-hin! If only I had eaten the venison before going for my blanket!"

Those tears no longer moved the hand of the Generous Giver. They were selfish tears. The Great Spirit does not heed them ever.

IKTOMI AND THE MUSKRAT

Beside a white lake, beneath a large grown willow tree, sat Iktomi on the bare ground. The heap of smouldering ashes told of a recent open fire. With ankles crossed together around a pot of soup, Iktomi bent over some delicious boiled fish.

Fast he dipped his black horn spoon into the soup, for he was ravenous. Iktomi had no regular meal times. Often when he was hungry he went without food.

Well hid between the lake and the wild rice, he looked nowhere save into the pot of fish. Not knowing when the next meal would be, he meant to eat enough now to last some time.

"How, how, my friend!" said a voice out of the wild rice. Iktomi started. He almost choked with his soup. He peered through the long reeds from where he sat with his long horn spoon in mid-air.

"How, my friend!" said the voice again, this time close at his side. Iktomi turned and there stood a dripping muskrat who had just come out of the lake.

"Oh, it is my friend who startled me. I wondered if among the wild rice some spirit voice was talking. How, how, my friend!" said Iktomi. The muskrat stood smiling. On his lips hung a ready "Yes, my friend," when Iktomi would ask, "My friend, will you sit down beside me and share my food?"

That was the custom of the plains people. Yet Iktomi sat silent. He hummed an old dance-song and beat gently on the edge of the pot with his buffalo-horn spoon. The muskrat began to feel awkward before such lack of hospitality and wished himself under water.

After many heart throbs Iktomi stopped drumming with his horn ladle, and looking upward into the muskrat's face, he said:

"My friend, let us run a race to see who shall win this pot of fish. If I win, I shall not need to share it with you. If you win, you shall have half of it." Springing to his feet, Iktomi began at once to tighten the belt about his waist.

"My friend Ikto, I cannot run a race with you! I am not a swift runner, and you are nimble as a deer. We shall not run any race together," answered the hungry muskrat.

For a moment Iktomi stood with a hand on his long protruding chin. His eyes were fixed upon something in the air. The muskrat looked out of the corners of his eyes without moving his head. He watched the wily Iktomi concocting a plot.

"Yes, yes," said Iktomi, suddenly turning his gaze upon the unwelcome visitor; "I shall carry a large stone on my back. That will slacken my usual speed; and the race will be a fair one."

Saying this he laid a firm hand upon the

muskrat's shoulder and started off along the edge of the lake. When they reached the opposite side Iktomi pried about in search of a heavy stone.

He found one half-buried in the shallow water. Pulling it out upon dry land, he wrapped it in his blanket.

"Now, my friend, you shall run on the left side of the lake, I on the other. The race is for the boiled fish in yonder kettle!" said Iktomi.

The muskrat helped to lift the heavy stone upon Iktomi's back. Then they parted. Each took a narrow path through the tall reeds fringing the shore. Iktomi found his load a heavy one. Perspiration hung like beads on his brow. His chest heaved hard and fast.

He looked across the lake to see how far the muskrat had gone, but nowhere did he see any sign of him. "Well, he is running low under the wild rice!" said he. Yet as he scanned the tall grasses on the lake shore, he saw not one stir as if to make way for the runner. "Ah, has he gone so fast ahead that the disturbed grasses in his trail have quieted again?" exclaimed Iktomi. With that thought he quickly dropped the heavy stone. "No more of this!" said he, patting his chest with both hands.

Off with a springing bound, he ran swiftly toward the goal. Tufts of reeds and grass fell flat under his feet. Hardly had they raised their heads when Iktomi was many paces gone.

Soon he reached the heap of cold ashes. Iktomi halted stiff as if he had struck an invisible cliff. His black eyes showed a ring of white about them as he stared at the empty ground. There was no pot of boiled fish! There was no water-man in sight! "Oh, if only I had shared my food like a real Dakota, I would not have lost it all! Why did I not know the muskrat would run through the water? He swims faster than I could ever run! That is what he has done. He has laughed at me for carrying a weight on my back while he shot hither like an arrow!"

Crying thus to himself, Iktomi stepped to the water's brink. He stooped forward with a hand on each bent knee and peeped far into the deep water.

"There!" he exclaimed, "I see you, my friend, sitting with your ankles wound around my little pot of fish! My friend, I am hungry. Give me a bone!"

"Ha! ha! ha!" laughed the water-man, the muskrat. The sound did not rise up out of the lake, for it came down from overhead. With his hands still on his knees, Iktomi turned his face upward into the great willow tree. Opening wide his mouth he begged, "My friend, my friend, give me a bone to gnaw!"

"Ha! ha!" laughed the muskrat, and leaning over the limb he sat upon, he let fall a small sharp bone which dropped right into Iktomi's throat. Iktomi almost choked to death before he could get it out. In the tree the muskrat sat laughing loud. "Next time, say to a visiting friend, 'Be seated beside me, my friend. Let me share with you my food.'"

IKTOMI AND THE COYOTE

Afar off upon a large level land, a summer sun was shining bright. Here and there over the rolling green were tall bunches of coarse gray weeds. Iktomi in his fringed buckskins walked alone across the prairie with a black bare head glossy in the sunlight. He walked through the grass without following any well-worn footpath.

From one large bunch of coarse weeds to another he wound his way about the great plain. He lifted his foot lightly and placed it gently forward like a wildcat prowling noiselessly through the thick grass. He stopped a few steps away from a very large bunch of wild sage. From shoulder to shoulder he tilted his head. Still farther he bent from side to side, first low over one hip and then over the other. Far forward he stooped, stretching his long thin neck like a duck, to see what lay under a fur coat beyond the bunch of coarse grass.

A sleek gray-faced prairie wolf! his pointed black nose tucked in between his four feet drawn snugly together; his handsome bushy tail wound over his nose and feet; a coyote fast asleep in the shadow of a bunch of grass!—this is what Iktomi spied. Carefully he raised one foot and cautiously reached out with his toes. Gently, gently he lifted the foot behind and placed it before the other. Thus he came nearer and nearer to the round fur ball lying motionless under the sage grass.

Now Iktomi stood beside it, looking at the closed eyelids that did not quiver the least bit. Pressing his lips into straight lines and nodding his head slowly, he bent over the wolf. He held his ear close to the coyote's nose, but not a breath of air stirred from it.

"Dead!" said he at last. "Dead, but not long since he ran over these plains! See! there in his paw is caught a fresh feather. He is nice fat meat!" Taking hold of the paw with the bird feather fast on it, he exclaimed, "Why, he is still warm! I'll carry him to my dwelling and have a roast for my evening meal. Ah-ha!" he laughed, as he seized the coyote by its two fore paws and its two hind feet and swung him over head across his shoulders. The wolf was large and the teepee was far across the prairie. Iktomi trudged along with his burden, smacking his hungry lips together. He blinked his eyes hard to keep out the salty perspiration streaming down his face.

All the while the coyote on his back lay gazing into the sky with wide open eyes. His long white teeth fairly gleamed as he smiled and smiled.

"To ride on one's own feet is tiresome, but to be carried like a warrior from a brave fight is great fun!" said the coyote in his heart. He had never been borne on any one's back before and the new experience delighted him. He lay there lazily on Iktomi's shoulders, now and then blinking blue winks. Did you never see a birdie blink a blue wink? This is how it first became a saying among the plains people. When a bird stands aloof watching your strange ways, a thin bluish white tissue slips quickly over his eyes and as quickly off again; so quick that you think it was only a mysterious blue wink. Sometimes when children grow drowsy they blink blue winks, while others who are too proud to look

with friendly eyes upon people blink in this cold bird-manner.

The coyote was affected by both sleepiness and pride. His winks were almost as blue as the sky. In the midst of his new pleasure the swaying motion ceased. Iktomi had reached his dwelling place. The coyote felt drowsy no longer, for in the next instant he was slipping out of Iktomi's hands. He was falling, falling through space, and then he struck the ground with such a bump he did not wish to breathe for a while. He wondered what Iktomi would do, thus he lay still where he fell. Humming a dance-song, one from his bundle of mystery songs, Iktomi hopped and darted about at an imaginary dance and feast. He gathered dry willow sticks and broke them in two against his knee. He built a large fire out of doors. The flames leaped up high in red and yellow streaks. Now Iktomi returned to the coyote who had been looking on through his eyelashes.

Taking him again by his paws and hind feet, he swung him to and fro. Then as the wolf swung toward the red flames, Iktomi let him go. Once again the coyote fell through space. Hot air smote his nostrils. He saw red dancing fire, and now he struck a bed of cracking embers. With a quick turn he leaped out of the flames. From his heels were scattered a shower of red coals upon Iktomi's bare arms and shoulders. Dumbfounded, Iktomi thought he saw a spirit walk out of his fire. His jaws fell apart. He thrust a palm to his face, hard over his mouth! He could scarce keep from shrieking.

Rolling over and over on the grass and rubbing the sides of his head against the ground, the coyote soon put out the fire on his fur. Iktomi's eyes were almost ready to jump out of his head as he stood cooling a burn on his brown arm with his breath.

Sitting on his haunches, on the opposite side of the fire from where Iktomi stood, the coyote began to laugh at him.

"Another day, my friend, do not take too much for granted. Make sure the enemy is stone dead before you make a fire!"

Then off he ran so swiftly that his long bushy tail hung out in a straight line with his back.

IKTOMI AND THE FAWN

In one of his wanderings through the wooded lands, Iktomi saw a rare bird sitting high in a tree-top. Its long fan-like tail feathers had caught all the beautiful colors of the rainbow. Handsome in the glistening summer sun sat the bird of rainbow plumage. Iktomi hurried hither with his eyes fast on the bird.

He stood beneath the tree looking long and wistfully at the peacock's bright feathers. At length he heaved a sigh and began: "Oh, I wish I had such pretty feathers! How I wish I were not I! If only I were a handsome feathered creature how happy I would be! I'd be so glad to sit upon a very high tree and bask in the summer sun like you!" said he suddenly, pointing his bony finger up toward the peacock, who was eyeing the stranger below, turning his head from side to side.

"I beg of you make me into a bird with green and purple feathers like yours!" implored Iktomi, tired now of playing the brave in beaded buck-skins. The peacock then spoke to Iktomi: "I have a magic power. My touch will change you in a moment into the most beautiful peacock if you can keep one condition."

"Yes! yes!" shouted Iktomi, jumping up and down, patting his lips with his palm, which caused his voice to vibrate in a peculiar fashion. "Yes! yes! I could keep ten conditions if only you would change me into a bird with long, bright tail feathers. Oh, I am so ugly! I am so tired of being myself! Change me! Do!"

Hereupon the peacock spread out both his wings, and scarce moving them, he sailed slowly down upon the ground. Right beside Iktomi he alighted. Very low in Iktomi's ear the peacock whispered, "Are you willing to keep one condition, though hard it be?"

"Yes! yes! I've told you ten of them if need be!" exclaimed Iktomi, with some impatience.

"Then I pronounce you a handsome feathered bird. No longer are you Iktomi the mischief-maker." Saying this the peacock touched Iktomi with the tips of his wings.

Iktomi vanished at the touch. There stood beneath the tree two handsome peacocks. While one of the pair strutted about with a head turned aside as if dazzled by his own bright-tinted tail feathers, the other bird soared slowly upward. He sat quiet and unconscious of his gay plumage. He seemed content to perch there on a large limb in the warm sunshine.

After a little while the vain peacock, dizzy with his bright colors, spread out his wings and lit on the same branch with the elder bird.

"Oh!" he exclaimed, "how hard to fly! Brightly tinted feathers are handsome, but I wish they were light enough to fly!" Just there the elder bird interrupted him. "That is the one condition. Never try to fly like other birds. Upon the day you try to fly you shall be changed into your former self."

"Oh, what a shame that bright feathers cannot fly into the sky!" cried the peacock. Already he grew restless. He longed to soar through space. He yearned to fly above the trees high upward to the sun.

"Oh, there I see a flock of birds flying thither! Oh! oh!" said he, flapping his wings, "I must try my wings! I am tired of bright tail feathers. I want to try my wings."

"No, no!" clucked the elder bird. The flock of chattering birds flew by with whirring wings. "Oop! oop!" called some to their mates.

Possessed by an irrepressible impulse the Iktomi peacock called out, "He! I want to come! Wait for me!" and with that he gave a lunge into the air. The flock of flying feathers wheeled about and lowered over the tree whence came the pea-cock's cry. Only one rare bird sat on the tree, and beneath, on the ground, stood a brave in brown buckskins.

"I am my old self again!" groaned Iktomi in a sad voice. "Make me over, pretty bird. Try me this once again!" he pleaded in vain.

"Old Iktomi wants to fly! Ah! We cannot wait for him!" sang the birds as they flew away.

Muttering unhappy vows to himself, Iktomi had not gone far when he chanced upon a bunch of long slender arrows. One by one they rose in the air and shot a straight line over the prairie. Others shot up into the blue sky and were soon lost to sight. Only one was left. He was making ready for his flight when Iktomi rushed upon him and wailed, "I want to be an arrow! Make me into an arrow! I want to pierce the blue Blue overhead. I want to strike yonder summer sun in its center. Make me into an arrow!"

"Can you keep a condition? One condition, though hard it be?" the arrow turned to ask.

"Yes! Yes!" shouted Iktomi, delighted.

Hereupon the slender arrow tapped him gently with his sharp flint beak. There was no Iktomi, but two arrows stood ready to fly. "Now, young arrow, this is the one condition. Your flight must always be in a straight line. Never turn a curve nor jump about like a young fawn," said the arrow magician. He spoke slowly and sternly.

At once he set about to teach the new arrow how to shoot in a long straight line.

"This is the way to pierce the Blue overhead," said he; and off he spun high into the sky.

While he was gone a herd of deer came trotting by. Behind them played the young fawns together. They frolicked about like kittens. They bounced on all fours like balls. Then they pitched forward, kicking their heels in the air. The Iktomi arrow watched them so happy on the ground. Looking quickly up into the sky, he said in his heart, "The magician is out of sight. I'll just romp and frolic with these fawns until he returns. Fawns! Friends, do not fear me. I want to jump and leap with you. I long to be happy as you are," said he. The young fawns stopped with stiff legs and stared at the speaking arrow with large brown wondering eyes. "See! I can jump as well as you!" went on Iktomi. He gave one tiny leap like a fawn. All of a sudden the fawns snorted with extended nostrils at what they beheld. There among them stood Iktomi in brown buckskins, and the strange talking arrow was gone.

"Oh! I am myself. My old self!" cried Iktomi, pinching himself and plucking imaginary pieces out of his jacket.

"Hin-hin-hin! I wanted to fly!"

The real arrow now returned to the earth. He alighted very near Iktomi. From the high sky he had seen the fawns playing on the green. He had seen Iktomi make his one leap, and the charm was broken. Iktomi became his former self.

"Arrow, my friend, change me once more!" begged Iktomi.

"No, no more," replied the arrow. Then away he shot through the air in the direction his comrades had flown.

By this time the fawns gathered close around Iktomi. They poked their noses at him trying to know who he was.

Iktomi's tears were like a spring shower. A new desire dried them quickly away. Stepping boldly to the largest fawn, he looked closely at the little brown spots all over the furry face.

"Oh, fawn! What beautiful brown spots on your face! Fawn, dear little fawn, can you tell me how those brown spots were made on your face?"

"Yes," said the fawn. "When I was very, very small, my mother marked them on my face with a red hot fire. She dug a large hole in the ground and made a soft bed of grass and twigs in it. Then she placed me gently there. She covered me over with dry sweet grass and piled dry cedars on top. From a neighbor's fire she brought hither a red, red ember. This she tucked carefully in at my head. This is how the brown spots were made on my face."

"Now, fawn, my friend, will you do the same for me? Won't you mark my face with brown, brown spots just like yours?" asked Iktomi, always eager to be like other people.

"Yes. I can dig the ground and fill it with dry grass and sticks. If you will jump into the pit, I'll cover you with sweet smelling grass and cedar wood," answered the fawn.

"Say," interrupted Ikto, "will you be sure to

cover me with a great deal of dry grass and twigs? You will make sure that the spots will be as brown as those you wear."

"Oh, yes. I'll pile up grass and willows once oftener than my mother did."

"Now let us dig the hole, pull the grass, and gather sticks," cried Iktomi in glee.

Thus with his own hands he aids in making his grave. After the hole was dug and cushioned with grass, Iktomi, muttering something about brown spots, leaped down into it. Lengthwise, flat on his back, he lay. While the fawn covered

him over with cedars, a far-away voice came up through them, "Brown, brown spots to wear forever!" A red ember was tucked under the dry grass. Off scampered the fawns after their mothers; and when a great distance away they looked backward. They saw a blue smoke rising, writhing upward till it vanished in the blue ether.

"Is that Iktomi's spirit?" asked one fawn of another.

"No! I think he would jump out before he could burn into smoke and cinders," answered his comrade.

Louis-Honoré Fréchette (1839–1908) was a French Canadian poet, play-wright, journalist, and writer of short fiction. He was also a politician for the Liberal Party of Montreal, although he only served in the Canadian Parliament for four years. Louis Fréchette was one of the most accomplished French Canadian writers of his time. He wrote both original stories and folktales, along with poetry and plays. His tales from the logging camps in Quebec are written in a vernacular typical of that time period but still today have a universal appeal. This story, "Marionettes," is part of a sequence of stories featuring his raconteur, Jos Violon, a man he knew in real life in his youth. Fréchette's stories rely heavily on the raconteur voice and the tradi-tional folk model. In "Marionettes," Fréchette demonstrates a very tradi-tional logging folktale of that time. Unlike the tall tales of Paul Bunyan in the United States that exaggerated accomplishments and boasted of all things (always bigger!), these French Canadian tales are focused on the religious fantastic, with a strong moralistic ending.

Marionettes

Louis Fréchette

Translated by Gio Clairval

CRICK-CRACK, CHILDREN! Tawkie, tawkoe, let's tawk! Ta cut a thick yarn thin, yield the stage ta Jos Violon. Ouch-ouch, tobacco pouch, if they don't listen theya off the couch. I know you've been dancin til père Jean Bilodeau's floor got worn down ta the slabs, so maybe 'tis time ta take a breather! Anyway you can see that our violliner is on his knees . . . No offense ta the chum. Obvi-ous, he ain't gotten our Fifi Labranche's stamina! Fifi Labranche? Methinks, you children haven't known Fifi Labranche, the violin player.

Yer too young ta have known him, and that's normal 'cause he died at Pointe-aux-Trembles, the year of the great cholera. What a rydah! He had some twist in his wrist ta make the youth dance. As they say, he was unreal! And when he had a bow at the end of his hand, one could run down the south coast from Baie-du-Fenvre ta Cap-Saint-Ignace and never meet, among old and young, one single fella ta match him.

Everyuns knew 'bout Fifi Labranche and his violin. Well, children, I was just sayin all this 'cause, one fall, I got ta be his partner. Not ta play music, mind you, because, even tho' they call me Jos Violon—a good name I've always borne as honorably as I could, thank God—nobody has ever wanted me ta play any instrument, not even a shawm with no holes.

Nope, Fifi Labranche and me, we'd become partners just ta cut some square timber. He was a swell lumberjack, our Fifi Labranche, and, as fer me, I've been known fer swingin da great axe at em oak, elm, red pine and white spruce, I was as good at loggin as him at playin reels and gigues. Honest, you could have hiked wicked far before someone could prove me wrong. That's what I'm sayin.

So, that winter the both of us set up our loggin camp somewhere near da Gatineau River, by the Baptist River, as they call it, with a gang of crooks a foreman of Master Wright's had pranced about through a parish called the Cedars, upstairs in da North. Eh, children, em travelers that tramp across the Cedars, they don't swear like the guys from Sorel, nope! They don't scurrilate the Good Lord and all the Saints of the calendar either, like em thugs from Trois-Rivières do. They don't stop ta squabble at any fencin picket they come by, like those hard fighters from Lanoraie.

But when it comes ta doin unearthly deeds, fer example, not many guys 'round here can hold up a candle ta em. Every night that God brings, on a raft of timber or in the woods, em scapegallows have one brewitchery or three at the ready.

Ah, those children of perdition!

I've seen some of em balance a quarter pork on the tips of their fingers, as if it was a pillow, all the way jabbin through prayers backwards, that no way could a Chrissian twig a damn word. I've seen 'un of those Barabbas chewin on firebrands, with all respect, like a plug of tobacco.

Anuther fella, one Pierre Cadoret, nicknamed "Rope Sheepskin," or, "The Rope," carried around a black hen. Whaddideedo with that? God only knows; or maybe the devil, because, every mornin at the break of dawn, that impious black hen crowed like a rooster, as if rulin over a whole chicken coop. You have my word as yer truthful Jos Violon, children! I heard that with my own two eyes, more than twenty times!

Some bunch of serious miscreants, I am tellin you, that's what they were. It rubbed my temper the wrong way, havin ta put up with that kind of scoundrels. I ain't no sacristy mouse, nope, sir!

But black hens and me is like chalk and cheese, patticularly with hens that crow like roosters.

Fer all these reasons, I wasn't likin that society at all. But I was paired up with Fifi Labranche, right? So I let the rest of the gang knock up their sacrileges between emselves; and after dinner the two of us played a little game of checkers, puffin on our pipes, ta kill time without throwin our souls inta Old Harry's clutches.

But it didn't count: you know, a bad clique is a bad clique. As Monsieur le Curé says, tell me what you peddle and I'll tell you what's killin you.

On Christmas Eve, the boss came ta see us:

"Listen up, ya two," he tells us. "'Tis 'cause you are two whitebacks from Pont-Lévis that you don't want ta have fun with da oders? You've got yer violin, right, Fifi? How come I can't hear it? Oh! Pull da tool out da coffer and play us a reel à quatre, a simple gigue, a voleuse, anythin you wish, provided it makes us waggle about. Listen, guys, we're goint have some music. Those who suffer from itchy toes have my permission ta get a remedy."

Fifi Labranche wasn't obstinate:

"Am not copin out," he says.

He gets his violin, rubs some rosin on da bow, sits on da corner of da table, chops off a bit of plug, spits inta his hands, and then, deed-a-reedle, forward ho, *boys*!

The stove glowed in the middle of the place; after half an hour, you could—I rib you not—wring out our shirts like dishcloths.

"Dis is what I call violin playin," the boss says, re-lightin his pipe: "Fifi, yer not reasonable not ta play more often."

"Agreed!" everyone else says, "Ya should play more often."

"Playin da fiddle when no 'uns dancin, dat's not a great job," goes Fifi.

"So what are we doin here?" asks one of our travelin chums, namely, the man with the black hen, a thin scrag-guy, so tall he'd duck ta pass under a door—The Rope, he was nicknamed. "This ain't dancin by ya? Whaddahwedeein then? We ain't shellin fava beans, I reckon."

"Ay, ya dance in da evenin 'cause tomorrow

'tis a holiday. If ya had ta chop wood tomorrow before dawn, ya'd not be flexin yer legs so easily. Wadd'ya think, Jos Violon?"

"Dabber Knack! I'd say, as fer as Am concerned, I'll spare my stems fer when Am goint turn in."

"Know what, hey?" says the Rope. "When men don't dance, ya got somethin else dancin."

"Who den? Cookin pots, surely? Tables, benches?"

"Da marionettes, that's what I mean."

"Marionettes?"

"Ay, da marionettes . . ."

Maybe you don't know what the marionettes are, children; oh, well, those are sorts of antichrist lights that show up in the North, when 'tis goint get freezzin. They crackle, so ta speak, like when you rub yer hands on a cat's back in the evenin. They stretch out, shrink, sprawl, spread like butter across da sky, you'll see nothin like that, as if the devil scrambled the stars like eggs ta make himself an omelet. That's what it is, the marionettes.

As fer Monsieur le Curé, he calls em *des horreurs de Morréal*, then he adds that they don't dance. Oh, well, dunno if they really are *des horreurs de Morréal* or from Trois-Rivières, but I did see some in Québec is all; and I can tell you that they do dance, oh, yeah, me, Jos Violon, am tellin you! 'Tis the devil that gets in the way, I believe, but they dance! I saw em dance, and I wasn't seein things. Fifi Labranche saw em, too, 'tis a fact 'cause 'tis him who made em dance, the proof bein that his violin was hexed fer three months long. Why, I muss tell you that, hearin the folks talk about the marionettes, the poor Fifi, who was a true believer, like mesel, started ta kick against the idea. "What den if there's no marionettes 'round here?" he says.

"When dey ain't here, ya make em come," says the Rope, "Easy-peasy."

"How d'ya make em come?"

"Why, when you know em words."

"What words?"

"Em words ta make da marionettes come."

"Ya know words ta make em come?"

"Ay, and ta make em dance, too. I learnt da words when I was little, from my gran-gran, who was a famous violliner, Ay, oh, *that* he was, back in da days."

"Can you get da marionettes ta come here tonight?"

"Sure! Da sky is clear. If ya play yer violin, I'll say da words, and ya'll see em comin."

"I'd like ta see that," says Fifi Labranche.

"Fifi," I say, "Beware, these ain't games fer good Chrissians."

"Yeah," he says, "it won't kill us for once."

"That's right, Fifi," everyone else said. "Let Jos Violon be a wimp, if he wants ta, but you hang out with da bon vivants."

"Fifi, Am tellin ya again, beware! You should not mingle with em spells. 'Tis the Devil's tricks ta ensnare you. You know the Rope . . . And on Christmas, too! . . ." But I'd just finished speakin that everyone had already gathered on the snow bank, gazin up, eyes ta the North, while Fifi Labranche tuned his violin. My my, never mind! I ended up doin what all the others were doin, sayin ta mesel: "So long as I'm just lookin on, nothin too bad is goin ta happen ta me."

We were havin fine, dry weather; not a whisper of wind, the smoke from our chimbly soared straight up like a paschal candle, and the stars blinked like critters threadin needles. We could hear twigs snappin in the woods, I kid you not, worse than em carters' whiplashes.

"Are ya ready, Fifi?" says the Rope.

"Ay," says my partner. "Whaddya want me ta play?"

"Play whatever ya want, just make it bouncy."

"Da Money Musk?"

"Da Money Musk it is!"

It sounded like the whistle of a spinnin top. The bow quivered in Fifi's hand like an eel at the tip of a boathook. And *zin! zin! zin!* . . . Our heels swiveled of their own accord on the packed snow. I believe the rascal had never played like that in his whole life. The Rope, eyes rolled backward, mumbled dunno what kind of sorcerer's litany, while gesticulatin with his thumb, makin signs in the air, in front, behind, ta the left, ta the right—ta the four corners of da world, as the sayin goes. And the Money Musk was still on. Fifi zin-zigged like a fiend.

All of a sudden, I sense a kinda icy frisson scratchin me between the shoulders: I'd just heard four or five of those cracklin, poppin noises like a cat's hide rubbed the wrong way. "Here em come!" da chums begin ta scream. "Here em come! Hurrah fer Da Rope! Keep it up, Fifi!"

At the same time one could make out some sorts of little greyish glimmers that spread out ta the North, as if someone had smudged the firmament with sulfur matches.

"Keep it up, Fifi, here em come!" continued the gang of the possessed. And indeed, the goddamned gleams were comin in, from here, from there, quite slow, creepin, slinkin, scatterin, twistin like threads of white smoke intertwined after dashes of heat.

"Keep it up Fifi!" screamed the gang of energumens.

The Rope, on his end, was keepin it up, too, cos here they were, little blazes then sparks then embers risin, fallin, crisscrossin, chasin one another like a saraband of wills-o'-the-wisp that played hide and seek, wreckin their own buddies with sticks of rotten timber. At times the glowin dimmed, and one could see almost nothin, and then, *crack*! the things flared up into streaks of blood-red lashes.

"Keep it up, Fifi, up!"

Fifi couldn't do any better, I'm tellin you. The arm was spinnin like a crank handle, and I noticed he'd started ta blanch. As fer me, my hair stood on end under my hard hat, like an angry tomcat's tail.

"Fifi, come away," I tell him, "come away! The devil's goint take someone, that's fer sure!"

But the sad wretch couldn't hear me anymore. He looked as possessed as the others and the Money Musk bounced off his bow like the screeches of feral cats flayed by a pack of lynxes. Ya've never heard anythin like that, children.

But it wasn't the finest of it yet, yer goint see soon.

While all my imps screamed their heads off,

oh, I couldn't believe it! em damned marionettes kick off pirouettin.

By da sacredest word, children! Jos Violon is no liar, you know that—now the evil spawns start ta dance—by all my wide-eyed conscience of the Good Lord—like grown-up people, they didn't miss one step, thank you very much!

And then they packed up, shoved one another and passed and fought and jumped one over the other, sometimes they fell back, and then brusquely stepped forward . . .

By-da-Jessum, children, those hussies called *horreurs de Morréal*, as Monsieur le Curé would say, came forth in rhythm with Fifi's Money Musk, and now they were comin right at us.

I told you already, methinks, that I was no chicken, and I'll give evidence of that; oh, well, seein all the circus—I won't hide it from you—without thinkin about it twice, I get da hell outa' there, hair standin on end, and I run wild ta hide inta the hut.

Five minutes later, four men carried in our poor Fifi, unconscious.

He remained one day without speakin, then three days without bein able ta lift his axe. He had, accordin ta the foreman, a wring in da tongue, then a torticollis in da arm. That's what the foreman said, but I knew better than that, c'm on!

All week long he was out of sorts: no way ta get him ta play a checkers match. He grumbled all alone in his corner, like a man who'd had, with all due respect, his bag of nether sentiments knocked upside down.

So, on New Year's Eve, the chums felt like dancin again.

"Hurrah, Fifi! Pull out da catgut, then brew us a little caper, 'tis time!" says the boss.

"You oughta move, else you congeal like curds, hey! Are ya ready, chummies?"

"Ay, here we go," the whole gang say, kickin off their shoes and spittin inta their hands. "Ho! loosen up our adzes!"

I was expecting some arm-twistin ta get the poor cripple ta play again, but nope. He takes out his violin, greases his bow, spits inta his hands in turn, and starts playin da Money Musk.

"Ah, well," say da dancers, "Enough with da Money Musk! We're no marionettes."

"'Tis strange." Fifi scratches his forehead. "I didn't want ta play this one. So, whadd'ya want? A simple gigue? A hornpipe?"

"A square dance, goodreel me! We need ta shake it tonight!"

"All right!" says Fifi. Then he resumes playin . . . the Money Musk . . .

"Listen, Fifi, are ya goin crazy? Or are ya mockin us with yer Money Musk? We're fed up with da Money Musk, d'ya catch?"

"Scoundrel's word! Dunno what's gotten inta me fingers," says Fifi. "I wanna play a square dance and it turns inta da Money Musk anyway."

"Ah you feelin like messin with us?"

"Am blowed if Am jokin."

"Oh, well, then start again—Dammit!—and pay attention, this time."

C'm on, here's Fifi stickin it out, bow in one hand and violin in the other, chin pressed against da tailpiece, and both eyes riveted on the E string, he resumes playin.

Everybody yelled, children:

"Whoa! . . ."

followed by a salvo of swear words. And fer good reason, the confounded Fifi was still playin da Money Musk.

"Sacrebent!" he says. "There's somethin criminal inside the ding; I swear Am doin all I can ta play a square dance, and then da god-ditched violin wants ta play da Money Musk only. 'Tis hexed, da piece of crime! Dis is a violin I've been playin wi' fer da last fifteen years. Here's what gives when you have da devil dance with his spawns . . . Ya beastly fiddle, yer done insultin me! Go play fer em hussies marionettes!"

And with these words, he grabs the mutinous instrument by the neck and mightily hurls it into da fireplace, where it'd have dissmashed into a thousand shards, fer sure, had we not been there ta snatch it, as the sayin goes, in midair.

Twice, durin that winter, did the poor Fifi Labranche take out his bow ta try playin a scatter of dances, but no way he could scratch that violin and produce anythin except fer the Money Musk.

One last time he set forth ta play some of those good old canticles meant for the white-haired guys among us who amble wicked slow, but nothin doin! The violin got goin of its own accord and played the Money Musk! One can't be more hexed than that, right?

Finally, it keeped on like that until springtime, when we were floatin down the Ottawa River with our raft of timber, Fifi Labranche had the opportunity ta have his violin blessed by the par-ish priest from Perrot Island, on one condition: that he would not make them marionettes dance ever again.

It wasn't that hard ta have him make such a promise, I can tell you that!

Anyways, after the exorcism, everythin worked like in the good ol' days. Fifi Labranche was able ta play any rigodon, either fashionable or played in the old style.

Here's what Jos Violon has seen, children, with his own ears!

Oh, well, believe me if you wish, but that depraved Fifi, ta make me look like a damn liar, invariably, never admitted right until the day he died that his violin had be hexed. He said it was a fib he'd come up with ta get rid of those who wanted him ta play at every turn, while he preferred ta play a good checkers game. Now, *that* is unbelievable! Rest assured nobody could make me believe such nonsense. Because I was there. I've seen everything, and if I can't say that of mesel, everyone will tell you that Jos Violon knows what he's talkin about.

After all this, the violin, the one Fifi Labranche owned, is still full of life, just like me; 'tis George Boutin, who inherited it. He can show it ta you, if you don't believe me.

And, ouch-ouch, tobacco-pouch! Far, for, fir, my story ends here!

Paul Scheerbart (1863–1915) was a German science fiction author and artist who is often described as a utopian for the refreshingly original ways in which he tried to truly see a positive future for humankind. Scheerbart was preoccupied with how imagination could influence science and how scientific discoveries could be used creatively. He often used real science in order to make his stories more realistic and to set a clear image in the minds of his audience. With his colored-glass architecture, floating cities, perpetual motion machines, humanoid worms, and use of quantum mechanics in his fiction, Scheerbart was nothing short of a visionary. His most popular works include *Glass Architecture* (1914), *Lesabéndio: An Asteroid Novel* (1913), and *The Gray Cloth with Ten Percent White* (1914). In 1915, Scheerbart strongly opposed the war, and it is rumored that he died of starvation after a hunger strike protesting it. *Dance of the Comets* was originally meant to be a scenario in one of Richard Strauss's ballets, but the project was never realized. Beautifully written, it is often read in tandem with Scheerbart's other short work, *The Stairway to the Sun* (1903), four fairy tales about morality, each set in its own universe.

Dance of the Comets: An Astral Pantomime in Two Acts

Paul Scheerbart

Translated by W. C. Bamberger

CAST

Three Large Comets	The Wizard
Seven Smaller Stars	The Poet
The Full Moon	Wandering Stars
The King	Harem Women
The First Wife of the King	Hangmen
The Second Wife of the King	Minstrels
A Zealous Maid	Courtiers
The Executioner	Servants
A Jester	

ACT 1

THE NIGHTINGALES

MANY BIRDCALLS can be heard—especially those of nightingales—quietly at first, and then growing louder and more raucous.

In the meantime, the curtain slowly rises, and a night sky with countless twinkling stars can be seen. On both sides of the stage, tall rosebush hedges, myrtle, and oleander shrubs gradually become visible. The white floor, irregularly tiled with pointed black stars, extends into the background; the scene gradually grows brighter.

Resting on a marble bench to the right is a poet holding a guitar. The poet has a neat blond beard, but his clothes are brown and gray and look neglected. He looks at the scenery and shakes his head, looks at the audience and is startled—he is a very young and quite foolish poet.

A shooting star slowly moves diagonally across the sky.

The poet hastily rises.

The space is quite dark. Only the white tiles are shining, so the pointed black stars emerge from the tiled floor quite clearly. Quiet music of the spheres is heard. The nightingales can still be heard, but more quietly than before. The poet sits back down on the marble bench and accompanies the music of the spheres with his guitar. A second and a third shooting star cross the sky. The nightingales fall silent.

The music of the spheres suddenly shifts to a hurried, whirling pace, even as it grows quieter and quieter.

THE JESTER APPEARS

The jester creeps toward the marble bench on tiptoe, startled by the sight of the poet. He puts his forefinger to his mouth to indicate that they must be silent. The nightingales sing, as if from a distance.

The jester is no longer young and hasn't shaved, and of course as a jester his clothing is brightly colored and checkered and tight-fitting.

The jester's face twitches as if he constantly wants to laugh—and knows he should refrain.

The poet slings his guitar on his back, and the jester takes his place next to the poet on the marble bench. They stare silently into space, where there are glittering stars, between which a number of light-blue, green, and red meteors come trickling through like snowflakes. The music of the spheres has grown calmer and at the same time richer and stronger.

Servants with tall, milk-white octahedral floor lamps that light up everything bring in a number of astronomical and astrological devices—quadrants, astrolabes, a large telescope, and a half-meter-tall, black celestial globe on which stars are indicated by diamonds. The globe is placed in the center of the stage.

The servants all wear white caps in the shape of spiked pentagonal stars; their clothing is elaborately pleated and boldly striped in primary colors.

The astronomical and astrological instruments are placed in front of the shrubs to the right and left.

The instruments gleam, and the globe gleams as well.

A GRIMACING INTERMEZZO

The jester caresses and kisses the instruments and spreads his arms before them with ludicrous rapture. He falls to his knees before the globe and folds his hands in mock prayer. The servants writhe with laughter, but let no sound escape their lips; terrible grimaces distort their faces.

A low rumble sounds through the music of the spheres.

The zealous maid appears in the background.

And what the jester, who remains on his knees before the globe, did out of ridicule, the maid now does with touching but amusing devotion. In her hand she holds a duster of long green feathers as a badge of her station as a maid. As she goes along, she uses the feather duster to clean the instruments.

The squatting servants make more faces. In the end the maid, once she had shown her veneration to all of the instruments, leaps with the help of two servants onto the globe and revolves there in blissful ecstasy, constantly reaching her hands upward as if to draw heaven's stars down to her.

The maid is wearing a light blue dress that goes down to her knees. The dress is covered with shining silver crescent moons. On her shoulders she wears two shiny silver full moons as epaulets.

The crescent moons, like the full moons, have faces. As headgear the maid wears a white crown of feathers; the feathers sway back and forth. Two shiny silver disk-shaped half-moons—also with faces—form two wings on the maid's back that follow the curved line of her body.

A servant suddenly jumps out of the bushes with his arms raised and claps his hands.

And all now stand as stiff and sober as poles—the jester and the poet included. The white lamps are two perfectly straight chains of light running to the right and to the left. The maid jumps down from the globe and disappears into the background.

THE KING AND HIS ENTOURAGE

The king appears.

The poet and the jester raise their right arms with their index fingers extended stiffly skyward and bow—this is the usual celestial greeting that is offered at court to the king at every possible opportunity.

The king has light blond curly locks and very little facial hair. He wears a long black velvet coat that goes down to his knees and is held closed by an emerald belt. There are also emeralds on his collar, on the cuffs of his shirt, on the sheath of his sword, and on the upper edges of his polished black boots. An emerald medal in the shape of a jagged star gleams on the right side of his chest, and the largest emeralds of all blaze in the king's gold crown. The king wears no rings. He, like all the kings of his time, is very satisfied with his environment; his attitude is carefree and a little weary—he is still a very young, very enthusiastic king.

The courtiers who make up the king's entourage belong to every race on the globe—most are new mixes of races. Because the story is of course set in the distant future, the costumes of the entourage are the freest composites of historical costumes with many fantastic elements: Polish fur hats are worn with Japanese robes, turbans with European frock coats and Scottish britches, Indian-style feathered headdresses with Hungarian hussars' uniforms, top hats with Chinese Mandarins' coats, etc., etc.

All of them are wearing brilliant star-shaped medals, some on their shoulder or chest, some on their hat or on their arms. Each—with the exception of the executioner—also carries a curved saber in a scabbard richly set with jewels. Their clothing is all quite colorful, but bright red is scrupulously avoided. Only the executioner wears a bright red cap with a cloth that hangs down in the back to protect his neck; his archaic Spanish top hat is bright red as well; his straight broadsword is in a bright red scabbard. The executioner also stands out because of his black gauntlets, his black complexion, and his pointed black beard.

The executioner is accompanied by the great wizard, walking with great dignity in his tall Assyrian cap and long caftan with broad sleeves. His hat and caftan are decorated with white constellations. From his cap three peacock feathers point upward over his forehead and ears. A long black beard flows down over the wizard's chest. After the ceremonial welcome of the king, during which a number of courtiers draw fancy lines and flourishes in the air with their right forefingers, mushroom-shaped stools are set out, on which the assembled gradually settle. But many courtiers remain standing near the king.

The music of the spheres plays haltingly.

THE HAREM ARRIVES

The king looks through the large telescope, caresses the celestial globe and the astronomical and astrological instruments, and unconsciously makes a few comic pantomime movements. The servants holding the lamps to the right and left sides bite their lips. Drum and timpani rolls sound from the right and left, and the minstrels emerge from the bushes.

The women of the harem enter from all sides, dancing. They greet the king, who has sat down on the marble bench, in the usual manner, with outstretched right index fingers. The king's two wives arrive last. They are wearing light green dresses that go down to their knees and are decorated with small golden-tailed comets. Each wife wears her own particular shade of light green.

They both wear crowns of golden comet tails.

Each of the other women of the harem wears a dress of a particular color; they go down to the knee and are trimmed with gold and silver stars and constellations. The women's dresses are monochrome but very bright, while the clothing of the courtiers is based on muted and tasteful color schemes.

All of the women wear gold or silver crescent moons with faces on their backs as wings and, the two queens excepted, dark stockings and no headdresses. The music of the spheres shifts into a violently whirling and provocative dance tempo.

The courtiers present celestial greetings to the women of the harem as well—but with their left hand and their left little finger.

THE LUNAR GAVOTTE

And the zealous maid comes running from the background like a whirlwind—followed by seven women in lunar Pierrot costumes.

The maid leaps onto the globe and like the seven Pierrots lifts her right index finger toward the heavens and holds it aloft for a long moment.

The maid now puts a hat on her head, a bright silver globe of the full moon with a face; her green feather duster is still in her left hand. The Pierrots—all seven of them in white—have golden full moons the size of a fist as buttons, somewhat larger ones on their shoulders, elbows, and knees and on the heels of their shoes—as well as golden moon hats and golden full moon wings in disk form.

The Pierrots dance a gavotte with the seven women in blue; the shades of blue are diverse, but none are the same as the maid's dress.

The maid conducts the gavotte using her feather duster as a baton. The minstrels play from the right and left sides by the tall lamps. The courtiers and the remaining women of the harem form a semicircle around the dancers, who frequently bow in the direction of the marble bench where the king sits with the executioner.

At times the king smiles—but it is a tired smile.

THE LEONID POLONAISE

After the maid, with the help of her seven Pierrots, has jumped down from the globe and again replaced her feathered crown with her moon hat, she asks permission to approach the executioner and now invites him to climb onto the globe— which he does, after some show of reluctance and with the help of some of the servants, while the women of the harem—and the Pierrots— remove their moon hats and set comet tails made of feathers on their heads.

All the women of the harem, hereinafter referred to as the shooting stars from the Leonid swarm, hold head-sized mirrors in their right hands that produce small sparkles; they call for the courtiers to present a polonaise. The king does not dance with them. Neither do the wizard, the poet, or the jester, all of whom remain near the king. The executioner looks quite powerless, and everyone smiles at him, but furtively.

The two queens lead the polonaise as the first pair.

The polonaise frequently winds around the globe, sideways and back and forth.

Suddenly, however, the hissing of a great number of comets slanting down from the sky can be heard under the sounds of the spheres; everyone is terribly frightened.

Terror disrupts order, and the polonaise abruptly dissolves as everyone runs to and fro out of fear. As the music of the spheres skitters along nervously the executioner tries to come down from the globe as quickly as possible. Because the servants are caught up in the general confusion the jester has to help the king's executioner down. The wizard and the poet arrive too late.

Everyone is frightened more by this interlude than by the unexpected meteor shower.

THE HOROSCOPE MINUET

The Pierrots now quickly chase the bewildered couples to the sides. The celestial globe is transformed into a terrestrial globe by means of a multicolored cloth that is meant to represent America. The king's first wife goes up onto the globe—and with the wizard's help, the lady on the terrestrial globe is given her horoscope by the seven Pierrots.

The servants with the milk-white lanterns form the wide arc of a semicircle behind the globe, pushing the courtiers, minstrels, and other women of the harem into the background on the right and left sides.

The Mercury Pierrot now has the traditional winged helmet on her head and a terrible laughing villain's mask in each hand.

The Mars Pierrot has a Polish Hussar's fur cap on her head and a large pistol in each hand.

The Jupiter Pierrot has the traditional long locks and beard of Zeus—and carries a scepter and orb in her hands.

The Saturn Pierrot wears a lustrous European top hat and a stiff collar consisting top and bottom of black and white rings, so that the collar resembles a target. The collar extends far beyond her shoulders and can easily be pushed forward with her chin onto her breast, so that at times the full rings can be seen.

The Moon Pierrot still wears the costume that was prescribed for the moon gavotte. The Sun Pierrot must often hold up with both hands her large mask of the face of the sun, which is heavily spotted with beauty marks.

The wizard continually changes the constellations; he is always seeking to improve them. While remaining in place, the Pierrots assiduously dance minuets, wherein they evoke their missing partners, and also occasionally perform assertive solo dances. After the first wife has been presented her horoscope, for which she gives thanks by doing a solo dance on the globe, the second is presented hers in a similar manner—though this proceeds a little more wildly. Finally, the king, who naturally finds all this magical dancing absurd and appalling, is also presented his horoscope. The king has the maid place his crown on the terrestrial globe.

In determining the constellation, however, the crown is knocked down by the Saturn Pierrot's collar—and the terrible hubbub that ensues ends the horoscope minuet. The jester straightens out the bent crown—and the king is very angry—his forehead wrinkles menacingly.

THE SATURN'S RINGS' ROUND DANCE

The king is very annoyed, so naturally everyone rushes to present the next number.

A near-frightened haste is apparent in the court and in the music; one is always a little frightened before the king—because everything arranged by the harem was intended to please the king, and to honor him, but it cannot be denied that some things that have happened may smack of mockery in regards to the king's astral proclivities.

And so the servants rush to present the great rings of Saturn. And out of the globe comes a black Saturn with two white rings and one gray. The rings are a little tilted—higher toward the back—on their firm supports.

And now the complete Saturn, like a wonder of the world, dances around—everyone hand in hand.

The Pierrots dance in the rings, while the maid dances on the globe.

Then the two queens dance together on the globe, while the women of the harem dance in gowns in the rings. Everyone except the two queens wears wide-brimmed Saturn hats, which are modeled on the large globe with the rings. The dances are performed more and more quickly, because the king is very impatient.

At one point he is comfortable and makes the poet and jester dance with them. Then, however, his good mood goes downhill with lightning speed.

The servants holding the lamps must also dance around Saturn.

Meanwhile, as the king once again looks very grim, the maid gives a signal for all to come to a standstill.

And everyone stands still. The nightingales sing. The music of the spheres is booming in the deepest bass range, while the king attentively studies the laces of his patent leather boots.

THE MAID'S WALTZ

The maid, atop the globe, pushes her Saturn hat down onto the nape of her neck and gives the servants another sign—and the three big rings of Saturn are individually removed over the head of the stooping maid and carried away.

The maid gives the minstrels leave to begin her waltz, jumps cheerfully down from the globe, and asks the king to dance—but he gives her the executioner as a dance partner. And soon a spirited waltz is begun by the courtiers and the women of the harem. A servant holding a tall lantern stands with his back to the globe and a circle forms around him. Unfortunately, a few arrogant dancers now take up some of the astronomical instruments—and this show of arrogance is such a success that soon all of the instruments, except the globe and the telescope, are taken up by those dancing the maid's waltz.

When the king sees this, he walks into the center and sternly prohibits any more dancing.

The instruments are set again in their rightful places at the right and left. The tall lamps, too, are soon returned to the right and left as before.

The king has placed his left hand on the globe and sadly lets his head fall to his chest.

The nightingales are very loud again.

The people are silent.

Soft music of the spheres undulates up and down.

Only a few of the harem women continue wearing their Saturn hats; most give them to the servants and sigh.

THE KING AND THE POET

The wizard reverently approaches the king. But the king asks for the poet.

As the poet stands before the king, he indicates his deep contempt for his court and his harem, then with a transfigured expression regards the stars in the heavens, and the astronomical instruments themselves—and lastly the poet's guitar. This pantomime is repeated a few times, with variations. The poet hesitantly copies the movements of the king—points his index finger at the court, harem, stars, instruments, king, and guitar—lastly at his own forehead—then slides the guitar off his shoulder and throws it at the feet of the king—then he turns his back.

The king is startled, the nightingales flap their wings, the quiet music of the spheres undulates up and down; a wavering goes through the ranks of the courtiers and the women of the harem tremble with excitement.

The king gently places his hand on the poet's left shoulder—but the poet shakes it off.

The king waves in his executioner.

THE EXECUTIONER

The executioner whistles for his bright red assistants to approach, and he pulls his straight broad sword from its scabbard.

The poet is surrounded by the assistant executioners and forced into a kneeling position. Chains rattle.

It grows very quiet on the stage; the only sounds are the gnashing of the courtiers' teeth and the rustle of the trembling women's dresses.

The executioner has his assistant burnish his straight broad sword; this is done with much ceremony. While everyone awaits the execution with horrified eyes, the music of the spheres grows louder—but it is still soft and whispering, like the whisper of distant reeds. The executioner takes his sword in hand, checks its sharpness and prepares to discharge his duties in the usual manner. Then the poet jumps over and kneels before the king—wrings his hands, jumps up again, and grasps the executioner's arm tightly, repeats both actions, and while doing so tears the peacock feathers from his cap and waves them unceasingly in the air—making spooky gestures.

And the king waves the executioner to his side—and places his sword back in its scabbard.

The executioner's assistants withdraw. The music of the spheres is thrilling and showy, like a magic garden.

The poet sits down on the tiled floor and rattles his chains.

THE WIZARD

The wizard takes his peacock feathers in his right hand, raises them and draws them through the air in magic helical lines, while continually walking backward.

And all the stars in the sky fall simultaneously, straight down from the sky.

An eerie buzzing and chirping music of the spheres sounds. The king becomes excited and sways with his trembling wives, courtiers, and servants, who all weep terrible tears and tear at their faces with their fingernails; those in the background do the same.

The poet crawls to the marble bench and sits down.

Every man and woman sways back and forth at the falling of the stars and through their arm movements show that they are having the sensation of being lifted into the sky, along with the tile floor and the nearby bushes.

THE STARS OF THE SKY

Colorful clouds of smoke rise at the front of the stage, and the king and his court are not visible. Large round star worlds—spheres one to five meters tall—slowly rise up through the smoke.

The music of the spheres grows wilder and wilder.

A laughing full moon with a large face soon appears, quite still in the midst of the smoke.

Comet tails bounce up and down like jumping jacks to the right and left of the full moon.

While the music of the spheres rages in a frenzy, the curtains are slowly drawn.

The frenzied music of the spheres ends with a drum roll.

ACT 2

THE DANCE OF THE THREE LARGE COMETS

The king remains as he was at the end of act 1, with his courtiers and his harem stage rear.

The stars of the sky are still falling straight down; the tiled floor, the nearby bushes, and the entire court are still rising higher into the sky.

The poet, still in chains, has now laid down on the bench to the right and is staring at the falling stars, unconcerned.

The servants with the tall lanterns are distributed irregularly, some at the sides, some at the back. The entire court has turned its back to the audience.

At the wizard's command some servants carry the celestial globe forward and place it there to the left of the large telescope. A large comet appears in the sky, and the stars in the sky stand still.

At the sight of the comet the women flee with bright cries; the men try to calm the women.

The king is up front, leaning against his celestial globe.

Meanwhile, the comet descends and gleams at the back of the stage.

Everyone stands like statues, with their mouths open in fear and horror.

The wizard soothes them by passing his peacock feathers over the heads of the frightened.

The comet comes forward and bows before the king, who regains his composure with difficulty.

The poet stands and bows to the comet and rattles his chains.

The two other comets arrive in succession, in the same way as the first, and their welcome to the king plays out exactly the same.

The music of the spheres sounds very mild, indulgent and soft.

The men and women gradually calm down; the wizard instructs the servants to spread colorful blankets on the tiles to the right and left.

And the women settle on the blankets.

The men arrange themselves, standing behind the women.

The king is leaning against his globe to the left of the executioner, who leans on his sword.

Right in front on the marble bench sit the poet and the jester.

The music of the spheres begins playing dance tunes.

And the comets dance.

The comets are represented by people whose heads are invisible. Their feet and human extremities are also invisible. In place of their heads, a beam like that of an electric headlight shoots into the air; smaller beams radiate from between their human shoulders. Their bodies are surrounded by feathers like glittering branches. The lights on their heads and between their shoulders are easy to move, and the glittering branches as easy to bend and manipulate as spiders' legs—they glisten as if coated with enamel in countless bright colors.

During the dance of the comets all the beams of light are repeatedly set at different angles to one another, often staying in one position only for a few seconds—whereby a twitchy element enters into the expression of the dance. The king follows the playful dancing with his body bent far forward.

The music of the spheres is bright.

THE DANCE OF THE THREE LARGE COMETS WITH THE SEVEN SMALLER STARS

The music of the spheres suddenly becomes very noisy.

And with bangs and booms the seven smaller stars appear in succession in the sky. They are more than double the size of the moon, and move independently, like the comets on the stage. The greeting of the king is done very casually—almost irreverently.

Two of the comets move to the right and left and one moves back, and they bend slightly forward, so that the beams from their heads come together in a crisscross pattern.

And under these three beams the seven smaller stars first dance alone.

Among the seven smaller stars the largest is no more than two meters high. Some of the stars are jagged, others cube-shaped, round, or square; some of their lights shine, as gleaming as colored diamonds, others like gold or silver or opal and pearl. Their movements primarily consist of revolving while sparkling and swaying back and forth, but they can quickly change their position and leap. Feet and human extremities are not to be noticeable on these smaller stars, either.

Finally, the comets dance together with the smaller stars; the show of color and light is endlessly lively. The comets, whose fingers are always spinning, use the stars to create a variety of brilliant ornaments that at first remain fixed, but subsequently act as a constantly rotating kaleidoscope—full of violent movement.

The dances are accompanied by the powerful music of the spheres; solemn organ notes frequently break through the dance tunes.

As the stars and comets suddenly come to a standstill—the comets with their head beams pointing straight up—the music of the spheres again becomes very gentle.

The courtiers and the ladies begin moving again—as if they had been freed from a spell.

THE PAS DE DEUX

The king's two wives find the lights of the astral dances extraordinarily pleasing—and both want to dance together with the comets and the stars. In pantomime they ask the king to permit them to do so.

The king nods and thinks about other matters with wide-open eyes.

As the women approach the comets, these move into the background of the stage and lay themselves flat on the floor so that very little of their bright tails can be seen.

The queens wonder why this has happened, and now want to dance with the seven small stars, but these move sideways and into the background, thereby greatly disturbing the courtiers and the women of the harem.

The two queens dance with the stars anyway, at first alone, to show them that they are certainly worthy of dancing with stars. The minstrels play along as well as they can; the music of the spheres sounds restrained and mocking.

Everyone is amazed.

In pantomime, the king asks the wizard how this has happened. The wizard shrugs.

The two queens break off their dancing; they are insulted and angry—very piqued.

THE PAS SEUL

The maid wishes to save the honor of the royal harem; she appears dressed in full-length sheer white robes. She is wearing a crescent-shaped snow-white hat, the horns of which extend down next to her ears. In her hands she has a long duster of snow-white feathers. Flickering colored lights color her for a time, giving her the look of a Scottish tartan.

The maid dances and displays her longing for the stars, which stand at the sides, half-concealed by the bushes. She offers a particularly poignant expression of longing to the comets lying in the background.

At times the comets briefly rise up, but always lie back down again. The maid often dances with her back to the audience, showing off the Scottish tartan to great advantage.

Only three or four of the servants with the tall lamps are to be seen, at the back or at the sides.

The stars remain in their places.

In the end the maid grows very sad and, shaking her head, crosses over to the king and falls sobbing at his feet. Her pain is so apparent that the courtiers cannot stifle their smiles.

The king smoothes both her cheeks and bends down to lift her up.

THE FRIENDSHIP PANTOMIME

The women of the harem are enormously agitated; they gesture emphatically and all rise, angrily ball up their colorful scarves and throw them at the heads of the servants and the courtiers.

And now all the women dance a dance meant to express their great desire for friendship, a dance that consists mainly of arm and finger movements.

Artful back and forth movements of their bodies are added, but their legs and feet remain motionless, and only occasionally move a few steps to change the dancers' position.

During this dance the comets and the stars are unable to move. The king laughs at his harem.

The minstrels no longer play.

The music of the spheres can again be heard. It sounds rough, unapproachable.

Irritated by the king, who will not stop laughing at them, the women of the harem try to force the celestial dancers to dance with them. However, they burn their fingers on them and quickly run to the center.

The king no longer laughs; at times he can be quite compassionate. He now goes back over to the marble bench, sits down, and again turns his attention to the laces of his patent leather boots.

THE DESPAIR PANTOMIME

The women sprinkle each other's burns with powder and bandage them with handkerchiefs and move around desperately, standing, sitting, and lying in rows; the colorful scarves are back.

The bodies and limbs are contorted this way and that, and a harmony of movement takes place that conveys an overall impression of pain. Faces are used to great effect.

And the wizard similarly expresses his despair over the aloofness of the celestial beings.

The wizard drops to one knee before the king and begs for mercy, shrugs, and suggests by way of his hand and arm movements that one cannot force celestial beings. These movements form a counterpoint to the desperate movements of the women of the harem.

The music of the spheres becomes a muffled growl.

The king indicates through a number of smiling gestures that he fully understands the stars. The king would not dance with his harem, either.

Then of course all of the courtiers have to laugh with arch cordiality. The women of course understand neither their king nor the laughter of the men.

The wizard bows seven times, smiling, before his king and clasps his hands together seven times as a sign of his gratitude.

THE PAS DE TROIS

On tiptoes, the jester creeps to the center of the stage, makes faces full of meaning, and confidently pantomimes in every way possible that as a jester he can certainly seduce the stars into dancing with him. After a wild clown dance, which the minstrels raucously accompany, the gold and silver stars approach the jester. When the trio begins to dance, the women try to applaud. With their burnt fingers, this of course is not possible.

The *Pas de trois*, however, comes to an abrupt conclusion just as the trio moves toward the background, when the two stars wedge the jester between them and rise into the air, taking him with them.

THE SABER PANTOMIME

This ascension releases the entire company from the script.

The courtiers believe it is now their duty to actively intervene.

As if by silent agreement, the courtiers all simultaneously display their immense indignation to the crowd: they draw their flashing sabers and brandish them in the air.

And a very lively, menacing saber pantomime develops. It is as if the courtiers with their flashing sabers are attacking the entire sky in order to win back the jester.

The wizard runs around desperately, wringing his hands, trying to calm those who have become excited and are genuflecting. After a great effort, he succeeds.

The comets straighten up a few times in surprise at the flashing of the sabers.

Marvelous metallic sounds are heard through the music of the spheres.

The king, his arms raised, has for a long while been staring up at the jester.

THE FULL MOON

Everything becomes quiet.

The nightingales sing again.

The music of the spheres whispers like a distant lullaby.

The wizard again raises his peacock feathers to the sky, and with them describes long incantatory lines. And following this incantation, a laughing full moon appears in the sky. He majestically descends from the higher regions. The full moon takes the stage and, to the singing of the nightingales, dances a droll waggling dance with small jumps that enables the entire court to regain their good mood. The courtiers' sabers fly back into their sheaths. The moon has a very funny face; it is the same one that appeared in the clouds at the end of the first act. The back of his head consists of nothing but dark violet curls that fly to and fro as he dances. His face is plump and golden yellow.

At the end of his dance, the moon expels the jester from his hair.

And while the moon, in the manner of celestial globes, stands calmly in the center of the stage, others help the jester back onto his feet—with both hands he grasps large tufts of dark violet hair.

THE MOON'S CURLS BACCHANAL

The jester distributes the moon's violet curls among the women of the harem, the courtiers, and the servants.

The curls possess an intoxicating power—so that everyone bounces about in absolutely mute exhilaration—and a genuine bacchanal is staged, in which only the wine is missing.

The king, the poet, the wizard, the maid, and a few individual men and women have refused the curls and are now standing about dolefully, while the intoxicated dance around the moon—in an unbridled and ludicrous manner—as the servants and the minstrels dance along.

The white octahedral lanterns flit through the air like fireflies.

The five smaller stars at first do not move, but as the ferocity of the bacchanal wanes they approach the moon and bow small bows. Everyone laughs.

The maid then wants to lodge herself in the moon's purple curls, but the moon shakes his head and the maid is thrown into the executioner's powerful arms. A strong resolution is born in the king: the king wants to be lifted skyward in the moon's hair. But as soon as he begins making serious preparations to do so, the moon opens his mouth and blows on the king so powerfully that he staggers backward.

And the full moon screams hideously loud, like a donkey braying, moves back, and, while a nightingale that lights on his nose is heard singing loudly, rises back up into the background with the stars—his violet hair apparently having room for at most one jester.

The king does not understand any of this, and the women of the harem and the courtiers do not understand, either—they clap their hands together over their heads and again stand as still as statues—the violet hair no longer affects them.

The bacchanal is at an end.

THE ABDUCTION

The comets in the background once again raise their heads a little, so that their head beams shine upward at a slant; they raise and lower the beams intermittently.

The king, using a number of pantomime gestures, asks what it was like to be in the sky.

The five smaller stars move into the background and float there individually, one after the other.

And the king is terribly agitated. While the courtiers and harem women lie exhausted on the tile floor, the king tries to detain the stars. He pantomimes entreating them with beseeching movements of his arms and bent knees. He wants them to remain with him at court.

And the five small stars do not stay. Fear seizes the king—he fears that the comets could leave him as well.

The wizard was supposed to have held the comets with his peacock feathers; that the wizard could not do.

The king wants the peacock feathers.

But the wizard will not hand over the feathers, and again gives his best pantomime of despair.

And the king is angry and beckons his executioner and his henchmen and takes the feathers by force. The wizard is handcuffed and made to kneel in company with the poet, while the king tries to summon the three comets with the peacock feathers.

And the feathers burn.

And the king will now behead the wizard and the poet if they are unable to compel the three large comets to remain.

And the pair must crane their necks and, rolling their eyes, shrug.

As the executioner again sharpens his sword and makes preparations to strike, the comets, with their head beams shining high and oscillating to and fro, stroll slowly to the foreground and free the two condemned men with their glittering spider fingers—the chains, clattering, fall away. The comets take the king, the executioner and the maid into their midst and go—despite the executioner's reluctance—into the background, and there, with the three, rise slowly into starry space.

The king becomes quite giddy with delight. He greets his court with his emerald crown as if it were a cap, thumbs his nose at his court, sticks out his tongue to those left behind, and laughs heartily.

The executioner is of course very angry, and the maid is of course utterly thrilled. The trio disappears up among the stars.

Clouds billow from the tiled floor and flames emerge. The stage sinks amid thunder and lightning, taking those who remained behind into the depths. Meanwhile, not far from the lamps, an old wall, as long as the stage is wide, slowly rises up out of the floor, a good meter high.

THE ENCHANTED

The music of the spheres is roaring; it often sounds like deep rocks being crushed.

And the planets appear—round globes in various colors, from one to five meters high. Black Saturn displays its gray rings at various angles.

The great globes slowly float up and down. In the background the laughing full moon passes through.

The voice of a nightingale sounds fervidly within the music of the spheres as long as the moon can be seen.

The clouds gradually disappear, and the fixed stars are visible. Some of these are much larger than usual and oddly shaped and tinted.

The king, the executioner, and the maid appear before the new front wall and, turning their backs on the audience, look at the planets with the greatest enchantment.

The executioner is soon weary of this admiration, but his two companions are not; they show their enthusiasm with expressive movements of their arms, heads, and bodies.

The three slowly pass along the wall from right to left. The two men are now unarmed.

THE INSANE

The round planets move to the side—new planets are emerging from the fixed stars.

The music of the spheres has been growing ever faster and hurtles along at its wildest tempo at this point.

The new planets are no longer shaped like spheres. They now take the form of giant diamonds and multifaceted phosphorescent crystal bodies. Some consist of shapeless tubular structures that shimmer like soap bubbles and are reminiscent of polyps, others resemble solidified flames—most are very gaudy and richly formed. From suns that resemble huge whitecaps, colorful lights strike out like headlights that shine through the new world of stars. All the stars move up and down, and the globe-shaped planets also reemerge and join the richly shaped planetary bodies. The planets frequently move deep into the background toward the fixed stars, so that there are always different stars in the foreground. The three people climb a narrow and bumpy stone staircase to the left, which continues back along the left side up to a rock, on the top of which are castle-like ruins with an upper room.

Because of the upper room's high stone balustrade, the three are at times obscured. Their enthusiasm has now exceeded all bounds, its bustle growing greater and greater—only the executioner plays the cold rationalist.

And so it is quite natural that they clash with one another and finally come to blows. Unfortunately, the executioner is the strongest, and after he has thrown them down behind the stone balustrade, he succeeds in throwing his two adversaries headlong into the world of the stars—first the king and then the maid. Immediately after this event the full moon appears above, his hair now standing on end—he descends very quickly, hurrying to the aid of the fallen. The nightingale can again be heard; she is back on the nose of the moon.

At the left, a rotund globe star pushes forward against the narrow stairs and casts them into the wings, together with the rock walkway and the executioner.

The sound of thunder comes through the music of the spheres.

THE STARS OF THE HEAVENS

Once again new planets emerge from the fixed stars—gaseous forms of light that pass through one another like shadows. There is a constant flickering of colorful flashes. This develops into an exhilarating, wavering abundance of tremendous lighting effects.

Comets resembling flaming swords dart through the chaotic realm.

Glowing ribbon meteors like fiery eels wind through everywhere.

The round and richly formed planets, which often float off to the side but rarely disappear entirely, are frequently lit in every possible color by the tails of the passing comets.

The music of the spheres reaches its greatest intensity and at times sounds like ancient rock being scratched by giant claws. Floating slowly up from below into this world of excited light, color, and form come the three great comets, the lights on their heads beaming straight up—the three comets again carry the three people they abducted into the sky, holding them in their glittering arms.

All the stars float to the sides and into the background to make room.

The comets, with the king, maid, and executioner who now all calmly turn their heads from side to side, float slowly upward into still higher spheres that are invisible. The music of the spheres grows ever quieter and softer.

The moon also rises from the depths and floats upward, smiling, following the comets and the people. When the moon is nearly up the curtain slowly falls.

And the music of the spheres resounds very softly, as if from a great distance.

And the voice of the nightingale also sounds, as if from a great distance.

FINIS

Arthur Machen (1863–1947), also known as Arthur Llewellyn Jones, was a Welsh author, translator, and actor who is considered the godfather of weird fiction. His work was a major influence on H. P. Lovecraft and raised the level of horror from what it was to a new height of terror and suspense. Most of his stories are set in medieval England or Wales in order to invoke an innate gothic mystery from antiquity. Indeed, Machen's contributions to fantasy fiction, in novels like *The Hill of Dreams* (1907), is much underrated because of his connection to weird fiction. First appearing in *Horlick's Magazine* in 1904, "The White People" is a horrifying tale about human sin, but also contains extremely original and potent evocations of witchcraft, folktales, and the fantastical.

The White People

Arthur Machen

PROLOGUE

"SORCERY AND SANCTITY," said Ambrose, "these are the only realities. Each is an ecstasy, a withdrawal from the common life."

Cotgrave listened, interested. He had been brought by a friend to this mouldering house in a northern suburb, through an old garden to the room where Ambrose the recluse dozed and dreamed over his books.

"Yes," he went on, "magic is justified of her children. There are many, I think, who eat dry crusts and drink water, with a joy infinitely sharper than anything within the experience of the 'practical' epicure."

"You are speaking of the saints?"

"Yes, and of the sinners, too. I think you are falling into the very general error of confining the spiritual world to the supremely good; but the supremely wicked, necessarily, have their portion in it. The merely carnal, sensual man can no more be a great sinner than he can be a great saint. Most of us are just indifferent, mixed-up creatures; we muddle through the world without realizing the meaning and the inner sense of things, and, consequently, our wickedness and our goodness are alike second-rate, unimportant."

"And you think the great sinner, then, will be an ascetic, as well as the great saint?"

"Great people of all kinds forsake the imperfect copies and go to the perfect originals. I have no doubt but that many of the very highest among the saints have never done a 'good action' (using the words in their ordinary sense). And, on the other hand, there have been those who have sounded the very depths of sin, who all their lives have never done an 'ill deed.'"

He went out of the room for a moment, and Cotgrave, in high delight, turned to his friend and thanked him for the introduction.

"He's grand," he said. "I never saw that kind of lunatic before."

Ambrose returned with more whisky and helped the two men in a liberal manner. He abused the teetotal sect with ferocity, as he handed the seltzer, and pouring out a glass of water for himself, was about to resume his monologue, when Cotgrave broke in—

"I can't stand it, you know," he said, "your paradoxes are too monstrous. A man may be a great sinner and yet never do anything sinful! Come!"

"You're quite wrong," said Ambrose. "I never make paradoxes; I wish I could. I merely said that a man may have an exquisite taste in Romanée Conti, and yet never have even smelt four ale. That's all, and it's more like a truism than a paradox, isn't it? Your surprise at my remark is due to the fact that you haven't realized what sin is. Oh, yes, there is a sort of connexion between Sin with the capital letter, and actions which are commonly called sinful: with murder, theft, adultery, and so forth. Much the same connexion that there is between the A, B, C and fine literature. But I believe that the misconception—it is all but universal—arises in great measure from our looking at the matter through social spectacles. We think that a man who does evil to *us* and to his neighbours must be very evil. So he is, from a social standpoint; but can't you realize that Evil in its essence is a lonely thing, a passion of the solitary, individual soul? Really, the average murderer, *quâ* murderer, is not by any means a sinner in the true sense of the word. He is simply a wild beast that we have to get rid of to save our own necks from his knife. I should class him rather with tigers than with sinners."

"It seems a little strange."

"I think not. The murderer murders not from positive qualities, but from negative ones; he lacks something which non-murderers possess. Evil, of course, is wholly positive—only it is on the wrong side. You may believe me that sin in its proper sense is very rare; it is probable that there have been far fewer sinners than saints. Yes, your standpoint is all very well for practical, social

purposes; we are naturally inclined to think that a person who is very disagreeable to us must be a very great sinner! It is very disagreeable to have one's pocket picked, and we pronounce the thief to be a very great sinner. In truth, he is merely an undeveloped man. He cannot be a saint, of course; but he may be, and often is, an infinitely better creature than thousands who have never broken a single commandment. He is a great nuisance to *us*, I admit, and we very properly lock him up if we catch him; but between his troublesome and unsocial action and evil—Oh, the connexion is of the weakest."

It was getting very late. The man who had brought Cotgrave had probably heard all this before, since he assisted with a bland and judicious smile, but Cotgrave began to think that his "lunatic" was turning into a sage.

"Do you know," he said, "you interest me immensely? You think, then, that we do not understand the real nature of evil?"

"No, I don't think we do. We over-estimate it and we under-estimate it. We take the very numerous infractions of our social 'bye-laws'— the very necessary and very proper regulations which keep the human company together—and we get frightened at the prevalence of 'sin' and 'evil.' But this is really nonsense. Take theft, for example. Have you any *horror* at the thought of Robin Hood, of the Highland caterans of the seventeenth century, of the moss-troopers, of the company promoters of our day?

"Then, on the other hand, we underrate evil. We attach such an enormous importance to the 'sin' of meddling with our pockets (and our wives) that we have quite forgotten the awfulness of real sin."

"And what is sin?" said Cotgrave.

"I think I must reply to your question by another. What would your feelings be, seriously, if your cat or your dog began to talk to you, and to dispute with you in human accents? You would be overwhelmed with horror. I am sure of it. And if the roses in your garden sang a weird song, you would go mad. And suppose the stones in the road began to swell and grow before your eyes, and if the pebble that you noticed at night had shot out stony blossoms in the morning?

"Well, these examples may give you some notion of what sin really is."

"Look here," said the third man, hitherto placid, "you two seem pretty well wound up. But I'm going home. I've missed my tram, and I shall have to walk."

Ambrose and Cotgrave seemed to settle down more profoundly when the other had gone out into the early misty morning and the pale light of the lamps.

"You astonish me," said Cotgrave. "I had never thought of that. If that is really so, one must turn everything upside down. Then the essence of sin really is—"

"In the taking of heaven by storm, it seems to me," said Ambrose. "It appears to me that it is simply an attempt to penetrate into another and higher sphere in a forbidden manner. You can understand why it is so rare. There are few, indeed, who wish to penetrate into other spheres, higher or lower, in ways allowed or forbidden. Men, in the mass, are amply content with life as they find it. Therefore there are few saints, and sinners (in the proper sense) are fewer still, and men of genius, who partake sometimes of each character, are rare also. Yes; on the whole, it is, perhaps, harder to be a great sinner than a great saint."

"There is something profoundly unnatural about sin? Is that what you mean?"

"Exactly. Holiness requires as great, or almost as great, an effort; but holiness works on lines that *were* natural once; it is an effort to recover the ecstasy that was before the Fall. But sin is an effort to gain the ecstasy and the knowledge that pertain alone to angels, and in making this effort man becomes a demon. I told you that the mere murderer is not *therefore* a sinner; that is true, but the sinner is sometimes a murderer. Gilles de Raiz is an instance. So you see that while the good and the evil are unnatural to man as he now is—to man the social, civilized being—evil is unnatural in a much deeper sense than good. The saint endeavours to recover a gift which he has lost; the

sinner tries to obtain something which was never his. In brief, he repeats the Fall."

"But are you a Catholic?" said Cotgrave.

"Yes; I am a member of the persecuted Anglican Church."

"Then, how about those texts which seem to reckon as sin that which you would set down as a mere trivial dereliction?"

"Yes; but in one place the word 'sorcerers' comes in the same sentence, doesn't it? That seems to me to give the key-note. Consider: can you imagine for a moment that a false statement which saves an innocent man's life is a sin? No; very good, then, it is not the mere liar who is excluded by those words; it is, above all, the 'sorcerers' who use the material life, who use the failings incidental to material life as instruments to obtain their infinitely wicked ends. And let me tell you this: our higher senses are so blunted, we are so drenched with materialism, that we should probably fail to recognize real wickedness if we encountered it."

"But shouldn't we experience a certain horror—a terror such as you hinted we would experience if a rose tree sang—in the mere presence of an evil man?"

"We should if we were natural: children and women feel this horror you speak of, even animals experience it. But with most of us convention and civilization and education have blinded and deafened and obscured the natural reason. No, sometimes we may recognize evil by its hatred of the good—one doesn't need much penetration to guess at the influence which dictated, quite unconsciously, the 'Blackwood' review of Keats—but this is purely incidental; and, as a rule, I suspect that the Hierarchs of Tophet pass quite unnoticed, or, perhaps, in certain cases, as good but mistaken men."

"But you used the word 'unconscious' just now, of Keats' reviewers. Is wickedness ever unconscious?"

"Always. It must be so. It is like holiness and genius in this as in other points; it is a certain rapture or ecstasy of the soul; a transcendent effort to surpass the ordinary bounds. So, surpassing these, it surpasses also the understanding, the faculty that takes note of that which comes before it. No, a man may be infinitely and horribly wicked and never suspect it. But I tell you, evil in this, its certain and true sense, is rare, and I think it is growing rarer."

"I am trying to get hold of it all," said Cotgrave. "From what you say, I gather that the true evil differs generically from that which we call evil?"

"Quite so. There is, no doubt, an analogy between the two; a resemblance such as enables us to use, quite legitimately, such terms as the 'foot of the mountain' and the 'leg of the table.' And, sometimes, of course, the two speak, as it were, in the same language. The rough miner, or 'puddler,' the untrained, undeveloped 'tiger-man,' heated by a quart or two above his usual measure, comes home and kicks his irritating and injudicious wife to death. He is a murderer. And Gilles de Raiz was a murderer. But you see the gulf that separates the two? The 'word,' if I may so speak, is accidentally the same in each case, but the 'meaning' is utterly different. It is flagrant 'Hobson Jobson' to confuse the two, or rather, it is as if one supposed that Juggernaut and the Argonauts had something to do etymologically with one another. And no doubt the same weak likeness, or analogy, runs between all the 'social' sins and the real spiritual sins, and in some cases, perhaps, the lesser may be 'schoolmasters' to lead one on to the greater—from the shadow to the reality. If you are anything of a Theologian, you will see the importance of all this."

"I am sorry to say," remarked Cotgrave, "that I have devoted very little of my time to theology. Indeed, I have often wondered on what grounds theologians have claimed the title of Science of Sciences for their favourite study; since the 'theological' books I have looked into have always seemed to me to be concerned with feeble and obvious pieties, or with the kings of Israel and Judah. I do not care to hear about those kings."

Ambrose grinned.

"We must try to avoid theological discussion," he said. "I perceive that you would be a bitter disputant. But perhaps the 'dates of the kings' have as much to do with theology as the hobnails of the murderous puddler with evil."

"Then, to return to our main subject, you think that sin is an esoteric, occult thing?"

"Yes. It is the infernal miracle as holiness is the supernal. Now and then it is raised to such a pitch that we entirely fail to suspect its existence; it is like the note of the great pedal pipes of the organ, which is so deep that we cannot hear it. In other cases it may lead to the lunatic asylum, or to still stranger issues. But you must never confuse it with mere social misdoing. Remember how the Apostle, speaking of the 'other side,' distinguishes between 'charitable' actions and charity. And as one may give all one's goods to the poor, and yet lack charity; so, remember, one may avoid every crime and yet be a sinner."

"Your psychology is very strange to me," said Cotgrave, "but I confess I like it, and I suppose that one might fairly deduce from your premisses the conclusion that the real sinner might very possibly strike the observer as a harmless personage enough?"

"Certainly; because the true evil has nothing to do with social life or social laws, or if it has, only incidentally and accidentally. It is a lonely passion of the soul—or a passion of the lonely soul—whichever you like. If, by chance, we understand it, and grasp its full significance, then, indeed, it will fill us with horror and with awe. But this emotion is widely distinguished from the fear and the disgust with which we regard the ordinary criminal, since this latter is largely or entirely founded on the regard which we have for our own skins or purses. We hate a murderer, because we know that we should hate to be murdered, or to have any one that we like murdered. So, on the 'other side,' we venerate the saints, but we don't 'like' them as we like our friends. Can you persuade yourself that you would have 'enjoyed' St. Paul's company? Do you think that you and I would have 'got on' with Sir Galahad?

"So with the sinners, as with the saints. If you met a very evil man, and recognized his evil; he would, no doubt, fill you with horror and awe; but there is no reason why you should 'dislike' him. On the contrary, it is quite possible that if you could succeed in putting the sin out of your mind you might find the sinner capital company, and in a little while you might have to reason yourself back into horror. Still, how awful it is. If the roses and the lilies suddenly sang on this coming morning; if the furniture began to move in procession, as in De Maupassant's tale!"

"I am glad you have come back to that comparison," said Cotgrave, "because I wanted to ask you what it is that corresponds in humanity to these imaginary feats of inanimate things. In a word—what is sin? You have given me, I know, an abstract definition, but I should like a concrete example."

"I told you it was very rare," said Ambrose, who appeared willing to avoid the giving of a direct answer. "The materialism of the age, which has done a good deal to suppress sanctity, has done perhaps more to suppress evil. We find the earth so very comfortable that we have no inclination either for ascents or descents. It would seem as if the scholar who decided to 'specialize' in Tophet, would be reduced to purely antiquarian researches. No palæontologist could show you a *live* pterodactyl."

"And yet you, I think, have 'specialized,' and I believe that your researches have descended to our modern times."

"You are really interested, I see. Well, I confess, that I have dabbled a little, and if you like I can show you something that bears on the very curious subject we have been discussing."

Ambrose took a candle and went away to a far, dim corner of the room. Cotgrave saw him open a venerable bureau that stood there, and from some secret recess he drew out a parcel, and came back to the window where they had been sitting.

Ambrose undid a wrapping of paper, and produced a green pocket-book.

"You will take care of it?" he said. "Don't leave it lying about. It is one of the choicer pieces in my collection, and I should be very sorry if it were lost."

He fondled the faded binding.

"I knew the girl who wrote this," he said. "When you read it, you will see how it illustrates the talk we have had to-night. There is a sequel, too, but I won't talk of that."

"There was an odd article in one of the reviews some months ago," he began again, with the air of a man who changes the subject. "It was written by a doctor—Dr. Coryn, I think, was the name. He says that a lady, watching her little girl playing at the drawing-room window, suddenly saw the heavy sash give way and fall on the child's fingers. The lady fainted, I think, but at any rate the doctor was summoned, and when he had dressed the child's wounded and maimed fingers he was summoned to the mother. She was groaning with pain, and it was found that three fingers of her hand, corresponding with those that had been injured on the child's hand, were swollen and inflamed, and later, in the doctor's language, purulent sloughing set in."

Ambrose still handled delicately the green volume.

"Well, here it is," he said at last, parting with difficulty, it seemed, from his treasure.

"You will bring it back as soon as you have read it," he said, as they went out into the hall, into the old garden, faint with the odour of white lilies.

There was a broad red band in the east as Cotgrave turned to go, and from the high ground where he stood he saw that awful spectacle of London in a dream.

THE GREEN BOOK

The morocco binding of the book was faded, and the colour had grown faint, but there were no stains nor bruises nor marks of usage. The book looked as if it had been bought "on a visit to London" some seventy or eighty years ago, and had somehow been forgotten and suffered to lie away out of sight. There was an old, delicate, lingering odour about it, such an odour as sometimes haunts an ancient piece of furniture for a century or more. The end-papers, inside the binding, were oddly decorated with coloured patterns and faded gold. It looked small, but the paper was fine, and there were many leaves, closely covered with minute, painfully formed characters.

I found this book (the manuscript began) in a drawer in the old bureau that stands on the landing. It was a very rainy day and I could not go out, so in the afternoon I got a candle and rummaged in the bureau. Nearly all the drawers were full of old dresses, but one of the small ones looked empty, and I found this book hidden right at the back. I wanted a book like this, so I took it to write in. It is full of secrets. I have a great many other books of secrets I have written, hidden in a safe place, and I am going to write here many of the old secrets and some new ones; but there are some I shall not put down at all. I must not write down the real names of the days and months which I found out a year ago, nor the way to make the Aklo letters, or the Chian language, or the great beautiful Circles, nor the Mao Games, nor the chief songs. I may write something about all these things but not the way to do them, for peculiar reasons. And I must not say who the Nymphs are, or the Dôls, or Jeelo, or what voolas mean. All these are most secret secrets, and I am glad when I remember what they are, and how many wonderful languages I know, but there are some things that I call the secrets of the secrets of the secrets that I dare not think of unless I am quite alone, and then I shut my eyes, and put my hands over them and whisper the word, and the Alala comes. I only do this at night in my room or in certain woods that I know, but I must not describe them, as they are secret woods. Then there are the Ceremonies, which are all of them important, but some are more delightful than others—there are the White Ceremonies, and the Green Ceremonies, and the Scarlet Ceremonies. The Scarlet Ceremonies are the best, but there is only one place where they can be performed properly, though there is a very nice imitation which I have done in other places. Besides these, I have the dances, and the Comedy, and I have done the Comedy sometimes when the others were looking, and they didn't understand anything about it. I was very little when I first knew about these things.

When I was very small, and mother was alive, I can remember remembering things before that, only it has all got confused. But I remember when I was five or six I heard them talking about me when they thought I was not noticing. They were saying how queer I was a year or two before, and how nurse had called my mother to come and listen to me talking all to myself, and I was saying words that nobody could understand. I was speaking the Xu language, but I only remember a very few of the words, as it was about the little white faces that used to look at me when I was lying in my cradle. They used to talk to me, and I learnt their language and talked to them in it about some great white place where they lived, where the trees and the grass were all white, and there were white hills as high up as the moon, and a cold wind. I have often dreamed of it afterwards, but the faces went away when I was very little. But a wonderful thing happened when I was about five. My nurse was carrying me on her shoulder; there was a field of yellow corn, and we went through it, it was very hot. Then we came to a path through a wood, and a tall man came after us, and went with us till we came to a place where there was a deep pool, and it was very dark and shady. Nurse put me down on the soft moss under a tree, and she said: "She can't get to the pond now." So they left me there, and I sat quite still and watched, and out of the water and out of the wood came two wonderful white people, and they began to play and dance and sing. They were a kind of creamy white like the old ivory figure in the drawing-room; one was a beautiful lady with kind dark eyes, and a grave face, and long black hair, and she smiled such a strange sad smile at the other, who laughed and came to her. They played together, and danced round and round the pool, and they sang a song till I fell asleep. Nurse woke me up when she came back, and she was looking something like the lady had looked, so I told her all about it, and asked her why she looked like that. At first she cried, and then she looked very frightened, and turned quite pale. She put me down on the grass and stared at me, and I could see she was shaking all over. Then she said I had been dreaming, but I knew I hadn't. Then she made me promise not to say a word about it to anybody, and if I did I should be thrown into the black pit. I was not frightened at all, though nurse was, and I never forgot about it, because when I shut my eyes and it was quite quiet, and I was all alone, I could see them again, very faint and far away, but very splendid; and little bits of the song they sang came into my head, but I couldn't sing it.

I was thirteen, nearly fourteen, when I had a very singular adventure, so strange that the day on which it happened is always called the White Day. My mother had been dead for more than a year, and in the morning I had lessons, but they let me go out for walks in the afternoon. And this afternoon I walked a new way, and a little brook led me into a new country, but I tore my frock getting through some of the difficult places, as the way was through many bushes, and beneath the low branches of trees, and up thorny thickets on the hills, and by dark woods full of creeping thorns. And it was a long, long way. It seemed as if I was going on for ever and ever, and I had to creep by a place like a tunnel where a brook must have been, but all the water had dried up, and the floor was rocky, and the bushes had grown over-head till they met, so that it was quite dark. And I went on and on through that dark place; it was a long, long way. And I came to a hill that I never saw before. I was in a dismal thicket full of black twisted boughs that tore me as I went through them, and I cried out because I was smarting all over, and then I found that I was climbing, and I went up and up a long way, till at last the thicket stopped and I came out crying just under the top of a big bare place, where there were ugly grey stones lying all about on the grass, and here and there a little twisted, stunted tree came out from under a stone, like a snake. And I went up, right to the top, a long way. I never saw such big ugly stones before; they came out of the earth some of them, and some looked as if they had been rolled

to where they were, and they went on and on as far as I could see, a long, long way. I looked out from them and saw the country, but it was strange. It was winter time, and there were black terrible woods hanging from the hills all round; it was like seeing a large room hung with black curtains, and the shape of the trees seemed quite different from any I had ever seen before. I was afraid. Then beyond the woods there were other hills round in a great ring, but I had never seen any of them; it all looked black, and everything had a voor over it. It was all so still and silent, and the sky was heavy and grey and sad, like a wicked voorish dome in Deep Dendo. I went on into the dreadful rocks. There were hundreds and hundreds of them. Some were like horrid-grinning men; I could see their faces as if they would jump at me out of the stone, and catch hold of me, and drag me with them back into the rock, so that I should always be there. And there were other rocks that were like animals, creeping, horrible animals, putting out their tongues, and others were like words that I could not say, and others like dead people lying on the grass. I went on among them, though they frightened me, and my heart was full of wicked songs that they put into it; and I wanted to make faces and twist myself about in the way they did, and I went on and on a long way till at last I liked the rocks, and they didn't frighten me any more. I sang the songs I thought of; songs full of words that must not be spoken or written down. Then I made faces like the faces on the rocks, and I twisted myself about like the twisted ones, and I lay down flat on the ground like the dead ones, and I went up to one that was grin-ning, and put my arms round him and hugged him. And so I went on and on through the rocks till I came to a round mound in the middle of them. It was higher than a mound, it was nearly as high as our house, and it was like a great basin turned upside down, all smooth and round and green, with one stone, like a post, sticking up at the top. I climbed up the sides, but they were so steep I had to stop or I should have rolled all the way down again, and I should have knocked against the stones at the bottom, and perhaps been killed. But I wanted to get up to the very top of the big round mound, so I lay down flat on my face, and took hold of the grass with my hands and drew myself up, bit by bit, till I was at the top. Then I sat down on the stone in the middle, and looked all round about. I felt I had come such a long, long way, just as if I were a hundred miles from home, or in some other country, or in one of the strange places I had read about in the "Tales of the Genie" and the "Arabian Nights," or as if I had gone across the sea, far away, for years and I had found another world that nobody had ever seen or heard of before, or as if I had somehow flown through the sky and fallen on one of the stars I had read about where everything is dead and cold and grey, and there is no air, and the wind doesn't blow. I sat on the stone and looked all round and down and round about me. It was just as if I was sitting on a tower in the middle of a great empty town, because I could see nothing all around but the grey rocks on the ground. I couldn't make out their shapes any more, but I could see them on and on for a long way, and I looked at them, and they seemed as if they had been arranged into patterns, and shapes, and figures. I knew they couldn't be, because I had seen a lot of them coming right out of the earth, joined to the deep rocks below, so I looked again, but still I saw nothing but circles, and small circles inside big ones, and pyramids, and domes, and spires, and they seemed all to go round and round the place where I was sitting, and the more I looked, the more I saw great big rings of rocks, getting bigger and bigger, and I stared so long that it felt as if they were all moving and turning, like a great wheel, and I was turning, too, in the middle. I got quite dizzy and queer in the head, and everything began to be hazy and not clear, and I saw little sparks of blue light, and the stones looked as if they were springing and dancing and twisting as they went round and round and round. I was frightened again, and I cried out loud, and jumped up from the stone I was sitting on, and fell down. When I got up I was so glad they all looked still, and I sat down on the top and slid down the mound, and went on again.

I danced as I went in the peculiar way the rocks had danced when I got giddy, and I was so glad I could do it quite well, and I danced and danced along, and sang extraordinary songs that came into my head. At last I came to the edge of that great flat hill, and there were no more rocks, and the way went again through a dark thicket in a hollow. It was just as bad as the other one I went through climbing up, but I didn't mind this one, because I was so glad I had seen those singular dances and could imitate them. I went down, creeping through the bushes, and a tall nettle stung me on my leg, and made me burn, but I didn't mind it, and I tingled with the boughs and the thorns, but I only laughed and sang. Then I got out of the thicket into a close valley, a little secret place like a dark passage that nobody ever knows of, because it was so narrow and deep and the woods were so thick round it. There is a steep bank with trees hanging over it, and there the ferns keep green all through the winter, when they are dead and brown upon the hill, and the ferns there have a sweet, rich smell like what oozes out of fir trees. There was a little stream of water running down this valley, so small that I could easily step across it. I drank the water with my hand, and it tasted like bright, yellow wine, and it sparkled and bubbled as it ran down over beautiful red and yellow and green stones, so that it seemed alive and all colours at once. I drank it, and I drank more with my hand, but I couldn't drink enough, so I lay down and bent my head and sucked the water up with my lips. It tasted much better, drinking it that way, and a ripple would come up to my mouth and give me a kiss, and I laughed, and drank again, and pretended there was a nymph, like the one in the old picture at home, who lived in the water and was kissing me. So I bent low down to the water, and put my lips softly to it, and whispered to the nymph that I would come again. I felt sure it could not be common water, I was so glad when I got up and went on; and I danced again and went up and up the valley, under hanging hills. And when I came to the top, the ground rose up in front of me, tall and steep as a wall, and there was nothing but the green wall and the sky. I thought of "for ever and for ever, world without end, Amen"; and I thought I must have really found the end of the world, because it was like the end of everything, as if there could be nothing at all beyond, except the kingdom of Voor, where the light goes when it is put out, and the water goes when the sun takes it away. I began to think of all the long, long way I had journeyed, how I had found a brook and followed it, and followed it on, and gone through bushes and thorny thickets, and dark woods full of creeping thorns. Then I had crept up a tunnel under trees, and climbed a thicket, and seen all the grey rocks, and sat in the middle of them when they turned round, and then I had gone on through the grey rocks and come down the hill through the stinging thicket and up the dark valley, all a long, long way. I wondered how I should get home again, if I could ever find the way, and if my home was there any more, or if it were turned and everybody in it into grey rocks, as in the "Arabian Nights." So I sat down on the grass and thought what I should do next. I was tired, and my feet were hot with walking, and as I looked about I saw there was a wonderful well just under the high, steep wall of grass. All the ground round it was covered with bright, green, dripping moss; there was every kind of moss there, moss like beautiful little ferns, and like palms and fir trees, and it was all green as jewellery, and drops of water hung on it like diamonds. And in the middle was the great well, deep and shining and beautiful, so clear that it looked as if I could touch the red sand at the bottom, but it was far below. I stood by it and looked in, as if I were looking in a glass. At the bottom of the well, in the middle of it, the red grains of sand were moving and stirring all the time, and I saw how the water bubbled up, but at the top it was quite smooth, and full and brimming. It was a great well, large like a bath, and with the shining, glittering green moss about it, it looked like a great white jewel, with green jewels all round. My feet were so hot and tired that I took off my boots and stockings, and let my feet down into the water, and the water was soft and cold, and when I got

up I wasn't tired any more, and I felt I must go on, farther and farther, and see what was on the other side of the wall. I climbed up it very slowly, going sideways all the time, and when I got to the top and looked over, I was in the queerest country I had seen, stranger even than the hill of the grey rocks. It looked as if earth-children had been playing there with their spades, as it was all hills and hollows, and castles and walls made of earth and covered with grass. There were two mounds like big beehives, round and great and solemn, and then hollow basins, and then a steep mounting wall like the ones I saw once by the seaside where the big guns and the soldiers were. I nearly fell into one of the round hollows, it went away from under my feet so suddenly, and I ran fast down the side and stood at the bottom and looked up. It was strange and solemn to look up. There was nothing but the grey, heavy sky and the sides of the hollow; everything else had gone away, and the hollow was the whole world, and I thought that at night it must be full of ghosts and moving shadows and pale things when the moon shone down to the bottom at the dead of the night, and the wind wailed up above. It was so strange and solemn and lonely, like a hollow temple of dead heathen gods. It reminded me of a tale my nurse had told me when I was quite little; it was the same nurse that took me into the wood where I saw the beautiful white people. And I remembered how nurse had told me the story one winter night, when the wind was beating the trees against the wall, and crying and moaning in the nursery chimney. She said there was, somewhere or other, a hollow pit, just like the one I was standing in, everybody was afraid to go into it or near it, it was such a bad place. But once upon a time there was a poor girl who said she would go into the hollow pit, and everybody tried to stop her, but she would go. And she went down into the pit and came back laughing, and said there was nothing there at all, except green grass and red stones, and white stones and yellow flowers. And soon after people saw she had most beautiful emerald earrings, and they asked how she got them, as she and her mother were quite poor. But she laughed, and said her earrings were not made of emeralds at all, but only of green grass. Then, one day, she wore on her breast the reddest ruby that any one had ever seen, and it was as big as a hen's egg, and glowed and sparkled like a hot burning coal of fire. And they asked how she got it, as she and her mother were quite poor. But she laughed, and said it was not a ruby at all, but only a red stone. Then one day she wore round her neck the loveliest necklace that any one had ever seen, much finer than the queen's finest, and it was made of great bright diamonds, hundreds of them, and they shone like all the stars on a night in June. So they asked her how she got it, as she and her mother were quite poor. But she laughed, and said they were not diamonds at all, but only white stones. And one day she went to the Court, and she wore on her head a crown of pure angel-gold, so nurse said, and it shone like the sun, and it was much more splendid than the crown the king was wearing himself, and in her ears she wore the emeralds, and the big ruby was the brooch on her breast, and the great diamond necklace was sparkling on her neck. And the king and queen thought she was some great princess from a long way off, and got down from their thrones and went to meet her, but somebody told the king and queen who she was, and that she was quite poor. So the king asked why she wore a gold crown, and how she got it, as she and her mother were so poor. And she laughed, and said it wasn't a gold crown at all, but only some yellow flowers she had put in her hair. And the king thought it was very strange, and said she should stay at the Court, and they would see what would happen next. And she was so lovely that everybody said that her eyes were greener than the emeralds, that her lips were redder than the ruby, that her skin was whiter than the diamonds, and that her hair was brighter than the golden crown. So the king's son said he would marry her, and the king said he might. And the bishop married them, and there was a great supper, and afterwards the king's son went to his wife's room. But just when he had his hand on the door, he saw a tall, black man, with a dreadful face, standing in front of the door, and a voice said—

Venture not upon your life. This is mine own wedded wife.

Then the king's son fell down on the ground in a fit. And they came and tried to get into the room, but they couldn't, and they hacked at the door with hatchets, but the wood had turned hard as iron, and at last everybody ran away, they were so frightened at the screaming and laughing and shrieking and crying that came out of the room. But next day they went in, and found there was nothing in the room but thick black smoke, because the black man had come and taken her away. And on the bed there were two knots of faded grass and a red stone, and some white stones, and some faded yellow flowers. I remembered this tale of nurse's while I was standing at the bottom of the deep hollow; it was so strange and solitary there, and I felt afraid. I could not see any stones or flowers, but I was afraid of bringing them away without knowing, and I thought I would do a charm that came into my head to keep the black man away. So I stood right in the very middle of the hollow, and I made sure that I had none of those things on me, and then I walked round the place, and touched my eyes, and my lips, and my hair in a peculiar manner, and whispered some queer words that nurse taught me to keep bad things away. Then I felt safe and climbed up out of the hollow, and went on through all those mounds and hollows and walls, till I came to the end, which was high above all the rest, and I could see that all the different shapes of the earth were arranged in patterns, something like the grey rocks, only the pattern was different. It was getting late, and the air was indistinct, but it looked from where I was standing something like two great figures of people lying on the grass. And I went on, and at last I found a certain wood, which is too secret to be described, and nobody knows of the passage into it, which I found out in a very curious manner, by seeing some little animal run into the wood through it. So I went after the animal by a very narrow dark way, under thorns and bushes, and it was almost dark when I came to a kind of open place in the middle. And there I saw the most wonderful sight I have ever seen, but it was only for a minute, as I ran away directly, and crept out of the wood by the passage I had come by, and ran and ran as fast as ever I could, because I was afraid, what I had seen was so wonderful and so strange and beautiful. But I wanted to get home and think of it, and I did not know what might not happen if I stayed by the wood. I was hot all over and trembling, and my heart was beating, and strange cries that I could not help came from me as I ran from the wood. I was glad that a great white moon came up from over a round hill and showed me the way, so I went back through the mounds and hollows and down the close valley, and up through the thicket over the place of the grey rocks, and so at last I got home again. My father was busy in his study, and the servants had not told about my not coming home, though they were frightened, and wondered what they ought to do, so I told them I had lost my way, but I did not let them find out the real way I had been. I went to bed and lay awake all through the night, thinking of what I had seen. When I came out of the narrow way, and it looked all shining, though the air was dark, it seemed so certain, and all the way home I was quite sure that I had seen it, and I wanted to be alone in my room, and be glad over it all to myself, and shut my eyes and pretend it was there, and do all the things I would have done if I had not been so afraid. But when I shut my eyes the sight would not come, and I began to think about my adventures all over again, and I remembered how dusky and queer it was at the end, and I was afraid it must be all a mistake, because it seemed impossible it could happen. It seemed like one of nurse's tales, which I didn't really believe in, though I was frightened at the bottom of the hollow; and the stories she told me when I was little came back into my head, and I wondered whether it was really there what I thought I had seen, or whether any of her tales could have happened a long time ago. It was so queer; I lay awake there in my room at the back of the house, and the moon was shining on the other side towards the river, so the bright light did not fall upon the wall. And the house was quite still. I had heard my father come upstairs, and just after the clock struck twelve, and after the house was still and empty, as if there was nobody alive in it. And though it was all dark and indistinct in my room, a pale glimmering kind of light shone in through the white blind, and once I got up and looked out, and there was a great black shadow of the house covering the garden, looking like a prison where men are hanged; and then beyond it was all white; and the wood shone white with black gulfs between the trees. It was still and clear, and there were no clouds on the sky. I wanted to think of what I had seen but I couldn't, and I began to think of all the tales that nurse had told me so long ago that I thought I had forgotten, but they all came back, and mixed up with the thickets and the grey rocks and the hollows in the earth and the secret wood, till I hardly knew what was new and what was old, or whether it was not all dreaming. And then I remembered that hot summer afternoon, so long ago, when nurse left me by myself in the shade, and the white people came out of the water and out of the wood, and played, and danced, and sang, and I began to fancy that nurse told me about something like it before I saw them, only I couldn't recollect exactly what she told me. Then I wondered whether she had been the white lady, as I remembered she was just as white and beautiful, and had the same dark eyes and black hair; and sometimes she smiled and looked like the lady had looked, when she was telling me some of her stories, beginning with "Once on a time," or "In the time of the fairies." But I thought she couldn't be the lady, as she seemed to have gone a different way into the wood, and I didn't think the man who came after us could be the other, or I couldn't have seen that wonderful secret in the secret wood. I thought of the moon: but it was afterwards when I was in the middle of the wild land, where the earth was made into the shape of great figures, and it was all walls, and mysterious hollows, and smooth round mounds, that I saw the great white moon come up over a round hill. I was wondering about all these things, till at last I got quite frightened, because I was afraid something had happened to me, and I remembered nurse's tale of the poor girl who went into the hollow pit, and was carried away at last by the black man. I knew I had gone into a hollow pit too, and perhaps it was the same, and I had done something dreadful. So I did the charm over again, and touched my eyes and my lips and my hair in a peculiar manner, and said the old words from the fairy language, so that I might be sure I had not been carried away. I tried again to see the secret wood, and to creep up the passage and see what I had seen there, but somehow I couldn't, and I kept on thinking of nurse's stories. There was one I remembered about a young man who once upon a time went hunting, and all the day he and his hounds hunted everywhere, and they crossed the rivers and went into all the woods, and went round the marshes, but they couldn't find anything at all, and they hunted all day till the sun sank down and began to set behind the mountain. And the young man was angry because he couldn't find anything, and he was going to turn back, when just as the sun touched the mountain, he saw come out of a brake in front of him a beautiful white stag. And he cheered to his hounds, but they whined and would not follow, and he cheered to his horse, but it shivered and stood stock still, and the young man jumped off the horse and left the hounds and began to follow the white stag all alone. And soon it was quite dark, and the sky was black, without a single star shining in it, and the stag went away into the darkness. And though the man had brought his gun with him he never shot at the stag, because he wanted to catch it, and he was afraid he would lose it in the night. But he never lost it once, though the sky was so black and the air was so dark, and the stag went on and on till the young man didn't know a bit where he was. And they went through enormous woods where the air was full of whispers and a pale, dead light came out

from the rotten trunks that were lying on the ground, and just as the man thought he had lost the stag, he would see it all white and shining in front of him, and he would run fast to catch it, but the stag always ran faster, so he did not catch it. And they went through the enormous woods, and they swam across rivers, and they waded through black marshes where the ground bubbled, and the air was full of will-o'-the-wisps, and the stag fled away down into rocky narrow valleys, where the air was like the smell of a vault, and the man went after it. And they went over the great mountains and the man heard the wind come down from the sky, and the stag went on and the man went after. At last the sun rose and the young man found he was in a country that he had never seen before; it was a beautiful valley with a bright stream running through it, and a great, big round hill in the middle. And the stag went down the valley, towards the hill, and it seemed to be getting tired and went slower and slower, and though the man was tired, too, he began to run faster, and he was sure he would catch the stag at last. But just as they got to the bottom of the hill, and the man stretched out his hand to catch the stag, it vanished into the earth, and the man began to cry; he was so sorry that he had lost it after all his long hunting. But as he was crying he saw there was a door in the hill, just in front of him, and he went in, and it was quite dark, but he went on, as he thought he would find the white stag. And all of a sudden it got light, and there was the sky, and the sun shining, and birds singing in the trees, and there was a beautiful fountain. And by the fountain a lovely lady was sitting, who was the queen of the fairies, and she told the man that she had changed herself into a stag to bring him there because she loved him so much. Then she brought out a great gold cup, covered with jewels, from her fairy palace, and she offered him wine in the cup to drink. And he drank, and the more he drank the more he longed to drink, because the wine was enchanted. So he kissed the lovely lady, and she became his wife, and he stayed all that day and all that night in the hill where she lived, and when he woke he found he was lying on the ground, close to where he had seen the stag first, and his horse was there and his hounds were there waiting, and he looked up, and the sun sank behind the mountain. And he went home and lived a long time, but he would never kiss any other lady because he had kissed the queen of the fairies, and he would never drink common wine any more, because he had drunk enchanted wine. And sometimes nurse told me tales that she had heard from her great-grandmother, who was very old, and lived in a cottage on the mountain all alone, and most of these tales were about a hill where people used to meet at night long ago, and they used to play all sorts of strange games and do queer things that nurse told me of, but I couldn't understand, and now, she said, everybody but her great-grandmother had forgotten all about it, and nobody knew where the hill was, not even her great-grandmother. But she told me one very strange story about the hill, and I trembled when I remembered it. She said that people always went there in summer, when it was very hot, and they had to dance a good deal. It would be all dark at first, and there were trees there, which made it much darker, and people would come, one by one, from all directions, by a secret path which nobody else knew, and two persons would keep the gate, and every one as they came up had to give a very curious sign, which nurse showed me as well as she could, but she said she couldn't show me properly. And all kinds of people would come; there would be gentle folks and village folks, and some old people and boys and girls, and quite small children, who sat and watched. And it would all be dark as they came in, except in one corner where some one was burning something that smelt strong and sweet, and made them laugh, and there one would see a glaring of coals, and the smoke mounting up red. So they would all come in, and when the last had come there was no door any more, so that no one else could get in, even if they knew there was anything beyond. And once a gentleman who was a stranger and had ridden a long way, lost his path at night, and his horse took him into the very middle of the wild country, where everything was upside down, and there were dreadful marshes and great stones everywhere, and holes underfoot, and the trees looked like gibbet-posts, because they had great black arms that stretched out across the way. And this strange gentleman was very frightened, and his horse began to shiver all over, and at last it stopped and wouldn't go any farther, and the gentleman got down and tried to lead the horse, but it wouldn't move, and it was all covered with a sweat, like death. So the gentleman went on all alone, going farther and farther into the wild country, till at last he came to a dark place, where he heard shouting and singing and crying, like nothing he had ever heard before. It all sounded quite close to him, but he couldn't get in, and so he began to call, and while he was calling, something came behind him, and in a minute his mouth and arms and legs were all bound up, and he fell into a swoon. And when he came to himself, he was lying by the roadside, just where he had first lost his way, under a blasted oak with a black trunk, and his horse was tied beside him. So he rode on to the town and told the people there what had happened, and some of them were amazed; but others knew. So when once everybody had come, there was no door at all for anybody else to pass in by. And when they were all inside, round in a ring, touching each other, some one began to sing in the darkness, and some one else would make a noise like thunder with a thing they had on purpose, and on still nights people would hear the thundering noise far, far away beyond the wild land, and some of them, who thought they knew what it was, used to make a sign on their breasts when they woke up in their beds at dead of night and heard that terrible deep noise, like thunder on the mountains. And the noise and the singing would go on and on for a long time, and the people who were in a ring swayed a little to and fro; and the song was in an old, old language that nobody knows now, and the tune was queer. Nurse said her great-grandmother had known some one who remembered a little of it, when she was quite a little girl, and nurse tried to sing some of it to me, and it was so strange a tune that I turned all cold and my flesh crept as if I had put my hand on something dead. Sometimes it was a man that sang and sometimes it was a woman, and sometimes the one who sang it did it so well that two or three of the people who were there fell to the ground shrieking and tearing with their hands. The singing went on, and the people in the ring kept swaying to and fro for a long time, and at last the moon would rise over a place they called the Tole Deol, and came up and showed them swinging and swaying from side to side, with the sweet thick smoke curling up from the burning coals, and floating in circles all around them. Then they had their supper. A boy and a girl brought it to them; the boy carried a great cup of wine, and the girl carried a cake of bread, and they passed the bread and the wine round and round, but they tasted quite different from common bread and common wine, and changed everybody that tasted them. Then they all rose up and danced, and secret things were brought out of some hiding place, and they played extraordinary games, and danced round and round and round in the moonlight, and sometimes people would suddenly disappear and never be heard of afterwards, and nobody knew what had happened to them. And they drank more of that curious wine, and they made images and worshipped them, and nurse showed me how the images were made one day when we were out for a walk, and we passed by a place where there was a lot of wet clay. So nurse asked me if I would like to know what those things were like that they made on the hill, and I said yes. Then she asked me if I would promise never to tell a living soul a word about it, and if I did I was to be thrown into the black pit with the dead people, and I said I wouldn't tell anybody, and she said the same thing again and again, and I promised. So she took my wooden spade and dug a big lump of clay and put it in my tin bucket, and told me to say if any one met us that I was going to make pies when I went home. Then we went on a little way till we came to a little brake growing right down into the road, and nurse stopped, and looked up the road and down it, and then peeped through the hedge into the field on the other side, and then she said, "Quick!" and we ran into the brake, and crept in and out among the bushes till we had gone a good way from the road. Then we sat down under a bush, and I wanted so much to know what nurse was going to make with the clay, but before she would begin she made me promise again not to say a word about it, and she went again and peeped through the bushes on every side, though the lane was so small and deep that hardly anybody ever went there. So we sat down, and nurse took the clay out of the bucket, and began to knead it with her hands, and do queer things with it, and turn it about. And she hid it under a big dock-leaf for a minute or two and then she brought it out again, and then she stood up and sat down, and walked round the clay in a peculiar manner, and all the time she was softly singing a sort of rhyme, and her face got very red. Then she sat down again, and took the clay in her hands and began to shape it into a doll, but not like the dolls I have at home, and she made the queerest doll I had ever seen, all out of the wet clay, and hid it under a bush to get dry and hard, and all the time she was making it she was singing these rhymes to herself, and her face got redder and redder. So we left the doll there, hidden away in the bushes where nobody would ever find it. And a few days later we went the same walk, and when we came to that narrow, dark part of the lane where the brake runs down to the bank, nurse made me promise all over again, and she looked about, just as she had done before, and we crept into the bushes till we got to the green place where the little clay man was hidden. I remember it all so well, though I was only eight, and it is eight years ago now as I am writing it down, but the sky was a deep violet blue, and in the middle of the brake where we were sitting there was a great elder tree covered with blossoms, and on the other side there was a clump of meadowsweet, and when I think of that day the smell of the meadowsweet and elder blossom seems to fill the room, and if I shut my eyes I can see the glaring blue sky, with little clouds very white floating across it, and nurse who went away long ago sitting opposite me and looking like the beautiful white lady in the wood. So we sat down and nurse took out the clay doll from the secret place where she had hidden it, and she said we must "pay our respects," and she would show me what to do, and I must watch her all the time. So she did all sorts of queer things with the little clay man, and I noticed she was all streaming with perspiration, though we had walked so slowly, and then she told me to "pay my respects," and I did everything she did because I liked her, and it was such an odd game. And she said that if one loved very much, the clay man was very good, if one did certain things with it, and if one hated very much, it was just as good, only one had to do different things, and we played with it a long time, and pretended all sorts of things. Nurse said her great-grandmother had told her all about these images, but what we did was no harm at all, only a game. But she told me a story about these images that frightened me very much, and that was what I remembered that night when I was lying awake in my room in the pale, empty darkness, thinking of what I had seen and the secret wood. Nurse said there was once a young lady of the high gentry, who lived in a great castle. And she was so beautiful that all the gentlemen wanted to marry her, because she was the loveliest lady that anybody had ever seen, and she was kind to everybody, and everybody thought she was very good. But though she was polite to all the gentlemen who wished to marry her, she put them off, and said she couldn't make up her mind, and she wasn't sure she wanted to marry anybody at all. And her father, who was a very great lord, was angry, though he was so fond of her, and he asked her why she wouldn't choose a bachelor out of all the handsome young men who came to the castle. But she only said she didn't love any of them very much, and she must wait, and if they pestered her, she said she would go and be a nun in a nunnery. So all the gentlemen said they would go away and wait for a year and a day, and when a year and a day were gone, they would come back again and ask her to say which one she would marry. So the day was appointed and they all went away; and the lady had promised that in a year and a day it would be her wedding day with one of them. But the truth was, that she was the queen of the people who danced on the hill on summer nights, and on the proper nights she would lock the door of her room, and she and her maid would steal out of the castle by a secret passage that only they knew of, and go away up to the hill in the wild land. And she knew more of the secret things than any one else, and more than any one knew before or after, because she would not tell anybody the most secret secrets. She knew how to do all the awful things, how to destroy young men, and how to put a curse on people, and other things that I could not understand. And her real name was the Lady Avelin, but the dancing people called her Cassap, which meant somebody very wise, in the old language. And she was whiter than any of them and taller, and her eyes shone in the dark like burning rubies; and she could sing songs that none of the others could sing, and when she sang they all fell down on their faces and worshipped her. And she could do what they called shib-show, which was a very wonderful enchantment. She would tell the great lord, her father, that she wanted to go into the woods to gather flowers, so he let her go, and she and her maid went into the woods where nobody came, and the maid would keep watch. Then the lady would lie down under the trees and begin to sing a particular song, and she stretched out her arms, and from every part of the wood great serpents would come, hissing and gliding in and out among the trees, and shooting out their forked tongues as they crawled up to the lady. And they all came to her, and twisted round her, round her body, and her arms, and her neck, till she was covered with writhing serpents, and there was only her head to be seen. And she whispered to them, and she sang to them, and they writhed round and round, faster and faster, till she told them to go. And they all went away directly, back to their holes, and on the lady's breast there would be a most curious, beautiful stone, shaped something like an egg, and coloured dark blue and yellow, and red, and green, marked like a serpent's scales. It was called a glame stone, and with it one could do all sorts of wonderful things, and nurse said her great-grandmother had seen a glame stone with her own eyes, and it was for all the world shiny and scaly like a snake. And the lady could do a lot of other things as well, but she was quite fixed that she would not be married. And there were a great many gentlemen who wanted to marry her, but there were five of them who were chief, and their names were Sir Simon, Sir John, Sir Oliver, Sir Richard, and Sir Rowland. All the others believed she spoke the truth, and that she would choose one of them to be her man when a year and a day was done; it was only Sir Simon, who was very crafty, who thought she was deceiving them all, and he vowed he would watch and try if he could find out anything. And though he was very wise he was very young, and he had a smooth, soft face like a girl's, and he pretended, as the rest did, that he would not come to the castle for a year and a day, and he said he was going away beyond the sea to foreign parts. But he really only went a very little way, and came back dressed like a servant girl, and so he got a place in the castle to wash the dishes. And he waited and watched, and he listened and said nothing, and he hid in dark places, and woke up at night and looked out, and he heard things and he saw things that he thought were very strange. And he was so sly that he told the girl that waited on the lady that he was really a young man, and that he had dressed up as a girl because he loved her so very much and wanted to be in the same house with her, and the girl was so pleased that she told him many things, and he was more than ever certain that the Lady Avelin was deceiving him and the others. And he was so clever, and told the servant so many lies, that one night he managed to hide in the Lady Avelin's room behind the curtains. And he stayed quite still and never moved, and at last the lady came. And she bent down under the bed, and raised up a stone, and there was a hollow place underneath, and out of it she took a waxen image, just like the clay one that I and nurse had made in the brake. And all the time her eyes were burning like rubies. And

she took the little wax doll up in her arms and held it to her breast, and she whispered and she murmured, and she took it up and she laid it down again, and she held it high, and she held it low, and she laid it down again. And she said, "Happy is he that begat the bishop, that ordered the clerk, that married the man, that had the wife, that fashioned the hive, that harboured the bee, that gathered the wax that my own true love was made of." And she brought out of an aumbry a great golden bowl, and she brought out of a closet a great jar of wine, and she poured some of the wine into the bowl, and she laid her mannikin very gently in the wine, and washed it in the wine all over. Then she went to a cupboard and took a small round cake and laid it on the image's mouth, and then she bore it softly and covered it up. And Sir Simon, who was watching all the time, though he was terribly frightened, saw the lady bend down and stretch out her arms and whisper and sing, and then Sir Simon saw beside her a handsome young man, who kissed her on the lips. And they drank wine out of the golden bowl together, and they ate the cake together. But when the sun rose there was only the little wax doll, and the lady hid it again under the bed in the hollow place. So Sir Simon knew quite well what the lady was, and he waited and he watched, till the time she had said was nearly over, and in a week the year and a day would be done. And one night, when he was watching behind the curtains in her room, he saw her making more wax dolls. And she made five, and hid them away. And the next night she took one out, and held it up, and filled the golden bowl with water, and took the doll by the neck and held it under the water. Then she said—

Sir Dickon, Sir Dickon, your day is done. You shall be drowned in the water wan.

And the next day news came to the castle that Sir Richard had been drowned at the ford. And at night she took another doll and tied a violet cord round its neck and hung it up on a nail. Then she said—

Sir Rowland, your life has ended its span. High on a tree I see you hang.

And the next day news came to the castle that Sir Rowland had been hanged by robbers in the wood. And at night she took another doll, and drove her bodkin right into its heart. Then she said—

Sir Noll, Sir Noll, so cease your life. Your heart piercèd with the knife.

And the next day news came to the castle that Sir Oliver had fought in a tavern, and a stranger had stabbed him to the heart. And at night she took another doll, and held it to a fire of charcoal till it was melted. Then she said—

Sir John, return, and turn to clay. In fire of fever you waste away.

And the next day news came to the castle that Sir John had died in a burning fever. So then Sir Simon went out of the castle and mounted his horse and rode away to the bishop and told him everything. And the bishop sent his men, and they took the Lady Avelin, and everything she had done was found out. So on the day after the year and a day, when she was to have been married, they carried her through the town in her smock, and they tied her to a great stake in the market-place, and burned her alive before the bishop with her wax image hung round her neck. And people said the wax man screamed in the burning of the flames. And I thought of this story again and again as I was lying awake in my bed, and I seemed to see the Lady Avelin in the market-place, with the yellow flames eating up her beautiful white body. And I thought of it so much that I seemed to get into the story myself, and I fancied I was the lady, and that they were coming to take me to be burnt with fire, with all the people in the town looking at me. And I wondered whether she cared, after all the strange things she had done, and whether it hurt very much to be burned at the stake. I tried again and again to forget nurse's stories, and to remember the secret I had seen that afternoon, and what was in the secret wood, but I could only see the dark and a glimmering in the dark, and then it went away, and I only saw myself running, and then a great moon came up white over a dark round hill. Then all the old stories came back again, and the queer rhymes that nurse used to sing to me; and there was one beginning "Halsy cumsy Helen musty," that she used to sing very softly when she wanted me to go to sleep. And I began to sing it to myself inside of my head, and I went to sleep.

The next morning I was very tired and sleepy, and could hardly do my lessons, and I was very glad when they were over and I had had my dinner, as I wanted to go out and be alone. It was a warm day, and I went to a nice turfy hill by the river, and sat down on my mother's old shawl that I had brought with me on purpose. The sky was grey, like the day before, but there was a kind of white gleam behind it, and from where I was sitting I could look down on the town, and it was all still and quiet and white, like a picture. I remembered that it was on that hill that nurse taught me to play an old game called "Troy Town," in which one had to dance, and wind in and out on a pattern in the grass, and then when one had danced and turned long enough the other person asks you questions, and you can't help answering whether you want to or not, and whatever you are told to do you feel you have to do it. Nurse said there used to be a lot of games like that that some people knew of, and there was one by which people could be turned into anything you liked, and an old man her great-grandmother had seen had known a girl who had been turned into a large snake. And there was another very ancient game of dancing and winding and turning, by which you could take a person out of himself and hide him away as long as you liked, and his body went walking about quite empty, without any sense in it. But I came to that hill because I wanted to think of what had happened the day before, and of the secret of the wood. From the place where I was sitting I could see beyond the town, into the opening I had found, where a little brook had led me into an unknown country. And I pretended I was following the brook over again, and I went all the way in my mind, and at last I found the wood, and crept into it under the bushes, and then in the dusk I saw something that made me feel as if I were filled with fire, as if I wanted to dance and sing and fly up into the air, because I was changed and wonderful. But what I saw was not changed at all, and had not grown old, and I wondered again and again how such things could happen, and whether nurse's stories were really true, because in the daytime in the open air everything seemed quite different from what it was at night, when I was frightened, and thought I was to be burned alive. I once told my father one of her little tales, which was about a ghost, and asked him if it was true, and he told me it was not true at all, and that only common, ignorant people believed in such rubbish. He was very angry with nurse for telling me the story, and scolded her, and after that I promised her I would never whisper a word of what she told me, and if I did I should be bitten by the great black snake that lived in the pool in the wood. And all alone on the hill I wondered what was true. I had seen something very amazing and very lovely, and I knew a story, and if I had really seen it, and not made it up out of the dark, and the black bough, and the bright shining that was mounting up to the sky from over the great round hill, but had really seen it in truth, then there were all kinds of wonderful and lovely and terrible things to think of, so I longed and trembled, and I burned and got cold. And I looked down on the town, so quiet and still, like a little white picture, and I thought over and over if it could be true. I was a long time before I could make up my mind to anything; there was such a strange fluttering at my heart that seemed to whisper to me all the time that I had not made it up out of my head, and yet it seemed quite impossible, and I knew my father and everybody would say it was dreadful rubbish. I never dreamed of telling him or anybody else a word about it, because I knew it would be of no use, and I should only get laughed at or scolded, so for a long time I was very quiet, and went about thinking and wondering; and at night I used to dream of amazing things, and sometimes I woke up in the early morning and held out my arms with a cry. And I was frightened, too, because there were dangers, and some awful thing would happen to me, unless I took great care, if the story were true. These old tales were always in my head, night and morning, and I went over them and told them to myself over and over again, and went for walks in the places where nurse had told them to me; and when I sat in the nursery by the fire in the evenings I used to fancy nurse was sitting in the other chair, and telling me some wonderful story in a low voice, for fear anybody should be listening. But she used to like best to tell me about things when we were right out in the country, far from the house, because she said she was telling me such secrets, and walls have ears. And if it was something more than ever secret, we had to hide in brakes or woods; and I used to think it was such fun creeping along a hedge, and going very softly, and then we would get behind the bushes or run into the wood all of a sudden, when we were sure that none was watching us; so we knew that we had our secrets quite all to ourselves, and nobody else at all knew anything about them. Now and then, when we had hidden ourselves as I have described, she used to show me all sorts of odd things. One day, I remember, we were in a hazel brake, overlooking the brook, and we were so snug and warm, as though it was April; the sun was quite hot, and the leaves were just coming out. Nurse said she would show me something funny that would make me laugh, and then she showed me, as she said, how one could turn a whole house upside down, without anybody being able to find out, and the pots and pans would jump about, and the china would be broken, and the chairs would tumble over of themselves. I tried it one day in the kitchen, and I found I could do it quite well, and a whole row of plates on the dresser fell off it, and cook's little work-table tilted up and turned right over "before her eyes," as she said, but she was so frightened and turned so white that I didn't do it again, as I liked her. And afterwards, in the hazel copse, when she had shown me how to make things tumble about, she showed me how to make rapping noises, and I learnt how to do that, too. Then she taught me rhymes to say on certain occasions, and peculiar marks to make on other occasions, and other things that her great-grandmother had taught her when she was a little girl herself. And these were all the things I was thinking about in those days after the strange walk when I thought I had seen a great secret, and I wished nurse were there for me to ask her about it, but she had gone away more than two years before, and nobody seemed to know what had become of her, or where she had gone. But I shall always remember those days if I live to be quite old, because all the time I felt so strange, wondering and doubting, and feeling quite sure at one time, and making up my mind, and then I would feel quite sure that such things couldn't happen really, and it began all over again. But I took great care not to do certain things that might be very dangerous. So I waited and wondered for a long time, and though I was not sure at all, I never dared to try to find out. But one day I became sure that all that nurse said was quite true, and I was all alone when I found it out. I trembled all over with joy and terror, and as fast as I could I ran into one of the old brakes where we used to go—it was the one by the lane, where nurse made the little clay man—and I ran into it, and I crept into it; and when I came to the place where the elder was, I covered up my face with my hands and lay down flat on the grass, and I stayed there for two hours without moving, whispering to myself delicious, terrible things, and saying some words over and over again. It was all true and wonderful and splendid, and when I remembered the story I knew and thought of what I had really seen, I got hot and I got cold, and the air seemed full of scent, and flowers, and singing. And first I wanted to make a little clay man, like the one nurse had made so long ago, and I had to invent plans and stratagems, and to look about, and to think of things beforehand, because nobody must dream of anything that I was doing or going to do, and I was too old to carry clay about in a tin bucket. At last I thought of a plan, and I brought the wet clay to the brake, and did everything that nurse had done, only I made a much finer image than the one she had made; and when it was finished I did everything that I could imagine and much more than she did, because it was the likeness of something far better. And a few days later, when I had done my lessons early, I went for the second time by the way of the little brook that had led me into a strange country. And I followed the brook, and went through the bushes, and beneath the low branches of trees, and up thorny thickets on the hill, and by dark woods full of creeping thorns, a long, long way. Then I crept through the dark tunnel where the brook had been and the ground was stony, till at last I came to the thicket that climbed up the hill, and though the leaves were coming out upon the trees, everything looked almost as black as it was on the first day that I went there. And the thicket was just the same, and I went up slowly till I came out on the big bare hill, and began to walk among the wonderful rocks. I saw the terrible voor again on everything, for though the sky was brighter, the ring of wild hills all around was still dark, and the hanging woods looked dark and dreadful, and the strange rocks were as grey as ever; and when I looked down on them from the great mound, sitting on the stone, I saw all their amazing circles and rounds within rounds, and I had to sit quite still and watch them as they began to turn about me, and each stone danced in its place, and they seemed to go round and round in a great whirl, as if one were in the middle of all the stars and heard them rushing through the air. So I went down among the rocks to dance with them and to sing extraordinary songs; and I went down through the other thicket, and drank from the bright stream in the close and secret valley, putting my lips down to the bubbling water; and then I went on till I came to the deep, brimming well among the glittering moss, and I sat down. I looked before me into the secret darkness of the valley, and behind me was the great high wall of grass, and all around me there were the hanging woods that made the valley such a secret place. I knew there was nobody here at all besides myself, and that no one could see me. So I took off my boots and stockings, and let my feet down into the water, saying the words that I knew. And it was not cold at all, as I expected, but warm and very pleasant, and when my feet were in it I felt as if they were in silk, or as if the nymph were kissing them. So when I had done, I said the other words and made the signs, and then I dried my feet with a towel I had brought on purpose, and put on my stockings and boots. Then I climbed up the steep wall, and went into the place where there are the hollows, and the two beautiful mounds, and the round ridges of land, and all the strange shapes. I did not go down into the hollow this time, but I turned at the end, and made out the figures quite plainly, as it was lighter, and I had remembered the story I had quite forgotten before, and in the story the two figures are called Adam and Eve, and only those who know the story understand what they mean. So I went on and on till I came to the secret wood which must not be described, and I crept into it by the way I had found. And when I had gone about halfway I stopped, and turned round, and got ready, and I bound the handkerchief tightly round my eyes, and made quite sure that I could not see at all, not a twig, nor the end of a leaf, nor the light of the sky, as it was an old red silk handkerchief with large yellow spots, that went round twice and covered my eyes, so that I could see nothing. Then I began to go on, step by step, very slowly. My heart beat faster and faster, and something rose in my throat that choked me and made me want to cry out, but I shut my lips, and went on. Boughs caught in my hair as I went, and great thorns tore me; but I went on to the end of the path. Then I stopped, and held out my arms and bowed, and I went round the first time, feeling with my hands, and there was nothing. I went round the second time, feeling with my hands, and there was nothing. Then I went round the third time, feeling with my hands, and the story was all true, and I wished that the years were gone by, and that I had not so long a time to wait before I was happy for ever and ever.

Nurse must have been a prophet like those we read of in the Bible. Everything that she said began to come true, and since then other things that she told me of have happened. That was how I came to know that her stories were true and that I had not made up the secret myself out of my own head. But there was another thing that happened that day. I went a second time to the secret place. It was at the deep brimming well, and when I was standing on the moss I bent over and looked in, and then I knew who the white lady was that I had seen come out of the water in the wood long ago when I was quite little. And I trembled all over, because that told me other things. Then I remembered how sometime after I had seen the white people in the wood, nurse asked me more about them, and I told her all over again, and she listened, and said nothing for a long, long time, and at last she said, "You will see her again." So I understood what had happened and what was to happen. And I understood about the nymphs; how I might meet them in all kinds of places, and they would always help me, and I must always look for them, and find them in all sorts of strange shapes and appearances. And without the nymphs I could never have found the secret, and without them none of the other things could happen. Nurse had told me all about them long ago, but she called them by another name, and I did not know what she meant, or what her tales of them were about, only that they were very queer. And there were two kinds, the bright and the dark, and both were very lovely and very wonderful, and some people saw only one kind, and some only the other, but some saw them both. But usually the dark appeared first, and the bright ones came afterwards, and there were extraordinary tales about them. It was a day or two after I had come home from the secret place that I first really knew the nymphs. Nurse had shown me how to call them, and I had tried, but I did not know what she meant, and so I thought it was all nonsense. But I made up my mind I would try again, so I went to the wood where the pool was, where I saw the white people, and I tried again. The dark nymph, Alanna, came, and she turned the pool of water into a pool of fire . . .

EPILOGUE

"That's a very queer story," said Cotgrave, handing back the green book to the recluse, Ambrose. "I see the drift of a good deal, but there are many things that I do not grasp at all. On the last page, for example, what does she mean by 'nymphs'?"

"Well, I think there are references throughout the manuscript to certain 'processes' which have been handed down by tradition from age to age. Some of these processes are just beginning to come within the purview of science, which has arrived at them—or rather at the steps which lead to them—by quite different paths. I have interpreted the reference to 'nymphs' as a reference to one of these processes."

"And you believe that there are such things?"

"Oh, I think so. Yes, I believe I could give you convincing evidence on that point. I am afraid you have neglected the study of alchemy? It is a pity, for the symbolism, at all events, is very beautiful, and moreover if you were acquainted with certain books on the subject, I could recall to your mind phrases which might explain a good deal in the manuscript that you have been reading."

"Yes; but I want to know whether you seriously think that there is any foundation of fact beneath these fancies. Is it not all a department of poetry; a curious dream with which man has indulged himself?"

"I can only say that it is no doubt better for the great mass of people to dismiss it all as a dream. But if you ask my veritable belief—that goes quite the other way. No; I should not say belief, but rather knowledge. I may tell you that I have known cases in which men have stumbled quite by accident on certain of these 'processes,' and have been astonished by wholly unexpected results. In the cases I am thinking of there could have been no possibility of 'suggestion' or subconscious action of any kind. One might as well suppose a schoolboy 'suggesting' the existence of Æschylus to himself, while he plods mechanically through the declensions.

"But you have noticed the obscurity," Ambrose went on, "and in this particular case it must have been dictated by instinct, since the writer never thought that her manuscripts would fall into other hands. But the practice is universal, and for most excellent reasons. Powerful and sovereign medicines, which are, of necessity, virulent poisons also, are kept in a locked cabinet. The child may find the key by chance, and drink herself dead; but in most cases the search

is educational, and the phials contain precious elixirs for him who has patiently fashioned the key for himself."

"You do not care to go into details?"

"No, frankly, I do not. No, you must remain unconvinced. But you saw how the manuscript illustrates the talk we had last week?"

"Is this girl still alive?"

"No. I was one of those who found her. I knew the father well; he was a lawyer, and had always left her very much to herself. He thought of nothing but deeds and leases, and the news came to him as an awful surprise. She was missing one morning; I suppose it was about a year after she had written what you have read. The servants were called, and they told things, and put the only natural interpretation on them—a perfectly erroneous one.

"They discovered that green book somewhere in her room, and I found her in the place that she described with so much dread, lying on the ground before the image."

"It was an image?"

"Yes, it was hidden by the thorns and the thick undergrowth that had surrounded it. It was a wild, lonely country; but you know what it was like by her description, though of course you will understand that the colours have been heightened. A child's imagination always makes the heights higher and the depths deeper than they really are; and she had, unfortunately for herself, something more than imagination. One might say, perhaps, that the picture in her mind which she succeeded in a measure in putting into words, was the scene as it would have appeared to an imaginative artist. But it is a strange, desolate land."

"And she was dead?"

"Yes. She had poisoned herself—in time. No; there was not a word to be said against her in the ordinary sense. You may recollect a story I told you the other night about a lady who saw her child's fingers crushed by a window?"

"And what was this statue?"

"Well, it was of Roman workmanship, of a stone that with the centuries had not blackened, but had become white and luminous. The thicket had grown up about it and concealed it, and in the Middle Ages the followers of a very old tradition had known how to use it for their own purposes. In fact it had been incorporated into the monstrous mythology of the Sabbath. You will have noted that those to whom a sight of that shining whiteness had been vouchsafed by chance, or rather, perhaps, by apparent chance, were required to blindfold themselves on their second approach. That is very significant."

"And is it there still?"

"I sent for tools, and we hammered it into dust and fragments."

"The persistence of tradition never surprises me," Ambrose went on after a pause. "I could name many an English parish where such traditions as that girl had listened to in her childhood are still existent in occult but unabated vigour. No, for me, it is the 'story' not the 'sequel,' which is strange and awful, for I have always believed that wonder is of the soul."

Gustav Meyer (1868–1932) was an Austrian author who published under the name Gustav Meyrink. He is among the most esteemed German-language writers of his time within the genre of supernatural fiction. He was a banker before he took to the pen. An arrest on charges of profiteering led to his bank being ruined. By the time of his release after he was found innocent, he was ostracized from the community. Meyrink then moved to Vienna, where he became an editor and began publishing satirical stories whose aim seems to have been to insult the wealthy and notable figures of the city, certainly earning him the title of gadfly. By the early twentieth century, though, he turned away from satire and began to work with more fantastical and phantasmagorical elements. The utterly unique "Blamol" (1903), reprinted here in a new translation, was one of the first stories to display his new interest. Meyrink's novel *The Golem* (1914), by far his best-known fiction, has been adapted to film numerous times.

Blamol

Gustav Meyrink

Translated by Gio Clairval

True, without error, certain and most true, I shall tell you: that which is below is as that which is above.

—Smaragdine Table

THE OLD SQUID SAT IN FRONT of a thick blue book found in a wrecked ship and slowly imbibed himself with ink.

Cloddwellers have no idea how busy a squid can be all day long.

This one had devoted himself to the study of medicine and from dawn till dusk two poor little starfish had to help him turn the pages—because they owed him so much money.

Around his midsection—where other people have a waist—he wore a golden pince-nez, part of a marine loot. The lenses—left and right—were placed far away and anyone who accidentally looked through them became disagreeably dizzy.

——Peace and quiet all around.

That's when a polyp came flying at him, bag-shaped snout stretched forward, tentacles trailing behind like a bundle of rods, and it dropped to lie near the book.—It waited until the old fellow glanced up, and then greeted him profusely, after which it unwrapped a tin box out of his body.

"You're the purple polyp from Turbot Alley, aren't you?" said the squid graciously. "Right, right, I knew your mother well, she was born *von Octopus*." (You, perch, bring me the *Polyps' Almanach de Gophalopoda*.) Well, what can I do for you, dear polyp?"

"The inscription,—uhm, uhm—read the inscription." The polyp coughed sheepishly (he had such a slimy pronunciation) and pointed to the tin can. The squid stared at the can and scrutinized the inscription like a prosecutor: "So, what do we have here?—Blamol!? That's an invaluable find. Certainly from the stranded Christmas steamer? 'Blamol—the new remedy— the more you take it, the healthier you become!'

"I want to open the thing immediately. You, perch, fetch me the two lobsters, you know, Coral Bank and Branch II, the brothers Scissors, but be quick about it."

No sooner had the green sea anemone, which was sitting nearby, heard about the new remedy than she immediately flitted up to the polyp:—Oh, she was so eager to take the remedy;—alas, so eager!

And with her many hundreds of prehensile tentacles, she performed a delightful bustle, so that the bystanders could not take their eyes off her.

—Holy shark!—was she beautiful! The mouth was a bit large, but that is so piquant on a woman.

Everybody was engrossed in her charms and overlooked the arrival of the two lobsters that diligently endeavored to slash the tin can with their claws, all the way speaking their Chechen dialect.

A light push, and the can fell apart.

Like a hailstorm, the white pills erupted from the tin and—lighter than cork—disappeared upward, as quick as lightning.

Everyone scrambled in excited confusion: "Stop, stop!"

But nobody was fast enough to grab anything. Only the sea anemone succeeded in catching a pill, quickly putting it in her mouth.

General displeasure: one would have liked to box the brothers Scissors 'round the ears.

"You, perch, you could have paid attention!— What are you my assistant for?"

It was a good ranting and scolding! Only the polyp could not utter a word, instead angrily slamming his clenched tentacles on a seashell so that the mother-of-pearl was crushed.

All of a sudden there was a deathly silence:— The sea anemone!

A blow must have hit her: she could not move a limb. Tentacles stretched out, she whimpered quietly.

With an air of importance, the squid swam along and commenced an unfathomable examination. With a pebble he tapped or pricked different tentacles. (Hm, hm, Babynskian Phenomenon, disruption of the pyramidal tracts.)

Finally, with the sharpness of a fin-edge, he crisscrossed the sea anemone's belly a few times, taking on an impenetrable gaze, then he straightened in a dignified motion and said: "Lateral sclerosis. The lady is paralyzed."

"Can we do something? What do you think?" cried the good seahorse. "Help her, help her. I'll rush to the pharmacy."

"Help?!—Are you crazy, sir? Do you think I studied medicine in order to cure diseases?" The squid became increasingly vehement. "It seems to me you are taking me for a barber, or do you want to mock me? You, perch—hat and cane—yes!"

One by one, they all swam away. "The things that can happen to anyone here, in this life. It's terrible, isn't it?"

Soon the place was empty, only from time to time did the perch return grudgingly to look for some lost or forgotten items.

At the bottom of the sea, the night stirred. Rays of light, of which nobody knows where they come from and where they disappear, floated like veils in the green water, shimmering so wearily as if they were never again to return.

The poor sea anemone lay immobile and watched them in bitter pain as they rose slowly, slowly upward.

Yesterday, by this time, she had been fast asleep in a safe hiding place.—And now?—To die outside, like an—animal!—Beads of air pearled on her forehead.

And tomorrow it is Christmas!!

She thought of her distant husband, who was wandering about, God knows where—Three months and already a seagrass widow! Truly, it would not have been a wonder if she had cheated on him.

Oh, if only the seahorse had stayed with her! She was so afraid!

It was getting so dark it was almost impossible to make out one's own tentacles.

Broad-shouldered darkness crept out from behind rocks and algae, devouring the blurred shadows of coral reefs.

Ghostly black bodies glided past—with glowing eyes and violet-lit fins—Night fish!—Evil rays and monkfish that stalk in the dark. Murderously lurking behind shipwrecks—

Coy and quiet as thieves, clams open up their shells and lure the late wanderer onto soft cushions for gruesome debauchery.

Far away, a dogfish barks.

—— A bright gleam flickers through the green algae: a luminous medusa guides drunken boozers home—Eeldandies and slovenly Moray-strumpets swimming fin-in-fin. Two silver-decked young salmon have stopped to look contemptuously at the exciting crowd. Rakish singing resounded:

"Among the green seagrass
I asked her
If she craved me.——
—Yes, she said.
Then down she bent—
and I pinched her.
Oh, among the green seagrass . . ."

"No, no, out of the way, Shoo—naughty salmon—Shoo!" an eel roared suddenly.

The silvery one continues: "Be quiet! You need to speak Viennish. That's because you're the only creature that does not live in the Danubian region, I suppose—"

"Pst, pst," soothed the medusa, "shame on you, look who comes!"

All of them fell silent and gazed timidly at a few slender, colorless figures that demurely moved in their direction.

"Lancet fish," someone whispered.

? ? ? ? ?

—— "Oh, these are high lords,—councilors, diplomats and such.—Yes, they are from birth destined to natural wonders: they have neither brain nor backbone."

Minutes of silent admiration, and then everyone swims peacefully off.

The noises die away.—The deathly hush deepens.

Time passes.—Midnight, the hour of terror.

Weren't those voices?—They cannot be shrimps,—so late now?—

The Night Watch makes the rounds: *Policecrabs!*—

How they are pawing with armored legs, crunching the sand, dragging their prisoners to secure places.

Woe to him who falls into their hands;—they do not shy away from any crime,—and their lies stand in court like oaths. Even the electric ray tingles when they approach.

The sea anemone's heartbeat halts in horror, she, a lady, lies there helpless, out in the open! What will happen if they see her? They will drag her to the judge, that perjurious crab,—the biggest crook in the whole deep sea—and then—and then—

They approach—now—one more step, and shame and ruin will sink their fangs in her belly.

The dark water quivers, the coral trees groan and tremble like seagrass, a pale light shining far away.

Crabs, rays, monkfish duck low and dart in wild flight across the sand as rocks break and whirl upward.

A bluish, glistening wall—as tall as the world—comes flying through the sea.

Nearer and nearer the phosphorescence hunts: the glowing giant fin of Tintorera, the demon of annihilation, sweeps along and rips abyssal glowing funnels into the foaming water.

Everything twists into crazed swirls. The sea anemone flies across bubbling expanses, up and down—over lands of emerald froth. Where are the crabs, where are shame and fear! Roaring destruction storms throughout the world. A bacchanal of death, a jubilant dance for the soul.

Her senses blink out, like dull light.

A terrible jolt. Whirling, and faster, faster, faster and faster, everything twirls backward and crashes to the bottom, all that the spinning funnels had wrested from the ground. A few armors break.

When the sea anemone finally emerged from unconsciousness after the fall, she found herself lying on a bed on soft algae.

The good seahorse—who had not gone to work for the day—leaned over her.

Cool morning water fanned her face, and she looked around. The chattering of barnacles and the cheerful bleating of a lamprey reached her.

"You're in my country cottage," the seahorse answered her questioning look, looking deep into her eyes. "Wouldn't you want to go back to sleep, my gracious lady? It would do you good!"

The sea anemone couldn't sleep for all she tried. An indescribable feeling of disgust pulled down the corners of her mouth.

"What a storm, last night! Everything is still spinning before my eyes," the seahorse continued. "By the way, can I tempt you with a bit of smoked ham, a piece of Sailor's speck?"

At the mere hearing of the word "ham," the sea anemone became so nauseated that she had to squeeze her lips tight. In vain. A choking sensation seized her (the seahorse glanced discreetly aside) and she vomited. The Blamol pill, undigested, came up, soared among air bubbles, and disappeared upward.

Thank God the seahorse had not noticed. The invalid suddenly felt well again, good as new.

She curled up comfortably.

Oh, wonder, she could curl up again, move her limbs like she used to. Delight and more delight! Beads of air filled the eyes of the overjoyed seahorse. "Christmas, it's really Christmas today," the cheering continued, "and I'll have to report to the squid what happened, right away. In the meantime, I trust you will sleep well."

"What do you find so wonderful about the sea anemone's sudden recovery, my dear seahorse?" asked the squid, with a benign smile. "You are an enthusiast, my young friend! Although I do not speak, in principle, with laypeople (you, perch, fetch a chair for the gentleman) about medical science, this time I shall make an exception and I shall seek to adapt my language to your comprehension as much as possible. So, you think Blamol is a poison and its effect is paralysis. Oh, what a mistake! Incidentally, Blamol has long been dismissed, it is a remedy of yesterday, today Idiotine Chloride is usually prescribed (in other words, medicine progresses inexorably). The fact that the illness coincided with the swallowing of the pill was mere coincidence—everything, it is a well-known fact, is coincidence—because, first of all, sub-lateral sclerosis has completely different causes, although discretion forbids me to mention them, and secondly, like all these remedies, Blamol does not work untill it is spat out. Even so, of course, it is only beneficial.

"And finally, as far as the healing is concerned—well, there's a definite case of auto-suggestion here. In reality (you see what I mean: *the thing in itself*, after Kant) the lady is just as sick as yesterday, even if she does not notice it. Autosuggestion often works, especially with people with inferior thinking. Of course I have said nothing of the sort, you know that I appreciate the ladies very highly: *Honor the women, They plait and weave*—As Schiller puts it.

"And now, my young friend, enough of this subject, it would just upset you unnecessarily—By the way, will you do me the great pleasure of this evening? It's Christmas and my marriage."

"Wha—? Marr . . ." the seahorse blurted out,

but he caught himself in time: "Oh, it will be an honor, Mister Mediconsult."

"Who is he marrying?" he asked the perch while floating away.

"You don't say: the lousy mussel??"

". . . Why not! Another marriage of convenience."

When, in the evening, the sea anemone, arriving a little late but with a radiant complexion, swam into the room, holding the seahorse's fin, the guests' jubilation seemed never to end. Everyone embraced her; even the veil snails and the cockles that acted as bridesmaids put their girlish shyness aside.

It was a brilliant party, of the kind only rich people can throw. The mussel's parents were billionaires and had even ordered marine luminescence. Four long banks of oysters had been laid out. After a full hour of feasting, more dishes were still brought to the tables. The perch never ceased to swim around, serving a hundred-year-old air salvaged from the cabin of a submerged wreck. She went about pouring from a shimmering pitcher (held, of course, upside down).

Everyone was already tipsy. The toasts dedicated to the mussel and her groom were completely lost in the popping of the corkpolyps and the clatter of the knifeshells.

The seahorse and the sea anemone sat at the far end of the table, completely in the shade, and in their merriment they paid little attention to what happened around them.

"He" sometimes furtively squeezed one of "her" tentacles, and then another, and she rewarded him with a provocative glance. Then toward the end of the meal the music ensemble played this beautiful song:

"Yes, to kiss, . . .
to frolick
with young gentl'men
is all the more for ladies
very modern,"

—and while the mischievous guests traded winks, no one could dismiss the impression that everyone here fantasized all sorts of tender relationships.

Louis-Honoré Fréchette (1839–1908) was a French Canadian poet, playwright, journalist, and writer of short fiction. This story, "Goblins: A Logging Camp Story," is another story featuring Jos Violon and lutins (elves or goblins). Some of the more famous recurring images of the folktales of the logging camps were *la bête à grand'queue / la Hère* (a wild beast), *fi-follet / fifolet / feux follets* (will-o'-the-wisp), and the *chasse-galerie* (the flying canoe). All of these images were religious in nature. In French Canada, a person turns into a werewolf after failing to go to church (specifically confession and Easter) for seven years. In most cases the person turned into a werewolf (how often depends on the teller—sometimes each night, or once a week—but not really related to the moon) can be turned back into a human simply by drawing a drop of their blood. They can be permanently cured by returning to church. *La bête à grand'queue* is a monster that pursues Catholics who fail to attend church/confession for seven years. *Fi-follets* are often also connected to religion (can turn into one after failing to go to church for fourteen years), but can also simply be lost souls. *Chasse-galerie* is the most intriguing. The flying canoe is essentially powered by the devil, and there are specific terms to use it (no drinking, no swearing, no invoking the name of God, no touching church steeples). The flying canoe is largely a combination of indigenous myths surrounding flying canoes and the European Wild Hunt. "Goblins" is a story that doesn't take place at a logging camp, but instead at a country farm.

Goblins: A Logging Camp Story

Louis Fréchette

Translated by Gio Clairval

GOBLINS, CHILDREN? Yer askin me if I know 'bout goblins? When 'un has traveled like I have, fer thirty good years in the woods, on timber rafts and in loggin camps, 'un's got to know, 'un thing leadin ta another, all 'bout those types. Ay, Jos Violon knows 'bout that, a little!

Needless to say it was precisely Jos Violon himself, our usual storyteller, who had the floor, and who was about to treat us to one of his winter camp stories, where he'd been an eyewitness when not having a central role in the events.

"What are the goblins already?" someone in the audience asked. "Are they people? Demons?"

"Bless my soul! That's more than I could ever

tell ya!" replied the veteran from the upper country. "All I know is that ya shouldn't mess with em. They ain't really maleficent, but when ya tease em, when ya badgerrupt / em too much, ya oughta watch out. They play tricks on ya, and not funny 'uns at all: take this young bride, they tramped her around on her weddin night, on hosseback, only ta bring her back breathless and almost unconscious at five o'clock in the mornin.

First of all, em goblins, everyone who's seen em, me included, will tell ya that, if they're not demons, they're little Jeesums even less. Imagine short ankle biters, eighteen inch tall, with only 'un eye in the middle of the forehead, noses like hazelnuts, bullfrog's mouths slashed up ta the ears, the arms and feet of a toad, bellies like tomatoes, and big pointy hats that make em look like spring mushrooms.

This 'un eye they have like that in the middle of their physiognomy burns like a real brand, and that's what sheds light for em, 'cause that tribe sleeps durin the day, but durin the night they ferret about, makin—with all due respect—frickin mess of things. They live below ground, under logs, between two rocks, but patticularly underneath pavin stones in the stables, 'cause, if they have a penchant fer somethin', it's fer em hossies.

Oh, when it comes ta tendin hosses, there's no hoss dealer in the whole Beauce ta match em. When they make friends with a hossie, the hoss's manger is always full, and then ya've got ta see the coat, how it glows! Like a mirror, children, even down under the belly, not ta mention mane and tail beautified like any pretty critter with long braids; ya've got ta have glimpsed the scene, like I did. Listen ta what I'm goint tell ya, if ya don't mind me takin the time ta light mesel a smoke.

And after having tidily lit his pipe at the candle, the old storyteller proffered his usual preamble: "Tawkie, tawko, let's tawk," etc., and began his story as he always did:

"So, I was tellin ya, children, that year we were winterin on the Oak River, in the service of old Gilmore, with a gang of lads from back home, rounded up in the hills above Pointe-Lévis and the Coves of Cap-Blanc.

Even though our timber yard was near Saint-Maurice, the père Gilmore had refused ta hire the louts from Trois-Rivières. He wanted decent workers, no blasphemers, no drunks, and no sorcerers. Those miscreants that worry the sky in their infernal flying canoe, those cantankerous types that speak ta the devil and sell the black hen, he was fed up with em.

So we were all good people, even tho' we had not the chance ta attend a Low Mass every mornin.

As ya surely know, children, the Oak River is not in the neighbor's backyard, as they say, but it's not in the back of nowhere either. Talkin 'bout Trois-Rivières, ya can get there easily in two days and a half: and, given that the trail is not too rough, ya can take hosses with ya, ta pull the cart.

The boss, before leavin', had garnished himsel with two. A big'un, black, half tamed, and a silver-grey little mare, smooth as silk. Hah name was Belzemir. An eel in the neck she had, children—and she was also a real whirl of dust on the road. It was so nice ta work with that little beast, I'm tellin ya! Everybody loved her. We vied with each other ta see who could steal a sugar lump from the caboose, ta give her.

Did I tell ya that the big Zeb Roberge was a part of our gang? Well, he was in charge of the stable, in other words, he took care of the animals every day. A good lad, as ya know, our Zeb Roberge. Given we came from the same place, we were a pair of friends, and, Sundays, when the weather was fine, we often went ta smoke our pipes at the stable threshold, takin care not ta start a fire, 'course.

"Père Jos," 'un day he tells me, "d'ya believe in goblins?"

"Ye askin if I believe in goblins?"

"Ay."

"Why are ya askin?"

"D'ya believe den?"

"Oh, it depends, I tell ya. It's not 'bout religion, the goblins, ya're under no obligation ta believe."

"That's what I thought, too," says Zeb Roberge, "I thought, 'It depends.' In dis case, listen!

It's not religion, dat's true, but, help me God . . . me, am startin ta believe all da same."

"In goblins?"

"In goblins!"

"Are ya kiddin me?"

"Not at all, I swear! Why, put yersel in me shoes, père Jos. Every Monday mornin, fer some time, whatever hour I get up, guess what I find in da stable?"

"Don't tell me . . ."

"As true as yer standin' right dere, I don't get it. Belzemir is already groomed, how come? Trough full of hay, manger full of rye, coat like silk, but she's also breathless, as if she's been runnin fifteen miles all in one go."

"Get out of here!"

"Cross my heart! The sight frazzled my gourd at first, but I didn't think 'bout it too much, 'cause I hadn't noticed da main course; in a lantern light ya can't see everythin, can ya? What set off the dinglin in my suspicion was what I heard, last Monday, France Lapointe sayin ta Pierre Fecteau: 'Lookie how da Big Zeb takes care of his Belzemir! Ya'd dink he's spendin' his Sundays dollin' her up and den pamperin' her some more!' Fact is, père Jos, da impish mare's hair, mane and tail, was all combed up, crinkled and crimpled, and den braided, I kid ya not, it was . . . criminal. So I said ta mesel: 'Here's somethin' odd. Gotta watch dat thing.'"

"Have ya been watchin good?"

"The whole week long, père Jos."

"So?"

"Nothin!"

"An' what 'bout Monday mornin?"

"Same, da mare with da skin on her belly stretched like drums, and da hair . . . Come see fer yersel, père Jos, it's still full of waves."

Take my word for it, children, eyeballin the actual sight, a sudden fright scurried down my back. Can't describe that hairdo as just "curly": I would have sworn that the impious filly was all pomaded up, as ta go dancin. Only things missin: a pair of ear-pendants and maybe a brooch. We were wonderin, the Big Zeb and mesel, what was goin on, when we heard, near the door, a voice

treatin us as fools. We turned 'round and it was Gingerbread.

Gingerbread (dunno if I mentioned it, children), a type who was always puffin on his pipe, a man from the Coves, who called himsel Baptiste Lanouette, nicknamed Gingerbread by his chums, who knows why. A good lad, I believe, but a bit shifty, the way I saw it. He tiptoed up ta us and whispered in our ears:

"Ya can see it's em goblins!"

"Uhun!"

"Can't ya see she's been cared fer by goblins? It's obvious, hey."

"I was just talkin' 'bout it with da père Jos," Zeb says.

"Tut-tut!" said Gingerbread, "Since when ya've become so white-livered? Surely dere's some spell of dat kind at da bottom o' da bag . . . I almost feel like sendin all my concern ta . . . Tell me, did em hurt ya since the beginnin o' da winter, em goblins? Nope! So let em be. They ain't harmful, or tricky. Just don't talk 'bout em. If ya don't mess with deir business, they'll be no problem at all. I know em, em goblins; I've seen plenty at my deceased father's home. He was a carter."

Well, I'm tellin ya, children, this business was chewin on me, bad.

"What he says makes sense," I tell Zeb Roberge, the next evenin. "And I wouldn't mind seein some of those goblins. It ain't really evil, it ain't dangerous, and I also heard that if ya nab one, ya become wicked rich. Ye roll in dough. Handfuls and handfuls of coins! Patticularly when it's a female.—That's what happened ta a big merchant of the Ouelle River—ya can exchange it fer a barrel full of gold. Now, Zeb, if we are smart enough, ya understand . . ."

At first, Zeb made a face, but when he heard 'bout the barrel full of gold, I sensed the thought was startin ta wrap iself 'round his temper. Finally, ta make it short, we decided ta hide in the stable, on Sunday evenin, ta spy the little devils when they'd come ta play their little tricks on our Belzemir.

As planned, Sunday evenin come, at seven and a half, here we are, the both of us, Zeb Roberge and me, crouchin in a corner, behind two bales of straw, while our lantern (we needed some light, right?) sat on the shelf, as if forgotten, behind the filly.

We didn't remain on the lookout fer long. It wasn't eight of clock yet when we heard like a sort of tiny bustle that seemed ta come from right under us. And here we were, shakin like leaves. No matter how brave ya are . . .

Jos Violon and a wimp are beasts of a different color, ya know that, but, well, dunno what kept me in place.

It must have been Zeb who held me back 'cause I noticed his hand was cold like ice cubes. I even thought him unconscious. Patticularly when I spotted, two steps away from our hidin place, guess what, children, 'un of the floor beams that was risin slow, slow, like somebody was pushin it up from underneath. It couldn't be rats. We jumped, as we should. And, *crack!* here's the beam fallin back in place. I thought I'd been dreamin.

"Didd'ya see that?" I say quietly ta Zeb.

His voice sounded like he'd barely the strength ta speak.

"Ay, père Jos. It's da end of us. Fer sure."

"Let's keep still!" I say, while Zeb, who had a wholesome fear 'o God, crossed hissel with his two hands.

Out of the big nothin, here's the floor beam that starts movin again. We looked on. This time the sight slammed us right in the eyeballs. It was all too visible in the glow of our lantern. First we glimpsed the top of a pointy hat, then a large brim half pushed over somethin' that glowed like ember, which looked like a lit pipe, but it was in fact that kind of flamin eye those folks have in the middle of the forehead. Barrin that detail, I almost believed it was Gingerbread with his cakehole-burner between his clenched teeth. That's what imagination can do ta a fella! I even believed I'd heard him mutter: "Drats. Da Zeb went and forgot ta put his lantern off."

I didn't stop ta think, but put my hand in my pocket ta grab my rosary. *Bang!* Here's my damned sprung-knife that biffs on the ground, Zeb screams, the pointy hat disappears, and I find

the door at full speed, my partner right behind me—he'd forgotten all 'bout em handfuls of coins and barrels full of gold. I'll sign my report thrice 'cause 'tis all true.

Ya can imagine, children, why we weren't keen on talkin 'bout our adventure. Nowhere in Hell were we goint annoy the infernal society we'd just glimpsed. We knew all we wanted ta know, right? It wasn't worth it puttin the whole circus hot on our trail. We let the business continue as it'd started.

Every Monday mornin, Zeb found Belzemir all groomed and curried. But it got much worse on New Year's Day: Belzemir was nowhere in sight! She resurfaced the mornin' after, fresh like a daisy. What happened ta her in the meantime? Ginjiabread, who'd been away huntin all day, swore on all the Saints that he'd seen her careenin in the distance, jumpin over trees as if the devil was carryin her off.

The followin days, I inquired 'bout the matter once or thrice, but each time I opened my mouth . . .

"Please, père Jos," said the big Zeb, "let's not talk 'bout it. 'Tis better dis way. Each time I set foot in da stable, I get weak at da knees, thinkin dat da frickin beam is 'bout ta rise and da damned pointy hat is goin' ta show up. It'll be a hundred years before I wander back ta dis place. Da all of Saint-Maurice is hexed, one would dink!"

Who was Jos Violon that he'd contradict the poor sod, children? Because, as true as yer here, dunno if it was the fault of the Trois-Rivières bein nearish, but I've never wintered around Saint-Maurice without somethin' unwholesome happenin in our camp.

Be it as it may, as Mr. *le Curé* would say, springtime come, we didn't need convincin to bugger off down the river. The rafts were ready, everybody lashed his little luggage down ta start our journey. Cloaks, helmets, snowshoes, tools, rifles, traps, Fifi Labranche's violin, Bram Lacouture's checkerboard, exetera, exetera!

The Boss tasked us, Zeb Roberge and me, ta bring the hosses. And off we went, in tow, with Belzemir attached between the shafts, and the tall black 'un followin. We were goin fast, when, in a place called the Fork, here's the mare takin ta the left at breakneck speed, instead of turnin right along the river.

Zeb draws in the reins, yanks at the curb chain, then pulls left, right, left, right—sev'ral times—ta no avail!

"Listen," I say, "we should let her have it her way. We'll find the river down the road apiece."

We covered at least five miles at that speed, and I was startin ta find the route long, when we glimpsed a house.

"All right!" I was 'bout ta say, "This is a good moment ta flex our manners!"

But as we opened our mouths, Belzemir stopped right in front of the door.

"Well," says Zeb Roberge, "looks like da silly mare knows da place; she's never trotted 'round here though."

As he finished sayin' these words, here's the door swingin' open, and a thin, clear voice sayin:

"Look who's here! It's Mr. Baptiste's mare!

She's smart, uh. She's recognized the place, even tho' she's come only a few times in daylight . . ."

"Shut up and close the door!" a big, harsh voice thundered, from the back of the house.

It smelled like goblinfolk, that much is sure.

The year after, guess who I stumbled upon, down in the Cul-de-Sac, in Quebec? Baptiste Lanouette, nicknamed Gingerbread, pipe glued to his cakehole, 'course, head adorned with a big pointy hat, which had me thinkin 'bout the 'un I'd spotted on the goblin's head, near the Oak River.

He told me that he had almost nabbed one of those, in the very stable where Zeb and I had seen our own, so that the goblin's hat had remained in his hands.

I'd recognized the thing right away, c'mon!

Damned Gingerbread! Just one more second, and he'd become a wickedly rich man.

If ya ever pass by the Coves of Cap-Blanc, children, ask about Baptiste Lanouette and talk ta him of these things. See if I lie.

Grazia Deledda (1871–1936) was an Italian (Sardinian) novelist and playwright known for her social realism. In 1926, Deledda won the Nobel Peace Prize in Literature. She was the first Italian woman to win the prize, and she continued to write with vigor after receiving this honor. Deledda was an intriguing person: she kept a pet crow and did not particularly like many of the perks that came with fame. In fact, Mussolini once asked her if he could do her a favor, and instead of asking for wealth, she asked for the release of a friend who was imprisoned for anti-Fascist activities. In 1936, Deledda lost a long battle with breast cancer. Yet she continued to publish posthumously, as additional manuscripts were found in her home. "Sowbread" (1908) is an unusual tale, in that it is told from the point of view of a plant.

Sowbread

Grazia Deledda

Translated by Gio Clairval

AS SOON AS HE BLOOMED, the cyclamen saw a spectacle that many famous poets have never seen. He saw a moonlit night in the mountains. The silence was so deep the cyclamen could hear the drops of water—collected by the leaves of an oak protecting the small flower—fall to the ground as if poured by small hands.

The night was terse and cold, the mountain black and white, like an immense sleeping ermine, its profile of a pale purple color sparkling against the blue sky. It was not too high, that mountain: the woods covered it to the top; the snow-blanketed rocks resembled blocks of marble in which a gigantic artist had attempted to sketch strange figures. There was one, for example, that looked like a huge wolf with its face turned to the sky; and a thread of smoke, coming out of the rock as if exhaled from the mouth of the beast, increased the illusion.

From its damp and sheltered corner, the cyclamen saw the rocks, the trees, the moon, and a blue background with the outlines of other distant mountains. The moon was setting behind these mountains. Everything existed in silent, pure coldness. The stars shimmered with unusual splendors: they seemed to be looking at each other, communicating a joy unknown to the inhabitants of the earth. The cyclamen felt a bit of this joy; and he, too, trembled on his stem; and he did not know what it was, and did not know that it was the joy that makes the diamond and the spring water sparkle: the joy of feeling pristine. And this happiness lasted a long time, much longer than most human pleasure: it lasted an hour.

Then the cyclamen saw a strange thing, more marvelous even than the white rocks, the black trees, the shining stars. He saw a shadow moving. The flower had believed that everything in its world was still, or just trembling: instead the shadow walked. And after the wonder, the cyclamen shook with dread. The shadow approached, growing larger, rising against the blue background, among the black trunks; and it was so tall that it hid a whole mountain and reached up to the moon. It was a man. From time to time the man stopped under the trees, doubled over, as if looking for something in the shadows at his feet. Arriving under the oak he crouched, and began to rummage through the rotting leaves that covered the ground. And the young flower knew that the man had found what he was looking for: a little cyclamen plant.

After his one hour of life, certain that he had seen all that is most beautiful and most terrible in the entire universe, the cyclamen resigned himself to die. The unfriendly shadow uprooted the seedling, leaving some of the feeding soil around the bulbs. The cyclamen then realized that the black shadow did not represent Death: on the contrary it seemed to him his life was going to be more intense, if not as happy as that which he experienced before. With all his family of leaves, with his unbroken brothers, the flower was riding high, and saw the sky, the stars, better, as he abandoned his birthplace, moving across the mountain.

Like the man who carried him on the palm of his hand, the cyclamen possessed the great power of movement, and he felt a deep gratitude for the one who brought him so much joy. Upon coming under the rock that looked like a wolf, the man entered a cave that looked like the heart of a wolf, black, harsh, full of smoke; and having laid the seedling on a rock ledge, he bent to rekindle the fire. The little flower's despair lasted but an instant, for he saw another wonderful thing. He saw a black oak trunk transform into fire, and the flames spring from the branches like large golden leaves shook by a burning breath.

The man lay down by the fire and from his corner the little flower saw him fall asleep and heard him talking in his dream. And the man's voice seemed to him another revelation. Then a whistle vibrated outside, a dog barked, the man raised his head.

Another man entered the cave: the newcomer was young, tall and dressed in red cloth and black skins; his face, swarthy, but with blue eyes and a reddish beard, had something sweet and wild at the same time.

"Compadre," he said, as soon as he entered, "I think we're going to catch the fox tonight."

The older man raised his face, questioning.

"I saw the trail!" said the young man.

The two men said nothing more, but the old man jolted to his feet, and they both listened for a long time. One hour passed, though, and outside the silence of the night was still intense and deep. For a moment the moon appeared at the cave entrance, like a pale face with curious gray eyes, and then disappeared. The white darkness of snow took over the night.

"Your fox is not coming," said the old man. "And I've got to take off! How is the little mistress?"

"Not good. Maybe she'll die tonight."

"And you didn't tell me! I've got to go back! Must bring her the flower."

"What flower?"

"A sowbread. Yesterday, in her fever, she asked for nothing else. She imagines he's embroidering a stole for Holy Mass and wants to copy the flower. We must please her. I'm off."

"A stole with a sowbread on it . . . ?" The young man gave a puzzled smile. Then he raised his head, whispering: "Did you hear that?"

A dog barked, another echoed in the distance. The two shepherds, leaping out of the cave, heard whistles, screams, shouts more hoarse and ferocious than the dogs' barking. The flame ceased to tremble, as if listening to the din, while the cyclamen closed his petals among his sleeping brothers. The two men returned, dragging between them a young man with a bruised face and thick, frizzy black hair. Bound with leather strings, the captive struggled desperately. The three men were silent, while their breathing, panting, almost hissing, revealed their anger. This scene, beautiful and terrible, evoked the cavemen's world, man fighting his fellow man.

The prisoner was taken to the end of the cave, tied better, with cowhide straps and a noose, the end rope fixed to the ground with a stone. He didn't protest but lowered his disheveled head to the rocky ground and closed his eyes: he seemed dead.

The old man stared at him in rage, shuddering. "One, two, three times you escaped the gallows. But now you won't decimate my flock anymore! I'm alerting the judge."

And after throwing a leather bag across his shoulders, forming a hump on his back, he strode out.

No sooner had the old man departed, than the prisoner opened his eyes and pulled his head up, listening. The footsteps could not be heard any longer. The young man with a reddish beard sat on the ground next to the fire, looking sad. The prisoner gazed at him and said a word: "Remember!"

The other remained silent and still. The thief repeated: "The authorities. Remember! Once, on the night of St. John, two boys from different villages watched a flock under the moon. They loved each other like brothers. The elder said: 'Should we become St. John's fellows?' And they swore to be brothers, for life and for death, and especially in the hour of danger. Then they grew up and each went his way. And once the elder went to steal and was caught and given in custody to the younger, who happened to be in the sheep pen. The first word, though, that the prisoner said, 'Remember!' was enough, because the other, regardless of the damage that would come to him, untied him and released him. Remember!"

The younger shepherd avoided the captive's eyes: "That was different! I wasn't a servant back then. Before the fellow comes the master."

"No, before the master comes the brother: and a St. John's fellow is a brother."

The other, eyes fixed on the flame, did not answer, but seemed lost in a dream.

"We are all subject to error," said the thief.

"Some do this and some do that! We are born with our destiny. And does your master have no flaws? He is the proudest man on earth. He's the one who's killing his daughter, your little mistress. And what is she guilty of? Doesn't everyone say that she's dying because she's in love with a priest? No? Ah, you say it's not like that? You say that the young man became a priest out of despair, because he was not given the girl's hand? Even so, she should have stopped loving him. Instead, she dies . . ."

"Ah, that's why . . . The stole . . . the sowbread flower!" The shepherd stood and untied the prisoner, who, without even saying "thank you," jumped up and ran away.

Left alone, the shepherd picked up the sowbread plant, ran out, leaped from rock to rock, went down a path, shouting, calling the old man by his name.

The latter answered from afar. And the voices of the two men, closer and closer, crisscrossed in the silence of the night.

"You forgot the flower!"

"You left that devil alone!"

"The flower . . ."

"Give me! Go back . . ."

"I thought of the little mistress . . ."

"Go, go back. Now!"

The seedling passed into the old man's hand, and it was as good as a warm, capacious planter. The old man walked quickly but safely down the path illuminated by snow glowing like a grayish twilight. Finally he reached the foot of the mountain, and the cyclamen discovered a place that was darker and sadder than the cave: it was a place inhabited by men, a village.

The old man knocked on a door; a woman came to open, dressed in yellow and black, very pale in the face.

"How's the little mistress? I brought her the flower she wanted to copy for an embroidery."

The woman gave a hissing cry and began tearing at her hair. "The little mistress is dead!"

The man did not utter a word but entered the vast kitchen and laid the seedling on the ottoman where the little mistress used to sit to sew and embroider. In the adjacent rooms women's cries resounded like the chanting of ancient preachers. The old man left.

And long hours passed. The fire went out in the hearth. A hooded man, dressed in dark velvet, came to sit on the ottoman and kept still for a long time, without weeping, without speaking. Then the red-bearded servant arrived, and began to tell the story of the thief and the cyclamen.

"While I was bringing the flower to the master, the thief found a way to untie himself and escaped. I tried to catch him, in vain: I ran all night. Now the old fool says that the fault is mine, and that he, the master, will send me away."

The man dressed in velvet did not understand the story of the cyclamen. "An embroidery? For whom?"

The pale servant turned red. He lowered his voice even more. "They say . . . the stole is for Priest Paulu's first mass . . ."

A fleeting blush colored the hooded man's dull face. He looked at the seedling, then, in a harsh voice, he said: "Return to the sheep pen."

The shepherd studied the man's face and, before leaving, whispered: "May the Lord grant you all the good . . . Master . . ." But the man dressed in velvet did not seem to hear the wish. As soon as he was alone he grabbed the seedling, and clenched his teeth angrily.

The cyclamen saw his end come.

The man dressed in velvet opened his fist, stared at the folded leaves, the languishing little flower, and wept. And so, before dying, the cyclamen, who had seen so many beautiful and terrible scenes, experienced a deep wonder, a shiver, a commotion similar to the one he had sensed while he was blooming. He seemed to see the stars again, he believed himself on the mountain again, feeling, within the confines of that man's hand, still happy and pure as in mother earth. And all this because he had collected among his petals the tears of a proud man.

Gilbert Keith Chesterton (1874–1936), or G. K. Chesterton, was an English writer known for his exuberant personality and his mastery of the ballad form. By the time of his death at the age of sixty-two, Chesterton wrote five novels, five plays, and more than two hundred short stories. His critical repertoire is just as impressive, if not more so. In fact, it is almost impossible to sum him up, and many of his contemporaries considered him a genius, including H. G. Wells. Many a tale begins with a remarkable first sentence and "The Angry Street" (1908) is no different.

The Angry Street

G. K. Chesterton

I CANNOT REMEMBER whether this tale is true or not. If I read it through very carefully I have a suspicion that I should come to the conclusion that it is not. But, unfortunately, I cannot read it through very carefully because, you see, it is not written yet. The image and idea of it clung to me through a great part of my boyhood; I may have dreamt it before I could talk; or told it to myself before I could read; or read it before I could remember. On the whole, however, I am certain that I did not read it. For children have very clear memories about things like that; and of the books of which I was really fond I can still remember not only the shape and bulk and binding, but even the position of the printed words on many of the pages. On the whole, I incline to the opinion that it happened to me before I was born.

At any rate, let us tell the story now with all the advantages of the atmosphere that has clung to it. You may suppose me, for the sake of argument, sitting at lunch in one of those quick-lunch restaurants in the City where men take their food so fast that it has none of the quality of food,

and take their half-hour's vacation so fast that it has none of the qualities of leisure. To hurry through one's leisure is the most unbusiness-like of actions. They all wore tall shiny hats as if they could not lose an instant even to hang them on a peg, and they all had one eye a little off, hypnotised by the huge eye of the clock. In short, they were the slaves of the modern bondage, you could hear their fetters clanking. Each was, in fact, bound by a chain; the heaviest chain ever tied to a man—it is called a watch-chain.

Now, among these there entered and sat down opposite to me a man who almost immediately opened an uninterrupted monologue. He was like all the other men in dress, yet he was startlingly opposite to them all in manner. He wore a high shiny hat and a long frock coat, but he wore them as such solemn things were meant to be worn; he wore the silk hat as if it were a mitre, and the frock coat as if it were the ephod of a high priest. He not only hung his hat up on the peg, but he seemed (such was his stateliness) almost to ask permission of the hat for doing so, and to apologise to the peg for making use of it. When he had sat down on a wooden chair with the air of one considering its feelings and given a sort of slight stoop or bow to the wooden table itself, as if it were an altar, I could not help some comment springing to my lips. For the man was a big, sanguine-faced, prosperous-looking man, and yet he treated everything with a care that almost amounted to nervousness.

For the sake of saying something to express my interest I said, "This furniture is fairly solid; but, of course, people do treat it much too carelessly."

As I looked up doubtfully my eye caught his, and was fixed as his was fixed, in an apocalyptic stare. I had thought him ordinary as he entered, save for his strange, cautious manner; but if the other people had seen him they would have screamed and emptied the room. They did not see him, and they went on making a clatter with their forks, and a murmur with their conversation.

But the man's face was the face of a maniac.

"Did you mean anything particular by that remark?" he asked at last, and the blood crawled back slowly into his face.

"Nothing whatever," I answered. "One does not mean anything here; it spoils people's digestion."

He leaned back and wiped his broad forehead with a big handkerchief; and yet there seemed to be a sort of regret in his relief. "I thought perhaps," he said in a low voice, "that another of them had gone wrong."

"If you mean another digestion gone wrong," I said, "I never heard of one here that went right. This is the heart of the Empire, and the other organs are in an equally bad way."

"No, I mean another street gone wrong," and he said heavily and quietly, "but as I suppose that doesn't explain much to you, I think I shall have to tell you the story. I do so with all the less responsibility, because I know you won't believe it. For forty years of my life I invariably left my office, which is in Leadenhall Street, at half-past five in the afternoon, taking with me an umbrella in the right hand and a bag in the left hand. For forty years two months and four days I passed out of the side door, walked down the street on the left-hand side, took the first turning to the left and the third to the right, from where I bought an evening paper, followed the road on the right-hand side round two obtuse angles, and came out just outside a Metropolitan Station, where I took a train home. For forty years two months and four days I fulfilled this course by accumulated habit: it was not a long street that I traversed, and it took me about four and a half minutes to do it. After forty years two months and four days, on the fifth day I went out in the same manner, with my umbrella in the right hand and my bag in the left, and I began to notice that walking along the familiar street tired me somewhat more than usual. At first I thought I must be breathless and out of condition; though this, again, seemed unnatural, as my habits had always been like clockwork. But after a little while I became convinced that the road was distinctly on a more steep incline than I had known previously; I was positively panting uphill.

"Owing to this no doubt the corner of the street seemed farther off than usual; and when I turned it I was convinced that I had turned down the wrong one. For now the street shot up quite a steep slant, such as one only sees in the hilly parts of London, and in this part there were no hills at all.

"Yet it was not the wrong street. The name written on it was the same; the shuttered shops were the same; the lampposts and the whole look of the perspective was the same; only it was tilted upward like a lid. Forgetting any trouble about breathlessness or fatigue I ran furiously forward, and reached the second of my accustomed turnings, which ought to bring me almost within sight of the station. And as I turned that corner I nearly fell on the pavement. For now the street went up straight in front of my face like a steep staircase or the side of a pyramid. There was not for miles around that place so much as a slope like that of Ludgate Hill. And this was a slope like that of the

Matterhorn. The whole street had lifted itself like a single wave, and yet every speck and detail of it was the same, and I saw in the high distance, as at the top of an Alpine pass, picked out in pink letters, the name over my paper shop.

"I ran on and on blindly now, passing all the shops, and coming to a part of the road where there was a long grey row of private houses. I had, I know not why, an irrational feeling that I was on a long iron bridge in empty space. An impulse seized me, and I pulled up the iron trap of a coal-hole. Looking down through it I saw empty space and the stars. When I looked up again a man was standing in his front garden, having apparently come out of his house; he was leaning over the railings and gazing at me. We were all alone on that nightmare road; his face was in shadow; his dress was dark and ordinary; but when I saw him standing so perfectly still I knew somehow that be was not of this world. And the stars behind his head were larger and fiercer than ought to be endured by the eyes of men.

"'If you are a kind angel,' I said, 'or a wise devil, or have anything in common with mankind, tell me what is this street possessed of devils.'

"After a long silence he said, 'What do you say it is?'

"'It is Bumpton Street, of course,' I snapped. 'It goes to Oldgate Station.'

"'Yes,' he admitted gravely, 'it goes there sometimes. Just now, however, it is going to heaven.'

"'To heaven?' I said. 'Why?'

"'It is going to heaven for justice,' he replied. 'You must have treated it badly. Remember always there is one thing that cannot be endured by anybody or anything. That one unendurable thing is to be overworked and also neglected. For instance, you can overwork women—everybody

does. But you can't neglect women—I defy you to. At the same time, you can neglect tramps and gipsies and all the apparent refuse of the State, so long as you do not overwork them.

"'But no beast of the field, no horse, no dog can endure long to be asked to do more than his work and yet have less than his honour.

"'It is the same with streets. You have worked this street to death, and yet you have never remembered its existence. If you had owned a healthy democracy, even of pagans, they would have hung this street with garlands and given it the name of a god. Then it would have gone quietly. But at last the street has grown tired of your tireless insolence; and it is bucking and rearing its head to heaven. Have you never sat on a bucking horse?'

"I looked at the long gray street, and for a moment it seemed to me to be exactly like the long gray neck of a horse flung up to heaven. But in a moment my sanity returned, and I said, 'But this is all nonsense. Streets go to the place they have to go to. A street must always go to its end.'

"'Why do you think so of a street?' he asked, standing very still.

"'Because I have always seen it do the same thing,' I replied, in reasonable anger. 'Day after day, year after year, it has always gone to Oldgate Station; day after . . .'

"I stopped, for he had flung up his head with the fury of the road in revolt.

"'And you?' he cried terribly. 'What do you think the road thinks of you? Does the road think you are alive? Are you alive? Day after day, year after year, you have gone to Oldgate Station . . .' Since then I have respected the things called inanimate!"

And bowing slightly to the mustard-pot, the man in the restaurant withdrew.

Edith Nesbit (1858–1924) was an English author and poet who published under the name E. Nesbit. She created worlds with a logic all their own, always with her trademark witty prose. She was also one of the founders of the Fellowship of New Life, which later became the Fabian Society, a group dedicated to creating a democratic socialist state in Great Britain. She began writing in the 1890s and published more than sixty children's books alone. Somewhat ironically, Nesbit was not a fan of children, although they are often the protagonists of her books. It is probable that her dislike of them aided her clear and genuine portrayal of them in her novels *The Wouldbegoods* (1901), *The Revolt of the Toys*, and *What Comes of Quarreling* (1902). Quite possibly the inspiration for C. S. Lewis's Chronicles of Narnia series, "The Aunt and Amabel" involves using a wardrobe as an entrance into another world.

The Aunt and Amabel

E. Nesbit

IT IS NOT PLEASANT to be a fish out of water. To be a cat in water is not what any one would desire. To be in a temper is uncomfortable. And no one can fully taste the joys of life if he is in a Little Lord Fauntleroy suit. But by far the most uncomfortable thing to be in is disgrace, sometimes amusingly called Coventry by the people who are not in it.

We have all been there. It is a place where the heart sinks and aches, where familiar faces are clouded and changed, where any remark that one may tremblingly make is received with stony silence or with the assurance that nobody wants to talk to such a naughty child. If you are only in disgrace, and not in solitary confinement, you will creep about a house that is like the one you have had such jolly times in, and yet as unlike it as a bad dream is to a June morning. You will long to speak to people, and be afraid to speak. You will wonder whether there is anything you can do that will change things at all. You have said you are sorry, and that has changed nothing. You will wonder whether you are to stay for ever in this desolate place, outside all hope and love and fun and happiness. And though it has happened before, and has always, in the end, come to an end, you can never be quite sure that this time it is not going to last for ever.

"It *is* going to last for ever," said Amabel, who was eight. "What shall I do? Oh whatever shall I do?"

What she *had* done ought to have formed the subject of her meditations. And she had done what had seemed to her all the time, and in fact still seemed, a self-sacrificing and noble act. She was staying with an aunt—measles or a new baby,

426

or the painters in the house, I forget which, the cause of her banishment. And the aunt, who was really a great-aunt and quite old enough to know better, had been grumbling about her head gardener to a lady who called in blue spectacles and a beady bonnet with violet flowers in it.

"He hardly lets me have a plant for the table," said the aunt, "and that border in front of the breakfast-room window—it's just bare earth—and I expressly ordered chrysanthemums to be planted there. He thinks of nothing but his greenhouse."

The beady-violet-blue-glassed lady snorted, and said she didn't know what we were coming to, and she would have just half a cup, please, with not quite so much milk, thank you very much.

Now what would you have done? Minded your own business most likely, and not got into trouble at all. Not so Amabel. Enthusiastically anxious to do something which should make the great-aunt see what a thoughtful, unselfish little girl she really was (the aunt's opinion of her being at present quite otherwise), she got up very early in the morning and took the cutting-out scissors from the work-room table drawer and stole, "like an errand of mercy," she told herself, to the greenhouse where she busily snipped off every single flower she could find. MacFarlane was at his breakfast. Then with the points of the cutting-out scissors she made nice deep little holes in the flower-bed where the chrysanthemums ought to have been, and struck the flowers in—chrysanthemums, geraniums, primulas, orchids, and carnations. It would be a lovely surprise for Auntie.

Then the aunt came down to breakfast and saw the lovely surprise. Amabel's world turned upside down and inside out suddenly and surprisingly, and there she was, in Coventry, and not even the housemaid would speak to her. Her great-uncle, whom she passed in the hall on her way to her own room, did indeed, as he smoothed his hat, murmur, "Sent to Coventry, eh? Never mind, it'll soon be over," and went off to the City banging the front door behind him.

He meant well, but he did not understand.

Amabel understood, or she thought she did, and knew in her miserable heart that she was sent to Coventry for the last time, and that this time she would stay there.

"I don't care," she said quite untruly. "I'll never try to be kind to anyone again." And that wasn't true either. She was to spend the whole day alone in the best bedroom, the one with the four-post bed and the red curtains and the large wardrobe with a looking-glass in it that you could see yourself in to the very ends of your strap-shoes.

The first thing Amabel did was to look at herself in the glass. She was still sniffing and sobbing, and her eyes were swimming in tears, another one rolled down her nose as she looked—that was very interesting. Another rolled down, and that was the last, because as soon as you get interested in watching your tears they stop.

Next she looked out of the window, and saw the decorated flower-bed, just as she had left it, very bright and beautiful.

"Well, it *does* look nice," she said. "I don't care what they say."

Then she looked round the room for something to read; there was nothing. The old-fashioned best bedrooms never did have anything. Only on the large dressing-table, on the left-hand side of the oval swing-glass, was one book covered in red velvet, and on it, very twistily embroidered in yellow silk and mixed up with misleading leaves and squiggles were the letters, A.B.C.

"Perhaps it's a picture alphabet," said Mabel, and was quite pleased, though of course she was much too old to care for alphabets. Only when one is very unhappy and very dull, anything is better than nothing. She opened the book.

"Why, it's only a time-table!" she said. "I suppose it's for people when they want to go away, and Auntie puts it here in case they suddenly make up their minds to go, and feel that they can't wait another minute. I feel like that, only it's no good, and I expect other people do too."

She had learned how to use the dictionary, and this seemed to go the same way. She looked up the names of all the places she knew.—Brighton where she had once spent a month, Rugby where her brother was at school, and Home, which was Amberley—and she saw the times when the trains left for these places, and wished she could go by those trains.

And once more she looked round the best bedroom which was her prison, and thought of the Bastille, and wished she had a toad to tame, like the poor Viscount, or a flower to watch growing, like Picciola, and she was very sorry for herself, and very angry with her aunt, and very grieved at the conduct of her parents—she had expected better things from them—and now they had left her in this dreadful place where no one loved her, and no one understood her.

There seemed to be no place for toads or flowers in the best room, it was carpeted all over even in its least noticeable corners. It had everything a best room ought to have—and everything was of dark shining mahogany. The toilet-table had a set of red and gold glass things—a tray, candlesticks, a ring-stand, many little pots with lids, and two bottles with stoppers. When the stoppers were taken out they smelt very strange, something like very old scent, and something like cold cream also very old, and something like going to the dentist's.

I do not know whether the scent of those bottles had anything to do with what happened. It certainly was a very extraordinary scent. Quite different from any perfume that I smell nowadays, but I remember that when I was a little girl I smelt it quite often. But then there are no best rooms now such as there used to be. The best rooms now are gay with chintz and mirrors, and there are always flowers and books, and little tables to put your teacup on, and sofas, and armchairs. And they smell of varnish and new furniture.

When Amabel had sniffed at both bottles and looked in all the pots, which were quite clean and empty except for a pearl button and two pins in one of them, she took up the A.B.C. again to look for Whitby, where her godmother lived. And it was then that she saw the extraordinary name "*Whereyouwantogoto*." This was odd—but the name of the station from which it started was still more extraordinary, for it was not Euston or Cannon Street or Marylebone.

The name of the station was "*Bigwardrobein-spareroom*." And below this name, really quite unusual for a station, Amabel read in small letters:

"Single fares strictly forbidden. Return tickets No Class Nuppence. Trains leave *Bigwardrobein-spareroom* all the time." And under that in still smaller letters—

"*You had better go now.*"

What would you have done? Rubbed your eyes and thought you were dreaming? Well, if you had, nothing more would have happened. Nothing ever does when you behave like that. Amabel was wiser. She went straight to the Big Wardrobe and turned its glass handle.

"I expect it's only shelves and people's best hats," she said. But she only said it. People often say what they don't mean, so that if things turn out as they don't expect, they can say "I told you so," but this is most dishonest to one's self, and being dishonest to one's self is almost worse than being dishonest to other people. Amabel would never have done it if she had been herself. But she was out of herself with anger and unhappiness.

Of course it wasn't hats. It was, most amazingly, a crystal cave, very oddly shaped like a railway station. It seemed to be lighted by stars, which is, of course, unusual in a booking office, and over the station clock was a full moon. The clock had no figures, only *Now* in shining letters all round it, twelve times, and the *Nows* touched, so the clock was bound to be always right. How different from the clock you go to school by!

A porter in white satin hurried forward to take Amabel's luggage. Her luggage was the A.B.C. which she still held in her hand.

"Lots of time, Miss," he said, grinning in a most friendly way, "I *am* glad you're going. You *will* enjoy yourself! What a nice little girl you are!"

This was cheering. Amabel smiled.

At the pigeon-hole that tickets come out of,

another person, also in white satin, was ready with a mother-of-pearl ticket, round, like a card counter.

"Here you are, Miss," he said with the kindest smile, "price nothing, and refreshments free all the way. It's a pleasure," he added, "to issue a ticket to a nice little lady like you." The train was entirely of crystal, too, and the cushions were of white satin. There were little buttons such as you have for electric bells, and on them "*Whatyouwantoeat*," "*Whatyouwantodrink*," "*Whatyouwantoread*," in silver letters.

Amabel pressed all the buttons at once, and instantly felt obliged to blink. The blink over, she saw on the cushion by her side a silver tray with vanilla ice, boiled chicken, and white sauce, almonds (blanched), peppermint creams, and mashed potatoes, and a long glass of lemonade—beside the tray was a book. It was Mrs. Ewing's *Bad-tempered Family*, and it was bound in white vellum.

There is nothing more luxurious than eating while you read—unless it be reading while you eat. Amabel did both: they are not the same thing, as you will see if you think the matter over.

And just as the last thrill of the last spoonful of ice died away, and the last full stop of the *Bad-tempered Family* met Amabel's eye, the train stopped, and hundreds of railway officials in white velvet shouted, "*Whereyouwantogoto!* Get out!"

A velvety porter, who was somehow like a silkworm as well as like a wedding handkerchief sachet, opened the door.

"Now!" he said, "come on out, Miss Amabel, unless you want to go to *Whereyoudon'twantogoto*."

She hurried out, on to an ivory platform.

"Not on the ivory, if you please," said the porter, "the white Axminster carpet—it's laid down expressly for you."

Amabel walked along it and saw ahead of her a crowd, all in white.

"What's all that?" she asked the friendly porter.

"It's the Mayor, dear Miss Amabel," he said, "with your address."

"My address is The Old Cottage, Amberley," she said, "at least it used to be"—and found herself face to face with the Mayor. He was very like Uncle George, but he bowed low to her, which was not Uncle George's habit, and said:

"Welcome, dear little Amabel. Please accept this admiring address from the Mayor and burgesses and apprentices and all the rest of it, of Whereyouwantogoto."

The address was in silver letters, on white silk, and it said:

"Welcome, dear Amabel. We know you meant to please your aunt. It was very clever of you to think of putting the greenhouse flowers in the bare flower-bed. You couldn't be expected to know that you ought to ask leave before you touch other people's things."

"Oh, but," said Amabel quite confused. "I did . . ."

But the band struck up, and drowned her words. The instruments of the band were all of silver, and the bandsmen's clothes of white leather. The tune they played was "Cheero!"

Then Amabel found that she was taking part in a procession, hand in hand with the Mayor, and the band playing like mad all the time. The Mayor was dressed entirely in cloth of silver, and as they went along he kept saying, close to her ear, "You have our sympathy, you have our sympathy," till she felt quite giddy.

There was a flower show—all the flowers were white. There was a concert—all the tunes were old ones. There was a play called *Put yourself in her place*. And there was a banquet, with Amabel in the place of honour.

They drank her health in white wine whey, and then through the Crystal Hall of a thousand gleaming pillars, where thousands of guests, all in white, were met to do honour to Amabel, the shout went up—"Speech, speech!"

I cannot explain to you what had been going on in Amabel's mind. Perhaps you know. Whatever it was it began like a very tiny butterfly in a box, that could not keep quiet, but fluttered, and fluttered, and fluttered. And when the Mayor rose and said:

"Dear Amabel, you whom we all love and understand; dear Amabel, you who were so unjustly punished for trying to give pleasure to an unresponsive aunt; poor, ill-used, ill-treated, innocent Amabel; blameless, suffering Amabel, we await your words," that fluttering, tiresome butterfly-thing inside her seemed suddenly to swell to the size and strength of a fluttering albatross, and Amabel got up from her seat of honour on the throne of ivory and silver and pearl, and said, choking a little, and extremely red about the ears—

"Ladies and gentlemen, I don't want to make a speech, I just want to say, 'Thank you,' and to say—to say—to say . . ."

She stopped, and all the white crowd cheered.

"To say," she went on as the cheers died down, "that I wasn't blameless, and innocent, and all those nice things. I ought to have thought. And they *were* Auntie's flowers. But I did want to please her. It's all so mixed. Oh, I wish Auntie was here!"

And instantly Auntie *was* there, very tall and quite nice-looking, in a white velvet dress and an ermine cloak.

"Speech," cried the crowd. "Speech from Auntie!"

Auntie stood on the step of the throne beside Amabel, and said:

"I think, perhaps, I was hasty. And I think Amabel meant to please me. But all the flowers that were meant for the winter . . . well—I was annoyed. I'm sorry."

"Oh, Auntie, so am I—so am I," cried Amabel, and the two began to hug each other on the ivory step, while the crowd cheered like mad, and the band struck up that well-known air, "If you only understood!"

"Oh, Auntie," said Amabel among hugs, "This is such a lovely place, come and see everything, we may, mayn't we?" she asked the Mayor.

"The place is yours," he said, "and now you can see many things that you couldn't see before.

We are The People who Understand. And now you are one of Us. And your aunt is another."

I must not tell you all that they saw because these things are secrets only known to The People who Understand, and perhaps you do not yet belong to that happy nation. And if you do, you will know without my telling you.

And when it grew late, and the stars were drawn down, somehow, to hang among the trees, Amabel fell asleep in her aunt's arms beside a white foaming fountain on a marble terrace, where white peacocks came to drink.

She awoke on the big bed in the spare room, but her aunt's arms were still round her.

"Amabel," she was saying, "Amabel!"

"Oh, Auntie," said Amabel sleepily, "I am so sorry. It *was* stupid of me. And I did mean to please you."

"It *was* stupid of you," said the aunt, "but I am sure you meant to please me. Come down to supper." And Amabel has a confused recollection of her aunt's saying that she was sorry, adding, "Poor little Amabel."

If the aunt really did say it, it was fine of her. And Amabel is quite sure that she did say it.

Amabel and her great-aunt are now the best of friends. But neither of them has ever spoken to the other of the beautiful city called "*Whereyouwantogoto.*" Amabel is too shy to be the first to mention it, and no doubt the aunt has her own reasons for not broaching the subject.

But of course they both know that they have been there together, and it is easy to get on with people when you and they alike belong to the *Peoplewhounderstand.*

If you look in the A.B.C. that your people have you will not find "*Whereyouwantogoto.*" It is only in the red velvet bound copy that Amabel found in her aunt's best bedroom.

Aleksey Mikhaylovich Remizov (1877–1957) was a Russian modernist writer with a passion for the bizarre. He started writing for periodicals, but his real fame came with the publication of *The Indefatigable Tambourine* (1910), a whimsical and grotesque narrative of provincial life. In the same year, he published one of his most popular works, *Sisters of the Cross*. Commonly known for his fairy tales and his symbolistic novels, he was adept at integrating the surreal into his work. Due to his experience with wrongful exile in 1897, Remizov stayed away from politics and emigrated to Berlin after the Bolsheviks came into power. "Sacrifice" is one of his earlier works, and in 1911 he published a novel by the same name. "Sacrifice" is a beautifully eloquent story of the gothic that flirts with the fantastical.

Sacrifice

Aleksey Remizov

Translated by Ekaterina Sedia

FIRST CHAPTER

TRULY, ANYONE WHO HAD ever visited Blagodatnoye would not be lying if they praised the old Borodin's homestead. And it was not without reason Blagodatnoye was called that: you could not imagine a better place, even though there were no grapevines in its gardens and birds of paradise were not singing in its branches, but it was so: it was as if God's grace was nurturing its very soil.

The old mansion with its stately columns, the maple allée, the orchards and the fields, the forest, the cattle, and the people—everything here delighted not only Blagodatnoye's neighbors but every visitor from far-away lands, any sneering close-cropped denizen of St. Petersburg, and every spoiled and unkempt Muscovite.

The house is in order, and a veritable cornucopia! Even bees would be jealous.

Mr. Borodin himself, Pyotr Nikolayevich, was a known eccentric and a joker, you wouldn't find another one like him. Wherever he went, in any company and fine society, hilarity followed him and never stopped. Whether they knew him or they didn't, they all roared with merriment, regardless.

Only the face of the gray-haired, never changing joker was odd: years went by, his fortieth birthday came and went, but his expression stayed the same, as if it was stamped over his unmoving frozen features once and forever. And it was even odder when everyone all but rolled on the floor busting their guts with laughter, as his face remained calm—neither a smile nor a titter, only terrible glimmers in his sunken dull eyes. And even stranger was his speech that made everyone so joyful, it had a mechanical echo to it, like a talking doll, and when once someone tried to record his jokes, on paper his words were simple and ordinary, and not at all funny.

And despite such, you would think, incongruous appearance of Pyotr Nikolayevich Borodin and inappropriateness of his jokes, no one seemed to think to ask: what's his secret and why is it so amusing and hilarious? Only once some lover of enigmas—there is always one—tried to explain him, aiming for the heart of the matter: there's a play of his features, and artful expressions and mimicry, and very amusing way of talking—yes, yes, of course, that must be it. Fortunately such explanations never made any impression: no one wanted to ask anything, and why would they? It was distracting and joyful, and what else would one want?

Pyotr Nikolayevich was not serving at any offices, and was not involved in any community affairs. Once he was elected the County Marshal of Nobility. Soon enough everyone had had enough of that memorable Borodin's marshaldom. Not because he did poorly or because of any disasters, but rather the contrary: no one remembers a merrier year. Every problem became an amusement and every task was so entertaining that at the end there was such confusion and so many discrepancies and silliness that it took a long while to straighten things out. And those who didn't know Pyotr Nikolayevich could have thought, God forbid, that he was a bit touched in the head (and it was rumored that someone in St. Petersburg said just that either in a salon or in a report). It was pure luck that everything had ended well.

Every living man has his eccentricities, everyone has his own manner. So Pyotr Nikolayevich is not an exception.

He also liked tidying up, everything to its place, and he did it so cunningly that after his tidying whatever he tidied could never be found again: many things, some of them quite neces-sary, disappeared in this manner. And he also liked straightening up by moving around the tables and the chairs, etageres, by re-hanging the paintings from one wall to another, by moving around the books in his library, and this is how he spent his days from morning until lunch. At dinner, he preferred scrumptious dishes, such as tripe, marrow, and shanks, and often didn't know his measure and overstuffed himself, and always complained about his stomach. He liked to light up the fires—he was always chilly—and with a long poker he walked from one hearth to the next, stirring the embers. He would talk to the help in the house and the serfs, but even though he talked business, everything came out as nonsense at the end. As a sad and undesirable consequence of that, no one was not only fearful of him but—can't keep this a secret!—no one had faith in Pyotr Nikolayevich. Also, joking and fooling around, he would promise impossible things, such as he would gift his land to any comer, even though not by a great measure, more like a step across and three steps in length—such jester's share. What else? Oh yes: he had a real passion for cutting chicken's throats, and he was as good as a chef: his hens didn't flap around and run about headless, as happens with awkward hands. And he also liked seeing the dead: and the more disgusting were the corpse's features, the stronger was the smell of decay, the more attractive he found them. Every time someone died in the village, the priest Father Ivan would let the Borodins know; they immediately tacked the horses and readied the carriage, and Ivan Nikolayevich dropped everything and flew to the house where the corpse happened to be.

Such frightful passions, as Aleksandra Pavlovna, his wife, would say when teasing her spoiled husband (whom, it should be said, she adored), Pyotr Nikolayemvich's excitements mostly dealt with such domestic details that wouldn't be worth even mentioning if it wasn't for one spurious rumor that stained the honor and reputation of the entire Blagodatnoye.

Two years ago an old friend of Pyotr Nikolayevich, also a former St. Petersburg lycee graduate, visited Blagodatnoye. He had not seen his friend since their St. Petersburg days. The reasons for his visit remained unclear: he did not announce them, and his valet spoke only vaguely in the manservants' quarters: either it was the matter of land shares or the General was surveying the provinces. But it wasn't that important: couldn't an old friend visit out of pure curiosity?

The guest was welcomed with open arms. Aleksandra Pavlovna met him and lamented that not everyone was around—the children scattered, and she worried that the visit would be dull. But the guest was so charming, and talked about their close friendship with Pyotr Nikolayevich back in St. Petersburg, and he didn't seem to be in need of much company as he waited for his friend's return. Pyotr Nikolayevich, unfortunately, was away since morning, visiting some corpse in the village, and returned home late at night. The friends reunited. And this is when the misfortune happened. The guest was visibly scared and shaken, that he was trembling in his boots. Either he did not recognize his friend—or he did recognize him but noticed such changes in him that his head spun—or maybe he noticed in his face, gait, and speech something so unexpected, impossible, unlikely—but who knows!—that the guest took a step back, and waving his arms, fainted.

Taciturn and sorrowful, glancing about with suspicion and agreeing with everything that anyone said, and with that pathetic smile of a man caught suddenly in between the plates of a vise that can squash one flat, the guest stayed a week, and one morning, babbling incoherently and waving about some upside-down papers, out of his mind, he rode out of Blagodatnoye only in his underclothes and left his luggage behind. And soon after his departure the rumors and the tongue-wagging started among the neighbors and even in the city.

They said that there was nothing exceptional about Blagodatnoye, that the famed Borodin mansion was a very average house, and come to think of it, had some flaws—one half very visibly renovated after the fire, and the garden was just a garden—sure, it was old and offered a lovely shade, but if you traveled around Russia you'd know that there were plenty of others just like it. As for fields and forests—what could you say?—the fields were spacious and the forest delightful, but nothing everyone hadn't seen before; as for people—they were, to be frank, trash: poor, with hardly any land, and one day they would move and then come back, and if there were any unrests, even if they didn't set the mansion on fire or poked the horses' eyes out (like they did to the neighbor Bessonov's horses), even they would still talk about burning down the mansion, wrecking everything, and taking Borodin's land. And when it came to Pyotr Nikolayevich, they said such God-awful nonsense that it's a shame to repeat that. And they told their friends and their enemies to avoid Blagodatnoye even under the most dire of circumstances: the place was cursed.

Some old friends advised Aleksandra Pavlovna to complain to the governor, but she would not hear of it. To her eyes, the rumors contained not a drop of truth, and there was no use in making waves. After all, who knows what some suspicious mind can imagine—they only want to make trouble. And the rumors stopped all by themselves by and by: maybe people were not as stupid as they seemed.

After the rumors all died down, everyone remembered that Blagodatnoye was an Eden on earth, the Borodin family was exemplary, and Pyotr Nikolayevich was a known eccentric and such a joker, you wouldn't find another one like him.

The head of the family was Aleksandra Pavlovna: the order and the abundance of Blagodatnoye was credited to her attentive eye alone. She was of strict temper, few of words, and Aleksandra Pavlovna kept everyone in line without them ever talking back: everyone was afraid of her, and respected her word. She got married early and for love, and from the first year of marriage their children started: one son and three daughters, all a year apart. Aleksandra Pavlovna's life went by in looking after the household and the finances, which, as the children grew older, grew more complicated and pressing, and her burdens seemed endless. But she was ready to carry a mountain on her shoulders, as long as her children and husband were content—and neither the children nor the husband ever complained.

At nights, happy and joyful, she would sit at her grand piano; her strong fingers, confidently touching the keys, brought forth a great and festive sound—and the tall rooms filled with grandeur and gaiety.

And if there were a desperate wanderer looking through the brightly lit windows from the outside, he would look at her with such envy, at her contentment with her home; and an unfortunate man would curse his lot if he ever met her happy gaze; and if a blind man ever heard her voice, with such resignation and faith he would follow her!

Rear Admiral Akhmatov, whose opinions by virtue of their perspicacity usually traveled to all the neighborhood nobility and were repeated even by the city fops, and who was also the youngest daughter Sonya's godfather, called Aleksandra Pavlovna a seductive brunette. And, as always, he was correct. And who would believe that this seductive brunette, who had belabored this exemplary home and her happy domestic life into existence, could had thought herself the most unfortunate among all people. In truth it happened many years ago, and since then her luck and happiness had erased all traces of the past misery and only contentment and self-assurance lived in her soul. It was fifteen years ago, one year after the day Sonya was born, that Blagodatnoye was just a step away from a great calamity—the mansion almost burned to the ground, Pyotr Nikolayevich nearly perished, and it was Aleksandra Pavlovna who saved them all.

In the fall and winter, when the children left, Aleksandra Pavlovna spent her days with her husband. She looked at him as she did twenty years earlier, with the same tender love, and saw him as he used to be twenty years ago, so in love; and the deep furrow clearly seen between her dark brows smoothed out. And he, dried out and long as a rod, gray, with a deathly pale face, stared with his unmoving eyes and their terrible sparks, and bared his teeth as he stood before her.

"I know no boredom," he would repeat a thousandth time, "everything is a breeze!" but it sounded like "I don't care, I don't desire anything" instead.

But she could not hear these terrible words, they sounded like the words he whispered the first time they kissed, and she, blinded by love, responded with all the passion of a well-tended woman.

If someone were to spy on them through the window, he would laugh heartily at this ridiculous scene, but who knows—maybe he would faint without saying a word, like that guest, the general, Pyotr Nikolayevich's old friend.

SECOND CHAPTER

There was a big to-do in Blagodatnoye: Liza, the oldest daughter who had graduated from the Institute last year, was to be married on St. Matryona's Day. Her fiancé was a well-known landowner, Rameykov. Everyone was excited for the wedding—they said the feast would be the biggest anyone had ever seen; at least, Pyotr Nikolayevich beheaded near every chicken.

Blagodatnoye was taking on a ceremonious appearance—the guests were arriving in droves and well in advance, and many nearly got conniptions from the merriment—Pyotr Nikolayevich was especially in the mood for tales and amusements. Aleksandra Pavlovna tripped all over herself—there was so much to do, and hardly enough hands to do it all.

Finally the whole family gathered: from Petersburg, their oldest son Misha, first-year student, had arrived; then Zina from Kiev where she was attending the Institute, and the schoolgirl Sonya from the county's seat. The momentous day was nigh.

And, to give credit where it was due, the wedding was a merry affair, although it was not without tomfoolery: after Pyotr Nikolayevich blessed the icons before the ceremony, he was going to give the newlyweds his fatherly address, but after a long pause he limited himself to just a single-word directive, quite strong and not to be repeated in polite company, and upon hearing that strong word the groom could barely keep upright, and the laughter was choking all those present. In church, Pyotr Nikolayevich whispered to the priest that the night before he dreamt of eggs in a hole, and even though Father Ivan did not know if such a dream was a bad omen, he thought it highly incongruous. And already everyone was in the mood, and Father Ivan guffawed so loud the entire church shook, and then his diakon busted laughing without any shame, and everyone started braying—a wedding or a circus, there was no telling.

After the post-nuptial dinner, the newlyweds left for Moscow. But Blagodatnoye kept on celebrating, and even Lent was not very lenten. By the time Yule rolled around, the young ones staged a play, they dressed up in costumes and paid each other visits as if it was a masquerade. The pond froze over, and there was skating and sledding, and on this improvised rink young people held skating races and contests.

Misha Borodin was considered the best skater. He was lithe and uncommonly flexible, with remarkable agility and skill he performed complex tricks and maneuvers. Sonya was not far behind, the girl quick as a flame, and her resonant and contagious laughter rang far in the winter nights. Everyone admired the two of them when hand in hand they raced down the hill and to the farthest willows. But Zina was very much like her sister Liza, and like Liza, she was quiet and restrained; some would have called her shy if she didn't have a bit of a temper. "Just like their mother," said aunties and uncles and old acquaintances who truly knew Aleksandra Pavlovna.

The Day of Baptism of the Lord approached. Misha's pals and the girls' girlfriends started to disperse—and it was time for the young Borodins to get ready for their departure, but they were so happy in their village that they didn't even want to think about leaving.

On Baptism's Eve, Misha and Sonya waited for the Star of the Magi to come out and ran to the rink where they were spending their last nights. The night was bright with succulent blue stars reflected in the snow, and so cold that the ice was creaking and their cheeks were pricked as if by needles. But they were glad to race and skate all night long.

After the rink they went for a ride in the empty fields, with Misha holding the reins. But as soon as they left the gates, the horses spooked. Sonya fell into the snow, and Misha was tossed out of the sled with such force that he hit his head on the fence. House servants came to their cries, someone ran to fetch the doctor. By the morning Misha was dead—such tragedy.

The day of the funeral the house felt empty and everyone was overwhelmed by grief and fatigue, the kind that keeps one from doing anything and yet one cannot sit still. By the end of the day, a telegram from Moscow came, summoning Aleksandra Pavlovna to come right away.

She left that night.

Sonya and Zina were greatly worried, but not Pyotr Nikolaye—he seemed to carry on as if nothing was the matter. He still beheaded chickens, maybe even a bit more than before; but they said it was because Zina caught a cold at the funeral, and required a special diet. He also requested a very large cow tongue to be served for lunch; such eccentricity!

Finally the news came from Moscow: Liza had hanged herself. What tragedy!

The Borodin crypt received the second body, and the heavy emptiness hung in the rooms. Aleksandra Pavlovna wandered about like a ghost.

She blamed herself for agreeing to the marriage—she always knew Rameykov was a frivolous man, and possibly dishonest—yes, dishonest—why didn't she talk Liza out of it? Liza would've listened to her. She could've convinced her, she heard some unsavory things people whispered about him, even in their mansion the day of the wedding.

But it was too late now: whether one forgave herself or didn't, there was no fixing this calamity. Aleksandra Pavlovna was ready to scream and howl.

Pyotr Nikolayevich meanwhile looked a bit fatigued, but that was hardly due to the fact of death. The death of his son as well as his daughter piqued his curiosity in the same way any dead body did, whether he knew the deceased or not. He was fatigued mostly from the lack of sleep: Liza's coffin was delivered to Blagodatnoye sealed shut, but he insisted that they opened it. After the lid came off, he uncovered his daughter's face by himself, and stood over her, never looking away, all night long.

The day after the funeral, he dozed in his chair, wearing his usual bottle-green robe.

Meanwhile Zina's condition grew worse. The doctors said she had something similar to diphtheria, and the entire Blagodatnoye hushed, waiting for the disease to break. Instead, her condition became critical, doctors called a consilium. She was hopeless.

Ever since the children were small, there was a certain order in the house, and they all had their chores: Liza took care of the flowers, Zina fed the parrot. Now the old valet Michey looked after the flowers, and the parrot screeched that it was hungry.

And one could see that Zina heard it and remembered, and suffered because of it, and she felt guilt that by staying in bed she was somehow violating the proper order and it would be better if they took her back to the city, but she couldn't say anything—her throat closed up. With her last strength she beckoned Sonya to give her paper and pencil, and with her weak hand she wrote one word: "parrot," and the pencil rolled from her fingers. With that, she passed. Such tragedy.

THIRD CHAPTER

The third Borodin coffin was carried out of the mansion. In church, after the rites, as Aleksandra Pavlovna was saying good-bye to her daughter, she looked one last time at that resigned face

with tightly closed eyelids, blue as steel, and her crusted over, long-suffering lips, Aleksandra Pavlovna suddenly remembered—not her recent contentment but the far-away, secret past that she had managed to forget for so many years. She howled and walked away from the coffin, bent into an old, old woman.

"Why would I think that I would bury them like this?" she cried and shook her head.

And instead of comfort, her conscience bent her down further, raked her skin with new furrows, and reminded her that there was no one else to blame, there was no one but herself, and it was she, she alone who was responsible for everything.

Sonya would not leave her mother's side, pressed against her and tried to comfort her, and then cried herself and stared with wide eyes—one could not help but worry about this frightened child.

"Mama, what are you saying?" she asked, startled by her own voice.

And her mother told her of the secret past that she had managed to forget for so long.

Fifteen years ago, when Sonya was just a year old, Aleksandra Pavlovna took her children and went to visit her mother—it was the first time she left Blagodatnoye since the wedding, leaving her mansion and her husband behind. And when she was away she had a dream: her husband entering the altar. She got scared—was he sick, was he dead? Next night, she had another dream: her wedding band broke. And again she got scared that her husband would die. And she decided to come back home.

"So I gathered everything, and got on my way," Aleksandra Pavlovna told Zina, "and all the way I keep praying to God, all the way home I pray to Him: if a misfortune to befall us, let Misha die, let Liza die, let Zina die, just let him live. I thought, they were little, it happens, I'd survive, I just need him alive. I never mentioned you—I could not. When I got home, I found out that there was a great fire, and Pyotr Nikolayevich was on death's door. God heard my prayer: he gave me back the mansion and your father. And now Misha is dead, Liza is dead, Zina is dead . . . how could I think that they would die when they were like this?"

Aleksandra Pavlovna suffered and would not let Sonya leave her side.

Pyotr Nikolayevich seemed concerned and bewildered; there was some thought that was gnawing at him, needling him. He could not carry on as usual and occupy himself the same way as before. At night he tried to move around the hutch in the dining room—moved it away from the wall and then just left it there as it was. Took a poker in his hand—but even the stoves did not hold his attention. A few times he came to Aleksandra Pavlovna's bedroom, sat on the edge of the bed, and then stood up, leaving his devastated wife and daughter.

"They all were lost—Misha, Liza, Zina, Sonya, and now everyone but Sonya are found," he muttered senselessly and terribly, addressing who knows who—maybe Michey or the potter Kuzma, or the housekeeper Darya Ivanovna who took over for Aleksandra Pavlovna for the time being.

Late at night, Pyotr Nikolayevich settled down and went to his study, followed by Michey who would not leave him alone, like an old nanny.

The mansion felt unsettled and filled with dread, all the corners grew cold. Where did everything go? Where was the peace, laughter, contentment? Three coffins—three deaths froze dead the warm fire in the Borodin hearth.

FOURTH CHAPTER

The events that only took one month—the string of Borodins' tragedies—was immediately taken up by local gossips.

"Clearly, something is not right," they said in the neighboring Chernyanka and Kostomarovka, and even Britany and Motovilovka and, of course, the city.

Why, what, how? And they started, and kept on it.

The entire Blagodatnoye existence was turned top to bottom and dissected, they remembered the Borodins' grannies and aunties, and even the things that never happened, and even the things that did happen but to someone else—say, the Muromtsevs. Everything was dragged into the sun—look, everyone, and judge, and we had known all this a long time ago.

They even latched onto that mysterious visiting General for some reason—that friend of Pyotr Nikolayevich that fled God knows why. So everyone decided that the General surely knew everything, and that he should be interrogated and then everything would be crystal-clear. Only where would you find him? No one knew where to start.

Someone said, "All St. Petersburg knows Pereverdeyev."

"So he's in St. Petersburg?"

"Of course!"

The governor dispatched an urgent request to St. Petersburg, and the certified response came right away. It said that there were plenty of generals there, and some even with such strange names that it could be a bit awkward in mixed company, but no Pereverdeyev. Perhaps Pereverzev?

And while they were finding out about that Pereverzev, judged and discussed forward and backward and sideways, someone steely, without asking, without reporting to anyone, already started his assured mission, someone merciless already walked in his seven-miles steps from far, far away to conduct his own trial and execution.

Without Aleksandra Pavlovna, nothing was quite proper, and she forced herself to pay attention to the daily minutiae, abandoning her heavy thoughts for a time. She did not feel she had the right to abandon her home, her husband, and her daughter to their fates—her husband, to whose love she offered such an enormous sacrifice; her daughter, to whose love she was ready to offer her entire sanity.

Wasn't she mistaken that she, when she prayed, sacrificed only the oldest three, and forgotten Sonya? And didn't forget, but intentionally omitted? Why didn't she name her? If she offered all four, wouldn't they all be alive today?

Or perhaps all four dead. But no, that couldn't be, because he who sacrifices all . . . why didn't she sacrifice all? That was the question that kept drilling in her mind and would not let her rest.

What if Sonya would die too? Didn't she just say that she would sacrifice all, meaning Sonya too? That was the question that chased her from room to room, like a woman possessed.

"Sonya, Sonya, where are you?" She would catch herself and start looking for her daughter that never strayed far from her anymore.

Her torment for her past, for her terrible deed, her torment for her only daughter, was tinged by her worry for her beloved husband, whose life was propped up by three precious deaths. Pyotr Nikolayevich barely moved, he rarely left his study, turned blue, his hair plastered down, and his dull skin, as if separated from the rest of his body, hung loose on him, like a sack.

The mansion, all the rooms, smelled rotten.

The mansion was an old building, and under the floors there were plenty of rats—generations of them, so it was possible that some ancient rat gave up the ghost, and that was the source of the intolerable smell. In the old days, Pyotr Nikolayevich would've found the source of the smell, they would've lifted the floors and disposed of the carcass, but nowadays everything fell by the wayside.

Everyone who happened to come by Blagodatnoye in those days felt that life could not go on like this, that sooner or later—and it didn't matter how, but there would be an escape. And they waited.

And they were supposed to wait three days and three nights. And two days and two nights had already passed.

Saturday evening Father Ivan came to the mansion for the nightlong service, and was very generous with his myrrh and smoked up the place thoroughly. After a repast he left, and everyone turned in soon after.

Afterward, valet Michey told about that night. "Late, I heard the master is calling me. 'Michey, bring me a young rooster, for Christ's sake, I won't forget your kindness.' And I say, 'Master, what do you want with a rooster at such an hour? It's night out.' And he only winked at me—like, you figure out what. I went to the coop, found a fat rooster, caught 'im, and brought him over. So I hand the rooster to the master, and offer him his knife. So he started cutting his throat—but he has no strength left, the rooster is still twitching. So he tried-tried, and finally finished the bird. A whole puddle of blood on the floor and all over 'im. And he seemed a bit better. 'Michey, wouldn't it be nice to see a dead one.' And I say, 'God keep you, what dead at this hour! No one heard of such a thing.' And I can feel like a cold hand down my back, and my hackles are goin' up. I can see he's not himself—shaking and teeth are clattering, and if something is choking him. 'Where is Sonya?' he asks, and looks at me . . . such a look, on my deathbed I'll remember, such look! 'In the mistress's bedroom, with the mistress.' Then the master calmed down a bit, so I went to lie down."

The housekeeper Darya Ivanovna remembered, "I woke up that night, I heard as if a cat was meowing. And I wonder—where did a cat come from? So I meowed back, and something hissed at me."

"The rooster was crowing," others remembered.

But even the rooster did not help—and what a fine rooster it was! The old man had barely any strength left, last breath in his throat. Pyotr Nikolayevich sat up. "Everyone was lost—Misha, Liza, Zina, and Sonya, and now all are found, only Sonya is missing!"

And there was only one swaddling thought in him, to find his Sonya immediately, this very second, and it forced him to his feet and led him. With the knife still in his hands, he crawled from his study to the bedroom.

The bedroom door stood ajar. The bedside lamp lit the room, and Sonya lay on the bed next to her mother, her face to the wall.

"Chicken, my little hen," the old man whispered as he crawled toward the bed.

Sonya woke up and sat, and saw her father, curled up and bent, covered in chicken blood; in utmost dread she stretched her swan-like neck.

"Chicken, little hen," he whispered, struggling to get to his feet.

And stood.

The swan neck, lit by the shimmering light of the lamp, stretched even more under the glinting knife. One moment more and the cherry necklace would've wound around the white swan. But there was no salvation for him—his last strength abandoned him, and the knife slid from his fingers along with his slimy skin.

The old man shuddered and crouched down, and everything in him—nose, mouth, ears—gathered in fat folds and with a loud pffttt! started flowing.

And flowed the thin sticky mush, cleaning the muck off the white bones.

Naked, eyeless skull, smiling so, white as a sugar lump, the skull shone in the light of the lamp.

And at that moment the flame blew the bedroom door open, pricked the sleeping mother with its red gaze, and the stupefied daughter, and the dead skull of the dead father, and licked the ceiling and rose like a red rooster over the roof.

The Borodin mansion burned.

William Edward Burghardt Du Bois (1868–1963), or W. E. B. Du Bois, was an African American writer, activist, and historian. He was a founding officer of the National Association for the Advancement of Colored People (NAACP) and was an integral part of the progression of racial equality in the United States. His collection of essays, *The Souls of Black Folk* (1903), remains a monument in American literature. Although he is most acclaimed for his scholarly work, Du Bois was also an avid fiction writer. A precursor of Afro-futurism, "The Princess Steel" is an unpublished work, but some date it back to his time at Atlanta University, roughly around 1910. The story was discovered in a box of additional stories by scholars Britt Rusert and Adrienne Brown. Somewhere between thirty and forty additional unpublished stories exist, many in a speculative vein.

The Princess Steel

W. E. B. Du Bois

"IT IS PERFECTLY CLEAR," said my wife, pointing to the sign on the door. "It is perfectly absurd," I answered and yet there it stood written: "Prof. Johnson, Laboratory in Sociology. Hours 9 until 3." We were on the top story of the new Whistler building, or rather tower, on Broadway, New York, and we had come on account of a rather queer advertisement, which we had seen the night before in the *Evening Post*. It had said "Professor Hannibal Johnson will exhibit the results of his great experiments in Sociology by the aid of the megascope at two tomorrow. A few interested parties will be admitted." Now my wife and I were interested in Sociology; we had studied together at Chicago, so diligently indeed that we had just married and were spending our honeymoon in New York. We had, too, certain pet theories in regard to sociological work and experiment and it certainly seemed very oppor-tune to hear almost immediately upon our arrival of a great lecturer in Sociology albeit his name, to our chagrin, was new to us. I was disposed to regard it as rather a joke but my wife took it seriously. We started therefore early the next morning, ascended to the forty-third story or rather "sailed up" as she said, chafed each other a bit and laughed until sure enough we came to the door.

We knocked and entered and then scarcely looking at the man at the door, we uttered an exclamation of wonder. The wall was dark with velvety material shrouding its contents in a great soft gloom except where, straight before us, the whole wall had been removed leaving one vast window full 40 by 20 feet, and through that burst suddenly on us the whole panorama of New York. We rushed forward and looked down on seething Broadway. "The river and cliffs of Manhattan!"

said my wife. Then with one accord, bethinking ourselves we turned to apologize to the silent professor and with surprise I saw that he was black. It never occurred to my little Southern wife that this was aught but a servant. She simply said, "Well, uncle, where is professor?" "I am he," he said and then it was our turn to be not only surprised but rather disagreeably shocked. He was a little man in well-brushed black broadcloth with a polished old mahogany face and bushy hair; he stepped softly and had even a certain air of ancient gentility about him. His voice was like the velvet on the walls and his movements precise and formal. One would not for a moment have hesitated to call him a gentleman had it not been for his color. His voice, his manner, everything showed training and refinement. Naturally my wife stiffened and drew back and yet she felt me smiling and hated to acknowledge the failure of our expedition. I was about to suggest going when I noticed that what I had taken to be a velvet-covered wall was in reality the velvet-bound backs of innumerable tall narrow books all of about the same size. I was struck with curiosity. "You have a fine library," I said tentatively. "It is the Great Chronicle," he said motioning us gently to chairs; we cautiously sat down.

"I discovered it," he said, "twenty-seven years ago. This is a chronicle of everyday facts, births, deaths, marriages, sickness, houses, schools, churches, organizations, the infirm, insane, blind, crimes, travel and migration, occupations, crops, things made and unmade—just the everyday facts of life but kept with surprising accuracy by a Silent Brotherhood for two hundred years. This treasure has come to me, and forms," he said, "the basis of my great discovery. See." We looked round the room—there were desks and papers, machines apparently for tabulating, a typewriter with a carriage full five feet long, and rolls of paper with figures; but past these he pointed to a great frame over which was stretched a thin transparent film, covered with tiny rectangular lines, and pierced with tiny holes. He pulled his chair nearer and spoke nervously and with intense preoccupation:

"A dot measured by height and breadth on a plane surface like this may measure a single human deed in two dimensions. Now place plane on plane, dot over dot and you have a history of these deeds in days and months and years; so far man has gone, though the Great Chronicle renders my work infinitely more accurate and extensive; but I go further: If now these planes be curved about one center and reflected to and fro we get a curve of infinite curvings which is—" —he paused impressively—"which is the Law of Life." I smiled at this but my wife looked interested; she had apparently forgotten his color.

The old man rose and reached up to the gloomy ceiling—we glanced and saw a network of levers and wires and a great bright silent wheel that whirled so steadily it seemed quite still till ever and again its cogs caught a black ball and sent it whirling till it stopped in the faint tinkle of a silvery bell. The old man seized a lever and swung his weight to it—click- click- clank—it said. We heard the slow tremulous sliding of a great mass. "Look," he said. We looked out the great window and there hanging before it we saw a vast solid crystal globe. I think I have never seen so perfect and beautiful a sphere. It was nearly fifty feet in diameter and seemed at arts like a great ball of light, a scintillating captive star glistening in the morning sunlight. "This," he said, "is the globe on which I plot my curves of life. You know in the Middle Age they used to use spheres like this—of course smaller and far less perfect—but that was mere playing with science just as their alchemy was but the play and folly of chemistry. Now my first series of experiments covering the last twenty years has been the plotting of the curves which will give me the Great Curve but—," and here he came nearer and almost whispered, "but when I would cast the great lines of this Curve I was continually hampered by curious counter-curves and shadows and crossings—which all my calculations could not eliminate. Then suddenly a hypothesis occurred to me. Human life is not alone on earth—there is an Over-life—nay—nay I mean nothing metaphysical or theological—I mean a social Over-life—a life of Over-men, Super-men, not merely Captains of Industry but field marshalls of the Zeitgeist, who today are guiding the world events and dominating the lives of men. It is a Life so near ourselves that we think it is ourselves, and yet so vast that we vaguely identify it with the universe. I am now seeking these shadowing curves of the Over-life. But I go further: I will not merely know this Over-life. I will see it with my Soul. And I have seen it," he cried triumphantly with burning eyes. Then, feverishly: "I want today to show you one of the Over-men—his deeds, his world, his life, or rather Life of lives—I can do it," he said and drew his chair nervously toward us and looked at us intently with his dark weak eyes. "I can do more than that," he said. "You know we can see the great that is far by means of the telescope and the small that is near by the means of the microscope. We can see the Far Great and the Near Small but not the Great Near." "Nor," I added, finding my voice for the first in a vain effort to break the spell, "the Far Small." He beamed— "Yes—yes, that's it," he said, "and that will come later—Now the Great Near! And that problem I have solved by the microscope megascope," and with one more swinging of the lever there swept down before the window a great tube, like a great golden trumpet with the flare toward us and the mouthpiece pointed toward the glittering sphere; laced round it ran silken cords like coiled electric wire ending in handles, globes, and collar-like appendages. "See," he said: and lo! on the burning sphere a snakelike shadow traced itself under his rapid fingering of the machinery—"it is the Curve of Steel—the sum of all the facts and quantities and times and lives that go to make Steel, that skeleton of the Modern World. We will look through here and if all is well behold the Over-world of steel and its Over-men."

I shook my head in vague assent and looked out of the corner of my eye at my wife for I saw that we [were] dealing with a crank, not with a scientist, and I was wondering just how far we should let it go. He, however, was working feverishly. He had placed three luxurious chairs before

the shining trumpet and arranged the pieces and the silken cords.

"Now," he said in a whisper almost fierce, "my first experiment will begin. We shall behold the Spirit of the wonderful metal which is the center of our modern life, and the inner life of the Over-life that dominates this vast industry—the great grim forces of men—in fact," and he lowered his voice, "We shall see the Over-men."

I smiled. The thin dark curve blazed on the flaming globe. With a sweeping bow he conducted us to the great tube which was now pointed on this light. Carefully he adjusted it. Then he raised the silken cords with what I now saw were head and eye and ear and hand pieces and placed them on my wife. She did not hesitate but eagerly stared into the tube. I did hesitate but at last followed suit. The things I touched seemed tremulous, alive, pulsing. "Now," said his hollow voice, "the experiment begins—Look—feel—see!"

A little tremor of half fear came over me. I put my foot out to touch my wife's toe but she seemed reconciled. We were hidden as it were from the outer-world in these tubes and earpieces, looking at the sphere which faced Broadway. At first I could see nothing—all was darkness. Then at last far, far away yet painfully distinct I saw Broadway—"the river and cliffs of Manhattan," as my wife had called it. I watched it idly, dreamily as it faded darker, and yet strangely more intense, and then suddenly lashed into murmuring darkness—then to black silence. The silence grew intense. Then came a vague quickening as of wandering winds beating and whirring over rock-ribbed moors. I could hear the lonely chirp of a cricket. The wind rose higher, the crickets chirped louder and lonelier; then I heard waters rushing on, nearer and nearer, swelling and roaring. Lights began to appear and I saw great crags beetling above the rushing waters. It seemed a narrow stream that struggled and foamed as it came down its broad straight way. The crags that soared above were crowned with great castles and up through the castles and under and over the crags ran ever threads—little silver threads that went out through the broad empty countryside, out far, far away until they seemed all to meet on a great misty hill to westward. "Those are the hills of Pittsburg," cried the hollow voice of the old man. I laughed. The idea of seeing Pittsburg from Broadway, and yet I strained my eyes. In the pale but glowing light that waxed more and more brilliant I could see distinctly, above the hills, the forming of a vast bluish radiance of silver hair, a pale blue face crowned with silver light, radiant like the rising of the moon. On went the rolling waters, the land around seemed to quiver, even the great crags. And the castles were not castles they were mills—Mills of the Gods, I whispered. Everywhere were moving things, first I thought them men, women and children—I even caught the babel of voices—but no—they were I came to feel but the things of this New World, the World of Steel; they came down the waters, they rolled along the land, they followed the silvery threads and came on and on until all seemed to choke through a great crag-like narrowing in the river, above which beetled the tallest and most sinister of the castles that seemed, with its great whirling wheel, a mighty Mill for some new meal. As yet I had seen nothing really alive, only the moving of Things until looking narrowly I saw below the castle just at the portcullis, where the great drawbridge stretched across the narrow throat of the gorge, the form of a huge armored knight. His visor was down and he sat on a horse, vast and silent, watching the ever moving mass of things that rolled past him down the gorge, through the great hopper of his mill where they left their Souls—while their Bodies went whirling drunkenly on. Sometimes the things choked in the grinding, and the water roared and foamed on the rocks, but then he would strike his spear angrily on the great Wheel and with frightened roar it whirled the faster as the stream moved on and the pile of ground and bolted Souls grew higher.

"Who is he?" I asked. "An Over-man—Immortal—All Powerful," came from a disembodied Voice. "Rhythmic with youth and age just as earth is with night and day, and yet never dying." "Look," I said, "See!" Across the plain beyond came tripping four armored knights. Their visors were down, their spears couched, their horses careering madly and their bannerets lying. The first knight threw a shrewd look over his shoulder, turned and gathered his arms. His eyes flashed darkly beneath his helmet. The clash was coming—there was fury in the air, when suddenly I heard the Voice: "Listen! You cannot understand this conflict until you hear of the story that goes before. His man here is the Lord of the Golden Way and what he has done and how he came to be here, commanding the silver threads and keeping toll over the Great River of Things, I know not, but I ween and so I have constructed in my own way a tale of his past which my little viewing and measuring of his life makes plausible. Listen. Once upon a time there lived an Over-man, Sir Guess of Londonton. He was a man of thought and study and ever his eager brains were pounding at the riddles of the world. As he wondered and wandered he found and captured the black Witch Knowal. Fearful she groveled before him. 'My husband is the Ogre, Evilhood, and if thou dost me no harm and bringest me to his cave I will make him tell thee a secret, a marvellous secret of a captive maid whom thou mayest loose and have.' So Sir Guess of Londonton took her to the Ogre and the Ogre said in thanks: 'To westward lie hills, and in the hills the Pit of Pittsburg, and in the pit dwelleth captive the dark Queen of the Iron Isles—she that of old came out of Africa. But she hath,' said the Ogre, 'a secret of which men have not dreamed. One of the greatest of the world's great secrets but not the greatest. When the Queen was captured she was heavy with child by the Sun-God; and when that daughter was born, fearing lest daughter like mother should be slaves to men, she hid the child, enchanting it, in her arm; but if thou goest, and callest her up from hell and strikest her right arm with the Golden Sword, then the enchanted daughter may be yours, she and her Treasure. More, too: if she be burned then and there, in the fires of Hell, she will become immortal and be the most wonderful princess of the princesses of the world, the Princess Steel!' 'She and her Treasure,' but she said not what the Treasure was. 'Where is the Golden Sword?' cried Sir Guess of Londonton, but Evilgood and Knowal were gone.

"So Sir Guess hastened away westward toward the Pit, seeking as he went word of the Golden Sword where-with he might strike the right arm of the queen. Now the Golden Sword belongs to the Lord of the Golden Way and the Lord warding the way of his winding river (a pitiful dwindling river in those poor days) saw the young wanderer and wormed his secret; he was amazed and interested and spoke sweetly to the young man and said, 'I will follow and help you, and when we have gained the Princess Steel, she shall work for us.' 'Nay, nay,' said Sir Guess, 'the princess herself shall be mine, but her Treasure I will give you'; and the Lord of the Golden Way gladly consented. So he unlocked the Golden Sword (now the Story of the Golden Sword has not been told as yet) and they traveled over great waters and wild lands, hills and vales and faced westward ever westward, until one twilight time they came to the Pit of Pittsburg. Great clouds hung over it, dashed with the red of the dying sun, strange murmurs rose from the earth, black smoke and yellow fire. They felt the very ground beneath them tremble and groan; almost they were afraid to enter, yet Sir Guess never doubted and followed by the Lord of the Golden Way at midnight they climbed the hill and crawling, climbing, squirming, dropped into the bottom of the Pit. Or ever they touched earth, with thundering scream, the great dark form of Queen Iron rose all about them and above, and bent over them and enveloped them. 'Who art thou that bravest me, here in my prison walls?' she said. 'I am Sir Guess of Londonton,' answered the knight bravely, 'and I have come to free the daughter whom thou hidest,' and with the word there came a wail upon the night that thrilled all earth and heaven, the wild and curdling cry of mother panting for child. She swept her hands across the black and lurid heavens, and grasped for the bold knight, clutched his fingers and as she clutched, the Iron gripped his soul.

Almost he died with the pain of that fierce grasp. His head whirred and his heartstrings hardened. Yet he gathered himself and left-handed raised the Golden Sword, while his companion crawled and whimpered to the dark,—twice he whirled the sword and it sang in the air, twice again it circled about the great dark head of the queen, and then the fifth time hissing it gripped and bit the flesh, gnawed and craunched the bone; it drank the dark oozing stream of her blood, till the swollen right arm burst, and out rolled and fell a dull, leaden, imagelike thing, inert, dead, heavy. Down shot the wounded woman with a great gasping cry that set the ocean twanging and hill a-trembling; up flew the fires of Hell. The two men rushed forward and seizing the gray image, rolled it in the soft cold clay, and straining and sweating, swung it above the fires that were bursting from below. It seethed and hissed and burned—it glowed and screamed and shivered; black fiends rose covered and beat back the flames. Off shot the leaden lid: a gleaming hissing scintillating brilliance flooded the cave; a great mist curtained the Incarnation and then when it fell away, the two knights staggered backward and sunk face forward to the dust.

"Naked she stood, lithe and yet nobly formed. Her flesh was the soft blue brilliance of the moon-light—her hair was the bright glistening of silver—her eyes the pale gold of the sunlight on a dying day—her face in its dark blue wonderful radiance seemed at first strange and uncanny; and yet there was in its brilliance a beauty such as mortal never wore. She stepped forward, poised, unconscious, listening. Above between the smoke and grime of the Pit peered the blue sky. She looked toward it, 'Mother,' she said softly. A little star paced slowly by. She hesitated—watching it greedily. 'Sister, sister?' she asked. Then quickly, swiftly she climbed, groping but ever more and more lightly, gliding, until at last she stood upon the mighty hill and raised her golden eyes toward the great blue dome of the sky beneath the twinkling radiance of the stars. The tears streamed down and she lifted her voice and sang: 'Life, Life, Life!' Then all silent she stood, enraptured, worshipful. Out of the east came light; a white gray brilliance began to unfold. She turned upon it wonderingly and watched it with great eyes; the east glowed and reddened and she cowered almost in terror;—long barbed spears of light lashed across the world and killed the stars; the winds waited, the birds sang, twittered, the princess trembled in wild confusion, until above the earth shot the great red glory of the sun. Then she rose and danced and in sudden great good laughter lifted up her voice and cried in ecstasy: 'Father, Father, the Prince of the Princess of Africa!' Ever she laughed and twirled and danced upon the hill until suddenly her eyes fell upon the crouched form of Sir Guess of Londonton and she stood very still. He seeing her for the first time in the broad brilliance and beholding that beautiful face, rose with a wonder in his soul; rose and half timidly, half beseechingly stretched his arms. She looked at him in fright, amaze and sympathy; a softness crept into her eyes. Her bosom heaved. She gathered the silver of her hair around her, shading her lithe limbs and heaving breasts, and then with sudden abandon cried, 'I love thee.' He started toward her. 'Hold.'

"It was the cry of the Lord of the Golden Way as he groped from out of the Pit, tired, dirty, fearsome. 'What will you?' asked the younger lord. 'Our bargain,' muttered the other. 'Where is it?' cried the youth—'Look fool! her hair is silver and her eyes are golden, and,' he whispered, 'mayhap there be jewels crusted on her heart.' For a moment they gazed at each other. 'Wouldst murder my bride for silver and gold?' cried Sir Guess. 'The Treasure,' growled the lord doggedly and his greedy eyes shifted and caught the gleam of the Golden Sword where it lay between them. He bent stealthily toward it. 'Back,' cried the other. 'We fight with iron and who so wins, his be the Princess, Treasure and All.' Out sprang the iron broad swords and made morning music on the hills. Three times the Lord of the Golden Way slipped to his knees and twice the younger, slighter man grazed death; finally lunging forward the Lord struck Sir Guess heavily upon his shoulder and the knight slipped and fell along the

mountain way; ere he could rise the Lord threw away his iron and seized the Golden Sword. Twice he twirled it and twice again and then with an oath drove it through helm and corselet and the younger warrior with gurgling burst of hot red blood, fell at the maiden's feet while the other sick with his fighting dropped fainting to his side. The maiden had at the first onset stood like a stone, then slowly she wakened, at first bewildered, then half confused at the quick wondrous dancing of the men. Then she became grave, excited, mad: her voice came forth in little sharp cries and faint sweet moans. Pain and sorrow wrote themselves on her face. She threw her hands, wildly unloosed and tossed her silvery hair until it went whirling like a great white misty web above her dark blue glowing face and golden eyes and to her face struggled the memory of other worlds and other battles; so from the face of a maiden it became a woman's face and with a woman's great bereaved cry she threw herself on her fallen lover, ripped off the helmet and tore aside the breastplate staunching the blood with her silvery hair, and lay panting and murmuring above him. Then the hair seemed to her coarse. She rose, hesitated and stood there all silver until she spied a thin round stone lying in the dust. With deft strength she clove a hole in its middle and gripping it lightly in her fingers wheeled and whirled it and so spun a strand of her hair to a long thin beautiful thread and wove it carefully round and round the bloody body in cunning fashion until it lay there hearsed in burning breathing silver.

"The Lord of the Golden Way awoke, gasped and painfully dragged himself to his knees. He saw the wonderful covering and he knew that the treasure he wanted was the spun hair of the maiden. The sweat of greed oozed on his forehead. He crept forward, stealthily, silently. The maiden never deigned to notice him but crouched there all clothed and gowned in her burning curls. She watched the wan cold face of her lover's, whispering to him and making mystic passes above his bier. Stealthily, silently the Lord crept on till he had seized lightly a single strand of her hair; then he slipped quickly and more quickly down the hill, toiling and trailing after him.

"Then came long days of work and sweat; he rigged a great wheel and spun the silken steel—clumsily and coarsely but finely enough to joy him to ecstasy. Upward he crept stealthily and seized another strand and spun it; and another and another; and then bold and ever bolder he seized a great curl and setting up a mighty loom wove to a great tough solid mat that rang and pealed till the Lord screamed with greed and joy. And yet ever the maid sat, silent, save for the mystic whispering; motionless, save for the mystic waving of her hand above the bier, there on hills over the Pit of the imprisonment to which her spun hair held her as it stretched across the world. 'I bent forward and watched her—There it was I first saw her,' said the Voice—that bluish radiance above the western hills, wondrous beautiful, all crowned in silvery cloud and I caught the low full voice in some language of all Languages:

"I watch and ward above my sleeping lord till he awake and then woe World! When I shake my curls a-loose."

I started for I too heard those mystic words and the answering voice of the old man, from afar: "What then? O Princess?" She laughed. Her laugh was like the beating of the billows on the bar, angry with softness. One hand lashed up and with a quick sharp grasp she pulled a single curl. I watched where the curl wended its way past Chicago, past Omaha, past the great plain and the sad mountain and the rough roaring of lands toward the sea and San Francisco; and suddenly the world whirled in San Francisco. The ire burst, the earth trembled, buildings fell, great cries rang round the world. Only the Steel stood

silent and grim in the treacherous innocence—I gasped in fear—again lashed that blue and fatal hand: another curl trembled and far down in Valparaiso the earth sighed and sank and staggered, and the steel stood cold and grim; again, and the Isles of the Sea quivered, a great ship shivered and dove to its death. Again—but I cried in horror, "Hold—hold O Princess—" the hand sank and low the voice came sad and full of awful sweetness. "I watch and ward above my sleeping Lord till he awake and then woe World! when I shake my curls a-loose." The voice ceased but on the plain where the Lord of the Golden Way held the mill and guarded the things that rolled thither on the silver threads, I heard the crash and roar of battle as the four robber knights bore down upon him. "How will it end?" I cried to the Voice at my side. "I know not nor shall we know in many hundred years. For a day to the Over-World is a thousand years to us and even the megascope is slave to Time."

I dropped the ends of the machine and sat back astonished. My wife sat looking at me curiously. "Well what on earth have you been doing?" she said. "Didn't you see—didn't you hear?" I cried. "I've been watching Broadway." "But the cliffs? Saw you not the cliffs and castles and the Lord?"—I hesitated. "I saw only the great towering cliff-like buildings," she said. "Did you not hear the roar of the waters?" "I heard the roar of passing wagons and the voices of men." "And the space above the hills? Did you not see that?" "I saw clouds and the rising moon—for really Robert, it's late and we must go—."

"It was not tuned delicately enough for her," said the old man—"Next time—" but we greeted him hurriedly and passed out.

Fernán Caballero was a pseudonym of Cecilia Böhl de Faber (1796–1877), a Spanish writer known for her gift for description. Her most popular novel was *The Seagull* (1849), and her short stories depict the legends, beliefs, and traditions of the Andalusian people, although she was not raised there. Even though she is not as popular as she once was, *The Seagull* was the precursor to Spanish realism, and her short folkloric stories, like "The Hump" (1911), are still household favorites in Spain.

The Hump

Fernán Caballero

Translated by Marian and James Womack

ONCE UPON A TIME there was a King who had an only daughter, whom he wished very much to marry off in order to ensure heirs to his kingdom. But the girl, who had been spoiled when young, was willful and did not wish to marry (although, if her father had been opposed to her marriage, then she would have been anxious to marry, and as soon as possible).

One day, as she was heading out to Mass, she met with a beggar, who was so old, so hunchbacked, so ugly, and so insistent that he made her sick, and she didn't want to give him any alms. The wretch, in order to take his revenge, threw a flea at her; and the Princess, who had never seen one of these disgusting creatures before, took it home to the palace, put it in a bottle and fed it on milk broth, until it was so big that it didn't fit in the bottle anymore. And so the Princess sent it off to be slaughtered, and ordered its hide to be tanned and used to make the skin for a tambourine, stretched over a hoop of fennel-stalk.

And then one day, when her father started off insisting again that she get married, she said that she would, but only to the man who could guess what her tambourine was made of.

"So be it," said her father, "but I swear, as I am a King and a Christian, you have to marry the man who guesses correctly, whoever he may be."

Once the news had spread that the Princess would marry the man who guessed what her tambourine was made of, there came from all four corners of the world Kings, Princes, Dukes, Marquises, Counts and very well-behaved knights, and each one of them, in order of noble precedence, took a look at the tambourine, and no one guessed what it was made of. The strangest thing about it was that, when it was struck, the sound that it made was very much like the cry that beggars gave to ask for alms, in the name of the Lord. And then the King gave permission for anyone who wanted, noble or not, to come and see if they could guess what the tambourine was made of.

And it so happened that among the Princes there was one, a very handsome one, to whom the King's daughter had taken a fancy, and when she was out on her balcony she saw him, and called out:

Fennel-stalk, and the skin of a flea:
They're what make my tambourine.

But the Prince did not hear what she shouted; the person who *did* hear was the horrible hunchback, to whom she had refused her alms. The old man, who was very crafty, understood what the words the Princess had said to the handsome Prince must mean, and so he went posthaste to the palace, and said that he had come to guess what the King's daughter's tambourine was made of, and no sooner was he standing in front of the court than he said:

Fennel-stalk, and the skin of a flea:
They're what make your tambourine.

Alas! He had guessed correctly, and there was no way round it. And the Princess, for all that she was against the idea, was handed over by her father to this horrid beggar, who had won the prize that the Princess had offered.

"Go, now, right away, with your husband," the King said, "and forget you ever had a father."

This Princess, ashamed and weeping, went away with her hunchback, and they walked and walked until they came to a river, which they had to cross.

"Take me on your back and start to wade. That's what wives are for," the old man said.

The Princess did what her husband said, but when she was halfway across the river she started to shake and jump in order to throw the beggar into the water. And she shook and jumped, and he fell to pieces: first the head, then the arms and legs; everything, in fact, apart from the hump, which stayed stuck to the Princess's back, as though it had been glued there.

Once she was over the river, she asked for directions, and she found out that her hump imitated her voice and copied whatever she said, as though she had an echoing crag instead of a hump stuck to her back. Some people laughed at her, and some people were angry because they thought she was making fun of them; and so she had no option but to pretend to be dumb. In this way, holding out her hand to beg for alms, she went walking until she came to a city that she guessed must be the kingdom of the Prince she had liked so much. She went to the palace and asked to be taken on as a serving maid, and they took her. The Prince saw her and thought she was very pretty, and he said:

"If she weren't dumb and hunchbacked, I might even marry the serving maid, because she's got a charming face."

The Prince's family was trying to marry him off, and the Princess felt ever more sad and jealous, as she was falling more in love with the Prince every day.

Once the marriage contracts were drawn up between the Prince and another Princess, ramrod straight and chattier than a parrot, the Prince set off with a great host to bring her back to the palace, and the whole palace was all of a hubbub preparing for the marriage feast. They set the dumb serving maid to frying pancakes.

As she fried, the maid said to her hump:

"Little hump, little hump, would you like a pancake?"

The hump, which, as it had come from an old man and was very greedy, said yes.

"Well, get up on my shoulder," the Princess said.

And she gave it a pancake.

And then she asked again:

"Little hump, little hump, would you like another pancake?"

The hump said that it would.

And she said:

"Well, get down into my lap."

The hump made a little leap and settled on the Princess's lap; but she was ready, and took the tongs and picked up the hump and threw it into the oil, where it was fried up like a pork scratching.

As soon as she was free of her hump, she went to her room, cleaned herself, combed her hair, and put on makeup and got dressed in a green and gold dress.

When the Prince returned, he was ecstatic to see the serving girl in a new dress, so clean and tidy, and without her hump.

His promised bride saw this, and said:

Just you look at her, all dressed in green:
Thinks she's a princess, thinks she's a queen.

To which the Princess, all high and mighty, replied:

No, just you look at her, with her flounces and
*   furs:*
Only just got here, and putting on airs.

As soon as the Prince had registered that the dumb serving maid could speak, and that there was no sign of her former hump, then he married her, and they had lots of children, and were very happy, and I was obscurely disappointed.

Edward Morgan Forster (1879–1970), who wrote as E. M. Forster, was an English novelist and critic who gained acclaim for his novels *Howards End* (1910) and *A Passage to India* (1924). During World War I, he lived in Egypt and published short stories under the pseudonym Pharos. Although lesser known, Forster's short stories are just as intriguing and sometimes groundbreaking. This work tends to showcase how the imagination can undermine one's sense of reality and morals, but also includes at least a couple classics of modern speculative fiction. Some critics believe that Forster was able to create such visceral scenarios because of his travels and his coming to terms with his sexuality. "The Celestial Omnibus" (1911) is about self-discovery that coincides with a magical awakening.

The Celestial Omnibus

E. M. Forster

I

THE BOY WHO RESIDED at Agathox Lodge, 28, Buckingham Park Road, Surbiton, had often been puzzled by the old sign-post that stood almost opposite. He asked his mother about it, and she replied that it was a joke, and not a very nice one, which had been made many years back by some naughty young men, and that the police ought to remove it. For there were two strange things about this sign-post: firstly, it pointed up a blank alley, and, secondly, it had painted on it in faded characters, the words, "To Heaven."

"What kind of young men were they?" he asked.

"I think your father told me that one of them wrote verses, and was expelled from the University and came to grief in other ways. Still, it was a long time ago. You must ask your father about

it. He will say the same as I do, that it was put up as a joke."

"So it doesn't mean anything at all?"

She sent him upstairs to put on his best things, for the Bonses were coming to tea, and he was to hand the cake-stand.

It struck him, as he wrenched on his tightening trousers, that he might do worse than ask Mr. Bons about the sign-post. His father, though very kind, always laughed at him—shrieked with laughter whenever he or any other child asked a question or spoke. But Mr. Bons was serious as well as kind. He had a beautiful house and lent one books, he was a churchwarden, and a candidate for the County Council; he had donated to the Free Library enormously, he presided over the Literary Society, and had Members of Parliament to stop with him—in short, he was probably the wisest person alive.

Yet even Mr. Bons could only say that the

sign-post was a joke—the joke of a person named Shelley.

"Off course!" cried the mother; "I told you so, dear. That was the name."

"Had you never heard of Shelley?" asked Mr. Bons.

"No," said the boy, and hung his head.

"But is there no Shelley in the house?"

"Why, yes!" exclaimed the lady, in much agitation. "Dear Mr. Bons, we aren't such Philistines as that. Two at the least. One a wedding present, and the other, smaller print, in one of the spare rooms."

"I believe we have seven Shelleys," said Mr. Bons, with a slow smile. Then he brushed the cake crumbs off his stomach, and, together with his daughter, rose to go.

The boy, obeying a wink from his mother, saw them all the way to the garden gate, and when they had gone he did not at once return to the house, but gazed for a little up and down Buckingham Park Road.

His parents lived at the right end of it. After No. 39 the quality of the houses dropped very suddenly, and 64 had not even a separate servants' entrance. But at the present moment the whole road looked rather pretty, for the sun had just set in splendour, and the inequalities of rent were drowned in a saffron afterglow. Small birds twittered, and the breadwinners' train shrieked musically down through the cutting—that wonderful cutting which has drawn to itself the whole beauty out of Surbiton, and clad itself, like any Alpine valley, with the glory of the fir and the silver birch and the primrose. It was this cutting that had first stirred desires within the boy— desires for something just a little different, he knew not what, desires that would return whenever things were sunlit, as they were this evening, running up and down inside him, up and down, up and down, till he would feel quite unusual all over, and as likely as not would want to cry. This evening he was even sillier, for he slipped across the road towards the sign-post and began to run up the blank alley.

The alley runs between high walls—the walls of the gardens of "Ivanhoe" and "Belle Vista" respectively. It smells a little all the way, and is scarcely twenty yards long, including the turn at the end. So not unnaturally the boy soon came to a standstill. "I'd like to kick that Shelley," he exclaimed, and glanced idly at a piece of paper which was pasted on the wall. Rather an odd piece of paper, and he read it carefully before he turned back. This is what he read:

S. AND C.R.C.C.
Alteration in Service.
Owing to lack of patronage the Company are regretfully compelled to suspend the hourly service, and to retain only the
Sunrise and Sunset Omnibuses,
which will run as usual. It is to be hoped that the public will patronize an arrangement which is intended for their convenience. As an extra inducement, the Company will, for the first time, now issue
Return Tickets!
(available one day only), which may be obtained of the driver. Passengers are again reminded that *no tickets are issued at the other end*, and that no complaints in this connection will receive consideration from the Company. Nor will the Company be responsible for any negligence or stupidity on the part of Passengers, nor for Hailstorms, Lightning, Loss of Tickets, nor for any Act of God.
For the Direction.

Now he had never seen this notice before, nor could he imagine where the omnibus went to. S. of course was for Surbiton, and R.C.C. meant Road Car Company. But what was the meaning of the other C.? Coombe and Maiden, perhaps, or possibly "City." Yet it could not hope to compete with the South-Western. The whole thing, the boy reflected, was run on hopelessly unbusiness-like lines. Why no tickets from the other end? And what an hour to start! Then he realized that unless the notice was a hoax, an omnibus must have been starting just as he was wishing the Bonses good-bye. He peered at the ground through the gathering dusk, and there he saw what might or might not be the marks of wheels. Yet nothing had come out of the alley. And he had never seen an omnibus at any time in the Buckingham Park Road. No: it must be a hoax, like the sign-posts, like the fairy tales, like the dreams upon which he would wake suddenly in the night. And with a sigh he stepped from the alley—right into the arms of his father.

Oh, how his father laughed! "Poor, poor Popsey!" he cried. "Diddums! Diddums! Diddums think he'd walky-palky up to Evvink!" And his mother, also convulsed with laughter, appeared on the steps of Agathox Lodge. "Don't, Bob!" she gasped. "Don't be so naughty! Oh, you'll kill me! Oh, leave the boy alone!"

But all that evening the joke was kept up. The father implored to be taken too. Was it a very tiring walk? Need one wipe one's shoes on the door-mat? And the boy went to bed feeling faint and sore, and thankful for only one thing— that he had not said a word about the omnibus. It was a hoax, yet through his dreams it grew more and more real, and the streets of Surbiton, through which he saw it driving, seemed instead to become hoaxes and shadows. And very early in the morning he woke with a cry, for he had had a glimpse of its destination.

He struck a match, and its light fell not only on his watch but also on his calendar, so that he knew it to be half-an-hour to sunrise. It was pitch dark, for the fog had come down from London in the night, and all Surbiton was wrapped in its embraces. Yet he sprang out and dressed himself, for he was determined to settle once for all which was real: the omnibus or the streets. "I shall be a fool one way or the other," he thought, "until I know." Soon he was shivering in the road under the gas lamp that guarded the entrance to the alley.

To enter the alley itself required some courage. Not only was it horribly dark, but he now realized that it was an impossible terminus for an omnibus. If it had not been for a policeman, whom he heard approaching through the fog, he would never have made the attempt. The next

moment he had made the attempt and failed. Nothing. Nothing but a blank alley and a very silly boy gaping at its dirty floor. It *was* a hoax. "I'll tell papa and mamma," he decided. "I deserve it. I deserve that they should know. I am too silly to be alive." And he went back to the gate of Agathox Lodge.

There he remembered that his watch was fast. The sun was not risen; it would not rise for two minutes. "Give the bus every chance," he thought cynically, and returned into the alley.

But the omnibus was there.

II

It had two horses, whose sides were still smoking from their journey, and its two great lamps shone through the fog against the alley's walls, changing their cobwebs and moss into tissues of fairyland. The driver was huddled up in a cape. He faced the blank wall, and how he had managed to drive in so neatly and so silently was one of the many things that the boy never discovered. Nor could he imagine how ever he would drive out.

"Please," his voice quavered through the foul brown air, "Please, is that an omnibus?"

"Omnibus est," said the driver, without turning round. There was a moment's silence. The policeman passed, coughing, by the entrance of the alley. The boy crouched in the shadow, for he did not want to be found out. He was pretty sure, too, that it was a Pirate; nothing else, he reasoned, would go from such odd places and at such odd hours.

"About when do you start?" He tried to sound nonchalant.

"At sunrise."

"How far do you go?"

"The whole way."

"And can I have a return ticket which will bring me all the way back?"

"You can."

"Do you know, I half think I'll come." The driver made no answer. The sun must have risen, for he unhitched the brake. And scarcely had the boy jumped in before the omnibus was off.

How? Did it turn? There was no room. Did it go forward? There was a blank wall. Yet it was moving—moving at a stately pace through the fog, which had turned from brown to yellow. The thought of warm bed and warmer breakfast made the boy feel faint. He wished he had not come. His parents would not have approved. He would have gone back to them if the weather had not made it impossible. The solitude was terrible; he was the only passenger. And the omnibus, though well-built, was cold and somewhat musty. He drew his coat round him, and in so doing chanced to feel his pocket. It was empty. He had forgotten his purse.

"Stop!" he shouted. "Stop!" And then, being of a polite disposition, he glanced up at the painted notice-board so that he might call the driver by name. "Mr. Browne! stop; O, do please stop!"

Mr. Browne did not stop, but he opened a little window and looked in at the boy. His face was a surprise, so kind it was and modest.

"Mr. Browne, I've left my purse behind. I've not got a penny. I can't pay for the ticket. Will you take my watch, please? I am in the most awful hole."

"Tickets on this line," said the driver, "whether single or return, can be purchased by coinage from no terrene mint. And a chronometer, though it had solaced the vigils of Charlemagne, or measured the slumbers of Laura, can acquire by no mutation the double-cake that charms the fangless Cerberus of Heaven!" So saying, he handed in the necessary ticket, and, while the boy said "Thank you," continued: "Titular pretensions, I know it well, are vanity. Yet they merit no censure when uttered on a laughing lip, and in an homonymous world are in some sort useful, since they do serve to distinguish one Jack from his fellow. Remember me, therefore, as Sir Thomas Browne."

"Are you a Sir? Oh, sorry!" He had heard of these gentlemen drivers. "It *is* good of you about the ticket. But if you go on at this rate, however does your bus pay?"

"It does not pay. It was not intended to pay. Many are the faults of my equipage; it is compounded too curiously of foreign woods; its cushions tickle erudition rather than promote repose; and my horses are nourished not on the evergreen pastures of the moment, but on the dried bents and clovers of Latinity. But that it pays!—that error at all events was never intended and never attained."

"Sorry again," said the boy rather hopelessly. Sir Thomas looked sad, fearing that, even for a moment, he had been the cause of sadness. He invited the boy to come up and sit beside him on the box, and together they journeyed on through the fog, which was now changing from yellow to white. There were no houses by the road; so it must be either Putney Heath or Wimbledon Common.

"Have you been a driver always?"

"I was a physician once."

"But why did you stop? Weren't you good?"

"As a healer of bodies I had scant success, and several score of my patients preceded me. But as a healer of the spirit I have succeeded beyond my hopes and my deserts. For though my draughts were not better nor subtler than those of other men, yet, by reason of the cunning goblets wherein I offered them, the queasy soul was ofttimes tempted to sip and be refreshed."

"The queasy soul," he murmured; "if the sun sets with trees in front of it, and you suddenly come strange all over, is that a queasy soul?"

"Have you felt that?"

"Why yes."

After a pause he told the boy a little, a very little, about the journey's end. But they did not chatter much, for the boy, when he liked a person, would as soon sit silent in his company as speak, and this, he discovered, was also the mind of Sir Thomas Browne and of many others with whom he was to be acquainted. He heard, however, about the young man Shelley, who was now quite a famous person, with a carriage of his own, and about some of the other drivers who are in the service of the Company. Meanwhile the light grew stronger, though the fog did not disperse.

It was now more like mist than fog, and at times would travel quickly across them, as if it was part of a cloud. They had been ascending, too, in a most puzzling way; for over two hours the horses had been pulling against the collar, and even if it were Richmond Hill they ought to have been at the top long ago. Perhaps it was Epsom, or even the North Downs; yet the air seemed keener than that which blows on either. And as to the name of their destination, Sir Thomas Browne was silent.

Crash!

"Thunder, by Jove!" said the boy, "and not so far off either. Listen to the echoes! It's more like mountains."

He thought, not very vividly, of his father and mother. He saw them sitting down to sausages and listening to the storm. He saw his own empty place. Then there would be questions, alarms, theories, jokes, consolations. They would expect him back at lunch. To lunch he would not come, nor to tea, but he would be in for dinner, and so his day's truancy would be over. If he had had his purse he would have bought them presents—not that he should have known what to get them.

Crash!

The peal and the lightning came together. The cloud quivered as if it were alive, and torn streamers of mist rushed past. "Are you afraid?" asked Sir Thomas Browne.

"What is there to be afraid of? Is it much farther?"

The horses of the omnibus stopped just as a ball of fire burst up and exploded with a ringing noise that was deafening but clear, like the noise of a blacksmith's forge. All the cloud was shattered.

"Oh, listen. Sir Thomas Browne! No, I mean look; we shall get a view at last. No, I mean listen; that sounds like a rainbow!"

The noise had died into the faintest murmur, beneath which another murmur grew, spreading stealthily, steadily, in a curve that widened but did not vary. And in widening curves a rainbow was spreading from the horses' feet into the dissolving mists.

"But how beautiful! What colours! Where will it stop? It is more like the rainbows you can tread on. More like dreams."

The colour and the sound grew together. The rainbow spanned an enormous gulf. Clouds rushed under it and were pierced by it, and still it grew, reaching forward, conquering the darkness, until it touched something that seemed more solid than a cloud.

The boy stood up. "What is that out there?" he called. "What does it rest on, out at that other end?"

In the morning sunshine a precipice shone forth beyond the gulf. A precipice—or was it a castle? The horses moved. They set their feet upon the rainbow.

"Oh, look!" the boy shouted. "Oh, listen! Those caves—or are they gateways? Oh, look between those cliffs at those ledges. I see people! I see trees!"

"Look also below," whispered Sir Thomas. "Neglect not the diviner Acheron."

The boy looked below, past the flames of the rainbow that licked against their wheels. The gulf also had cleared, and in its depths there flowed an everlasting river. One sunbeam entered and struck a green pool, and as they passed over he saw three maidens rise to the surface of the pool, singing, and playing with something that glistened like a ring.

"You down in the water——" he called.

They answered, "You up on the bridge——" There was a burst of music. "You up on the bridge, good luck to you. Truth in the depth, truth on the height."

"You down in the water, what are you doing?"

Sir Thomas Browne replied: "They sport in the mancipiary possession of their gold"; and the omnibus arrived.

III

The boy was in disgrace. He sat locked up in the nursery of Agathox Lodge, learning poetry for a punishment. His father had said, "My boy! I can pardon anything but untruthfulness," and had caned him, saying at each stroke, "There is *no* omnibus, *no* driver, *no* bridge, *no* mountain; you are a *truant*, *guttersnipe*, a *liar*." His father could be very stern at times. His mother had begged him to say he was sorry. But he could not say that. It was the greatest day of his life, in spite of the caning, and the poetry at the end of it.

He had returned punctually at sunset—driven not by Sir Thomas Browne, but by a maiden lady who was full of quiet fun. They had talked of omnibuses and also of barouche landaus. How far away her gentle voice seemed now! Yet it was scarcely three hours since he had left her up the alley.

His mother called through the door. "Dear, you are to come down and to bring your poetry with you."

He came down, and found that Mr. Bons was in the smoking-room with his father. It had been a dinner party.

"Here is the great traveller!" said his father grimly. "Here is the young gentleman who drives in an omnibus over rainbows, while young ladies sing to him." Pleased with his wit, he laughed.

"After all," said Mr. Bons, smiling, "there is something a little like it in Wagner. It is odd how, in quite illiterate minds, you will find glimmers of Artistic Truth. The case interests me. Let me plead for the culprit. We have all romanced in our time, haven't we?"

"Hear how kind Mr. Bons is," said his mother, while his father said, "Very well. Let him say his Poem, and that will do. He is going away to my sister on Tuesday, and she will cure him of this alley-slopering." (Laughter.) "Say your Poem."

The boy began. "'Standing aloof in giant ignorance.'"

His father laughed again—roared. "One for you, my son! 'Standing aloof in giant ignorance!' I never knew these poets talked sense. Just describes you. Here, Bons, you go in for poetry. Put him through it, will you, while I fetch up the whisky?"

"Yes, give me the Keats," said Mr. Bons. "Let him say his Keats to me."

So for a few moments the wise man and the ignorant boy were left alone in the smoking-room.

"'Standing aloof in giant ignorance, of thee I dream and of the Cyclades, as one who sits ashore and longs perchance to visit——'"

"Quite right. To visit what?"

"'To visit dolphin coral in deep seas,'" said the boy, and burst into tears.

"Come, come! why do you cry?"

"Because—because all these words that only rhymed before, now that I've come back they're me."

Mr. Bons laid the Keats down. The case was more interesting than he had expected. "*You?*" he exclaimed, "This sonnet, *you?*"

"Yes—and look further on: 'Aye, on the shores of darkness there is light, and precipices show untrodden green.' It *is* so, sir. All these things are true."

"I never doubted it," said Mr. Bons, with closed eyes.

"You—then you believe me? You believe in the omnibus and the driver and the storm and that return ticket I got for nothing and——"

"Tut, tut! No more of your yarns, my boy. I meant that I never doubted the essential truth of Poetry. Some day, when you read more, you will understand what I mean."

"But Mr. Bons, it *is* so. There *is* light upon the shores of darkness. I have seen it coming. Light and a wind."

"Nonsense," said Mr. Bons.

"If I had stopped! They tempted me. They told me to give up my ticket—for you cannot come back if you lose your ticket. They called from the river for it, and indeed I was tempted, for I have never been so happy as among those precipices. But I thought of my mother and father, and that I must fetch them. Yet they will not come, though the road starts opposite our house. It has all happened as the people up there warned me, and Mr. Bons has disbelieved me like every one else. I have been caned. I shall never see that mountain again."

"What's that about me?" said Mr. Bons, sitting up in his chair very suddenly.

"I told them about you, and how clever you were, and how many books you had, and they said, 'Mr. Bons will certainly disbelieve you.'"

"Stuff and nonsense, my young friend. You grow impertinent. I—well—I will settle the matter. Not a word to your father. I will cure you. To-morrow evening I will myself call here to take you for a walk, and at sunset we will go up this alley opposite and hunt for your omnibus, you silly little boy."

His face grew serious, for the boy was not disconcerted, but leapt about the room singing, "Joy! joy! I told them you would believe me. We will drive together over the rainbow. I told them that you would come." After all, could there be anything in the story? Wagner? Keats? Shelley? Sir Thomas Browne? Certainly the case was interesting.

And on the morrow evening, though it was pouring with rain, Mr. Bons did not omit to call at Agathox Lodge.

The boy was ready, bubbling with excitement, and skipping about in a way that rather vexed the President of the Literary Society. They took a turn down Buckingham Park Road, and then—having seen that no one was watching them—slipped up the alley. Naturally enough (for the sun was setting) they ran straight against the omnibus.

"Good heavens!" exclaimed Mr. Bons. "Good gracious heavens!"

It was not the omnibus in which the boy had driven first, nor yet that in which he had returned. There were three horses—black, gray, and white, the gray being the finest. The driver, who turned round at the mention of goodness and of heaven, was a sallow man with terrifying jaws and sunken eyes. Mr. Bons, on seeing him, gave a cry as if of recognition, and began to tremble violently.

The boy jumped in.

"Is it possible?" cried Mr. Bons. "Is the impossible possible?"

"Sir; come in, sir. It is such a fine omnibus. Oh, here is his name—Dan some one."

Mr. Bons sprang in too. A blast of wind immediately slammed the omnibus door, and the shock jerked down all the omnibus blinds, which were very weak on their springs.

"Dan . . . Show me. Good gracious heavens! we're moving."

"Hooray!" said the boy.

Mr. Bons became flustered. He had not intended to be kidnapped. He could not find the door-handle, nor push up the blinds. The omnibus was quite dark, and by the time he had struck a match, night had come on outside also. They were moving rapidly.

"A strange, a memorable adventure," he said, surveying the interior of the omnibus, which was large, roomy, and constructed with extreme regularity, every part exactly answering to every other part. Over the door (the handle of which was outside) was written, "Lasciate ogni baldanza voi che entrate"—at least, that was what was written, but Mr. Bons said that it was Lashy arty something, and that baldanza was a mistake for speranza. His voice sounded as if he was in church. Meanwhile, the boy called to the cadaverous driver for two return tickets. They were handed in without a word. Mr. Bons covered his face with his hand and again trembled. "Do you know who that is!" he whispered, when the little window had shut upon them. "It is the impossible."

"Well, I don't like him as much as Sir Thomas Browne, though I shouldn't be surprised if he had even more in him."

"More in him?" He stamped irritably. "By accident you have made the greatest discovery of the century, and all you can say is that there is more in this man. Do you remember those vellum books in my library, stamped with red lilies? This—sit still, I bring you stupendous news!— *this is the man who wrote them*."

The boy sat quite still. "I wonder if we shall see Mrs. Gamp?" he asked, after a civil pause.

"Mrs.——?"

"Mrs. Gamp and Mrs. Harris. I like Mrs. Harris. I came upon them quite suddenly. Mrs. Gamp's bandboxes have moved over the rainbow so badly. All the bottoms have fallen out, and two of the pippins off her bedstead tumbled into the stream."

"Out there sits the man who wrote my vellum books!" thundered Mr. Bons, "and you talk to me of Dickens and of Mrs. Gamp?"

"I know Mrs. Gamp so well," he apologized. "I could not help being glad to see her. I recognized her voice. She was telling Mrs. Harris about Mrs. Prig."

"Did you spend the whole day in her elevating company?"

"Oh, no. I raced. I met a man who took me out beyond to a race-course. You run, and there are dolphins out at sea."

"Indeed. Do you remember the man's name?"

"Achilles. No; he was later. Tom Jones."

Mr. Bons sighed heavily. "Well, my lad, you have made a miserable mess of it. Think of a cultured person with your opportunities! A cultured person would have known all these characters and known what to have said to each. He would not have wasted his time with a Mrs. Gamp or a Tom Jones. The creations of Homer, of Shakespeare, and of Him who drives us now, would alone have contented him. He would not have raced. He would have asked intelligent questions."

"But, Mr. Bons," said the boy humbly, "you will be a cultured person. I told them so."

"True, true, and I beg you not to disgrace me when we arrive. No gossiping. No running. Keep close to my side, and never speak to these Immortals unless they speak to you. Yes, and give me the return tickets. You will be losing them."

The boy surrendered the tickets, but felt a little sore. After all, he had found the way to this place. It was hard first to be disbelieved and then to be lectured. Meanwhile, the rain had stopped, and moonlight crept into the omnibus through the cracks in the blinds.

"But how is there to be a rainbow?" cried the boy.

"You distract me," snapped Mr. Bons. "I wish to meditate on beauty. I wish to goodness I was with a reverent and sympathetic person."

The lad bit his lip. He made a hundred good resolutions. He would imitate Mr. Bons all the visit. He would not laugh, or run, or sing, or do any of the vulgar things that must have disgusted his new friends last time. He would be very careful to pronounce their names properly, and to remember who knew whom. Achilles did not know Tom Jones—at least, so Mr. Bons said. The Duchess of Malfi was older than Mrs. Gamp—at least, so Mr. Bons said. He would be self-conscious, reticent, and prim. He would never say he liked any one. Yet when the Wind flew up at a chance touch of his head, all these good resolutions went to the winds, for the omnibus had reached the summit of a moonlit hill, and there was the chasm, and there, across it, stood the old precipices, dreaming, with their feet in the everlasting river. He exclaimed, "The mountain! Listen to the new tune in the water! Look at the camp fires in the ravines," and Mr. Bons, after a hasty glance, retorted, "Water? Camp fires? Ridiculous rubbish. Hold your tongue. There is nothing at all."

Yet, under his eyes, a rainbow formed, compounded not of sunlight and storm, but of moonlight and the spray of the river. The three horses put their feet upon it. He thought it the finest rainbow he had seen, but did not dare to say so, since Mr. Bons said that nothing was there. He leant out—the window had opened—and sang the tune that rose from the sleeping waters.

"The prelude to Rhinegold?" said Mr. Bons suddenly. "Who taught you these *leit motifs*?" He, too, looked out of the window. Then he behaved very oddly. He gave a choking cry, and fell back on to the omnibus floor. He writhed and kicked. His face was green.

"Does the bridge make you dizzy?" the boy asked.

"Dizzy!" gasped Mr. Bons. "I want to go back. Tell the driver."

But the driver shook his head.

"We are nearly there," said the boy, "They are asleep. Shall I call? They will be so pleased to see you, for I have prepared them."

Mr. Bons moaned. They moved over the lunar rainbow, which ever and ever broke away behind their wheels. How still the night was! Who would be sentry at the Gate?

"I am coming," he shouted, again forgetting the hundred resolutions. "I am returning—I, the boy."

"The boy is returning," cried a voice to other voices, who repeated, "The boy is returning."

"I am bringing Mr. Bons with me."

Silence.

"I should have said Mr. Bons is bringing me with him."

Profound silence.

"Who stands sentry?"

"Achilles."

And on the rocky causeway, close to the springing of the rainbow bridge, he saw a young man who carried a wonderful shield.

"Mr. Bons, it is Achilles, armed."

"I want to go back," said Mr. Bons.

The last fragment of the rainbow melted, the wheels sang upon the living rock, the door of the omnibus burst open. Out leapt the boy—he could not resist—and sprang to meet the warrior, who, stooping suddenly, caught him on his shield.

"Achilles!" he cried, "let me get down, for I am ignorant and vulgar, and I must wait for that Mr. Bons of whom I told you yesterday."

But Achilles raised him aloft. He crouched on the wonderful shield, on heroes and burning cities, on vineyards graven in gold, on every dear passion, every joy, on the entire image of the Mountain that he had discovered, encircled, like it, with an everlasting stream. "No, no," he protested, "I am not worthy. It is Mr. Bons who must be up here."

But Mr. Bons was whimpering, and Achilles trumpeted and cried, "Stand upright upon my shield!"

"Sir, I did not mean to stand! something made me stand. Sir, why do you delay? Here is only the great Achilles, whom you knew."

Mr. Bons screamed, "I see no one. I see nothing. I want to go back." Then he cried to the driver, "Save me! Let me stop in your chariot. I have honoured you. I have quoted you. I have bound you in vellum. Take me back to my world."

The driver replied, "I am the means and not the end. I am the food and not the life. Stand by yourself, as that boy has stood. I cannot save you. For poetry is a spirit; and they that would worship it must worship in spirit and in truth."

Mr. Bons—he could not resist—crawled out of the beautiful omnibus. His face appeared, gaping horribly. His hands followed, one gripping the step, the other beating the air. Now his shoulders emerged, his chest, his stomach. With a shriek of "I see London," he fell—fell against the hard, moonlit rock, fell into it as if it were water, fell through it, vanished, and was seen by the boy no more.

"Where have you fallen to, Mr. Bons? Here is a procession arriving to honour you with music and torches. Here come the men and women whose names you know. The mountain is awake, the river is awake, over the race-course the sea is awaking those dolphins, and it is all for you. They want you——"

There was the touch of fresh leaves on his forehead. Some one had crowned him.

TELOS

From the *Kingston Gazette,
Surbiton Times,* and *Paynes Park Observer.*

The body of Mr. Septimus Bons has been found in a shockingly mutilated condition in the vicinity of the Bermondsey gasworks. The deceased's pockets contained a sovereign-purse, a silver cigar-case, a bijou pronouncing dictionary, and a couple of omnibus tickets. The unfortunate gentleman had apparently been hurled from a considerable height. Foul play is suspected, and a thorough investigation is pending by the authorities.

Emily Pauline Johnson (1861–1913), known by the literary community as either E. Pauline Johnson or Tekahionwake, was a Canadian poet who often performed her poetry onstage. Her mother was English and her father was a member of the Mohawk tribe, and Johnson considered herself Indian above all else. At the time she began her writing career, most Indigenous writers were men who focused on critical essays about history and politics. She, however, cared more about the creative world of fiction and poetry and how it could be used to showcase the lives of Indigenous peoples. She performed her poetry in Canada, the United States, and even in London, and today her work is viewed as a landmark of Indigenous feminism. "The Legend of the Ice Babies" first appeared in 1911 in *Mother's Magazine*.

The Legend of the Ice Babies

E. Pauline Johnson

AS YOU JOURNEY across Canada from east to west, and have been absorbed in the beauty of the St. Lawrence, the Great Lakes, the prairies, the Rockies, the Selkirks, and finally the fiercely rugged grandeur of the Frazer River, as you are nearing the rim of the gentle Pacific, you will pass through one of the most fruitful valleys in all the Great Dominion. Orchards and vineyards, gardens and blossoming flowers stretch on every side, and in the misty distance there circles a band of bubbling mountains, and great armies of the giant Douglas firs and cedars that only the Western slope could ever give birth to. Through this valley stretches many a lazy arm of the sea, but there are also to be found several beautiful little fresh-water lakes. One in particular is remarkably lovely. It is small, and the shores so precipitous that winds seldom ruffle its clear blue-green waters. The majestic old forest trees, the mosses, the trailing vines, the ferns and bracken crowd so

closely down to the margin that they are mirrored in the lake in all their rich coloring and exquisite design. In looking on this secluded beauty one instinctively feels the almost sanctity of purity that can be found only in the undefiled forest lands. Nature has not been molested, and the desecrating hand of man has not yet profaned it. A happy chance had taken me along the shores of this perfect little gem, molded in its rocky setting, and one day when the Klootchman and I sat together on the sands watching the Pacific as it slept under an autumn sun, I spoke to her of the little fresh-water jewel up in the Chilliwack Valley.

"You have seen it?" she asked with great interest. I nodded.

"I am very glad. We Squamish women love it. The mothers love it most. We call it the Lake of the Ice Babies."

I remarked on the beauty of the name, and

then on its oddity. "For," I said, "surely it does not freeze there!"

"Yes," she replied, "it always freezes over at least once in the winter, if only for a day. The lake is so still there is no wind now to keep it open from the frost."

I caught at the word "now." "Was there ever a wind there?" I ventured, for one must voice his thoughts delicately if one hopes to extract a tradition from my good old reticent Klootchman.

"Yes, once it used to be very stormy, terrible gales would get imprisoned in that cup of the mountains, and they would sweep round and round, lashing up the waters of the lake like a chained wild animal," she answered. Then she added that ever-present pitiful remark: "But that was long ago—before the white man came." It has been the redskin's cry for more than a century, that melancholy "Before the white man came."

Presently she picked up a handful of silver sand, and while she trailed it leisurely from palm to palm, threading it between her thin, dark fingers, her voice fell into the sonorous monotone, the half whisper, half chant, in which she loved to relate her quaint stories, while I sat beside her sun-bathed and indolent, and listened to the

"LEGEND OF THE ICE BABIES"

"There were two of them, two laughing, toddling little children but just released from the bands of their cradle baskets. Girls, both of them, and cousins, of the same age, happy-hearted and playful, and the treasures of their mothers' lives. It was a warm, soft day of late autumn, a day like this, when not a leaf stirred, not a wave danced, that the wandering band of Squamish encamped in the bluffs about the little lake, and prepared to stay the night. The men cut branches and built a small lodge. The women gathered firewood and cooked venison and grouse, and the children and babies played about, watching their elders, and sometimes replenishing the camp fires. The evening wore on, and with the twilight came a gentle ris-

ing wind, that whispered at first through the pines and cedars like a mother singing very softly to her sleeping child. Then the wind-voice grew louder, it began to speak harshly. The song in it died, and the mighty voices of the trees awoke like the war cry of many tribes in battle. The little lake began to heave and toss, then lash itself into a fury; whirlpools circled, waves rose and foamed and fought each other. The gale was shut within the cup of shores and could not release itself.

"In the stir of fitting the camp for the night, and protecting the frail lodge against destruction, the two girl babies were unnoticed, and hand in hand they wandered with halting childish steps to the brink of the shore. Before them the waves arose and fell, frothed and whirled like some playful wild thing, and their little hands longed to grasp the curling eddies, the long lines of combers and breakers. Laughingly the babies slid down the fern-covered banks, and stepped into the shallow waters at the margin, then wandered out over the surface of the lake, frolicking and playing in the tossing waves and whirlpools, but neither little body sank. The small feet skimmed the angry waters like feathers dropped from the wings of some passing bird, for under those dancing innocent feet the Saghalie Tyee had placed the palms of his hands, and the soft baby soles rested and romped in an anchorage greater than the most sheltered harbor in all the vast Pacific coast.

From the shores their mothers watched them, first in an agony of fear, then with wonder, then with reverence.

"'The great Tyee holds them in his hand,' spoke one with whispered awe.

"'Listen, he speaks.'

"'Will you give these babies to rue, oh, mothers of the Squamish?' said a voice from above the clouds. 'To me to keep for you, always as babies, always as laughing, happy little ones, or will you take them back to yourselves and the shore, to have them grow away from their innocence, their childhood; to have them suffer in heart and body as women must ever suffer, to have them grow ill with age, old with pain and years, and then to die, to leave you lonely, and to go where you may not follow and care for them and love them? Which will you, oh, mothers of the Squamish? If you love yourselves best, you shall have your babies again. If you love your babies most, you will give them to me.'

"And the two mothers answered as one voice: 'Keep them always as babies, always innocent, always happy—take them, oh, Great Tyee, for we love them more than we love ourselves!'

"The winds began to sob lower. The waves ceased swirling, the roar of tempestuous waters calmed to whispers, then lulled into perfect tranquility, but the babies still played and laughed on its blue surface. The hands of the Saghalie Tyee still upheld them.

"That night the lake froze from shore to shore. When morning dawned, the two mothers were 'wakened by a voice that spoke very gently, but it came from invisible lips, and they knew it to be a message from the Tyee of the Happy Hunting Grounds. 'The babies are yours forever,' he said, 'although I, the Saghalie Tyee of all men, shall keep them in the hollow of my hands. I have bridged the waters with eternal stillness, for their little bodies are young and tender, their little feet too soft for rough waves, their little hands too frail to battle rough winds. No storm shall ever again fret this lake, no gale churn its surface to fury. I have tempered their little world to their baby needs, and they shall live in shelter for all time. Rise, oh, mothers of the Squamish, and look upon your gifts to me, which I shall keep in trust for you forever.'

"The women arose, and creeping to the door of the lodge beheld their babies dancing on the frail, clear ice far out across the lake. They could see the baby smiles, hear the baby laughter, and they knew their mother-hearts would never mourn for their children's lost innocence, or lost babyhood. And each year since that time, when the first frosts of late autumn touch the little lake with a film of ice, the babies come to play and laugh like elves of the air, upon its shining surface. They have never grown older, never grown less innocent. They are pure as the ice their soft, small feet touch with dancing step, and so they will remain for all time."

The silver sands were still filtering between her brown fingers as the Klootchman ended the tale, and I still lay watching the sunlight glint on the lazy Pacific, and wondering if it, too, were not the dancing feet of some long-ago children.

"Do people ever see these ice babies now?" I asked dreamily.

"Only those who are nearing the country of the Great Tyee," she replied. "As one nears that land one becomes again as a little child, one's eyes grow innocent, one's heart trusting, one's life blameless, as they go down the steep shores of age to the quiet, windless, waveless lake where they must rest forever in the hollows of the Great Tyee's hands, for he has kept these pure Ice babies there for many hundreds of years because he wishes his Indian children to become like them before they cross the lake to the Happy Hunting Grounds on the far shore."

She was silent for a moment, then added: "I am growing old, Tillicum (friend), perhaps I shall see them—soon."

William Hope Hodgson (1877–1918) was an English author, photographer, sailor, and bodybuilder. Being a bodybuilder and also a personal trainer for a time may make him sui generis among weird fantasy writers. Although perhaps less known today, Hodgson's fantasy, horror, and science fiction presaged much of the modern work done in these genres. His most popular works include *The House on the Borderland* (1908), *The Night Land* (1912), excerpted here, and the story suite *Carnacki the Ghost-Finder* (1913). Hodgson died at the age of forty while serving in World War I. *The House on the Borderland*, by departing from the traditional Gothic literature of the period, became an early twentieth-century example of radically fey fantasy. "The Last Redoubt" is a potent excerpt of the nameless narrator's exploration of a classic science-fantasy land forever shrouded in darkness.

The Last Redoubt

(EXCERPT FROM *THE NIGHT LAND*)

William Hope Hodgson

SINCE MIRDATH, My Beautiful One, died and left me lonely in this world, I have suffered an anguish, and an utter and dreadful pain of longing, such as truly no words shall ever tell; for, in truth, I that had all the world through her sweet love and companionship, and knew all the joy and gladness of Life, have known such lonesome misery as doth stun me to think upon.

Yet am I to my pen again; for of late a wondrous hope has grown in me, in that I have, at night in my sleep, waked into the future of this world, and seen strange things and utter marvels, and known once more the gladness of life; for I have learned the promise of the future, and have visited in my dreams those places where in the womb of Time, she and I shall come together, and part, and again come together—breaking asunder most drearly in pain, and again reuniting after strange ages, in a glad and mighty wonder.

And this is the utter strange story of that which I have seen, and which, truly, I must set out, if the task be not too great; so that, in the setting out thereof, I may gain a little ease of the heart; and likewise, mayhap, give ease of hope to some other poor human, that doth suffer, even as I have suffered so dreadful with longing for Mine Own that is dead.

And some shall read and say that this thing was not, and some shall dispute with them; but to them all I say naught, save "Read!" And having read that which I set down, then shall one and all have looked towards Eternity with me—unto its very portals. And so to my telling:

To me, in this last time of my visions, of which I would tell, it was not as if I *dreamed*; but, as it were, that I *waked* there into the dark, *in the future of this world*. And the sun had died; and for me thus newly waked into that Future, to look back upon this, our Present Age, was to look back into dreams that my soul knew to be of reality; but which to those newly seeing eyes of mine, appeared but as a far vision, strangely hallowed with peacefulness and light.

Always, it seemed to me when I awaked into the Future, into the Everlasting Night that lapped this world, that I saw near to me, and girdling me all about, a blurred greyness. And presently this, the greyness, would clear and fade from about me, even as a dusky cloud, and I would look out upon a world of darkness, lit here and there with strange sights. And with my waking into that Future, I waked not to ignorance; but to a full knowledge of those things which lit the Night Land; even as a man wakes from sleep each morning, and knows immediately he wakes, the names and knowledge of the Time which has bred him, and in which he lives. And the same while, a knowledge I had, as it were sub-conscious, of this Present—this early life, which now I live so utterly alone.

In my earliest knowledge of *that* place, I was a youth, seventeen years grown, and my memory tells me that when first I waked, or came, as it might be said, to myself, in that Future, I stood in one of the embrasures of the Last Redoubt—that great Pyramid of grey metal which held the last millions of this world from the Powers of the Slayers.

And so full am I of the knowledge of that Place, that scarce can I believe that none here know; and because I have such difficulty, it may be that I speak over familiarly of those things of which I know; and heed not to explain much that it is needful that I should explain to those who must read here, in this our present day. For there, as I stood and looked out, I was less the man of years of *this* age, than the youth of *that*, with the

natural knowledge of *that* life which I had gathered by living all my seventeen years of life there; though, until that my first vision, I (of this Age) knew not of that other and Future Existence; yet woke to it so naturally as may a man wake here in his bed to the shining of the morning sun, and know it by name, and the meaning of aught else. And yet, as I stood there in the vast embrasure, I had also a knowledge, or memory, of this present life of ours, deep down within me; but touched with a halo of dreams, and yet with a conscious longing for One, known even there in a half memory as Mirdath.

As I have said, in my earliest memory, I mind that I stood in an embrasure, high up in the side of the Pyramid, and looked outwards through a queer spy-glass to the North-West. Aye, full of youth and with an adventurous and yet half-fearful heart.

And in my brain was, as I have told, the knowledge that had come to me in all the years of my life in the Redoubt; and yet until that moment, this *Man of this Present Time* had no knowledge of that future existence; and now I stood and had suddenly the knowledge of a life already spent in that strange land, and deeper within me the misty knowings of this our present Age, and, maybe, also of some others.

To the North-West I looked through the queer spy-glass, and saw a landscape that I had looked upon and pored upon through all the years of that life, so that I knew how to name this thing and that thing, and give the very distances of each and every one from the "Centre-Point" of the Pyramid, which was that which had neither length nor breadth, and was made of polished metal in the Room of Mathematics, where I went daily to my studies.

To the North-West I looked, and in the wide field of my glass, saw plain the bright glare of the fire from the Red Pit, shine upwards against the underside of the vast chin of the North-West Watcher—The Watching Thing of the North-West. . . . "That which hath Watched from the Beginning, and until the opening of the Gateway of Eternity" came into my thoughts, as I looked through the glass . . . the words of Aesworpth, the *Ancient* Poet (though incredibly *future* to this our time). And suddenly they seemed at fault; for I looked deep down into my being, and saw, as dreams are seen, the sunlight and splendour of *this* our Present Age. And I was amazed.

And here I must make it clear to all that, even as I waked from *this* Age, suddenly into *that* life, so must I—*that* youth there in the embrasure—have awakened then to the knowledge of *this* far-back life of ours—seeming to him a vision of the very beginnings of eternity, in the dawn of the world. Oh! I do but dread I make it not sufficient clear that I and he were both *I*—the same soul. He of that far date seeing vaguely the life that *was* (that I do now live in this present Age); and I of this time beholding the life that I yet shall live. How utterly strange!

And yet, I do not know that I speak holy truth to say that I, in that future time, had *no* knowledge of *this* life and Age, before that awakening; for I woke to find that I was one who stood apart from the other youths, in that I had a dim knowledge—visionary, as it were, of the past, which confounded, whilst yet it angered, those who were the men of learning of that age; though of this matter, more anon. But this I do know, that from that time, onwards, my knowledge and assuredness of the Past was tenfold; for this my memory of that life told me.

And so to further my telling. Yet before I pass onwards, one other thing is there of which I shall speak—In the moment in which I waked out of that youthfulness, into the assured awareness of *this* our Age, in that moment the hunger of this my love flew to me across the ages; so that what had been but a memory-dream, grew to the pain of *Reality*, and I knew suddenly that I *lacked*; and from that time onwards, I went, listening, as even now my life is spent.

And so it was that I (fresh-born in that future time) hungered strangely for My Beautiful One with all the strength of that new life, knowing that she had been mine, and might live again, even as I. And so, as I have said, I hungered, and found that I listened.

And now, to go back from my digression, it was, as I have said, I had amazement at perceiving, in memory, the unknowable sunshine and splendour of this age breaking so clear through my hitherto most vague and hazy visions; so that the ignorance of Aesworpth was shouted to me by the things which now I *knew*.

And from that time, onward, for a little space, I was stunned with all that I knew and guessed and felt; and all of a long while the hunger grew for that one I had lost in the early days—she who had sung to me in those faery days of light, that *had been* in verity. And the especial thoughts of that age looked back with a keen, regretful wonder into the gulf of forgetfulness.

But, presently, I turned from the haze and pain of my dream-memories, once more to the inconceivable mystery of the Night Land, which I viewed through the great embrasure. For on none did it ever come with weariness to look out upon all the hideous mysteries; so that old and young watched, from early years to death, the black monstrosity of the Night Land, which this our last refuge of humanity held at bay.

To the right of the Red Pit there lay a long, sinuous glare, which I knew as the Vale of Red Fire, and beyond that for many dreary miles the blackness of the Night Land; across which came the coldness of the light from the Plain of Blue Fire.

And then, on the very borders of the Unknown Lands, there lay a range of low volcanoes, which lit up, far away in the outer darkness, the Black Hills, where shone the Seven Lights, which neither twinkled nor moved nor faltered through Eternity; and of which even the great spy-glass could make no understanding; nor had any adventurer from the Pyramid ever come back to tell us aught of them. And here let me say, that down in the Great Library of the Redoubt, were the histories of all those, with their discoveries, who had ventured out into the monstrousness of the Night Land, risking not the life only, but the spirit of life.

And surely it is all so strange and wonderful to set out, that I could almost despair with the contemplation of that which I must achieve; for there is so much to tell, and so few words given to man by which he may make clear that which lies beyond the sight and the present and general knowings of Peoples.

How shall you ever know, as I know in verity, of the greatness and reality and terror of the thing that I would tell plain to all; for we, with our puny span of recorded life must have great histories to tell, but the few bare details we know concerning years that are but a few thousands in all; and I must set out to you in the short pages of this my life there, a sufficiency of the life that had been, and the life that was, both within and without that mighty Pyramid, to make clear to those who may read, the truth of that which I would tell; and the histories of that great Redoubt dealt not with odd thousands of years; but with very millions; aye, away back into what they of that Age conceived to be the early days of the earth, when the sun, maybe, still gloomed dully in the night sky of the world. But of all that went before, nothing, save as myths, and matters to be taken most cautiously, and believed not by men of sanity and proved wisdom.

And I . . . how shall I make all this clear to you who may read? The thing cannot be; and yet I must tell my history; for to be silent before so much wonder would be to suffer of too full a heart; and I must even ease my spirit by this my struggle to tell to all how it was with me, and how it will be. Aye, even to the memories which were the possession of that far future youth, who was indeed I, of his childhood's days, when his nurse of that Age swung him, and crooned impossible lullabies of this mythical sun which, according to those future fairy-tales, had once passed across the blackness that now lay above the Pyramid.

Such is the monstrous futureness of this which I have seen through the body of that far-off youth.

And so back to my telling. To my right, which was to the North, there stood, very far away, the House of Silence, upon a low hill. And in that House were many lights, and no sound. And so had it been through an uncountable Eternity of

Years. Always those steady lights, and no whisper of sound—not even such as our distance-microphones could have discovered. And the danger of this House was accounted the greatest danger of all those Lands.

And round by the House of Silence, wound the Road Where The Silent Ones Walk. And concerning this Road, which passed out of the Unknown Lands, nigh by the Place of the Ab-humans, where was always the green, luminous mist, nothing was known; save that it was held that, of all the works about the Mighty Pyramid, it was, alone, the one that was bred, long ages past, of healthy human toil and labour. And on this point alone, had a thousand books, and more, been writ; and all contrary, and so to no end, as is ever the way in such matters.

And as it was with the Road Where The Silent Ones Walk, so it was with all those other monstrous things . . . whole libraries had there been made upon this and upon that; and many a thousand million mouldered into the forgotten dust of the earlier world.

I mind me now that presently I stepped upon the central travelling-roadway which spanned the one thousandth plateau of the Great Redoubt. And this lay six miles and thirty fathoms above the Plain of the Night Land, and was somewhat of a great mile or more across. And so, in a few minutes, I was at the South-Eastern wall, and looking out through The Great Embrasure towards the Three Silver-fire Holes, that shone before the Thing That Nods, away down, far in the South-East. Southward of this, but nearer, there rose the vast bulk of the South-East Watcher—The Watching Thing of the South-East. And to the right and to the left of the squat monster burned the Torches; maybe half-a-mile upon each side; yet sufficient light they threw to show the lumbered-forward head of the never-sleeping Brute.

To the East, as I stood there in the quietness of the Sleeping-Time on the One Thousandth Plateau, I heard a far, dreadful sound, down in the lightless East; and, presently, again—a strange, dreadful laughter, deep as a low thunder among the mountains. And because this sound came odd whiles from the Unknown Lands beyond the Valley of The Hounds, we had named that far and never-seen Place "The Country Whence Comes The Great Laughter." And though I had heard the sound, many and oft a time, yet did I never hear it without a most strange thrilling of my heart, and a sense of my littleness, and of the utter terror which had beset the last millions of the world.

Yet, because I had heard the Laughter oft, I paid not over-long attention to my thoughts upon it; and when, in a little it died away into that Eastern Darkness, I turned my spy-glass upon the Giants' Pit, which lay to the South of the Giants' Kilns. And these same Kilns were tended by the giants, and the light of the Kilns was red and fitful, and threw wavering shadows and lights across the mouth of the pit; so that I saw giants crawling up out of the pit; but not properly seen, by reason of the dance of the shadows. And so, because ever there was so much to behold, I looked away, presently, to that which was plainer to be examined.

To the back of the Giants' Pit was a great, black Headland, that stood vast, between the Valley of The Hounds (where lived the monstrous Night Hounds) and the Giants. And the light of the Kilns struck the brow of this black Headland; so that, constantly, I saw things peer over the edge, coming forward a little into the light of the Kilns, and drawing back swiftly into the shadows. And thus it had been ever, through the uncounted ages; so that the Headland was known as The Headland From Which Strange Things Peer; and thus was it marked in our maps and charts of that grim world.

And so I could go on ever; but that I fear too weary; and yet, whether I do weary, or not, I must tell of this country that I see, even now as I set my thoughts down, so plainly that my memory wanders in a hushed and secret fashion along its starkness, and amid its strange and dread habitants, so that it is but by an effort I realise me that my body is not there in this very moment that I write. And so to further tellings:

Before me ran the Road Where The Silent Ones Walk; and I searched it, as many a time in my earlier youth had I, with the spy-glass; for my heart was always stirred mightily by the sight of those Silent Ones.

And, presently, alone in all the miles of that night-grey road, I saw one in the field of my glass—a quiet, cloaked figure, moving along, shrouded, and looking neither to right nor left. And thus was it with these beings ever. It was told about in the Redoubt that they would harm no human, if but the human did keep a fair distance from them; but that it were wise never to come close upon one. And this I can well believe.

And so, searching the road with my gaze, I passed beyond this Silent One, and past the place where the road, sweeping vastly to the South-East, was lit a space, strangely, by the light from the Silver-fire Holes. And thus at last to where it swayed to the South of the Dark Palace, and thence Southward still, until it passed round to the Westward, beyond the mountain bulk of the Watching Thing in the South—the hugest monster in all the visible Night Lands. My spy-glass showed it to me with clearness—a living hill of watchfulness, known to us as The Watcher of the South. It brooded there, squat and tremendous, hunched over the pale radiance of the Glowing Dome.

Much, I know, had been writ concerning this Odd, Vast Watcher; for it had grown out of the blackness of the South Unknown Lands a million years gone; and the steady growing nearness of it had been noted and set out at length by the men they called Monstruwacans; so that it was possible to search in our libraries, and learn of the very coming of this Beast in the olden-time.

And, while I mind me, there were even then, and always, men named Monstruwacans, whose duty it was to take heed of the great Forces, and to watch the Monsters and the Beasts that beset the great Pyramid, and measure and record, and have so full a knowledge of these same that, did one but sway a head in the darkness, the same matter was set down with particularness in the Records.

And, so to tell more about the South Watcher.

A million years gone, as I have told, came it out from the blackness of the South, and grew steadily nearer through twenty thousand years; but so slow that in no one year could a man perceive that it had moved.

Yet it had movement, and had come thus far upon its road to the Redoubt, when the Glowing Dome rose out of the ground before it—growing slowly. And this had stayed the way of the Monster; so that through an eternity it had looked towards the Pyramid across the pale glare of the Dome, and seeming to have no power to advance nearer.

And because of this, much had been writ to prove that there were other forces than evil at work in the Night Lands, about the Last Redoubt. And this I have always thought to be wisely said; and, indeed, there to be no doubt to the matter, for there were many things in the time of which I have knowledge, which seemed to make clear that, even as the Forces of Darkness were loose upon the End of Man; so were there other Forces out to do battle with the Terror; though in ways most strange and unthought of by the human mind. And of this I shall have more to tell anon.

And here, before I go further with my telling, let me set out some of that knowledge which yet remains so clear within my mind and heart. Of the coming of these monstrosities and evil Forces, no man could say much with verity; for the evil of it began before the Histories of the Great Redoubt were shaped; aye, even before the sun had lost all power to light; though, it must not be a thing of certainty, that even at this far time the invisible, black heavens held no warmth for this world; but of this I have no room to tell; and must pass on to that of which I have a more certain knowledge.

The evil must surely have begun in the Days of the Darkening (which I might liken to a story which was believed doubtfully, much as we of this day believe the story of the Creation). A dim record there was of olden sciences (that are yet far off in our future) which, disturbing the unmeasurable Outward Powers, had allowed to pass the Barrier of Life some of those Monsters and Ab-human creatures, which are so wondrously cushioned from us at this normal present. And thus there had materialized, and in other cases developed, grotesque and horrible Creatures, which now beset the humans of this world. And where there was no power to take on material form, there had been allowed to certain dreadful Forces to have power to affect the life of the human spirit. And this growing very dreadful, and the world full of lawlessness and degeneracy, there had banded together the sound millions, and built the Last Redoubt; there in the twilight of the world—so it seems to us, and yet to them (bred at last to the peace of usage) as it were the Beginning; and this I can make no clearer; and none hath right to expect it; for my task is very great, and beyond the power of human skill.

And when the humans had built the great Pyramid, it had one thousand three hundred and twenty floors; and the thickness of each floor was according to the strength of its need. And the whole height of this pyramid exceeded seven miles, by near a mile, and above it was a tower from which the Watchmen looked (these being called the Monstruwacans). But where the Redoubt was built, I know not; save that I believe in a mighty valley, of which I may tell more in due time.

And when the Pyramid was built, the last millions, who were the Builders thereof, went within, and made themselves a great house and city of this Last Redoubt. And thus began the Second History of this world. And how shall I set it all down in these little pages! For my task, even as I see it, is too great for the power of a single life and a single pen. Yet, to it!

And, later, through hundreds and thousands of years, there grew up in the Outer Lands, beyond those which lay under the guard of the Redoubt, mighty and lost races of terrible creatures, half men and half beast, and evil and dreadful; and these made war upon the Redoubt; but were beaten off from that grim, metal mountain, with a vast slaughter. Yet, must there have been many such attacks, until the electric circle was put about the Pyramid, and lit from the Earth-

Current. And the lowest half-mile of the Pyramid was sealed; and so at last there was a peace, and the beginnings of that Eternity of quiet watching for the day when the Earth-Current shall become exhausted.

And, at whiles, through the forgotten centuries, had the Creatures been glutted time and again upon such odd bands of daring ones as had adventured forth to explore through the mystery of the Night Lands; for of those who went, scarce any did ever return; for there were eyes in all that dark; and Powers and Forces abroad which had all knowledge; or so we must fain believe.

And then, so it would seem, as that Eternal Night lengthened itself upon the world, the power of terror grew and strengthened. And fresh and greater monsters developed and bred out of all space and Outward Dimensions, attracted, even as it might be Infernal sharks, by that lonely and mighty hill of humanity, facing its end—so near to the Eternal, and yet so far deferred in the minds and to the senses of those humans. And thus hath it been ever.

And all this but by the way, and vague and ill told, and set out in despair to make a little clear the beginnings of that State which is so strange to our conceptions, and yet which had become a Condition of Naturalness to Humanity in that stupendous future.

Thus had the giants come, fathered of bestial humans and mothered of monsters. And many and diverse were the creatures which had some human semblance; and intelligence, mechanical and cunning; so that certain of these lesser Brutes had machinery and underground ways, having need to secure to themselves warmth and air, even as healthy humans; only that they were incredibly inured to hardship, as they might be wolves set in comparison with tender children. And surely, do I make this thing clear?

And now to continue my telling concerning the Night Land. The Watcher of the South was, as I have set to make known, a monster differing from those other Watching Things, of which I have spoken, and of which there were in all four. One to the North-West, and one to the South-East, and of these I have told; and the other twain lay brooding, one to the South-West, and the other to the North-East; and thus the four watchers kept ward through the darkness, upon the Pyramid, and moved not, neither gave they out any sound. Yet did we know them to be mountains of living watchfulness and hideous and steadfast intelligence.

And so, in a while, having listened to the sorrowful sound which came ever to us over the Grey Dunes, from the Country of Wailing, which lay to the South, midway between the Redoubt and the Watcher of the South, I passed upon one of the moving roadways over to the South-Western side of the Pyramid, and looked from a narrow embrasure thence far down into the Deep Valley, which was four miles deep, and in which was the Pit of the Red Smoke.

And the mouth of this Pit was one full mile across, and the smoke of the Pit filled the Valley at times, so that it seemed but as a glowing red circle amid dull thunderous clouds of redness. Yet the red smoke rose never much above the Valley; so that there was clear sight across to the country beyond. And there, along the further edge of that great depth, were the Towers, each, maybe, a mile high, grey and quiet; but with a shimmer upon them.

Beyond these, South and West of them, was the enormous bulk of the South-West Watcher, and from the ground rose what we named the Eye Beam—a single ray of grey light, which came up out of the ground, and lit the right eye of the monster. And because of this light, that eye had been mightily examined through unknown thousands of years; and some held that the eye looked through the light steadfastly at the Pyramid; but others set out that the light blinded it, and was the work of those Other Powers which were abroad to do combat with the Evil Forces. But however this may be, as I stood there in the embrasure, and looked at the thing through the spy-glass, it seemed to my soul that the Brute looked straightly at me, unwinking and steadfast, and fully of a knowledge that I spied upon it. And this is how I felt.

To the North of this, in the direction of the West, I saw The Place Where the Silent Ones Kill; and this was so named, because there, maybe ten thousand years gone, certain humans adventuring from the Pyramid, came off the Road Where The Silent Ones Walk, and into that place, and were immediately destroyed. And this was told by one who escaped; though he died also very quickly, for his heart was frozen. And this I cannot explain; but so it was set out in the Records.

Far away beyond The Place Where the Silent Ones Kill, in the very mouth of the Western Night was the Place of the Ab-humans, where was lost the Road Where The Silent Ones Walk, in a dull green, luminous mist. And of this place nothing was known; though much it held the thoughts and attentions of our thinkers and imaginers; for some said that there was a Place Of Safety, differing from the Redoubt (as we of this day suppose Heaven to differ from the Earth), and that the Road led thence; but was barred by the Ab-humans. And this I can only set down here; but with no thought to justify or uphold it.

Later, I travelled over to the North-Eastern wall of the Redoubt, and looked thence with my spy-glass at the Watcher of the North-East—the Crowned Watcher it was called, in that within the air above its vast head there hung always a blue, luminous ring, which shed a strange light downwards over the monster—showing a vast, wrinkled brow (upon which a whole library had been writ); but putting to the shadow all the lower face; all save the ear, which came out from the back of the head, and belled towards the Redoubt, and had been said by some observers in the past to have been seen to quiver; but how that might be, I knew not; for no man of our days had seen such a thing.

And beyond the Watching Thing was The Place Where the Silent Ones Are Never, close by the great road; which was bounded upon the far side by The Giant's Sea; and upon the far side of that, was a Road which was always named The Road by the Quiet City; for it passed along that place where burned forever the constant and never-moving lights of a strange city; but no glass had ever shown life there; neither had any light ever ceased to burn.

And beyond that again was the Black Mist. And here, let me say, that the Valley of the Hounds ended towards the Lights of the Quiet City.

And so have I set out something of that land, and of those creatures and circumstances which beset us about, waiting until the Day of Doom, when our Earth-Current should cease, and leave us helpless to the Watchers and the Abundant Terror.

And there I stood, and looked forth composedly, as may one who has been born to know of such matters, and reared in the knowledge of them. And, anon, I would look upward, and see the grey, metalled mountain going up measureless into the gloom of the everlasting night; and from my feet the sheer downward sweep of the grim, metal walls, six full miles, and more, to the plain below.

And one thing (aye! and I fear me, many) have I missed to set out with particularness:

There was, as you do know, all around the base of the Pyramid, which was five and one-quarter miles every way, a great circle of light, which was set up by the Earth-Current, and burned within a transparent tube; or had that appearance. And it bounded the Pyramid for a clear mile upon every side, and burned for ever; and none of the monsters had power ever to pass across, because of what we did call The Air Clog that it did make, as an invisible Wall of Safety. And it did give out also a more subtile vibration, that did affect the weak Brain-Elements of the monsters and the Lower Men-Brutes. And some did hold that there went from it a further vibration of a greater subtileness that gave a protecting against the Evil Forces. And some quality it had truly thiswise; for the Evil Powers had no ability to cause harm to any within. Yet were there some dangers against which it might not avail; but these had no cunning to bring harm to any *within* the Great Redoubt who had wisdom to meddle with no dreadfulness. And so were those last millions guarded until the Earth-Current should be used to its end. And this circle is that which I have called the Electric Circle; though with failure to explain. But there it was called only, The Circle.

And thus have I, with great effort, made a little clear that grim land of night, where, presently, my listening heard one calling across the dark. And how that this grew upon me, I will set out forthwith.

Lyman Frank Baum, better known as L. Frank Baum (1856–1919), was an American author best known for his children's series about the land of Oz. Baum published his first collection for young readers, *Mother Goose in Prose*, in 1897, and soon after he shocked the world with a tale about a girl named Dorothy. He wrote more than sixty books in his lifetime, and his Oz series was continued after his death by several other authors. The character of Jack Pumpkinhead first appeared in the second Oz book and remained a main character in all of the Oz books since then. "Jack Pumpkinhead and the Sawhorse" is one of the six *Little Wizard Stories of Oz* (1913). The character has appeared on the stage, in film, and even in comic books. He has also inspired authors such as Neil Gaiman, who based his character Mervyn Pumpkinhead the handyman on Baum's good-natured Jack.

Jack Pumpkinhead and the Sawhorse

L. Frank Baum

IN A ROOM OF THE ROYAL PALACE of the Emerald City of Oz hangs a Magic Picture, in which are shown all the important scenes that transpire in those fairy dominions. The scenes shift constantly and by watching them, Ozma, the girl Ruler, is able to discover events taking place in any part of her kingdom.

One day she saw in her Magic Picture that a little girl and a little boy had wandered together into a great, gloomy forest at the far west of Oz and had become hopelessly lost. Their friends were seeking them in the wrong direction and unless Ozma came to their rescue the little ones would never be found in time to save them from starving.

So the Princess sent a message to Jack Pumpkinhead and asked him to come to the palace. This personage, one of the queerest of the queer inhabitants of Oz, was an old friend and companion of Ozma. His form was made of rough sticks fitted together and dressed in ordinary clothes. His head was a pumpkin with a face carved upon it, and was set on top a sharp stake which formed his neck.

Jack was active, good-natured and a general favorite; but his pumpkin head was likely to spoil with age, so in order to secure a good supply of heads he grew a big field of pumpkins and lived in the middle of it, his house being a huge pumpkin hollowed out. Whenever he needed a new head he picked a pumpkin, carved a face on it and stuck it upon the stake of his neck, throwing away the old head as of no further use.

The day Ozma sent for him Jack was in prime condition and was glad to be of service in rescuing the lost children. Ozma made him a map, showing just where the forest was and how to get to it and the paths he must take to reach the little ones. Then she said:

"You'd better ride the Sawhorse, for he is swift and intelligent and will help you accomplish your task."

"All right," answered Jack, and went to the royal stable to tell the Sawhorse to be ready for the trip.

This remarkable animal was not unlike Jack Pumpkinhead in form, although so different in shape. Its body was a log, with four sticks stuck into it for legs. A branch at one end of the log served as a tail, while in the other end was chopped a gash that formed a mouth. Above this were two small knots that did nicely for eyes. The Sawhorse was the favorite steed of Ozma and to prevent its wooden legs from wearing out she had them shod with plates of gold.

Jack said "Good morning" to the Sawhorse and placed upon the creature's back a saddle of purple leather, studded with jewels.

"Where now?" asked the horse, blinking its knot eyes at Jack.

"We're going to rescue two babes in the wood," was the reply. Then he climbed into the saddle and the wooden animal pranced out of the stable, through the streets of the Emerald City and out upon the highway leading to the western forest where the children were lost.

Small though he was, the Sawhorse was swift and untiring. By nightfall they were in the far west and quite close to the forest they sought. They passed the night standing quietly by the roadside. They needed no food, for their wooden bodies never became hungry; nor did they sleep, because they never tired. At daybreak they continued their journey and soon reached the forest.

Jack now examined the map Ozma had given him and found the right path to take, which the Sawhorse obediently followed. Underneath the trees all was silent and gloomy and Jack beguiled the way by whistling gayly as the Sawhorse trotted along.

The paths branched so many times and in so many different ways that the Pumpkinhead was often obliged to consult Ozma's map, and finally the Sawhorse became suspicious.

"Are you sure you are right?" it asked.

"Of course," answered Jack. "Even a Pumpkinhead whose brains are seeds can follow so clear a map as this. Every path is plainly marked, and here is a cross where the children are."

Finally they reached a place, in the very heart of the forest, where they came upon the lost boy and girl. But they found the two children bound fast to the trunk of a big tree, at the foot of which they were sitting.

When the rescuers arrived, the little girl was sobbing bitterly and the boy was trying to comfort her, though he was probably frightened as much as she.

"Cheer up, my dears," said Jack, getting out of the saddle. "I have come to take you back to your parents. But why are you bound to that tree?"

"Because," cried a small, sharp voice, "they are thieves and robbers. That's why!"

"Dear me!" said Jack, looking around to see who had spoken. The voice seemed to come from above.

A big grey squirrel was sitting upon a low branch of the tree. Upon the squirrel's head was a circle of gold, with a diamond set in the center of it. He was running up and down the limbs and chattering excitedly.

"These children," continued the squirrel, angrily, "robbed our storehouse of all the nuts we had saved up for winter. Therefore, being King of all the Squirrels in this forest, I ordered them arrested and put in prison, as you now see them. They had no right to steal our provisions and we are going to punish them."

"We were hungry," said the boy, pleadingly, "and we found a hollow tree full of nuts, and ate them to keep alive. We didn't want to starve when there was food right in front of us."

"Quite right," remarked Jack, nodding his pumpkin head. "I don't blame you one bit, under the circumstances. Not a bit."

Then he began to untie the ropes that bound the children to the tree.

"Stop that!" cried the King Squirrel, chattering and whisking about. "You mustn't release our prisoners. You have no right to."

But Jack paid no attention to the protest. His wooden fingers were awkward and it took him some time to untie the ropes. When at last he succeeded, the tree was full of squirrels, called together by their King, and they were furious at losing their prisoners. From the tree they began to hurl nuts at the Pumpkinhead, who laughed at them as he helped the two children to their feet.

Now, at the top of this tree was a big dead limb, and so many squirrels gathered upon it that suddenly it broke away and fell to the ground. Poor Jack was standing directly under it and when the limb struck him it smashed his pumpkin head into a pulpy mass and sent Jack's wooden form tumbling, to stop with a bump against a tree a dozen feet away.

He sat up, a moment afterward, but when he felt for his head it was gone. He could not see; neither could he speak. It was perhaps the greatest misfortune that could have happened to Jack Pumpkinhead, and the squirrels were delighted. They danced around in the tree in great glee as they saw Jack's plight.

The boy and girl were indeed free, but their protector was ruined. The Sawhorse was there, however, and in his way he was wise. He had seen the accident and knew that the smashed pumpkin would never again serve Jack as a head. So he said to the children, who were frightened at this accident to their newfound friend:

"Pick up the Pumpkinhead's body and set it on my saddle. Then mount behind it and hold on. We must get out of this forest as soon as we can, or the squirrels may capture you again. I must guess at the right path, for Jack's map is no lon-

ger of any use to him since that limb destroyed his head."

The two children lifted Jack's body, which was not at all heavy, and placed it upon the saddle. Then they climbed up behind it and the Sawhorse immediately turned and trotted back along the path he had come, bearing all three with ease. However, when the path began to branch into many paths, all following different directions, the wooden animal became puzzled and soon was wandering aimlessly about, without any hope of finding the right way. Toward evening they came upon a fine fruit tree, which furnished the children a supper, and at night the little ones lay upon a bed of leaves while the Sawhorse stood watch, with the limp, headless form of poor Jack Pumpkinhead lying helpless across the saddle.

Now, Ozma had seen in her Magic Picture all that had happened in the forest, so she sent the little Wizard, mounted upon the Cowardly Lion, to save the unfortunates. The Lion knew the forest well and when he reached it he bounded straight through the tangled paths to where the Sawhorse was wandering, with Jack and the two children on his back.

The Wizard was grieved at the sight of the headless Jack, but believed he could save him. He first led the Sawhorse out of the forest and restored the boy and girl to the arms of their anxious friends, and then he sent the Lion back to Ozma to tell her what had happened.

The Wizard now mounted the Sawhorse and supported Jack's form on the long ride to the pumpkin field. When they arrived at Jack's house the Wizard selected a fine pumpkin—not too ripe—and very neatly carved a face on it. Then he stuck the pumpkin solidly on Jack's neck and asked him:

"Well, old friend, how do you feel?"

"Fine!" replied Jack, and shook the hand of the little Wizard gratefully. "You have really saved my life, for without your assistance I could not have found my way home to get a new head. But I'm all right, now, and I shall be very careful not to get this beautiful head smashed." And he shook the Wizard's hand again.

"Are the brains in the new head any better than the old ones?" inquired the Sawhorse, who had watched Jack's restoration.

"Why, these seeds are quite tender," replied the Wizard, "so they will give our friend tender thoughts. But, to speak truly, my dear Sawhorse, Jack Pumpkinhead, with all his good qualities, will never be noted for his wisdom."

Edgar Rice Burroughs (1875–1950) was a prolific American writer who contributed greatly to the adventure and science fiction genres. Before he began his writing career, Burroughs served his country as a cowboy, a gold miner, and a railroad policeman. He even applied for a position in the Chinese Army; his application was promptly rejected. Interestingly, Burroughs failed at everything he did until the day he submitted a partial manuscript to *All-Story Magazine* in 1911. *Under the Moons of Mars*, his first story starring Captain John Carter, is still acclaimed as the turning point in twentieth-century science fiction, and he continued his masterpiece with the sequel *The Gods of Mars*, another thrilling science-fantasy adventure in the series. "The Plant Men" (1913) is the first chapter of this book.

The Plant Men

(EXCERPT FROM *THE GODS OF MARS*)

Edgar Rice Burroughs

AS I STOOD UPON THE BLUFF before my cottage on that clear cold night in the early part of March, 1886, the noble Hudson flowing like the gray and silent specter of a dead river below me, I felt again the strange, compelling influence of the mighty god of war, my beloved Mars, which for ten long and lonesome years I had implored with outstretched arms to carry me back to my lost love.

Not since that other March night in 1866, when I had stood without that Arizona cave in which my still and lifeless body lay wrapped in the similitude of earthly death had I felt the irresistible attraction of the god of my profession.

With arms outstretched toward the red eye of the great star I stood praying for a return of that strange power which twice had drawn me through the immensity of space, praying as I had prayed on a thousand nights before during the long ten years that I had waited and hoped.

Suddenly a qualm of nausea swept over me, my senses swam, my knees gave beneath me, and I pitched headlong to the ground upon the very verge of the dizzy bluff.

Instantly my brain cleared and there swept back across the threshold of my memory the vivid picture of the horrors of that ghostly Arizona cave; again, as on that far-gone night, my muscles refused to respond to my will and again, as though even here upon the banks of the placid Hudson, I could hear the awful moans and rustling of the fearsome thing which had lurked and threatened me from the dark recesses of the cave, I made the same mighty and superhuman effort to break the bonds of the strange anaesthesia which held me, and again came the sharp click as of the sudden parting of a taut wire, and I stood naked and free beside the staring, lifeless thing that had so recently pulsed with the warm, red lifeblood of John Carter.

With scarcely a parting glance I turned my eyes again toward Mars, lifted my hands toward his lurid rays, and waited.

Nor did I have long to wait; for scarce had I turned ere I shot with the rapidity of thought into the awful void before me. There was the same instant of unthinkable cold and utter darkness that I had experienced twenty years before, and then I opened my eyes in another world, beneath the burning rays of a hot sun, which beat through a tiny opening in the dome of the mighty forest in which I lay.

The scene that met my eyes was so un-Martian that my heart sprang to my throat as the sudden fear swept through me that I had been aimlessly tossed upon some strange planet by a cruel fate.

Why not? What guide had I through the track-less waste of interplanetary space? What assur-ance that I might not as well be hurtled to some far-distant star of another solar system, as to Mars?

I lay upon a close-cropped sward of red grass-like vegetation, and about me stretched a grove of strange and beautiful trees, covered with huge and gorgeous blossoms and filled with brilliant, voiceless birds. I call them birds since they were winged, but mortal eye ne'er rested on such odd, unearthly shapes.

The vegetation was similar to that which cov-ers the lawns of the red Martians of the great waterways, but the trees and birds were unlike anything that I had ever seen upon Mars, and then through the further trees I could see that most un-Martian of all sights—an open sea, its blue waters shimmering beneath the brazen sun.

As I rose to investigate further I experienced the same ridiculous catastrophe that had met my first attempt to walk under Martian conditions. The lesser attraction of this smaller planet and the reduced air pressure of its greatly rarefied atmosphere, afforded so little resistance to my earthly muscles that the ordinary exertion of the mere act of rising sent me several feet into the air and precipitated me upon my face in the soft and brilliant grass of this strange world.

This experience, however, gave me some slightly increased assurance that, after all, I might indeed be in some, to me, unknown corner of Mars, and this was very possible since during my ten years' residence upon the planet I had explored but a comparatively tiny area of its vast expanse.

I arose again, laughing at my forgetfulness, and soon had mastered once more the art of attuning my earthly sinews to these changed conditions.

As I walked slowly down the imperceptible slope toward the sea I could not help but note the park-like appearance of the sward and trees. The grass was as close-cropped and carpet-like as some old English lawn and the trees themselves showed evidence of careful pruning to a uniform height of about fifteen feet from the ground, so that as one turned his glance in any direction the forest had the appearance at a little distance of a vast, high-ceiled chamber.

All these evidences of careful and systematic cultivation convinced me that I had been fortu-nate enough to make my entry into Mars on this second occasion through the domain of a civi-lized people and that when I should find them I would be accorded the courtesy and protection that my rank as a Prince of the house of Tardos Mors entitled me to.

The trees of the forest attracted my deep admiration as I proceeded toward the sea. Their great stems, some of them fully a hundred feet in diameter, attested their prodigious height, which I could only guess at, since at no point could I penetrate their dense foliage above me to more than sixty or eighty feet.

As far aloft as I could see the stems and branches and twigs were as smooth and as highly polished as the newest of American-made pianos. The wood of some of the trees was as black as ebony, while their nearest neighbors might perhaps gleam in the subdued light of the forest as clear and white as the finest china, or, again, they were azure, scarlet, yellow, or deepest purple.

And in the same way was the foliage as gay and variegated as the stems, while the blooms that clustered thick upon them may not be described in any earthly tongue, and indeed might challenge the language of the gods.

As I neared the confines of the forest I beheld before me and between the grove and the open sea, a broad expanse of meadow land, and as I was about to emerge from the shadows of the trees a sight met my eyes that banished all romantic and poetic reflection upon the beauties of the strange landscape.

To my left the sea extended as far as the eye could reach, before me only a vague, dim line indicated its further shore, while at my right a mighty river, broad, placid, and majestic, flowed between scarlet banks to empty into the quiet sea before me.

At a little distance up the river rose mighty perpendicular bluffs, from the very base of which the great river seemed to rise.

But it was not these inspiring and magnificent evidences of Nature's grandeur that took my immediate attention from the beauties of the forest. It was the sight of a score of figures moving slowly about the meadow near the bank of the mighty river.

Odd, grotesque shapes they were; unlike anything that I had ever seen upon Mars, and yet, at a distance, most manlike in appearance. The larger specimens appeared to be about ten or twelve feet in height when they stood erect, and to be proportioned as to torso and lower extremities precisely as is earthly man.

Their arms, however, were very short, and from where I stood seemed as though fashioned much after the manner of an elephant's trunk, in that they moved in sinuous and snakelike undulations, as though entirely without bony structure, or if there were bones it seemed that they must be vertebral in nature.

As I watched them from behind the stem of a huge tree, one of the creatures moved slowly in my direction, engaged in the occupation that seemed to be the principal business of each of them, and which consisted in running their oddly shaped hands over the surface of the sward, for what purpose I could not determine.

As he approached quite close to me I obtained an excellent view of him, and though I was later to become better acquainted with his kind, I may say that that single cursory examination of this awful travesty on Nature would have proved quite sufficient to my desires had I been a free agent. The fastest flier of the Heliumetic Navy could not quickly enough have carried me far from this hideous creature.

Its hairless body was a strange and ghoulish blue, except for a broad band of white which encircled its protruding, single eye: an eye that was all dead white—pupil, iris, and ball.

Its nose was a ragged, inflamed, circular hole in the centre of its blank face; a hole that resembled more closely nothing that I could think of other than a fresh bullet wound which has not yet commenced to bleed.

Below this repulsive orifice the face was quite blank to the chin, for the thing had no mouth that I could discover.

The head, with the exception of the face, was covered by a tangled mass of jet-black hair some eight or ten inches in length. Each hair was about the bigness of a large angleworm, and as the thing moved the muscles of its scalp this awful head-covering seemed to writhe and wriggle and crawl about the fearsome face as though indeed each separate hair was endowed with independent life.

The body and the legs were as symmetrically human as Nature could have fashioned them, and the feet, too, were human in shape, but of monstrous proportions. From heel to toe they were fully three feet long, and very flat and very broad.

As it came quite close to me I discovered that its strange movements, running its odd hands over the surface of the turf, were the result of its peculiar method of feeding, which consists in cropping off the tender vegetation with its razor-like talons and sucking it up from its two mouths, which lie one in the palm of each hand, through its arm-like throats.

In addition to the features which I have already described, the beast was equipped with a massive tail about six feet in length, quite round where it joined the body, but tapering to a flat, thin blade toward the end, which trailed at right angles to the ground.

By far the most remarkable feature of this most remarkable creature, however, were the two tiny replicas of it, each about six inches in length, which dangled, one on either side, from its armpits. They were suspended by a small stem which seemed to grow from the exact tops of their heads to where it connected them with the body of the adult.

Whether they were the young, or merely portions of a composite creature, I did not know.

As I had been scrutinizing this weird monstrosity the balance of the herd had fed quite close to me and I now saw that while many had the smaller specimens dangling from them, not all were thus equipped, and I further noted that the little ones varied in size from what appeared to be but tiny unopened buds an inch in diameter through various stages of development to the full-fledged and perfectly formed creature of ten to twelve inches in length.

Feeding with the herd were many of the little fellows not much larger than those which remained attached to their parents, and from the young of that size the herd graded up to the immense adults.

Fearsome-looking as they were, I did not know whether to fear them or not, for they did not seem to be particularly well equipped for fighting, and I was on the point of stepping from my hiding-place and revealing myself to them to note the effect upon them of the sight of a man when my rash resolve was, fortunately for me, nipped in the bud by a strange shrieking wail, which seemed to come from the direction of the bluffs at my right.

Naked and unarmed, as I was, my end would have been both speedy and horrible at the hands of these cruel creatures had I had time to put my resolve into execution, but at the moment of the shriek each member of the herd turned in the direction from which the sound seemed to come, and at the same instant every particular snake-like hair upon their heads rose stiffly perpendicular as if each had been a sentient organism looking or listening for the source or meaning of the wail. And indeed the latter proved to be the truth, for this strange growth upon the craniums of the plant men of Barsoom represents the thousand ears of these hideous creatures, the last remnant of the strange race which sprang from the original Tree of Life.

Instantly every eye turned toward one member of the herd, a large fellow who evidently was the leader. A strange purring sound issued from the mouth in the palm of one of his hands, and at the same time he started rapidly toward the bluff, followed by the entire herd.

Their speed and method of locomotion were both remarkable, springing as they did in great leaps of twenty or thirty feet, much after the manner of a kangaroo.

They were rapidly disappearing when it occurred to me to follow them, and so, hurling caution to the winds, I sprang across the meadow in their wake with leaps and bounds even more prodigious than their own, for the muscles of an athletic Earth man produce remarkable results when pitted against the lesser gravity and air pressure of Mars.

Their way led directly toward the apparent source of the river at the base of the cliffs, and as I neared this point I found the meadow dotted with huge boulders that the ravages of time had evidently dislodged from the towering crags above.

For this reason I came quite close to the cause of the disturbance before the scene broke upon my horrified gaze. As I topped a great boulder I saw the herd of plant men surrounding a little group of perhaps five or six green men and women of Barsoom.

That I was indeed upon Mars I now had no

doubt, for here were members of the wild hordes that people the dead sea bottoms and deserted cities of that dying planet.

Here were the great males towering in all the majesty of their imposing height; here were the gleaming white tusks protruding from their massive lower jaws to a point near the center of their foreheads, the laterally placed, protruding eyes with which they could look forward or backward, or to either side without turning their heads, here the strange antennae–like ears rising from the tops of their foreheads; and the additional pair of arms extending from midway between the shoulders and the hips.

Even without the glossy green hide and the metal ornaments which denoted the tribes to which they belonged, I would have known them on the instant for what they were, for where else in all the universe is their like duplicated?

There were two men and four females in the party and their ornaments denoted them as members of different hordes, a fact which tended to puzzle me infinitely, since the various hordes of green men of Barsoom are eternally at deadly war with one another, and never, except on that single historic instance when the great Tars Tarkas of Thark gathered a hundred and fifty thousand green warriors from several hordes to march upon the doomed city of Zodanga to rescue Dejah Thoris, Princess of Helium, from the clutches of Than Kosis, had I seen green Martians of different hordes associated in other than mortal combat.

But now they stood back to back, facing, in wide-eyed amazement, the very evidently hostile demonstrations of a common enemy.

Both men and women were armed with long-swords and daggers, but no firearms were in evidence, else it had been short shrift for the gruesome plant men of Barsoom.

Presently the leader of the plant men charged the little party, and his method of attack was as remarkable as it was effective, and by its very strangeness was the more potent, since in the science of the green warriors there was no defense for this singular manner of attack, the like of which it soon was evident to me they were as unfamiliar with as they were with the monstrosities which confronted them.

The plant man charged to within a dozen feet of the party and then, with a bound, rose as though to pass directly above their heads. His powerful tail was raised high to one side, and as he passed close above them he brought it down in one terrific sweep that crushed a green warrior's skull as though it had been an eggshell.

The balance of the frightful herd was now circling rapidly and with bewildering speed about the little knot of victims. Their prodigious bounds and the shrill, screeching purr of their uncanny mouths were well calculated to confuse and terrorize their prey, so that as two of them leaped simultaneously from either side, the mighty sweep of those awful tails met with no resistance and two more green Martians went down to an ignoble death.

There were now but one warrior and two females left, and it seemed that it could be but a matter of seconds ere these, also, lay dead upon the scarlet sward.

But as two more of the plant men charged, the warrior, who was now prepared by the experiences of the past few minutes, swung his mighty long-sword aloft and met the hurtling bulk with a clean cut that clove one of the plant men from chin to groin.

The other, however, dealt a single blow with his cruel tail that laid both of the females crushed corpses upon the ground.

As the green warrior saw the last of his companions go down and at the same time perceived that the entire herd was charging him in a body, he rushed boldly to meet them, swinging his long-sword in the terrific manner that I had so often seen the men of his kind wield it in their ferocious and almost continual warfare among their own race.

Cutting and hewing to right and left, he laid an open path straight through the advancing plant men, and then commenced a mad race for the forest, in the shelter of which he evidently hoped that he might find a haven of refuge.

He had turned for that portion of the forest which abutted on the cliffs, and thus the mad race was taking the entire party farther and farther from the boulder where I lay concealed.

As I had watched the noble fight which the great warrior had put up against such enormous odds my heart had swelled in admiration for him, and acting as I am wont to do, more upon impulse than after mature deliberation, I instantly sprang from my sheltering rock and bounded quickly toward the bodies of the dead green Martians, a well-defined plan of action already formed.

Half a dozen great leaps brought me to the spot, and another instant saw me again in my stride in quick pursuit of the hideous monsters that were rapidly gaining on the fleeing warrior, but this time I grasped a mighty long-sword in my hand and in my heart was the old blood lust of the fighting man, and a red mist swam before my eyes and I felt my lips respond to my heart in the old smile that has ever marked me in the midst of the joy of battle.

Swift as I was I was none too soon, for the green warrior had been overtaken ere he had made half the distance to the forest, and now he stood with his back to a boulder, while the herd, temporarily balked, hissed and screeched about him.

With their single eyes in the center of their heads and every eye turned upon their prey, they did not note my soundless approach, so that I was upon them with my great long-sword and four of them lay dead ere they knew that I was among them.

For an instant they recoiled before my terrific onslaught, and in that instant the green warrior rose to the occasion and, springing to my side, laid to the right and left of him as I had never seen but one other warrior do, with great circling strokes that formed a figure eight about him and that never stopped until none stood living to oppose him, his keen blade passing through flesh and bone and metal as though each had been alike thin air.

As we bent to the slaughter, far above us rose that shrill, weird cry which I had heard once before, and which had called the herd to the attack upon their victims. Again and again it rose, but we were too much engaged with the fierce and powerful creatures about us to attempt to search out even with our eyes the author of the horrid notes.

Great tails lashed in frenzied anger about us, razor-like talons cut our limbs and bodies, and a green and sticky syrup, such as oozes from a crushed caterpillar, smeared us from head to foot, for every cut and thrust of our longswords brought spurts of this stuff upon us from the severed arteries of the plant men, through which it courses in its sluggish viscidity in lieu of blood.

Once I felt the great weight of one of the monsters upon my back and as keen talons sank into my flesh I experienced the frightful sensation of moist lips sucking the lifeblood from the wounds to which the claws still clung.

I was very much engaged with a ferocious fellow who was endeavouring to reach my throat from in front, while two more, one on either side, were lashing viciously at me with their tails.

The green warrior was much put to it to hold his own, and I felt that the unequal struggle could last but a moment longer when the huge fellow discovered my plight, and tearing himself from those that surrounded him, he raked the assailant from my back with a single sweep of his blade, and thus relieved I had little difficulty with the others.

Once together, we stood almost back to back against the great boulder, and thus the creatures were prevented from soaring above us to deliver their deadly blows, and as we were easily their match while they remained upon the ground, we were making great headway in dispatching what remained of them when our attention was again attracted by the shrill wail of the caller above our heads.

This time I glanced up, and far above us upon a little natural balcony on the face of the cliff stood a strange figure of a man shrieking out his shrill signal, the while he waved one hand in the direction of the river's mouth as though beckoning to some one there, and with the other pointed and gesticulated toward us.

A glance in the direction toward which he was looking was sufficient to apprise me of his aims and at the same time to fill me with the dread of dire apprehension, for, streaming in from all directions across the meadow, from out of the forest, and from the far distance of the flat land across the river, I could see converging upon us a hundred different lines of wildly leaping creatures such as we were now engaged with, and with them some strange new monsters which ran with great swiftness, now erect and now upon all fours.

"It will be a great death," I said to my companion. "Look!"

As he shot a quick glance in the direction I indicated he smiled.

"We may at least die fighting and as great warriors should, John Carter," he replied.

We had just finished the last of our immediate antagonists as he spoke, and I turned in surprised wonderment at the sound of my name.

And there before my astonished eyes I beheld the greatest of the green men of Barsoom; their shrewdest statesman, their mightiest general, my great and good friend, Tars Tarkas, Jeddak of Thark.

Hermann Hesse (1877–1962) was a German novelist and poet who explored the power of the individual in discovering their purpose and identity. His 1919 novel, *Demian*, came about as the result of his personal psychoanalysis and placed him on the literary map. Hesse also became intrigued by the idea of the duality of human nature and he explored this idea in various modes of writing. His last novel, *The Glass Bead Game*, was published in 1943, yet he continued to write essays, short stories, and poetry. In 1946, Hesse won a much-deserved Nobel Prize in Literature. "Strange News from Another Star" (1915) was published soon after the start of World War I and combines Hesse's interests in psychology with the reality of the world he was living in.

Strange News from Another Star

Hermann Hesse

IN ONE OF THE SOUTHERN PROVINCES of our beautiful planet there was a horrible catastrophe. An earthquake, accompanied by terrible thunderstorms and floods, caused great destruction to three large villages and all their gardens, fields, forests, and farms. Many people and animals were killed, and saddest of all, the villagers lacked enough flowers to make wreaths for the dead and adorn their graves in the appropriate way.

Of course, the people took care of everything else that had to be done. Immediately after the horrible event, messengers rushed through the neighboring regions carrying pleas for aid and charity, and from all the towers of the entire province, chanters could be heard singing those stirring and deeply touching verses known for ages as the "Salutation to the Goddess of Compassion." It was impossible for anyone listening to these chants to resist them. Large groups of rescuers and helpers came right away from all

the towns and cities, and those unfortunate people who had lost the roofs over their heads were overwhelmed by kind invitations and took refuge in the dwellings of relatives, friends, and strangers. Food and clothes, wagons and horses, tools, stones, and wood, and many other useful things were brought from all over. The old men, women, and children were comforted, consoled, and led away to shelters by kindly hands. The injured were carefully washed and bandaged. And while some people were still searching for victims of the quake under the ruins, others had already begun to clear away the fallen roofs, to prop up the wobbly walls with beams, and to prepare everything necessary for the quick reconstruction of the villages. Still, a cloud of horror from the accident hung in the air, and the dead were a reminder to everyone that this was a time of mourning and austere silence. Yet a joyful readiness and a certain vibrant festive mood could also be detected in all the faces and voices of the people, for they were inspired by their common action and zeal and the certainty that they were all doing something unusual and necessary, something beautiful and deserving of thanks. Initially people had worked in silence and awe, but cheerful voices and the soft sounds of singing could soon be heard here and there. As one might well imagine, two ancient proverbs were among the favorites that were sung: "Blessed are those who bring help to those who have recently been overcome by need. Don't they drink the good deed as a parched garden drinks the first rainfall, and shouldn't they respond with flowers of gratitude?" and "The serenity of God flows from common action."

However, it was just then that they discovered they did not have enough flowers for the burials. To be sure, the first dead bodies to be found had been buried and adorned with flowers and branches gathered from the destroyed gardens. Then the people began fetching all the flowers in the vicinity. But as luck would have it, they were in a special dilemma because the three destroyed villages had been the ones with the largest and most beautiful gardens of flowers during this time of year. It was here that visitors came each year to see the narcissus and crocuses because they could not be found anywhere else in such immense quantities. Moreover, they were always cultivated with great care in remarkably different colors. Yet all this had now been devastated and ruined. So the people were in a quandary—they did not know how to follow the customary rites regarding the burial of the dead. Tradition required that before burial each human being and each animal be adorned lavishly with flowers of the season, and that the burial ritual be all the richer and more resplendent, the more sudden and more sorrowful that death had struck.

The Chief Elder of the province, who was one of the first to appear with help in his wagon, soon found himself so overwhelmed by questions, requests, and complaints that he had difficulty keeping his composure. But he took heart. His eyes remained bright and friendly; his voice was clear and polite; and under his white beard his lips never lost the silent, kind smile for one moment—something that suited him as a wise councilor.

"My friends," he said, "a calamity has struck that was most likely sent by the gods to test us. Of course, whatever has been destroyed here, we shall be able to rebuild for our brothers and give it all back to them, and I thank the gods that I've been able to experience in my old age how you all stopped whatever you were doing and came here to help. But where are we going to find the flowers to adorn all these dead people and celebrate their transformation in a beautiful and reverent manner? As long as we are alive and well, we must make sure that not a single one of these weary pilgrims be buried without their rightful floral tribute. Don't you all agree?"

"Yes," they cried. "We all agree."

"I knew it," said the Elder in his fatherly voice. "Now I want to tell you, my friends, what we must do. We must carry all the remains that cannot be buried today to the large summer temple high in the mountains, where snow is still on the ground. They will be safe there and will not decompose before we can fetch flowers for them. Only one person can really help us obtain so many flowers at this time of the year, and that is the King. Therefore one of us must be sent to the King to request his assistance."

And again the people all nodded and cried out, "Yes, yes, to the King!"

"So be it," the Elder continued, and everyone was pleased to see his pleasant smile glistening from beneath his white beard. "But whom shall we send to the King? He must be young and robust because he shall travel far on our best horse. Furthermore, he must be handsome and kind and have sparkling eyes, so that the King's heart will not be able to resist him. He needn't say much, but his eyes must be able to speak. Clearly, it would be best if we sent a child, the handsomest child in the community. But how could he possibly undertake such a journey? You must help me, my friends, and if there is anyone here who wants to volunteer to be the messenger, or if you know somebody suitable for this task, please tell me."

The Elder stopped and looked around with his bright eyes, but nobody stepped forward. Not a single voice could be heard. When he repeated his question a second and then a third time, a young man suddenly emerged from the crowd. He was sixteen years old, practically still a boy, and he fixed his eyes on the ground and blushed as he greeted the Elder.

As soon as the Elder looked at him, he realized that the young man was the perfect messenger. So he smiled and said, "It's wonderful that you want to be our messenger. But why is it that, among all those people, you should be the one to volunteer?"

The young man raised his eyes to the old man and said, "If there is no one else here who wants to go, then I should be the one to go."

Someone from the crowd shouted, "Send him, Elder. We know him. He comes from our village, and the earthquake destroyed his flower garden, which was the most beautiful in the region."

The Elder gave the young man a friendly look and asked, "Are you sad about what happened to your flowers?"

The young man responded very softly, "Yes, I'm sorry, but that is not why I've volunteered. I had a dear friend and also a splendid young horse, my favorite, and both were killed by the earthquake. Now they are lying in our hall, and we must have flowers so that they can be buried."

The Elder blessed the young man by placing his hands on his head, and the best horse was soon brought out for him. Immediately the young man sprang onto the horse's back, slapped it on the neck, and nodded farewell to the people. Then he dashed out of the village and headed straight across the wet and ravaged fields.

The young man rode the entire day, and in order to reach the distant capital and see the King as soon as he could, he took the path over the mountains. In the evening, as it began to turn dark, he led his horse by the reins up a steep path through the forest and rocks.

A large dark bird, a kind that the young man had never seen before, flew ahead of him, and he followed it until the bird landed on the roof of a small open temple. The young man left his horse and walked through wooden pillars into the simple sanctuary. There he found a sacrificial altar, but it was only a solid block made of a black stone not usually found in that region. On it was an obscure symbol of a deity that the messenger did not recognize—a heart that was being devoured by a wild bird.

He paid tribute to the deity by offering a bluebell flower that he had plucked at the foot of the mountain and stuck in the lapel of his coat. Thereafter he lay down in a corner of the temple, for he was very tired and wanted to sleep.

However, he could not fall asleep as easily as he was accustomed to at home each evening. Perhaps it was the bluebell on the stone, or the black stone itself, or something else, but whatever it was, something odd disturbed him by exuding a penetrating and scintillating aroma. Furthermore, the eerie symbol of the god glimmered like a ghost in the dark hall, and the strange bird sat on the roof and vigorously flapped its gigantic wings from time to time so that it seemed as if a storm were brewing.

Eventually the young man got up in the middle of the night, went outside the temple, and looked up at the bird, which raised and lowered its wings.

"Why aren't you sleeping?" asked the bird.

"I don't know," the young man replied. "Perhaps it's because I've suffered."

"What exactly have you suffered?"

"My friend and my favorite horse were both killed."

"Is dying so bad?" the bird asked disdainfully.

"Oh, no, great bird, it's not so bad. It's only a farewell. But that's not the reason why I'm sad. The bad thing is that we cannot bury my friend and my splendid horse because we no longer have any flowers."

"There are worse things than that," said the bird, ruffling its feathers indignantly.

"No, bird, there is certainly nothing worse than this. Whoever is buried without a floral tribute cannot be reborn the way his heart desires. And whoever buries his dead people without celebrating the floral tribute will continue to see their shadows in his dreams. You see, I already cannot sleep anymore because my dead people are still without flowers."

The bird rasped and screeched with its bent beak, "Young boy, you know nothing about suffering if this is all that you've experienced. Haven't you ever heard about the great evils? About hatred, murder, and jealousy?"

As he listened to these words, the young man thought he was dreaming. Then he collected himself and said discreetly, "Yes, bird, I can remember. These things are written in the old stories and tales. But they have nothing to do with reality, or perhaps it was that way once upon a time in the world before there were flowers and gods that are good. Who in the world still thinks about such things as that now?"

The bird laughed softly with its raspy voice. Then it stretched itself taller and said to the boy, "And now you want to go to the King, and I'm to show you the way?"

"Oh, you already know!" the young man joyfully exclaimed. "Yes, I'd appreciate it if you'd lead me there."

Then the great bird floated silently to the ground, spread out its wings without making a sound, and ordered the young man to leave his horse behind and fly with him to the King. In response, the messenger sat down on the bird's back and prepared himself for the ride.

"Shut your eyes," the bird commanded, and the young man did as he was told, and they flew through the darkness of the sky silently and softly like the flight of an owl. The messenger could hear only the cold wind roaring in his ears, and they flew and flew the entire night.

When it was early morning, they came to a stop, and the bird cried out, "Open your eyes!" The young man opened his eyes and saw that he was standing at the edge of a forest. Beneath him was a plain that glistened so brightly in the early hours that its light blinded him.

"You'll find me here in the forest again," the bird announced, whereupon he shot into the sky like an arrow and soon disappeared into the blue.

A strange feeling came over the young messenger as he began wandering from the forest into the broad plain. Everything around him was so different and changed that he did not know whether he was awake or dreaming. Meadows and trees were just as they were at home. The sun shone, and the wind played in the fresh grass. But there were no people or animals, no houses or gardens to be seen. Rather, it appeared that an earthquake had taken its toll here just as in the young man's home country, for ruins of buildings, broken branches, uprooted trees, wrecked fences, and lost farm equipment were spread all over the ground. Suddenly he saw a dead man lying in the middle of a field. He had not been buried and was horribly decomposed. The young man felt a deep revulsion at the sight of the dead body, and nausea swelled up within him, for he had never seen anything like it. The dead man's face was not even covered and seemed to have already been ravaged by the birds in its decayed condition. So the young man plucked some green leaves and flowers, and with his face turned away, he covered the visage of the dead man with them.

An inexpressible, disgusting, and stifling smell hung in the tepid air and seemed glued to the entire plain. Again the young man saw a corpse lying in the grass, with ravens circling overhead. There was also a horse without its head, and bones from humans and animals, and they all lay abandoned in the sun. There seemed to have been no thought of a floral tribute and burial. The young man feared that an incredible catastrophe had caused the death of every single person in this country, and that there were so many dead that he would never be able to pick enough flowers to cover their faces. Full of dread, with half-closed eyes, he wandered farther. The stench of carrion and blood swept toward him from all sides, and an even stronger wave of unspeakable misery and suffering rose from a thousand different piles of corpses and rubble. The messenger thought that he was caught in an awful dream. Perhaps it was a warning from the divine powers, he thought, because his own dead were still without their floral tribute and burial. Then he recalled what the mysterious bird had said to him the night before on the temple roof, and he thought he heard its sharp voice once more claiming, "There are much worse things."

Now he realized that the bird had carried him to another planet and that everything he saw was real and true. He remembered the feeling he had experienced when he had occasionally listened to ghastly tales of primeval times. It was this same exact feeling that he had now—a horrid chill, and behind the chill a quiet, pleasant feeling of comfort, for all this was infinitely far away from him and had long since passed. Everything here was like a horror story. This whole strange world of atrocity, corpses, and vultures seemed to have no meaning or order. In fact, it seemed subject to incomprehensible laws, insane laws, according to which bad, foolish, and nasty things occurred instead of beautiful and good things.

In the meantime he noticed a live human being walking across the field, a farmer or hired hand, and he ran quickly toward him, calling out. When the young man approached, he was horrified, and his heart was overcome by compassion, for this farmer was terribly ugly and no longer resembled anything like a child of the sun. He seemed more like a man accustomed to thinking only about himself and to seeing only false, ugly, and horrible things happen everywhere, like a man who lived constantly in ghastly nightmares. There was not a trace of serenity or kindness in his eyes and in his entire face and being, no gratitude or trust. This unfortunate creature seemed to be without the least bit of virtue.

But the young man pulled himself together and approached the man with great friendliness, as though the man had been marked by misfortune. He greeted him in brotherly fashion and spoke to him with a smile. The ugly man stood as though paralyzed, looking bewildered with his large, bleary eyes. His voice was rough and without music, like the growl of a primitive creature. But it was impossible for him to resist the young man's cheerful and trustworthy look. And after he had stared at the stranger for a while, the farmer expressed a kind of smile or grin on his rugged and crude face—ugly enough, but gentle and astonished, like the first little smile of a reborn soul that has just risen from the lowest region of the earth.

"What do you want from me?" the man asked the young stranger.

The young man responded according to the custom of his native country: "I thank you, friend, and I beg you to tell me whether I can be of service to you."

When the farmer did not reply but only stared and smiled with embarrassment, the messenger said to him, "Tell me, friend, what is going on here? What are all these horrible and terrible things?" And he pointed all around him.

The farmer had difficulty understanding him, and when the messenger repeated his question, the farmer said, "Haven't you ever seen this before? This is war. This is a battlefield." He pointed to a dark pile of ruins and cried, "That was my house." And when the stranger looked into his murky eyes with deep sympathy, the farmer lowered them and looked down at the ground.

"Don't you have a king?" the young man asked, and when the farmer said yes, he asked further, "Where is he?"

The man pointed to a small, barely visible encampment in the distance. The messenger said farewell by placing his hand on the man's forehead, then departed. In response, the farmer felt his forehead with both hands, shook his heavy head with concern, and stared after the stranger for a long time.

The messenger walked and walked over rubble and past horrifying sights until he arrived at the encampment. Armed men were standing here and there or scurrying about. Nobody seemed to notice him, and he walked between the people and the tents until he found the largest and most beautiful tent, which belonged to the King. Once there, he entered.

The King was sitting on a simple low cot inside the tent. Next to him lay his coat, and behind him in deep shadow crouched his servant, who had fallen asleep. The King himself sat bent over in deep thought. His face was handsome and sad; a crop of gray hair hung over his tan forehead. His sword lay before him on the ground.

The young man greeted the King silently with sincere respect, just as he would have greeted his own King, and he remained standing with his arms folded across his chest until the King glanced at him.

"Who are you?" he asked severely, drawing his dark eyebrows together, but his glance focused on the pure and serene features of the stranger, and the young man regarded him with such trust and friendliness that the King's voice grew milder.

"I've seen you once before," he said, trying to recall. "You resemble somebody I knew in my childhood."

"I'm a stranger," said the messenger.

"Then it was a dream," remarked the King softly. "You remind me of my mother. Say something to me. Tell me why you are here."

The young man began: "A bird brought me here. There was an earthquake in my country. We want to bury our dead, but there are no flowers."

"No flowers?" said the King.

"No, no more flowers at all. And it's terrible, isn't it, when people want to bury their dead and the floral tribute cannot be celebrated? After all, it's important for people to experience their transformation in glory and joy."

Suddenly it occurred to the messenger that there were many dead people on the horrible field who had not yet been buried, and he held his breath while the King regarded him, nodded, and sighed deeply.

"I wanted to seek out our King and request that he send us many flowers," the messenger continued. "But as I was in the temple on the mountain, a great bird came and said he wanted to bring me to the King, and he carried me through the skies to you. Oh, dear King, it was the temple

of an unknown deity on whose roof the bird sat, and this god had a most peculiar symbol on his altar—a heart that was being devoured by a wild bird. During the night, however, I had a conversation with that great bird, and it is only now that I understand its words, for it said that there is much more suffering and many more terrible things in the world than I knew. And now I am here and have crossed the large field and have seen endless suffering and misfortune during this short time—oh, much more than there is in our most horrible tales. So now I've come to you, oh King, and I would like to ask you if I can be of any service to you."

The King, who listened attentively, tried to smile, but his handsome face was so serious and bitter and sad that he could not.

"I thank you," he said. "You've already been of service to me. You've reminded me of my mother. I thank you for this."

The young man was disturbed because the King could not smile. "You're so sad," he said. "Is it because of this war?"

"Yes," said the King.

The young man had the feeling that the King was a noble man who was deeply depressed, and he could not refrain from breaking a rule of courtesy and asking him a straightforward question: "But tell me, please, why are you waging such wars on your planet? Who's to blame for all this? Are you yourself responsible?"

The King stared at the messenger for a long time. He seemed indignant and angry at the audacity of this question. However, he was not able to maintain his gloomy look as he peered into the bright and innocent eyes of the stranger.

"You're a child," said the King, "and there are things that you can't understand. The war is nobody's fault. It occurs by itself, like thunder and lightning. All of us who must fight wars are not the perpetrators. We are only their victims."

"Then you must all die very easily?" the young man asked. "In my country death is not at all feared, and most people go willingly to their death. Many approach their transformation with joy. But nobody would ever dare to kill another human being. It must be different on your planet."

"People are indeed killed here," said the King, shaking his head. "But we consider it the worst of crimes. Only in war are people permitted to kill because nobody kills for his own advantage. Nobody kills out of hate or envy. Rather, they do what society demands of them. Still, you'd be mistaken if you believed that my people die easily. You just have to look into the faces of our dead, and you can see that they have difficulty dying. They die hard and unwillingly."

The young man listened to all this and was astounded by the sadness and gravity in the lives of the people on this planet. He would have liked to ask many more questions, but he had a clear sense that he would never grasp the complex nature of all these obscure and terrible things. Indeed, he felt no great desire now to understand them. Either these sorrowful people were creatures of an inferior order, or they had not been blessed by the light of the gods and were still ruled by demons. Or perhaps a singular mishap was determining the course of life on this planet. It seemed to him much too painful and cruel to keep questioning the King, compelling him to provide answers and make confessions that could only be bitter and humiliating for him. He was sorry for these people—people who lived in gloom and dread of death and nevertheless killed each other in droves. These people, whose faces took on ignoble, crude countenances like that of the farmer, or who had expressions of deep and terrible sorrow like that of the King. They seemed to him to be rather peculiar—and almost ridiculous, to be ridiculous and foolish in a disturbing and shameful way.

There was one more question, however, that the young man could not repress. Even if these poor creatures were backward, children behind the times, sons of a latter-day planet without peace; even if their lives ran their course as a convulsive cramp and ended in desperate slaughter; even if they let their dead lie on the fields and perhaps even ate them—for horror tales were told about such things occurring in primeval

times—they must still have a presentiment of the future, a dream of the gods, some spark of soul in them. Otherwise this entire unpleasant world would be only a meaningless mistake.

"Forgive me, King," the young man said with a flattering voice. "Forgive me if I ask you one more question before I leave your strange country."

"Go ahead," replied the King, who was perplexed by this stranger, for the young man seemed to have a sensitive, mature, and insightful mind in many ways, but in others he seemed to be a small child whom one had to protect and was not to be taken seriously.

"My foreign King," spoke the messenger, "you've made me sad. You see, I've come from another country, and the great bird on the temple roof was right. There is infinitely more misery here than I could have imagined. Your life seems to be a dreadful nightmare, and I don't know whether you are ruled by gods or demons. You see, King, we have a legend—I used to believe that it was all fairy-tale rubbish and empty smoke. It is a legend about how such things as war and death and despair were common in our country at one time. These terrible words, which we have long since stopped using in our language, can be read in collections of our old tales, and they sound awful to us and even a little ridiculous. Today I've learned that these tales are all true, and I see you and your people dying and suffering what I've known only from the terrible legends of primeval times. But now tell me, don't you have in your soul a sort of intimation that you're not doing the right thing? Don't you have a yearning for bright, serene gods, for sensible and cheerful leaders and mentors? Don't you ever dream in your sleep about another, more beautiful life where nobody is envious of others, where reason and order prevail, where people treat other people only with cheerfulness and consideration? Have you never thought that the world might be a totality, and that it might be beneficial and salutary to honor this unity of all things? Don't you know anything about what we at home call music and divine worship and blessedness?"

As he listened to these words, the King's head sank, and when he raised it again, his face had been transformed, and it glowed radiantly with a smile, even though there were tears in his eyes.

"Beautiful boy," said the King, "I don't know for certain whether you're a child, a sage, or perhaps a god. But I can tell you that we sense all this and cradle it in our souls, all that you have mentioned. We have intimations of happiness, freedom, and gods. Indeed, we have a legend about a wise man who lived long ago and who perceived the unity of the worlds as harmonious music of the heavenly spheres. Does this answer suffice? You may be, you see, a blessed creature from another world, or you may even be God Himself. Whatever the case may be, you have no happiness in your heart, no power, no will that does not live as a presentiment, a reflection, a distant shadow in our hearts, too."

Suddenly the King stood up, and the young man was surprised, for the King's face was soaked in a bright, clear smile for a moment like the first rays of the sun.

"Go now," he cried to the messenger. "Go, and let us fight and murder! You've made my heart soft. You've reminded me of my mother. Enough, enough of this, you dear handsome boy. Go now, and flee before the next battle begins! I'll think of you when the blood flows and the cities burn, and I'll think of the world as a whole, and how our folly and fury and ruthlessness cannot separate us from it. Farewell, and give my regards to your planet, and give my regards to your deity, whose symbol is a heart being devoured by a wild bird. I know this heart, and I know the bird very well. And don't forget, my handsome friend from a distant land: When you think of your friend, the poor King in war, do not think of him as he sat on the cot plunged in deep sorrow. Think of him with tears in his eyes and blood on his hands and how he smiled!"

The King raised the flap of the tent with his own hand so as not to wake the servant, and he let the stranger out. The young man crossed the plain again steeped in thought, and as he went, he saw a large city blazing in flames on the horizon

in the evening light. He climbed over dead people and the decayed carcasses of horses until it grew dark and he reached the edge of the forest.

Suddenly the great bird swooped down from the clouds and took the young man on its wings, and they flew through the night silently and softly like the flight of the owl.

When the young man awoke from a restless sleep, he lay in the small temple in the mountains, and his horse stood before the temple in the wet grass, greeting the day with a neigh. However, the messenger recalled nothing of the great bird and his flight to a foreign planet, nothing of the King and the battlefield. All this remained only as a shadow in his soul, a tiny, obscure pain, as if from a sharp thorn. It hurt, just as sympathy hurts when nothing can be done, just as a little unfulfilled wish can torment us in dreams until we finally encounter the person we have secretly loved, with whom we want to share our joy and whose smile we wish to see.

The messenger mounted his horse and rode the entire day until he came to the capital, where he was admitted to the King. And he proved to be the right messenger, for the King received him with a greeting of grace by touching his forehead and remarking, "Your request was fulfilled before I even heard it."

Soon thereafter the messenger received a charter from the King that placed all the flowers of the whole country at his command. Companions and messengers went with him to the villages to pick them up. Joined by wagons and horses, they took a few days to go around the mountain on the flat country road that led back to his province and community. The young man led the wagons and carts, horses and donkeys, all loaded with the most beautiful flowers from gardens and greenhouses that were plentiful in the north. There were enough flowers to place wreaths on the bodies of the dead and to adorn their graves lavishly, as well as enough to plant a memorial flower, a bush, and a young tree for each dead person, as custom demanded. And the pain caused by the death of his friend and his favorite horse subsided in the young man and turned into silent, serene memories after he adorned and buried them and planted two flowers, two bushes, and two fruit trees over their graves.

Now that he had done what he had desired and fulfilled his obligations, the memory of that journey through the night began to stir in his soul, and he asked his friends and relatives to permit him to spend a day all alone. So he sat under the Tree of Contemplation one whole day and night. There he unfolded, clean and unwrinkled in his memory, the images of all that he had seen on the foreign planet. One day later on, he went to the Elder, requested a private talk with him, and told him all that had happened.

The Elder sat and pondered everything as he listened. Then he asked, "Did you see all this with your eyes, my friend, or was it a dream?"

"I don't know," said the young man. "I believe that it may have been a dream. However, with your permission, may I say that it seems to me there is hardly a difference whether I actually experienced everything in reality. A shadow of sadness has remained within me, and a cool wind from that other planet continues to blow upon me, right into the midst of the happiness of my life. That is why I am asking you, my honorable Elder, what to do about this."

"Return to the mountains tomorrow," the Elder said, "and go up to the place where you found the temple. The symbol of that god seems odd to me, for I've never heard of it before. It may well be that he is a god from another planet. Or perhaps the temple and its god are so old that they belong to the epoch of our earliest ancestors, to those days when there are supposed to have been weapons, fear, and dread of death among us. Go to that temple, my dear boy, and bring flowers, honey, and song."

The young man thanked the Elder and followed his advice. He took a bowl of honey, such as was customarily presented to honored guests at the first festival of the bees in early summer, and carried his lute with him. In the mountains he found the place where he had once picked the bluebell, and he found the steep rocky path in the forest that led up the mountain, where he had recently gone on foot leading his horse. However, he could not find the place of the temple or the temple itself, the black sacrificial stone, the wooden pillars, the roof, or the great bird on the roof. He could not find them on that day, nor on the next, and nobody he asked knew anything about the kind of temple that he described. So he returned to his home, and when he walked by the Shrine of Lovely Memories, he went inside and offered the honey, played the lute and sang, and told the god of lovely memories all about his dream, the temple and the bird, the poor farmer, and the dead bodies on the battlefield. And most of all, he told about the King in his war tent. Afterward he returned to his dwelling with a light heart, hung the symbol of the unity of the world in his bedroom, and recuperated from the events of the past few days in deep sleep. The next morning he helped his neighbors remove the last traces of the earthquake from the gardens and fields, singing as they worked.

Franz Kafka (1883–1924) was a Jewish novelist born in what is now the Czech Republic, although he wrote in German. Before his death, Kafka asked that all his unpublished works be destroyed but his literary executor, the writer Max Brod, ignored his wishes and published many instead. If Brod had listened, the world would have never known the novels *The Trial* (1925), *The Castle* (1926), or *Amerika* (1927). Kafka did not publish much during his lifetime due to his job at an insurance company; he simply did not have as much time as he would have liked to write, and at the time he died in 1924 was underappreciated by the literary community. *The Metamorphosis* is by far his most renowned work. The novella has been made into a play and a comic by R. Crumb, and in 2009 it was adapted into a film told from the eyes of Elsa, Gregor's older sister.

The Metamorphosis

Franz Kafka

Translated by Ian Johnston

ONE MORNING, as Gregor Samsa was waking up from anxious dreams, he discovered that in his bed he had been changed into a monstrous verminous bug. He lay on his armor-hard back and saw, as he lifted his head up a little, his brown, arched abdomen divided up into rigid bow-like sections. His blanket perched high on this belly could hardly stay in place; it seemed about to slide off completely. His numerous legs, pitifully thin in comparison to the rest of his circumference, flickered helplessly before his eyes.

"What's happened to me?" he thought. It was no dream. His room, a proper room for a human being, only somewhat too small, lay quietly between the four well-known walls. Above the table, on which an unpacked collection of sample cloth goods was spread out—Samsa was a trav-

eling salesman—hung the picture which he had cut out of an illustrated magazine a little while ago and set in a pretty gilt frame. It was a picture of a woman with a fur hat and a fur boa. She sat erect, lifting up in the direction of the viewer a solid fur muff into which her entire forearm had disappeared.

Gregor's glance then turned to the window. The dreary weather—you could hear the raindrops falling on the metal window ledge—made him quite melancholy. "Why don't I keep sleeping for a little while longer and forget all this foolishness?" he thought. But this was entirely impractical, for he was used to sleeping on his right side; and in his present state he could not get himself into this position. No matter how hard he threw himself onto his right side, he always rolled onto his back again. He must have tried it a hundred times, closing his eyes so that he would not have to see the wriggling legs, and gave up only when he began to feel a light, dull pain in his side that he had never felt before.

"O God," he thought, "what a demanding job I've chosen! Day in, day out, on the road. The stresses of selling are much greater than the actual work going on at head office, and, in addition to that, I still have to cope with the problems of traveling, the worries about train connections, irregular bad food, temporary and constantly changing human interactions, which never come from the heart. To hell with it all!" He felt a slight itching on the top of his abdomen. He slowly pushed himself on his back closer to the bedpost so that he could lift his head more easily, and found the itchy part, which was entirely covered with small white spots. He did not know what to make of them and wanted to feel the place with a leg, but he retracted it immediately, for the contact felt like a cold shower all over him.

He slid back again into his earlier position. "This getting up early," he thought, "makes a man quite idiotic. A man must have his sleep. Other traveling salesmen live like harem women. For instance, when I come back to the inn during the course of the morning to write up the necessary orders, these gentlemen are just sitting down to breakfast. If I were to try that with my boss, I'd be fired on the spot. Still, who knows whether that mightn't be really good for me. If it weren't for my parents' sake, I'd have quit ages ago. I would've gone to the boss and told him just what I think from the bottom of my heart. He would've fallen right off his desk! How weird it is for him to sit up at that desk, talking down to the employee from way up there—and even more weird because the boss has trouble hearing, so the employee has to step up quite close to him. Anyway, I haven't completely given up that hope yet. Once I've got together the money to pay off my parents' debt to him—that should take another five or six years—I'll do it for sure. Then I'll make my big break. In any case, right now I have to get up. My train leaves at five o'clock."

He looked over at the alarm clock ticking away on the chest of drawers. "Good God!" he thought. It was half past six, and the hands were going quietly on. It was even past the half hour, already nearly quarter to. Could the alarm have failed to ring? You could see from the bed that it was properly set for four o'clock. Certainly it had rung. Yes, but was it possible to sleep peacefully through that noise which made the furniture shake? Now, it is true he had not slept peacefully, but evidently he had slept all the more deeply. Still, what should he do now? The next train left at seven o'clock. To catch that one, he would have to go in a mad rush. The case of samples was not packed up yet, and he really did not feel particularly bright and lively. And even if he caught the train, there was no avoiding a blow-up with the boss; the firm's errand boy would have waited for the five o'clock train and reported the news of his absence long ago. He was the boss's minion, without backbone or intelligence. Well then, what if he reported in sick? But that would be extremely embarrassing and suspicious, because during his five years' service Gregor had not been sick even once. The boss would certainly come with the doctor from the health insurance company and would reproach his parents for their lazy son and cut short all objections by asking for the insurance doctor's comments; for this doctor, everyone was completely healthy but really lazy about work. And besides, would the doctor in this case be totally wrong? Apart from a really excessive drowsiness after the long sleep, Gregor, in fact, felt quite well and even had a really strong appetite.

As he was thinking all this over in the greatest haste, without being able to make the decision to get out of bed—the alarm clock was indicating exactly quarter to seven—there was a cautious knock on the door by the head of the bed. "Gregor," a voice called—it was his mother— "it's quarter to seven. Don't you want to be on your way?" That soft voice! Gregor was startled when he heard his own voice answering. It was clearly and unmistakably the voice he'd had before, but in it was intermingled, as if from below, an irrepressible, painful squeaking, which left the words positively distinct only in the first moment and distorted them in the reverberation, so that anyone listening did not know if he had heard correctly. Gregor wanted to answer in detail and explain everything, but in these circumstances he confined himself to saying, "Yes, yes, thank you, Mother. I'm getting up right away." Because of the wooden door the change in Gregor's voice was not really noticeable outside, so his mother calmed down with this explanation and shuffled off. However, as a result of the short conversation, the other family members became aware that Gregor was unexpectedly still at home, and already his father was knocking on one side door, weakly but with his fist. "Gregor, Gregor," he called out, "what's going on?" And, after a short while, he urged him on again in a deeper voice: "Gregor! Gregor!" At the other side door, however, his sister knocked lightly. "Gregor? Are you all right? Do you need anything?" Gregor directed answers in both directions: "I'll be ready right away." He made an effort with the most careful articulation and inserted long pauses between the individual words to remove everything remarkable from his voice. His father turned back to his breakfast. However, his sister whispered, "Gregor, open the door—I beg you." Gregor had no intention of opening the door; he congratulated himself on his precaution, acquired from traveling, of locking all doors during the night, even at home.

First he wanted to stand up quietly and undisturbed, get dressed, above all have breakfast, and only then consider further action, for—he noticed this clearly—by thinking things over in bed he would not reach a reasonable conclusion. He remembered that before now in bed he had often felt some light pain or other, which was perhaps the result of an awkward lying position, and which later, once he stood up, turned out to be purely imaginary, and he was eager to see how his present fantasies would gradually dissipate. That the change in his voice was nothing other than the onset of a cold, an occupational illness of commercial travelers, of that he had not the slightest doubt.

It was very easy to throw aside the blanket. He needed only to push his stomach out a little, and it fell by itself. But to continue was difficult, particularly because he was so unusually wide. He needed arms and hands to push himself upright. Instead of these, however, he had only many small limbs, which were incessantly moving with very different motions and which, in addition, he was unable to control. If he wanted to bend one of them, then it was the first to extend itself, and if he finally succeeded doing what he wanted with this limb, in the meantime all the others, as if left free, moved around in an excessively painful agitation. "But I must not stay in bed uselessly," said Gregor to himself.

At first he wanted to get out of bed with the lower part of his body, but this lower part—which, by the way, he had not yet looked at and which he also could not picture clearly—proved itself too difficult to move. The attempt went so slowly. When, having become almost frantic, he finally hurled himself forward with all his force and without thinking, he chose his direction incorrectly, and he hit the lower bedpost hard. The violent pain he felt revealed to him that the lower part of his body was at the moment probably the most sensitive.

Thus, he tried to get his upper body out of the bed first and turned his head carefully toward the edge of the bed. He managed to do this easily, and in spite of its width and weight his body mass at last slowly followed the turning of his head. But as he finally extended his head beyond the bed into the air, he became anxious about moving forward any further in this manner, for if he allowed himself eventually to fall by this process, it would really take a miracle to prevent his head from getting injured. And at all costs he must not lose consciousness right now. He preferred to remain in bed.

But after a similar effort it was no different. He lay there again, sighing as before, and once again saw his small limbs fighting one another, if anything even worse than earlier, and did not see any chance of imposing quiet and order on this arbitrary movement. He told himself again that he could not possibly remain in bed and that it might be the most reasonable thing to sacrifice everything if there was even the slightest hope of getting himself out of bed in the process. At the same time, however, he did not forget to keep reminding himself periodically of the fact that calm—indeed the calmest—reflection might be much better than confused decisions. At such moments, he directed his gaze as precisely as he could toward the window, but unfortunately a glance at the morning mist, which concealed even the other side of the narrow street, offered little to make him more confident or cheerful. "It's already seven o'clock," he told himself at the latest sounds from the alarm clock, "already seven o'clock and still such a fog." And for a little while longer he lay quietly with weak breathing, as if perhaps waiting for normal and natural conditions to re-emerge out of the complete stillness.

But then he said to himself, "Before it strikes a quarter past seven, whatever happens I must be completely out of bed. Besides, by then someone from the office will arrive to inquire about me, because the office will open before seven o'clock." And he made an effort then to rock his entire body length out of the bed with a uniform motion. If he let himself fall out of the bed in this way, his head, which in the course of the fall he intended to lift up sharply, would probably remain uninjured. His back seemed to be hard; nothing would really happen to that as a result of the fall onto the carpet. His greatest reservation was a worry about the loud noise which the fall must create and which presumably would arouse, if not fright, then at least concern on the other side of all the doors. Nevertheless, he had to take that chance.

As Gregor was already in the process of lifting himself half out of bed—the new method was more of a game than an effort; he needed only to rock with a series of jerks—it struck him how easy all this would be if someone were to come to his aid. Two strong people—he thought of his father and the servant girl—would have been quite sufficient. They would only have had to push their arms under his arched back to get him out of the bed, to bend down with their load, and then merely to exercise patience so that he could complete the flip onto the floor, where his diminutive legs would then, he hoped, acquire a purpose. Now, quite apart from the fact that the doors were locked, should he really call out for help? In spite of all his distress, he was unable to suppress a smile at this idea.

He had already got to the point where, by rocking more strongly, he was making it very difficult for himself to keep his balance, and very soon he would finally have to make a final decision, for in five minutes it would be a quarter past seven. Then there was a ring at the door of the apartment. "That's someone from the office," he told himself, and he almost froze, while his small limbs only danced around all the faster. For one moment everything remained still. "They aren't opening the door," Gregor said to himself, caught up in some absurd hope. But of course then, as usual, the servant girl with her firm tread went to the door and opened it. Gregor needed to hear only the first word of the visitor's greeting to recognize immediately who it was, the manager himself. Why was Gregor the only one condemned to work in a firm where the slightest lapse would attract the greatest suspicion? Were all the employees collectively, one and all, scoundrels? Among them was there then no truly devoted person who, if he failed to use just a couple of hours in the morning for office work, would become abnormal from pangs of conscience and really be in no state to get out of bed? Would it not have been enough to let an apprentice make inquiries, if such questioning was even necessary? Must the manager himself come, and in the process must it be demonstrated to the entire innocent family that the investigation of this suspicious circumstance could be entrusted only to the intelligence of the manager? More as a consequence of the excited state in which this idea put Gregor than as a result of any actual decision, he swung himself with all his might out of the bed. There was a loud thud, but not a real crash. The fall was absorbed somewhat by the carpet and, in addition, his back was more elastic than Gregor had thought. For that reason the dull noise was not quite so conspicuous. But he had not held his head up with sufficient care and had bumped it. He turned his head, irritated and in pain, and rubbed it on the carpet.

"Something has fallen in there," said the manager in the next room on the left. Gregor tried to imagine to himself whether anything similar to what was happening to him today could have also happened at some point to the manager. At least one had to concede the possibility of such a thing. However, as if to give a rough answer to this question, the manager now, with a squeak of his polished boots, took a few determined steps in the next room. From the neighboring room on the right the sister was whispering to inform Gregor: "Gregor, the manager is here." "I know," said Gregor to himself. But he did not dare make his voice loud enough so that his sister could hear.

"Gregor," his father now said from the neighboring room on the left, "Mr. Manager has come and is asking why you did not leave on the early train. We don't know what we should tell him. Besides, he also wants to speak to you personally. So please open the door. He will be good enough to forgive the mess in your room." In the middle of all this, the manager called out in a friendly way, "Good morning, Mr. Samsa." "He is not well," said his mother to the manager, while his father was still talking at the door, "He is not well, believe me, Mr. Manager. Otherwise how would Gregor miss a train? The young man has nothing in his head except business. I'm almost angry that he never goes out in the evening. Right now he's been in the city eight days, but he's been at home every evening. He sits here with us at the table and reads the newspaper quietly or studies his travel schedules. Working with wood can be quite a diversion for him; he busies himself with fretwork. For instance, he cut out a small frame over the course of two or three evenings. You'd be amazed how pretty it is. It's hanging right inside the room. You'll see it immediately, as soon as Gregor opens the door. Anyway, I'm happy that you're here, Mr. Manager. By ourselves, we would never have made Gregor open

the door. He's so stubborn, and he's certainly not well, although he denied that this morning." "I'm coming right away," said Gregor slowly and deliberately, without moving, so as not to lose one word of the conversation. "My dear lady, I cannot explain it to myself in any other way," said the manager; "I hope it is nothing serious. On the other hand, I must also say that we business people, luckily or unluckily, however one looks at it, very often simply have to overcome a slight indisposition for business reasons." "So can Mr. Manager come in to see you now?" asked his father impatiently and knocked once again on the door. "No," said Gregor. In the neighboring room on the left an awkward stillness descended. In the neighboring room on the right the sister began to sob.

Why did his sister not go to the others? She had probably just got up out of bed now and had not even started to get dressed yet. Then why was she crying? Because he was not getting up and letting the manager in, because he was in danger of losing his position, and because then his boss would badger his parents once again with the old demands? Those were probably unnecessary worries right now. Gregor was still here and was not thinking at all about abandoning his family. At the moment he was lying right there on the carpet, and no one who knew about his condition would have seriously demanded that he let the manager in. In any case, Gregor would not be casually dismissed right away because of this small discourtesy, for which he would find an easy and suitable excuse later on. It seemed to Gregor that it would be far more reasonable to leave him in peace at the moment, instead of disturbing him with crying and exhortations. But the others were distressed by their uncertainty, which excused their behavior.

"Mr. Samsa!" The manager was now shouting, his voice raised. "What's the matter? You are barricading yourself there in your room, answering with only a yes and a no, you are making serious and unnecessary trouble for your parents, and you are neglecting—I mention this only incidentally—your commercial duties in a truly unheard-of manner. I am speaking here in the name of your parents and your employer, and I am requesting you in all seriousness to give an immediate and clear explanation. I am amazed. I am amazed. I thought I knew you as a calm, reasonable person, and now you appear suddenly to want to start parading around in strange moods. The Chief indicated to me earlier this very day a possible explanation for your neglect—it concerned the collection of cash entrusted to you a short while ago—but in truth I almost gave him my word of honor that this explanation could not be correct. However, now I see here your unimaginable pig-headedness, and I am totally losing any desire to speak up for you in the slightest. And your position is not at all the most secure. Originally I intended to mention all this to you privately, but since you are letting me waste my time here uselessly, I don't know why the matter shouldn't come to the attention of your parents as well. Your productivity has been very unsatisfactory recently. Of course, it's not the time of year to produce exceptional sales, we recognize that, but a time of year for producing no sales, there is no such thing at all, Mr. Samsa, and such a thing must not be permitted."

"But, Mr. Manager," called Gregor, beside himself and, in his agitation, forgetting everything else, "I'm opening the door immediately, this very moment. A slight indisposition, a dizzy spell, has prevented me from getting up. I'm still lying in bed right now. But I'm quite refreshed once again. I'm in the midst of getting out of bed. Just have patience for a short moment! Things are not yet going as well as I thought. But things are all right with me. How suddenly this can overcome someone! Only yesterday evening everything was fine with me. My parents certainly know that. Actually just yesterday evening I had a small premonition. People must have seen that in me. Why did I not report that to the office? But people always think that they'll get over sickness without having to stay at home. Mr. Manager! Take it easy on my parents! There is really no basis for the criticisms which you're now making against me. Nobody has said a word to me about any of this. Perhaps you have not seen the latest orders I sent in. Besides, I'm setting out on a new sales trip on the eight o'clock train; the few hours' rest have made me stronger. Mr. Manager, there's no need for you to wait here any longer. I will be at the office in person right away. Please have the goodness to report that and to convey my respects to the Chief."

While Gregor was quickly blurting all this out, hardly aware of what he was saying, he had moved close to the chest of drawers without effort, probably as a result of the practice he had already had in bed, and now he was trying to raise himself up on it. Actually, he wanted to open the door. He really wanted to let himself be seen and to speak with the manager. He was keen to see what the others who had been asking about him just now would say when they saw him. If they were startled, then Gregor would no longer be burdened by responsibility and could be calm. But if they accepted everything quietly, then he would have no reason to get excited; if he got a move on, he could really be at the station around eight o'clock. At first he slid down a few times on the smooth chest of drawers. But at last he gave himself a final swing and stood upright there. He was no longer at all aware of the pains in his lower body, no matter how they might still sting. Now he let himself fall against the back of a nearby chair, on the edge of which he braced himself with his small limbs. By doing this he gained control over himself and kept quiet, for he could now hear the manager.

"Did you understand even a single word?" the manager asked the parents. "Is he playing the fool with us?" "For God's sake," cried the mother, already in tears, "perhaps he's very ill, and we're upsetting him. Grete! Grete!" she yelled. "Mother?" called the sister from the other side. They were making themselves understood through Gregor's room. "You must go to the doctor right away. Gregor is sick. Hurry to the doctor. Did you hear Gregor speak just now?" "That was an animal's voice," said the manager, remarkably quiet in comparison to the mother's cries. "Anna! Anna!" yelled the father through the hall into the kitchen, clapping his hands. "Fetch a locksmith right away!" The two young women were already running through the hall with swishing skirts—how had his sister dressed herself so quickly?—and pulling open the doors of the apartment. You couldn't hear the doors closing at all. They probably had left them open, as is customary in an apartment where a great misfortune has taken place.

However, Gregor had become much calmer. All right, people did not understand his words any more, although they seemed clear enough to him, clearer than previously, perhaps because his ears had gotten used to them. But at least people now thought that things were not completely all right with him and were prepared to help him. The confidence and assurance with which the first arrangements had been carried out made him feel good. He felt himself included once again in the circle of humanity and was expecting from both the doctor and the locksmith, without differentiating between them with any real precision, splendid and surprising results. In order to make his voice as clear as possible for the critical conversation which was imminent, he coughed a little. He certainly took care to do this in a really subdued way, since it was possible that even this noise would sound like something different from a human clearing of the throat. He no longer trusted his judgment. Meanwhile in the next room it had become very quiet. Perhaps his parents were sitting with the manager at the table whispering; perhaps they were all leaning against the door and listening.

Gregor pushed himself slowly toward the door, with the help of the easy chair. Then he let go of the chair, threw himself against the door, held himself upright against it—the balls of his tiny limbs had a little sticky stuff on them—and rested there momentarily from his exertion. Next he made an effort to turn the key in the lock with his mouth. Unfortunately it seemed that he had no real teeth. How then was he to grab hold of the key? But to make up for that his jaws were naturally very strong; with their help he managed to get the key actually moving. He did not notice that he was obviously inflicting some damage on himself; a brown fluid was coming out of his mouth, flowing over the key, and dripping onto the floor. "Just listen," said the manager in the next room. "He's turning the key." For Gregor that was a great encouragement. But they should all have called out to him, including his father and mother. "Come on, Gregor," they should have shouted, "keep going, keep working on the lock!" Imagining that all his efforts were being followed with suspense, he bit down on the key unthinkingly with all the force he could muster. As the key turned more, he danced around the lock. Now he was holding himself upright only with his mouth, and he had to alternate as necessary between hanging onto the key and pressing it down again with the whole weight of his body. The quite distinct click of the lock as it finally snapped open really woke Gregor up. Breathing heavily he said to himself, "So I didn't need the locksmith," and he set his head against the door handle to open the door completely.

Because he'd had to open the door in this way, it swung open really wide without him yet being visible. He first had to edge himself slowly around the door frame, very carefully, of course, if he did not want to fall awkwardly on his back right at the entrance into the room. He was still preoccupied with this difficult movement and had no time to pay attention to anything else, when he heard the manager exclaim a loud "Oh!"—it sounded like the wind whistling—and now he saw him, nearest to the door, pressing his hand against his open mouth and moving slowly back, as if an invisible constant force were pushing him away. His mother—in spite of the presence of the manager she was standing here with her hair sticking up on end, still a mess from the night—first looked at his father with her hands clasped, then went two steps toward Gregor and collapsed right in the middle of her skirts, which were spread out all around her, her face sunk on her breast, completely concealed. His father clenched his fist with a hostile expression, as if he wished to push Gregor back into his room, then looked uncertainly around the living room, covered his eyes with his hands, and cried so that his mighty breast shook.

At this point Gregor had still not taken one step into the room; he was leaning his body from the inside against the firmly bolted wing of the door, so that only half his body was visible, as well as his head, tilted sideways, with which he peeped over at the others. Meanwhile it had become much brighter. Standing out clearly from the other side of the street was a section of the endless gray-black house situated opposite—it was a hospital—with its severe regular windows breaking up the facade. The rain was still coming down, but only in large individual drops visibly and firmly thrown down one by one onto the ground. Countless breakfast dishes were standing piled around on the table, because for his father breakfast was the most important meal time in the day, one which he prolonged for hours by reading various newspapers. Directly across on the opposite wall hung a photograph of Gregor from the time of his military service; it was a picture of him as a lieutenant; smiling and worry free, with his hand on his sword, he demanded respect for his bearing and uniform. The door to the hall was ajar, and since the door to the apartment was also open, you could see out into the landing of the apartment and the start of the staircase going down.

"Now," said Gregor, well aware that he was the only one who had kept his composure, "I'll get dressed right away, pack up the collection of samples, and set off. You'll allow me to set out on my way, will you not? You see, Mr. Manager, I am not pig-headed, and I am happy to work. Traveling is exhausting, but I couldn't live without it. Where are you going, Mr. Manager? To the office? Really? Will you report everything truthfully? A person can be incapable of work momentarily, but that's precisely the best time to remember the earlier achievements and to consider that later, after the obstacles have been removed, the person will certainly work all the more diligently and intensely. I am really so indebted to Mr. Chief—you know that perfectly well. On the other hand, I am concerned about my parents and my sister. I'm in a fix, but I'll work myself out of it again. Don't make things more difficult for me than they already are. Speak up on my behalf in the office! People don't like traveling salesmen. I know that. People think they earn pots of money and thus lead a fine life. People never have any special reason to think through this judgment more clearly. But you, Mr. Manager, you have a better perspective on what's involved than other people—even, I tell you in total confidence, a better perspective than Mr. Chief himself, who in his capacity as the employer may easily shade his decisions at the expense of an employee. You also know well enough that the traveling salesman who is outside the office almost the entire year can become so easily a victim of gossip, coincidences, and groundless complaints, against which it's totally impossible for him to defend himself. For the most part he doesn't hear about them at all, and if he does it's only when he's at home and exhausted after finishing a trip. Then he gets to feel in his own body the nasty consequences, which can't be thoroughly traced back to their origins. Mr. Manager, don't leave without speaking a word indicating to me that you'll at least concede that I'm a little in the right!"

But at Gregor's first words the manager had already turned away, and now he looked back with pursed lips at Gregor over his twitching shoulders. During Gregor's speech he had not been still for a moment but had kept moving away toward the door, without taking his eyes off Gregor, but really gradually, as if there were a secret ban on leaving the room. He was already in the hall, and given the sudden movement with which he finally pulled his foot out of the living room, you could have believed that he had just burned his sole. In the hall, however, he stretched his right hand out away from his body toward the staircase, as if some almost supernatural relief was waiting for him there.

Gregor realized that he must not under any circumstances allow the manager to go away in this frame of mind, if his position in the firm was not to be placed in the greatest danger. His parents did not understand all this very well. Over the long years, they had developed the conviction that Gregor was set up for life in this firm and, in addition, they had so much to do nowadays with their present troubles that all foresight was foreign to them. But Gregor had this foresight. The manager must be detained, calmed down, convinced, and finally won over. The future of Gregor and his family really depended on it! If only his sister had been there! She was clever. She had already cried while Gregor was still lying quietly on his back. And the manager, always a friend of the ladies, would certainly let himself be guided by her. She would have closed the door to the apartment and talked him out of his fright in the hall. But his sister was not even there. Gregor had to deal with it himself. Without thinking that as yet he did not know anything about his present ability to move, and without thinking that his speech possibly—indeed probably—had once again not been understood, he left the wing of the door, pushed himself through the opening, and tried to go over to the manager, who was already holding the handrail on the landing tight, gripping with both hands in a ridiculous way. But as Gregor looked for something to steady himself, with a small scream he immediately fell down onto his numerous little legs. Scarcely had this happened, when he felt for the first time that morning a general physical well-being. The small limbs had firm floor under them; they obeyed perfectly, as he noticed to his joy, and even strove to carry him forward in the direction he wanted. Right away he believed that the final amelioration of all his suffering was immediately at hand. But at the very moment when he lay on the floor rocking in a restrained manner quite close to and directly across from his mother, who seemed to have totally sunk into herself, she suddenly sprang right up with her arms spread far apart and her fingers extended and cried out, "Help, for God's sake, help!" She held her head bowed down, as if she wanted to view Gregor better, but then she ran senselessly back, contradicting that gesture, forgetting that behind her stood the table with all the dishes on it. When she reached the table, she sat down heavily on it, as if absent-

mindedly, and did not appear to notice at all that next to her coffee was pouring out onto the carpet in a full stream from the large, overturned pot.

"Mother, Mother," said Gregor quietly and looked over toward her. The manager had momentarily vanished completely from his mind. On the other hand, when he saw the flowing coffee Gregor could not stop himself snapping his jaws in the air a few times. At that his mother screamed all over again, hurried from the table, and collapsed into the arms of his father, who was rushing toward her. But Gregor had no time right now for his parents—the manager was already on the staircase. With his chin on the banister, the manager looked back for the last time. Gregor made a running start to catch up to him if possible. But the manager must have suspected something, because he made a leap down over a few stairs and disappeared, still shouting "Aah!" The sound echoed throughout the entire stairwell. Unfortunately this flight of the manager seemed to bewilder his father completely. Earlier he had been relatively calm. Now instead of running after the manager himself, or at least not hindering Gregor from his pursuit, with his right hand he grabbed hold of the cane that the manager had left behind on a chair with his hat and overcoat. With his left hand, the father grabbed a large newspaper from the table and, stamping his feet on the floor, he set out to drive Gregor back into his room by waving the cane and the newspaper. No request of Gregor's was of any use; no request would even be understood. No matter how willing he was to turn his head respectfully, his father just stomped all the harder with his feet. Across the room from him his mother had pulled open a window, in spite of the cool weather, and leaning out with her hands on her cheeks, she pushed her face far outside the window. Between the lane and the stairwell a strong draft came up, the curtains on the window flew around, the newspapers on the table rustled, and individual sheets fluttered down over the floor. His father relentlessly pushed his way forward, hissing like a wild man. Now, Gregor still had no practice at all in going backward—it was really very slow going. If Gregor only had been allowed to turn himself around, he would have been in his room right away, but he was afraid to make his father impatient by the time-consuming process of turning around, and each moment he faced the threat of a mortal blow on his back or his head from the cane in his father's hand. Finally Gregor had no other option, for he noticed with horror that he did not understand yet how to maintain his direction going backward. And so he began, amid constantly anxious sideways glances in his father's direction, to turn himself around as quickly as possible, although in truth he could only do this very slowly. Perhaps his father noticed his good intentions, for he did not disrupt Gregor in this motion, but with the tip of the cane from a distance he even directed Gregor's rotating movement now and then. If only his father had not hissed so unbearably! Because of that Gregor totally lost his head. He was already almost totally turned around, when, always with this hissing in his ear, he just made a mistake and turned himself back a little. But when he finally was successful in getting his head in front of the door opening, it became clear that his body was too wide to go through any further. Naturally his father, in his present mental state, had no idea of, say, opening the other wing of the door a bit to create a suitable passage for Gregor to get through. His single fixed thought was that Gregor must get into his room as quickly as possible. He would never have allowed the elaborate preparations Gregor required to raise himself up and perhaps in this way get through the door. Perhaps with his excessive noise he was now driving Gregor forward as if there were no obstacle. Behind Gregor the sound at this point was no longer like the voice of only a single father. Now it was really no longer a joke, and Gregor forced himself, come what might, into the doorway. One side of his body lifted up. He lay at an angle in the door opening. His one flank was all raw from the scraping. On the white door ugly blotches were left. Soon he was stuck fast and would not have been able to move any more on his own. The tiny legs on one side hung twitching in the air above,

and the ones on the other side were pushed painfully into the floor. Then his father gave him one really strong liberating push from behind, and he scurried, bleeding severely, far into his room. The door was slammed shut with the cane, and then finally it was quiet.

II

Gregor first woke up from his heavy swoon-like sleep in the evening twilight. He would certainly have woken up soon afterward even without any disturbance, for he felt himself sufficiently rested and wide awake; but it appeared to him as if a hurried step and a cautious closing of the door to the hall might have roused him. Light from the electric streetlamps lay pale here and there on the ceiling of his room and on the higher parts of the furniture, but down around Gregor it was dark. He pushed himself slowly toward the door, still groping awkwardly with his feelers, which he now learned to value for the first time, to check what was happening. His left side seemed one single long unpleasantly stretched scar, and he really had to hobble on his two rows of legs. In addition, one small leg had been seriously wounded in the course of the morning incident—it was almost a miracle that only one had been hurt—and dragged lifelessly behind.

By the door he first noticed what had really lured him there: it was the smell of something to eat. A bowl stood there, filled with sweetened milk, in which swam tiny pieces of white bread. He almost laughed with joy, for he had an even greater hunger than in the morning, and he immediately dipped his head almost over his eyes down into the milk. But he soon drew it back again in disappointment, not just because it was difficult for him to eat on account of his delicate left side—he could eat only if his entire panting body worked in a coordinated way—but also because the milk, which had always been his favorite drink and which his sister had certainly placed there for that reason, did not appeal to him at all. He turned away from the bowl almost with aversion and crept back into the middle of the room.

In the living room, as Gregor saw through the crack in the door, the gas was lit, but where, on other occasions at this time of day, his father was accustomed to read the afternoon newspaper in a loud voice to his mother and sometimes also to his sister, at the moment no sound was audible. Perhaps this reading aloud, about which his sister had always spoken and written to him, had recently fallen out of their general routine. But it was so still all around, in spite of the fact that the apartment was certainly not empty. "What a quiet life the family leads," said Gregor to himself, and, as he stared fixedly out in front of him into the darkness, he felt a great pride that he had been able to provide such a life for his parents and his sister in such a beautiful apartment. But how would things go if now all tranquility, all prosperity, all contentment should come to a horrible end? In order not to lose himself in such thoughts, Gregor preferred to set himself moving, so he crawled up and down in his room.

Once during the long evening one side door and then the other door were opened just a tiny crack and quickly closed again. Someone presumably had felt they needed to come in but had then thought better of it. Gregor immediately took up a position by the living room door, determined to bring in the hesitant visitor somehow or other, or at least to find out who it might be. But now the door was not opened anymore; Gregor waited in vain. Earlier, when the door had been barred, they had all wanted to come in to him; now, when he had opened one door and when the others had obviously been opened during the day, no one came any more, and now the keys were stuck in the locks on the outside.

The light in the living room was turned off only late at night, and it was now easy to establish that his parents and his sister had stayed awake all this time, for one could hear them clearly as all three moved away on tiptoe. Now it was certain that no one would come in to Gregor any more until the morning. Thus, he had a long time to think undisturbed about how he should reor-

ganize his life from scratch. But the high, open room, in which he was compelled to lie flat on the floor, made him anxious, without his being able to figure out the reason, for he had lived in the room for five years. With a half-unconscious turn and not without a little shame he scurried under the couch, where, in spite of the fact that his back was a little cramped and he could no longer lift up his head, he felt very comfortable right away and was sorry only that his body was too wide to fit completely under the couch.

There he remained the entire night, which he spent partly in a state of semi-sleep, out of which his hunger constantly woke him with a start, but partly in a state of worry and murky hopes, which all led to the conclusion that for the time being he would have to keep calm and with patience and the greatest consideration for his family tolerate the troubles which in his present condition he was now forced to cause them.

Already early in the morning—it was still almost night—Gregor had an opportunity to test the power of the decisions he had just made, for his sister, almost fully dressed, opened the door from the hall into his room and looked eagerly inside. She did not find him immediately, but when she noticed him under the couch—God, he had to be somewhere or other, for he could hardly fly away—she got such a shock that, without being able to control herself, she slammed the door shut once again from the outside. However, as if she was sorry for her behavior, she immediately opened the door again and walked in on her tiptoes, as if she was in the presence of a serious invalid or a total stranger. Gregor had pushed his head forward just to the edge of the couch and was observing her. Would she really notice that he had left the milk standing, not indeed from any lack of hunger, and would she bring in something else to eat more suitable for him? If she did not do it on her own, he would sooner starve to death than call her attention to the fact, although he had a really powerful urge to dash out from under the couch, throw himself at his sister's feet, and beg her for something or other good to eat. But his sister noticed right away with astonishment that the bowl was still full, with only a little milk spilled around it. She picked it up immediately, not with her bare hands but with a rag, and took it out of the room. Gregor was extremely curious what she would bring as a substitute, and he pictured to himself very different ideas about it. But he never could have guessed what his sister, out of the goodness of her heart, in fact, did. To test his taste, she brought him an entire selection, all spread out on an old newspaper. There were old half-rotten vegetables, bones from the evening meal, covered with a white sauce which had almost solidified, some raisins and almonds, cheese which Gregor had declared inedible two days earlier, a slice of dry bread, a slice with butter, and a slice of salted bread smeared with butter. In addition to all this, she put down the bowl—probably designated once and for all as Gregor's—into which she had poured some water. And out of her delicacy of feeling, since she knew that Gregor would not eat in front of her, she went away very quickly and even turned the key in the lock, so that Gregor could now know that he might make himself as comfortable as he wished. Gregor's small limbs buzzed now that the time for eating had come. His wounds must, in any case, have already healed completely. He felt no handicap on that score. He was astonished at that, and thought about how more than a month ago he had cut his finger very slightly with a knife—and this wound had still hurt the day before yesterday. "Am I now going to be less sensitive?" he thought, already sucking greedily on the cheese, which had strongly attracted him right away, more than all the other foods. Quickly and with his eyes watering with satisfaction, he ate one after the other the cheese, the vegetables, and the sauce. The fresh food, by contrast, did not taste good to him. He could not even bear the smell and carried the things he wanted to eat a little distance away. By the time his sister slowly turned the key as a sign that he should withdraw, he was long finished with everything and now lay lazily in the same spot. The noise immediately startled him, in spite of the fact that he was already almost asleep, and he scurried back

again under the couch. But it cost him great self-control to remain under the couch, even for the short time his sister was in the room, because his body had filled out somewhat on account of the rich meal and in the narrow space there he could scarcely breathe. In the midst of minor attacks of asphyxiation, he looked at her with somewhat protruding eyes, as his unsuspecting sister swept up with a broom, not just the remnants, but even the foods which Gregor had not touched at all, as if these were also now useless, and as she dumped everything quickly into a bucket, which she closed with a wooden lid, and then carried all of it out of the room. She had hardly turned around before Gregor had already dragged himself out from under the couch, stretched out, and let his body expand.

In this way Gregor now got his food every day, once in the morning, when his parents and the servant girl were still asleep, and a second time after the common noon meal, for his parents were asleep then for a little while, and the servant girl was sent off by his sister on some errand or other. They certainly would not have wanted Gregor to starve to death, but perhaps they could not have endured finding out what he ate (other than by hearsay). Perhaps his sister also wanted to spare them what was possibly only a small grief, for they were really suffering quite enough already.

What sorts of excuses people had used on that first morning to get the doctor and the locksmith out of the house again Gregor was completely unable to ascertain. Since they could not understand him, no one, not even his sister, had imagined that he might be able to understand others, and thus, when his sister was in his room, he had to be content with listening now and then to her sighs and invocations to the saints. Only later, when she had grown somewhat accustomed to everything—naturally there could never be any talk of her growing completely accustomed to it—Gregor sometimes caught a comment which was intended to be friendly or could be interpreted as such. "Well, today it tasted good to him," she said, if Gregor had really cleaned up what he had to eat; whereas, in the reverse situation, which gradually repeated itself more and more frequently, she used to say almost sadly, "Now everything has been left again."

But while Gregor could get no new information directly, he did hear a good deal from the room next door, and as soon as he heard voices, he scurried over right away to whichever door it was and pressed his entire body against it. In the early days especially, there was no conversation which was not concerned with him in some way or other, even if only surreptitiously. For two days at all meal times discussions could be heard of how they should now conduct themselves. They also talked about the same subject in the times between meals, for there were always at least two family members at home, since no one really wanted to remain in the house alone and people could not under any circumstances leave the apartment completely empty. In addition, on the very first day the servant girl—it was not completely clear what and how much she knew about what had happened—on her knees had begged his mother to let her go immediately. When she said goodbye about fifteen minutes later, she thanked them for the dismissal with tears in her eyes, as if she was receiving the greatest favor which people had ever shown her there, and, without anyone demanding it from her, she swore a fearful oath not to reveal anything to anyone, not even the slightest detail.

Now his sister had to team up with his mother to do the cooking, although that did not create much trouble because people were eating almost nothing. Again and again Gregor listened as one of them vainly invited another one to eat and received no answer other than "Thank you. I've had enough" or something like that. And perhaps they had stopped having anything to drink, too. His sister often asked his father whether he wanted to have a beer and gladly offered to fetch it herself, and when his father was silent, she said, in order to remove any reservations he might have, that she could send the caretaker's wife to get it. But then the father would finally say a resounding "No," and nothing more would be spoken about it.

Already during the first day his father laid out all the financial circumstances and prospects to his mother and to his sister as well. From time to time he stood up from the table and pulled out of the small lockbox salvaged from his business, which had collapsed five years previously, some document or other or some notebook. The sound was audible as he opened up the complicated lock and, after removing what he was looking for, locked it up again. Some of the father's explanations were the first enjoyable thing that Gregor had the chance to listen to since his imprisonment began. He had thought that his father had been left with nothing at all from that business; at least his father had told him nothing to contradict that view, and Gregor in any case had not asked him about it. At the time Gregor's only concern had been to do everything he could in order to allow his family to forget as quickly as possible the business misfortune which had brought them all into a state of complete hopelessness. And so at that point he had started to work with a special intensity; from a minor assistant he had become, almost overnight, a traveling salesman, who naturally had entirely different possibilities for earning money and whose successes at work were converted immediately into the form of cash commissions, which could be set out on the table at home for his astonished and delighted family. Those had been beautiful days, and they had never come back since, at least not with the same splendor, in spite of the fact that Gregor later earned so much money that he was in a position to bear the expenses of the entire family, costs which he, in fact, did bear. They had become quite accustomed to it, both the family and Gregor as well. They took the money with thanks, and he happily surrendered it, but there was no longer any special warmth about it. Only his sister had remained still close to Gregor, and it was his secret plan to send her next year to the Conservatory, regardless of the great expense which that necessarily involved and which would be made up in other ways. In contrast to Gregor, she loved music very much and knew how to play the violin charmingly. Now and then during

Gregor's short stays in the city the Conservatory was mentioned in conversations with his sister, but always merely as a beautiful dream, whose realization was unimaginable; their parents never listened to these innocent expectations with pleasure. But Gregor thought about them with scrupulous consideration and intended to announce his proposal solemnly on Christmas Eve.

In his present situation, such completely futile ideas would go through his head while he pushed himself right up against the door and listened. Sometimes in his general exhaustion he could not listen anymore and let his head bang listlessly against the door, but he immediately pulled himself together once more, for even the small sound which he made by this motion would be heard nearby and silence everyone. "There he goes on again," his father would say after a while, clearly turning toward the door, and only then would the interrupted conversation gradually be resumed again.

Gregor soon found out clearly enough—for his father tended to repeat himself from time to time in his explanations, partly because he had not personally concerned himself with these matters for a long time now, and partly because his mother did not understand everything right away the first time—that, in spite of all bad luck, an amount of money, although a very small one, was still available from the old times and that the interest, which had not been touched, had in the intervening time accumulated a little. In addition to this, the money which Gregor had brought home every month—he had kept only a few crowns for himself—had not been completely spent and had grown into a small capital amount. Gregor, behind his door, nodded eagerly, rejoicing over this unanticipated foresight and frugality. True, with this excess money, he could really have paid off more of the father's debt to his employer and the day on which he could be rid of this position would have been a lot closer, but now things were doubtless better the way his father had arranged them.

At the moment, however, this money was not nearly sufficient to permit the family to live off the interest payments. Perhaps the savings would be enough to maintain the family for one or at most two years, that was all. Thus, it only really added up to an amount that one should not draw upon and that should be set aside for an emergency. They had to earn money to live on. Now, it's true his father was indeed a healthy man, but he was old and had not worked for five years and thus could not be counted on for very much. He had in these five years, the first holidays of his laborious but unsuccessful life, put on a good deal of fat and thus had become really heavy. And should his old mother now be expected to work for money? A woman who suffered from asthma, for whom wandering through the apartment was even now a great strain and who spent every second day on the sofa by the open window, having trouble with her breathing? Should his sister earn money, a girl who was still a seventeen-year-old child and whose earlier lifestyle—consisting of dressing herself nicely, sleeping in late, helping around the house, taking part in a few modest enjoyments and, above all, playing the violin—had been so very delightful? When it came to talking about this need to earn money, Gregor would at first always let go of the door and throw himself on the cool leather sofa nearby, quite hot from shame and sorrow.

Often he lay there all night long, not sleeping at all, just scratching on the leather for hours at a time. Or he would take on the very difficult task of pushing a chair over to the window. Then he would creep up on the windowsill and, braced on the chair, lean against the window to look out, obviously with some memory or other of the liberating sense which looking out the window used to bring him in earlier times. For, in fact, from day to day he perceived things with less and less clarity, even things that were only a short distance away. The hospital across the street, the all-too-frequent sight of which he had previously cursed, was not visible at all anymore, and if he had not been very well aware that he lived in the quiet but completely urban Charlotte Street, he could have believed that from his window he was peering out at a featureless wasteland, in which the gray heaven and the gray earth had merged and were indistinguishable. His observant sister had only to notice a couple of times that the chair stood by the window; then, after cleaning up the room, she would each time push the chair back right against the window again. She even began to leave the inner casements open.

If Gregor had only been able to speak to his sister and thank her for everything that she had to do for him, he would have tolerated her service more easily. As it was, he suffered under it. To her credit, the sister sought to cover up the awkwardness of everything as much as possible, and, as time went by, she naturally became more successful at it. But with the passing of time Gregor also came to understand everything much more clearly. Even the way she would come in was terrible for him. As soon as she entered, she ran straight to the window, without taking the time to shut the door—in spite of the fact that at other times she was very careful to spare anyone the sight of Gregor's room—and yanked the window open with eager hands, as if she were almost suffocating, and remained for a while by the window breathing deeply, even when it was very cold. With all her noisy rushing about she frightened Gregor twice every day. The entire time he trembled under the couch, and yet he knew very well that she would certainly have spared him all this gladly if it had only been possible for her to remain with the window closed in a room where Gregor lived.

On one occasion—about one month had already gone by since Gregor's transformation, and there was no particular reason any more for his sister to be startled at Gregor's appearance— she arrived a little earlier than usual and came upon Gregor as he was still looking out the window, immobile and positioned as if to frighten someone. It would not have come as a surprise to Gregor if she had not come in, since his position was preventing her from opening the window immediately. But not only did she not step inside; she even stepped back and shut the door. A stranger really could have concluded from this that Gregor had been lying in wait for her and wanted to bite her. Of course, Gregor immediately concealed himself under the couch, but he had to wait until noon before his sister returned, and she seemed much less calm than usual. From this he realized that his appearance was still intolerable to her and should remain intolerable to her in future—and that she really must have to exert a lot of self-control not to run away from a glimpse of only the small part of his body which stuck out from under the couch. In order to spare her even this sight, one day he dragged the bedsheet on his back up onto the couch—this task took him four hours—and arranged it in such a way that he was now completely concealed and his sister, even if she bent down, could not see him. If this sheet was not necessary as far as she was concerned, then she could certainly have removed it, for it was clear enough that Gregor could not derive any pleasure from isolating himself away so completely. But she left the sheet just as it was, and Gregor believed he even caught a look of gratitude when, on one occasion, he carefully lifted up the sheet a little with his head to check as his sister took stock of the new arrangement.

In the first two weeks his parents could not bring themselves to visit him, and he often heard how they fully acknowledged his sister's present work; whereas, earlier they had often got annoyed at his sister because she had seemed to them a somewhat useless girl. Now both his father and his mother frequently waited in front of Gregor's door while his sister cleaned up inside. As soon as she came out, she had to explain in great detail how things looked in the room, what Gregor had eaten, how he had behaved this time, and whether perhaps a slight improvement was perceptible. As it happened, his mother comparatively soon had wanted to visit Gregor, but his father and his sister had restrained her, at first with reasons which Gregor listened to very attentively and which he completely endorsed. Later, however, they had to hold her back forcefully. When she then cried "Let me go to Gregor. He's my unfortunate son! Don't you understand that I have to go to him?" Gregor then thought that perhaps it would be a good thing if his mother came in, not every day, of course, but maybe once a week. She understood everything much better than his sister, who, in spite of all her courage, was still merely a child and, in the last analysis, had perhaps undertaken such a difficult task only out of childish recklessness.

Gregor's wish to see his mother was soon realized. While during the day Gregor, out of consideration for his parents, did not want to show himself by the window, he could not crawl around very much on the few square meters of the floor. He found it difficult to bear lying quietly during the night, and soon eating no longer gave him the slightest pleasure. So for diversion he acquired the habit of crawling back and forth across the walls and ceiling. He was especially fond of hanging from the ceiling. The experience was quite different from lying on the floor. It was easier to breathe, a slight vibration went through his body, and in the midst of the almost happy amusement which Gregor found up there, it could happen that, to his own surprise, he let go and hit the floor. However, now he naturally controlled his body quite differently than before, and he did not injure himself in such a great fall. Now, his sister noticed immediately the new amusement which Gregor had found for himself—for as he crept around he left behind here and there traces of his sticky stuff—and so she got the idea of making the area where Gregor could creep around as large as possible and thus of removing the furniture which got in the way, especially the chest of drawers and the writing desk. But she was in no position to do this by herself. She did not dare to ask her father to help, and the servant girl would certainly not have assisted her, for although this girl, about sixteen years old, had courageously remained since the dismissal of the previous cook, she had begged for the privilege of being allowed to stay permanently confined to the kitchen and of having to open the door only in answer to a special summons. Thus, his sister had no other choice but to involve his mother, choosing a time when his father was absent. His mother approached Gregor's room with cries of excited joy, but she fell silent at the

door. Of course, his sister first checked whether everything in the room was in order. Only then did she let his mother enter. Gregor had, with the greatest haste, drawn the sheet down even further and wrinkled it more. The whole thing really looked just like a coverlet thrown carelessly over the couch. On this occasion, Gregor also held back from spying out from under the sheet. For now, he refrained from looking at his mother and was merely happy that she had now come. "Come on. You can't see him," said his sister and evidently led his mother by the hand. Now Gregor listened as these two weak women shifted the heavy old chest of drawers from its position. His sister constantly took on herself the greatest part of the work, without listening to the warnings of his mother, who was afraid that she would strain herself. The work lasted a very long time. After about a quarter of an hour had already gone by, his mother said it would be better if they left the chest of drawers where it was, because, in the first place, it was too heavy. They would not be finished before his father's arrival, and leaving the chest of drawers in the middle of the room would block all Gregor's pathways, but, in the second place, they could not be at all certain that Gregor would be pleased with the removal of the furniture. To Gregor's mother the reverse seemed likely to be true. The sight of the empty walls pierced her right to the heart; and why should Gregor not feel the same? He had been accustomed to the room furnishings for a long time and without them would feel himself abandoned in an empty room. "And is it not the case," his mother concluded very quietly, almost whispering, as if she wished to prevent Gregor, whose exact location she really did not know, from hearing even the sound of her voice—for she was convinced that he did not understand her words—"and isn't it a fact that by removing the furniture we'd be showing that we were giving up all hope of an improvement and leaving him to his own resources without any consideration? I think it would be best if we tried to keep the room exactly in the condition it was in before, so that, when Gregor returns to us, he finds everything unchanged and can forget the intervening time all the more easily."

As he heard his mother's words Gregor realized that the lack of all immediate human contact, together with the monotonous life surrounded by the family over the course of these two months, must have confused his understanding, because otherwise he could not explain to himself how he, in all seriousness, could have been so keen to have his room emptied. Was he really eager to let the warm room, comfortably furnished with pieces he had inherited, be turned into a cavern in which he would, of course, then be able to crawl about in all directions without disturbance, but at the same time with a quick and complete forgetting of his human past as well? Was he then at this point already on the verge of forgetting and was it only the voice of his mother, which he had not heard for a long time, that had aroused him? Nothing was to be removed—everything must remain. In his condition he could not function without the beneficial influences of his furniture. And if the furniture prevented him from carrying out his senseless crawling about all over the place, then there was no harm in that, but rather a great benefit.

But his sister unfortunately thought otherwise. She had grown accustomed, certainly not without justification, to acting as a special expert when discussing matters concerning Gregor with their parents, and so now the mother's advice was for his sister sufficient reason to insist on the removal, not only of the chest of drawers and the writing desk, which were the only items she had thought about at first, but also of all the rest of the furniture, with the exception of the indispensable couch. Of course, it was not only childish defiance and her recent very unexpected and hard-won self-confidence which led her to this demand. She had also actually observed that Gregor needed a great deal of room to creep about; the furniture, on the other hand, as far as one could see, was not the slightest use. But perhaps the enthusiastic sensibility of young women of her age also played a role. This feeling sought release at every opportunity, and with it Grete now felt tempted by the desire to make Gregor's situation even more terrifying, so that then she would be able to do even more for him than she had up to now. For surely no one except Grete would ever trust themselves to enter a room in which Gregor ruled the empty walls all by himself.

And so she did not let herself be dissuaded from her decision by her mother, who in her sheer agitation seemed uncertain of herself in the room as it was. She soon fell quiet, and helped his sister with all the energy she could muster to get the chest of drawers out of the room. Now, Gregor could still do without the chest of drawers if need be, but the writing desk really had to stay. And scarcely had the women left the room with the chest of drawers, groaning as they pushed it, when Gregor stuck his head out from under the sofa to see how he could intervene, cautiously and with as much consideration as possible. But unfortunately it was his mother who came back into the room first; Grete had her arms wrapped around the chest of drawers in the next room and was rocking it back and forth by herself, of course without moving it from its position. But his mother was not used to the sight of Gregor; just seeing him could have made her ill, and so, frightened, Gregor scurried backward right to the other end of the sofa. However, he could no longer prevent the front of the sheet from moving a little. That was enough to catch his mother's attention. She came to a halt, stood still for a moment, and then went back to Grete.

Although Gregor kept repeating to himself over and over that really nothing unusual was going on, that only a few pieces of furniture were being rearranged, he soon had to admit to himself that the movements of the women to and fro, their quiet conversations, and the scraping of the furniture on the floor affected him like a great commotion stirred up on all sides. He was pulling in his head and legs and pressing his body into the floor so firmly that he had to tell himself unequivocally he would not be able to endure all this much longer. They were cleaning out his room, taking away from him everything he cherished; they had already dragged out the chest of drawers in which the fret saw and other tools were kept, and they were now loosening the writing desk which was fixed tight to the floor, the desk on which he, as a business student, as a high school student, indeed even as an elementary school student, had written out his assignments. At that moment he really did not have any more time to consider the good intentions of the two women, whose existence he had in any case almost forgotten, because in their exhaustion they were working really silently; the heavy stumbling of their feet was the only sound to be heard.

And so he scuttled out—the women were just propping themselves up on the writing desk in the next room in order to take a short breather. He changed the direction of his path four times. He really did not know what he should rescue first. Then he saw hanging conspicuously on an otherwise empty wall the picture of the woman dressed in nothing but fur. He quickly scurried up over it and pressed himself against the glass which held it in place and which made his hot abdomen feel good. At least this picture, which Gregor for the moment completely concealed— surely no one would now take this away. He twisted his head toward the door of the living room to observe the women as they came back in.

They had not allowed themselves very much rest and were coming back right away. Grete had placed her arm around her mother and held her tightly. "So what shall we take now?" said Grete and looked around her. Then her glance met Gregor's from the wall. She kept her composure only because her mother was there. She bent her face toward her mother in order to prevent her from looking around, and said, although in a trembling voice and too quickly, "Come, wouldn't it be better to go back to the living room for just another moment?" Grete's purpose was clear to Gregor: she wanted to take his mother to a safe place and then chase him down from the wall. Well, let her just try! He squatted on his picture and did not hand it over. He would sooner spring into Grete's face.

But Grete's words had immediately made the mother very uneasy. She walked to the side, caught sight of the enormous brown splotch on the flowered wallpaper, and, before she became truly aware that what she was looking at was Gregor, screamed out in a high-pitched raw voice "Oh God, oh God" and fell with outstretched arms, as if she was surrendering everything, down onto the couch. She lay there motionless. "Gregor, you . . ." cried out his sister with a raised fist and an urgent glare. Since his transformation these were the first words she had directed right at him. She ran into the room next door to bring some spirits—anything with which she could revive her mother from her fainting spell. Gregor wanted to help as well—there was time enough to save the picture—but he was stuck fast on the glass and had to tear himself loose forcibly. Then he too scurried into the next room, as if he could give his sister some advice, as in earlier times. He had to stand there idly behind her, while she rummaged about among various small bottles. Still, she was frightened when she turned around. A bottle fell onto the floor and shattered. A splinter of glass wounded Gregor in the face, and some corrosive medicine or other dripped over him. Now, without lingering any longer, Grete took as many small bottles as she could hold and ran with them in to her mother. She slammed the door shut with her foot. Gregor was now shut off from his mother, who was perhaps near death, thanks to him. He could not open the door; he did not want to chase away his sister, who had to remain with the mother. At this point he had nothing to do but wait. Overwhelmed with self-reproach and worry, he began to creep and crawl over everything: walls, furniture, and ceiling. Finally, in his despair, as the entire room started to spin around him, he fell onto the middle of the large table.

A short time elapsed. Gregor lay there limply. All around was still. Perhaps that was a good sign. Then there was a ring at the door. The servant girl was naturally shut up in her kitchen, and therefore Grete had to go to open the door. His father had arrived. "What's happened?" were his first words. Grete's appearance had told him everything. Grete replied with a dull voice; evidently she was pressing her face against her father's chest: "Mother fainted, but she's getting better now. Gregor has broken loose." "Yes, I expected that," said his father, "I always warned you of that, but you women don't want to listen." It was clear to Gregor that the father had badly misunderstood Grete's all-too-brief message and was assuming that Gregor had committed some violent crime or other. Thus, Gregor now had to find his father to calm him down, for he had neither the time nor the ability to explain things to him. And so he rushed away to the door of his room and pushed himself against it, so that his father could see right away as he entered from the hall that Gregor fully intended to return at once to his room, that it was not necessary to drive him back, but that one only needed to open the door, and he would disappear immediately.

But his father was not in the mood to observe such niceties. "Ah!" he yelled as soon as he entered, with a tone as if he were at once angry and pleased. Gregor pulled his head back from the door and raised it in the direction of his father. He had not really pictured his father as he now stood there. Of course, what with his new style of creeping all around, he had in the past while neglected to pay attention to what was going on in the rest of the apartment, as he had used to do; he really should have grasped the fact that he would encounter different conditions. And yet, and yet, was that still his father? Was that the same man who had lain exhausted and buried in bed in earlier days when Gregor was setting out on a business trip; who had received him on the evenings of his return in a sleeping gown and armchair, totally incapable of standing up; who had only lifted his arms as a sign of happiness; and who in their rare strolls together a few Sundays a year and on the most important holidays made his way slowly forward between Gregor and his mother—who themselves moved slowly—even a bit more slowly than them, bundled up in his old coat, working hard to move forward and always setting down his walking stick carefully; and who, when he had wanted to say something, had almost always stood still and gathered his entourage around him? Now he was standing up really straight, dressed in a tight-fitting blue uniform with gold buttons, like the ones doormen wear in a banking company. Above the high stiff collar of his jacket his firm double chin stuck out prominently, beneath his bushy eyebrows the glance of his black eyes was fresh and alert, and his usually disheveled white hair was combed down into a shining and carefully exact part. He threw his cap, on which a gold monogram, probably the symbol of a bank, was affixed, in an arc across the entire room onto the sofa and, thrusting back the edges of the long coat of his uniform, with his hands in his trouser pockets and a grim face, moved right up to Gregor. He really did not know what he had in mind, but he raised his feet uncommonly high anyway, and Gregor was astonished at the gigantic size of the soles of his boots. Gregor did not linger on that point; he had known even from the first day of his new life that, as far as he was concerned, his father considered the only appropriate response to be the most forceful one. And so he scurried away from his father, stopped when his father remained standing, and scampered forward again when his father stirred a little. In this way they made their way around the room repeatedly, without anything decisive taking place. In fact, because of the slow pace, it did not look like a chase. Gregor remained on the floor for the time being, especially since he was afraid that his father could interpret a flight up onto the wall or the ceiling as an act of real malice. At any event, Gregor had to tell himself that he could not keep up this running around for a long time, because whenever his father took a single step, he had to go through a large number of movements. Already he was starting to feel short of breath, just as in his earlier days when his lungs had been quite unreliable. As he now staggered around in this way, trying to gather all his energy for running, hardly able to keep his eyes open and feeling so listless that he had no notion at all of any escape other than by running and had almost already forgotten that the walls were available to him, although here they were obstructed by carefully carved furniture full of sharp points and spikes—at that moment something or other thrown casually flew close by and rolled in front of him. It was an apple. Immediately a second one flew after it. Gregor stood still in fright. Further running away was useless, for his father had decided to bombard him. From the fruit bowl on the sideboard his father had filled his pockets, and now, without for the moment taking accurate aim, he was throwing apple after apple. These small red apples were rolling around on the floor, as if electrified, and colliding with each other. A weakly thrown apple grazed Gregor's back but skidded off harmlessly. However, another thrown immediately after that one drove into his back really hard. Gregor wanted to drag himself onward, as if he could make the unexpected and incredible pain go away if he changed his position. But he felt as if he was nailed in place and lay stretched out, completely confused in all his senses. Only with his final glance did he notice how the door of his room was pulled open; and how, right in front of his screaming sister, his mother ran out in her underbodice (for his sister had loosened her clothing in order to give her some freedom to breathe in her fainting spell); and how his mother then ran up to his father—on the way her loosened petticoats slipping toward the floor one after the other—and how, tripping over them, she hurled herself onto the father and, throwing her arms around him, in complete union with him—but at this moment Gregor's powers of sight gave way—as her hands reached around the father's neck, and she begged him to spare Gregor's life.

III

Gregor's serious wound, from which he suffered for over a month—since no one ventured to remove the apple, it remained in his flesh as a visible reminder—seemed by itself to have reminded the father that, in spite of Gregor's present unhappy and hateful appearance, he was a member of the family and should not be treated as an enemy. It was, on the contrary, a requirement of family duty to suppress one's aversion and to endure—nothing else, just endure.

If, through his wound, Gregor had now also apparently lost for good his ability to move and for the time being needed many, many minutes to crawl across his room, like an aged invalid—so far as creeping up high was concerned, that was unimaginable—nevertheless, for this worsening of his condition, in his view he did get completely satisfactory compensation, because every day toward evening the door to the living room, which he was in the habit of keeping a sharp eye on even one or two hours beforehand, was opened, so that he, lying down in the darkness of his room, invisible from the living room, could see the entire family at the illuminated table and listen to their conversation, to a certain extent with their common permission, a situation quite different from what had happened before.

Of course, it was no longer the animated social interaction of former times—of the sort which Gregor had always thought about with a certain longing in small hotel rooms, when, tired out, he had had to throw himself into the damp bedclothes. For the most part what went on now was only very quiet. After the evening meal, the father soon fell asleep in his armchair. The mother and sister warned each other to be quiet. Bent far over the light, the mother sewed fine undergarments for a fashion shop. The sister, who had taken on a job as a salesgirl, in the evening studied stenography and French, so as perhaps to obtain a better position later on. Sometimes the father woke up and, as if he was quite ignorant that he had been asleep, said to the mother, "How long you have been sewing again today!" and went right back to sleep, while the mother and the sister smiled tiredly to each other.

With a sort of stubbornness the father refused to take off his servant's uniform even at home, and while his sleeping gown hung unused on the coat hook, the father dozed completely dressed in his place, as if he was always ready for his responsibility and even here was waiting for the voice of his superior. As a result, in spite of all the care from the mother and sister, his uniform, which even at the start was not new, grew dirty, and Gregor looked, often for the entire evening, at this clothing, with stains all over it and with its gold buttons always polished, in which the old man, though he must have been very uncomfortable, nonetheless was sleeping peacefully.

As soon as the clock struck ten, the mother tried gently to encourage the father to wake up and then to persuade him to go to bed, on the grounds that he could not get a proper sleep here and that the father, who had to report for service at six o'clock, really needed a good sleep. But in his stubbornness, which had gripped him since he had become an employee, he always insisted on staying even longer by the table, although he regularly fell asleep and then could be prevailed upon only with the greatest difficulty to trade his chair for the bed. No matter how much the mother and sister might at that point work on him with small admonitions, for a quarter of an hour he would remain shaking his head slowly, his eyes closed, without standing up. The mother would pull him by the sleeve and speak flattering words into his ear; the sister would leave her work to help her mother, but that would not have the desired effect on the father. He would merely settle himself even more deeply into his armchair. Only when the two women grabbed him under the armpits would he throw his eyes open, look back and forth at the mother and sister, and habitually say, "This is a life. This is the peace and quiet of my old age." And propped up by both women, he would heave himself up elaborately, as if for him it was the greatest trouble, allow himself to be led to the door by the women, wave them away, and proceed on his own from that point, while the mother quickly threw down her sewing implements and the sister her pen in order to run after the father and help him some more.

In this overworked and exhausted family who had time any longer to worry about Gregor more than was absolutely necessary? The household was constantly getting smaller. The servant girl had been let go. A huge bony cleaning woman with white hair flying all over her head now came in the morning and evening to do the heaviest work. The mother took care of everything else, in addition to her considerable sewing work. It even happened that various pieces of family jewelery, which previously the mother and sister had been overjoyed to wear on social and festive occasions, were sold, as Gregor found out in the evening from the general discussion of the prices they had fetched. But the greatest complaint was always that they could not leave this apartment, which was much too big for their present means, since it was impossible to imagine how Gregor might be moved. Gregor fully recognized that it was not just consideration for him which was preventing a move, for he could have been transported easily in a suitable box with a few air holes. The main thing holding the family back from a change in living quarters was far more their complete hopelessness and the idea that they had been struck by a misfortune like no one else in their entire circle of relatives and acquaintances. What the world demands of poor people they now carried out to an extreme degree. The father brought breakfast to the petty officials at the bank; the mother sacrificed herself for the undergarments of strangers; the sister behind her desk was at the beck and call of customers. But the family's energies did not extend any further. And the wound in Gregor's back began to pain him all over again, when his mother and sister, after they had escorted the father to bed, now came back, let their work lie, moved close together, and sat cheek to cheek and when his mother would now say, pointing to Gregor's room, "Close the door, Grete," and when Gregor was again in the darkness, while close by the women mingled their tears or, quite dry eyed, stared at the table.

Gregor spent his nights and days with hardly any sleep. Sometimes he thought that the next time the door opened he would take over the family arrangements just as he had earlier. In his imagination appeared again, after a long time, his boss and the manager, the chief clerk and the apprentices, the excessively dense custodian, two or three friends from other businesses, a chambermaid from a hotel in the provinces (a loving, fleeting memory), a cashier from a hat shop, whom he had seriously but too slowly courted— they all appeared mixed in with strangers or people he had already forgotten, but instead of helping him and his family, they were all unapproachable, and he was happy to see them disappear. But sometimes he was in no mood to worry about his family. He could be filled with sheer anger over the wretched care he was getting, even though he could not imagine anything which he might have an appetite for. Still, he made plans about how he could get into the pantry to take there what he at all accounts deserved, even if he was not hungry. Without thinking any more about what might give Gregor special pleasure, the sister very quickly kicked some food or other, whatever she felt like, into his room in the morning and at noon, before she ran off to her shop. And in the evening, quite indifferent to whether the food had perhaps only been tasted or—what happened most frequently—remained entirely undisturbed, she whisked it out with one sweep of her broom. The task of cleaning his room, which she now always carried out in the evening, could not have been done any more quickly. Streaks of dirt ran along the walls; here and there lay tangles of dust and garbage. At first, when his sister arrived, Gregor positioned himself in a particularly filthy corner as a way of making some sort of protest. But he could well have stayed there for weeks without his sister's doing the job any better. In fact, she saw the dirt as well as he did, but she had decided just to let it stay. In this business, with a touchiness which was quite new to her and which had generally taken over the entire family, she kept watch to see that the cleaning of Gregor's room remained reserved for her. His mother had once undertaken a major cleanup of his room, which she had only completed successfully after using a few buckets of water. The extensive dampness made Gregor sick, however, and he lay spread out, embittered and immobile, on the couch. But the mother did not escape punishment. For in the evening the sister had hardly observed the change in Gregor's room before she ran into the living room mightily offended and, in spite of her mother's hand lifted high in entreaty, broke out in a fit of crying. Her parents—the father had, of course, woken up with a start in his armchair—at first looked at her astonished and helpless, but then they started to get agitated as well. Turning to his right, the father heaped reproaches on the mother that she had not left the cleaning of Gregor's room to the sister and, turning to his left, he shouted at the sister that she would never again be allowed to clean Gregor's room, while the mother tried to pull the father, beside himself in his excitement, into the bedroom. The sister, shaken by her crying fit, pounded on the table with her tiny fists, and Gregor hissed at all this, angry that no one thought about shutting the door and sparing him the sight of this commotion.

But even when the sister, exhausted from her daily work, had grown tired of caring for Gregor as she had before, even then the mother did not have to come at all in her place. And Gregor did not have to be neglected. For now the cleaning woman was there. This old widow, whose strong bony frame had enabled her to survive the worst a long life can offer, had no real horror of Gregor. Without being in the least curious, she had once accidentally opened Gregor's door. At the sight of Gregor, who, totally surprised, began to scamper here and there, although no one was chasing him, she remained standing with her hands folded across her stomach staring at him. Since then she would never fail to open the door furtively a little every morning and evening and look in on Gregor. At first, she also called him to her with words that she probably thought were friendly, like "Come on over here, old dung beetle!" or "Hey, look at the old dung beetle!" Addressed in such a manner, Gregor made no answer, but remained motionless in his place, as if the door had not been opened at all. If only, instead of allowing this cleaning woman to disturb him uselessly whenever she felt like it, they had given her orders to clean up his room every day! Once in the early morning—a hard downpour, perhaps already a sign of the coming spring, struck the windowpanes—when the cleaning woman started up once again with her usual conversation, Gregor was so bitter that he turned toward her, as if for an attack, although slowly and weakly. But instead of being afraid of him, the cleaning woman merely lifted up a chair standing close by the door and, as she stood there with her mouth wide open, her intention was clear: she would close her mouth only when the chair in her hand had been thrown down on Gregor's back. "This goes no further, all right?" she asked, as Gregor turned himself around again, and she placed the chair calmly back in the corner.

Gregor ate hardly anything anymore. Only when he chanced to move past the food which had been prepared did he, as a game, take a bit into his mouth, hold it there for hours, and generally spit it out again. At first he thought it might be his sadness over the condition of his room that kept him from eating, but he very soon became reconciled to the alterations in his room. People had grown accustomed to discard in there things which they could not put anywhere else, and at this point there were many such items, now that they had rented one room of the apartment to three lodgers. These solemn gentlemen—all three had full beards, as Gregor once found out through a crack in the door—were meticulously intent on tidiness, not only in their own room but, since they had now rented a room here, in the entire household, particularly in the kitchen. They simply did not tolerate any useless, let alone any dirty, stuff. Moreover, for the most part they had brought with them their own pieces of furniture. Thus, many items had become superfluous, but these were not really things one could sell or things people wanted to throw out. All these pieces ended up in Gregor's room, even the box of ashes and the garbage pail from the kitchen. The cleaning woman, always in a great hurry, simply flung anything that was for the moment useless into Gregor's room. Fortunately Gregor generally saw only the relevant object and the hand which held it. The cleaning woman perhaps was intending, when time and opportunity allowed, to take the stuff out again or to throw everything out all at once, but in fact the things remained lying there, wherever they had ended up at the first throw, unless Gregor squirmed his way through the accumulation of junk and moved them. At first he was forced to do this because otherwise there was no room for him to creep around; later he did it with a growing pleasure, although after such movements, tired to death and feeling wretched, he did not budge again for hours.

Because the lodgers sometimes also took their evening meal at home in the common living room, the door to it stayed shut on many evenings. But Gregor had no trouble at all going without the open door. Already on many evenings when it was open he had not availed himself of it, but, without the family noticing, was stretched out in the darkest corner of his room. However, on one occasion the cleaning woman had left the door to the living room slightly ajar, and it remained open even when the lodgers came in, as evening fell and the lights were put on. They sat down at the head of the table—where in earlier days the mother, the father, and Gregor had eaten—unfolded their serviettes, and picked up their knives and forks. The mother immediately appeared in the door with a dish of meat and right behind her the sister with a dish piled high with potatoes. The food gave off a lot of steam. The gentlemen lodgers bent over the plates set before them, as if they wanted to check them before eating, and in fact the one who sat in the middle—for the other two he seemed to serve as the authority—cut off a piece of meat still on the serving dish, obviously to establish whether it was sufficiently tender and whether or not it should be sent back to the kitchen. He was satisfied, and mother and sister, who had looked on in suspense, began to breathe easily and to smile.

The family itself ate in the kitchen. In spite of that, before the father went into the kitchen, he came into the living room and with a single bow, cap in hand, made a tour of the table. The lodgers rose up collectively and murmured something into their beards. Then, when they were alone, they ate almost in complete silence. It seemed odd to Gregor that, out of all the many different sorts of sounds of eating, what was always audible was their chewing teeth, as if by that Gregor should be shown that people needed their teeth to eat and that nothing could be done even with the most handsome toothless jawbone. "I really do have an appetite," Gregor said to himself sorrowfully, "but not for these things. How these lodgers stuff themselves, and I am dying of hunger!"

On this very evening the violin sounded from the kitchen. Gregor did not remember ever hearing it all through this period. The lodgers had already ended their night meal, the middle one had pulled out a newspaper and had given each of the other two a page, and they were now leaning back, reading and smoking. When the violin started playing, they became attentive, got up, and went on tiptoe to the hall door, at which they remained standing pressed up against one another. They must have been audible from the kitchen, because Gregor's father called out, "Perhaps the gentlemen don't like the playing? It can be stopped at once." "On the contrary," stated the lodger in the middle, "might the young woman not come in to us and play in the room here, where it is really much more comfortable and cheerful?" "Oh, certainly," cried Gregor's father, as if he were the one playing the violin. The men stepped back into the room and waited. Soon his father came with the music stand, his mother with the sheet music, and his sister with the violin. His sister calmly prepared everything for the recital. His parents, who had never previously rented a room and therefore behaved with exaggerated politeness to the lodgers, dared not sit on their own chairs. His father leaned against the door, his right hand stuck between two buttons of his buttoned-up uniform. His mother, however, accepted a chair offered by one of the lodgers. Since she let the chair stay where the gentleman had chanced to put it, she sat to one side in a corner.

His sister began to play. His father and mother, one on each side, followed attentively the movements of her hands. Attracted by the playing, Gregor had ventured to advance a little further forward, and his head was already in the living room. He scarcely wondered about the fact that recently he had had so little consideration for the others. Earlier, consideration for his family had been something he was proud of. And for that very reason he would have had at this moment more reason to hide away, because as a result of the dust which lay all over his room and flew around with the slightest movement, he was totally covered in dirt. On his back and his sides he carted around with him threads, hair, and remnants of food. His indifference to everything was much too great for him to lie on his back and scour himself on the carpet, as he had done earlier several times a day. Now, in spite of his condition he had no timidity about inching forward a bit on the spotless floor of the living room.

In any case, no one paid him any attention. The family was all caught up in the violin playing. The lodgers, by contrast, having initially placed themselves, hands in their trouser pockets, behind the music stand much too close to his sister, so that they could all see the sheet music, something that must certainly have bothered his sister, soon drew back to the window conversing in low voices with bowed heads, where they then remained, anxiously observed by the father. It now seemed abundantly clear that, having assumed they were to hear a beautiful or entertaining violin recital, they were disappointed; they had had enough of the entire performance and were allowing their peace and quiet to be disturbed only out of politeness. In particular, the way in which they all blew the smoke from their cigars out of their noses and mouths up into the air led one to conclude that they were very tense. And yet his sister was playing so beautifully. Her face was turned to the side, her eyes following the score intently and sadly. Gregor crept forward still a little further, keeping his head close against the floor in order to be able to catch her gaze if possible. Was he a beast that music so captivated him? It was as if the way to the unknown nourishment he craved was revealing itself. He was determined to press forward right up to his sister, to tug at her dress, and to indicate to her in this way that she might still come with her violin into his room, because here no one valued the recital as he longed to value it. He did not wish to let her go from his room any more, at least not while he was still alive. His frightening appearance would for the first time become useful for him. He wanted to be at all the doors of his room simultaneously and snarl back at the attackers. However, his sister should not be compelled but would remain with him voluntarily. She would sit next to him on the sofa, bend down her ear to him, and he would then confide in her that he had firmly intended to send her to the Conservatory and that, if his misfortune had not arrived in the interim, he would have declared all this last Christmas—had Christmas really already come and gone?—and would have brooked no argument. After this explanation his sister would break out in tears of emotion, and Gregor would lift himself up to her shoulder and kiss her throat, which she, from the time she had been going to work, had left exposed without a ribbon or a collar.

"Mr. Samsa!" called out the middle lodger to the father and, without uttering a further word, pointed his index finger at Gregor as he was moving slowly forward. The violin fell silent. The middle lodger smiled, first shaking his head at his friends, and then looked down at Gregor once more. Rather than driving Gregor back, his father seemed to consider it more important for the time being to calm down the lodgers, although they were not at all upset and Gregor seemed to entertain them more than the violin recital. His father hurried over to them and with outstretched arms tried to push them into their own room and at the same time to block their view of Gregor with his own body. At this point they really did become somewhat irritated, although it was hard to tell whether that was because of his father's behavior or because of the knowledge they had just acquired—that they had a neighbor like Gregor and had not been aware of it. They demanded explanations from his father, raised their arms to make their points, tugged agitatedly at their beards, and moved back toward their room quite slowly. In the meantime, his sister, suddenly left on her own, had felt overwhelmed by the unexpected breaking off of the recital. She had held onto the violin and bow in her limp hands for a little while and had continued to look at the sheet music as if she were still playing. All at once she pulled herself together, placed the instrument in her mother's lap—the mother was still sitting in her chair having trouble breathing, her lungs laboring hard—and had run into the next room, which the lodgers, pressured by the father, were already approaching more rapidly. One could observe how under his sister's practiced hands the covers and pillows on the beds were thrown high and then rearranged. Even before the lodgers had reached the room, she had finished fixing the beds and was slipping out. His father seemed once again so gripped by his stubbornness that he forgot about the respect that, after all, he must show his lodgers. He pressed on and on, until right in the door of the room the middle gentleman stamped loudly with his foot and thus brought Gregor's father to a standstill. "I hereby declare," the middle lodger said, raising his hand and casting his glance both on Gregor's mother and sister, "that considering the disgraceful conditions prevailing in this apartment and family"—with this he spat decisively on the floor—"I immediately cancel my room. I will, of course, pay nothing at all for the days which I have lived here; on the contrary, I shall think about whether or not I will initiate some sort of action against you, something which— believe me—would be very easy to establish." He fell silent and looked directly in front of him, as if he was waiting for something. In fact, his two friends immediately joined in with their opinions, "We also give immediate notice." At that he seized the door handle and with a bang slammed the door shut.

Gregor's father groped his way tottering to his chair and let himself fall into it. It looked as if he were stretching out for his usual evening snooze, but the heavy nodding of his head, which appeared as if it had no support, showed that he was not sleeping at all. Gregor had lain motionless the entire time in the spot where the lodgers had caught him out. Disappointment with the collapse of his plan and perhaps also weakness brought on by his severe hunger made it impossible for him to move. He was afraid and reasonably certain that they might launch a combined attack against him at any moment, and he waited. He was not even startled when the violin fell from his mother's lap, out from under her trembling fingers, and gave off a reverberating tone.

"My dear parents," said his sister, banging her hand on the table by way of an introduction, "things cannot go on any longer in this way. If you don't understand that, well, I do. I will not utter my brother's name in front of this monster, and thus I say only that we must try to get rid of it. We have tried what is humanly possible to take care of it and to be patient. I believe that no one can criticize us in the slightest."

"She is right in a thousand ways," said his father to himself. His mother, who was still incapable of breathing properly, began to cough numbly with her hand held up over her mouth and a manic expression in her eyes.

His sister hurried over to her mother and held her forehead. His sister's words seemed to have led his father to certain reflections. He sat upright, played with his service hat among the plates, which still lay on the table from the lodgers' evening meal, and looked now and then at the motionless Gregor.

"We must try to get rid of it," his sister now said decisively to his father, for his mother, in her coughing fit, was not listening to anything. "It is killing you both. I see it coming. When people have to work as hard as we all do, they can't also tolerate this endless torment at home. I just can't go on any more." And she broke out into such a crying fit that her tears flowed down onto her mother's face. She wiped them off her mother with mechanical motions of her hands.

"Child," said her father sympathetically and with obvious appreciation, "then what should we do?"

Gregor's sister only shrugged her shoulders as a sign of the perplexity which, in contrast to her previous confidence, had now come over her while she was crying.

"If he understood us," said his father in a half-questioning tone. His sister, in the midst of her sobbing, shook her hand energetically as a sign that there was no point thinking of that.

"If he understood us," repeated his father and by shutting his eyes he absorbed the sister's conviction of the impossibility of this point, "then perhaps some compromise would be possible with him. But as it is . . ."

"It has to go," cried his sister. "That is the only way, Father. You must try to get rid of the idea that this is Gregor. The fact that we have believed this for so long, that is our real misfortune. But how can it be Gregor? If it were Gregor, he would have long ago realized that a life among human beings is not possible for such a creature and would have gone away voluntarily. Then we would not have a brother, but we could go on living and honor his memory. But this animal plagues us. It drives away the lodgers and obviously wants to take over the entire apartment and leave us to spend the night in the alley. Just look, Father," she suddenly cried out, "he's already starting up again." With a fright which was totally incomprehensible to Gregor, his sister left his mother, literally pushed herself away from her chair, as if she would sooner sacrifice her mother than remain in Gregor's vicinity, and rushed behind her father who, excited merely by her behavior, also stood up and half raised his arms in front of Gregor's sister as though to protect her.

But Gregor did not have any notion of wishing to create problems for anyone and certainly not for his sister. He had just started to turn himself around in order to creep back into his room, quite a startling sight, since, as a result of his ailing condition, he had to guide himself through the difficulty of turning around with his head, in this process lifting and striking it against the floor several times. He paused and looked around. His good intentions seemed to have been recognized. The fright had lasted only for a moment. Now they looked at him in silence and sorrow. His mother lay in her chair, with her legs stretched out and pressed together, her eyes almost shut from weariness. His father and sister sat next to one another. His sister had laid her hand around her father's neck.

"Now perhaps I can actually turn myself around," thought Gregor and began the task again. He couldn't stop puffing at the effort and had to rest now and then. No one was urging him on; it was all left to him on his own. When he had finished turning around, he immediately began to head straight back toward his room. He was astonished at the great distance which separated him from his room and did not understand in the least how in his weakness he had covered the same distance a short time before, almost without noticing it. Always intent only on creeping along quickly, he hardly paid any attention to the fact that no word or cry from his family interrupted him. Only when he was already in the doorway did he turn his head, not completely, because he felt his neck growing stiff. At any rate, he still saw that behind him nothing had changed. Only his sister was standing up. His last glimpse brushed over his mother, who was now completely asleep.

He was only just inside his room when the door was pushed shut very quickly, bolted fast, and barred. Gregor was startled by the sudden commotion behind him, so much so that his little limbs bent double under him. It was his sister who had been in such a hurry. She was already standing up, had waited, and then had sprung forward nimbly. Gregor had not heard anything of her approach. She cried out "Finally!" to her parents, as she turned the key in the lock.

"What now?" Gregor asked himself and looked around him in the darkness. He soon made the discovery that he could no longer move at all. He was not surprised at that. On the contrary, it struck him as unnatural that up to this point he had actually been able to move around with these thin little legs. Despite everything he felt relatively content. True, he had pains throughout his entire body, but it seemed to him that they were gradually becoming weaker and weaker and would finally go away completely. He hardly noticed the rotten apple in his back and the inflamed surrounding area, which were now entirely covered with soft dust. He remembered his family with deep feelings of love. In this whole business, his own conviction that he had to disappear was, if possible, even more firmly held than his sister's. He remained in this state of empty and peaceful reflection until the tower clock struck three in the morning. He lived long enough to see everything outside the window beginning to grow brighter. Then without his willing it, his head sank all the way down, and from his nostrils his last breath flowed weakly out.

Early in the morning the cleaning woman came. In her sheer energy and haste she banged all the doors—in precisely the way people had already frequently asked her not to do—so much so that once she arrived a quiet sleep was no longer possible anywhere in the entire apartment. In her customary brief visit to Gregor she at first found nothing unusual. She thought he lay so immobile there on purpose and was playing the offended party. She gave him credit for as complete an understanding as possible. Since she happened to be holding the long broom in her hand, she tried to tickle Gregor with it from the door. When that was quite unsuccessful, she became irritated and poked Gregor a little, and only when she had shoved him from his place without any resistance did she take notice. When she realized the true state of affairs, her eyes grew large and she whistled to herself. However, she didn't restrain herself for long. She pulled open the door of the bedroom and yelled in a loud voice into the darkness, "Come and look. It's kicked the bucket. It's lying there. It's completely snuffed it!"

The Samsas sat upright in their double bed and had to get over their fright at the cleaning woman before they managed to grasp her message. But then Mr. and Mrs. Samsa climbed very quickly out of bed, one on either side. Mr. Samsa threw the bedspread over his shoulders,

Mrs. Samsa came out only in her nightshirt, and like this they stepped into Gregor's room. Meanwhile, the door of the living room, where Grete had been sleeping since the lodgers had arrived on the scene, had also opened. She was fully clothed, as if she had not slept at all; her white face also seemed to indicate that. "Dead?" said Mrs. Samsa and looked questioningly at the cleaning woman, although she could have checked everything on her own—and indeed it was all clear enough even without checking anything. "I should say so," said the cleaning woman and, by way of proof, poked Gregor's body with the broom a considerable distance more to the side. Mrs. Samsa made a movement as if she wished to restrain the broom but did not do it. "Well," said Mr. Samsa, "now we can give thanks to God." He crossed himself, and the three women followed his example. Grete, who did not take her eyes off the corpse, said, "Just look how thin he was. He has eaten nothing for such a long time. The meals which came in here came out again exactly the same." In fact, Gregor's body was completely flat and dry. That was apparent really for the first time, now that he was no longer raised on his small limbs and nothing else distracted one from looking.

"Grete, come and join us for a moment," said Mrs. Samsa with a melancholy smile, and Grete went, not without looking back at the corpse, following her parents into the bedroom. The cleaning woman shut the door and opened the window wide. In spite of the early morning, the fresh air was partly tinged with warmth. It was already almost the end of March.

The three lodgers stepped out of their room and looked around for their breakfast, astonished that they had been forgotten. The middle one of the gentlemen asked the cleaning woman grumpily, "Where is the breakfast?" However, she laid her finger to her lips and then quickly and silently indicated to the lodgers that they could come into Gregor's room. So they came and stood in the room, which was already quite bright, around Gregor's corpse, their hands in the pockets of their somewhat worn jackets.

Then the door of the bedroom opened, and Mr. Samsa appeared in his uniform, with his wife on one arm and his daughter on the other. All were a little tear stained. Now and then Grete pressed her face into her father's arm.

"Get out of my apartment immediately," said Mr. Samsa and pointed to the door, without letting go of the women. "What do you mean?" said the middle lodger, somewhat dismayed and with a sugary smile. The two others kept their hands behind them and constantly rubbed them against each other, as if in joyful anticipation of a great squabble which must end up in their favor. "I mean exactly what I say," replied Mr. Samsa, and, with his two female companions, went directly up to the lodger. The latter at first stood there motionless and looked at the floor, as if matters were arranging themselves in a new way in his head. "All right, then we'll go," he said and looked up at Mr. Samsa as if, suddenly overcome by humility, he was even asking fresh permission for this decision. Mr. Samsa merely nodded briefly and repeatedly to him with his eyes open wide. Following that, with long strides the lodger did actually go out into the hall. His two friends had already been listening for a while with their hands quite still, and now they hopped smartly after him, as if afraid that Mr. Samsa could step into the hall ahead of them and disturb their reunion with their leader. In the hall all three of them took their hats from the coat rack, pulled their canes from the umbrella stand, bowed silently, and left the apartment. In what turned out to be an entirely groundless mistrust, Mr. Samsa stepped with the two women out onto the landing, leaned against the railing, and looked over as the three lodgers slowly but steadily made their way down the long staircase, disappeared on each floor in a certain turn of the stairwell, and in a few seconds reappeared again. The further down they went, the more the Samsa family lost interest in them, and when a butcher's assistant with a tray on his head came up to meet them and then with a proud bearing ascended the stairs high above them, Mr. Samsa, together with the women, soon left the banister, and they all returned, as if relieved, back into their apartment.

They decided to pass that day resting and going for a stroll. Not only had they earned this break from work, but there was no question that they really needed it. And so they sat down at the table and wrote three letters of apology: Mr. Samsa to his supervisor, Mrs. Samsa to her client, and Grete to her proprietor. During the writing the cleaning woman came in to say that she was going off, for her morning work was finished. The three people writing at first merely nodded, without glancing up. Only when the cleaning woman was still unwilling to depart, did they look up annoyed. "Well?" asked Mr. Samsa. The cleaning woman stood smiling in the doorway, as if she had a great stroke of luck to report to the family but would only do it if she was questioned thoroughly. The almost upright small ostrich feather in her hat, which had irritated Mr. Samsa during her entire service with them, swayed lightly in all directions. "All right then, what do you really want?" asked Mrs. Samsa, whom the cleaning lady respected more than the others. "Well," answered the cleaning woman, smiling so happily she couldn't go on speaking right away, "you mustn't worry about throwing out that rubbish from the next room. It's all taken care of." Mrs. Samsa and Grete bent down to their letters, as though they wanted to go on writing. Mr. Samsa, who saw that the cleaning woman would now want to describe everything in detail, decisively prevented her with an outstretched hand. Since she was not allowed to explain, she remembered the great hurry she was in, and called out, clearly insulted, "Bye bye, everyone," then turned around furiously and left the apartment with a fearful slamming of the door.

"This evening she'll be given notice," said Mr. Samsa, but he got no answer from either his wife or from his daughter, because the cleaning woman seemed to have once again upset the tranquility they had just attained. The women got up, went to the window, and remained there, with their arms about each other. Mr. Samsa turned around in his chair in their direction and observed them quietly for a while. Then he called out, "All right, come here then. Let's set aside these old matters once and for all. And have a little consideration for me." The women attended to him at once. They rushed to him, caressed him, and quickly ended their letters.

Then all three left the apartment together, something they had not done for months now, and took the electric tram into the open air outside the city. The car in which they were sitting by themselves was wholly flooded by the warm sun. Leaning back comfortably in their seats, they talked to each other about future prospects, and they discovered that on closer observation these were not at all bad, for the three of them had not really questioned each other about their employment at all. Each of their positions was extremely favorable and offered especially promising future prospects. The greatest improvement in their situation at this point, of course, would have to come from a change of dwelling. They would now like to rent a smaller and cheaper apartment but better situated and generally more practical than the present one, which Gregor had chosen. While they amused themselves chatting in this way, it struck Mr. and Mrs. Samsa, almost at the same moment, as they looked at their daughter, who was getting more animated all the time, how she had blossomed recently, in spite of all the troubles which had made her cheeks pale, into a beautiful and voluptuous young woman. Growing more silent and almost unconsciously understanding each other in their glances, they thought that the time was now at hand to seek out a good honest man for her. And it was something of a confirmation of their new dreams and good intentions when at the end of their journey their daughter stood up first and stretched her young body.

Lord Dunsany (1878–1957) was born Edward John Moreton Drax Plunkett, the eighteenth baron of Dunsany. Known for his fantasy, Lord Dunsany was a master wordsmith who could create entire universes in his novels and short stories. Not content with working in one genre, Dunsany also wrote stage and radio plays. Most of his tales were published between 1905 and 1919. Because he influenced such writers as J. R. R. Tolkien, Ursula K. Le Guin, and H. P. Lovecraft, it would be accurate to say that his work was as influential to fantasy fiction as Edgar Allan Poe's work was to horror and detective fiction. *The Book of Wonder* (1916), from which this tale is taken, was Dunsany's fifth collection of short stories and is a vital part of any fantasy enthusiast's collection.

The Hoard of the Gibbelins

Lord Dunsany

THE GIBBELINS EAT, as is well known, nothing less good than man. Their evil tower is joined to Terra Cognita, to the lands we know, by a bridge. Their hoard is beyond reason; avarice has no use for it; they have a separate cellar for emeralds and a separate cellar for sapphires; they have filled a hole with gold and dig it up when they need it. And the only use that is known for their ridiculous wealth is to attract to their larder a continual supply of food. In times of famine they have even been known to scatter rubies abroad, a little trail of them to some city of Man, and sure enough their larders would soon be full again.

Their tower stands on the other side of that river known to Homer—*ho rhoos okeanoio*, as he called it—which surrounds the world. And where the river is narrow and fordable the tower was built by the Gibbelins' gluttonous sires, for they liked to see burglars rowing easily to their steps.

Some nourishment that common soil has not the huge trees drained there with their colossal roots from both banks of the river.

There the Gibbelins lived and discreditably fed.

Alderic, Knight of the Order of the City and the Assault, hereditary Guardian of the King's Peace of Mind, a man not unremembered among makers of myth, pondered so long upon the Gibbelins' hoard that by now he deemed it his. Alas that I should say of so perilous a venture, undertaken at dead of night by a valorous man, that its motive was sheer avarice! Yet upon avarice only the Gibbelins relied to keep their larders full, and once in every hundred years sent spies into the cities of men to see how avarice did, and always the spies returned again to the tower saying that all was well.

It may be thought that, as the years went on

and men came by fearful ends on that tower's wall, fewer and fewer would come to the Gibbelins' table: but the Gibbelins found otherwise.

Not in the folly and frivolity of his youth did Alderic come to the tower, but he studied carefully for several years the manner in which burglars met their doom when they went in search of the treasure that he considered his. *In every case they had entered by the door.*

He consulted those who gave advice on this quest; he noted every detail and cheerfully paid their fees, and determined to do nothing that they advised, for what were their clients now? No more than examples of the savoury art, and mere half-forgotten memories of a meal; and many, perhaps, no longer even that.

These were the requisites for the quest that these men used to advise: a horse, a boat, mail armour, and at least three men-at-arms. Some said, "Blow the horn at the tower door"; others said, "Do not touch it."

Alderic thus decided: he would take no horse down to the river's edge, he would not row along it in a boat, and he would go alone and by way of the Forest Unpassable.

How pass, you may say, the unpassable? This was his plan: there was a dragon he knew of who if peasants' prayers are heeded deserved to die, not alone because of the number of maidens he cruelly slew, but because he was bad for the crops; he ravaged the very land and was the bane of a dukedom.

Now Alderic determined to go up against him. So he took horse and spear and pricked till he met the dragon, and the dragon came out against him breathing bitter smoke. And to him Alderic shouted, "Hath foul dragon ever slain true knight?" And well the dragon knew that this had never been, and he hung his head and was silent, for he was glutted with blood. "Then," said the knight, "if thou wouldst ever taste maiden's blood again thou shalt be my trusty steed, and if not, by this spear there shall befall thee all that the troubadours tell of the dooms of thy breed."

And the dragon did not open his ravening mouth, nor rush upon the knight, breathing out fire; for well he knew the fate of those that did these things, but he consented to the terms imposed, and swore to the knight to become his trusty steed.

It was on a saddle upon this dragon's back that Alderic afterwards sailed above the unpassable forest, even above the tops of those measureless trees, children of wonder. But first he pondered that subtle plan of his which was more profound than merely to avoid all that had been done before; and he commanded a blacksmith, and the blacksmith made him a pickaxe.

Now there was great rejoicing at the rumour of Alderic's quest, for all folk knew that he was a cautious man, and they deemed that he would succeed and enrich the world, and they rubbed their hands in the cities at the thought of largesse; and there was joy among all men in Alderic's country, except perchance among the lenders of money, who feared they would soon be paid. And there was rejoicing also because men hoped that when the Gibbelins were robbed of their hoard, they would shatter their high-built bridge and break the golden chains that bound them to the world, and drift back, they and their tower, to the moon, from which they had come and to which they rightly belonged. There was little love for the Gibbelins, though all men envied their hoard.

So they all cheered, that day when he mounted his dragon, as though he was already a conqueror, and what pleased them more than the good that they hoped he would do to the world was that he scattered gold as he rode away; for he would not need it, he said, if he found the Gibbelins' hoard, and he would not need it more if he smoked on the Gibbelins' table.

When they heard that he had rejected the advice of those that gave it, some said that the knight was mad, and others said he was greater than those what gave the advice, but none appreciated the worth of his plan.

He reasoned thus: for centuries men had been well advised and had gone by the cleverest way, while the Gibbelins came to expect them to come by boat and to look for them at the door whenever their larder was empty, even as a man looketh for a snipe in a marsh; but how, said Alderic, if a snipe should sit in the top of a tree, and would men find him there? Assuredly never! So Alderic decided to swim the river and not to go by the door, but to pick his way into the tower through the stone. Moreover, it was in his mind to work below the level of the ocean, the river (as Homer knew) that girdles the world, so that as soon as he made a hole in the wall the water should pour in, confounding the Gibbelins, and flooding the cellars, rumoured to be twenty feet in depth, and therein he would dive for emeralds as a diver dives for pearls.

And on the day that I tell of he galloped away from his home scattering largesse of gold, as I have said, and passed through many kingdoms, the dragon snapping at maidens as he went, but being unable to eat them because of the bit in his mouth, and earning no gentler reward than a spurthrust where he was softest. And so they came to the swart arboreal precipice of the unpassable forest. The dragon rose at it with a rattle of wings. Many a farmer near the edge of the world saw him up there where yet the twilight lingered, a faint, black, wavering line; and mistaking him for a row of geese going inland from the ocean, went into their houses cheerily rubbing their hands and saying that winter was coming, and that we should soon have snow. Soon even there the twilight faded away, and when they descended at the edge of the world it was night and the moon was shining. Ocean, the ancient river, narrow and shallow there, flowed by and made no murmur. Whether the Gibbelins banqueted or whether they watched by the door, they also made no murmur. And Alderic dismounted and took his armour off, and saying one prayer to his lady, swam with his pickaxe. He did not part from his sword, for fear that he meet with a Gibbelin. Landed the other side, he began to work at once, and all went well with him. Nothing put out its head from any window, and all were lighted so that nothing within could see him in the dark. The blows of his pickaxe were dulled in the deep walls. All night he worked, no sound came to molest him, and at dawn the last rock swerved and tumbled inwards, and the river poured in after. Then Alderic took a stone, and went to the bottom step, and hurled the stone at the door; he heard the echoes roll into the tower, then he ran back and dived through the hole in the wall.

He was in the emerald-cellar. There was no light in the lofty vault above him, but, diving through twenty feet of water, he felt the floor all rough with emeralds, and open coffers full of them. By a faint ray of the moon he saw that the water was green with them, and, easily filling a satchel, he rose again to the surface; and there were the Gibbelins waist-deep in the water, with torches in their hands! And, without saying a word, *or even smiling*, they neatly hanged him on the outer wall—and the tale is one of those that have not a happy ending.

Abraham Grace Merritt (1884–1943) or A. Merritt, was a real estate developer born in Beverly, New Jersey, and an editor of *The American Weekly*. Though his style was nothing groundbreaking, he was a crafter of worlds. Merritt had the ability to shape a beautiful, realistic universe, and this may be the only reason his stories were popular. The publication of his tale "The Moon Pool" (1918) is when people really began to take notice. He was able to blend fantastic elements into very realistic stories, and readers sometimes believed that they were reading true accounts. Abraham Merritt took his writing seriously and often revised a story and published a new iteration multiple times. "Thru the Dragon Glass" (1917), also published as "Through the Dragon Glass," was his first published story.

Through the Dragon Glass

A. Merritt

HERNDON HELPED LOOT the Forbidden City when the Allies turned the suppression of the Boxers into the most gorgeous burglar-party since the days of Tamerlane. Six of his sailor-men followed faithfully his buccaneering fancy. A sympathetic Russian highness whom he had entertained in New York saw to it that he got to the coast and his yacht. That is why Herndon was able to sail through the Narrows with as much of the Son of Heaven's treasures as the most accomplished laborer in Peking's mission vineyards.

Some of the loot he gave to charming ladies who had dwelt or were still dwelling on the sunny side of his heart. Most of it he used to fit up those two astonishing Chinese rooms in his Fifth Avenue house. And a little of it, following a vague religious impulse, he presented to the Metropolitan Museum. This, somehow, seemed to put the stamp of legitimacy on his part of the pillage—

like offerings to the gods and building hospitals and peace palaces and such things.

But the Dragon Glass, because he had never seen anything quite so wonderful, he set up in his bedroom where he could look at it the first thing in the morning, and he placed shaded lights about it so that he could wake up in the night and look at it! Wonderful? It is more than wonderful, the Dragon Glass! Whoever made it lived when the gods walked about the earth creating something new every day. Only a man who lived in that sort of atmosphere could have wrought it. There was never anything like it.

I was in Hawaii when the cables told of Herndon's first disappearance. There wasn't much to tell. His man had gone to his room to awaken him one morning—and Herndon wasn't there. All his clothes were, though. Everything was just as if Herndon ought to be somewhere in the house— only he wasn't.

A man worth ten millions can't step out into thin air and vanish without leaving behind him the probability of some commotion, naturally. The newspapers attend to the commotion, but the columns of type boiled down to essentials contained just two facts—that Herndon had come home the night before, and in the morning he was undiscoverable.

I was on the high seas, homeward bound to help the search, when the wireless told the story of his reappearance. They had found him on the floor of his bedroom, shreds of a silken robe on him, and his body mauled as though by a tiger. But there was no more explanation of his return than there had been of his disappearance.

The night before he hadn't been there—and in the morning there he was. Herndon, when he was able to talk, utterly refused to confide even in his doctors. I went straight through to New York, and waited until the men of medicine decided that it was better to let him see me than have him worry any longer about not seeing me.

Herndon got up from a big invalid chair when I entered. His eyes were clear and bright, and there was no weakness in the way he greeted me, nor in the grip of his hand. A nurse slipped from the room.

"What was it, Jim?" I cried. "What on earth happened to you?"

"Not so sure it was on earth," he said. He pointed to what looked like a tall easel hooded with a heavy piece of silk covered with embroidered Chinese characters. He hesitated for a moment and then walked over to a closet. He drew out two heavy bore guns, the very ones, I remembered, that he had used in his last elephant hunt.

"You won't think me crazy if I ask you to keep one of these handy while I talk, will you, Ward?" he asked rather apologetically. "This looks pretty real, doesn't it?"

He opened his dressing gown and showed me his chest swathed in bandages. He gripped my shoulder as I took without question one of the guns. He walked to the easel and drew off the hood.

"There it is," said Herndon.

And then, for the first time, I saw the Dragon Glass!

There never has been anything like that thing! Never! At first all you saw was a cool, green, glimmering translucence, like the sea when you are swimming under water on a still summer day and look up through it. Around its edges ran flickers of scarlet and gold, flashes of emerald, shimmers of silver and ivory. At its base a disk of topaz rimmed with red fire shot up dusky little vaporous yellow flames.

Afterward you were aware that the green translucence was an oval slice of polished stone. The flashes and flickers became dragons. There were twelve of them. Their eyes were emeralds, their fangs were ivory, their claws were gold. There were scaled dragons, and each scale was so inlaid that the base, green as the primeval jungle, shaded off into vivid scarlet, and the scarlet into tips of gold. Their wings were of silver and vermilion, and were folded close to their bodies.

But they were alive, those dragons. There was never so much life in metal and wood since Al-Akram, the Sculptor of ancient Ad, carved the first crocodile, and the jealous Almighty breathed life into it for a punishment!

And last you saw that the topaz disk that sent up the little yellow flames was the top of a metal sphere around which coiled a thirteenth dragon, thin and red, and biting its scorpion-tipped tail.

It took your breath away, the first glimpse of the Dragon Glass. Yes, and the second and third glimpse, too—and every other time you looked at it.

"Where did you get it?" I asked, a little shakily.

Herndon said evenly: "It was in a small hidden crypt in the Imperial Palace. We broke into the crypt quite by"—he hesitated—"well, call it accident. As soon as I saw it I knew I must have it. What do you think of it?"

"Think!" I cried. "Think! Why, it's the most marvelous thing that the hands of man ever made! What is that stone? Jade?"

"I'm not sure," said Herndon. "But come here. Stand just in front of me."

He switched out the lights in the room. He turned another switch, and on the glass opposite me three shaded electrics threw their rays into its mirror-like oval.

"Watch!" said Herndon. "Tell me what you see!"

I looked into the glass. At first I could see nothing but the rays shining farther, farther—back into infinite distances, it seemed. And then.

"Good God!" I cried, stiffening with horror. "Jim, what hellish thing is this?"

"Steady, old man," came Herndon's voice. There was relief and a curious sort of joy in it. "Steady; tell me what you see."

I said: "I seem to see through infinite distances—and yet what I see is as close to me as though it were just on the other side of the glass. I see a cleft that cuts through two masses of darker green. I see a claw, a gigantic, hideous claw that stretches out through the cleft. The claw has seven talons that open and close—open and close. Good God, such a claw, Jim! It is like the claws that reach out from the holes in the lama's hell to grip the blind souls as they shudder by!"

"Look, look farther, up through the cleft, above the claw. It widens. What do you see?"

I said: "I see a peak rising enormously high and cutting the sky like a pyramid. There are flashes of flame that dart from behind and outline it. I see a great globe of light like a moon that moves slowly out of the flashes; there is another moving across the breast of the peak; there is a third that swims into the flame at the farthest edge—"

"The seven moons of Rak," whispered Herndon, as though to himself. "The seven moons that bathe in the rose flames of Rak which are the fires of life and that circle Lalil like a diadem. He upon whom the seven moons of Rak have shone is bound to Lalil for this life, and for ten thousand lives."

He reached over and turned the switch again. The lights of the room sprang up.

"Jim," I said, "it can't be real! What is it? Some devilish illusion in the glass?"

He unfastened the bandages about his chest.

"The claw you saw had seven talons," he answered quietly. "Well, look at this."

Across the white flesh of his breast, from left shoulder to the lower ribs on the right, ran seven healing furrows. They looked as though they had been made by a gigantic steel comb that had been drawn across him. They gave one the thought they had been ploughed.

"The claw made these," he said as quietly as before.

"Ward," he went on, before I could speak, "I wanted you to see—what you've seen. I didn't know whether you would see it. I don't know whether you'll believe me even now. I don't suppose I would if I were in your place—still—"

He walked over and threw the hood upon the Dragon Glass.

"I'm going to tell you," he said. "I'd like to go through it—uninterrupted. That's why I cover it.

"I don't suppose," he began slowly—"I don't suppose, Ward, that you've ever heard of Rak the Wonder-Worker, who lived somewhere back at the beginning of things, nor how the Greatest Wonder-Worker banished him somewhere outside the world?"

"No," I said shortly, still shaken by the sight.

"It's a big part of what I've got to tell you," he went on. "Of course you'll think it rot, but—I came across the legend in Tibet first. Then I ran across it again—with the names changed, of course—when I was getting away from China.

"I take it that the gods were still fussing around close to man when Rak was born. The story of his parentage is somewhat scandalous. When he grew older Rak wasn't satisfied with just seeing wonderful things being done. He wanted to do them himself, and he—well, he studied the method. After a while the Greatest Wonder-Worker ran across some of the things Rak had made, and he found them admirable—a little too admirable. He didn't like to destroy the lesser wonder-worker because, so the gossip ran, he felt a sort of responsibility. So he gave Rak a place somewhere—outside the world—and he gave him power over every one out of so many millions of births to lead or lure or sweep that soul into his domain so that he might build up a people—and over his people Rak was given the high, the low, and the middle justice.

"And outside the world Rak went. He fenced his domain about with clouds. He raised a great mountain, and on its flank he built a city for the men and women who were to be his. He circled the city with wonderful gardens, and he placed in the gardens many things, some good and some very—terrible. He set around the mountain's brow seven moons for a diadem, and he fanned behind the mountain a fire which is the fire of life, and through which the moons pass eternally to be born again." Herndon's voice sank to a whisper.

"Through which the moons pass," he said. "And with them the souls of the people of Rak. They pass through the fires and are born again— and again—for ten thousand lives. I have seen the moons of Rak and the souls that march with them into the fires. There is no sun in the land—only the new-born moons that shine green on the city and on the gardens."

"Jim," I cried impatiently. "What in the world are you talking about? Wake up, man! What's all that nonsense got to do with this?"

I pointed to the hooded Dragon Glass.

"That," he said. "Why, through that lies the road to the gardens of Rak!"

The heavy gun dropped from my hand as I stared at him, and from him to the glass and back again. He smiled and pointed to his bandaged breast.

He said: "I went straight through to Peking with the Allies. I had an idea what was coming, and I wanted to be in at the death. I was among the first to enter the Forbidden City. I was as mad for loot as any of them. It was a maddening sight, Ward. Soldiers with their arms full of precious stuff even Morgan couldn't buy; soldiers with wonderful necklaces around their hairy throats and their pockets stuffed with jewels; soldiers with their shirts bulging treasures the Sons of Heaven had been hoarding for centuries! We were

Goths sacking imperial Rome. Alexander's hosts pillaging that ancient gemmed courtesan of cities, royal Tyre! Thieves in the great ancient scale, a scale so great that it raised even thievery up to something heroic.

"We reached the throne-room. There was a little passage leading off to the left, and my men and I took it. We came into a small octagonal room. There was nothing in it except a very extraordinary squatting figure of jade. It squatted on the floor, its back turned toward us. One of my men stooped to pick it up. He slipped. The figure flew from his hand and smashed into the wall. A slab swung outward. By a—well, call it a fluke, we had struck the secret of the little octagonal room!

"I shoved a light through the aperture. It showed a crypt shaped like a cylinder. The circle of the floor was about ten feet in diameter. The walls were covered with paintings, Chinese characters, queer-looking animals, and things I can't well describe. Around the room, about seven feet up, ran a picture. It showed a sort of island floating off into space. The clouds lapped its edges like frozen seas full of rainbows. There was a big pyramid of a mountain rising out of the side of it. Around its peak were seven moons, and over the peak—a face!

"I couldn't place that face and I couldn't take my eyes off it. It wasn't Chinese, and it wasn't of any other race I'd ever seen. It was as old as the world and as young as tomorrow. It was benevolent and malicious, cruel and kindly, merciful and merciless, saturnine as Satan and as joyous as Apollo. The eyes were as yellow as buttercups, or as the sunstone on the crest of the Feathered Serpent they worship down in the Hidden Temple of Tuloon. And they were as wise as Fate.

"'There's something else here, sir,' said Martin—you remember Martin, my first officer. He pointed to a shrouded thing on the side. I entered, and took from the thing a covering that fitted over it like a hood. It was the Dragon Glass!

"The moment I saw it I knew I had to have it—and I knew I would have it. I felt that I did not want to get the thing away any more than the thing itself wanted to get away. From the first I thought of the Dragon Glass as something alive. Just as much alive as you and I are. Well, I did get it away. I got it down to the yacht, and then the first odd thing happened.

"You remember Wu-Sing, my boat steward? You know the English Wu-Sing talks. Atrocious! I had the Dragon Glass in my stateroom. I'd forgotten to lock the door. I heard a whistle of sharply indrawn breath. I turned, and there was Wu-Sing. Now, you know that Wu-Sing isn't what you'd call intelligent-looking. Yet as he stood there something seemed to pass over his face, and very subtly change it. The stupidity was wiped out as though a sponge had been passed over it. He did not raise his eyes, but he said, in perfect English, mind you; 'Has the master augustly counted the cost of his possession?'

"I simply gaped at him.

"'Perhaps,' he continued, 'the master has never heard of the illustrious Hao-Tzan? Well, he shall hear.'

"Ward, I couldn't move or speak. But I know now it wasn't sheer astonishment that held me. I listened while Wu-Sing went on to tell in polished phrase the same story that I had heard in Tibet, only there they called him Rak instead of Hao-Tzan. But it was the same story.

"'And,' he finished, 'before he journeyed afar, the illustrious Hao-Tzan caused a great marvel to be wrought. He called it the Gateway.' Wu-Sing waved his hand to the Dragon Glass. 'The master has it. But what shall he who has a Gateway do but pass through it? Is it not better to leave the Gateway behind—unless he dare go through it?'

"He was silent. I was silent, too. All I could do was wonder where the fellow had so suddenly got his command of English. And then Wu-Sing straightened. For a moment his eyes looked into mine. They were as yellow as buttercups, Ward, and wise, wise! My mind rushed back to the little room behind the panel. Ward—the eyes of Wu-Sing were the eyes of the face that brooded over the peak of the moons!

"And all in a moment, the face of Wu-Sing dropped back into its old familiar stupid lines. The eyes he turned to me were black and clouded. I jumped from my chair.

"'What do you mean, you yellow fraud!' I shouted. 'What do you mean by pretending all this time that you couldn't talk English?'

"He looked at me stupidly, as usual. He whined in his pidgin that he didn't understand; that he hadn't spoken a word to me until then. I couldn't get anything else out of him, although I nearly frightened his wits out. I had to believe him. Besides, I had seen his eyes. Well, I was fair curious by this time, and I was more anxious to get the glass home safely than ever.

"I got it home. I set it up here, and I fixed those lights as you saw them. I had a sort of feeling that the glass was waiting—for something. I couldn't tell just what. But that it was going to be rather important, I knew—"

He suddenly thrust his head into his hands, and rocked to and fro.

"How long, how long," he moaned, "how long, Santhu?"

"Jim!" I cried. "Jim! What's the matter with you?"

He straightened. "In a moment you'll understand," he said.

And then, as quietly as before: "I felt that the glass was waiting. The night I disappeared I couldn't sleep. I turned out the lights in the room; turned them on around the glass and sat before it. I don't know how long I sat, but all at once I jumped to my feet. The dragons seemed to be moving! They were moving! They were crawling round and round the glass. They moved faster and faster. The thirteenth dragon spun about the topaz globe. They circled faster and faster until they were nothing but a halo of crimson and gold flashes. As they spun, the glass itself grew misty, mistier, mistier still, until it was nothing but a green haze. I stepped over to touch it. My hand went straight on through it as though nothing were there.

"I reached in—up to the elbow, up to the

shoulder. I felt my hand grasped by warm little fingers. I stepped through—"

"Stepped through the glass?" I cried.

"Through it," he said, "and then—I felt another little hand touch my face. I saw Santhu!

"Her eyes were as blue as the cornflowers, as blue as the big sapphire that shines in the forehead of Vishnu, in his temple at Benares. And they were set wide, wide apart. Her hair was blue-black, and fell in two long braids between her little breasts. A golden dragon crowned her, and through its paws slipped the braids. Another golden dragon girded her. She laughed into my eyes, and drew my head down until my lips touched hers. She was lithe and slender and yielding as the reeds that grow before the Shrine of Hathor that stands on the edge of the Pool of Djeeba. Who Santhu is or where she came from—how do I know? But this I know—she is lovelier than any woman who ever lived on earth. And she is a woman!

"Her arms slipped from about my neck and she drew me forward. I looked about me. We stood in a cleft between two great rocks. The rocks were a soft green, like the green of the Dragon Glass. Behind us was a green mistiness. Before us the cleft ran only a little distance. Through it I saw an enormous peak jutting up like a pyramid, high, high into a sky of chrysoprase. A soft rose radiance pulsed at its sides, and swimming slowly over its breast was a huge globe of green fire. The girl pulled me toward the opening. We walked on silently, hand in hand. Quickly it came to me—Ward, I was in the place whose pictures had been painted in the room of the Dragon Glass!

"We came out of the cleft and into a garden. The Gardens of Many-Columned Iram, lost in the desert because they were too beautiful, must have been like that place. There were strange, immense trees whose branches were like feathery plumes and whose plumes shone with fires like those that clothe the feet of Indra's dancers. Strange flowers raised themselves along our path, and their hearts glowed like the glow-worms that are fastened to the rainbow bridge to Asgard. A wind sighed through the plumed trees, and lumi-nous shadows drifted past their trunks. I heard a girl laugh, and the voice of a man singing.

"We went on. Once there was a low wailing far in the garden, and the girl threw herself before me, her arms outstretched. The wailing ceased, and we went on. The mountain grew plainer. I saw another great globe of green fire swing out of the rose flashes at the right of the peak. I saw another shining into the glow at the left. There was a curious trail of mist behind it. It was a mist that had tangled in it a multitude of little stars. Everything was bathed in a soft green light— such a light as you would have if you lived within a pale emerald.

"We turned and went along another little trail. The little trail ran up a little hill, and on the hill was a little house. It looked as though it was made of ivory. It was a very odd little house. It was more like the Jain pagodas at Brahmaputra than anything else. The walls glowed as though they were full of light. The girl touched the wall, and a panel slid away. We entered, and the panel closed after us.

"The room was filled with a whispering yellow light. I say whispering because that is how one felt about it. It was gentle and alive. A stairway of ivory ran up to another room above. The girl pressed me toward it. Neither of us had uttered a word. There was a spell of silence upon me. I could not speak. There seemed to be nothing to say. I felt a great rest and a great peace—as though I had come home. I walked up the stairway and into the room above. It was dark except for a bar of green light that came through the long and narrow window. Through it I saw the mountain and its moons. On the floor was an ivory head-rest and some silken cloths. I felt suddenly very sleepy. I dropped to the cloths, and at once was asleep.

"When I awoke the girl with the cornflower eyes was beside me! She was sleeping. As I watched, her eyes opened. She smiled and drew me to her—

"I do not know why, but a name came to me. 'Santhu!' I cried. She smiled again, and I knew that I had called her name. It seemed to me that

I remembered her, too, out of immeasurable ages. I arose and walked to the window. I looked toward the mountain. There were now two moons on its breast. And then I saw the city that lay on the mountain's flank. It was such a city as you see in dreams, or as the tale-tellers of El-Bahara fashion out of the mirage. It was all of ivory and shining greens and flashing blues and crimsons. I could see people walking about its streets. There came the sound of little golden bells chiming.

"I turned toward the girl. She was sitting up, her hands clasped about her knees, watching me. Love came, swift and compelling. She arose—I took her in my arms—

"Many times the moons circled the mountains, and the mist held the little, tangled stars passing with them. I saw no one but Santhu; no thing came near us. The trees fed us with fruits that had in them the very essences of life. Yes, the fruit of the Tree of Life that stood in Eden must have been like the fruit of those trees. We drank of green water that sparkled with green fires, and tasted like the wine Osiris gives the hungry souls in Amenti to strengthen them. We bathed in pools of carved stone that welled with water yellow as amber. Mostly we wandered in the gardens. There were many wonderful things in the gardens. They were very unearthly. There was no day nor night. Only the green glow of the ever-circling moons. We never talked to each other. I don't know why. Always there seemed nothing to say.

"Then Santhu began to sing to me. Her songs were strange songs. I could not tell what the words were. But they built up pictures in my brain. I saw Rak the Wonder-Worker fashioning his gardens, and filling them with things beautiful and things—evil. I saw him raise the peak, and knew that it was Lalil; saw him fashion the seven moons and kindle the fires that are the fires of life. I saw him build his city, and I saw men and women pass into it from the world through many gateways.

"Santhu sang—and I knew that the marching stars in the mist were the souls of the people of Rak which sought rebirth. She sang, and I saw myself ages past walking in the city of Rak with Santhu beside me. Her song wailed, and I felt myself one of the mist-entangled stars. Her song wept, and I felt myself a star that fought against the mist, and, fighting, break away—a star that fled out and out through immeasurable green space—

"A man stood before us. He was very tall. His face was both cruel and kind, saturnine as Satan and joyous as Apollo. He raised his eyes to us, and they were yellow as buttercups, and wise, so wise! Ward, it was the face above the peak in the room of the Dragon Glass! The eyes that had looked at me out of Wu-Sing's face! He smiled on us for a moment and then—he was gone!

"I took Santhu by the hand and began to run. Quite suddenly it came to me that I had enough of the haunted gardens of Rak; that I wanted to get back to my own land. But not without Santhu. I tried to remember the road to the cleft. I felt that there lay the path back. We ran. From far behind came a wailing. Santhu screamed—but I knew the fear in her cry was not for herself. It was for me. None of the creatures of that place could harm her who was herself one of its creatures. The wailing drew closer. I turned.

"Winging down through the green air was a beast, an unthinkable beast, Ward! It was like the winged beast of the Apocalypse that is to bear the woman arrayed in purple and scarlet. It was beautiful even in its horror. It closed its scarlet and golden wings, and its long, gleaming body shot at me like a monstrous spear.

"And then—just as it was about to strike—a mist threw itself between us! It was a rainbow mist, and it was—cast. It was cast as though a hand had held it and thrown it like a net. I heard the winged beast shriek its disappointment, Santhu's hand gripped mine tighter. We ran through the mist.

"Before us was the cleft between the two green rocks. Time and time again we raced for it, and time and time again that beautiful shining horror struck at me—and each time came the thrown mist to baffle it. It was a game! Once I heard a laugh, and then I knew who was my hunter. The master of the beast and the caster of the mist. It was he of the yellow eyes—and he was playing me—playing me as a child plays with a cat when he tempts it with a piece of meat and snatches the meat away again and again from the hungry jaws!

"The mist cleared away from its last throw, and the mouth of the cleft was just before us. Once more the thing swooped—and this time there was no mist. The player had tired of the game! As it struck, Santhu raised herself before it. The beast swerved—and the claw that had been stretched to rip me from throat to waist struck me a glancing blow. I fell—fell through leagues and leagues of green space.

"When I awoke I was here in this bed, with the doctor men around me and this—" He pointed to his bandaged breast again.

"That night when the nurse was asleep I got up and looked into the Dragon Glass, and I saw—the claw, even as you did. The beast is there. It is waiting for me!"

Herndon was silent for a moment.

"If he tires of the waiting he may send the beast through for me," he said. "I mean the man with the yellow eyes. I've a desire to try one of these guns on it. It's real, you know, the beast is—and these guns have stopped elephants."

"But the man with the yellow eyes, Jim," I whispered—"who is he?"

"He," said Herndon—"why, he's the Wonder-Worker himself!"

"You don't believe such a story as that!" I cried. "Why, it's—it's lunacy! It's some devilish illusion in the glass. It's like the—crystal globe that makes you hypnotize yourself and think the things your own mind creates are real. Break it, Jim! It's devilish! Break it!"

"Break it!" he said incredulously. "Break it? Not for the ten thousand lives that are the toll of Rak! Not real? Aren't these wounds real? Wasn't Santhu real? Break it! Good God, man, you don't know what you say! Why, it's my only road back to her! If that yellow-eyed devil back there were only as wise as he looks, he would know he didn't have to keep his beast watching there. I want to go, Ward; I want to go and bring her back with me. I've an idea, somehow, that he hasn't—well, full control of things. I've an idea that the Greatest Wonder-Worker wouldn't put wholly in Rak's hands the souls that wander through the many gateways into his kingdom. There's a way out, Ward; there's a way to escape him. I won away from him once, Ward. I'm sure of it. But then I left Santhu behind. I have to go back for her. That's why I found the little passage that led from the throne-room. And he knows it, too. That's why he had to turn his beast on me.

"And I'll go through again, Ward. And I'll come back again—with Santhu!"

But he has not returned. It is six months now since he disappeared for the second time. And from his bedroom, as he had done before. By the will that they found—the will that commended that in event of his disappearing as he had done before and not returning within a week I was to have his house and all that was within it—I came into possession of the Dragon Glass. The dragons had spun again for Herndon, and he had gone through the gateway once more. I found only one of the elephant guns, and I knew that he had had time to take the other with him.

I sit night after night before the glass, waiting for him to come back through it—with Santhu. Sooner or later they will come. That I know.

E. F. Benson (1867–1940) was an English writer who tried his hand at novels, biographies, short stories, and even archaeology. His first novel, *Dodo* (1893), was somewhat controversial for its portrayal of polite society, and not long after Benson explored horror in a different way: through the palpable terror of his supernatural tales. The uncanny also figures into a later novel, *David Blaize and the Blue Door* (1918), in yet a third mode. The novel, excerpted here, reads much like Lewis Carroll's *Alice's Adventures in Wonderland* and seems to take place in a dream, filled with the nonsensical and the absurd. This was in itself a departure from the same character written about in a realistic way—with normal depictions of schoolboy life—in his prior novel *David Blaize* (1916). Somewhat underrated today, Benson's body of work is extraordinary for its quality and range.

David Blaize and the Blue Door

(EXCERPT)

E. F. Benson

DAVID WAS NOW JUST "turned six," as Nannie expressed it, and knew that he had only about four years more in front of him before he began to lapse into that drowsy state of grown-uppishness which begins when boys are ten or thereabouts, and lasts, getting worse and worse, till they are twenty or seventy or anything else. If he was going to find the real world of which he caught glimpses now and then, he must do so without losing much time. There was probably a door into it, and for a long time he had hoped that it was the door in the ground by the lake. But one day he had found that door open, and it was an awful disappointment to see that it only contained a tap and a round opening, to which presently the gardener fixed a long curly pipe. When he turned the tap, the pipe gave some jolly chuckling noises, and began to stream with water at its far end. That was very delightful, and consoled David a little for the disappointment.

Then one night he had a clue. He had just lain down in his bed, when he heard a door beginning to behave as doors do when they think they are quite alone, and nobody is looking. Then, as you know, they unlatch themselves, and begin walking to and fro on their hinges, hitting themselves against their frames. This often happened to the nursery door when he came downstairs in the morning, after he was quite sure he had shut it. His mother therefore sent him up to shut it again, and sure enough the door was always open, having undone itself to go for a walk on its hinges.

But on this night he thought that the sound of the door came from under his pillow, but he very carelessly fell asleep just as he was listening in order to make sure, and the next thing he knew was that Nannie was telling him it was morning. Again, on the very next night he had only just put his head on the pillow when the door began banging. It sounded muffled, and there was no doubt this time that it came from under his pillow. He sat up in bed, broad awake, and pulled his pillow away. By the light of the flame-cats who were dancing to-night, he could see the smooth white surface of his bolster, but, alas, there was no door there.

David was now quite sure that somewhere under his pillow was the door he was looking for. One time he had allowed himself to go to sleep before finding it, and the other time he had got too much awake. So on the third night he took the pin-partridge to bed with him, in the hope that it would keep him just awake enough, by pricking him with the head of its pin-leg. The pin-partridge had, of course, come out of Noah's Ark, and in the course of some terrible adventures had lost a leg. So Nannie had taken a pin, and driven it into the stump, so that it could stand again. The pin-leg was rather longer than the wooden one, which made the partridge lean a little to one side, as if it was listening to the agreeable conversation of the animal next it.

Sure enough, on this third night, David had only just lain down, with the pin-partridge in one hand, and the pin ready to scratch his leg to keep him just awake enough, when the door began banging again, just below his pillow. He listened a little while, pressing the pin-head against his calf so that it hurt a little, but not enough to wake him up hopelessly, and moved his head about till he was sure that his ear was directly above the door. Then very quietly he pushed his pillow aside, and there, in the middle of his bolster was a beautiful shining blue door with a gold handle, swinging gently to and fro, as if it was alone. He got up, pushed it open and entered. For fear of some dreadful misfortune happening, like finding his mother on the other side of it, who might send

him back to shut it, he closed it very carefully and softly. He found that there was a key hanging up on the wall beside it, and to his great joy it fitted the keyhole. He locked it, and put the key back on its nail, so that when he came back he could let himself out, and in the meantime nobody could possibly reach him.

CHAPTER II

The passage into which the blue door opened was very like the nursery passage at home, and it was certainly night, because the flame-cats were dancing on the walls, which only happened after dark. Yet there was no fire burning anywhere, which was rather puzzling, but soon David saw that these were real cats, not just the sort of unreal ones which demanded a fire to make them dance at all. Some were red, some were yellow, some were emerald green with purple patches, and instead of having a band or a piano to dance to, they all squealed and purred and growled, making such a noise that David could not hear himself speak. So he stamped his foot and said "Shoo!" at which the dance suddenly came to an end, and all the cats sat down, put one hind-leg in the air, and began licking themselves.

"If you please," said David, "will you tell me where to go next?"

Every cat stopped licking itself, and looked at him. Some cat behind him said:

"Lor! it's the boy from the nursery."

David turned round. All the cats had begun licking themselves again, except a large tabby, only instead of being black and brown, it was the colour of apricot jam and poppies.

"Was it you who spoke?" said David.

"Set to partners!" said the tabby, and they all began dancing again.

"Shoo, you silly things," said David, stamping again. "I don't want to stop your dancing, except just to be told where I'm to go, and what I'm to do if I'm hungry."

The dancing stopped again.

"There is a pot of mouse-marmalade somewhere," said the tabby, "only you mustn't take more than a very little bit. It's got to last till February."

"But I don't like mouse-marmalade," said David.

"I never said you did," said the tabby. "Where's the cook?"

"Gone to buy some new whiskers," said another. "She put them too close to the fire, which accounts for the smell of burning."

"Then all that can be done is to set to partners, and hope for the best," said the tabby.

"If any one dances again," said David, "before you tell me the way, and where I shall find a shop with some proper food in it, not mousey, I shall turn on the electric light."

"Fiddle-de-dee!" said the tabby, and they all began singing

"Hey diddle-diddle
The cat and the fiddle."

at the top of their voices.

David was getting vexed with them all, and he looked about for the electric light. But there were no switches by the door, as there ought to have been, but only a row of bottles which he knew came out of his father's laboratory. But the stopper in one of them was loose, and a fizzing noise came out of it. He listened to it a minute, with his ear close to it, and heard it whispering, "*It's me! it's me! it's me!*"

"And when he's got, it, he doesn't know what to do with it!" said the tabby contemptuously.

David hadn't the slightest idea. He was only sure that the bottle had something to do with the electric light, and he took it up and began shaking it, as Nannie did to his medicine bottle. To his great delight, he saw that, as he shook it, the cats grew fainter and fainter, and the passage lighter and lighter.

The tabby spoke to him in a tremulous voice.

"You're shocking us frightfully," she said. "Please, don't. You may have all the mouse-marmalade as soon as the cook comes back with her whiskers. She's been gone a long time. And if you don't like it, you really know where everything else is. There's the garden outside, and then

the lake, and then the village. It's all just as usual, except that everything is real here. But whatever you do, don't shock us any more."

The passage had grown quite bright by now, and there were only a few of the very strongest cats left. So, as he was a kind boy, he put down the bottle again, which began fizzing and whispering:

"*Pleased to have met you: pleased to have met you: pleased to have met you.*"

"I don't know why you couldn't have told me that at first," said David to the tabby.

"Nor do I. It was my poor head. The dancing gets into it, and makes it turn round and square, one after the other. May we go on?"

The cats began to recover as he stopped shaking the bottle, and he walked on round the corner where the game cupboard stood against the wall. All the games were kept there, the Noah's Ark, and the spillikins, and the Badminton, and the Happy Families, and the oak-bricks, and the lead soldiers; and, as usual, the door of it was slightly open, because, when all the games were put away, even Nannie could not shut it tight. To-night there was an extraordinary stir going on in it, everything was slipping about inside, and, as David paused to see what was happening, a couple of marbles rolled out. But, instead of stopping on the carpet, they continued rolling faster and faster, and he heard them hopping downstairs in the direction of the garden door.

"I don't want to play games just yet," he said to himself, "there is so much to explore, but I must see what they are doing."

He opened the door a little wider, and heard an encouraging voice, which he knew must be Noah's, come from inside.

"That's right," it said; "now we can see what we're doing. Is my ulster buttoned properly this time, missus? Last night, when you buttoned it for me, you did it wrong, you did, and I caught cold in my ankle, I did. It's been sneezing all day, it has."

"I never saw such trouble as you men are," said Mrs. Noah. "Get up, you silly, and don't sit on Shem's hat. I've been looking for it everywhere."

David stooped down and looked in. He had a sort of idea that he was invisible, and wouldn't disturb anybody. There was the ark, with all its windows open, and the family were dressing. It consisted of two compartments, in the second of which lived the animals, one on the top of each other right up to the roof. There was no door in it, but the roof lifted off. At present it was tightly closed and latched, and confused noises of lions roaring and elephants trumpeting and cows mooing, dogs barking, and birds singing came from inside. Sometimes there was ordinary talk too, for the animals had all learned English from David as well as knowing their own animal tongue, and the Indian elephant spoke Hindustanee in addition. He was slim and light blue, and was known as the "Elegant Elephant," in contrast to a stout black one who never spoke at all. All this David thought that he and Nannie had made up, but now he knew that it was perfectly true. And he stood waiting to see what would happen next.

The hubbub increased.

"If that great lamb would get off my chest," said the elegant elephant, "I should be able to get up. Why don't they come and open the roof?"

"Not time yet," said the cow. "The family are still dressing. But it's a tight fit to-night. I'm glad the pin-partridge isn't here scratching us all."

"Where's it gone?" said the elephant.

"David took it to bed; more fool he," said the cow.

"He couldn't be much more of a fool than he is," grunted the pig. "He knows nothing about us really."

At this moment David heard an irregular kind of hopping noise coming down the passage, and, just as he turned to look, the pin-partridge ran between his legs. It flew on to the roof of the ark, and began pecking at it.

"Let me in," it shouted. "I believe it's the first of September. What cads you fellows are not to let me in!"

"You always think it's the first of September," said the cow. "Now look at me; I'm milked every day, which must hurt me much more than being shot once."

"Not if it's properly done," said the partridge. "I know lots of cows who like it."

"But it's improperly done," said the cow. "David knows less about milking than anybody since the flood. You wait till I catch him alone, and see if I can't teach him something about tossing."

This sounded a very awful threat, and David, who knew that it was best to take cows as well as bulls by the horns, determined on a bold policy.

"If I hear one word more about tossing, I shan't let any of you out," he said.

There was dead silence.

"Who's that?" said the cow in a trembling voice, for she was a coward as well as a cow.

"It's me!" said David.

There was a confused whispering within.

"We can't stop here all night."

"Say you won't toss him."

"You can't anyhow, because your horns are both broken."

"Less noise in there," said Noah suddenly, from the next compartment.

The cow began whimpering.

"I'm a poor old woman," she said, "and everybody's very hard on me, considering the milk and butter I've given you."

"Chalk and water and margarine," said the pin-partridge, who had been listening with his ear to the roof. "Do say you won't toss him. I can't see him, but he's somewhere close to me."

"Very well. I won't toss him. Open the roof, boy."

David was not sure that Noah would like this, as he was the ark-master, but he felt that his having said that he would keep the roof shut unless the cow promised, meant that he would open it if she did, and so he lifted the roof about an inch.

At that moment Noah's head appeared. He was standing on Shem's head, who was standing on Ham's head, who was standing on Japheth's head, who was standing on his mother's head. They always came out of their room in this way, partly in order to get plenty of practice in case of fire, and partly because they couldn't be certain that the flood had gone down, and were afraid that if they opened the door, which is the usual way of leaving a room, the water might come in. When Noah had climbed on to the top of the wall, he pulled Shem after him, who pulled Ham, who pulled Japheth, who pulled Mrs. Noah, and there they all stood like a row of sparrows on a telegraph wire, balancing themselves with great difficulty.

"Who's been meddling with my roof?" asked Noah, in an angry voice. "I believe it's that pin-partridge."

The pin-partridge trembled so violently at this that he fell off the roof altogether, quite forgetting that he could fly. But the moment he touched the ground, he became a full-sized partridge.

"No, I didn't," he said. "There's that boy somewhere about, but I can't see him. He got through the blue door to-night."

David now knew that he was invisible, but though it had always seemed to him that it must be the most delicious thing in the world to be able to be visible or invisible whenever you chose, he found that it was not quite so jolly to have become invisible without choosing, and not to have the slightest idea how to become visible again. It gave him an empty kind of feeling like when he was hungry long before the proper time.

"The cats saw me," he said, joining in, for he knew if he couldn't be seen, he could be heard.

"Of course they did," said Noah, "because they can see in the dark when everything is invisible. That's why they saw you. You needn't think that you're the only thing that is invisible. I suppose you think it's grand to be invisible."

"When I was a little boy," said Ham, "I was told that little boys should be seen and not heard. This one is heard and not seen. I call that a very poor imitation of a boy. I dare say he isn't a real one."

"I've been quite ordinary up to now," said David. "It seems to have come on all of a sudden. And I don't think it's at all grand to be invisible. I would be visible this minute if I knew how."

"I want to get down," said Mrs. Noah, swaying backwards and forwards because her stand was broken.

"You'll get down whether you want to or not, ma," said Shem irritably, "if you go swaying about like that. Don't catch hold of me now. I've got quite enough to do with keeping my balance myself."

"Why don't you get down?" asked David, who wanted to see what would happen next.

"I haven't seen the crow fly yet," said Noah. "We can't get down till the crow has flown."

"What did the crow do?" asked David.

"It didn't. That's why we're still here," said Japheth.

"Some people," said Noah, "want everything explained to them. When the cock crows it shows it's morning, and when the crow flies it shows it's night. We can't get down until."

"But what would happen if you did get down?" said David.

"Nobody knows," said Noah. "I knew once, and tied a knot in my handkerchief about it, so that I could remember, but the handkerchief went to the wash, and they took out the knot. So I forgot."

"If you tied another knot in another handkerchief, wouldn't you remember again?" asked David.

"No. That would not be the same knot. I should remember something quite different, which I might not like at all. That would never do."

"One, two, three," said Mrs. Noah, beating time, and they all began to sing:

"Never do, never do,
Never, never, never do."

Most of the animals in the ark joined in, and they sang it to a quantity of different tunes. David found himself singing too, but the only tune he could remember was "Rule Britannia," which didn't fit the words very well. By degrees the others stopped singing, and David was left quite alone to finish his verse feeling rather shy, but knowing that he had to finish it whatever happened. When he had done, Noah heaved a deep sigh.

"That is the loveliest thing I ever heard in my life," he said. "Are you open to an engagement to sing in the ark every evening? Matinées of course, as well, for which you would have to pay extra."

This was a very gratifying proposal, but David did not quite understand about the paying.

"I should have to pay?" he asked.

"Why, of course. You'd have to pay a great deal for a voice like that. You mustn't dream of singing like that for nothing. It would fill the ark."

"I should say it would empty it," said Mrs. Noah snappishly.

"I don't know if I'm rich enough," said David, not taking any notice of this rude woman.

"Go away at once then," said Mrs. Noah. "I never give to beggars."

Just then there was a tremendous rattle from the ark, as if somebody was shaking it.

"It's the crow," shouted Ham. "The crow's just going to fly. Get out of the way, boy."

The crow forced its way through the other animals, balanced itself for a moment on the edge of the ark, and flew off down the passage, squawking. The moment it left the ark it became ordinary crow-size again, and at the same moment David suddenly saw his one hand still holding up the lid of the ark, and knew that he had become visible. That was a great relief, but he had no time to think about it now, for so many interesting things began happening all at once. The Noah family jumped from the edge of the ark, and the moment their stands touched the ground, they shot up into full-sized human beings, with hats and ulsters on, and large flat faces with two dots for eyes, one dot for a nose, and a line for a mouth. They glided swiftly about on their stands, like people skating, and seemed to be rather bad at guiding themselves, for they kept running into each other with loud wooden crashes, and into the animals that were pouring out of the ark in such numbers that it really was difficult to avoid everybody. Occasionally they were knocked down, and then lay on their backs with their eyes winking very quickly, and their mouths opening and shutting, like fish out of water, till somebody picked them up.

David got behind the cupboard door to be out of the way of the animals and all the other things that came trooping from the shelves. Luckily the nursery passage seemed to have grown much bigger, or it could never have held everybody, for the animals also shot up to their full size as soon as they left the ark. But they kept their colours and their varnish and though David had been several times to the Zoological Gardens, there was nothing there half so remarkable as the pale blue elephant or the spotted pigs, to take only a few examples. Every animal here was so much brighter in colour, and of course their conversation made them more interesting. On they trooped with the Noahs whirling in and out, towards the steps to the garden door, and when they were finished with, the "Happy Families," all life-size, too, followed them. There were Mrs. Dose, the doctor's wife, with her bottle, and Miss Bones, the butcher's daughter, gnawing her bone in a very greedy manner, and Master Chip, the carpenter's son, with his head supported in the pincers. He had no body, you will remember, and walked in a twisty manner, very upright and soldier-like, on the handles of them. The lead soldiers followed them with the band playing, and the cannons shooting peas in all directions, only the peas were as big as cannon-balls, and shot down whole regiments of their own men, and many of the hindmost of the happy families. But nobody seemed to mind, but picked themselves up again at once. Often the whole band was lying on their backs together, but they never ceased playing for a moment. The battledores and shuttlecocks came next, the shuttlecocks hitting the battledores in front of them, which flew down the passage high over the heads of the soldiers, and waited there, standing on their handles till the shuttlecocks came up and hit them again. After this came David's clockwork train, which charged into everything that was in its way, and cut a lane for itself through soldiers, happy families, and animals alike. It had a cow-catcher in front of the engine, which occasionally picked people up, instead of running over them, and when David saw it last, before it plunged down the stairs, it had Mr. Soot, the chimney-sweep, and the Duke of Wellington, and the llama all lying on it, jumbled up together, and kicking furiously.

While he was watching this extraordinary scene, the cupboard doors banged to again, and he saw that there was a large label on one of them:—

NO ADMITTANCE EXCEPT BY PRESENTING YOUR CALLING-CARD AND VERY LITTLE THEN.

And on the other was this:

NO BOTTLES OR FOLLOWERS OR ANYTHING ELSE. RING ALSO.

David studied this for a minute or two. He did not want to go in, but he wanted to know how. He hadn't got a calling-card—at least he never had before he came through the blue door, but so many odd things had happened since, that he was not in the least surprised when he put his hand in his pocket to find it quite full of calling-cards, on which was printed his name, only it was upside down. So he naturally turned the card upside down to get the name un-upside-down, but, however he turned it, his name was still upside down. If he looked at it very closely as he turned it, he could see the letters spin round like wheels, and it always remained like this:

˙ƎZIⱯ˥ꓭ ꓷIⱯꓯꓷ

The other trouser-pocket was also quite full of something, and he drew out of it hundreds of other calling-cards. On one was printed "The Elegant Elephant, R.S.V.P.," on another "Master Ham, P.P.C.," on another "The Duke of Wellington, W.P.," on another "The Engine Driver, R.A.M.C.," on another "Miss Battledore, W.A.A.C." Everybody had been calling on him.

"Whatever am I to do?" thought David. "Shall I have to return all these calls? It will take me all my time, and I shall see nothing. Besides"—and he looked round and saw that the passage was completely empty, and had shrunk to its usual size again—"Besides, I don't know where they've all gone."

He looked at the cupboard doors again, and found that they had changed while he had been looking at the cards. They were now exactly like the big front door at home, which opened in the middle, and had a hinge at each side. In front of it was a doormat, in the bristles of which was written

GO AWAY.

Now David was the sort of boy who often wanted to do something, chiefly because he was told not to, in order to see what happened, and this doormat made him quite determined to go in. It was no use trying the left-hand side of the door, partly because neither bottles nor followers nor anything was admitted, and partly because you had to ring also, and there wasn't any bell. But there seemed just a chance of getting in by the right-hand part of the door, and he went up to it and knocked. To his great surprise he heard a bell ring inside as soon as he had knocked, which seemed to explain "ring also." The bell did not sound like an electric bell, but was like the servants' dinner bell. As soon as it had stopped, he heard a voice inside the door say very angrily:

"Give me my tuffet at once."

There was a pause, and David heard the noise of some furniture being moved, and the door flew open.

"What's your name?" said the butler. "And have you got a calling-card?"

David gave him one of his cards, and he looked at it and turned it upside down.

"It's one of them dratted upside-downers," he said, "and it sends the blood to the head something awful."

He gave a heavy sigh, and bent down and stood on his head.

"Now I can read it," he said. "Are you David or Blaize? If David, where's Blaize, and if Blaize, where's David?"

"I'm both," said David.

"You can't be both of them," said the butler. "And I expect you're neither of them. And why didn't you go away?"

"You've given me too much curds," said a voice behind the door. "I've told you before to find some way to weigh the whey. It's a curd before. Take it away!"

"That must be Miss Muffet," thought David. "There's a girl creeping into it after all. I wonder if she makes puns all the time. I wish I hadn't knocked."

"No, I'm rationed about puns," said Miss Muffet, as if he had spoken aloud, "and I've had my week's allowance now. But a margin's allowed for margarine. Butter—margarine," she said in explanation.

"I saw that," said David.

"No, you didn't: you heard it. Now, come in and shut the door, because the tuffet's blowing about. And the moment you've shut the door, shut your eyes too, because I'm not quite ready. I'll sing to you my last ballad while you're waiting. I shall make it up as I go along."

Accordingly David shut the door, and then his eyes, and Miss Muffet began to sing in a thin cracked voice:

"As it fell out upon a day
When margarine was cheap,
It filled up all the grocers' shops
In buckets wide and deep.

Ah, well-a-day! ah, ill-a-day!
Matilda bought a heap.
And it fell out upon a day
When margarine was dear,
Matilda bought a little more
And made it into beer.

Ah, well-a-day! ah, ill-a-day!
It tasted rather queer.
As it fell out upon a day
There wasn't any more;
Matilda took her bottled beer
And poured it on the floor.

Ah, well-a-day! ah, ill-a-day!
And that was all I saw."

"Poor thing!" said Miss Muffet. "Such a brief and mysterious career. Now you may open your eyes."

David did so, and found himself in a large room, with all the furniture covered up as if the family was away. The butler was still standing on his head, squinting horribly at David's card, and muttering to himself, "He can't be both, and he may be neither. He may be either, but he can't be both." In the middle of the room was a big round seat, covered with ribands which were still blowing about in the wind, and on it was seated a little old lady with horn spectacles, eating curds and whey out of a bowl that she held on her knees.

"Come and sit on the tuffet at once," she said, "and then we'll pretend that there isn't room for the spider. Won't that be a good joke? I like a bit of chaff with my spider. I expect the tuffet will bear, won't it? But I can't promise you any curds."

"Thank you very much," said David politely, "but I don't like curds."

"No more do I," said Miss Muffet. "I knew we should agree."

"Then why do you eat them?" asked David.

"For fear the spider should get them. Don't you adore my tuffet? It's the only indoor tuffet in the world. All others are out-door tuffets. But they gave me this one because most spiders are out-of-door spiders. By the way, we haven't been introduced yet. Where's that silly butler?"

"Here," said the butler. He was lying down on the floor now, and staring at the ceiling.

"Introduce us," said Miss Muffet. "Say Miss Muffet, David Blaize—David Blaize, Miss Muffet. Then whichever way about it happens, you're as comfortable as it is possible to be under the circumstances, or even above them, where it would naturally be colder."

"I don't quite see," said David.

"Poor Mr. Blaize. Put a little curds and whey in your eyes. That's the way. Dear me, there's another pun."

"You made it before," said David.

"I know. It counts double this time. But as I was saying, a little curds and whey—oh! it's tipped up again. What restless things curds are!"

She had not been looking at her bowl, and for several minutes now a perfect stream of curds and whey had been pouring from it over her knees and along the floor, to where the butler lay. He was still repeating, "Miss Muffet, David Blaize—David Blaize, Miss Muffet." Sometimes, by way of variety, he said, "Miss Blaize—David Muffet," but as nobody attended, it made no difference what he said.

"It always happens when I get talking," she said. "And now we know each other, I may be permitted to express a hope that you didn't expect to find me a little girl?"

"No, I like you best as you are," said David quickly.

"It isn't for want of being asked that I've remained Miss Muffet," said she. "And it isn't from want of being answered. But give me a little pleasant conversation now and then, and one good frightening away every night, and I'm sure I'll have no quarrel with anybody; and I hope nobody hasn't got none with me. How interesting it must be for you to meet me, when you've read about me so often. It's not nearly so interesting for me, of course, because you're not a public character."

"Does the spider come every night, or every day, whatever it is down here?" asked David.

"Yes, sooner or later," said Miss Muffet cheerfully, "but the sooner he comes, the sooner I get back again, and the later he comes the longer I have before he comes. So there we are."

She stopped suddenly, and looked at the ceiling.

"Do my eyes deceive me?" she whispered, "or is that the s——? No; my eyes deceive me, and I thought they would scorn the action, the naughty things. Perhaps you would like to peep at my furniture underneath the sheets. It will pass the time for you, but be ready to run back to the tuffet, when you hear the spider coming. Really, it's very tiresome of him to be so late."

David thought he had never seen such an odd lot of furniture. Covered up in one sheet was a stuffed horse, in another a beehive, in another a mowing-machine. They were all priced in plain figures, and the prices seemed to him equally extraordinary, for while the horse was labelled "Two shillings a dozen," and the mowing-machine "Half a crown a pair," the beehive cost ninety-four pounds empty, and eleven and six-pence full. David supposed the reason for this was that if the beehive was full, there would be bees buzzing about everywhere, which would be a disadvantage.

"When I give a party," said Miss Muffet, "as I shall do pretty soon if the spider doesn't come, and take all the coverings off my furniture, the effect is quite stupendous. Dazzling in fact, my dear. You must remember to put on your smoked spectacles."

David was peering into the sheet that covered the biggest piece of furniture of all. He could only make out that it was like an enormous box on wheels, and cost ninepence. Then the door in it swung open, and he saw that it was a bathing-machine. On the floor of it was sitting an enormous spider.

"Does she expect me?" said the spider hoarsely. "I'm not feeling very well."

David remembered that he had to run back to the tuffet, but it seemed impolite not to ask the spider what was the matter with it. It had a smooth kind face, and was rather bald.

"My web caught cold," said the spider. "But I'll come if she expects me."

David ran back to the tuffet.

"He's not very well," he said, "but he'll come if you expect him."

"The kind good thing!" said Miss Muffet. "Now I must begin to get frightened. Will you help me? Say "Bo!" and make faces with me in the looking-glass, and tell me a ghost story. Bring me the looking-glass, silly," she shouted to the butler.

He took one down from over the chimney-piece, and held it in front of them, while David and Miss Muffet made the most awful faces into it.

"That's a beauty," said Miss Muffet, as David squinted, screwed up his nose, and put his tongue out. "Thank you for that one, my dear. It gave me quite a start. You are really remarkably ugly. Will you feel my pulse, and see how I am getting on. Make another face: I'm used to that one. Oh, I got a beauty then: it terrified me. And begin your ghost story quickly."

David had no idea where anybody's pulse was, so he began his ghost story.

"Once upon a time," he said, "there was a ghost that lived in the hot-water tap."

"Gracious, how dreadful!" said Miss Muffet. "What was it the ghost of?"

"It wasn't the ghost of anything," said David. "It was just a ghost."

"But it must have been 'of' something," said Miss Muffet. "The King is the King of England, and I'm Miss Muffet of nothing at all. But you must have an 'of.'"

"This one hadn't," said David firmly. "It was just a ghost. It groaned when you turned the hot water on, and it squealed when you turned it off."

"This will never do," said Miss Muffet. "I'm getting quite calm again, like a kettle going off the boil. Make another face. Oh, now it's too late!"

There came a tremendous cantering sound behind them, and Miss Muffet opened her mouth and screamed so loud that her horn spectacles broke into fragments.

"Here he comes!" she said. "O-oh, how frightened I am!"

She gave one more wild shriek as the spider leaped on to the tuffet, and began running about the room with the most amazing speed, the spider cantering after her. They upset the bathing-machine, and knocked the stuffed horse down, they dodged behind the butler, and sent the beehive spinning, and splashed through the curds and whey, which formed a puddle on the floor. Then the door through which David had entered flew open, and out darted Miss Muffet with the spider in hot pursuit. Her screaming, which never stopped for a moment, grew fainter and fainter.

The butler gave an enormous yawn.

"Cleaning up time," he said, and took a mop from behind the door, and dipped it into the pool of curds and whey. When it was quite soaked, he twisted it rapidly round and round, and a shower of curds and whey deluged David. As it fell on him, it seemed to turn to snow. It was snowing heavily from the roof too, and snow was blowing in through the door. Then he saw that it wasn't a door at all, but the opening of a street, and that the walls were the walls of houses. It was difficult to see distinctly through the snowstorm, but he felt as if he knew where he was.

Franz Blei (1871–1942) was an Austrian playwright, essayist, and critic who also translated many works into German. From 1908 to 1910, Blei edited the journal *Hyperion*, which was the first to publish work by Franz Kafka (who later became Blei's good friend). Many of his works were erotic and religious, so *The Big Bestiary of Modern Literature* (1918), excerpted here, can be considered somewhat on the border of his usual mode of writing. When first published, *The Bestiarium* was not well received and, for a time, caused Blei to be excluded from the German book market. For the second edition, Blei adopted the name "Peregrin Steinhövel." Today, many critics see it as an amusing literary history brimming with sardonic detail. But it is also a historical document, a kind of snapshot of the literary landscape. Some of the entries showcased feature now-obscure writers but are included because of Blei's delightful and pointed gift for satire. Like any encyclopedia, excerpted or not, the *Bestiary* is meant to be dipped into, not read straight through. Until now only a thousand-word excerpt had been translated into English.

The Big Bestiary of Modern Literature

Franz Blei

Translated by Gio Clairval

SECTION I (INTRODUCTION)

PREFACE TO THE FIRST EDITION

UNDETERRED BY so many predecessors, I have in this bestiary made the attempt to give a short, as well as vivid and accurate, description of the living animals that the Lord was pleased to bring into the book world, inasmuch as they walk the lands of the German Language—for better and for worse. If we human beings, observing the specimens of this fauna, find it more difficult than ever to recognize the usefulness and purpose of God's creations, then we should berate ourselves and not the Creator, because, being able to perceive much of the very meaningfulness of His work, we should also assume that even that which seems to be useless has a precise meaning. Given the short span, not only of our own lives but also of the objects of our observations, not to mention our limited means of comprehension, we should not be obsessed with the vain pursuit of deciphering God's each and every intent.

And allow me to say one more thing to the skeptics who doubt the order immanent in the person of our Lord: that we shall not think ourselves heretical if we imagine God resting from His laborious day-and-night works, and, finding Himself in a merry mood, deciding to fashion our literary fauna, whose description I present here to the hypocrites as well as to my readers and friends, after trying *sine ira*, but *multo studio* to determine the species, the appearance, and lifestyle of each animal. I think I am now entitled to say that I have not overlooked any beasts of importance or notoriety and that I have gathered them all quite comfortably within the cage of my bestiary, or, more precisely, in this zoo— for imprisoning all these beasts in a single cage would mean to brave the extraordinary incompatibility of these animals. I would lock them up together only if I were interested in their mutual extermination, assuming God's role, which is far from my intention. Nevertheless, should the reader reckon that an animal—or more—is missing in this bestiary, I feel confident to affirm that said animal is only familiar to the reader or his family, possibly as a local pet.

Otherwise, I choose not to mention such beasts for the following reason. There is a widespread microbe, the *Bacillus imbecillus*, which has many thousands of names in common life, but is always the same strain of bacteria that affects thick-skinned individuals of all social statuses and classes. At first the victim, thanks to the thick skin, only feels a pleasant tickling, but soon the infected person falls into complete dementia. This *Bacillus imbecillus* should be associated with the class of pathogens more than the animal kingdom; therefore it belongs to bacteriology and would be out of place in a bestiary.

I have knowingly left out some species—very few—so that learned reviewers can fully enjoy the pleasure of proving this to me, thus reaffirming the necessity of their existence. The animal lover as well as the animal hater also will immediately notice with pleasure the benefit of this succinctly written bestiary. This work renounces the verbose but pointless appendices that are peculiar to all the Natural History compendia about our literary fauna, instead offering easy-to-remember short phrases.

That being said, I agree with my dear friend Dr. Negelinus in thinking that this bestiary will soon be of no practical use, only to be valued as an antique curiosity. After all, there is every sign of an imminent terrestrial catastrophe, and then the little of the past that remains after this second deluge will be abandoned by most of the literary animals still living, with only sparse fragments available in paleontological museums. It is unlikely that a new Noah will come forth, who would good-naturedly want to build a saving ark for these creatures. Thus, the more urgent my task was to describe our animals while still alive.

As the reader will notice, I have abstained from any criticism of our creatures. We have to accept them as God created them, to Him alone the honor and the responsibility. In general, I only want to briefly comment on a recent heated debate: the question of whether our animals possess intelligence or not. There is no doubt that our ancient, extinct literary wildlife possessed intelligence to a great extent. Today's animals, with very few exceptions, do not distinguish themselves for their intellect. Nevertheless, a new term has been invented to characterize our living beasts: it is the word "Intellectual." The word was likely minted after the expression *canis a non canendo* (a dog is called a dog because it can't sing). The truth is, our present-day animals, with a few exceptions, are quite emotional and not intelligent at all. Indeed, it can be observed that they act under the influence of undefined feelings; they have nothing but feelings and no common sense, not even in their particular fields of activity. To put it bluntly, they let themselves be ensnared by anyone who can skillfully spread some birdlime. Here is what some of our animals claim they will not do: think. They are therefore not to be called "intellectuals," but more aptly "emotives" or "sensitivists," who succumb to every opportunity they can grasp by means of their emotions. That which they sometimes call "thoughts" are in fact feelings. Our literary animals share this common error with today's people.

More eruditorum, I am bound by the duty to thank those who have earned merits with this bestiary, in so far as they, like Hagenbecke with the fauna literarica, often with considerable sacrifices of time, money, patience and strength, have demonstrated interest in this endeavor, whether by discovering animals, or helping them to survive, or at least providing for the possibility of comfortable viewing via crates, preserves, cages, and containers. In particular, I would like to thank for such useful help, first of all, the dean of our literary crowd, a latter-day Hagenbecke, the equally intelligent and insightful Mr. S. Fischer-Berlin, then the multifaceted Mr. G. Müller-Munich, the always curious Mr. K. Wolff-Munich, the daring E. Rowohlt-Berlin, the cordial GH Meyer-Munich, the cautious A. Kippenberg-Leipzig, the persistent G. Kiepenheuer-Potsdam, the lively P. Cassirer-Berlin, and of course Herr Reiß. I thank all these gentlemen for doing their part in bringing some order to the collection of peculiar creatures issued from God's many-forming hand, as we humans need order in our ignorance of the higher divine sense pervading the Creation on Earth. I must also thank my friend, Dr. Negelinus. I must thank him for his contribution based on special studies, in particular the description of the Fackelkraus, or Kinky Hare.

SECTION II (ENTRIES)

(ABRIDGED)

Altenberg, also "Peter," exists for unknown reasons because of the mysterious whim that induced God to create a beast consisting only of a single organ: a hyperoptic, perspicacious eye made of a thousand facets—like a fly's—each of which captures reality by fragmenting the visible world into minuscule images of great sharpness. Onto such a strange creature was of course bestowed only a short life. But against Nature and contrary to God's purpose, this Eye, swollen with pride, fashioned something resembling a body. The beast became as result somewhat weak, as was to be expected, and the Eye known as Peter was tormented by a damning stream of annoyances, which resulted in damages to the Eye itself. Peter the Eye became so engrossed in the production of his own digestive system, that in the end he was able to see nothing more than the transient content of his own intestines: the Eye no longer reflected the surrounding world, but only the color of his excrements.

The **Bahr (Hermann)**. There is one and only one, and this single item is kept in Salzburg. Its once sharp smell has changed into the gentler odor of holiness, and the beast's horns, along with its fangs, have fallen off long ago, since the Bahr began to fear the Devil. In exchange for this loss, both mane and beard have grown over and over, which gives the creature a venerable appearance. The hiker who strolls across the Bahr's reservation in the Unterberg Mountain can spot this unique specimen or even chat with it, for the Bahr is an exceedingly talkative creature, and, lacking a companion, it usually speaks to itself. Its wardens, like the very pious priest, A. B. C. Schmitz, always fear that the Bahr may kill itself, not after a bad fall but because of its continuous blabbering. In truth, the Bahr has fallen over more than once, without sustaining injuries, and anyway the beast falls on its knees at least twice a day. This sign of senile degenerescence is mistaken for piety by the devout Salzburgerians. Such a pious behavior, so rare among animals, never ceases to amaze the populace. A Capuchin monk, therefore, took the Bahr with him to Holy Mass, and the beast behaved in church exactly like its God-fearing minister, so that one could not say if the Bahr followed a Capuchin or a Capuchin followed the Bahr. All in all, the Bahr, during this pious visit, let its venerable mane fall over its small, sharp, and wise eyes.

Becher, or Beaker [possibly Ulrich Becher; unclear -ed.]. This thing does not belong in the

Bestiary. The "Becher" is in fact a rocket used in modern fireworks, hence the alternative names "beaker" and "rocket-bird." The latter appellation is the probable reason why this rocket is mistakenly kept as a pet. The only thing this item has in common with living beings is that this thing never works as its Creator wants. Loaded with any possible and impossible charges, the Beaker either does not ignite at all or it goes off at the wrong time; the rocket flies toward the audience instead of upward and vanishes with a puff, leaving behind—instead of a beautiful umbrella of sparks—a terrible stench.

The **Benn (Gottfried)** is a small venomous lancet fish, which is mostly found in the corpses of drowned people. If such cadavers are fished out in broad daylight, the Benn happily slithers either out the rear passage or the private parts. The Benn can also try to creep back inside the body through the same channels.

Bie (Oskar). The Bie is a crab with stringy moustaches and the apparent shape of a mollusk. This creature has lived for decades in the columns of daily newspapers, without losing an ounce of its innocence. The Bie feeds on dance and music. It builds a leaf-shaped, rapidly calcified shell once a month from the waste of German literature, and this shell the faux mollusk carries about with sudden backward movements. During this phase of its life, the Bie is very much appreciated by fishermen.

The **Bierbaum (Otto Julius)**, also called "Beertree," or even Birnbaum (the "pear tree"), as pronounced by the inhabitants of the Saxon-Meissen, was a plant made of cardboard, bookbinder glue, *papier à main*, and flyleaf. Its fruits were those sugar syrupy crunchy bonbons made of tragacanth gum. Children used to lick the fruit and cry, "How sweet!" This paper pear-tree was a beloved centerpiece on stage at the turn of the twentieth century puppet theater during the German cultural boom. Old and young sang folk songs and old favorites in the shadow cast by its paper-clad leaves and danced with grace, arching and bending their legs, both Christians and Jews as well as Berliners, mischievous and impish, "à la Bieder" or "à la Meier," with their ornate productions of ring-around-the-rosy—circling reverently the trunk mounted on cardboard, as it symbolized the German Oak. It was impossible to make more poetic an impression than standing under the Beertree in 1902. The ax of war did not strike down the plant. A long time before, the cardboard tree had already been put away deep in the junk-room of German Poetry.

Blei (Franz), or the Lead. The Lead is a fish, smoothly diving and floating in all the fresh waters one can find, owing its name—middle high German *blî*, old high German *blîo* = clear—to the transparency of its skin, the exceptionally smooth and thin hide through which the food becomes visible with all its color. One can always see what the Lead has just eaten, and if the color of the food is lively, the Lead becomes entirely invisible, and only the food remains to be seen. Our fish eats a very varied diet, but always fastidiously picked, which is why, in analogy to the pig, this creature is called "the truffle fish" due to its ability to track down the most exquisite treats. Captured and trapped in a bowl, the Lead often serves as decoration in ladies' boudoirs, and, because it gets easily bored, it creates quite perfect tricks for the spectator's amusement, using fins and tail. But that is truly a misuse of this freedom-loving fish, which is unfairly prevented from hunting for its own pleasure and dietary needs. A curious friendship is maintained by the Lead with the Carthusian Crab, as well as with the Red Pike, but the nature of these friendships is not yet sufficiently understood to be part of a definitive report. Especially since the true Carthusian Crab is very rare and the most nonsensical fables circulate about the Red Pike's lifestyle.

Paul Bourget. In its green youth, an impeccably ironed, fashionable trouser crease proclaimed that the pants' content would hold its promise. For a short time. So, for a long time, all the salons were dominated by crowds of iron-pressed trousers—those places where, for generations, people have known that no thighs or calves exist any more, only pant creases. At the very last, and shortly before the inevitable kinks could appear even in the best-quality trousers, this tailored piece, as it always happens in France, turned into a tailcoat and entered the Museum of Fine Arts.

The **Brod** [The Bread], or also **Maxbrod**, is the last fashionable pet in the synagogues. It is harmless and takes food from the hand, even when irritated. From this fact one can form a conclusion as to its suitability as a religious animal. Some want to predict that the Maxbrod will one day enjoy the same veneration as the Martin Buber, the famous sacred animal of the Jews. But the small, not at all imposing Maxbrod lacks the stature to fulfill the function, so a greater effort is needed here. In other words, the size of the garden trellis is not augmented when you cut through the climbing twine and take the arch apart. In other words:

$$\text{BŘEZINA} = 2 \times 2 = \tau \left(\frac{d\sigma}{d\tau}\right)_0 + \frac{\tau^2}{2}\left(\frac{d^2\sigma}{d\tau^2}\right)_0 + \cdots$$
$$(d\sigma_1 + d\sigma_2) = 4.$$

The **Browning (Robert).** So was called the giant whose one leg was much shorter than the other. This made his gait eccentric, the more so as he walked like a real Englishman, which he was. Not like the dwarf Tennyson, who had of a giant the one gigantic leg, and always took himself seriously, but whom our giant just considered stubborn, which he was.

The **Burte (Hermann).** This is a Black Forest hart, and a solitude lover. He is endowed with an inordinate number of antlers, which are interlocked like crosses. His own strength impresses him greatly. His voice is so powerful the can make his own echo resound no less than seven times.

The **Chesterton (G. K.)** uses its legs only when he thinks nobody is paying attention. In public, the Chesterton makes a point of always standing on its head, and has perfected this position to a virtuosity that allows the beast to run at any pace whilst on the head: the Chesterton can stroll, walk, stagger, swagger, march, bounce, jump, run—any possible gait—on its head. To the faithful's great distress, the Chesterton, *la tête terrible* not *la bête terrible*, loves to display its nimbleness on all occasions, particularly in churches during worship. The Chesterton believes its particular on-the-head position offers the irrefutable proof of God's existence.

Cabell (James Branch). This is the victory scream of a magical American horse. Its soul is limitless and its thought encompasses the entire horizon. Even though its body gleams like malleable silver, its hardness surpasses that of steel. Inconsequentially, our springy horse's cry sounds like laughter. Perhaps the Cabell was the same Centaur that swam across the ocean two-thousand years ago, and then happened upon the land where houses are as tall as forests. The nation where the Great Pan was resurrected as Whitman—oh, yes, Cabell is that Centaur.

Conrad (Michael Georg). The Conrad belongs to Paleontology as it is long extinct and only a few bone fragments remain. The items displayed in the Munich museum confirm the assumption that this creature was a microcephalic dwarf bull, with a wooly, flax-yellow mane sprouting around its ears. German-nationalistic associations used its horns to fabricate drinking horns, but these proved to be useless, because as soon as any beverage touched these recipients, the liquid vaporized into foaming bubbles.

The **Courthsmahler (Hedwig)** is a louse that lays a million eggs in a second. She prefers to do this in cinema booths, where she is sure to find protection and sustenance for her numerous offspring. In department stores, the oldest shopwomen spread Courthsmahler's eggs on slices of bread as a caviar ersatz.

The **Däubler (Theodor)** is a robust jellyfish that lives in the Adriatic Sea and is predominantly silver gray, but can also change color at will. The organization of its intestinal threads is extremely intricate. Often, this creature does not know itself and becomes too involved in efforts to unravel its own complexity. In doing so, the Däubler ends up trapped in the folds of its own bowels, forever losing the ability to change colors.

The **Döblin (Alfred)**. This is the name of an admirable and magnificently built beast, which stands and strides firmly upon its four legs. He has the peculiar habit—which manifests itself on a few occasions, and always for a short duration—of standing on his left front paw, placing his head between his legs, to gaze at the world upside down. This position gives him the impression that the world is extremely filthy, either because it is so, or only because of the proximity of our animal's nether regions. The Döblin quickly rectifies this position on his left paw because it does not suit his temperament, and if we can then see this creature for what it really is, as he strolls happily down his good, straightforward path: a strong, enduring, excellent animal.

The **Einstein (Albert)** is part of the study of comets, inasmuch as the Einstein is a tailed celestial object or wandering star in the metaphysical heaven, from which, at times, in an inexplicable manner—as its path is unpredictable—it strays into the earth's atmosphere. Here it ignites with sparks and roars. Its appearance above our planet is catastrophic for bourgeois brains, the mushy substance of which boils with anger upon spotting the Einstein so near to Earth. The Einstein is therefore forced to continue its metaphysical course, whose trajectory is unknown, even by his sharpest observer Rowohlt.

The **Paulernst** is the name of a persistent type of tapeworm, which still continues to be expelled by the corpse of the well-known, long dead Friedrich Hebbel. The tapeworm's droppings are perfectly harmless, but if someone happens to see one of them, she may be seized by horripilation of an inconceivable intensity, which is expressed in spasmodic yawning. To demonstrate the complete harmlessness of these excretions, the well-known Munich zoologist Georg Mueller collected a few samples. But he could not cure anyone from their delusion. Perhaps this will only happen when the complete collection of the Paulernst's droppings becomes available, but this may not be possible, for our Paulernst is a very long tapeworm.

The **Eulenberg (Herbert)**, or "the Owls' Mountain." The Eulenberg is a wretched jinxed bird of the owl family. This bird has tried to build its artistic nest in the ruins of baroque, rococo, or Biedermeier palaces, or other castle styles. But since it has always been discovered and driven out, it has renounced the project of building a nest of his own, and since then it has been living inside the limits of other birds' shadows. Permission was granted to him to live in this place, even though there is no one in the sun, and he is also allowed on occasion to defile his refuge within someone else's shadow in an abominable manner.

The **Eucken (Rudolf Christoph)**. This enigmatic word can be found engraved on all the cowbells of German Ideal-Idealism. The ringing of these engraved bells is recognizable by a hollow, beautiful sound. The animals adorned with these Euckens are designated in the Austrian butchers' lingo as "little knuckels," meaning that their flesh is very lean and can be eaten without roasting.

The **Fackelkraus (Karl Kraus)**, or "Kinky Torch," has a nature contrary to Nature, as this beast is born from the waste of the enemies it wants to destroy. Because of its unclean birth, the Fackelkraus is always having fits of rage. The F. is distinguished by its ability to imitate people's voices, in various ways: it imitates the voices of prophets and poets to feel their equal and to be taken for one of them, but other people can be impersonated, too, to mock and destroy them. Before the (Frank) Wedekind's extinction, our Kinky Torch was its friend and stood on a raised podium to observe the Wedekind's mating rituals and also its bodily excretions. The F. then applauded with thunderlike noises in order to be heard. When it explodes in fury, this beast becomes extremely malicious, to the point of toxicity, whenever it suspects that others could be heard in its stead. This the beast can't abide. In order to prevent others from being heard, our creature either praises its competitors, or it derides them. In both cases the F. uses a high-pitched, sonorous screeching voice, to make sure everyone can hear. It must be remembered that the Kinky Torch has no nature intrinsic to itself, for it is nothing but a voice, and as a consequence only exists for as long as someone listens. Knowing this and fearing death, like every living creature does, it has skillfully practiced so that its voice will be heard for long periods of time. In anger, the F.'s voice is particularly elaborate, because, for fear of being ignored, the animal screams at new, never-heard-before octaves. If it realizes that someone is listening, the F. becomes very proud of itself and starts all over again. Fashioned out of its enemies' excrements, the breath of a Kinky Torch offends every nose. But because the creature believes that by destroying bodily waste it can destroy enemies, it angrily eats enormous amounts of turds. That is why the Kinky Torch is a useful animal, even though only people born without olfaction can endure its vicinity, because the outstanding Fackelkraus can destroy vast amounts of excrement.

The **Frank (Leonhard)**. The Frank is a shellfish without a shell, despite the fact that the harsh environment the Frank lives in should require a shell to protect its very soft, delicate body. Unfortunately, the softness extends to the Frank's mind, and does not allow our beast to form a firm shell by exuding a hard substance, of which it is in theory capable. All that the Frank can do is to gaze with dove eyes at the encroaching and punishing surroundings, and pray that they may become as beneficent as the Frank is. One must believe that the Lord is pleased to have created a Saint Francis of the Beasts.

The **Friedell (Egon)**. Not to be confused with the Ferret [*Frettchen*], as our beast is more akin to the archaic Enu, a Megatherium from the group of Polisponges. Feeds mainly on Chesterton, Kierkegaard, Shaw, Hegel, Nietzsche and other herbs. With its great head, the F. digests everything perfectly; the noises emitted by this creature during digestion are widely feared, as from a distance they can be mistaken for humor.

Hackel (Eduard). This is the name of the god on whom the freethinker takes oaths. For here a human being has truly become God, by grace of nothing outside his insistence on telling the German what Darwin made damn sure not to tell the English, that the human is descended from a monkey. An enthusiastic German humankind climbed on the tree of such knowledge and applauded with all four legs. After some time of this awe-inspiring spectacle, some meaning had to come into the matter. And so the human ape invented Monism. And because this was happening in Protestant countries, monistic Sunday preachers soon appeared—naturally from the Land of Saxony. The monists recognize one another by the well-displayed genealogical tree.

The **Hamsun (Knut)**, the most beautiful of the living Saurians, is a perfect music-box mechanism created by Nature. Despite the alligator size and the apparent awkwardness of the limbs, and despite the Hamsun's predilection for brooding in a state of pensive tranquility, this beast possesses an incredible and improbable agility. Very shy, he lives hidden among the rocks. As it is told, it was actually only a single researcher who discovered this species when a stone quarry was blown up, and the Hamsun stood in a cloud of dust and steam. The legend was born that our animal was in reality a simple, honest, and fair-looking person skilled in geometry, with sparks of almost feminine genius. But this legend is likely to have been invented in a big city. Not even a Nobel prize succeeded in luring the Hamsun out of its cave. The beast has too large a mouth, which makes him suffer. It is an organ which, in the case of reptiles, allows these creatures to survive in different elements, but in any case it is developed in the shape of a pharynx. Since the Hamsun is shy, humble and modest, its large mouth mortifies it a great deal. For just at the moment when one cannot deny this animal's beauty . . . the gaze lingers on the disproportionate maw.

The **Gehauptmann (Gerhart Hauptmann)**. The Gehauptmann is the most corpulent quadruped of the German fauna, with an exceptionally small head, which grows smaller as the beast ages, while the body grows larger. The original form of this body can no longer be recognized. It is astonishing that four feet can bear all these humps, bulges, valleys, excesses, bumps, and tumors. In some parts of this body small feathers sprout, in others there are hairs; elsewhere, the skin is completely bare; in yet other places, it has sunken, or is petrified. The irregularity of our animal's surface probably explains the fact that in some parts of his body debris have accumulated, which he carries patiently, and in another place a small meadow grows. Yes, there has been a tiny coal miners' village for a time. But the Gehaupt. is so monstrous that its brain does not even notice what's going on. Our beast only eats vegetables, in astronomical quantities. Meat makes it sick. Its little head often remains entirely invisible; often it abstains from performing any function. The above might explain the tremendous growth and the uncertain, fluctuating gait of our Gehauptmann.

The **Hesse (Hermann)**. This is a lovely forest turtledove that cannot be found in her natural habitat any longer. Thanks to her gracious appearance, she has become a favorite caged bird, charming the beholder by the way she behaves, as if she still lived freely in her forest. In this way she gives to the city-dweller the impression of being in the wilderness, and the illusion is increased by tiny odoriferous glands, from which our Hesse secretes a smell that gently recalls the coniferous resinous scent.

The **Hofmannsthal (Hugo von)**. This gazelle-like animal with beautiful fur, exceptionally spindle-shanked—solely created for the reason of having him parade proudly—is the product of an interesting cross-breed between an Italian greyhound bitch (from the breeder d'Annunzio) and a dog of the English Northumberland variety Swinburne. His birth was saluted with such amazement that—to use an expression usually applied to humans—he was compared to a wonder boy, which he remained as he aged, by virtue of this exceptional admiration, and even at eighty years of age, until death took him. This very precious, fragile species can breathe only artificial air, which is why every specimen has a subtly exquisite scent. The Hofmannsthal's taste is so refined, given the fragility of his crossbred stomach, that he often eats nothing at all for months, so as not to bring to the most delicate intestines the danger of constipation, which is his secret pain. At such times he takes to lamenting from his silver terrace in a plaintive voice on the melancholy of a Sunday afternoon in July. Sometimes the Hofmannsthal expresses the desire for a trip to a rural hay meadow, where he can take a few humorous jumps, which makes the bystanders tear up with sadness, while the Hofmannsthal finds this frolicking very funny, even though he soon becomes exhausted. Back in the time the ladies called him Cherub, and this graceful beast still responds to this name, on the one hand, out of amiability, on the other from melancholy. It is one of our most beautiful animals.

Ibsen (Henrik). He was an apothecary apprentice. Pinching and turning the tablets between his fingertips, he became pensive, pondering about the people who ingested his preparations. And he was amazed at the fact that the customers gobbled down those tablets. So he began to sell his own recipes, the labels of which he received from the Parisian company *Dumas Fils*. The French company was well established in the small town, and granted credit to the little pharmacist who had created his own business. The raw materials of his remedies he procured in many ways, but especially from England. When his shipments remained stored in the small windowless warehouse of his northern town for too long, the tablets were covered in a thin coat of mildew, which however tasted just right to the Germans, to which he exclusively exported for some time. At first, secretly, then more boldly, and finally very ostentatiously, any German woman who was more or less misunderstood took Nora—or Heddapills. This trend made the fortune of a Swedish exporter who was able to sell tablets of better quality, which caused the little Norwegian pharmacist to fall out of fashion. The Ibsen con-

sidered this matter in his little shop, and came to the conclusion: *nosce te Ibsen*. And he quietly began to unravel the fraud he had perpetrated.

The Kafka (Franz). The Kafka is a very rarely seen, magnificent moon-blue mouse that does not eat meat, but feeds on bitter herbs. Its gaze is entrancing, because this mouse has human eyes.

Kipling (Rudyard). Thus was named the great cannon that was for the first time fired over the Queen's tomb, and the echo of which was heard by the Boers as well as the Hindus, the Canadians, and the Australians. Finally, in 1914, the Kipling tore at everybody's eardrums in every sense of the word. The fact that a little child from Lissau pissed his pants out of fear did not help the Kipling's cause.

The Maupassant (Guy de). A Diver bird of the Gaviidae family, which brings pearls from the depths with infinite grace. These depths, however, must not be deeper than the *profondeurs du cœur*, or depths of the heart, as they were fathomed in Paris, 1880.

The Mallarmé (Stéphane). A fragile insect of amethyst-blue color, with spiritual features. It is enclosed in a piece of glass-transparent amber, which is unique given its crystalline structure. The amazing thing is that an insect would survive in such airtight, confined space.

The Meyrink (Gustav). The Meyrink is the only mooncalf that fell to the earth and was captured alive. Exhibitions were initially forbidden as the frightful sight provoked a few premature births, but today the Meyrink is temporarily put on display by his catcher and pregnant women are now allowed to see the exhibit. In the meantime, the women have grown accustomed to the horrific shape, so that they can endure the view, even with a smile of satisfaction. Austrian-Hungarian officers and National-German deputies wanted to ban the public exhibition of the Meyrink altogether, claiming that the one big eye distorted their reflection, as they put it. The owner of the specimen, however, proved that the reflection was not distorted at all, but those particular objects distorted the Meyrink's eye. The number of visitors has diminished since many lunar calves have been spotted running about. We cannot be certain that those specimens fell from the moon, but they surely have fallen on their heads.

The **Morgenstern (Christian)** [The Morningstar] is, as everyone knows, the same as the Evening Star. It is only a matter of the time at which one gazes lovingly at the star, to name it as one thing or the other. In the morning, our Morning Star would have all sorts of beautiful and universal feelings, but in the evening he would no longer experience those moods. So, instead, he rehashed the same sentiments by means of satire, only to fall back into his stellar clichés the next morning.

The **Mombert (Alfred)**. The Mombert is an invertebrate, and it is remarkable that this creature was able to transform its fairly small brain mass into ganglia. This exploit has had an influence on the animal's vocal expression, which bears a striking resemblance to the babble of certain German lyricists. This peaceful and solitary animal has not taken any new nourishment since its first meal, and continues to ruminate only on that old food.

The **Hansmüller**. Thus the little Moritz Benedict called his kite, which he used to fly mostly Sundays on Firs Street. Since little Moritz had a lot of rope, the Hansmüller flew very high, so that children thought him a bird, while he was only a bunch of old newspapers glued together. Later on, the rope broke, and the Hansmüller fell on the roof of an old theater, where our kite is sometimes seen flapping in the wind. Now even the children know that the Hansmüller consists only of paper cuts.

The **Thomasmann** and the **Heinrichmann**. Both these animals belong to a family of medium-sized xylophages. They are of different colors but similar in their nature and mode of life. They are always found on the same tree, but living on the opposite extremities, since these two wood beetles cannot stand each other. If the Thomasmann drills from down up, then the Heinrichmann pierces from top down. If one finds the lime tree delicious, the other thinks it rotten, and vice versa. The strange thing is that they are always wrong about the tree. They believe they are exploring an oak tree, when they are sitting on a door made of pinewood. If they are convinced they are sauntering up a spruce, it might well be a limewood chest of drawers. Nonetheless, the fact remains that they loathe each other. It is only when the two beetles are placed on a wooden fountain pen that they cease scoffing, instead engaging in their preferred activity, diligently sliding up and down, always in opposite directions. As for their colors, the Thomasmann flaunts black-and-white striped wings, while those of the Heinrichmann are blue-white-red, with sometimes the red spots disappearing rapidly when humans approach. These red small dots can also be removed by rubbing lightly.

The **Robertmüller**. Providing an exact description of this ruthlessly hunted animal is rendered more difficult by the fact that the Robertmüller often changes his point of view, and does not always know exactly where he stands. To be precise, it should be emphasized, however, that his outlook is always from his own perspective. The Robertmüller is an American-trained racedog with wings. This dog flutters and runs in zigzags and nobody can catch him. Similar to the Celtic bloom of the Shaw, which grows on spectral

Cymric shafts and changes its smell overnight, our animal is difficult to determine. Some say he is not an animal at all, but such impression might be one of his tricks. Others think that he descends from the Jensen, although his forepaws were not conceived for grasping, but were subject to a metaphysical tension that enabled the Robertmüller to spring into the air or into the future. Zoologists are still debating whether the deterioration of the beast's forepaws is an advantage or a weakness.

Mencken (H. L.). This is the name of the most important living American zoologist, which means that—since Lowell was American, but not important—not only is the Mencken the most important, but also the very first one. Given his argute humor, it is regrettable that he has to deal with no better fauna than the mostly ridiculous North American, which is led by Presbyterian parishioners (and that is ninety percent of all U.S. citizens) into arid pastures.

The **Meredith (George).** This is an Anglo-Celtic synonym for unicorn. All the others, those that in this Christian age tried to assume this pagan beast's allure, were pantomime costumes and cardboard cutouts. Only the Meredith was a natural unicorn, which like a god fathered gigantic females. The most famous among them is Diana. At times, the Meredith entangled his horn in telegraph wires, and had to free himself with many jokes, but without losing his graceful posture for a moment. When the Meredith was shown in Protestant Germany, the poetically trained Germany shied away from the mythical beast, for Germany only knew and loved the unicorn painted by Böcklin, with a virgin for good measure, and titled: "Silence in the forest."

Munchausen. This is the name given to a heraldic joke which represents a creature composed of all heraldic animals. Inside the Munchausen has been inserted a music box which, activated by a string, makes a clarion melody.

The **Musil (Robert).** The Musil is a noble animal of powerful and harmonious build. Notable is the Musil's habit to hibernate, despite its being appropriately assigned to the small family of the Fallow deer, in which hibernation is not customary. After every year of his life, the Musil sleeps for five years in an inaccessible forest. The lethargy seems to be necessary because of this animal's unusual muscular power joined to the high-strung quality of his nervous system, which the Musil manifests during his waking year.

Nietzsche (Friedrich Wilhelm). He is perhaps the most important zoologist of the Natural History park. Not only because he identified George Sand as a creative writing handbook—"And how self-satisfied she may have lain there"—and Zola as "the delight in stinking." Such sidelong glances at the insubstantial, in events of secondary importance, only demonstrate the impossibility of apprehending the incalculable distance between the animaliterate and the real writer, and fall like depth charges from an unknown surface into their own abyss. Hate against all that is prejudiced, when one has come to bring the sword, is what differentiates the positive person from the mere living being. And the positive person despises the art that arises from innate gifts, the talents, the art of the actor that moves across his space through continuous transformations, while time flows untapped by the gawkers' souls as their minds cannot fathom how to grasp it. Thus, even the Europeans, and particularly the Germans, these gifted among the Jews, have become anything into which they can transform at the eleventh hour; they have become Christians, even Buddhists—but they are nothing at all. They do nothing seriously, these Germans. They play Nation and confession, war and peace, pit Potsdam against Weimar, Weimar against Potsdam, in accordance with the date in a symbolic Versailles: 1871 or 1918; and so they progress through purely external metamorphosis, by modulation, keeping their essential cores undisturbed, tethered to a still and stubborn time in space. But the fact is that they began somewhere with something, and to become serious in the end requires a life of paradoxes, for mere information does not suffice: Cesare Borgia as Pope. The zoologist Nietzsche's evil reveals itself in the gladiatorial net in which the German buffoon ends up entangled, and it is the first concrete thing. Make this net a mirror, and one would look at one's reflection and finally find pleasure in the thought of being imprisoned within the glass; this German who says "no" out of comfort, theatrical showiness, coquetry of the mind, would say "yes" to the very last things, in time. And Nietzsche, who makes fun of history, called this evil with the sweetest names, the most seductive for Nordic ears: he called it South, Italy, Bizet . . . And he was jealous of this south of the spirit, as of a geographical south—"I have seen broken lines in Sorrento." Yes, the human being bending under the metaphysical guilt of the act of acting, Wagner or the German, or the European, to coalesce the flow of pure being into a concrete being, must do a very dangerous thing, a monstrous thing. How? Would this person's conversion to the cross first happen in and through the Antichrist? (What did Nietzsche expect from Wagner?) In order for the ahasverish being to break out of his destiny, isn't his first conscious "no" to Good, a latter-day saint, his first "yes" to life? The Cross as the premature, as the arrogated and the arrogance against an unknown life, as yet not possible, as yet historically not achievable, as the prejudice that we already have history, which should be baptized, as a religion, perhaps of the very last day, certainly not the present day: it remains as an impossible task the great rebus, against a perhaps already confirmed, yet premature, and thus immoral judgment on the instincts, a judgment from mouths singing on a Christian tone, making music before they have a language, there remains only the Herculean work of anticipating the Antichristian, in order to create a counter-antiquity in the liberal present, to allow a fullness of time, again and again.

Nietzsche's evil is the historical *ens realissimum*, which alone can receive its own reality and consistency; it is the Renaissance of the demiurgical ages, the same phenomenon of humanism and the Reformation, here as antiquity, resurfaced as the Old Covenant; Renaissance as the "mystical" idea of all "education" in order to repeat the demiurgical "fullness of time," the individual's self-knowledge and self-conquest, but as a historical act, not on the path of historicism: Cesare Borgia as a pope, Paul's identity of both prosecutor and apostle, and even in the Judaism of the traitor and "most credulous," and in the Antichrist! The experiencing and overcoming of the demiurgic period as a hypothetical negation of the Logos, here torn into the eternal moment and into the historical present, in order to prepare for the completed knowledge of his theological overreach in the Church, in order to render its danger with the indifferentism without which the Advent neither fulfilled its concept in time nor in the soul: this is at the same time the presumption of the most noble and profound eschatological mystery and its integration into the individual— the Antichrist as the provocation of Christ. The last things and forms projected into the future have been discovered by the boldest Protestant as heuristic principles for the highest need of faith, to be turned by the almost superhuman against himself, against the phantomatic quality within the Übermensch, those principles representing the only and foremost aphrodisiacs used to achieve the *amor Dei*.

Peladan (Joséphin). Peladans are called the cheap bazar articles that are sold in shops for tourists on rue Rivoli in Paris, particularly to Saxon couples on honeymoon. The things are made of undefined, but anyway cheap material. There is Richard Wagner's head as a cigar cutter, the Flying Persian as a box for sewing spools,

Siegfried who Blows the Horn as a cane handle, Isolde as a cigar holder, etc. The couples who purchase these items see in these Peladans a marriage of Gallic wit and German emotional depth.

The **Polgar (Alfred)**. This is a fine, silent, silvery-gray mouse, particularly agreeable to behold when the wise animal runs over the tuneless lyre of time, carefree in a studied way, producing a little tinkling filled with longing and dust. Most consider the Polgar to be harmless, but our investigation has shown that the delicate powder gnawed by our animal from the house foundations contains, in a very finely dispersed and weakened condition, ecrasite (an explosive material unaffected by moisture, shocks, or fire). The *Polgar viennensis* builds small nests of thought called philigranitic works of art, because of their strange blend of fragility and long-lasting filigree, made of tiny absurdities and malaises, inevitable newspaper sheets, lyrism and witticisms, along with beautiful red-blood corpuscles of a better life.

The **Ringelnatz (Joachim)**. He came swimming under the bordeaux-colored oceans, between bottle and battle, God only knows whence. He abruptly dropped in the deepest part of the ocean the highest peak of a joke. Perhaps the Ringelnatz descends from the wanderer Rimbaud's loins, somewhere between Abyssinia, the Lower Rhine, and the rest of the world.

Rabindranatagore is the name of India reduced to the level of Europe. In the long run, the weak remainders of the Indian wall could not resist the onslaught of English Biblical societies, American theosophists, Saxon natural apostles, French Bergsonians, and Prussian monists. Dying India produces by herself that from which she died, and this process is called Rabindranatagore.

The **Rilke (Maria Rainer)**. Zoologists and botanists are currently disputing among themselves whether Rilke belongs to the animal or plant kingdom. The Botanists, who do not wish to deal with the Rilke, assign the beast to Zoology. The Zoologists, who do not wish to deal with this creature either, assign it to Botany or to Agriculture; and the zoologists say that the Rilke lacks the right blood, which legitimates their turning the thing away, and again the botanists say that the Rilke has an animal's dentition, which the species uses to repair lines of poetry of any length wherever there is no articulation, either melodic or rhythmic. And this strange part at least should be admitted. Strange, too, is the circumstance that the Rilke is only female, although certain external sexual characteristics, such as facial hair, have a male character. Still, these characteristics, like the Rilke's beard, are gently, sadly downturned, as if they do not want to be there, as their presence can only cause embarrassment. These features are also contrasted by the high-pitched feminine voice of the Rilke, which tends to die out in a whisper. Like the **Werfel**, the Rilke is popular as a parlor pet, but more for older ladies because of the Rilke's sexual cleanliness, a purity which triggers the delightful word "heavenly," so loved by those ladies. Among seven such ladies you can always meet the Rilke as the seventh. In order to emphasize her gender, she likes to put on a bonnet, which, as the ladies exclaim, is "heavenly." Because of this continuous exaltation, our beast has gotten into the pedantic habit of putting her nose into theological books, Marian legends, and the like.

Ruskin (John). This is the name of a prophet, who, sometimes, without any sexual motivation, would turn into an English nanny, and, as such, played out every ecclesiastical art against the Church. Governor Ruskin suffered from a chronic moral headache. The prophet wrote with his right hand what the governess' left hand did not want to write. In Germany he is only appreciated in his capacity as a nanny, for here we are moral, honest, chaste, and so on and so forth.

Shaw (George Bernard). It is the name of a gardener who turned himself into a buck. The Shaw is, in fact, a zoologist who fancies the animal guise, although he always ends up transforming back into a gardener. While performing comical cartwheels, he takes the drollery out of them by trying to explain their meaning. For some time, it was debated whether "Shaw" was a pseudonym for Trebitsch, because of a certain philological incommensurability. Until it was ascertained that the Trebitsch cannot even pronounce the name of Shaw, let alone carry it.

Schnitzler (Arthur) is the name of a racehorse that runs in the Freudenau, out of the Fischer stable. This horse was in its glory days a favorite with all the ladies and the little darlings of Vienna because of his melancholy temperament. People would bet on Schnitzler out of sympathy, even if everyone knew in advance that he would not even place. Because Schnitzler was so popular, and the little darlings' granddaughters continued to go to the Freudenau, it was agreed in the Jockeys' Club, that Schnitzler, whenever he ran, in any race, would always be third, even if he gave up after the first lap. Long may he run.

Steiner (Rudolph) [der Stein: the stone]. "*Saxa loquuntur*," claims that part of humankind who, after purchasing the price of admission cashed in by old Noah, climbs onto the ark, whose future lies not on water, but on the Steiner. The salesman lures: Quickly, quickly! It's going to rain, and the flocks run. *In hoc petro* [sic]—"You are Peter and on this rock I will build my church"— capitalism was built, what he may call his church, and, behold, the stone multiplied and became the Steiner. And all the debris and the mud of the foundered, trodden souls gathered around him, or her, or it—this enormous joint stock religious company, which dismantled everything into pieces, everything that had ever been thought and formed as religious—distorted, diluted, baked, and chewed for toothless mouths. Such was Sophia, to whom Theos was to give his blessing. But God's blessing was only for Steiner, as formerly it was for Cohn.

The Steffen (Albert). This is an apocalyptic animal and currently exists as only one specimen, more fabled than scientifically observed. But his existence is not to be doubted. The Steffen has only one eye, but can move it from a place on his strangely shaped body to any other place. He keeps his sex hidden. He has wings, but these are so attached that he cannot fly. He has legs but he does not make much use of them for reasons not yet ascertained. Most of the time the Steffen crouches, plants his one eye in the middle of his face, and lets a whole world reflect strangely in the pupil.

The Stehr (Hermann). This is the name of a large maggot that has been discovered in the **Gehauptmann**'s coffin. His conspicuous size led to the assumption that he had only accidentally entered this peculiar environment. It has therefore been attempted to place the Stehr, very carefully, in other living conditions, which was achieved, albeit rarely. But the Stehr has remained a maggot.

The Storm (Theodor). One cannot say of him that it is long dead, for this creature has never existed other than in a stuffed form. Truly, it never possessed something called "internal organs." To stuff the Storm, the taxidermist filled the smooth gray-yellow skin with sea grass, heather, gull feathers, and the like, which gave the Storm a stale smell, for which the Storm is still valued today in the houses of brave German Nordic vicars. That particular smell is the essence of the Storm. One calls this odor "mood." The fragrance was extracted, fixed with zero percent alcohol and brought into the market in bottles of all formats. The most famous of these colognes was once Jorn Uhl, and this was for some time the most popular mouthwash of the German mind, and the Germans used it to wash their deepest, toothless hollows.

The **Swinburne (Algernon Charles)**. This large enchanted English bird sang once before the rising of a sun that never rose—an oversight. He once sang in front of the crucifix *against* the crucifix—a misunderstanding. The miracle of this bird is that it is, nevertheless, full of extraordinary melodies, and has, in human terms, a style that no human being ever possessed at the time or later on. This style is so inimitable that the Swinburne himself could not imitate it when he tried to, after growing old.

Tennyson (Alfred). Sometimes an elderly mime plays *Enoch Arden* with a musical accompaniment—no other works remain of this provincial Virgil. He was *poeta laureatus*; no one laughed at this appellation, for it suited him; he thought exactly what his queen thought, and he only put his thoughts into words in the best style. He was always terribly serious about what an Englishman, as the Chesterton says, has to do to assume a horrible appearance. He had a lot to say, but he had far more words than necessary; therefore, if he talked for a long time, he no longer knew what he was talking about.

The **Tolstoy (Leo)**. Originally the Tolstoy was a steppe horse, but already selectively bred. He was first ridden by Grusinian, Circassian, and Cossacks chiefs. Later, he belonged to the regular heavy cavalry of Literature. In the north and south of Time and Space, he participated in all the great campaigns, including those which lasted several volumes. Stringy, lean, but fiery, always ready to cartwheel and quaff champagne from buckets as a fierce steppe horse should, but always hovering at the manger and even a little spoiled, the Tolstoy followed his logical destiny of becoming the company trumpet-major's steed. In battle he had carried winners on his back; in his old age he whinnied in a kind and subdued tone while his dung balls were revered as golden apples. This animal's most striking feature is his superior mind. All his life, he refused to understand that the sparks came from his hooves hitting the ground; that his upturned nose and small head were gruff, devoid of beauty, and even unpleasant, particularly when he rolled his big naive eyes until they protruded, giving him a gloomy stare; and that his long tail, left untrimmed, belonged to a Gobi desert of the spirit; he also refused to acknowledge that he was only a glum reminder of the vast wealth of Asiatic desert horses. With the tip of this tail, he whipped his loins in a Christian manner, believing he was lambasting the world and transforming it in the process, which showcased the limitations of his horsey narrow-mindedness. But the sparks which had once sprung from his hooves remain unforgotten.

The **Unruh (Fritz Von?)** [the balance]. The Unruh is a dainty frog that usually lives in ponds and feeds on small water skeeters. It is, however, equipped with an inflatable pharyngeal cavity, with which it may sing, but which it also needs to fill with air, albeit only occasionally. To this end, the frog must seek out dry land, even though this species of Anuran lacks the ability to survive out of water. The Unruh, drawing in clean air, expands its pharynx to the size of a child's head, attracting the passers-by's attention. Thereafter, our frog redoubles its efforts to draw air, causing its throat to enlarge to the size of a watermelon. Luckily, the Unruh loses its balance, because of the out-of-proportion air bubble, and rolls back into the water, where its throat immediately empties. When in its element, the Unruh is a delicate little frog.

———

The **Vollmöller (Karl)**. The Vollmöller is a sea serpent, of which only part is visible on the surface of the water. How long the Vollmöller is, no one knows, but the assertion that it is longer than eighty centimeters is to be rejected as exaggerated.

The **Walser (Robert)**. This is a pulchritudinous, graceful, and whimsical animal from the family of the squirrels. On the highest trees one cannot spot it (nor does our animal make any attempt to get up there). Yet the Walser's naive and mischievous grace gives the average-sized trees a joyous liveliness.

Wassermann (Jakob) [Aquarius], also called Mogen Jaakob, is a small—but not too small— star in the constellation of Pisces, and can be seen particularly well from the high-positioned Beer-Hofmann observatory. It is equidistant from Vienna and Dostoyevsky, respectively, to the north and south of these two poles, and was made famous by a mysterious music of the spheres, which, as if emanated from Yahweh himself, gave the Germans—the new chosen people—in other words the absolute Germans, their final ahasverish name: Madness. This mysterious name was also found in a meteorite of incommensurable size, which, on closer inspection, turned out to be a mixture of graphite, ink, paper, moss, ambition, and binding strings.

The **Werfel (Franz)**, as round as a ball, lacks the ability to curl up like an hedgehog, whereas he can expand. From the hedgehog, it has the pikes, only these are very delicate and soft and sometimes they curve inwardly, which hurts the animal. This contradiction between the appearance and the essence of the Werfel makes this round, soft, and somewhat lazy animal a very popular mundane porcupine at today's cultural gatherings. One can hardly find a social circle where he is not on display. Therefore, the person who is unfamiliar with the nature of the Werfel's spikes marvels at seeing this sharp-pointed grenade showcased on the palm of one hand, while the other strokes the sting-sharp creature like a cat, and, in fact, doing so seems to induce very pleasant sensations. That being said, the Werfel is loved for the sake of a different ability with which God has endowed him: he can sing like Caruso and likes doing so, happily and often, especially when he hears noise around him. If, for instance, a war rumbles, the Werfel sings. If the songs were printed, it would be easy to fill a 308-page-long octavo volume with them. On account of his tenor voice, which distinguishes itself in arias and trills, the Werfel is greatly envied by other animals, who seek to imitate him.

The **Wevonscholz**. This is a useful bird, given its propensity to consume the bits of tapeworm that come out of the Friedrich Hebbel (and also the Paulernst), which all other animals find indigestible. Instead, the Wevonscholz gobbles down every little piece with much satisfaction. Sometimes this bird sings quite beautifully. And it might sing even better if it fed on any other food.

Whitman (Walt). Thus is the Great Pan named, who never died, because he alone among the gods was immortal, although often times he disappeared into the deepest cave of the earth. On the old man's wrinkled hand, a butterfly rests, and the insect knows exactly what the Whitman is: a branch from the world tree, from which was hewed out the cross planted on a mound of shards.

The **Wilde (Oscar)** was a famous and much-talked-about cutout silhouette from the end of the last century. The silhouette was reminiscent of the costume of a man in tights, in which the wild Wilde, a beauty of a predator—in other words, the negation of negation—loved to show up, with Lord Brummel's grace, to be admired by the ancestors of our snobs. The Emperor Nero in a similar manner liked to dress as a comedian, to be more than an emperor, to be everything, to be Proteus himself. Faithfully, Wilde partook in the false universalism of an epoch, of a system full of hypocrisy: one can seem what one is, or one can play the role of what one would have wanted to be. It is only through terrible excesses that laws which still exist are capable of suffusing the social classes barriers with reverential fear, inasmuch as the same laws can instill the foreboding of fateful events into men terrified by their fate. To such legal excesses, the Wilde also fell victim—a vain sacrifice, for the same caste he had tried both to imitate and transform, condemned the Wilde by donning the judge's robe, shedding the silhouette in tights.

Zola (Emile) owned a sprawling factory for the production of social schematics. His situation machines would punch people out smoothly and cleanly through continuous-flow manufacturing. Other machines, which laminated the truth on the causality chain, would collect processed people and assemble them into theater companies that were taught to act on experimental stages, as naturally as Nature itself. A small moon made of silver paper added the required amount of sentimentality.

The **Steffzweig (Stefan Zweig)** must be mentioned in this bestiary, since it is still regarded as a living being by a few. Still, the Steffzweig is an artifact, made to celebrate the occasion of a Viennese poet's congress, with feathers, skin, hair, etc., from each and every kind of European beasts. It is, so to speak, a volapük* animal. At present, only in remote lands, and in certain Geneva circles, does anyone believe in the Steffzweig's existence. Some claim to have seen the Steffzweig in a Leipzig home, on 7 Short Street, under a small glass bell. In the last few years we have heard of an Arnzweig as a real animal. Ascertaining the Arnzweig's existence has proved to be impossible so far, since it occurs solely in Zion. Nor is it possible to determine this country's geographical position. Breaking news report that the Arnzweig is a good, honest animal created by God.

---

* Volapük is a constructed language, created in 1879–1880 by Johann Martin Schleyer, a Roman Catholic priest in Baden, Germany. Schleyer felt that God had told him in a dream to create an international language. The vocable "volapuk" is composed of "vola," from the English "world," and "pük," from the English "speech."

Horacio Silvestre Quiroga Forteza (1878–1937), or Horacio Quiroga, was a playwright and poet born in Salto, Uruguay. He began writing in prose and verse but soon realized that his calling was leading him toward the short story form. Many of his stories were set in the jungle and inhabited the viewpoints of both humans and animals in their struggle to survive. Quiroga was also adept at portraying mental illness and hallucinations. He loved to travel and often went to the jungle in order to get more material for his stories. *Stories of the Jungle* (1918) and *The Decapitated Chicken and Other Stories* (1925) are his two major collections, but his novel *Anaconda* (1921) is generally considered his greatest work. "The Alligator War" first appeared in Quiroga's collection *Stories of the Jungle*.

The Alligator War

Horacio Quiroga

Translated by Arthur Livingston

IT WAS A VERY BIG RIVER in a region of South America that had never been visited by white men; and in it lived many, many alligators—perhaps a hundred, perhaps a thousand. For dinner they ate fish, which they caught in the stream, and for supper they ate deer and other animals that came down to the water side to drink. On hot afternoons in summer they stretched out and sunned themselves on the bank. But they liked nights when the moon was shining best of all. Then they swam out into the river and sported and played, lashing the water to foam with their tails, while the spray ran off their beautiful skins in all the colors of the rainbow.

These alligators had lived quite happy lives for a long, long time. But at last one afternoon, when they were all sleeping on the sand, snoring and snoring, one alligator woke up and cocked

his ears—the way alligators cock their ears. He listened and listened, and, to be sure, faintly, and from a great distance, came a sound: *Chug! Chug! Chug!*

"Hey!" the alligator called to the alligator sleeping next to him. "Hey! Wake up! Danger!"

"Danger of what?" asked the other, opening his eyes sleepily, and getting up.

"I don't know!" replied the first alligator.

The other alligator listened: *Chug! Chug! Chug!*

In great alarm the two alligators went calling up and down the river bank: "Danger! Danger!" And all their sisters and brothers and mothers and fathers and uncles and aunts woke up and began running this way and that with their tails curled up in the air. But the excitement did not serve to calm their fears. *Chug! Chug! Chug!* The noise was growing louder every moment; and at last, away off down the stream, they could see something moving along the surface of the river, leaving a trail of gray smoke behind it and beating the water on either side to foam: *Chush! Chush! Chush!*

The alligators looked at each other in the greatest astonishment: "What on earth is that?"

But there was one old alligator, the wisest and most experienced of them all. He was so old that only two sound teeth were left in his jaws—one in the upper jaw and one in the lower jaw. Once, also, when he was a boy, fond of adventure, he had made a trip down the river all the way to the sea.

"I know what it is," said he. "It's a whale. Whales are big fish, they shoot water up through their noses, and it falls down on them behind."

At this news, the little alligators began to scream at the top of their lungs, "It's a whale! It's a whale! It's a whale!" and they made for the water intending to duck out of sight.

But the big alligator cuffed with his tail a little alligator that was screaming nearby with his mouth open wide. "Dry up!" said he. "There's nothing to be afraid of! I know all about whales! Whales are the afraidest people there are!" And the little alligators stopped their noise.

But they grew frightened again a moment afterward. The gray smoke suddenly turned to an inky black, and the *Chush! Chush! Chush!* was now so loud that all the alligators took to the water, with only their eyes and the tips of their noses showing at the surface.

Cho-ash-h-h! Cho-ash-h-h! Cho-ash-h-h! The strange monster came rapidly up the stream. The alligators saw it go crashing past them, belching great clouds of smoke from the middle of its back, and splashing into the water heavily with the big revolving things it had on either side.

It was a steamer, the first steamer that had ever made its way up the Parana. *Chush! Chush! Chush!* It seemed to be getting further away again. *Chug! Chug! Chug!* It had disappeared from view.

One by one, the alligators climbed up out of the water onto the bank again. They were all quite cross with the old alligator who had told them wrongly that it was a whale.

"It was not a whale!" they shouted in his ear—for he was rather hard of hearing. "Well, what was it that just went by?"

The old alligator then explained that it was a steamboat full of fire; and that the alligators would all die if the boat continued to go up and down the river.

The other alligators only laughed, however. Why would the alligators die if the boat kept going up and down the river? It had passed by without so much as speaking to them! That old alligator didn't really know so much as he pretended to! And since they were very hungry they all went fishing in the stream. But alas! There was not a fish to be found! The steamboat had frightened every single one of them away.

"Well, what did I tell you?" said the old alligator. "You see: we haven't anything left to eat! All the fish have been frightened away! However—let's just wait till tomorrow. Perhaps the boat won't come back again. In that case, the fish will get over their fright and come back so that we can eat them." But the next day, the steamboat came crashing by again on its way back down the river, spouting black smoke as it had done before, and setting the whole river boiling with its paddle wheels.

"Well!" exclaimed the alligators. "What do you think of that? The boat came yesterday. The boat came today. The boat will come tomorrow. The fish will stay away; and nothing will come down here at night to drink. We are done for!"

But an idea occurred to one of the brighter alligators: "Let's dam the river!" he proposed. "The steamboat won't be able to climb a dam!"

"That's the talk! That's the talk! A dam! A dam! Let's build a dam!" And the alligators all made for the shore as fast as they could.

They went up into the woods along the bank and began to cut down trees of the hardest wood they could find—walnut and mahogany, mostly. They felled more than ten thousand of them altogether, sawing the trunks through with the kind of saw that alligators have on the tops of their tails. They dragged the trees down into the water and stood them up about a yard apart, all the way across the river, driving the pointed ends deep into the mud and weaving the branches together. No steamboat, big or little, would ever be able to pass that dam! No one would frighten the fish away again! They would have a good dinner the following day and every day! And since it was late at night by the time the dam was done, they all fell sound asleep on the river bank.

Chug! Chug! Chug! Chush! Chush! Chush! Cho-ash-h-h-h! Cho-ash-h-h-h! Cho-ash-h-h-h!

They were still asleep, the next day, when the boat came up; but the alligators barely opened their eyes and then tried to go to sleep again. What did they care about the boat? It could make all the noise it wanted, but it would never get by the dam!

And that is what happened. Soon the noise from the boat stopped. The men who were steering on the bridge took out their spy-glasses and began to study the strange obstruction that had been thrown up across the river. Finally a small boat was sent to look into it more closely. Only then did the alligators get up from where they were sleeping, run down into the water, and swim out behind the dam, where they lay floating and looking downstream between the piles. They could not help laughing, nevertheless, at the joke they had played on the steamboat!

The small boat came up, and the men in it saw how the alligators had made a dam across the river. They went back to the steamer, but soon after, came rowing up toward the dam again.

"Hey, you, alligators!"

"What can we do for you?" answered the alligators, sticking their heads through between the piles in the dam.

"That dam is in our way!" said the men.

"Tell us something we don't know!" answered the alligators.

"But we can't get by!"

"I'll say so!"

"Well, take the old thing out of the way!"

"Nosireesir!"

The men in the boat talked it over for a while and then they called:

"Alligators!"

"What can we do for you?"

"Will you take the dam away?"

"No!"

"No?"

"No!"

"Very well! See you later!"

"The later the better," said the alligators.

The rowboat went back to the steamer, while the alligators, as happy as could be, clapped their tails as loud as they could on the water. No boat could ever get by that dam, and drive the fish away again!

But the next day the steamboat returned; and when the alligators looked at it, they could not say a word from their surprise: it was not the same boat at all, but a larger one, painted gray like a mouse! How many steamboats were there, anyway? And this one probably would want to pass the dam! Well, just let it try! No, sir! No steamboat, little or big, would ever get through that dam!

"They shall not pass!" said the alligators, each taking up his station behind the piles in the dam.

The new boat, like the other one, stopped some distance below the dam; and again a little boat came rowing toward them. This time there were eight sailors in it, with one officer. The officer shouted:

"Hey, you, alligators!"

"What's the matter?" answered the alligators.

"Going to get that dam out of there?"

"No!"

"No?"

"No!"

"Very well!" said the officer. "In that case, we shall have to shoot it down!"

"Shoot it up if you want to!" said the alligators.

And the boat returned to the steamer.

But now, this mouse-gray steamboat was not an ordinary steamboat: it was a warship, with armor plate and terribly powerful guns. The old alligator who had made the trip to the river mouth suddenly remembered, and just in time to shout to the other alligators: "Duck for your lives! Duck! She's going to shoot! Keep down deep under water."

The alligators dived all at the same time, and headed for the shore, where they halted, keeping all their bodies out of sight except for their noses and their eyes. A great cloud of flame and smoke burst from the vessel's side, followed by a deafening report. An immense solid shot hurtled through the air and struck the dam exactly in the middle. Two or three tree trunks were cut away into splinters and drifted off downstream. Another shot, a third, and finally a fourth, each tearing a great hole in the dam. Finally the piles were entirely destroyed; not a tree, not a splinter, not a piece of bark, was left; and the alligators, still sitting with their eyes and noses just out of water, saw the warship come steaming by and blowing its whistle in derision at them.

Then the alligators came out on the bank and held a council of war. "Our dam was not strong enough," said they; "we must make a new and much thicker one."

So they worked again all that afternoon and night, cutting down the very biggest trees they could find, and making a much better dam than they had built before. When the gunboat appeared the next day, they were sleeping soundly and had to hurry to get behind the piles of the dam by the time the rowboat arrived there.

"Hey, alligators!" called the same officer.

"See who's here again!" said the alligators, jeeringly.

"Get that new dam out of there!"

"Never in the world!"

"Well, we'll blow it up, the way we did the other!"

"Blaze away, and good luck to you!"

You see, the alligators talked so big because they were sure the dam they had made this time would hold up against the most terrible cannon balls in the world. And the sailors must have thought so, too; for after they had fired the

first shot a tremendous explosion occurred in the dam. The gunboat was using shells, which burst among the timbers of the dam and broke the thickest trees into tiny, tiny bits. A second shell exploded right near the first, and a third near the second. So the shots went all along the dam, each tearing away a long strip of it till nothing, nothing, nothing was left. Again the warship came steaming by, closer in toward shore on this occasion, so that the sailors could make fun of the alligators by putting their hands to their mouths and holloing.

"So that's it!" said the alligators, climbing up out of the water. "We must all die, because the steamboats will keep coming and going, up and down, and leaving us not a fish in the world to eat!"

The littlest alligators were already whimpering; for they had had no dinner for three days; and it was a crowd of very sad alligators that gathered on the river shore to hear what the old alligator now had to say.

"We have only one hope left," he began. "We must go and see the Sturgeon! When I was a boy, I took that trip down to the sea along with him. He liked the salt water better than I did, and went quite a way out into the ocean. There he saw a sea fight between two of these boats; and he brought home a torpedo that had failed to explode. Suppose we go and ask him to give it to us. It is true the Sturgeon has never liked us alligators; but I got along with him pretty well myself. He is a good fellow, at bottom, and surely he will not want to see us all starve!"

The fact was that some years before an alligator had eaten one of the Sturgeon's favorite grandchildren; and for that reason the Sturgeon had refused ever since to call on the alligators or receive visits from them. Nevertheless, the alligators now trooped off in a body to the big cave under the bank of the river where they knew the Sturgeon stayed, with his torpedo beside him. There are sturgeons as much as six feet long, you know, and this one with the torpedo was of that kind.

"Mr. Sturgeon! Mr. Sturgeon!" called the alligators at the entrance of the cave. No one of them dared go in, you see, on account of that matter of the sturgeon's grandchild.

"Who is it?" answered the Sturgeon.

"We're the alligators," the latter replied in a chorus.

"I have nothing to do with alligators," grumbled the Sturgeon crossly.

But now the old alligator with the two teeth stepped forward and said:

"Why, hello, Sturgy. Don't you remember Ally, your old friend that took that trip down the river, when we were boys?"

"Well, well! Where have you been keeping yourself all these years?" said the Sturgeon, surprised and pleased to hear his old friend's voice. "Sorry, I didn't know it was you! How goes it? What can I do for you?"

"We've come to ask you for that torpedo you found, remember? You see, there's a warship keeps coming up and down our river scaring all the fish away. She's a whopper, I'll tell you, armor plate, guns, the whole thing! We made one dam and she knocked it down. We made another and she blew it up. The fish have all gone away and we haven't had a bite to eat in near onto a week. Now you give us your torpedo and we'll do the rest!"

The Sturgeon sat thinking for a long time, scratching his chin with one of his fins. At last he answered:

"As for the torpedo, all right! You can have it in spite of what you did to my eldest son's firstborn. But there's one trouble: who knows how to work the thing?"

The alligators were all silent. Not one of them had ever seen a torpedo.

"Well," said the Sturgeon, proudly, "I can see I'll have to go with you myself. I've lived next to that torpedo a long time. I know all about torpedoes."

The first task was to bring the torpedo down to the dam. The alligators got into line, the one behind taking in his mouth the tail of the one in front. When the line was formed it was fully a quarter of a mile long. The Sturgeon pushed the torpedo out into the current, and got under it so as to hold it up near the top of the water on his back. Then he took the tail of the last alligator in his teeth, and gave the signal to go ahead. The Sturgeon kept the torpedo afloat, while the alligators towed him along. In this way they went so fast that a wide wake followed on after the torpedo; and by the next morning they were back at the place where the dam was made.

As the little alligators who had stayed at home reported, the warship had already gone by upstream. But this pleased the others all the more. Now they would build a new dam, stronger than ever before, and catch the steamer in a trap, so that it would never get home again.

They worked all that day and all the next night, making a thick, almost solid dike, with barely enough room between the piles for the alligators to stick their heads through. They had just finished when the gunboat came into view.

Again the rowboat approached with the eight men and their officer. The alligators crowded behind the dam in great excitement, moving their paws to hold their own with the current; for this time, they were downstream.

"Hey, alligators!" called the officer.

"Well?" answered the alligators.

"Still another dam?"

"If at first you don't succeed, try, try, again!"

"Get that dam out of there!"

"No, sir!"

"You won't?"

"We won't!"

"Very well! Now you alligators just listen! If you won't be reasonable, we are going to knock this dam down, too. But to save you the trouble of building a fourth, we are going to shoot every blessed alligator around here. Yes, every single last alligator, women and children, big ones, little ones, fat ones, lean ones, and even that old codger sitting there with only two teeth left in his jaws!"

The old alligator understood that the officer was trying to insult him with that reference to his two teeth, and he answered:

"Young man, what you say is true. I have only two teeth left, not counting one or two others that are broken off. But do you know what those two teeth are going to eat for dinner?" As he said this the old alligator opened his mouth wide, wide, wide.

"Well, what are they going to eat?" asked one of the sailors.

"A little dude of a naval officer I see in a boat over there!"—and the old alligator dived under water and disappeared from view.

Meantime the Sturgeon had brought the torpedo to the very center of the dam, where four alligators were holding it fast to the river bottom waiting for orders to bring it up to the top of the water. The other alligators had gathered along the shore, with their noses and eyes alone in sight as usual.

The rowboat went back to the ship. When he saw the men climbing aboard, the Sturgeon went down to his torpedo.

Suddenly there was a loud detonation. The warship had begun firing, and the first shell struck and exploded in the middle of the dam. A great gap opened in it.

"Now! Now!" called the Sturgeon sharply, on seeing that there was room for the torpedo to go through. "Let her go! Let her go!"

As the torpedo came to the surface, the Sturgeon steered it to the opening in the dam, took aim hurriedly with one eye closed, and pulled at the trigger of the torpedo with his teeth. The propeller of the torpedo began to revolve, and it started off upstream toward the gunboat.

And it was high time. At that instant a second shot exploded in the dam, tearing away another large section.

From the wake the torpedo left behind it in the water the men on the vessel saw the danger they were in, but it was too late to do anything about it. The torpedo struck the ship in the middle, and went off.

You can never guess the terrible noise that torpedo made. It blew the warship into fifteen thousand million pieces, tossing guns, and smoke-

stacks, and shells and rowboats—everything, hundreds and hundreds of yards away.

The alligators all screamed with triumph and made as fast as they could for the dam. Down through the opening bits of wood came floating, with a number of sailors swimming as hard as they could for the shore. As the men passed through, the alligators put their paws to their mouths and holloed, as the men had done to them three days before. They decided not to eat a single one of the sailors, though some of them deserved it without a doubt. Except that when a man dressed in a blue uniform with gold braid came by, the old alligator jumped into the water off the dam, and snap! snap! ate him in two mouthfuls.

"Who was that man?" asked an ignorant young alligator, who never learned his lessons in school and never knew what was going on.

"It's the officer of the boat," answered the Sturgeon. "My old friend, Ally, said he was going to eat him, and eaten him he has!"

The alligators tore down the rest of the dam, because they knew that no boats would be coming by that way again.

The Sturgeon, who had quite fallen in love with the gold lace of the officer, asked that it be given him in payment for the use of his torpedo. The alligators said he might have it for the trouble of picking it out of the old alligator's mouth, where it had caught on the two teeth. They gave him also the officer's belt and sword. The Sturgeon put the belt on just behind his front fins, and buckled the sword to it. Thus togged out, he swam up and down for more than an hour in front of the assembled alligators, who admired his beautiful spotted skin as something almost as pretty as the coral snake's, and who opened their mouths wide at the splendor of his uniform. Finally they escorted him in honor back to his cave under the river bank, thanking him over and over again, and giving him three cheers as they went off.

When they returned to their usual place they found the fish had already returned. The next day another steamboat came by; but the alligators did not care, because the fish were getting used to it by this time and seemed not to be afraid. Since then the boats have been going back and forth all the time, carrying oranges. And the alligators open their eyes when they hear the *chug! chug!* *chug!* of a steamboat and laugh at the thought of how scared they were the first time, and of how they sank the warship.

But no warship has ever gone up the river since the old alligator ate the officer.

Francis Stevens was the pseudonym of the influential American author Gertrude Barrows Bennett (1884–1948). Her first publication, "The Curious Experience of Thomas Dunbar" (1904), was published under her own name, but it would be her only publication for over a decade. Only after the deaths of both her husband and her father did Bennett return to writing as a means of income. She usually read her grim tales to her daughter, who offered her suggestions, and in 1917 her novella *The Nightmare* appeared in an issue of *All-Story Weekly*. The editor of the magazine decided on the name Francis Stevens for Bennett after turning down Bennett's own suggestion. Bennett's tales often include some evil or madness that must be overcome. Her stories did more than provide for her family; they gave her acclaim, and she has been said to be the inventor of dark fantasy. "Friend Island" is set in a future where women have become the dominant sex and was considered a feminist tale at the time.

Friend Island

Francis Stevens

IT WAS UPON THE WATERFRONT that I first met her, in one of the shabby little tea shops frequented by able sailoresses of the poorer type. The uptown, glittering resorts of the Lady Aviators' Union were not for such as she.

Stern of feature, bronzed by wind and sun, her age could only be guessed, but I surmised at once that in her I beheld a survivor of the age of turbines and oil engines—a true sea-woman of that elder time when woman's superiority to man had not been so long recognized. When, to emphasize their victory, women in all ranks were sterner than today's need demands.

The spruce, smiling young maidens—enginewomen and stokers of the great aluminum rollers, but despite their profession, very neat in gold-braided blue knickers and boleros—these looked askance at the hard-faced relic of a harsher day, as they passed in and out of the shop.

I, however, brazenly ignoring similar glances at myself, a mere male intruding on the haunts of the world's ruling sex, drew a chair up beside the veteran. I ordered a full pot of tea, two cups, and a plate of macaroons and put on my most ingratiating air. Possibly my unconcealed admiration and interest were wiles not exercised in vain. Or the macaroons and tea, both excellent, may have loosened the old sea-woman's tongue. At any rate, under cautious questioning, she had soon launched upon a series of reminiscences well beyond my hopes for color and variety.

"When I was a lass," quoth the sea-woman, after a time, "there was none of this high-flying, gilt-edged, leather-stocking luxury about the sea.

We sailed by the power of our oil and gasoline. If they failed on us, like as not 'twas the rubber ring and the rolling wave for ours."

She referred to the archaic practice of placing a pneumatic affair called a life-preserver beneath the arms, in case of that dreaded disaster, now so unheard of, shipwreck.

"In them days there was still many a man bold enough to join our crews. And I've knowed cases," she added condescendingly, "where just by the muscle and brawn of such men some poor sailor lass has reached shore alive that would have fed the sharks without 'em. Oh, I ain't so down on men as you might think. It's the spoiling of them that I don't hold with. There's too much preached nowadays that man is fit for nothing but to fetch and carry and do nurse-work in big child-homes. To my mind, a man who hasn't the nerve of a woman ain't fitted to father children, let alone raise 'em. But that's not here nor there. My time's past, and I know it, or I wouldn't be setting here gossipin' to you, my lad, over an empty teapot."

I took the hint, and with our cups replenished, she bit thoughtfully into her fourteenth macaroon and continued.

"There's one voyage I'm not likely to forget, though I live to be as old as Cap'n Mary Barnacle, of the *Shouter*. 'Twas aboard the old *Shouter* that this here voyage occurred, and it was her last and likewise Cap'n Mary's. Cap'n Mary, she was then that decrepit, it seemed a mercy that she should go to her rest, and in good salt water at that.

"I remember the voyage for Cap'n Mary's sake, but most I remember it because 'twas then that I come the nighest in my life to committin' matrimony. For a man, the man had nerve; he was nearer bein' companionable than any other man I ever seed; and if it hadn't been for just one little event that showed up the—the *mannishness* of him, in a way I couldn't abide, I reckon he'd be keepin' house for me this minute."

"We cleared from Frisco with a cargo of silkateen petticoats for Brisbane. Cap'n Mary was always strong on petticoats. Leather breeches or even half-skirts would ha' paid far better, they being more in demand like, but Cap'n Mary was three-quarters owner, and says she, land women should buy petticoats, and if they didn't it wouldn't be the Lord's fault nor hers for not providing 'em.

"We cleared on a fine day, which is an ill sign—or was, then when the weather and the seas o' God still counted in the trafficking of the humankind. Not two days out we met a whirling, mucking bouncer of a gale that well nigh threw the old *Shouter* a full point off her course in the first wallop. She was a stout craft, though. None of your featherweight, gas-lightened, paper-thin alloy shells, but toughened aluminum from stern to stern. Her turbine drove her through the combers at a forty-five knot clip, which named her a speedy craft for a freighter in them days.

"But this night, as we tore along through the creaming green billows, something unknown went 'way wrong down below.

"I was forward under the shelter of her long over-sloop, looking for a hairpin I'd dropped somewheres about that afternoon. It was a gold hairpin, and gold still being mighty scarce when I was a girl, a course I valued it. But suddenly I felt the old *Shouter* give a jump under my feet like a plane struck by a shell in full flight. Then she trembled all over for a full second, frightened like. Then, with the crash of doomsday ringing in my ears, I felt myself sailing through the air right into the teeth o' the shrieking gale, as near as I could judge. Down I come in the hollow of a monstrous big wave, and as my ears doused under I thought I heard a splash close by. Coming up, sure enough, there close by me was floating a new, patent, hermetic, thermo-ice-chest. Being as it was empty, and being as it was shut up air-tight, that ice-chest made as sweet a life-preserver as a woman could wish in such an hour. About ten foot by twelve, it floated high in the raging sea. Out on its top I scrambled, and hanging on by a handle I looked expectant for some of my poor fellow-women to come floating by. Which they never did, for the good reason that the *Shouter* had blowed up and went below, petticoats, Cap'n Mary and all."

"What caused the explosion?" I inquired.

"The Lord and Cap'n Mary Barnacle can explain," she answered piously. "Besides the oil for her turbines, she carried a power of gasoline for her alternative engines, and likely 'twas the cause of her ending so sudden like. Anyways, all I ever seen of her again was the empty ice-chest that Providence had well-nigh hove upon my head. On that I sat and floated, and floated and sat some more, till by-and-by the storm sort of blowed itself out, the sun come shining—this was next morning—and I could dry my hair and look about me. I was a young lass, then, and not bad to look upon. I didn't want to die, any more than you that's sitting there this minute. So I up and prays for land. Sure enough toward evening a speck heaves up low down on the horizon. At first I took it for a gas liner, but later found it was just a little island, all alone by itself in the great Pacific Ocean.

"Come, now, here's luck, thinks I, and with that I deserts the ice-chest, which being empty, and me having no ice to put in it, not likely to have in them latitudes, is of no further use to me. Striking out I swum a mile or so and set foot on dry land for the first time in nigh three days.

"Pretty land it were, too, though bare of human life as an iceberg in the Arctic.

"I had landed on a shining white beach that run up to a grove of lovely, waving palm trees. Above them I could see the slopes of a hill so high and green it reminded me of my own old home, up near Couquomgomoc Lake in Maine. The whole place just seemed to smile and smile at me. The palms waved and bowed in the sweet breeze, like they wanted to say, 'Just set right down and make yourself to home. We've been waiting a long time for you to come.' I cried, I was that happy to be made welcome. I was a young lass then, and sensitive-like to how folks treated me. You're laughing now, but wait and see if or not there was sense to the way I felt.

"So I up and dries my clothes and my long, soft hair again, which was well worth drying, for I had far more of it than now. After that I walked along a piece, until there was a sweet little path meandering away into the wild woods.

"Here, thinks I, this looks like inhabitants. Be they civil or wild, I wonder? But after traveling the path a piece, lo and behold it ended sudden like in a wide circle of green grass, with a little spring of clear water. And the first thing I noticed was a slab of white board nailed to a palm tree close to the spring. Right off I took a long drink, for you better believe I was thirsty, and then I went to look at this board. It had evidently been tore off the side of a wooden packing box, and the letters was roughly printed in lead pencil.

"'Heaven help whoever you be,' I read. 'This island ain't just right. I'm going to swim for it. You better too. Good-by. Nelson Smith.' That's what it said, but the spellin' was simply awful. It all looked quite new and recent, as if Nelson Smith hadn't more than a few hours before he wrote and nailed it there.

"Well, after reading that queer warning I begun to shake all over like in a chill. Yes, I shook like I had the ague, though the hot tropic sun was burning down right on me and that alarming board. What had scared Nelson Smith so much that he had swum to get away? I looked all around real cautious and careful, but not a single frightening thing could I behold. And the palms and the green grass and the flowers still smiled that peaceful and friendly like. 'Just make yourself to home,' was wrote all over the place in plainer letters than those sprawly lead pencil ones on the board.

"Pretty soon, what with the quiet and all, the chill left me. Then I thought, 'Well, to be sure, this Smith person was just an ordinary man, I reckon, and likely he got nervous of being so alone. Likely he just fancied things which was really not. It's a pity he drowned himself before I come, though likely I'd have found him poor company. By his record I judge him a man of but common education.'

"So I decided to make the most of my welcome, and that I did for weeks to come. Right near the spring was a cave, dry as a biscuit box, with a nice floor of white sand. Nelson had lived there too, for there was a litter of stuff—tin cans—empty—scraps of newspapers and the like. I got to calling him Nelson in my mind, and then Nelly, and wondering if he was dark or fair, and how he come to be cast away there all alone, and what was the strange events that drove him to his end. I cleaned out the cave, though. He had devoured all his tin-canned provisions, however he come by them, but this I didn't mind. That there island was a generous body. Green milk-coconuts, sweet berries, turtle eggs and the like was my daily fare.

"For about three weeks the sun shone every day, the birds sang and the monkeys chattered. We was all one big, happy family, and the more I explored that island the better I liked the company I was keeping. The land was about ten miles from beach to beach, and never a foot of it that wasn't sweet and clean as a private park.

"From the top of the hill I could see the ocean, miles and miles of blue water, with never a sign of a gas liner, or even a little government running-boat. Them running-boats used to go most every-where to keep the seaways clean of derelicts and the like. But I knowed that if this island was no more than a hundred miles off the regular courses of navigation, it might be many a long day before I'd be rescued. The top of the hill, as I found when first I climbed up there, was a wore-out cra-ter. So I knowed that the island was one of them volcanic ones you run across so many of in the seas between Capricorn and Cancer.

"Here and there on the slopes and down through the jungly tree-growth, I would come on great lumps of rock, and these must have came up out of that crater long ago. If there was lava it was so old it had been covered up entire with green growing stuff. You couldn't have found it without a spade, which I didn't have nor want."

"Well, at first I was happy as the hours was long. I wandered and clambered and waded and swum, and combed my long hair on the beach, having fortunately not lost my side-combs nor the rest of my gold hairpins. But by-and-by it begun to get just a bit lonesome. Funny thing, that's a feeling that, once it starts, it gets worse and worser so quick it's perfectly surprising. And right then was when the days begun to get gloomy. We had a long, sickly hot spell, like I never seen before on an ocean island. There was dull clouds across the sun from morn to night. Even the little monkeys and parrakeets, that had seemed so gay, moped and drowsed like they was sick. All one day I cried, and let the rain soak me through and through—that was the first rain we had—and I didn't get thorough dried even dur-ing the night, though I slept in my cave. Next morning I got up mad as thunder at myself and all the world.

"When I looked out the black clouds was bil-lowing across the sky. I could hear nothing but great breakers roaring in on the beaches, and the wild wind raving through the lashing palms.

"As I stood there a nasty little wet monkey dropped from a branch almost on my head. I grabbed a pebble and slung it at him real vicious. 'Get away, you dirty little brute!' I shrieks, and with that there come a awful blinding flare of light. There was a long, crackling noise like a bunch of Chinese fireworks, and then a sound as if a whole fleet of *Shouters* had all went up together.

"When I come to, I found myself 'way in the back of my cave, trying to dig further into the rock with my finger nails. Upon taking thought, it come to me that what had occurred was just a lightning-clap, and going to look, sure enough there lay a big palm tree right across the glade. It was all busted and split open by the lightning, and the little monkey was under it, for I could see his tail and his hind legs sticking out.

"Now, when I set eyes on that poor, crushed little beast I'd been so mean to, I was terrible ashamed. I sat down on the smashed tree and considered and considered. How thankful I had ought to have been. Here I had a lovely, plenteous island, with food and water to my taste, when it might have been a barren, starvation rock that was my lot. And so, thinking, a sort of gradual peaceful feeling stole over me. I got cheerfuller and cheerfuller, till I could have sang and danced for joy.

"Pretty soon I realized that the sun was shining bright for the first time that week. The wind had stopped hollering, and the waves had died to just a singing murmur on the beach. It seemed kind o' strange, this sudden peace, like the cheer in my own heart after its rage and storm. I rose up, feeling sort of queer, and went to look if the little monkey had came alive again, though that was a fool thing, seeing he was laying all crushed up and very dead. I buried him under a tree root, and as I did it a conviction come to me.

"I didn't hardly question that conviction at all. Somehow, living there alone so long, perhaps my natural womanly intuition was stronger than ever before or since, and so I *knowed*. Then I went and pulled poor Nelson Smith's board off from the tree and tossed it away for the tide to carry off. That there board was an insult to my island!"

The sea-woman paused, and her eyes had a far-away look. It seemed as if I and perhaps even the macaroons and tea were quite forgotten.

"Why did you think that?" I asked, to bring her back. "How could an island be insulted?"

She started, passed her hand across her eyes, and hastily poured another cup of tea.

"Because," she said at last, poising a macaroon in mid-air, "because that island—that particular island that I had landed on—had a heart!

"When I was gay, it was bright and cheerful. It was glad when I come, and it treated me right until I got that grouchy it had to mope from sympathy. It loved me like a friend. When I flung a rock at that poor little drenched monkey critter, it backed up my act with an anger like the wrath o' God, and killed its own child to please me! But it got right cheery the minute I seen the wrongness of my ways. Nelson Smith had no business to say, 'This island ain't just right,' for it was a righter place than ever I seen elsewhere. When I cast away that lying board, all the birds begun to sing like mad. The green milk-coconuts fell right and left. Only the monkeys seemed kind o' sad like still, and no wonder. You see, their own

mother, the island, had rounded on one o' them for my sake!

"After that I was right careful and considerate. I named the island Anita, not knowing her right name, or if she had any. Anita was a pretty name, and it sounded kind of South Sea like. Anita and me got along real well together from that day on. It was some strain to be always gay and singing around like a dear duck of a canary bird, but I done my best. Still, for all the love and gratitude I bore Anita, the company of an island, however sympathetic, ain't quite enough for a human being. I still got lonesome, and there was even days when I couldn't keep the clouds clear out of the sky, though I will say we had no more tornadoes.

"I think the island understood and tried to help me with all the bounty and good cheer the poor thing possessed. None the less my heart give a wonderful big leap when one day I seen a blot on the horizon. It drawed nearer and nearer, until at last I could make out its nature."

"A ship, of course," said I, "and were you rescued?"

"'Tweren't a ship, neither," denied the sea-woman somewhat impatiently. "Can't you let me spin this yarn without no more remarks and fool questions? This thing what was bearing down so fast with the incoming tide was neither more nor less than another island!

"You may well look startled. I was startled myself. Much more so than you, likely. I didn't know then what you, with your book-learning, very likely know now—that islands sometimes float. Their underparts being a tangled-up mess of roots and old vines that new stuff's growed over, they sometimes break away from the mainland in a brisk gale and go off for a voyage, calm as a old-fashioned, eight-funnel steamer. This one was uncommon large, being as much as two miles, maybe, from shore to shore. It had its palm trees and its live things, just like my own Anita, and I've sometimes wondered if this drifting piece hadn't really been a part of my island once—just its daughter like, as you might say.

"Be that, however, as it might be, no sooner

did the floating piece get within hailing distance than I hears a human holler and there was a man dancing up and down on the shore like he was plumb crazy. Next minute he had plunged into the narrow strip of water between us and in a few minutes had swum to where I stood.

"Yes, of course it was none other than Nelson Smith!

"I knowed that the minute I set eyes on him. He had the very look of not having no better sense than the man what wrote that board and then nearly committed suicide trying to get away from the best island in all the oceans. Glad enough he was to get back, though, for the coconuts was running very short on the floater what had rescued him, and the turtle eggs wasn't worth mentioning. Being short of grub is the surest way I know to cure a man's fear of the unknown."

"Well, to make a long story short, Nelson Smith told me he was a aeronauter. In them days to be an aeronauter was not the same as to be an aviatress is now. There was dangers in the air, and dangers in the sea, and he had met with both. His gas tank had leaked and he had dropped into the water close by Anita. A case or two of provisions was all he could save from the total wreck.

"Now, as you might guess, I was crazy enough to find out what had scared this Nelson Smith into trying to swim the Pacific. He told me a story that seemed to fit pretty well with mine, only when it come to the scary part he shut up like a clam, that aggravating way some men have. I give it up at last for just man-foolishness, and we begun to scheme to get away.

"Anita moped some while we talked it over. I realized how she must be feeling, so I explained to her that it was right needful for us to get with our kind again. If we stayed with her we should probably quarrel like cats, and maybe even kill each other out of pure human cussedness. She cheered up considerable after that, and even, I thought, got a little anxious to have us leave. At any rate, when we begun to provision up the little floater, which we had anchored to the big island

by a cable of twisted bark, the green nuts fell all over the ground, and Nelson found more turtle nests in a day than I had in weeks.

"During them days I really got fond of Nelson Smith. He was a companionable body, and brave, or he wouldn't have been a professional aeronauter, a job that was rightly thought tough enough for a woman, let alone a man. Though he was not so well educated as me, at least he was quiet and modest about what he did know, not like some men, boasting most where there is least to brag of.

"Indeed, I misdoubt if Nelson and me would not have quit the sea and the air together and set up housekeeping in some quiet little town up in New England, maybe, after we had got away, if it had not been for what happened when we went. I never, let me say, was so deceived in any man before nor since. The thing taught me a lesson and I never was fooled again.

"We was all ready to go, and then one morning, like a parting gift from Anita, come a soft and favoring wind. Nelson and I run down the beach together, for we didn't want our floater to blow off and leave us. As we was running, our arms full of coconuts, Nelson Smith stubbed his bare toe on a sharp rock, and down he went. I hadn't noticed, and was going on.

"But sudden the ground begun to shake under my feet, and the air was full of a queer, grinding, groaning sound, like the very earth was in pain.

"I turned around sharp. There sat Nelson, holding his bleeding toe in both fists and giving vent to such awful words as no decent sea-going lady would ever speak nor hear to!

"'Stop it, stop it!' I shrieked at him, but 'twas too late.

"Island or no island, Anita was a lady, too! She had a gentle heart, but she knowed how to behave when she was insulted.

"With one terrible, great roar a spout of smoke and flame belched up out o' the heart of Anita's crater hill a full mile into the air!

"I guess Nelson stopped swearing. He couldn't have heard himself, anyways. Anita was talking now with tongues of flame and such roars as would have bespoke the raging protest of a continent.

"I grabbed that fool man by the hand and run him down to the water. We had to swim good and hard to catch up with our only hope, the floater. No bark rope could hold her against the stiff breeze that was now blowing, and she had broke her cable. By the time we scrambled aboard great rocks was falling right and left. We couldn't see each other for a while for the clouds of fine gray ash.

"It seemed like Anita was that mad she was flinging stones after us, and truly I believe that such was her intention. I didn't blame her, neither!

"Lucky for us the wind was strong and we was soon out of range.

"'So!' says I to Nelson, after I'd got most of the ashes out of my mouth, and shook my hair clear of cinders. 'So, that was the reason you up and left sudden when you was there before! You aggravated that island till the poor thing druv you out!'

"'Well,' says he, and not so meek as I'd have admired to see him, 'how could I know the darn island was a lady?'

"'Actions speak louder than words,' says I. 'You should have knowed it by her ladylike behavior!'

"'Is volcanoes and slingin' hot rocks ladylike?' he says. 'Is snakes ladylike? T'other time I cut my thumb on a tin can, I cussed a little bit. Say—just a li'l' bit! An' what comes at me out o' all the caves, and out o' every crack in the rocks, and out o' the very spring o' water where I'd been drinkin'? Why snakes! *Snakes*, if you please, big, little, green, red, and sky-blue-scarlet! What'd I do? Jumped in the water, of course. Why wouldn't I? I'd ruther swim and drown than be stung or swallowed to death. But how was I t' know the snakes come outta the rocks because I cussed?'

"'You, couldn't,' I agrees, sarcastic. 'Some folks never knows a lady till she up and whangs 'em over the head with a brick. A real, gentle, kind-like warning, them snakes were, which you would not heed! Take shame to yourself, Nelly,' says I, right stern, 'that a decent little island like Anita can't associate with you peaceable, but you must hurt her sacredest feelings with language no lady would stand by to hear!'

"I never did see Anita again. She may have blew herself right out of the ocean in her just wrath at the vulgar, disgustin' language of Nelson Smith. I don't know. We was took off the floater at last, and I lost track of Nelson just as quick as I could when we was landed at Frisco.

"He had taught me a lesson. A man is just full of mannishness, and the best of 'em ain't good enough for a lady to sacrifice her sensibilities to put up with.

"Nelson Smith, he seemed to feel real bad when he learned I was not for him, and then he apologized. But apologies weren't no use to me. I could never abide him, after the way he went and talked right in the presence of me and my poor, sweet lady friend, Anita!"

Now I am well versed in the lore of the sea in all ages. Through mists of time I have enviously eyed wild voyagings of sea rovers who roved and spun their yarns before the stronger sex came into its own, and ousted man from his heroic pedestal. I have followed—across the printed page—the wanderings of Odysseus. Before Gulliver I have burned the incense of tranced attention; and with reverent awe considered the history of one Munchausen, a baron. But alas, these were only men!

In what field is not woman our subtle superior?

Meekly I bowed my head, and when my eyes dared lift again, the ancient mariness had departed, leaving me to sorrow for my surpassed and outdone idols. Also with a bill for macaroons and tea of such incredible proportions that in comparison therewith I found it easy to believe her story!

Stella Benson (1892–1933) was an English poet, novelist, and travel writer. Although absent from the literary canon, Stella Benson was an unsung hero of the twentieth century to her contemporaries. She began writing poetry at the age of fourteen and may have inherited her love for the written word from an aunt, Mary Cholmondeley, who was a novelist. Much of her work was inspired by her suffragist beliefs and included the themes of isolation and tragedy that mirrored her experiences in World War I, as well as the lives of women she met on her travels. Her third novel, *Living Alone* (1919), is full of odd and witty tales. Benson claims that *Living Alone*, excerpted here, is a book only for the magically inclined minority, and once someone reads "Magic Comes to a Committee" they'll understand why.

Magic Comes to a Committee

(EXCERPT FROM *LIVING ALONE*)

Stella Benson

CHAPTER I

MAGIC COMES TO A COMMITTEE

THIS IS NOT A REAL BOOK. *It does not deal with real people, nor should it be read by real people. But there are in the world so many real books already written for the benefit of real people, and there are still so many to be written, that I cannot believe that a little alien book such as this, written for the magically inclined minority, can be considered too assertive a trespasser.*

There were six women, seven chairs, and a table in an otherwise unfurnished room in an unfashionable part of London. Three of the women were of the kind that has no life apart from committees. They need not be mentioned in detail. The names of two others were Miss Meta Mostyn Ford and Lady Arabel Higgins. Miss Ford was a good woman, as well as a lady. Her hands were beautiful because they paid a manicurist to keep them so, but she was too righteous to powder her nose. She was the sort of person a man would like his best friend to marry. Lady Arabel was older: she was virtuous to the same extent as Achilles was invulnerable. In the beginning, when her soul was being soaked in virtue, the heel of it was fortunately left dry. She had a husband, but no apparent tragedy in her life. These two women were obviously not native to their surroundings. Their eyelashes brought Bond Street—or at least

572

Kensington—to mind; their shoes were mudless; their gloves had not been bought in the sales. Of the sixth woman the less said the better.

All six women were there because their country was at war, and because they felt it to be their duty to assist it to remain at war for the present. They were the nucleus of a committee on War Savings, and they were waiting for their Chairman, who was the Mayor of the borough. He was also a grocer.

Five of the members were discussing methods of persuading poor people to save money. The sixth was making spots on the table with a pen.

They were interrupted, not by the expected Mayor, but by a young woman, who came violently in by the street door, rushed into the middle of the room, and got under the table. The members, in surprise, pushed back their chairs and made ladylike noises of protest and inquiry.

"They're after me," panted the person under the table.

All seven listened to thumping silence for several seconds, and then, as no pursuing outcry declared itself, the Stranger arose, without grace, from her hiding-place.

To anybody except a member of a committee it would have been obvious that the Stranger was of the Cinderella type, and bound to turn out a heroine sooner or later. But perception goes out of committees. The more committees you belong to, the less of ordinary life you will understand. When your daily round becomes nothing more than a daily round of committees you might as well be dead.

The Stranger was not pretty; she had a broad, curious face. Her clothes were much too good to throw away. You would have enjoyed giving them to a decayed gentlewoman.

"I stole this bun," she explained frankly. "There is an uninterned German baker after me."

"And why did you steal it?" asked Miss Ford, pronouncing the H in "why" with a haughty and terrifying sound of suction.

The Stranger sighed. "Because I couldn't afford to buy it."

"And why could you not afford to buy the bun?" asked Miss Ford. "A big strong girl like you."

You will notice that she had had a good deal of experience in social work.

The Stranger said: "Up till ten o'clock this morning I was of the leisured classes like yourselves. I had a hundred pounds."

Lady Arabel was one of the kindest people in the world, but even she quivered at the suggestion of a common leisure. The sort of clothes the Stranger wore Lady Arabel would have called "too dretful." If one is well dressed one is proud, and may look an angel in the eye. If one is really shabby one is even prouder, one often goes out of one's way to look angels in the eye. But if one wears a squirrel fur "set," and a dyed dress that originally cost two and a half guineas, one is damned.

"You have squandered all that money?" pursued Miss Ford.

"Yes. In ten minutes."

A thrill ran through all six members. Several mouths watered.

"I am ashamed of you," said Miss Ford. "I hope the baker will catch you. Don't you know that your country is engaged in the greatest conflict in history? A hundred pounds . . . you might have put it in the War Loan."

"Yes," said the Stranger, "I did. That's how I squandered it."

Miss Ford seemed to be partially drowned by this reply. One could see her wits fighting for air.

But Lady Arabel had not committed herself, and therefore escaped this disaster. "You behaved foolishly," she said. "We are all too dretfully anxious to subscribe what we can spare to the War Loan, of course. But the State does not expect more than that of us."

"God bless it," said the Stranger loudly, so that everybody blushed. "Of course it doesn't. But it is fun, don't you think, when you are giving a present, to exceed expectations?"

"The State—" began Lady Arabel, but was

nudged into silence by Miss Ford. "Of course it's all untrue. Don't let her think we believe her."

The Stranger heard her. Such people do not only hear with their ears. She laughed.

"You shall see the receipt," she said.

Out of her large pocket she dragged several things before she found what she sought. The sixth member noticed several packets labelled MAGIC, which the Stranger handled very carefully. "Frightfully explosive," she said.

"I believe you're drunk," said Miss Ford, as she took the receipt. It really was a War Loan receipt, and the name and address on it were: "Miss Hazeline Snow, The Bindles, Pymley, Gloucestershire."

Lady Arabel smiled in a relieved way. She had not long been a social worker, and had not yet acquired a taste for making fools of the undeserving. "So this is your name and address," she said.

"No," said the Stranger simply.

"This is your name and address," said Lady Arabel more loudly.

"No," said the Stranger. "I made it up. Don't you think 'The Bindles, Pymley,' is too darling?"

"Quite drunk," repeated Miss Ford. She had attended eight committee meetings that week.

"S—s—s—sh, Meta," hissed Lady Arabel. She leaned forward, not smiling, but pleasantly showing her teeth. "You gave a false name and address. My dear, I wonder if I can guess why."

"I dare say you can," admitted the Stranger. "It's such fun, don't you think, to get no thanks? Don't you sometimes amuse yourself by sending postal orders to people whose addresses look pathetic in the telephone book, or by forgetting to take away the parcels you have bought in poor little shops? Or by standing and looking with ostentatious respect at boy scouts on the march, always bearing in mind that these, in their own eyes, are not little boys trotting behind a disguised curate, but British Troops on the Move? Just two pleased eyes in a crowd, just a hundred pounds dropped from heaven into poor Mr. Bonar Law's wistful hand. . . ."

Miss Ford began to laugh, a ladylike yet nasty laugh. "You amuse me," she said, but not in the kind of way that would make anybody wish to amuse her often.

Miss Ford was the ideal member of committee, and a committee, of course, exists for the purpose of damping enthusiasms.

The Stranger's manners were somehow hectic. Directly she heard that laughter the tears came into her eyes. "Didn't you like what I was saying?" she asked. Tears climbed down her cheekbones.

"Oh!" said Miss Ford. "You seem to be— if not drunk—suffering from some form of hysteria."

"Do you think youth is a form of hysteria?" asked the Stranger. "Or hunger? Or magic? Or—"

"Oh, don't recite any more lists, for the Dear Sake!" implored Miss Ford, who had caught this rather pretty expression where she caught her laugh and most of her thoughts—from contemporary fiction. She had a lot of friends in the writing trade. She knew artists too, and an actress, and a lot of people who talked. She very nearly did something clever herself. She continued: "I wish you could see yourself, trying to be uplifting between the munches of a stolen bun. You'd laugh too. But perhaps you never laugh," she added, straightening her lips.

"How d'you mean—laugh?" asked the Stranger. "I didn't know that noise was called laughing. I thought you were just saying 'Ha—ha.'"

At this moment the Mayor came in. As I told you, he was a grocer, and the Chairman of the committee. He was a bad Chairman, but a good grocer. Grocers generally wear white in the execution of their duty, and this fancy, I think, reflects their pureness of heart. They spend their days among soft substances most beautiful to touch; and sometimes they sell honest-smelling soaps; and sometimes they chop cheeses, and thus reach the glory of the butcher's calling, without its painfulness. Also they handle shining tins, marvellously illustrated.

Mayors and grocers were of course nothing to Miss Ford, but Chairmen were very important. She nodded curtly to the Mayor and grocer, but she pushed the seventh chair towards the Chairman.

"May I just finish with this applicant?" she asked in her thin inclusive committee voice, and then added in the direction of the Stranger: "It's no use talking nonsense. We all see through you, you cannot deceive a committee. But to a certain extent we believe your story, and are willing, if the case proves satisfactory, to give you a helping hand. I will take down a few particulars. First your name?"

"M—m," mused the Stranger. "Let me see, you didn't like Hazeline Snow much, did you? What d'you think of Thelma . . . Thelma Bennett Watkins? . . . You know, the Rutlandshire Watkinses, the younger branch—"

Miss Ford balanced her pen helplessly. "But that isn't your real name."

"How d'you mean—real name?" asked the Stranger anxiously. "Won't that do? What about Iris . . . Hyde? . . . You see, the truth is, I was never actually christened . . . I was born a conscientious objector, and also—"

"Oh, for the Dear Sake, be silent!" said Miss Ford, writing down "Thelma Bennett Watkins," in self-defence. "This, I take it, is the name you gave at the time of the National Registration."

"I forget," said the Stranger. "I remember that I put down my trade as Magic, and they registered it on my card as 'Machinist.' Yet Magic, I believe, is a starred profession."

"What is your trade really?" asked Miss Ford.

"I'll show you," replied the Stranger, unbuttoning once more the flap of her pocket.

She wrote a word upon the air with her finger, and made a flourish under the word. So flowery was the flourish that it spun her round, right round upon her toes, and she faced her watchers again. The committee jumped, for the blind ran up, and outside the window, at the end of a strange perspective of street, the trees of some far square were as soft as thistledown against a lemon-coloured sky. A sound came up the street. . . .

The forgotten April and the voices of lambs pealed like bells into the room. . . .

Oh, let us flee from April! We are but swimmers in seas of words, we members of committees, and to the song of April there are no words. What do we know, and what does London know, after all these years of learning?

Old Mother London crouches, with her face buried in her hands; and she is walled in with her fogs and her loud noises, and over her head are the heavy beams of her dark roof, and she has the barred sun for a skylight, and winds that are but hideous draughts rush under her door. London knows much, and every moment she learns a new thing, but this she shall never learn—that the sun shines all day and the moon all night on the silver tiles of her dark house, and that the young months climb her walls, and run singing in and out between her chimneys. . . .

Nothing else happened in that room. At least nothing more important than the ordinary manifestations attendant upon magic. The lamp had tremulously gone out. Coloured flames danced about the Stranger's head. One felt the thrill of a purring cat against one's ankles, one saw its green eyes glare. But these things hardly counted.

It was all over. The Mayor was heard cracking his fingers, and whispering "Puss, Puss." The lamp relighted itself. Nobody had known that it was so gifted.

The Mayor said: "Splendid, miss, quite splendid. You'd make a fortune on the stage." His tongue, however, seemed to be talking by itself, without the assistance of the Mayor himself. One could see that he was shaken out of his usual grocerly calm, for his feverish hand was stroking a cat where no cat was.

Black cats are only the showy properties of magic, easily materialised, even by beginners, at will. It must be confusing for such an orderly animal as the cat to exist in this intermittent way, never knowing, so to speak, whether it is there or not there, from one moment to another.

The sixth member took a severely bitten pen

from between her lips, and said: "Now you mention it, I think I'll go down there again for the week-end. I can pawn my ear-rings."

Nobody of course took any notice of her, yet in a way her remark was logical. For that singing Spring that had for a moment trespassed in the room had reminded her of very familiar things, and for a few seconds she had stood upon a beloved hill, and had looked down between beech trees on a far valley, like a promised land; and had seen in the valley a pale river and a dark town, like milk and honey.

As for Miss Ford, she had become rather white. Although the blind had now pulled itself down, and dismissed April, Miss Ford continued to look at the window. But she cleared her throat and said hoarsely: "Will you kindly answer my questions? I asked you what your trade was."

"It's too dretful of me to interrupt," said Lady Arabel suddenly. "But, do you know, Meta, I feel we are wasting this committee's time. This young person needs no assistance from us." She turned to the Stranger, and added: "My dear, I am dretfully ashamed. You must meet my son Rrchud. . . . My son Rrchud knows. . . ."

She burst into tears.

The Stranger took her hand.

"I should like awfully to meet Rrchud, and to get to know you better," she said. She grew very red. "I say, I should be awfully pleased if you would call me Angela."

It wasn't her name, but she had noticed that something of this sort is always said when people become motherly and cry.

Then she went away.

"Lawdy," said the Mayor. "I didn't expect she'd go out by the door, somehow. Look—she's left some sort of hardware over there in the corner."

It was a broomstick.

CHAPTER II

THE COMMITTEE COMES TO MAGIC

I don't suppose for a moment that you know Mitten Island: it is a difficult place to get to; you have to change buses seven times, going from Kensington, and you have to cross the river by means of a ferry. On Mitten Island there is a model village, consisting of several hundred houses, two churches, and one shop.

It was the sixth member who discovered, after the committee meeting, that the address on the forsaken broomstick's collar was: Number 100 Beautiful Way, Mitten Island, London.

The sixth member, although she was a member of committees, was neither a real expert in, nor a real lover of, Doing Good. In Doing Good, I think, we have got into bad habits. We try in groups to do good to the individual, whereas, if good is to be done, it would seem more likely, and more consonant with precedent, that the individual might do it to the group. Without the smile of a Treasurer we cannot unloose our purse-strings; without the sanction of a Chairman we have no courage; without Minutes we have no memory. There is hardly one of us who would dare to give a flannelette nightgown to a Factory Girl who had Stepped Aside, without a committee to lay the blame on, should the Factory Girl, fortified by the flannelette nightgown, take Further Steps Aside.

The sixth member was only too apt to put her trust in committees. Herself she did not trust at all, though she thought herself quite a good creature, as selves go. She had come to London two years ago, with a little trunk and a lot of good intentions as her only possessions, and she had paid the inevitable penalty for her earnestness. It is a sad thing to see any one of naturally healthy and rebellious tendency stray into the flat path of Charity. Gay heedless young people set their unwary feet between the flowery borders of that path, the thin air of resigned thanks breathed by the deserving poor mounts to their heads like wine; committees lie in wait for them on every side; hostels and settlements entice them fatally to break their journey at every mile; they run rejoicing to their doom, and I think shall eventually find themselves without escape, elected eternal life-members of the Committee that sits around the glassy sea.

The sixth member was saved by a merciful inefficiency of temperament from attaining the vortex of her whirlpool of charity. To be in the vortex is, I believe, almost always to see less. The bull's eye is generally blind.

The sixth member was a person who, where Social Work was concerned, did more or less as she was told, without doing it particularly well. The result, very properly, was that all the work which a committee euphemistically calls "organising work" was left to her. Organising work consists of sitting in buses bound for remote quarters of London, and ringing the bells of people who are almost always found to be away for a fortnight. The sixth member had been ordered to organise the return of the broomstick to its owner.

Perhaps it would be more practical to call the sixth member Sarah Brown.

The bereaved owner of the broomstick was washing her hair at Number 100 Beautiful Way, Mitten Island. She was washing it behind the counter of her shop. She was the manageress of the only shop on Mitten Island. It was a general shop, but made a speciality of such goods as Happiness and Magic. Unfortunately Happiness is rather difficult to get in war-time. Sometimes there was quite a queue outside the shop when it opened, and sometimes there was a card outside, saying politely: "Sorry, it's no use waiting. I haven't any." Of course the shop also sold Sunlight Soap, and it was with Sunlight Soap that the shop-lady was washing her hair, because it was Sunday, and this was a comparatively cheap amusement. She had no money. She had meant to go down to the offices of her employer after breakfast, to borrow some of the salary that would be due to her next week. But then she found that she had left her broomstick somewhere. As a rule Harold—for that was the broomstick's name—was fairly independent, and could find his way home alone, but when he got mislaid and left in strange hands, and particularly when kindly finders took him to Scotland Yard, he often lost his head. You, in your innocence, are suggesting that his owner might have borrowed another broom-stick from stock. But you have no idea what arduous work it is, breaking in a wild broomstick to the saddle. It sometimes takes days, and is not really suitable work for a woman, even in war-time. Often the brutes are savage, and always they are obstinate. The shop-lady could not afford to go to the City by Tube, not to mention the ferry fare, which was rather expensive and erratic, not being L.C.C. Of course a flash of lightning is generally available for magic people. But it is considered not only unpatriotic but bad form to use lightning in war-time.

The shop was not expecting customers on Sunday, but its manageress had hardly got her head well into the basin when somebody entered. She stood up dripping.

"Is Miss Thelma Bennett Watkins at home?" asked Sarah Brown, after a pause, during which she made her characteristic effort to remember what she had come for.

"No," said the other. "But do take a seat. We met last night, you may remember. Perhaps you wouldn't mind lending me one-and-twopence to buy two chops for our luncheon. I've got an extra coupon. There's tinned salmon in stock, but I don't advise it."

"I've only got sevenpence, just enough to take me home," answered Sarah Brown. "But I can pawn my ear-rings."

I dare say you have never been in a position to notice that there is no pawn-shop on Mitten Island. The inhabitants of model villages always have assured incomes and pose as lilies of the field. Sarah Brown and her hostess sat down on the counter without regret to a luncheon consisting of one orange, found by the guest in her bag and divided, and two thin captain biscuits from stock. They were both used to dissolving visions of impossible chops, both were cheerfully familiar with the feeling of light tragedy which invades you towards six o'clock P.M., if you have not been able to afford a meal since breakfast.

"Now look here," said Sarah Brown, as she plunged her pocket-knife into the orange. "Would you mind telling me—are you a fairy, or a third-floor-back, or anything of that sort? I won't register it, or put it on the case-paper, I promise, though if you are superhuman in any way I shall be seriously tempted."

"I am a Witch," said the witch.

Now witches and wizards, as you perhaps know, are people who are born for the first time. I suppose we have all passed through this fair experience, we must all have had our chance of making magic. But to most of us it came in the boring beginning of time, and we wasted our best spells on plesiosauri, and protoplasms, and angels with flaming swords, all of whom knew magic too, and were not impressed. Witches and wizards are now rare, though not so rare as you think. Remembering nothing, they know nothing, and are not bored. They have to learn everything from the very beginning, except magic, which is the only really original sin. To the magic eye, magic alone is commonplace, everything else is unknown, unguessed, and undespised. Magic people are always obvious—so obvious that we veteran souls can rarely understand them,—they are never subtle, and though they are new, they are never Modern. You may tell them in your cynical way that to-day is the only real day, and that there is nothing more unmentionable than yesterday except the day before. They will admire your cleverness very much, but the next moment you will find the witch sobbing over Tennyson, or the wizard smiling at the quaint fancies of Sir Edwin Landseer. You cannot really stir up magic people with ordinary human people. You and I have climbed over our thousand lives to a too dreadfully subtle eminence. In our day—in our many days—we have adored everything conceivable, and now we have to fall back on the inconceivable. We stand our idols on their heads, it is newer to do so, and we think we prefer them upside down. Talking constantly, we reel blindfold through eternity, and perhaps if we are lucky, once or twice in a score of lives, the blindfolding handkerchief slips, and we wriggle one eye free, and see gods like trees walking. By Jove, that gives us enough to talk about for two or three lives! Witches and wizards are not blinded by having a Point of View. They just look, and are very much surprised and interested.

All witches and wizards are born strangely and die violently. They are descended always from old mysterious breeds, from women who wrought domestic magic and perished for its sake, and from men who wrought other magic among lost causes and wars without gain, and fell and died, still surprised, still interested, with their faces among flowers. All men who die so are not wizards, nor are all martyred and adventuring women witches, but all such bring a potential strain of magic into their line.

"A witch," said Sarah Brown. "Of course. I have been trying to remember what broomsticks reminded me of. A witch, of course. I have always wished to be friends with a witch."

The witch was unaware that the proper answer to this was: "Oh, my Dear, *do* let's. Do you know I had quite a *crush* on you from the first minute." She did not answer at all, and Sarah Brown, who was tired of proper answers, was not sorry. Nevertheless the pause seemed a little empty, so she filled it herself, saying pedantically: "Of course I don't believe friendship is an end in itself. Only a means to an end."

"I don't know what you mean," said the witch, after wrestling conscientiously with this remark for a minute. "Do tell me—do you know yourself, or are you just saying it to see what it means?"

Sarah Brown was obviously damped by this, and the witch added kindly: "I bet you twopence you don't know what this place is."

"A shop," said Sarah Brown, who was sitting on the counter.

"It is a sort of convent and monastery mixed," replied the witch. "I am connected with it officially. I undertook to manage it, yet I forget what the proper word for me is. Not undertaker, is it?"

"Superintendent or secretary," suggested Sarah Brown moodily.

"Superintendent, I think," said the witch. "At least I know Peony calls me Soup. Do you live alone?"

"Yes."

"Then you ought to live here. This is the only place in the world of its kind. The name of this house is Living Alone. I'll read you the prospectus."

She fell suddenly upon her knees and began fighting with a drawer. The drawer was evidently one of the many descendants of the Sword Excalibur—none but the appointed hand could draw it forth. The witch, after a struggle, passed this test, and produced a parchment covered with large childish printing in red ink.

"My employer made up this," said the witch. "And the ferryman wrote it out for us."

This is the prospectus:

The name of this house is Living Alone.

It is meant to provide for the needs of those who dislike hotels, clubs, settlements, hostels, boarding-houses, and lodgings only less than their own homes; who detest landladies, waiters, husbands and wives, charwomen, and all forms of lookers after. This house is a monastery and a convent for monks and nuns dedicated to unknown gods. Men and women who are tired of being laboriously kind to their bodies, who like to be a little uncomfortable and quite uncared for, who love to live from week to week without speaking, except to confide their destinations to bus-conductors, who are weary of woolly decorations, aspidistras, and the eternal two generations of roses which riot among blue ribbons on hireling wall-papers, who are ignorant of the science of tipping and thanking, who do not know how to cook yet hate to be cooked for, will here find the thing they have desired, and something else as well.

There are six cells in this house, and no common sitting-room. Guests wishing to address each other must do so on the stairs, or in the shop. Each cell has whitewashed walls, and contains a small deal table, one wooden chair, a hard bed, a tin bath, and a little inconvenient fireplace. No guest may bring into the house more than can be carried out again in one large suit-case. Carpets, rugs, mirrors, and any single garment costing more than three guineas, are prohibited. Any guest proved to have made use of a taxi, or to have travelled anywhere first class, or to have bought cigarettes or sweets costing more than three shillings a hundred or eighteenpence a pound respectively, or to have paid more than three and sixpence (war-tax included) for a seat in any place of entertainment, will be instantly expelled. Dogs, cats, goldfish, and other superhuman companions are encouraged.

Working guests are preferred, but if not at work, guests must spend at least eighteen hours out of the twenty-four entirely alone. No guest may entertain or be entertained except under special license obtainable from the Superintendent.

There is a pump in the back yard. There is no telephone, no electric light, no hot water system, no attendance, and no modern comfort whatever. Tradesmen are forbidden to call. There is no charge for residence in this house.

"It certainly sounds an unusual place," admitted Sarah Brown. "Is the house always full?"

"Never," said the witch. "A lot of people can swallow everything but the last clause. We have at present one guest, called Peony."

She replaced the prospectus in the drawer, which she then tried to shut. While she was engaged in this thundering endeavour, Sarah Brown noticed that the drawer was full of the little paper packets which she had seen the day before in the witch's possession.

"What do you do with your magic?" she asked.

"Oh, many things. Chiefly I use it as an ingredient for happiness, sometimes to remind people, and sometimes to make them forget. It seems to me that some people take happiness rather tragically."

"I find," said Sarah Brown, rather sententiously, "that I always owe my happiness to earth, never to heaven."

"How d'you mean heaven?" said the witch. "I know nothing about heaven. When I used to work in the City, I bought a little book about heaven to read in the Tube every morning. I thought I should grow daily better. But I couldn't see that I did."

Sarah Brown was naturally astonished to meet any one who did not know all about heaven. But she continued the pursuit of her ideas on happiness. Sarah Brown meant to write a book some day, if she could find a really inspiring exercise-book to start in. She thought herself rather good at ideas—poor Sarah Brown, she simply had to be confident about something. She was only inwardly articulate, I think, not outwardly at all, but sometimes she could talk about herself.

"Heaven has given me wretched health, but never gave me youth enough to make the wretchedness adventurous," she went on. "Heaven gave me a thin skin, but never gave me the natural and comforting affections. Heaven probably meant to make a noble woman of me by encrusting me in disabilities, but it left out the necessary nobility at the last moment; it left out, in fact, all the compensations. But luckily I have found the compensations for myself; I just had to find something. Men and women have given me everything that such as I could expect. I have never met with reasonless enmity, never met with meanness, never met with anything more unbearable than natural indifference, from any man or woman. I have been, I may say, a burden and a bore all over the world; I have been an ill and fretful stranger within all men's gates; I have asked much and given nothing; I have never been a friend. Nobody has ever expected any return from me, yet nothing was grudged. Landladies, policemen, chorus girls, social bounders, prostitutes, the natural enemies, one would say, of such as I, have given me kindness, and often much that they could not easily spare, and always amusement and distraction. . . ."

"Ah, how you interest and excite me," said the witch, whose attention had been frankly wandering. "You are exactly the sort of person we want in this house."

"But—ill?" said Sarah Brown pessimistically. "Oh, witch, I have been so wearisome to every one, so constantly ill. The first thing I get to know about a new hostess or a landlady is always the colour of her dressing-gown by candlelight, or whether she has one."

"Illnesses are never bad here," said the witch. "I bet you twopence I've got something in the shop that would make you well. Three fingers of happiness, neat and hot, at night—"

"But, witch—oh, witch—this is the worst of all. My ears are failing me—I think I am going deaf. . . ."

"You can hear what I say," said the witch.

"Yes, I can hear what you say, but when most people talk I am like a prisoner locked up; and every day there are more and more locked doors between me and the world. You do not know how horrible it is."

"Oh, well," said the witch, "as long as you can hear magic you will not lack a key to your prison. Sometimes it's better not to hear the other things. You are the ideal guest for the House of Living Alone."

"I'll go and fetch David my Dog and Humphrey my Suit-case," said Sarah Brown.

At that moment a taxi was heard to arrive at the other side of the ferry, and the ferryman's voice was heard shouting: "All right, all right, I'll be there in half a tick."

"I hope this isn't Peony in a taxi," said the witch. "I get so tired of expelling guests. She's been drawing her money, which may have been tempting."

They listened.

They heard someone alight from the ferryboat, and the voice of Miss Meta Mostyn Ford asking the ferryman: "Do you know anything about a young woman of the name of Watkins, living at Number 100 Beautiful Way—"

"No, he doesn't," shouted the witch, opening the shop door. "But do step in. We met yesterday, you may remember. I'll ask the ferryman to get half-a-dozen halfpenny buns for tea, if you will be so kind as to lend me threepence. We don't bake ourselves."

"I have had tea, thank you," said Miss Ford. "I have just come from a little gathering of friends on the other side of the river, and I thought I would call here on my way home. I had noted your address—"

She started as she came in and saw Sarah Brown, and added in her committee voice: "I had noted your address, because I never mind how much trouble I take in following up a promising case."

Sarah Brown, on first hearing that trenchant voice, had lost her head and begun to hide under the counter. But the biscuit-tins refused to make room, so she drew herself up and smiled politely.

"How good of you to go to a little gathering of friends," said the witch, obviously trying to behave like a real human person. "I never do, except now and then by mistake. And even then I only stay when there are grassy sandwiches to eat. Once there were grassy sandwiches mixed with bits of hard-boiled egg, and then I stayed to supper. You didn't have such luck, I see, or you would look happier."

"I don't go to my friends for their food, but for their ideas," said Miss Ford.

Sarah Brown was gliding towards the door.

"Oh, don't go," said the witch, who did not recognise tact when she met it. "I have sent Harold the Broomstick for your Dog David and your Suit-case Humphrey. He is an excellent packer and very clean in his person and work. Please, please, don't go. Do you know, I live in constant dread of being left alone with a clever person."

"I must apologise for my intrusion, in that case," said Miss Ford, with dignity. "I repeat, I only came because I saw yours was an exceptional case."

There was a very long silence in the growing dusk. The moon could already be seen through the glass door, rising, pushing vigorously aside the thickets of the crowded sky. A crack across the corner of the glass was lighted up, and looked like a little sprig of lightning, plucked from a passing storm and preserved in the glass.

Miss Ford suddenly began to talk in a very quick and confused way. Any sane hearer would have known that she was talking by mistake, that she was possessed by some distressingly Anti-Ford spirit, and that nothing she might say in parenthesis like this ought to be remembered against her.

"Oh, God," said Miss Ford, "I have come because I am hungry, hungry for what you spoke of last night, in the dark. . . . You spoke of an April sea—clashing of cymbals was the expression you used, wasn't it? You spoke of a shore of brown diamonds flat to the ruffled sea . . . and white sandhills under a thin veil of grass . . . and tamarisks all blown one way. . . ."

"Well?" said the witch.

"Well," faltered Miss Ford. "I think I came to ask you . . . whether you knew of nice lodgings there . . . plain wholesome bath . . . respectable cooking, hot and cold . . ."

Her voice faded away pathetically.

There was a sudden shattering, as the door burst open, and a dog and a suit-case were swept in by a brisk broomstick.

"I am so sorry, Miss Watkins," said Miss Ford stiffly. Her face was scarlet—neat and formal again now, but scarlet.—"I am so sorry if I have talked nonsense. I am rather run down, I think, too much work, four important meetings yesterday. I sometimes think I shall break down. I have such alarming nerve-storms."

She looked nervously at Sarah Brown. It is always tiresome to meet fellow-members of committees in private life, especially if one is in a mood for having nerve-storms. People may be excellent in a philanthropic way, of course, and yet impossible socially.

But Sarah Brown had heard very little. She always found Miss Ford's voice difficult. She was on her knees asking her dog David what it had felt like, coming. But David was still too much dazed to say much.

"You must not think," said Miss Ford, "that because I am a practical worker I have no understanding of Inner Meanings. On the contrary, I have perhaps wasted too much of my time on spiritual matters. That is why I take quite a personal and special interest in your case. I had a great friend, now in the trenches, alas, who possessed Power. He used to come to my Wednesdays—at least I used to invite him to come, but he was dreamy like you and constantly mistook the date. He helped me enormously, and I miss him. . . . Well, the truest charity should be anything but formal, I think, and I saw at a glance that your case was exceptional, and that you also were Occult—"

"How d'you mean—occult?" asked the witch. "Do you mean just knowing magic?"

"A strange mixture," mused Miss Ford self-consciously. It is impossible to muse aloud without self-consciousness. "A strange and rather interesting mixture of naïveté and power. The question is—power to what extent? Miss Watkins, I want you to come to one of my Wednesdays to meet one or two people who might possibly help you to a job—lecturing, you know. Lectures on hypnotism or spiritualism, with experiments, are always popular. You certainly have Power, you only want a little advertisement to be a real help to many people."

"How d'you mean—advertisement?" asked the witch. "This new advertisement stunt is one of the problems that tire my head. I am awfully worried by problems. The world seems to be ruled by posters now. People look to the hoardings for information about their duty. Why don't we paste up the ten commandments on all the walls and all the buses, and be done with it?"

"Now listen, Miss Watkins," persisted Miss Ford. "I want you to meet Bernard Tovey, the painter, and Ivy MacBee, who founded the Aspiration Club, and Frere, the editor of *I Wonder*, and several other regular Wednesday friends of mine, all interested in the Occult. It would be a real opportunity for you."

"I am afraid you will be very angry with me," said the witch presently in a hollow voice. "If I was occult last night—I'm awfully sorry, but it must have been a fluke. I seem to have said so much last night without knowing it. I'm afraid I was showing off a little."

The painful tears of confession were in her eyes, but she added, changing the subject: "Do you live alone?"

"Yes, absolutely," said Miss Ford. "My friends call me a perfect hermit. I hardly ever have visitors in my spare room, it makes so much work for my three maids."

"I suppose you wouldn't care to divorce your three maids and come and live here," suggested the witch. "I could of course cure you of the nerve-storms you speak of. Or rather I could help you to have nerve-storms all the time, without any stagnant grown-upness in between. Then you wouldn't notice the nerve-storms. This house is a sort of nursing home and college combined. I'll read you the prospectus."

"Very amusing," said Miss Ford, after waiting a minute to see if there was any more of the prospectus. She had quite recovered herself, and was wearing the brisk acute expression that deceived her into claiming a sense of humour. "But why all those uncomfortable rules? And why that discouragement of social intercourse? I am afraid the average person of the class you cater for does not recognise the duty of social intercourse."

"This house," replied the witch, "caters for people who are outside averages. The ferryman says that people who are content to be average are lowering the general standard. I wish you could have met Peony, the only guest up to now, but she is out, and may be a teeny bit drunk when she comes in. She has gone to draw her money."

"What sort of money?" asked Miss Ford, who was always interested in the sources of income of the Poor.

"Soldier's allotment. Unmarried wife."

The expression of Miss Ford's face tactfully wiped away this bald unfortunate statement from the surface of the conversation. "And how do you make your boarding-house pay," she asked, "if there is no charge for residence?"

"How d'you mean—pay?" asked the witch. "Pay whom? And what with? Look here, if you will come and live here you shall have a little

Wednesday every week on the stairs, under license from me. Harold the Broomstick is apt to shirk cleaning the stairs, but as it happens, he is keeping company with an O-Cedar Mop in Kentish Town, and I've no doubt she would come over and do the stairs thoroughly every Tuesday night. Besides, we have overalls in stock at only two and eleven three——"

"Oh, I like your merry mood," said Miss Ford, laughing heartily. "You must remember to talk like that when you come to my Wednesdays. Most of my friends are utter Socialists, and believe in bridging as far as possible the gulf between one class and another, so you needn't feel shy or awkward."

The splashing of the ferry-boat was once more heard, and then the shop quaked a little as a heavy foot alighted on the landing-stage. The ferryman was heard saying: "I don't know any party of that name, but I believe the young woman at the shop can help you."

Lady Arabel Higgins entered the shop.

"What, Meta, you here? And Sarah Brown? What a too dretfully funny coincidence. Well, Angela dear, I made a note of your address yesterday, and then lost the note—too dretfully like me. So I rang up the Mayor, and he said he also had made a note, and he would come and show me the way. But I didn't wait for him. I wanted to talk to you about—"

"Well, I must truly be going," interrupted Sarah Brown. "I'll just nip across to the Brown Borough and find a pawn-shop, being hungry."

"There is no need for any one to move on my account," said Lady Arabel. "You all heard what Angela said last night in her little address to the committee in the dark. I don't know why she addressed her remarks particularly at me, but as she did so, there is no secret in the matter. Of course, just at first, it seemed dretful to me that any one should know or speak about it. I cannot understand how you knew, Angela; I am trying not to understand. . . ."

She took up a thin captain biscuit and bit it absent-mindedly. It trembled in her hand like a leaf.

"Yes, it is true that Rrchud isn't like other women's boys. You know it, Meta. Angela evidently knows it, and—at least since yesterday—I know that I know it. His not being able to read or write—I always knew in my heart that my old worn-out tag—'We can't all be literary geniuses'—didn't meet the case. His way of disappearing and never explaining. . . . Do you know, I have only once seen him with other boys, doing the same as other boys, and that was when I saw him marching with hundreds of real boys . . . in 1914. . . . It was the happiest day I ever had, I thought after all that I had borne a real boy. Well, then, as you know, he couldn't get a commission, couldn't even get his stripe, poor darling. He deserted twice—pure absence of mind—it was always the same from a child—'I wanted to see further,' he'd say, and of course worse in the trenches. Why, you know it all, Angela dear—at least, perhaps not quite all. I should like to tell you—because you said that about the splendour of being the mother of Rrchud. . . .

"Pinehurst—my husband, he is a doctor, you know—had that same passion for seeing further. He was often ill in London. I said it was asthma, but he said it was not being able to see far enough. We were in America for Rrchud's birth, and Pinehurst insisted on going West. I took the precaution of having a good nurse with me. Pinehurst said the East was full of little obstacles, and people's eyes had sucked all the secrets out of the horizon, he said. I like Cape Cod, but he said there was always a wall of sea round those flat wet places. We stayed in a blacksmith's spare room on the desert of Wyoming, but even that horizon seemed a little higher than we, and one clear day, in a pink sunrise, we saw something that might have been a dream, my dears, and might have been the Rockies. Pinehurst couldn't stand that, we pushed west—so tahsome. We climbed a little narrow track up a mountain, in a light buggy that a goldminer lent us. Oh, of course, you'll think us mad, Meta, but, do you know, we actually found the world's edge, a place with no horizon; we looked between ragged pine trees, and saw over the shoulders of great old violet mountains—we saw right down into the stars for ever. . . . There was a tower of rocks—rose-red rocks in sloping layers—sunny hot by day, my dears, and a great shelter by night. You know, the little dark clouds walk alone upon the mountain tops at sunset—as you said, Angela—they are like trees, and sometimes like faces, and sometimes like the shadows of little bent gipsies. . . . I used to look at the mountains and think: 'What am I about, to be so worried and so small, in sight of such an enormous storm of mountains under a gold sky?' I think of those rocks often at night, standing just as we left them, all by themselves, under that unnatural moon,—it was an unnatural moon on the edge of the world there,—all by themselves, with no watching eyes to spoil them, as Pinehurst used to say, not even one's own eyes. . . . You'll say that adventure—my one adventure—was impossible, Meta. Yes, it was. Rrchud was an impossible boy, born on an impossible day, in an impossible place. Ah, my poor Rrchud. . . . My dears, I am talking dretful nonsense. We were mad. You'd have to know Pinehurst, really, to understand it. Ah, we can never find our mountain again. I can never forgive Pinehurst. . . ."

"You can never repay Pinehurst," said the witch.

Lady Arabel did not seem to hear. For a long time there was nothing to be heard but Sarah Brown, murmuring to her Dog David. You must excuse her, and remember that she lived most utterly alone. She was locked inside herself, and the solitary barred window in her prison wall commanded only a view of the Dog David.

Rrchud's mother said at last: "I really came to tell you that Rrchud came back on leave unexpectedly last night. Of course you must meet him—"

"Rrchud home!" exclaimed Miss Ford. "How odd! I was just telling Miss Watkins about his Power, and how strongly she reminded me of him. Do tell him to keep Wednesday afternoon free."

Lady Arabel, ignoring Miss Ford by mistake, said to the witch: "Will you come on Tuesday to tea or supper?"

"Supper, please," said the witch instantly. Tact, I repeat, was a stranger to her, so she added: "I will bring Sarah Brown too. I bet you twopence she hasn't had a decent meal for days."

And then the Mayor arrived. The witch saw at once that there was some secret understanding between him and her that she did not understand. Her magic escapades often left her in this position. However, she winked back hopefully. But she was not a skilled winker. Everybody— even the Dog David—saw her doing it, and Miss Ford looked a little offended.

Yefim Davidovich Zozulya (1891–1941) was a Russian journalist and writer known for his satire and black humor. Zozulya began writing at the age of eighteen and in 1923 cofounded the journal *Ogonyok* and later organized a book series called Library Ogonyok. Zozulya's "The Dictator: A Story of Ak and Humanity" is a tale in which the citizens who had originally agreed to a totalitarian government were then forced to prove that they deserved to exist. Inventive and unique, this political satire resulted in Zozulya's arrest on more than one occasion. Upon his death in 1941, he left a number of unfinished short stories. Although his work attained some popularity before World War II, most of his work has not been republished and has gone untranslated into English until *The Big Book of Science Fiction* (2016). His "Gramophone of the Ages" is an anti-utopic story that illustrates the beauty of silence. This is the first time this story has been translated into English.

Gramophone of the Ages

Yefim Zozulya

Translated by Ekaterina Sedia

1. KUKS FINALLY REACHED HIS GOAL

IT IS HARDLY POSSIBLE to thoroughly describe the appearance of Kuks the inventor and his work study, especially that particularly felicitous morning his old friend Tilibom came to visit.

"What happened?" Tilibom opened his arms in wonderment. "Kuks, look at your nostrils turned inside-out, your red eyes, gray hair, and trembling hands! Look in the mirror! What happened to you?"

"I am so happy!" Kuks closed his eyes, drowning in a smile. "For the first time in my life, I am perfectly happy. Of course I haven't slept for sixteen nights straight and am completely out of my mind, but regardless, I am happy. You're say-ing my nostrils are turned inside out? It seems possible—for eight days I've been sniffing a compound of my invention. But today, I am happy."

Sarcastic Tilibom, smiling slyly, said, "Have you finally finished your Gramophone of the Ages?"

"You guessed it, Tilibom," the scientist responded in his usual mild way. "You guessed right! Of course you don't believe me now, but today I have prevailed. Yes, Gramophone of the Ages is finished. Completely finished."

Tilibom not only didn't believe his friend, but he also felt sincere pity for him. He was quite sick of the forty-year story of this woebegone invention. Kuks had spent forty years trying to prove his theory that human voices, as well as other sounds, are recorded as invisible bumps on all inanimate objects near which they originated. Those bumps, according to Kuks's theory, are preserved for millennia, and new sounds merely deposit on top of the old ones, creating layers—just like dust, sand, and many minerals in nature.

To prove his theory, Kuks had promised to create an apparatus that would decode these deposits of sounds. This apparatus, combined with a perfected and more complex gramophone was meant to restore words of people long dead— billions of words of bygone generations . . .

The task Kuks had set for himself was so grandiose and daring that two kings (Kuks started his work ten years before the total and universal socialist takeover in Europe) subsidized him, and a third king, more impatient than the other two, put him in jail. He was freed thanks to the insistence of the queen, who was known for her kindness, and transferred to a mental hospital.

Nothing discouraged Kuks, and once he was free from the subsidies, jail, and mental institutions, kept working on his invention, and, as the reader would soon see, reached his goal after all.

The Gramophone of Ages was complete. Kuks was not lying.

2. THE AMAZING INVENTION

Kuks's old face, troughed with years, work, and suffering of a genius, was lit by a wandering tired smile.

Tilibom stood still and felt his skepticism melting like ice cream under the spring sun.

There was something in Kuks's distracted smile more convincing than mere facts and in any case more convincing than words.

Tilibom capitulated. "Come on, Kuks, show me the apparatus."

But too late! Kuks had already fallen asleep.

The happy inventor slept for thirty-five hours straight and was woken up by his own scream. He

dreamed that someone was breaking, and stomping on, his wondrous invention.

He jumped up from the deep chair in which he slept, rubbed his eyes, and looked around: in his study, there was no one, and his apparatus, the creation of which had cost him almost his entire life, sat still, with an innocent, secretive, and indifferent look of any machine.

Kuks telephoned Tilibom to summon him, and the two friends embarked on examining and testing the wondrous apparatus.

Kuks grew unusually animated as he ran around the Gramophone of the Ages and addressed every screw as if it was alive. "Calm down, you." He wagged his finger at a tiny cog that looked like a half-opened mouth of an idiot. "I triumphed over you, aha! Sixteen years you defied me, and now I am your master, ha ha! Now you know your place. See, patience and labor conquer all."

The appearance of the Gramophone was unpleasant: it resembled a giant spider, with snakelike pipes winding all around it.

From its sides, wide vise-like levers stuck out like dead fish heads. Everywhere black wire was sticking up, like tough unshaven beard, and next to the tiny white dome crowning the contraption with its single blue eye, a large lopsided shell was tied on, like an ear.

"How do you like it?" Kuks rubbed his hands in excitement.

"It's all right, an interesting doohickey," Tilibom answered, noncommittal.

3. "THE GRAMOPHONE OF THE AGES" AT WORK

The tentacles, levers, and pipes of the apparatus were adapted for fitting into its case. Once there, the Gramophone had the appearance of a normal photo camera, and was quite easy to carry around.

"Where should we start?" asked Kuks.

"Wherever you want. But we have to do some robust testing. There is no hurry, no one is paying us! And not like you need a patent: you just have to present this to the Academy, but we can't do that without a good thorough trial."

Tilibom's jokes were not very original—no one used money for a long time now, just like the patents, and even quips about them had stopped being funny.

"It's great that there's no money though." Kuks sighed. "Much better than getting handouts from kings and fat cats, be they forever cursed, and then having to go to their galas and birthday parties and mince among their hangers-on, fools and nobodies, having to smile and congratulate them, to lower yourself with flattery. Ah, this is how I wasted my youth! Such frivolous nonsense . . ."

"That's enough, old friend! We have business at hand, let's get started!"

"I already listened to everything in my study . . . I even heard what the masons were saying as they laid down these walls."

"What were they saying?"

"Judging by the content of their discussions, this house was built twenty or thirty years before socialism triumphed. First of all, they of course swore. Then two argued about the party line disagreements. Then they came to blows. Two face slaps were quite resonant, and the machine picked them up very clearly. Then the building remained unfinished for quite a while—it served as an embrasure, or a barricade, or some-such. The machine deafeningly shoots, screams, moans, weeps, in many voices. I think that the building was empty for five years or so, during the Revolution and the following wars and the manufacturing lull right after, but it was finished soon after all that. They finished it with songs and laughter, with bracing sonorant sounds of willing, joyful labor . . . I listened to the sound biography of the construction, this symphony of the rising building with great interest . . . but come on, so many interesting discoveries still await us!"

"Well, if you are telling the truth, try the apparatus in your dining room, I have to hear it right away! This sounds like a fairy tale," Tilibom said, frantic. "You already heard your study and I want to hear your dining room."

"All right." Kuks brought over his apparatus, fussed with it, stepped aside, and invited Tilibom to sit down.

"The Gramophone of the Ages" shook, hissed, and started . . .

Words—dozens, hundreds, thousands—wound onto the thin, plaintive, unending moan of the metal cylinder.

Everyday words, conversations, exclamations, footfalls, slamming doors, laughter, sobs . . .

Then suddenly a loud child's cry.

"That's my Nadya weeping," Kuks said softly. "When Manya, my wife, passed away. And this—this is the voice of my deceased, can you recognize her?"

Tilibom, pale and perturbed by the miracle, nodded. He stood and listened, his mouth hanging open. The shell of the machine spat out words and sentences. "Hello! Have a sit, please. It's a bit stuffy, I'll crack the window."

"My husband is so busy."

"Always so, so busy."

"Nadya! Nadya! Dress warm."

Thousands of mundane exchanges, but both listened with bated breath.

And then—strong and brash voice of young Tilibom. "Maria Andreyevna, Manya, Manechka, I love you! Love you so much! I cannot stand to see that old fool, your husband, that insane . . . I feel such pity for you. Manya, I love . . . you."

Tilibom buried his face in his hands.

Kuks stared at the floor. The machine continued to weave an unending ribbon of words, sentences—so clear, merciless, terrifying, and innocent. Different.

In that living stenography there was, by the way, this moment: "Who was here? That bastard Tilibom again? I am so sick of his talentless snout! So sick!" (That was Kuks saying that relatively recently.)

Five hours passed without them even noticing. The friends grew weary.

Both heard many unflattering things about themselves, said at various times by the other. Tilibom tried to seduce his friend's wife more than once, but it turned out that she was seduced by other friends . . .

Soon all that was eclipsed by other people, those who used to live in this house earlier. And against the backdrop of the life sounds—misery and joy, laughter and despair—personal hurts and betrayals seemed insignificant and small.

"Your hand!" Kuks smiled kindly as he approached Tilibom. "See, we are worth each other. But let's forget all that. This is the past. Twenty years we have been living in the socialist utopia, and yet we continue to be so small, so underhanded. . . . But our children are different already. Your son, Tilibom, is not like you at all."

"Yes, Kuks, my son is different, and the next generation will be spectacular. Even now, in just twenty years, the makeup of the future people has changed already. We, Kuks, will think it strange, but that's to be expected. The future people will be more naive than we are, healthier and stronger and more pure . . . but most importantly, happier."

"This is not all, and not quite," Kuks added. "The future humans will be smarter than we are, despite their naivete. Yes, my friend, simply more intelligent. You are mistaken thinking that you are so clever with your spectacular cynicism. But cynicism is the greatest indiscrimination, mixed with the deepest indifference, and both are birthed only of weakness, of impotence. The new humans won't need to be cynical; they will be intelligent, generous and proud, because above all they will be strong. Look at some of the young people's faces—their eyes are so clear, their moral cores are so solid, their features are distinct, and their souls are sensitive."

"Yes, oh yes!" Tilibom rejoiced that an unpleasant conversation took such an unexpected turn. "The new people will be resplendent. And even we, old dogs, just for their mere proximity are becoming better and more sensible. If your damn 'Gramophone of the Ages' exposed us twenty years ago, would we be so calm?"

The friends stared at the floor for a while, deep dark wrinkles furrowing their weary faces. In these wrinkles, there was an invisible and great change happening—a new thought, a new life was plowing the old dirt, looking for fertile soil for new seedlings . . .

"Who knows," Tilibom sighed, thoughtful. "Perhaps we don't need hundreds of years to overcome human weaknesses, the ones we thought were so ingrained."

"Of course, a lot less," Kuks agreed.

4. PEOPLE ASPIRED TO GREATNESS BUT LIFE WAS ALREADY BEAUTIFUL

In year 19__ during the tenth year of pan-European socialism, a law was passed that forbade any rooms or building that did not allow in the natural sunlight. Thousands of old, dank, and dark houses were demolished; some of the sturdy ones were refitted with glass roofs and ceilings, and the most sunless ones were equipped with special mirrors that transferred sunlight.

And that year sun shone like never before, and, like never before, it illuminated and gladdened. The city, drowning in greenery and mirrors, seemed a sea of light and joy from an aeroplane, and on the ground that impression grew even more bright and vividly colored.

The dawn was greeted by the factory horns and whistles, and orchestras. Some factory chimneys in some of the city's neighborhoods still had the installations from the 1920 hungry and heroic Petersburg. Each apparatus produced a single powerful note, and all of the chimneys together deafeningly played fine melodies. Nowadays, only a few neighborhoods still had these installations, and they had their own special fans—the old revolutionaries.

The new generation started their own orchestras, using the same principle. Each building—residential or business—had a powerful relay of musical scales, harmonious with the scales in the neighboring houses.

And so this bright, powerful music greeted the sun, woke up the workers, and sent them on their way to work, lunch break, and home.

The factories and workshops were cozy nests, fitted with every convenience, and inviting to joyful labor and creativity.

The city was governed by the councils—but because they were so numerous, being a council member did not excuse one from work. The order was protected by the rotation of ordinary citizens, after the police has been abolished. Criminality shrank to unheard-of in human history lows: in the largest cities there were no more than ten murders a year, and most of those were the crimes of passion, or committed by those with pathologies. Every year the numbers decreased. The courts were nearly obsolete; they were replaced in 19__ by much softer "Abilities and Callings Chambers," in which people were brought for lazy, unproductive work. They were trying to figure out the causes of such abnormal attitude toward labor, and tried to find in each accused his true calling and find him a more fitting and fulfilling work.

For the most retrograde, there were special "Experience Workshops," in which the students tried their hand at different endeavors. The question of abilities and callings was one of the most pernicious problems in socialist daily life. Even back in 1919 in the young and still feeble Socialist Russian Republic, all workers of social occupations were asked what were their professional inclinations, and what they would like to do. That question was more complex than anyone had expected, and the complete solution was not yet found after the first twenty years of the socialist society. Quite sizable groups had trouble finding themselves.

But how could the society help them?

One of the following chapters will offer the reader some idea of the "Abilities Chambers,"

since the scientist Kuks, famous for his dedication to his work, was among those helping others to develop this important for work and creativity quality.

5. KUKS DOES NOT SEPARATE FROM "THE GRAMOPHONE OF THE AGES" AND HIS INVENTION BECOMES FAMOUS IN THE CITY BEFORE THE ACADEMY

Kuks became one with the apparatus. He would not let it go, and Tilibom was close behind.

"Look, what genius, what delight!" Kuks said with admiration.

Indeed, the second half of the twentieth century was a bright epoch, and streets and houses were filled with joy, ease, and peace.

Wide sidewalks were alive with a mass of people.

This era had created a new type of person: the city dweller of this epoch was sturdy and lean, lithe and light-footed. The shapes of clothes were distinguished by their streamlined simplicity—there was not a trace of the complicated jackets and tailcoats people used to wear in the beginning of this tumultuous century, clothes that made men look like birds, and women—dressed in their multicolored rags—like dolls. Every heart, every soul, every pair of eyes rejoiced looking at the new men and women, the loose shapes of their garments, at their happy faces, clear eyes, and white teeth of the girls.

Suddenly the streets flooded with something vibrant, multivoiced, fresh, and delightful—children.

There were several thousand of them; tanned and half-naked, joyful, singing and laughing, they were heading outside of the city for a hike and lessons. Those who were still little, weak, or tired, rode on greenery- and flowers-wreathed carts.

Bracing, wild and joyful air emanated from the rapid procession of the children. As they went, the procession grew larger—the children who lived separately in the enormous "Children's

Palaces" were joined by those who visited their parents for a sleepover.

Kuks and Tilibom saw the morning march of the children many times before, but every time they admired it anew. Just like an old forest denizen, who had long become accustomed to its fresh air, still relishes breathing it with full chest and finds word to express his admiration.

"Great! So wonderful!" Kuks and Tilibom burst out in turn.

"I wonder what this street was like before?" Kuks said, glancing at the Gramophone. "Was it always like this?"

"Let's hear it then."

Kuks took the apparatus out of its case and wound it up.

The passersby at first did not pay any mind to the two old men and their machine. They thought it was a demonstration of some strange oration or a play. They couldn't place the source of the sounds emanating from the strange shell, resembling an ear.

A few adolescents gathered around the apparatus, but they could barely understand what they were hearing.

"Gramophone of the Ages" once again strung thousands and tens of thousands of words and sounds over the the quiet, plaintive squeak of the cylinder.

Everything was so mundane, so normal for the old, bygone reality.

Someone was being beaten. Someone screamed. Someone chased a thief and arrested him.

Yelling and swearing gave way to the calls of coach drivers and pedestrians. Plaintive songs and pleas of the beggars often cut through the usual sounds of street life. After three hours of the apparatus' work, the old men heard the screams of people being murdered and violated. It was a pogrom . . .

After a while, the apparatus attracted a curious crowd.

"What play is that?" they asked Kuks.

Kuks chuckled bitterly. "It's not a play, citi-

zens! It's life! The very life of this street, its biography. In a few days, the Academy of Sciences will accept 'Gramophone of the Ages,' and from this prototype many copies will be made, and you will be able to learn the history of every stone, every clod of earth. Citizens, stones are the silent witnesses of the terrible human history. But they are silent just for the time being. Surely you heard the expression 'the stones will cry out'? Now they are crying out. Listen how much misery and desperation, human tears and human blood is known to every stone of the old world order, and listen how they speak, those very stones, when science gives them a way of telling what they know."

People stared at Kuks and only dimly understood his speech. He spoke for a while, sincerely and passionately, but they still could not grasp his meaning.

Wild screams ripped from the shell, moans and bitter humiliations of the beggars, so ordinary back in the day; the shouts of the policemen and the dull din of the tormented serfs, working against their will to exhaustion.

People heard the living terrible sounds of the bygone lives as if they were just a nightmare.

The old people understood and went quickly by, and the young ones lingered, looking around with surprise, their faces grimacing in pain and disgust.

6. IN THE "ABILITIES AND CALLINGS CHAMBER"

Tilibom gave up completely.

"You are a great man, Kuks," he said. "I am won over by your invention. But you know, human history is terrifying. In books and even in pictures it's not nearly as horrible as in the living sounds. Yesterday, when you were not around, I availed myself to the apparatus and listened to my own apartment. In the stairwell, there is a large, porous, chipped stone. Curse it, but I swear to you, it used to be an executioner's block, or else I was delirious and hallucinating. Screams. Can you see, just screams and moans of the tortured, beheaded, slashed . . . Then I went to the garden with the apparatus, and there it was the same: everywhere there was crying, yelling, slapping, taunting, violence . . . And only once in a while there would be some trite words of love. Sparse, repetitive love confessions and violence—this is the main axis of human history. When you read about it, it's not so bad, but when you hear their live voices, all these groans, screams, and pleading, it is terrible, inexplicable, and scary. You are a great man, Kuks, because you made inanimate objects speak."

Kuks thanked him for the compliment, and added, "That is all great, but I am not yet sure what use 'Gramophone of the Ages' will find. You see, people don't get it. In socialist schools they teach them how to build the future, rather than familiarize the students with the details of the past. Obviously they don't have time to pay attention to old things. My apparatus, I imagine, would only be an aid to the historians, and we better forget about widespread use."

"That's understandable, Kuks! Interest in the sick and corrupt past can only cause a sick and corrupt present, but if the present is joyful and beautiful . . ."

"Tomorrow I'll turn the apparatus to the Academy. But today I'd like to do an experiment in the "Abilities Chamber." I have classes there today; come with me, if you'd like."

"Let's go."

The "Abilities and Callings Chamber" was a large hall, occupied mostly by specialized equipment and devices. All workers who were unhappy with their labor, who felt indifferent toward their work, came here.

They asked the specialists to help them figure out the causes and give advice, and in some cases suggest whether they should take up another occupation, and what kind. The Chamber itself was an entryway to several buildings, united under the name of "Experience Workshops."

The Experience Workshops were a wondrous sight. All sorts of work was being done there, and the results were at times spectacular: a poor plumber would turn out to be a talented actor, a terrible actor harbored a calling for canning herring, and a teacher had a knack for beekeeping.

The volume of work for the Chamber and the Workshops grew smaller every year, since the perfected schools lessened its burden by helping the students figure out their abilities and decide on the fitting profession.

Kuks was assigned to talk to a tall, sulking young man, with a widely developed jaw and narrow sunken eyes. The young man was incredibly strong—his uncommon strength showed in his long, knotted arms with heavy muscle bulges.

"Have a seat. What do you do?"

"I am a mason. I pulverize stones into gravel."

"How long have you been doing that?"

"Four years, since the termination of my education."

"Why is your work a burden to you?"

"I get sad when I work, and it decreases my productivity."

"Were you interested in your work before?"

"I was."

"What were you experiencing during work then?"

"In the beginning, I could not break apart especially hard stones, and I tried to learn that skill. It was pleasing, to see a gigantic stone shatter to smithereens with two or three blows of my hammer. After a while, this pleasant feeling dulled. So I had to amuse myself somehow during work. I imagined that the stones had faces, and if I liked the face, I would put the stone aside, and if not—I would shatter it. One day, a giant stone reminded me of a snarling, disgusting cur, and I broke it ferociously. And I feel that this work is awakening my worst instincts . . . The most pleasant part of my work is when I imagine an interesting face and I try to carve features into it—nose, eyes . . . but then I become less productive, and I lag behind all my comrades."

"You should take up the art of sculpture, this much is clear. Once you start doing that, you will feel right in your proper place."

The mason excitedly thanked Kuks and headed to the Experience Workshop, to apply to the sculpture program.

"See what became of the judiciary courts in socialist society?" Kuks smiled at Tilibom. "I wonder what those youths would say if they learned about the courts of old? There is an old courthouse nearby; now it's just a museum, and no one will prevent us from listening to the memories of its walls, ceilings, and wooden floors."

Kuks invited a few visitors of the Chamber to come along, and headed with them to the museum.

"Gramophone of the Ages" worked better than ever before.

Kuks and Tilibom sat transfixed.

One bright, terrifying scene from the court replaced another. The thundering orations of the prosecutors, witnesses' testimonies, judges' rejoinders, cries of the accused and of the convicted—everything was terrifyingly fascinating.

Like a moment, a few hours flew by.

When Kuks and Tilibom came to, they traded bewildered looks—none of the young people remained.

They probably grew bored and left, preoccupied with their lives and their work, with figuring out their abilities, their healthy and vivacious thirst for creative fulfillment.

7. EVENING

Ceremoniously the enormous red sun was setting.

The laborers had long ago returned home from their factories, workshops, and offices. The streets were being watered, and above the roofs, mechanical music of the buildings poured in pleasant waves.

On the tall building of "The Nightly Cine-Newspaper" the workers readied to print the most important news of the day on the darkened sky; they were waiting for the sun to set completely.

Young people scattered to gardens and parks, and their laughter filled the alleys. The moving flying theaters amused and distracted the passersby. Sometimes the public would join the actors, and the crowd put together and acted out an improvised play, and the spectators and the performers delighted together, their voices joining in shared jubilation.

When the sky grew dark, it displayed many important daily items: the manufacturing output, which was of interest to everyone, because everyone owned the means of production; the latest innovations developed in various spheres; the outlook and directives for the next day; and the news received from other cities and countries.

Those so inclined could attend hundreds of cinema theaters, showing the work events from the previous day, the life of the entire city and its offices, and much more.

Some went to watch the updates from schools and children's communes, others—from factories, yet others—of theaters. And some were interested in watching the goings-on in the streets filmed just the day before.

Philharmonic orchestras played, choirs sang.

There were also "Quiet Neighborhoods," where those who desired complete rest could retire to.

Kuks and Tilibom sat on the roof of the enormous building where Kuks' apartment was. The old men silently read the evening celestial newspaper, and then discussed, like all the other city denizens, what they had read.

"Not a word about my invention, ha ha," Kuks chuckled.

"Any day we'll read about it," Tilibom comforted his friend. "Soon we'll read about it, and your mug will be in every cinema."

8. THE ACADEMY OF SCIENCES SCANDAL

Finally the testing of the "Gramophone of the Ages" was done, and it was time to turn it in to the Academy of Sciences.

Kuks did it not without excitement.

The Academy had gathered the cream of human genius and knowledge. Because they were to investigate the new invention, they invited the representatives from every prominent Academy of Sciences in Europe.

They tested the "Gramophone of the Ages" the entire week.

The trial run of the wondrous apparatus caused, unfortunately, two misfortunes. One of the scientists, the creator of "New Ethics," was present when the apparatus ran in the garden, under an ancient oak tree.

It turned out that a man was executed by a firing squad under that oak, and the plea of the condemned was truly terrible: Go ahead, shoot, just not in the face!

That request of some man killed by no one knew who made such a sad impression that the sensitive creator of the New Ethics started striking his head against the ground and, as his further behavior clarified, had gone insane.

The second misfortune was no less tragic.

When the apparatus started to reproduce with merciless clarity the scene of a landowner torturing his serf in another garden, and the garden came alive with hair-raising screams of the tormented, an old revolutionary present among the scientists lunged at the apparatus, threw it on the ground, and started stomping on it with his feet.

In the overall din, it was impossible to hear what the agitated revolutionary was yelling.

Kuks lay on the ground in a deep swoon.

Once he came to and calmed down a bit, they invited him to join the scientists' gathering.

Weary and broken, he entered the hall, expecting sympathy and thinking of whether the apparatus could be fixed.

But to his surprise, no one offered any sympathy, and no one even objected to the apparatus's destruction.

"Your invention, citizen," they told him, "is great, but unfortunately it is completely useless. Let us forever curse the old order! We don't need its moans, we don't need its horrors. We don't want to listen to its dreadful voices. Let it be cursed forever! Kuks, look out of the window. Today is a celebration. Look at our children, listen to their voices—healthy and happy, listen and tell us: isn't it a sacrilege to simultaneously hear the horrors coming out of your demonic machine? You are a genius, Kuks, but in the name of our new joyful order sacrifice your genius. Don't torment us. We don't want to know and hear the bygone world we left behind forever."

Kuks wanted to object that he did not agree, that even today he saw many imperfections that could be removed precisely by his machine, but he was spent, objected weakly, and no one listened to him.

9. THE SAD FATE OF "GRAMOPHONE OF THE AGES"

Kuks gathered his mutilated apparatus and trudged home. At home, Tilibom was waiting for him.

Kuks told him about his ordeal. Tilibom listened and said, "But they are right, Kuks! You know, ever since I learned about the Gramophone, I lost my inner peace. I am bewildered. I am sad. I cry often. I started doubting you and your friendship. I did not tell you, but I ran the apparatus in my apartment, and heard many underhanded things you were kind enough to say in my house while I was absent."

"Then please explain, weren't you trying to seduce my dearly departed wife, Manya?"

"Yes, it is so. We are worth each other, of course. The old order with its hypocrisy, lies, betrayals, and underhandedness isn't entirely burned out from our souls, but we probably should not revive it in our memories."

Kuks stayed silent.

"And besides the personal grossness," Tilibom continued, "my ears are constantly filled with moans, screams, swearing, and curses the old world was brimming with, and with which now every stone is crying out, thanks to your infernal machine—and every piece of drywall, every inanimate object. Oh, I am happy that 'Gramophone of the Ages' is no more! I am very happy."

Kuks kept quiet.

Once Tilibom had left, he lay on a couch and gave himself to thinking.

The mutilated "Gramophone of the Ages" sat on the floor. A few cylinders, driven by inertia, kept moving, and occasional random phrases and words, picked up at different times, kept spewing forth.

The old order was breathing its last breath inside the machine, cursed out and spoke out the dull, mundane words of its cruelty, boredom, banality, and ennui.

"Punch you in the face," bluntly barked the machine.

"Shut up!"

"Oh hello, it's been a long time!"

"Leave me alone, I have no change. God will provide."

"Ow! No, daddy, please don't hit me, I won't do it again!"

"Bastard! Cur! Piece of . . . keep working, dog!"

"Silence!"

"I'll shoot you like an animal!"

"I love you, Linochka . . . I adore you!"

"Here's your tip, waiter."

And so on, and so on.

Disconnected words and sentences, but all equally dreadful, in all languages, kept spilling from the machine. Kuks jumped to his feet and started stomping on the machine, to further its demise, like that revolutionary at the Academy.

Then he stopped, scratched his bald pate, and said, softly, "Yes, let the past disappear. We don't need . . . no more."

David Lindsay (1876–1945) was an English writer who was influenced by the work of Jules Verne as well as Norse mythology, but in a much different way than E. R. Eddison. While Eddison focused on the storytelling and mythology of Norse sagas, Lindsay was drawn to the exploration of existence through philosophy. He was highly intellectual and had a passion for writing, but unfortunately he never achieved any kind of success with his books. *A Voyage to Arcturus* is considered by many to be a masterpiece; however, it sold less than six hundred copies when first published in 1920. His subsequent novels, *The Haunted Woman*, *Sphinx*, and *The Ancient Tragedy* (published as *Devil's Tor* after so many rejections), had a similar lack of success, both critically and in sales. This left him penniless as well as a tragic, pessimistic figure. *A Voyage to Arcturus* remains an inspiration to generations of writers of the fantastic, including C. S. Lewis and J. R. R. Tolkien. Indeed, it is truly one of the most imaginative and unique novels of the twentieth century. This selection is a chapter from this thought-provoking novel where we follow Maskull, a man who seeks adventure, traveling to the planet Tormance in the Arcturus star system.

Joiwind

(EXCERPT FROM *A VOYAGE TO ARCTURUS*)

David Lindsay

IT WAS A DENSE NIGHT when Maskull awoke from his profound sleep. A wind was blowing against him, gentle but wall-like, such as he had never experienced on earth. He remained sprawling on the ground, as he was unable to lift his body because of its intense weight. A numbing pain, which he could not identify with any region of his frame, acted from now onward as a lower, sympathetic note to all his other sensations. It gnawed away at him continuously; sometimes it embittered and irritated him, at other times he forgot it.

He felt something hard on his forehead. Putting his hand up, he discovered there a fleshy protuberance the size of a small plum, having a cavity in the middle, of which he could not feel the bottom. Then he also became aware of a large knob on each side of his neck, an inch below the ear.

From the region of his heart, a tentacle had

budded. It was as long as his arm, but thin, like whipcord, and soft and flexible.

As soon as he thoroughly realised the significance of these new organs, his heart began to pump. Whatever might, or might not, be their use, they proved one thing—that he was in a new world.

One part of the sky began to get lighter than the rest. Maskull cried out to his companions, but received no response. This frightened him. He went on shouting out, at irregular intervals—equally alarmed at the silence and at the sound of his own voice. Finally, as no answering hail came, he thought it wiser not to make too much noise, and after that he lay quiet, waiting in cold blood for what might happen.

In a short while he perceived dim shadows around him, but these were not his friends.

A pale, milky vapour over the ground began to succeed the black night, while in the upper sky rosy tints appeared. On earth, one would have said that day was breaking. The brightness went on imperceptibly increasing for a very long time.

Maskull then discovered that he was lying on sand. The colour of the sand was scarlet. The obscure shadows he had seen were bushes, with black stems and purple leaves. So far, nothing else was visible.

The day surged up. It was too misty for direct sunshine, but before long the brilliance of the light was already greater than that of the midday sun on earth. The heat, too, was intense, but Maskull welcomed it—it relieved his pain and diminished his sense of crushing weight. The wind had dropped with the rising of the sun.

He now tried to get onto his feet, but succeeded only in kneeling. He was unable to see far. The mists had no more than partially dissolved, and all that he could distinguish was a narrow circle of red sand dotted with ten or twenty bushes.

He felt a soft, cool touch on the back of his neck. He started forward in nervous fright and, in doing so, tumbled over onto the sand. Looking up over his shoulder quickly, he was astounded to see a woman standing beside him.

She was clothed in a single flowing, pale green garment, rather classically draped. According to earth standards she was not beautiful, for, although her face was otherwise human, she was endowed—or afflicted—with the additional disfiguring organs that Maskull had discovered in himself. She also possessed the heart tentacle. But when he sat up, and their eyes met and remained in sympathetic contact, he seemed to see right into a soul that was the home of love, warmth, kindness, tenderness, and intimacy. Such was the noble familiarity of that gaze, that he thought he knew her. After that, he recognised all the loveliness of her person. She was tall and slight. All her movements were as graceful as music. Her skin was not of a dead, opaque colour, like that of an earth beauty, but was opalescent; its hue was continually changing, with every thought and emotion, but none of these tints was vivid—all were delicate, half-toned, and poetic. She had very long, loosely plaited, flaxen hair. The new organs, as soon as Maskull had familiarised himself with them, imparted something to her face that was unique and striking. He could not quite define it to himself, but subtlety and inwardness seemed added. The organs did not contradict the love of her eyes or the angelic purity of her features, but nevertheless sounded a deeper note—a note that saved her from mere girlishness.

Her gaze was so friendly and unembarrassed that Maskull felt scarcely any humiliation at sitting at her feet, naked and helpless. She realised his plight, and put into his hands a garment that she had been carrying over her arm. It was similar to the one she was wearing, but of a darker, more masculine colour.

"Do you think you can put it on by yourself?"

He was distinctly conscious of these words, yet her voice had not sounded.

He forced himself up to his feet, and she helped him to master the complications of the drapery.

"Poor man—how you are suffering!" she said, in the same inaudible language. This time he discovered that the sense of what she said was received by his brain through the organ on his forehead.

"Where am I? Is this Tormance?" he asked. As he spoke, he staggered.

She caught him, and helped him to sit down. "Yes. You are with friends."

Then she regarded him with a smile, and began speaking aloud, in English. Her voice somehow reminded him of an April day, it was so fresh, nervous, and girlish. "I can now understand your language. It was strange at first. In the future I'll speak to you with my mouth."

"This is extraordinary! What is this organ?" he asked, touching his forehead.

"It is named the 'breve.' By means of it we read one another's thoughts. Still, speech is better, for then the heart can be read too."

He smiled. "They say that speech is given us to deceive others."

"One can deceive with thought, too. But I'm thinking of the best, not the worst."

"Have you seen my friends?"

She scrutinised him quietly, before answering. "Did you not come alone?"

"I came with two other men, in a machine. I must have lost consciousness on arrival, and I haven't seen them since."

"That's very strange! No, I haven't seen them. They can't be here, or we would have known it. My husband and I—"

"What is your name, and your husband's name?"

"Mine is Joiwind—my husband's is Panawe. We live a very long way from here; still, it came to us both last night that you were lying here insensible. We almost quarrelled about which of us should come to you, but in the end I won." Here she laughed. "I won, because I am the stronger-hearted of the two; he is the purer in perception."

"Thanks, Joiwind!" said Maskull simply.

The colors chased each other rapidly beneath her skin. "Oh, why do you say that? What pleasure is greater than loving-kindness? I rejoiced at the opportunity. . . . But now we must exchange blood."

"What is this?" he demanded, rather puzzled.

"It must be so. Your blood is far too thick and heavy for our world. Until you have an infusion of mine, you will never get up."

Maskull flushed. "I feel like a complete ignoramus here. . . . Won't it hurt you?"

"If your blood pains you, I suppose it will pain me. But we will share the pain."

"This is a new kind of hospitality to me," he muttered.

"Wouldn't you do the same for me?" asked Joiwind, half smiling, half agitated.

"I can't answer for any of my actions in this world. I scarcely know where I am. . . . Why, yes—of course I would, Joiwind."

While they were talking it had become full day. The mists had rolled away from the ground, and only the upper atmosphere remained fog-charged. The desert of scarlet sand stretched in all directions, except one, where there was a sort of little oasis—some low hills, clothed sparsely with little purple trees from base to summit. It was about a quarter of a mile distant.

Joiwind had brought with her a small flint knife. Without any trace of nervousness, she made a careful, deep incision on her upper arm. Maskull expostulated.

"Really, this part of it is nothing," she said, laughing. "And if it were—a sacrifice that is no sacrifice—what merit is there in that? . . . Come now—your arm!"

The blood was streaming down her arm. It was not red blood, but a milky, opalescent fluid.

"Not that one!" said Maskull, shrinking. "I have already been cut there." He submitted the other, and his blood poured forth.

Joiwind delicately and skilfully placed the mouths of the two wounds together, and then kept her arm pressed tightly against Maskull's for a long time. He felt a stream of pleasure entering his body through the incision. His old lightness and vigour began to return to him. After about five minutes a duel of kindness started between them; he wanted to remove his arm, and she to continue. At last he had his way, but it was none too soon—she stood there pale and dispirited.

She looked at him with a more serious expression than before, as if strange depths had opened up before her eyes.

"What is your name?"

"Maskull."

"Where have you come from, with this awful blood?"

"From a world called Earth. . . . The blood is clearly unsuitable for this world, Joiwind, but after all, that was only to be expected. I am sorry I let you have your way."

"Oh, don't say that! There was nothing else to be done. We must all help one another. Yet, somehow—forgive me—I feel polluted."

"And well you may, for it's a fearful thing for a girl to accept in her own veins the blood of a strange man from a strange planet. If I had not been so dazed and weak I would never have allowed it."

"But I would have insisted. Are we not all brothers and sisters? Why did you come here, Maskull?"

He was conscious of a slight degree of embarrassment. "Will you think it foolish if I say I hardly know?—I came with those two men. Perhaps I was attracted by curiosity, or perhaps it was the love of adventure."

"Perhaps," said Joiwind. "I wonder . . . These friends of yours must be terrible men. Why did they come?"

"That I can tell you. They came to follow Surtur."

Her face grew troubled. "I don't understand it. One of them at least must be a bad man, and yet if he is following Surtur—or Shaping, as he is called here—he can't be really bad."

"What do you know of Surtur?" asked Maskull in astonishment.

Joiwind remained silent for a time, studying his face. His brain moved restlessly, as though it were being probed from outside. "I see . . . and yet I don't see," she said at last. "It is very difficult. . . . Your God is a dreadful Being—bodyless, unfriendly, invisible. Here we don't worship a God like that. Tell me, has any man set eyes on your God?"

"What does all this mean, Joiwind? Why speak of God?"

"I want to know."

"In ancient times, when the earth was young and grand, a few holy men are reputed to have walked and spoken with God, but those days are past."

"Our world is still young," said Joiwind. "Shaping goes among us and converses with us. He is real and active—a friend and lover. Shaping made us, and he loves his work."

"Have *you* met him?" demanded Maskull, hardly believing his ears.

"No. I have done nothing to deserve it yet. Some day I may have an opportunity to sacrifice myself, and then I may be rewarded by meeting and talking with Shaping."

"I have certainly come to another world. But why do you say he is the same as Surtur?"

"Yes, he is the same. We women call him Shaping, and so do most men, but a few name him Surtur."

Maskull bit his nail. "Have you ever heard of Crystalman?"

"That is Shaping once again. You see, he has many names—which shows how much he occupies our minds. Crystalman is a name of affection."

"It's odd," said Maskull. "I came here with quite different ideas about Crystalman."

Joiwind shook her hair. "In that grove of trees over there stands a desert shrine of his. Let us go and pray there, and then we'll go on our way to Poolingdred. That is my home. It's a long way off, and we must get there before Blodsombre."

"Now, what is Blodsombre?"

"For about four hours in the middle of the day Branchspell's rays are so hot that no one can endure them. We call it Blodsombre."

"Is Branchspell another name for Arcturus?"

Joiwind threw off her seriousness and laughed. "Naturally we don't take our names from you, Maskull. I don't think our names are very poetic, but they follow nature."

She took his arm affectionately, and directed

their walk towards the tree-covered hills. As they went along, the sun broke through the upper mists and a terrible gust of scorching heat, like a blast from a furnace, struck Maskull's head. He involuntarily looked up, but lowered his eyes again like lightning. All that he saw in that instant was a glaring ball of electric white, three times the apparent diameter of the sun. For a few minutes he was quite blind.

"My God!" he exclaimed. "If it's like this in early morning you must be right enough about Blodsombre." When he had somewhat recovered himself he asked, "How long are the days here, Joiwind?"

Again he felt his brain being probed.

"At this time of the year, for every hour's daylight that you have in summer, we have two."

"The heat is terrific—and yet somehow I don't feel so distressed by it as I would have expected."

"I feel it more than usual. It's not difficult to account for it; you have some of my blood, and I have some of yours."

"Yes, every time I realise that, I—Tell me, Joiwind, will my blood alter, if I stay here long enough?—I mean, will it lose its redness and thickness, and become pure and thin and light-coloured, like yours?"

"Why not? If you live as we live, you will assuredly grow like us."

"Do you mean food and drink?"

"We eat no food, and drink only water."

"And on that you manage to sustain life?"

"Well, Maskull, our water is good water," replied Joiwind, smiling.

As soon as he could see again he stared around at the landscape. The enormous scarlet desert extended everywhere to the horizon, excepting where it was broken by the oasis. It was roofed by a cloudless, deep blue, almost violet, sky. The circle of the horizon was far larger than on earth. On the skyline, at right angles to the direction in which they were walking, appeared a chain of mountains, apparently about forty miles distant. One, which was higher than the rest, was shaped like a cup. Maskull would have felt inclined to

believe he was travelling in dreamland, but for the intensity of the light, which made everything vividly real.

Joiwind pointed to the cup-shaped mountain. "That's Poolingdred."

"You didn't come from there!" he exclaimed, quite startled.

"Yes, I did indeed. And that is where we have to go to now."

"With the single object of finding me?"

"Why, yes."

The colour mounted to his face. "Then you are the bravest and noblest of all girls," he said quietly, after a pause. "Without exception. Why, this is a journey for an athlete!"

She pressed his arm, while a score of unpaintable, delicate hues stained her cheeks in rapid transition. "Please don't say any more about it, Maskull. It makes me feel unpleasant."

"Very well. But can we possibly get there before midday?"

"Oh, yes. And you mustn't be frightened at the distance. We think nothing of long distances here—we have so much to think about and feel. Time goes all too quickly."

During their conversation they had drawn near the base of the hills, which sloped gently, and were not above fifty feet in height. Maskull now began to see strange specimens of vegetable life. What looked like a small patch of purple grass, above five feet square, was moving across the sand in their direction. When it came near enough he perceived that it was not grass; there were no blades, but only purple roots. The roots were revolving, for each small plant in the whole patch, like the spokes of a rimless wheel. They were alternately plunged in the sand, and withdrawn from it, and by this means the plant proceeded forward. Some uncanny, semi-intelligent instinct was keeping all the plants together, moving at one pace, in one direction, like a flock of migrating birds in flight.

Another remarkable plant was a large, feathery ball, resembling a dandelion fruit, which they encountered sailing through the air. Joiwind caught it with an exceedingly graceful movement of her arm, and showed it to Maskull. It had roots and presumably lived in the air and fed on the chemical constituents of the atmosphere. But what was peculiar about it was its colour. It was an entirely new colour—not a new shade or combination, but a new primary colour, as vivid as blue, red, or yellow, but quite different. When he inquired, she told him that it was known as "ulfire." Presently he met with a second new colour. This she designated "jale." The sense impressions caused in Maskull by these two additional primary colors can only be vaguely hinted at by analogy. Just as blue is delicate and mysterious, yellow clear and unsubtle, and red sanguine and passionate, so he felt ulfire to be wild and painful, and jale dreamlike, feverish, and voluptuous.

The hills were composed of a rich, dark mould. Small trees, of weird shapes, all differing from each other, but all purple-coloured, covered the slopes and top. Maskull and Joiwind climbed up and through. Some hard fruit, bright blue in colour, of the size of a large apple, and shaped like an egg, was lying in profusion underneath the trees.

"Is the fruit here poisonous, or why don't you eat it?" asked Maskull.

She looked at him tranquilly. "We don't eat living things. The thought is horrible to us."

"I have nothing to say against that, theoretically. But do you really sustain your bodies on water?"

"Supposing you could find nothing else to live on, Maskull—would you eat other men?"

"I would not."

"Neither will we eat plants and animals, which are our fellow creatures. So nothing is left to us but water, and as one can really live on anything, water does very well."

Maskull picked up one of the fruits and handled it curiously. As he did so another of his newly acquired sense organs came into action. He found that the fleshy knobs beneath his ears were in some novel fashion acquainting him with the inward properties of the fruit. He could not only see, feel, and smell it, but could detect its intrinsic nature. This nature was hard, persistent and melancholy.

Joiwind answered the questions he had not asked.

"Those organs are called 'poigns.' Their use is to enable us to understand and sympathise with all living creatures."

"What advantage do you derive from that, Joiwind?"

"The advantage of not being cruel and selfish, dear Maskull."

He threw the fruit away and flushed again.

Joiwind looked into his swarthy, bearded face without embarrassment and slowly smiled. "Have I said too much? Have I been too familiar? Do you know why you think so? It's because you are still impure. By and by you will listen to all language without shame."

Before he realised what she was about to do, she threw her tentacle round his neck, like another arm. He offered no resistance to its cool pressure. The contact of her soft flesh with his own was so moist and sensitive that it resembled another kind of kiss. He saw who it was that embraced him—a pale, beautiful girl. Yet, oddly enough, he experienced neither voluptuousness nor sexual pride. The love expressed by the caress was rich, glowing, and personal, but there was not the least trace of sex in it—and so he received it.

She removed her tentacle, placed her two arms on his shoulders and penetrated with her eyes right into his very soul.

"Yes, I wish to be pure," he muttered. "Without that what can I ever be but a weak, squirming devil?"

Joiwind released him. "This we call the 'magn,'" she said, indicating her tentacle. "By means of it what we love already we love more, and what we don't love at all we begin to love."

"A godlike organ!"

"It is the one we guard most jealously," said Joiwind.

The shade of the trees afforded a timely screen from the now almost insufferable rays of Branchspell, which was climbing steadily upward to the zenith. On descending the other side of the little hills, Maskull looked anxiously for traces of Nightspore and Krag, but without result. After staring about him for a few minutes he shrugged his shoulders; but suspicions had already begun to gather in his mind.

A small, natural amphitheatre lay at their feet, completely circled by the tree-clad heights. The centre was of red sand. In the very middle shot up a tall, stately tree, with a black trunk and branches, and transparent, crystal leaves. At the foot of this tree was a natural, circular well, containing dark green water.

When they had reached the bottom, Joiwind took him straight over to the well.

Maskull gazed at it intently. "Is this the shrine you talked about?"

"Yes. It is called Shaping's Well. The man or woman who wishes to invoke Shaping must take up some of the gnawl water, and drink it."

"Pray for me," said Maskull. "Your unspotted prayer will carry more weight."

"What do you wish for?"

"For purity," answered Maskull, in a troubled voice.

Joiwind made a cup of her hand, and drank a little of the water. She held it up to Maskull's mouth. "You must drink too." He obeyed. She then stood erect, closed her eyes, and, in a voice like the soft murmurings of spring, prayed aloud.

"Shaping, my father, I am hoping you can hear me. A strange man has come to us weighed down with heavy blood. He wishes to be pure. Let him know the meaning of love, let him live for others. Don't spare him pain, dear Shaping, but let him seek his own pain. Breathe into him a noble soul."

Maskull listened with tears in his heart.

As Joiwind finished speaking, a blurred mist came over his eyes, and, half buried in the scarlet sand, appeared a large circle of dazzlingly white pillars. For some minutes they flickered to and fro between distinctness and indistinctness, like an object being focused. Then they faded out of sight again.

"Is that a sign from Shaping?" asked Maskull, in a low, awed tone.

"Perhaps it is. It is a time mirage."

"What can that be, Joiwind?"

"You see, dear Maskull, the temple does not yet exist but it will do so, because it must. What you and I are now doing in simplicity, wise men will do hereafter in full knowledge."

"It is right for man to pray," said Maskull. "Good and evil in the world don't originate from nothing. God and Devil must exist. And we should pray to the one, and fight the other."

"Yes, we must fight Krag."

"What name did you say?" asked Maskull in amazement.

"Krag—the author of evil and misery—whom you call Devil."

He immediately concealed his thoughts. To prevent Joiwind from learning his relationship to this being, he made his mind a blank.

"Why do you hide your mind from me?" she demanded, looking at him strangely and changing colour.

"In this bright, pure, radiant world, evil seems so remote, one can scarcely grasp its meaning." But he lied.

Joiwind continued gazing at him, straight out of her clean soul. "The world is good and pure, but many men are corrupt. Panawe, my husband, has travelled, and he has told me things I would almost rather have not heard. One person he met believed the universe to be, from top to bottom, a conjurer's cave."

"I should like to meet your husband."

"Well, we are going home now."

Maskull was on the point of inquiring whether she had any children, but was afraid of offending her, and checked himself.

She read the mental question. "What need is there? Is not the whole world full of lovely children? Why should I want selfish possessions?"

An extraordinary creature flew past, uttering a plaintive cry of five distinct notes. It was not a bird, but had a balloon-shaped body, paddled by five webbed feet. It disappeared among the trees.

Joiwind pointed to it, as it went by. "I love that beast, grotesque as it is—perhaps all the more for its grotesqueness. But if I had children of my own, would I still love it? Which is best—to love two or three, or to love all?"

"Every woman can't be like you, Joiwind, but it is good to have a few like you. Wouldn't it be as well," he went on, "since we've got to walk through that sun-baked wilderness, to make turbans for our heads out of some of those long leaves?"

She smiled rather pathetically. "You will think me foolish, but every tearing off of a leaf would be a wound in my heart. We have only to throw our robes over our heads."

"No doubt that will answer the same purpose, but tell me—weren't these very robes once part of a living creature?"

"Oh, no—no, they are the webs of a certain animal, but they have never been in themselves alive."

"You reduce life to extreme simplicity," remarked Maskull meditatively, "but it is very beautiful."

Climbing back over the hills, they now without further ceremony began their march across the desert.

They walked side by side. Joiwind directed their course straight toward Poolingdred. From the position of the sun, Maskull judged their way to lie due north. The sand was soft and powdery, very tiring to his naked feet. The red glare dazed his eyes, and made him semi-blind. He was hot, parched, and tormented with the craving to drink; his undertone of pain emerged into full consciousness.

"I see my friends nowhere, and it is very queer."

"Yes, it is queer—if it is accidental," said Joiwind, with a peculiar intonation.

"Exactly!" agreed Maskull. "If they had met with a mishap, their bodies would still be there. It begins to look like a piece of bad work to me. They must have gone on, and left me. . . . Well, I am here, and I must make the best of it. I will trouble no more about them."

"I don't wish to speak ill of anyone," said Joiwind, "but my instinct tells me that you are better away from those men. They did not come here for your sake, but for their own."

They walked on for a long time. Maskull was beginning to feel faint. She twined her magn lovingly around his waist, and a strong current of confidence and well-being instantly coursed through his veins.

"Thanks, Joiwind! But am I not weakening *you*?"

"Yes," she replied, with a quick, thrilling glance. "But not much—and it gives me great happiness."

Presently they met a fantastic little creature, the size of a new-born lamb, waltzing along on three legs. Each leg in turn moved to the front, and so the little monstrosity proceeded by means of a series of complete rotations. It was vividly coloured, as though it had been dipped into pots of bright blue and yellow paint. It looked up with small, shining eyes, as they passed.

Joiwind nodded and smiled to it. "That's a personal friend of mine, Maskull. Whenever I come this way, I see it. It's always waltzing, and always in a hurry, but it never seems to get anywhere."

"It seems to me that life is so self-sufficient here that there is no need for anyone to get anywhere. What I don't quite understand is how you manage to pass your days without ennui."

"That's a strange word. It means, does it not, craving for excitement?"

"Something of the kind," said Maskull.

"That must be a disease brought on by rich food."

"But are you never dull?"

"How could we be? Our blood is quick and light and free, our flesh is clean and unclogged, inside and out. . . . Before long I hope you will understand what sort of question you have asked."

Farther on they encountered a strange phenomenon. In the heart of the desert a fountain rose perpendicularly fifty feet into the air, with a cool and pleasant hissing sound. It differed, however, from a fountain in this respect—that the water of which it was composed did not return to the ground but was absorbed by the atmosphere at the summit. It was in fact a tall, graceful column of dark green fluid, with a capital of coiling and twisting vapours.

When they came closer, Maskull perceived that this water column was the continuation and termination of a flowing brook, which came down from the direction of the mountains. The explanation of the phenomenon was evidently that the water at this spot found chemical affinities in the upper air, and consequently forsook the ground.

"Now let us drink," said Joiwind.

She threw herself unaffectedly at full length on the sand, face downward, by the side of the brook, and Maskull was not long in following her example. She refused to quench her thirst until she had seen him drink. He found the water heavy, but bubbling with gas. He drank copiously. It affected his palate in a new way—with the purity and cleanness of water was combined the exhilaration of a sparkling wine, raising his spirits—but somehow the intoxication brought out his better nature, and not his lower.

"We call it 'gnawl water,'" said Joiwind. "This is not quite pure, as you can see by the colour. At Poolingdred it is crystal clear. But we would be ungrateful if we complained. After this you'll find we'll get along much better."

Maskull now began to realise his environment, as it were for the first time. All his sense organs started to show him beauties and wonders that he had not hitherto suspected. The uniform glaring scarlet of the sands became separated into a score of clearly distinguished shades of red. The sky was similarly split up into different blues. The radiant heat of Branchspell he found to affect every part of his body with unequal intensities. His ears awakened; the atmosphere was full of murmurs, the sands hummed, even the sun's rays had a sound of their own—a kind of faint Aeolian harp. Subtle, puzzling perfumes assailed his nostrils. His palate lingered over the memory of the gnawl water. All the pores of his skin were tickled and soothed by hitherto unperceived currents of air. His poigns explored actively the inward nature of everything in his immediate vicinity. His magn touched Joiwind, and drew from her person a stream of love and joy. And lastly by means of his breve he exchanged thoughts with her in silence. This mighty sense symphony stirred him to the depths, and throughout the walk of that endless morning he felt no more fatigue.

When it was drawing near to Blodsombre, they approached the sedgy margin of a dark green lake, which lay underneath Poolingdred.

Panawe was sitting on a dark rock, waiting for them.

Maurice Renard (1875–1939) was a French writer who served as a soldier during World War I. It was during his military service that he discovered the work of H. G. Wells and soon began crafting his own science fiction and horror stories. Renard's literary career began with his collection *Phantoms and Puppets* (1905). His first novel, *Doctor Lerne* (1908), although clearly inspired by Wells, was also evidence of a unique voice. It melds the fantastic with horror and set the tone for many of Renard's later work. In 1920, he published *The Hands of Orlac*, a cautionary tale about receiving organ transplants from strangers. Now considered a classic, the novel has been adapted to film three times. Renard also published a novel that was banned by many libraries and seen as sacrilegious by the church: *The Monkey* (1925), cowritten with Albert-Jean, that explored cloning. The somewhat mystical and mysterious story reprinted here is among his most enduring.

Sound in the Mountain

Maurice Renard

Translated by Gio Clairval

ONLY ON THE SECOND DAY did Florent Max hear the sound. The morning before, as he passed by, he hadn't paid attention: the whispering blended with the mountain's uncountable murmurs. In the evening, when he was going home, he recalled the vague memory of something like buzzing flies, or a subterranean torrent.

The second day, he stopped to listen.

Florent Max had left his mountain cabin before dawn. Paint-box flung around his neck, folding easel tucked under his arm, he ascended the mule path toward his favorite spot, and the unfinished work that awaited him.

The landscape painter advanced slowly. Morning doled out her first rays of light. The surrounding splendors revealed themselves in the imperceptible growth of clarity. Florent Max, doubling over, studied his ankle boots' progression on the stones.

He moved forward with no enthusiasm, out of necessity and habit. Art? Beauty? Nature? A childish waste of time! . . . He was forty-five. *That* worried him. *Old!* he thought. *Old!* It had happened all of a sudden. He'd catcalled this beautiful girl, and she'd thrown that word in his face just by sizing him up, her cursory glance full of contempt. *Old.* And right there, as if the girl's eye had cast a spell on him, he'd pictured himself crowned with salt and pepper, hidden behind a wrinkled mask, smothered in fat, laden to the bones with arthritis and ice—in other words, all that he actually was.

Old? Who, him? He'd accomplished nothing. He hadn't done anything, loved anyone, arrived anywhere!

Lost in the horror of his recent discovery, he darkly considered every angle. Knees that bent with telling stiffness. Kidneys of perceptible size, weighing him down—particularly on the left, and he was aware of his early-hour face needing, as he would say, "a little ironing out."

Ah, if only I'd done something of consequence, he thought. *No dice! Love? No dice! Blame the war. They say it lasted five years. Yeah, right. It's like Rip's night. A one-century-long night.*

We left young, but a day lasted thrice, no, four times as long, and we came back old. Old!

A rebellious thought stopped him, eyes transfixed. It was morning, speckled with gold, and it was springtime. Spring. Youth. The rising sun stretched its beams, bold, conquering. Over there rosy peaks, blurred with dawny mists, shimmered like a virgin's cheeks. Everything was new and fresh.

I'm at odds with all this now. How come? . . . I've tasted nothing . . . What's it all about? Two halves, one made of projects and the other of regrets? Are we here to transition, without realizing it, from the shame of being too young to the shame of being too old? If only I were famous. Glory compensates for many disappointments . . . A famous man has no age . . .

The corners of his lips turned downward, like an antique drama mask.

I'm a loser. Painting, I still care about painting. Not that much, though . . . Oh, well. But the rest . . . I'm alone. My masters are gone. My successors, absent. And love! I've wasted my time with Marie. Twenty-five years together. We're of an age. For a woman, it's too late for anything new. To me, she's the nightmarish relic of a lost idyll . . .

Then:

Will I live looking back in regret? My youth, my youth is eating me from the inside like a glittering cancer. And this. I traveled fantastic landscapes as a blind man. And now. What am I now? There are vegetable people, people like fruits, people like flowers. If it is so, I'm over.

Then:

Still, still . . .

And then:

Be honest, old man. You've been sleeping in the train. Ancient? Not yet. But "old" to young women, yes. A childless, penniless man without a name. And this organic dissolution beginning with the first gray hair . . . Death is just a sudden acceleration.

Florent Max followed the path among brambles and bushes. To his left, the ravine dropped from a vertiginous height, and, at the bottom of the precipice, the slope opposite rebounded with magnificent élan, projecting the forest above like a screen of blue greenery.

Wallowing in his melancholy mood, the painter drifted along a different trail that slanted upward in a sea of boulders and brushes.

"Too much soul, sir, too much soul."

Proud of this four-pence Shakespearean line, he listened. Stillness enhanced the silence. A deaf man would have known there was nothing to hear. Not a screeching grasshopper, not a fly buzzing over a flower.

The painter strained to listen, turning his head from side to side.

"How strange! I'm sure it wasn't tinnitus. The thing made the noise of a clover field in the sun."

And he began ferreting everywhere.

The ravine opposed him with obsidian blackness blended of vines and shrubs.

He decided to go back to the spot where he'd heard the sound distinctly.

After some fumbling and groping, Florent Max found the noise: it was audible from a very small patch of ground. If he moved half a step in any direction, the stubborn thing vanished from his hearing range. Had he lowered his head as he passed the spot, he would have missed the murmuring. It was so peculiar he compared it to a buzzing object placed behind several obstacles pierced by a hair-thin interstice. This comparison falls short, but it doesn't really matter.

Ready to perform to some invisible audience, he pursed his lips stage left, stage right.

Hardly had this tomfoolery begun than astonishment froze Florent Max's countenance. Picture someone who believed himself the victim of a practical joke, only to discover he was wrong. Damn wrong.

He couldn't help looking up, even if he knew that *no telegraph lines climbed the mountain.* Gaping, he questioned the rock, the sky . . . but of course he saw no electric cables. What he was hearing, though, resembled a nest of telegraph wires spanning the void. It was like approaching an ear to hollow wood, to catch the howling tide of a faraway crowd, the rumble of rioting people overflowing an immense square, in some mysterious place.

There was no heavenly organ playing, no celestial harp. There was only their music, floating in mid-air from a fixed point. The aerial sound sustained a chord of multiple musical notes, rich with agreeable tunes. Yes, it came from the right, from the incline . . . He moved in that direction, and the music vanished. He moved back, and the sound blossomed like an otherworldly flower sprouted from a soil of silence.

Florent Max studied the incline. Forty yards away. The slope shot upward, stopping the slanting sunbeams with its formidable vertical wall, lumpy, cyclopean. The painter thought that an echo ricocheted on that surface. A particular echo, like in a crypt. He then noticed that the incline formed a large round hollow, the interior of a spherical niche, a concave reflector. A vault opened in front of him instead of hanging overhead. Surely the concavity concentrated an echo into a single spot. It was the foyer of an acoustic mirror. Or so he decided. So the mirror reflected sounds that came from the opposite direction. But behind him only forest covered the mountain, and there was nothing there, at any rate nothing that could produce that sound. It wasn't the noise of a swarm, or torrents, or telegraphic wires, or clover fields, nor was it some concert created by the wind.

The other side of the ravine, he thought, only sent the marvelous harmony back to this wall, after receiving it from an unknown source . . . It came from afar, by a string of ricochets, reflections, resonances. That must be it. Did it travel by way of air? Beneath the ground? From a distant place for sure.

He could hear voices, whispers, breaths, the sounds of light feet, the rustling of mousseline silk . . . or wings. An organic murmur. The chattering of a lively crowd.

So beautiful, he thought, *as beautiful as a distant memory.*

He blinked. A low-pitched, melodious note had risen over the pedal's humming.

How to explain that such a perpetual symphony was being played, instead of the din of ordinary human life? He decided that, by some fortuitous circumstance, he had encountered a city that existed elsewhere. Like Venice. Devoid of horses and cars. He'd visited Venice, and the memory of Piazza San Marco haunted him. But he had to abandon this theory. The distant memory didn't originate in that city: those jingling sounds playing at regular intervals weren't reminiscent of Venice. And the voices spoke no Italian.

He shuddered when he was able to discern the first accents. Two voices approached. He thought a couple of superior creatures moved over the crest of the ravine, stepping across the void. After a moment, the image was gone. The two voices remained for a few delicious moments until they faded, too, like minutes of shared happiness, which always end in separation.

So beautiful, he repeated. *As beautiful as my life when I was young.*

His throat tightened. A sentiment akin to pain convulsed his eyebrows into an expression that had no theatrical fakeness. He was about to cry, and he didn't try to hold back his tears.

Other voices floated close. He was standing a step or two away from the speakers!

He hollered then, but suavely, to avoid scaring the strangers away. No reactions signaled that his calls had been heard. He didn't try again, contenting himself with listening.

He made a fine figure, a bulky man standing on the rim of a ravine, hand curled like a conch shell around his ear, scanning the landscape with the stupid gaze of those who see nothing because they're trying to use all their senses minus sight.

I would need, he thought, *an instrument to listen with both ears.*

For the time being he rolled up a sheet of paper to use it as an acoustic horn, which didn't improve his appearance.

He was caught in his delight, bewitched, happy.

That day, he didn't feel like painting. Florent Max stood at the edge of that ravine. He ate the cold cuts Marie had enveloped for him in brown paper, and spent the afternoon listening to the sounds.

Night approached. He set off, overexcited, heat on his cheeks. He had to turn in. Marie would make herself sick with worry. But tomorrow . . .

What if the whispers disappeared? A string of echoes can be easily broken.

He would procure a manual of Acoustics.

Did the sound travel through the atmosphere? Or through the terrestrial mass?

The place existed somewhere. He needed to know, to find that forum of happiness. He had to go there. He could not live elsewhere. He could not.

Why did his mind insist on "remembering"? What was Florent Max remembering?

Joy filled him like a goddess possessing her lover, puffing up his chest as if a human shape could not contain her whole. Still he had yet to hear the supreme voice! The superior being that would accept him by her side.

He ran down the rocky path without seeing anything, hearing anything but the memory of those marvelous echoes. Life played her victory song for him. The world had changed.

Marie asked, "What happened? Are you sick? You're so red in the face! And you're late."

Florent Max shook himself awake, as if he'd been dreaming. Should he tell her? He, who had climbed down the mountain like a hero descending the Hartz, he who had almost encountered another species, should he break the incomparable news?

Experience advised against telling. Jealousy ordered to keep his mouth shut. The treasure he'd discovered, he would not share. The whispers were his. He owned them. Nobody else would taste that happiness.

He answered by a groan.

Marie studied him.

The table was set with a blue-checkered cloth. They ate in silence. His body was there, but his mind transported him to that solitary ravine, over to the mysterious dimension whence the sounds came.

All of a sudden, he stood and began walking about.

"What's the matter with you?" Marie's voice trembled.

"Shut up!"

The reminiscence. He had it! That fantastic city of domes and minarets, those suspended gardens, that serene multitude of palaces and columns glittering through the mist. He'd had this vision as a little boy. He remembered. He remembered.

He remembers. He is ten. He's sitting in that armchair of red velvet lined with a tapestry band. Before his eyes, the marvelous city. In his lap, a book. Is it a serious book or a collection of tales? He can't remember. He had taken the book from his father's library, whose destiny was to be reduced to cinders by the Germans. After thirty-five years, he can still see the text. How could he forget? It was one of his childhood's enchantments.

This is what the book said:

"At two in the afternoon, our caravan resumed its journey. A murderous heat engulfed us, and the air fluttered so strongly the desert seemed to be shaken by marine waves. The sky filled with treacherous images created by refractions on the hot layers of the atmosphere. Oases materialized. Mountainous chains soared, to disappear in an instant. These mirages were sometimes reversed, and sometimes doubled. They lured us with apparitions reflected in calm rivers.

"One of these illusions was so enchanting we thought ourselves at the Opera House. In a moonlight brighter than sunshine we entered the most beautiful of cities. We glimpsed a terrace with walls and balustrades mirrored on the surface of a lake. Edifices of exquisite architecture surrounded the place. A profusion of domed houses with ribbed balconies stretched to the horizon. Thin spires and turrets pierced the sky, more numerous than masts in a crowded port. A steeple soared above the terrace, topped by a gleaming disc that released a blinding light whenever a sort of gigantic hammer struck it. We thought the disc worked like an oversized drum. For a moment, we perceived the hustling movement of a busy place, but we couldn't observe the passers-by, as the vision faded too quickly.

"Our curiosity piqued, we surmised that this city was the reflection of a real place, but despite every one of us had crossed the four corners of the world, nobody could recognize it. We had glimpsed the capital of an empire hidden in the mystery of Africa, or a civilization that existed on some plane of existence separate from ours. Such hypotheses, however, sounded like nonsense, and our companions chose to think that the heat and thirst caused us to hallucinate."

Florent Max compared the description of the "tympanum" with the *jingling sounds playing at regular intervals* that punctuated the music from the ravine. Two impressions created certainty in his mind: the story was no tale; the mirage was no hallucination. The city existed. Because a man had seen its reflection and another man had heard its echo.

But where was it?

The style of the narration didn't seem archaic. The book had probably been written around the beginning of the nineteenth century, or the end of the eighteenth. Had some kingdom been discovered since? Not really. A few tribes. Villages made of adobe. Hadn't everything been discovered already? Still, the city must have been somewhere. Physical laws proved it!

Florent Max knew he would never find the book, not his own, not another. He had no title, no author.

At the same time, the thought struck him that the city was out of reach, that he had to give up the project of finding the place, that he should content himself with listening to the adorable sound, without trying to discover its origin.

That's when he had the idea of purchasing the ravine and having a house built there, with an elegant room for him to recline in, at the exact place where the whispers came alive. He would lounge there, a cigarette—

"Darling, please, tell me what is going on . . ."

He was going to say: "What is going on is that your voice screeches like a broken rattle." But he saw her, elbows on the table. She seemed so affectionate, and so unhappy. And he thought that his voice, too, would sound like a rattle. He pitied her, because he pitied himself a great deal. He took her into his arms and, cheek-to-cheek, he said:

"*Ma petite Marie*, forgive me . . . I'm afraid I'm not aging gracefully."

But now the thought of growing old, he accepted it.

The day after, he left as usual, before the first light, but he told Marie that he would surely come home late in the night as he intended to do a few studies *au clair de la lune* up in the mountain. He reached the ravine at the break of dawn. Venus still shone in the sky. His heart thumped in his chest, and the cold chilled his limbs. He halted, as tense as a lover who fears to find the door bolted. His head probed the air with tiny movements, he faltered, gave a little smile.

There it was, the whispering.

He listened, watching the stars, but Venus vanished, drowned in light, and Florent Max remained alone with the sound. He couldn't discern any variations, any changes from the quiet of night to the busy hours of the morning. The city lived on a different time, far away from the ordinary lives of humankind.

The high-pitched gong vibrated. Florent Max pulled out his watch. A red star resounded and died with a slow diminuendo. He counted seven minutes and three seconds between the tingling sounds. Wherever that world was, time existed in the same way. Maybe the two worlds weren't that different. Maybe the other dimension was accessible.

One day, he heard a voice that detached itself clearly against the background of whispers. Another day, the murmuring grew to reach an extraordinary intensity. The gong clanged as strong as the low-pitched bell of a cathedral, and the beautiful voice brushed against his skin like a kiss. But an ice-cold gale dissipated it. Temperature and humidity influenced the quality of the sound.

He pictured the whispering like a bunch of rays. The niche in the vertical wall turned a little to face the sky, and there the acoustic rays rebounded to span the valley. There, there, just before the forest, the echo faded. Finally, he devised a method to study the phenomenon. He should try tracing the direction the sound took across the ravine.

The morning he should have completed his calculations, as he climbed the path, two detona-tions, followed by a third, split the quiet. He had heard about the project of widening the path to let automobiles reach the plateau above, but he hadn't thought his ravine would be touched.

When he arrived at the usual place, he already knew. All day he looked for the sound, but he couldn't find it. The felicitous coincidence of angles and right lines that allowed the whisper-ing to become audible was broken.

The last place, the precise spot where the echo disappeared into the forest, he left for the end. There started a daring bridge in the air, which carried the sound over from the other dimension. The night found him at the edge of the ravine.

Marie found him lying on a bramble, which hadn't softened his fall. He looked like something honorable, très *clair de lune*. He wasn't old any longer. Like others before him, he had come to believe that hope is better than memory.

Ryūnosuke Akutagawa (1892–1927) was a Japanese writer of eerie tales who also went by the names of Chōkōdō Shujin and Gaki. Akutagawa's evocation of the fantastical and uncanny was unique, and much of his work still feels sui generis. He is among the most translated Japanese writers and quite a few of his 150 stories have inspired writers, mangakas, and film directors for generations. His later tales were less popular, as they lacked some of the dark, macabre intensity of his early works, but nonetheless, they are still an important part of the literary canon of Japan's Taishō era. In fact, the lurid fable of a novel, *Kappa* (1927), created a whole new creature of Japanese folklore. "Sennin" (1922), reprinted here in a new translation, is a sly, clever tale.

Sennin

(IMMORTAL)

Ryūnosuke Akutagawa

Translated by Gio Clairval

LISTEN TO ME, you all. Given that I am presently in Osaka, I would like to tell you a story that happened in this same city.

In the olden days, a man came to Osaka to find work as a servant. I do not know the man's real name, but given that he was offering to serve as a valet, legend has preserved him simply as Gonsuké, a generic appellation given to hired hands.

So Gonsuké pushed past the fluttering fabric of the *noren*, into an employment office and uttered his request to a clerk who held a long *kiseru* bamboo pipe clenched between his teeth. "You see, sir, I'm offering my services as help, but I'd like to transcend my human condition and become an immortal *sennin*, too, so I'm asking you to find me masters who could teach me the new trade as well."

The clerk was left speechless in surprise.

"Did you hear me, sir?" Gonsuké asked, and repeated his request word for word.

"I'm really sorry, believe me, but . . ." said the

clerk, who meanwhile had resumed smoking his tobacco, inhaling large puffs. "Your demand to work as a *sennin* has no precedents here. I would advise inquiring at some other office."

Visibly upset, Gonsuké shifted forward on his knees—he was wearing blue working trousers with a tiny pattern on them—moving nearer, in order to argue his case better.

"The matter is in slightly different terms. Let's see, what is written on the *noren* in your doorway? Doesn't it read '*any* placement'? This surely means that you must be able to satisfy *any* request for a job. Or maybe you have written a lie on your *noren*?" From his point of view, he had good reason to be outraged.

"That writing is by no means a lie. If you must insist on your demand to find a position as a servant, meanwhile learning to become a *sennin*, too, kindly come back tomorrow. Within this very day I shall start looking for someone who may suit your expectations."

The clerk thought this response was the only possible way to get the visitor to leave. In reality, he did not expect to find any household that could teach our man the way of the immortal *sennin*, assuming they would even hire him as a servant. No sooner had Gonsuké left than the clerk set forth toward the house of a physician who lived nearby. After explaining chapter and verse, the clerk asked, puzzled, "What do you make of this, Doctor? To whom should I turn to find, on such short notice, someone who would teach that servant to become a *sennin*?"

Upon hearing this question, even the physician seemed perplexed. He pondered for a moment, arms crossed on his chest, eyes fixed on a pine that loomed solitary in the garden. His wife, on the other hand, a quick-witted little woman known as the Old Fox did not hesitate to intrude into the conversation.

"Send him here. In a couple of years we will make a true *sennin* of him."

"Really? That would be wonderful, and you would do me a great favor indeed. In fact, I was under the impression that there were a few affinities between a physician and a *sennin*," said the naïve clerk.

Then he bowed several times before leaving, quite satisfied.

The physician looked at the clerk's retreating back and then drily addressed his wife. "What got into you that you should say such nonsense?" he scolded her. "I'm curious to see what you're going to tell that poor hick in a couple of years, when he'll start complaining that we have taught him nothing about the way of the immortal *sennin*."

Instead of apologizing, the wife burst into laughter.

"Shut up yourself. If it was up to you and your ridiculous honesty, we would have nothing to put on the table in this dog-eat-dog world." With these words, she silenced him.

The following day, as agreed, that poor hick of a Gonsuké showed up with the clerk. Maybe because he was reporting to his employers for the first time, Gonsuké wore over his *hakama* a *haori* covered in coats of arms, even though all his efforts to look his best failed to make him appear any different from an ordinary peasant. And the servant's appearance was extremely disappointing to the physician, who had been expecting someone more unusual and now, in his surprise, stared wide-eyed at the wannabe *sennin*, as if he'd been gazing at some exotic deer from India.

"Well, I'm told you wish at all costs to become a *sennin*. How did this wish come about?" he asked warily.

"There is no precise reason. Well, seeing the Osaka castle it came to me that the powerful man dwelling inside it, surely a much-revered man, will have to die sooner or later, as we all do, even the mighty and glorious, because we are fragile and ephemeral, we are nothing in this world."

"So you're willing to do anything to become a *sennin*," cut in the physician's sly wife, without wasting time.

"Precisely, ma'am. I'm willing to do anything to become a *sennin*."

"Then you'll enter into our service this same day, and you will work for twenty years. After this period, we will teach you the way of the immortal."

"Really? It's the greatest favor you can do me."

"In exchange for that, we shall not pay you any money for twenty years."

"That's all right. That's all right. I accept everything. I have no objection."

And so Gonsuké worked as a servant in the physician's house for twenty years. He drew water, cut wood, cooked, cleaned. The medicine box balancing on his shoulder, he also accompanied the doctor on his rounds. And given that he never asked for coin, he was the best servant in Japan, a true prodigy.

Twenty years passed. Gonsuké, again decked out in *haori* complete with coats of arms, stood before his masters. Dignified, he expressed his deep gratitude for being looked after during all these years.

"We have reached the point where, as you promised, you are about to reveal to me how to become a *sennin*, capable to defeat old age and death."

The physician, hearing these words, was ill at ease. That poor man had served him and his wife for twenty years without pay, and now it seemed disloyal to disclose to him that they knew nothing about the teachings allowing someone to become an immortal.

Finding no solution, the doctor looked away and quickly said: "My wife, she's the expert, and she will teach you."

The Old Fox, however, remained confident and composed.

"I shall teach you to become immortal, but you must promise that you will do everything I tell you to do, no matter how difficult it may seem. Even the impossible. Otherwise, you will not become a *sennin*, and you shall have to work for us for twenty more years, without a salary, if you wish to avoid the gods' punishment that will reduce you to ashes on the spot."

"I understand. I am ready to do anything, even the impossible."

Happy and content, he waited for the instructions.

The woman ordered, "Climb up the pine tree in the garden."

Since the Old Fox had not the slightest idea of what the teachings to become immortal entailed, she intended to order him to accomplish tasks he would invariably fail, which would entitle her to have an unpaid servant at her disposal for twenty more years.

Gonsuké, hearing her command, did not hesitate to climb up the pine.

"Higher, you must climb higher."

The woman, standing on the edge of the porch, craned her neck to gaze at Gonsuké dangling in the tree. Still he climbed. His *haori* flapped in the wind over the highest branches.

"Now release the right hand."

Gonsuké clung to a sturdy branch with his left hand and slowly released his right hand.

"The other hand, too!"

"Hey! He will fall to the ground," said her husband the doctor, joining her at the porch railing. "It's full of stones under the tree," he protested, anxious. "He won't survive his fall."

"It's not the moment to make a scene. Trust me, for once . . ." To her servant, she cried, "Come on now, release your grip entirely!"

Gonsuké hesitated. Up there, without clinging to anything, he could only fall to his death. But then he let go. In no time, he and his *haori* broke off the pine tree.

And then, and then, instead of plummeting down, he remained mysteriously suspended in midair, stock-still, like a marionette in the morning sky.

"Oh, thank you, thank you so much! I'm a real *sennin* now."

He bowed ceremoniously, floating in the blue sky wrapped in silence, and then, taking gentle steps, he rose higher until he disappeared behind the clouds.

Strangely enough, no one heard about the physician and his wife ever again. The pine tree remained in their garden for a long time, up to the day when one Yodoya Tatsugoro, who wished to enjoy the sight of the branches covered in snow, had the tree uprooted and transported into his own garden, and by that time the pine had grown very, very tall.

Eric Rücker Eddison (1882–1945), who wrote fantasy as E. R. Eddison, was an English author. He is best known for his creation of secondary worlds, such as Zimiamvia, the setting for his Zimiamvian trilogy. His work was admired by J. R. R. Tolkien and C. S. Lewis, and he often joined them as a visitor to the Inklings group, an informal gathering of writers who enjoyed talking about fantasy literature. Later writers, such as Michael Moorcock and Ursula K. Le Guin, would also claim his work as a source of inspiration. Eddison was fascinated by Icelandic sagas and had translated many stories. This is an excerpt from his most famous novel, *The Worm Ouroboros*.

Koshtra Pivrarcha

(EXCERPT FROM *THE WORM OUROBOROS*)

E. R. Eddison

OF THE COMING OF THE *Lords of Demonland to Morna Moruna, whence they beheld the Zimiamvian Mountains, seen also by Gro in years gone by; and of the wonders seen by them and perils undergone and deeds done in their attempt on Koshtra Pivrarcha, the which alone of all Earth's mountains looketh down upon Koshtra Belorn; and none shall ascend up into Koshtra Belorn that hath not first looked down upon her.*

Now it is to be said of Lord Juss and Lord Brandoch Daha that they, finding themselves parted from their people in the fog, and utterly unable to find them, when the last sound of battle had died away wiped and put up their bloody swords and set forth at a great pace eastward. Only Mivarsh fared with them of all their following. His lips were drawn back a little, showing his teeth, but he carried himself proudly as one who being resolved to die walks with a quiet mind to his destruction. Day after day they journeyed, sometimes in clear weather, sometimes in mist or sleet, over the changeless desert, without a landmark, save here a little sluggish river, or here a piece of rising ground, or a pond, or a clump of rocks: small things which faded from sight amid the waste ere they were passed by a half-mile's distance. So was each day like yesterday, drawing to a morrow like to it again. And always fear walked at their heel and sat beside them sleeping: clanking of wings heard above the wind, a brooding hush of menace in the sunshine, and noises out of the void of darkness as of teeth chattering. So came they on the twentieth day to Morna Moruna, and stood at even in the sorrowful twilight by the little round castle, silent on Omprenne Edge.

From their feet the cliffs dropped sheer.

Strange it was, standing on that frozen lip of the Moruna, as on the limit of the world, to gaze southward on a land of summer, and to breathe faint summer airs blowing up from blossoming trees and flower-clad alps. In the depths a carpet of huge tree-tops clothed a vast stretch of country, through the midst of which, seen here and there in a bend of silver among the woods, the Bhavinan bore the waters of a thousand secret mountain solitudes down to an unknown sea. Beyond the river the deep woods, blue with distance, swelled to feathery hilltops with some sharper-featured loftier heights bodying cloudily beyond them. The Demons strained their eyes searching the curtain of mystery behind and above those foot-hills; but the great peaks, like great ladies, shrouded themselves against their curious gaze, and no glimpse was shown them of the snows.

Surely to be in Morna Moruna was to be in the death chamber of some once lovely presence. Stains of fire were on the walls. The fair gallery of open wood-work that ran above the main hall was burnt through and partly fallen in ruin, the blackened ends of the beams that held it jutting blindly in the gap. Among the wreck of carved chairs and benches, broken and worm-eaten, some shreds of figured tapestries rotted, the home now of beetles and spiders. Patches of colour, faded lines, mildewed and damp with the corruption of two hundred years, lingered to be the memorials, like the mummied skeleton of a king's daughter long ago untimely dead, of sweet gracious paintings on the walls. Five nights and five days the Demons and Mivarsh dwelt in Morna Moruna, inured to portents till they marked them as little as men mark swallows at their window. In the still night were flames seen, and flying forms dim in the moonlit air; and in moonless nights unstarred, moans heard and gibbering accents: prodigies beside their beds, and ridings in the sky, and fleshless fingers plucking at Juss unseen when he went forth to make question of the night.

Cloud and mist abode ever in the south, and only the foot-hills showed of the great ranges beyond Bhavinan. But on the evening of the sixth day before Yule, it being the nineteenth of December when Betelgeuze stands at midnight on the meridian, a wind blew out of the north-west with changing fits of sleet and sunshine. Day was fading as they stood above the cliff. All the forest land was blue with shades of approaching night: the river was dull silver: the wooded heights afar mingled their outlines with the towers and banks of turbulent deep blue vapour that hurtled in ceaseless passage through the upper air. Suddenly a window opened in the clouds to a space of clean wan wind-swept sky high above the shaggy hills. Surely Juss caught his breath in that moment, to see those deathless ones where they shone pavilioned in the pellucid air, far, vast, and lonely, most like to creatures of unascended heaven, of wind and of fire all compact, too pure to have aught of the gross elements of earth or water. It was as if the rose-red light of sundown had been frozen to crystal and these hewn from it to abide to everlasting, strong and unchangeable amid the welter of earthborn mists below and tumultuous sky above them. The rift ran wider, eastward and westward, opening on more peaks and sunset-kindled snows. And a rainbow leaning to the south was like a sword of glory across the vision.

Motionless, like hawks staring from that high place of prospect, Juss and Brandoch Daha looked on the mountains of their desire.

Juss spake, haltingly as one talking in a dream. "The sweet smell, this gusty wind, the very stone thy foot standeth on: I know them all before. There's not a night since we sailed out of Lookinghaven that I have not beheld in sleep these mountains and known their names."

"Who told thee their names?" asked Lord Brandoch Daha.

"My dream," Juss answered. "And first I dreamed it in mine own bed in Galing when I came home from guesting with thee last June. And they be true dreams that are dreamed there." And he said, "Seest thou where the foothills part to a dark valley that runneth deep into the chain, and the mountains are bare to view from crown to foot? Mark where, beyond the nearer range, bleak-visaged precipices, cobweb-streaked with huge snow corridors, rise to a rampart where the rock towers stand against the sky. This is the great ridge of Koshtra Pivrarcha, and the loftiest of those spires his secret mountaintop."

As he spoke, his eye followed the line of the eastern ridge, where the towers, like dark gods going down from heaven, plunge to a parapet which runs level above a curtain of avalanche-fluted snow. He fell silent as his gaze rested on the sister peak that east of the gap flamed skyward in wild cliffs to an airy snowy summit, soft-lined as a maiden's cheek, purer than dew, lovelier than a dream.

While they looked the sunset fires died out upon the mountains, leaving only pale hues of death and silence. "If thy dream," said Lord Brandoch Daha, "conducted thee down this Edge, over the Bhavinan, through yonder woods and hills, up through the leagues of ice and frozen rock that stand betwixt us and the main ridge, up by the right road to the topmost snows of Koshtra Belorn: that were a dream indeed."

"All this it showed me," said Juss, "up to the lowest rocks of the great north buttress of Koshtra Pivrarcha, that must first be scaled by him that would go up to Koshtra Belorn. But beyond those rocks not even a dream hath ever climbed. Ere the light fades, I'll show thee our pass over the nearer range." He pointed where a glacier crawled betwixt shadowy walls down from a torn snow-field that rose steeply to a saddle. East of it stood two white peaks, and west of it a sheer-faced and long-backed mountain like a citadel, squat and dark beneath the wild sky-line of Koshtra Pivrarcha that hung in air beyond it.

"The Zia valley," said Juss, "that runneth into Bhavinan. There lieth our way: under that dark bastion called by the Gods Tetrachnampf."

On the morrow Lord Brandoch Daha came to Mivarsh Faz and said, "It is needful that this day we go down from Omprenne Edge. I would for no sake leave thee on the Moruna, but 'tis no walking matter to descend this wall. Art thou a cragsman?"

"I was born," answered he, "in the high valley of Perarshyn by the upper waters of the Beirun in Impland. There boys scarce toddle ere they can climb a rock. This climb affrights me not, nor those mountains. But the land is unknown and terrible, and many loathly ones inhabit it, ghosts and eaters of men. O devils transmarine, and my friends, is it not enough? Let us turn again, and if the Gods save our lives we shall be famous for ever, that came unto Morna Moruna and returned alive."

But Juss answered and said, "O Mivarsh Faz, know that not for fame are we come on this journey. Our greatness already shadoweth all the world, as a great cedar tree spreading his shadow in a garden; and this enterprise, mighty though it be, shall add to our glory only so much as thou mightest add to these forests of the Bhavinan by planting of one more tree. But so it is, that the great King of Witchland, practising in darkness in his royal palace of Carcë such arts of gram-marie and sendings magical as the world hath not been grieved with until now, sent an ill thing to take my brother, the Lord Goldry Bluszco, who is dear to me as mine own soul. And They that dwell in secret sent me word in a dream, bidding me, if I would have tidings of my dear brother, inquire in Koshtra Belorn. Therefore, O Mivarsh, go with us if thou wilt, but if thou wilt not, why, fare thee well. For nought but my death shall stay me from going thither."

And Mivarsh, bethinking him that if the mantichores of the mountains should devour him along with those two lords, that were yet a kindlier fate than all alone to abide those things he wist of on the Moruna, put on the rope, and after commending himself to the protection of his gods followed Lord Brandoch Daha down the rotten slopes of rock and frozen earth at the head of a gully leading down the cliff.

For all that they were early afoot, yet was it high noon ere they were off the rocks. For the peril of falling stones drove them out from the gully's bed first on to the eastern buttress and after, when that grew too sheer, back to the western wall. And in an hour or twain the gully's bed grew shallow and it narrowed to an end, whence Brandoch Daha gazed between his feet to where, a few spear's lengths below, the smooth slabs curved downward out of sight and the eye leapt straight from their clean-cut edge to shimmering tree-tops that showed tiny as mosses beyond the unseen gulf of air. So they rested awhile; then returning a little up the gully forced a way out on to the face and made a hazardous traverse to a mew gully westward of the first, and so at last plunged down a long fan of scree and rested on soft fine turf at the foot of the cliffs.

Little mountain gentians grew at their feet; the pathless forest lay like the sea below them; before them the mountains of the Zia stood supreme: the white gables of Islargyn, the lean dark finger of Tetrachnampf nan Tshark lying back above the Zia Pass pointing to the sky, and west of it, jutting above the valley, the square bastion of Tetrachnampf nan Tsurm. The greater mountains were for the most part sunk behind this nearer range, but Koshtra Belorn still towered above the Pass. As a queen looking down from her high window, so she overlooked those green woods sleeping in the noon-day; and on her forehead was beauty like a star. Behind them where they sat, the escarpment reared back in cramped perspective, a pile of massive buttresses cleft with ravines leading upward from that land of leaves and waters to the hidden wintry flats of the Moruna.

That night they slept on the fell under the stars, and next day, going down into the woods, came at dusk to an open glade by the waters of the broad-bosomed Bhavinan. The turf was like a cushion, a place for elves to dance in. The far bank full half a mile away was wooded to the water with silver birches, dainty as mountain nymphs, their limbs gleaming through the twilight, their reflections quivering in the depths of the mighty river. In the high air day lingered yet, a faint warmth tingeing the great outlines of the mountains, and westward up the river the young moon stooped above the trees. East of the glade a

little wooded eminence, no higher than a house, ran back from the river bank, and in its shoulder a hollow cave.

"How smiles it to thee?" said Juss. "Be sure we shall find no better place than this thou seest to dwell in until the snows melt and we may on. For though it be summer all the year round in this fortunate valley, it is winter on the great hills, and until the spring we were mad to essay our enterprise."

"Why then," said Brandoch Daha, "turn we shepherds awhile. Thou shalt pipe to me, and I'll foot thee measures shall make the dryads think they ne'er went to school. And Mivarsh shall be a goat-foot god to chase them; for to tell thee truth country wenches are long grown tedious to me. O, 'tis a sweet life. But ere we fall to it, bethink thee, O Juss: time marcheth, and the world waggeth: what goeth forward in Demonland till summer be come and we home again?"

"Also my heart is heavy because of my brother Spitfire," said Juss. "Oh, 'twas an ill storm, and ill delays."

"Away with vain regrettings," said Lord Brandoch Daha. "For thy sake and thy brother's fared I on this journey, and it is known to thee that never yet stretched I out mine hand upon aught that I have not taken it, and had my will of it."

So they made their dwelling in that cave beside deep-eddying Bhavinan, and before that cave they ate their Yule feast, the strangest they had eaten all the days of their lives: seated, not as of old, on their high seats of ruby or of opal, but on mossy banks where daisies slept and creeping thyme; lighted not by the charmed escarbuncle of the high presence chamber in Galing, but by the shifting beams of a brushwood fire that shone not on those pillars crowned with monsters that were the wonder of the world but on the mightier pillars of the sleeping beechwoods. And in place of that feigned heaven of jewels self-effulgent beneath the golden canopy at Galing, they ate pavilioned under a charmed summer night, where the great stars of winter, Orion, Sirius, and the Little Dog, were raised up near the zenith, yielding their known courses in the southern sky to Canopus and the strange stars of the south. When the trees spake, it was not with their winter voice of bare boughs creaking, but with whisper of leaves and beetles droning in the fragrant air. The bushes were white with blossom, not with hoar-frost, and the dim white patches under the trees were not snow, but wild lilies and wood anemones sleeping in the night.

All the creatures of the forest came to that feast, for they were without fear, having never looked upon the face of man. Little tree-apes, and popinjays, and titmouses, and coalmouses, and wrens, and gentle round-eyed lemurs, and rabbits, and badgers, and dormice, and pied squirrels, and beavers from the streams, and storks, and ravens, and bustards, and wombats, and the spider-monkey with her baby at her breast: all these came to gaze with curious eye upon those travellers. And not these alone, but fierce beasts of the woods and wildernesses: the wild buffalo, the wolf, the tiger with monstrous paws, the bear, the fiery-eyed unicorn, the elephant, the lion and she-lion in their majesty, came to behold them in the firelight in that quiet glade.

"It seems we hold court in the woods to-night," said Lord Brandoch Daha. "It is very pleasant. Yet hold thee ready with me to put some fire-brands amongst 'em if need befall. 'Tis likely some of these great beasts are little schooled in court ceremonies."

Juss answered, "And thou lovest me, do no such thing. There lieth this curse upon all this land of the Bhavinan, that whoso, whether he be man or beast, slayeth in this land or doeth here any deed of violence, there cometh down a curse upon him that in that instant must destroy and blast him for ever off the face of the earth. Therefore it was I took away from Mivarsh his bow and arrows when we came down from Omprenne Edge, lest he should kill game for us and so a worse thing befall him."

Mivarsh harkened not, but sat all a-quake, looking intently on a crocodile that came ponderously out upon the bank. And now he began to scream with terror, crying, "Save me! let me fly! give me my weapons! It was foretold me by a wise woman that a cocadrill-serpent must devour me at last!" Whereat the beasts drew back uneasily, and the crocodile, his small eyes wide, startled by Mivarsh's cries and violent gestures, lurched with what speed he might back into the water.

Now in that place Lord Juss and Lord Brandoch Daha and Mivarsh Faz abode for four moons' space. Nothing they lacked of meat and drink, for the beasts of the forest, finding them well disposed, brought them of their store. Moreover, there came flying from the south, about the ending of the year, a martlet which alighted in Juss's bosom and said to him, "The gentle Queen Sophonisba, fosterling of the Gods, had news of your coming. And because she knoweth you both mighty men of your hands and high of heart, therefore by me she sent you greeting."

Juss said, "O little martlet, we would see thy Queen face to face, and thank her."

"Ye must thank her," said the bird, "in Koshtra Belorn."

Brandoch Daha said, "That shall we fulfil. Thither only do our thoughts intend."

"Your greatness," said the martlet, "must approve that word. And know that it is easier to lay under you all the world in arms than to ascend up afoot into that mountain."

"Thy wings were too weak to lift me, else I'd borrow them," said Brandoch Daha.

But the martlet answered, "Not the eagle that flieth against the sun may alight on Koshtra Belorn. No foot may tread her, save of those blessed ones to whom the Gods gave leave ages ago, till they become that the patient years await: men like unto the Gods in beauty and in power, who of their own might and main, unholpen by magic arts, shall force a passage up to her silent snows."

Brandoch Daha laughed. "Not the eagle?" he cried, "but thou, little flitter-jack?"

"Nought that hath feet," said the martlet. "I have none."

The Lord Brandoch Daha took it tenderly in his hand and held it high in the air, looking to the high lands in the south. The birches swaying by the Bhavinan were not more graceful nor the distant mountain-crags behind them more untameable to behold than he. "Fly to thy Queen," he said, "and say thou spakest with Lord Juss beside the Bhavinan and with Lord Brandoch Daha of Demonland. Say unto her that we be they that were for to come; and that we, of our own might and main, ere spring be well turned summer, will come up to her in Koshtra Belorn to thank her for her gracious sendings."

Now when it was April, and the sun moving among the signs of heaven was about departing out of Aries and entering into Taurus, and the melting of the snows in the high mountains had swollen all the streams to spate, filling the mighty river so that he brimmed his banks and swept by like a tide-race, Lord Juss said, "Now is the season propitious for our crossing of the flood of Bhavinan and setting forth into the mountains."

"Willingly," said Lord Brandoch Daha. "But shall's walk it, or swim it, or take to us wings? To me, that have many a time swum back and forth over Thunderfirth to whet mine appetite ere I brake my fast, 'tis a small matter of this river stream howso swift it runneth. But with our harness and weapons and all our gear, that were far other matter."

"Is it for nought we are grown friends with them that do inhabit these woods?" said Juss. "The crocodile shall bear us over Bhavinan for the asking."

"It is an ill fish," said Mivarsh; "and it sore dislikes me."

"Then here thou must abide," said Brandoch Daha. "But be not dismayed, I will go with thee. The fish may bear us both at a draught and not founder."

"It was a wise woman foretold it me," answered Mivarsh, "that such a kind of serpent must be my bane. Yet be it according to your will."

So they whistled them up the crocodile; and first the Lord Juss fared over Bhavinan, riding on the back of that serpent with all his gear and weapons of war, and landed several hundred paces down stream for the stream was very strong; and thereafter the crocodile returning to the north bank took the Lord Brandoch Daha and Mivarsh Faz and put them across in like manner. Mivarsh put on a gallant face, but rode as near the tail as might be, fingering certain herbs from his wallet that were good against serpents, his lips moving in urgent supplication to his gods. When they were come ashore they thanked the crocodile and bade him farewell and went their way swiftly through the woods. And Mivarsh, as one new loosed from prison, went before them with a light step, singing and snapping his fingers.

Now had they for three days or four a devious journey through the foot-hills, and thereafter made their dwelling for forty days' space in the Zia valley, above the gorges. Here the valley widens to a flat-floored amphitheatre, and lean limestone crags tower heavenward on every side. High in the south, couched above great gray moraines, the Zia glacier, wrinkle-backed like some dragon survived out of the elder chaos, thrusts his snout into the valley. Here out of his caves of ice the young river thunders, casting up a spray where rainbows hover in bright weather. The air blows sharp from the glacier, and alpine flowers and shrubs feed on the sunlight.

Here they gathered them good store of food. And every morning they were afoot before the sunrise, to ascend the mountains and make sure their practice ere they should attempt the greater peaks. So they explored all the spurs of Tetrachnampf and Islargyn, and those peaks themselves; the rock peaks of the lower Nuanner range overlooking Bhavinan; the snow peaks east of Islargyn: Avsek, Kiurmsur, Myrsu, Byrshnargyn, and Borch Mehephtharsk, loftiest of the range, by all his ridges, dwelling a week on the moraines of the Mehephtharsk glacier above the upland valley of Foana; and westward the dolomite group of Burdjazarshra and the great wall of Shilack.

Now were their muscles by these exercises grown like bands of iron, and they hardy as mountain bears and sure of foot as mountain goats. So on the ninth day of May they crossed the Zia Pass and camped on the rocks under the south wall of Tetrachnampf nan Tshark. The sun went down, like blood, in a cloudless sky. On either hand and before them, the snows stretched blue and silent. The air of those high snowfields was bitter cold. A league and more to the south a line of black cliffs bounded the glacier-basin. Over that black wall, twelve miles away, Koshtra Belorn and Koshtra Pivrarcha towered against an opal heaven.

While they supped in the fading light, Juss said, "The wall thou seest is called the Bamers of Emshir. Though over it lieth the straight way to Koshtra Pivrarcha, yet is it not our way, but an ill way. For, first, that barrier hath till now been held unclimbable, and so proven even by half-gods that alone assayed it."

"I await not thy second reason," said Brandoch Daha. "Thou hast had thy way until now, and now thou shalt give me mine in this, to come with me to-morrow and show how thou and I make of such barriers a puff of smoke if they stand in the path between us and our fixed ends."

"Were it only this," answered Juss, "I would not gainsay thee. But not senseless rocks alone are we set to deal with if we take this road. Seest thou where the Barriers end in the east against yonder monstrous pyramid of tumbled crags and hanging glaciers that shuts out our prospect east-away? Menksur men call it, but in heaven it hath a more dreadful name: Ela Mantissera, which is to say, the Bed of the Mantichores. O Brandoch Daha, I will climb with thee what unscaled cliff thou list, and I will fight with thee against the most grisfullest beasts that ever grazed by the Tartarian streams. But both these things in one moment of time, that were a rash part and a foolish."

But Brandoch Daha laughed, and answered him, "To nought else may I liken thee, O Juss, but to the sparrow-camel. To whom they said, 'Fly,' and it answered, 'I cannot, for I am a camel'; and when they said, 'Carry,' it answered, 'I cannot, for I am a bird.'"

"Wilt thou egg me on so much?" said Juss.

"Ay," said Brandoch Daha, "if thou wilt be assish."

"Wilt thou quarrel?" said Juss.

"Thou knowest me," said Brandoch Daha.

"Well," said Juss, "thy counsel hath been right once and saved us, for nine times that it hath been wrong, and my counsel saved thee from an evil end. If ill behap us, it shall be set down that it had from thy peevish will original." And they wrapped them in their cloaks and slept.

On the morrow they rose betimes and set forth south across the snows that were crisp and hard from the frosts of the night. The Barriers, as it were but a stone's-throw removed, stood black before them; starlight swallowed up size and distance that showed only by walking, as still they walked and still that wall seemed no nearer nor no larger. Twice and thrice they dipped into a valley or crossed a raised-up fold of the glacier; till they stood at break of day below the smooth blank wall frozen and bleak, with never a ledge in sight great enough to bear snow, barring their passage southward.

They halted and ate and scanned the wall before them. And ill to do with it seemed. So they searched for an ascent, and found at last a spot where the glacier swelled higher, a mile or less from the western shoulder of Ela Mantissera. Here the cliff was but four or five hundred feet high; yet smooth enow and ill enow to look on; yet their likeliest choice.

Some while it was ere they might get a footing on that wall, but at length Brandoch Daha, standing on Juss's shoulder, found him a hold where no hold showed from below, and with great travail fought a passage up the rock to a stance some hundred feet above them, whence sitting sure on a broad ledge great enough to hold six or seven folk at a time he played up Lord Juss on the rope and after him Mivarsh. An hour and a half it cost them for that short climb.

"The north-east buttress of Ill Stack was children's gruel to this," said Lord Juss.

"There's more aloft," said Lord Brandoch Daha, lying back against the precipice, his hands clasped behind his head, his feet a-dangle over the ledge. "In thine ear, Juss: I would not go first on the rope again on such a pitch for all the wealth of Impland."

"Wilt repent and return?" said Juss.

"If thou'lt be last down," he answered. "If not, I'd liever risk what waits untried above us. If it prove worse, I am confirmed atheist."

Lord Juss leaned out, holding by the rock with his right hand, scanning the wall beside and above them. An instant he hung so, then drew back. His square jaw was set, and his teeth glinted under his dark moustachios something fiercely, as a thunder-beam betwixt dark sky and sea in a night of thunder. His nostrils widened, as of a war-horse at the call of battle; his eyes were like the violet levin-brand, and all his body hardened like a bowstring drawn as he grasped his sharp sword and pulled it forth grating and singing from its sheath.

Brandoch Daha sprang afoot and drew his sword, Zeldornius's loom. "What stirreth?" he cried. "Thou look'st ghastly. That look thou hadst when thou tookest the helm and our prows swung westward toward Kartadza Sound, and the fate of Demonland and all the world beside hung in thine hand for wail or bliss."

"There's little sword-room," said Juss. And again he looked forth eastward and upward along the cliff. Brandoch Daha looked over his shoulder. Mivarsh took his bow and set an arrow on the string.

"It hath scented us down the wind," said Brandoch Daha.

Small time was there to ponder. Swinging from hold to hold across the dizzy precipice, as an ape swingeth from bough to bough, the beast drew near. The shape of it was as a lion, but bigger and taller, the colour a dull red, and it had prickles lancing out behind, as of a porcupine; its face a man's face, if aught so hideous might be conceived of human kind, with staring eye-balls, low wrinkled brow, elephant ears, some wispy mangy likeness of a lion's mane, huge bony chaps, brown blood-stained gubber-tushes grinning betwixt bristly lips. Straight for the ledge it made, and as they braced them to receive it,

with a great swing heaved a man's height above them and leaped down upon their ledge from aloft betwixt Juss and Brandoch Daha ere they were well aware of its changed course. Brandoch Daha smote at it a great swashing blow and cut off its scorpion tail; but it clawed Juss's shoulder, smote down Mivarsh, and charged like a lion upon Brandoch Daha, who, missing his footing on the narrow edge of rock, fell backwards a great fall, clear of the cliff, down to the snow an hundred feet beneath them.

As it craned over, minded to follow and make an end of him, Juss smote it in the hinder parts and on the ham, shearing away the flesh from the thigh bone, and his sword came with a clank against the brazen claws of its foot. So with a horrid bellow it turned on Juss, rearing like a horse; and it was three heads greater than a tall man in stature when it reared aloft, and the breadth of its chest like the chest of a bear. The stench of its breath choked Juss's mouth and his senses sickened, but he slashed it athwart the belly, a great round-armed blow, cutting open its belly so that the guts fell out. Again he hewed at it, but missed, and his sword came against the rock, and was shivered into pieces. So when that noisome vermin fell forward on him roaring like a thousand lions, Juss grappled with it, running in beneath its body and clasping it and thrusting his arms into its inward parts, to rip out its vitals if so he might. So close he grappled it that it might not reach him with its murthering teeth, but its claws sliced off the flesh from his left knee downward to the ankle bone, and it fell on him and crushed him on the rock, breaking in the bones of his breast. And Juss, for all his bitter pain and torment, and for all he was well nigh stifled by the sore stink of the creature's breath and the stink of its blood and puddings blubbering about his face and breast, yet by his great strength wrastled with that fell and filthy man-eater. And ever he thrust his right hand, armed with the hilt and stump of his broken sword, yet deeper into its belly until he searched out its heart and did his will upon it, slicing the heart asunder like a lemon and severing and tearing all the great vessels about the heart until the blood gushed about him like a spring. And like a caterpillar the beast curled up and straightened out in its death spasms, and it rolled and fell from that ledge, a great fall, and lay by Brandoch Daha, the foulest beside the fairest of all earthly beings, reddening the pure snow with its blood. And the spines that grew on the hinder parts of the beast went out and in like the sting of a new-dead wasp that goes out and in continually. It fell not clean to the snow, as by the care of heaven was fallen Brandoch Daha, but smote an edge of rock near the bottom, and that strook out its brains. There it lay in its blood, gaping to the sky.

Now was Juss stretched face downward as one dead, on that giddy edge of rock. Mivarsh had saved him, seizing him by the foot and drawing him back to safety when the beast fell. A sight of terror he was, clotted from head to toe with the beast's blood and his own. Mivarsh bound his wounds and laid him tenderly as he might back against the cliff, then peered down a long while to know if the beast were dead indeed.

When he had gazed downward earnestly so long that his eyes watered with the strain, and still the beast stirred not, Mivarsh prostrated himself and made supplication saying aloud, "O Shlimphli, Shiamphi, and Shebamri, gods of my father and my father's fathers, have pity of your child, if as I dearly trow your power extendeth over this far and forbidden country no less than over Impland, where your child hath ever worshipped you in your holy places, and taught my sons and my daughters to revere your holy names, and made an altar in mine house, pointed by the stars in manner ordained from of old, and offered up my seventh-born son and was minded to offer up my seventh-born daughter thereon, in meekness and righteousness according to your holy will; but this I might not do, since you vouchsafed me not a seventh daughter, but six only. Wherefore I beseech you, of your holy names' sake, strengthen my hand to let down this my companion safely by the rope, and thereafter bring me safely down from this rock, howsoever he be a devil and an unbeliever; O save his life, save both their lives. For I am sure that if these be not saved alive, never shall your child return, but in this far land starve and die like an insect that dureth but for a day."

So prayed Mivarsh. And belike the high Gods were moved to pity of his innocence, hearing him so cry for help unto his mumbo-jumbos, where no help was; and belike they were not minded that those lords of Demonland should there die evilly before their time, unhonoured, unsung. Howsoever, Mivarsh arose and made fast the rope about Lord Juss, knotting it cunningly beneath the arms that it might not tighten in the lowering and crush his breast and ribs, and so with much ado lowered him down to the foot of the cliff. Thereafter came Mivarsh himself down that perilous wall, and albeit for many a time he thought his bane was upon him, yet by good cragsmanship spurred by cold necessity he gat him down at last. Being down, he delayed not to minister to his companions, who came to themselves with heavy groaning. But when Lord Juss was come to himself he did his healing art both on himself and on Lord Brandoch Daha, so that in a while they were able to stand upon their feet, albeit something stiff and weary and like to vomit. And it was by then the third hour past noon.

While they rested, beholding where the beast mantichora lay in his blood, Juss spake and said, "It is to be said of thee, O Brandoch Daha, that thou to-day hast done both the worst and the best. The worst, when thou wast so stubborn set to fare upon this climb which hath come within a little of spilling both thee and me. The best, whenas thou didst smite off his tail. Was that by policy or by chance?"

"Why," said he, "I was never so poor a man of my hands that I need turn braggart. 'Twas handiest to my sword, and it disliked me to see it wagging. Did aught lie on it?"

"The sting of his tail," answered Juss, "were competent for thine or my destruction, and it grazed but our little finger."

"Thou speakest like a book," said Brandoch Daha. "Else might I scarce know thee for my noble friend, being betrayed with blood as a buffalo with mire. Be not angry with me, if I am most at ease to windward of thee."

Juss laughed. "If thou be not too nice," he said, "go to the beast and dabble thyself too with the blood of his bowels. Nay, I mock not; it is most needful. These be enemies not of mankind only, but each of other; walking every one by himself, loathing every one his kind living or dead, so that in all the world there abideth nought loathlier unto them than the blood of their own kind, the least smell whereof they do abhor as a mad dog abhorreth water. And 'tis a clinging smell. So are we after this encounter most sure against them."

That night they camped at the foot of a spur of Avsek, and set forth at dawn down the long valley eastward. All day they heard the roaring of mantichores from the desolate flanks of Ela Mantissera that showed now no longer as a pyramid but as a long-backed screen, making the southern rampart of that valley. It was ill going, and they somewhat shaken. Day was nigh gone when beyond the eastern slopes of Ela they came where the white waters of the river they followed thundered together with a black water rushing down from the south-west. Below, the river ran east in a wide valley dropping afar to tree-clad depths. In the fork above the watersmeet the rocks enclosed a high green knoll, like some fragment of a kindlier clime that over-lived into an age of ruin.

"Here, too," said Juss, "my dream walked with me. And if it be ill crossing there where this stream breaketh into a dozen branching cataracts a little above the watersmeet, yet well I think 'tis our only crossing." So, ere the light should fade, they crossed that perilous edge above the waterfalls, and slept on the green knoll.

That knoll Juss named Throstlegarth, after a thrush that waked them next morning, singing in a little wind-stunted mountain thorn that grew among the rocks. Strangely sounded that homely song on the cold mountain side, under the unhallowed heights of Ela, close to the confines of those enchanted snows which guard Koshtra Belorn.

No sight of the high mountains had they from Throstlegarth, nor, for a long while, from the bed of that straight steep glen of the black waters up which now their journey lay. Rugged spurs and buttresses shut them in. High on the left bank above the cataracts they made their way, buffeted by the wind that leaped and charged among the crags, their ears sated with the roaring sound of waters, their eyes filled with the spray blown upward. And Mivarsh followed after them. Silent they fared, for the way was steep and in such a wind and such a noise of torrents a man must shout lustily if he would be heard. Very desolate was that valley, having a dark aspect and a ghastful, such as a man might look for in the infernal glens of Pyriphlegethon or Acheron. No living thing they saw, save at whiles high above them an eagle sailing down the wind, and once a beast's form running in the hollow mountain side. This stood at gaze, lifting up its foul human platter-face with glittering eyes bloody and great as saucers; scented its fellow's blood, started, and fled among the crags.

So fared they for the space of three hours, and so, coming suddenly round a shoulder of the hill, stood on the upper threshold of that glen at the gates of a flat upland valley. Here they beheld a sight to darken all earth's glories and strike dumb all her singers with its grandeur. Framed in the crags of the hillsides, canopied by blue heaven, Koshtra Pivrarcha stood before them. So huge he was that even here at six miles' distance the eye might not at a glance behold him, but must sweep back and forth as over a broad landscape from the ponderous roots of the mountain where they sprang black and sheer from the glacier, up the vast face, where buttress was piled upon buttress and tower upon tower in a blinding radiance of ice-hung precipice and snow-filled gully, to the lone heights where like spears menacing high heaven the white teeth of the summit-ridge cleft the sky. From right to left he filled nigh a quarter of the heavens, from the graceful peak of Ailinon looking over his western shoulder, to where on the east the snowy slopes of Jalchi shut in the prospect, hiding Koshtra Belorn.

They camped that evening on the left moraine

of the High Glacier of Temarm. Long spidery streamers of cloud, filmy as the gauze of a lady's veil, blew eastward from the spires on the ridge, signs of wild weather aloft.

Juss said, "Glassy clear is the air. That forerunneth not fair weather."

"Well, time shall wait for us if need be," said Brandoch Daha. "So mightily my desire crieth unto me from those horns of ice that, having once looked on them, I had as lief die as leave them unclimbed. But of thee, O Juss, I make some marvel. Thou wast bidden inquire in Koshtra Belorn, and sure she were easier won than Koshtra Pivrarcha, going behind Jalchi by the snowfields and so avoiding her great western cliffs."

"There is a saw in Impland," answered Juss, "'Ware of a tall wife.' Even so there lieth a curse on any that shall attempt Koshtra Belorn that hath not first looked down upon her; and he shall have his death or ever he have his will. And from one point only of earth may a man look down on Koshtra Belorn; and 'tis from yonder unascended tooth of ice where thou seest the last beam burn. For that is the topmost pinnacle of Koshtra Pivrarcha. And it is the highest point of the stablished earth."

They were silent a minute's space. Then Juss spake: "Thou wast ever greatest amongst us as a mountaineer. Which way likes thee best for our climbing up him?"

"O Juss," said Brandoch Daha, "on ice and snow thou art my master. Therefore give me thy rede. For mine own choice and pleasure, I have settled it this hour and more: namely to ascend into the gap between the two mountains, and thence turn westward up the east ridge of Pivrarcha."

"It is the fearsomest climb to look on," said Juss, "and belike the grandest, and for both counts I had wagered it thy choice. That gap hight the Gates of Zimiamvia. It, and the Koshtra glacier that runneth up to it, lieth under the weird I told thee of. It were our death to adventure there ere we had looked down upon Koshtra Belorn; which done, the charm is broke for us, and from that time forth it needeth but our own

might and skill and a high heart to accomplish whatsoever we desire."

"Why then, the great north buttress," cried Brandoch Daha. "So shall she not behold us as we climb, until we come forth on the highest tooth and overlook her and tame her to our will."

So they supped and slept. But the wind cried among the crags all night long, and in the morning snow and sleet blotted out the mountains. All day the storm held, and in a lull they struck camp and came down again to Throstlegarth, and there abode nine days and nine nights in wind and rain and battering hail.

On the tenth day the weather abated, and they went up and crossed the glacier and lodged them in a cave in the rock at the foot of the great north buttress of Koshtra Pivrarcha. At dawn Juss and Brandoch Daha went forth to survey the prospect. They crossed the mouth of the steep snow-choked valley that ran up to the main ridge betwixt Ashnilan on the west and Koshtra Pivrarcha on the east, rounded the base of Ailinon, and climbed from the west to a snow saddle some three thousand feet up the ridge of that mountain, whence they might view the buttress and choose their way for their attempt.

"'Tis a two days' journey to the top," said Lord Brandoch Daha. "If night on the ridge freeze us not to death, I dread no other hindrance. That black rib that riseth half a mile above our camp, shall take us clean up to the crest of the buttress, striking it above the great tower at the northern end. If the rocks be like those we camped on, hard as diamond and rough as a sponge, they shall not fail us but by our own neglect. As I live, I ne'er saw their like for climbing."

"So far, well," said Juss.

"Above," said Brandoch Daha, "I'd drive thee a chariot until we come to the first great kick o' the ridge. That must we round, or ne'er go further, and on this side it showeth ill enough, for the rocks shelve outward. If they be iced, there's work indeed. Beyond that, I'll prophesy nought, O Juss, for I can see nought clear save that the ridge is hacked into clefts and steeples. How we may overcome them must be put to the proof. It is too high and too far to know. This only: where we would go, there have we gone until now. And by that ridge lieth, if any way there lieth, the way to this mountain top that we crossed the world to climb."

Next day with the first paling of the skies they arose all three and set forth southward over the crisp snows. They roped at the foot of the glacier that came down from the saddle, some five thousand feet above them, where the main ridge dips between Ashnilan and Koshtra Pivrarcha. Ere the brighter stars were swallowed in the light of morning they were cutting their way among the labyrinthine towers and chasms of the ice-fall. Soon the new daylight flooded the snowfields of the High Glacier of Temarm, dyeing them green and saffron and palest rose. The snows of Islargyn glowed far away in the north to the right of the white dome of Emshir. Ela Mantissera blocked the view north-eastward. The buttress that bounded their valley on the east plunged it in shadow blue as a summer sea. High on the other side the great twin peaks of Ailinon and Ashnilan, roused by the warm beams out of their frozen silence of the night, growled at whiles with avalanches and falling stones.

Juss was their leader in the ice-fall, guiding them now along high knife-edges that fell away on either hand to unsounded depths, now within the very lips of those chasms, along the bases of the ice-towers. These, five times a man's height, some square, some pinnacled, some shattered or piled with the ruins of their kind, leaned above the path, as ready to fall and overwhelm the climbers and dash their bones for ever down to those blue-green secret places of frost and silence where the chips of ice chinked hollow as Juss pressed onward, cutting his steps with Mivarsh's axe. At length the slope eased and they walked out on the unbroken surface of the glacier, and passing by a snow-bridge over the great rift betwixt the glacier and the mountain side came two hours before noon to the foot of the rock-rib that they had scanned from Ailinon.

Now was Brandoch Daha to lead them. They climbed face to the rock, slowly and without rest, for sound and firm as the rocks were the holds were small and few and the cliffs steep. Here and there a chimney gave them passage upward, but the climb was mainly by cracks and open faces of rock, a trial of main strength and endurance such as few might sustain for a short while only: but this wall was three thousand feet in height. By noon they gained the crest, and there rested on the rocks too weary to speak, looking across the avalanche-swept face of Koshtra Pivrarcha to the corniced parapet that ended against the western precipices of Koshtra Belorn.

For some way the ridge of the buttress was broad and level. Then it narrowed suddenly to the width of a horse's back, and sprang skyward two thousand feet and more. Brandoch Daha went forward and climbed a few feet up the cliff. It bulged out above him, smooth and holdless. He tried it once and again, them came down saying, "Nought without wings."

Then he went to the left. Here hanging glaciers overlooked the face from on high, and while he gazed an avalanche of iceblocks roared down it. Then he went to the right, and here the rocks sloped outward, and the sloping ledges were piled with rubbish and the rocks rotten and slippery with snow and ice. So having gone a little way he returned, and, "O Juss," he said, "wilt take it right forth, and that must be by flying, for hold there is none: or wilt go east and dodge the avalanche: or west, where all is rotten and slither and a slip were our destruction?"

So they debated, and at length decided on the eastern road. It was an ill step round the jutting corner of the tower, for little hold there was, and the rocks were undercut below, so that a stone or a man loosed from that place must fall clear at a bound three or four thousand feet to the Koshtra glacier and there be dashed in pieces. Beyond, wide ledges gave them passage along the wall of the tower, that now swept inward, facing south. Far overhead, dazzling white in the sunshine, the broken glacier-edges and splinters jutted against the blue, and icicles greater than a man hung glittering from every ledge: a sight heavenly fair, whereof they yet had little joy, hastening as they had not hastened in their lives before to be out of the danger of that ice-swept face.

Suddenly was a noise above them like the crack of a giant whip, and looking up they beheld against the sky a dark mass which opened like a flower and spread into a hundred fragments. The Demons and Mivarsh hugged the cliffs where they stood, but there was little cover. All the air was filled with the shrieking of the stones, as they swept downwards like fiends returning to the pit, and with the crash of them as they dashed against the cliffs and burst in pieces. The echoes rolled and reverberated from cliff to distant cliff, and the limbs of the mountain seemed to writhe as under a scourge. When it was done, Mivarsh was groaning for pain of his left wrist sore hurt with a stone. The others were scatheless.

Juss said to Brandoch Daha, "Back, howsoever it dislike thee."

Back they went; and an avalanche of ice crashed down the face which must have destroyed them had they proceeded. "Thou dost misjudge me," said Brandoch Daha, laughing. "Give me where my life lieth on mine own might and main; then is danger meat and drink to me, and nought shall turn me back. But here on this cursed cliff, on the ledges whereof a cripple might walk at ease, we be the toys of chance. And it were pure folly to abide upon it a moment longer."

"Two ways be left us," said Juss. "To turn back, and that were our shame for ever; and to essay the western traverse."

"And that should be the bane of any save of me and thee," said Brandoch Daha. "And if our bane, why, we shall sleep sound."

"Mivarsh," said Juss, "is nought so bounden to this adventure. He hath bravely held by us, and bravely stood our friend. Yet here we be come to such a pass, I sore misdoubt me if it were less danger of his life to come with us than seek safety alone."

But Mivarsh put on a hardy face. Never a word he spake, but nodded his head, as who should say, "Forward."

"First I must be thy leech," said Juss. And he bound up Mivarsh's wrist. And because the day was now far spent, they camped under the great tower, hoping next day to reach the top of Koshtra Pivrarcha that stood unseen some six thousand feet above them.

Next morning, when it was light enough to climb, they set forth. For two hours' space on that traverse not a moment passed but they were in instant peril of death. They were not roped, for on those slabbery rocks one man had dragged a dozen to perdition had he made a slip. The ledges sloped outward; they were piled with broken rock and mud; the soft red rock broke away at a hand's touch and plunged at a leap to the glacier below. Down and up and along, and down and up and up again they wound their way, rounding the base of that great tower, and came at last by a rotten gully safe to the ridge above it.

While they climbed, white wispy clouds which had gathered in the high gullies of scilinon in the morning had grown to a mass of blackness that hid in the mountains to the west. Great streamers ran from it across the gulf below, joined and boiled upward, lifting and sinking like a full-tided sea, rising at last to the high ridge where the Demons stood and wrapping them in a cloak of vapour with a chill wind in its folds, and darkness in broad noon-day. They halted, for they might not see the rocks before them. The wind grew boisterous, shouting among the splintered towers. Snow swept powdery and keen across the ridge. The cloud lifted and plunged again like some great bird shadowing them with its wings. From its bosom the lightning flared above and below. Thunder crashed on the heels of the lightning, sending the echoes rolling among distant cliffs. Their weapons, planted in the snow, sizzled with blue flame; Juss had counselled laying them aside lest they should perish holding them. Crouched in a hollow of the snow among the rocks of that high ridge of Koshtra Pivrarcha, Lord Juss and Lord Brandoch Daha and Mivarsh Faz weathered that night of terror. When night came they knew not, for the storm brought darkness on them hours before sun-down. Blinding snow and sleet and fire and thunder, and wild winds shrieking in the gullies till the firm mountain seemed to rock, kept them awake. They were near frozen, and scarce desired aught but death, which might bring them ease from that hellish roundelay.

Day broke with a weak gray light, and the storm died down. Juss stood up weary beyond speech. Mivarsh said, "Ye be devils, but of myself I marvel. For I have dwelt by snow mountains all my days, and many I wot of that have been benighted on the snows in wild weather. And not one but was starved by reason of the cold. I speak of them that were found. Many were not found, for the spirits devoured them."

Whereat Lord Brandoch Daha laughed aloud, saying, "O Mivarsh, I fear me that in thee I have but a graceless dog. Look on him, that in hardihood and bodily endurance against all hardships of frost or fire surpasseth me as greatly as I surpass thee. Yet is he weariest of the three. Wouldst know why? I'll tell thee: all night he hath striven against the cold, chafing not himself only but me and thee to save us from frost-bite. And be sure nought else had saved thy carcase."

By then was the mist grown lighter, so that they might see the ridge for a hundred paces or more where it went up before them, each pinnacle standing out shadowy and unsubstantial against the next succeeding one more shadowy still. And the pinnacles showed monstrous huge through the mist, like mountain peaks in stature.

They roped and set forth, scaling the towers or turning them, now on this side now on that; sometimes standing on teeth of rock that seemed cut off from all earth else, solitary in a sea of shifting vapour; sometimes descending into a deep gash in the ridge with a blank wall rearing aloft on the further side and empty air yawning to left and right. The rocks were firm and good, like those they had first climbed from the glacier. But they went but a slow pace, for the climbing was difficult and made dangerous by new snow and by the ice that glazed the rocks.

As the day wore the wind was fallen, and all was still when they stood at length before a ridge of hard ice that shot steeply up before them like the edge of a sword. The east side of it on their left was almost sheer, ending in a blank precipice that dropped out of sight without a break. The western slope, scarcely less steep, ran down in a white even sheet of frozen snow till the clouds engulfed it.

Brandoch Daha waited on the last blunt tooth of rock at the foot of the ice-ridge. "The rest is thine," he cried to Lord Juss. "I would not that any save thou should tread him first, for he is thy mountain."

"Without thee I had never won up hither," answered Juss; "and it is not fitting that I should have that glory to stand first upon the peak when thine was the main achievement. Go thou before."

"I will not," said Lord Brandoch Daha. "And it is not so."

So Juss went forward, smiting with his axe great steps just below the backbone of the ridge on the western side, and Lord Brandoch Daha and Mivarsh Faz followed in the steps.

Presently a wind arose in the unseen spaces of the sky, and tore the mist like a rotten garment. Spears of sunlight blazed through the rifts. Distant sunny lands shimmered in the unimaginable depths to the southward, seen over the crest of a tremendous wall that stood beyond the abyss: a screen of black rock buttresses seamed with a thousand gullies of glistening snow, and crowned as with battlements with a row of mountain peaks, savage and fierce of form, that made the eye blink for their brightness: the lean spires of the summit-ridge of Koshtra Pivrarcha. These, that the Demons had so long looked up to as in distant heaven, now lay beneath their feet. Only the peak they climbed still reared itself above them, clear now and near to view, showing a bare beetling cliff on the north-east, overhung by a cornice of snow. Juss marked the cornice, turned him again to his step-cutting, and in half an hour from the breaking of the clouds stood on that unascended pinnacle, with all earth beneath him.

They went down a few feet on the southern side and sat on some rocks. A fair lake studded with islands lay bosomed in wooded and crag-girt hills at the foot of a deep-cut valley which ran down from the Gates of Zimiamvia. Ailinon and

Ashnilam rose near by in the west, with the delicate white peak of Akra Garsh showing between them. Beyond, mountain beyond mountain like the sea.

Juss looked southward where the blue land stretched in fold upon fold of rolling country, soft and misty, till it melted in the sky. "Thou and I," said he, "first of the children of men, now behold with living eyes the fabled land of Zimiamvia. Is that true, thinkest thou, which philosophers tell us of that fortunate land: that no mortal foot may tread it, but the blessed souls do inhabit it of the dead that be departed, even they that were great upon earth and did great deeds when they were living, that scorned not earth and the delights and the glories thereof, and yet did justly and were not dastards nor yet oppressors?"

"Who knoweth?" said Brandoch Daha, resting his chin in his hand and gazing south as in a dream. "Who shall say he knoweth?"

They were silent awhile. Then Juss spake saying, "If thou and I come thither at last, O my friend, shall we remember Demonland?" And when he answered him not, Juss said, "I had rather row on Moommere under the stars of a summer's might, than be a King of all the land of Zimiamvia. And I had rather watch the sunrise on the Scarf, than dwell in gladness all my days on an island of that enchanted Lake of Ravary, under Koshtra Belorn."

Now the curtain of cloud that had hung till now about the eastern heights was rent into shreds, and Koshtra Belorn stood like a maiden before them, two or three miles to eastward, facing the slanting rays of the sun. On all her vast precipices scarce a rock showed bare, so encrusted were they with a dazzling robe of snow. More lovely she seemed and more graceful in her airy poise than they had yet beheld her. Juss and Brandoch Daha rose up, as men arise to greet a queen in her majesty. In silence they looked on her for some minutes.

Then Brandoch Daha spake, saying, "Behold thy bride, O Juss."

Pinkhus Kahanovich (1884–1950) was a philosopher, critic, and writer who wrote in Yiddish under the pen name of Der Nister (literally meaning: "The Hidden One"). He was born in the city of Berdychiv, in what is now Ukraine. In 1920 he went into brief exile, first to Lithuania and then Germany. He returned to the Soviet Union in 1925. In 1950, he was arrested in conditions of secrecy and died shortly thereafter in a prison hospital. His grave, near the Siberian city of Vorkuta, was only recently identified. To date the only book-length translations of his work into English are of the social-realist novel *The Family Mashber* and *Regrowth*, a collection of posthumously published short stories. His work was said to be inspired by the stories of Rabbi Nachman, a teacher of the kabbalah (Jewish mysticism). His style was considered unique for the Yiddish language, as it included Jewish mysticism alongside other world religions. Although he had several books published, his two-volume collection *Gedakht* ("Imagined") was his first successful literary project. This story is from that collection, for the first time translated into English.

At the Border

Der Nister

Translated by Joseph Tomaras

AT THE BORDER between the town and the desert, there is someone who keeps watchful guard on the desert boundary, who appears to be a sort of wild beast, and she is eternally watchful and guarding.

—What do you expect from the desert?

—Someone is coming from there, and will show himself—she says.

—Who?

—She holds herself back from responding. . . . But it comes out, at the end of the day, when she is tired from patrolling, and worn out from always looking around; when she seats herself on a stone, and her face is marked by care and turns sorrowfully toward the desert; when you find yourself near her, and remain standing by her to give her a break from her watch, and you ask: "For whom are you waiting?" She takes a long, drawn-out look face-to-face with the questioner, then she takes in the questioner's face and whole body in a glance, then she turns toward the desert and, looking down, she begins to speak:

—For whom am I waiting? For the two-humped camel from the desert.

—And what is the camel carrying?

—No rider and no herdsman. No merchandise and no travelers. Just two candles upon its humps . . .

—What do you mean?

—The beast begins her story:

Far out in the desert, beneath an enormous sand-dune, lived the last of the giants. The giant pledged to make his way back to the homeland of his ancestors, to excavate their temples and their gods, to bring them back to life and power. He had wandered over half the world, until he came to the desert and went to sleep beneath that dune. . . . They say that he found the gods inside that dune, and the storytellers claim that on an evening when the dune is shrouded in darkness and is overtaken by the desert's dusky winds, you can see his walking stick wrapped in his coat left resting at its peak. He put them up there, and forgot where he left them, and looked around the dune, never finding them. And he yearns, and he waits, impatiently; one night, when his legs stretch, and his head rises from out of the peak, the dune will explode to bits. He will open his eyes, and no shadow will pass over them. Not the slightest whistle of the winds will escape detection by his ears. But for a while, they did not hear and did not see. Only once, upon some evening, after great exertions and much seeking, did he hear a voice coming from the very peak of the dune, and this is what the voice said to him:

"Giant, you will not bring back the rule of your gods, nor shall the line of your ancestors be made powerful, for you shall find no mate and cannot bring a new generation into being."

Hearing this, the giant thought to himself: Where could he find a mate, since he was the last of the line of giants? Where could he turn, when his race had nearly died out, and the people of the town were unlike him, and looked upon him as a monstrosity, a wild, primeval relic? Whenever he walked through the town, his head blocked out the sun, and whenever he ran through it, his feet brought accidents and catastrophes. He had devoured forests and flocks of livestock, destroyed cities and fields. People were like mites to him; they would hide themselves from him in holes in the ground and the cracks between stones. So

he thought: To whom could he turn? Who could advise him? The voice of the dune had spoken to him only once, and would not busy itself with his troubles any more. He was furious. He looked all around him in the desert: Perhaps someone would come to him after all, perhaps something would be revealed to him in the distance. But the desert was desert, and nothing else, so he sat alone in his place. His eyes could find nothing beside himself in all that space, nothing beside the horizon and the skies, in which not even birds were to be seen. Again he waited for some time, sitting with care and attention, so worn down and saddened, until finally he noticed the noise of wings around his head. He lifted his head, and he saw a bird, a gigantic bird of great wingspan, wheeling over his head, flying around and around in a perfect circle. Then the bird descended from its heights and remained hovering near him, and began to speak to him:

"Giant, do not worry, do not be sad! Your mate is already waiting for you, but she is very far away from you. I have brought to you, from the place where she can be found, a letter from her."

The giant saw a letter that the bird had dropped at his feet, folded and sealed, and fell to the earth to grab it. He opened it up to read it, and this is what he read:

"To the last of the Giants, wherever he may not be and wherever he may not be found, whether at sea or on shore, in a village or in the desert: I wish you great peace, blessings, and treasure! We should get to know one another. At the corner of the desert where the wilderness meets the sea, at the stony shore, we survive and remain. Our ancestors ruled as kings for a long time, until they died out, wiped themselves out by killing one another in battles, leaving us as the remainder of the race of giants only one daughter; she lives high in a tower, with three windows, of which one faces the sea, a second toward dry land, and a third faces up to the heavens above. And from there she rules and issues decrees, through one window, upon the sea and upon the fish of the sea, from the second, upon the land and upon the livestock and wild beasts of the land, and from the third, upon the winds and storms and all manner of birds in the air above. All the creatures hear her and obey her decrees, and she alone follows her gods and abides by their commandments. Thus have the gods commanded her: What she shall sit through and what she shall endure, for the tower of empire is getting old, and no one is repairing it; termites have been found in its walls, and holes have already been eaten through. . . . She is still young, but her youth is passing without sweetness. Her body is strong, and she can give birth to a new generation of giants. So the gods have advised her: They know with certainty that there is still a male giant remaining, somewhere at sea or upon the land, but somewhere far away and thus in the same circumstance as her, living alone and searching for his other half. He searches, but has not found his mate—so she should seek after him, and bring him to her tower. She has followed the advice of her gods, turning to the birds and asking the swiftest, most skillful of flyers: who shall find the giant for me? One came forward to accept the mission. From the young empress he has taken a letter, to fly all over the world searching for the giant, at sea and on land, leaving no spot unexamined. And you, who now reads this letter that the bird has brought to your feet, you are the one, the only one, called upon to take the daughter of giants as your mate. She says to you: Come to me. Love and riches await you, you the only one, the long-awaited one."

Having finished reading, the giant looked up again at where the bird was, and saw the bird once again flying above and around the spot. So he asked the bird:

"And how do you get to the daughter of giants?"

"By foot."

"In which direction should I go?"

"This way, as the bird flies."

The bird stopped looking down at the giant and lifted himself higher into the sky, then flew a few more circles around the giant's head, and then, straightening himself out, pointed himself toward a horizon and flew away. The giant lifted

himself from where he was seated, turned his face in the direction that the bird had flown, then turned his whole body in that direction, and with his very first step, departed the sand dune for the very last time. He turned to look at its peak, and addressed these words to the dune:

"Dune, I say to you, I swear to you, just as I rested beneath you and at your foot, so shall my gods rest upon your highest peak, and my firstborn, the first to issue from my loins, shall serve upon you as a High Priest, the first High Priest and most loyal servant of you, great mountain!"

So he said, and the giant took his first step, and with that step, covered what would be a day's journey for a man; then with the other foot, another day's journey, and once again the first foot. And then the giant made for himself, in the midst of the desert, a sort of tent, out of sticks and branches, sheets and rags, and the whole structure was weak as a hut and sagging toward the earth, which in the middle of the desert, in the great lonely expanse of the desert, was just pitiful. The tent was too small for the giant to see out of it, or else he would have seen, through the opening of the tent, a sort of a person, hidden by and rising from the earth. The person was wrapped in a dark cloak from head to toe, face and eyes invisible. When the giant finally noticed this person, he wondered: Who can that be, and what are they doing here in the desert? He bent over to yell downward:

"Who is there?"

"The leper," came the answer in a voice from the ground, weak and dampened from being wrapped in a cloak.

"And what are you doing here in the desert?"

"There is no place for me in the town."

"And where has the leper come from?"

"From the daughter of giants, who lives at the corner of the desert."

"What did you say?"

"Please bend down lower, closer to me, I don't have the strength to yell any louder."

And the giant bent over, laying his head and half his body on the ground, while the leper stood up and began to tell this story:

—At the edge of the desert and the shore of the sea, there is a palace, where there lives the last daughter of giants, the remainder of the old race of giants, and she lives there alone, she has no mate. Her youth is passing in unhappiness and loneliness, she spends her time alone with the walls around her, day and night she has no joy in her life, and she doesn't know what to do with herself. She has retained all her hereditary powers, though, and to this day she speaks to the birds as her ancestors did before her, and they serve her following all her commands. She called upon them and sent the best and swiftest, to go and to fly to the ends of the earth to find her destined one, her other half, her giant. He flew and he flew, searching for a long time, and he found nothing, no one, and finally he turned around to come back home, and he met me on the way. Back then I was young, and also a giant, and I was also searching for my mate, my other half. He was pleased to meet me, hailed me, showed me the way, and told me a great deal—about her life and her suffering alone in the palace. I stood up and made my way following the bird. I was coming to her, to her youth and her home, filling up with love for her. I spent some time with her, got to know her, and readied myself to become her lordly husband. . . . And I did, finally, I became her husband. And one night, when the moon reigned in the sky and sea and shined in upon us through the window, and she and I were together, and there was not another creature in the palace besides us two, I saw her, lying in bed in the light of the moon, and I was terrified. She looked at me in total silence with her two eyes, and her eyes were cold. Her face looked as though there was nothing there to see at all, as if I were invisible, not there at all. So I turned to her and asked her: What are you thinking? What are you feeling? She did not answer me. So I asked her again: What is the matter with you? What are you looking at that way? Who are you thinking of? She looked down at me and answered, "Of another, a better one, not you who is lying there."

"What do you mean?" I asked her.

"Enough!" she said, not looking at me, and as if she were speaking against her will.

"Why?"

"You are small and covered in running sores."

And it was true: After her words I looked at myself and saw how small I was beside her, almost nothing, what a needless, alien, used-up remainder of a person I had become; she was beautiful and uncannily silent, while beside her I was covered over with pustulent sores. . . . I got up, got down out of the bed, and left her lying there by herself. I looked at her once more, at her indifference, her alienation from me, her contempt and desire to be left alone, for me to leave. I thought a bit, thought and soon I understood: a witch! I was under the spell of a witch! I got out of the room as quick as I could, out of the palace, into the fresh air. I went to the sea and stood there in the power of the moon. From the sea, I could see, toward the shore, where the water was not deep, there was a camel standing on all fours with water up to its knees and a wound on its head. It stood silently, masticating nothingness, taken up with itself and whatever spell it was under. I went to the camel, as if I had found a friend, a companion in suffering, a neighbor in the water. I turned to it and asked it a question:

"What do you think, camel?"

"I think it is not the first time, and that you are not her first suitor."

"What is to be done?"

"Go to the desert."

"And do what?"

"Find others like you, and turn them around from the path they are taking."

I listened to the camel and got on its back, and it carried me out of the sea and across the shore, onto the sand and into the desert, where I settled in a tent, and warned every passerby who was going that way of what awaited that way— and that is all.

And so the leper ended his story, and remained silently wrapped in his cloak, and in his going silent, standing with head bowed, with his body and his silent standing he waited upon the giant who was standing over him.

"And what do you say I should do now?"

"Don't go."

"And the bird who called upon me?"

"It is one of her messengers."

After some more minutes of silence, the giant rose from his bent position and turned his head toward the horizon where the bird had flown before. He looked for the bird, seeking it out with his eyes, but did not find it, thus passing a bit more time. It flew back, returning to the giant.

"What do you want, giant?"

"I want to know the truth."

"What truth?"

"About the daughter of giants, and your message."

"It is the truth."

"And what the leper has said?"

"The words of a leper."

"Do you have a sign for me?"

"The camel."

"Where?"

"There!"

And a camel had shown itself standing next to the giant, its back uplifted and its head and face turned toward a corner of the sky. It looked so thoughtful, ready, waiting at attention to answer any of the giant's questions.

"And what do you say, camel, about the leper?"

"I don't know him."

"And who brought him here?"

"Not I, and none from my kind, none of those like me . . ."

"Leper!" The giant shouted, lifting his foot over the leper's body and head, ready to plant it down upon him. "Leper!!" He raised his voice and then brought his foot down with great force. . . . And the leper was annihilated. The giant returned to his makeshift desert hut and gathered the rags and sticks, and used them to build a gravesite, a memorial—"There he lies, the liar." And the giant continued on his way.

———

So the giant traveled another day through the desert, and then a second, with no impediment, nor any sign of change, along his way. The desert remained desert, and no way out was to be seen. So at twilight he laid himself down upon the sand and called out to the bird, his wayfinder, leader, and his vanguard, and commanded: "Bird, show yourself!" The bird returned flying from a distant corner of the sky, his wings dull in the advancing darkness. Then holding himself humbly before the giant, in the last rays of sun cast upon the desert, he made his way toward the giant, asking:

"Giant, what is your command?"

"How far is it still to the giantess's tower?"

"Not far now. You can get yourself ready."

"For what?"

"For night and what comes after it."

Since the giant had laid down, stretched out upon the desert sands with legs and limbs relaxed, his eyes closed and sleep cast its spell upon him soon enough. When he was fully asleep, he started to dream: The lost mountain of the gods, the dune that formerly sheltered him, had once again come to life. On top of the mountain, at its peak, there was a temple, a newly built temple, shining and renewed and open today for a holy day, a festival . . . and now it is night, and outside it is dark and tenebrous, but inside the temple all is illuminated, and the lights of the festival shine through the windows of the temple onto the slopes of the mountain outside. . . . And the temple is empty; there is just one servant at its threshold, opening the treasures and readying the temple for pilgrims and entering priests. And the pilgrims can be seen approaching the mountain from all around, gathered around on every side at its foot, coming by foot and by caravan, all carrying candles in their hands, protecting the flames from being extinguished by the winds. They come up the mountain in groups and enter the temple, walking through its portal, stunned silent by its insides. And the pilgrims multiply, women carrying children, elders led by the young, and all enter the illuminated temple carrying their candles. Upon an altar against the eastern wall, opposite the entrance, an old High Priest reveals himself, dressed entirely in white. He stands silently before the congregation, stands silently and then begins to speak to them:

"In the name of the temple, and in the name of its gods, I declare the temple reopened and renewed! For this we have one of us to thank, who was one of the last remainders of our kind, he who strived for this, who worked for this renewal, and thanks to his will and his effort we are gathered here today, we have returned here once again. Come forward, and honor the temple."

And the congregation heard the High Priest, and bent at the knees with their lights in their hands, and the High Priest lifted his hands in silent prayer, the congregation still kneeling silently, taking the prayer and the silence upon their heads.

"And now," said the High Priest. "Rise and take heed."

And the congregation rose from its knees and from the ground, and all were looking at the High Priest, and all were waiting for his word. And the High Priest called out again, saying:

"In the name of the temple and of its gods, we make this offering to our benefactor upon his wedding night, may there be two candles, unlit, for him and for his mate, for him and for the daughter of giants so long awaited."

And from the podium of the altar, which was full of burning candles, the High Priest took two candles which had not been lit, which were not burning: large and long, waxen, and with brand-new wicks, he held one in each hand, his arms stretched forth toward the congregation, and he called out again, saying:

"May he continue and may he take strength, our benefactor and the builder of our temple, unto the wedding canopy and his first night with his bride, and as he finds his destined one and is reunited with his other half, so shall the two candles have their wicks alit, one shall burn the other and they shall become one fire, and a message shall go forth unto the people, and the people shall see the candles and they shall know: The ancient race has risen again, the old gods have come back to life, and the family of giants are once again in power."

And the giant heard this for he was among the congregation. He came out from among the congregation and approached the old High Priest upon the altar, reached out his hand and took one of the candles away, carrying it to the back of the sanctuary.

And when the giant reached the back with the candle, he saw that the temple had gone completely dark. All the candles had been put out as at the end of the festival, and an air of mourning had come over the walls of the temple. It was as if the entire congregation had been wrapped and covered in a dark shadow, and remained in darkness, having extinguished each candle in their own hands. So, too, had all the candles on the altar begun to flicker out. The temple had gone silent. And he saw upon the altar that in place of the High Priest who had been there before, was instead a bent-over person, wrapped in a crude cloak completely covering both its body and head, and from beneath that covering its voice could be heard, weakly, saying:

"And the giant, he should not think, he should not imagine, that what he has seen here he has seen true, that what passes here before his eyes shall come to pass in truth. . . . It is just a dream, a self-deception. He should accept what he does not want to accept, that he who now speaks, speaks the truth, and the leper spoke the truth. The giant has smashed the leper but not his truth! He does not want to hear it, but so it is. . . ."

And then the temple and all that had filled the temple vanished before the eyes of the giant; the congregation was gone, and silence, emptiness, and night reigned once more upon the dune. At its peak, the memorial-tent of the leper stood in silence, and the leper beside it. . . . The giant woke up, trembling.

"Bird!" he shouted. "Where are you?"

The giant had startled himself awake with his own shout, opening his eyes wide open. He looked around at his surroundings, near and far, on all sides. To his disappointment he found a gray dawn, silent and deserted, with nothing living in his surroundings, not a single creature showing itself all around. Everything was still asleep, or dead silent. The giant called again for the bird, and the bird shouted back. He came back flying out of the gray sky, drowsily, presenting himself to the giant like a sleepwalker, asking, "What do you want?"

"I had a dream."

"I know."

"What do you know?"

"It's nothing."

"And the two candles?"

"There they are!"

The bird pointed to the camel, who was coming from the direction of the rising sun. After some time had passed, the camel arrived next to the bird and the giant bearing two large, long, unlit, waxen candles, one on each of his two humps. They were resting against each other, crossed over the camel's humps, and the camel bore them in camelian silence. The camel waited for the giant to rise from the ground, so they could resume their travels.

And the giant stood, having consoled himself from the night's upsetting dream, and the bird was already flying in the distance once again to show the way, and the camel was also moving from his place, the giant following along, resolved upon another day of travel.

For the third and last time, the leper met the giant on his way, and this is how it happened: After the giant had been traveling for some time, and the desert was no longer all that could be seen, when he could finally begin to see a corner of the sea and the tower in the distance, a mirage appeared to the giant in the middle of the bright desert. In the sunlight reflected from the sand it appeared to the giant as though there were a large town, with walls and buildings and alleyways, full of the tumult of people in the streets. People rushing about and banging into one another, people making haste and shunning their fellows, and all bearing the burdens of business. Suddenly a plaza opened up within the city—a large, one

might even say, gigantic plaza—where a great mob of people could assemble. But the plaza remained empty for the time being, no one gathering there, no one appearing. Only after it was completely emptied did people begin to trickle in; they came out from every corner, street, and alleyway and began to gather. Those who before were occupied with their solitary affairs were now gathered into masses, and gradually the plaza was filled completely by a great assembly, until it was completely crammed. The plaza was black with people, and a black mood had overtaken the crowd. In the middle an elevated platform could be seen, and one could not tell if it had been built from wooden boards, or was a pile of sand. From there, a person looked out and around from above the assembly. He waited a bit for everyone to settle down, a minute or two, looked around as he waited, and then, to grab the attention of the crowd, he stretched out his hand upward and began to speak:

"People of the great assembly, a festival has been proclaimed for us, great events are overtaking us, and it is this: A giant has been seen in the desert, one who has until now lived alone in the desert, the last remaining of his kind, so he thought, but now he has met his mate, and today the two of them will mate; that means a new generation, regeneration of his kind, the race of his ancient ancestors, and great giants going forth from their land. That means great giants coming to our town, and a new regime coming to rule over our heads. The giant's throne will be built tall enough to reach the skies, so that his head will be crowned by the sun itself. And you shall be under the protection of the Crown of Giants, and no enemy shall attack you. Even the enemy's pioneering scouts will not dare to cross the border. . . . Hear the news and understand, hear it and rejoice in what you have been told!"

The audience heard him out, and then remained silent. After the man's speech, the crowd did not budge a hairbreadth from where they stood; no one raised their voice, and no expressions of joy erupted from any portion of the audience. The audience was so silent, in such tense readiness, that suddenly when a voice did cry out, from outside the plaza, it echoed through it from every corner. The echoing shout: We don't want him! We don't need him! We are not waiting for him, and he should leave the sun alone!

"We don't need him! We don't want him!" It came from every wall and corner, and also from voices within the crowd itself. "We don't need him! He is a stranger to us! The giant, he will trod on our heads! He will destroy our buildings! He will steal our sun and consign us to the darkness! We don't need him!"

Each person in the crowd bowed to the ground to pick up handfuls of dirt, sand, dust, clods of earth, and stones, and waving their full hands at the person on the platform they turned toward him shouting:

"Where is he?" as if in one tremendous, bellowing voice.

"There!" The person pointed to the giant standing in the desert. "There he is, and do what you will to him! He is in your hands!"

The people tried throwing whatever they had, stones, dust, making a great tumult within the crowd. Some were trod underfoot by their fellows, others hit with stones, and all came to some sort of injury one way or the other, but they kept drawing closer and closer to the giant, until suddenly—the vision dissolved and nothing remained of the crowd, the plaza was completely emptied—completely cleared out, not a soul to be seen anywhere but one alone upon the platform, the town crier from before, who looked to the giant as though he were standing face to face with him. They were in the plaza by themselves, silently looking one another over. Now that he was alone, the town crier looked sad, a bit bereft, and turning silently toward the giant, he began to speak:

"Giant, where are you going? Where are your giant steps taking you?"

"Over there, where the bird is leading me," answered the giant.

"Toward what?"

"To renew the ancient powers of the giants and bless the town with my might."

"Who wants that?"

"I want it, and I must have it!"

"And the people?"

"The leper!"

The person had begun to remove the veils and clothing which had hidden his face and head from the giant . . . and truly it was his old acquaintance, the leper from before, standing in front of the giant, bent over and wrapped in a mantle. The giant beheld him with surprise, anger, and disgust. . . . But the leper did not remain, nor any of the desert mirage, for it all dissolved around the giant—the city, the streets of the city, and every trace was soon gone—the sun was already setting in the desert, and the giant looked around himself in shock, looking for some trace of the leper. With his eyes wide open, he had lost track of the desert, his exit from the desert, and his destination. . . . Then he caught a taste of the sea on the breeze, which turned his attention toward the sea and with it, he could soon detect a trace of the shoreline, and on the shore, the tower, an old, solitary tower with windows turned toward both sea and desert. . . . It was darkening, and the flag on top of the tower was being lowered, and the giant saw it, and turned his footsteps toward the tower.

He saw that the bird had perched in one of the windows of the tower, and with a tired wing was knocking on a windowpane. The window opened. A head looked out of the window—a large head, belonging to the daughter of giants, whom his body had pursued from across the desert. He revealed himself, putting himself into a beam of light, so that she could see who was coming. And the sea was quiet, and the giant also saw, by the coast at the very start of the road, the camel from before, still carrying the large, waxen candles on his humps, candles that still had never been lit.

And the giant entered the tower. How he and the daughter of giants met, how they greeted one another and what they did with one another, no one has seen, for no one was there who can say.

For she had a chamber within a chamber, and no one was allowed to enter that chamber ever, and it was always locked, only opened when she was ready. There were a table and lamp, and the lamp was never lit, not until this first meeting.

They were in that room together. For an hour, maybe, silence. And then another hour, and all that could be heard was a humming. . . . Night had fallen, and stars could be seen in the sky—and the tower and its lamp were illuminated with a festive light. . . . Then late night came, and the sea woke from its sleep, speaking, and the camel was still standing on the shore, listening to what the sea had to say. The camel stepped into the sea, and turned toward the tower, waiting upon the lamp. Finally, the lamp was extinguished. . . . And all was again quiet there where the tower stood, old and decaying, but the darkness had been renewed, so that it was if it had never before been quite so dark before. . . . The sea sighed, and then breathed out heavily. The camel remained standing, silently, looking out for signs of night's end. This is how it spent the entire night. When the morning star appeared, it looked down again at the sea and the desert. It took them both in, in one glance, and said a blessing on each. . . . Then the tower's sea-facing window opened, and from the window a voice could be heard:

"The night is over and a fortunate night for us, and the time has come for the candles on the humps of the camel."

This meant the candles that still leaned upon one another on the camel's humps. When the morning star cast its light upon them, it lit both the wicks. Their flames united into a single fire, and the camel, startled, raced from the water onto the shore and passed the beach, and in this way, with a burning fire on its back in the silence of the dawn, it turned his face toward the desert. But it wanted to get *out* of the desert, to the town, to carry the light and the message, and set off on the road toward us.

And that is what I am waiting for, for that camel; I am looking for that camel at the border, and soon enough, when it has crossed the desert, the time will come.

So says the beast.

W. B. Laughead (1882–1958) was an American logger and the manager of advertising at the Red River Lumber Company. One day in 1914, as he was working on a promotional pamphlet, he decided to use an old logger folktale, the tale of Paul Bunyan. The folk hero originally appeared in print in 1906 but was an obscure character known only by loggers and their families. It was Laughead's ingenuity that brought Bunyan out of obscurity and into the role of folk hero. Laughead defined the appearance and characteristics of the character and added characters such as Babe the Blue Ox and her caretaker Brimstone Bill. *The Marvelous Exploits of Paul Bunyan* (1922) was an edited version of Laughead's first work and reached a larger audience than its predecessor. Although the tales are entertaining, it is worth noting that they were meant to promote new logging technology and thus were also basically advertisements that promoted a very conservative agenda.

The Marvelous Exploits of Paul Bunyan

AS TOLD IN THE CAMPS OF THE WHITE PINE LUMBERMEN FOR GENERATIONS DURING WHICH TIME THE LOGGERS HAVE PIONEERED THE WAY THROUGH THE NORTH WOODS FROM MAINE TO CALIFORNIA COLLECTED FROM VARIOUS SOURCES AND EMBELLISHED FOR PUBLICATION

W. B. Laughead

PUBLISHED FOR THE AMUSEMENT OF OUR FRIENDS BY THE RED RIVER LUMBER COMPANY MINNEAPOLIS, WESTWOOD, CAL., CHICAGO, LOS ANGELES, SAN FRANCISCO

SCHOLARS SAY He is the Only American Myth.

Paul Bunyan is the hero of lumbercamp whoppers that have been handed down for generations.

These stories, never heard outside the haunts of the lumberjack until recent years, are now being collected by learned educators and literary authorities who declare that Paul Bunyan is "the only American myth."

The best authorities never recounted Paul Bunyan's exploits in narrative form. They made their statements more impressive by dropping them casually, in an offhand way, as if in reference to actual events of common knowledge.

To overawe the greenhorn in the bunk shanty, or the paper-collar stiffs and home guards in the saloons, a group of lumberjacks would remember meeting each other in the camps of Paul Bunyan. With painful accuracy they established the exact time and place, "on the Big Onion the winter of the blue snow" or "at Shot Gunderson's camp on the Tadpole the year of the sourdough drive." They elaborated on the old themes and new stories were born in lying contests where the heights of extemporaneous invention were reached.

In these conversations the lumberjack often took on the mannerisms of the French Canadian. This was apparently done without special intent and no reason for it can be given except for a similarity in the mock seriousness of their statements and the anti-climax of the bulls that were made, with the braggadocio of the habitant. Some investigators trace the origin of Paul Bunyan to Eastern Canada. Who can say?

Paul Bunyan came to Westwood, California, in 1913 at the suggestion of some of the most prominent loggers and lumbermen in the country. When the Red River Lumber Company announced their plans for opening up their forests of Sugar Pine and California White Pine, friendly advisors shook their heads and said,

"Better send for Paul Bunyan."

Apparently here was the job for a Superman,— quality-and-quantity-production on a big scale and great engineering difficulties to be overcome. Why not Paul Bunyan? This is a White Pine job and here in the High Sierras the winter snows lie deep, just like the country where Paul grew up. Here are trees that dwarf the largest "cork pine" of the Lake States and many new stunts were planned for logging, milling and manufacturing a product of supreme quality—just the job for Paul Bunyan.

The Red River people had been cutting White Pine in Minnesota for two generations; the crews that came west with them were old heads and every one knew Paul Bunyan of old. Paul had followed the White Pine from the Atlantic seaboard west to the jumping-off place in Minnesota, why not go the rest of the way?

Paul Bunyan's picture had never been published until he joined Red River and this likeness, first issued in 1914 is now the Red River trademark. It stands for the quality and service you have the right to expect from Paul Bunyan.

When and where did this mythical Hero get his start? Paul Bunyan is known by his mighty works, his antecedents and personal history are lost in doubt. You can prove that Paul logged off North Dakota and grubbed the stumps, not only by the fact that there are no traces of pine forests in that State, but by the testimony of oldtimers who saw it done. On the other hand, Paul's parentage and birth date are unknown. Like Topsy, he jes' growed.

Nobody cared to know his origin until the professors got after him. As long as he stayed around the camps his previous history was treated with the customary consideration and he was asked no questions, but when he broke into college it was all off. Then he had to have ancestors, a birthday and all sorts of vital statistics.

Now Paul is a regular myth and students of folklore make scientific research of "The Paul Bunyan Legend."

His first appearance in print was in the booklets published by The Red River Lumber Company in 1914 and 1916, these stories are reprinted in the present volume, with additions. Paul has followed the wanderings of pioneering workmen and performed new wonders in the oil fields, on big construction jobs and in the wheat fields but the stories in this book deal only with his work in the White Pine camps where he was born and raised. Care has been taken to preserve the atmosphere of the old style camps.

So now we will get on with Paul's doings and in the language of the four-horse skinner, "Let's dangle!"

Babe, the big blue ox constituted Paul Bunyan's assets and liabilities. History disagrees as to when, where and how Paul first acquired this bovine locomotive but his subsequent record is reliably established. Babe could pull anything that had two ends to it.

Babe was seven axehandles wide between the eyes according to some authorities; others equally dependable say forty-two axehandles and a plug of tobacco. Like other historical contradictions this comes from using different standards. Seven of Paul's axehandles were equal to a little more than forty-two of the ordinary kind.

When cost sheets were figured on Babe, Johnny Inkslinger found that upkeep and overhead were expensive but the charges for operation and depreciation were low and the efficiency was very high. How else could Paul have hauled logs to the landing a whole section (640 acres) at a time? He also used Babe to pull the kinks out of the crooked logging roads and it was on a job of this kind that Babe pulled a chain of three-inch links out into a straight bar.

They could never keep Babe more than one night at a camp for he would eat in one day all the feed one crew could tote to camp in a year. For a snack between meals he would eat fifty bales of hay, wire and all and six men with picaroons were kept busy picking the wire out of his teeth. Babe was a great pet and very docile as a general thing but he seemed to have a sense of humor and frequently got into mischief. He would sneak up behind a drive and drink all the water out of the river, leaving the logs high and dry. It was impossible to build an ox-sling big enough to hoist Babe off the ground for shoeing, but after they logged off Dakota there was room for Babe to lie down for this operation.

Once in a while Babe would run away and be gone all day roaming all over the Northwestern country. His tracks were so far apart that it was impossible to follow him and so deep that a man falling into one could only be hauled out with difficulty and a long rope. Once a settler and his wife and baby fell into one of these tracks and the son got out when he was fifty-seven years old and reported the accident. These tracks, today form the thousands of lakes in the "Land of the Sky-Blue Water."

Because he was so much younger than Babe and was brought to camp when a small calf, Benny was always called the Little Blue Ox although he was quite a chunk of an animal. Benny could not, or rather, would not haul as much as Babe nor was he as tractable but he could eat more.

Paul got Benny for nothing from a farmer near Bangor, Maine. There was not enough milk for the little fellow so he had to be weaned when three days old. The farmer only had forty acres of hay and by the time Benny was a week old he had to dispose of him for lack of food. The calf was undernourished and only weighed two tons when Paul got him. Paul drove from Bangor out to his headquarters camp near Devil's Lake, North Dakota, that night and led Benny behind the sleigh. Western air agreed with the little calf and every time Paul looked back at him he was two feet taller.

When they arrived at camp Benny was given a good feed of buffalo milk and flapjacks and put into a barn by himself. Next morning the barn was gone. Later it was discovered on Benny's back as he scampered over the clearings. He had outgrown his barn in one night.

Benny was very notional and would never pull a load unless there was snow on the ground so after the spring thaws they had to white wash the logging roads to fool him.

Gluttony killed Benny. He had a mania for pancakes and one cook crew of two hundred men was kept busy making cakes for him. One night he pawed and bellowed and threshed his tail about till the wind of it blew down what pine Paul had left standing in Dakota. At breakfast time he broke loose, tore down the cook shanty and began bolting pancakes. In his greed he swallowed the red-hot stove. Indigestion set in and nothing could save him. What disposition was made of his body is a matter of dispute. One oldtimer claims that the outfit he works for bought a hind quarter of the carcass in 1857 and made corned beef of it. He thinks they have several carloads of it left.

Another authority states that the body of Benny was dragged to a safe distance from the North Dakota camp and buried. When the earth was shoveled back it made a mound that formed the Black Hills in South Dakota.

The custodian and chaperon of Babe, the Big Blue Ox, was Brimstone Bill. He knew all the tricks of that frisky giant before they happened.

"I know oxen," the old bullwhacker used to say, "I've worked 'em and fed 'em and doctored 'em ever since the ox was invented. And Babe, I know that pernicious old reptyle same as if I'd abeen through him with a lantern."

Bill compiled "The Skinner's Dictionary," a handbook for teamsters, and most of the terms used in directing draft animals (except mules) originated with him. His early religious training accounts for the fact that the technical language of the teamster contains so many names of places and people spoken of in the Bible.

The buckskin harness used on Babe and Benny when the weather was rainy was made by Brimstone Bill. When this harness got wet it would stretch so much that the oxen could travel clear to the landing and the load would not move from the skidway in the woods. Brimstone would fasten the harness with an anchor Big Ole made for him and when the sun came out and the harness shrunk the load would be pulled to the landing while Bill and the oxen were busy at some other job.

The winter of the Blue Snow, the Pacific Ocean froze over and Bill kept the oxen busy hauling regular white snow over from China. M. H. Keenan can testify to the truth of this as he worked for Paul on the Big Onion that winter. It must have been about this time that Bill made the first ox yokes out of cranberry wood.

Feeding Paul Bunyan's crews was a complicated job. At no two camps were conditions the same. The winter he logged off North Dakota he had 300 cooks making pancakes for the Seven Axemen and the little Chore-boy. At headquarters on the Big Onion he had one cook and 462 cookees feeding a crew so big that Paul himself never knew within several hundred either way, how many men he had.

At Big Onion camp there was a lot of mechanical equipment and the trouble was a man who could handle the machinery cooked just like a machinist too. One cook got lost between the flour bin and the root cellar and nearly starved to death before he was found.

Cooks came and went. Some were good and others just able to get by. Paul never kept a poor one very long. There was one jigger who seemed to have learned to do nothing but boil. He made soup out of everything and did most of his work with a dipper. When the big tote-sled broke through the ice on Bull Frog Lake with a load of split peas, he served warmed up, lake water till the crew struck. His idea of a lunch box was a jug or a rope to freeze soup onto like a candle. Some cooks used too much grease. It was said of one of these that he had to wear calked shoes to keep from sliding out of the cook-shanty and rub sand on his hands when he picked anything up.

There are two kinds of camp cooks, the Baking Powder Bums and the Sourdough Stiffs. Sourdough Sam belonged to the latter school. He made everything but coffee out of Sourdough. He had only one arm and one leg, the other members having been lost when his sourdough barrel blew up. Sam officiated at Tadpole River headquarters, the winter Shot Gunderson took charge.

After all others had failed at Big Onion camp, Paul hired his cousin Big Joe who came from three weeks below Quebec. This boy sure put a mean scald on the chuck. He was the only man who could make pancakes fast enough to feed the crew. He had Big Ole, the blacksmith, make him a griddle that was so big you couldn't see across it when the steam was thick. The batter, stirred in drums like concrete mixers was poured on with cranes and spouts. The griddle was greased by boys who skated over the surface with hams tied to their feet. They had to have boys to stand the heat.

At this camp the flunkeys wore roller skates and an idea of the size of the tables is gained from the fact that they distributed the pepper with four-horse teams.

Sending out lunch and timing the meals was

rendered difficult by the size of the works which required three crews—one going to work, one on the job and one coming back. Joe had to start the bull-cook out with the lunch sled two weeks ahead of dinner time. To call the men who came in at noon was another problem. Big Ole made a dinner horn so big that no one could blow it but Big Joe or Paul himself. The first time Joe blew it he blew down ten acres of pine. The Red River people wouldn't stand for that so the next time he blew straight up but this caused severe cyclones and storms at sea so Paul had to junk the horn and ship it East where later it was made into a tin roof for a big Union Depot.

When Big Joe came to Westwood with Paul, he started something. About that time, you may have read in the papers about a volcanic eruption at Mt. Lassen, heretofore extinct for many years. That was where Big Joe dug his bean-hole and when the steam worked out of the bean kettle and up through the ground, everyone thought the old hill had turned volcano. Every time Joe drops a biscuit they talk of earthquakes.

It was always thought that the quality of the food at Paul's camps had a lot to do with the strength and endurance of the men. No doubt it did, but they were a husky lot to start with. As the feller said about fish for a brain food, "It won't do you no good unless there is a germ there to start with."

There must have been something to the food theory for the chipmunks that ate the prune pits got so big they killed all the wolves and years later the settlers shot them for tigers.

A visitor at one of Paul's camps was astonished to see a crew of men unloading four-horse logging sleds at the cook-shanty. They appeared to be rolling logs into a trap door from which poured clouds of steam.

"That's a heck of a place to land logs," he remarked.

"Them ain't logs," grinned a bull-cook, "them's sausages for the teamsters' breakfast."

At Paul's camp up where the little Gimlet empties into the Big Auger, newcomers used to kick because they were never served beans. The bosses and the men could never be interested in beans. E. E. Terrill tells us the reason:

Once when the cook quit they had to detail a substitute to the job temporarily. There was one man who was no good anywhere. He had failed at every job. Chris Crosshaul, the foreman, acting on the theory that every man is good somewhere, figured that this guy must be a cook, for it was the only job he had not tried. So he was put to work and the first thing he tackled was beans. He filled up a big kettle with beans and added some water. When the heat took hold the beans swelled up till they lifted off the roof and bulged out the walls. There was no way to get into the place to cook anything else, so the whole crew turned in to eat up the half-cooked beans. By keeping at it steady they cleaned them up in a week and rescued the would-be-cook. After that no one seemed to care much for beans.

It used to be a big job to haul prune pits and coffee grounds away from Paul's camps. It required a big crew of men and either Babe or Benny to do the hauling. Finally, Paul decided it was cheaper to build new camps and move every month.

The winter Paul logged off North Dakota with the Seven Axemen, the Little Chore Boy and the 300 cooks, he worked the cooks in three shifts—one for each meal. The Seven Axemen were hearty eaters; a portion of bacon was one side of a 1,600-pound pig. Paul shipped a stern-wheel steamboat up Red River and they put it in the soup kettle to stir the soup.

Like other artists, cooks are temperamental and some of them are full of cussedness but the only ones who could sass Paul Bunyan and get away with it were the stars like Big Joe and Sourdough Sam. The lunch sled,—most popular institution in the lumber industry! Its arrival at the noon rendezvous has been hailed with joy by hungry men on every logging job since Paul invented it. What if the warm food freezes on your tin plate, the keen cold air has sharpened your appetite to enjoy it. The crew that toted lunch for Paul Bunyan had so far to travel and so many to feed they hauled a complete kitchen on the lunch sled, cooks and all.

When Paul invented logging he had to invent all the tools and figure out all his own methods. There were no precedents. At the start his outfit consisted of Babe and his big axe.

No two logging jobs can be handled exactly the same way so Paul adapted his operations to local conditions. In the mountains he used Babe to pull the kinks out of the crooked logging roads; on the Big Onion he began the system of hauling a section of land at a time to the landings and in North Dakota he used the Seven Axemen.

At that time marking logs was not thought of, Paul had no need for identification when there were no logs but his own. About the time he started the Atlantic Ocean drive others had come into the industry and although their combined cut was insignificant compared to Paul's, there was danger of confusion, and Paul had most to lose.

At first Paul marked his logs by pinching a piece out of each log. When his cut grew so large that the marking had to be detailed to the crews, the "scalp" on each log was put on with an axe, for even in those days not every man could nip out the chunk with his fingers.

The Grindstone was invented by Paul the winter he logged off North Dakota. Before that Paul's axemen had to sharpen their axes by rolling rocks downhill and running alongside of them. When they got to "Big Dick," as the lumberjacks called Dakota, hills and rocks were so hard to find that Paul rigged up the revolving rock.

This was much appreciated by the Seven Axemen as it enabled them to grind an axe in a week, but the grindstone was not much of a hit with the Little Chore Boy whose job it was to turn it. The first stone was so big that working at full speed, every time it turned around once it was payday.

The Little Chore Boy led a strenuous life. He was only a kid and like all youngsters putting in their first winter in the woods, he was put over the jumps by the oldtimers. His regular work

was heavy enough, splitting all the wood for the camp, carrying water and packing lunch to the men, but his hazers sent him on all kinds of wild goose errands to all parts of the works, looking for a "left-handed peavy" or a "bundle of cross-hauls."

He had to take a lot of good-natured rough-neck wit about his size for he only weighed 800 pounds and a couple of surcingles made a belt for him. What he lacked in size he made up in grit and the men secretly respected his gameness. They said he might make a pretty good man if he ever got any growth, and considered it a necessary education to give him a lot of extra chores.

Often in the evening, after his day's work and long hours put in turning the grindstone and keeping up fires in the camp stoves—that required four cords of wood apiece to kindle a fire, he could be found with one of Big Ole's small 600-pound anvils in his lap pegging up shoes with railroad spikes.

It was a long time before they solved the problem of turning logging sleds around in the road. When a sled returned from the landing and put on a load they had to wait until Paul came along to pick up the four horses and the load and head them the other way. Judson M. Goss says he worked for Paul the winter he invented the round turn.

All of Paul's inventions were successful except when he decided to run three ten-hour shifts a day and installed the Aurora Borealis. After a number of trials, the plan was abandoned because the lights were not dependable.

"The Seven Axemen of the Red River" they were called because they had a camp on Red River with the three-hundred cooks and the Little Chore Boy. The whole State was cut over from the one camp and the husky seven chopped from dark to dark and walked to and from work.

Their axes were so big it took a week to grind one of them. Each man had three axes and two helpers to carry the spare axes to the river when they got red hot from chopping. Even in those days they had to watch out for forest fires. The axes were hung on long rope handles. Each axe-man would march through the timber whirling his axe around him till the hum of it sounded like one of Paul's for-and-aft mosquitoes, and at every step a quarter-section of timber was cut.

The height, weight and chest measurement of the Seven Axemen are not known. Authorities differ. History agrees that they kept a cord of four-foot wood on the table for toothpicks. After supper they would sit on the deacon seat in the bunk shanty and sing "Shanty Boy" and "Bung Yer Eye" till the folks in the settlements down on the Atlantic would think another nor'wester was blowing up.

Some say the Seven Axemen were Bay Chaleur men; others declare they were all cousins and came from down Machias way. Where they came from or where they went to blow their stake after leaving Paul's camp no one knows but they are remembered as husky lads and good fellows around camp.

After the Seven Axemen had gone down the tote road, never to return, Paul Bunyan was at a loss to find a method of cutting down trees that would give him anything like the output he had been getting. Many trials and experiments followed and then Paul invented the two-man Saw.

The first saw was made from a strip trimmed off in making Big Joe's dinner horn and was long enough to reach across a quarter section, for Paul could never think in smaller units. This saw worked all right in a level country, in spite of the fact that all the trees fell back on the saw, but in rough country only the trees on the hill tops were cut. Trees in the valleys were cut off in the tops and in the pot holes the saw passed over the trees altogether.

It took a good man to pull this saw in heavy timber when Paul was working on the other end. Paul used to say to his fellow sawyer, "I don't care if you ride the saw, but please don't drag your feet." A couple of cousins of Big Ole's were given the job and did so well that ever afterward in the Lake States the saw crews have generally been Scandinavians.

It was after this that Paul had Big Ole make the "Down-Cutter." This was a rig like a mowing machine. They drove around eight townships and cut a swath 500 feet wide.

Paul Bunyan's Trained Ants are proving so successful that they may replace donkeys and tractors on the rugged slopes of the Sierras. Inspired by his success with Bees and Mosquitoes, Paul has developed a breed of Ants that stand six feet tall and weigh 200 pounds.

To overcome their habit of hibernating all Winter, Paul supplied the Ants with Mackinaws made with three pairs of sleeves or legs. They eat nothing but Copenhagen Snuff. The Ants (or Uncles as they prefer to be called) can run to the Westwood shops with a damaged locomotive quicker than the Wrecking Crew can come out. They do not patronize bootleggers or require time off to fix their automobiles.

Lucy, Paul Bunyan's cow was not, so far as we can learn, related to either Babe or Benny. Statements that she was in any way their mother are without basis in fact. The two oxen had been in Paul's possession for a long time before Lucy arrived on the scene.

No reliable data can be found as to the pedigree of this remarkable dairy animal. There are no official records of her butterfat production nor is it known where or how Paul got her.

Paul always said that Lucy was part Jersey and part wolf. Maybe so. Her actions and methods of living seemed to justify the allegation of wolf ancestry, for she had an insatiable appetite and a roving disposition. Lucy ate everything in sight and could never be fed at the same camp with Babe or Benny. In fact, they quit trying to feed her at all but let her forage her own living. The Winter of the Deep Snow, when even the tallest White Pines were buried, Brimstone Bill outfitted Lucy with a set of Babe's old snowshoes and a pair of green goggles and turned her out to graze on the snowdrifts. At first she had some trouble with the new foot gear but once she learned to run them and shift gears without wrecking herself, she answered the call of the limitless snow fields and ran away all over North America until Paul decorated her with a bell borrowed from a buried church.

In spite of short rations, she gave enough milk to keep six men busy skimming the cream. If she had been kept in a barn and fed regularly she might have made a milking record. When she fed on the evergreen trees and her milk got so strong of White Pine and Balsam that the men used it for cough medicine and liniment, they quit serving the milk on the table and made butter out of it. By using this butter, to grease the logging roads when the snow and ice thawed off, Paul was able to run big logging sleds all summer.

The family life of Paul Bunyan, from all accounts, has been very happy. A charming glimpse of Mrs. Bunyan is given by Mr. E. S. Shepard of Rhinelander, Wis., who tells of working in Paul's camp on Round River in '62, the Winter of the Black Snow. Paul put him wheeling prune pits away from the cook camp. After he had worked at this job for three months Paul had him haul them back again as Mrs. Bunyan, who was cooking at the camp, wanted to use them to make the hot fires necessary to cook her famous soft-nosed pancakes.

Mrs. Bunyan, at this time used to call the men to dinner by blowing into a woodpecker hole in an old hollow stub that stood near the door. In this stub there was a nest of owls that had one short wing and flew in circles. When Mr. Shepard made a sketch of Paul, Mrs. Bunyan, with wifely solicitude for his appearance, parted Paul's hair with a hand axe and combed it with an old cross-cut saw.

From other sources we have fragmentary glimpses of Jean, Paul's youngest son. When Jean was three weeks old he jumped from his cradle one night and seizing an axe, chopped the four posts out from under his father's bed. The incident greatly tickled Paul, who used to brag about it to anyone who would listen to him. "The boy is going to be a great logger someday," he would declare with fatherly pride.

The last we heard of Jean he was working for a lumber outfit in the South, lifting logging trains past one another on a single-track railroad.

What is camp without a dog? Paul Bunyan loved dogs as well as the next man but never would have one around that could not earn its keep. Paul's dogs had to work, hunt or catch rats. It took a good dog to kill the rats and mice in Paul's camp for the rodents picked up scraps of the buffalo milk pancakes and grew to be as big as two-year-old bears.

Elmer, the moose terrier, practiced up on the rats when he was a small pup and was soon able to catch a moose on the run and finish it with one shake. Elmer loafed around the cook camp and if the meat supply happened to run low the cook would put the dog out the door and say, "Bring in a moose." Elmer would run into the timber, catch a moose and bring it in and repeat the performance until, after a few minutes work, the cook figured he had enough for a mess and would call the dog in.

Sport, the reversible dog was really the best hunter. He was part wolf and part elephant hound and was raised on bear milk. One night when Sport was quite young, he was playing around in the horse barn and Paul, mistaking him for a mouse, threw a band axe at him. The axe cut the dog in two but Paul, instantly realizing what had happened, quickly stuck the two halves together, gave the pup first aid and bandaged him up. With careful nursing the dog soon recovered and then it was seen that Paul in his haste had twisted the two halves so that the hind legs pointed straight up. This proved to be an advantage for the dog learned to run on one pair of legs for a while and then flop over without loss of speed and run on the other pair. Because of this he never tired and anything he started after got caught. Sport never got his full growth. While still a pup he broke through four feet of ice on Lake Superior and was drowned.

As a hunter, Paul would make old Nimrod himself look like a city dude lost from his guide. He was also a good fisherman. Old-timers tell of seeing Paul as a small boy, fishing off the Atlantic

Coast. He would sail out early in the morning in his three-mast schooner and wade back before breakfast with his boat full of fish on his shoulder.

About this time, he got his shotgun that required four dishpans full of powder and a keg of spikes to load each barrel. With this gun he could shoot geese so high in the air they would spoil before reaching the ground.

Tracking was Paul's favorite sport and no trail was too old or too dim for him to follow. He once came across the skeleton of a moose that had died of old age and, just for curiosity, picked up the tracks of the animal and spent the whole afternoon following its trail back to the place where it was born.

The shaggy dog that spent most of his time pretending to sleep in front of Johnny Inkslinger's counter in the camp office was Fido, the watch dog. Fido was the bug-bear (not bearer, just bear) of the greenhorns. They were told that Paul starved Fido all winter and then, just before payday, fed him all the swampers, barn boys, and student bullcooks. The very marrow was frozen in their heads at the thought of being turned into dog food. Their fears were groundless for Paul would never let a dog go hungry or mistreat a human being. Fido was fed all the watch peddlers, tailors' agents, and camp inspectors and thus served a very useful purpose.

It is no picnic to tackle the wilderness and turn the very forest itself into a commercial commodity delivered at the market. A logger needs plenty of brains and back bone.

Paul Bunyan had his setbacks the same as every logger only his were worse. Being a pioneer, he had to invent all his stuff as he went along. Many a time his plans were upset by the mistakes of some swivel-headed strawboss or incompetent foreman. The winter of the blue snow, Shot Gunderson had charge in the Big Tadpole River country. He landed all of his logs in a lake and in the spring when ready to drive he boomed the logs three times around the lake before he discovered there was no outlet to it. High hills surrounded the lake and the drivable stream was ten miles away. Apparently, the logs were a total loss.

Then Paul came on the job himself and got busy. Calling in Sourdough Sam, the cook who made everything but coffee out of sourdough, he ordered him to mix enough sourdough to fill the big watertank. Hitching Babe to the tank he hauled it over and dumped it into the lake. When it "riz," as Sam said, a mighty lava-like stream poured forth and carried the logs over the hills to the river. There is a landlocked lake in Northern Minnesota that is called "Sourdough Lake" to this day.

Chris Crosshaul was a careless cuss. He took a big drive down the Mississippi for Paul and when the logs were delivered in the New Orleans boom it was found that he had driven the wrong logs. The owners looked at the barkmarks and refused to accept them. It was up to Paul to drive them back upstream.

No one but Paul Bunyan would ever tackle a job like that. To drive logs upstream is impossible, but if you think a little thing like an impossibility could stop him, you don't know Paul Bunyan. He simply fed Babe a good big salt ration and drove him to the upper Mississippi to drink. Babe drank the river dry and sucked all the water upstream. The logs came up river faster than they went down.

Big Ole was the Blacksmith at Paul's headquarters camp on the Big Onion. Ole had a cranky disposition but he was a skilled workman. No job in iron or steel was too big or too difficult for him. One of the cooks used to make doughnuts and have Ole punch the holes. He made the griddle on which Big Joe cast his pancakes and the dinner horn that blew down ten acres of pine. Ole was the only man who could shoe Babe or Benny. Every time he made a set of shoes for Babe they had to open up another Minnesota iron mine. Ole once carried a pair of these shoes a mile and sunk knee deep into solid rock at every step. Babe cast a shoe while making a hard pull one day, and it was hurled for a mile and tore down forty acres of pine and injured eight Swedes that were swamping out skidways. Ole was also a mechanic and built the Downcutter, a rig like a mowing machine that cut down a swath of trees 500 feet wide.

In the early days, whenever Paul Bunyan was broke between logging seasons, he traveled around like other lumberjacks doing any kind of pioneering work he could find. He showed up in Washington about the time The Puget Construction Co. was building Puget Sound and Billy Puget was making records moving dirt with droves of dirt throwing badgers. Paul and Billy got into an argument over who had shoveled the most. Paul got mad and said he'd show Billy Puget and started to throw the dirt back again. Before Billy stopped him, he had piled up the San Juan Islands.

When a man gets the reputation in the woods of being a "good man" it refers only to physical prowess. Frequently he is challenged to fight by "good men" from other communities.

There was Pete Mufraw. "You know Joe Mufraw?" "Oui, two Joe Mufraw, one named Pete." That's the fellow. After Pete had licked everybody between Quebec and Bay Chaleur he started to look for Paul Bunyan. He bragged all over the country that he had worn out six pair of shoe-pacs looking for Paul. Finally, he met up with him.

Paul was plowing with two yoke of steers and Pete Mufraw stopped at the brush-fence to watch the plow cut its way right through rocks and stumps. When they reached the end of the furrow Paul picked up the plow and the oxen with one arm and turned them around. Pete took one look and then wandered off down the trail muttering, "Hox an' hall! She's lift hox an' hall."

Paul Bunyan started traveling before the steam cars were invented. He developed his own means of transportation and the railroads have never been able to catch up. Time is so valuable to Paul he has no time to fool around at sixty miles an hour.

In the early days he rode on the back of Babe, the Big Blue Ox. This had its difficulties because he had to use a telescope to keep Babe's hind legs in view and the hooves of the ox created such havoc that after the settlements came into different parts of the country there were heavy damage claims to settle every trip.

Snowshoes were useful in winter but one trip on the webs cured Paul of depending upon them for transcontinental hikes. He started from Minnesota for Westwood one Spring morning. There was still snow in the woods so Paul wore his snowshoes. He soon ran out of the snow belt but kept right on without reducing speed. Crossing the desert, the heat became oppressive, his mackinaws grew heavy and the snowshoes dragged his feet but it was too late to turn back.

When he arrived in California he discovered that the sun and hot sand had warped one of his shoes and pulled one foot out of line at every step, so instead of traveling on a bee line and hitting Westwood exactly, he came out at San Francisco. This made it necessary for him to travel an extra three hundred miles north. It was late that night when he pulled into Westwood and he had used up a whole day coming from Minnesota.

Paul's fast foot work made him a "good man on the round stuff" and in spite of his weight he had no trouble running around on the floating logs, even the small ones. It was said that Paul could spin a log till the bark came off and then run ashore on the bubbles. He once threw a peavy handle into the Mississippi at St. Louis and standing on it, poled up to Brainerd, Minnesota. Paul was a "white water bucko" and rode water so rough it would tear an ordinary man in two to drink out of the river.

Johnny Inkslinger was Paul's headquarters clerk. He invented bookkeeping about the time Paul invented logging. He was something of a genius and perfected his own office appliances to increase efficiency. His fountain pen was made by running a hose from a barrel of ink and with it he could "daub out a walk" quicker than the recipient of the pay-off could tie the knot in his tussick rope.

One winter Johnny left off crossing the "t's"

and dotting the "i's" and saved nine barrels of ink. The lumberjacks accused him of using a split pencil to charge up the tobacco and socks they bought at the wanagan but this was just bunkshanty talk (is this the origin of the classic term "the bunk"?) for Johnny never cheated anyone.

Have you ever encountered the Mosquito of the North Country? You thought they were pretty well-developed animals with keen appetites, didn't you? Then you can appreciate what Paul Bunyan was up against when he was surrounded by the vast swarms of the giant ancestors of the present race of mosquitoes, getting their first taste of human victims. The present mosquito is but a degenerate remnant of the species. Now they rarely weigh more than a pound or measure more than fourteen or fifteen inches from tip to tip.

Paul had to keep his men and oxen in the camps with doors and windows barred. Men armed with pikepoles and axes fought off the insects that tore the shakes off the roof in their efforts to gain entrance. The big buck mosquitoes fought among themselves and trampled down the weaker members of the swarm and to this alone Paul Bunyan and his crew owe their lives.

Paul determined to conquer the mosquitoes before another season arrived. He thought of the big Bumble Bees back home and sent for several yoke of them. These, he hoped would destroy the mosquitoes. Sourdough Sam brought out two pair of bees, overland on foot. There was no other way to travel for the flight of the beasts could not be controlled. Their wings were strapped with surcingles, they checked their stingers with Sam and walking shoes were provided for them. Sam brought them through without losing a bee.

The cure was worse than the original trouble. The Mosquitoes and the Bees made a hit with each other. They soon intermarried and their off-spring, as often happens, were worse than their parents. They had stingers fore-and-aft and could get you coming or going.

Their bee blood caused their downfall in the long run. Their craving for sweets could only be satisfied by sugar and molasses in large quantities, for what is a flower to an insect with a ten-gallon stomach? One day the whole tribe flew across Lake Superior to attack a fleet of ships bringing sugar to Paul's camps. They destroyed the ships but ate so much sugar they could not fly and all were drowned.

One pair of the original bees were kept at headquarters camp and provided honey for the pancakes for many years.

If Paul Bunyan did not invent Geography he created a lot of it. The Great Lakes were first constructed to provide a water hole for Babe the Big Blue Ox. Just what year his work was done is not known but they were in use prior to the Year of the Two Winters.

The Winter Paul Bunyan logged off North Dakota he hauled water for his ice roads from the Great Lakes. One day when Brimstone Bill had Babe hitched to one of the old water tanks and was making his early morning trip, the tank sprung a leak when they were halfway across Minnesota. Bill saved himself from drowning by climbing Babe's tail but all efforts to patch up the tank were in vain so the old tank was abandoned and replaced by one of the new ones. This was the beginning of the Mississippi River and the truth of this is established by the fact that the old Mississippi is still flowing.

The cooks in Paul's camps used a lot of water and to make things handy, they used to dig wells near the cook shanty. At headquarters on the Big Auger, on top of the hill near the mouth of the Little Gimlet, Paul dug a well so deep that it took all day for the bucket to fall to the water, and a week to haul it up. They had to run so many buckets that the well was forty feet in diameter. It was shored up with tamarac poles and when the camp was abandoned Paul pulled up this cribbing. Travelers who have visited the spot say that the sand has blown away until 178 feet of the well is sticking up into the air, forming a striking landmark.

The Winter of the Deep Snow everything

was buried. Paul had to dig down to find the tops of the tallest White Pines. He had the snow dug away around them and lowered his sawyers down to the base of the trees. When the tree was cut off he hauled it to the surface with a long parbuckle chain to which Babe, mounted on snowshoes, was hitched. It was impossible to get enough stovepipe to reach to the top of the snow, so Paul had Big Ole make stovepipe by boring out logs with a long six-inch auger.

The year of the Two Winters they had winter all summer and then in the fall it turned colder. One day Big Joe set the boiling coffeepot on the stove and it froze so quick that the ice was hot. That was right after Paul had built the Great Lakes and that winter they froze clear to the bottom. They never would have thawed out if Paul had not chopped out the ice and hauled it out on shore for the sun to melt. He finally got all the ice thawed but he had to put in all new fish.

The next spring was the year the rain came up from China. It rained so hard and so long that the grass was all washed out by the roots and Paul had a great time feeding his cattle. Babe had to learn to eat pancakes like Benny. That was the time Paul used the straw hats for an emergency ration.

When Paul's drive came down, folks in the settlements were astonished to see all the river-pigs wearing huge straw hats. The reason for this was soon apparent. When the fodder ran out every man was politely requested to toss his hat into the ring. Hundreds of straw hats were used to make a lunch for Babe.

When Paul Bunyan took up efficiency engineering he went at the job with all his customary thoroughness. He did not fool around clocking the crew with a stopwatch, counting motions and deducting the ones used for borrowing chews, going for drinks, dodging the boss and preparing for quitting time. He decided to cut out labor altogether.

"What's the use," said Paul, "of all this sawing, swamping, skidding, decking, grading and icing roads, loading, hauling and landing? The object of the game is to get the trees to the land-ing, ain't it? Well, why not do it and get it off your mind?"

So he hitched Babe to a section of land and snaked in the whole 640 acres at one drag. At the landing the trees were cut off just like shearing a sheep and the denuded section hauled back to its original place. This simplified matters and made the work a lot easier. Six trips a day, six days a week just cleaned up a township for section 37 was never hauled back to the woods on Saturday night but was left on the landing to wash away in the early spring when the drive went out.

Documentary evidence of the truth of this is offered by the United States government surveys. Look at any map that shows the land subdivisions and you will never find a township with more than thirty-six sections.

The foregoing statement, previously published, has caused some controversy. Mr. T. S. Sowell of Miami, Florida, wrote to us citing the townships in his State that have sections numbered 37 to 40. He said that the government survey had been complicated by the old Spanish land grants. We put the matter up to Paul Bunyan and from his camp near Westwood came this reply:

Red River Advertising Department.

Dear Sir: Yes sir, I remember those sections and a lot of bother they made me too. One winter when I was starting the White Pine business and snaking sections down to the Atlantic Ocean, a man from Florida came along and ordered a bunch of sections delivered down to his place. He wanted to see if he could grow the same kind of White Pine down there. I yarded out a nice bunch of sections and next summer when my drive was in and I wasn't busy I took a crew of Canada Boys and Mainites and poled them down the coast. When I come to collect they said this man was gone looking for a Fountain of Youth or some fool thing.

I don't know what luck he had with his White Pine ranch. I never seen them again. I had a lot of other things to tend to and clean forgot it till you sent me Mr. Sowell's letter. Maybe that man was a Spaniard I don't know.

Yours respectively,
P. BUNYAN.

From 1917 to 1920 Paul Bunyan was busy toting the supplies and building camps for a bunch of husky young fellow-Americans who had a contract on the other side of the Atlantic, showing a certain prominent European (who is now logging in Holland) how they log in the United States.

After his service overseas with the A. E. F., Paul couldn't get back to the States quick enough. Airplanes were too slow so Paul embarked in his Bark Canoe, the one he used on the Big Onion the year he drove logs upstream. When he threw the old paddle into high he sure rambled and the sea was covered with dead fish that broke their backs trying to watch him coming and going.

As he shoved off from France, Paul sent a wireless to New York but passed the Statue of Liberty three lengths ahead of the message. From New York to Westwood he traveled on skis. When the home folks asked him if the Allegheny Mountains and the Rockies had bothered him, Paul replied, "I didn't notice any mountains but the trail was a little bumpy in a couple of spots."

In the forests of the Red River Lumber Company Paul Bunyan can cut his lumber for many future years in the region where Nature found conditions exactly suited to the growth of pine of the finest texture and largest size.

Early in the closing decade of the nineteenth century the Red River people took a long look into the future. Foreseeing the exhaustion of their Minnesota white pine, which came a quarter of a century later, they set out to find the pine that would take its place. Their search covered several years and reached all the important stands in the western States. This was well in advance of the westward movement of the industry and Red River had the pioneer's opportunity for choice and rejection.

Sugar Pine, "cork pine's big brother," is botanically and physically true white pine, with all the family virtues. It is the largest of all pines.

California Pine is the trade name for pinus ponderosa or western yellow pine from certain regions where conditions of growth have so modified the nature of the wood that it is more like white pine than it is like its botanical brothers that grow elsewhere. Some say this change is due to volcanic soil. Whatever the cause, California Pine from Red River's forest is exceptionally light, brightly colored, soft and even textured and second only to Sugar Pine in size.

Red River "Paul Bunyan's" California Pine and Sugar Pine meet the strict requirements of trades that have made white pine their standard. Where freedom from distortion is essential, as for example piano actions, organ pipes, foundry patterns and the best sash and doors, Red River pines are used. They finish economically with paints, stains and enamels and are highly valued as cores for fine hardwood veneers. They work easily, smoothly and cleanly with edged tools and do not nail-split.

The durability of these California pines is shown by their sound condition in California buildings that have stood for generations, many of them in regions where climatic conditions are more conducive to decay than in the middle western and eastern states.

Paul Bunyan tackled a real problem when he came to Westwood. The site of the mill and town was unbroken forest in 1913, sixty mountainous miles from the nearest railroad. Trails were graded into passable roads and materials and machinery were freighted in. When the railroad arrived in 1914 the first mill was in operation and the town well under construction. Town and plant had been detailed on the drafting boards in Minneapolis. Sanitary sewers, water system, electric lights and telephones were extended as the forest was cleared and Westwood, with a population of 5,000, enjoys all the facilities of a modern American community.

The electrically operated sawmill has an annual capacity of 250 million board feet. Dry kilns, one of the largest plywood factories in the country, sash and door factory and re-manufacturing departments round out production of a complete line of lumber products.

Red River operates its own logging railroad, 20 miles of which are electrified, hydro-electric plants and the foundry and machine shops, where many units of the logging and plant machinery are designed and built.

Back in the early days, when his camps were so far from anywhere that the wolves following the tote-teams got lost in the woods, Paul Bunyan made no attempt to keep in touch with the trade. What's the use when every letter that comes in is about things that happened the year before?

Since he came to Westwood Paul has renewed old friendships, formed new ones and kept close contact with the world. Everyone expects great things of Paul Bunyan and with the Red River outfit back of him he has the chance of his life to make good. Continuous production keeps a full assortment of stock on hand. Customers in all parts of America find Westwood a dependable source of supply.

Aleksandr Grin (1880–1932) was born Aleksandr Stepanovich Grinevsky in Kirov Oblast, Russia. With his first publication in 1906, Grin began publishing mainly poetry and short stories. His work was exotic and romantic at a time when most Russian writers used satire to dissect the political climate. A *domovoi* is a protective, typically unseen house spirit and in Slavic culture is sometimes called the "master" of the house. And as in many Slavic folktales, a family could bribe this spirit with milk. "Talkative Domovoi" is reminiscent of *Scarlet Sails*, Grin's most iconic novel, because it is also set in an unnamed fantasy land.

Talkative Domovoi

Aleksandr Grin

Translated by Ekaterina Sedia

I stood by the window, whistling a song about Annie.
> —E. W. Hornung

I

THE DOMOVOI SUFFERING a toothache—doesn't it seem like libeling the being whose services are sought by so many witches and miracle-workers that you'd think he could scarf sugar by the barrel? But it was so, it was the truth—small and sad domovoi sat by the cold stove, its fire long forgotten. He shook his head rhythmically, held onto his bandaged cheek and moaned pitifully, like a child, and suffering pulsed in his red and cloudy eyes.

The rain was pouring outside, and I entered this abandoned house to wait out the weather and saw him . . . he forgot to disappear as would be proper.

"It doesn't even matter," he told me in a voice resembling a combative parrot, "no one will believe that you saw me anyway."

Just in case, I folded my fingers into the sign of a snail's horns, and said, "Don't worry. You won't receive neither a silver coin shot nor a spell from me. But the house is empty."

"And yet how hard is it to leave it despite that," the little domovoi argued. "Just listen. I'll tell you but only because my teeth hurt—I feel better when I talk . . . much better, oy. My dear friend, it was just one hour—and this is why I got stranded here. You see, it is important to understand the whys and the hows. Mine—my kin . . ." He signed plaintively. "Mine—I mean, ours—they all are already brushing horses' tails on the other side of the mountains, they all left here. But I cannot, because I have to understand.

"Look around—there are holes in the walls and the ceiling, but imagine that everything is aglow with warmest, shiniest copperware, the curtains are white and gauzy, and there are as many flowers inside as in the meadows and the forest; the floor is polished, the cold stove you are sitting on like it's a grave marker is red-hot, and the dinner bubbling in pots is exhaling scrumptious steam.

"There used to be mines not far from here—granite pits. And in this house, there used to live a husband and a wife—a rarest pair. His name was Philipp, and hers—Annie. She was twenty years old, and he was twenty-five. Look, look, do you like this?" The domovoi grabbed at a tiny flower that sprang in the dirt that accumulated over the years in the crack of the windowsill, and ceremoniously handed it to me. "This is what she was like. I loved her husband too, but I liked her better—she was so domestic . . . and we like people who are just like us, we find charm in that. Sometimes she would go to the nearby creek and try to catch fish with her bare hands, or strike a great stone at the crossroads and listen how long it would take to go silent, and laughed at the yellow sun dapples on the wall. Don't think her strange—there is magic in things like that, a great knowledge, but only us, goat-legged can read the signs of a great soul; people are not insightful.

"'Annie!' the husband would call joyfully when he came home for lunch from the mine where he was a bookkeeper. 'I am not alone—I brough Ralph with me.' He made this joke so often that Annie smiled and without hesitation set the table for two. And they would meet as if they were just discovering each other—she ran to meet him, and he brought her back in his arms.

"At night, he would take out Ralph's letters—Ralph was his friend he spent many years of his youth with before he met Annie, and he read them out loud. Annie would rest her head on her folded arms and half-listen to the familiar words about the sea and the shining of miraculous rays on the other side of our enormous earth, about volcanoes and pearl-divers, storms and great battles in the shade of gigantic forest trees. And every word resonated like a heavy singing stone at the crossroads, which makes a drawn-out peal every time it is struck.

"'He will arrive soon,' Philipp would say. 'He will visit us when his three-masted *Sinbad* sails to Gres. From there, it is just an hour by train and another hour from the train station to our house.'

"Sometimes Annie would ask a question about Ralph's life, and then Philipp would launch into tales of Ralph's bravery and oddness and generosity, and his fate resembling a fairy tale: poverty and striking gold, how he bought his ship, the lace of the legends spun from ship's rigging, seafoam, games and trade, danger and surprises. Eternal game. Eternal excitement.

Eternal music of the sea and the shore.

"I never heard them fight—and I hear everything. I never saw them look at each other coldly—and I see everything. 'I'm sleepy,' she would say at night, and he would wrap her up in a blanket and carry her to bed like a child. As she was falling asleep, she would ask, 'Phil, who's whispering in the treetops? Who's walking on the roof? Whose face do I see reflected in the creek next to yours?' And he would answer, looking into her half-closed eyes with worry,

"'There's a crow on the roof, the wind blowing through the trees, stones are shining in the creek—go to sleep, and don't walk around barefoot.'

"He would then sit at his desk to finish his latest report, wash his face, prepare the logs for the morning fire, and when he went to bed he fell asleep immediately and always forgot his dreams. And he never went to the crossroads to strike the singing stone, where fairies spin magnificent carpets from dust and moonrays."

II

All right, so listen. There isn't much left of this story of three people who so perplexed the domovoi.

"It was a sunny day, a full blooming of the

earth, when Philipp, his ledger in hand, was taking stock of the granite pit daily output, and Annie, coming home from the station where she did her shopping, stopped by her stone and made it sing with the strikes of her house keys. Now, the stone was a shard from a great mountain, taller than your waist. When you strike it, it rings for a long time, quieter and quieter, and just when you think it went silent, you can press your ear against it and still hear its almost silent voice inside.

"Our forest roads are gardens. Their beauty grasps your heart, the flowers and boughs over your head are watching the sun through their fingers. The sun changes color and your eyes too get tired of it and wander about aimlessly, as its yellow and lilac and dark-green colors dapple the white sand. There is nothing better on such a day than cold water.

"Annie stopped and listened to the forest singing in her very chest, and struck the stone again, smiling every time the new wave of sound caught up and drowned the previous, dying one. She never thought she was being watched, but a man came around the turn of the road and approached her. His steps grew slower until he stopped; she was still smiling when she looked up and saw him—she didn't start or step back, as if he always was there.

"He was tanned—very tanned, and the sea has carved his face into sharpness, like a running wave. And it was beautiful because it reflected an untamed and gentle soul, and his dark eyes looked into Annie's, growing darker and brighter, and her pale eyes looked mildly back.

"You would be correct in thinking that I always followed her—there are snakes in the forest.

"The stone had fallen silent some time ago and they still looked, smiling, wordless, silent. He stretched his hand toward her and she—slowly— extended hers to meet his. He took her head into his hands carefully, so carefully that I was afraid to breathe, and kissed her lips. Her eyes closed.

"Then they stepped away from each other, the stone separating them. Annie turned to see Philipp, coming their way. 'Look, Philipp! Ralph's finally here.'

"Philipp couldn't get a word out at first. Finally, he tossed his hat into the air and shouted, 'Ralph! I see you already met Annie. Look, it's her!' His kind, rough face shone with excitement. 'Ralph, you'll stay with us, we'll show you around. And finally we'll talk and catch up. Look, my friend, my wife . . . she also was waiting for you.'

"Annie rested her hand on her husband's shoulder and looked at him with her warmest, most generous expression, and then looked at their visitor with the same gaze, as if both were equally dear to her.

"'Phil, I'll have to go back,' Ralph said. 'I mixed up your address and thought I was taking the wrong road . . . this is why I left my luggage at the station. I have to go get it.'

"They made plans to meet later and each went their own way. And that's all, hunter, murderer of my friends, I know about it. And I don't understand. Maybe you can explain this to me."

"Did Ralph come back?"

"They waited for him but he wrote from the station that he ran into an acquaintance who offered him a lucrative opportunity he could not turn down."

"What about them?"

"Died . . . Died a long time ago, maybe thirty years. Cold water on a hot day—she was the first, caught a cold. He walked behind her coffin, half-gray, and then disappeared. Locked himself in the room with the firepit, I hear. But before that—what happened? My teeth hurt and I cannot understand."

"And it will be so," I said, politely, shaking his hairy unwashed paw good-bye. "Only we, five-fingered, can read the signs of the heart; domovois are not insightful."

Aleksandr Grin (1880–1932) was a Russian writer who wrote under the name Grin. His full name was Aleksandr Stepanovich Grinevsky. He was a fan of the adventure stories of Robert Louis Stevenson as well as Jules Verne. He created a world called Grinlandia in his most famous work of fiction, *Scarlet Sails*, what some have called the Russian *Treasure Island*. He wrote a lot of fiction set in this fantasy world. He was also influenced by the work of Edgar Allan Poe, and it was rumored he used to carry a photograph of the American writer with him wherever he went. He wrote several well-received novels, as well as more than three hundred short stories. "The Ratcatcher" is one of his longer stories, translated into English for the first time.

The Ratcatcher

Aleksandr Grin

Translated by Ekaterina Sedia

There, over still waters, stands Chillon
There, in the dungeon, seven columns
Covered in centuries-old moss . . .

I

IN THE SPRING OF THE YEAR 1920, specifically in March, specifically on the twenty-second—let's give the accuracy its due, so we may join the lap of sworn documentarists, without which the curious reader would probably start asking questions of the publishers—I went to the market. I went to the market on March 22 of, I repeat, the year 1920. It was the Sennaya Market. I cannot tell you that I positioned myself on a certain corner, nor can I remember what the newspapers were writing about on that day. I did not stand on a corner but instead paced back and forth in front of the ruined building of the market. I was selling a few books—the last of my possessions.

Cold and wet snow, sifting over the heads in the crowd like a cloud of white sparks, gave the scene a repellent air. Fatigue and chill illuminated all faces. I had no luck. I walked around for over two hours, and only three persons asked what I wanted for my books, but even they found my price of five pounds of bread exceedingly high. Meanwhile, it was getting darker—the circumstance most unfortunate for selling books. I stopped on the sidewalk and leaned against a wall.

To my right, there was an old woman in a

hooded cloak and an old black hat with glass beads. With a clockwork shaking of her head, she offered in her knotted fingers two baby bonnets, ribbons, and a stack of yellowed shirt collars. To my left, securing a warm gray kerchief under her chin with her free hand, stood with a rather independent expression a young woman, holding the same wares as I—books. Her small, quite sturdy, shoes, a skirt falling quietly all the way to the toe—unlike those knee-length squirmy skirts that even old women started wearing those days—her flannel jacket and old warm gloves with the fingertips peeking through the holes, and also her demeanor as she looked at the passersby—without a smile or enticements, sometimes angling her long lashes at the books, and how she held them, how she suppressed a sigh with a small grunt when a passerby, having glanced at her hands and then face, walked off, as if surprised and stuffing his mouth with sunflower seeds—everything about her was endearing.

We are curious about people who fit our idea of a person in certain circumstances, and so I asked the girl if her small enterprise was going well. She coughed lightly, turned her head to draw her attentive gray-blue eyes at me, and said, "Same as yours."

We exchanged observations about selling things in general, and at first she only spoke enough to be understood. Then, a man in blue glasses and jodhpurs bought her *Don Quixote*, and she livened up.

"No one knows that I take the books to sell," she said, trustingly showing me a counterfeit bill, wedged among others by the thoughtful citizen, and waving it about absentmindedly. "I mean, I don't steal them, I take them from the shelves when Father is asleep. When Mother was dying. We sold everything then, almost everything. We had no bread or firewood or kerosene. You understand? But my father will be angry if he finds out that I come here. So I come and bring books on the sly. I miss the books, but what can you do? Thank god, we have so many. Do you have a lot too?"

"N-n-no," I said, with the shiver—I already caught a cold and was rasping a bit. "I don't think I have a lot. At least these are all I have."

She looked at me with naive attention—just like peasant children watch a visiting official drinking tea—and, with her bare fingertips, touched the collar of my shirt. It, as well as the collar of my light coat, was missing buttons; I lost them and had never sewn on their replacements, since I have not cared enough about myself for quite a long while already, have given up on my past as well as the future.

"You'll catch a cold," she said, automatically clutching her own kerchief tighter, and I understood that her father loved her, that she was spoiled and frivolous, but kind. "You'll catch a cold because you run around with your collar whipped open. Come closer, citizen."

She stuffed her books under her arm and walked under the arched gates. There I lifted my head with a stupid smile and let her near my throat. She was well built but significantly shorter than I, and once she found all the necessities with the same mysterious, absent expression women have when they fuss with their pins, she put her books on a stoop, made a small effort somewhere under her jacket, and, breathing with great concentration and importance, pinned the edges of my shirt and my coat together with a safety pin.

"Tender like a calf," a stout woman walking by said.

"Well!" The girl critically examined her handiwork. "That's it. You can go for a walk now."

I laughed and wondered. I haven't seen much of such simplicity. We either don't believe in it or don't see it, and we only see it when things are quite bad.

I took her hand and shook it, and thanked her, and asked her name.

"It won't take long to say, but why?" she said, looking at me with pity. "Not worth it. Although write down our phone number; maybe I'll ask you to sell some books."

I wrote it down, smiling, watching her index finger tracing the air as she enunciated each digit like a schoolmarm. Then a crowd running from the horseback-mounted raid surrounded and separated us; I dropped my books and when I picked them up, she was already gone. The alarm was not major enough to leave the market altogether, and an old man in round glasses and a goatee bought my books a few minutes later. He didn't offer much, but I was glad regardless. Only as I was approaching my house did I realize that I also sold the book with the phone number in it and had now irreversibly forgotten it.

II

At first I took it with a light consternation of any minor loss. Still not slaked hunger shielded my perceptions. I thoughtfully boiled the potatoes in the room with waterlogged, rotten windows. I had a small iron stove. As for firewood . . . in those days, many ventured into the attics, and so did I—walked along the slanted darkness of the roofs like a thief, listening to the wind blaring in the chimneys, and spying a pale splotch of the sky through the broken window as the snowflakes settled over the debris. I found splinters remaining from the times they axed down the beams, old window frames, fallen-apart sills and carried it all back to my basement room, listening on the stairwell landings for the clanking of the front door key, letting out a late visitor.

Behind the wall lived a washerwoman; I spent entire days listening to the strong movement of her hands in the washtub, producing the sound reminiscent of the rhythmic chewing of a horse. In the same room, like the clock gone mad, a sewing machine often clanked into deep night. A bare table, a bare bed, a stool, a cup without a saucer, a frying pan, and a kettle I used to boil my potatoes—but enough of these reminders. The spirit of the everyday turns away from the mirror, which the precisely educated people keep pointing at it, and their profanities under the new orthography are as proficient as the old one.

When the night fell, I remembered the mar-

ket and vividly relived every moment as I studied my safety pin. Carmen did not do much—she only tossed a flower at a lazy soldier. No more was committed today. For a long while I had been thinking about meeting someone—first looks, first words. They are memorable and always carve their impression if there is nothing superfluous. There is a perfect purity of such characteristic moments, which could be entirely converted into sentences or a drawing—this is the part of life that gives rise to the arts. A true event, encased in an untroubled simplicity of a natural and true voice, which we hope for with our every step, is always filled with magic. So little, but so fully realized is such an impression.

And this is why I returned to the safety pin again and again, repeating from memory what was said by me and by the girl. Then I grew tired, lay down and came to, but as soon as I got up I fell unconscious. It was the beginning of the typhus, and in the morning, they took me to the hospital. But I had enough memory and wits to put my safety pin into a tin box where I kept my tobacco, and not to separate from it until the end.

III

With a fever of 41 degrees my delirium took shape of visitations. People from whom I have not heard in several years came to see me. I had long conversations with all of them, and asked every one of them to bring me some sour milk. But as if they all conspired with each other, they kept telling me that sour milk was forbidden by the doctor. Meanwhile I secretly waited to spy among their faces, blinking in and out as if in banya fog, the new sister of mercy—who, I reasoned, must be no other than the girl with the safety pin. From time to time she walked past behind the wall among the tall flowers, in a golden crown against the golden sky. How mildly, how joyfully her eyes shone! Even when she made no appearance, her unseen presence filled the ward, flickering with suppressed lights, and from time to time I pushed the safety pin in its box with my fingers. By the morning, five of us were dead and the red-cheeked orderlies carried them out, and my thermometer showed 36 and a fraction, after which a sober and merry recovery followed. I was discharged from the hospital three months later, when I could walk although with some pain in my legs, and I found myself homeless. My room was already given to an invalid, and I was morally incapable of going from office to office to solicit new housing.

Maybe now would be a good time to mention a few things about my appearance, using as reference the letter my friend Repin wrote to the journalist Fingal. I quote it only to aid the reader's imagination, and not to further my vanity. "His complexion is dark," Repin wrote, "with a reluctant to everything expression of his regularly proportioned face, he cuts his hair short, speaks slowly and with an effort." This was all true, but such a manner of speaking was not a consequence of illness—it stemmed from the sorrowful sensation, rarely even acknowledged by ourselves, that our internal life is of interest to a very few. However, I was fixedly curious about every other soul, and this is why I expressed myself little and listened more. And this is why when several people gathered, animatedly determined to interrupt each other as much as possible, to attract maximum attention to themselves, I usually withdrew to the side.

For three weeks I slept in the apartments of my friends and friends' friends, in a course of a compassionate relay. I slept on floors and sofas, on the kitchen stove and on empty crates, on chairs pushed together, and once on an ironing board. During this time I saw plenty of interesting things, the glory of life resolutely fighting for warmth, people dear to it, and food. I saw the stove being stoked by a china hutch, the kettle being boiled over a lamp; I saw horsemeat cooked in coconut oil and on stolen newels from ruined buildings. But all of it—and more, and much greater than this—is already described by many quills, shredding the novelty to bits, and we won't

capture it. Other events are pulling me along— the ones that happened to me.

IV

By the end of the third week I contracted acute insomnia. How it started is hard to say, I only remember that I fell asleep with greater and greater difficulty, and woke up earlier. During that time, a random encounter led me to a dubious shelter. As I was walking along the Moika Canal and amusing myself with the sights of fishing—a peasant with a net on a long rod sedately followed the granite embankment, occasionally lowering his contraption into the water and pulling out a handful of tiny fish—I met a store owner from whom I used to buy groceries; the man now had an office job of some sort. He was admitted to a multitude of homes on some official household managerial footing. I did not recognize him right away: not an apron, not a cotton shirt with a Turkish pattern, nor mustache nor beard; the former shopkeep wore severe military garb, was cleanly shaven, and resembled an Englishman, but with a Yaroslavl tint. Even though he was carrying a very thick briefcase, he lacked the power to just house me wherever he pleased, but he did offer me the empty quarters of the Central Bank, where 260 rooms stood like pond water, quiet and empty.

"Vatican," I said, slightly recoiling at the thought of such apartments. "But isn't anyone living there? Or maybe someone does come by, and if they do, will the janitor call the police?"

"Oh," the ex-shopkeep said. "That house is not far; let's go and see for yourself."

He took me through a large yard, crossed by arched gates of different yards, looked around, and, as there was nobody there, headed confidently to the dark corner, where the back staircase led us upward. He stopped on the third landing in front of an ordinary apartment door; there was trash stuck under it. The landing was thickly littered with soiled paper. It seemed uninhabited silence from behind the door seeped through the keyhole in slabs of nothingness. There the shop-keep showed me how to open the door without a key: pull the door handle, shake and press it upward, and then two halves swung open, since there was no latch.

"There is a key," the shopkeep said, "but not with me. Who knows this secret, can enter easily. Just don't tell anyone the secret, and you can lock the doors from the inside as well as the outside, just slam them shut. If you need to leave, peek at the staircase first—there is a small window for that (indeed, at the face height in the wall near the door there was a spy hole with broken glass). I won't come in with you. You are an educated man, you'll see how to arrange yourself best; just know that you can hide an entire regiment in there. Feel free to stay for three nights or so; as soon as I find some other housing for you, I'll notify you immediately. And to that effect—please excuse the delicate subject, but everyone needs to eat and drink—please accept this as a loan until your circumstances improve."

He slung flat a fat wallet and pressed into my silently limp hand, as if paying the doctor for a visit, several bills, repeated his instructions and left, and I closed the door and sat down on a crate. Meanwhile the silence we always hear inside us—the reminder of life's sounds—already beckoned me, like a forest. It was hiding behind the half-closed door of the neighboring room. I stood up and started exploring.

I passed from door to door of tall, large rooms like a man stepping on new ice. It was spacious and resonant all around me. As soon as I left one set of doors, I already saw others in front of me and to the sides, leading to the diminishing light of the farther away, darker entrances. Paper was strewn about on the parquet floors like dirty spring snow; its abundances reminded one of the heaps on the sidewalks of shoveled streets. In some rooms one had to walk on its wobbly debris, knee-high, starting at the very doors.

Paper in every variation, of every purpose and color, spread its omniscient commotion with a truly magnificent scale. It swept up the walls in snowdrifts, hung onto the sills, flowed in white floods from one square of parquet flooring onto the next, streaming out of the wardrobes, filling the corners, occasionally forming barriers and plowed fields. Notebooks, forms, ledgers, dust jackets, numbers and rulers, texts printed and handwritten—the contents of thousands of cabi-nets everted before my eyes—my gaze wandered, intimidated by the magnitude of the spectacle. All rustles, all footfalls, and even my own breath sounded as if pressing against my ears—so grand, so engrossingly acute was this empty silence. The entire time the dull smell of dust followed me; the windows were double-paned. As I glanced through their evening glass, I saw either the trees by the canal or the roofs of the annexes or the facade of Nevsky Palace. It told me that these quarters circled the entire city block, but its size, owing to the frequent and tedious tactility of its space, sectioned by the constant walls and door-ways, felt like the trek of many days of walking—the feeling opposite to what we mean when we say Little Street or Little Square. Even when I first started my exploration, I compared this place to a labyrinth. Everything was monotone—heaps of trash, occasional emptiness, marked by windows and doorways, and the expectation of many other doors devoid of human commotion. So would a man move, if he could, inside the mirrored realm when two mirrors repeat to the point of numb-ness the space they captured, and all that would be missing was his own face looking through the doorway like a frame.

I have traversed no more than twenty rooms but I was already disoriented and started to note signs as not to get completely lost: a slab of dry-wall on the floor; a broken bureau over there, and here a torn-out door panel propped against the wall; the windowsill buried under lilac ink-wells; heaps of used blotting paper; a fireplace; an occasional cabinet or an upturned chair. But even these signs started to repeat: as I looked back, I noticed with surprise that I occasionally happened somewhere where I had already visited, and only realized that I was mistaken by noticing an array of additional objects. Sometimes I happened upon a steel safe with its door hanging open like an empty stove, a telephone that looked more like a post box or a mushroom on a birch; a folding ladder; I even found a black hat form that included itself in this inventory for some unknown reason.

The dusk already caressed the depth of the halls, glowing white with paper in a distance, the nexuses and hallways grew indistinct in the dusk and the clouded light twisted the parquet into rhombic patterns across doorways, but the walls adjacent to windows still shone in places with the tense glow of the sunset. The memory of what I left behind as I passed coagulated like milk the moment new entrances opened up before me, and I, at my core, only knew and remembered that I was walking on trash and paper through the rows of walls. In one place, I had to climb upward, kneading the heaps of slippery manila folders with my feet; the noise as if through the bushes. As I walked I kept glancing back with trepidation—so thick, inseparable from me was the smallest sound, that I felt as if I was dragging bunches of dried-up brooms on my shoes, listening if all this walking would catch someone else's hearing. At first, I trod on the neural matter of the bank, stomping on black grains of the numbers with a sense that I was violating the harmony of orchestral notes, heard from Alaska to Niagara. I was not looking for these comparisons: they, called forth by the unforgettable sights, materialized and disappeared like a chain of figures made of smoke. I felt like I was walking on the bottom of an aquarium after the water had been drained from it, or among the ice floes, or—and this was the most distinct and gloomy impression—that I was meandering through past centuries turned into the present. I walked the length of the inner corridor, so twistedly long that one could ride a bicycle along it. At the end of it there was a set of stairs, and I walked up to the next floor and descended a different flight of stairs, having passed a moderately sized hall crowded with armature. I could see orbs of matte glass, tulip-

and bell-shaped lampshades, serpentine bronze chandeliers, coils of wire, heaps of china and copperware.

The next confused passage took me to the archives, where in the crowded darkness of bookshelves, slicing the space in parallel rows connecting the floor and the ceiling, the passage was impossible. A mess of copied books rose all the way to my chest and higher; I was unable to take a good look around—so jumbled together everything was.

I took the side door and followed the semi-dusk of whitewashed walls, until I saw a large arch spinning between the vestibule and the grand central hall, lined with two rows of black columns. The alabaster rails ran along the tops of the columns in a giant rectangle; I could hardly discern the ceiling. A person suffering from fear of open spaces would've left covering his face—so far away was the other end of this space that could accommodate throngs, where the opposite doors were black rectangles no bigger than playing cards. A thousand people could dance here. In the center there was a fountain, and its masks, with mockingly or tragically open mouths, seemed a mound of real heads. Abutting the columns, a long counter unfurled, guarded by a matte glass barrier and red lettering indicating cashiers' and bookkeepers' offices. Broken dividers and ruined cubicles, the desks pushed against the walls were almost invisible, swallowed by the hall's enormousness. It took an effort for a human gaze to collect these objects indicating gutted life. I stood immobile, taking it all in. I started to develop the taste for this spectacle, to understand its style. Once again I understood the elation of a great conflagration's eyewitness. The temptation of destruction sang its romantic insights—it was as if a unique landscape, terrain, or even an entire country. Its coloring naturally transitioned my impression into a suggestion, similar to a musical suggestion of the original motif. It was difficult to imagine that at some point a multitude of thousands moved through here, with thousands of concerns in their thoughts and briefcases. Everything was now stamped with decay and silence. But the air of unheard of daring blew from door to door—a magnificent, unstoppable force of nature, crushing everything as easily as a foot flattens an eggshell. This impression sowed a peculiar mental itch, pulling my thoughts toward catastrophes with the same magnetic force that pushes us to look into an abyss.

It seemed that a single echoing idea surrounded every form here, and followed like ringing in one's ears—a thought that resembled a motto:

"Finished and is silent."

V

Finally I grew weary. I could barely discern the passages and the stairwells. I was hungry. I could not possibly hope to find an exit to go out and buy something to eat. In one of the kitchens I slaked my thirst with some tap water—to my amazement the water ran, although weakly, and this insignificant sign of life refreshed me on its own. Then I started to choose a room. It took a few more minutes, until I came across an office with a single door, a fireplace, and a telephone. The furniture was largely absent, and the only thing one could lie or sit upon was a scalped and legless sofa, bristling in all directions with flayed leather, springs, and horse hair. In the alcove in one of the walls there was a tall hazelnut cabinet—locked. I smoked a cigarette or two, until I reached a relative mental equilibrium, and prepared for my rest.

It was a long time since I had experienced the joy of exhaustion—deep and restful sleep. During the daylight I thought of the nightfall with the caution of a man carrying a vessel overflowing with water, trying not to get irritated, almost certain that this time my fatigue would win over the tedious alert consciousness. But the closer it would get to midnight, the more my senses confirmed their unnatural keenness; a dark liveliness, like flashes of magnium in the dusk, wound my nerves into a resonant to a smallest impression, taut string, and it was if I woke from day into the

night, with its long journey inside a restless heart. My fatigue would dissipate, my eyes pricked as if by dry sand; every incipient thought immediately developed in every possible complexity of its implications, and the imminent long and idle hours made me indignant, like compulsory and fruitless labor I could not avoid. With my every fiber, I summoned sleep. In the morning, with my body as if filled with hot water, I sucked in the mendacious presence of sleep in pretend yawning, but the moment I would close my eyes I would immediately experience the senselessness of this situation, like does everyone who closes his eyes during daylight. I had tried every remedy: staring at motes on the walls, counting, immobility, repetition of a single phrase—and all in vain.

I had a candle stub with me, an absolutely indispensable thing in the days when the staircases were never lit. Albeit dimly, it illuminated the cold height of my enclosure, and I filled the gouges in the couch with paper and constructed a headrest from books. My coat was my blanket. I needed to light the fireplace, so I could watch the fire. Besides, even though it was summer, it was not particularly warm. At least I had something to do, and it cheered me up. Soon sheaves of ledgers and bills burned in the roomy fireplace in a strong flame, crumbling into ash through the grate. The firelight pushed apart the dusk of the open doorway, spreading into a still shining puddle in a distance.

But fruitlessly secretive this fire burned. It did not illuminate the habitual objects that we study in the fantastical light of red and yellow embers, and find there an inner warmth and light of our souls. It was harsh, like a thief's bonfire. I lay, propping my head with my numb arm, without any desire to doze off. All my efforts toward it would be an actor's pretense when he yawns as the crowd watches and lies in bed. Besides, I was hungry and to silence my hunger I smoked often.

I lay, lazily watching the fire and the cabinet. Then it occurred to me that the cabinet must be locked not without a reason. But what could possibly be hidden in it, if not sheaves of dead papers? What could possibly not yet be taken from there? My sad experiment with a trove of burned-out electric bulbs in one such cabinet made me suspect that this cabinet was locked without intention, just because someone thrifty turned the key. And nonetheless I stared at the massive doors, solid like the front gates of the building, and thought of food. I was not very seriously hoping to find anything edible. My stomach drove me blindly, always forcing me to think in its own stenciled pattern—just like it summons forth saliva at the sight of food. To entertain myself I wandered through a few of the adjacent rooms, and rifled through in the light of my candle nub, and after I did not find even a bread crust, I returned, beckoned by the cabinet ever more. In the fireplace the last of the ashes were dimly burning out. My reasoning dealt with vagrants such as myself. Could someone have locked in a loaf of bread, or maybe a kettle and some tea and sugar? Diamonds and gold would be kept elsewhere, quite obviously. I thought I was in my right to open the cabinet, because of course I would never touch any valuables were I to find them, but as for the edible stuffs, whatever the law said on the matter, I now had a claim.

As I lit my way, I was not too eager to critique my own assertion so as not to accidentally lose my moral ground. I picked up a steel ruler, guided its tip into the keyhole, pressed against the lock, and pulled backward. The latch rang and came off, the cabinet creaked and opened, and I stepped back, as I saw the improbable. I threw the ruler on the ground in an abrupt movement, I shook and did not cry out only because I lacked the strength. I was stunned, as if by icy water dumped over my head from a barrel.

VI

The first tremor of discovery was at the same time the tremor of an instantaneous but terrible doubt. But this was no derangement of the senses. I saw a cache of valuable foodstuffs—six shelves, stretching into the depths of the cabinet, groaning under the heft of their load. It was com-

prised of everything that had grown rare—the choice groceries of a wealthy, well-fed household, the very taste and smell of which had become a hazy memory. I pulled a desk closer and started my survey.

First I closed the doors, shy of the empty spaces like suspicious eyes; I even stepped out to listen for footfalls of someone, who like myself wandered among these walls. The silence was my cue.

I started my survey at the top. The top, sixth and fifth shelves, were occupied by four large baskets, from which, as soon as I touched them, a large rust-colored rat jumped out and flopped to the floor with a nauseating shriek. My hand spasmed as I stood, petrified with disgust. My next movement provoked the escape of two more vile creatures as they skittered between my feet like large lizards. I shook the baskets and banged on the side of the cabinet and jumped immediately back—would there be a deluge of these sinuous, gloomy little bodies, twisting their tails? But the rats, if there were any more, must have escaped through the back of the cabinet into the fissures in the wall—the cabinet stood still.

Of course, I was surprised by the manner of keeping provisions in places where mice (Murinae) and rats (*Mus decumanus*) must have felt at home. But my delight outstripped all ruminations, they could barely squeeze through this whirlwind apotheosis, like water through the dam. Let no one tell me that the senses connected to food are base; that our appetite makes humanity equal with amphibians. In the moments such as I experienced, our entire being is transported, and our joy is no less radiant than at a sight of a dawn from the mountaintops. The soul marches along with the band music. I was already drunk with the sight of my treasures, especially since every basket held an assortment of homogenous, but varied if put together, delights. One basket contained cheeses—a collection of cheeses from dry blue to Rochester and brie. The second, no less hefty, smelled like a meat grocer's shop; its hams, sausages, smoked tongues, and stuffed turkeys gave way to the next basket, filled with battery of canned goods. The fourth was engorged with mounds of eggs. I knelt, to examine the lower shelves. There I discovered eight hunks of sugar; a tea chest; an oaken barrel with copper hoops filled with coffee; baskets of tea biscuits, cakes, and toasts. Two lowest shelves resembled a restaurant basement, since their only contents were the wine bottles in the arrangement and abundance of a cord of firewood. Their labels mentioned every taste, every brand, every accolade and achievement of their winemakers.

It was prudent if not hurry up then at least start eating, since, clearly, the treasure with the fresh appearance of a well-planned cache, could not have been abandoned out of somebody's desire to cheer up an unexpected visitor of this place with such an enormous find. During the day or night, but a man could just show up and start yelling and raising his arms, if not something more dangerous—say, a knife. Everything indicated the dark stab of a coincidence. There were many things I should've been wary of in this place, since I had stood against the unknown. Meanwhile the hunger spoke its own language, and I, having closed the cabinet, sat on the cadaver of the couch, surrounded by provisions on large sheets of paper I used instead of plates. I ate the most substantial foods, that is toast, ham, eggs, and cheese, chasing it with tea biscuits and washing the lot down with Port. At first I could not hold back shivers and nervous uneasy laugh, but once I calmed down somewhat, when I somewhat accepted possessing all these scrumptious morsels, not even fifteen minutes ago mere fantasies, then I took possession of my movements and thoughts. Satiety happened quickly, much quicker than I expected when I just started eating, as the result of my excitement, strenuous even for my appetite. But I was too exhausted to simply resign, and my satiety offered succor without the usual mental dullness that accompanies the everyday consumption of voluminous courses. After I ate all that I took and then thoroughly destroyed the remains of my feast, I felt that this evening was good.

Meanwhile as much as I strained myself with conjectures, they only scratched the surface of the event like a dull knife, leaving its gist hidden from the unenlightened eye. As I walked the sleeping enormousness of the bank, I possibly have quite accurately deduced how my shopkeep was connected to this paperwork Klondike: it was possible to remove and carry out hundreds of trainloads of wrapping paper, so valued by the shop clerks for its ability to skew the weighing of groceries. Besides, the electric cords and small armature could be exchanged for more than a handful of bills: it was no coincidence that the wiring and the outlets were cut out from most of the walls I examined. This is why I did not peg him for the owner of the hidden provisions; he probably kept his elsewhere. But I could not progress a single step past this point as all my ruminations were baseless. My find had not been touched by anyone in quite a while, as proven by the traces of rats; their teeth left vast gouges on cheeses and hams.

I was sated and I examined the cabinet again, discovering some things I had missed in the first flash of discovery. Among the baskets there were packages with knives, forks, and napkins; behind the hunks of sugar, a large silver samovar hid; one chest clinked with colliding glasses, champagne flutes, and etched glassware. It looked like the society that gathered here did so in pursuit of either debauched or conspiratorial aims, counting on isolation and secrecy—perhaps some influential organization, with knowledge by and help from the housing association. If it was so, I had to keep alert. I tidied the cabinet the best I could, hoping that the small amounts I consumed for supper would not be missed. However (and I did not feel guilty) I took a few things, wrapped them and another bottle of wine in a tight package, and hid it under an avalanche of paper near a bend of the twisting corridor.

Of course in those moments I lacked the inclination to not only sleep but to even lie down. I lit a blond, fragrant cigarette, made with fibrous tobacco, with a long holder—my only find I fully gave its due, filling all my pockets with delightful cigarettes. I was in a state of intoxicating, musical anticipation, a man who had a long chain of loud improbabilities awaiting him. In this brilliant turmoil, I remembered the girl in a gray kerchief who pinned my collar closed with a safety pin—could I ever forget this motion? She was the only person of whom I thought in beautiful and touching words. It is useless to quote them, since the moment one sounds them out they lose their enchanting air. This girl, whose name I did not even know, disappeared, leaving a trace similar to a streak of light running across water to the setting sun. Such a meek effect she made with her simple safety pin and the sound of her focused breathing as she rose on tiptoe. This is truly what white magic is; since the girl, like I, was in need, I fervently wanted to spoil her with my blinding discovery. But I did not know where she was and I could not call her. Even if my charitable memory would cry out the forgotten number, it would not help here, even with the abundance of telephones to which my eyes inexorably turned: they did not work—could not work, for reasons all too obvious. I stared at one of the apparatuses with a certain pernicious doubt, in which the rational thought took no part whatsoever. I reached for it playfully. The urge to commit an act of silliness would not let go, and, like all nighttime nonsense, festooned itself with ephemera of the sleepless fantasies. I had convinced myself that I would remember the number if only I took the physical position of talking on the phone. And those mysterious wall fungi with a caoutchouc mouth and a metal ear always seemed to me objects not entirely knowable—a kind of superstition, inspired among other things by *The Atmosphere* by Flammarion, with its story about lightning. I highly recommend to everyone to reread this book and contemplate the peculiarities of the electrical storms, and especially the actions of ball lightning capable, for example, of hanging a frying pan or a shoe on the knife handle of the knife it previously drove into the wall; or re-tiling a roof in such a way that all the tiles are laid in the precise reverse order; and not to mention the photographs on the bodies of those killed by the lightning, the photographs of their surroundings at the moment where the tragedy happened. They are always faint blue, like the old daguerreotypes. "Kilowatts" and "amperes" mean little to me. In my case, the apparatus was the case for a premonition, without the strange languid haziness that usually accompanies most of the absurdities we commit. And so, I can explain to you now, I was akin to an iron rod in front of a magnet.

I picked up the receiver. It seemed colder to me than it actually was, numb, facing the indifferent wall. I put it to my ear expecting not much more than from a broken watch, and pressed the button. Was it the ringing in my ears or an aural memory, but I trembled when I heard the buzzing of a fly, the insect-like vibration of the wires, which, under these conditions, was the very absurdity I strove for.

The persnickety urge to comprehend, like the decay that wears even a marble sculpture, strips any experience with a secret source of its immediate impact. The desire to comprehend the incomprehensible was not among my assets, but I did test my impression. I took the receiver away from my ear and reproduced that characteristic sound in my imagination, but it only reappeared once I listened to the receiver once more. The sound did not waver, did not cease, did not wane, and did not increase; the invisible space hummed in the receiver, as it was supposed to, awaiting contact. Strange impressions took hold of me, strange like the humming of the telephone wire in this dead house. I saw the knots of entangled wires, torn by gale winds and connecting at imperceptible nexuses of their own chaos; bouquets of electrical sparks shooting out of hunched backs of cats jumping from roof to roof; magnetic flashes of tram lines; the fabric and the heart of matter in the shape of sharp angles of a futurist drawing. These thoughts-visions lasted no longer than a single heartbeat; my heart reared up, beating, drumming out the sensations of night forces in some untranslatable language.

Then from the walls an image of that girl, clear like a new moon, arose. Could I have expected that the impression of her would be so viable and enduring? A force of a hundred people bound and hummed in me when, staring at the rubbed out numbers of the apparatus, I led my memory through the snowstorm of integers, vainly trying to conjure up a combination that would restore the lost phone number.

Sly, inconstant memory! It swears to never forget neither numbers nor days nor details, nor a dear face, and when we doubt it it responds with a look of innocence. But the time comes, and the naive one realizes that he made a deal with a shameless ape, who would trade a precious diamond ring for a handful of nuts. The features of the remembered face are incomplete and hazy, the important number is missing digits, and uselessly he clutches his head in his hands, tormented by a slippery memory. But if we remembered, if we could recall everything—what mind would be able to withstand without price the entire life beheld in one instance, especially the remembrances of feelings?

I senselessly repeated digits, moving my lips to grasp their trustworthiness. Finally an array reminiscent of the forgotten number flashed—107-21. "One hundred and seven, twenty-one," I enunciated, probing, but did not know with certainty if I was mistaken again. A sudden doubt blinded me when I pushed the button the second time, but it was too late: the buzzing filled into a roar, something pinged and shifted in the telephone distance, and right against the skin of my cheek a tired female contralto said, "Station." "Station!" it repeated impatiently, but even then I would not speak right away—my throat constricted so coldly!—because in the depths of my heart I was still merely playing a game.

Whatever the case, if I bound and summoned these spirits—call them "Atmosphere" or "Kilowatts" of the society of year 86—I spoke and I was answered. The wheels of a broken watch turned the gears. Above my head, the steel rays of its hands started moving. Whoever gave the pendulum its push, the mechanism started to turn. "One hundred seven twenty-one," I said

dully, watching my candle growing short among the rubbish. "Group A," the displeased answer followed, and the roar was clapped down with a distant movement of a weary wrist.

At these moments, I felt mentally overheated. My finger pressed the very button with the letter A on it; it not only meant that the phone worked but also confirmed the miraculous reality of the entangled wires—a detail remarkable for the impatient soul. As I tried to connect A, I pressed B. Then in the tonality of the electrical current set free, as if a door suddenly swung open, sharp voices barged in, as if from a gramophone loudspeaker—the unknown screamers, beating in my hand holding the receiver. They interrupted each other with the impatience and harshness of people arguing in the streets. Their mixed exclamations were like the concerto of rooks: "Ah-la-la-la-la!" an unknown being yowled against a baritone of someone else's measured and slow speech, separated with pauses and punctuation, and a cloying expression. "I cannot offer . . ."—"If you see . . ."—"Someday . . ."—"I am telling you that . . ."—"You are listening . . ."—"Size thirty and five . . ."—"Over . . ."—"The car has been sent . . ."—"I don't understand any of this . . ."—"Hang up the phone . . ." And into this marketplace trance weakly, like the mosquito whining, crept moans, distant weeping, laughter, cries, violin scales, the shuffle of slow footfalls, rustles, and whispers. Where, in which streets did these words of worry and reproach and pleas and complaints sound? Finally, a businesslike movement clanged, the voices fell silent, and into the hum of the wires entered the same voice. "Group B."

"A! I need A," I said. "The wires are mixed up." After a silence in which the hum fell quiet twice, a new voice announced, with a lilt and softer, "Group A."

"One hundred and seven twenty-one," I enunciated as clearly as I could.

"One hundred and eight zero one," the phone girl said thoroughly and indifferently, and I barely held back the deadly correction—the mistake certainly restored the forgotten number: I recognized it the moment I heard it, as one discerns a familiar face in the passerby.

"Yes yes," I said in extreme excitement, running high along the rim of a vertiginous abyss. "Yes, exactly—one hundred and eight zero one."

Everything froze inside and around me. The sound of the connection squeezed my heart with a rising icy wave; I did not even hear the usual "Dialing now" and "You are connected"—I do not remember what had been said. I listened to birds, trilling compelling songs. Swooning, I leaned against the wall. Then, after a pause— such cruelty—fresh, fresh like fresh air, a reasonable and small voice cautiously said, "I am trying. I am speaking into a non-functioning telephone because you heard a ring? Who is it?" She spoke apparently not expecting an answer, just in case, in a tone of lighthearted scolding.

I said, almost screamed, "I am the one who spoke to you at the market and left with your safety pin. I was selling books. Please remember, I beg you. I don't have the name—please tell me it is you."

"How strange." The voice coughed thoughtfully. "Wait, don't hang up. I am pondering. Old man, have you ever seen such a thing?"

The latter was not addressed to me. A male voice answered her indistinctly, probably from another room.

"I remember our meeting," she again addressed my ear. "But I don't remember the pin you're talking about. Oh yes! I did not realize your memory is so robust. But it is so strange to talk to you—our phone has been turned off. What happened? Where are you calling from?"

"Can you hear me well?" I answered, avoiding to name the place where I was located, as if I didn't get that question, and once I received her assurance, I continued, "I am not sure how much longer we can talk. There are reasons why I cannot dwell on it. Like you, I don't know many things. So please tell me your address right away—I do not have it."

For a while the current hummed evenly, as if my last words had interrupted the transmission.

Again the distance stretched like a solid wall— the repellent disappointment and embarrassed longing almost sent me into a long and inappropriate tirade on the nature of phone conversations, preventing us from free expressions of nuances of the most simple and natural emotions. In some cases, face and the words are inalienable. Perhaps she was contemplating the same during the silence, and then I heard, "What for? But all right. Here, write it down." She said "write it down" not without certain slyness. "Write this down. My address: 5th line, 97, apartment 11. But why, why do you need my address? To be honest, I don't understand. I am usually home in the evenings. . . ."

The voice continued unhurried but had grown quiet and dull, as if trapped in a chest. I could hear her—she seemed to be expounding on something—but without discerning words. Her speech grew more distant and blurred, until it sounded like the drumming of raindrops—and finally the barely perceived pulse of the current indicated that it had stopped. There was no connection and the apparatus remained dumbly silent. In front of me, there was the wall, the case, the receiver. The night rain was drumming on the windowpanes. I pressed the button; it clanged and stopped. The resonator died; the enchantment departed.

But I heard, I spoke, what happened could not have not happened. The impressions of these minutes flooded and left in a whirlwind, and I was still filled with its echoes and I sat down, suddenly exhausted, as if I had just run up a steep staircase. Meanwhile I was in the mere beginning of the events. Their development began with the knock of distant footfalls.

VII

Still very far away from me—was it at the very beginning of my trek?—and maybe on the other side, quite a long way from the first sound I caught, the mysterious footsteps sounded. One could tell that it was someone alone, stepping lively and lightly, taking a familiar route in the dark and possibly lighting their way with a hand-held flashlight or a candle. However in my mind I saw him hurrying cautiously in the dark; he walked looking around and behind him. I didn't know why I imagined that. I sat immobile and panicked, as if grabbed from afar by a pair of giant pliers. I was filled with anticipation to the point of pain in my temples, I was in distress robbing me of any ability of counteraction. I would be calm or at least would've grown calmer were the footfalls to grow more distant, but I heard them more and more clearly, closer to me, and I was held as if in a stupor by this languidly long walk across the empty building, tormenting my hearing. The premonition that I would not be able to escape the meeting touched my consciousness repulsively; I stood and then sat again, unsure of what to do. My pulse followed the rhythms and pauses of the footfalls precisely, and once it was able to overcome the glum dullness of the body, the heart started beating with full force, and I felt my existence in its every contraction. My intentions got confused; I hesitated whether to put out the candle or leave it burning, and it was not a rational thought—but the very possibility of any action seemed to me a good way of avoiding the dangerous meeting. I had no doubt that the meeting would be dangerous and alarming. I had felt calm among these uninhabited walls, and longed to hold on to this night's illusion. Once I stepped outside the doors, trying to step silently, to see whether I could hide in any of the adjacent rooms, as if the room I sat in, my back blocking the candle light from my nub, was already marked for visitation and someone knew that I am in it. I abandoned the idea, realizing that as I move about, I would act as a roulette player, who would see with consternation, once he changed numbers, that he only lost because he was unfaithful to its chosen digit. It would be most prudent to sit and wait, after I put out the fire. I did so, and waited in the dark.

Meanwhile there was no doubt left that the distance between me and the unknown intruder was shrinking with every beat of my pulse. He was walking now not farther away than five or six walls, gliding from door to door with a smooth alacrity of featherweight body. I tensed, entrapped by the footfalls, bound to the speeding, like an automobile, collision of meeting glances—eye to eye, and I prayed to God that his would not have a mad smudge of the white above the darkly shining pupils. I was no longer waiting but knowing that I would see him; my instinct took over reason and was telling me the truth, nudging its blind snout into the sharp edge of fear. Ghosts entered the darkness. I saw a furry creature from the dark corner of the nursery, a gloomy phantom, and—most terrifying, scarier than a fall from a great height—I feared that behind my door the footsteps would fall silent, there would be no one there, and this absence would touch my face with a gust of air. There was no time to imagine a man such as myself. The meeting careened closer; there was nowhere to conceal myself. Then the footfalls went silent, stopped so close to the door, and for the longest time I heard nothing but the skittering of mice in the paper heaps, and I could barely hold back a scream. I imagined that someone, hunched over, was creeping through the door, intent to grab. The stupor of meaningless exclamation, resounding on the dark, threw me forward, my arms outstretched in front of me—and I recoiled, covering my face. The light shone, throwing the entire visible expanse from door to door. It became as light as day. I felt a sort of nervous shock but, after a moment's hesitation, went forth. Behind the nearest wall, a woman's voice said, "Come here." Then a soft, pert laugh.

With all my shock, I did not expect such an end to the torture I had just endured for likely an hour. "Who is calling?" I asked softly, cautiously moving toward the door behind which the unknown woman revealed her presence with such a beautiful and gentle voice. When I heard her, I imagined her appearance matching the aural delight of her voice and trustingly stepped forth, listening to her repeated words, "Come, come over here!"

But there was no one behind the door. Matte orbs and chandeliers shone under the ceilings, sowing the nighttime brilliance among the black windows. And so, asking and always getting the reply from behind the next wall, "Come, come quickly!"—I examined five or six rooms, catching once my own reflection in the mirror, attentively looking from one void to the next. Then I imagined that the shadows in the mirrors are filled with crouching, creeping one after another women in mantillas and shawls they held against their faces, obscuring the features, and only their black eyes under the slyly arched brows smiled, shone, and flickered mysteriously. But I was wrong—I turned around too quickly for even the most agile creatures to escape. Tired and excited but still wary of something truly threatening among the starkly lit emptiness, I finally said sharply, "Show yourself or I will not go any further. Who are you and why are you calling me?"

Before she answered, the echo crumpled my voice into a hazy and dull hum.

Solicitous concern was audible in the words of the mysterious woman when she called me again from an unseen corner. "Hurry, do not stop, come, come along, no arguing." It seemed that these words were spoken near me—resonant like splashing water and resounding as if half-whispered into my ear but I hurried in vain, in my impatient fugue throwing the doors open, rounding the bends, hoping to catch somewhere the movement of the slipping-away woman— and everywhere I only met emptiness, doors, light. It went on like the game of hide-and-seek, and several times I heaved a frustrated sigh, not knowing whether to keep on going or to stop, stop decisively until I saw who I was speaking to from this distance. If I fell silent, the voice sought me; it sounded more and more soulful and urgent, always pointing the direction and softly exclaiming ahead, behind a new wall, "Here, hurry to me!"

As sensitive as I was to the nuances of voices in general but especially in these circumstances of extreme tension, I caught in those calls, in those insistent invitations of the inaudibly fleeing woman neither cruelty nor deceit; even though her behavior was more than strange, I did not suspect any danger or anything truly foul, since I did not know the circumstances that caused it. It seemed more reasonable to suspect the urgent need to show me something in a great hurry, when time was very short. If I made a mistake and entered a wrong room, following the rustling, rapid breathing and another musical beckoning, I was directed and corrected with a soft, "Here!" I was too far along to turn back. I was dangerously engrossed in the unknown, almost running across the vast parquet expanses, my eyes always following the direction of the voice.

"I am here," the voice finally said in the tone indicating the end of the story. It was in the intersection of a corridor and a staircase of just a few steps leading into another corridor just a bit higher.

"All right, but this is the last time," I warned. She waited for me at the beginning of the corridor to my right, where the light was dimmer; I heard her breathing and, after I ascended the stairs, stared into the darkness, irate. Of course she tricked me again. Both walls of the corridor were piled high with books, leaving only a narrow passage. In the light of a single lamp weakly illuminating just the stairs and the beginning of the way, I could potentially miss a person at a distance.

"Then where are you?" I said, peering into the darkness. "Stop, you're in such a hurry. Come closer."

"I can't," the voice said softly. "But can't you see? I am here. I got tired and had to sit down. Come to me."

In fact, I did hear her quite close. I just had to round the bend. Behind it there was darkness, marked at the end with a pale spot of the door. I stumbled over some books, my foot slipped, I teetered, and as I fell I knocked over a stack of ledgers. It plummeted somewhere, down from a great height. I fell on my hands, and felt only empty air under them, almost going over the precipice myself; my involuntary cry was answered by the roar of the book avalanche. I survived only by falling just a bit before approaching the edge. If the surprise and fear held back the realization of that moment, then the laughter—a mirthful, cold titter on the other side of the trap—immediately explained my role. The laughter grew distant, falling quieter with the last cruel note, and I no longer heard it.

I did not jump to my feet, did not crawl away noisily, as it would be extraneous in my presumed fall; once I understood the trick, I did not even move, letting the other party's impression settle in the direction desirable for them. But I had to take a look at the bed prepared for me. There were no signs of surveillance, and I, with great caution, lit a match and saw the rectangular chute of the broken-through floor. The light did not reach the bottom, but judging by the pause between the push and the din of the books that fell through, I determined the height of the fall at about twelve meters. It meant the floor of the story below was destroyed symmetrically with the top hole, forming a double chute. I was in someone's way. I realized that I had weighty evidence to that effect, but I could not understand how the most birdlike woman could fly over this massive opening, which had no edge that could be used for crossing; the width of it was well over two meters.

I waited until the incident had lost its dangerous immediacy and crawled back, to where the light reached enough to be able to discern the walls, and stood up then. I was reluctant to go back into the illuminated spaces. But now I was also unable to leave the scene where I almost performed the finale of the fifth act. I touched things too serious to be able to continue going forth. Unsure of where to begin, I carefully walked back, sometimes hiding behind the buttresses of the walls, to verify that there was no one there. By one such buttress there was a sink, and the faucet dripped water. There was a towel, with wet traces of just-dried hands; the towel still moved. Someone left here maybe a mere ten paces ahead of me, unnoticed by me (as I was by him) by sheer chance. It would not be wise to tempt these places any longer. Stunned by tension brought about by the sight of the towel, touched almost in front of me, I retreated, bating my breath, and with

relief spotted a narrow side door in the shade of a buttress, almost completely blocked by papers. With some effort, I pulled it open just enough to squeeze through. I disappeared into that passage as if into the wall, and entered a well-lit, silent and empty passageway, very narrow, with a bend very near me, but I did not dare look around it. I stood leaning against the wall in the alcove of a door nailed shut.

No sound, no occurrence that could be perceived by senses would have evaded me in those moments, so internally sharpened and attuned I was, gathered into hearing and breathing. But it seemed as if life on earth had died—such silence stared into my eyes with a still light of this white dead-end passageway. It seemed that everything living had left it—or lay low. I started to grow overwhelmed, to reach with the impatience of desperation for any kind of noise, but away from the torpid light, binding my heart with its silence. And then suddenly more than enough sounds needed for reassurance erupted—you could call it "stillness in the storm"—many footsteps sounded behind the wall, far below me. I distinguished voices and exclamations. These sounds of the beginning of an unknown excitement were joined by the sounds of tuning instruments: an acutely shrieking violin; a cello, a flute, and a contrabass stretched a few disjointed notes, muffled by the sounds of moving furniture.

In the middle of the night—I did not know what time it was—these signs of life three stories deep, after my experience with the chute, sounded like a new threat to me. If I were to walk tirelessly, I could've perhaps found a way out of this endless house, but not now when I could not be sure what waited for me behind the nearest door. But I could only know my situation once I determined what was happening downstairs. Listening intently, I calculated the distance between myself and the sounds; it was rather sizable, and located across the wall opposite from me, and down.

I stood in my doorway niche for a long while, until I grew bold enough to come out and investigate my options. I moved quietly ahead, and noticed a small opening in the wall, no bigger than a tiny spy window with glass. It was above my head, just high enough to touch. Nearby was a folding ladder, of a kind that the painters use when they whitewash ceilings. I dragged the ladder over carefully, never touching the walls or making any noise, and leaned it against the opening. The glass was caked with dust from the inside as well as out, but once I cleaned it with my palm, as much and as well as I could, I was able to see but as if through smoke. My guess based on my earlier hearing was confirmed: I was looking into that very central hall of the bank I visited the evening before, but I could not see down, the window was facing the top tiers. The extravagant sculpted ceiling hung very near; the balustrade on this side was eye-level and concealed the depths, and only the distant columns on the opposite side were visible barely halfway up. The entire tier was deserted, but meanwhile downstairs, tormenting with its invisibility, some lively merriment took place. I heard laughter, exclamations, moving chairs, garbled snippets of conversations, a soothing hum of the doors. Confident clinking of china, coughing and blowing of noses, strings of heavy and light footsteps and musical and sly intonations—yes, it was a banquet, a ball, a fete, a party, a jubilee—anything but the former cold and enormous emptiness, with echo muffled by the dust. The chandeliers carried the glint of the fiery pattern downward, and even though my hiding spot was lit, the even brighter light of the hall rested on my hand.

Almost certain that no one would come here, to this corner more likely related to the attic than the thoroughfare of the lower passage, I dared to remove the glass. Its frame, kept in place by two bent nails, wobbled. I turned the nails out and took out the barrier. The din was now distinct, like wind in my face; while I was getting accustomed to its character, the music started playing some café chantant number but strangely soft, unable or unwilling to let loose. The orchestra played with muted strings, as if ordered to do so. However, the voices it was muffling grew louder, making a natural effort and reaching all the way

to my sanctuary still wrapped in their meaning. As far as I could discern, the interests of various groups in the hall gravitated toward suspicious deals, although without a clear indication of their connections. Some phrases sounded like neighing, others—cruel shrieks; weighty, businesslike laughter mixed with hisses. Women's voices had a dark and tense timbre, occasionally sliding toward tempting playfulness with debauched intonations of loose women. Occasionally someone's solemn remark moved the conversation to discussing prices of gold and of precious stones; other words made one flinch, hinting murder or some other crime of no less decisive outlines. Argot of the jail, shamelessness of nighttime streets, the outward sheen of a daring intrigue and lively wordiness of a soul looking around nervously were mixed with the sound of the other orchestra, to which the first one fed high-pitched playful phrases.

There was a pause; several doors opened in the depths of the remote lower stories, and it seemed as if some new players appeared. It was immediately confirmed with solemn shouts. After a few muffled exchanges the warnings and invitations to pay attention thundered. Meanwhile, someone's speech was already flowing there, quietly, crawling along like a beetle in pine needles, dripping in streaks.

"Cheers to the Redeemer!" the chorus pronounced in a roar. "Death to the Ratcatcher!"

"Death!" darkly rang the women's voices. The echoes resonated in a loud howl and fell silent. Even though I was enormously engrossed in what I heard, I don't know why but I turned around, as if I felt someone's stare on my back; and only drew a deep breath—there was no one behind me. I still had time to figure out how to disappear: behind the bend two walked by, never suspecting my presence. They stopped. Their light shadow lay across the floor, but glancing at it, I could only see a blob. They spoke with the certainty of interlocutors confident that they were alone. It was a continuation, and apparently the trajectory of the conversation had stopped on their way here on some unknown question, that now received a response. I remembered every word of this vague and sharp answer.

"He will die," the unknown said, "but not at once. Here's the address: Fifth Line, ninety-seven, apartment eleven. His daughter is with him. This will be the great deed of the Redeemer. The Redeemer arrived from afar. His journey is arduous, and they await him in many cities. Tonight, everything must be ended. Go and examine the passage. If there is nothing to threaten the Redeemer, the Ratcatcher will be dead, and we will see his empty eyes!"

VIII

I listened to the end of the vengeful tirade with one foot already on the floor, since the moment I heard the exact address of my unknown girl, whose name I did not have a chance to find out, my instinct led me blindly down—to flee, hide, and fly to be her herald to the 5th Line. With any sensible doubt, the numbers and the name of the street could not tell me whether there was another family living in that apartment—it was enough for me to think of her and to know that she was there. In this frightful state of torturous rush, as if from a fire, I miscalculated my last step down; the ladder slid from the wall with a crack, my presence was revealed, and at first I stayed still, like a fallen sack. The lights immediately went out; the music fell silent, and a furious scream led my way in my blind dash along the narrow corridor, until I hit my chest against the door which I used to infiltrate here. With unexplainable strength, I pushed it open against the heaps of trash covering it, and ran into the memorable hallway with the trap. Salvation! The dawn with its first haze had begun, showing the outlines of the doors, and I could run until I was out of breath. Instinctively I looked for ways up rather than down, scaling short stairwells and abandoned passageways in a single leap. Sometimes I tossed about, circling in one spot, or ran into a dead end. It was terrible, like a bad dream—especially since I was being followed; I heard hurried steps behind me and

in front, that psychologically oppressive noise I could never escape. It followed with the irregularity of city traffic, sometimes so close that I jumped, or else followed evenly along at some distance, as if promising at any moment to cut across and intercept me. I grew weak, dumb with fear and the constant thundering of resonant floors. But then I was flying along the garrets. The last staircase I had noticed led to the ceiling, to the square attic opening, and I climbed it with the sense of an immediate blow rising behind my back—everyone seemed to be rushing toward me so. I found myself in the suffocating darkness of the attic, and immediately pushed everything that shone whitely in the dusk over the closed trapdoor—a stack of window frames, and only the force of desperation was able to move them with a single effort. They fell across and along, forming with their overlapping an impenetrable forest. Once that was done, I ran for the attic window, the gray spot of which was obscured by wooden boards and stacked barrels. The way was littered—I jumped over beams, crates, bricks, among the holes and chimneys, dense like the woods. Finally I reached the window. The freshness of open space breathed in its deep sleep. Behind a distant roof there was a pink, smudged shadow; no smoke rose from the chimneys, there was not a sound of passersby. I climbed out and crawled to the rain gutter. It was wobbly and its brackets whined when I started my descent. About halfway down, the cold iron of it was covered in dew and I slid down and had to catch myself at the joint. Finally my feet touched the sidewalk; I hurried toward the river, fearful to find the bridges drawn open, and as soon as I caught my breath, I took off running.

IX

The moment I rounded the corner, I had to stop, when I saw a crying little boy of about seven, his sweet face pale from tears; he rubbed his eyes with his tiny fists plaintively and whimpered. With concern, natural for anyone at such an encounter, I leaned to him, asking, "Little boy, where are you from? Were you abandoned? How did you happen here?"

He sobbed and remained silent, looking up at me and terrifying me with his stare. His skinny body shook, his little feet were dirty and bare. As much as I was driven to the place of danger, I could not abandon a child, especially since he kept quiet, from fatigue or fear, and only trembled and recoiled at my every question, as if from a threat. I stroked his hair and looked into his tear-filled eyes, but he could only hang his head and cry. "Little friend," I said, having decided to knock on some doors to see if anyone would take the child in. "Wait here, I'll be back soon, and we'll find your wayward mommy." But to my surprise, he seized my hand, not letting go. There was something base and wild in his effort; he even skidded along the sidewalk a bit when I jerked my hand away with sudden suspicion. His lovely face was twisted, squeezed into a tense grimace. "Hey you!" I shouted, trying to wrestle my hand free. "Let go!" And I pushed him away. No longer crying and still silent, he stared at me with his enormous black eyes; then he stood and, tittering a bit, walked so fast that I started in surprise. "Who are you?" I yelled with a threat in my voice. He giggled and, picking up the pace, disappeared around the corner, and I still stared for a while in that direction, feeling like I had just been bitten, until I remembered myself and ran as quickly as a man chasing a tram. My breath caught and I had to stop twice, and walked for a bit, then ran again, and when out of breath walked in an insane gait, as quick as a run.

I reached Konnogvardeysky Boulevard when a girl passed me, glancing at me with an expression of a straining memory. She was about to keep walking when I recognized her with an internal push, the delight of salvation. My call and her exclamation rang out in unison, and she stopped with an expression of sweet annoyance.

"But it's you!" she said. "I can't believe I did not recognize you! I almost walked by until I saw your agitation. How tormented you look, how pale!"

A great bewilderment yet a great calm descended over me. I looked at this nearly lost face with faith in complex and meaningful coincidences, with a radiant and acute shyness. I was so overwhelmed, so internally startled by her in my journey to find her; but the end of my trek had been already presented to me by my impatient imagination, and now I felt torn—it would be sweeter for me to have found her there.

"Listen," I told her, not looking away from her trusting eyes, "I was rushing to your place. It's not too late."

She interrupted me and led me aside by my sleeve. "Now it's too early," she said meaningfully. "Or late, however you want to look at it. It's light out, but it is still night. And you should come by in the evening, do you hear? And I will tell you everything. I thought a lot about our relationship. Please know: I love you."

It was as if the clock had stopped. That moment, my heart no longer beat with hers. She could not, should not have said this. With a sigh I let go of the small fresh hand holding mine and stepped back. She looked at me, her face ready to tremble with impatience. That expression skewed her features—tenderness became dullness, her eyes darted sharply.

I breathed a hollow laugh and wagged my finger. "No, you won't trick me," I said. "She is there. She is sleeping now, and I will wake her. Go away, foul creature, whoever you are."

Flutter of a handkerchief quickly thrown before my very face was the last thing I saw clearly. Then there were narrow spaces between trees, sometimes showing a running female figure, sometimes indicating that it was I who was running as hard as possible. The clocktower of the square was already visible. The gates were down and the bridges were just starting to rise; far away, by the opposite embankment, a black tugboat was spewing smoke, straining the cable of the barge. I jumped over the gates and crossed the bridge at the last moment, when the rift had already split the tram rails. My flying leap was met by the swearing and screaming of the watchmen, but, barely glancing at the shining sliver of water below, I was already far from them and I ran until I reached the gates.

X

Then, or rather a bit later, the moment from which I could reconstruct going backward my desperate and dimmed act, took place. First of all I saw the girl, standing by the door, listening, her hand extended toward me as people do when asking or demanding for us to sit still. She wore a summer coat; her face looked alarmed and sad. She was sleeping just before I got there. I knew that, but the circumstances of my arrival slipped away from me, like water in a closed fist, the moment I tried to string everything together. Obeying her alarmed gesture, I kept sitting quietly, waiting for the results of her intent listening. I tried to discern its meaning in vain. Just a bit more and I could have made the decisive effort to overcome my extreme weakness, I wanted to ask what was happening now in this large room when, as if guessing my intention, the girl turned her head, frowning and wagging her finger. Then I remembered that her name was Susie, that someone who exited here called her by that name and told her, "We need absolute silence." Was I sleeping or just scattered? Trying to solve this question, I looked down to see that the bottom of my coat was torn. But it was undamaged when I hurried here. My confusion became surprise. Then everything shook and as if drained out, stirring up the light; blood rushed to my head and a deafening crack, like a gunshot next to my ear, then a shout, "Halt!" someone behind the door yelled. I jumped up, sucking in air. From behind the door, a man in a gray housecoat appeared, showing the girl, who took a step back, a small board on which, crushed by an arced wire, a giant black rat, broken in two, hung. Its teeth were bared, its tail limp.

My memory was jolted from its terrifying state by the blow and the scream, and it crossed the dark void. I immediately grasped and held on too much. My senses spoke. My internal gaze returned to the beginning of the scene, reliving the chain of my efforts. I remembered climbing over the gates, too afraid to knock lest I attracted a new danger, how I crossed the doorway and rang the doorbell for the third story. But the argument behind the doors—the argument that went long and worrisome, when a man's and a woman's voice argued whether to let me in—I had forgotten completely. I only restored it later.

All these not completely fitting images appeared with the speed of a glance through a window. The old man carrying the rat trap had a dense gray cap of short hair, round like the cup of an acorn. Sharp nose, shaven thin lips wearing an intractable expression, bright pale eyes and tufts of sideburns on his pink face, ending in the forward-jutting chin, sunken into a blue scarf, would be of interest to a portraitist, a connoisseur of strong character lines.

He said, "You are seeing the so-called black Guinea rat. Its bite is very dangerous. It causes a slow rot of the living body, turning the one so bitten into an assemblage of tumors and boils. This rodent species is quite rare in Europe, but sometimes steamships carry them here. The "free passage" you heard of last night, is an artificial gap I created near my kitchen to experiment with different trap designs; two last days the passage has indeed been free, since I was too engrossed in Aert Aertus's *The Cellar of a King Rat*, a book quite rare. It was printed in Germany four hundred years ago. The author was burned at the stake for heresy in Bremen. Your tale. . . ."

Then I already told them everything I meant to. But I still had some doubts. I asked, "Did you take any precautions? Do you know the nature of this danger, since I don't quite understand it?"

"Precautions?" Susie said. "Which precautions are you talking about?"

"Danger," the old man started but stopped as soon as he glanced at Susie. "I don't understand."

There was a slight impasse as the three of us traded expectant looks.

"I am saying," I started, uncertain, "that you must be careful. I think I already said this but forgive me, I cannot quite remember what I did say. It seems to me now that I was in a deep swoon."

The girl looked at her father and then at me, with a puzzled smile. "How can it be?"

"He is tired, Susie," the old man said. "I know insomnia. Everything was said, and the measures have been taken. If I call this rat," he dropped the trap at my feet with the satisfied mien of a hunter, "if I call it 'The Redeemer,' you will understand."

"It's a joke," I objected, "and a joke of course appropriate for the profession of a Ratcatcher." As I said it, I remembered a small plaque under the doorbell. It said:

"RATCATCHER"—Extermination of rats and mice—I. Iensen. Phone 1-08-01

I saw it when I entered.

"You are joking, since I don't think that this Redeemer would cause you too much trouble."

"He is not joking," said Susie. "He knows."

I compared these two gazes, to which I responded with a smile of vain guesses—the gaze of youth, filled with genuine conviction, and the gaze of old but clear eyes, filled with hesitation at whether to continue the conversation in this manner.

"I will let Aert Aertus tell you something about these matters for me." The Ratcatcher left and returned with an old book bound in leather, with a red edge. "Here's an excerpt you can laugh at or contemplate, whatever you please."

"*This treacherous and glum creature possesses the abilities of a human mind. It also commands the mysteries of the underground where it dwells. It has the power to change its appearance, showing itself as a human being with arms and legs, wearing clothes, having a face, eyes, movements similar to a man, and not at all inferior to his—like his complete but false image. Rats can also inflict incurable disease, using the ways available only to them.*

They are aided by death, famine, war, floods, and invasions. Then they gather under the sigils of mys-terious transformations, acting as people, and you would talk to them without knowing who they are. They steal and sell with gains surprising for an honest laborer, and they fool with their shiny clothes and soft speech. They kill and burn, swindle and lie in wait; they surround themselves with luxury, eat and drink their fill, and have everything in abundance. Gold and silver are their favorite spoils, as well as gemstones they keep in treasuries underground."

"But enough reading," said the Ratcatcher, "and you of course have already guessed why I translated this particular passage. You were surrounded by rats."

But I already knew. Sometimes we prefer to keep quiet to let the new impression, uncertain and torn by other considerations, find a reliable foothold. Meanwhile the furniture covers shone under the daylight spilling from the windows, and the first voices of the street sounded clear, as if they were in the room. Again I was sinking into oblivion. The faces of the girl and her father grew distant, becoming hazy apparitions limned by transparent fog. "Susie, what's wrong with him?" a loud question rang out. The girl came closer, hovering somewhere near me but I could not see where exactly because I could not turn my head. Suddenly my forehead grew warm from a woman's hand pressing against it, just as the surroundings, their lines twisted and blurred, disappeared in a chaotic mental avalanche. Wild, deep sleep abducted me. I heard her voice, "He is sleeping"—the words to which I woke up after thirty nonexistent hours.

I had been carried to the crammed neighboring room, onto a real bed, after which I learned that I "was very light for a man." Someone took pity on me; a room in the neighboring apartment was given to me the very next day. There is no accounting for the future. But it is up to me to make it akin to the moment when I felt the warm hand on my forehead. I must earn trust.

And now—not another word.

Robert Ervin Howard (1906–1936), or Robert E. Howard, was born in Peaster, Texas, and had a passion for oral storytelling. He began writing around the age of nine and made his first professional sale at eighteen. Despite having a professional career of only twelve years, Howard's passion for words led him to write more than one hundred short stories. Many know him as the creator of Conan the Barbarian, the wanderer Solomon Kane, and the Godfather of the fantasy subgenre known as sword and sorcery. He was a dynamic storyteller and thus little wonder that his characters remain popular, many of which have been featured in films. "The Shadow Kingdom" was originally published in 1929 in the magazine *Weird Tales*. Part of Howard's popular Kull of Atlantis series and set in the fictional Thurian Age, it is an immensely creative work brimming with suspense and paranoia.

The Shadow Kingdom

Robert E. Howard

1. A KING COMES RIDING

THE BLARE OF THE TRUMPETS grew louder, like a deep golden tide surge, like the soft booming of the evening tides against the silver beaches of Valusia. The throng shouted, women flung roses from the roofs as the rhythmic chiming of silver hosts came clearer and the first of the mighty array swung into view in the broad, white street that curved round the golden-spired Tower of Splendor.

First came the trumpeters, slim youths, clad in scarlet, riding with a flourish of long, slender golden trumpets; next the bowmen, tall men from the mountains; and behind these the heavily armed footmen, their broad shields clashing in unison, their long spears swaying in perfect rhythm to their stride. Behind them came the mightiest soldiery in all the world, the Red Slayers, horsemen, splendidly mounted, armed in red from helmet to spur. Proudly they sat their steeds, looking neither to right nor to left, but aware of the shouting for all that. Like bronze statues they were, and there was never a waver in the forest of spears that reared above them.

Behind those proud and terrible ranks came the motley files of the mercenaries, fierce, wild-looking warriors, men of Mu and of Kaa-u and of the hills of the east and the isles of the west. They bore spears and heavy swords, and a compact group that marched somewhat apart were the bowmen of Lemuria. Then came the light foot of the nation, and more trumpeters brought up the rear.

A brave sight, and a sight which aroused a fierce thrill in the soul of Kull, king of Valusia. Not on the Topaz Throne at the front of the regal Tower of Splendor sat Kull, but in the saddle, mounted on a great stallion, a true warrior king. His mighty arm swung up in reply to the salutes as the hosts passed. His fierce eyes passed the gorgeous trumpeters with a casual glance, rested longer on the following soldiery; they blazed with a ferocious light as the Red Slayers halted in front of him with a clang of arms and a rearing of steeds, and tendered him the crown salute. They narrowed slightly as the mercenaries strode by. They saluted no one, the mercenaries. They walked with shoulders flung back, eyeing Kull boldly and straightly, albeit with a certain appreciation; fierce eyes, unblinking; savage eyes, staring from beneath shaggy manes and heavy brows.

And Kull gave back a like stare. He granted much to brave men, and there were no braver in all the world, not even among the wild tribesmen who now disowned him. But Kull was too much the savage to have any great love for these. There were too many feuds. Many were age-old enemies of Kull's nation, and though the name of Kull was now a word accursed among the mountains and valleys of his people, and though Kull had put them from his mind, yet the old hates, the ancient passions still lingered. For Kull was no Valusian but an Atlantean.

The armies swung out of sight around the gem-blazing shoulders of the Tower of Splendor and Kull reined his stallion about and started toward the palace at an easy gait, discussing the review with the commanders that rode with him, using not many words, but saying much.

"The army is like a sword," said Kull, "and must not be allowed to rust." So down the street they rode, and Kull gave no heed to any of the whispers that reached his hearing from the throngs that still swarmed the streets.

"That is Kull, see! Valka! But what a king! And what a man! Look at his arms! His shoulders!"

And an undertone of more sinister whispering:

"Kull! Ha, accursed usurper from the pagan isles." "Aye, shame to Valusia that a barbarian sits on the Throne of Kings."

Little did Kull heed. Heavy-handed had he seized the decaying throne of ancient Valusia and with a heavier hand did he hold it, a man against a nation.

After the council chamber, the social palace where Kull replied to the formal and laudatory phrases of the lords and ladies, with carefully hidden grim amusement at such frivolities; then the lords and ladies took their formal departure and Kull leaned back upon the ermine throne and contemplated matters of state until an attendant requested permission from the great king to speak, and announced an emissary from the Pictish embassy.

Kull brought his mind back from the dim mazes of Valusian statecraft where it had been wandering, and gazed upon the Pict with little favor. The man gave back the gaze of the king without flinching. He was a lean-hipped, massive-chested warrior of middle height, dark, like all his race, and strongly built. From strong, immobile features gazed dauntless and inscrutable eyes.

"The chief of the Councilors, Ka-nu of the tribe right hand of the king of Pictdom, sends greetings and says: 'There is a throne at the feast of the rising moon for Kull, king of kings, lord of lords, emperor of Valusia.'"

"Good," answered Kull. "Say to Ka-nu the Ancient, ambassador of the western isles, that the king of Valusia will quaff wine with him when the moon floats over the hills of Zalgara."

Still the Pict lingered. "I have a word for the king, not"—with a contemptuous flirt of his hand—"for these slaves."

Kull dismissed the attendants with a word, watching the Pict warily.

The man stepped nearer, and lowered his voice:

"Come alone to feast tonight, lord king. Such was the word of my chief."

The king's eyes narrowed, gleaming like gray sword steel, coldly.

"Alone?"

"Aye."

They eyed each other silently, their mutual tribal enmity seething beneath their cloak of formality. Their mouths spoke the cultured speech, the conventional court phrases of a highly polished race, a race not their own, but from their eyes gleamed the primal traditions of the elemental savage. Kull might be the king of Valusia and the Pict might be an emissary to her courts, but there in the throne hall of kings, two tribesmen glowered at each other, fierce and wary, while ghosts of wild wars and world-ancient feuds whispered to each.

To the king was the advantage and he enjoyed it to its fullest extent. Jaw resting on hand, he eyed the Pict, who stood like an image of bronze, head flung back, eyes unflinching.

Across Kull's lips stole a smile that was more a sneer.

"And so I am to come—alone?" Civilization had taught him to speak by innuendo and the Pict's dark eyes glittered, though he made no reply. "How am I to know that you come from Ka-nu?"

"I have spoken," was the sullen response.

"And when did a Pict speak truth?" sneered Kull, fully aware that the Picts never lied, but using this means to enrage the man.

"I see your plan, king," the Pict answered imperturbably. "You wish to anger me. By Valka, you need go no further! I am angry enough. And I challenge you to meet me in single battle—spear, sword or dagger, mounted or afoot. Are you king or man?"

Kull's eyes glinted with the grudging admiration a warrior must needs give a bold foeman, but he did not fail to use the chance of further annoying his antagonist.

"A king does not accept the challenge of a nameless savage," he sneered, "nor does the emperor of Valusia break the Truce of Ambassadors. You have leave to go. Say to Ka-nu I will come alone."

The Pict's eyes flashed murderously. He fairly shook in the grasp of the primitive blood-lust; then, turning his back squarely upon the king of Valusia, he strode across the Hall of Society and vanished through the great door.

Again Kull leaned back upon the ermine throne and meditated.

So the chief of the Council of Picts wished him to come alone? But for what reason? Treachery? Grimly Kull touched the hilt of his great sword. But scarcely. The Picts valued too greatly the alliance with Valusia to break it for any feudal reason. Kull might be a warrior of Atlantis and hereditary enemy of all Picts, but too, he was king of Valusia, the most potent ally of the Men of the West.

Kull reflected long upon the strange state of affairs that made him ally of ancient foes and foe of ancient friends. He rose and paced restlessly across the hall, with the quick, noiseless tread of a lion. Chains of friendship, tribe and tradition had he broken to satisfy his ambition. And, by Valka, god of the sea and the land, he had realized that ambition! He was king of Valusia—a fading, degenerate Valusia, a Valusia living mostly in dreams of bygone glory, but still a mighty land and the greatest of the Seven Empires. Valusia—Land of Dreams, the tribesmen named it, and sometimes it seemed to Kull that he moved in a dream. Strange to him were the intrigues of court and palace, army and people. All was like a masquerade, where men and women hid their real thoughts with a smooth mask. Yet the seizing of the throne had been easy—a bold snatching of opportunity, the swift whirl of swords, the slaying of a tyrant of whom men had wearied unto death, short, crafty plotting with ambitious statesmen out of favor at court—and Kull, wandering adventurer, Atlantean exile, had swept up to the dizzy heights of his dreams: he was lord of Valusia, king of kings. Yet now it seemed that the seizing was far easier than the keeping. The sight of the Pict had brought back youthful associations to his mind, the free, wild savagery of his boyhood. And now a strange feeling of dim unrest, of unreality, stole over him as of late it had been doing. Who was he, a straightforward man of the seas and the mountain, to rule a race strangely and terribly wise with the mysticisms of antiquity? An ancient race—

"I am Kull!" said he, flinging back his head as a lion flings back his mane. "I am Kull!"

His falcon gaze swept the ancient hall. His self-confidence flowed back. . . . And in a dim nook of the hall a tapestry moved slightly.

2. THUS SPAKE THE SILENT HALLS OF VALUSIA

The moon had not risen, and the garden was lighted with torches aglow in silver cressets when Kull sat down on the throne before the table of Ka-nu, ambassador of the western isles. At his right hand sat the ancient Pict, as much unlike an emissary of that fierce race as a man could be. Ancient was Ka-nu and wise in statecraft, grown old in the game. There was no elemental hatred in the eyes that looked at Kull appraisingly; no tribal traditions hindered his judgments. Long associations with the statesmen of the civilized nations had swept away such cobwebs. Not: who and what is this man? was the question ever foremost in Ka-nu's mind, but: can I use this man, and how? Tribal prejudices he used only to further his own schemes.

And Kull watched Ka-nu, answering his conversation briefly, wondering if civilization would make of him a thing like the Pict. For Ka-nu was soft and paunchy. Many years had stridden across the sky-rim since Ka-nu had wielded a sword. True, he was old, but Kull had seen men older than he in the forefront of battle. The Picts were a long-lived race. A beautiful girl stood at Ka-nu's elbow, refilling his goblet, and she was kept busy. Meanwhile Ka-nu kept up a running fire of jests and comments, and Kull, secretly contemptuous of his garrulity, nevertheless missed none of his shrewd humor.

At the banquet were Pictish chiefs and statesmen, the latter jovial and easy in their manner, the warriors formally courteous, but plainly hampered by their tribal affinities. Yet Kull, with a tinge of envy, was cognizant of the freedom and ease of the affair as contrasted with like affairs of the Valusian court. Such freedom prevailed in the rude camps of Atlantis—Kull shrugged his shoulders. After all, doubtless Ka-nu, who had seemed to have forgotten he was a Pict as far as time-hoary custom and prejudice went, was right and he, Kull, would better become a Valusian in mind as in name.

At last when the moon had reached her zenith, Ka-nu, having eaten and drunk as much as any three men there, leaned back upon his divan with a comfortable sigh and said, "Now, get you gone, friends, for the king and I would converse on such matters as concern not children. Yes, you too, my pretty; yet first let me kiss those ruby lips—so; no, dance away, my rose-bloom."

Ka-nu's eyes twinkled above his white beard as he surveyed Kull, who sat erect, grim and uncompromising.

"You are thinking, Kull," said the old statesman, suddenly, "that Ka-nu is a useless old reprobate, fit for nothing except to guzzle wine and kiss wenches!"

In fact, this remark was so much in line with his actual thoughts, and so plainly put, that Kull was rather startled, though he gave no sign.

Ka-nu gurgled and his paunch shook with his mirth. "Wine is red and women are soft," he remarked tolerantly. "But—ha! ha!—think not old Ka-nu allows either to interfere with business."

Again he laughed, and Kull moved restlessly. This seemed much like being made sport of, and the king's scintillant eyes began to glow with a feline light.

Ka-nu reached for the wine-pitcher, filled his beaker and glanced questioningly at Kull, who shook his head irritably.

"Aye," said Ka-nu equably, "it takes an old head to stand strong drink. I am growing old, Kull, so why should you young men begrudge me such pleasures as we oldsters must find? Ah me, I grow ancient and withered, friendless and cheerless."

But his looks and expressions failed far of bearing out his words. His rubicund countenance fairly glowed, and his eyes sparkled, so that his white beard seemed incongruous. Indeed, he looked remarkably elfin, reflected Kull, who felt vaguely resentful. The old scoundrel had lost all of the primitive virtues of his race and of Kull's race, yet he seemed more pleased in his aged days than otherwise.

"Hark ye, Kull," said Ka-nu, raising an admonitory finger, "'tis a chancy thing to laud a young man, yet I must speak my true thoughts to gain your confidence."

"If you think to gain it by flattery—"

"Tush. Who spake of flattery? I flatter only to disguard."

There was a keen sparkle in Ka-nu's eyes, a cold glimmer that did not match his lazy smile. He knew men, and he knew that to gain his end he must smite straight with this tigerish barbarian, who, like a wolf scenting a snare, would scent out unerringly any falseness in the skein of his wordweb.

"You have power, Kull," said he, choosing his words with more care than he did in the council rooms of the nation, "to make yourself mightiest of all kings, and restore some of the lost glories of Valusia. So. I care little for Valusia—though the women and wine be excellent—save for the fact that the stronger Valusia is, the stronger is the Pict nation. More, with an Atlantean on the throne, eventually Atlantis will become united—"

Kull laughed in harsh mockery. Ka-nu had touched an old wound.

"Atlantis made my name accursed when I went to seek fame and fortune among the cities of the world. We—they—are age-old foes of the Seven Empires, greater foes of the allies of the Empires, as you should know."

Ka-nu tugged his beard and smiled enigmatically.

"Nay, nay. Let it pass. But I know whereof I speak. And then warfare will cease, wherein there is no gain; I see a world of peace and prosperity— man loving his fellow man—the good supreme. All this can you accomplish—if you live!"

"Ha!" Kull's lean hand closed on his hilt and he half rose, with a sudden movement of such dynamic speed that Ka-nu, who fancied men as some men fancy blooded horses, felt his old blood leap with a sudden thrill. Valka, what a warrior! Nerves and sinews of steel and fire, bound together with the perfect co-ordination, the fighting instinct, that makes the terrible warrior.

But none of Ka-nu's enthusiasm showed in his mildly sarcastic tone.

"Tush. Be seated. Look about you. The gardens are deserted, the seats empty, save for ourselves. You fear not me?"

Kull sank back, gazing about him warily.

"There speaks the savage," mused Ka-nu. "Think you if I planned treachery I would enact it here where suspicion would be sure to fall upon me? Tut. You young tribesmen have much to learn. There were my chiefs who were not at ease because you were born among the hills of Atlantis, and you despise me in your secret mind because I am a Pict. Tush. I see you as Kull, king of Valusia, not as Kull, the reckless Atlantean, leader of the raiders who harried the western isles. So you should see in me, not a Pict but an international man, a figure of the world. Now to that figure, hark! If you were slain tomorrow who would be king?"

"Kaanuub, baron of Blaal."

"Even so. I object to Kaanuub for many reasons, yet most of all for the fact that he is but a figurehead."

"How so? He was my greatest opponent, but I did not know that he championed any cause but his own."

"The night can hear," answered Ka-nu obliquely. "There are worlds within worlds. But you may trust me and you may trust Brule, the Spear-slayer. Look!" He drew from his robes a bracelet of gold representing a winged dragon coiled thrice, with three horns of ruby on the head.

"Examine it closely. Brule will wear it on his arm when he comes to you tomorrow night so that you may know him. Trust Brule as you trust yourself, and do what he tells you to. And in proof of trust, look ye!"

And with the speed of a striking hawk, the ancient snatched something from his robes, something that flung a weird green light over them, and which he replaced in an instant.

"The stolen gem!" exclaimed Kull, recoiling. "The green jewel from the Temple of the Serpent! Valka! You! And why do you show it to me?"

"To save your life. To prove my trust. If I betray your trust, deal with me likewise. You hold my life in your hand. Now I could not be false to you if I would, for a word from you would be my doom."

Yet for all his words the old scoundrel beamed merrily and seemed vastly pleased with himself.

"But why do you give me this hold over you?" asked Kull, becoming more bewildered each second.

"As I told you. Now, you see that I do not intend to deal you false, and tomorrow night when Brule comes to you, you will follow his advice without fear of treachery. Enough. An escort waits outside to ride to the palace with you, lord."

Kull rose. "But you have told me nothing."

"Tush. How impatient are youths!" Ka-nu looked more like a mischievous elf than ever. "Go you and dream of thrones and power and kingdoms, while I dream of wine and soft women and roses. And fortune ride with you, King Kull."

As he left the garden, Kull glanced back to see Ka-nu still reclining lazily in his seat, a merry ancient, beaming on all the world with jovial fellowship.

A mounted warrior waited for the king just without the garden and Kull was slightly surprised to see that it was the same that had brought Ka-nu's invitation. No word was spoken as Kull swung into the saddle nor as they clattered along the empty streets.

The color and the gayety of the day had given way to the eerie stillness of night. The city's antiquity was more than ever apparent beneath the bent, silver moon. The huge pillars of the mansions and palaces towered up into the stars. The broad stairways, silent and deserted, seemed to climb endlessly until they vanished in the shadowy darkness of the upper realms. Stairs to the stars, thought Kull, his imaginative mind inspired by the weird grandeur of the scene.

Clang! clang! clang! sounded the silver hoofs on the broad, moon-flooded streets, but otherwise there was no sound. The age of the city, its incredible antiquity, was almost oppressive to the king; it was as if the great silent buildings laughed at him, noiselessly, with unguessable mockery. And what secrets did they hold?

"You are young," said the palaces and the temples and the shrines, "but we are old. The world was wild with youth when we were reared. You and your tribe shall pass, but we are invincible, indestructible. We towered above a strange world, ere Atlantis and Lemuria rose from the sea; we still shall reign when the green waters sigh for many a restless fathom above the spires of Lemuria and the hills of Atlantis and when the isles of the Western Men are the mountains of a strange land.

"How many kings have we watched ride down these streets before Kull of Atlantis was even a dream in the mind of Ka, bird of Creation? Ride on, Kull of Atlantis; greater shall follow you; greater came before you. They are dust; they are forgotten; we stand; we know; we are. Ride, ride on, Kull of Atlantis; Kull the king, Kull the fool!"

And it seemed to Kull that the clashing hoofs took up the silent refrain to beat it into the night with hollow re-echoing mockery; "Kull-the-king! Kull-the-fool!"

Glow, moon; you light a king's way! Gleam, stars; you are torches in the train of an emperor! And clang, silver-shod hoofs; you herald that Kull rides through Valusia.

Ho! Awake, Valusia! It is Kull that rides, Kull the king!

"We have known many kings," said the silent halls of Valusia.

And so in a brooding mood Kull came to the palace, where his bodyguard, men of the Red Slayers, came to take the rein of the great stallion and escort Kull to his rest. There the Pict, still sullenly speechless, wheeled his steed with a savage wrench of the rein and fled away in the dark like a phantom; Kull's heightened imagination pictured him speeding through the silent streets like a goblin out of the Elder World.

There was no sleep for Kull that night, for it was nearly dawn and he spent the rest of the night hours pacing the throne-room, and pondering over what had passed. Ka-nu had told him nothing, yet he had put himself in Kull's complete power. At what had he hinted when he had said the baron of Blaal was naught but a figurehead? And who was this Brule who was to come to him by night, wearing the mystic armlet of the dragon? And why? Above all, why had Ka-nu shown him the green gem of terror, stolen long ago from the Temple of the Serpent, for which the world would rock in wars were it known to the weird and terrible keepers of that temple, and from whose vengeance not even Ka-nu's ferocious tribesmen might be able to save him? But Ka-nu knew he was safe, reflected Kull, for the statesman was too shrewd to expose himself to risk without profit. But was it to throw the king off his guard and pave the way to treachery? Would Ka-nu dare let him live now? Kull shrugged his shoulders.

3. THEY THAT WALK THE NIGHT

The moon had not risen when Kull, hand to hilt, stepped to a window. The windows opened upon the great inner gardens of the royal palace, and the breezes of the night, bearing the scents of spice trees, blew the filmy curtains about. The king looked out. The walks and groves were deserted; carefully trimmed trees were bulky shadows; fountains nearby flung their slender sheen of silver in the starlight and distant fountains rippled steadily. No guards walked those gardens, for so closely were the outer walls guarded that it seemed impossible for any invader to gain access to them.

Vines curled up the walls of the palace, and even as Kull mused upon the ease with which they might be climbed, a segment of shadow detached itself from the darkness below the window and a bare, brown arm curved up over the sill. Kull's great sword hissed halfway from the sheath; then the king halted. Upon the muscular forearm gleamed the dragon armlet shown him by Ka-nu the night before.

The possessor of the arm pulled himself up over the sill and into the room with the swift, easy motion of a climbing leopard.

"You are Brule?" asked Kull, and then stopped in surprise not unmingled with annoyance and suspicion; for the man was he whom Kull had taunted in the Hall of Society; the same who had escorted him from the Pictish embassy.

"I am Brule, the Spear-slayer," answered the Pict in a guarded voice; then swiftly, gazing closely in Kull's face, he said, barely above a whisper:

"Ka nama kaa lajerama!"

Kull started. "Ha! What mean you?"

"Know you not?"

"Nay, the words are unfamiliar; they are of no language I ever heard—and yet, by Valka!—somewhere—I have heard—"

"Aye," was the Pict's only comment. His eyes swept the room, the study room of the palace. Except for a few tables, a divan or two and great shelves of books of parchment, the room was barren compared to the grandeur of the rest of the palace.

"Tell me, king, who guards the door?"

"Eighteen of the Red Slayers. But how come you, stealing through the gardens by night and scaling the walls of the palace?"

Brule sneered. "The guards of Valusia are blind buffaloes. I could steal their girls from under their noses. I stole amid them and they saw me not nor heard me. And the walls—I could scale them without the aid of vines. I have hunted tigers on the foggy beaches when the sharp east breezes blew the mist in from seaward and I have climbed the steeps of the western sea mountain. But come—nay, touch this armlet."

He held out his arm and, as Kull complied wonderingly, gave an apparent sigh of relief.

"So. Now throw off those kingly robes; for

there are ahead of you this night such deeds as no Atlantean ever dreamed of."

Brule himself was clad only in a scanty loincloth through which was thrust a short, curved sword.

"And who are you to give me orders?" asked Kull, slightly resentful.

"Did not Ka-nu bid you follow me in all things?" asked the Pict irritably, his eyes flashing momentarily. "I have no love for you, lord, but for the moment I have put the thought of feuds from my mind. Do you likewise. But come."

Walking noiselessly, he led the way across the room to the door. A slide in the door allowed a view of the outer corridor, unseen from without, and the Pict bade Kull look.

"What see you?"

"Naught but the eighteen guardsmen."

The Pict nodded, motioned Kull to follow him across the room. At a panel in the opposite wall Brule stopped and fumbled there a moment. Then with a light movement he stepped back, drawing his sword as he did so. Kull gave an exclamation as the panel swung silently open, revealing a dimly lighted passageway.

"A secret passage!" swore Kull softly. "And I knew nothing of it! By Valka, someone shall dance for this!"

"Silence!" hissed the Pict.

Brule was standing like a bronze statue as if straining every nerve for the slightest sound; something about his attitude made Kull's hair prickle slightly, not from fear but from some eerie anticipation. Then beckoning, Brule stepped through the secret doorway which stood open behind them. The passage was bare, but not dust-covered as should have been the case with an unused secret corridor. A vague, gray light filtered through somewhere, but the source of it was not apparent. Every few feet Kull saw doors, invisible, as he knew, from the outside, but easily apparent from within.

"The palace is a very honeycomb," he muttered. "Aye. Night and day you are watched, king, by many eyes."

The king was impressed by Brule's manner.

The Pict went forward slowly, warily, half-crouching, blade held low and thrust forward. When he spoke it was in a whisper and he continually flung glances from side to side.

The corridor turned sharply and Brule warily gazed past the turn.

"Look!" he whispered. "But remember! No word! No sound—on your life!"

Kull cautiously gazed past him. The corridor changed just at the bend to a flight of steps. And then Kull recoiled. At the foot of those stairs lay the eighteen Red Slayers who were that night stationed to watch the king's study room. Brule's grip upon his mighty arm and Brule's fierce whisper at his shoulder alone kept Kull from leaping down those stairs.

"Silent, Kull! Silent, in Valka's name!" hissed the Pict. "These corridors are empty now, but I risked much in showing you, that you might then believe what I had to say. Back now to the room of study." And he retraced his steps, Kull following; his mind in a turmoil of bewilderment.

"This is treachery," muttered the king, his steel gray eyes a-smolder, "foul and swift! Mere minutes have passed since those men stood at guard."

Again in the room of study Brule carefully closed the secret panel and motioned Kull to look again through the slit of the outer door. Kull gasped audibly. For without stood the eighteen guardsmen!

"This is sorcery!" he whispered, half-drawing his sword. "Do dead men guard the king?"

"Aye!" came Brule's scarcely audible reply; there was a strange expression in the Pict's scintillant eyes. They looked squarely into each other's eyes for an instant, Kull's brow wrinkled in a puzzled scowl as he strove to read the Pict's inscrutable face. Then Brule's lips, barely moving, formed the words; "The-snake-that-speaks!"

"Silent!" whispered Kull, laying his hand over Brule's mouth. "That is death to speak! That is a name accursed!"

The Pict's fearless eyes regarded him steadily.

"Look, again. King Kull. Perchance the guard was changed."

"Nay, those are the same men. In Valka's name, this is sorcery—this is insanity! I saw with my own eyes the bodies of those men, not eight minutes agone. Yet there they stand."

Brule stepped back, away from the door, Kull mechanically following.

"Kull, what know ye of the traditions of this race ye rule?"

"Much—and yet, little. Valusia is so old—" "Aye," Brule's eyes lighted strangely, "we are but barbarians—infants compared to the Seven Empires. Not even they themselves know how old they are. Neither the memory of man nor the annals of the historians reach back far enough to tell us when the first men came up from the sea and built cities on the shore. But Kull, men were not always ruled by men!" The king started. Their eyes met. "Aye, there is a legend of my people—" "And mine!" broke in Brule. "That was before we of the isles were allied with Valusia. Aye, in the reign of Lion-fang, seventh war chief of the Picts, so many years ago no man remembers how many. Across the sea we came, from the isles of the sunset, skirting the shores of Atlantis, and falling upon the beaches of Valusia with fire and sword. Aye, the long white beaches resounded with the clash of spears, and the night was like day from the flame of the burning castles. And the king, the king of Valusia, who died on the red sea sands that dim day—" His voice trailed off; the two stared at each other, neither speaking; then each nodded.

"Ancient is Valusia!" whispered Kull. "The hills of Atlantis and Mu were isles of the sea when Valusia was young."

The night breeze whispered through the open window. Not the free, crisp sea air such as Brule and Kull knew and reveled in, in their land, but a breath like a whisper from the past, laden with musk, scents of forgotten things, breathing secrets that were hoary when the world was young.

The tapestries rustled, and suddenly Kull felt like a naked child before the inscrutable wisdom of the mystic past. Again the sense of unreality swept upon him. At the back of his soul stole dim, gigantic phantoms, whispering monstrous things. He sensed that Brule experienced similar thoughts. The Pict's eyes were fixed upon his face with a fierce intensity. Their glances met. Kull felt warmly a sense of comradeship with this member of an enemy tribe. Like rival leopards turning at bay against hunters, these two savages made common cause against the inhuman powers of antiquity. Brule again led the way back to the secret door. Silently they entered and silently they proceeded down the dim corridor, taking the opposite direction from that in which they previously traversed it. After a while the Pict stopped and pressed close to one of the secret doors, bidding Kull look with him through the hidden slot.

"This opens upon a little-used stair which leads to a corridor running past the study-room door."

They gazed, and presently, mounting the stair silently, came a silent shape.

"Tu! Chief councilor!" exclaimed Kull. "By night and with bared dagger! How, what means this, Brule?"

"Murder! And foulest treachery!" hissed Brule. "Nay"—as Kull would have flung the door aside and leaped forth—"we are lost if you meet him here, for more lurk at the foot of those stairs. Come!"

Half running, they darted back along the passage. Back through the secret door Brule led, shutting it carefully behind them, then across the chamber to an opening into a room seldom used. There he swept aside some tapestries in a dim corner nook and, drawing Kull with him, stepped behind them. Minutes dragged. Kull could hear the breeze in the other room blowing the window curtains about, and it seemed to him like the murmur of ghosts. Then through the door, stealthily, came Tu, chief councilor of the king. Evidently he had come through the study room and, finding it empty, sought his victim where he was most likely to be.

He came with upraised dagger, walking silently. A moment he halted, gazing about the apparently empty room, which was lighted dimly by a single candle. Then he advanced cautiously, apparently at a loss to understand the absence of the king. He stood before the hiding-place—and "Slay!" hissed the Pict.

Kull with a single mighty leap hurled himself into the room. Tu spun, but the blinding, tiger-ish speed of the attack gave him no chance for defense or counterattack. Sword steel flashed in the dim light and grated on bone as Tu toppled backward, Kull's sword standing out between his shoulders.

Kull leaned above him, teeth bared in the kill-er's snarl, heavy brows a scowl above eyes that were like the gray ice of the cold sea. Then he released the hilt and recoiled, shaken, dizzy, the hand of death at his spine.

For as he watched, Tu's face became strangely dim and unreal; the features mingled and merged in a seemingly impossible manner. Then, like a fading mask of fog, the face suddenly vanished and in its stead gaped and leered a monstrous ser-pent's head! "Valka!" gasped Kull, sweat beading his forehead, and again; "Valka!"

Brule leaned forward, face immobile. Yet his glittering eyes mirrored something of Kull's horror.

"Regain your sword, lord king," said he. "There are yet deeds to be done."

Hesitantly Kull set his hand to the hilt. His flesh crawled as he set his foot upon the terror which lay at their feet, and as some jerk of mus-cular reaction caused the frightful mouth to gape suddenly, he recoiled, weak with nausea. Then, wrathful at himself, he plucked forth his sword and gazed more closely at the nameless thing that had been known as Tu, chief councilor. Save for the reptilian head, the thing was the exact coun-terpart of a man.

"A man with the head of a snake!" Kull mur-mured. "This, then, is a priest of the serpent god?"

"Aye. Tu sleeps unknowing. These fiends can take any form they will. That is, they can, by a magic charm or the like, fling a web of sorcery about their faces, as an actor dons a mask, so that they resemble anyone they wish to."

"Then the old legends were true," mused the king; "the grim old tales few dare even whisper, lest they die as blasphemers, are no fantasies. By Valka, I had thought—I had guessed—but it seems beyond the bounds of reality. Ha! The guardsmen outside the door—"

"They too are snake-men. Hold! What would you do?"

"Slay them!" said Kull between his teeth.

"Strike at the skull if at all," said Brule. "Eighteen wait without the door and perhaps a score more in the corridors. Hark ye, king, Ka-nu learned of this plot. His spies have pierced the inmost fastnesses of the snake priests and they brought hints of a plot. Long ago he discovered the secret passageways of the palace, and at his command I studied the map thereof and came here by night to aid you, lest you die as other kings of Valusia have died. I came alone for the reason that to send more would have roused suspicion. Many could not steal into the palace as I did. Some of the foul conspiracy you have seen. Snake-men guard your door, and that one, as Tu, could pass anywhere else in the palace; in the morning, if the priests failed, the real guards would be holding their places again, nothing knowing, nothing remembering; there to take the blame if the priests succeeded. But stay you here while I dispose of this carrion."

So saying, the Pict shouldered the fright-ful thing stolidly and vanished with it through another secret panel. Kull stood alone, his mind a-whirl. Neophytes of the mighty serpent, how many lurked among his cities? How might he tell the false from the true? Aye, how many of his trusted councilors, his generals, were men? He could be certain—of whom?

The secret panel swung inward and Brule entered.

"You were swift."

"Aye!" The warrior stepped forward, eyeing the floor. "There is gore upon the rug. See?"

Kull bent forward; from the corner of his eye he saw a blur of movement, a glint of steel. Like a loosened bow he whipped erect, thrusting upward. The warrior sagged upon the sword, his own clattering to the floor. Even at that instant

Kull reflected grimly that it was appropriate that the traitor should meet his death upon the sliding, upward thrust used so much by his race.

Then, as Brule slid from the sword to sprawl motionless on the floor, the face began to merge and fade, and as Kull caught his breath, his hair a-prickle, the human features vanished and there the jaws of a great snake gaped hideously, the terrible beady eyes venomous even in death.

"He was a snake priest all the time!" gasped the king. "Valka! What an elaborate plan to throw me off my guard! Ka-nu there, is he a man? Was it Ka-nu to whom I talked in the gardens? Almighty Valka!" as his flesh crawled with a horrid thought; "are the people of Valusia men or are they all serpents?"

Undecided he stood, idly seeing that the thing named Brule no longer wore the dragon armlet. A sound made him wheel.

Brule was coming through the secret door.

"Hold!" Upon the arm upthrown to halt the king's hovering sword gleamed the dragon armlet. "Valka!" The Pict stopped short. Then a grim smile curled his lips.

"By the gods of the seas! These demons are crafty past reckoning. For it must be that one lurked in the corridors, and seeing me go carrying the carcass of that other, took my appearance. So, I have another to do away with."

"Hold!" there was the menace of death in Kull's voice; "I have seen two men turn to serpents before my eyes. How may I know if you are a true man?"

Brule laughed. "For two reasons, King Kull. No snake-man wears this"—he indicated the dragon armlet—"nor can any say these words," and again Kull heard the strange phrase; "Ka nama kaa lajerama."

"Ka nama kaa lajerama," Kull repeated mechanically. "Now, where, in Valka's name, have I heard that? I have not! And yet—and yet—"

"Aye, you remember, Kull," said Brule. "Through the dim corridors of memory those words lurk; though you never heard them in this life, yet in the bygone ages they were so terribly impressed upon the soul mind that never dies,

that they will always strike dim chords in your memory, though you be reincarnated for a million years to come. For that phrase has come secretly down the grim and bloody eons, since when, uncounted centuries ago, those words were watchwords for the race of men who battled with the grisly beings of the Elder Universe. For none but a real man of men may speak them, whose jaws and mouth are shaped different from any other creature. Their meaning has been forgotten but not the words themselves."

"True," said Kull. "I remember the legends. Valka!" He stopped short, staring, for suddenly, like the silent swinging wide of a mystic door, misty, unfathomed reaches opened in the recesses of his consciousness and for an instant he seemed to gaze back through the vastness that spanned life and life; seeing through the vague and ghostly fogs dim shapes reliving dead centuries—men in combat with hideous monsters, vanquishing a planet of frightful terrors. Against a gray, ever-shifting background moved strange nightmare forms, fantasies of lunacy and fear; and man, the jest of the gods, the blind, wisdomless striver from dust to dust, following the long bloody trail of his destiny, knowing not why, bestial, blundering, like a great murderous child, yet feeling somewhere a spark of divine fire . . . Kull drew a hand across his brow, shaken; these sudden glimpses into the abysses of memory always startled him.

"They are gone," said Brule, as if scanning his secret mind; "the bird-women, the harpies, the bat-men, the flying fiends, the wolf-people, the demons, the goblins—all save such as this being that lies at our feet, and a few of the wolf-men. Long and terrible was the war, lasting through the bloody centuries, since first the first men, risen from the mire of apedom, turned upon those who then ruled the world.

"And at last mankind conquered, so long ago that naught but dim legends come to us through the ages. The snake-people were the last to go, yet at last men conquered even them and drove them forth into the waste lands of the world, there to mate with true snakes until some day, say the sages, the horrid breed shall vanish utterly. Yet the Things returned in crafty guise as men grew soft and degenerate, forgetting ancient wars. Ah, that was a grim and secret war! Among the men of the Younger Earth stole the frightful monsters of the Elder Planet, safeguarded by their horrid wisdom and mysticisms, taking all forms and shapes, doing deeds of horror secretly. No man knew who was a true man and who was false. No man could trust any man. Yet by means of their own craft they formed ways by which the false might be known from the true. Men took for a sign and a standard the figure of the flying dragon, the winged dinosaur, a monster of past ages, which was the greatest foe of the serpent. And men used those words which I spoke to you as a sign and symbol, for as I said, none but a true man can repeat them. So mankind triumphed. Yet again the fiends came after the years of forgetfulness had gone by—for man is still an ape in that he forgets what is not ever before his eyes. As priests they came; and for that men in their luxury and might had by then lost faith in the old religions and worships, the snake-men, in the guise of teachers of a new and truer cult, built a monstrous religion about the worship of the serpent god. Such is their power that it is now death to repeat the old legends of the snake-people, and people bow again to the serpent god in new form; and blind fools that they are, the great hosts of men see no connection between this power and the power men overthrew eons ago. As priests the snake-men are content to rule—and yet—" He stopped.

"Go on." Kull felt an unaccountable stirring of the short hair at the base of his scalp.

"Kings have reigned as true men in Valusia," the Pict whispered, "and yet, slain in battle, have died serpents—as died he who fell beneath the spear of Lion-fang on the red beaches when we of the isles harried the Seven Empires. And how can this be, Lord Kull? These kings were born of women and lived as men! This—the true kings died in secret—as you would have died tonight—and priests of the Serpent reigned in their stead, no man knowing."

Kull cursed between his teeth. "Aye, it must be. No one has ever seen a priest of the Serpent and lived, that is known. They live in utmost secrecy."

"The statecraft of the Seven Empires is a mazy, monstrous thing," said Brule. "There the true men know that among them glide the spies of the Serpent, and the men who are the Serpent's allies—such as Kaanuub, baron of Blaal— yet no man dares seek to unmask a suspect lest vengeance befall him. No man trusts his fellow and the true statesmen dare not speak to each other what is in the minds of all. Could they be sure, could a snake-man or plot be unmasked before them all, then would the power of the Serpent be more than half broken; for all would then ally and make common cause, sifting out the traitors. Ka-nu alone is of sufficient shrewdness and courage to cope with them, and even Ka-nu learned only enough of their plot to tell me what would happen—what has happened up to this time. Thus far I was prepared; from now on we must trust to our luck and our craft. Here and now I think we are safe; those snake-men without the door dare not leave their post lest true men come here unexpectedly. But tomorrow they will try something else, you may be sure. Just what they will do, none can say, not even Ka-nu; but we must stay at each other's sides, King Kull, until we conquer or both be dead. Now come with me while I take this carcass to the hiding-place where I took the other being."

Kull followed the Pict with his grisly burden through the secret panel and down the dim corridor. Their feet, trained to the silence of the wilderness, made no noise. Like phantoms they glided through the ghostly light, Kull wondering that the corridors should be deserted; at every turn he expected to run full upon some frightful apparition. Suspicion surged back upon him; was this Pict leading him into ambush? He fell back a pace or two behind Brule, his ready sword hovering at the Pict's unheeding back. Brule should die first if he meant treachery. But if the Pict was aware of the king's suspicion, he showed no sign. Stolidly he tramped along, until they came to a room, dusty and long unused, where moldy tapestries hung heavy. Brule drew aside some of these and concealed the corpse behind them.

Then they turned to retrace their steps, when suddenly Brule halted with such abruptness that he was closer to death than he knew; for Kull's nerves were on edge.

"Something moving in the corridor," hissed the Pict. "Ka-nu said these ways would be empty, yet—"

He drew his sword and stole into the corridor, Kull following warily.

A short way down the corridor a strange, vague glow appeared that came toward them. Nerves a-leap, they waited, backs to the corridor wall; for what they knew not, but Kull heard Brule's breath hiss through his teeth and was reassured as to Brule's loyalty.

The glow merged into a shadowy form. A shape vaguely like a man it was, but misty and illusive, like a wisp of fog, that grew more tangible as it approached, but never fully material. A face looked at them, a pair of luminous great eyes, that seemed to hold all the tortures of a million centuries. There was no menace in that face, with its dim, worn features, but only a great pity—and that face—that face—

"Almighty gods!" breathed Kull, an icy hand at his soul; "Eallal, king of Valusia, who died a thousand years ago!"

Brule shrank back as far as he could, his narrow eyes widened in a blaze of pure horror, the sword shaking in his grip, unnerved for the first time that weird night. Erect and defiant stood Kull, instinctively holding his useless sword at the ready; flesh a-crawl, hair a-prickle, yet still a king of kings, as ready to challenge the powers of the unknown dead as the powers of the living.

The phantom came straight on, giving them no heed; Kull shrank back as it passed them, feeling an icy breath like a breeze from the arctic snow. Straight on went the shape with slow, silent footsteps, as if the chains of all the ages were upon those vague feet, vanishing about a bend of the corridor.

"Valka!" muttered the Pict, wiping the cold beads from his brow; "that was no man! That was a ghost!"

"Aye!" Kull shook his head wonderingly. "Did you not recognize the face? That was Eallal, who reigned in Valusia a thousand years ago and who was found hideously murdered in his throne-room—the room now known as the Accursed Room. Have you not seen his statue in the Fame Room of Kings?"

"Yes, I remember the tale now. Gods, Kull! that is another sign of the frightful and foul power of the snake priests—that king was slain by snake-people and thus his soul became their slave, to do their bidding throughout eternity! For the sages have ever maintained that if a man is slain by a snake-man his ghost becomes their slave."

A shudder shook Kull's gigantic frame. "Valka! But what a fate! Hark ye"—his fingers closed upon Brule's sinewy arm like steel—"hark ye! If I am wounded unto death by these foul monsters, swear that ye will smite your sword through my breast lest my soul be enslaved."

"I swear," answered Brule, his fierce eyes lighting. "And do ye the same by me, Kull."

Their strong right hands met in a silent sealing of their bloody bargain.

4. MASKS

Kull sat upon his throne and gazed broodily out upon the sea of faces turned toward him. A courtier was speaking in evenly modulated tones, but the king scarcely heard him. Close by, Tu, chief councilor, stood ready at Kull's command, and each time the king looked at him, Kull shuddered inwardly. The surface of court life was as the unrippled surface of the sea between tide and tide. To the musing king the affairs of the night before seemed as a dream, until his eyes dropped to the arm of his throne. A brown, sinewy hand rested there, upon the wrist of which gleamed a dragon armlet; Brule stood beside his throne and ever the Pict's fierce secret whisper brought him back from the realm of unreality in which he moved.

No, that was no dream, that monstrous interlude. As he sat upon his throne in the Hall of Society and gazed upon the courtiers, the ladies, the lords, the statesmen, he seemed to see their faces as things of illusion, things unreal, existent only as shadows and mockeries of substance. Always he had seen their faces as masks, but before he had looked on them with contemptuous tolerance, thinking to see beneath the masks shallow, puny souls, avaricious, lustful, deceitful; now there was a grim undertone, a sinister meaning, a vague horror that lurked beneath the smooth masks. While he exchanged courtesies with some nobleman or councilor, he seemed to see the smiling face fade like smoke and the frightful jaws of a serpent gaping there. How many of those he looked upon were horrid, inhuman monsters, plotting his death, beneath the smooth mesmeric illusion of a human face?

Valusia—land of dreams and nightmares—a kingdom of the shadows, ruled by phantoms who glided back and forth behind the painted curtains, mocking the futile king who sat upon the throne—himself a shadow.

And like a comrade shadow Brule stood by his side, dark eyes glittering from immobile face. A real man, Brule! And Kull felt his friendship for the savage become a thing of reality and sensed that Brule felt a friendship for him beyond the mere necessity of statecraft.

And what, mused Kull, were the realities of life? Ambition, power, pride? The friendship of man, the love of women—which Kull had never known—battle, plunder, what? Was it the real Kull who sat upon the throne or was it the real Kull who had scaled the hills of Atlantis, harried the far isles of the sunset, and laughed upon the green roaring tides of the Atlantean sea? How could a man be so many different men in a lifetime? For Kull knew that there were many Kulls and he wondered which was the real Kull. After

all, the priests of the Serpent went a step further in their magic, for all men wore masks, and many a different mask with each different man or woman; and Kull wondered if a serpent did not lurk under every mask. So he sat and brooded in strange, mazy thought ways, and the courtiers came and went and the minor affairs of the day were completed, until at last the king and Brule sat alone in the Hall of Society save for the drowsy attendants.

Kull felt a weariness. Neither he nor Brule had slept the night before, nor had Kull slept the night before that, when in the gardens of Ka-nu he had had his first hint of the weird things to be. Last night nothing further had occurred after they had returned to the study room from the secret corridors, but they had neither dared nor cared to sleep. Kull, with the incredible vitality of a wolf, had aforetime gone for days upon days without sleep, in his wild savage days but now his mind was edged from constant thinking and from the nerve-breaking eeriness of the past night. He needed sleep, but sleep was furthest from his mind.

And he would not have dared sleep if he had thought of it. Another thing that had shaken him was the fact that though he and Brule had kept a close watch to see if, or when, the study-room guard was changed, yet it was changed without their knowledge; for the next morning those who stood on guard were able to repeat the magic words of Brule, but they remembered nothing out of the ordinary. They thought that they had stood at guard all night, as usual, and Kull said nothing to the contrary. He believed them true men, but Brule had advised absolute secrecy, and Kull also thought it best.

Now Brule leaned over the throne, lowering his voice so not even a lazy attendant could hear: "They will strike soon, I think, Kull. A while ago Ka-nu gave me a secret sign. The priests know that we know of their plot, of course, but they know not, how much we know. We must be ready for any sort of action. Ka-nu and the Pictish chiefs will remain within hailing distance now until this is settled one way or another. Ha, Kull, if it comes to a pitched battle, the streets and the castles of Valusia will run red!"

Kull smiled grimly. He would greet any sort of action with a ferocious joy. This wandering in a labyrinth of illusion and magic was extremely irksome to his nature. He longed for the leap and clang of swords, for the joyous freedom of battle.

Then into the Hall of Society came Tu again, and the rest of the councilors.

"Lord king, the hour of the council is at hand and we stand ready to escort you to the council room."

Kull rose, and the councilors bent the knee as he passed through the way opened by them for his passage, rising behind him, and following. Eyebrows were raised as the Pict strode defiantly behind the king, but no one dissented. Brule's challenging gaze swept the smooth faces of the councilors with the defiance of an intruding savage.

The group passed through the halls and came at last to the council chamber. The door was closed, as usual, and the councilors arranged themselves in the order of their rank before the dais upon which stood the king. Like a bronze statue, Brule took up his stand behind Kull.

Kull swept the room with a swift stare. Surely no chance of treachery here. Seventeen councilors there were, all known to him; all of them had espoused his cause when he ascended the throne.

"Men of Valusia—" he began in the conventional manner, then halted, perplexed. The councilors had risen as a man and were moving toward him. There was no hostility in their looks, but their actions were strange for a council room. The foremost was close to him when Brule sprang forward, crouched like a leopard.

"Ka nama kaa lajerama!" his voice crackled through the sinister silence of the room and the foremost councilor recoiled, hand flashing to his robes; and like a spring released, Brule moved and the man pitched headlong and lay still while his face faded and became the head of a mighty snake.

"Slay, Kull!" rasped the Pict's voice. "They be all serpent-men!"

The rest was a scarlet maze. Kull saw the familiar faces dim like fading fog and in their places gaped horrid reptilian visages as the whole band rushed forward. His mind was dazed but his giant body faltered not.

The singing of his sword filled the room, and the onrushing flood broke in a red wave. But they surged forward again, seemingly willing to fling their lives away in order to drag down the king. Hideous jaws gaped at him; terrible eyes blazed into his unblinkingly; a frightful fetid scent pervaded the atmosphere—the serpent scent that Kull had known in southern jungles. Swords and daggers leaped at him and he was dimly aware that they wounded him. But Kull was in his element; never before had he faced such grim foes but it mattered little; they lived, their veins held blood that could be spilt and they died when his great sword cleft their skulls or drove through their bodies. Slash, thrust, thrust and swing. Yet had Kull died there but for the man who crouched at his side, parrying and thrusting. For the king was clear berserk, fighting in the terrible Atlantean way, that seeks death to deal death; he made no effort to avoid thrusts and slashes, standing straight up and ever plunging forward, no thought in his frenzied mind but to slay. Not often did Kull forget his fighting craft in his primitive fury, but now some chain had broken in his soul, flooding his mind with a red wave of slaughter-lust. He slew a foe at each blow, but they surged about him, and time and again Brule turned a thrust that would have slain, as he crouched beside Kull, parrying and warding with cold skill, slaying not as Kull slew with long slashes and plunges, but with short overhand blows and upward thrusts.

Kull laughed, a laugh of insanity. The frightful faces swirled about him in a scarlet blaze. He felt steel sink into his arm and dropped his sword in a flashing arc that cleft his foe to the breastbone. Then the mists faded and the king saw that he and Brule stood alone above a sprawl of hideous crimson figures who lay still upon the floor.

"Valka! what a killing!" said Brule, shaking the blood from his eyes. "Kull, had these been warriors who knew how to use the steel, we had died here. These serpent priests know naught of swordcraft and die easier than any men I ever slew. Yet had there been a few more, I think the matter had ended otherwise."

Kull nodded. The wild berserker blaze had passed, leaving a mazed feeling of great weariness. Blood seeped from wounds on breast, shoulder, arm and leg. Brule, himself bleeding from a score of flesh wounds, glanced at him in some concern.

"Lord Kull, let us hasten to have your wounds dressed by the women."

Kull thrust him aside with a drunken sweep of his mighty arm.

"Nay, we'll see this through ere we cease. Go you, though, and have your wounds seen to—I command it."

The Pict laughed grimly. "Your wounds are more than mine, lord king—" he began, then stopped as a sudden thought struck him. "By Valka, Kull, this is not the council room!"

Kull looked about and suddenly other fogs seemed to fade. "Nay, this is the room where Eallal died a thousand years ago—since unused and named 'Accursed.'"

"Then by the gods, they tricked us after all!" exclaimed Brule in a fury, kicking the corpses at their feet. "They caused us to walk like fools into their ambush! By their magic they changed the appearance of all—"

"Then there is further deviltry afoot." said Kull, "for if there be true men in the councils of Valusia they should be in the real council room now. Come swiftly."

And leaving the room with its ghastly keepers they hastened through halls that seemed deserted until they came to the real council room. Then Kull halted with a ghastly shudder. From the council room sounded a voice speaking, and the voice was his!

With a hand that shook he parted the tapestries and gazed into the room. There sat the councilors, counterparts of the men he and Brule had just slain, and upon the dais stood Kull, king of Valusia.

He stepped back, his mind reeling.

"This is insanity!" he whispered. "Am I Kull? Do I stand here or is that Kull yonder in very truth, and am I but a shadow, a figment of thought?"

Brule's hand clutching his shoulder, shaking him fiercely, brought him to his senses.

"Valka's name, be not a fool! Can you yet be astounded after all we have seen? See you not that those are true men bewitched by a snake-man who has taken your form, as those others took their forms? By now you should have been slain, and yon monster reigning in your stead, unknown by those who bowed to you. Leap and slay swiftly or else we are undone. The Red Slayers, true men, stand close on each hand and none but you can reach and slay him. Be swift!"

Kull shook off the onrushing dizziness, flung back his head in the old, defiant gesture. He took a long, deep breath as does a strong swimmer before diving into the sea; then, sweeping back the tapestries, made the dais in a single lion-like bound. Brule had spoken truly. There stood men of the Red Slayers, guardsmen trained to move quick as the striking leopard; any but Kull had died ere he could reach the usurper. But the sight of Kull, identical with the man upon the dais, held them in their tracks, their minds stunned for an instant, and that was long enough. He upon the dais snatched for his sword, but even as his fingers closed upon the hilt, Kull's sword stood out behind his shoulders and the thing that men had thought the king pitched forward from the dais to lie silent upon the floor.

"Hold!" Kull's lifted hand and kingly voice stopped the rush that had started, and while they stood astounded he pointed to the thing which lay before them—whose face was fading into that of a snake. They recoiled, and from one door came Brule and from another came Ka-nu.

These grasped the king's bloody hand and Ka-nu spoke: "Men of Valusia, you have seen with your own eyes. This is the true Kull, the mightiest king to whom Valusia has ever bowed. The power of the Serpent is broken and ye be all true men. King Kull, have you commands?"

"Lift that carrion," said Kull, and men of the guard took up the thing.

"Now follow me," said the king, and he made his way to the Accursed Room. Brule, with a look of concern, offered the support of his arm but Kull shook him off.

The distance seemed endless to the bleeding king, but at last he stood at the door and laughed fiercely and grimly when he heard the horrified ejaculations of the councilors.

At his orders the guardsmen flung the corpse they carried beside the others, and motioning all from the room Kull stepped out last and closed the door.

A wave of dizziness left him shaken. The faces turned to him, pallid and wonderingly, swirled and mingled in a ghostly fog. He felt the blood from his wounds trickling down his limbs and he knew that what he was to do, he must do quickly or not at all.

His sword rasped from its sheath.

"Brule, are you there?"

"Aye!" Brule's face looked at him through the mist, close to his shoulder, but Brule's voice sounded leagues and eons away.

"Remember our vow, Brule. And now, bid them stand back."

His left arm cleared a space as he flung up his sword. Then with all his waning power he drove it through the door into the jamb, driving the great sword to the hilt and sealing the room forever.

Legs braced wide, he swayed drunkenly, facing the horrified councilors. "Let this room be doubly accursed. And let those rotting skeletons lie there forever as a sign of the dying might of the Serpent. Here I swear that I shall hunt the serpent-men from land to land, from sea to sea, giving no rest until all be slain, that good triumph and the power of Hell be broken. This thing I swear-I-Kull-king-of-Valusia."

His knees buckled as the faces swayed and swirled. The councilors leaped forward, but ere they could reach him, Kull slumped to the floor, and lay still, face upward.

The councilors surged about the fallen king, chattering and shrieking. Ka-nu beat them back with his clenched fists, cursing savagely.

"Back, you fools! Would you stifle the little life that is yet in him? How, Brule, is he dead or will he live?"—to the warrior who bent above the prostrate Kull.

"Dead?" sneered Brule irritably. "Such a man as this is not so easily killed. Lack of sleep and loss of blood have weakened him—by Valka, he has a score of deep wounds, but none of them mortal. Yet have those gibbering fools bring the court women here at once."

Brule's eyes lighted with a fierce, proud light.

"Valka, Ka-nu, but here is such a man as I knew not existed in these degenerate days. He will be in the saddle in a few scant days and then may the serpent-men of the world beware of Kull of Valusia. Valka! But that will be a rare hunt! Ah, I see long years of prosperity for the world with such a king upon the throne of Valusia."

Hirai Tarō (1894–1965), known to the literary world as Edogawa Ranpo, was a Japanese author and translator commonly acknowledged as a master of crime and mystery fiction. Ranpo even created the Japanese Gothic mystery, influenced by the work of Edgar Allan Poe. He was the first Japanese author to ever pen a story about a vampire in one of the books of his Akechi series, *Vampire* (1930). In 1955, the Mystery Writers of Japan decided to give an award in his honor. The Edogawa Ranpo award is presented annually to an unpublished mystery novel. "The Man Traveling with the Brocade Portrait" is one of the most unusual fantasy stories in this volume and showcases Ranpo's mastery.

The Man Traveling with the Brocade Portrait

Edogawa Ranpo

Translated by Michael Tangeman

IF THIS STORY IS NOT A DREAM of mine or a hallucination brought on by a temporary state of insanity, then surely the man traveling with the brocade portrait was himself insane. Yet, like a dreamer who is permitted to peek at a world other than our own or a lunatic who hears and sees what the rest of us cannot, it may well be that I happened to catch a glimpse—if only for an instant—of something that lies beyond the field of vision in our world, and by using the bizarre mechanism of the atmosphere as my lens, I peered into a corner of a realm that exists outside our own. The date escapes me, but it was a warm, overcast day. I had set out to see the famous mirages at the seashore at Uozu. Now I was on my way home.

Close friends always interrupt me when I get to this point in the story.

"Hey, wait a minute," they ask incredulously. "When did you ever go to Uozu?"

Well, put it that way, and I suppose I can't produce evidence to demonstrate categorically I was there on such and such a day. Maybe it was a dream after all. But never before had I experienced a dream in which the colors were so vivid. The scenes in most dreams are, like those in black-and-white movies, devoid of color. But the one from that night when I took the train home alone from Uozu to Tokyo is burned into my memory as vividly as one might remember the eye of a snake. And at the heart of that dream is the gaudy portrait I saw that night, brocade puffed up and stuffed from inside, fabric woven in brilliant hues of purple and red. The dream was so powerful that it makes me wonder if we'll be able to see the dream of films made in color come true.

The trip was the first time I had ever seen a mirage. I imagined a mirage would look like an old-fashioned painting in which the beautiful Dragon Palace of the God of the Sea floated majestically among bubbles rising from a giant clam. But seeing the real thing took me completely by surprise. It came to me as a shock. The experience bordered on fear, and it made me break into oily sweat.

A breathless throng had gathered among the stretch of pine trees that ran along the sandy beach. People looked no bigger than dried beans scattered on a tray as they stood there taking in the expanse of both sea and sky that filled our field of vision. I had never seen the sea so quiet. It was silent as a deaf-mute. The calm was all the more unexpected since I had always thought the Sea of Japan as being terribly rough. The gray sea, which was smooth and without a wave or a ripple, reminded me of a vast marsh that stretches on and on without end. Unlike the Pacific Ocean, the Sea of Japan has no horizon. Instead the water seemed to meld into the sky and become an identical, indistinct gray haze of indeterminate thickness. So that, just when I thought I was looking at the upper reaches of the haze—that is, what I mistook for sky—all of a sudden a large, white sailboat floated across it like a ghost wing through a mist. I was startled to realize I was staring at the surface of water!

The mirage looked like drops of India ink, dripped one by one on a piece of milky white film. Slowly but steadily the black droplets spread across the surface of the film until it became a gigantic movie screen projected on vast, open sky.

Viewed through these two different layers of sky, each with its own refracting lens, the distant forests of the Nōtō Peninsula were like a black-bug that one examines through a microscope yet to be adjusted and brought into focus. An indistinct yet grossly enlarged image appeared to be suspended over the heads of the spectators on the beach. It resembled a strangely shaped black cloud, and it really did appear to exist there in the sky. Yet, oddly enough, the distance between it and the spectators was indistinct and impossible to gauge. At first, the mirage was a big cumulonimbus floating high above the sea. But then it seemed to change. It became a weird sort of haze that pressed within a foot of the viewer's face. Or still closer—like a blur that flits across the cornea of the eye. What was important was the indistinctness. The inability to gauge distance was what gave it the air of something unimaginable . . . of something weird . . . of something insane.

The vaguely shaped, giant jet-black triangles of the mirage were piled on top of the other, but then, in the blink of an eye, they fell apart and arrayed themselves horizontally as if they were a row of box cars linked together like a train. In turn they broke into smaller pieces, becoming the treetops in a stand of Lebanese cedars. They stood there, still and immovable, until they transformed themselves again—abracadabra—into radically different shapes.

If the magic of a mirage possesses the power to drive a person insane, then surely I was under its spell as I boarded the train in Uozu and headed home for Tokyo. Having spent more than two hours riveted to the spot as I watched a series of seductive and unearthly transfigurations in the sky, there was no question I was not fully myself that long night I spent on the train. My state of mind was completely different from what it would have been on an ordinary day. Perhaps it was akin to temporary insanity—like the hysteria that sets in when a phantom spirit or robber accosts one out of the blue and leaves one in fear for one's life.

I boarded the train at Uozu Station bound for Ueno Station in Tokyo at about six p.m. I don't know if it was by strange coincidence or merely a normal event on trains in the area, but the second-class car where I sat (at the time there were still first-, second-, and third-class cars) was, save for myself, as empty as a church. Only one other passenger had boarded ahead of me, and he was hunkered down on a seat in the far corner of the car.

The train ran on and on, its monotonous, mechanical sounds reverberating along the lonely shoreline with its steep cliffs and sandy bays. A dark, blood-colored sun floated lazily over the depths of the haze as it set over the marshlike sea. A white sail, which appeared to be abnormally large, scudded through the haze as if it were moving in a dream. It was a windless, stiflingly hot day, and windows in the car were open here and there. Yet even the gentle breeze, which slipped in like a legless ghost, did little to stir the air. The many short tunnels and the thin slats on row after row of snow fences broke the endless gray expanse of sky and sea into stripes as we passed them.

By the time we passed the cliffs at Oyashirazu, the lamplight in the car and the light left in the sky appeared to cancel each other out, and darkness closed in on us aboard the train. It was then that the only other passenger in the car, the man sitting in the far corner, abruptly stood up and spread a large black cloth over the seat. Then he took an object of two to three feet in length—it had been turned toward the window—and began wrapping it up in the cloth. His actions gave me a decidedly eerie feeling.

I felt certain the flat object was a framed picture, and it appeared there was special significance to the fact the man had propped it up to face toward the train window. I was convinced that earlier he had deliberately removed the object from the cloth and placed it in the window to face the outside. Based on the quick glimpse I stole when he rewrapped it, I could tell the picture, which was executed in the most brilliant combination of colors, had a marvelously raw, vital quality to it. There was something not of this world about it—or at least not of our everyday world.

I took a second look at the bearer of the strange package. As peculiar as the object in his possession may have seemed, I was more surprised by its owner, who looked very strange indeed. He was an old-fashioned type the likes of which one sees only in faded photographs from our fathers' youth. He was dressed in a black suit with a narrow collar and pointy shoulders. Yet the suit looked strangely appropriate given the man's height and his long legs. It even made him look dapper. He had a long, narrow face, and aside from his eyes that seemed to burn a tad too brightly, he was handsome and his features well proportioned. His neatly parted hair shone with a black, luxurious sheen, making me think at first glance he was about forty years old. Upon closer examination, however, I noticed a considerable number of wrinkles on his face. He seemed to age twenty years in a single leap. He could have been sixty easily. The contrast between his pitch-black hair and the maze of wrinkles etched across his pale face was striking enough that it took my breath away. It struck me as most peculiar and unsettling.

As the man finished carefully wrapping up the picture, he happened to look in my direction just as I was observing his every move. Our eyes locked. The corners of his lips turned nervously upward into a faint and awkward smile. Without stopping to think, I returned his greeting by nodding in his direction.

During the short period of time it took the train to race through the next two or three local stations, we sat in our respective corners of the car, repeating the game of nervously looking out the window if our eyes happened to meet. Outside everything was pitch black. Even if I pushed my face against the window, there was nothing to see but darkness, except for the occasional running lights of fishing boats that bobbed at a distance on the sea. In the endless dark, our long, narrow car rattled on and on as if it existed in its own little world. Inside the dimly lit compartment I felt as if every living being in the world had disappeared without a trace, leaving only the two of us behind. No passengers boarded our second-class car at any station, and neither porter nor conductor appeared. Now that I think about it, this too strikes me as most bizarre.

I grew increasingly leery and frightened of the strange man who looked, simultaneously, both forty and sixty and who possessed the demeanor of a magician from the West. Fear has a way of growing infinitely and overtaking one physically when there is nothing to dispel it. The hair on the back of my neck stood on end, and no longer able to bear the suspense, I finally stood up and boldly walked over to the man sitting at the opposite end of the car. The more detestable and fearsome he became, the more I wanted to approach him.

Without so much as a word I lowered myself into the seat directly opposite him. As I drew nearer, a strange, tumultuous feeling welled up inside me. If he seemed not-of-this-world, then I too might be a phantom. My eyes became narrow slits, and I held my breath as I studied his odd, heavily wrinkled face.

The man seemed to welcome me with his eyes from the instant I left my seat, and as I stared at his face, he gestured with his chin at the frame sitting beside him. It was as though he had been waiting for me. He eschewed the usual preliminary niceties and asked, as if it were the most natural question in the world,

"Is this what interests you?" His tone was so matter-of-fact that it gave me pause. "Would you care to take a look at it?" His manner was very polite.

I sat there in total silence. I was at a loss for words. He repeated the question.

"Would you be kind enough to show it to me?" I was enchanted by his manner and found myself uttering this odd request in spite of the fact that I had left my seat intending *not* to look at the man's picture.

"I'd be delighted. I have been wondering when you would ask. I felt certain you'd come and take a look."

As he spoke, the man—perhaps it would be more appropriate to say "the old man"—deftly undid the large cloth with his long fingers and propped the framelike object against the window. But this time he turned it to face the inside of the car.

Why was it that I unconsciously closed my eyes after taking a quick glance at the picture? To this day I do not know why, but I felt an inexpli-cable, overwhelming urge to do so. I closed my eyes for a mere second or two, but when I looked again what I saw was a vision so strange that it was unlike anything I had ever seen. Even now I do not have words to describe what was so eerie about it.

The artist's exaggerated use of perspective allowed the viewer to peer into a series of rooms inside a palace the likes of which one sees on the stage of the Kabuki theater. It was quite a spectacle—the tatami mats were brand-new and still somewhat green; the paneled ceiling stretched into the depths of the painting; the tempera colors, especially the indigo, had been applied quite heavily—even grossly. In the foreground to the left, the window of a room constructed in the style of a *shoin*, or gentleman's study, was roughly sketched in using heavy black brush strokes. A writing desk, also in black, was drawn in beneath the window. It too was done in a hand unconcerned with getting the angles correct. Perhaps you'll find it easier to understand if I describe the backdrop as done in the style typical of votive plaques one sees at a temple.

Two figures, both about a foot high, floated against this background. I say "floated" because they were the only part of the painting not done in tempera paints. Instead they were constructed of silk brocade that had been applied a layer at a time to create two raised or padded figures. An elderly gentleman, who had white hair and wore an outdated Western suit made of black velvet, sat stiffly at the center. (I noticed he was, oddly enough, a perfect match for the man who carried the painting, even down to the cut of his suit.) Meanwhile, his companion was a smooth-skinned beauty of seventeen or eighteen who had her hair done in the *yuiwata* style and who wore a black satin sash over a red long-sleeved kimono dyed in a dappled pattern. She was leaning coquettishly against the old man's knees. The two of them looked like they belonged in a love scene on the stage.

It goes without saying that the juxtaposition of an old man with an amorous-looking young maiden struck me as most peculiar, although that was not what made me call them "eerie." No, it was the elaborate craftsmanship of the brocade that had been carefully executed and stood in stark contrast to the artlessness of the background of the portrait. White silk had been used to create a feeling of depth and to depict even the tiniest wrinkles on the man's face. Strands of human hair had been woven one by one into the material for the girl's hair, which was coiffed like that of a real person. Doubtless, the hair on the old man's head was also genuine and had been applied with equal care. The seams of his suit were realistically cut and sewn, and the buttons—not one of them bigger than a grain of millet—attached in all the right places. The swell of the girl's bosom, the elegantly sensuous curves of the area about her thighs, the splash of scarlet crepe, the glimpse of flesh tones, the nails that grew from her fingertips like sea shells—all in all, the raised brocade was so meticulously crafted that, were one to inspect it with a magnifying glass, he'd see the craftsman included every pore and dewy hair.

I had seen raised brocade work only once before in the shape of faces of Kabuki actors mounted on battledores used at New Year's. While some of the actors' faces were elaborately designed, they were no comparison for this portrait, which was so minutely crafted. The brocade portrait of the old man with the pretty young girl was probably the work of a true master of the art. Still, that was not what I found eerie.

Given the age of the painting and the paint flaking here and there, the materials used to make the girl's red kimono and the old man's black velvet suit had faded to the point where they were a pale shadow of how they originally looked. Nonetheless, the two figures retained an indescribable—indeed almost lethally poisonous—quality about them. Their faces possessed a vitality that glowed like a burning flame and seared its way deep into the viewer's eye. Still, that is not what was particularly eerie about it.

Forced to describe it, I would have to say I felt the two people in the portrait were still alive.

There are only one, maybe two, moments in a performance of the Bunraku puppet theater when a master puppeteer succeeds in breathing the breath of a god into a puppet and making the doll truly come alive. Even then, such moments last for a mere second or two. Just like the puppet that comes momentarily alive on the stage, the brocade figures appeared to have been affixed to the backdrop of the painting at the very moment when they were most alive and before the breath of life could escape from them. It looked as though they would go on living there forever.

When the man on the train saw the startled expression on my face, he gave a shout for joy. He sounded so confident about what he had to say. "Aha, I think you *are* finally getting my point!"

As he spoke, he took out a key and carefully unlocked a black leather case that hung from his shoulder. He removed an ancient pair of binoculars from the case and offered them to me.

"Take a look at the painting through these. No, you're too close where you are now. Excuse me for ordering you about, but would you mind trying it from over there? Good. That should be about right."

It was a most peculiar request, but I did as I was told because curiosity was getting the best of me. I did as the man asked. I got up from my seat and walked five or six paces. The man grasped the frame in both hands and held it up to the overhead light in the car so that I could see it better. As I look back on it now, I think what a strange spectacle it was! Why, it was sheer madness.

The binoculars appeared to have been imported to Japan thirty or forty years earlier. They resembled the ones we often saw depicted on signs at the optician's office when we were children—drawings of magnifying glasses with irregularly shaped prisms. Much like the suit of clothes on the old man in the painting, they had a classic, nostalgic look about them. The brass backing on the case shone in places where the leather was worn from frequent use.

I turned the binoculars over in my hands and fiddled with the adjustments out of sheer fascination. By and by I raised them to my eyes with both hands. It was then that all of a sudden—and I do mean suddenly—the man on the train gave such a shout that I almost dropped them.

"No! Don't! You've got them backwards. You mustn't look through them backwards. You mustn't."

He was white as a sheet. His eyes were as big as saucers, and he was frantically waving his hands. Why was it so awful to look through the binoculars backwards? I was puzzled by the old man's strange behavior. It made no sense.

"Oh, I see. . . . Yes, I've got them turned around."

I did not give much attention to the peculiar expression on the man's face because I was so intent on looking through the binoculars. I turned them around, quickly lifted them to my face, and examined the people in the brocade picture.

As I focused the lens, and the two circles of light slowly blended into one, the image, which initially was like a vague rainbow, grew sharper. The upper half of the girl's torso from her breasts to the top of her head loomed surprisingly large. It filled my entire field of vision, as if there were nothing else in the world to see.

It is difficult for me to convey the manner in which the image presented itself because I have not witnessed anything like it before—or since. The best I can do is to describe a similar kind of feeling. Perhaps it can be likened to viewing a pearl diver from the side of a boat after she dives into the sea. While at the bottom, her naked body looks exactly like swaying sea grasses on account of it being filtered through the complex undulations of the layers of blue water. It moves in unnaturally supple ways. The outline of it is out of focus, and the woman diver takes on the whitish figure of a ghost. But as she rises smoothly and quickly toward the boat, the layers of dark blue water fade and lose their rich color. Her shape becomes clearly visible and distinct, and when her head finally pops above the surface, it is like one's eyes have suddenly opened after a deep sleep. The white ghost of the watery depths

reveals herself in her true form as a human being. That's how the girl in the painting looked to me as I peered through the binoculars. She began to move like a life-size human being.

Another world existed at the opposite end of the old-fashioned, nineteenth-century prism of the binocular lenses. It was a world quite apart from anything we might imagine today. It was the world in which the erotic young woman with the *yuiwata* hairdo and the white-haired man in the old-fashioned suit lived out their strange lives. I knew it was wrong of me to spy on them, yet I felt compelled to. It was as if I were made to do so by a worker of spells and magic. As I look back on it now, it was with the strangest, most inexplicable feeling that I gazed upon the bizarre world I saw in the painting. It was as though I were possessed.

No, it was not that the girl moved physically. But my overall impression of her was drastically different from what I had seen with my naked eye. Seen through the lenses, she brimmed with life. Her pale face was slightly flushed with a touch of peach, and a heart beat within her breast. (I actually heard it beating.) It seemed to me that she generated a vitality so intense that it penetrated through the layers of her kimono.

After I let my eyes run the full length of her body, I turned my attention to the happy-looking, white-haired man. He too was alive inside the world of the binoculars. He looked pleased to have his arm around a young woman who looked forty years his junior. At the same time, it was strange that the hundreds of wrinkles on his face were born, it seemed, not of happiness but of sorrow. That may have been because I was standing too close—a distance of a mere foot away. As a result, his face looked excessively large. But the longer and more carefully I studied it, the more convinced I became that the peculiar expression on his face was one of fear and bitterness.

I began to feel I was having a nightmare. To look through the binoculars any longer became unbearable. Without thinking, I lowered them. I let my eyes run wildly over my surroundings. Yes,

I was still aboard the railway car of a passenger train as it made its way through the lonely night, and the brocade portrait and the man who held it looked just as they had before. Outside the train window everything was pitch dark. I heard the monotonous repetition of the wheels on the train tracks—just as before. I felt sure I'd awakened from a nightmare.

"You, my good sir, have a very peculiar look on your face, if I may be so bold as to say so."

The man put the picture by the window, sat down, and then motioned with his hand for me to sit in the seat across from him. He looked deep into my face.

"Something's gone wrong with my head," I said. "It's gotten all fogged up." I meant my reply to serve as a cover for my feelings of awkwardness.

He was hunched in his seat, and he let his long, thin fingers fidget atop his knees as if he were tapping out a secret code as he thrust his face closer to mine. In the faintest of whispers he said,

"They're alive, aren't they?"

He bent still farther forward as if he had another, even more important, message to impart. He looked into my face with eyes so wide open and glimmering I thought they might bore their way into my head.

"Would you care to hear their story?" he asked in a whisper.

I wondered if the swaying of the train and the clatter of the wheels kept me from hearing him correctly.

"Did you say 'their story'?"

"That's right—'their story,' " he replied in a whisper. "Although it's really the story of only one of them, the white-haired old man."

"A story from his youth?" I found myself saying the most uncharacteristic and odd sort of things that night.

"He was twenty-five at the time."

"I'd be honored if you would share it with me."

I did not hesitate. I urged him on much as one asks to hear a story about a real, live human being. The wrinkles on the man's face deepened. He seemed delighted at my reply.

"Aha, then you will listen to it, won't you?"

With that he began to tell his singularly strange and wondrous tale.

"I remember it precisely because it was the most unforgettable moment in my life. My older brother got to looking like that," he said, pointing to the old man in the picture, "on the night of April 27, 1895. That was the spring of the twenty-eighth year of Meiji. At the time my brother and I were still living with our parents. The house was in the third *chōme* of Nihonbashi-dōri. Our father was a merchant who ran a dry goods store. The events of the story took place not long after the 'Twelve-Story Tower'—that's what people called it in the vernacular—was erected in Asakusa, the site of the famous temple, arcade, and amusement district in the old part of Tokyo. The tower's real name was Ryōunkaku, 'The Cloud Scraper,' and it was the tallest building in Japan at the time. My brother loved to climb the steps to the top of it every day. He was one of those people who never tired of newfangled gadgets, especially exotic items imported from abroad. Take this pair of binoculars, for instance. He found them in the storefront of a strange-looking curio shop in Chinatown in Yokohama. He was told they once belonged to the captain of a foreign ship. He paid what at the time, he said, was an exorbitant sum to get hold of them."

Whenever the man said "my older brother," he would cast a glance in the direction of the man in the painting, or he would point to him as if his brother were sitting next to him. He had confused his actual brother, who existed in his memory, with the white-haired gentleman in the picture. In fact, the way he talked made me feel as if a third party were present—and that the brocade figures in the painting were alive and listening to him tell their story. Still stranger was the fact that I didn't find this the least bit odd. Somehow or other we had transcended the laws of nature and had entered a different world altogether—a world out of sync with our own.

"Did you ever climb the Twelve-Story Tower? Ah, you didn't! That's too bad. I wonder, what magician of an architect built it. It was a truly remarkable and unusual building. An Italian engineer designed the facade, you know. Think about it. Back in those days the amusement park in Asakusa was known for the Human Spider Sideshow . . . the Women Fencers . . . acrobats who balanced themselves on large balls . . . tops that danced on fountain sprays . . . and all kinds of peep shows. The most exotic exhibit was a model of Mount Fuji called 'The Maze,' and then there were the 'Hidden Cedars of Yajin' too. But that was the ultimate in what the park had to offer, in those days. And that's why, my friend, you'd have been taken by surprise to find an unbelievably tall brick tower had suddenly shot up into the air one day. At over ninety feet, it was almost a city block long in height. It was incredibly tall, and on top of the tower was an octagonal platform shaped like a pointed Chinese hat. All you had to do was find a slight rise anywhere in Tokyo, and you could see what everyone called the 'Red Ghost.'

"As I was saying, it was in the spring of 1895 that my brother came into possession of the binoculars. Not long after that, a change seemed to come over him that affected him both physically and mentally. Father would say, 'Why, the fool's gone mad.' He was quite worried. As you can imagine, I too was devoted to my older brother, and his odd behavior also drove me to distraction. Perhaps I should explain that he virtually stopped eating. He never talked to anyone in the house. He shut himself up in his room and did nothing but brood. He became terribly gaunt, and his face took on the gray pall of someone suffering from tuberculosis. Only his eyes moved—he watched us like a hawk. Of course, he didn't have the best complexion to begin with, but it was sad to see him grow so pale. But even in this weakened state, he left the house every day without fail as if he were going to work. He left around noon and stayed out until dusk. He wouldn't say a word if we asked where he was going. Mother got quite upset. She tried every possible means to get him to reveal the source of his depression, but he never said a word. Things continued like this for almost a month.

"Then one day I secretly followed him to find out exactly where he was going. We were all so worried, and I did it at my mother's request, you see. The day was overcast and unpleasant like today. My brother left shortly after noon with the pair of binoculars slung over his shoulder and wearing a new Western-style suit made of black velvet. He himself had the suit tailored, and black velvet was considered extremely fashionable or 'high collar,' as people said in those days. He ambled toward the horse-drawn tramway that ran on Nihonbashi-dōri. I followed him so as not to be seen. Are you following me, my friend?

"My brother waited for the tram bound for Ueno and leapt aboard it when it arrived at the stop. I couldn't follow him on the next car like you can do today because there weren't many streetcars back then, you see. I had to use a bit of money that Mother had given me to hire a rickshaw. It is no great feat for a rickshaw runner to keep a tram in sight if he has any strength at all. That's how I was able to follow my brother.

"When he got off, I left the rickshaw and went on foot for a distance. Wouldn't you know, he led me to the famous Temple of the Goddess of Mercy in Asakusa. He passed through the gate to the temple—with its two big, glaring guardian kings—but then he skipped the temple altogether and headed straight into the crowd that swirled around the sideshow stalls behind the main hall of the temple. It was like he was parting the waves as he walked. He passed under the stone gate of the Twelve-Story Tower, and paying the admission fee, he disappeared under the sign at the entrance that read 'Ryōunkaku—the Cloud Scraper.' Never in my wildest dreams would I have thought he was coming here day after day. I was flabbergasted. I wasn't even twenty at the time. I still thought like a child. I got the crazy idea in my head that my brother had gotten bewitched by the Red Ghost of the Twelve-Story Tower.

"Our father had taken us there once, and we had climbed the steps to the top. But I had never gone back. I had a strange feeling about the place, but there was my brother, and he was climbing the stairs. What could I do but follow him, staying one dimly lit story behind? The windows along the stairs were tall and skinny, and the brick walls very thick. That made the tower as cold as a cellar. Japan was in the midst of a war with China, and oil paintings of the principal battles had been hung along the walls in a long, endless row. At the time oil paintings were still quite rare in Japan. Japanese soldiers yelled as they charged, their faces as fearsome as wolves. Using bayonets affixed to their rifles, they gouged out the innards of the enemy. The writhing purple-faced and purple-lipped Chinese troops used both hands to staunch the heavy flow of blood that spurted from their bodies. Decapitated pigtailed heads flew through the air like balloons.

"Such were the scenes portrayed in the unspeakably garish and blood-drenched paintings that glowed in the dim light that filtered through the windows of the tower. Meanwhile, the gloomy set of stone stairs continued to wind like a snail's shell endlessly up and up alongside the paintings and windows.

"There were no walls to the platform atop the tower. There was only the octagonal railing that created a walkway with a spectacular view. When I finally made my way to the top of the stairs and the darkness suddenly gave way to bright light, I was startled at how much time I had spent in the dark before reaching the platform. The clouds in the sky appeared low enough to reach out and touch. As I looked at the city, the roofs of Tokyo were like trash that had been raked together into a big pile. Meanwhile, the battery along the bay at Shinagawa reminded me of tiny landscape stones arranged in a bonsai tray. I felt dizzy as I dared to look down. I could see the great hall of the temple at the bottom of the tower. The sideshow stalls looked like small toys. All I could see of the people walking below were their heads and feet.

"Ten or so sightseers with a most uncomfortable look on their faces were huddled together whispering anxiously and looking at Tokyo Bay in the direction of Shinagawa. There, alone and apart from them, stood my brother. He was looking intently through the binoculars at the temple grounds down below. Seen from behind, his

black velvet suit stood out all the more distinctly against the sea of clouds in the whitish, overcast sky. Moreover, at this height there was no danger of him being confused with the teeming masses down below. I knew it was my brother standing across the way. He looked so heavenly sublime—like the subject in a Western oil painting. I hesitated to say anything to him.

"But I was on a mission for my mother. I knew I couldn't wait any longer. I approached him from the rear.

"'What are you looking at?'

"He spun around in a state of shock. There was an embarrassed look on his face, but he said nothing.

"'Mother and Father are terribly worried about you. They don't understand where you disappear to every day. So this is it? And can you tell me why? Just tell me the reason. We've always been pals.'

"Fortunately, nobody was close by. I pressed my case.

"He was silent for the longest while. But, when I pressed him again and again, he finally gave in and told me the secret he had kept hidden for the past month.

"As for the source of the anguish in his heart—well, that too is another equally strange story.

"About a month before, while he was looking at the temple grounds with his binoculars from the top of the tower, he said he caught sight of a girl's face in the crowd below. She was unbelievably beautiful—a real 'out-of-this-world' beauty—and he felt strangely moved by the brief glimpse he had of her in the binoculars. As a general rule, he had been indifferent to the opposite sex, but this girl was the exception. So overcome was he at the sight of her that a great chill passed through him.

"He had caught only a single glimpse of her that day. In fact, he was so taken by surprise at the sight of her that he inadvertently pulled the glasses away from his face. But, when he went to take a second look—and he went nearly crazy trying to find her—the lenses never chanced on her face again. You see, objects are really far away even if binoculars make them look very close. Moreover, given the size of the crowd down below, there was little likelihood of his finding her again. Although you find something once, there's no guarantee it can be found a second time.

"He said he could not forget her. Being a terribly introverted type, he began to suffer from a case of old-fashioned love sickness. Modern people may laugh, but people back then were more sensitive and genteel. It was an era in which men frequently fell head over heels in love after only one look at a woman they'd seen on the street. It goes without saying that the business of finding the girl became his sole occupation. He stopped eating, and every day he dragged his weak and undernourished frame to the temple grounds, climbed the stairs of the twelve-story tower, and spent his time peering through the binoculars in the vain hope of seeing the girl again. Love is a strange and wondrous thing, isn't it?

"No sooner did he tell me his story than he began looking feverishly through the binoculars. I found myself in complete sympathy with him. Although he had less than even one chance in a thousand, and his efforts were a waste of time, I did not have the heart to tell him to give up. I was moved to tears by his sad state of affairs. And then.

"Aahh, even to this day I can't forget how seductively beautiful the spectacle was! If I close my eyes, it comes back to me, even though it happened thirty-five years ago. The image is so vivid. It's like a dream, and all of the colors rush into my head.

"As I said before, all I could see was the sky as I stood behind him. His thin, suited frame set against the hazy layers of clouds seemed to rise to the fore like a figure in a painting, and as masses of clouds swept over the tower, his body seemed to float in space. Suddenly, as if fireworks had been set off, innumerable spheres of red, blue, and purple rose into the white sky. They were soft and round, like bubbles, each competing to fly higher into the air. Words don't do it justice, but it really was like a painting—if not some kind of omen or foreshadowing. In any event, I was filled

with a strange and indescribable sense of wonder. I quickly looked down to see what had happened. I discovered a vendor had carelessly allowed his rubber balloons to escape into the air all at once. Back then, rubber balloons were relatively rare. It seemed odd to see so many of them all at once even though I now understood the reason why.

"My brother became very agitated. It was most peculiar, and I don't think it was on account of the balloons. His pale face flushed bright red, and his breathing grew more rapid. He stepped toward me and grabbed my hand.

"'Come on, let's go! We'll be too late if we don't hurry!'

"I asked him the reason why as he pulled me pell-mell down the stairs of the tower. He said he had found the girl. She was sitting in a room—the sort of large room where one received or entertained guests—and there were new tatami mats on the floor. She was right where he expected her to be.

"The place was a large house to the rear of the temple. A large pine tree marked the spot. When we arrived, the tree was there all right, but no building was in sight. It was as if a mischievous fox spirit had been at work, and it had bewitched us into coming. I felt sure my brother had let himself be deluded by his hopes. Still, he seemed so pitiful, looking wilted and full of despair, that we went around and made inquiries at the neighboring teahouses in order to make him feel better. The girl was nowhere to be found.

"We became separated while we were searching the area. After making the rounds of all the teahouses, I went back to the pine tree where I had seen different vending stalls. Among them was one that offered a stereoscopic picture show, and the proprietor was cracking a whip in the air to drum up business. Who did I see crouched over the viewing glasses used to peep into the stall but my brother?!? He was totally absorbed in watching the scenes of the story as they appeared one after the other in front of the stereoscopic lenses. When I tapped him on the shoulder and asked what he was doing, he whirled around with a look of total surprise written across his face. I'll never forget how shocked he looked. How shall I put it? It was as though he were lost in a dream. The muscles in his face had gone slack, and his eyes were set on a faraway place. Even his voice sounded strangely vacuous.

"'She's in there,' he said, pointing to the inside of the peep show mechanism.

"I immediately paid the fee and looked through the viewing glasses. Inside were a series of panels that illustrated the story of the infamous O-shichi. She was the greengrocer's daughter who, smitten with a handsome young man, lit her parents' house on fire so that the family had to evacuate to nearby Kisshōji temple, where the acolyte named Kichisa resided. I came in on the episode in which O-shichi was now ensconced at the temple. The panel appeared, and it depicted her leaning coquettishly toward Kichisa in the temple lecture hall. I shall never forget it. At precisely that moment, the proprietor and his wife raised their husky voices in unison, and cracking the whip in time to the narration, they sang the line in the story that goes 'now knee to knee, she spoke to him with her eyes.' It seems this peculiar line of narrative had special appeal for my brother. He appeared to repeat it over and over to himself in his head.

"The figures mounted on the panel were done in brocade relief, and they were surely the work of a master. The vitality evident in O-shichi's face was amazing. I too thought she was alive. For the first time I completely understood why my brother had been so taken with the girl. It made perfect sense.

"With a far-off look in his eyes, he said, 'I can't give her up even though I know she's the work of an artist and made only of brocade. It's sad, but I can't let her go. Even if it's only once, I want to step into the picture and talk to her like her companion Kichisa.' He stood rooted to the spot and made no attempt to move. Come to think of it, the top of the picture show stall was open to the sky to allow light to flow inside and illuminate the panels. My brother must have been looking down from the top of the tower at just the right angle when he saw the picture of the girl that was inside the peep show mechanism.

"The sun was going down, and fewer people were about. Two or three children in pageboy haircuts were loitering about the stall as if they had a lingering desire to take a peek inside. Around noon the sky had turned gray and overcast. By now low clouds hung over the horizon. It looked as though it might rain at any minute. It was the sort of unpleasant weather that makes one feel pinned down by the weight of the sky— yes, just the sort of weather calculated to drive one crazy. Deep inside my head, I heard a low, rumbling noise. It was like someone beating a big taiko drum very slowly. Meanwhile, my brother stood there simply gazing into the distance. He looked as though he could stay that way forever. We must have stood on the spot for over an hour.

"When the sun set and the gas lamps on the stage for the acrobats began to flicker bright and beautiful farther down the arcade, my brother suddenly seized me by the chest. The expression on his face was that of a man who has awakened from a deep sleep. He said something most peculiar.

"'I've figured it out! And it means I have a favor to ask. Take the binoculars, turn them around, and put the larger end of the lenses to your eyes. Now look at me.'

"I asked him why.

"'Don't fuss about it. Just do it, all right?'

"The truth be told, I never cared much for lenses, glasses, and the like. Whether it's a pair of binoculars or a microscope—to bring distant objects right up to your face or to make tiny bugs look as big as beasts does not appeal to me. There's something spooky about the whole business. I hadn't looked through my brother's prized pair of binoculars very often, but on the rare occasion when I toyed with them, I always felt there was something weirdly magical about the way they worked. Here we were, standing in the middle of a deserted spot behind the temple, and my brother was asking me to reverse the binoculars and look at him!?! The whole thing struck me as slightly demented, if not as tempting fate. But he desperately wanted me to do it. I had no choice. I looked at him through the large end of the binoculars. Although he was no more than eight or nine feet away, he appeared about two feet tall. The smaller he became, the more distinctly his shape floated in the gloom. There was no way to include anything else in the frame of the lens but him. All I could see was my brother in his natty black suit in miniature form. He grew progressively smaller because he was backing away from me step by step. Finally, he was about the size of a cute-looking doll that was a foot tall. He seemed to float in space until—before I knew it—he had melted into the darkness and disappeared.

"I was so scared. (You think I'm too old to say such a thing, but at the time I felt my hair stand on end.) I jerked the binoculars away from my face, and running in the direction from which my brother had disappeared, I called after him. '*Nii-san.*' '*Nii-san.*' I could not find him no matter what. I looked high and low. He could not have gone far. There hadn't been enough time. Yet he was nowhere in sight.

"And that, my friend, is the story of how my brother disappeared from the face of the earth. Since that time I have grown more and more wary of touching these magical binoculars. I have no idea who the ship captain was who originally owned them, but there is something about them and the fact that they once belonged to a foreigner that gives me a special dislike for them. I don't know about other binoculars, but as for this pair—never, ever turn them around and look through the larger end. I firmly believe terrible misfortune will be the inevitable result. Now you'll understand why I was so brusque with you when you started to hold them the wrong way.

"But, getting back to my brother, I returned exhausted to the picture show stall after searching for him for quite a long time. That was when it dawned on me. He had put the magical powers of the binoculars to work on account of his passion for the girl in the panel. He had reduced

himself to her size and quietly slipped into the world of the raised brocade figures. At least that is my theory. I asked the proprietor, who had yet to close shop for the evening, to show me the scene of O-shichi and Kichisa in the lecture hall at Kisshōji temple. Exactly as I had predicted, my brother was in the panel, mounted on it in raised brocade. Using the light cast by a *kandelaar* hand lamp that I held over the panel, I could see he had taken the place of the handsome young acolyte Kichisa. My brother was smiling contentedly to himself as he held O-shichi in his arms.

"But I was not sad. In fact, I was so happy that I wept tears of joy for my brother, who had finally attained his heart's desire. I had the proprietor make me a hard and fast promise that he would never sell the panel to anyone but me—I would buy it regardless of the cost. (Strangely enough, he never noticed that my brother, dressed in a natty Western suit, had taken Kichisa's place.) I ran home as fast as I could, but when I explained what happened in detail to my mother, she scoffed at me. Both she and my father wondered if I had lost my mind. They would not believe me no matter how hard I pleaded with them. 'Now isn't he being funny?' they said, and then they laughed at me. 'Ha ha ha ha ha ha.'"

The man on the train began to laugh as if he had told a joke. Oddly enough, I found myself sympathizing with him. We both had a hearty laugh together.

"They had it in their heads that a human being could never be transformed into—of all things!—a piece of raised brocade. But doesn't the fact that my brother was not again seen on the face of the earth prove he had become part of the painting? They came to the grossly mistaken conclusion that he had run away from home even though it made no sense at all. In the end, I wheedled money out of my mother, and in spite of protests from the family, I obtained the painting and set out on a trip. I traveled to Hakone, and from there I went to Kamakura. You see—I wanted to give my brother a honeymoon. When I ride a train like I'm doing now, I can't help but think of those earlier days. I prop the picture in the window, just as I did this evening, to show my brother and his lover the scenery outside. I can imagine how happy he must feel. And what about her? How could she reject such a true expression of love? They blush in embarrassment like real newlyweds. They press closer and closer to each other and engage in endless pillow talk.

"Father closed his shop in Tokyo after my brother disappeared and retired to his hometown near Toyama, where I have lived all this while. It's been over thirty years since the day we were last at Asakusa Park, so I wanted to take this trip with my brother to show him how much Tokyo has changed.

"What's saddest of all, my friend, is that because the girl was the work of human hands, she will never grow old no matter how long she lives, but my brother is doomed to age like you and me, his transformation notwithstanding. It was too extreme a change, and only so many years are allotted to the human lifespan. See for yourself. My brother, who was once a pretty young lad of twenty-five, now has a shock of white hair on his head and a face covered in unsightly wrinkles. He must be bitterly unhappy. The girl beside him will always remain young and beautiful, where he continues to age so foully. It's frightening. The expression on his face is terribly sad. He has been looking unhappy for the past several years.

"I am overcome with pity whenever I think of him."

Already growing old himself, the old man on the train tearfully looked at the old man in the picture. But then, as if suddenly awakening from a reverie, he added—

"Ah, I see I've talked far too long. Yet you understand me, don't you? You won't be like other people and say I'm crazy. If I've convinced you, then it was worthwhile talking with you. By now my brother and the young girl are probably very tired. I dare say I've embarrassed them by making them sit in front of you while I told their story. Well, I shall let them take a rest."

With that, he quietly wrapped the frame in the large black cloth. Perhaps it was a figment of my imagination, but in that instant, it seemed as though the faces in the painting softened however slightly. The corners of the lips moved ever so subtly, and the two of them gave me a shy parting smile.

The old man sank into silence. I too fell silent. The train continued to chug toward Tokyo in the darkness.

After about ten minutes, the wheels began to turn more slowly, and two or three lanterns came into view outside as the train pulled into a small station in the middle of the mountains. Who knew where we were? There was only one station attendant, and he was standing on the platform by himself.

"Well, I will be spending the night here with a relative," the old man traveling with the brocade portrait announced.

He stood up abruptly with the picture under one arm and got off the train. As I looked out the window, I saw his tall, thin frame (was it not identical to that of the old man in the painting?) move toward the exit and hand his ticket to the station attendant at what passed for a wicket at the small station. With that, he disappeared, melting into the darkness.

Vladimir (Vladimirovich) Nabokov (1899–1977) was an iconic and influential Russian American novelist and critic who wrote in both Russian and English. The son of wealthy parents who tried to establish democracy in Russia, Nabokov began writing poetry at the age of thirteen, and after graduating from Cambridge in 1922, he returned to Russia—only to leave again when his politically prominent father was assassinated. His travels took him from Berlin to Paris to the United States, each time just a step ahead of the Nazis. His list of notable works includes the controversial *Lolita* (1955), *Invitation to a Beheading* (1938), *Despair* (1934), and *Pale Fire*. Nabokov also translated his Russian-era work into English once he was established in the United States. "A Visit to the Museum," both humorous and creepy, is an eerie tale about a Russian émigré.

A Visit to the Museum

Vladimir Nabokov

Translated by Dmitri Nabokov

SEVERAL YEARS AGO a friend of mine in Paris—a person with oddities, to put it mildly—learning that I was going to spend two or three days at Montisert, asked me to drop in at the local museum where there hung, he was told, a portrait of his grandfather by Leroy. Smiling and spreading out his hands, he related a rather vague story to which I confess I paid little attention, partly because I do not like other people's obtrusive affairs, but chiefly because I had always had doubts about my friend's capacity to remain this side of fantasy. It went more or less as follows: after the grandfather died in their St. Petersburg house back at the time of the Russo-Japanese War, the contents of his apartment in Paris were sold at auction. The portrait, after some obscure peregrinations, was acquired by the museum of

Leroy's native town. My friend wished to know if the portrait was really there; if there, if it could be ransomed; and if it could, for what price. When I asked why he did not get in touch with the museum, he replied that he had written several times, but had never received an answer.

I made an inward resolution not to carry out the request—I could always tell him I had fallen ill or changed my itinerary. The very notion of seeing sights, whether they be museums or ancient buildings, is loathsome to me; besides, the good freak's commission seemed absolute nonsense. It so happened, however, that, while wandering about Montisert's empty streets in search of a stationery store, and cursing the spire of a long-necked cathedral, always the same one, that kept popping up at the end of every street, I was caught in a violent downpour which immediately went about accelerating the fall of the maple leaves, for the fair weather of a southern October was holding on by a mere thread. I dashed for cover and found myself on the steps of the museum.

It was a building of modest proportions, constructed of many-colored stones, with columns, a gilt inscription over the frescoes of the pediment, and a lion-legged stone bench on either side of the bronze door. One of its leaves stood open, and the interior seemed dark against the shimmer of the shower. I stood for a while on the steps, but, despite the overhanging roof, they were gradually growing speckled. I saw that the rain had set in for good, and so, having nothing better to do, I decided to go inside. No sooner had I trod on the smooth, resonant flagstones of the vestibule than the clatter of a moved stool came from a distant corner, and the custodian—a banal pensioner with an empty sleeve—rose to meet me, laying aside his newspaper and peering at me over his spectacles. I paid my franc and, trying not to look at some statues at the entrance (which were as traditional and as insignificant as the first number in a circus program), I entered the main hall.

Everything was as it should be: gray tints, the sleep of substance, matter dematerialized. There was the usual case of old, worn coins resting in the inclined velvet of their compartments. There was, on top of the case, a pair of owls, Eagle Owl and Long-eared, with their French names reading "Grand Duke" and "Middle Duke" if translated. Venerable minerals lay in their open graves of dusty papier-mâché; a photograph of an astonished gentleman with a pointed beard dominated an assortment of strange black lumps of various sizes. They bore a great resemblance to frozen frass, and I paused involuntarily over them, for I was quite at a loss to guess their nature, composition, and function. The custodian had been following me with felted steps, always keeping a respectful distance; now, however, he came up, with one hand behind his back and the ghost of

the other in his pocket, and gulping, if one judged by his Adam's apple.

"What are they?" I asked.

"Science has not yet determined," he replied, undoubtedly having learned the phrase by rote. "They were found," he continued in the same phony tone, "in 1895, by Louis Pradier, Municipal Councillor and Knight of the Legion of Honor," and his trembling finger indicated the photograph.

"Well and good," I said, "but who decided, and why, that they merited a place in the museum?"

"And now I call your attention to this skull!" the old man cried energetically, obviously changing the subject.

"Still, I would be interested to know what they are made of," I interrupted.

"Science . . ." he began anew, but stopped short and looked crossly at his fingers, which were soiled with dust from the glass.

I proceeded to examine a Chinese vase, probably brought back by a naval officer; a group of porous fossils; a pale worm in clouded alcohol; a red-and-green map of Montisert in the seventeenth century; and a trio of rusted tools bound by a funereal ribbon—a spade, a mattock, and a pick. To dig in the past, I thought absentmindedly, but this time did not seek clarification from the custodian, who was following me noiselessly and meekly, weaving in and out among the display cases. Beyond the first hall there was another, apparently the last, and in its center a large sarcophagus stood like a dirty bathtub, while the walls were hung with paintings.

At once my eye was caught by the portrait of a man between two abominable landscapes (with cattle and "atmosphere"). I moved closer and, to my considerable amazement, found the very object whose existence had hitherto seemed to me but the figment of an unstable mind. The man, depicted in wretched oils, wore a frock coat, whiskers, and a large pince-nez on a cord; he bore a likeness to Offenbach, but, in spite of the work's vile conventionality, I had the feeling one could make out in his features the horizon of a resemblance, as it were, to my friend. In one corner, meticulously traced in carmine against a black background, was the signature *Leroy* in a hand as commonplace as the work itself.

I felt a vinegarish breath near my shoulder, and turned to meet the custodian's kindly gaze. "Tell me," I asked, "supposing someone wished to buy one of these paintings, whom should he see?"

"The treasures of the museum are the pride of the city," replied the old man, "and pride is not for sale."

Fearing his eloquence, I hastily concurred, but nevertheless asked for the name of the museum's director. He tried to distract me with the story of the sarcophagus, but I insisted. Finally he gave me the name of one M. Godard and explained where I could find him.

Frankly, I enjoyed the thought that the portrait existed. It is fun to be present at the coming true of a dream, even if it is not one's own. I decided to settle the matter without delay. When I get in the spirit, no one can hold me back. I left the museum with a brisk, resonant step, and found that the rain had stopped, blueness had spread across the sky, a woman in besplattered stockings was spinning along on a silver-shining bicycle, and only over the surrounding hills did clouds still hang. Once again the cathedral began playing hide-and-seek with me, but I outwitted it. Barely escaping the onrushing tires of a furious red bus packed with singing youths, I crossed the asphalt thoroughfare and a minute later was ringing at the garden gate of M. Godard. He turned out to be a thin, middle-aged gentleman in high collar and dickey, with a pearl in the knot of his tie, and a face very much resembling a Russian wolfhound; as if that were not enough, he was licking his chops in a most doglike manner, while sticking a stamp on an envelope, when I entered his small but lavishly furnished room with its malachite inkstand on the desk and a strangely familiar Chinese vase on the mantel. A pair of fencing foils hung crossed over the mirror, which reflected the narrow gray back of his head. Here

and there photographs of a warship pleasantly broke up the blue flora of the wallpaper.

"What can I do for you?" he asked, throwing the letter he had just sealed into the wastebasket. This act seemed unusual to me; however, I did not see fit to interfere. I explained in brief my reason for coming, even naming the substantial sum with which my friend was willing to part, though he had asked me not to mention it, but wait instead for the museum's terms.

"All this is delightful," said M. Godard. "The only thing is, you are mistaken—there is no such picture in our museum."

"What do you mean there is no such picture? I have just seen it! *Portrait of a Russian Nobleman* by Gustave Leroy."

"We do have one Leroy," said M. Godard when he had leafed through an oilcloth notebook and his black fingernail had stopped at the entry in question. "However, it is not a portrait but a rural landscape: *The Return of the Herd*."

I repeated that I had seen the picture with my own eyes five minutes before and that no power on earth could make me doubt its existence.

"Agreed," said M. Godard, "but I am not crazy either. I have been curator of our museum for almost twenty years now and know this catalogue as well as I know the Lord's Prayer. It says here *Return of the Herd* and that means the herd is returning, and, unless perhaps your friend's grandfather is depicted as a shepherd, I cannot conceive of his portrait's existence in our museum."

"He is wearing a frock coat," I cried. "I swear he is wearing a frock coat!"

"And how did you like our museum in general?" M. Godard asked suspiciously. "Did you appreciate the sarcophagus?"

"Listen," I said (and I think there was already a tremor in my voice), "do me a favor—let's go there this minute, and let's make an agreement that if the portrait is there, you will sell it."

"And if not?" inquired M. Godard.

"I shall pay you the sum anyway."

"All right," he said. "Here, take this red-and-blue pencil and using the red—the red, please—put it in writing for me."

In my excitement I carried out his demand. Upon glancing at my signature, he deplored the difficult pronunciation of Russian names. Then he appended his own signature and, quickly folding the sheet, thrust it into his waistcoat pocket.

"Let's go," he said, freeing a cuff.

On the way he stepped into a shop and bought a bag of sticky-looking caramels which he began offering me insistently; when I flatly refused, he tried to shake out a couple of them into my hand. I pulled my hand away. Several caramels fell on the sidewalk; he stopped to pick them up and then overtook me at a trot. When we drew near the museum we saw the red tourist bus (now empty) parked outside.

"Aha," said M. Godard, pleased. "I see we have many visitors today."

He doffed his hat and, holding it in front of him, walked decorously up the steps.

All was not well at the museum. From within issued rowdy cries, lewd laughter, and even what seemed like the sound of a scuffle. We entered the first hall; there the elderly custodian was restraining two sacrilegists who wore some kind of festive emblems in their lapels and were altogether very purple-faced and full of pep as they tried to extract the municipal councillor's merds from beneath the glass. The rest of the youths, members of some rural athletic organization, were making noisy fun, some of the worm in alcohol, others of the skull. One joker was in rapture over the pipes of the steam radiator, which he pretended was an exhibit; another was taking aim at an owl with his fist and forefinger. There were about thirty of them in all, and their motion and voices created a condition of crush and thick noise.

M. Godard clapped his hands and pointed at a sign reading "VISITORS TO THE MUSEUM MUST BE DECENTLY ATTIRED." Then he pushed his way, with me following, into the second hall. The whole company immediately swarmed after us. I steered Godard to the portrait; he froze before it, chest inflated, and then stepped back a bit, as if admiring it, and his feminine heel trod on somebody's foot.

"Splendid picture," he exclaimed with genuine sincerity. "Well, let's not be petty about this. You were right, and there must be an error in the catalogue."

As he spoke, his fingers, moving as it were on their own, tore up our agreement into little bits which fell like snowflakes into a massive spittoon.

"Who's the old ape?" asked an individual in a striped jersey, and, as my friend's grandfather was depicted holding a glowing cigar, another funster took out a cigarette and prepared to borrow a light from the portrait.

"All right, let us settle on the price," I said, "and, in any case, let's get out of here."

"Make way, please!" shouted M. Godard, pushing aside the curious.

There was an exit, which I had not noticed previously, at the end of the hall and we thrust our way through to it.

"I can make no decision," M. Godard was shouting above the din. "Decisiveness is a good thing only when supported by law. I must first discuss the matter with the mayor, who has just died and has not yet been elected. I doubt that you will be able to purchase the portrait but nonetheless I would like to show you still other treasures of ours."

We found ourselves in a hall of considerable dimensions. Brown books, with a half-baked look and coarse, foxed pages, lay open under glass on a long table. Along the walls stood dummy soldiers in jackboots with flared tops.

"Come, let's talk it over," I cried out in desperation, trying to direct M. Godard's evolutions to a plush-covered sofa in a corner. But in this I was prevented by the custodian. Flailing his one arm, he came running after us, pursued by a merry crowd of youths, one of whom had put on his head a copper helmet with a Rembrandtesque gleam.

"Take it off, take it off!" shouted M. Godard, and someone's shove made the helmet fly off the hooligan's head with a clatter.

"Let us move on," said M. Godard, tugging

at my sleeve, and we passed into the section of Ancient Sculpture.

I lost my way for a moment among some enormous marble legs, and twice ran around a giant knee before I again caught sight of M. Godard, who was looking for me behind the white ankle of a neighboring giantess. Here a person in a bowler, who must have clambered up her, suddenly fell from a great height to the stone floor. One of his companions began helping him up, but they were both drunk, and, dismissing them with a wave of the hand, M. Godard rushed on to the next room, radiant with Oriental fabrics; there hounds raced across azure carpets, and a bow and quiver lay on a tiger skin.

Strangely, though, the expanse and motley only gave me a feeling of oppressiveness and imprecision, and, perhaps because new visitors kept dashing by or perhaps because I was impatient to leave the unnecessarily spreading museum and amid calm and freedom conclude my business negotiations with M. Godard, I began to experience a vague sense of alarm. Meanwhile we had transported ourselves into yet another hall, which must have been really enormous, judging by the fact that it housed the entire skeleton of a whale, resembling a frigate's frame; beyond were visible still other halls, with the oblique sheen of large paintings, full of storm clouds, among which floated the delicate idols of religious art in blue and pink vestments; and all this resolved itself in an abrupt turbulence of misty draperies, and chandeliers came aglitter and fish with translucent frills meandered through illuminated aquariums. Racing up a staircase, we saw, from the gallery above, a crowd of gray-haired people with umbrellas examining a gigantic mock-up of the universe.

At last, in a somber but magnificent room dedicated to the history of steam machines, I managed to halt my carefree guide for an instant. "Enough!" I shouted. "I'm leaving. We'll talk tomorrow."

He had already vanished. I turned and saw, scarcely an inch from me, the lofty wheels of a sweaty locomotive. For a long time I tried to find the way back among models of railroad stations. How strangely glowed the violet signals in the gloom beyond the fan of wet tracks, and what spasms shook my poor heart! Suddenly everything changed again: in front of me stretched an infinitely long passage, containing numerous office cabinets and elusive, scurrying people. Taking a sharp turn, I found myself amid a thousand musical instruments; the walls, all mirror, reflected an enfilade of grand pianos, while in the center there was a pool with a bronze Orpheus atop a green rock. The aquatic theme did not end here as, racing back, I ended up in the Section of Fountains and Brooks, and it was difficult to walk along the winding, slimy edges of those waters.

Now and then, on one side or the other, stone stairs, with puddles on the steps, which gave me a strange sensation of fear, would descend into misty abysses, whence issued whistles, the rattle of dishes, the clatter of typewriters, the ring of hammers, and many other sounds, as if, down there, were exposition halls of some kind or other, already closing or not yet completed. Then I found myself in darkness and kept bumping into unknown furniture until I finally saw a red light and walked out onto a platform that clanged under me—and suddenly, beyond it, there was a bright parlor, tastefully furnished in Empire style, but not a living soul, not a living soul. . . . By now I was indescribably terrified, but every time I turned and tried to retrace my steps along the passages, I found myself in hitherto unseen places—a greenhouse with hydrangeas and broken windowpanes with the darkness of artificial night showing through beyond; or a deserted laboratory with dusty alembics on its tables. Finally I ran into a room of some sort with coatracks monstrously loaded down with black coats and astrakhan furs; from beyond a door came a burst of applause, but when I flung the door open, there was no theater, but only a soft opacity and splendidly counterfeited fog with the perfectly convincing blotches of indistinct streetlights. More than convincing! I advanced, and immediately a joyous and unmistakable sensation of reality at last replaced all the unreal trash amid which I had just been dashing to and fro. The stone beneath my feet was real sidewalk, powdered with wonderfully fragrant, newly fallen snow, in which the infrequent pedestrians had already left fresh black tracks. At first the quiet and the snowy coolness of the night, somehow strikingly familiar, gave me a pleasant feeling after my feverish wanderings. Trustfully, I started to conjecture just where I had come out, and why the snow, and what were those lights exaggeratedly but indistinctly beaming here and there in the brown darkness. I examined and, stooping, even touched a round spur stone on the curb, then glanced at the palm of my hand, full of wet granular cold, as if hoping to read an explanation there. I felt how lightly, how naively I was clothed, but the distinct realization that I had escaped from the museum's maze was still so strong that, for the first two or three minutes, I experienced neither surprise nor fear. Continuing my leisurely examination, I looked up at the house beside which I was standing and was immediately struck by the sight of iron steps and railings that descended into the snow on their way to the cellar. There was a twinge in my heart, and it was with a new, alarmed curiosity that I glanced at the pavement, at its white cover along which stretched black lines, at the brown sky across which there kept sweeping a mysterious light, and at the massive parapet some distance away. I sensed that there was a drop beyond it; something was creaking and gurgling down there. Further on, beyond the murky cavity, stretched a chain of fuzzy lights. Scuffling along the snow in my soaked shoes, I walked a few paces, all the time glancing at the dark house on my right; only in a single window did a lamp glow softly under its green-glass shade. Here, a locked wooden gate. . . . There, what must be the shutters of a sleeping shop. . . . And by the light of a streetlamp whose shape had long been shouting to me its impossible message, I made out the ending of a sign—" . . . INKA SAPOG" (". . . OE REPAIR")—but no, it was not the snow

that had obliterated the "hard sign" at the end. "No, no, in a minute I shall wake up," I said aloud, and, trembling, my heart pounding, I turned, walked on, stopped again. From somewhere came the receding sound of hooves, the snow sat like a skullcap on a slightly leaning spur stone and indistinctly showed white on the woodpile on the other side of the fence, and already I knew, irrevocably, where I was. Alas, it was not the Russia I remembered, but the factual Russia of today, forbidden to me, hopelessly slavish, and hopelessly my own native land. A semiphantom in a light foreign suit, I stood on the impassive snow of an October night, somewhere on the Moyka or the Fontanka Canal, or perhaps on the Obvodny, and I had to do something, go somewhere, run; desperately protect my fragile, illegal life. Oh, how many times in my sleep I had experienced a similar sensation! Now, though, it was reality. Everything was real—the air that seemed to mingle with scattered snowflakes, the still unfrozen canal, the floating fish house, and that peculiar squareness of the darkened and the yellow windows. A man in a fur cap, with a briefcase under his arm, came toward me out of the fog, gave me a startled glance, and turned to look again when he had passed me. I waited for him to disappear and then, with a tremendous haste, began pulling out everything I had in my pockets, ripping up papers, throwing them into the snow and stamping them down. There were some documents, a letter from my sister in Paris, five hundred francs, a handkerchief, cigarettes; however, in order to shed all the integument of exile, I would have to tear off and destroy my clothes, my linen, my shoes, everything, and remain ideally naked; and, even though I was already shivering from my anguish and from the cold, I did what I could.

But enough. I shall not recount how I was arrested, nor tell of my subsequent ordeals. Suffice it to say that it cost me incredible patience and effort to get back abroad, and that, ever since, I have forsworn carrying out commissions entrusted one by the insanity of others.

Karel Čapek (1890–1938) was a prolific Czech writer who donned many hats in his lifetime. His early short stories such as "The Luminous Depths" (1916) and "The Garden of Krakonoš" (1918) could be considered philosophical. In later works, Čapek presented a series of suspect utopias featuring scientific discoveries that ultimately lead to rebellion. One such work is a play titled *Rossum's Universal Robots* (1920), which introduced the public to the term "robot." Another famous work is the early science-fantasy novel *The War with the Newts*. He also wrote stories satirizing complacency, greed, and man's understanding of the self. "The Water Sprite's Tale" (1932) is one of many fairy tales that combine satire with the fantastic and is part of the collection *Nine Fairy Tales & One More Thrown in for Good Measure*, delightfully illustrated by his brother, Josef Čapek. The language and wordplay are phenomenal and reflective of the nimble, clever aspects of Čapek's fiction.

The Water Sprite's Tale

Karel Čapek

Translated by Dagmar Hermann

CHILDREN, IF YOU BELIEVE that there are no water sprites, you are wrong. Why, there are so many different sorts and kinds, you wouldn't believe your eyes! Just to give you an example, I need only mention the one who lived near my hometown, in the river Úpa, under the sluice. Then there was the one in Haviovice who used to dwell near the wooden bridge, and there was yet another who resided in the Radec brook. That one was a German sprite who spoke not a word of Czech. Once he came to my father's office to have his tooth pulled and, in return, gave my dad a basket full of silver and pink pikes neatly covered with a nettle to keep them fresh. He was a water sprite, no doubt, for when he got up from the chair, he left a puddle on the seat. There was

also the one next to my grandpa's mill, in Hronov, who kept sixteen horses under the sluice. That's why the engineers used to say that at that particular spot the river had sixteen horsepower. The sixteen white horses kept on pulling, the water mill went on spinning, and when one night our grandpa died, the water sprite quietly unharnessed the sixteen horses, and for three days the wheel stopped dead in its spokes. In large rivers there are water sprites who own even more horses, perhaps fifty, or maybe one hundred. On the other hand, there are also those poor ragamuffins who haven't even a wooden toy horse to play with.

Of course, a water sprite magnate in Prague, in the river Moldau, would be quite affluent, and a gentleman of fine standing. He might even own a motorboat and, in summer, he would vacation at the seashore. For in Prague, even an ordinary, second-rate water sprite has more money than there are shells in the sand, and he darts around in a flashy car spattering mud all around.

Then again, there are those petty little hucksters who barely have a puddle, no larger than the palm of your hand, and in it a frog, three mosquitoes, and two water bugs; or their business is located in such a miserable trickle that if a mouse ran across it, he wouldn't even dampen his tummy. Some can barely lure a passing paper boat, and, if they are lucky, they may catch a baby diaper that the stream snatched from a mother while she was washing it. How awful!

Now the Rožmberk water sprite, for instance, has perhaps twenty thousand carp, as well as some scrod, catfish, mackerel, and toothy pike. There is no justice in this world, that's for sure!

Water sprites are loners by nature, but once or twice a year, during high tide, they will all gather and hold what you would call a district meeting. The ones who hail from our area always meet in the deep waters along Hradec Králové meadows, for there the country is nice and flat, with beautiful pools, backwater reaches, and river beds cushioned with the finest grade of mud. As is the case with liniment, the mud must be yellow or slightly brownish, for if it is red, or gray, it will not be supple enough. What a lovely, dank place their conference ground is! There they sit and share the news: About the old water sprite George who was forced into moving from Hilldry because of some newly enforced regulation; about the price increase of pots and ribbon that was scandalous, to say the least! If a water sprite intends to make a catch, he now must spend thirty crowns on ribbons, another three on a small pot, and the pot turns out to be trash in the bargain. It would be better to quit the whole blasted business and take up a different trade altogether. They also talk about Faltys the redhead, from Jaroměř, who went into business selling mineral waters; and about the lame Slepánek who has become a plumber and makes water pipes; and about the others who made ends meet in different trades. Obviously, a water sprite can only take up a trade that relates to water: you understand that, of course, children, don't you? So, for instance, he can perfect any of the water crafts, become a waterman, and end up working on a ferry in, say, Waterloo. He can also grow watercress, water lilies, or watermelons. He may become a painter of watercolors. On the other hand, he can become a professional water polo player, too. He need not be well known, nor well-to-do, to pretend that he is well bred, but then again, he might be as well. At any rate, some water must be in it!

So you see, there are plenty of trades left open for water sprites. That's also why their numbers are dwindling. The roll call at every annual meeting is accompanied by sad comments, like "Again, we have lost five of us. If the trend continues, friends, our trade will slowly die out."

"Times are changing," said the old Kreuzmann, the Trutnov water sprite. "Today is different from yesterday. Goodness, it must be thousands and thousands of years now since the whole of Bohemia was under water, and man, water man, to be exact, for people weren't around as yet. That's right, those were different times . . . darn it, where was I?"

"In Bohemia, under water," cued Greeney, the water sprite from Skalice.

"That's it," said Kreuzmann, and continued. "The whole of Bohemia was under the water, and Žaltman too, of course, and so was Red Mountain, and Crow Mountain, and all the other mountains, and any of you fellas could have crossed the country under water, I'd say from as far as Brno, to Prague, directly. Even Snow Mountain was hidden a fathom deep. Those were the days, my friends . . ."

"They were," recalled Kulda, the water sprite from Ratiboř. "And we weren't such loners and recluses then. We had underwater cities built of water bricks, furniture made of hard water, and featherbeds made of soft rainwater. We used hot water for heating our homes. And there was no bottom to the water, nor embankment, nor even surface. Only water and us."

"That's right," agreed Fox from Froggy Bottom marsh, nicknamed the Croaker. "And what gorgeous water that was! One could slice it like butter, roll it into balls, spin it into yarn, and twist it into ropes. Back then, water was like steel, like flax, like glass, like down. It was thick as cream, solid as oak, and warm as a fur coat. Everything was made of water. Goodness! Where can you find water like that today? Not even in America!" Croaker spat, then spat again, till he made quite a deep pool.

"It used to be . . ." Kreuzmann mused. "Water was absolutely beautiful, but it also was, how shall I put it? It was mute."

"How is that?" asked Greeney, who wasn't as old as the rest of them.

"What do you mean, how's that? It was silent," said Fox the Croaker.

"It had no voice. It couldn't talk yet. It was as quiet and mute as it turns now when it freezes. Quiet as midnight after the snow has fallen and not a thing stirs. When it's so still, so silently still you nearly quiver, your head popping out of the water, listening. When the endless silence wrings your heart—that's how quiet it was when water was mute."

"Then how come it isn't mute anymore?" asked Greeney, who was only seven thousand years old.

"Let me tell you," said Fox. "My great-grandfather said it happened some million years ago. There once lived a water sprite—what was his name, what was it? Reeds, no, it wasn't Reeds. Minařík, no, wrong again. Hampl, no, not Hampl. Pavlásek, no, it wasn't Pavlásek. Fiddlesticks! What was his name again?"

"Arion," said Kreuzmann.

"That's it, Arion," agreed Fox. "Arion was his name. I had it on the tip of my tongue. Now this Arion had a unique gift, a God-given talent of sorts. He spoke and sang so beautifully that he made your heart throb and cry with joy. What a musician he was!"

"Poet," corrected Kulda.

"Musician or poet, never mind," Fox replied. "He knew how to perform, let me tell you that.

Great-grandpa said that this Arion needed only to hum the first measures of a tune, and everybody around him began to sob. He harbored a great grief in his heart, Arion. No one knows how great. Nobody knows what ill had befallen him, but his heart must have been broken to make him sing so beautifully and with such anguish. As he sang and wailed in the deep waters, every trickle quivered like a trembling tear, and as his song sailed through the water, every droplet caught a bit of its tune. That's why water isn't mute anymore. That's why it jingles and tingles, rustles and murmurs, trickles and bubbles, splashes, hums, drones, groans and wails, roars and booms, sighs, moans, laughs, plays as if on a silver harp, warbles like a nightingale, rumbles like an organ, blasts like a French horn, and speaks like a man in joy or in sorrow. Since that time, water has spoken all the many languages in the world and can say things so strange and wonderful that no one, man, least of all, understands them. Yet, before Arion taught the water to sing, it was mute as the sky."

"It wasn't Arion, though, who set the sky into the water," said the old Kreuzmann. "That happened later, during my father's time, Lord preserve his memory forever. Croakoax did it, out of love."

"How did that happen?" asked Greeney.

"I'll tell you how. Listen. Croakoax fell in love. He saw Princess Croakanne, and his heart was aflame. Croakanne was beautiful indeed. She had a yellow tummy, tiny frog's legs, a frog's mouth stretching from ear to ear, and she was all wet and cold. A beauty. There are none left like her."

"And what happened then?" inquired Greeney, eagerly.

"What do you think happened? Croakanne was beautiful and she was proud. She just puffed up, and said, 'Croak.' Croakoax went mad with desire. 'If you marry me,' he told her, 'I'll give you anything you wish for.' 'Then bring me the blue of the sky,' she said."

"What did he do then?" Greeney queried.

"What could he have done? He remained under the water and moaned, 'Croak, croaaaak.' He wanted to take his own life. To that end, he jumped from the water into the air, trying to drown in it. No one before him had jumped into the air. Croakoax was the first."

"And what did he do in the air?"

"Nothing. He looked up, and lo, blue sky was above. He looked down, and behold, blue sky was below, as well. Croakoax marveled. That happened at a time when no one knew that water reflected the sky. When Croakoax saw the blue sky in the water, bewildered, he uttered, 'Croak,' and fell into the water again. Then he took Croakanne on his back, and jumped with her into the air. Seeing the blue sky reflected in the water, Croakanne filled with joy and exclaimed, 'Croak, croak,' for Croakoax had brought her the blue from the sky."

"What happened then?"

"Nothing. They lived happily ever after and had oodles of tadpoles. Ever since, water sprites crawl out of the water to remind themselves that the sky is in their home. When one leaves home, whoever he may be, and looks back, just as Croakoax did when he looked into the water, he will understand that his home is there, where the real sky extends. The real, blue, beautiful sky."

"Who said so?"

"Croakoax did."

"Long live Croakoax!"

"Long live Croakanne!"

Just then, a man came walking by and thought to himself: "Boy, how the frogs are croaking today!" He grabbed a pebble and threw it into the marsh. The water sprites jumped in. They wouldn't have another meeting before the year was over. The water splattered high and splashed, then all was quiet.

Lao She is the pseudonym of the Chinese author Shu Sheyu (1899–1966). But even the name Shu Sheyu is not the name he was born with; that would be Shu Qingchun. She was an elementary school principal and after reading Dickens' novels, he was inspired to pen his own. She's first novel was *Philosophy of Lao Zhang* (1926), serialized in a literary magazine. Many of his novels, often banned in China, documented how diligence and fortitude could change one's circumstances in a cruel world. One such novel, *Rickshaw* (1936), was illegally bowdlerized in the translation *Rickshaw Boy* (1945), which became more popular in the United States than the original version. She was badly beaten as a dissident during the Cultural Revolution and committed suicide in 1966. Written in reaction to the Japanese invasion of Manchuria, the novel *Cat Country* (1932), an example of science fantasy, has been translated into numerous languages and is said to be one of the earliest examples of Chinese speculative fiction. "The Capital of Cat Country" is a short excerpt from She's popular work.

The Capital of Cat Country

Lao She

Translated by William A. Lyell

AS SOON AS I SET EYES on Cat City, for some reason or other, a sentence took form in my mind: this civilization will soon perish! It certainly wasn't because I knew all there was to know about the civilization of Cat Country that I thought this—the experience I had in the reverie forest had only been enough to stimulate my curiosity and make me want to understand everything. Nor was it because I viewed the civilization of Cat Country as a mere tragic interlude prepared for my entertainment and diversion. It was rather that I had hoped to utilize my sojourn in Cat Country to fully comprehend the inner workings of at least this one civilization and thus

enrich my experience of life. I knew that it was possible that a whole civilization or even a whole race might perish, for the history of mankind on my own planet, Earth, was not entirely wreathed in roses. And since perusing the history of mankind had been at times enough to make me shed tears, imagine my feelings at the prospect of seeing a civilization breathe its last before my very eyes!

The life of a man, like a candle, seems to glow again with its former brilliance just before going out; similarly, an entire civilization on the point of extinction is not without a final, ephemeral splendor. And yet there is a difference: a civiliza-

715

tion on the edge of oblivion is not so conscious of its own imminent demise as is a lone man. It is almost as though the creative process itself had marked the civilization for extinction so that the good—and there are always a few good people left, even in a country that's about to expire—suffer the same fate as the evil. And perhaps in such a civilization, the few good people left will begin to experience a certain shortness of breath, will begin to draw up their wills, and will even moan over the impending fate of their civilization. But their sad cries, matched against the funeral dirge of their own death-bound culture, will be but as the chirps of lingering cicadas against a cruel autumn wind.

And while Cat City was full of life, behind this lively façade one was conscious of a skeletal hand, a hand that seemed ever ready to tear the skin and flesh away from the Cat People to leave nothing but a wasteland of bleached bones. And yet, despite all of this, Cat City was one of the liveliest places I have ever seen.

The arrangement of the city itself was the simplest that I'd yet encountered. There was nothing you could really call a street, for other than an apparently endless line of dwellings, there was just a kind of highway or, perhaps one ought to say, empty-square. If one kept in mind what the layout of a Cat Country army camp was like, one could well imagine the layout of the city: an immense open square with a row of houses down the middle, totally devoid of color and utterly drowned in Cat People. This was what they called "Cat City." There were crowds of people, but one couldn't tell exactly what they were doing. No one walked in a straight line, and everyone got in each other's way. Fortunately the streets were wide, and when it was no longer possible to go forward, people could switch to walking sideways as they crowded past one another.

It was as though the single row of houses formed a breakwater against which a tide of people pounded. I still don't know whether they had house numbers or not. But if we assume they did—then a man who wanted to go from number five to number ten would have to zig-zag his

way for at least three miles. Once outside his own door, he'd be crowded into a sideways progress and simply float along on the tide until he arrived at his destination. If by chance the direction of the tide should change before he got there, he'd be crowded home again. However, if he hit things just right, he would probably make it to number ten. But, of course, one can't always be sure of hitting things just right, and occasionally he might be crowded back and forth so much that he would be taken even farther from his destination and might well fail to even make it home that day.

There was a reason that the city had just one row of buildings. I worked that reason out somewhat as follows. I assumed that in the beginning there must have been several rather narrow streets. Crowding about in the narrow lanes had doubtless resulted in wasting a good deal of time, and had probably cost a number of lives to boot. You see, in the eyes of the Cat People, yielding the right of way was considered to be most disgraceful, and keeping to one side of the street was seen as incompatible with their freedom-loving spirit. Thus, if they had built houses on both sides of the street, they would be forever bottled up between them, and it is likely that the bottleneck wouldn't break up before one row of the houses had collapsed under the pressure of the crowd. And thus it was, I concluded, that they had built their houses in one long line, making the streets on either side infinitely wide. While they hadn't completely solved the problem of crowding quite yet, at least no more lives were lost. To be sure, crowding ten miles out and back in the course of a short trip took you out of your way a bit, but it didn't place you in any mortal danger. Therefore we can cite this new and less dangerous arrangement as another piece of testimony to the humane spirit of the Cat People.

Furthermore, crowding along in this manner wasn't all that unpleasant. Besides, when people crowded you off your feet and carried you along in the press, you were, in effect, getting free transportation. In all honesty, I must admit that this explanation is merely my own hypothesis and I dare not vouch for its correctness. To make a solid case for my theory, I'd have to go back and see whether or not I could, in fact, find traces of the old streets that I assume were there previously.

If it were simply a matter of crowding, it wouldn't have been all that unusual. But I discovered that the tide didn't merely roll to the left and right, but even had its risings and fallings! As I was watching the Cat City crowd, a pebble on the road caught someone's eye and an entire group of Cat People suddenly squatted down to examine it, thus occasioning an eddy on the surface of the tide. It was as though, come hell or high water, they just had to see that pebble. Soon they changed from a squatting position to a sitting one, and all around them more and more people began to squat; making the eddy grow larger and larger. Those in back, of course, could not see the stone, and, as they pushed forward, those who had been seated were crowded to their feet again. The more people crowded, the higher up those who'd been sitting in front were pushed, until they were finally on top of their neighbors' heads. Suddenly, everyone forgot the pebble, stood up, and threw their heads back to watch those who now rested on their neighbors' heads, thus filling the eddy up again.

As though decreed by fate, two old friends happened to meet at the edge of the eddy that had just filled in. They immediately sat down for a chat and those around them also sat down to listen in on the conversation. This, of course, occasioned another eddy. Then the bystanders who were listening in began chipping in with their opinions and before long, a brawl ensued, causing the eddy to expand suddenly. As the fighting continued, the eddy kept getting larger and larger until it reached the edge of another eddy that had formed when two old men decided to play a game of chess on the street. Now the two eddies became one, and as more and more people began to watch the chess game, the brawl died out. But before the bystanders had a chance to start chipping in, the chess-game-eddy was possessed of a fleeting stability.

This cat-tide was interesting enough itself, but the best was yet to come. A large crack suddenly appeared in the tide that reminded one of the parting of the Red Sea when the Israelites crossed it. Had it not been for a similar miracle, I can't possibly imagine how Scorpion's reverie leaf formation could have got through the tide intact, since its destination—Scorpion's home—was smack dab in the center of Cat City.

Backtracking a bit, let me explain how it was that this miracle came about. One would have expected that as Scorpion's formation neared the city, they would have devised some way of skirting the edges of that sea of cats while they jockeyed for a position from which they might work their way to his home. But no! With seven of them bearing Scorpion on their heads, they plunged headlong into the cat-surf! Then music was struck up. At first I thought it was a signal for the pedestrians to clear a right of way. But as soon as they heard the music, rather than shrinking back, the people all began crowding over in the direction of the reverie leaf formation until they were packed as tight as sardines in a can. I thought it would be a miracle if Scorpion's men ever made it through.

But Scorpion was much more capable than I had imagined. *Bump-ba clump-, dump-dump, bump-ba dump-clump-dump*—lively as a roll of drums in a Chinese military opera, the clubs of the soldiers came down on the heads of the Cat People and a crack began to appear in the cat-tide. Thus Scorpion made his own Red Sea miracle. Strange to say, the people's eagerness to see what was going on was not abated one whit by the clubs, although they did fall back to open up a path as they kept smiling at the formation. The clubs, however, didn't stop merely because of this friendly reception, but continued with a *bump-ba dump-dump-clump*. By dint of careful observation, I was able to make out a difference between the city cats and the country cats: the city cats had a bald spot where a part of the skull had been replaced by a steel plate at the center of the head, which also doubled as a drum—clear evidence they had long experience of having their heads drummed by soldiers while watching exciting public spectacles, for experience is never the product of a single, fortuitous occurrence.

Originally, I'd thought the soldiers were beating heads as they walked along merely to open up a path; but it turned out that this drum playing also served another purpose. You see, the victims of all this drum playing were not exactly angels themselves. None of those who were hindmost were willing to stay at the back, and would push, kick, crowd, and even bite in order to make their way in the world and become foremost. Those who were already foremost, on the other hand, kicked back with their heels, poked back with their elbows, and leaned back hard in order to keep the hindmost in their proper place. Now the soldiers didn't beat those who were in the front rows exclusively; they also reached out with their clubs and played a *bump-ba dump-dump-dump* on the cat-heads in back. Thus all the heads hurt and this made them forget somewhat the pain they were causing each other. And so the soldiers' drumming served to reduce the hostility the spectators felt—for each other. One may call this method "treating pain with pain."

I was completely wrapped up in watching them. To tell the truth, they exerted a compelling, though melancholy, attraction over me. It seemed that I just had to watch them. I was so taken up with observing them that I didn't pay attention to what the row of houses in the center of the square was like. I already knew that whatever they were like, they certainly couldn't be beautiful, for a foul stench continuously emanated from them. Now it may be possible for beauty to exist in the midst of filth, but I for one don't think so. I can't conceive, for instance, of a Taj Mahal resplendent beneath a coat of black mud and foul water. The people on the street didn't do much to improve things either. Whenever I approached them, they immediately cried out and shrank back as far as the throng would allow; but then they would quickly rush back toward me again, a clear indication that the fear and respect that city dwellers felt for foreigners was not quite as intense as that of the country folk. Having dissipated their fear and surprise by crying out, the city dwellers then felt brave enough to come up to me and give me the once-over. If I'd stood still on the road, I would certainly never have been able to move again, for they'd have surrounded me so closely that you wouldn't have been able to get a drop of water between us.

Ten thousand fingers kept pointing at me. The Cat People are very straightforward: if they see anything fresh and new, they simply point it right out with their fingers. Still unable to completely rid myself of the vanity of a human being from Earth, I was most uncomfortable. I longed to take wing and fly away to some quiet, peaceful spot where I might sit and rest for a while. My courage was gone and I simply didn't dare to raise my head. Although I am not a poet, I still possess a certain degree of the poet's sensitivity, and it seemed that these fingers and eyes were about to watch me away or, point me away like a melting piece of ice. They made me feel like a thing, with no personality left. But there are two sides to everything, and my not daring to raise my head also had its advantages. The road was uneven, covered with potholes and strewn with stinking lumps of mud. If I were to walk with my head up, I would make the lower half of my body as dirty as a pig. In spite of their very long history, it seemed that the Cat People had never once repaired their roads.

Fortunately, I finally arrived at Scorpion's house. It was only at this point that I had understood that the houses in Cat City were not much better than that little hole I'd lived in in the reverie forest.

Christine Quintasket (1884–1936), better known by her pen name Mourning Dove, was a Native American author. Quintasket often noted that she was constantly punished for not being able to speak English in school, but also was influenced by reading mass market romance novels of the time. Her novel *Cogewea, The Half Blood: A Depiction of the Great Montana Cattle Range* (1927) was the first novel published by a Native American woman. This novel about a woman of mixed race made Mourning Dove extremely popular and remains her most celebrated work. The tales reprinted here are from *Coyote Stories*, a collection written after Mourning Dove heard oral tales from reservation elders.

Coyote Stories

Mourning Dove

THE SPIRIT CHIEF NAMES THE ANIMAL PEOPLE

HAH-AH' EEL-ME'-WHEM, the great Spirit Chief, called the Animal People together. They came from all parts of the world. Then the Spirit Chief told them there was to be a change, that a new kind of people was coming to live on the earth.

"All of you *Chip-chap-tiqulk*—Animal People—must have names," the Spirit Chief said. "Some of you have names now, some of you haven't. But tomorrow all will have names that shall be kept by you and your descendants forever. In the morning, as the first light of day shows in the sky, come to my lodge and choose your names. The first to come may choose any name that he or she wants. The next person may take any other name. That is the way it will go until all the names are taken. And to each person I will give work to do."

That talk made the Animal People very ex-cited. Each wanted a proud name and the power to rule some tribe or some part of the world, and everyone determined to get up early and hurry to the Spirit Chief's lodge.

Sin-ka-lip'—Coyote—boasted that no one would be ahead of him. He walked among the people and told them that, that he would be the first. Coyote did not like his name; he wanted another. Nobody respected his name, Imitator, but it fitted him. He was called *Sin-ka-lip'* because he liked to imitate people. He thought that he could do anything that other persons did, and he pretended to know everything. He would ask a question, and when the answer was given he would say:

"I knew that before. I did not have to be told."

Such smart talk did not make friends for Coyote. Nor did he make friends by the foolish things he did and the rude tricks he played on people.

"I shall have my choice of the three biggest names," he boasted. "Those names are: *Kee-lau-*

naw, the Mountain Person—Grizzly Bear, who will rule the four-footed people; *Milka-noups*—Eagle, who will rule the birds, and *En-tee-tee-ueh*, the Good Swimmer—Salmon. Salmon will be the chief of all the fish that the New People use for food."

Coyote's twin brother, Fox, who at the next sun took the name *Why-ay'-looh*—Soft Fur, laughed. "Do not be so sure, *Sin-ka-lip'*," said Fox. "Maybe you will have to keep the name you have. People despise that name. No one wants it."

"I am tired of that name," Coyote said in an angry voice. "Let someone else carry it. Let some old person take it—someone who cannot win in war. I am going to be a great warrior. My smart brother, I will make you beg of me when I am called Grizzly Bear, Eagle, or Salmon."

"Your strong words mean nothing," scoffed Fox. "Better go to your *swool'-hu* (tepee) and get some sleep, or you will not wake up in time to choose any name."

Coyote stalked off to his tepee. He told himself that he would not sleep any that night; he would stay wide awake. He entered the lodge, and his three sons called as if with one voice:

"*Le-ee'-oo*!" ("Father!")

They were hungry, but Coyote had brought them nothing to eat. Their mother, who after the naming day was known as *Pul'-laqu-whu*—Mole, the Mound Digger—sat on her foot at one side of the doorway. Mole was a good woman, always loyal to her husband in spite of his mean ways, his mischief-making, and his foolishness. She never was jealous, never talked back, never replied to his words of abuse. She looked up and said:

"Have you no food for the children? They are starving. I can find no roots to dig."

"*Eh-ha*!" Coyote grunted. "I am no common person to be addressed in that manner. I am going to be a great chief tomorrow. Did you know that? I will have a new name. I will be Grizzly Bear. Then I can devour my enemies with ease. And I shall need you no longer. You are growing too old and homely to be the wife of a great warrior and chief."

Mole said nothing. She turned to her corner of the lodge and collected a few old bones, which she put into a *klek'-chin* (cooking-basket). With two sticks she lifted hot stones from the fire and dropped them into the basket. Soon the water boiled, and there was weak soup for the hungry children.

"Gather plenty of wood for the fire," Coyote ordered. "I am going to sit up all night."

Mole obeyed. Then she and the children went to bed.

Coyote sat watching the fire. Half of the night passed. He got sleepy. His eyes grew heavy. So he picked up two little sticks and braced his eyelids apart. "Now I can stay awake," he thought, but before long he was fast asleep, although his eyes were wide open.

The sun was high in the sky when Coyote awoke. But for Mole he would not have wakened then. Mole called him. She called him after she returned with her name from the Spirit Chief's lodge. Mole loved her husband. She did not want him to have a big name and be a powerful chief. For then, she feared, he would leave her. That was why she did not arouse him at day-break. Of this she said nothing.

Only half-awake and thinking it was early morning, Coyote jumped at the sound of Mole's voice and ran to the lodge of the Spirit Chief. None of the other *Chip-chap-tiqulk* were there. Coyote laughed. Blinking his sleepy eyes, he walked into the lodge. "I am going to be *Kee-lau-naw*," he announced in a strong voice. "That shall be my name."

"The name Grizzly Bear was taken at dawn," the Spirit Chief answered.

"Then I shall be *Milka-noups*," said Coyote, and his voice was not so loud.

"Eagle flew away at sunup," the other replied.

"Well, I shall be called *En-tee-tee-ueh*," Coyote said in a voice that was not loud at all.

"The name Salmon also has been taken," explained the Spirit Chief. "All the names except your own have been taken. No one wished to steal your name."

Poor Coyote's knees grew weak. He sank down beside the fire that blazed in the great tepee, and the heart of *Hah-ah' Eel-me'-whem* was touched.

"*Sin-ka-lip'*," said that Person, "you must keep your name. It is a good name for you. You slept long because I wanted you to be the last one here. I have important work for you, much for you to do before the New People come. You are to be chief of all the tribes.

"Many bad creatures inhabit the earth. They bother and kill people, and the tribes cannot increase as I wish. These *En-alt-na Skil-ten*—People-Devouring Monsters—cannot keep on like that. They must be stopped. It is for you to conquer them. For doing that, for all the good things you do, you will be honored and praised by the people that are here now and that come afterward. But, for the foolish and mean things you do, you will be laughed at and despised. That you cannot help. It is your way.

"To make your work easier, I give you *squas-tenk'*. It is your own special magic power. No one else ever shall have it. When you are in danger, whenever you need help, call to your power. It will do much for you, and with it you can change yourself into any form, into anything you wish.

"To your twin brother, *Why-ay'-looh*, and to others I have given *shoo'-mesh*. It is strong power. With that power Fox can restore your life should you be killed. Your bones may be scattered but, if there is one hair of your body left, Fox can make you live again. Others of the people can do the same with their *shoo'-mesh*. Now, go, *Sin-ka-lip'*! Do well the work laid for your trail!"

Well, Coyote was a chief after all, and he felt good again. After that day his eyes were different. They grew slant from being propped open that night while he sat by his fire. The New People, the Indians, got their slightly slant eyes from Coyote.

After Coyote had gone, the Spirit Chief thought it would be nice for the Animal People and the coming New People to have the benefit of the spiritual sweat-house. But all of the Animal People had names, and there was no one to take the name of Sweat-house—*Quil'-sten*, the Warmer. So the wife of the Spirit Chief took the name. She wanted the people to have the sweat-house, for she pitied them. She wanted them to have a place to go to purify themselves, a place where they could pray for strength and good luck and strong medicine-power, and where they could fight sickness and get relief from their troubles.

The ribs, the frame poles, of the sweat-house represent the wife of *Hah-ah' Eel-me'-whem*. As she is a spirit, she cannot be seen, but she always is near. Songs to her are sung by the present generation. She hears them. She hears what her people say, and in her heart there is love and pity.

COYOTE JUGGLES HIS EYES

As he was walking through the timber one morning, Coyote heard someone say: "I throw you up and you come down in!"

Coyote thought that was strange talk. It made him curious. He wanted to learn who was saying that, and why. He followed the sound of the voice, and he came upon little *Zst-skaka'-na*—Chickadee—who was throwing his eyes into the air and catching them in his eye-sockets. When he saw Coyote peering at him from behind a tree, Chickadee ran. He was afraid of Coyote.

"That is my way, not yours," Coyote yelled after him.

Now, it wasn't Coyote's way at all, but Coyote thought he could juggle his eyes just as easily as Chickadee juggled his, so he tried. He took out his eyes and tossed them up and repeated the words used by the little boy: "I throw you up and you come down in!" His eyes plopped back where they belonged. That was fun. He juggled the eyes again and again.

Two ravens happened to fly that way. They saw what Coyote was doing, and one of them said: "*Sin-ka-lip'* is mocking someone. Let us steal his eyes and take them to the Sun-dance. Perhaps then we can find out his medicine-power."

"Yes, we will do that," agreed the other raven. "We may learn something."

As Coyote tossed his eyes the next time, the ravens swooped, swift as arrows from a strong bow. One of them snatched one eye and the other raven caught the other eye.

"Quoh! Quoh! Quoh!" they laughed and flew away to the Sun-dance camp.

Oh, but Coyote was mad! He was crazy with rage. When he could hear the ravens laughing no longer, he started in the direction they had gone. He hoped somehow to catch them and get back his eyes. He bumped into trees and bushes, fell into holes and gullies, and banged against boulders. He soon was bruised all over, but he kept on going, stumbling along. He became thirsty, and he kept asking the trees and bushes what kind they were, so that he could learn when he was getting close to water. The trees and bushes answered politely, giving their names. After a while he found he was among the mountain bushes, and he knew he was near water. He came soon to a little stream and satisfied his thirst. Then he went on and presently he was in the pine timber. He heard someone laughing. It was *Kok'-qhi Ski'-kaka*—Bluebird. She was with her sister, *Kwas'-kay*—Bluejay.

"Look, sister," said Bluebird. "There is *Sin-ka-lip'* pretending to be blind. Isn't he funny?"

"Do not mind *Sin-ka-lip'*," advised Bluejay. "Do not pay any attention to him. He is full of mean tricks. He is bad."

Coyote purposely bumped into a tree and rolled over and over toward the voices. That made little Bluebird stop her laughing. She felt just a little bit afraid.

"Come, little girl," Coyote called. "Come and see the pretty star that I see!"

Bluebird naturally was very curious, and she wanted to see that pretty star, but she hung back, and her sister warned her again not to pay attention to Coyote. But Coyote used coaxing words; told her how bright the star looked.

"Where is the star?" asked Bluebird, hopping a few steps toward Coyote.

"I cannot show you while you are so far away," he replied. "See, where I am pointing my finger!"

Bluebird hopped close, and Coyote made one quick bound and caught her. He yanked out her eyes and threw them into the air, saying:

"I throw you up and you come down in!" and the eyes fell into his eye-sockets.

Coyote could see again, and his heart was glad. "When did you ever see a star in the sunlight?" he asked Bluebird, and then ran off through the timber.

Bluebird cried, and Bluejay scolded her for being so foolish as to trust Coyote. Bluejay took two of the berries she had just picked and put them into her sister's eye-sockets, and Bluebird could see as well as before. But, as the berries were small, her new eyes were small, too. That is why Bluebird has such berrylike eyes.

While his new eyes were better than none at all, Coyote was not satisfied. They were too little. They did not fit very well into his slant sockets. So he kept on hunting for the ravens and the Sun-dance camp. One day he came to a small tepee. He heard someone inside pounding rocks together. He went in and saw an old woman pounding meat and berries in a stone mortar. The old woman was *Su-see-wass*—Pheasant. Coyote asked her if she lived alone.

"No," she said, "I have two granddaughters. They are away at the Sun-dance. The people there are dancing with Coyote's eyes."

"Aren't you afraid to be here alone?" Coyote asked. "Isn't there anything that you fear?"

"I am afraid of nothing but the *stet'-chee-hunt* (stinging-bush)," she said.

Laughing to himself, Coyote went out to find a stinging-bush. In a swamp not far away he found several bushes of that kind. He broke off one of those nettle bushes and carried it back to the tepee. Seeing it, Pheasant cried:

"Do not touch me with the *stet'-chee-hunt*! Do not touch me! It will kill me!"

But Coyote had no mercy in his heart, no pity. He whipped poor Pheasant with the stinging-bush until she died. Then, with his flint knife, he skinned her, and dressed himself in her skin. He looked almost exactly like the old woman. He hid her body and began to pound meat in the stone mortar. He was doing that when the granddaughters came home. They were laughing. They told how they had danced over Coyote's eyes. They did not recognize Coyote in their grandmother's skin, but Coyote knew them. One was little Bluebird and the other was Bluejay. Coyote smiled. "Take me with you to the Sun-dance, granddaughters," he said in his best old-woman's voice.

The sisters looked at each other in surprise, and Bluejay answered: "Why, you did not want to go with us when the morning was young."

"Grandmother, how strange you talk!" said Bluebird.

"That is because I burned my mouth with hot soup," said Coyote.

"And, Grandmother, how odd your eyes look!" Bluejay exclaimed. "One eye is longer than the other!"

"My grandchild, I hurt that eye with my cane," explained Coyote.

The sisters did not find anything else wrong with their grandmother, and the next morning the three of them started for the Sun-dance camp. The sisters had to carry their supposed grandmother. They took turns. They had gone part way when Coyote made himself an awkward burden and almost caused Bluejay to fall. That made Bluejay angry, and she threw Coyote to

the ground. Bluebird then picked him up and carried him. As they reached the edge of the Sun-dance camp, Coyote again made himself an awkward burden, and Bluebird let him fall. Many of the people in the camp saw that happen. They thought the sister were cruel, and the women scolded Bluebird and Bluejay for treating such an old person so badly.

Some of the people came over and lifted Coyote on his feet and helped him into the Sun-dance lodge. There the people were dancing over Coyote's eyes, and the medicine-men were passing the eyes to one another and holding the eyes up high for everyone to see. After a little Coyote asked to hold the eyes, and they were handed to him.

He ran out of the lodge, threw his eyes into the air, and said: "I throw you up and you come down in!"

His eyes returned to their places, and Coyote ran to the top of a hill.

There he looked back and shouted: "Where are the maidens who had Coyote for a grandmother?"

Bluejay and Bluerbird were full of shame. They went home carrying Pheasant's skin, which Coyote had thrown aside. They searched and found their grandmother's body and put it back in the skin, and Pheasant's life was restored. She told them how Coyote had killed her with the stinging bush.

Zora Neale Hurston (1891–1960) was born in Notasulga, Alabama. Many hear her name and think of her novel, *Their Eyes Were Watching God* (1937), but she was also a sociologist and a folklorist. She even tried her hand as a playwright when she collaborated with Langston Hughes on a play that was never finished titled *The Mule-Bone: A Comedy of Negro Life in Three Acts.* Hurston spent most of her written words portraying the struggles of African Americans living in a racist society. At the time of her death, Zora Neale Hurston was not a public figure, but toward the later end of the twentieth century, her popularity soared, which caused many of her collections to be published posthumously. Uncle Monday is a shape-shifter and conjurer of central Florida, and as Hurston traveled collecting regional tales, she came upon his story.

Uncle Monday

Zora Neale Hurston

PEOPLE TALK A WHOLE LOT about Uncle Monday, but they take good pains not to let him hear none of it. Uncle Monday is an out-and-out conjure doctor. That in itself is enough to make the people handle him carefully, but there is something about him that goes past hoodoo. Nobody knows anything about him, and that's a serious matter in a village of less than three hundred souls, especially when a person has lived there for forty years and more.

Nobody knows where he came from nor who his folks might be. Nobody knows for certain just when he did come to town. He was just there one morning when the town awoke. Joe Lindsay was the first to see him. He had some turtle lines set down on Lake Belle. It is a hard lake to fish because it is entirely surrounded by a sooky marsh that is full of leeches and moccasins. There is plenty of deep water once you pole a boat out beyond the line of cypress pines, but there are so many alligators out there that most people don't think the trout are worth the risk. But Joe had baited some turtle lines and thrown them as far as he could without wading into the marsh. So next morning he went as early as he could see light to look after his lines. There was a turtle head on every line, and he pulled them up cursing the 'gators for robbing his hooks. He says he started on back home, but when he was a few yards from where his lines had been set something made him look back, and he nearly fell dead. For there was an old man walking out of the lake between two cypress knees. The water there was too deep for any wading, and besides, he says the man was not wading, he was walking vigorously as if he were on dry land.

Lindsay says he was too scared to stand there and let the man catch up with him, and he was too scared to move his feet; so he just stood there and saw the man cross the marshy strip and come down the path behind him. He says he felt the hair rise on his head as the man got closer to him, and somehow he thought about an alligator slipping up on him. But he says that alligators were in the front of his mind that morning because first, he had heard bull 'gators fighting and bellowing all night long down in this lake, and then his turtle lines had been robbed. Besides, everybody knows that the father of all 'gators lives in Belle Lake.

The old man was coming straight on, taking short quick steps as if his legs were not long enough for his body, and working his arms in unison. Lindsay says it was all he could do to stand his ground and not let the man see how scared he was, but he managed to stand still anyway. The man came up to him and passed him without looking at him seemingly. After he had passed, Lindsay noticed that his clothes were perfectly dry, so he decided that his own eyes had fooled him. The old man must have come up to the cypress knees in a boat and then crossed the marsh by stepping from root to root. But when he went to look, he found no convenient roots for anybody to step on. Moreover, there was no boat on the lake either.

The old man looked queer to everybody, but still no one would believe Lindsay's story. They said that he had seen no more than several others—that is, that the old man had been seen coming from the direction of the lake. That was the first that the village saw of him, way back in the late eighties, and so far, nobody knows any more about his past than that. And that worries the town.

Another thing that struck everybody unpleasantly was the fact that he never asked a name nor a direction. Just seemed to know who everybody was and called each and every one by their right name. Knew where everybody lived too. Didn't earn a living by any of the village methods. He didn't garden, hunt, fish, nor work for the white folks. Stayed so close in the little shack that he had built for himself that sometimes three weeks would pass before the town saw him from one appearance to another.

Joe Clarke was the one who found out his name was Monday. No other name. So the town soon was calling him Uncle Monday. Nobody can say exactly how it came to be known that he was a hoodoo man. But it turned out that that was what he was. People said he was a good one too. As much as they feared him he had plenty of trade. Didn't take him long to take all the important cases away from Ant Judy, who had had a monopoly for years.

He looked very old when he came to the town. Very old, but firm and strong. Never complained of illness.

But once Emma Lou Pittman went over to his shack early in the morning to see him on business and ran back with a fearsome tale. She said that she noticed a heavy trail up to his door an across the steps as if a heavy, bloody body had been dragged inside. The door was cracked a little and she could hear a great growling and snapping of mighty jaws. It wasn't exactly a growling either, it was more a subdued howl in a bass tone. She shoved the door a little and peeped inside to see if some varmint was in there attacking Uncle Monday. She figured he might have gone to sleep with the door ajar and a catamount, or a panther, or a bob-cat might have gotten in. He lived near enough to Blue Sink Lake for a 'gator to have come in the house but she didn't remember ever hearing of them tracking anything but dogs.

But no; no varmint was inside there. The noise she heard was being made by Uncle Monday. He was lying on a pallet of pine-straw in such agony that his eyes were glazed over. His right arm was horribly mangled. In fact, it was all but torn away from right below the elbow. The side of his face was terribly torn too. She called him but he didn't seem to hear her. So she hurried back for some men to come and do something for him. The men came as fast as their legs would bring them, but the house was locked from the outside and there was no answer to their knocking. Mrs. Pittman would have been made out an awful liar if it were not for the trail of blood. So they concluded that Uncle Monday had gotten hurt somehow and had dragged himself home; or had been dragged by a friend. But who could the friend have been?

Nobody saw Uncle Monday for a month after that. Every day or so, someone would drop by to see if hide or hair could be found of him. A full month passed before there was any news. The town had about decided that he had gone away as mysteriously as he had come.

But one evening around dusk-dark Sam Merchant and Jim Gooden were on their way home from a squirrel hunt around Lake Belle. They swore that, as they rounded the lake and approached the footpath that leads toward the village, they saw what they thought was the great 'gator that lives in the lake crawl out of the marsh. Merchant wanted to take a shot at him for his hide and teeth, but Gooden reminded him that they were loaded with bird shot, which would not even penetrate a 'gator's hide, let alone kill it. They say the thing they took for the 'gator then struggled awhile, pulling off something that looked like a long black glove. Then he scraped a hole in the soft ground with his paws and carefully buried the glove which had come from his right paw. Then without looking either right or left; he stood upright and walked on toward the village. Everybody saw Uncle Monday come thru the town, but still Merchant's tale was hard to swallow. But, by degrees, people came to believe that Uncle Monday could shed any injured member of his body and grow a new one in its place. At any rate, when he reappeared his right hand and arm bore no scars.

The village is even skeptical about his dying. Once Joe Clarke said to Uncle Monday, "I'god, Uncle Monday, aint you skeered to stay way off by yo'self, old as you is?"

Uncle Monday asked, "Why would I be skeered?"

"Well, you liable to take sick in de night sometime, and you'd be dead befo' anybody would know you was even sick."

Uncle Monday got up off the nail keg and said in a voice so low that only the men right close to him could hear what he said "I have been dead for many a year. I have come back from where you are going." Then he walked away with his quick short steps and his arms bent at the elbow keeping time with his feet

It is believed that he has the singing stone, which is the greatest charm, the most powerful "hand" in the world. It is a diamond and comes from the mouth of a serpent (which is thought of as something different from an ordinary snake) and is the diamond of diamonds. It not only lights your home without the help of any other light, but it also warns its owner of approach.

The serpents who produce these stones live in the deep waters of Lake Maitland. There is a small island in this lake and a rare plant grows there, which is the only food of this serpent. She only comes to nourish herself in the height of a violent thunderstorm, when she is fairly certain that no human will be present.

It is impossible to kill or capture her unless nine healthy people have gone before to prepare the way with THE OLD ONES, and then more will die in the attempt to conquer her. But it is not necessary to kill or take her to get the stone. She has two. One is embedded in her head, and the other she carries in her mouth. The first one cannot be had without killing the serpent, but the second one may be won from her by trickery.

Since she carries this stone in her mouth, she cannot eat until she has put it down. It is her pilot, that warns her of danger. So when she comes upon the island to feed, she always vomits the stone and covers it with earth before she goes to the other side of the island to dine.

To get this diamond, dress yourself all over in black velvet. Your assistant must be dressed in the same way. Have a velvet-covered bowl along. Be on the island before the storm reaches its height, but leave your helper in the boat and warn him to be ready to pick you up and flee at a moment's notice.

Climb a tall tree and wait for the coming of the snake. When she comes out of the water, she will look all about her on the ground to see if anyone is about. When she is satisfied that she is alone, she will vomit the stone, cover it with dirt, and proceed to her feeding ground. Then, as soon as you feel certain that she is busy eating, climb down the tree as swiftly as possible, cover the mound hiding the stone with the velvet-lined bowl, and flee for your life to the boat. The boatman must fly from the island with all possible speed. For as soon as you approach the stone it will ring like chiming bells and the serpent will hear it. Then she will run to defend it. She will return to the spot, but the velvet-lined bowl will make it invisible to her. In her wrath she will knock down grown trees and lash the island like a hurricane. Wait till a calm fair day to return for the stone. She never comes up from the bottom of the lake in fair weather. Furthermore, a serpent who has lost her mouth-stone cannot come to feed alone after that. She must bring her mate. The mouth-stone is their guardian and when they lose it they remain in constant danger unless accompanied by one who has the singing stone.

They say that Uncle Monday has a singing stone, and that is why he knows everything without, being told.

Whether he has the stone or not, nobody thinks of doubting his power as a hoodoo man. He is feared, but sought when life becomes too powerful for the powerless. Mary Ella Shaw backed out on Joe-Nathan Moss the day before the wedding was to have come off. Joe-Nathan had even furnished the house and bought rations. His people, her people, everybody tried to make her marry the boy. He loved her so, and besides he had put out so much of his little cash to fix for the marriage. But Mary Ella just wouldn't. She had seen Caddie Brewton, and she was one of the kind who couldn't keep her heart still after her eye had wandered.

So Joe-Nathan's mama went to see Uncle Monday. He said, "Since she is the kind of woman that lets her mind follow her eye, we'll have to let the snake-bite cure itself. You go on home. Never no man will keep her. She kin grab the world full of men, but she'll never keep one any longer than from one full moon to the other."

Fifteen years have passed. Mary Ella has been married four times. She was a very pretty girl, and men just kept coming, but not one man has ever stayed with her longer than the twenty-eight days. Besides her four husbands, no telling how many men she has shacked up with for a few weeks at a time. She has eight children by as many different men, but still no husband.

John Wesley Hogan was another driver of sharp bargains in love. By his own testimony and experience, all women from eight to eighty were his meat, but the woman who was sharp enough to make him marry her wasn't born and her mama was dead. They couldn't frame him and they couldn't scare him.

Mrs. Bradley came to him nevertheless about her Dinkie. She called him out from his workplace and said, "John Wesley, you know I'm a widder-woman and I aint got no husband to go to de front for me, so I reckon I got to do de talkin' for me and my chile. I come in de humblest way I know how to ast you to go 'head and marry my chile befo' her name is painted on de signposts of scorn."

If it had not made John Wesley so mad, it would have been funny to him. So he asked her scornfully, "'Oman, whut you take me for? You better git outa my face wid dat mess! How you reckon I know who Dinkie been foolin roun wid? Don't try to come dat mess over *me*. I been all over de North. I aint none of yo' fool. You must think I'm Big Boy. They kilt Big Boy shootin after Fat Sam so there aint no mo' fools in de world. Ha, ha! All de wimmen *I* done seen! I'll tell you like de monkey tole de elephant—don't bull me, big boy! If you want Dinkie to git married off so bad, go grab one of dese country clowns. I aint yo' man. Taint no use you goin runnin to de high-sheriff neither. I got witness to prove Dinkie knowed more'n I do."

Mrs. Bradley didn't bother with the sheriff. All he could do was to make John Wesley marry Dinkie; but by the time the interview was over that wasn't what the stricken mother wanted. So she waited till dark, and went on over to Uncle Monday.

Everybody says you don't have to explain things to Uncle Monday. Just go there, and you will find that he is ready for you when you arrive. So he set Mrs. Bradley down at a table, facing a huge mirror hung against the wall. She says he had a loaded pistol and a huge dirk lying on the table before her. She looked at both of the weapons, but she could not decide which one she wanted to use. Without a word, he handed her a gourd full of water and she took a swallow. As soon as the water passed over her tongue she seized the gun. He pointed toward the looking-glass. Slowly the form of John Wesley formed in the glass and finally stood as vivid as life before her. She took careful aim and fired. She was amazed that the mirror did not shatter. But there was a loud report, a cloud of bluish smoke and the figure vanished.

On the way home, Brazzle told her that John Wesley had dropped dead, and Mr. Watson had promised to drive over to Orlando in the morning to get a coffin for him.

ANT JUDY BICKERSTAFF

Uncle Monday wasn't the only hoodoo doctor around there. There was Ant Judy Bickerstaff. She was there before the coming of Uncle Monday. Of course it didn't take long for professional jealousy to arise. Uncle Monday didn't seem to mind Ant Judy, but she resented him, and she couldn't hide her feelings.

This was natural when you consider that before his coming she used to make all the "hands" around there, but he soon drew off the greater part of the trade.

Year after year this feeling kept up. Every now and then some little incident would accentuate the rivalry. Monday was sitting on top of the heap, but Judy was not without her triumphs.

Finally she began to say that she could reverse anything that he put down. She said she could not only reverse it, she could throw it back on *him*, let alone his client. Nobody talked to him about her boasts. People never talked to him except on business anyway. Perhaps Judy felt safe in her boasting for this reason.

Then one day she took it in her head to go fishing. Her children and grandchildren tried to discourage her. They argued with her about her great age and her stiff joints. But she had her grandson to fix her a trout pole and a bait pole and set out for Blue Sink, a lake said to be bottomless by the villagers. Furthermore, she didn't set out till near sundown. She didn't want any company. It was no use talking, she felt that she just must go fishing in Blue Sink.

She didn't come home when dark came and her family worried a little. But they reasoned she had probably stopped at one of her friends' houses to rest and gossip, so they didn't go to hunt her right away. But when the night wore on and she didn't return, the children were sent out to locate her.

She was not in the village; a party was organized to search Blue Sink for her. It was after nine o'clock at night when the party found her. She was in the lake. Lying in shallow water and keeping her old head above the water by supporting it on her elbow. Her son Ned said that he saw a huge alligator dive away as he shined the torch upon his mother's head.

They bore Ant Judy home and did everything they could for her. Her legs were limp and useless and she never spoke a word, not a coherent word for three days. It was more than a week before she could tell how she came to be in the lake.

She said that she hadn't really wanted to go fishing. The family and the village could witness that she never had fooled round the lakes. But that afternoon she *had* to go. She couldn't say why, but she knew she must go. She baited her hooks and stood waiting for a bite. She was afraid to sit down on the damp ground on account of her rheumatism. She got no bites. When she saw the sun setting she wanted to come home, but somehow she just couldn't leave the spot. She was afraid, terribly afraid down there on the lake; but she couldn't leave.

When the sun was finally gone and it got dark, she says she felt a threatening powerful evil all around her. She was fixed to the spot. A small but powerful whirlwind arose right under her feet. Something terrific struck her and she fell into the water. She tried to climb out, but found that she could not use her legs. She thought of 'gators and otters, and leeches and gar-fish, and began to scream, thinking maybe somebody would hear her and come to her aid.

Suddenly a bar of red light fell across the lake from one side to the other. It looked like a fiery sword. Then she saw Uncle Monday walking across the lake to her along this flaming path. On either side of the red road swam thousands of alligators, like an army behind its general.

The light itself was awful. It was red, but she never had seen any red like it before. It jumped and moved all the time, but always it pointed straight across the lake to where she lay helpless in the water. The lake is nearly a mile wide, but Ant Judy says Uncle Monday crossed it in less than a minute and stood over her. She closed her eyes from fright, but she saw him right on thru her lids.

After a brief second she screamed again. Then he growled and leaped at her. "Shut up!" he snarled. "Part your lips just one more time and it will be your last breath! Your bragging tongue has brought you here and you are going to stay here until you acknowledge my power. So you can throw back my work, eh? I put you in this lake; show your power and get out. You will not die, and you will not leave this spot until you give consent in your heart that I am your master. Help will come the minute you knuckle under."

She fought against him. She felt that once she was before her own altar she could show him something. He glowered down upon her for a spell and then turned and went back across the lake the way he had come. The light vanished behind his feet. Then a huge alligator slid up beside her where she lay trembling and all her strength went out of her. She lost all confidence in her powers. She began to feel if only she might either die or escape from the horror, she would never touch another charm again. If only she could escape the maw of the monster beside her! Any other death but that. She wished that Uncle Monday would come back so that she might plead with him for deliverance. She opened her mouth to call, but found that speech had left her. But she saw a light approaching by land. It was the rescue party.

Ant Judy never did regain the full use of her legs, but she got to the place where she could hobble about the house and yard. After relating her adventure on Lake Blue Sink she never called the name of Uncle Monday again.

The rest of the village, always careful in that respect, grew almost as careful as she. But sometimes when they would hear the great bull 'gator, that everybody knows lives in Lake Belle, bellowing on cloudy nights, some will point the thumb in the general direction of Uncle Monday's house and whisper, "The Old Boy is visiting the home folks tonight."

María Teresa León (1903–1988) was a Spanish writer and activist who was determined to break down barriers her entire life. She was a feminist and often contributed articles to magazines that dealt with culture and women's rights. She used the pen name Isabel Inghirami for these articles. Isabel Inghirami was the name of a wayward widow in the book *Maybe Yes, Maybe No* (1910) by the Italian author Gabriele d'Annunzio. It is quite possible that León felt a bond with the character, as she chose to live her life in a way that opposed the norm. In 1933, León started the literary journal *Octubre* with her second husband, Rafael Alberti, a poet. The couple was exiled to Paris in 1940, and the project abandoned, but León never ceased writing, hoping that soon her work would receive recognition. The story "Rose-Cold, Moon Skater" first appeared in a collection of the same name.

Rose-Cold, Moon Skater

María Teresa León

Translated by Marian and James Womack

The fir trees skate on the ice.
R. A.

KNOCK, KNOCK.

"Who's that, bothering me so early?"

"Moo! It's me."

And in through the window came the cow that the stars use as their messenger: a bluish cow, with two red patches and little golden horns. A cow who knows every balcony in the city and how to get in through all of them.

"Rose-Cold, let's go. It's time. There's snow on the Moon. They're saving a crater and some lemon sorbet for you."

"Hurry up, quickly! Let's go to the Moon, you blunt-headed cow!"

They went up to the clouds on the white

smoke from a chimney-pot. And from there, they climbed through a window onto the Moon.

The window of the Moon's house was covered in frost. It was a little pine cabin, where you couldn't fit anything more than just your face. The wolves took it down to the earth one day to frighten little children, but no one was frightened. It was just the scarecrows that noticed. Ever since then, there have been straw men wearing hats in the gardens, set up to make the moon laugh, and the birds, and the children.

Rose-Cold, first-class skater, winner of titles at every possible distance, who had invented the sport of filling corridors with snow confetti in order to be able to use her skis and skates before winter had come, and who was bored of looking at spiders, greeted the Moon. And the Moon said:

"Rose-Cold, I've organized a little competition for you. The Four Seasons Cup. All the signs of the Zodiac are invited, as well as the Great Bear. We might even get some shooting stars coming through. Look at how much snow there is on the railings. I've asked the North and the South Pole to fill my house with snow. The comets, with their broom-tails, will move it all around and cover everything. All the volcanoes are already covered, and the Dream Peak, and the petrified circuses. The competitors will be: Smoke from Trains and Smoke from Factories; Steam from Horses and Oxen; Human Sighs; Dogs Barking, and Glances at Balloons on Quiet Evenings. Would you like to meet them?"

Rose-Cold started to quake. They were much faster than her, these competitors were.

Smoke from Trains came.

"Hello, Rose-Cold. Do you remember me?"

"I think so, Mr. Smoke. I see you every evening between the thistles and the telegraph poles. Sometimes you reach the thyme bushes, and go head to head with the cows."

"I'll be faster than you, Rose-Cold."

Steam from Horses and Oxen came along.

"How did you get up to the Moon?" Rose-Cold asked.

"We came here on a simoom, I think, or else on the topmost seat of a Ferris wheel, alongside a woman who was always asking what time it was. I don't remember too well."

"And what is that, always stretching, stretching and turning red?"

"We are Human Sighs. Be nice to us."

"You look ridiculous, so skinny and disproportionate."

Now Smoke from Factories came in, wearing a red scarf, and knocking everything down that was in his path, pushing the stars that watched him out of place.

"You weren't waiting for me; you wanted to start without me. I think that's not on. Is this why I give you my chimneys, why I let your rays rest a little? No, no, and again no. I can't allow this to happen. That's it, no more beautiful smoke twisting in the skies."

"No one forgot about you. They were just introducing themselves," Rose-Cold said.

"Oh, is that you, moon-skater? Prepare to have your socks knocked off."

And the Smoke tried a little training walk.

"Are you happy that so many of your friends come to me to die?" the Moon asked.

"To die?"

"Of course, they die here; they've just used up all their strength back on Earth. The water that sleeps in the rocks evaporates when the moon is on the wane, and I gather it all; and the water in still ponds, with all its choruses of frogs; and all the bonfires on St. John's Eve; and all the smoke from the houses by the shore, lit up at night, calling their sailors home. Everything comes to the Moon, and everything falls silent here, falls silent for ever."

"So?"

"Come on, Rose-Cold. The Great Bear is shivering impatiently, and out there in the stands the Three Marias are chatting to Sirius and Altair. Aldebaran has said he'll be along a little later, when he can convince Boötes of something or other, and the Milky Way is asking for a discount to get in with all her children."

Rose-Cold wanted to leave. The stars made the snow shine. The pine trees slid around, looking for a good vantage point.

Rose-Cold called to the cow.

"Come on, dear little cow, you know I can't skate; I've just put my foot in an ice-hole and I've twisted my ankle."

Everyone was very shocked at this. They sent the seals flopping across the ice: they are much more stable because they move more slowly.

"Send for the doctors!"

The walruses came, with their white spectacles, in a sledge with a green flag.

"Ow, ow!"

They looked at her foot. They looked at it all over. The Moon, very sad, called for the reindeer:

"Send for the reindeer!"

The reindeer came, wearing surgeons' aprons and with rubber gloves on their hooves.

They spoke to one another in Latin.

"What is it?"

"Nothing. No, Miss Moon; I mean there's nothing wrong with her."

"Ow, ow! I got a snowflake in my eye!" shouted Rose-Cold.

"Send for the Aurora Borealis!"

The Aurora Borealis had a remedy made from distilled water that he poured down an albatross's beak.

"It's nothing." He stroked her hair. "It's nothing. You'll be able to run the Four Seasons Cup before you know it."

"Come here, my little cow, you who love children so much. Call for the Wild Mistral Wind; I want to give him an errand."

"The stars are getting impatient and are calling for whisky to warm themselves up."

"Oh, let them drink whatever they want! Little cow, call for the Wild Mistral Wind."

The Moon was furious, and argued with Smoke from Factories, which turned red with anger. The Mistral came.

"Oh, Wild Mistral Wind, call the pine trees over with your soft hands; wake them up; tell them that Rose-Cold will die on the Moon if they don't help her."

The doctors gathered together again.

"Nothing, Miss Moon. There's nothing wrong with her."

The stars were spinning round now, just to have something to do. Their orbiting made them dizzy, and they got cross.

The pine trees started to climb up from the earth. They got to the tops of mountains. Long chains of ice hung from their watch-pockets. The Mistral whispered:

"They are here, Rose-Cold."

"Oh, Wild Wind, good Wild Wind, call the winter wolves. Put them on your shoulders, and quickly, because Rose-Cold needs them."

And the wolves came, with their long tails dragging behind, like soldiers with their sabers, and they stood behind the rows of seats.

"You are fine now, Rose-Cold. Put on your skates."

"Little cow, before I do that, bring me my handkerchief, where my mirror is folded away."

Moon moved her horns quickly to get all the skaters together. They made a very surprising line. Each one had chosen his own color. Human Sighs, in their kitsch way, had decided to go in pink. A meteorite announced that the games had begun. The benches shook.

"Run! Good! Faster! Run, Smoke from Factories!"

Dogs Barking ran past quickly, and Glances at Balloons on Quiet Evenings passed by almost unseen.

"Go for it! Go on, Rose-Cold!"

They were going to beat her. The scarf, the skirt, the scarf . . . the scarf . . . the skirt . . .

"Rose-Cold! Rose-Cold!"

The scarf . . . the skirt slid down to the craters. Rose-Cold climbed up out of it. She was exhausted. She threw her mirror down onto the snow. The pines opened their arms to her. They caught Factory Smoke and Train Steam in their arms, and Horse Sweat, and Evaporation from Pools. The wolves leapt among the tree trunks and captured Dogs Barking and the Glances at Balloons. It was only the Sighs that carried on running, all in pink, sadly climbing a slope. They found the mirror at the top and stopped to look at themselves.

Rose-Cold reached the finishing line, pushed along by a friendly wind. A beautiful constellation gave her the Four Seasons Cup. The Moon gave her a necklace made of lightning stones, and the stars gave her cinema tickets.

"Little Cow, I'm tired; take me back to Earth."

The cow left her on her balcony. And it was already morning when the cow went back to the Moon, carried in a chicken's beak.

Bruno Schulz (1892–1942) was a writer and art teacher considered among the greatest Polish writers of his time. Known to be shy, rarely leaving his hometown, he wrote stories filled with vitality and curiosity about what he did know. *Cinnamon Shops*, also known as *The Street of Crocodiles* (1934), and *Sanatorium Under the Sign of the Hourglass* (1937) are two hard-to-classify collections written in a beautiful and luminous way. Not only did his writing and artwork have an influence on the culture, even his death inspired novels. Schulz was Jewish, and most believe that he was killed by an SS officer in a ghetto. This officer killed Schulz for no reason other than the fact that he did not like another officer who protected Schulz. In 1992, UNESCO announced the Year of Bruno Schulz, which commemorated the fiftieth anniversary of his death and the one hundredth anniversary of his birth.

A Night of the High Season

Bruno Schulz

Translated by John Curran Davis

EVERYBODY KNOWS that whimsical time, in the course of mundane and ordinary years, occasionally will bring forth from its womb other years, odd years, degenerate years, somewhere in which, like a little sixth finger upon a hand, a spurious thirteenth month sprouts up. Spurious, we say; for seldom will it grow to full size. Like late begotten children, it lags behind in its development, a hunchback month, a half-wilted offshoot, and more conjectured than real.

The intemperance of summer's age is to blame for it, its licentious, belated vitality. It often happens, though August has already gone by, that summer's thick and hoary stem continues to burgeon, by force of habit, and from its touchwood it pushes out those wilding days, barren and idiotic weed days, and for good measure it throws in cabbage-stump days for free—empty and inedible, white, bewildered and unnecessary days.

They sprout up, irregular and misshapen, formless and fused together, like the fingers of a monstrous hand, sprouting buds and coiled up into a fist.

Others liken those days to apocrypha, slipped in furtively between the chapters of the great book of the year, to palimpsests inserted secretly among its pages, or to those white, unprinted sheets upon which one's eyes, having read their fill and now replete with content, might be drained of visions and relinquish colors, ever paler on those empty pages, reposing on their nothingness before being drawn into the labyrinths of new adventures and chapters.

Ah, that old, yellowed romance of the year!

That great, crumbling book of the calendar! It lies forgotten, somewhere in the archives of time, where its contents continue to grow between the covers, endlessly swollen by months of garrulousness, a rapid autogeny of gibberish, all the storytelling and the reveries that multiply within it. Ah! And in writing down these stories of mine, arranging these tales of my father in the used up margin of its text, do I not yield to the secret hope that, someday, they will strike root imperceptibly between the faded leaves of that most magnificent, scattering book; that they will fall into the great rustle of its pages, which will enfold them?

The matters of which we shall speak here took place then, in the thirteenth, supernumerary and somewhat spurious month of that year, on those dozen or so empty pages of the great chronicle of the calendar.

The mornings were strangely pungent and invigorating then. From a serene and cooler pace of time, an entirely new taste in the air, a change in the consistency of the light, it was plain to see that a different run of days had arrived, a new region of the Holy Year. One's voice resonated beneath those skies with the sonorousness and freshness of a still new and unoccupied apartment, its aroma of lacquer and paint, incipient and speculative matters. That new echo was tested with a strange stirring of emotion, sliced into with curiosity, like a ring cake on some cool and sober morning, on the eve of a journey.

My father was sitting once more in the rear office of the shop, a vaulted little chamber crisscrossed like a beehive into multi-cellular registries and endlessly shedding its layers of papers, letters, and invoices. The cross-ruled and empty existence of that room sprang from the rustling of those pages, the endless shuffling of those documents, and from the incessant sifting of those letters, with their innumerous company headings, an apotheosis was created in the air in the form of a factory town as birds in flight see it—bristling with smoking chimneys, surrounded by stacks of coins, its limits described by the flourishes and meanderings of grandiloquent &s and Sons.

There sat Father on a high stool, as if in an aviary, while the dovecotes of the filing cabinets rustled their paper sheaves and all of their birds' nests and tree-hollows chimed throughout with a twittering of numbers.

The depths of the great shop were darkened and enriched every day with new supplies of cloth, serge, velvet, and cord. On those dark shelves, in those storehouses and repositories of cool, felty hues, the dark and mellow pageantry of things yielded its hundredfold interest, and autumn's abundant capital was increased and consolidated. That capital grew larger and darker there, distributed ever more widely on the shelves as if in the galleries of some great theater, replenished and supplemented each morning with new consignments of merchandise, which arrived with the cool of the dawn in boxes and crates carried in on the great, bear-like shoulders of groaning, bearded porters, in mists of autumn freshness and vodka. The shop assistants unpacked those new supplies of lavish, deep-blue hues. They filled with them, neatly plugged with them, all of the chinks and gaps in the tall cupboards. It was a colossal register of all possible autumnal hues, ordered into layers and sorted into shades, running up and down as if on a ringing flight of stairs, a scale of all variegated octaves. It began at the bottom, where it plaintively and timidly ventured alto slides and semitones; it passed to the faded ashes of the distance, to Gobelin blues, and rising to the heights in ever broader harmonies, it arrived at deep royal azures, the indigo of distant forests, the plush of murmuring parks, and from there it entered the rustling shade of wilting gardens, through all of their ochres, rich reds, russets and sepias, finally to arrive at a dark aroma of mushrooms, a waft of touchwood in the depths of an autumn night, to the muted accompaniment of the deepest double basses.

My father walked along those arsenals of the cloth autumn. He placated and silenced those hulks and their rising force, the calm power of the Season. He wanted to keep those reserves of stowed-away hues intact for as long as possible. He was reluctant to break up that endowment fund of the autumn and exchange it for ready cash. But he knew, he sensed, that the time was at hand and an autumn gale, ravaging and warm, would soon blow over those cupboards, and they would empty. There would be no restraining their outflow, those torrents of colourfulness about to burst over the whole town.

For the time of the High Season was approaching, and the streets were growing busy. At six o'clock in the evening, the town blossomed with fervor. The houses blushed; the people wandered, animated by some inner fire, glaringly made up and painted, their eyes shining with some beautiful and evil, festival fever.

In the side streets, in quiet alleyways leading nowhere now but into an evening district, the town was empty. Only the children were playing on the little squares, beneath their balconies. They played breathlessly, raucously, and nonsensically. They put tiny balloons to their lips, to inflate them, and suddenly, glaringly, to scowl themselves into great, gurgling, swashing excrescences, or to cock-a-doodle-doo themselves into stupid cockerel masks, autumn apparitions, red and crowing, colorful, fantastic and absurd. So puffed up and crowing, they seemed about to soar into the air in long, colored chains, to be strung over the town like autumn V formations of birds, fantastic flotillas of tissue-paper and autumnal weather, or they rode, screaming, on noisy little carts, which resounded with a colored rattling of wheels, spokes and poles. Loaded up with their screams, those carts rolled to the bottom of the street, all the way down to a yellow evening brook that surged in a crevice, where they fell to pieces in a wreckage of splinters, wheels and sticks.

And as the children's games grew noisier and more confused, the town's blushes deepened and were flushed with crimson. The whole world suddenly began to wilt and blacken, and an hallucinatory twilight rapidly seeped out and infected everything. That pestilence of the twilight spread everywhere; it passed insidiously and venomously from place to place, and whatever it touched quickly moldered, blackened, and crumbled into dust. The people fled the twilight in silent panic, but that leprosy caught up

with them at once, breaking out in a dark rash on their foreheads, and their faces were lost, falling away in great, shapeless smears as they ran, without features now, without eyes, casting off mask after mask until the twilight teemed with those discarded masks and dominoes, tumbling in the wake of their flight. Then everything began to develop a patina of putrefying black bark, infected scabs of darkness peeling away in great flakes. But as everything down below fell into confusion and ruin in that silent turmoil, in the panic of its hasty schedule, the silent alarum of sunset remained up above, rising ever higher and higher, trembling with the tinkling of a million silent bluebells, surging with the ascent of a million silent skylarks, all flying together into one great, silver infinity. And suddenly it was nighttime, holy night, still growing, the gusts of wind that swelled it still gathering their strength. In its multifarious labyrinth, bright nests were carved out—shops, great colored lanterns, heaped up with merchandise and filled with a bustle of customers. Through the bright panes of those lanterns, the ritual of autumn shopping could be discerned, noisy and full of bizarre ceremony.

That great, voluminous autumn night, dilated by the wind, its shadows lengthening, concealed bright pockets in its dark folds, pouches of colored trinkets and gaudy merchandise, a grocer's shop miscellany of chocolates and biscuits. Botched from confectionery boxes, brightly wallpapered with advertisements for chocolate bars, filled with tablets of soap, cheerful rubbish, golden trifles, tinfoil, trumpets, wafers, and colored mints, those kiosks and stalls were stations of frivolity, rattle-boxes of blitheness strewn along the creepers of an enormous, labyrinthine night flapping in the winds.

Huge, dark crowds flowed in noisy confusion in the darkness, the shuffling of a thousand feet and the uproar of a thousand mouths, a teeming, tangled migration dragging along the arteries of the autumnal town. And that river flowed on, full of turmoil and dark looks, broken into conversations and shreds of gossip, a great pulp of rumors, laughter and tumult, as if dried autumnal poppy heads were moving in a crowd and scattering their seeds—rattlebox-heads, doorknocker-people.

Restless, tinged with blushes, his eyes shining, my father wandered about the brightly lit shop, listening intently. Through the display window and portal, the noise of the town, the muffled hubbub of the flowing throng, arrived from afar. Above the silence of the shop, pendent from its great vault, a paraffin lamp shone brightly, and silently chased the last trace of shadow from every nook and cranny. The vast, empty floor crackled softly in its light, calculating, down and across, all of its gleaming squares, its chessboard of great tiles, which spoke to one another in a silence of crackles and replied, now here, now there, with a loud crack. But the layers of cloth lay quiet, voiceless in their felty downiness, passing looks back and forth behind Father's back, all along the walls, exchanging silent, knowing signs from cupboard to cupboard.

Father listened. His ears seemed to grow elongated in that nocturnal silence, to branch out beyond the window like a fantastic coral, an undulating red polyp in the sediment of the night. He listened and he heard. He heard with growing unease the distant tide of the approaching crowd. He looked around the empty shop in dismay, searching for the shop assistants, but those dark, red-haired angels had flown away somewhere. He was left alone, in fear of the crowd that soon would swamp the silence of the shop in a raucous, plundering multitude and divide it among themselves, auction off all of that rich autumn accumulated throughout the years in its great, secluded storehouse. Where were the shop assistants? Where were those handsome cherubs who ought to defend the dark cloth ramparts? Father had the awful suspicion that, somewhere deep inside the house, they were sinning with the daughters of men. Standing motionless, filled with foreboding, his eyes shining in the bright silence of the shop, he heard with his inner ear what was going on deep inside the house, in the rear chambers of that great, colored lantern. Room after room, chamber after chamber, the house opened up before him like a house of cards.

He saw the shop assistants' pursuit of Adela through all of those empty and brightly lit rooms, upstairs, downstairs, until at last she gave them the slip and fell into the bright kitchen, which she barricaded with the credenza. She stood breathless, shiny and amused, smiling and fluttering her great eyelashes.

The shop assistants giggled, crouching at the door. The kitchen window was open onto a great, black night filled with reveries and confusion, its black, half-open panes ablaze with a reflex of distant illumination. Here and there, shining pots and demijohns stood in perfect stillness, their greasy glaze gleaming in the silence. Adela, her eyelids fluttering, cautiously leaned her tinged, rouged face out of the window. She was looking in the dark courtyard for the shop assistants, certain of their ambush. And she saw them. They were making their way in cautious single file along a narrow ledge at first-floor level, along a wall red in a glow of distant illumination, and stealing up to the window. Father shrieked with fury and despair. But just then, the uproar of voices grew very loud, and suddenly the bright shop window was populated with faces—up close and contorted with laughter, garrulous faces flattening their noses onto the glistening panes. Father turned scarlet with distress. He jumped onto the counter, and as the crowd laid siege to that fortress, as that raucous throng stormed the shop, he leaped in a single bound onto a shelf piled high with bales of cloth, and suspended high above the crowd, blew with all his might into a huge shofar and trumpeted the alert. But it was no sound of angels hurrying to his aid that came to fill that vault. In reply to each wail of his trumpet there came only the great, laughing chorus of the crowd.

"Jakub, trade with us! Jakub, sell to us!" they called out in unison, and those continually repeated cries fell into the rhythm of a chorus, which slowly became the melody of a refrain sung by every throat. My father conceded defeat. He jumped down from the high ledge and ran, shrieking, toward the barricades of cloth. He was grown gigantic with anger, his face bulging into a purple fist. He ran at the cloth ramparts like a prophet of war and began to rage against them. He pushed with all his might into the huge bales of wool and prised them from their places. He pushed his way with his whole body under the enormous bales of cloth and heaved them onto the counter, where they fell with a dull flop. The bales flew out into enormous banners, unwinding and fluttering in the air. The shelves burst forth from all sides with explosions of drapery, waterfalls of cloth, as if smote with Moses' rod.

The cupboards' reserves poured out, surging, flowing in broad rivers. The shelves' colorful contents were disgorged; they grew; they increased; they flooded all of the counters and desks. The walls of the shop disappeared under the mighty formations of that cloth cosmogony, those mountain ranges towering into lofty peaks.

Wide valleys opened between those mountainsides, and the contours of continents thundered amid a broad pathos of uplands. The shop's expanse widened into a panorama of an autumn landscape, full of lakes and distances, and against the backdrop of that scene, Father walked between the folds and valleys of a fantastic Canaan. He walked with great strides, his hands outspread prophetically in the clouds, and with inspired strokes he fashioned a country.

But down below, on the foothills of that Sinai grown out of Father's anger, the multitudes were gesticulating and transgressing, worshipping Baal, and trading. They grasped whole handfuls of those soft folds; they draped themselves in that colored cloth; they wound themselves up in improvised carnival masks and mantles, and chattered profusely, albeit unintelligibly.

My father, grown tall with anger, rose over those groups of traders. With a powerful word he reproved their idolatry from on high. Seized by despair, he clambered onto the high gallery of the cupboards and ran madly over the beams of their shelves, over the clattering planks of their bare scaffolding, pursued by an image of shameless licentiousness which he sensed behind his back, deep inside the house. The shop assistants had now reached the iron balcony at the kitchen window, and clinging to the balustrade, had seized Adela by the waist and were pulling her out of the window, her eyelids fluttering and her slender legs in silk stockings trailing behind her.

And as my father's gestures of fur—in his mortification at the odiousness of sin—became as one with the menace of the landscape, Baal's carefree multitude down below began to succumb to immoderate gaiety. Some parodistic passion, some pestilence of laughter, had taken possession of that mob. But how could one expect solemnity of them, that multitude of doorknockers and nutcrackers! How could one expect those hand-mills, incessantly grinding out a colored pulp of words, to comprehend Father's great concerns? Deaf to the thunder of his prophetic anger, those dealers in their silk frogged coats squatted in small clusters around the folded foothills of the material, where they thrashed out, effusively and amid laughter, the merits of the merchandise. Those black marketeers eagerly besmirched the noble substance of the landscape; they ground it up into a hash of idle talk, and all but consumed it.

Elsewhere stood groups of Jews in colored gabardines and huge fur kalpaks, before the high waterfalls of bright material. These were the men of the High Council, gentlemen venerable and full of solemnity, stroking their long, well-kept beards and conducting quiet, diplomatic conversations. But even in the midst of that ceremonious talk there was a flash of smiling irony in the looks that they exchanged.

Among those groups, the vulgar multitude wound its way, an amorphous crowd, a mob without faces or identities. They began to fill the gaps in the landscape; they carpeted its background with bluebells and rattle-boxes of mindless chattering. They were a clownish element, a crowd of Pulcinellas and Arlecchinos, dancing with abandon, who reduced to absurdity with their clownish pranks, lacking as they did the serious intentions of traders, the occasional transactions that were entered into. But gradually, grown bored with their clownishness, that cheerful little multitude began to disband among the further regions of the landscape and slowly became lost there amid its stone curves and valleys. Perhaps they had fallen somewhere, one after the other, between the folds and crevices of that terrain, like children in the corners and nooks of an apartment who are weary of revelry on the night of a ball.

Meanwhile, the Town Fathers, the men of the Great Sanhedrin, strolled in solemn and dignified groups, conducting quiet and profound disputes. Dispersed throughout that great, mountainous country, they wandered in twos and threes on its remote, winding roads, and that whole desert upland was populated with their dark, tiny silhouettes, above which a dark and heavy sky sagged, cloudy and folded, ploughed into long, parallel furrows, silver and white slices, exhibiting in its profundities the ever more distant layers of its stratification.

The lamplight created an artificial day in that country, a strange day, a day with no morning or evening.

My father slowly grew calm. His anger settled, cooled down in the layers and strata of the landscape. He was now sitting in the galleries of the high shelves and gazing out into an immense country passing into autumn. He could see people out fishing on distant lakes. Those fishermen sat in pairs in little cockleshell boats, casting their nets into the water. Boys on the banks carried baskets on their heads, filled with a flapping, silvery catch.

Then he noticed groups of wanderers in the distance, turning their heads to the sky and pointing at something with upraised hands.

And the sky broke out in a colorful, teeming rash; it spilled over with undulating smears, which grew, developed, and rapidly filled the sky with a strange multitude of birds. They circled and wheeled in great, overlapping spirals, and the whole sky was filled with their soaring flights, the flapping of their wings and the majestic lines of their quiet gliding. Some were floating, like enormous storks, unmoving on calmly outspread wings, whilst others, reminiscent of colorful plumes waving in barbarian adulation, flapped clumsily and heavily to remain aloft on currents of warm air. Others, finally, inept conglomerations of wings, huge legs and plucked necks, called to mind badly stuffed vultures and condors with sawdust spilling out of them. Among them were two-headed birds, many-winged birds, and cripples, hobbling in the air in ungainly one-winged flight. The sky began to resemble an old fresco, full of abnormities and fantastic beasts, which circled, crossed each other's paths, and returned once more in colorful ellipses.

My father, bathed in sudden radiance, hoisted himself aloft by the joists. He stretched out his hands, calling to the birds with an old incantation. Filled with emotion, he recognized them: it was the remote, forgotten progeny of that avian generation which Adela, once upon a time, had driven off to every fringe of the sky. And now it had returned, degenerate and luxuriant, that artificial progeny, that internally wasted avian tribe. Grown preposterously huge, a stupidly shot up manifestation, they were empty and lifeless inside. All the energy of those birds had gone into their plumage, expanded into fantasticality. They resembled some museum of disused species—rejects of bird paradise. Some were flying on their backs; they had heavy, ungainly beaks, like padlocks or zip fasteners, weighted down with colored excrescences, and they were blind. How that unexpected return affected Father! How he marveled at their avian instinct, their attachment to their Master, whom that banished tribe had kept like a legend in their souls, finally to return after many generations to their primæval homeland, on the last day before the extinction of their tribe.

But those blind, paper birds could no longer recognize Father. He called to them in vain with the old incantation, in forgotten avian speech. They heard him not, nor did they see him.

Suddenly stones began to whistle through the air. It was the jesters, the stupid and mindless tribe. They had begun to aim projectiles into the fantastic avian sky.

In vain, Father called the alert. In vain, he tried to warn them with imploring gestures. They could not catch his words. They could not make him out. And the birds fell. Each one, struck by a projectile, drooped ponderously and sagged in the air. Before they hit the ground they were nothing but ill-proportioned clumps of feathers.

That upland was strewn in the blinking of an eye with that strange, fantastic carrion. Before Father could reach the site of the massacre, the whole magnificent avian brood lay dead, scattered over the rocks. Only now, at close quarters, could Father perceive how utterly paltry was that impoverished generation, how truly comical its tawdry anatomy. They were enormous bunches of feathers, old carcasses stuffed any old how. Many had no discernible head, since that club-shaped part of their body bore no indications of a soul. Some were coated with fur, clotted with a pelage, like bison, and they stunk abominably. Others were reminiscent of hunchbacked, bald and sickly camels. And others, finally, were apparently made of a kind of paper, empty inside, albeit magnificently colored on the outside. And some, at close quarters, were shown to be nothing more than huge peacock tails, colored fans, into which, by incomprehensible means, some semblance of life had been breathed.

I saw my father's woeful return. The artificial day had already begun to take on the hues of an ordinary morning. In the ravaged shop, the highest shelves were replete with the colors of a morning sky. Among the fragments of a dead landscape painting, in the devastated wings of a nocturnal stage, Father saw the shop assistants rising from their sleep. They rose from among the bales of cloth and yawned to the sunshine. Upstairs in the kitchen, Adela, warm from sleep, her hair tousled, was grinding coffee in a mill, pressing it to her white bosom, from which the grindings derived their sheen and their heat. The cat washed itself in the sunshine.

Fernand Demoustier (1906–1945), who wrote under the name Fernand Dumont, was a Belgian poet and writer best known for his surrealist works. In 1940, he wrote an essay, "Treatise on Fairies," for his newborn daughter that discusses various aspects of fairies and the fairy world. "The Influence of the Sun" was one of his best-known pieces, for a writer who today is largely forgotten. His work was admired by André Breton, the founder of the surrealism movement. He perished in Bergen-Belsen, a concentration camp, during World War II.

The Influence of the Sun

Fernand Dumont

Translated by Gio Clairval

RECENTLY THE SURPRISING STORY has been going around of a couple who decided to live without in the least taking into consideration what could be happening, thought, or said in the town where chance had brought them together despite most categorical opposition from their parents. They must have been, so people declare, in a best-of-three match with the sun, for it was impossible to meet them in any season without seeing on their faces, hands, and hair that special light generally there only on persons returning from vacation.

Certain individuals, who had had the extraordinary privilege of getting into their home on one pretext or another, affirmed that it was full of and even cluttered with shining objects of strange shape for which they had not been able to discover the use or necessity. Others claimed that certain rooms on the first floor (into which they had not had occasion to go, but had been able to steal a glance, on the sly, thanks to a door

having been left accidentally half open) offered a spectacle such as you could not conceive, they were arranged in such a singular way, were decorated with such inexplicably phosphorescent wall paintings, and had such an unusual and novel appearance that, really, one had to give up trying to describe them.

These people were closely questioned all the same, but, as was to be expected, their contradictory and confused explanations, far from allaying curiosity, aggravated it to the point where soon, all over town, people no longer spoke of anything else. Those who were most curious, the very ones who, for personal reasons they could not admit to, had always defended the principle of the inviolability of the home, went so far as to advocate use of the worst pretexts, so as to be done with this aggravating enigma.

It did no good.

The bogus beggars, the obsequious canvassers, the make-believe bailiffs ran into the polite but categorical refusal of an obstinately closed door. And so they had to bow to the facts, whether they liked it or not, but with that unconfessed confidence they persist in placing in the outcome of events, with that secret hope that in the end events one day will take a favorable turn; but the days slipped by one after the other without bringing the least response that that immense collective curiosity could feed on, and nothing, in truth, was more exasperating than finding oneself everywhere in the presence of that couple, telling oneself that all one had to do was question them to get to the bottom of the matter, and doing no more than tell oneself so and repeat it to oneself, for no one would have risked doing this, since the couple seemed to have, in the highest degree, that attitude made up of coldness, indifference, and disdain which instantly discourages the most determined of people.

Then people tried not to think about it any more, to tell themselves they had been the sport of an illusion or victims of a bad joke, that after all those two were like everybody else and that one would have to be very credulous to lend an attentive ear to such talk, but all that was to no avail, it was no use crying "hoax," speaking of other matters, opening a newspaper or going for a walk, people discovered with some amazement that it was impossible not to think of it any more.

People were on the point of seizing control when, one day, as if they had guessed it was important to strike an attitude, the couple moved among the crowd letting something like a long scarf float behind them, a wake in which all who passed could not but think of the silence, scarcely interrupted by the distant crowing of the first rooster, of an April dawn in an orchard full of dew.

The news spread like wildfire and gave rise, as you can imagine, to the most diversified comments. While some claimed it was a matter of the purely chemical production of a perfume with the distillation of which the shining objects glimpsed in the secret house must have something to do, others, on the basis of vague considerations of a psychic order, gave free rein to their confusional thought, deducing with a rough appearance of truth, that everyone was facing a manifestation of an immaterial order that must be connected with the well-known phenomenon of thought transference, and most with their customary pettiness, persisted in locating the importance of the whole question in the wretched point of knowing whether the phenomenon was material or not, in centering all their hopes on getting this trifling thing dear, incapable as they were of realizing for a single instant the overwhelming significance of this thing that had never come about before.

If it was quickly established through many witnesses that they were dealing with a phenomenon perceptible to everybody, no one proved capable of explaining its origin and nature.

The depositions did not provide the conclusive element. Most of them betrayed almost total indigence so far as investigative means are concerned, but they made it possible nevertheless to establish that the phenomenon, fluid or perfume, acted in the same way upon everybody. No one spoke of dusk, or of a pine forest, of a farmyard, or of a September mist. The measure of agreement was surprising. It made no difference whether it was midwinter, whether one was in the midst of a crowd, in the hubbub of an intersection initialed by railroad switches, it made no difference whether one was taken up with the most absorbing preoccupations, with the most animated conversations, with the most secret women, all one needed was to pass through the couple's wake, as the earth passes through the cone of shadow during an eclipse, to find oneself in the presence of that reverie which encroaches like bindweed.

The authorities remained defenseless for, even showing that notorious bad faith they never fail to manifest toward anything that, in any way, can look like disturbing established order, it was still practically impossible for them to give the couple's movements the felonious interpretation that could have justified the inquisitorial measures impatiently demanded.

However, more scandalously beautiful than an indecent assault, more provocative than a shout of laughter in a lighted church, more indifferent than the path of a cyclone, the couple moved about the town letting that unforgettable atmosphere float behind them that corresponds exactly, I have said, to the silence (scarcely interrupted by the distant crowing of the first rooster) of the dawn of a very fine April day in an orchard full of dew. Then people decided to appeal to specialists and were astonished to find that not a single one existed in the whole world. Thanks to their insistence, a few mystified psychiatrists made it known that they would immediately hold an extraordinary convention in the town, with the purpose of examining the question, but the very morning of their arrival a thick fog suddenly came down over the town.

As it was the season for fogs, everyone thought this a mere coincidence, quite annoying no doubt, but a mere coincidence, yes, pure chance, in short . . .

The learned men landed in fog so dense that getting them without mishap to a downtown hotel gave all the trouble in the world. Local people of consequence apologized profusely and suggested that the obviously disappointed visitors devote the whole day to hearing the best witnesses, while they waited for more favorable conditions—which could not be long coming—for the experiments proper. So it was done, but the next day all the windows in town opened early in the morning upon an impenetrable screen of white mist. This was all the harder to understand because milkmen and market-gardeners from the surrounding countryside reported that, when they had set out, the sky had been splendidly starry. During the morning, the suburban motormen declared that the sun was shining brightly everywhere over the outskirts, and at noon a reading of the weather forecast, listened to in silence, gave rise to the conviction that it was not a mere coincidence.

People were beginning to live under the yellowish light of anguish.

They felt the urge to shout that it was not true, that the couple had nothing to do with that fog stretching before their exhausted eyes, that it was necessary at all cost for this not to be true. People felt the crazy urge to rip it apart, to destroy it, to tear it away, find anything at all to drive it off, invent a storm, telephone the sun. Only in their imagination could they be rid of it and find their town once again familiar, transparent, easy to live in. And yet, as happens when people find themselves facing a succession of unforeseen events in which they do not manage to make up their minds to admit the existence of a causal relationship that seems at the same time demonstrated by the facts and contradicted by their unusual character, people still hesitated to establish this feature, this slender causal thread between the couple and the fog, people still hesitated to erect that narrow footbridge over the comfortable precipice of positive realities, people still hesitated to register the short and terrifying conclusion, even with the most explicit reservations, people still hesitated, for it appeared only too dearly, all in all, that official recognition of the marvelous would give the signal for the final collapse of all values currently prevailing.

People still tried to be reasonable, to appeal to old good sense; old men would pretend to recall comparable situations and, in front of an open fire, shutters closed, under the lamplight, between two pipes of tobacco, people would once again find the little zone of bluish calm, as pleasant to the heart as an island to a shipwrecked man, but it was shrinking visibly and in the streets, if the fog had lifted, they would have been able to ascertain that the terror of living had inscribed its name everywhere on the walls.

At the end of the third day, the authorities held an emergency meeting and decided the only measure to take, to check this monstrous enterprise of demoralization, was to proceed to arrest the couple. Everything was prepared in secret, down to the smallest detail, and the most thorough precautions were taken to assure the success of this operation that was set for the following morning. And so, how stupefied they all were when they perceived in the early morning that the fog had dissipated completely. They had become so accustomed to it that they had difficulty believing their eyes, while the sun, still very low over the horizon, seemed to shine with singular brightness.

Already the authorities were beginning to ask themselves what on earth had managed to dictate those extreme measures that nothing, all of a sudden, seemed to justify any more, and they were beginning to hesitate, to tell themselves it was perhaps premature to act, that it would be wise to require additional information without which they ran the risk of leaving themselves open to derision from all sides. But the crowd was growing and its presence alone prescribed action, the long-repressed desire to violate an aggravating mystery and, above all, their preoccupation with not contradicting themselves in public, coupled with the petty vanity of playing an apparently courageous role, carried the day fairly easily.

They set off, then, with a little incoercible band of anguish around their hearts, and, when they were in sight of the couple's house, they saw it was already surrounded by a semicircle of interested spectators and heard at once that it was impossible to approach any closer, on account of the extraordinary heat given off by the house. This was all the more difficult to understand because no smoke, no flame, no sign at all permitted the eye to bow to the facts. The dwelling looked absolutely normal. However, the circle was widening more and more, pushed back by that invisible furnace and the light, the light that a while ago was already strangely bright, the light slowly became so dazzling, so terribly blinding that the street had to be evacuated and they had to shut themselves up hurriedly in the houses. From time to time, volunteers went out to reconnoiter, despite the entreaties of those around them, but not one returned.

Then no one ventured out any more and, after endless hours, night slowly came down on a deserted town.

Toward dawn windows were half-opened and, as nothing aroused suspicion, a few persons went down into the street and approached the house stealthily, hugging the walls.

The heat had abated and, as it was still very dark, they thought at first they were the sport of an hallucination, but a little later they realized this was not at all the case and then began to shout at the top of their voices for everyone to come, that there was not the slightest danger any more, that everyone absolutely must come to see this extraordinary thing.

The house was now nothing but an immense block of an incredibly transparent substance, softly luminous, something like crystal, but infinitely more pure than the one we know and, inside, beyond that admirable shell of which no breath could tarnish the brightness, the couple could be seen coming and going as in one of those dazzling dreams after which one retains, always, a painful hankering, they could be seen coming and going against a background of very old legend, much smaller than life size, splendid and shining as ever.

Soon the couple made their way slowly toward the mystery of a bluish forest and, at the very moment when they were about to be lost from sight, those who, to see better, had leaned against the shell fell crashing into a horrible piece of waste ground where, among the nettles and rubbish, an exceedingly rare rose was opening, for it was of the sadly prophetic color of the last dusk we shall be permitted to see before we depart this life.

Hagiwara Sakutarō (1886–1942) was a Japanese poet who began writing poetry at age fifteen, for literary magazines. He refused to become a doctor like his father and soon left college and traveled to Tokyo, where he studied the mandolin. Sadly, his lack of a steady occupation caused him to lose his first love, but she appeared in a number of his poems afterward, even after his marriage to another woman. His first book of poetry, *Howling at the Moon* (1917), transformed modern Japanese verse. That book along with *Blue Cat* (1923) firmly established Sakutarō's reputation as a poet. Most of his poetry focused on mental uncertainty and questions of identity while conveying an interesting melancholy tone. "The Town of Cats" (1935) is Sakutarō's only short story and an amazing narrative of ambiguity and the surreal fantastical. Although Haruki Murakami disavows the story as an influence on parts of his novel *IQ84* (2009), perhaps they conjured up elements from the same collective subconscious.

The Town of Cats

Hagiwara Sakutarō

Translated by Jeffrey Angles

I

THE QUALITY THAT INCITES the desire for travel has gradually disappeared from my fantasies. Before, however, symbols of travel were all that filled my thoughts. Just to picture a train, steamboat, or town in an unfamiliar foreign land was enough to make my heart dance. But experience has taught me that travel presents nothing more than identical objects moving in identical spaces: No matter where one goes, one finds the same sort of people living in similar villages and repeating the same humdrum lives. One finds merchants in every small country town spending their days clicking abacuses and watching the dusty white road outside. In every municipal office, government officials smoke and think about what they will have for lunch. They live out insipid, monotonous lives in which each new day is identical to the last, gradually watching themselves grow old as the days go by. Now the thought of travel projects onto my weary heart an infinitely tedious landscape like that of a paulownia tree growing in a vacant lot, and I feel a dull loathing for human life in which this sameness repeats itself everywhere. Travel no longer holds any interest or romance for me.

In the past, I often undertook wondrous voyages in my own personal way. Let me explain. I would reach that unique moment in which

744

humankind sometimes finds itself able to soar—
that special moment outside of time and space,
outside the chain of cause and effect—and I
would adroitly navigate the borderline between
dreams and reality to play in an uninhibited world
of my own making.—Having said this much, I
doubt I need to explain my secret further. Let me
simply add that, in undertaking these hallucinatory trips, I generally preferred to use the likes of
morphine and cocaine, which can be ingested in
a simple shot or dose, instead of opium, which is
hard to obtain in Japan and requires troublesome
tools and provisions.

There is not enough room here to describe in
detail the lands that I traveled in those dreams of
narcotic ecstasy, but I will tell you that the trips
frequently took me wandering through wetlands
where little frogs gathered, through polar coasts
where penguins live, and on and on. The landscapes in those dreams were filled with brilliant
primary hues. The sea and sky were always as
clear and blue as glass. Even after returning to
normal, I would cling to those visions and relive
them again and again in the world of reality.

These drug-induced voyages took a terrible
toll on my health. I grew increasingly drawn
and pale by the day, and my skin deteriorated
as if I had aged terribly. By and by, I began to
pay more attention to my health. Following my
doctor's advice, I started taking walks through
my neighborhood. Every day, I would cover the
distance of forty or fifty *chō*, walking anywhere
from thirty minutes to an hour. One day while I
was out taking my exercise, I happened upon a
new way to satisfy my eccentric wanderlust. I was
walking through the usual area around my home.
Normally, I do not deviate from my established
ph, but for some reason that day, I slipped into
an un____ alley, and going the wrong way, lost
all sense of di____.

All in all, I h__ __ have no innate sense of direction. My __ability to keep track of the points of
the __npass is terribly deficient. As a result, I
am ful at remembering my way anywhere, and
if o someplace even slightly unfamiliar, in no
ti I end up completely lost. To make matters

worse, I have a habit of getting absorbed in my
thoughts as I walk. If an acquaintance happens
to greet me along the way, I will pass by in total
obliviousness. Because I am so bad at keeping
track of directions, I can lose my way even in a
place that I know perfectly well, such as my own
neighborhood. I can be so close to my destination that people laugh at me when I ask how to
get there. Once I walked tens of times around
the hedge surrounding the very house in which
I have lived for years. Though the gate was right
before my eyes, my lack of a sense of direction
made it impossible for me to find it. My family
insisted a fox must have bewitched me.

Psychologists would probably account for this
bewitching as a disturbance of the inner ear. I say
this because the experts claim that the function
of sensing direction belongs to the semicircular
canals located in the ear.

In any case, I was completely lost and bewildered. I made a random guess and rushed down
the street in search of my house. After going in
circles several times in a neighborhood of suburban estates surrounded by trees, suddenly I came
upon a bustling street. It was a lovely little neighborhood, but I had no idea where I was!

The roads had been swept clean, and the flagstones were wet with dew. All of the shops were
neat and tidy, all with different types of unusual
merchandise lined up in polished show windows.
A flowering tree flourished by the eaves of a coffee shop, bringing an artistic play of light and
shadow to the borough. The red mailbox at the
street crossing was also beautiful, and the young
woman in the cigarette shop was as bright and
sweet as a plum.

I had never seen such an aesthetically charming place! Where in Tokyo could I possibly be?
But I was unable to recall the layout of the city. I
figured I could not have strayed far from home
because so little time had elapsed. It was perfectly
clear that I was within the territory where I ordinarily strolled, only a half hour or so from home,
or at least not too far from it. But how could this
place be so close without my having known it?

I felt as if I was dreaming. I wondered if perhaps what I was seeing was not a real town but a reflection or silhouette of a town projected on a screen. Then, just as suddenly, my memory and common sense returned. Examining my surroundings again, I realized I was seeing an ordinary, familiar block in my neighborhood. The mailbox was at the intersection as always, and the young lady with the gastric disorder sat in the cigarette shop. The same out-dated, dusty merchandise yawned from the space that it occupied in the store windows. On the street, the eaves of the coffee shop were boorishly decorated with an arch of artificial flowers. This was nowhere new. It was my familiar, boring neighborhood.

In the blink of an eye, my reaction to my surroundings had altered completely. The mysterious and magical transformation of this place into a beautiful town had occurred simply because I had mixed up my directions. The mailbox that always stood at the south end of the block seemed to be on the opposite, northern approach. The tradesmen's houses on the left side of the street had shifted to the right. The changes sufficed to make the entire neighborhood look new and different. In that brief moment that I spent in the unknown, illusory town, I noticed a sign above a store. I swore to myself that I had seen a picture just like it on a signboard somewhere else.

When my memory was back in working order, all of the directions reversed themselves. Until a moment before, the crowds on my left had been on the right, and I discovered that, though I had been walking north, I was now headed south. In that instant when my memory returned to normal, the needle of my compass spun around, and the cardinal directions switched positions. The whole universe changed, and the mood of the town that manifested itself before me became utterly different. The mysterious neighborhood that I had seen a moment before existed in some universe of opposite space where the compass was reversed.

After this accidental discovery, I made it a point to lose my bearings in order to travel again to such mysterious places. The deficiency on my part that I described before was especially helpful in allowing me to undertake these travels, but even people with a normal, sound sense of direction may at times experience the same special places that I have. For instance, imagine yourself returning home on a train late at night. First, the train leaves the station, and then the tracks carry you straight east to west. Some time later, you wake from a dream-filled nap. You realize the train has changed directions at some point and is now moving west to east. You reason this cannot be right, and in the reality you perceive, the train is moving away from your destination. To double-check, you look out the window. The intermediary stations and landscapes to which you are accustomed are all entirely new. The world looks so different that you cannot recognize a single place. But you arrive in the end. When you step down on the familiar train platform, you awaken from the illusion and regain an accurate sense of direction. And once that sense is regained, strange landscapes and sights transform themselves into boring familiarities as unremarkable and ordinary as ever.

In effect, you see the same landscape, first from the reverse and then from the front, as you are accustomed to seeing it. One can think of a thing as having two separate sides. Just by changing your perspective, the other side will appear. Indeed there is no metaphysical problem more mysterious than the notion that a given phenomenon can possess a "secret, hidden side." When I was a boy a long time ago, and I used to examine a framed picture that hung on the walls of the house, I wondered all the while what worlds lay hidden on the reverse side of the framed landscape. I removed the frame repeatedly to peer at the back side of the painting. Those childhood thoughts have now turned into a riddle that remains impossible for me to solve even as an adult.

But the story that I am about to tell may contain a hint for solving the riddle. Should my strange tale lead you, my readers, to imagine a world of the fourth dimension hidden behind things and external manifestations—a verse existing on the reverse side of the landscape—

then this tale will seem completely real to you. If, however, you are unable to imagine the existence of such a place, then what follows will seem like the decadent hallucinations of an absurd poet whose nerves have been shattered by a morphine addiction.

In any event, I shall gather my courage and write. I am not a novelist, and therefore I do not know the intricacies of drama and plot that will excite readers. All that I can do is give a straight-forward account of the realities I experienced.

II

I was staying in the Hokuetsu region at a hot spring resort in a town that I shall call K. September was nearly over, the equinox already past. Being in the mountains, we were well into autumn. All of the guests who had come from the city to escape the summer heat had returned home, leaving only a handful of visitors to quietly nurse their illnesses in the healing waters of the spa. The autumn shade had grown long, and the leaves of the trees were scattered across the lonely courtyard of our inn. I would don a flannel kimono and spend time pursuing my daily ritual of walking alone along the back mountain roads.

There were three towns a short distance from the hot spring. Perhaps I should not call them towns they were so small. Two of them were like a little cluster of country homes, about the size of what would pass as a village elsewhere. The third, however, was a compact country settlement that sold the necessities of daily living. It even had restaurants like those one finds in the city. I shall call this town, the most prosperous of the three, U. Each of the three towns connected directly to the hot spring via a road, and every day at pre-scribed times, horse-drawn coaches traveled back and forth between them. A small, narrow-gauge railway had been laid to U, so I often made the trip to it on the train to shop and have a drink, with the ladies. But simply riding the train was enough to bring me tremendous pleasure. The cute, toylike railway would weave through groves of deciduous trees and gorges that revealed views of entire valleys.

One day, I got off the train midway, and I began walking toward U. I wanted to take a lei-surely walk alone over the mountain crests with their commanding views. The road cut an irregu-lar path through the woods, following the direc-tion of the tracks nearby. Autumn flowers were in bloom here and there. The surface of the red earth glistened, and the trunks of felled trees were scattered across the ground. While watch-ing the clouds float across the sky, I thought of the old folklore that survives there in the mountains. In these backwoods areas, with their primitive taboos and superstitions, one can still hear many legends and folk-tales. In fact, many of the local people believe the stories even to this day. The maids and the locals visiting our inn told me sev-eral strange stories in voices tinged with fear and disgust. They said the spirits of dogs possessed the inhabitants of one particular settlement, while cats possessed the inhabitants of another. Those possessed by dog-spirits ate only meat. Those possessed by cat-spirits lived on nothing but fish.

The people in the surrounding areas called these odd settlements "the possessed villages," and they were careful to avoid contact with them. Once a year, the people of the allegedly possessed villages would select a black, moonless night to hold a festival. It was strictly forbidden for any-one outside the village to observe what ensued during those mysterious rites, if by some rare chance an outsider happened to glimpse the pro-ceedings, he would invariably bite his tongue and say nothing. The rumors about the villages ran rampant: the denizens of the villages were privy to special magic; they were hiding a vast fortune of unknown origin; and so on. After recounting these stories, the locals would add that one of the villages was located quite close to the hot spring, only it wasn't very long ago that the inhabitants had deserted the town. They had up and left, but it was common speculation that they continued to live their secret life in a community somewhere else. As irrefutable proof, the people telling the story cited the experiences of others who had seen the *okura*, the true form of the malevolent spirits.

All these stories proved to me was how stubbornly superstitious farming people can be. Conscious of it or not, the villagers were forcing their own fears and realities on me. Because their stories interested me for anthropological reasons, however, I listened carefully. Secretive village practices and taboos like those they described can be found throughout Japan. One likely theory is that the people engaging in these practices were the descendants of immigrants from foreign countries with different customs and habits, and even today they continued to worship the clan gods of their ancestors. Another possibility is that the villages were holdovers from the seventeenth century, when believers in Christianity, persecuted by the Tokugawa government, went into hiding and practiced their religion in secret.

There are countless things in this vast universe that humankind does not know. As the Latin poet Horace once noted, the intellect of the mind knows nothing. Instead, people use it to make common sense of the world and have myths that explain things in everyday terms. Still, the secrets of the universe continue to transcend the quotidian. All philosophers must, therefore, doff their hats to the poets when they discover that the path of reason takes them only so far. The universe that lies beyond common sense and logic—the universe that is known intuitively to the poet—belongs to the metaphysical.

While indulging in these speculations, I walked through the autumn mountains. The narrow road continued for some time, then disappeared into the depths of the woods. The railroad tracks, the sole thing I relied on to guide me to my destination, were nowhere in sight. I had lost my way.

"I'm lost!"

These lonely words rose in my heart as I came to my senses and left my contemplations behind. Immediately I became uneasy and began to look frantically for the road. I backtracked in an attempt to find it. Instead, I became all the more turned around. I ended up in an inescapable labyrinth of countless paths. The paths led deeper into the mountains and then disappeared into the brambles. I wasted a great deal of time. Not once did I see a single soul—not even a woodcutter. Becoming increasingly upset, I paced about impatiently like a dog trying to scout out its way. At long last, I discovered a narrow but clear path marked by feet and hooves. Following it intently, I descended little by little toward the base of the mountain. I figured I could relax once I made it to the base of one of the mountains and found a house.

I arrived at the foot of the mountain some hours later. There, I discovered a world of human habitation beyond anything that I could have anticipated in my wildest dreams. Instead of poor farmers, I had come upon a beautiful, prosperous town. An acquaintance of mine once told me about a trip he had taken on the Trans-Siberian railroad. He said the passengers would travel for days and days through desolate, uninhabited plains that stretched as far as the eye could see. As a result, when the train finally stopped, even the tiniest station looked like one of the most animated, prosperous cities in the world. The surprise that I felt was probably similar to what my friend had experienced. There in the low, flat plain at the base of the mountain stood rows and rows of buildings.

Towers and lofty buildings shone in the sun. The sight was so impressive that I could hardly believe such a marvelous metropolis really existed there in the remote mountains.

Feeling as if I was seeing an image projected by a magic lantern onto a screen in front of me, I slowly approached the town. At some point, though, I crossed over into the projection and became part of the mysterious town itself. Starting down a narrow alley, I passed through some dark, confusing, cramped pathways, but then suddenly I walked into the center of a bustling avenue, almost as if I were emerging from a womb into the world. The city that I saw was so special, so unusual! The rows of shops and other buildings were designed with an unusual, artistic feel. They acted, as it were, like the building blocks for the communal aesthetic that pervaded the entire town. The whole place was beautiful, but the beauty did not seem to have been consciously created. The artistic feel had evolved naturally as the town gradually weathered and developed an elegant patina that reflected its age, this elegant depth spoke with grace and gentility of the town's old history and the long memories of the towns-people.

The town was so tightly knit that the main avenue was only a dozen or a dozen and a half feet across. Other smaller streets were pressed into the space between the eaves of the buildings so that they became deep, narrow passages that wound about like paths in a labyrinth. Roads descended down flagstone-covered slopes or passed under the shadow of second-story bay windows, creating dark tunnels. As in southern climes, flowering trees grew near the wells located here and there throughout the town. A ubiquitous, deep shade filled the whole place, leaving everything as tranquil as the shadow of a laurel tree. What appeared to be the houses of courtesans stood in a row, and from deep inside an enclosed garden came the quiet sound of elegant music.

On the main avenue, I found many Western-style houses with glass windows instead of the sliding wooden and paper doors found in Japan. A red-and-white-striped pole stuck out from the eaves of a hairdresser's shop, along with a painted sign that read in English, "Barbershop." There were also traditional Japanese-style inns and shops that did laundry in the neighborhood. Near an intersection stood a photography studio with glass windows that reflected the sunny autumn sky with the lonely stoicism of a weather observatory. In the front of a watch shop sat the store's bespectacled owner working quietly and intently.

The streets were thronged with hustling crowds, yet the people created little noise. A refined, hushed silence reigned over the place,

casting a pall that was as profound as a deep sleep. The town was silent, I realized, because there were no noisy horse-drawn carriages charging by, only pedestrians. But that wasn't all. The crowds were also quiet. Everyone—both men and women—had an air about them that was genteel and discreet, elegant and calm. The women were especially lovely and graceful, and even a bit coquettish. The people shopping in the stores and stopping in the street to talk also spoke politely in harmonious, soft voices. As a result, instead of appealing to the sense of hearing, their voices seemed to present meaning in an almost tactile fashion, something soft to the touch. The voices of the women had the especially sweet and rapturous charm of a gentle stroke passing over the surface of one's skin. People and things came and went like shadows.

I realized right away that the atmosphere of the town was an artificial creation whose existence relied on the subtle attentions of its inhabitants. It was not just its buildings. The entire system of individual nerves that came together to create its atmosphere was focused on one single, central aesthetic plan. In everything from the slightest stirrings in the air, there was strict adherence to the aesthetic laws of contrast, symmetry, harmony, and equilibrium. These aesthetic laws entailed, however, extremely complicated differential equations that, requiring tremendous effort, made all of the nerves of the town quiver and strain. For instance, even uttering a word slightly too high in pitch was forbidden, for it would shatter the harmony of the entire town. When the inhabitants did anything—when they walked down the street, moved their hands, ate, drank, thought, or even chose the pattern of their clothing—they had to give painstaking attention to their actions to make sure they harmonized with the reigning atmosphere and did not lose the appropriate degrees of contrast and symmetry with their environs. The whole town was a perilously fragile structure of thin crystal. A loss of balance, even for a moment, would have dashed the entire thing to smithereens. A subtle mathematical structure of individual supports was necessary to maintain stability, and a complex of individual connections governed by the laws of contrast and symmetry strained to support the whole.

However frightening this might be, such was the truth about the town. One careless mishap would mean the collapse and destruction of the entire place. Trepidation and fear had stretched the nerves of the whole town dangerously thin. The plan of this town, which seemed so aesthetically inclined on the surface, went beyond a mere matter of taste. It hid a more frightening and acute problem.

This realization suddenly made me extremely anxious. The air surrounding me was electrically charged, and in it I felt the anguish of the inhabitants' nerves stretched to the breaking point. The peculiar beauty and dreamlike serenity of the town had now become hushed and uncanny. I felt as if I were unraveling a code to discover some frightening secret. A vague premonition, the color of a pale fear, washed over my heart, though I could not quite understand what it was trying to tell me. All of my senses were fully alert. I perceived all of the colors, scents, sounds, tastes, and meanings of the things surrounding me in infinitesimal detail. The stench of corpses filled the air, and the barometric pressure rose with each passing instant. All of the things that manifested themselves around me seemed to portend some evil. Something strange was about to happen! Something had to happen!

But the town did not change. The street was full of elegant people going to and fro, walking quietly without making a sound, just as they had moments ago. From somewhere in the distance, I heard a continuous, low, mournful note that sounded like the stroking of the strings of a *kokyū*. Like someone haunted by a strange omen in the moments before a great earthquake, I experienced an anxious premonition—mere steps away from me, a person falls . . . and the harmony on which the entire town is based collapses, throwing everything into utter chaos!

I struggled with this horrifying vision like someone having a nightmare and trying frantically to awaken. With each passing second, the sky turned bluer and more transparent. The pressure of the electrically charged air rose higher and higher. The buildings bent precariously, growing long and sickly thin. Here and there, they distended into bizarre, turretlike forms. The roofs became strangely bony and deformed like the long, thin legs of a chicken.

"It's happening!"

The words escaped my lips as my chest thumped with fear. Just then, a small black rat or something like it dashed into the center of the road. I saw it with extraordinary delineation and clarity. What on earth was going on? I was seized by the strange, sudden notion that it would destroy the harmony of the entire town.

Right then . . . the whole universe stopped dead, and an infinite quiet settled over everything. What next!?!

An unimaginably strange and horrifying sight appeared before me. Great packs of cats materialized everywhere, filling all the roads around me! Cats, cats, cats, cats, cats, cats, and more cats! Everywhere I looked there was nothing but cats! Whiskered cat faces rose in the windows of all the houses, filling the panes like pictures in frames.

I shuddered. I held my breath from fright and nearly passed out. This wasn't the human world! Was there nothing in this world but cats? What on earth had happened? Was this world real? Something had to be wrong with me. Either I was seeing an illusion or I had gone mad! My senses had lost their balance. The universe was collapsing around me.

I was terrified. Some final, frightening destruction would surely be closing in on me. I closed my eyes, and fear rushed through the darkness inside me.

But, suddenly, my senses returned. As my heart began to slow its furious beat, I opened my eyes again to examine the world of reality that now surrounded me.

The inexplicable vision of all those cats had vanished. There was nothing out of the ordinary about the town. Hollow, deserted windows stretched open their empty mouths. The traffic moved by uneventfully as the white clay of the dull streets roasted in the sun. Nowhere was there even a shadow of a cat. The town had undergone a complete change in feeling. Everywhere there were rows of plain old shops. Walking the dry, midday streets were the same tired, dusty people who live in every country. The mysterious, perplexing town of a moment ago had vanished without a trace. An entirely separate world had appeared, almost as if a playing card had been turned over to reveal its other side. It was nothing but an ordinary, commonplace country town. Wasn't it the same old town of U that I knew so well? There at the barbershop, facing the midday traffic outside the shop window, was a row of barber chairs that had no customers. On the left side of the dilapidated town yawned a clock shop that never sold anything, its door shut as always. Everything was just like I remembered it—a never-changing, humdrum town in the country.

Once my mind cleared, I understood everything. I had foolishly allowed myself to succumb again to my perceptual malady, to my disturbance of the semicircular canals. Getting turned around in the mountains, I had completely lost any sense of direction. Though I thought I was descending the other side of the mountain, I went the wrong way and ended up here in the town of U. Also, I had wandered into the heart of it from a direction opposite to that I arrived from on the train. All of my assumptions as to my whereabouts were completely backward, and my mistaken impressions were showing me a world with the directions all turned around. I was looking at a separate universe of another dimension, at the back side of the landscape where up and down, front and back, and the four cardinal directions were all reversed. As popular parlance would have it, I had been "bewitched by a fox."

III

My tale ends here, but the end of this story is the point of departure for my strange, unresolved enigma. The Chinese philosopher Zhuangzi once dreamed he was a butterfly. When he woke, he questioned his own identity, wondering if he was the butterfly in the dream or the person he was at that moment.

This ancient riddle has remained unsolved across the ages. Is the universe of illusion only visible to those who have been bewitched by foxes? Or is it visible to those with clear intellect and good sense? Where does the metaphysical world exist in relationship to the ordinary landscape? Is it the reverse of what we ordinarily see? Is it in front? Perhaps there is no one who can answer these riddles.

That magical town outside the bounds of the human world remains lodged in my memory. I still remember the vision of that bizarre feline town with the silhouettes of cats appearing so vividly in every window, under all the eaves, and in every gathering on the street. Even today, more than ten years later, I still relive the terror of that day by just thinking about it. I see it all over again as if it were right there in front of my eyes.

People smile coldly at my tale. They say it is the demented illusion of a poet or a nonsensical hallucination born of absentminded daydreaming. Still, I continue to insist that I did see a town of nothing but cats. I did see a town where cats took on human form and crowded the streets. Though reasoning and logic tell me otherwise, I am absolutely sure that, somewhere in this universe, I did encounter such a place. Nothing is more certain to me than this. The entire population of the world can stand before me and snicker, but I will not abandon my faith in that strange settlement described in the legends of the backwoods. Somewhere, in some corner of this universe, a town is inhabited solely by the spirits of cats. Sure enough, it does exist.

Leonora Carrington (1917–2011) was a British-born Mexican painter and writer in the Surrealist movement. Her tales are whimsical and humorous but also often, simultaneously, creepy and uncomfortable. The symbolism she used often reflects her life and her emotions at the time and gave everything she wrote a dreamlike quality. Many stories feature starvation or bizarre feasts, such as the one in "The Debutante" (1937). Finally collected in one volume in 2017, Carrington's stories, some originally published in French, are just as memorable as her paintings, each one surprising and emotional. They were also a major influence on post–World War II fantasists such as Angela Carter.

The Debutante

Leonora Carrington

WHEN I WAS A DEBUTANTE I often went to the zoological garden. I went so often that I was better acquainted with animals than with the young girls of my age. It was to escape from the world that I found myself each day at the zoo. The beast I knew best was a young hyena. She knew me too. She was extremely intelligent; I taught her French and in return she taught me her language. We spent many pleasant hours in this way.

For the first of May my mother had arranged a ball in my honor. For entire nights I suffered: I had always detested balls, above all those given in my own honor.

On the morning of May first, 1934, very early, I went to visit the hyena. "What a mess of shit," I told her. "I must go to my ball this evening."

"You're lucky," she said. "I would go happily. I do not know how to dance, but after all, I could engage in conversation."

"There will be many things to eat," said I. "I

have seen wagons loaded entirely with food coming up to the house."

"And you complain!" replied the hyena with disgust. "As for me, I eat only once a day, and what rubbish they stick me with!"

I had a bold idea; I almost laughed. "You have only to go in my place."

"We do not look enough alike, otherwise I would gladly go," said the hyena, a little sad.

"Listen," said I, "in the evening light one does not see very well. If you were disguised a little, no one would notice in the crowd. Besides, we are almost the same size. You are my only friend; I implore you."

She reflected upon this sentiment. I knew that she wanted to accept. "It is done," she said suddenly.

It was very early; not many keepers were about. Quickly I opened the cage and in a moment we were in the street. I took a taxi; at the house, everyone was in bed. In my room, I brought out the gown I was supposed to wear that evening. It was a little long, and the hyena walked with difficulty in my high-heeled shoes. I found some gloves to disguise her hands which were too hairy to resemble mine. When the sunlight entered, she strolled around the room several times—walking more or less correctly. We were so very occupied that my mother, who came to tell me good morning, almost opened the door before the hyena could hide herself under my bed. "There is a bad odor in the room," said my mother, opening the window. "Before this evening you must take a perfumed bath with my new salts."

"Agreed," said I. She did not stay long; I believe the odor was too strong for her. "Do not be late for breakfast," she said, as she left the room.

The greatest difficulty was to find a disguise for the hyena's face. For hours and hours we sought an answer: she rejected all of my proposals. At last she said, "I think I know a solution. You have a maid?"

"Yes," I said, perplexed.

"Well, that's it. You will ring for the maid and when she enters we will throw ourselves upon her and remove her face. I will wear her face this evening in place of my own."

"That's not practical," I said to her. "She will probably die when she has no more face; someone will surely find the corpse and we will go to prison."

"I am hungry enough to eat her," replied the hyena.

"And the bones?"

"Those too," she said.

"Then it's settled?"

"Only if you agree to kill her before removing her face. It would be too uncomfortable otherwise."

"Good; it's all right with me." I rang for Marie, the maid, with a certain nervousness. I would not have done it if I did not detest dances

so much. When Marie entered I turned to the wall so as not to see. I admit that it was done quickly. A brief cry and it was over. While the hyena ate, I looked out the window. A few minutes later, she said: "I cannot eat anymore; the two feet are left, but if you have a little bag I will eat them later in the day."

"You will find in the wardrobe a bag embroidered with fleurs de lys. Remove the handkerchiefs inside it and take it." She did as I indicated.

At last she said: "Turn around now and look, because I am beautiful!" Before the mirror, the hyena admired herself in Marie's face. She had eaten very carefully all around the face so that what was left was just what was needed. "Surely, it's properly done," said I.

Toward evening, when the hyena was all dressed, she declared: "I am in a very good mood. I have the impression that I will be a great success this evening." When the music below had been heard for some time, I said to her: "Go now, and remember not to place yourself at my mother's side: she will surely know that it is not I. Otherwise I know no one. Good luck." I embraced her as we parted, but she smelled very strong.

Night had fallen. Exhausted by the emotions of the day, I took a book and sat down by the open window. I remember that I was reading *Gulliver's Travels* by Jonathan Swift. It was perhaps an hour later that the first sign of misfortune announced itself. A bat entered through the window, emitting little cries. I am terribly afraid of bats, I hid behind a chair, my teeth chattering. Scarcely was I on my knees when the beating of the wings was drowned out by a great commotion at my door. My mother entered, pale with rage. "We were coming to seat ourselves at the table," she said, "when the thing who was in your place rose and cried: 'I smell a little strong, eh? Well, as for me, I do not eat cake.' With these words she removed her face and ate it. A great leap and she disappeared out the window."

Fritz Reuter Leiber, Jr. (1910–1992), or Fritz Leiber, was an American writer born in Chicago who also performed as an actor and was a poet and playwright. His earlier fiction was characterized by horror, but later he began writing more fantastical pieces, including satirical science fiction. He published his first story, "Two Sought Adventure" (1939), after he had already begun his acting career. Leiber was a pivotal figure in the development of modern fantasy, horror, and science fiction—in part by setting his horror in modern settings. Leiber later retitled "Two Sought Adventure," the story reprinted here, to "The Jewels in the Forest." The story introduced strangely believable characters that would reappear in almost forty more stories over a span of fifty years. This is the tale that galvanized his shift from acting to writing. It is also the tale that began the saga of Fahfrd and the Gray Mouser, two of the most famous characters in all of heroic fantasy.

The Jewels in the Forest

Fritz Leiber

IT WAS THE YEAR OF THE BEHEMOTH, the Month of the Hedgehog, the Day of the Toad. A hot, late summer sun was sinking down toward evening over the somber, fertile land of Lankhmar. Peasants toiling in the endless grain fields paused for a moment and lifted their earth-stained faces and noted that it would soon be time to commence lesser chores. Cattle cropping the stubble began to move in the general direction of home. Sweaty merchants and shopkeepers decided to wait a little longer before enjoying the pleasures of the bath. Thieves and astrologers moved restlessly in their sleep, sensing that the hours of night and work were drawing near.

At the southernmost limit of the land of Lankhmar, a day's ride beyond the village of Soreev, where the grain fields give way to rolling forests of maple and oak, two horsemen cantered leisurely along a narrow, dusty road. They presented a sharp contrast. The larger wore a tunic of unbleached linen, drawn tight at the waist by a very broad leather belt. A fold of linen cloak was looped over his head as a protection against the sun. A longsword with a pomegranate-shaped golden pommel was strapped to his side. Behind his right shoulder a quiver of arrows jutted up. Half sheathed in a saddlecase was a thick yew bow, unstrung. His great, lean muscles, white skin, copper hair, green eyes, and above all the pleasant yet untamed expression of his massive countenance, all hinted at a land of origin colder, rougher, and more barbarous than that of Lankhmar.

Even as everything about the larger man suggested the wilderness, so the general appearance of the smaller man—and he was considerably smaller—spoke of the city. His dark face was that of a jester. Bright, black eyes, snub nose, and little lines of irony about the mouth. Hands of a conjurer. Something about the set of his wiry frame betokening exceptional competence in street fights and tavern brawls. He was clad from head to foot in garments of gray silk, soft and curiously loose of weave. His slim sword, cased in gray mouseskin, was slightly curved toward the tip. From his belt hung a sling and a pouch of missiles.

Despite their many dissimilarities, it was obvious that the two men were comrades, that they were united by a bond of subtle mutual understanding, woven of melancholy, humor, and many another strand. The smaller rode a dappled gray mare; the larger, a chestnut gelding.

They were nearing a point where the narrow road came to the end of a rise, made a slight turn and wound down into the next valley. Green walls of leaves pressed in on either side. The heat was considerable, but not oppressive. It brought to mind thoughts of satyrs and centaurs dozing in hidden glades.

Then the gray mare, slightly in the lead, whinnied. The smaller man tightened his hold on the reins, his black eyes darting quick, alert glances, first to one side of the road and then to the other. There was a faint scraping sound, as of wood on wood.

Without warning the two men ducked down, clinging to the side harness of their horses. Simultaneously came the musical twang of bowstrings, like the prelude of some forest concert, and several arrows buzzed angrily through the spaces that had just been vacated. Then the mare and the gelding were around the turn and galloping like the wind, their hooves striking up great puffs of dust.

From behind came excited shouts and answers as the pursuit got underway. There seemed to have been fully seven or eight men in the ambuscade—squat, sturdy rogues wearing chainmail shirts and steel caps. Before the mare and the gelding had gone a stone's throw down the road, they were out and after, a black horse in the lead, a black-bearded rider second.

But those pursued were not wasting time. The larger man rose to a stand in his stirrups, whipping the yew bow from its case. With his left hand he bent it against the stirrup, with his right he drew the upper loop of the string into place. Then his left hand slipped down the bow to the grip and his right reached smoothly back over his shoulder for an arrow. Still guiding his horse with his knees, he rose even higher and turned in his saddle and sent an eagle-feathered shaft whirring. Meanwhile his comrade had placed a small leaden ball in his sling, whirled it twice about his head, so that it hummed stridently, and loosed his cast.

Arrow and missile sped and struck together. The one pierced the shoulder of the leading horseman and the other smote the second on his steel cap and tumbled him from his saddle. The pursuit halted abruptly in a tangle of plunging and rearing horses. The men who had caused this confusion pulled up at the next bend in the road and turned back to watch.

"By the Hedgehog," said the smaller, grinning wickedly, "but they will think twice before they play at ambuscades again!"

"Blundering fools," said the larger. "Haven't they even learned to shoot from their saddles? I tell you, Gray Mouser, it takes a barbarian to fight his horse properly."

"Except for myself and a few other people," replied the one who bore the feline nickname of Gray Mouser. "But look, Fafhrd, the rogues retreat bearing their wounded, and one gallops far ahead. *Tcha*, but I dinted black beard's pate for him. He hangs over his nag like a bag of meal. If he'd have known who we were, he wouldn't have been so hot on the chase."

There was some truth to this last boast. The names of the Gray Mouser and the Northerner Fafhrd were not unknown in the lands around Lankhmar—and in proud Lankhmar, too. Their taste for strange adventure, their mysterious comings and goings, and their odd sense of humor were matters that puzzled almost all men alike.

Abruptly Fafhrd unstrung his bow and turned forward in his saddle.

"This should be the very valley we are seeking," he said. "See, there are the two hills, each with two close-set humps, of which the document speaks. Let's have another look at it, to test my guess."

The Gray Mouser reached into his capacious leather pouch and withdrew a page of thick vellum, ancient and curiously greenish. Three edges were frayed and worn; the fourth showed a clean and recent cut. It was inscribed with the intricate hieroglyphs of Lankhmarian writing, done in the black ink of the squid. But it was not to these that the Mouser turned his attention, but to several faint lines of diminutive red script, written into the margin. These he read.

"Let kings stack their treasure houses ceiling-high, and merchants burst their vaults with hoarded coin, and fools envy them. I have a treasure that outvalues theirs. A diamond as big as a man's skull. Twelve rubies each as big as the skull of a cat. Seventeen emeralds each as big as the skull of a mole. And certain rods of crystal and bars of orichalcum. Let Overlords swagger jewel-bedecked and queens load themselves with gems, and fools adore them. I have a treasure that will outlast theirs. A treasure house have I builded for it in the far southern forest, where the two hills hump double, like sleeping camels, a day's ride beyond the village of Soreev.

"A great treasure house with a high tower, fit for a king's dwelling—yet no king may dwell there. Immediately below the keystone of the chief dome my treasure lies hid, eternal as the glittering stars. It will outlast me and my name, I, Urgaan of Angarngi. It is my hold on the future. Let fools seek it. They shall win it not. For although my treasure house be empty as air, no deadly creature in rocky lair, no sentinel outside anywhere, no pitfall, poison, trap, or snare, above and below the whole place bare, of demon or devil not a hair, no serpent lethal-fanged yet fair, no skull with mortal eye a-glare, yet have I left a guardian there. Let the wise read this riddle and forbear."

"The man's mind runs to skulls," muttered the Mouser. "He must have been a gravedigger or a necromancer."

"Or an architect," observed Fafhrd thoughtfully, "in those past days when graven images of the skulls of men and animals served to bedeck temples."

"Perhaps," agreed the Mouser. "Surely the writing and ink are old enough. They date at least as far back as the Century of the Wars with the East—five long lifespans."

The Mouser was an accomplished forger, both of handwriting and of objects of art. He knew what he was talking about.

Satisfied that they were near the goal of their quest, the two comrades gazed through a break in the foliage down into the valley. It was shaped like the inside of a pod—shallow, long, and narrow. They were viewing it from one of the narrow ends. The two peculiarly humped hills formed the long sides. The whole of the valley was green with maple and oak, save for a small gap toward the middle. That, thought the Mouser, might mark a peasant's dwelling and the cleared space around it.

Beyond the gap he could make out something dark and squarish rising a little above the treetops. He called his companion's attention to it, but they could not decide whether it was indeed a tower such as the document mentioned, or just a peculiar shadow, or perhaps even the dead, limbless trunk of a gigantic oak. It was too far away.

"Almost sufficient time has passed," said Fafhrd, after a pause, "for one of those rogues to have sneaked up through the forest for another shot at us. Evening draws near."

They spoke to their horses and moved on slowly. They tried to keep their eyes fixed on the thing that looked like a tower, but since they were descending, it almost immediately dropped out of sight below the treetops. There would be no further chance of seeing it until they were quite close at hand.

The Mouser felt a subdued excitement running through his flesh. Soon they would discover if there was a treasure to be had or not. A diamond as big as a man's skull . . . rubies . . . emeralds . . . He found an almost nostalgic delight in prolonging and savoring to the full this last, leisurely stage of their quest. The recent ambuscade served as a necessary spice.

He thought of how he had slit the interesting-looking vellum page from the ancient book on architecture that reposed in the library of the rapacious and overbearing Lord Rannarsh. Of how, half in jest, he had sought out and interrogated several peddlers from the South. Of how he had found one who had recently passed through a village named Soreev. Of how that one had told him of a stone structure in the forest south of Soreev, called by the peasants the House of Angarngi and reputed to be long deserted. The peddler had seen a high tower rising above the trees. The Mouser recalled the man's wizened, cunning face and chuckled. And that brought to mind the greedy, sallow face of Lord Rannarsh, and a new thought occurred to him.

"Fafhrd," he said, "those rogues we just now put to flight—what did you take them for?"

The Northerner grunted humorous contempt.

"Run-of-the-manger ruffians. Waylayers of fat merchants. Pasture bravos. Bumpkin bandits!"

"Still, they were all well armed, and armed alike—as if they were in some rich man's service. And that one who rode far ahead. Mightn't he have been hastening to report failure to some master?"

"What is your thought?"

The Mouser did not reply for some moments.

"I was thinking," he said, "that Lord Rannarsh is a rich man and a greedy one, who slavers at the thought of jewels. And I was wondering if he ever read those faint lines of red lettering and made a copy of them, and if my theft of the original sharpened his interest."

The Northerner shook his head.

"I doubt it. You are oversubtle. But if he did, and if he seeks to rival us in this treasure quest, he'd best watch each step twice—and choose servitors who can fight on horseback."

They were moving so slowly that the hooves of the mare and the gelding hardly stirred up the dust. They had no fear of danger from the rear. A well-laid ambuscade might surprise them, but not a man or horse in motion. The narrow road wound along in a purposeless fashion. Leaves brushed their faces, and occasionally they had to swing their bodies out of the way of encroaching branches. The ripe scent of the late summer forest was intensified now that they were below the rim of the valley. Mingled with it were whiffs of wild berries and aromatic shrubs. Shadows imperceptibly lengthened.

"Nine chances out of ten," murmured the Mouser dreamily, "the treasure house of Urgaan of Angarngi was looted some hundred years ago, by men whose bodies are already dust."

"It may be so," agreed Fafhrd. "Unlike men, rubies and emeralds do not rest quietly in their graves."

This possibility, which they had discussed several times before, did not disturb them now, or make them impatient. Rather did it impart to their quest the pleasant melancholy of a lost hope. They drank in the rich air and let their horses munch random mouthfuls of leaves. A jay called shrilly from overhead and off in the forest a catbird was chattering, their sharp voices breaking in on the low buzzing and droning of the insects. Night was drawing near. The almost-horizontal rays of the sun gilded the treetops. Then Fafhrd's sharp ears caught the hollow lowing of a cow.

A few more turns brought them into the clearing they had spied. In line with their surmise, it proved to contain a peasant's cottage—a neat little low-eaved house of weathered wood, situated in the midst of an acre of grain. To one side was a bean patch; to the other, a woodpile which almost dwarfed the house. In front of the cottage stood a wiry old man, his skin as brown as his homespun tunic. He had evidently just heard the horses and turned around to look.

"Ho, father," called the Mouser, "it's a good day to be abroad in, and a good home you have here."

The peasant considered these statements and then nodded his head in agreement.

"We are two weary travelers," continued the Mouser.

Again the peasant nodded gravely.

"In return for two silver coins will you give us lodging for the night?"

The peasant rubbed his chin and then held up three fingers.

"Very well, you shall have three silver coins," said the Mouser, slipping from his horse. Fafhrd followed suit.

Only after giving the old man a coin to seal the bargain did the Mouser question casually, "Is there not an old, deserted place near your dwelling called the House of Angarngi?" The peasant nodded.

"What's it like?"

The peasant shrugged his shoulders.

"Don't you know?"

The peasant shook his head.

"But haven't you ever seen the place?" The Mouser's voice carried a note of amazement he did not bother to conceal.

He was answered by another head-shake.

"But, father, it's only a few minutes' walk from your dwelling, isn't it?"

The peasant nodded tranquilly, as if the whole business were no matter for surprise.

A muscular young man, who had come from behind the cottage to take their horses, offered a suggestion.

"You can see tower from other side the house. I can point her out."

At this the old man proved he was not completely speechless by saying in a dry, expressionless voice: "Go ahead. Look at her all you want."

And he stepped into the cottage. Fafhrd and the Mouser caught a glimpse of a child peering around the door, an old woman stirring a pot, and someone hunched in a big chair before a tiny fire.

The upper part of the tower proved to be barely visible through a break in the trees. The last rays of the sun touched it with deep red. It looked about four or five bowshots distant. And then, even as they watched, the sun dipped under and it became a featureless square of black stone.

"She's an old place," explained the young man vaguely. "I been all around her. Father, he's just never bothered to look."

"You've been inside?" questioned the Mouser.

The young man scratched his head.

"No. She's just an old place. No good for anything."

"There'll be a fairly long twilight," said Fafhrd, his wide green eyes drawn to the tower as if by a lodestone. "Long enough for us to have a closer look."

"I'd show the way," said the young man, "save I got water to fetch."

"No matter," replied Fafhrd. "When's supper?"

"When the first stars show."

They left him holding their horses and walked straight into the woods. Immediately it became much darker, as if twilight were almost over, rather than just begun. The vegetation proved to be somewhat thicker than they had anticipated. There were vines and thorns to be avoided. Irregular, pale patches of sky appeared and disappeared overhead.

The Mouser let Fafhrd lead the way. His mind was occupied with a queer sort of reverie about the peasants. It tickled his fancy to think how they had stolidly lived their toilsome lives, generation after generation, only a few steps from what might be one of the greatest treasure-troves in the world. It seemed incredible. How could people sleep so near jewels and not dream of them? But probably they never dreamed.

So the Gray Mouser was sharply aware of few things during the journey through the woods, save that Fafhrd seemed to be taking a long time—which was strange, since the barbarian was an accomplished woodsman.

Finally a deeper and more solid shadow loomed up through the trees, and in a moment they were standing in the margin of a small, boulder-studded clearing, most of which was occupied by the bulky structure they sought.

Abruptly, even before his eyes took in the details of the place, the Mouser's mind was filled with a hundred petty perturbations. Weren't they making a mistake in leaving their horses with those strange peasants? And mightn't those rogues have followed them to the cottage? And wasn't this the Day of the Toad, an unlucky day for entering deserted houses? And shouldn't they have a short spear along, in case they met a leopard? And wasn't that a whippoorwill he heard crying on his left hand, an augury of ill omen?

The treasure house of Urgaan of Angarngi was a peculiar structure. The main feature was a large, shallow dome, resting on walls that formed an octagon. In front, and merging into it, were two lesser domes. Between these gaped a great square doorway. The tower rose asymmetrically from the rear part of the chief dome. The eyes of the Mouser sought hurriedly through the dimming twilight for the cause of the salient peculiarity of the structure, and decided it lay in the utter simplicity. There were no pillars, no outjutting cornices, no friezes, no architectural ornaments of any sort, skull-embellished or otherwise. Save for the doorway and a few tiny windows set in unexpected places, the House of Angarngi was a compact mass of uniformly dark gray stones most closely joined.

But now Fafhrd was striding up the short flight of terraced steps that led toward the open door, and the Mouser followed him, although he would have liked to spy around a little longer. With every step he took forward he sensed an odd reluctance growing within him. His earlier mood of pleasant expectancy vanished as suddenly as if he'd stepped into quicksand. It seemed to him that the black doorway yawned like a toothless mouth. And then a little shudder went through him, for he saw the mouth had a tooth—a bit of ghostly white that jutted up from the floor. Fafhrd was reaching down toward the object.

"I wonder whose skull this may be?" said the Northerner calmly.

The Mouser regarded the thing, and the scattering of bones and fragments of bone beside it.

His feeling of uneasiness was fast growing toward a climax, and he had the unpleasant conviction that, once it did reach a climax, something would happen. What was the answer to Fafhrd's question? What form of death had struck down that earlier intruder? It was very dark inside the treasure house. Didn't the manuscript mention something about a guardian? It was hard to think of a flesh-and-blood guardian persisting for three hundred years, but there were things that were immortal or nearly immortal. He could tell that Fafhrd was not in the least affected by any premonitory disquietude, and was quite capable of instituting an immediate search for the treasure. That must be prevented at all costs. He remembered that the Northerner loathed snakes.

"This cold, damp stone," he observed casually. "Just the place for scaly, cold-blooded snakes."

"Nothing of the sort," replied Fafhrd angrily. "I'm willing to wager there's not a single serpent inside. Urgaan's note said, 'No deadly creature in rocky lair,' and to cap that, 'no serpent lethal-fanged yet fair.'"

"I am not thinking of guardian snakes Urgaan may have left here," the Mouser explained, "but only of serpents that may have wandered in for the night. Just as that skull you hold is not one set there by Urgaan 'with mortal eye a-glare,' but merely the brain-case of some unfortunate wayfarer who chanced to perish here."

"I don't know," Fafhrd said, calmly eyeing the skull.

"Its orbits might glow phosphorescently in absolute dark."

A moment later he was agreeing it would be well to postpone the search until daylight returned, now that the treasure house was located. He carefully replaced the skull.

As they reentered the woods, the Mouser heard a little inner voice whispering to him, *Just in time. Just in time.* Then the sense of uneasiness departed as suddenly as it had come, and he began to feel somewhat ridiculous. This caused him to sing a bawdy ballad of his own invention, wherein demons and other supernatural agents were ridiculed obscenely. Fafhrd chimed in good-naturedly on the choruses.

It was not as dark as they expected when they reached the cottage. They saw to their horses, found they had been well cared for, and then fell to the savory mess of beans, porridge, and pot herbs that the peasant's wife ladled into oak bowls. Fresh milk to wash it down was provided in quaintly carved oak goblets. The meal was a satisfying one and the interior of the house was neat and clean, despite its stamped earthen floor and low beams, which Fafhrd had to duck.

There turned out to be six in the family, all told. The father, his equally thin and leathery wife, the older son, a young boy, a daughter, and a mumbling grandfather, whom extreme age confined to a chair before the fire. The last two were the most interesting of the lot.

The girl was in the gawkish age of mid-adolescence, but there was a wild, coltish grace in the way she moved her lanky legs and slim arms with their prominent elbows. She was very shy, and gave the impression that at any moment she might dart out the door and into the woods.

In order to amuse her and win her confidence, the Mouser began to perform small feats of leg-erdemain, plucking copper coins out of the ears of the astonished peasant, and bone needles from the nose of his giggling wife. He turned beans into buttons and back again into beans, swallowed a large fork, made a tiny wooden manikin jig on the palm of his hand, and utterly bewildered the cat by pulling what seemed to be a mouse out of its mouth.

The old folks gaped and grinned. The little boy became frantic with excitement. His sister watched everything with concentrated interest, and even smiled warmly when the Mouser presented her with a square of fine, green linen he had conjured from the air, although she was still too shy to speak.

Then Fafhrd roared sea-chanteys that rocked the roof and sang lusty songs that set the old grandfather gurgling with delight. Meanwhile the Mouser fetched a small wineskin from his saddlebags, concealed it under his cloak, and filled the oak goblets as if by magic. These rapidly fuddled the peasants, who were unused to so potent a beverage, and by the time Fafhrd had finished telling a bloodcurdling tale of the frozen north, they were all nodding, save the girl and the grandfather.

The latter looked up at the merry-making adventurers, his watery eyes filled with a kind of impish, senile glee, and mumbled, "You two be right clever men. Maybe you be beast-dodgers." But before this remark could be elucidated, his eyes had gone vacant again, and in a few moments he was snoring.

Soon all were asleep, Fafhrd and the Mouser keeping their weapons close at hand, but only variegated snores and occasional snaps from the dying embers disturbed the silence of the cottage.

The Day of the Cat dawned clear and cool. The Mouser stretched himself luxuriously and, catlike, flexed his muscles and sucked in the sweet, dewy air. He felt exceptionally cheerful and eager to be up and doing. Was not this his day, the day of the Gray Mouser, a day in which luck could not fail him?

His slight movements awakened Fafhrd and together they stole silently from the cottage so as not to disturb the peasants, who were oversleeping with the wine they had taken. They refreshed their faces and hands in the wet grass and visited their horses. Then they munched some bread, washed it down with drafts of cool well water flavored with wine, and made ready to depart.

This time their preparations were well thought out. The Mouser carried a mallet and a stout iron pry-bar, in case they had to attack masonry, and made certain that candles, flint, wedges, chisels, and several other small tools were in his pouch. Fafhrd borrowed a pick from the peasant's implements and tucked a coil of thin, strong rope in his belt. He also took his bow and quiver of arrows.

The forest was delightful at this early hour. Bird cries and chatterings came from overhead, and once they glimpsed a black, squirrel-like animal scampering along a bough. A couple of chipmunks scurried under a bush dotted with red berries. What had been shadow the evening before was now a variety of green-leafed beauty. The two adventurers trod softly.

They had hardly gone more than a bowshot into the woods when they heard a faint rustling behind them. The rustling came rapidly nearer, and suddenly the peasant girl burst into view. She stood breathless and poised, one hand touching a treetrunk, the other pressing some leaves, ready to fly away at the first sudden move. Fafhrd and the Mouser stood as stock-still as if she were a doe or a dryad. Finally she managed to conquer her shyness and speak.

"You go there?" she questioned, indicating the direction of the treasure house with a quick, ducking nod. Her dark eyes were serious.

"Yes, we go there," answered Fafhrd, smiling.

"Don't." This word was accompanied by a rapid head-shake.

"But why shouldn't we, girl?" Fafhrd's voice was gentle and sonorous, like an integral part of the forest. It seemed to touch some spring within the girl that enabled her to feel more at ease. She gulped a big breath and began.

"Because I watch it from edge of the forest, but never go close. Never, never, never. I say to myself there be a magic circle I must not cross. And I say to myself there be a giant inside. Queer and fearsome giant." Her words were coming rapidly now, like an undammed stream. "All gray he be, like the stone of his house. All gray—eyes and hair and fingernails, too. And he has a stone club as big as a tree. And he be big, bigger than you, twice as big." Here she nodded at Fafhrd. "And with his club he kills, kills, kills. But only if you go close. Every day, almost, I play a game with him. I pretend to be going to cross the magic circle. And he watches from inside the door, where I can't see him, and he thinks I'm going to cross. And I dance through the forest all around the house, and he follows me, peering from the little windows. And I get closer and closer to the circle, closer and closer. But I never cross. And he be very angry and gnash his teeth, like rocks rubbing rocks, so that the house shakes. And I run, run, run away. But you mustn't go inside. Oh, you mustn't."

She paused, as if startled by her own daring. Her eyes were fixed anxiously on Fafhrd. She seemed drawn toward him. The Northerner's reply carried no overtone of patronizing laughter.

"But you've never actually seen the gray giant, have you?"

"Oh, no. He be too cunning. But I say to myself he must be there inside. I know he be inside. And that's the same thing, isn't it? Grandfather knows about him. We used to talk about him, when I was little. Grandfather calls him the beast. But the others laugh at me, so I don't tell."

Here was another astounding peasant-paradox, thought the Mouser with an inward grin. Imagination was such a rare commodity with them that this girl unhesitatingly took it for reality.

"Don't worry about us, girl. We'll be on the watch for your gray giant," he started to say, but he had less success than Fafhrd in keeping his voice completely natural or else the cadence of his words didn't chime so well with the forest setting.

The girl uttered one more warning. "Don't go inside, oh, please," and turned and darted away. The two adventurers looked at each other and smiled. Somehow the unexpected fairy tale, with its conventional ogre and its charmingly naive narrator added to the delight of the dewy morning. Without a comment they resumed their soft-stepping progress. And it was well that they went quietly, for when they had gotten within a stone's throw of the clearing, they heard low voices that seemed to be in grumbling argument. Immediately they cached the pick and pry-bar and mallet under a clump of bushes, and stole forward, taking advantage of the natural cover and watching where they planted their feet.

On the edge of the clearing stood half a dozen stocky men in black chain-mail shirts, bows on their backs, shortswords at their sides. They were immediately recognizable as the rogues who had laid the ambuscade. Two of them started for the treasure house, only to be recalled by a comrade. Whereupon the argument apparently started afresh.

"That red-haired one," whispered the Mouser after an unhurried look. "I can swear I've seen him in the stables of Lord Rannarsh. My guess was right. It seems we have a rival."

"Why do they wait, and keep pointing at the house?" whispered Fafhrd. "Is it because some of their comrades are already at work inside?"

The Mouser shook his head. "That cannot be. See those picks and shovels and levers they have rested on the ground? No, they wait for someone—for a leader. Some of them want to examine the house before he arrives. Others counsel against it. And I will bet my head against a bowling ball that the leader is Rannarsh himself. He is much too greedy and suspicious to entrust a treasure quest to any henchmen."

"What's to do?" murmured Fafhrd. "We cannot enter the house unseen, even if it were the wise course, which it isn't. Once in, we'd be trapped."

"I've half a mind to loose my sling at them right now and teach them something about the art of ambuscade," replied the Mouser, slitting his eyes grimly. "Only then the survivors would flee into the house and hold us off until, mayhap, Rannarsh came, and more men with him."

"We might circle part way around the clearing," said Fafhrd, after a moment's pause, "keeping to the woods. Then we can enter the clearing unseen and shelter ourselves behind one of the small domes. In that way we become masters of the doorway, and can prevent their taking cover inside. Thereafter I will address them suddenly and try to frighten them off, you meanwhile staying hid and giving substance to my threats by making enough racket for ten men."

This seemed the handiest plan to both of them, and they managed the first part of it without a hitch. The Mouser crouched behind the small dome, his sword, sling, daggers, and a couple of sticks of wood laid ready for either noise-making or fight. Then Fafhrd strode briskly forward, his bow held carelessly in front of him, an arrow fitted to the string. It was done so casually that it was a few moments before Rannarsh's henchmen

noticed him. Then they quickly reached for their own bows and as quickly desisted when they saw that the huge newcomer had the advantage of them. They scowled in irritated perplexity.

"Ho, rogues!" began Fafhrd. "We allow you just as much time as it will take you to make yourselves scarce, and no more. Don't think to resist or come skulking back. My men are scattered through the woods. At a sign from me they will feather you with arrows."

Meanwhile the Mouser had begun a low din and was slowly and artistically working it up in volume. Rapidly varying the pitch and intonation of his voice and making it echo first from some part of the building and then from the forest wall, he created the illusion of a squad of bloodthirsty bowmen. Nasty cries of "Shall we let fly?" "You take the redhead," and "Try for the belly shot; it's surest," kept coming now from one point and now another, until it was all Fafhrd could do to refrain from laughing at the woebegone, startled glances the six rogues kept darting around. But his merriment was extinguished when, just as the rogues were starting to slink shamefacedly away, an arrow arched erratically out of the woods, passing a spear's length above his head.

"Curse that branch!" came a deep, guttural voice the Mouser recognized as issuing from the throat of Lord Rannarsh. Immediately after, it began to bark commands.

"At them, you fools! It's all a trick. There are only the two of them. Rush them!"

Fafhrd turned without warning and loosed point-blank at the voice, but did not silence it. Then he dodged back behind the small dome and ran with the Mouser for the woods.

The six rogues, wisely deciding that a charge with drawn swords would be overly heroic, followed suit, unslinging their bows as they went. One of them turned before he had reached sufficient cover, nocking an arrow. It was a mistake. A ball from the Mouser's sling took him low in the forehead, and he toppled forward and was still.

The sound of that hit and fall was the last

heard in the clearing for quite a long time, save for the inevitable bird cries, some of which were genuine, and some of which were communications between Fafhrd and the Mouser. The conditions of the death-dealing contest were obvious. Once it had fairly begun, no one dared enter the clearing, since he would become a fatally easy mark; and the Mouser was sure that none of the five remaining rogues had taken shelter in the treasure house. Nor did either side dare withdraw all its men out of sight of the doorway, since that would allow someone to take a commanding position in the top of the tower, providing the tower had a negotiable stair. Therefore it was a case of sneaking about near the edge of the clearing, circling and counter-circling, with a great deal of squatting in a good place and waiting for somebody to come along and be shot.

The Mouser and Fafhrd began by adopting the latter strategy, first moving about twenty paces nearer the point at which the rogues had disappeared. Evidently their patience was a little better than that of their opponents. For after about ten minutes of nerve-racking waiting, during which pointed seed pods had a queer way of looking like arrowheads, Fafhrd got the red-haired henchman full in the throat just as he was bending his bow for a shot at the Mouser. That left four besides Rannarsh himself. Immediately the two adventurers changed their tactics and separated, the Mouser circling rapidly around the treasure house and Fafhrd drawing as far back from the open space as he dared.

Rannarsh's men must have decided on the same plan, for the Mouser almost bumped into a scar-faced rogue as soft-footed as himself. At such close range, bow and sling were both useless—in their normal function. Scarface attempted to jab the barbed arrow he held into the Mouser's eye. The Mouser weaved his body to one side, swung his sling like a whip, and felled the man senseless with a blow from the horn handle. Then he retreated a few paces, thanked the Day of the Cat that there had not been two of them, and took to the trees as being a safer, though slower method

of progress. Keeping to the middle heights, he scurried along with the sure-footedness of a rope walker, swinging from branch to branch only when it was necessary, making sure he always had more than one way of retreat open.

He had completed three-quarters of his circuit when he heard the clash of swords a few trees ahead. He increased his speed and was soon looking down on a sweet little combat. Fafhrd, his back to a great oak, had his broadsword out and was holding off two of Rannarsh's henchmen, who were attacking with their shorter weapons. It was a tight spot and the Northerner realized it. He knew that ancient sagas told of heroes who could best four or more men at swordplay. He also knew that such sagas were lies, providing the hero's opponents were reasonably competent.

And Rannarsh's men were veterans. They attacked cautiously but incessantly, keeping their swords well in front of them and never slashing wildly. Their breath whistled through their nostrils, but they were grimly confident, knowing the Northerner dared not lunge strongly at one of them because it would lay him wide open to a thrust by the other. Their game was to get one on each side of him and then attack simultaneously.

Fafhrd's counter was to shift position quickly and attack the nearer one murderously before the other could get back in range. In that way he managed to keep them side by side, where he could hold their blades in check by swift feints and crosswise sweeps. Sweat beaded his face and blood dripped from a scratch on his left thigh. A fearsome grin showed his white teeth, which occasionally parted to let slip a base, primitive insult.

The Mouser took in the situation at a glance, descended rapidly to a lower bough, and poised himself, aiming a dagger at the back of one of Fafhrd's adversaries. He was, however, standing very close to the thick trunk, and around this trunk darted a horny hand tipped with a short sword. The third henchman had also thought it wise to take to the trees. Fortunately for the Mouser, the man was uncertain of his footing and therefore his thrust, although well aimed, came a shade slow. As it was the little gray-clad man only managed to dodge by dropping off.

Thereupon he startled his opponent with a modest acrobatic feat. He did not drop to the ground, knowing that would put everyone at the mercy of the man in the tree. Instead, he grabbed hold of the branch on which he had been standing, swung himself smartly up again, and grappled. Steadying themselves now with one hand, now another, they drove for each other's throats, ramming with knees and elbows whenever they got a chance. At the first onset both dagger and sword were dropped, the latter sticking point-down in the ground directly between the two battling henchmen and startling them so that Fafhrd almost got home an attack.

The Mouser and his man surged and teetered along the branch away from the trunk, inflicting little damage on each other since it was hard to keep balance. Finally they slid off at the same time, but grabbed the branch with their hands. The puffing henchman aimed a vicious kick. The Mouser escaped it by yanking up his body and doubling up his legs. The latter he let fly violently, taking the henchman full in the chest, just where the ribs stop. The unfortunate retainer of Rannarsh fell to the ground, where he had the wind knocked out of him a second time.

At the same moment one of Fafhrd's opponents tried a trick that might have turned out well. When his companion was pressing the Northerner closely, he snatched for the short-sword sticking in the ground, intending to hurl it underhanded as if it were a javelin. But Fafhrd, whose superior endurance was rapidly giving him an advantage in speed, anticipated the movement and simultaneously made a brilliant counterattack against the other man. There were two thrusts, both lightninglike, the first a feint at the belly, the second a slicing stab that sheared through the throat to the spine. Then he whirled around and, with a quick sweep, knocked both weapons out of the hands of the first man, who looked up in bewilderment and promptly collapsed into a sitting position, panting in utter exhaustion, though with enough breath left to cry, "Mercy!"

To cap the situation, the Mouser dropped lightly down, as if out of the sky. Fafhrd automatically started to raise his sword, for a backhand swipe. Then he stared at the Mouser for as long a time as it took the man sitting on the ground to give three tremendous gasps. Then he began to laugh, first uncontrollable snickers and later thundering peals. It was a laughter in which the battle-begotten madness, completely sated anger, and relief at escape from death were equally mingled.

"Oh, by Glaggerk and by Kos!" he roared. "By the Behemoth! Oh, by the Cold Waste and the guts of the Red God! Oh! Oh! Oh!" Again the insane bellowing burst out. "Oh, by the Killer Whale and the Cold Woman and her spawn!" By degrees the laughter died away, choking in his throat. He rubbed his forehead with the palm of his hand and his face became starkly grave. Then he knelt beside the man he had just slain, and straightened his limbs, and closed his eyes, and began to weep in a dignified way that would have seemed ridiculous and hypocritical in anyone but a barbarian.

Meanwhile the Mouser's reactions were nowhere near as primitive. He felt worried, ironic, and slightly sick. He understood Fafhrd's emotions, but knew that he would not feel the full force of his own for some time yet, and by then they would be deadened and somewhat choked. He peered about anxiously, fearful of an anticlimactic attack that would find his companion helpless. He counted over the tally of their opponents. Yes, the six henchmen were all accounted for. But Rannarsh himself, where was Rannarsh? He fumbled in his pouch to make sure he had not lost his good-luck talismans and amulets. His lips moved rapidly as he murmured two or three prayers and cantrips. But all the while he held his sling ready, and his eyes never once ceased their quick shifting.

From the middle of a thick clump of bushes he heard a series of agonized gasps, as the man he had felled from the tree began to regain his wind.

The henchman whom Fafhrd had disarmed, his face ashy pale from exhaustion rather than fright, was slowly edging back into the forest. The Mouser watched him carelessly, noting the comical way in which the steel cap had slipped down over his forehead and rested against the bridge of his nose. Meanwhile the gasps of the man in the bushes were taking on a less agonized quality. At almost the same instant, the two rose to their feet and stumbled off into the forest.

The Mouser listened to their blundering retreat. He was sure that there was nothing more to fear from them. They wouldn't come back. And then a little smile stole into his face, for he heard the sounds of a third person joining them in their flight. That would be Rannarsh, thought the Mouser, a man cowardly at heart and incapable of carrying on single-handed. It did not occur to him that the third person might be the man he had stunned with his sling handle.

Mostly just to be doing something, he followed them leisurely for a couple of bowshots into the forest. Their trail was impossible to miss, being marked by trampled bushes and thorns bearing tatters of cloth. It led in a beeline away from the clearing. Satisfied, he returned, going out of his way to regain the mallet, pick, and pry-bar.

He found Fafhrd tying a loose bandage around the scratch on his thigh. The Northerner's emotions had run their gamut and he was himself again. The dead man for whom he had been somberly grieving now meant no more to him than food for beetles and birds. Whereas for the Mouser it continued to be a somewhat frightening and sickening object.

"And now do we proceed with our interrupted business?" the Mouser asked.

Fafhrd nodded in a matter-of-fact manner and rose to his feet. Together they entered the rocky clearing. It came to them as a surprise how little time the fight had taken. True, the sun had moved somewhat higher, but the atmosphere was still that of early morning. The dew had not dried yet. The treasure house of Urgaan of Angarngi stood massive, featureless, grotesquely impressive.

"The peasant girl predicted the truth with-out knowing it," said the Mouser with a smile. "We played her game of 'circle-the-clearing and don't-cross-the-magic circle,' didn't we?"

The treasure house had no fears for him today. He recalled his perturbations of the previous evening, but was unable to understand them. The very idea of a guardian seemed somewhat ridiculous. There were a hundred other ways of explaining the skeleton inside the doorway.

So this time it was the Mouser who skipped into the treasure house ahead of Fafhrd. The interior was disappointing, being empty of any furnishings and as bare and unornamented as the outside walls. Just a large, low room. To either side square doorways led to the smaller domes, while to the rear a long hallway was dimly apparent, and the beginnings of a stair leading to the upper part of the main dome.

With only a casual glance at the skull and the broken skeleton, the Mouser made his way toward the stair.

"Our document," he said to Fafhrd, who was now beside him, "speaks of the treasure as resting just below the keystone of the chief dome. Therefore we must seek in the room or rooms above."

"True," answered the Northerner, glancing around. "But I wonder, Mouser, just what use this structure served. A man who builds a house solely to hide a treasure is shouting to the world that he has a treasure. Do you think it might have been a temple?"

The Mouser suddenly shrank back with a sibilant exclamation. Sprawled a little way up the stair was another skeleton, the major bones hanging together in lifelike fashion. The whole upper half of the skull was smashed to bony shards paler than those of a gray pot. "Our hosts are overly ancient and indecently naked," hissed the Mouser, angry with himself for being startled. Then he darted up the stairs to examine the grisly find. His sharp eyes picked out several objects among the bones. A rusty dagger, a tarnished gold ring that looped a knucklebone, a handful of horn buttons, and a slim, green-eaten copper cylinder. The last awakened his curiosity. He picked it up, dislodging hand-bones in the process, so that they fell apart, rattling dryly. He pried off the cap of the cylinder with his dagger point, and shook out a tightly rolled sheet of ancient parchment. This he gingerly unwound. Fafhrd and he scanned the lines of diminutive red lettering by the light from a small window on the landing above.

Mine is a secret treasure. Orichalcum have I, and crystal, and blood-red amber. Rubies and emeralds that demons would war for, and a diamond as big as the skull of a man. Yet none have seen them save I. I, Urgaan of Angarngi, scorn the flattery and the envy of fools. A fittingly lonely treasure house have I built for my jewels. There, hidden under the keystone, they may dream unperturbed until earth and sky wear away. A day's ride beyond the village of Soreev, in the valley of the two double-humped hills, lies that house, trebly-domed and single-towered. It is empty. Any fool may enter. Let him. I care not.

"The details differ slightly," murmured the Mouser, "but the phrases have the same ring as in our document."

"The man must have been mad," asserted Fafhrd, scowling. "Or else why should he carefully hide a treasure and then, with equal care, leave directions for finding it?"

"We thought our document was a memorandum or an oversight," said the Mouser thoughtfully. "Such a notion can hardly explain two documents." Lost in speculation, he turned toward the remaining section of the stair, only to find still another skull grinning at him from a shadowy angle. This time he was not startled, yet he experienced the same feeling that a fly must experience when, enmeshed in a spider's web, it sees the dangling, empty corpses of a dozen of its brothers. He began to speak rapidly.

"Nor can such a notion explain three or four or mayhap a dozen such documents. For how came these other questers here, unless each had found a written message? Urgaan of Angarngi may have been mad, but he sought deliberately to lure men here. One thing is certain: this house conceals—or did conceal—some deadly trap. Some guardian. Some giant beast, say. Or perhaps the very stones distill a poison. Perhaps

hidden springs release sword blades which stab out through cracks in the walls and then return."

"That cannot be," answered Fafhrd. "These men were killed by great, bashing blows. The ribs and spine of the first were splintered. The second had his skull cracked open. And that third one there. See! The bones of his lower body are smashed."

The Mouser started to reply. Then his face broke into an unexpected smile. He could see the conclusion to which Fafhrd's arguments were unconsciously leading—and he knew that that conclusion was ridiculous. What thing would kill with great, bashing blows? What thing but the gray giant the peasant girl had told them about? The gray giant twice as tall as a man, with his great stone club—a giant fit only for fairy tales and fantasies.

And Fafhrd returned the Mouser's smile. It seemed to him that they were making a great deal of fuss about nothing. These skeletons were suggestive enough, to be sure, but did they not represent men who had died many, many years ago—centuries ago? What guardian could outlast three centuries? Why, that was a long enough time to weary the patience of a demon! And there were no such things as demons, anyhow. And there was no earthly use in mucking around about ancient fears and horrors that were as dead as dust. The whole matter, thought Fafhrd, boiled down to something very simple. They had come to a deserted house to see if there was a treasure in it.

Agreed upon this point, the two comrades made their way up the remaining section of stair that led to the dimmer regions of the House of Angarngi. Despite their confidence, they moved cautiously and kept sharp watch on the shadows lying ahead. This was wise.

Just as they reached the top, a flash of steel spun out of the darkness. It nicked the Mouser in the shoulder as he twisted to one side. There was a metallic clash as it fell to the stone floor. The Mouser, gripped by a sudden spasm of anger and fright, ducked down and dashed rapidly through the door from which the weapon had come, straight at the danger, whatever it was.

"Dagger-tossing in the dark, eh, you slick-bellied worm?" Fafhrd heard the Mouser cry, and then he, too, had plunged through the door.

Lord Rannarsh cowered against the wall, his rich hunting garb dusty and disordered, his black, wavy hair pushed back from his forehead, his cruelly handsome face a sallow mask of hate and extreme terror. For the moment the latter emotion seemed to predominate and, oddly enough, it did not appear to be directed toward the men he had just assailed, but toward something else, something unapparent.

"O gods!" he cried. "Let me go from here. The treasure is yours. Let me out of this place. Else I am doomed. The thing has played at cat and mouse with me. I cannot bear it. I cannot bear it!"

"So now we pipe a different tune, do we?" snarled the Mouser. "First dagger-tossing, then fright and pleas!"

"Filthy coward tricks," added Fafhrd. "Skulking here safe while your henchmen died bravely."

"Safe? Safe, you say? O gods!" Rannarsh almost screamed. Then a subtle change became apparent in his rigid-muscled face. It was not that his terror decreased. If anything, that became greater. But there was added to it, over and above, a consciousness of desperate shame, a realization that he had demeaned himself ineradicably in the eyes of these two ruffians. His lips began to writhe, showing tight-clenched teeth. He extended his left hand in a gesture of supplication.

"Oh, mercy, have mercy," he cried piteously, and his right hand twitched a second dagger from his belt and hurled it underhand at Fafhrd.

The Northerner knocked aside the weapon with a swift blow of his palm, then said deliberately, "He is yours, Mouser. Kill the man."

And now it was cat against cornered rat. Lord Rannarsh whipped a gleaming sword from its gold-worked scabbard and rushed in, cutting, thrusting, stabbing. The Mouser gave ground slightly, his slim blade flickering in a defensive counterattack that was wavering and elusive, yet deadly. He brought Rannarsh's rush to a standstill. His blade moved so quickly that it seemed to weave a net of steel around the man. Then it leaped forward three times in rapid succession. At the first thrust it bent nearly double against a concealed shirt of chain mail. The second thrust pierced the belly. The third transfixed the throat. Lord Rannarsh fell to the floor, spitting and gagging, his fingers clawing at his neck. There he died.

"An evil end," said Fafhrd somberly, "although he had fairer play than he deserved, and handled his sword well. Mouser, I like not this killing, although there was surely more justice to it than the others."

The Mouser, wiping his weapon against his opponent's thigh, understood what Fafhrd meant. He felt no elation at his victory, only a cold, queasy disgust. A moment before he had been raging, but now there was no anger left in him. He pulled open his gray jerkin and inspected the dagger wound in his left shoulder. A little blood was still welling from it and trickling down his arm.

"Lord Rannarsh was no coward," he said slowly. "He killed himself, or at least caused his own death, because we had seen him terrified and heard him cry in fright."

And at these words, without any warning whatsoever, stark terror fell like an icy eclipse upon the hearts of the Gray Mouser and Fafhrd. It was as if Lord Rannarsh had left them a legacy of fear, which passed to them immediately upon his death. And the unmanning thing about it was that they had no premonitory apprehension, no hint of its approach. It did not take root and grow gradually greater. It came all at once, paralyzing, overwhelming. Worse still, there was no discernible cause. One moment they were looking down with something of indifference upon the twisted corpse of Lord Rannarsh. The next moment their legs were weak, their guts were cold, their spines prickling, their teeth clicking, their hearts pounding, their hair lifting at the roots.

Fafhrd felt as if he had walked unsuspecting into the jaws of a gigantic serpent. His barbaric mind was stirred to the deeps. He thought of the grim god Kos brooding alone in the icy silence of the Cold Waste. He thought of the masked powers Fate and Chance, and of the game they play for the blood and brains of men. And he did not will these thoughts. Rather did the freezing fear seem to crystallize them, so that they dropped into his consciousness like snowflakes.

Slowly he regained control over his quaking limbs and twitching muscles. As if in a nightmare, he looked around him slowly, taking in the details of his surroundings. The room they were in was semicircular, forming half of the great dome. Two small windows, high in the curving ceiling, let in light.

An inner voice kept repeating, *Don't make a sudden move. Slowly. Slowly. Above all, don't run. The others did. That was why they died so quickly. Slowly. Slowly.*

He saw the Mouser's face. It reflected his own terror. He wondered how much longer this would last, how much longer he could stand it without running amok, how much longer he could passively endure this feeling of a great invisible paw reaching out over him, span by span, implacably.

The faint sound of footsteps came from the room below. Regular and unhurried footsteps. Now they were crossing into the rear hallway below. Now they were on the stairs. And now they had reached the landing, and were advancing up the second section of the stairs.

The man who entered the room was tall and frail and old and very gaunt. Scant locks of intensely black hair straggled down over his high-domed forehead. His sunken cheeks showed clearly the outlines of his long jawbone, and waxy skin was pulled tight over his small nose. Fanatical eyes burned in deep, bony sockets. He wore the simple, sleeveless robe of a holy man. A pouch hung from the cord round his waist.

He fixed his eyes upon Fafhrd and the Gray Mouser.

"I greet you, you men of blood," he said in a hollow voice. Then his gaze fell with displeasure upon the corpse of Rannarsh.

"More blood has been shed. It is not well."

And with the bony forefinger of his left hand he traced in the air a curious triple square, the sign sacred to the Great God.

"Do not speak," his calm, toneless voice continued, "for I know your purposes. You have come to take treasure from this house. Others have sought to do the same. They have failed. You will fail. As for myself, I have no lust for treasure. For forty years I have lived on crusts and water, devoting my spirit to the Great God." Again he traced the curious sign. "The gems and ornaments of this world and the jewels and gauds of the world of demons cannot tempt or corrupt me. My purpose in coming here is to destroy an evil thing.

"I"—and here he touched his chest—"I am Arvlan of Angarngi, the ninth lineal descendant of Urgaan of Angarngi. This I always knew, and sorrowed for, because Urgaan of Angarngi was a man of evil. But not until fifteen days ago, on the Day of the Spider, did I discover from ancient documents that Urgaan had built this house, and built it to be an eternal trap for the unwise and venturesome. He has left a guardian here, and that guardian has endured.

"Cunning was my accursed ancestor, Urgaan, cunning and evil. The most skillful architect in all Lankhmar was Urgaan, a man wise in the ways of stone and learned in geometrical lore. But he scorned the Great God. He longed for improper powers. He had commerce with demons, and won from them an unnatural treasure. But he had no use for it. For in seeking wealth and knowledge and power, he lost his ability to enjoy any good feeling or pleasure, even simple lust. So he hid his treasure, but hid it in such a way that it would wreak endless evil on the world, even as he felt men and one proud, contemptuous, cruel woman—as heartless as this fane—had wreaked evil upon him. It is my purpose and my right to destroy Urgaan's evil.

"Seek not to dissuade me, lest doom fall upon you. As for me, no harm can befall me. The hand of the Great God is poised above me, ready to ward off any danger that may threaten his faithful servant. His will is my will. Do not speak, men of blood! I go to destroy the treasure of Urgaan of Angarngi."

And with these words, the gaunt holy man walked calmly on, with measured stride, like an apparition, and disappeared through the narrow doorway that led into the forward part of the great dome.

Fafhrd stared after him, his green eyes wide, feeling no desire to follow or to interfere. His terror had not left him but it was transmuted. He was still aware of a dreadful threat, but it no longer seemed to be directed against him personally.

Meanwhile, a most curious notion had lodged in the mind of the Mouser. He felt that he had just now seen, not a venerable holy man, but a dim reflection of the centuries-dead Urgaan of Angarngi. Surely Urgaan had that same high-domed forehead, that same secret pride, that same air of command. And those locks of youthfully black hair, which contrasted so ill with the aged face also seemed part of a picture looming from the past. A picture dimmed and distorted by time, but retaining something of the power and individuality of the ancient original.

They heard the footsteps of the holy man proceed a little way into the other room. Then for the space of a dozen heartbeats there was complete silence. Then the floor began to tremble slightly under their feet, as if the earth were quaking, or as if a giant were treading near. Then there came a single quavering cry from the next room, cut off in the middle by a single sickening crash that made them lurch. Then, once again, utter silence.

Fafhrd and the Mouser looked at one another in blank amazement—not so much because of what they had just heard but because, almost at the moment of the crash, the pall of terror had lifted from them completely. They jerked out their swords and hurried into the next room.

It was a duplicate of the one they had quitted, save that instead of two small windows, there were three, one of them near the floor. Also, there was but a single door, the one through which they had just entered. All else was closely mortised stone—floor, walls, and hemidomed ceiling.

Near the thick center wall, which bisected the dome, lay the body of the holy man. Only "lay" was not the right word. Left shoulder and chest were mashed against the floor. Life was fled. Blood puddled around.

Fafhrd's and the Mouser's eyes searched wildly for a being other than themselves and the dead man and found none—no, not one gnat hovering amongst the dust motes revealed by the narrow shafts of sunlight shooting down through the windows. Their imaginations searched as wildly and as much in vain for a being that could strike such a man-killing blow and vanish through one of the three tiny orifices of the windows. A giant, striking serpent with a granite head . . .

Set in the wall near the dead man was a stone about two feet square, jutting out a little from the rest. On this was boldly engraved, in antique Lankhmarian hieroglyphs: "Here rests the treasure of Urgaan of Angarngi."

The sight of that stone was like a blow in the face to the two adventurers. It roused every ounce of obstinacy and reckless determination in them. What matter that an old man sprawled smashed beside it? They had their swords! What matter they now had proof some grim guardian resided in the treasure house? They could take care of themselves! Run away and leave that stone unmoved, with its insultingly provocative inscription? No, by Kos, and the Behemoth! They'd see themselves in Nehwon's hell first!

Fafhrd ran to fetch the pick and the other large tools, which had been dropped on the stairs when Lord Rannarsh tossed his first dagger. The Mouser looked more closely at the jutting stone. The cracks around it were wide and filled with a dark, tarry mixture. It gave out a slightly hollow sound when he tapped it with his sword hilt. He calculated that the wall was about six feet thick at this point—enough to contain a sizable cavity. He tapped experimentally along the wall in both directions, but the hollow ring quickly ceased. Evidently the cavity was a fairly small one. He noted that the crevices between all the other stones were very fine, showing no evidence of any cementing substance whatsoever. In fact, he couldn't be sure that they weren't false crevices, superficial cuts in the surface of solid rock. But that hardly seemed possible. He heard Fafhrd returning, but continued his examination.

The state of the Mouser's mind was peculiar. A dogged determination to get at the treasure overshadowed other emotions. The inexplicably sudden vanishing of his former terror had left certain parts of his mind benumbed. It was as if he had decided to hold his thoughts in leash until he had seen what the treasure cavity contained. He was content to keep his mind occupied with material details, and yet make no deductions from them.

His calmness gave him a feeling of at least temporary safety. His experiences had vaguely convinced him that the guardian, whatever it was, which had smashed the holy man and played cat and mouse with Rannarsh and themselves, did not strike without first inspiring a premonitory terror in its victims.

Fafhrd felt very much the same way, except that he was even more single-minded in his determination to solve the riddle of the inscribed stone.

They attacked the wide crevices with chisel and mallet. The dark tarry mixture came away fairly easily, first in hard lumps, later in slightly rubbery, gouged strips. After they had cleared it away to the depth of a finger, Fafhrd inserted the pick and managed to move the stone slightly. Thus the Mouser was enabled to gouge a little more deeply on that side. Then Fafhrd subjected the other side of the stone to the leverage of the pick. So the work proceeded, with alternate pryings and gougings.

They concentrated on each detail of the job with unnecessary intensity, mainly to keep their imaginations from being haunted by the image of a man more than two hundred years dead. A man with high-domed forehead, sunken cheeks, nose of a skull—that is, if the dead thing on the floor was a true type of the breed of Angarngi. A man who had somehow won a great treasure, and then hid it away from all eyes, seeking to obtain nei-

ther glory nor material profit from it. Who said he scorned the envy of fools, and who yet wrote many provocative notes in diminutive red lettering in order to inform fools of his treasure and make them envious. Who seemed to be reaching out across the dusty centuries, like a spider spinning a web to catch a fly on the other side of the world.

And yet, he was a skillful architect, the holy man had said. Could such an architect build a stone automaton twice as tall as a tall man? A gray stone automaton with a great club? Could he make a hiding place from which it could emerge, deal death, and then return? No, no, such notions were childish, not to be entertained! Stick to the job in hand. First find what lay behind the inscribed stone. Leave thoughts until afterward.

The stone was beginning to give more easily to the pressure of the pick. Soon they would be able to get a good purchase on it and pry it out.

Meanwhile an entirely new sensation was growing in the Mouser—not one of terror at all, but of physical revulsion. The air he breathed seemed thick and sickening. He found himself disliking the texture and consistency of the tarry mixture gouged from the cracks, which somehow he could only liken to wholly imaginary substances, such as the dung of dragons or the solidified vomit of the behemoth. He avoided touching it with his fingers, and he kicked away the litter of chunks and strips that had gathered around his feet. The sensation of queasy loathing became difficult to endure.

He tried to fight it, but had no more success than if it had been seasickness, which in some ways it resembled. He felt unpleasantly dizzy. His mouth kept filling with saliva. The cold sweat of nausea beaded his forehead. He could tell that Fafhrd was unaffected, and he hesitated to mention the matter; it seemed ridiculously out of place, especially as it was unaccompanied by any fear or fright. Finally the stone itself began to have the same effect on him as the tarry mixture, filling him with a seemingly causeless, but none the less sickening revulsion. Then he could bear it no longer. With a vaguely apologetic nod to Fafhrd, he dropped his chisel and went to the low window for a breath of fresh air.

This did not seem to help matters much. He pushed his head through the window and gulped deeply. His mental processes were overshadowed by the general indifference of extreme nausea, and everything seemed very far away. Therefore when he saw that the peasant girl was standing in the middle of the clearing, it was some time before he began to consider the import of the fact. When he did, part of his sickness left him; or at least he was enabled to overpower it sufficiently to stare at her with gathering interest.

Her face was white, her fists were clenched, her arms held rigid at her sides. Even at the distance he could catch something of the mingled terror and determination with which her eyes were fixed on the great doorway. Toward this doorway she was forcing herself to move, one jerking step after another, as if she had to keep screwing her courage to a higher pitch. Suddenly the Mouser began to feel frightened, not for himself at all, but for the girl. Her terror was obviously intense, and yet she must be doing what she was doing— braving her "queer and fearsome gray giant"— for his sake and Fafhrd's. At all costs, he thought, she must be prevented from coming closer. It was wrong that she be subjected for one moment longer to such a horribly intense terror.

His mind was confused by his abominable nausea, yet he knew what he must do. He hurried toward the stairs with shaky strides, waving Fafhrd another vague gesture. Just as he was going out of the room he chanced to turn up his eyes, and spied something peculiar on the ceiling. What it was he did not fully realize for some moments.

Fafhrd hardly noticed the Mouser's movements, much less his gestures. The block of stone was rapidly yielding to his efforts. He had previously experienced a faint suggestion of the Mouser's nausea, but perhaps because of his greater single-mindedness, it had not become seriously bothersome. And now his attention was wholly concentrated on the stone. Persistent prying had edged it out a palm's breadth from the wall. Seizing it firmly in his two powerful hands, he tugged it from one side to the other, back and forth. The dark, viscous stuff clung to it tenaciously, but with each sidewise jerk it moved forward a little.

The Mouser lurched hastily down the stairs, fighting vertigo. His feet kicked bones and sent them knocking against the walls. What was it he had seen on the ceiling? Somehow, it seemed to mean something. But he must get the girl out of the clearing. She mustn't come any closer to the house. She mustn't enter.

Fafhrd began to feel the weight of the stone, and knew that it was nearly clear. It was damnably heavy—almost a foot thick. Two carefully gauged heaves finished the job. The stone overbalanced. He stepped quickly back. The stone crashed ponderously on the floor. A rainbow glitter came from the cavity that had been revealed. Fafhrd eagerly thrust his head into it.

The Mouser staggered toward the doorway. It was a bloody smear he had seen on the ceiling. And just above the corpse of the holy man. But why should that be? He'd been smashed against the floor, hadn't he? Was it blood splashed up from his lethal clubbing? But then why smeared? No matter. The girl. He must get to the girl. He must. There she was, almost at the doorway. He could see her. He felt the stone floor vibrating slightly beneath his feet. But that was his dizziness, wasn't it?

Fafhrd felt the vibration, too. But any thought he might have had about it was lost in his wonder at what he saw. The cavity was filled to a level just below the surface of the opening, with a heavy metallic liquid that resembled mercury, except that it was night-black. Resting on this liquid was a more astonishing group of gems than Fafhrd had ever dreamed of.

In the center was a titan diamond, cut with a myriad of oddly angled facets. Around it were two irregular circles, the inner formed of twelve rubies, each a decahedron, the outer formed of seventeen emeralds, each an irregular octahedron. Lying between these gems, touching some of them, sometimes connecting them with each other, were thin, fragile-looking bars of crystal, amber, greenish tourmaline, and honey-pale orichalcum. All these objects did not seem to be floating in the metallic liquid so much as resting upon it, their weight pressing down the surface into shallow depressions, some cup-shaped, others troughlike. The rods glowed faintly, while each of the gems glittered with a light that Fafhrd's mind strangely conceived to be refracted starlight.

His gaze shifted to the mercurous heavy fluid, where it bulged up between, and he saw distorted reflections of stars and constellations which he recognized, stars and constellations which would be visible now in the sky overhead, were it not for the concealing brilliance of the sun. An awesome wonder engulfed him. His gaze shifted back to the gems. There was something tremendously meaningful about their complex arrangement, something that seemed to speak of overwhelming truths in an alien symbolism. More, there was a compelling impression of inner movement, of sluggish thought, of inorganic consciousness. It was like what the eyes see when they close at night—not utter blackness, but a shifting, fluid pattern of many-colored points of light. Feeling that he was reaching impiously into the core of a thinking mind, Fafhrd gripped with his right hand for the diamond as big as a man's skull.

The Mouser blundered through the doorway. There could be no mistaking it now. The close-mortised stones were trembling. That bloody smear, as if the ceiling had champed down upon the holy man, crushing him against the floor, or as if the floor had struck upward. But there was the girl, her terror-wide eyes fastened upon him, her mouth open for a scream that did not come. He must drag her away, out of the clearing.

But why should he feel that a fearful threat was now directed at himself as well? Why should he feel that something was poised above him, threatening? As he stumbled down the terraced steps, he looked over his shoulder and up. The tower.

The tower! It was falling. It was falling toward him. It was dipping at him over the dome. But there were no fractures along its length. It was not breaking. It was not falling. It was bending.

Fafhrd's hand jerked back, clutching the great, strangely faceted jewel, so heavy that he had difficulty in keeping his hold upon it. Immediately the surface of the metallic, star-reflecting fluid was disturbed. It bobbled and shook. Surely the whole house was shaking, too. The other jewels began to dart about erratically, like water insects on the surface of a puddle. The various crystalline and metallic bars began to spin, their tips attracted now to one jewel and now to another, as if the jewels were lodestone and the bars iron needles. The whole surface of the fluid was in a whirling, jerking confusion that suggested a mind gone mad because of loss of its chief part.

For an agonizing instant the Mouser stared up in amazement—frozen at the clublike top of the tower, hurling itself down upon him. Then he ducked and lunged forward at the girl, tackling her, rapidly rolling over and over with her. The tower top struck a sword's length behind them, with a thump that jolted them momentarily off the ground. Then it jerked itself up from the pit-like depression it had made.

Fafhrd tore his gaze away from the incredible, alien beauty of the jewel-confused cavity. His right hand was burning. The diamond was hot. No, it was cold beyond belief. By Kos, the room was changing shape! The ceiling was bulging downward at a point. He made for the door, then stopped dead in his tracks. The door was closing like a stony mouth. He turned and took a few steps over the quaking floor toward the small, low window. It snapped shut, like a sphincter. He tried to drop the diamond. It clung painfully to the inside of his hand. With a snap of his wrist he whipped it away from him. It hit the floor and began to bounce about, glaring like a living star.

The Mouser and the peasant girl rolled toward the edge of the clearing. The tower made two more tremendous bashes at them, but both went yards wide, like the blows of a blind madman. Now they were out of range. The Mouser lay sprawled on his side, watching a stone house that hunched and heaved like a beast, and a tower that bent double as it thumped grave-deep pits into the ground. It crashed into a group of boulders and its top broke off, but the jaggedly fractured end continued to beat the boulders in wanton anger, smashing them into fragments. The Mouser felt a compulsive urge to take out his dagger and stab himself in the heart. A man had to die when he saw something like that.

Fafhrd clung to sanity because he was threatened from a new direction at every minute and because he could say to himself, "I know. I know. The house is a beast, and the jewels are its mind. Now that mind is mad. I know. I know." Walls, ceiling, and floor quaked and heaved, but their movements did not seem to be directed especially at him. Occasional crashes almost deafened him. He staggered over rocky swells, dodging stony advances that were half bulges and half blows, but that lacked the speed and directness of the tower's first smash at the Mouser. The corpse of the holy man was jolted about in grotesque mechanical reanimation.

Only the great diamond seemed aware of Fafhrd. Exhibiting a fretful intelligence, it kept bounding at him viciously, sometimes leaping as high as his head. He involuntarily made for the door as his only hope. It was champing up and down with convulsive regularity.

Watching his chance, he dived at it just as it was opening, and writhed through. The diamond followed him, striking at his legs. The carcass of Rannarsh was flung sprawling in his path. He jumped over it, then slid, lurched, stumbled, fell down stairs in earthquake, where dry bones danced. Surely the beast must die, the house must crash and crush him flat. The diamond leaped for his skull, missed, hurtled through the air, and struck a wall. Thereupon it burst into a great puff of iridescent dust.

Immediately the rhythm of the shaking of the house began to increase. Fafhrd raced across the heaving floor, escaped by inches the killing embrace of the great doorway, plunged across the clearing—passing a dozen feet from the spot where the tower was beating boulders into crushed rock—and then leaped over two pits in the ground. His face was rigid and white. His eyes were vacant. He blundered bull-like into two or three trees, and only came to a halt because he knocked himself flat against one of them.

The house had ceased most of its random movements, and the whole of it was shaking like a huge dark jelly. Suddenly its forward part heaved up like a behemoth in death agony. The two smaller domes were jerked ponderously a dozen feet off the ground, as if they were the paws. The tower whipped into convulsive rigidity. The main dome contracted sharply, like a stupendous lung. For a moment it hung there, poised. Then it crashed to the ground in a heap of gigantic stone shards. The earth shook. The forest resounded. Battered atmosphere whipped branches and leaves. Then all was still. Only from the fractures in the stone a tarry, black liquid was slowly oozing, and here and there iridescent puffs of air suggested jewel-dust.

Along a narrow, dusty road two horsemen were cantering slowly toward the village of Soreev in the southernmost limits of the land of Lankhmar. They presented a somewhat battered appearance. The limbs of the larger, who was mounted on a chestnut gelding, showed several bruises, and there was a bandage around his thigh and another around the palm of his right hand. The smaller man, the one mounted on a gray mare, seemed to have suffered an equal number of injuries.

"Do you know where we're headed?" said the latter, breaking a long silence. "We're headed for a city. And in that city are endless houses of stone, stone towers without numbers, streets paved with stone, domes, archways, stairs. Tcha, if I feel then as I feel now, I'll never go within a bowshot of Lankhmar's walls."

His large companion smiled.

"What now, little man? Don't tell me you're afraid of earthquakes?"

John Collier (1901–1980) was a British author and screenwriter. Collier actually set out to be a poet, yet it was not his calling and he turned to the novels and short stories for which he is best known. His biting, macabre stories often appeared in *The New Yorker*, including "Perfect Murder" (1934), "Another American Tragedy" (1940), and "Think No Evil" (1958). "Evening Primrose" (1940) is a haunting tale, and it may be his most famed story. It has been adapted many times, including into a recording read by none other than Vincent Price and a television musical created by Stephen Sondheim.

Evening Primrose

John Collier

IN A PAD OF HIGHLIFE BOND, *bought by Miss Sadie Brodribb at Bracey's for 25s*

MARCH 21

Today I made my decision. I would turn my back for good and all upon the bourgeois world that hates a poet. I would leave, get out, break away—

And I have done it. I am free! Free as the mote that dances in the sunbeam! Free as a house-fly crossing first-class in the *Queen Mary*! Free as my verse! Free as the food I shall eat, the paper I write upon, the lamb's-wool-lined softly slithering slippers I shall wear.

This morning I had not so much as a car-fare. Now I am here, on velvet. You are itching to learn of this haven: you would like to organize trips here, spoil it, send your relations-in-law, perhaps even come yourself. After all, this journal will hardly fall into your hands till I am dead. I'll tell you.

I am at Bracey's Giant Emporium, as happy as a mouse in the middle of an immense cheese, and the world shall know me no more.

Merrily, merrily shall I live now, secure behind a towering pile of carpets, in a corner-nook which I propose to line with eiderdowns, angora vestments, and the Cleopatrsean tops in pillows. I shall be cosy.

I nipped into this sanctuary late this afternoon, and soon heard the dying footfalls of closing time. From now on, my only effort will be to dodge the night-watchman. Poets can dodge.

I have already made my first mouse-like exploration. I tiptoed as far as the stationery department, and, timid, darted back with only these writing materials, the poet's first need. Now I shall lay them aside, and seek other necessities: food, wine, the soft furniture of my couch, and a natty smoking-jacket. This place stimulates me. I shall write here.

DAWN, NEXT DAY

I suppose no one in the world was ever more astonished and overwhelmed than I have been tonight. It is unbelievable. Yet I believe it. How interesting life is when things get like that!

I crept out, as I said I would, and found the great shop in mingled light and gloom. The central well was half illuminated; the circling galleries towered in a pansy Piranesi of toppling light and shade. The spidery stairways and flying bridges had passed from purpose into fantasy. Silks and velvets glimmered like ghosts, a hundred pantie-clad models offered simpers and embraces to the desert air. Rings, clips, and bracelets glittered frostily in a desolate absence of Honey and Daddy.

Creeping along the transverse aisles, which were in deeper darkness, I felt like a wandering thought in the dreaming brain of a chorus girl down on her luck. Only, of course, their brains are not so big as Bracey's Giant Emporium. And there was no man there.

None, that is, except the night-watchman. I had forgotten him. As I crossed the open space on the mezzanine floor, hugging the lee of a display of sultry shawls, I became aware of a regular thudding, which might almost have been that of my own heart. Suddenly burst upon me that is came from outside. It was footsteps away, and they were only a few paces away. Quick as a flash I seized a flamboyant mantilla, whirled it about me, and stood with one arm outflung, like a Carmen petrified in a gesture of disdain.

I was successful. He passed me, jingling his little machine on its chain, humming his little tune, his eyes scaled with refractions of the blaring day. "Go, worldling!" I whispered, and permitted myself a soundless laugh.

It froze on my lips. My heart faltered. A new fear seized me.

I was afraid to move. I was afraid to look round. I felt I was being watched, by something that could see right through me. This was a very different feeling from the ordinary emergency caused by the very ordinary night-watchman. My conscious impulse was the obvious one, to glance behind me. But my eyes knew better. I remained absolutely petrified, staring straight ahead.

My eyes were trying to tell me something that my brain refused to believe. They made their point. I was looking straight into another pair of eyes, human eyes, but large, flat, luminous. I have seen such eyes among the nocturnal creatures, which creep out under the artificial blue moonlight in the zoo.

The owner was only a dozen feet away from me. The watchman had passed between us, nearer him than me. Yet he had not been seen. I must have been looking straight at him for several minutes at a stretch. I had not seen him either.

He was half reclining against a low dais where, on a floor of russet leaves, and flanked by billows of glowing home-spun, the fresh-faced waxen girls modeled spectator sports suits in herringbones, checks, and plaids. He leaned against the skirt of one of these Dianas; its folds concealed perhaps his ear, his shoulder, and a little of his right side. He, himself, was clad in dim but large-patterned Shetland tweeds of the latest cut, suede shoes, a shirt of a rather broad *motif* in olive, pink, and grey. He was as pale as a creature found under a stone. His long thin arms ended in hands that hung floatingly, more like trailing, transparent fins, or wisps of chiffon, than ordinary hands.

He spoke. His voice was not a voice, a mere whistling under the tongue. "Not bad, for a beginner!"

I grasped that he was complimenting me, rather satirically, on my own, more amateurish, feat of camouflage. I stuttered. I said, "I'm sorry. I didn't know anyone else lived here." I noticed, even as I spoke, that I was imitating his own whistling sibilant utterance.

"Oh, yes," he said. "*We* live here. It's delightful."

"We?"

"Yes, all of us. Look."

We were near the edge of the first gallery. He swept his long hand round, indicating the whole well of the shop. I looked. I saw nothing. I could hear nothing, except the watchman's thudding step receding infinitely far along some basement aisle.

"Don't you see?"

You know the sensation one has, peering into the half-light of a vivarium? One sees bark, pebbles, a few leaves, nothing more. And then, suddenly, a stone breathes—it is a toad; there is a chameleon, another, a coiled adder, a mantis among the leaves. The whole case seems crepitant with life. Perhaps the whole world is. One glances at one's sleeve, one's feet.

So it was with the shop. I looked, and it was empty. I looked, and there was an old lady, clambering out from behind the monstrous clock. There were three girls, elderly ingénues, incredibly emaciated, simpering at the entrance of the perfumery. Their hair was a fine floss, pale as gossamer. Equally brittle and colorless was a man with the appearance of a colonel of southern extraction, who stood regarding me while he caressed moustachios that would have done credit to a crystal shrimp. A chintzy woman, possibly of literary tastes, swam forward from the curtains and drapes.

They came thick about me, fluttering, whistling, like a waving of gauze in the wind. Their eyes were wide and flatly bright. I saw there was no color to the iris.

"How raw he looks!"

"A detective! Send for the Dark Men!"

"I'm not a detective. I am a poet. I have renounced the world."

"He is a poet. He has come over to us. Mr. Roscoe found him."

"He admires us."

"He must meet Mrs. Vanderpant."

I was taken to meet Mrs. Vanderpant: she proved to be the Grand Old Lady of the store, almost entirely transparent.

"So you are a poet, Mr. Snell? You will find inspiration here. I am quite the oldest inhabitant. Three mergers and a complete rebuilding, but they didn't get rid of me!"

"Tell how you went out by daylight, dear Mrs. Vanderpant, and nearly got bought for Whistler's *Mother*."

"That was in pre-war days. I was more robust then. But at the cash desk they suddenly remembered there was no frame. And when they came back to look at me—"

"—She was gone."

Their laughter was like the stridulation of the ghosts of grasshoppers.

"Where is Ella? Where is my broth?"

"She is bringing it, Mrs. Vanderpant. It will come."

"Tiresome little creature! She is our foundling, Mr. Snell, She is not quite our sort."

"Is that so, Mrs. Vanderpant? Dear, dear!"

"I lived alone here, Mr. Snell, for many years. I took refuge here in the terrible times in the eighties. I was a young girl then, a beauty, people were kind enough to say, but poor Papa lost his money. Bracey's meant a lot to a young girl, in the New York of those days, Mr. Snell. It seemed to me terrible that I should not be able to come here in the ordinary way. So I came here for good. I was quite alarmed when others began to come in, after the crash of 1907. But it was the dear Judge, the Colonel, Mrs. Bilbee—"

I bowed. I was being introduced.

"Mrs. Bilbee writes plays. *And* of a very old Philadelphia family. You will find us quite nice here, Mr. Snell."

"I feel it a great privilege, Mrs. Vanderpant."

"And of course, all our dear *young* people came in '29. *Their* poor papas jumped from skyscrapers."

I did a great deal of bowing and whistling. The introductions took a long time. Who would have thought so many people lived in Bracey's?

"And here at last is Ella with my broth."

It was then I noticed that the young people were not so young after all, in spite of their smiles, their little ways, their *ingenue* dress. Ella was in her teens. Clad only in something from the shop-soiled counter, she nevertheless had the appearance of a living flower in a French cemetery, or a mermaid among polyps.

"Come, you stupid thing!"

"Mrs. Vanderpant is waiting."

Her pallor was not like theirs, not like the pallor of something that glistens or scuttles when you turn over a stone. Hers was that of a pearl.

Ella! Pearl of this remotest, most fantastic cave! Little mermaid, brushed over, pressed down by objects of a deadlier white—tentacles—! I can write no more.

MARCH 28

Well, I am rapidly becoming used to my new and half-lit world, to my strange company. I am learning the intricate laws of silence and camouflage which dominate the apparently casual strollings and gatherings of the midnight clan. How they detest the night-watchman, whose existence imposes these laws on their idle festivals!

"Odious, vulgar creature! He reeks of the coarse sun!"

Actually, he is quite a personable young man, very young for a night-watchman, so young that I think he must have been wounded in the war. But they would like to tear him to pieces.

They are very pleasant to me, though. They are pleased that a poet should have come among them. Yet I cannot like them entirely. My blood is a little chilled by the uncanny ease with which even the old ladies can clamber spider-like from balcony to balcony. Or is it because they are unkind to Ella?

Yesterday we had a bridge party. Tonight Mrs. Bilbee's little play, *Love in Shadowland*, is going to be presented. Would you believe it?—another colony, from Wanamaker's, is coming over *en masse* to attend. Apparently people live in all

stores. This visit is considered a great honor, for there is an intense snobbery in these creatures. They speak with horror of a social outcast who left a high-class Madison Avenue establishment, and now leads a wallowing, beachcomberish life in a delicatessen. And they relate with tragic emotion the story of the man in Altman's, who conceived such a passion for a model plaid dressing jacket that he emerged and wrested it from the hands of a purchaser. It seems that all the Altman colony, dreading an investigation, were forced to remove beyond the social pale, into a five-and-dime. Well, I must get ready to attend the play.

APRIL 14

I have found an opportunity to speak to Ella. I dared not before: here one has a sense always of pale eyes secretly watching. But last night, at the play, I developed a fit of hiccups. I was somewhat sternly told to go and secrete myself in the basement, among the garbage cans, where the watchman never comes.

There, in the rat-haunted darkness, I heard a stifled sob. "What's that? Is it you? Is it Ella? What ails you, child? Why do you cry?"

"They wouldn't even let me see the play."

"Is that all? Let me console you."

"I am so unhappy."

She told me her tragic little story. What do you think? When she was a child, a little tiny child of only six, she strayed away and fell asleep behind a counter, while her mother tried on a new hat. When she woke, the store was in darkness.

"And I cried, and they all came round, and took hold of me. 'She will tell, if we let her go,' they said. Some said, 'Call in the Dark Men.' 'Let her stay here,' said Mrs. Vanderpant. 'She will make me a nice little maid.'"

"Who are these Dark Men, Ella? They spoke of them when I came here."

"Don't you know? Oh, it's horrible! It's horrible!"

"Tell me, Ella. Let us share it."

She trembled. "You know the morticians, 'Journey's End,' who go to houses when people die?"

"Yes, Ella."

"Well, in that shop, just like here, and at Gimbel's, and at Bloomingdale's, there are people living, people like these."

"How disgusting! But what can they live upon, Ella, in a funeral home?"

"Don't ask me! Dead people are sent there, to be embalmed. Oh, they are terrible creatures! Even the people here are terrified of them. But if anyone dies, or if some poor burglar breaks in, and sees these people, and might tell—"

"Yes? Go on."

"Then they send for the others, the Dark Men."

"Good heavens!"

"Yes, and they put the body in Surgical Supplies—or the burglar, all tied up, if it's a burglar—and they send for these others, and then they all hide, and in they come, these others—Oh! they're like pieces of blackness. I saw them once. It was terrible."

"And then?"

"They go in, to where the dead person is, or the poor burglar. And they have wax there—and all sorts of things. And when they're gone there's just one of these wax models left, on the table. And then our people put a frock on it, or a bathing suit, and they mix it up with all the others, and nobody ever knows."

"But aren't they heavier than the others, these wax models? You would think they'd be heavier."

"No. They're not heavier. I think there's a lot of them—gone."

"Oh dear! So they were going to do that to you, when you were a little child?"

"Yes, only Mrs. Vanderpant said I was to be her maid."

"I don't like these people, Ella."

"Nor do I. I wish I could see a bird."

"Why don't you go into the pet-shop?"

"It wouldn't be the same. I want to see it on a twig, with leaves."

"Ella, let us meet often. Let us creep away down here and meet. I will tell you about birds, and twigs and leaves."

MAY 1

For the last few nights the store has been feverish with the shivering whisper of a huge crush at Bloomingdale's. Tonight was the night.

"Not changed yet? We leave on the stroke of two." Roscoe had appointed himself, been appointed, my guide or my guard.

"Roscoe, I am still a greenhorn. I dread the streets."

"Nonsense, there is nothing to it! We slip out by two's and three's, stand on the sidewalk, pick up a taxi. Were you never out late in the old days? If so, you must have seen us, many a time."

"Good heavens, I believe I have! And often wondered where you came from. And it was from here! But, Roscoe, my brow is burning, I find it hard to breathe. I fear a cold."

"In that case you must certainly remain behind. Our whole party would be disgraced in the unfortunate event of a sneeze."

I had relied on their rigid etiquette, so largely based on fear of discovery, and I was right. Soon they were gone, drifting out like leaves aslant in the wind. At once I dressed in flannel slacks, canvas shoes, and a tasteful sport shirt, all new in stock today. I found a quiet spot, safely off the track beaten by the night-watchman. There, in a model's lifted hand, I set a wide fern frond culled from the florist's shop, and at once had a young, spring tree. The carpet was sandy, sandy as a lakeside beach. A snowy napkin; two cakes, each with a cherry on it; I had only to imagine the lake and to find Ella.

"Why, Charles, what's this?"

"I'm a poet, Ell, and when a poet meets a girl like you he thinks of a day in the country. Do you see this tree? Let's call it *our* tree. There's the lake—the prettiest lake imaginable. Here is grass, and there are flowers. There are birds, too, Ella. You told me you like birds."

"Oh, Charles, you're so sweet. I feel I hear them singing."

"And here's our lunch. But before we eat, go behind the rock there, and see what you find."

I heard her cry out in delight when she saw the summer dress I had put there for her. When she came back the spring day smiled to see her, and the lake shone brighter than before. "Ella, let us have lunch. Let us have fun. Let us have a swim. I can just imagine you in one of those new bathing suits."

"Let's just sit here, Charles, and talk."

So we sat and talked and the time was gone like a dream. We might have stayed there, forgetful of everything, had it not been for the spider.

"Charles, what are you doing?"

"Nothing, my dear. Just a naughty little spider, crawling over your knee. Purely imaginary, of course, but that sort are sometimes the worst. I had to try to catch him."

"Don't, Charles! It's late. It's terribly late. They'll be back any minute. I'd better go home."

I took her home to the kitchenware on the sub-ground floor, and kissed her good-day. She offered me her cheek. This troubles me.

MAY 10

"Ella, I love you."

I said it to her just like that. We have met many times. I have dreamt of her by day. I have not even kept up my journal. Verse has been out of the question.

"Ella, I love you. Let us move into the trousseau department. Don't look so dismayed, darling. If you like, we will go right away from here. We will live in the refreshment rooms in Central Park. There are thousands of birds there."

"Please—please don't talk like that."

"But I love you with all my heart."

"You mustn't."

"But I find I must. I can't help it. Ella, you don't love another?"

She wept a little. "Oh, Charles, I do."

"Love another, Ella? One of these? I thought you dreaded them all. It must be Roscoe. He is the only one that's any way human. We talk of art, life, and such things. And he has stolen your heart!"

"No, Charles, no. He's just like the rest, really. I hate them all. They make me shudder."

"Who is it, then?"

"It's him."

"Who?"

"The night-watchman."

"Impossible!"

"No. He smells of the sun."

"Oh, Ella, you have broken my heart."

"Be my friend, though."

"I will. I'll be your brother. How did you fall in love with him?"

"Oh, Charles, it was so wonderful. I was thinking of birds, and I was careless. Don't tell on me, Charles, they'll punish me."

"No. No. Go on."

"I was careless, and there he was, coming round the corner. And there was no place for me, I had this blue frock on. There were only some wax models in their underthings."

"Please go on."

"I couldn't help it, Charles. I slipped off my dress, and stood still."

"I see."

"And he stopped just by me, Charles. And he looked at me. And he touched my cheek."

"Did he notice nothing?"

"No. It was cold. But Charles, he said—he said—'Say, honey, I wish they made 'em like you on Eighth Avenue.' Charles, wasn't that a lovely thing to say?"

"Personally, I should have said Park Avenue."

"Oh, Charles, don't get like these people here. Sometimes I think you're getting like them. It doesn't matter what street, Charles; it was a lovely thing to say."

"Yes, but my heart's broken. And what can you do about him? Ella, he belongs to another world."

"Yes, Charles, Eighth Avenue. I want to go there. Charles, are you truly my friend?"

"I'm your brother, only my heart's broken."

"I'll tell you. I will. I'm going to stand there again. So he'll see me."

"And then?"

"Perhaps he'll speak to me again."

"My dearest Ella, you are torturing yourself. You are making it worse."

"No, Charles. Because I shall answer him. He will take me away."

"Ella, I can't bear it."

"Ssh! There is someone coming. I shall see birds—real birds, Charles—and flowers growing. They're coming. You must go."

MAY 13

The last three days have been torture. This evening I broke. Roscoe had joined me. He sat eyeing me for a long time. He put his hand on my shoulder.

He said, "You're looking seedy, old fellow. Why don't you go over to Wanamaker's for some skiing?"

His kindness compelled a frank response. "It's deeper than that. Roscoe. I'm done for. I can't eat, I can't sleep. I can't write, man, I can't ever write."

"What is it? Day starvation?"

"Roscoe—it's love."

"Not one of the staff, Charles, or the customers? That's absolutely forbidden."

"No, it's not that, Roscoe. But just as hopeless."

"My dear old fellow, I can't bear to see you like this. Let me help you. Let me share your trouble."

Then it all came out. It burst out. I trusted him. I think I trusted him. I really think I had no intention of betraying Ella, of spoiling her escape, of keeping her here till her heart turned towards me. If I had, it was subconscious. I swear it.

But I told him all. All. He was sympathetic, but I detected a sly reserve in his sympathy. "You will respect my confidence, Roscoe? This is to be a secret between us."

"As secret as the grave, old chap."

And he must have gone straight to Mrs. Vanderpant. This evening the atmosphere has changed. People flicker to and fro, smiling nervously, horribly, with a sort of frightened sadistic exaltation. When I speak to them they answer evasively, fidget, and disappear. An informal dance has been called off. I cannot find Ella. I will creep out. I will look for her again.

LATER

Heaven! It has happened. I went in desperation to the manager's office, whose glass front overlooks the whole shop. I watched till midnight. Then I saw a little group of them, like ants bearing a victim. They were carrying Ella. They took her to the surgical department. They took other things.

And, coming back here, I was passed by a flittering, whispering horde of them, glancing over their shoulders in a thrilled ecstasy of panic, making for their hiding places. I, too, hid myself. How can I describe the dark inhuman creatures that passed me, silent as shadows? They went there—where Ella is.

What can I do? There is only one thing. I will find the watchman. I will tell him. He and I will save her. And if we are overpowered—Well, I will leave this on a counter. Tomorrow, if we live, I can recover it.

If not, look in the windows. Look for three new figures: two men, one rather sensitive-looking, and a girl. She has blue eyes, like periwinkle flowers, and her upper lip is lifted a little.

Look for us.

Smoke them out! Obliterate them! Avenge us!

Clark Ashton Smith (1893–1961) was a self-educated American poet and author who often had a difficult time selling his short stories to pulp magazines because they could be seen as too poetic. "The Coming of the White Worm" first appeared in an issue of *Stirring Science Stories* eight years after Smith had finished it. Although he published numerous short stories and poems, Smith only wrote one novel: his *The Immortals of Mercury* (1932) is a tale about a man who finds himself at the mercy of immortals. Like many artists ahead of their time, Smith gained more popularity after his death than he ever did in his lifetime. "The Coming of the White Worm" is from the eighth book in Smith's Hyperborea series, Hyperborea being a prehistoric universe of Smith's making. Interestingly, his Hyperborea series had the worst sales of all his fantasy collections during his lifetime, quite possibly due to his poetic style.

The Coming of the White Worm

Clark Ashton Smith

EVAGH THE WARLOCK, dwelling beside the boreal sea, was aware of many strange and untimely portents in mid-summer. Frorely burned the sun above Mhu Thulan from a welkin clear and wannish as ice. At eve the aurora was hung from zenith to earth, like an arras in a high chamber of gods. Wan and rare were the poppies and small the anemones in the cliff-sequestered vales lying behind the house of Evagh; and the fruits in his walled garden were pale of rind and green at the core. Also, he beheld by day the unseasonable flight of great multitudes of fowl, going southward from the hidden isles beyond Mhu Thulan; and by night he heard the distressful clamor of other passing multitudes. And always, in the loud wind and crying surf, he harkened to the weird whisper of voices from realms of perennial winter.

Now Evagh was troubled by these portents, even as the rude fisher-folk on the shore of the haven below his house were troubled. Being a past-master of all sortilege, and a seer of remote and future things, he made use of his arts in an effort to divine their meaning. But a cloud was upon his eyes through the daytime; and a darkness thwarted him when he sought illumination in dreams. His most cunning horoscopes were put to naught; his familiars were silent or answered him equivocally; and confusion was amid all his geomancies and hydromancies and haruspications. And it seemed to Evagh that an unknown power worked against him, mocking and making impotent in such fashion the sorcery that none had defeated heretofore. And Evagh knew, by certain tokens perceptible to wizards, that the power was an evil power, and its boding was of bale to man.

Day by day, through the middle summer, the fisher-folk went forth in their coracles of elk-hide and willow, casting their seines. But in the seines they drew dead fishes, blasted as if by fire or extreme cold; and they drew living monsters, such as their eldest captains had never beheld: things triple-headed and tailed and finned with horror; black, shapeless things that turned to a liquid foulness and ran away from the net; or headless things like bloated moons with green, frozen rays about them; or things leprous-eyed and bearded with stiffly-oozing slime.

Then, out of the sea-horizoned north, where ships from Cerngoth were wont to ply among the Arctic islands, a galley came drifting with idle oars and aimlessly veering helm. The tide beached it among the boats of the fishermen, which fared no longer to sea but were drawn up on the sands below the cliff-built house of Evagh. And, thronging about the galley in awe and wonder, the fishers beheld its oarsmen still at the oars and its captain at the helm. But the faces and hands of all were stark as bone, and were white as the flesh of leprosy; and the pupils of their open eyes had faded strangely, being indistinguishable now from the whites; and a blankness of horror was within them, like ice in deep pools that are fast frozen to the bottom. And Evagh himself, descending later, also beheld the galley's crew, and pondered much concerning the import of this prodigy.

Loath were the fishers to touch the dead men; and they murmured, saying that a doom was upon the sea, and a curse upon all sea-faring things and people. But Evagh, deeming that the bodies would rot in the sun and would breed pestilence, commanded them to build a pile of driftwood about the galley; and when the pile had risen above the bulwarks, hiding from view the dead rowers, he fired it with his own hands.

High flamed the pile, and smoke ascended black as a storm-cloud, and was borne in windy volumes past the tall towers of Evagh on the cliff. But later, when the fire sank, the bodies of the oarsmen were seen sitting amid the mounded embers; and their arms were still outstretched in the attitude of rowing, and their fingers were clenched; though the oars had now dropped away from them in brands and ashes. And the captain of the galley stood upright still in his place: though the burnt helm had fallen beside him. Naught but the raiment of the marble corpses had been consumed; and they shone white as moon-washed marble above the charrings of wood; and nowhere upon them was there any blackness from the fire.

Deeming this thing an ill miracle, the fishers were all aghast, and they fled swiftly to the uppermost rocks. There remained with Evagh only his two servants, the boy Ratha and the ancient crone Ahilidis, who had both witnessed many of his conjurations and were thus well inured to sights of magic. And, with these two beside him, the sorcerer awaited the cooling of the brands.

Quickly the brands darkened; but smoke arose from them still throughout the noon and afternoon; and still they were over-hot for human treading when the hour drew toward sunset. So Evagh bade his servants to fetch water in urns from the sea and cast it upon the ashes and charrings. And after the smoke and the hissing had died, he went forward and approached the pale corpses. Nearing them, he was aware of a great coldness, such as would emanate from trans-Arctic ice; and the coldness began to ache in his hands and ears, and smote sharply through the mantle of fur. Going still closer, he touched one of the bodies with his forefinger-tip; and the finger, though lightly pressed and quickly withdrawn, was seared as if by flame.

Evagh was much amazed: for the condition of the corpses was a thing unknown to him heretofore; and in all his science of wizardry there was naught to enlighten him. He bethought him that a spell had been laid upon the dead: an ensorcelling such as the wan polar demons might weave, or the chill witches of the moon might devise in their caverns of snow. And he deemed it well to retire for the time, lest the spell should now take effect upon others than the dead.

Returning to his house ere night, he burned at each door and window the gums that are most offensive to the northern demons; and at each angle where a spirit might enter, he posted one of his own familiars to guard against all intrusion. Afterwards, while Ratha and Ahilidis slept, he perused with sedulous care the writings of Pnom, in which are collated many powerful exorcisms. But ever and anon, as he read again, for his comfort, the old rubrics, he remembered ominously the saying of the prophet Lith, which no man had understood: "There is One that inhabits the place of utter cold, and One that respireth where none other may draw breath. In the days to come He shall issue forth among the isles and cities of men, and shall bring with Him as a white doom the wind that slumbereth in his dwelling."

Though a fire burned in the chamber, piled with fat pine and terebinth, it seemed that a deadly chill began to invade the air toward midnight. Then, as Evagh turned uneasily from the parchments of Pnom, and saw that the fires blazed high as if in no need of replenishment, he heard the sudden turmoil of a great wind full of sea-birds eerily shrieking, and the cries of land-fowl driven on helpless wings, and over all a high laughter of diabolic voices. Madly from the north the wind beat upon his square-based towers; and birds were cast like blown leaves of autumn against the stout-paned windows; and devils seemed to tear and strain at the granite walls. Though the room's door was shut and the windows were tight-closed, an icy gust went round and round, circling the table where Evagh sat, snatching the broad parchments of Pnom from beneath his fingers, and plucking at the lamp-flame.

Vainly, with numbing thoughts, he strove to recall that counter-charm which is most effective against the spirits of the boreal quarter. Then, strangely, it seemed that the wind fell, leaving a mighty stillness about the house. The chill gust was gone from the room, the lamp and the fire burned steadily, and something of warmth returned slowly into the half-frozen marrow of Evagh.

Soon he was made aware of a light shining beyond his chamber windows, as if a belated moon had now risen above the rocks. But Evagh knew that the moon was at that time a thin crescent, declining with eventide. It seemed that the light shone from the north, pale and frigid as fire of ice; and going to the window he beheld a great beam that traversed all the sea, coming as if from the hidden pole. In that light the rocks were paler than marble, and the sands were whiter than sea-salt, and the huts of the fishermen were as white tombs. The walled garden of Evagh was full of the beam, and all the green had departed from its foliage and its blossoms were like flowers of snow. And the beam fell bleakly on the lower walls of his house, but left still in shadow the wall of that upper chamber from which he looked.

He thought that the beam poured from a pale cloud that had mounted above the sea-line, or else from a white peak that had lifted skyward in the night; but of this he was uncertain. Watching, he saw that it rose higher in the heavens but climbed not upon his walls. Pondering in vain the significance of the mystery, he seemed to hear in the air about him a sweet and wizard voice. And, speaking in a tongue that he knew not, the voice uttered a rune of slumber. And Evagh could not resist the rune, and upon him fell such a numbness of sleep as overcomes the outworn watcher in a place of snow.

Waking stiffly at dawn, he rose up from the floor where he had lain, and witnessed a strange marvel. For, lo, in the harbour there towered an iceberg such as no vessel had yet sighted in all its sea-faring to the north, and no legend had told of among the dim Hyperborean isles. It filled the broad haven from shore to shore, and sheered up to a height immeasurable with piled escarpments and tiered precipices; and its pinnacles hung like towers in the zenith above the house of Evagh. It was higher than the dread mountain Achoravomas, which belches rivers of flame and liquid stone that pour unquenched through Tscho Vulpanomi to the austral main. It was steeper than the mountain Yarak, which marks the site of the boreal pole; and from it there fell a wan glittering on sea and land. Deathly and terrible was the glittering, and Evagh knew that this was the light he had beheld in the darkness.

Scarce could he draw breath in the cold that was on the air; and the light of the huge iceberg seared his eyeballs with an exceeding froreness. Yet he perceived an odd thing, that the rays of the glittering fell indirectly and to either side of his house; and the lower chambers, where Ratha and Ahilidis slept, were no longer touched by the beam as in the night; and upon all his house there was naught but the early sun and the morning shadows.

On the shore below he saw the charrings of the beached galley, and amid them the white corpses incombustible by fire. And along the sands and rocks, the fisher-folk were lying or standing upright in still, rigid postures, as if they had come forth from their hiding-places to behold the pale beam and had been smitten by a magic sleep. And the whole harbour-shore, and the garden of Evagh, even to the front threshold of his house, was like a place where frost has fallen thickly over all.

Again he remembered the saying of Lith; and with much foreboding he descended to the ground story. There, at the northern windows, the boy Ratha and the hag Ahilidis were leaning with faces turned to the light. Stiffly they stood, with wide-open eyes, and a pale terror was in their regard, and upon them was the white death of the galley's crew. And, nearing them, the sorcerer was stayed by the terrible chillness that smote upon him from their bodies.

He would have fled from the house, knowing his magic wholly ineffectual against this thing. But it came to him that death was in the direct falling of the rays from the iceberg, and, leaving the house, he must perforce enter that fatal light. And it came to him also that he alone, of all who dwelt on that shore, had been exempted from the

death. He could not surmise the reason of his exemption; but in the end he deemed it best to remain patiently and without fear, waiting whatever should befall.

Returning to his chamber he busied himself with various conjurations. But his familiars had gone away in the night, forsaking the angles at which he had posted them; and no spirit either human or demoniacal made reply to his questions. And not in any way known to wizards could he learn aught of the iceberg or divine the least inkling of its secret.

Presently, as he labored with his useless cantrips, he felt on his face the breathing of a wind that was not air but a subtler and rarer element cold as the moon's ether. His own breath forsook him with agonies unspeakable, and he fell down on the floor in a sort of swoon that was near to death. In the swoon he was doubtfully aware of voices uttering unfamiliar spells. Invisible fingers touched him with icy pangs; and about him came and went a bleak radiance, like a tide that flows and ebbs and flows again. Intolerable was the radiance to all his senses; but it brightened slowly, with briefer ebbings; and in time his eyes and his flesh were tempered to endure it. Full upon him now was the light of the iceberg through his northern windows; and it seemed that a great Eye regarded him in the light. He would have risen to confront the Eye; but his swoon held him like a palsy.

After that, he slept again for a period. Waking, he found in all his limbs their wonted strength and quickness. The strange light was still upon him, filling all his chamber; and peering out he witnessed a new marvel. For, lo, his garden and the rocks and sea-sands below it were visible no longer. In their stead were level spaces of ice about his house, and tall ice-pinnacles that rose like towers from the broad battlements of a fortress. Beyond the verges of the ice he beheld a sea that lay remotely and far beneath; and beyond the sea the low looming of a dim shore.

Terror came to Evagh now, for he recognized in all this the workings of a sorcery plenipotent and beyond the power of all mortal wizards. For plain it was that his high house of granite stood no longer on the coast of Mhu Thulan, but was based now on some upper crag of the iceberg. Trembling, he knelt then and prayed to the Old Ones, who dwell secretly in subterrene caverns, or abide under the sea or in the supermundane spaces. And even as he prayed, he heard a loud knocking at the door of his house.

In much fear and wonder he descended and flung wide the portals. Before him were two men, or creatures who had the likeness of men. Both were strange of visage and bright-skinned, and they wore for mantles such rune-woven stuffs as wizards wear. The runes were uncouth and alien; but when the men bespoke him he understood something of their speech, which was in a dialect of the Hyperborean isles.

"We serve the One whose coming was foretold by the prophet Lith," they said. "From spaces beyond the limits of the north he hath come in his floating citadel, the ice-mountain Yikilth, to voyage the mundane oceans and to blast with a chill splendour the puny peoples of humankind. He hath spared us alone amid the inhabitants of the broad isle Thulask, and hath taken us to go with him in his sea-faring upon Yikilth. He hath tempered our flesh to the rigour of his abode, and hath made respirable for us the air in which no mortal man may draw breath. Thee also he hath spared and hath acclimated by his spells to the coldness and the thin ether that go everywhere with Yikilth. Hail, O Evagh, whom we know for a great wizard by this token: since only the mightiest of warlocks are thus chosen and exempted."

Sorely astonished was Evagh; but seeing that he had now to deal with men who were as himself, he questioned closely the two magicians of Thulask. They were named Dooni and Ux Loddhan, and were wise in the lore of the elder gods. The name of the One that they served was Rlim Shaikorth, and he dwelt in the highest summit of the ice-mountain. They told Evagh nothing of the nature or properties of Rlim Shaikorth; and concerning their own service to this being they avowed only that it consisted of such worship as is given to a god, together with the repudiation of all bonds that had linked them heretofore to mankind. And they told Evagh that he was to go with them before Rlim Shaikorth, and perform the due rite of obeisance, and accept the bond of final alienage.

So Evagh went with Dooni and Ux Loddhan and was led by them to a great pinnacle of ice that rose unmeltable into the wan sun, beetling above all its fellows on the flat top of the berg. The pinnacle was hollow, and climbing therein by stairs of ice, they came at last to the chamber of Rlim Shaikorth, which was a circular dome with a round block at the center, forming a dais. And on the dais was that being whose advent prophet Lith had foretold obscurely.

At sight of this entity, the pulses of Evagh were stilled for an instant by terror; and, following quickly upon the terror, his gorge rose within him through excess of loathing. In all the world there was naught that could be likened for its foulness to Rlim Shaikorth. Something he had of the semblance of a fat white worm; but his bulk was beyond that of the sea-elephant. His half-coiled tail was thick as the middle folds of his body; and his front reared upward from the dais in the form of a white round disk, and upon it were imprinted vaguely the lineaments of a visage belonging neither to beast of the earth nor ocean-creature. And amid the visage a mouth curved uncleanly from side to side of the disk, opening and shutting incessantly on a pale and tongueless and toothless maw. The eye-sockets of Rlim Shaikorth were close together between his shallow nostrils; and the sockets were eyeless, but in them appeared from moment to moment globules of a blood-coloured matter having the form of eyeballs; and ever the globules broke and dripped down before the dais. And from the ice-floor of the dome there ascended two masses like stalagmites, purple and dark as frozen gore, which had been made by the ceaseless dripping of the globules.

Dooni and Ux Loddhan prostrated themselves before the being, and Evagh deemed it well to follow their example. Lying prone on the ice, he heard the red drops falling with a splash as of heavy tears; and then, in the dome above him, it seemed that a voice spoke; and the voice was like the sound of some hidden cataract in a glacier hollow with caverns.

"Behold, O Evagh," said the voice. "I have preserved thee from the doom of thy fellow-men, and have made thee as they that inhabit the bourn of coldness, and they that inhale the airless void. Wisdom ineffable shall be thine, and mastery beyond the conquest of mortals, if thou wilt but worship me and become my thrall. With me thou shalt voyage amid the kingdoms of the north, and shalt pass among the green southern islands, and see the white falling of death upon them in the light from Yikilth. Our coming shall bring eternal frost on their gardens, and shall set upon their people's flesh the seal of that gulf whose rigor paleth one by one the most ardent stars, and putteth rime at the core of suns. All this thou shalt witness, being as one of the lords of death, supernal and immortal; and in the end thou shalt return with me to that world beyond the uttermost pole, in which is mine abiding empire. For I am he whose coming even the gods may not oppose."

Now, seeing that he was without choice in the matter, Evagh professed himself willing to yield worship and service to the pale worm. Beneath the instruction of Dooni and Ux Loddhan, he performed the sevenfold rite that is scarce suitable for narration here, and swore the threefold vow of unspeakable alienation.

Thereafter, for many days and nights, he sailed with Rlim Shaikorth adown the coast of Mhu Thulan. Strange was the manner of that voyaging, for it seemed that the great iceberg was guided by the sorcery of the worm, prevailing ever against wind and tide. And always, by night or day, like the beams of a deathly beacon, the chill splendour smote afar from Yikilth. Proud galleys were overtaken as they fled southward, and their crews were blasted at the oars; and often ships were caught and embedded in the new bastions of ice that formed daily around the base of that ever-growing mountain.

The fair Hyperborean ports, busy with mari-time traffic, were stilled by the passing of Rlim Shaikorth. Idle were their streets and wharves, idle was the shipping in their harbours, when the pale light had come and gone. Far inland fell the rays, bringing to the fields and gardens a blight of trans-Arctic winter; and forests were frozen and the beasts that roamed them were turned as if into marble, so that men who came long afterward to that region found the elk and bear and mammoth still standing in all the postures of life. But, dwelling upon Yikilth, the sorcerer Evagh was immune to the icy death; and, sitting in his house or walking abroad on the berg, he was aware of no sharper cold than that which abides in summer shadows.

Now, beside Dooni and Ux Loddhan, the sorcerers of Thulask, there were five other wizards that went with Evagh on that voyage, having been chosen by Rlim Shaikorth. They too had been tempered to the coldness by Yikilth, and their houses had been transported to the berg by unknown enchantment. They were outlandish and uncouth men, called Polarians, from islands nearer the pole than broad Thulask; and Evagh could understand little of their ways; and their sorcery was foreign to him, and their speech was unintelligible; nor was it known to the Thulaskians.

Daily the eight wizards found on their tables all the provender necessary for human sustenance; though they knew not the agency by which it was supplied. All were united in the worship of the white worm; and all, it seemed, were content in a measure with their lot, and were fain of that unearthly lore and dominion which the worm had promised them. But Evagh was uneasy at heart, and rebelled in secret against his thralldom to Rlim Shaikorth; and he beheld with revulsion the doom that went forth eternally from Yikilth upon lovely cities and fruitful ocean-shores. Ruthfully he saw the blasting of flower-girdled Cerngoth, and the boreal stillness that descended on the thronged streets of Leqquan, and the frost that seared with sudden whiteness the garths and orchards of the sea-fronting valley of Aguil. And sorrow was in his heart for the fishing-coracles and the biremes of trade and warfare that floated manless after they had met Yikilth.

Ever southward sailed the great iceberg, bearing its lethal winter to lands where the summer sun rode high. And Evagh kept his own counsel, and followed in all ways the custom of Dooni and Ux Loddhan and the others. At intervals that were regulated by the motions of the circumpolar stars, the eight wizards climbed to that lofty chamber in which Rlim Shaikorth abode perpetually, half-coiled on his dais of ice. There, in a ritual whose cadences corresponded to the falling of those eye-like tears that were wept by the worm, and with genuflections timed to the yawning and shutting of his mouth, they yielded to Rlim Shaikorth the required adoration. Sometimes the worm was silent, and sometimes he bespoke them, renewing vaguely the promises he had made. And Evagh learned from the others that the worm slept for a period at each darkening of the moon; and only at that time did the sanguine tears suspend their falling, and the mouth forbear its alternate closing and gaping.

At the third repetition of the rites of worship, it came to pass that only seven wizards climbed to the tower. Evagh, counting their number, perceived that the missing man was one of the five outlanders. Afterwards, he questioned Dooni and Ux Loddhan regarding this matter, and made signs of inquiry to the four northrons; but it seemed that the fate of the absent warlock was a thing mysterious to them all. Nothing was seen or heard of him from that time; and Evagh, pondering long and deeply, was somewhat disquieted. For, during the ceremony in the tower chamber, it had seemed to him that the worm was grosser of bulk and girth than on any prior occasion.

Covertly he asked what manner of nutriment was required by Rlim Shaikorth. Concerning this, there was much dubiety and dispute: for Ux Loddhan maintained that the worm fed on nothing less unique than the hearts of white Arctic bears; while Dooni swore that his rightful nourishment was the liver of whales. But, to their

knowledge, the worm had not eaten during their sojourn upon Yikilth; and both averred that the intervals between his times of feeding were longer than those of any terrestrial creature, being computable not in hours or days but in whole years.

Still the iceberg followed its course, ever vaster and more prodigious beneath the heightening sun; and again, at the star-appointed time, which was the forenoon of every third day, the sorcerers convened in the presence of Rlim Shaikorth. To the perturbation of all, their number was now but six; and the lost warlock was another of the outlanders. And the worm had greatened still more in size; and the increase was visible as a thickening of his whole body from head to tail.

Deeming these circumstances an ill augury, the six made fearful supplication to the worm in their various tongues, and implored him to tell them the fate of their absent fellows. And the worm answered; and his speech was intelligible to Evagh and Ux Loddhan and Dooni and the three northrons, each thinking that he had been addressed in his native language.

"This matter is a mystery concerning which ye shall all receive enlightenment in turn. Know this: the two that have vanished are still present; and they and ye also shall share even as I have promised in the ultramundane lore and empery of Rlim Shaikorth."

Afterwards, when they had descended from the tower, Evagh and the two Thulaskians debated the interpretation of this answer. Evagh maintained that the import was sinister, for truly their missing companions were present only in the worm's belly; but the others argued that these men had undergone a more mystical translation and were now elevated beyond human sight and hearing. Forthwith they began to make ready with prayer and austerity, in expectation of some sublime apotheosis which would come to them in due turn. But Evagh was still fearful; and he could not trust the equivocal pledges of the worm; and doubt remained with him.

Seeking to assuage his doubt and peradventure to find some trace of the lost Polarians, he made search of the mighty berg, on whose battlements his own house and the houses of the other warlocks were perched like the tiny huts of fishers on ocean-cliffs. In this quest the others would not accompany him, fearing to incur the worm's displeasure. From verge to verge of Yikilth he roamed unhindered, as if on some broad plateau with peaks and horns; and he climbed perilously on the upper scarps, and went down into deep crevasses and caverns where the sun failed and there was no other light than the strange luster of that unearthly ice. Embedded here in the walls, as if in the stone of nether strata, he saw dwellings such as men had never built, and vessels that might belong to other ages or worlds; but nowhere could he detect the presence of any living creature; and no spirit or shadow gave response to the necromatic evocations which he uttered oftentimes as he went along the chasms and chambers.

So Evagh was still apprehensive of the worm's treachery; and he resolved to remain awake on the night preceding the next celebration of the rites of worship; and at eve of that night he assured himself that the other wizards were all housed in their separate mansions, to the number of five. And, having ascertained this, he set himself to watch without remission the entrance of Rlim Shaikorth's tower, which was plainly visible from his own windows.

Weird and chill was the shining of the berg in the darkness; for a light as of frozen stars was effulgent at all times from the ice. A moon that was little past the full arose early on the orient seas. But Evagh, holding vigil at his window till midnight, saw that no visible form emerged from the tall tower, and none entered it. At midnight there came upon him a sudden drowsiness, such as would be felt by one who had drunk some opiate wine; and he could not sustain his vigil any longer but slept deeply and unbrokenly throughout the remainder of the night.

On the following day there were but four sorcerers who gathered in the ice-dome and gave homage to Rlim Shaikorth. And Evagh saw that two more of the outlanders, men of bulk and stature dwarfish beyond their fellows, were now missing.

One by one thereafter, on nights preceding the ceremony of worship, the companions of Evagh vanished. The last Polarian was next to go; and it came to pass that only Evagh and Ux Loddhan and Dooni went to the tower; and then Evagh and Ux Loddhan went alone. And terror mounted daily in Evagh, for he felt that his own time drew near; and he would have hurled himself into the sea from the high ramparts of Yikilth, if Ux Loddhan, who perceived his intention, had not warned him that no man could depart therefrom and live again in solar warmth and terrene air, having been habituated to the coldness and thin ether. And Ux Loddhan, it seemed, was wholly oblivious to his doom, and was fain to impute an esoteric significance to the ever-growing bulk of the white worm and the vanishing of the wizards.

So, at that time when the moon had waned and darkened wholly, it occurred that Evagh climbed before Rlim Shaikorth with infinite trepidation and loath, laggard steps. And, entering the dome with downcast eyes, he found himself to be the sole worshipper.

A palsy of fear was upon him as he made obeisance; and scarcely he dared to lift his eyes and regard the worm. But even as he began to perform the customary genuflections, he became aware that the red tears of Rlim Shaikorth no longer fell on the purple stalagmites; nor was there any sound such as the worm was wont to make by the perpetual opening and shutting of his mouth. And venturing at last to look upward, Evagh beheld the abhorrently swollen mass of the monster, whose thickness was such as to overhang the dais' rim; and he saw that the mouth and eyeholes of Rlim Shaikorth were closed as if in slumber; and thereupon he recalled how the wizards of Thulask had told him that the worm slept for an interval at the darkening of each moon; which was a thing he had forgotten temporarily in his extreme dread and apprehension.

Now was Evagh sorely bewildered, for the rites he had learned from his fellows could be fittingly performed only while the tears of Rlim Shaikorth fell down and his mouth gaped and closed and gaped again in measured alternation. And none had instructed him as to what rites were proper and suitable during the slumber of the worm. And, being in much doubt, he said softly:

"Wakest thou, O Rlim Shaikorth?"

In reply, he seemed to hear a multitude of voices that issued obscurely from out the pale, tumid mass before him. The sound of the voices was weirdly muffled, but among them he distinguished the accents of Dooni and Ux Loddhan; and there was a thick muttering of outlandish words which Evagh knew for the speech of the five Polarians; and beneath this he caught, or seemed to catch, innumerable undertones that were not the voices of men or beasts, nor such sounds as would be emitted by earthly demons. And the voices rose and clamored, like those of a throng of prisoners in some profound oubliette.

Anon, as he listened in horror ineffable, the voice of Dooni became articulate above the others; and the manifold clamor and muttering ceased, as if a multitude were hushed to hear its own spokesman. And Evagh heard the tones of Dooni, saying:

"The worm sleepeth, but we whom the worm hath devoured are awake. Direly has he deceived us, for he came to our houses in the night, devouring us bodily one by one as we slept under the enchantment he had wrought. He has eaten our souls even as our bodies, and verily we are part of Rlim Shaikorth, but exist only as in a dark and noisome dungeon; and while the worm wakes we have no separate or conscious being, but are merged wholly in the ultraterrestrial being of Rlim Shaikorth.

"Hear then, O Evagh, the truth we have learned from our oneness with the worm. He has saved us from the white doom and has taken us upon Yikilth for this reason, because we alone of all mankind, who are sorcerers of high attainment and mastery, may endure the lethal ice-change and become breathers of the airless void, and thus, in the end, be made suitable for the provender of such as Rlim Shaikorth.

"Great and terrible is the worm, and the place wherefrom he cometh and whereto he returneth is not to be dreamt of by living men. And the worm is omniscient, save that he knows not the waking of them he has devoured, and their awareness during his slumber. But the worm, though ancient beyond the antiquity of worlds, is not immortal and is vulnerable in one particular. Whosoever learneth the time and means of his vulnerability and hath heart for this undertaking, may slay him easily. And the time for the deed is during his term of sleep. Therefore we adjure thee now by the faith of the Old Ones to draw the sword thou wearest beneath thy mantle and plunge it in the side of Rlim Shaikorth: for such is the means of his slaying.

"Thus alone, O Evagh, shall the going forth of the pale death be ended; and only thus shall we, thy fellow-sorcerers, obtain release from our blind thralldom and incarceration; and with us many that the worm hath betrayed and eaten in former ages and upon distant worlds. And only by the doing of this thing shalt thou escape the wan and loathly mouth of the worm, nor abide henceforward as a doubtful ghost among other ghosts in the evil blackness of his belly. But know, however, that he who slayeth Rlim Shaikorth must necessarily perish in the slaying."

Evagh, being wholly astounded, made question of Dooni and was answered readily concerning all that he asked. And often-times the voice of Ux Loddhan replied to him; and sometimes there were unintelligible murmurs as outcries from certain others of those foully enmewed phantoms. Much did Evagh learn of the worm's origin and essence; and he was told the secret of Yikilth, and the manner wherein Yikilth had floated down from trans-Arctic gulfs to voyage the seas of Earth. Ever, as he listened, his abhorrence greatened: though deeds of dark sorcery and conjured devils had long indurated his flesh and soul, making him callous to more than common horrors. But of that which he learned it were ill to speak now.

At length there was silence in the dome; for the worm slept soundly, and Evagh had no longer any will to question the ghost of Dooni; and they that were imprisoned with Dooni seemed to wait and watch in a stillness of death.

Then, being a man of much hardihood and resolution, Evagh delayed no more but drew from its ivory sheath the short but well-tempered sword of bronze which he carried always at his baldric. Approaching the dais closely, he plunged the blade in the over-swelling mass of Rlim Shai-korth. The blade entered easily with a slicing and tearing motion, as if he had stabbed a monstrous bladder, and was not stayed even by the broad pommel; and the whole right hand of Evagh was drawn after it into the wound.

He perceived no quiver or stirring of the worm, but out of the wound there gushed a sudden torrent of black liquescent matter, swiftening and deepening irresistibly till the sword was caught from Evagh's grasp as if in a mill-race. Hotter far than blood, and smoking with strange steam-like vapors, the liquid poured over his arms and splashed his raiment as it fell. Quickly the ice was a-wash about his feet; but still the fluid welled as if from some inexhaustible spring of foulness; and it spread everywhere in pools and runlets that came together.

Evagh would have fled then; but the sable liquid, mounting and flowing, was above his ankles when he neared the stair-head; and it rushed adown the stairway before him like a cataract in some steeply pitching cavern. Hotter and hotter it grew, boiling, bubbling; while the current strengthened, and clutched at him and drew him like malignant hands. He feared to essay the downward stairs; nor was there any place now in all the dome where he could climb for refuge. He turned, striving against the tide for bare foothold, and saw dimly through the reeking vapours the throned mass of Rlim Shaikorth. The gash had widened prodigiously, and a stream surged from it like the waters of a broken weir, billowing outward around the dais; and yet, as if in further proof of the worm's unearthly nature, his bulk was in no wise diminished thereby. And still the black liquid came in an evil flood; and it rose swirling about the knees of Evagh; and

the vapours seemed to take the forms of a myriad press of phantoms, wreathing obscurely together and dividing once more as they went past him. Then, as he tottered and grew giddy on the stair-head, he was swept away and was hurled to his death on the ice-steps far below.

That day, on the sea to eastward of middle Hyperborea, the crews of certain merchant galleys beheld an unheard-of thing. For, lo, as they sped north, returning from far ocean-isles with a wind that aided their oars, they sighted in the late forenoon a monstrous iceberg whose pinnacles and crags loomed high as mountains. The berg shone in part with a weird light; and from its loftiest pinnacle poured an ink-black torrent; and all the ice-cliffs and buttresses beneath were a-stream with rapids and cascades and sheeted falls of the same blackness, that fumed like boiling water as they plunged oceanward; and the sea around the iceberg was clouded and streaked for a wide interval as if with the dark fluid of the cuttlefish.

The mariners feared to sail closer; but, full of awe and marvelling, they stayed their oars and lay watching the berg; and the wind dropped, so that their galleys drifted within view of it all that day. They saw that the berg dwindled swiftly, melting as though some unknown fire consumed it; and the air took on a strange warmth, and the water about their ships grew tepid. Crag by crag the ice was runneled and eaten away; and huge portions fell off with a mighty splashing; and the highest pinnacle collapsed; but still the blackness poured out as from an unfathomable fountain. The mariners thought, at whiles, that they beheld houses running seaward amid the loosened fragments; but of this they were uncertain because of those ever-mounting vapors. By sunset-time the berg had dimished to a mass no larger than a common floe; yet still the welling blackness overstreamed it; and it sank low in the wave; and the weird light was quenched altogether. Thereafter, the night being moonless, it was lost to vision; and a gale rose, blowing strongly from the south; and at dawn the sea was void of any remnant.

Concerning the matters related above, many

and various legends have gone forth throughout Mhu Thulan and all the extreme Hyperboreal kingdoms and archipelagoes, even to the southmost isle of Oszhtror. The truth is not in such tales: for no man has known the truth heretofore. But I, the sorcerer Eibon, calling up through my necromancy the wave-wandering specter of Evagh, have learned from him the veritable history of the worm's advent. And I have written it down in my volume with such omissions as are needful for the sparing of mortal weakness and sanity. And men will read this record, together with much more of the elder lore, in days long after the coming and melting of the great glacier.

Marcel Aymé (1902–1967) was a French novelist, playwright, and screenwriter. Although his early novels are pastoral comedies, his later works, such as *The Green Mare* (1933) and *The Transient Hour* (1948), are more absurd. The absurdity of his shorter works caused them to be ignored for a long time even though they fit comfortably alongside the fables and fairy tales of other French writers such as Charles Perrault and Jean de la Fontaine. Aymé was a masterful storyteller, and his technique was in a class of its own. "The Man Who Could Walk Through Walls" (1943) has become such an influential part of French culture that it has been adapted to film twice. In 1989, the story inspired actor and sculptor Jean Marais to create a bronze sculpture of the protagonist at the Place Marcel Aymé, Montmartre.

The Man Who Could Walk Through Walls

Marcel Aymé

Translated by Sophie Lewis

IN MONTMARTRE, on the third floor of 75b Rue d'Orchampt, there lived an excellent gentleman called Dutilleul, who possessed the singular gift of passing through walls without any trouble at all. He wore pince-nez and a small black goatee, and was a lowly clerk in the Ministry of Records. In winter he would take the bus to work, and in fine weather he would make the journey on foot, in his bowler hat.

Dutilleul had just entered his forty-third year when he discovered his power. One evening, a brief electricity cut caught him in the hallway of his small bachelor's apartment. He groped for a while in the darkness and, when the lights came back on, found himself outside on the third-floor landing. Since his front door was locked from the inside, the incident gave him food for thought and, despite the objections of common sense, he decided to go back inside just as he had come out, by passing through the wall. This peculiar skill, apparently unrelated to any aspiration of his, rather disturbed him. So, the next day being Saturday, he took advantage of his English-style five-day week to visit a local doctor and explain his case. The doctor was soon persuaded that Dutilleul was telling the truth and, following a full examination, located the cause of the problem in a helicoid hardening of the strangulary wall in the thyroid gland. He prescribed sustained overexertion and a twice-yearly dose of one powdered tetravalent pirette pill, a mixture of rice flour and centaur hormones.

Having taken the first pill, Dutilleul put the medicine away in a drawer and forgot about it. As for the intensive overexertion, as a civil servant his rate of work was governed by practices that permitted no excess, nor did his leisure time, divided between reading the newspapers and tending his stamp collection, involve him in any excessive expenditure of energy either. A year later, therefore, his ability to walk through walls remained intact, but he never used it, apart from inadvertently, being uninterested in adventure and resistant toward the seductions of his imagination. He never even thought of entering his home by any route other than the front door and then only after having opened it by means of key and lock. Perhaps he would have grown old in the comfort of his habits, never tempted to put his gift to the test, had an extraordinary event not suddenly turned his life upside down. Being called to other duties, his deputy chief clerk Monsieur Mouron was replaced by a certain Monsieur Lécuyer, a man of abrupt speech who wore a nailbrush mustache. From his first day, the new deputy chief clerk looked unfavorably on Dutilleul's wearing of pince-nez with a chain and a black goatee, and made a show of treating him like an irritating, shabby old thing. But the worst of it was that he intended to introduce reforms of considerable scope into his department—just the thing to disturb his subordinate's peace. For twenty years now, Dutilleul had commenced his official letters with the following formula: "With reference to your esteemed communication of the nth of this month and, for the record, to all previous exchange of letters, I have the honor to inform you that . . ." A formula for which Monsieur Lécuyer intended to substitute another, much more American in tone: "In reply to your letter of n, I inform you that . . ." Dutilleul could not get used to these new epistolary fashions. In spite of himself, he would go back to his traditional ways, with a machinelike obstinacy that earned him the deputy clerk's growing hostility. The atmosphere inside the Ministry of Records

became almost oppressive. In the morning he would come in to work full of apprehension, and in bed in the evenings, it often happened that he stayed awake thinking for a whole fifteen minutes before falling asleep.

Disgusted by this backward thinking that was threatening the success of his reforms, Monsieur Lécuyer had banished Dutilleul to a badly lit cubbyhole that led off his own office. It was reached by a low and narrow door in the corridor and still displayed in capital letters the inscription: BROOM CUPBOARD. Dutilleul resigned himself to accepting this unprecedented humiliation, but at home, reading a news item on some bloodthirsty crime, he found himself picturing Monsieur Lécuyer as the victim.

One day, the deputy clerk burst into Dutilleul's cubbyhole brandishing a letter and began to bellow:

"Rewrite this tripe! Rewrite this piece of unspeakable dross that brings shame on my department!"

Dutilleul tried to protest, but Monsieur Lécuyer raged on, calling him a procedure-addicted cockroach and, before storming out, crumpled the letter in his hand and threw it in Dutilleul's face. Dutilleul was modest but proud. Sitting alone in his cubbyhole, he grew rather hot under the collar and suddenly felt a flash of inspiration. Leaving his seat, he stepped into the wall that divided his office from that of the deputy clerk—but stepped carefully, in such a way that only his head emerged on the other side. Sitting at his desk, his hand still shaking, Monsieur Lécuyer was shifting a comma in an underling's draft that had been submitted for his approbation, when he heard a cough inside his office. Looking up, with an unspeakable fright, he found Dutilleul's head mounted on the wall like a hunting trophy. But the head was still alive. Through its pince-nez, the head flashed a look of hatred at him. Even better, the head began to speak.

"Sir," it said, "you are a ruffian, a boor, and a scoundrel."

Gaping in horror, Monsieur Lécuyer was

unable to tear his eyes from this apparition. At last, hefting himself out of his armchair, he leaped into the corridor and ran around to the cubbyhole. Dutilleul, pen in hand, was sitting in his usual place, in a peaceful, hard-working attitude. The deputy clerk gave him a long stare and then, after stammering a few words, went back to his office. Hardly had he sat down when the head reappeared on the wall.

"Sir, you are a ruffian, a boor, and a scoundrel."

In the course of that day alone, the frightful head appeared on the wall twenty-three times and kept up the same frequency in the days that followed. Dutilleul, who had acquired a degree of skill in this game, was no longer satisfied with simply insulting the deputy clerk. He uttered obscure threats, exclaiming for example in a sepulchral voice, punctuated by truly demonic laughter:

"Werewolf! Werewolf! Hair of a beast!" (laughter) "A horror is lurking the owls have unleashed!" (laughter)

On hearing which, the poor deputy clerk grew even paler and even more choked, and his hair stood up quite straight on his head while down his back dribbled horrid cold sweat. On the first day he lost a pound in weight. In the following week, apart from melting away almost visibly, he began to eat his soup with a fork and to give passing policemen full military salutes. At the beginning of the second week, an ambulance came to collect him at home and took him to a mental asylum.

Delivered from Monsieur Lécuyer's tyranny, Dutilleul was free to return to his cherished formalities: "With reference to your esteemed communication of the nth of this month . . ." And yet, he was not satisfied. There was a craving inside him, a new, imperious urge—it was nothing less than the urge to walk through walls. Of course this was easily satisfied, for example at home, and there indeed he went ahead. But a man in possession of brilliant gifts cannot long be content to exercise them in pursuit of mediocre goals.

Besides, walking through walls cannot constitute an end in itself. It is the beginning of an adventure, which calls for a sequel, for elaboration and, in the end, for some reward. Dutilleul quite understood this. He felt within him a need for expansion, a growing desire to fulfill and surpass himself, and a stab of longing, which was something like the call of what lay through the wall. Unfortunately, he lacked an objective. He looked for inspiration in the newspaper, particularly in the politics and sports sections, since he felt these were honorable activities, but finally realizing that they offered no outlets for people who walk through walls, he made do with the most promising of the "in brief" news items.

The first break-in that Dutilleul carried out was at a large credit institution on the right bank of the river. After walking through a dozen walls and partitions, he forced a number of safes, filled his pockets with banknotes, and, before leaving, autographed the scene of his theft in red chalk with the pseudonym The Werewolf, with a very elegant flourish that was reproduced the next day in all the newspapers. By the end of the week, The Werewolf's name had become spectacularly famous. Public sympathy was unreservedly on the side of this superior burglar who was so cleverly mocking the police. He distinguished himself each succeeding night with the accomplishment of a new exploit, whether at the expense of a bank or a jeweler or some wealthy individual. There was not one among the dreamy type of Parisienne or country miss who did not passionately wish they belonged body and soul to the terrible Werewolf. After the theft of the famous Burdigala diamond and the burglary at the state pawnbroker's, which took place in the same week, the fervor of the masses reached the point of delirium. The Minister for the Interior was forced to resign, bringing the Minister for Records down with him. In spite of this, Dutilleul became one of the richest men in Paris, always came to work on time, and was talked of as a strong candidate for the *palmes académiques*, for his contribution to French culture. In the mornings at the Ministry of Records, he enjoyed listening to colleagues discussing his exploits of the night before. "This Werewolf," they said, "is amazing, a superman, a genius." Hearing such praise, Dutilleul blushed pink with embarrassment and, behind his pince-nez and chain, his eyes shone with warmth and gratitude.

One day, this sympathetic atmosphere won him over so completely that he felt he could not keep his secret for much longer. With some residual shyness, he considered his colleagues, gathered around a newspaper that announced his theft at the Bank of France, and declared in modest tones: "You know, I am The Werewolf." Hearty laughter greeted Dutilleul's confession and won him the mocking nickname "Werewolf." That evening, as they were leaving the Ministry, his colleagues made him the butt of endless jokes, and his life seemed less sweet.

A few days later, The Werewolf was caught by a night patrol in a jeweler's shop on the Rue de la Paix. He had added his signature to the counter and had begun to sing a drinking song while smashing various display cases with the help of a solid gold chalice. It would have been easy for him to sink into a wall and so escape the night patrol, but all the evidence suggests that he wanted to be arrested—probably solely in order to disconcert his colleagues, whose incredulity had mortified him. Indeed they were very surprised when the next day's papers ran a photograph of Dutilleul on their front pages. They bitterly regretted having misjudged their brilliant comrade and paid homage to him by all growing small goatees. Carried away by remorse and admiration, some were even tempted to try their hand at their friends' and acquaintances' wallets and heirloom watches.

It will doubtless be supposed that letting oneself get caught by the police simply in order to surprise a few colleagues shows a great deal of frivolity, unworthy of an exceptional man, but the obvious motivations count for very little with this kind of resolution. In giving up his liberty, Dutilleul believed he was giving in to an arrogant desire for revenge, while in truth he was simply slipping down the slope of his destiny. For a man who walks through walls, there can be no dazzling career if he hasn't at least once seen the inside of a prison.

When Dutilleul entered the premises of La Santé Prison, he felt that fate was spoiling him. The thickness of the walls was a veritable feast. Only a day after his incarceration, the astonished guards found that the prisoner had hammered a nail into his cell wall on which now hung a gold watch belonging to the warden. He either could not or would not reveal how this item had come into his possession. The watch was returned to its owner and, the following day, found once more at The Werewolf's bedside, along with the first volume of *The Three Musketeers* borrowed from the warden's personal library. The staff at La Santé grew very tense. Furthermore, the guards were complaining of kicks in their backsides of inexplicable provenance. It seemed that the walls no longer had ears but feet. The Werewolf's detention had lasted a week when, on entering his office one morning, the warden found the following letter on his desk:

Dear Warden, With reference to our interview of the seventeenth of this month and, for the record, to your general instructions dating from fifteenth of May of the previous year, I have the honor to inform you that I have just finished reading the second volume of *The Three Musketeers* and that I intend to escape tonight between eleven twenty-five and eleven thirty-five. I remain, dear Warden, yours respectfully, The Werewolf.

In spite of the close surveillance to which he was subjected that night, Dutilleul escaped at half-past eleven. Broadcast to the public the following morning, the news stirred deep admiration up and down the country. Nevertheless, after this latest feat, which had brought his popularity to even greater heights, Dutilleul hardly seemed concerned about secrecy and moved around Montmartre without any precautions. Three days after his escape, a little before noon, he was arrested on Rue Caulaincourt at the Café du Rêve, where he was enjoying a glass of white wine with lemon among friends.

Marched back to La Santé and triple-locked into a murky cell, The Werewolf escaped that very evening and went to sleep in the warden's own apartment, in the guest bedroom. The next morning at about nine o'clock, he called the maid for his breakfast and allowed himself to be plucked from his bed, without resisting, by belatedly alerted guards. Outraged, the warden set a guard at the door of Dutilleul's cell and put him on dry bread. Around noon, the prisoner went to lunch in a nearby restaurant and then, after his coffee, called the warden.

"Hello! Warden sir, I'm a little embarrassed but a moment ago, as I was leaving, I forgot to take your wallet with me, so here I am stuck for cash in this restaurant. Would you be so good as to send someone to pay the bill?"

The warden rushed over himself, so furious that he overflowed with threats and oaths. Personally offended, Dutilleul escaped the next night, this time never to return. He took the precaution of shaving off his black goatee and replacing his lorgnette and chain with tortoiseshell spectacles. A sports cap and a loud checked suit with plus fours completed his transformation. He set himself up in a small apartment on Avenue Junot to which, since his first arrest, he had sent a selection of furnishings and his most prized objects. He was getting tired of the fuss over his fame and, since his stay in La Santé, he had become rather blasé about the pleasure of walking through walls. The thickest, the proudest of them now seemed to him mere Japanese screens, and he dreamed of plunging into the heart of some immense pyramid. While planning a journey to Egypt, he continued to live a very peaceful life, dividing his time between his stamp collection, the cinema, and long strolls around Montmartre. His metamorphosis was so complete that, beardless and bespectacled, he could walk right past his best friends without being recognized by any of them.

Only the painter Gen Paul, who picked up the least physiological change in the old denizens of the neighborhood, at last managed to discover Dutilleul's true identity. One morning, finding himself face-to-face with Dutilleul at the corner of the Rue de l'Abreuvoir, he could not stop himself from saying, in his rough way:

"Well stone me, I see you've decked y'self out in fine new whistles to put the todd off the scent." (Which in common parlance means more or less: "I see you've disguised yourself as a gentleman in order to confuse the detectives.")

"Ah!" murmured Dutilleul. "You've recognized me!"

This troubled him and he decided to hasten his departure for Egypt. It was the afternoon of that very same day that he fell in love with a blonde beauty whom he bumped into twice in fifteen minutes on the Rue Lepic. Straightaway he forgot his stamp collection and Egypt and the Pyramids. For her part, the blonde had looked at him with genuine interest. Nothing speaks more eloquently to the imagination of today's young woman than plus fours and a pair of tortoiseshell spectacles. She will scent her big break, and dream of cocktails and nights in California. Unfortunately, Dutilleul was informed by Gen Paul, the beauty was married to a man both brutal and jealous. This suspicious husband, who happened to have a wild and disreputable lifestyle, regularly deserted his wife between ten at night and four in the morning, double-locked in her room, with all her shutters also padlocked. During the day he kept her under close supervision, sometimes even following her through the streets of Montmartre.

"Always on the lookout, him. S'just a great bob who can't stand the thought of other Bengals fishing in his pond."

But Gen Paul's warning only fired up Dutilleul even more. Bumping into the young lady on Rue Tholozé the next day, he dared to follow her into a creamery and, while she was waiting to be served, he said that he loved her most respectfully, that he knew about everything—the dreadful husband, the locked door and the shutters, but that he would see her that very evening in her bedroom. The blonde blushed, her milk jug trembled in her hand and, her eyes moist with yearning, she sighed softly: "Alas! Monsieur, it is impossible."

On the evening of this glorious day, by around ten o'clock, Dutilleul was keeping watch in Rue Norvins, observing a robust outer wall behind which stood a small house, the only signs of which were the weathervane and a chimney. A door in the wall opened and a man emerged who, after carefully locking the door behind him, walked off down the hill towards Avenue Junot. Dutilleul watched him vanish from view, far away at a bend in the road below, then counted to ten. Then he leaped forward, strode through the wall like an athlete, and, after dashing through every obstacle, finally penetrated the bedroom belonging to the beautiful recluse. She welcomed him rapturously and they made love until late into the night.

The following morning, Dutilleul was annoyed to wake up with a nasty headache. It did not bother him badly and he wasn't going to let such a minor thing keep him from his next rendezvous. Still, when he happened to find a few pills scattered at the back of a drawer, he gulped down one that morning and one in the afternoon. By evening, his headache was bearable and in his elation he managed to forget it completely. The young woman was waiting for him with an impatience fanned by memories of the night before, and that night they made love until three o'clock in the morning.

When he was leaving, while walking through the partitions and walls of the house, Dutilleul had the unfamiliar feeling that they were rubbing on his hips and at his shoulders. Nevertheless, he thought it best not to pay much attention to this. Besides, it was only on entering the outer wall that he really met with considerable resistance. It felt as though he were moving through a substance that, while still fluid, was growing sticky and, at every effort he made, taking on greater density. Having managed to push himself right into the wall, he realized that he was no longer moving forward and, horrified, remembered the two pills he had taken during the day. Those pills, which he had thought were aspirin, in fact contained the powder of tetravalent pirette that the doctor had prescribed him the year before. The medication's effects combined with that of intensive overexertion were now, suddenly, being realized.

Dutilleul was as if transfixed within the wall. He is still there today, incorporated into the stonework. Nighttime revelers walking down Rue Norvins at an hour when the buzz of Paris dies down can hear a muffled voice that seems to reach them from beyond the tomb and which they take for the moans of the wind as it blows through the crossroads of Montmartre. It is Werewolf Dutilleul, lamenting the end of his glorious career and the sorrows of a love cut short. On some winter nights, the painter Gen Paul may happen to take down his guitar and venture out into the sonorous solitude of Rue Norvins to console the poor prisoner with a song, and the notes of his guitar, rising from his swollen fingers, pierce to the heart of the wall like drops of moonlight.

John Ronald Reuel Tolkien (1892–1973) was an English writer, artist, and professor better known as J. R. R. Tolkien. Tolkien's high fantasy novels *The Hobbit* (1937), the posthumously published collection *The Silmarillion* (1977), and *The Lord of the Rings* (1954–1955) are his best-known works. Tolkien spent much of his adult life teaching Old and Middle English at Oxford and the Universities of Leeds. Writing was done in private simply as a way to amuse himself and pass the time. *The Hobbit* was one such story. The fame of this novel led to the publication of *The Lord of the Rings* as well as a cornucopia of short stories. "Leaf by Niggle" (1945) first appeared in the *Dublin Review* magazine but can be found in many of Tolkien's collections. It is unique and, strangely, the only story that Tolkien ever wrote in one sitting. Additionally, he barely edited the piece before sending it off for publication and believed himself to be similar to Niggle in a number of ways.

Leaf by Niggle

J. R. R. Tolkien

THERE WAS ONCE A LITTLE MAN called Niggle, who had a long journey to make. He did not want to go, indeed the whole idea was distasteful to him; but he could not get out of it. He knew he would have to start some time, but he did not hurry with his preparations.

Niggle was a painter. Not a very successful one, partly because he had many other things to do. Most of these things he thought were a nuisance; but he did them fairly well, when he could not get out of them: which (in his opinion) was far too often. The laws in his country were rather strict. There were other hindrances, too. For one thing, he was sometimes just idle, and did nothing at all. For another, he was kind-hearted, in a way. You know the sort of kind heart: it made him uncomfortable more often than it made him

do anything; and even when he did anything, it did not prevent him from grumbling, losing his temper, and swearing (mostly to himself). All the same, it did land him in a good many odd jobs for his neighbour, Mr. Parish, a man with a lame leg. Occasionally he even helped other people from further off, if they came and asked him to. Also, now and again, he remembered his journey, and began to pack a few things in an ineffectual way: at such times he did not paint very much.

He had a number of pictures on hand; most of them were too large and ambitious for his skill. He was the sort of painter who can paint leaves better than trees. He used to spend a long time on a single leaf, trying to catch its shape, and its sheen, and the glistening of dewdrops on its edges. Yet he wanted to paint a whole tree, with all of its leaves in the same style, and all of them different.

There was one picture in particular which bothered him. It had begun with a leaf caught in the wind, and it became a tree; and the tree grew, sending out innumerable branches, and thrusting out the most fantastic roots. Strange birds came and settled on the twigs and had to be attended to. Then all round the Tree, and behind it, through the gaps in the leaves and boughs, a country began to open out; and there were glimpses of a forest marching over the land, and of mountains tipped with snow. Niggle lost interest in his other pictures; or else he took them and tacked them on to the edges of his great picture. Soon the canvas became so large that he had to get a ladder; and he ran up and down it, putting in a touch here, and rubbing out a patch there. When people came to call, he seemed polite enough, though he fiddled a little with the pencils on his desk. He listened to what they said, but underneath he was thinking all the time about his big canvas, in the tall shed that had been built for it out in his garden (on a plot where once he had grown potatoes).

He could not get rid of his kind heart. "I wish I was more strong-minded!" he sometimes said to himself, meaning that he wished other people's troubles did not make him feel uncomfortable. But for a long time he was not seriously perturbed. "At any rate, I shall get this one picture done, my real picture, before I have to go on that wretched journey," he used to say. Yet he was beginning to see that he could not put off his start indefinitely. The picture would have to stop just growing and get finished.

One day, Niggle stood a little way off from his picture and considered it with unusual attention and detachment. He could not make up his mind what he thought about it, and wished he had some friend who would tell him what to think. Actually it seemed to him wholly unsatisfactory, and yet very lovely, the only really beautiful picture in the world. What he would have liked at that moment would have been to see himself walk in, and slap him on the back, and say (with obvious sincerity):

"Absolutely magnificent! I see exactly what you are getting at. Do get on with it, and don't bother about anything else! We will arrange for a public pension, so that you need not."

However, there was no public pension. And one thing he could see: it would need some concentration, some *work*, hard uninterrupted work, to finish the picture, even at its present size. He rolled up his sleeves, and began to concentrate. He tried for several days not to bother about other things. But there came a tremendous crop of interruptions. Things went wrong in his house; he had to go and serve on a jury in the town; a distant friend fell ill; Mr. Parish was laid up with lumbago; and visitors kept on coming. It was springtime, and they wanted a free tea in the country: Niggle lived in a pleasant little house, miles away from the town. He cursed them in his heart, but he could not deny that he had invited them himself, away back in the winter, when he had not thought it an "interruption" to visit the shops and have tea with acquaintances in the town. He tried to harden his heart; but it was not a success. There were many things that he had not the face to say *no* to, whether he thought them duties or not; and there were some things he was compelled to do, whatever he thought. Some of his visitors hinted that his garden was rather neglected, and that he might get a visit from an Inspector. Very few of them knew about his picture, of course; but if they had known, it would not have made much difference. I doubt if they would have thought that it mattered much. I dare say it was not really a very good picture, though it may have had some good passages. The Tree, at any rate, was curious. Quite unique in its way. So was Niggle; though he was also a very ordinary and rather silly little man.

At length Niggle's time became really precious. His acquaintances in the distant town began to remember that the little man had got to make a troublesome journey, and some began to calculate how long at the latest he could put off starting. They wondered who would take his house, and if the garden would be better kept.

The autumn came, very wet and windy. The little painter was in his shed. He was up on the ladder, trying to catch the gleam of the westering sun on the peak of a snow-mountain, which he had glimpsed just to the left of the leafy tip of one of the Tree's branches. He knew that he would have to be leaving soon: perhaps early next year. He could only just get the picture finished, and only so so, at that: there were some corners where he would not have time now to do more than hint at what he wanted.

There was a knock on the door. "Come in!" he said sharply, and climbed down the ladder. He stood on the floor twiddling his brush. It was his neighbour, Parish: his only real neighbour, all other folk lived a long way off. Still, he did not like the man very much: partly because he was so often in trouble and in need of help; and also because he did not care about painting, but was very critical about gardening. When Parish looked at Niggle's garden (which was often) he saw mostly weeds; and when he looked at Niggle's pictures (which was seldom) he saw only green and grey patches and black lines, which seemed to him nonsensical. He did not mind mentioning the weeds (a neighbourly duty), but he refrained from giving any opinion of the pictures. He thought this was very kind, and he did not realize that, even if it was kind, it was not kind enough. Help with the weeds (and perhaps praise for the pictures) would have been better.

"Well, Parish, what is it?" said Niggle.

"I oughtn't to interrupt you, I know," said Parish (without a glance at the picture). "You are very busy, I'm sure."

Niggle had meant to say something like that himself, but he had missed his chance. All he said was: "Yes."

"But I have no one else to turn to," said Parish.

"Quite so," said Niggle with a sigh: one of those sighs that are a private comment, but which are not made quite inaudible. "What can I do for you?"

"My wife has been ill for some days, and I am getting worried," said Parish. "And the wind has blown half the tiles on my roof, and water is pouring into the bedroom. I think I ought to get the doctor. And the builders, too, only they take so long to come. I was wondering if you had any wood and canvas you could spare, just to patch me up and see me through for a day or two." Now he did look at the picture.

"Dear, dear!" said Niggle. "You *are* unlucky. I hope it is no more than a cold that your wife has got. I'll come round presently, and help you move the patient downstairs."

"Thank you very much," said Parish, rather coolly. "But it is not a cold, it is a fever. I should not have bothered you for a cold. And my wife is in bed downstairs already. I can't get up and down with trays, not with my leg. But I see you are busy. Sorry to have troubled you. I had rather hoped you might have been able to spare the time to go for the doctor, seeing how I'm placed: and the builder too, if you really have no canvas you can spare."

"Of course," said Niggle; though other words were in his heart, which at the moment was merely soft without feeling at all kind. "I could go. I'll go, if you are really worried."

"I am worried, very worried. I wish I was not lame," said Parish.

So Niggle went. You see, it was awkward. Parish was his neighbour, and everyone else a long way off. Niggle had a bicycle, and Parish had not, and could not ride one. Parish had a lame leg, a genuine lame leg which gave him a good deal of pain: that had to be remembered, as well as his sour expression and whining voice. Of course, Niggle had a picture and barely time to finish it. But it seemed that this was a thing that Parish had to reckon with and not Niggle. Parish, however, did not reckon with pictures; and Niggle could not alter that. "Curse it!" he said to himself, as he got out his bicycle.

It was wet and windy, and daylight was waning. "No more work for me today!" thought Niggle, and all the time that he was riding, he was either swearing to himself, or imagining the strokes of his brush on the mountain, and on the spray of leaves beside it, that he had first imagined in the spring. His fingers twitched on the handlebars.

Now he was out of the shed, he saw exactly the way in which to treat that shining spray which framed the distant vision of the mountain. But he had a sinking feeling in his heart, a sort of fear that he would never now get a chance to try it out.

Niggle found the doctor, and he left a note at the builder's. The office was shut, and the builder had gone home to his fireside. Niggle got soaked to the skin, and caught a chill himself. The doctor did not set out as promptly as Niggle had done. He arrived next day, which was quite convenient for him, as by that time there were two patients to deal with, in neighbouring houses. Niggle was in bed, with a high temperature, and marvellous patterns of leaves and involved branches forming in his head and on the ceiling. It did not comfort him to learn that Mrs. Parish had only had a cold, and was getting up. He turned his face to the wall and buried himself in leaves.

He remained in bed some time. The wind went on blowing. It took away a good many more of Parish's tiles, and some of Niggle's as well: his own roof began to leak. The builder did not come. Niggle did not care; not for a day or two. Then he crawled out to look for some food (Niggle had no wife). Parish did not come round: the rain had got into his leg and made it ache; and his wife was busy mopping up water, and wondering if "that Mr. Niggle" had forgotten to call at the builder's. Had she seen any chance of borrowing anything useful, she would have sent Parish round, leg or no leg; but she did not, so Niggle was left to himself.

At the end of a week or so Niggle tottered out to his shed again. He tried to climb the ladder, but it made his head giddy. He sat and looked at the picture, but there were no patterns of leaves or visions of mountains in his mind that day. He could have painted a far-off view of a sandy desert, but he had not the energy.

Next day he felt a good deal better. He climbed the ladder, and began to paint. He had just begun to get into it again, when there came a knock on the door.

"Damn!" said Niggle. But he might just as well have said "Come in!" politely, for the door opened all the same. This time a very tall man came in, a total stranger.

"This is a private studio," said Niggle. "I am busy. Go away!"

"I am an Inspector of Houses," said the man, holding up his appointment-card, so that Niggle on his ladder could see it. "Oh!" he said.

"Your neighbour's house is not satisfactory at all," said the Inspector.

"I know," said Niggle. "I took a note to the builders a long time ago, but they have never come. Then I have been ill."

"I see," said the Inspector. "But you are not ill now."

"But I'm not a builder. Parish ought to make a complaint to the Town Council, and get help from the Emergency Service."

"They are busy with worse damage than any up here," said the Inspector. "There has been a flood in the valley, and many families are homeless. You should have helped your neighbour to make temporary repairs and prevent the damage from getting more costly to mend than necessary. That is the law. There is plenty of material here: canvas, wood, waterproof paint."

"Where?" asked Niggle indignantly.

"There!" said the Inspector, pointing to the picture.

"My picture!" exclaimed Niggle.

"I dare say it is," said the Inspector. "But houses come first. That is the law."

"But I can't . . .." Niggle said no more, for at that moment another man came in. Very much like the Inspector he was, almost his double: tall, dressed all in black.

"Come along!" he said. "I am the Driver."

Niggle stumbled down from the ladder. His fever seemed to have come on again, and his head was swimming; he felt cold all over.

"Driver? Driver?" he chattered. "Driver of what?"

"You, and your carriage," said the man. "The carriage was ordered long ago. It has come at last. It's waiting. You start today on your journey, you know."

"There now!" said the Inspector. "You'll have

to go; but it's a bad way to start on your journey, leaving your jobs undone. Still, we can at least make some use of this canvas now."

"Oh, dear!" said poor Niggle, beginning to weep. "And it's not, not even finished!"

"Not finished?" said the Driver. "Well, it's finished with, as far as you're concerned, at any rate. Come along!"

Niggle went, quite quietly. The Driver gave him no time to pack, saying that he ought to have done that before, and they would miss the train; so all Niggle could do was to grab a little bag in the hall. He found that it contained only a paint-box and a small book of his own sketches: neither food nor clothes. They caught the train all right. Niggle was feeling very tired and sleepy; he was hardly aware of what was going on when they bundled him into his compartment. He did not care much: he had forgotten where he was supposed to be going, or what he was going for. The train ran almost at once into a dark tunnel.

Niggle woke up in a very large, dim railway station. A Porter went along the platform shouting, but he was not shouting the name of the place; he was shouting *Niggle!*

Niggle got out in a hurry, and found that he had left his little bag behind. He turned back, but the train had gone away.

"Ah, there you are!" said the Porter. "This way! What! No luggage? You will have to go to the Workhouse."

Niggle felt very ill, and fainted on the platform. They put him in an ambulance and took him to the Workhouse Infirmary.

He did not like the treatment at all. The medicine they gave him was bitter. The officials and attendants were unfriendly, silent, and strict; and he never saw anyone else, except a very severe doctor, who visited him occasionally. It was more like being in a prison than in a hospital. He had to work hard, at stated hours: at digging, carpentry, and painting bare boards all one plain colour. He was never allowed outside, and the windows all looked inwards. They kept him in the dark for hours at a stretch, "to do some thinking," they said. He lost count of time. He did not even

begin to feel better, not if that could be judged by whether he felt any pleasure in doing anything. He did not, not even in getting into bed.

At first, during the first century or so (I am merely giving his impressions), he used to worry aimlessly about the past. One thing he kept on repeating to himself, as he lay in the dark: "I wish I had called on Parish the first morning after the high winds began. I meant to. The first loose tiles would have been easy to fix. Then Mrs. Parish might never have caught cold. Then I should not have caught cold either. Then I should have had a week longer." But in time he forgot what it was that he had wanted a week longer for. If he worried at all after that, it was about his jobs in the hospital. He planned them out, thinking how quickly he could stop that board creaking, or rehang that door, or mend that table-leg. Probably he really became rather useful, though no one ever told him so. But that, of course, cannot have been the reason why they kept the poor little man so long. They may have been waiting for him to get better, and judging "better" by some odd medical standard of their own.

At any rate, poor Niggle got no pleasure out of life, not what he had been used to call pleasure. He was certainly not amused. But it could not be denied that he began to have a feeling of—well, satisfaction: bread rather than jam. He could take up a task the moment one bell rang, and lay it aside promptly the moment the next one went, all tidy and ready to be continued at the right time. He got through quite a lot in a day, now; he finished small things off neatly. He had no "time of his own" (except alone in his bed-cell), and yet he was becoming master of his time; he began to know just what he could do with it. There was no sense of rush. He was quieter inside now, and at resting-time he could really rest.

Then suddenly they changed all his hours; they hardly let him go to bed at all; they took him off carpentry altogether and kept him at plain digging, day after day. He took it fairly well. It was a long while before he even began to grope in the back of his mind for the curses that he had practically forgotten. He went on digging, till his back seemed broken, his hands were raw, and he felt that he could not manage another spadeful. Nobody thanked him. But the doctor came and looked at him.

"Knock off!" he said. "Complete rest—in the dark."

Niggle was lying in the dark, resting completely; so that, as he had not been either feeling or thinking at all, he might have been lying there for hours or for years, as far as he could tell. But now he heard Voices: not voices that he had ever heard before. There seemed to be a Medical Board, or perhaps a Court of Inquiry, going on close at hand, in an adjoining room with the door open, possibly, though he could not see any light.

"Now the Niggle case," said a Voice, a severe voice, more severe than the doctor's.

"What was the matter with him?" said a Second Voice, a voice that you might have called gentle, though it was not soft—it was a voice of authority, and sounded at once hopeful and sad. "What was the matter with Niggle? His heart was in the right place."

"Yes, but it did not function properly," said the First Voice. "And his head was not screwed on tight enough: he hardly ever thought at all. Look at the time he wasted, not even amusing himself! He never got ready for his journey. He was moderately well-off, and yet he arrived here almost destitute, and had to be put in the paupers' wing. A bad case, I am afraid. I think he should stay some time yet."

"It would not do him any harm, perhaps," said the Second Voice. "But, of course, he is only a little man. He was never meant to be anything very much; and he was never very strong. Let us look at the Records. Yes. There are some favourable points, you know."

"Perhaps," said the First Voice; "but very few that will really bear examination."

"Well," said the Second Voice, "there are these. He was a painter by nature. In a minor way, of course; still, a Leaf by Niggle has a charm of its own. He took a great deal of pains with leaves, just for their own sake. But he never thought that that made him important. There is no note in the Records of his pretending, even to himself, that it excused his neglect of things ordered by the law."

"Then he should not have neglected so many," said the First Voice.

"All the same, he did answer a good many Calls."

"A small percentage, mostly of the easier sort, and he called those Interruptions. The Records are full of the word, together with a lot of complaints and silly imprecations."

"True; but they looked like interruptions to him, of course, poor little man. And there is this: he never expected any Return, as so many of his sort call it. There is the Parish case, the one that came in later. He was Niggle's neighbour, never did a stroke for him, and seldom showed any gratitude at all. But there is no note in the Records that Niggle expected Parish's gratitude; he does not seem to have thought about it."

"Yes, that is a point," said the First Voice; "but rather small. I think you will find Niggle often merely forgot. Things he had to do for Parish he put out of his mind as a nuisance he had done with."

"Still, there is this last report," said the Second Voice, "that wet bicycle-ride. I rather lay stress on that. It seems plain that this was a genuine sacrifice: Niggle guessed that he was throwing away his last chance with his picture, and he guessed, too, that Parish was worrying unnecessarily."

"I think you put it too strongly," said the First Voice. "But you have the last word. It is your task, of course, to put the best interpretation on the facts. Sometimes they will bear it. What do you propose?"

"I think it is a case for a little gentle treatment now," said the Second Voice.

Niggle thought that he had never heard anything so generous as that Voice. It made Gentle Treatment sound like a load of rich gifts, and the summons to a King's feast. Then suddenly Niggle felt ashamed. To hear that he was considered a case for Gentle Treatment overwhelmed him, and made him blush in the dark. It was like being publicly praised, when you and all the audience knew that the praise was not deserved. Niggle hid his blushes in the rough blanket.

There was a silence. Then the First Voice spoke to Niggle, quite close. "You have been listening," it said.

"Yes," said Niggle.

"Well, what have you to say?"

"Could you tell me about Parish?" said Niggle. "I should like to see him again. I hope he is not very ill? Can you cure his leg? It used to give him a wretched time. And please don't worry about him and me. He was a very good neighbour, and let me have excellent potatoes very cheap, which saved me a lot of time."

"Did he?" said the First Voice. "I am glad to hear it."

There was another silence. Niggle heard the Voices receding. "Well, I agree," he heard the First Voice say in the distance. "Let him go on to the next stage. Tomorrow, if you like."

Niggle woke up to find that his blinds were drawn, and his little cell was full of sunshine. He got up, and found that some comfortable clothes had been put out for him, not hospital uniform. After breakfast the doctor treated his sore hands, putting some salve on them that healed them at once. He gave Niggle some good advice, and a bottle of tonic (in case he needed it). In the middle of the morning they gave Niggle a biscuit and a glass of wine; and then they gave him a ticket.

"You can go to the railway station now," said the doctor. "The Porter will look after you. Good-bye."

Niggle slipped out of the main door, and blinked a little. The sun was very bright. Also he had expected to walk out into a large town, to match the size of the station; but he did not. He was on the top of a hill, green, bare, swept by a keen invigorating wind. Nobody else was about. Away down under the hill he could see the roof of the station shining.

He walked downhill to the station briskly, but without hurry. The Porter spotted him at once.

"This way!" he said, and led Niggle to a bay, in which there was a very pleasant little local train standing: one coach, and a small engine, both very bright, clean, and newly painted. It looked as if this was their first run. Even the track that lay in front of the engine looked new: the rails shone, the chairs were painted green, and the sleepers gave off a delicious smell of fresh tar in the warm sunshine. The coach was empty.

"Where does this train go, Porter?" asked Niggle.

"I don't think they have fixed its name yet," said the Porter. "But you'll find it all right." He shut the door.

The train moved off at once. Niggle lay back in his seat. The little engine puffed along in a deep cutting with high green banks, roofed with blue sky. It did not seem very long before the engine gave a whistle, the brakes were put on, and the train stopped. There was no station, and no signboard, only a flight of steps up the green embankment. At the top of the steps there was a wicket-gate in a trim hedge. By the gate stood his bicycle; at least, it looked like his, and there was a yellow label tied to the bars with NIGGLE written on it in large black letters.

Niggle pushed open the gate, jumped on the bicycle, and went bowling downhill in the spring sunshine. Before long he found that the path on which he had started had disappeared, and the bicycle was rolling along over a marvellous turf. It was green and close; and yet he could see every blade distinctly. He seemed to remember having seen or dreamed of that sweep of grass somewhere or other. The curves of the land were familiar somehow. Yes: the ground was becoming level, as it should, and now, of course, it was beginning to rise again. A great green shadow came between him and the sun. Niggle looked up, and fell off his bicycle.

Before him stood the Tree, his Tree, finished.

If you could say that of a Tree that was alive, its leaves opening, its branches growing and bending in the wind that Niggle had so often felt or guessed, and had so often failed to catch. He gazed at the Tree, and slowly he lifted his arms and opened them wide.

"It's a gift!" he said. He was referring to his art, and also to the result; but he was using the word quite literally.

He went on looking at the Tree. All the leaves he had ever laboured at were there, as he had imagined them rather than as he had made them; and there were others that had only budded in his mind, and many that might have budded, if only he had had time. Nothing was written on them, they were just exquisite leaves, yet they were dated as clear as a calendar. Some of the most beautiful—and the most characteristic, the most perfect examples of the Niggle style—were seen to have been produced in collaboration with Mr. Parish: there was no other way of putting it.

The birds were building in the Tree. Astonishing birds: how they sang! They were mating, hatching, growing wings, and flying away singing into the Forest, even while he looked at them. For now he saw that the Forest was there too, opening out on either side, and marching away into the distance. The Mountains were glimmering far away.

After a time Niggle turned towards the Forest. Not because he was tired of the Tree, but he seemed to have got it all clear in his mind now, and was aware of it, and of its growth, even when he was not looking at it. As he walked away, he discovered an odd thing: the Forest, of course, was a distant Forest, yet he could approach it, even enter it, without its losing that particular charm. He had never before been able to walk into the distance without turning it into mere surroundings. It really added a considerable attraction to walking in the country, because, as you walked, new distances opened out; so that you now had doubled, treble, and quadruple distances, doubly, trebly, and quadruply enchanting. You could go on and on, and have a whole country in a garden,

or in a picture (if you preferred to call it that). You could go on and on, but not perhaps for ever. There were the Mountains in the background. They did get nearer, very slowly. They did not seem to belong to the picture, or only as a link to something else, a glimpse through the trees of something different, a further stage: another picture.

Niggle walked about, but he was not merely pottering. He was looking round carefully. The Tree was finished, though not finished with— "Just the other way about to what it used to be," he thought—but in the Forest there were a number of inconclusive regions, that still needed work and thought. Nothing needed altering any longer, nothing was wrong, as far as it had gone, but it needed continuing up to a definite point. Niggle saw the point precisely, in each case.

He sat down under a very beautiful distant tree—a variation of the Great Tree, but quite individual, or it would be with a little more attention—and he considered where to begin work, and where to end it, and how much time was required. He could not quite work out his scheme.

"Of course!" he said. "What I need is Parish. There are lots of things about earth, plants, and trees that he knows and I don't. This place cannot be left just as my private park. I need help and advice: I ought to have got it sooner."

He got up and walked to the place where he had decided to begin work. He took off his coat. Then, down in a little sheltered hollow hidden from a further view, he saw a man looking round rather bewildered. He was leaning on a spade, but plainly did not know what to do. Niggle hailed him. "Parish!" he called.

Parish shouldered his spade and came up to him. He still limped a little. They did not speak, just nodded as they used to do, passing in the lane; but now they walked about together, arm in arm. Without talking, Niggle and Parish agreed exactly where to make the small house and garden, which seemed to be required.

As they worked together, it became plain that

Niggle was now the better of the two at ordering his time and getting things done. Oddly enough, it was Niggle who became most absorbed in building and gardening, while Parish often wandered about looking at trees, and especially at the Tree.

One day Niggle was busy planting a quickset hedge, and Parish was lying on the grass near by, looking attentively at a beautiful and shapely little yellow flower growing in the green turf. Niggle had put a lot of them among the roots of his Tree long ago. Suddenly Parish looked up: his face was glistening in the sun, and he was smiling.

"This is grand!" he said. "I oughtn't to be here, really. Thank you for putting in a word for me."

"Nonsense," said Niggle. "I don't remember what I said, but anyway it was not nearly enough."

"Oh yes, it was," said Parish. "It got me out a lot sooner. That Second Voice, you know: he had me sent here; he said you had asked to see me. I owe it to you." "No. You owe it to the Second Voice," said Niggle. "We both do."

They went on living and working together: I do not know how long. It is no use denying that at first they occasionally disagreed, especially when they got tired. For at first they did sometimes get tired. They found that they had both been provided with tonics. Each bottle had the same label: *A few drops to be taken in water from the Spring, before resting.*

They found the Spring in the heart of the Forest; only once long ago had Niggle imagined it, but he had never drawn it. Now he perceived that it was the source of the lake that glimmered, far away and the nourishment of all that grew in the country. The few drops made the water astringent, rather bitter, but invigorating; and it cleared the head. After drinking they rested alone; and then they got up again and things went on merrily. At such times Niggle would think of wonderful new flowers and plants, and Parish always knew exactly how to set them and where they would do best. Long before the tonics were finished they had ceased to need them. Parish lost his limp.

As their work drew to an end they allowed themselves more and more time for walking about, looking at the trees, and the flowers, and the lights and shapes, and the lie of the land. Sometimes they sang together; but Niggle found that he was now beginning to turn his eyes, more and more often, towards the Mountains.

The time came when the house in the hollow, the garden, the grass, the forest, the lake, and all the country was nearly complete, in its own proper fashion. The Great Tree was in full blossom.

"We shall finish this evening," said Parish one day. "After that we will go for a really long walk."

They set out next day, and they walked until they came right through the distances to the Edge. It was not visible, of course: there was no line, or fence, or wall; but they knew that they had come to the margin of that country. They saw a man, he looked like a shepherd; he was walking towards them, down the grass-slopes that led up into the Mountains.

"Do you want a guide?" he asked. "Do you want to go on?"

For a moment a shadow fell between Niggle and Parish, for Niggle knew that he did now want to go on, and (in a sense) ought to go on; but Parish did not want to go on, and was not yet ready to go.

"I must wait for my wife," said Parish to Niggle. "She'd be lonely. I rather gathered that they would send her after me, some time or other, when she was ready, and when I had got things ready for her. The house is finished now, as well as we could make it; but I should like to show it to her. She'll be able to make it better, I expect: more homely. I hope she'll like this country, too." He turned to the shepherd. "Are you a guide?" he asked. "Could you tell me the name of this country?"

"Don't you know?" said the man. "It is Niggle's Country. It is Niggle's Picture, or most of it: a little of it is now Parish's Garden."

"Niggle's Picture!" said Parish in astonishment. "Did *you* think of all this, Niggle? I never knew you were so clever. Why didn't you tell me?"

"He tried to tell you long ago," said the man;

"but you would not look. He had only got canvas and paint in those days, and you wanted to mend your roof with them. This is what you and your wife used to call Niggle's Nonsense, or That Daubing."

"But it did not look like this then, not *real*," said Parish.

"No, it was only a glimpse then," said the man; "but you might have caught the glimpse, if you had ever thought it worth while to try."

"I did not give you much chance," said Niggle. "I never tried to explain. I used to call you Old Earth-grubber. But what does it matter? We have lived and worked together now. Things might have been different, but they could not have been better. All the same, I am afraid I shall have to be going on. We shall meet again, I expect: there must be many more things we can do together. Good-bye!" He shook Parish's hand warmly: a good, firm, honest hand it seemed. He turned and looked back for a moment. The blossom on the Great Tree was shining like flame. All the birds were flying in the air and singing. Then he smiled, and nodded to Parish, and went off with the shepherd.

He was going to learn about sheep, and the high pasturages, and look at a wider sky, and walk ever further and further towards the Mountains, always uphill. Beyond that I cannot guess what became of him. Even little Niggle in his old home could glimpse the Mountains far away, and they got into the borders of his picture; but what they are really like, and what lies beyond them, only those can say who have climbed them.

"I think he was a silly little man," said Councillor Tompkins. "Worthless, in fact; no use to Society at all."

"Oh, I don't know," said Atkins, who was nobody of importance, just a schoolmaster. "I am not so sure: it depends on what you mean by *use*."

"No practical or economic use," said Tompkins. "I dare say he could have been made into a serviceable cog of some sort, if you schoolmasters knew your business. But you don't, and so we get useless people of his sort. If I ran this country I should put him and his like to some job that they're fit for, washing dishes in a communal kitchen or something, and I should see that they did it properly. Or I would put them away. I should have put *him* away long ago."

"Put him away? You mean you'd have made him start on the journey before his time?"

"Yes, if you must use that meaningless old expression. Push him through the tunnel into the great Rubbish Heap: that's what I mean."

"Then you don't think painting is worth anything, not worth preserving, or improving, or even making use of?"

"Of course, painting has uses," said Tompkins. "But you couldn't make use of his painting. There is plenty of scope for bold young men not afraid of new ideas and new methods. None for this old-fashioned stuff. Private daydreaming. He could not have designed a telling poster to save his life. Always fiddling with leaves and flowers. I asked him why, once. He said he thought they were pretty! Can you believe it? He said *pretty*! 'What, digestive and genital organs of plants?' I said to him; and he had nothing to answer. Silly footler."

"Footler," sighed Atkins. "Yes, poor little man, he never finished anything. Ah well, his canvases have been put to 'better uses,' since he went. But I am not sure, Tompkins. You remember that large one, the one they used to patch the damaged house next door to his, after the gales and floods? I found a corner of it torn off, lying in a field. It was damaged, but legible: a mountain-peak and a spray of leaves. I can't get it out of my mind."

"Out of your what?" said Tompkins.

"Who are you two talking about?" said Perkins, intervening in the cause of peace: Atkins had flushed rather red.

"The name's not worth repeating," said Tompkins. "I don't know why we are talking about him at all. He did not live in town."

"No," said Atkins; "but you had your eye on his house, all the same. That is why you used to go and call, and sneer at him while drinking his tea. Well, you've got his house now, as well as the one in town, so you need not grudge him his name. We were talking about Niggle, if you want to know, Perkins."

"Oh, poor little Niggle!" said Perkins. "Never knew he painted."

That was probably the last time Niggle's name ever came up in conversation. However, Atkins preserved the odd corner. Most of it crumbled; but one beautiful leaf remained intact. Atkins had it framed. Later he left it to the Town Museum, and for a long while "Leaf: by Niggle" hung there in a recess, and was noticed by a few eyes. But eventually the Museum was burnt down, and the leaf, and Niggle, were entirely forgotten in his old country.

"It is proving very useful indeed," said the Second Voice. "As a holiday, and a refreshment. It is splendid for convalescence; and not only for that, for many it is the best introduction to the Mountains. It works wonders in some cases. I am sending more and more there. They seldom have to come back."

"No, that is so," said the First Voice. "I think we shall have to give the region a name. What do you propose?"

"The Porter settled that some time ago," said the Second Voice. "*Train for Niggle's Parish in the bay:* he has shouted that for a long while now. Niggle's Parish. I sent a message to both of them to tell them."

"What did they say?"

"They both laughed. Laughed—Mountains rang with it!"

Acknowledgments

The editors would like to thank all other anthology editors who, out of love of literature, have labored to curate and present to readers the best fiction from all over the world. We also owe a huge debt of gratefulness to our team of translators who helped bring stories (and sometimes authors) into English for the first time, as well as for their new translations of stories previously translated into English. Thank you, Gio Clairval, Ekaterina Sedia, Minsoo Kang, Marian Womack, James Womack, and Joseph Tomaras. We would also like to thank the translators of the past, whose work is represented within these pages.

This book would not have been possible without the assistance, guidance, and support of several people we want to thank: Julie Nováková, Dominik Parisien, Johanna Sinisalo, John Coulthart, Scott Nicolay, Matthew Cheney, Eric Schaller, and Larry Nolen. Thanks for additional research to Chyina Powell, Edward Gauvin, Liam Henneghan, Michael Shreve, James Machin, and all the readers out there who have shared their favorites with us over the years.

We would also like to extend our gratitude to the many agents, editors, publishers, and other representatives who continue to advocate for writers and stories we love and want to share with our readers, including: Marc Lowenthal of Wakefield Press, Sara Kramer of NYRB, Daniel Seton of Pushkin Press, Richard Curtis Literary Agency, Ray Russell of Tartarus Press, CASiana Enterprises (Literary Estate of Clark Ashton Smith), Paul De Angelis Book Development, Dr. Margery Fee of the University of British Columbia, Dr. Carol Gerson of the Simon Fraser University, Dr. Wai Chee Dimock from Yale University, Sara Patel from PMLA, Dr. Danielle Kovacs from Special Collections and University Archives, UMass Amherst Libraries, the David Graham Du Bois Trust, the J. R. R. Tolkien Estate, and the Zora Neale Hurston Trust.

And of course, our heartfelt appreciation to our editor Tim O'Connell and all the good folks at Vintage, as well as our agent Sally Harding and everyone at the CookeMcDermid Agency.

Permissions

Akutagawa, Ryūnosuke: "Sennin" by Ryūnosuke Akutagawa. Translation copyright © 2018 by Gio Clairval. Originally published in Japanese in 1922. This new translation published by permission of the translator.

Alcott, Louisa May: "The Frost-King" by Louisa May Alcott. Originally published in *Flower Fables* by George W. Briggs & Co. in 1855.

Andersen, Hans Christian: "The Will-o'-the-Wisps Are in Town" by Hans Christian Andersen. Originally published in Danish as "Lygtemaendene ere i Byen, sagde Mosekonen" in 1865.

Anonymous: "The Story of Jeon Unchi" by Anonymous. Translation copyright © 2018 by Minsoo Kang. Originally published in Korean circa 1847. This new translation published by permission of the translator.

Aymé, Marcel: "The Man Who Could Walk Through Walls" by Marcel Aymé. Original French text copyright © 1943 by Éditions Gallimard. English translation copyright © 2012 by Sophie Lewis. Originally published in French as *Le Passe-muraille* in 1943. Reprinted by permission of Pushkin Press and the translator.

Baum, L. Frank: "Jack Pumpkinhead and the Sawhorse" by L. Frank Baum. Originally published as *Oz Books in Miniature, No. 5* in 1913, and subsequently published in *Little Wizard Stories of Oz* by Reilly & Britton Co. in 1914.

Benson, E. F.: "David Blaize and the Blue Door" by E. F. Benson. Excerpt from *David Blaize and the Blue Door*, originally published by Hodder and Stoughton Limited in 1918.

Benson, Stella: "Magic Comes to a Committee" by Stella Benson. Excerpt from *Living Alone*, originally published by Macmillan and Co., Limited in 1919.

About the Translators

Gio Clairval, after living in Paris for most of her life, moved to Scotland and then to Italy, and now from her windows she can see her pet, a giant pike, frolicking in the waters of Lake Como. Her stories have appeared in magazines such as *Weird Tales*, *Galaxy's Edge*, *Lightspeed* (Fantasy), and *Postscripts* and in several anthologies, including *The Lambshead Cabinet of Curiosities* (HarperCollins), *Kisses by Clockwork* (Ticonderoga Publications), *punkPunk!* (DogHorn Publishing), and *Caledonia Dreamin'* (Eibonvale Press). She also translates literary classics (Kafka, Blei, Meyrink, Strobl, Flaubert, Jarry, Fréchette, Bernanos, Cortazar, Deledda, and Buzzati, among others) into English.

Minsoo Kang is the author of the history books *Sublime Dreams of Living Machines: The Automaton in the European Imagination* and *Invincible and Righteous Outlaw: The Korean Hero Hong Gildong in Literature, History, and Culture* and the short story collection *Of Tales and Enigmas* and is the translator of the Penguin Classics edition of the Korean novel *The Story of Hong Gildong*. His stories have appeared in *Magazine of Fantasy & Science Fiction*, *Fantastic Stories of the Imagination*, *Azalea*, *Entropy*, *Lady Churchill's Rosebud Wristlet*, and the anthologies *Where the Stars Rise* and *Shanghai Steam*. His story "A Fearful Symmetry" was included in *The Year's Best Fantasy and Horror 2007* and "The Sacrifice of the Hanged Monkey" in *The Year's Best Science Fiction and Fantasy 2018*. Originally from South Korea, he has also lived in Austria, New Zealand, Iran, Brunei, and Germany. He served in the South Korean army and earned his Ph.D. in European history at UCLA. He is currently an associate professor of history at the University of Missouri–Saint Louis.

Ekaterina Sedia resides in the Pinelands of New Jersey. Her critically acclaimed and award-nominated novels, *The Secret History of Moscow*, *The Alchemy of Stone*, *The House of Discarded Dreams*, and *Heart of Iron*, were published by Prime Books. Her short stories have appeared in *Analog*, *Baen's Universe*, *Subterranean*, and *Clarkesworld*, as well as in numerous anthologies, including *Haunted Legends* and *Magic in the Mirrorstone*. She is also the editor of the anthologies *Paper Cities* (World Fantasy Award winner), *Running with the Pack*, *Bewere the Night*, and *Bloody Fabulous*, as well as *The Mammoth Book of Gaslit Romance* and *Wilful Impropriety*. Her short story collection, *Moscow But Dreaming*, was released by Prime Books in December 2012. She also cowrote a script for *Yamasong: March of the Hollows*, a fantasy feature-length puppet film voiced by Nathan Fillion, George Takei, Abigail Breslin, and Whoopi Goldberg, to be released by Dark Dunes Productions.

Joseph Tomaras lives in southern Maine and writes fiction, more or less speculative, some of which has been published. He is currently engaged in translating Der Nister's full "Gedakht" collection of short stories (1922–1923). He also reads voluminously in Spanish, German, Portuguese, French, Modern Greek, Hebrew, and, of course, Yiddish.

James Womack is a translator and poet. He has translated widely from Spanish and Russian, including works by Vladimir Mayakovsky, Sergio del Molino, Roberto Arlt, Silvina Ocampo, and Boris Savinkov. He currently teaches Spanish translation at Cambridge University. His second collection of poems, *On Trust: A Book of Lies*, was published in 2017, and his anthology of verses of Vladimir Mayakovsky, *"Vladimir Mayakovsky" and Other Poems*, came out in 2016.

Marian Womack is a translator, author, and editor. She is a graduate of the Cambridge University Creative Writing Master Degree and a postgraduate researcher at the Anglia Ruskin Centre for Science Fiction and Fantasy. Her *Lost Objects*, a collection of tales about ghosts and nature, was published by Luna Press in 2018.

About the Editors

Ann VanderMeer currently serves as an acquiring editor for Tor.com and *Weird Fiction Review* and is the editor-in-residence for Shared Worlds. She was the editor-in-chief for *Weird Tales* for five years, during which time she was nominated three times for the Hugo Award, winning one. Along with multiple nominations for the Shirley Jackson Award, she also has won a World Fantasy Award and a British Fantasy Award for coediting *The Weird: A Compendium of Strange and Dark Stories*. Other projects have included *Best American Fantasy*, three Steampunk anthologies, and a humor book, *The Kosher Guide to Imaginary Animals*. Her latest anthologies include *The Time Traveler's Almanac*; *Sisters of the Revolution*, an anthology of feminist speculative fiction; *The Bestiary*, an anthology of original fiction and art; and *The Big Book of Science Fiction*.

New York Times bestselling writer Jeff VanderMeer has been called "the weird Thoreau" by *The New Yorker* for his engagement with ecological issues. His most recent novel, *Borne*, received widespread critical acclaim for its exploration of animal and human life in a post-scarcity landscape. VanderMeer's prior work includes the Southern Reach trilogy (*Annihilation*, *Authority*, and *Acceptance*), which has been translated into thirty-five languages. *Annihilation* was made into a film by Paramount Pictures and won the Nebula Award and Shirley Jackson Award. VanderMeer's nonfiction has appeared in *The New York Times*, the *Los Angeles Times*, *The Atlantic*, *Slate*, *Salon*, and *The Washington Post*, among others. A three-time winner of the World Fantasy Award, he has also edited or coedited many iconic fiction anthologies, taught at the Yale Writers' Conference, lectured at MIT, Brown, and the Library of Congress, been the writer-in-residence for Hobart and William Smith Colleges, and serves as the codirector of Shared Worlds, a unique teen writing camp located at Wofford College. His forthcoming novel is the first in the Adventures of Jonathan Lambshead series (FSG Kids). With his wife, Ann VanderMeer, he has edited more than a dozen anthologies.

Editorial Consultant:

Dominik Parisien is the coeditor, with Navah Wolfe, of *Robots vs. Fairies* and *The Starlit Wood: New Fairy Tales*, which won the Shirley Jackson Award and was a finalist for the World Fantasy Award, the British Fantasy Award, and the Locus Award. He is also the coeditor, with Elsa Sjunneson-Henry, of *Disabled People Destroy Science Fiction*. His fiction, poetry, and nonfiction have appeared in *The Fiddlehead, Uncanny Magazine,* and *Exile: The Literary Quarterly*, as well as other magazines and anthologies. He is a disabled French Canadian and lives in Toronto.

Editorial Assistant:

Chyina Powell began reading in the confines of her home in Akron, Ohio, at an early age. She loved the way that she could relate to stories and how they were able to take her on a journey. Soon she began creating worlds of her own, writing short stories and poetry in her free time. By the time she was in high school, she found a passion in helping others with their own worlds. Now that she has completed her schooling, she hopes to become a full-time editor, as well as work on her own speculative fiction pieces.